Stories to Caution the World

警世通言

Stories to Caution the World

A MING DYNASTY COLLECTION

VOLUME 2

Compiled by Feng Menglong (1574–1646)
Translated by Shuhui Yang and Yunqin Yang

UNIVERSITY OF WASHINGTON PRESS
SEATTLE AND LONDON

Publication of *Stories to Caution the World* has been generously supported by Bates College.

Printed in the United States of America

12 11 10 09 08 07 06 05   5 4 3 2 1

University of Washington Press
P.O. Box 50096, Seattle, WA 98145
www.washington.edu/uwpress

Library of Congress Cataloging-in-Publication Data
Feng, Menglong, 1574–1646.
[Jing shi tong yan. English]
Stories to caution the world : a Ming dynasty collection / compiled by Feng Menglong ; translated by Shuhui Yang and Yunqin Yang.
p. cm.
ISBN 0-295-98552-6 (hardback : alk. paper)
I. Yang, Shuhui. II. Yang, Yunqin. III. Title.
PL2698.F4J5613 2005
895.1'346—dc22 2005010013

The paper used in this publication is acid-free and 90 percent recycled from at least 50 percent post-consumer waste. It meets the minimum requirements of American National Standard for Information Sciences—Permanence of Paper for Printed Library Materials, ANSI Z39.48-1984.

To our parents and sisters

Contents

Acknowledgments

This translation benefited greatly from the help of Professor Robert Hegel, two anonymous readers, and Lorri Hagman. We wish to express our profound gratitude for their enthusiastic encouragement and many valuable suggestions for improvement. We also wish to thank our copyeditor, Laura Iwasaki, for her meticulous preparation of the manuscript for press, and Bates College for its generous financial support.

Introduction

Stories to Caution the World (Jingshi tongyan), more commonly known in English as *Comprehensive Words to Warn the World,* was published in Jinling, present-day Nanjing, in 1624. It is the second of three celebrated Ming dynasty (1368–1644) collections of stories; the first is *Stories Old and New* (Gujin xiaoshuo; 1620), and the third is *Constant Words to Awaken the World* (Xingshi hengyan; 1627). Each collection contains forty stories, and since *Stories Old and New* is also known as *Illustrious Words to Instruct the World* (Yushi mingyan), the three books are most often referred to collectively as the *Sanyan* (Three words), from the Chinese character *yan* at the end of each title.[1]

The *Sanyan* collections were edited by Feng Menglong (1574–1646), the most knowledgeable connoisseur of popular literature of his time. He came from a well-to-do, educated family in exceptionally prosperous Suzhou Prefecture, one of the great cultural centers of Ming (1368–1644) China. Feng acquired the preliminary academic degree of *shengyuan* when he was about twenty but apparently had no further luck in the civil service examinations, in spite of his erudition and great literary fame. Finally, in 1630, at the age of fifty-six or fifty-seven, he seems to have lost hope that he would pass the examinations and decided instead to take the alternative route to office by accepting the status of tribute student.[2] He then served one term as assistant instructor in Dantu County (about ninety miles northwest of Suzhou), probably from 1631 to 1634, before he was promoted to a minor position as magistrate of Shouning County, Fujian.[3] He held this office for four years and proved to be an honest, caring, and efficient administrator, as is registered in the *County History of Shouning* (Shouning xian zhi), compiled in the early Qing period (1644–1911). The county history also tells us that Feng "venerated literary studies more than anything else" (*shou shang wenxue*) during his service.[4] Feng's last political involvement, toward the end of his life, was his association with the Southern Ming government in its desperate resistance against the crushing forces of the Manchus. He died soon afterward in 1646 at the age of seventy-two.

Feng Menglong was one of the most prolific writers of his time. The books he published could literally be "piled up to reach his own height" (*zhuzuo dengshen*), a phrase traditionally used by critics to praise exceptionally productive writers,[5] and they covered such a wide range of interests and literary genres that Feng has been described as "presenting himself in two distinct personae, or . . . in a range of personae between two extremes."[6] At one extreme, he appears in some of his works as the wit, the ribald humorist, the bohemian, the drinker, and the romantic lover. This is the Feng Menglong who compiled *Treasury of Jokes* (Xiaofu) and published two volumes of folk songs (*Guazhir* and *Hill Songs*), mostly on erotic or ribald themes, and whose passionate love affair with the famous Suzhou courtesan Hou Huiqing is revealed in some of his poems. At the other extreme is Feng Menglong the patriot, orthodox scholar, and ardent examination candidate, who authored at least three handbooks on the Confucian classic *The Spring and Autumn Annals,* wrote a similar handbook on the *Four Books,* and published many patriotic tracts as a consequence of his participation in Southern Ming resistance activities. These two personae may seem to be mutually exclusive, yet in his fiction as well as his plays, Feng Menglong often reveals elements of both in a single text.[7]

Modern scholars generally agree, however, that Feng Menglong's greatest contribution to literature is in the field of vernacular fiction, particularly his collecting and editing of the three *Sanyan* books of 120 vernacular short stories. This genre, known as *huaben,* is believed to have developed, along with the vernacular novel, during the Song (960–1279) and Yuan (1260–1368) dynasties and reached maturity in the late Ming. As a passionate champion of popular literature, Feng managed to rescue from oblivion a significant proportion of the early *huaben* stories by making them available to the public again. But preservation of existing stories was by no means Feng Menglong's only concern—he probably was more interested in giving prestige to this new literary genre and establishing it socially. In the preface to *Stories Old and New,* he places vernacular fiction on a par with the highly esteemed classical tales of the Tang dynasty (618–907):

> *Literature and the arts have been so vigorously advanced by the imperial court of this Ming dynasty that each and every school is flourishing; in vernacular fiction alone, there is no lack of writings of a quality far above those of the Song. It is a mistake to believe, as some do, that such works lack the charm of those of the Tang. One who has a love for the peach need not forsake the apricot. Fine linen, silk gauze, plush, brocade—each has its proper occasion for wear.*

In order to elevate the status of the vernacular story, Feng Menglong also claims, in the same preface, that the origin of all fiction is the grand tradition of historiography, and he ascribes more educational and moral power to the *huaben* story than to *The Analects of Confucius* (Lunyu).[8] With the aim of substantiating such claims, Feng is believed, not surprisingly, to have extensively modified some of the stories he had collected and incorporated many of his own stories and those of some friends into the *Sanyan* collections, although he does not acknowledge authorship in the preface.[9] According to Patrick Hanan, who applied rigorous stylistic criteria in his studies of the dating and authorship of Chinese vernacular stories, Feng Menglong is the probable author of nineteen stories in *Stories Old and New,* sixteen in *Stories to Caution the World,* and one or two in *Constant Words to Awaken the World.*[10]

A less drastic but more obvious aspect of Feng's "editing" is his rearrangement into pairs of the stories in the three collections. The thematically and grammatically parallel pairing of titles may be an attempt to parody the parallelism of classical poetry and belles lettres prose (the two most honored literary genres of Feng's time) or may simply represent his effort to elevate the vernacular short story.[11] However, on the textual level, it is clear that stories were composed with their pairings in mind.[12] The paired stories often share features of subject matter or plot line, and they occasionally contrast or comment on each other.

One of the most interesting and controversial characteristics of Chinese vernacular fiction is its "storyteller's rhetoric." This is part of what Patrick Hanan refers to as the "simulated context," or "the context of situation in which a piece of fiction claims to be transmitted."[13] In the *Sanyan* stories (and in other Chinese vernacular fiction as well), this simulacrum almost always takes the form of a professional storyteller addressing his audience. The storyteller-narrator asks questions of his simulated audience, converses with them, makes explicit references to his own stories, and intersperses his narrative with verses and poems. The narrator usually begins his talk with one or more prologue stories or poems, which supposedly allows time for his audience to gather before he presents the main piece in his performance.

Of course, in written literature, this storyteller's pose is only a pretense in which "the author and reader happily acquiesce in order that the fiction can be communicated."[14] It was a way to "naturalize, by reference to the familiar situation of hearing stories told in the vernacular by professional storytellers, the unfamiliar process of writing and reading fiction in vernacular Chinese."[15] But this formal feature, plus a misunderstanding of the term *huaben,* led many scholars of Chinese literature to subscribe, until a couple of decades ago, to the "prompt-book" theory, which held that the Chinese vernacular story developed directly from the prompt-books of marketplace storytellers in the Song dynasty and that the pre-*Sanyan* texts were genuine prompt-books written for performance in the Song and Yuan or early Ming periods.[16] W. L. Idema, however, argues that the storyteller's manner was developed deliberately in literati imitations by Feng Menglong and others. According to Idema, the conspicuous use of this rhetorical stance in the *Sanyan* collections was "a consequence mainly of Feng Menglong's reinterpretation of the genre and due to his overall rewritings."[17] In other words, Feng's editing of the collections included a systematic elaboration of this storyteller's rhetoric, which became a hallmark of the *huaben* story as he conceived of it.

This, however, is not to deny the presence of elements of oral folk literature in the *Sanyan* stories. Most contain anecdotes or episodes known even to the illiterate, which suggests that the editor looked to storytelling for raw materials as well as for rhetorical formulas. And we may assume that traces of the marketplace storyteller and the values he represented would unavoidably have remained in these *huaben* stories in spite of Feng Menglong's often meticulous editing. Idema argues that professional storytelling was but one of the many factors that helped to shape traditional Chinese fiction.[18] Small wonder that the *Sanyan* collections provide for us such a vivid panoramic view of the bustling world of imperial China before the end of the Ming; we see not only scholars, emperors, ministers, and generals but also a gallery of ordinary men and women in their everyday surroundings—merchants and artisans, prostitutes and courtesans, matchmakers and fortune-tellers, monks and nuns, servants and maids, thieves and impostors. We learn about their joys and sorrows, likes and dislikes, their views of life and death, and even their visions of the netherworld and the supernatural.

Thus, the *Sanyan* stories are necessarily overdetermined texts, historically, ideologically, and formally. They can justifiably be taken as an intersection of complex cultural determinations, with generic mixture and multiple voices making different and sometimes conflicting claims. This complexity of multiple voices in *Stories to Caution the World* has never been fully presented to the English reader. Of the forty stories in this collection, only fourteen have been published in English translation, appearing separately in journals and anthologies of Chinese literature instead of being arranged in pairs and in the original sequence. Moreover, in these previous translations, the storyteller's rhetoric, the verses, and the prologue stories often were deleted.[19] The interlinear and marginal comments, generally believed to have been made by Feng Menglong himself, are omitted even in modern Chinese editions of the collection.[20] This volume represents the first effort to translate the second of the seventeenth-century *Sanyan* collections in its entirety. In doing so, we hope not only to provide the English reader with a fuller picture of the complex social environment of imperial China but, more important, to show the intricate interactions among different voices in the texts, especially between the voice of the conventional storyteller-narrator and that of the literati editor Feng Menglong.

Shuhui Yang

Translators' Note

This translation follows the text of the 1624 *Jianshantang* edition of *Jingshi tongyan* as reprinted in the 1987 facsimile edition by Shanghai Guji Chubanshe. In this translation, the interlinear and marginal comments in the original text appear in italic within parentheses in roman text and in roman within parentheses in italic text.

Chinese proper names are rendered in the *pinyin* system. For the convenience of those readers who are more accustomed to the Wade-Giles system of romanization, we have provided the following short list of difficult consonants:

c = ts'
q = ch'
x = hs
z = tz
zh = ch

Information about previous translations of stories in this collection (in varying degrees of completeness and accuracy) is provided in the endnotes for individual stories.

Frequently Encountered Chinese Terms

chi, a unit of measurement, translated as "foot"
jin, translated as "catty," equals half a kilogram
jinshi, one who passed the imperial civil service examinations at the metropolitan (the highest) level
li, approximately one third of a mile
liang, translated as "tael," equals one sixteenth of a *jin*
mu, roughly one sixth of an acre
shi, a married woman known by her maiden name (e.g., Wang-shi)
xiucai, translated as "scholar," a successful candidate at the local level
zhuangyuan, a *jinshi* who ranked first in the palace examination, in which the emperor interviewed those who passed the imperial civil service examination at the metropolitan level
zi, translated as "courtesy name," the name by which an educated person was addressed by people of his or her own generation, probably used more often than an official name

For our translation of the first collection, *Stories Old and New,* published by the University of Washington Press in 2000, we obtained copies of illustrations from the 1620 Chinese edition of *Stories Old and New* from the Imperial Diet Library of Japan. Much to our regret, however, we were not able to obtain reproducible copies of illustrations for this volume.

Chronology of Chinese Dynasties

Xia	ca. 2100–ca. 1600 B.C.E.
Shang (Yin)	ca. 1600–ca. 1028 B.C.E.
Zhou	ca. 1027–ca. 256 B.C.E.
Western Zhou	ca. 1027–771 B.C.E.
Eastern Zhou	770–256 B.C.E.
Spring and Autumn	770–476 B.C.E.
Warring States	475–221 B.C.E.
Qin	221–207 B.C.E.
Han	206 B.C.E.–220 C.E.
Western Han	206 B.C.E.–8 C.E.
Xin	9–25
Eastern Han	25–220
Three Kingdoms	220–80
Wei	220–65
Shu	221–63
Wu	222–80
Six Dynasties (Wu, Eastern Jin, Former Song, Southern Qi, Southern Liang, and Southern Chen)	222–589
Jin	265–420
Western Jin	265–316
Eastern Jin	317–420
Southern and Northern Dynasties	420–589
Southern Dynasties	
Former Song	420–79
Southern Qi	479–502
Southern Liang	502–57
Southern Chen	557–89
Northern Dynasties	
Northern Wei	386–534
Eastern Wei	534–50
Western Wei	535–56
Northern Qi	550–77
Northern Zhou	557–81

Sui	581–618
Tang	618–907
Five Dynasties and Ten Kingdoms	907–79
Five Dynasties	
Later Liang	907–23
Later Tang	923–36
Later Jin	936–46
Later Han	947–50
Later Zhou	951–60
Ten Kingdoms	907–79
Liao (Khitan)	916–1125
Song	960–1279
Northern Song	960–1126
Southern Song	1127–1279
Xixia (Tangut)	1038–1227
Jin (Jurchen)	1115–1234
Yuan (Mongol)	1260–1368
Ming	1368–1644
Qing (Manchu)	1644–1911

Stories to Caution the World

警世通言

Stories to Caution the World

PUBLISHER'S NOTE

[IN THE 1624 EDITION]

Even those committed to the most rigorous scholarship have always included unofficial histories in their studies. It is no wonder, then, that the lower classes find popular historical romances most appealing. However, for those profit-driven individuals who offend decency by seeking out only narratives that are lewd and obscene, this publishing house has nothing but the utmost disdain. Under personal instructions from the Master of the Pingping Studio, we dare not fill these volumes with anything other than words that caution and enlighten the world. As was the wish of the late venerable one dedicated to the edification of the mind, we hope that these volumes will be looked upon favorably by members of the literati as well.

The Jianshan Publishing House of Jinling [present-day Nanjing]

Preface [to the 1624 edition]

Do all historical romances give true accounts of history? The answer is "Not necessarily." Are they all untrue, then? "Not necessarily." Should all that is untrue be done away with, and only what is true be preserved? "Not necessarily, either."

The Six Classics,[1] *The Analects* [of Confucius], and *Mencius,* about which commentaries abound, are, in summary, nothing but exhortations for ministers to be loyal, children to be filial, officials to be judicious, friends to be trustworthy, husbands to be honorable, wives to be chaste, scholars to be paragons of virtue, and families to do good deeds. The classics state the universal truths, and the histories serve the same purpose through narrating the events. Yet, the universal truths are explained to a world inhabited not exclusively by venerable men who diligently compare notes with each other in their moral pursuits, and the histories are narrated to a world consisting not exclusively of erudite scholars of impeccable moral behavior. And since villagers, children, ordinary women, and peddlers are easily stirred to joy or wrath by what others do rightly or wrongly, take guidance in their actions from stories about the operations of karma, and gain knowledge from hearsay and gossip, popular historical romances can well serve as supplements where the classics and the histories are found lacking.

One may say, "Just as home-brewed wine and meat bought from the village market are not good enough for the banquet table, such romances are nothing but vulgar absurdities."

Alas! The *fu* prose poems [about fictional characters] "Daren fu" (The Mighty One) and "Zixu fu" (Sir Fantasy), with the words of advice voiced toward the very end, stand unrivaled in their moral elevation.[2] Real historical figures do not have to be tied to real events, nor do real historical events have to be attributed to real names. What is real can be added to the archives of the imperial libraries, and what is unreal can inspire, edify, and profoundly move the audience. There is truth in what is real, but there is also truth in what is unreal. If there is no offense against decency, no deviation from the teachings of the sages, and no breach of the morals taught by classics such as *The Book of Songs* and *The Book of History,* why should such romances be done away with?

A neighbor's boy cut his finger when helping out in the kitchen. To comments of surprise that he did not let out cries of pain, the boy replied, "I just came back from Xuanmiao Temple, where I heard a storyteller tell about how Guan Yu [d.

220] of *The Romance of the Three Kingdoms* went on talking and laughing when a surgeon was scraping infection from a bone in his arm. Now, this little pain of mine is really nothing!" From the fact that a story about Guan Yu fills a boy with such courage, we can infer that stories about filial piety, loyalty, fidelity, and righteousness do foster these virtues in the audience, and that they strike deep chords in the audience and awaken their genuine feelings. When such stories are compared with the writings of those venerable men and erudite scholars of impeccable moral behavior, writings that are stylish and ornate but without feeling and substance, who can tell which are real and which are unreal?

I met a most extraordinary gentleman from west of the Long Mountains at the House on the Hill amid Rosy Clouds, a man with whom I formed a profound friendship the very first time we met.[3] We talked about our travels, and then, in the course of drinking, he produced several newly printed volumes of books and said, "These volumes are not really complete as yet, but would you be so kind as to give them a title?" Upon reading the volumes, I found them to consist mostly of words not unlike those spoken by monks in explanation of the operations of karma to save the souls of the people in this world. Just like home-brewed wine and meat bought from the village market, they provide nourishment for the masses. I therefore gave the volumes the title *Stories to Caution the World* [lit., Comprehensive words to caution the world] and urged that they be published.

Recluse Sans Souci of Yuzhang [present-day Nanchang, Jiangxi]
The twelfth month of the fourth year of the Tianqi reign period [1624]

I

Yu Boya Smashes His Zither in Gratitude to an Appreciative Friend

What a lie that Bao Shu was cheated out of his silver!
Who recognized Boya's talent in playing the zither?
An evil lot are those claiming friendship nowadays,
Unworthy of loving thoughts over seas and lakes.

When it comes to friendship, none since ancient times has measured up to that between Guan Yiwu [d. 645 B.C.E.] and Bao Shuya [also known as Bao Shu].[1] When both were engaged in business dealings, they divided their profits between them. Though Guan Yiwu took the larger share of the profits, Bao did not think Guan was a greedy man, for he knew Guan to be poor. Later, when Guan Yiwu became a prisoner, it was Bao who came to his rescue and recommended that he be made prime minister of the state of Qi [during the Spring and Autumn period]. Such is the stuff of which true friendships are made.

Now there are different kinds of friends. Those who are bound together by deeds of kindness are friends who truly know each other; those who show utter devotion to each other are friends of the heart; those who find much in common with each other are friends truly appreciative of each other. They all fall into the general category of friendship.

I now propose to tell a story about a certain Yu Boya. Dear audience, those of you who would like to hear it, please lend me your ears. Those who do not want to hear it are free to do whatever you wish. Truly,

What is meant for an appreciative ear
Is not to be wasted on just anyone.

As the story goes, during the Spring and Autumn and the Warring States period, there lived a man named Yu Rui, courtesy name Boya, in Yingdu, capital of the state of Chu, in what is now Jingzhou Prefecture in Huguang.[2]

Though a native of the state of Chu, Yu Boya was destined for a career as an official in the state of Jin, where he rose to be a senior grand master. By order of the king of Jin, he went on an official visit to Chu. It was actually a mission that he had solicited. He did so partly because, with his superior abilities, he was sure that he would acquit himself well as the king's emissary and partly because he could take the opportunity to visit his hometown, thus accomplishing two purposes at the same time. So he traveled by land to Yingdu, where he had an audience with the king of Chu and transmitted to him the message from the king of Jin, whereupon the king of Chu laid out a feast in his honor, treating him with great courtesy.

Yingdu being his hometown, Boya naturally went to visit the family graves and meet with relatives and friends. However, now that he was serving another state and was bearing orders from his king, he refrained from staying longer. As soon as his official business was over, he bade a respectful adieu to the king of Chu, who gave him gifts of gold, colored silk, and a canopied four-horse carriage.

Now, because he had been away from Chu for twelve years and missed the scenic rivers and mountains of his home state, Boya wished to make a big detour by water on his return journey so as to see the sights to his heart's content. He therefore said to the king of Chu, not in all honesty, "I have an unfortunate affliction that makes the rapid speed of carriages too much for me to bear. I humbly request permission to go by boat instead, which would make it easier for me to undergo treatment." The king of Chu approved Boya's request and ordered the navy to provide him with two big boats, one for his exclusive use as the emissary from the state of Jin and the other, of a lower ranking, for his servants and the luggage. Magnificent boats they were, with brocade canopies, tall masts, and decorated oars made of fragrant wood. The ministers of the court escorted Boya and his entourage all the way to the riverbank before they bade him farewell.

To satisfy his wish to see the sights,
He thought nothing of the distance.

Romantic scholar that he was, Boya found the sights to be all that he had hoped to enjoy. With sails unfurled, the boats rode on the undulating green waves, the distant wooded mountains and clear waters within full view. Before many days had passed, he found himself and his entourage at the mouth of Hanyang River. It was the fifteenth night of the eighth lunar month, the night of the Mid-autumn Festival. Suddenly, a storm sprang up. With waves leaping high and rain pouring down in sheets, the boats had to be moored at the foot of a hill. A while later, the wind died down, the waves subsided, the rain stopped, and the clouds cleared, revealing a bright, rain-washed moon that shone with double its usual brightness.

Sitting alone in the cabin and feeling bored, Yu Boya told his page boy, "Put some incense in that incense burner. I'm going to play my zither to express my feelings." Thereupon, the page boy lit the incense and put the zither case on the table. Boya opened the case, took out the zither, tuned it, and began to play. Before he had finished a piece, a string broke with a sharp twang. Startled, Boya told the page boy to ask the head boatman what kind of place this was. The head boatman replied,

"This is just the foot of a hill where the storm took us. There are some grass and trees around, but no houses." (*True enough.*)

Much taken by surprise, Boya thought to himself, "So, this is a deserted hill. If it were a town or a village where some intelligent person eager to learn listened secretly to my music, that would explain why the music suddenly changed in tone and why the string snapped. But in this deserted place at the foot of a hill, how can there be anyone listening to my music? Ah yes, I know. It must be an assassin sent by some enemy of mine, or it could be some robbers waiting here for the night to deepen before coming onto the boat to get my possessions." So thinking, he said to the attendants by his side, "Go ashore and look around for me. If there's no one in the depths of the willow grove, then search in the reeds."

Thus instructed, the men called out to other servants, and they all assembled, ready to use the gangplank to get to the rocky shore. At this moment, a man's voice was heard from the shore, saying, "The gentleman in the boat need not be suspicious. I am not a robber but a woodcutter. I had finished cutting firewood for the day and was on my way home after dark when I was caught in a bad storm. My rain gear not being enough to protect me from the rain, I found shelter by a rock. Then I heard the gentleman play the zither and stayed to listen."

Boya burst into laughter. "Imagine a woodcutter in the hills having the audacity to say he listens to music! Well, I won't even bother to find out whether that claim is true or not. Now, my men, tell him to leave."

Instead of leaving, the man on the rocky shore said loudly, "Sir, you've got it all wrong! Haven't you heard the sayings 'In a neighborhood of ten households, there are bound to be loyal and trustworthy people' and 'If there is a gentleman in the room, another gentleman will come to the door'? You, sir, in your contempt for these backwoods, think that no one around here would listen to music. Well, if so, there shouldn't be a zither player at the foot of a deserted hill, either."

Impressed by the man's refined speech, Boya began to think that this woodcutter might truly have been listening to his music. He told his men to quiet down and went to the cabin door. His displeasure having given way to delight, he asked, "Since the gentleman on the rocky shore has been standing and listening to my playing for quite some time, does he, by any chance, know what I was playing?"

"If I didn't know," said the man, "I wouldn't have stayed and listened. What you have been playing, sir, is a melody set to what Confucius wrote in memory of [his student] Yan Hui. The lines go like this, 'How tragic that Yan Hui died so early; / Memories of him have whitened my hair. / By living happily in poverty,'— and at this point, a string on your zither snapped before the fourth line could be played. But I remember the fourth line. It says, 'A good name he left for posterity.'"

Overjoyed upon hearing this, Boya said, "You are indeed a gentleman of culture. But it is difficult to talk with you across such a distance." Turning to his men, he said, "Put out the gangplank and the handrail and invite the gentleman to come aboard for a chat."

The servants put out the gangplank, and the man boarded the boat. He was indeed a woodcutter, with a broad-brimmed bamboo hat, a straw cape, a carrying pole with its load, an ax tied to his waist, and straw sandals on his feet. The servants, who had little appreciation for refined speech, assumed a contemptuous look at the sight of a mere woodcutter. (*Those who worship money and bully the poor and the humble don't know the good from the bad and, as such, will never rise above the servant class.*) "Hey, woodcutter!" they called out. "When you go into the cabin, be sure to kowtow to our master, and be respectful when you answer his questions. He's a highly placed official, you know."

The woodcutter was by no means of the common run. "You don't have to be so rude," he said. "Now, let me get myself ready before I go in." So saying, he took off his bamboo hat, under which was a blue cloth cap. Then he took off his straw cape, revealing a blue cloth shirt, a long bag worn around his waist, and a pair of cloth pants. All calm and collected, he put his cape and hat, his load and its carrying pole, and his ax outside the cabin door. (*What great composure! He has lost his respect for Boya by now.*) He removed his sandals, shook off the muddy water, put them on his feet again, and walked into the cabin, which was brightly lit by the candles on the emissary's writing desk.

The woodcutter bowed deeply with one hand cupped in the other before his chest but did not drop to his knees. "Greetings, sir," said he.

Being a minister in the court of Jin, Yu Boya, as a rule, would not deign to glance at a common laborer who was not wearing a robe. Now, he was afraid that to leave his seat and return the greeting would be beneath his dignity as an official, and yet, since he had already invited the man onto the boat, he could not very well drive him out. Left with no alternative, Boya lifted a hand slightly and said, "You, my good man, need not stand on ceremony." He then told his page boy to bring a seat. The page boy put a small stool in a spot usually assigned to lower-ranking people. Disregarding the usual decorum due to a guest, Boya said to the woodcutter, pushing out his lips, "You may sit." By addressing the man simply as "you," he made no secret of his unwillingness to play the good host.

Without any of the usual obligatory words of demurral, the woodcutter sat down in a dignified manner.

Slightly annoyed that the man had sat down without saying any polite words, Boya refrained from asking the man's name, nor did he instruct the servants to serve tea. After sitting silently for quite some time, he spoke up out of curiosity, "So, you are the one who was listening to my music?"

"Yes, sir."

"Let me ask you something. Since you were listening to my playing, you must know something about the history of the zither. Who invented the zither? What good does the zither do?"

Before he had finished with his questions, the head boatman came in to report that, the wind being favorable and the moonlight as bright as day, they were ready to be on their way. But Boya said, "Wait a moment."

The woodcutter said, "I thank you, sir, for being so kind as to ask me a few questions, but if I ramble on too long, I'm afraid I will prevent you from taking advantage of the favorable wind."

Boya said with a smile, "I'm just not sure if you know anything about the zither. If what you say makes sense, I won't mind even losing my official title, let alone being delayed on my journey."

"In that case," said the woodcutter, "I will make bold to speak out of turn. The first zither was made by Fuxi.[3] He saw the essence of the five planets fly through the air and fall on a *wutong* tree.[4] Then a phoenix descended onto the same tree. The phoenix, the king of all birds, eats only bamboo seeds, perches only on *wutong* trees, and drinks only from sweet springs. Knowing that *wutong* provides good timber, Fuxi thought that a musical instrument made of wood containing cosmic essences would produce the most elegant music. And so he ordered that the tree be cut down.

"The thirty-three-foot-tall tree, in harmony with the thirty-three layers of heaven, was cut into three segments, representing heaven, earth, and people respectively.[5] Fuxi tapped the upper segment, but finding the sound too delicate and soft, he put it aside. He then took up the bottom segment, tapped it, and, finding the sound too coarse and thick, put it aside as well. When he tapped the middle segment, he discovered that the sound was neither too delicate and soft nor too coarse and thick. The timber was put into an ever-running stream to soak for seventy-two days, in harmony with the seventy-two divisions of the year.[6] When the time was up, it was taken out of the water, dried in the shade, and, on a chosen auspicious hour of an auspicious day, was made by Liu Ziqi, the master craftsman, into a musical instrument.

"Because it produced the kind of music heard only in the Jasper Pool, it was named the jasper zither.[7] It is three feet six and one-tenth inches long, in harmony with the three hundred and sixty-one degrees of the cosmic circumference; eight inches wide in front, in harmony with the eight solar terms of the year;[8] four inches wide at the back, in harmony with the four seasons; and two inches thick, in harmony with the two elements of heaven and earth. It has a Golden Boy head, a Jade Maiden waist,[9] a fairy's back, a dragon's pond, a phoenix's pool,[10] jade tuning pegs, and gold frets. The frets are twelve in number, in harmony with the twelve months. There is also another fret in the middle, which stands for the leap month. There were originally five strings, which, on a cosmic scale, stood for the five phases of metal, wood, water, fire, and earth, but on the zither itself they also represent the five musical notes.

"During the time of Yao and Shun, the five-string zither was played to accompany the singing of the poem 'The South Wind,' and peace reigned throughout the land.[11] Later, when King Wen of the Zhou dynasty was incarcerated in Youli

Prison, he added a string to his zither so as to enhance the dolefulness of the tone and express mourning for his son Boyikao. That added string came to be called King Wen's [lit. trans. of *wen* is "civilian"] string. Thereafter, King Wu of Zhou, while surrounded by singers and dancers between campaigns against King Zhou of the Shang dynasty, added another string to the zither to enhance the forcefulness of the tone. That string came to be called King Wu's [lit. trans. of *wu* is "military"] string. The zither with the original five strings plus the two added strings then became known as the Wen and Wu seven-stringed zither.

"As for the zither: there are six things to be avoided, seven situations in which it should not be played, and eight superior qualities that it alone possesses.

"What are the six things to be avoided? They are severe cold, scorching heat, strong winds, torrential rain, sudden peals of thunder, and heavy snow.

"What are the seven situations in which the zither should not be played? When there is a death, when other musical instruments are being played, when one is busy with miscellaneous things, when one has not washed oneself clean, when one is not properly attired, when no incense is being burned, and when no appreciative listener is present.

"What are its eight superior qualities? Well, in short, they are its delicacy, uniqueness, serenity, elegance, dolefulness, grandeur, sweetness, and lingering vibrations.

"When the zither is played to perfection, a roaring tiger that hears it will quiet down and a screaming monkey that hears it will stop its cries. This is what refined music can do."

Boya was impressed by the man's eloquence but thought he might have been merely reciting what he had learned by rote. But then another thought struck him, "Even if he memorized all this by rote, it's a very creditable effort. Let me test him further."

This time not addressing the man simply as "you" (*Now, watch how Boya gradually changes his tone.*), he asked again, "Since you, my friend, know so much about music, let me ask you another question. Once, when Confucius was playing the zither in a room, Yan Hui entered from outside. Puzzled when he detected a trace of a thought about killing in the rumbling notes, Yan Hui questioned Confucius about it. Confucius replied, 'A moment ago, when I was playing, I saw a cat chasing a rat. I hoped that the cat would get the rat and was afraid that it would miss its prey. And this thought about killing came through in the music.' This shows what a profound master of music the sage's student was. If I play the zither while thinking about something, would you, my friend, be able to guess what it is?"

The woodcutter replied, "I will 'try to surmise what is in another man's thoughts,' as is said in *The Book of Songs.* Please play something, sir, and I will try my best to guess. If I fail to guess right, please do not take offense."

Boya replaced the broken string and thought for a while before playing a few strains, thinking of high mountains. The woodcutter said in praise, "How beautiful! How majestic! You, sir, were thinking of high mountains."

Boya did not reply. After another few moments of concentration, he started playing again, this time thinking of flowing water. The woodcutter again broke into praises. "How beautiful! What a magnificent torrent! You, sir, were thinking of flowing water."

Astounded that the man had guessed right both times, Boya pushed the zither aside, stood up, and exchanged formal greetings as a host with his guest, Ziqi the woodcutter. (*According to* The Atlas, *there is a Boya Terrace in Haiyan County, Jiaxing Prefecture, Zhejiang. To one side of the terrace is the Listening to Zither Bridge. This could very well be the place where Zhong Ziqi listened to Boya play the zither. Generally speaking, stories are not accurate records of facts. Neither is this one. It proposes only to make the point that an appreciative friend is hard to come by.*)

"How discourteous of me!" Boya exclaimed over and over again. "Buried in the rock is a piece of fine jade. If people are judged only by their appearance, wouldn't many talents of the land go unrecognized? What, may I ask, is your honorable name?"

The woodcutter raised himself slightly from his seat and replied, "My surname is Zhong, my given name Hui, and my humble courtesy name Ziqi."

With hands respectfully folded before his chest, Boya said, "Please accept my greetings, Mr. Zhong Ziqi."

"May I ask your name, sir?" said Ziqi in his turn. "And where do you serve, sir?"

"My humble name is Yu Rui. I serve as an official in the court of the state of Jin. I am here in this country as an emissary."

"So, you are none other than His Honor Yu Boya himself."

Boya moved Ziqi to a seat reserved for a guest of honor, and he himself sat as the host at the head of the table. He then bade the page boy serve tea and, after tea, some wine.

"I may be a poor host, but let's have a chat over a cup of wine."

"What an honor for me," said Ziqi.

The page boy took away the zither, and the two men sat down for wine. Boya asked again, "Judging from your accent, I believe Mr. Zhong is a native of Chu, but where is your honorable residence?"

"Not far from here, in the Ma'an Mountains, there's a place called Village of Worthy Men. That's where my humble home is."

Boya nodded. "Truly a village where worthy men gather," he commented. "What is your occupation?"

"Nothing more than cutting firewood for a living."

Boya said with a smile, "Well, Ziqi my friend, this humble official shouldn't be speaking out of turn either, but with your ability, why not seek fame and glory and find a position in a royal court and a place in the annals of history? My humble opinion is that you should not waste your talents among woods and rivers in the company of woodcutters and herdsmen and end up rotting with the grass and the trees."

"To be honest," said Ziqi, "I have my aged parents to take care of, and I have no siblings to help me do it. So I will continue to cut firewood for a living until my parents live out the rest of their days. I cannot bring myself to exchange even one day of taking care of my parents with the highest official title in the land."

"Such great filial piety is quite exceptional," said Boya.

They drank a while longer, toasting each other by turns.

Ziqi never lost his composure, not when he was being insulted earlier, nor when he was treated with much respect (*Well-made comment.*), which gained him even more respect and affection from Boya.

"May I ask your age?" said Boya.

"I have frittered away twenty-seven years."

"This humble official is older by ten years. If Ziqi is not disdainful, I would like us to pledge brotherhood, to do justice to our appreciation of each other and our friendship." (*Who else would be willing to do this?*)

"You are quite mistaken, sir. You are a famous official in your country, whereas I, Zhong Hui, am but a lowly woodcutter in a poor village. How would I dare aspire to claim connections with you and make demands on your kind attention?"

"I may have acquaintances all over the land, but how many among them understand my heart? In my busy, mundane life as an official, I consider it my greatest fortune to get to know such a worthy man as you. If you think I judge people by wealth and status, you are not doing me justice!" Thereupon he bade the page boy build up the flame in the incense burner, light some joss sticks of superior quality, and, in that very cabin, the two men performed the eight-bow ritual of pledged brotherhood, Boya as the older brother and Ziqi the younger. They pledged to address each other henceforth as brothers and never to betray each other in life or in death.

The ceremony over, more wine was heated and served. Ziqi insisted that Boya take the seat of honor, a courtesy Boya did not decline. Cups and chopsticks changed places, and Ziqi left the guest's seat. Addressing each other as brothers, they went on talking. (*From discourtesy to suspicion, to trust, to affection, and eventually to inseparable devotion, the friendship of the ancients is truly unmatchable.*) Indeed,

You never tire of a guest who shares your mind,
Nor of one with an appreciative ear.

In the course of their animated conversation, the moon paled, the stars dimmed, and the first faint glow of dawn lit the eastern sky. All the boatmen rose, readied the ropes and the sails, and prepared to set sail. Ziqi stood to bid Boya farewell.

Offering a cup of wine to Ziqi, Boya held the latter's hand and said with a sigh, "My good brother, I met you too late in my life, and now we have to part in such haste!"

When Ziqi heard this, tears fell from his eyes into the cup in spite of himself. He finished the wine in one gulp, filled another cup with wine, and offered it to Boya in return. Neither of them could bear the thought of parting.

"I'm not ready to part with you yet, my brother," said Boya. "I would like to invite you to leave with me and then stay with me for a few days. Would that be agreeable to you?"

"It's not that I don't want to go, my brother," said Ziqi, "but I have my parents to look after. [As Confucius says,] 'While your parents are alive, do not travel far.'"[12]

"But you can go home, tell them about it, and come to visit me in Jinyang.[13] By telling them about it, you will be 'making your whereabouts known to them.'"[14]

"I don't want to promise lightly because I do not want to go back on my words later. If I give you my promise, I will certainly fulfill it. (*Words of* [illegible].) Should my parents not approve my request, I would only be giving you false hopes while you wait for me thousands of li away, and I would be committing an even greater wrong."

"What a true gentleman my good brother is! All right, then, I'll come to see you next year."

"When will you be arriving next year, my good brother?" asked Ziqi. "Tell me, so that I know when to wait for you."

Counting on his fingers, Boya said, "Yesterday was the Mid-autumn Festival. With daybreak, it's now the sixteenth day of the eighth month. My good brother, I will be coming to visit you on the fifteenth or sixteenth day of the second month of next autumn. If I fail to arrive by the twenty-first day of that month or by the last month of autumn, I'll be breaking my promise, and I'll be no gentleman." He then turned to his page boy and said, "Tell the scribe to write down in the engagement book my good brother Zhong's address and the date of my visit next year."

Ziqi said, "In that case, I will stand by the river to wait for you on the fifteenth and sixteenth days of the second month of next autumn. I will do so without fail. Now, it's already light. I should be going."

"Not so fast, my good brother," said Boya.

He bade the page boy bring over two ingots of gold, and without wrapping them, he held them in his hands and said, "My good brother, this is a small gift from me, to be used toward supporting your parents. Please don't think that this is inadequate for a scholar's parents." Ziqi did not think it appropriate to decline the offer, so he accepted the gift.

After another bow of farewell, he left the cabin with tears in his eyes. He picked up his carrying pole, put his cape and hat in the load, attached the ax to his waistband, walked up the gangplank, holding onto the handrail, and went ashore. Boya saw him off at the bow of the boat, and they bade each other a tearful farewell.

We shall say no more of Ziqi's return home for the moment but will continue our story with Boya, who sounded the drum for the boats to set sail. However beautiful the scenery along the river, Boya had lost all interest in sightseeing. All his thoughts were with the one who understood his music. Several days later, he left the boat and continued the rest of the journey on land. Wherever he stopped, he was provided with horse carriages for transportation, for local officials knew him to be a senior grand master in the state of Jin, not someone to be slighted. So he traveled in this manner all the way back to Jinyang, where he reported to the king about the mission, but of this, no more.

Time flew. Quite unnoticeably, autumn, winter, and spring went by, and summer rolled around. Ziqi was never absent from Boya's thoughts, even for one day. With the Mid-autumn Festival drawing near, he asked the king of Jin for leave to return to his hometown, and the king approved the request. Boya gathered his things together and went, as before, by river in a big detour. Once on board, he told the boatmen to tell him the name of every place where the boat was to moor. As coincidence would have it, exactly on the fifteenth night of the eighth month, the boatmen came to report, "We are near the Ma'an Mountains."

Vaguely recalling the place where the boat had moored last year when he met Ziqi, Boya told the boatmen to stop there, cast the anchor to the bottom of the river and drive in a wooden stake next to the shore so they could tie the boat to it. It was a clear night, and a moonbeam shone through the portiere of the cabin door. Boya had a page boy roll up the portiere and walked out to stand at the bow, where he gazed up at the handle of the Big Dipper. The vast expanse of the water, lit as bright as day, joined the sky at the horizon. His thoughts went back to this time last year when, with the rain just over and the moon shining brightly, he had met his true friend, and this happened to be a glorious night as well. His friend had promised to wait for him at the riverside, but why was there no trace of him? Could he have broken his promise?

After waiting for a while longer, he thought, "Ah, I know. There are so many boats coming and going, and I'm not in the one I had last year. How can I expect my brother to see me right away? Last year, my zither playing caught his attention. Tonight, let me play my zither again. When my brother hears it, he'll surely come to greet me." So thinking, he bade the page boy bring a table to the bow of the boat and put the zither on the table.

With incense burning and his seat in place, Boya opened the zither case, tuned the strings, and started playing, but the notes sounded mournful. He stopped. "Ah," he said to himself, "the notes are so mournful. This must mean that one of my brother's parents has passed away. Last year, he did say that his parents were quite advanced in years. Either his father or his mother must have died. Being the filial son that he is, he has his priorities and would rather break a promise to me than be remiss in his duties toward his parents. That's why he chose not to come. After daybreak tomorrow, I'll go up on the rocky shore and visit him at home."

He had the page boy take away the zither table and retired to his cabin for the night. But he was awake the whole night through, waiting for a daybreak that just would not come. As soon as the moon's shadow on the portiere vanished and the sun appeared at the top of the hills, Boya rose, straightened his clothes, told his page boy to follow him, and took out two hundred taels of gold. "My brother will need this for the funeral if he's in mourning," he said to himself.

In one jump, he landed on the rocks and began walking along a woodcutters' path, which took him to the mouth of a valley more than ten li away. He stopped and stood still.

"Why have you stopped, Master?" asked the page boy.

"There is one mountain to the south and another one to the north, and there is one road leading to the east and another one leading to the west. From the mouth of the valley, I can take either of these two thoroughfares, but I wonder which one leads to the Village of Worthy Men. Let's wait for someone who knows the area well and ask him for directions before continuing on our way."

Boya sat down on a rock to rest a little, and the page boy stood behind him. Soon, an old man came into view, walking slowly down the road on Boya's left-hand side. His beard flowing like threads of jade, his silvery hair tied up in a knot, he wore a bamboo hat and farmers' clothes. In his left hand he carried a rattan walking stick, and in his right hand, a bamboo basket. The old man advanced slowly in Boya's direction. Boya rose, adjusted his clothes, and stepped forward with a bow.

Unhurriedly, the old man put down the basket and returned the greeting. He raised his walking stick with both hands, saying, "What can I do for you, sir?"

"Could you tell me which of these two roads leads to the Village of Worthy Men?"

"Well, the two roads lead to two different villages, both called Village of Worthy Men. The one to the left is the Upper Village of Worthy Men, and the one to the right is the Lower Village of Worthy Men. They are separated by a thirty-li thoroughfare. You, sir, having just come out of the mouth of the valley, are at the very midpoint of the road, which stretches fifteen li to the east and fifteen li to the west. Now, which village do you have in mind?"

Boya was at a loss for words. He thought to himself, "My brother is an intelligent man, but how could he have been so careless? That night when we met, he should have told me clearly that there are two Villages of Worthy Men, one upper and one lower."

While Boya was in the midst of these reflections, the old man said, "You look thoughtful, sir. Whoever gave you directions must have spoken only about the Village of Worthy Men, without specifying whether it's the upper one or the lower one. That's why you, sir, are at a loss."

"Exactly," said Boya.

"There are about ten to twenty families in these two villages. They are mostly people who chose to live here in seclusion. I have been living in these mountains longer than others. As the saying goes, 'After thirty years of life in the same neighborhood, you form ties everywhere.' My neighbors are either my relatives or my friends. You, sir, must be visiting a friend. If you could tell me your friend's name, I'll tell you where he lives."

"I'm looking for the Zhong family."

At the mention of the Zhong family, tears fell from the old man's age-dimmed eyes. "Please visit any other household but the Zhongs."

"Why?" asked Boya, startled.

"Which member of the Zhong family do you want to see, sir?"

"Ziqi."

The old man burst into loud sobs. "Ziqi, Zhong Hui, was my son. On his way home, late on the fifteenth night of the eighth month last year, he met Mr. Yu Boya, senior grand master of the state of Jin. They chatted and found that they had much in common. Before he left, he was given two ingots of gold as a gift. My son then bought books and applied himself to his studies. I am such an old and stupid man that I did not stop him. By day, he chopped firewood and carried heavy loads; by night, he labored at his studies, exhausting himself both mentally and physically until he contracted consumption and died after a few months."

At these words, Boya felt as if his insides had split open. His tears flowing like a gushing spring, he let out a loud cry, fell to the ground by the cliff, and fainted.

Mr. Zhong Senior put his hands around Boya and, turning to the page boy, asked, "Who might this gentleman be?"

The page boy whispered into the old man's ear, "He is none other than Master Yu Boya."

"So, he is my son's good friend." So saying, Mr. Zhong Senior raised Boya up. Upon coming to, Boya sat on the ground, foaming at the mouth, beating his chest with both hands, and crying bitterly. "My good brother," he wailed, "last night when my boat cast anchor, I blamed you for having broken your promise. Little did I know that you had already become a ghost in the Nine Springs.[15] What a short life for a man of such talent!"

Mr. Zhong Senior wiped away his tears and said some comforting words.

When he finished weeping, Boya rose and saluted Mr. Zhong Senior anew, not as just any elderly man, but as an uncle, as if the two clans had been friends for generations.

"Uncle," said Boya, "is your son's coffin still at home or is it already buried in an open space?"

"It's a long story. My wife and I sat by his bedside before he died, and these were his last words: 'How long one gets to live is a matter dictated by divine will. While living, your son has failed to provide good support for you. After I die, please bury me by the river at the foot of the Ma'an Mountains because I wish to keep the promise I made to Yu Boya, grand master of Jin.' I have fulfilled my son's last wish. To the right of the path that you, sir, just traveled along is a mound of newly dug earth, and that is my son Zhong Hui's grave. Today being the one hundredth day after his death, here I am, carrying a string of paper coins to be burned at his grave. I certainly did not expect to run into you here, sir!"

"In that case," said Boya, "I'll go with you, Uncle, so that I can bow to the grave." So saying, he instructed the page boy: "Carry the bamboo basket for Grandpa."

Supporting himself on his walking stick, Mr. Zhong Senior led the way, followed by Boya, with the page boy bringing up the rear. Upon reentering the mouth of the valley, Boya saw that there was indeed a mound of newly dug earth to the left of the path.

Boya adjusted his clothes and bowed deeply. "My good brother," said he, "in life you were an intelligent man. After death, you will be a deity responsive to prayers. Accept this bow from me, your unworthy brother, as my final farewell!" After bowing, he burst into loud wails again, wails that caught the attention of people all around this hilly region. Passersby as well as local residents, hearing that a court minister was here to mourn Zhong Ziqi, flocked to the grave and vied with one another for a better view. (*How vulgar, these rubberneckers!*)

Since he had not brought any sacrificial items, Boya found that he lacked the means to express his condolences. He told the page boy to take the zither from its case and put it on the stone altar. He then sat cross-legged in front of the grave and tearfully began to play. Hearing the clear, ringing notes of the zither, the onlookers clapped their hands and, laughing, went their separate ways.

"Uncle," said Boya, "I am overcome by grief when I play the zither to mourn my brother, your son. Why did these people laugh?"

Mr. Zhong Senior replied, "These are rustic people with no understanding of music. They laughed because they thought music is for entertainment."

"I see. Do you, Uncle, know what I've been playing?"

"I was quite studious when I was young, but now that I'm old and all my five senses are working only half as well as they used to, I have long since lost my ability to appreciate music."

"In that case, let me recite to you the short lyrics that I improvised to express my condolences for your son."

"I would be pleased to hear them," said the old man.

So Boya began to recite:

"I met you last spring at the riverside;[16]
I am here again, but where might my true friend be?
The sight of your grave gives me pangs of grief,
Pangs of grief that bring tears to my eyes.
Happily I came, sadly I go;
Gloomy clouds gather on the riverbanks.

"Ziqi! Ziqi! My good brother!
Our bond was worth a thousand pieces of gold;
We had more to talk about than the world could hold.
After this song of mine comes to an end,
I shall never play the zither again;
For you dies this three-foot jasper zither!"

Boya drew a small knife from inside his robe, cut the strings of the zither, raised it with both hands, and smashed it with all his might against the stone altar. The zither broke into pieces, and the jade tuning pegs and gold frets scattered everywhere.

Aghast, Mr. Zhong Senior asked, "Why did you smash your zither?"

And this was Boya's reply:

"The zither smashed, the phoenix's tail grew cold.[17]
Now that Ziqi's gone, for whom can I play?
All call themselves friends and give you a smile,
But to find a true friend is all too hard."

Mr. Zhong Senior said, "I see. How sad! How sad!"

"Do you, Uncle, live in the Upper Village or the Lower Village?"

"My humble home is the eighth house down the road in the Upper Village. Why do you still want to know?"

"I am too grief-stricken to follow you home, Uncle, but I have here forty [*sic*] taels of gold, half of which I wish to give to you on behalf of your son, for your daily subsistence. The other half is for you to buy a few *mu* of land with which to earn enough income to pay for the annual sacrificial rites at your son's grave. After I return to my court, I will submit a memorial to ask for retirement. After I retire, I will come to the Upper Village of Worthy Men to escort you and my aunt to my humble home, where you will live for the rest of your lives. I am Ziqi, and Ziqi is me. (*Such is the friendship between the ancients. The rich, frivolous men of today should be shamed to death.*) Uncle, please don't reject me as an outsider." So saying, he had his page boy bring out the gold, and he himself handed it to Mr. Zhong Senior. Weeping bitterly, he prostrated himself on the ground. Mr. Zhong Senior returned the courtesy with a salute. Boya lingered for a while longer before they bade farewell to each other.

This story is titled "Yu Boya Smashes His Zither in Gratitude to an Appreciative Friend." A poet of later times had this to say in praise:

Snobs mingle with snobs,
Nor do scholars value true friends.
Boya's loyalty after Ziqi's death
Lives on in the story of the smashed zither.

2

Zhuang Zhou Drums on a Bowl and Attains the Great Dao

Wealth and rank are but short-lived dreams;
Fame and glory are but floating clouds.
Your kith and kin may not be forever,
For tender love may change to burning hate.

Do not put the golden cangue on your neck,[1]
Nor bind yourself with a jade padlock.
Free yourself from the desires of the mundane world;
Enjoy your days, and abide by your lot.

The above lyric poem to the tune of "The Moon over the West River" exhorts people to sever ties of misplaced love and set themselves free, although ties between father and son and those between brothers cannot be severed because they are branches on the same tree. Confucianism, Daoism, and Buddhism may have their differences, but none denies the virtues of filial piety and fraternal love. As for the children and grandchildren, well, you can't very well make sure that everything works out exactly as you wish for the generations that come after you. There is a saying that puts it well:

Your children will have their own share of fortune;
Don't serve them meekly like beasts of burden.

As for husband and wife, even though they are tied by a red thread around their waists and a red string around their ankles, they are, after all, separable, just as skin is from flesh.[2] As another saying puts it so well,

Husband and wife are birds in the same woods;
When day breaks at last, they fly their separate ways.

In our contemporary world, human relationships are at sixes and sevens. Although there isn't much aberration in the observance of relationships between father and son and between brothers, people do dote overly on their children, and yet, the love for children is far exceeded by that between husband and wife. Goodness knows how many husbands, wallowing in the pleasures of the boudoir and listening to nothing but their wives' pillow talk, have been bewitched by women and done things in violation of filial piety and fraternal love. Such men are by no means men of wisdom.

I now propose to tell a story about Zhuang Zhou drumming on a bowl.[3] I do so not with the intention of provoking marital strife but simply to exhort people to know what is good from what is stupid and what is true from what is false and to tone down the passion that consumes them most. Gradually, much to their own advantage, their six senses will be purified, and Daoist thoughts will arise in their minds.[4] A poet of olden times, watching a farmer transplanting rice seedlings, intoned a quatrain that is full of insight:

Green seedlings in hand, you plant them one by one;
Head bent down, you see the sky in the water.
The six senses cleansed, you acquire the Dao;[5]
To back up is in fact to move ahead.[6]

As the story goes, toward the end of the Zhou dynasty, there lived a very wise man named Zhuang Zhou, courtesy name Zixiu, who was a native of Meng County in the state of Song.[7] While serving as an official in Qiyuan,[8] he studied under a great sage, the founder of Daoism, named Li Er, courtesy name Boyang. Born with white hair on his head, the sage was called Laozi [The Old Master] by all and sundry.

In one of his frequent daytime naps, Zhuang Zhou dreamed that he was a butterfly merrily flapping its wings in a garden among flowers and grass. Upon waking up, he still felt that his arms were fluttering like wings. He found it all very strange, and from that time on, the dream often came back to him. One day, during a recess in a lecture by Laozi on *The Book of Changes,* he told his teacher about his dreams. Being the great sage that he was, Laozi knew all about Zhuang Zhou's previous, current, and future lives and revealed to Zhuang that in his previous life, when the primeval chaos was first separated into heaven and earth, he had been a white butterfly. (*How absurd! What a far-fetched explanation!*) [As Laozi recounted,] heaven begot water and then wood. When wood flourished and flowers thrived, the white butterfly gathered the essences of all the hundred flowers and, nourished by the vital elements of the sun, the moon, and the climate, attained eternal life, with its wings as big as wheels. Later, while playing at the Jasper Pool,[9] it stole some pistils from the immortal peach blossoms, for which it was pecked to death by the green phoenix, guardian of flowers serving the Queen Mother of the Immortals. But the dead butterfly's spirit did not dissolve. It was reincarnated into the body of Zhuang Zhou of the mortal world. It was with such extraordinary natural endowments, in addition to a firm determination to follow the Dao, that he was now studying, as a disciple of Laozi, the teachings of quiescence and nonaction.

Enlightened by Laozi's account of his previous life, Zhuang felt as if he had just woken up from a dream, and his arms began to feel airborne, like the fluttering wings of a butterfly. Thereafter, he looked upon the vicissitudes of life in this world as nothing more than floating clouds and flowing water and freed himself from the trammels of care and worry.

Knowing that Zhuang Zhou had attained enlightenment, Laozi imparted to him all the secrets contained in the five-thousand-character *Daodejing.*[10] Zhuang Zhou assiduously intoned and studied the text, and he devoted himself to the cultivation of the Dao until he acquired the magic of self-replication, body concealment, and metamorphosis. (*So, the magic of self-replication, body concealment, and metamorphosis is contained in the* Daodejing. *Too bad it's quite beyond the ken of average people.*)

Zhuang Zhou then resigned from his position as an official in Qiyuan, took leave of Laozi, and began a wandering life in quest of the Dao.

Though a disciple of the teachings of quiescence and purification of the senses, he had not cut himself off from the ties of marriage. In fact, he had been married to three wives, one after another. The first one had died from illness. As for the second, he had divorced her on grounds of misdemeanor. Our story is about the third wife, who was from the Tian clan that ruled the state of Qi.

During Zhuang Zhou's wanderings in the state of Qi, the patriarch of the Tian clan was impressed by Zhuang's character and married his daughter to Zhuang. Now this Tian-shi was more beautiful than the two previous wives—her skin as fair as ice and snow, and her movements as graceful as those of a fairy maiden. Though not a man who succumbed easily to feminine charm, Zhuang Zhou was very fond of her and was as happy in this union as a fish in water.

King Wei of Chu, upon hearing about Zhuang's reputation as a man of worth, sent a messenger to him with an offer of the position of chief of protocol. The messenger also brought gifts of two thousand taels of gold, a thousand bolts of colorful silk, and a carriage drawn by four horses. With a sigh, Zhuang Zhou said, "An ox raised for sacrificial purposes, finding itself covered with brocade and fed fine fodder, gloats over its glory when it sees a farm ox hard at work, plowing the fields. But by the time it is led into the temple to face the ax, how it wishes, in vain, to be a farm ox!" With that, he rejected the offer and went back with his wife to the state of Song, to live the life of a recluse in the Nanhua Mountains in Caozhou.[11]

One day, on a tour at the foot of a mountain, Zhuang Zhou saw one deserted grave after another. He said with a sigh, "As the saying goes, 'The old and the young become indistinguishable. The wise and the foolish go the same way.' Can a body be resurrected once it is laid in the grave?" After heaving sigh upon sigh, he resumed his steps. Suddenly, he saw a new grave, with the earth at the top still wet. A young woman in mourning white was sitting by the grave, fanning it with a white silk fan in her hand. (*How very strange!*)

Zhuang Zhou asked in amazement, "Who is the person buried in the grave, madam? Why are you fanning the earth? You must have a reason for doing so."

The woman did not stand up and kept fanning away at the grave, giving, in that sweet little voice of hers, a reply that defied all reason. Truly, it was enough to

> *Twist a thousand mouths from too much laughing,*
> *And put to greater shame the one saying it.*

This is what the woman said: "Buried in the grave are my dead husband's bones. He was very much in love with me and couldn't bear the thought of parting with me upon death. Before dying, he told me that should I want to remarry, I must wait until the funeral was over and the earth on the grave was dry. Because it takes time for the earth on a newly dug grave to dry, I'm fanning it to make it dry faster."

Smiling, Zhuang Zhou thought to himself, "What an impatient woman! And she had the nerve to say that they had been in love! What would she be up to if they had never been in love?" So thinking, he said, "Madam, nothing can be easier than drying some newly dug earth. Your arms are too soft and delicate. You just don't have enough strength for this fanning job. Please let my unworthy self lend you my arm." (*Naughty Mr. Zhuang!*)

It was not until this moment that the woman stood up. With a deep curtsy, she said, "Many thanks to you, sir!" With both hands, she passed the white silk fan to Zhuang Zhou, who then began to apply his Daoist magic. He fanned the top of the grave a few times in quick succession. Immediately, all the moisture evaporated and the earth dried up.

Radiant with smiles, the woman said, "Thank you, sir, for all this trouble." With her dainty hand, she took a silver hairpin from her temple and gave it along with the silk fan to Mr. Zhuang as tokens of her gratitude. Zhuang Zhou declined the hairpin but accepted the fan, and, merrily, the woman took herself off.

Zhuang Zhou returned home, feeling quite upset. Sitting in his room and looking at the silk fan, he intoned the following quatrain:

> *"If not so fated, lovers will never meet,*
> *But once they do, when will their cursed love end?*
> *Had you known that no love lasts beyond the grave,*
> *You would have cut off all love before your death."*

Hearing Zhuang Zhou's laments, Tian-shi walked up to him from behind to ask what it was all about. As he was a cultured gentleman, Mr. Zhuang was respectfully addressed by his wife as "sir." Tian-shi said, "What are you lamenting, sir? Where did you get this fan?"

Zhuang Zhou told her about the woman fanning the grave so that the earth would dry quickly and she could remarry. "She gave me this fan as a gift," he concluded, "to thank me for helping her fan the grave."

Tian-shi burst into righteous indignation. "What a bad woman!" she cried over and over again, her face raised toward the sky. Then she addressed Zhuang Zhou, saying, "Such a heartless woman! The world has hardly ever seen the likes of her!"

At these words, Zhuang Zhou intoned another poem:

> *"Before you die, they all profess wifely love;*
> *After you're gone, they all rush to fan the graves.* (Sheer exaggeration!)
> *You may draw dragons and tigers—*
> *But how do you draw their bones?*
> *You may know people's faces—*
> *But how do you know their hearts?"*

Tian-shi exploded with rage. As an old saying put it, "Resentment makes you renounce ties of kinship; rage makes you forget all rules of decorum." Carried away with anger, she cast all polite manners to the winds and spit into her husband's face, saying, "There are good people, and there are foolish people. How can you so lightly dismiss all women as being alike? Aren't you being unfair to good women just because of some bad ones? That was quite an offensive remark, you know."

"Don't talk so big," countered Zhuangzi. "If I, Zhuang Zhou, should unfortunately die, am I to understand that you, in your blooming youth, will be able to get through even three to five years of widowhood?"

Tian-shi shot back, "As the saying goes, 'A loyal minister serves only one sovereign; a chaste woman serves only one husband.' Have you ever seen a woman from a good family accept two offers of marriage and sleep in the beds of two households? If the misfortune you spoke of does befall me, I will never do anything so shameful, never for the rest of my life, let alone a mere three to five years! Even in my dreams I am something of a woman of moral rectitude!" (*There has to be something suspicious about those with clever tongues.*)

"You never can tell! You never can tell!" said Zhuang.

Tian-shi countered with this tirade: "Women of moral rectitude are superior to men. Now *you* are a heartless one. You took in another wife when your first wife died and then divorced the second one and took in a third. You assume that everyone else would stoop to your level. Now *I,* as a woman, am firmly committed to *the* one in my life, just as one saddle serves only one horse. How would I ever allow myself to be a subject of gossip and let future generations hold me up to ridicule? You certainly are not dying; what right do you have to accuse me so unjustly?" (*It was this last remark that gave Zhuangzi the idea.*) So saying, she snatched the silk fan away from him and tore it to pieces.

"All this anger is quite uncalled for," said Zhuang. "I only hope you'll be able to live up to your words." With that, the argument came to an end.

A few days later, Zhuang Zhou was suddenly taken ill, and he got worse day by day. To Tian-shi, who sat sobbing by his bed, he said, "Being as ill as I am, I'll soon be parted from you forever. Too bad the silk fan was torn to pieces the other day. If it were still here, wouldn't it come in handy when you want to fan the grave?"

"Don't be so suspicious of me, sir," said Tian-shi. "I'm an educated woman with an understanding of decorum. I swear that I have no other wish than to serve only one man until I die. If you don't believe me, I'm more than willing to die right here before your eyes, so that you'll know for sure that I mean what I say."

"Yes, now that I do see you as a woman of moral rectitude, I can rest easy in death." With these words, he stopped breathing.

Stroking the corpse, Tian-shi burst into loud wails. As was the usual practice in such situations, she went around asking for the neighbors' help in preparing the burial clothes, the coffin, and the funeral rites. Clad in mourning white from head to toe, she was truly distraught with grief and cried bitterly day and night. Memories of Zhuang's love so overwhelmed her that she lost all desire for food and sleep.

Some of the farmers in the neighborhood, knowing that this Mr. Zhuang was a recluse living in the mountains in retirement from the world of fame, came to express their condolences, but funeral ceremonies in those parts were by no means the grand events they were in the cities.

On the seventh day, there suddenly arrived a young scholar with a complexion as fair as if by powder and lips as red as if with rouge. A more handsome and dashing young man could hardly be found. Wearing a purple robe, a black hat, an embroidered waistband, and red boots, and followed by an old servant, he claimed to be a member of the royal house of Chu, here because Mr. Zhuang had, some years before, promised to take him on as a disciple. Upon learning that Mr. Zhuang had died, he said, "What a loss!" With that, he immediately took off his purple robe, had the servant take out a white robe from their luggage, and put it on. "Master Zhuang," he said, with four bows to the coffin, "though this disciple of yours is not predestined to benefit from your teachings face-to-face, I wish to keep vigil for you for a hundred days to fulfill our bond as teacher and student."

After another four tearful bows, he rose and asked to see Tian-shi, who declined this request at first.

"According to tradition," said the young man, "women do not avoid the presence of their husbands' close friends, let alone their husbands' students, and I was Mr. Zhuang's student."

Resignedly, Tian-shi went out of the hall of mourning, greeted the young man of Chu, and exchanged some amenities with him. The good looks of the young man stirred tender feelings in her. Too bad, she thought, that she had no excuse to get to know him better.

The young man said, "Though my teacher is gone, I admire him so much that I will never forget him. I'd like to stay in your house for a hundred days, partly to keep vigil over my deceased teacher's coffin and partly for an opportunity to read any writings he might have left behind, so that I may benefit from his teachings."

"Being a good friend of the family," said Tian-shi, "you are welcome to stay here for as long as you wish."

Right away, a meal was set out in the young man's honor. After the meal, Tian-shi offered him *The Book of Nanhua* by Zhuangzi and the five-thousand-character *Daodejing* by Laozi. The young man thanked her heartily.

The center of the mourning hall was occupied by the memorial tablet for the deceased, so the young man took up quarters in the left section of the hall. Every day, Tian-shi went to that section of the hall, ostensibly to mourn the deceased, but actually to strike up some conversation with the young man. Gradually, a kind of familiarity began to develop between them, with exchanges of significant glances in a passion that was quite beyond control. If the young man was in love, Tian-shi was doubly so. Luckily, they were living in secluded mountains where no tongue would wag even if some impropriety were committed. But regrettably for her, the death was still too recent, and a marriage proposal could hardly be initiated by a woman.

A few more days went by. It was now about half a month after Zhuangzi's death. The woman found her passion too fiery to control. Surreptitiously, she summoned the visitor's old servant into her room, where she served him good wine, said nice things to him, and then asked, calmly, "Is your master betrothed?"

"Not yet."

"What kind of woman does your master have in mind for a wife?"

"My master said," replied the old servant, a little under the influence of the wine, "that he would be most happy with someone as pretty as you are."

"Did he really say that? You're not lying?"

"How could an old man like me lie?"

"In that case, I'd like to ask you to be the matchmaker. If your master doesn't object, I will gladly serve him as a wife."

"My master has said to me that this would be a good marriage, but he was your deceased husband's student, so he's afraid people might talk."

"My deceased husband only promised that he would teach your master. That doesn't make your master his student. Also, we have few neighbors in these deserted mountains. Who will be talking? Grandpa, you must tactfully pull off this job. You'll surely be invited to the wedding feast."

The old servant gave his promise. He was on the point of leaving when the woman called him back and said, "If he agrees, come back to my room, regardless of the hour, and let me know. I will be waiting here for a reply."

After the old servant left, the woman waited expectantly. Dozens of times she peeped into the hall of mourning. How she wished she could tie a thin string around the dashing young man's shapely feet and pull him into her room for a tight embrace! (*What a vivid description of the woman's burning desires!*)

When dusk set in, the woman's impatience got the better of her. In the darkness, she walked into the hall of mourning and listened for movements in the left section of the hall. Suddenly, she heard a noise from the table with the memorial tablet. She gave a start, thinking that it must have been the dead soul manifesting its presence. She hastened into the inner room to get a candle. By the candlelight, she saw that it was the old servant lying stiff on the table in a drunken stupor. Not daring to scold him or wake him up, she had no choice but to return to her own room, where she passed a wakeful night, counting the hours that went by.

The following day, she saw the old servant pottering about without coming to her with a reply. Itching with suspense, she summoned the old man into her room again and asked him about the matter.

"Can't be done!" said the servant.

"Why not? Didn't you relay to him what I said last night?"

"I did, but my master does have a point. He said, 'The problem is not with her looks, of course. And, since I was never officially taken on as a student, my scruples in this connection can also be disregarded. But there are three concerns that prevent me from accepting her offer.'"

"What three concerns?"

"My master said, 'With that unlucky thing—the coffin—placed right in the middle of the hall, how can I bring myself to hold a wedding ceremony with her? And it's quite an unseemly sight, too. Second, Master Zhuang and she were a loving couple. Moreover, he was a famous man of virtue and wisdom. My learning is not anywhere near his level. I'm afraid that she would look down on me. Third, my luggage has not arrived yet. I'm here quite empty-handed and unable to pay for all the expenses of betrothal gifts, the wedding feast, and so forth. These are the three reasons why I'm saying no.'"

"But there's no need to worry about these three things," the woman rejoined. "The coffin isn't rooted to the ground, is it? At the back of the house, there's a vacant room in bad condition. I'll just have a few farmhands move the coffin there. So the first concern is taken care of.

"About the second concern, how was my deceased husband ever a famous man of virtue and wisdom? He had failed to run an orderly household; that's why he divorced his wife and came to be called a heartless man. King Wei of Chu heard of his undeserved reputation and, out of admiration, sent him lavish gifts and invited him to be prime minister, but he himself knew all too well that he wasn't qualified for the job, and that's why he took refuge in this place. ([Illegible] . . . *a hero. She belongs to the kind of people with a penchant for vicious slander. How pathetic!*) Some time ago, when he was walking alone at the foot of the hill, he saw a widow fanning her deceased husband's grave so that she could remarry after the earth dried up. Taking liberties with that woman, my husband grabbed her silk fan, fanned the grave for her, and then brought the fan back home. I tore it to pieces. With such a man who exasperated me like this just a few days before he died, what love was there to speak of? Your young master, as studious as he is, will surely go far. Moreover, as he is from a royal background and I am from the distinguished Tian family, we will be well matched in status. The very fact that he's now in this place means that this is a match made in heaven.

"As for the third concern, about expenses for betrothal gifts and the wedding feast, I will take care of everything. I have no need for betrothal gifts, and I can easily afford the feast. On top of that, I'll also give your master twenty taels of silver out of my own private savings for him to make new clothes. Now go again and tell him what I said. Today is a lucky day for a wedding. If he says yes, the wedding can be held this very evening."

The old servant took the twenty taels of silver and went to relay the message to his master, who resignedly gave his consent. When the old servant told the woman about this, she went wild with joy. With alacrity, she removed her white mourning garments, applied her makeup, put on brightly colored clothes, and told the old servant to engage farmhands in the neighborhood to carry the coffin containing Zhuang Zhou's body into the dilapidated room at the back of the house. The hall was then swept clean in preparation for the wedding feast. There is a poem that bears witness:

The pretty widow—how charming she looks!
The handsome young man—what a dashing flirt!
One saddle for one horse—whose words were they?
Her thoughts tonight—be wedded anew!

That night, the woman prepared the bridal chamber, and the hall of mourning was ablaze with lights. The couple—he wearing a hat and a robe, she in a brocade blouse and an embroidered skirt—stood by the nuptial candles, looking as resplendent as if made of jade and gilded with gold. After they made their ceremonial bows, they went lovingly hand in hand into the bridal chamber, where they drank the nuptial wine. They were heading for the bed, ready to undress for the night, when the bridegroom, his brows knit tightly in a frown, stopped short in his tracks and collapsed to the floor. His hands clutching at his chest, he complained of a sharp chest pain.

In her love for the young man, Tian-shi cast aside all the scruples of a newlywed. She held him in her arms, rubbed his chest, and asked him how he was feeling, but in his extreme pain, speech was beyond him. Foaming at the mouth, he was on the verge of death. The old servant cowered in fear.

"Have there been attacks like this before?" asked Tian-shi.

The old servant replied on his master's behalf, "Yes, frequently, once every year or two. There's no medicine for it, but there is one cure that works in no time."

"What is it?" Tian-shi asked eagerly.

"The physician of the royal family gave him a prescription that works wonders. As soon as he swallows the brains from a living human being with some warm wine, the pain goes away. (*Naughty! Naughty!*) Every time he had an attack like this, his father, the old prince, would ask for the king's approval to have a convict awaiting execution trussed up and killed in order to get his brains. But where to get a human being's brains in these mountains? Oh, he's going to die this time, for sure!"

"A living person's brains are certainly out of the question," said Tian-shi, "but will a dead man's brains do?" (*There she goes!*)

The old servant replied, "According to the physician of the royal family, within forty-nine days of death, the brains have not yet dried up and can be used for that purpose."

"My husband has been dead for only about twenty days. Why not open the coffin and take his brains?"

"But you, madam, may not be willing to do this," said the old servant.

"Your master and I are now husband and wife. A wife has the duty to serve her husband with every fiber of her being. Since I don't begrudge him anything I have, why should I deny him what a heap of dead bones can offer?"

So saying, she ordered the old servant to attend to the young man while she herself found a firewood ax. With the ax in her right hand and a lamp in her left, she went to the dilapidated room at the back of the house. She put the lamp above the coffin lid and, fixing her eyes on the head of the coffin, raised the ax with both hands and brought it down with all the force she could muster. How is it that a coffin yielded to a woman of little strength? Let me explain. Being a man who rose above worldly concerns, Zhuang Zhou had opted for a simple funeral with a coffin made of *tong*-wood planks only three inches thick. With one hack of the ax, there went one piece of wood. Another hack, and the lid of the coffin split open. Lo and behold! With a sigh, Mr. Zhuang pushed open what remained of the lid and sat up.

However ruthless of heart, Tian-shi was, after all, but a woman. She was so frightened that her legs gave way under her, her heart pounded, and the ax fell to the floor without her knowing it.

"Wife," said Zhuangzi, "help me get out."

The woman saw nothing for it but to help Zhuang out of the coffin. Holding the lamp, Zhuangzi led the way, and the woman followed him into the hall. Thinking that the young man of Chu was in the hall with his servant, she was breathless with fear. For each step forward, she took two steps back. Upon arriving in the hall, she saw that the decorations were still there, as splendid as before, but the master and servant were nowhere in sight. Though apprehensive, the woman felt relieved nonetheless and, trying to lie her way out of it, said to Zhuang, "Since you died, I've been grieving day and night. I heard a noise in the coffin just a moment ago, and, thinking of the many stories about resurrections of the dead in ancient times, I began to hope that you would also come back to life. That's why I hacked at the coffin with an ax. Thanks to heaven and earth, you did indeed come back to life! What a lucky woman I am!"

"I thank you, wife, for your kindness. I have one question, though. The mourning period isn't over. Why are you in a brocade blouse and an embroidered skirt?"

The woman again prevaricated, saying, "To open the coffin is a happy event. I didn't dare let my mourning clothes clash with the good luck. That's why I put on brocade and silk, for good luck."

"All right! All right! But why is the coffin not in the main hall but discarded in that miserable room? Don't tell me that's also for good luck!"

The woman was struck speechless.

At the sight of the fine spread on the feast table, Zhuang Zhou asked no questions but ordered that wine be heated and brought to him. Letting himself go, he filled his horn-shaped vessel to the brim and drank one vessel after another.

Lacking good sense, the woman still hoped to regain her husband's affection and resume their conjugal life. She positioned herself near the wine flask and, acting the part of a spoiled coquette and mouthing tender and sweet words, tried to coax Zhuang into going to bed with her.

In a state of drunkenness, Zhuang Zhou asked for paper and a brush-pen and wrote the following quatrain:

We have settled the debts of our cursed love;
Now you're eager to love, but I am not.
To be your husband again is perhaps
To bring your ax down on top of my head!

When the woman read these lines, shame was written all over her face. Speech failed her. Zhuang wrote another quatrain:

What love is there between husband and wife?
Drawn to another man, she forgets her own.
The coffin was barely closed when down came the ax;
She beats the woman who fanned the grave dry.

Zhuang said again, "Let me show you two men." The woman turned to look in the direction of Zhuang's pointing finger, and whom should she see but the young man of Chu and his old servant, walking into the room at a leisurely pace. She gave a start. Turning around, she found Zhuang Zhou gone. Turning back again, she realized that the young man and his servant were gone, too. In fact, there was no young man of Chu or his old servant. It was Zhuang Zhou who had assumed their forms, using his magic of self-replication and body concealment.

As if in a trance, the woman felt a burning shame. She took off her embroidered waistband and hanged herself from a rafter. Alas! She gave up the ghost, and this time, the death was for real.

Seeing that the woman was dead and gone, Zhuangzi untied the knot, took her down, and put her body in the broken coffin. With an earthen bowl in hand to serve as a musical instrument, he leaned against the coffin and began to sing, drumming away on the bowl to keep time. And this is what he sang:

"Nature unwittingly gave life to her and me,
I not her husband, she not my wife.
By chance we met and lived under one roof;
When the hour comes, we unite, we part.
The unkind shift their love when their spouses die;
The truth laid bare, death is the only choice.

In life, she got to pick and choose;
In death, she returned to the void.
She mourned me by wielding the mighty ax;
I mourn her with this little song of mine.
The sound of the ax brought me back to life.
Do the notes of this song fall on her ears?
Well! Let me smash the bowl and stop beating time.
Who is she? And who am I?"

After the song, he intoned a quatrain:

"When you died, I buried your remains;
When I died, you married someone else.
If last time I had really died,
What a farce it all would have been!"

With a hearty laugh, he smashed the bowl and lit a fire that spread from the main hall to the other rooms and burned the whole house down. The coffin was also reduced to ashes. Only the *Daodejing* and *The Book of Nanhua* were indestructible. They were picked up by some local resident in the mountains and were passed down to this day. Zhuangzi spent his time wandering over the length and breadth of the land and never married again. By some accounts, he followed Laozi after meeting him at the Hangu Pass, whereupon he acquired the Dao, and became an immortal.[12] There is a poem that says,

Wu Qi the wife-killer should have known better;[13]
Xun Can's deep grief is just as laughable.[14]
Follow the example of bowl-beating Zhuang.
How free from care! How free from restraints!

3

Three Times Wang Anshi Tries to Baffle Academician Su

The sea turtle scorns the frog in the well;
The roc wings its way around the heavens.
For every smart one, there's someone smarter;
Never be smug and sing your own praises.

The four lines above exhort people to be modest and respectful of others and to guard against conceit. The ancients put it well: "Conceit spells loss; modesty brings benefit." There is also a proverb about four things that one should never do to an extreme. What are they?

Power should not be exercised to the utmost;
Fortune should not be enjoyed to the utmost;
Advantage should not be taken to the utmost;
Clever brains should not be racked to the utmost.

Consider how the powerful and influential people of today, instead of performing good deeds, often go wherever their whims and impulses lead them and bring affliction to other people. Seeing that others resignedly keep them at a distance out of fear, much as one would avoid going near poisonous snakes and ferocious beasts, they brim over with smugness, believing themselves to be the winners. Little do they know that there is a time when even the most furious tidal waves in the eighth month die down. Taking advantage of the favorable wind, they ride the surging waves in full sail over dangerous shoals. What a thrill it is! But they never give a thought to the fact that it is easier to go than to return.

In olden times, King Jie of the Xia dynasty and King Zhou of the Shang dynasty, Sons of Heaven though they were, ended up in disgrace.[1] One was banished to Nanchao [in present-day Chao County, Anhui], and the other was executed and his head was paraded on a Taibai banner. What crimes did Jie and Zhou commit? For the most part, they took advantage of their exalted positions to tyrannize the lowly and used their might to bully the weak. In short, they abused power. Had Jie and Zhou been commoners, would they have done so many evil deeds? (*Sound argument.*) That is why the proverb says that power should not be exercised to the utmost.

How do you explain the line "Fortune should not be enjoyed to the utmost?" Well, as is often said, "Take good care of your clothes, and you shall have clothes aplenty. Waste not your food, and you shall have food galore." Another proverb says, "Having lived out your span of life, you die; having used up your means, you perish." In the Jin dynasty, there was a certain Grand Commandant Shi Chong, who, in a competition with Wang Kai, an imperial kinsman, to show off their wealth, had pots washed with wine, generated heat with candles instead of firewood, and erected a brocade wall that stretched for fifty li. Even the lavatories were embellished with satin and silk gauze curtains that gave off a fragrance that assailed the nostrils. The servants and page boys were dressed in clothes made of asbestos fabric so expensive that one article of clothing cost a thousand pieces of gold. Concubines were bought at about ten bushels of pearls each. Later, Shi Chong died at the hands of King Lun of Zhao, his head severed from his body. This was divine retribution for his excessive enjoyment of his good fortune.[2]

What about the line "Advantage should not be taken to the utmost?" Well, if a merchant made a calculation error in his own favor, he may very well smile with delight, but he may not know that the error can cause a lowly peddler and his family to go hungry. And how much good does it do to gain such petty advantages anyway? A poet of olden times had this to say about taking advantage of others:

I will use your quilts as if they were mine;
At my disposal your blankets will also be.
When you have money, I'll help you use it;
If I run out of money, I will use yours.
On my way uphill, your hands support my feet;
On my way downhill, I lean on your shoulders.
If I have a son, he marries your daughter;
If you have a daughter, she sleeps by my side.
If you keep these words, I'll die after you;
If I break my words, you'll die before me.

If this advice is put into practice, everyone will want to follow suit. What fool would obligingly be taken advantage of? But, unbeknownst to you, your momentary gain will compromise your fortune and shorten your span of life. Therefore, Buddhism teaches that to suffer even the least bit of loss is to be blessed with boundless fortune in return. There is a poem in testimony:

You rejoice over every petty gain;
You grieve when things go against your plan.
If no gains and no losses,
Then no joys and no sorrows.

Storyteller, you've explained the first three lines well enough, but as for the last line, a clever head is really more than anything one could wish for. Why can't clever brains be racked to the utmost?

Well, there are, in this world, more things than you can ever see, more books than you can ever read, and more truths than you can ever understand. It is better to appear less smart than you are than the other way around. Let me now tell a story of a man who was the smartest man there ever has been. For all his intelligence, however, he had his few moments of foolishness and left us with this jewel of a story—a story that will serve as a lesson for all young men who are inclined to boast about their talent. Who was this most intelligent man?

He was a master of poetry and prose,
Full of humor and good at solving riddles.
If not another Confucius reborn,
He was surely a Yan Hui come back to life.[3]

As the story goes, during the reign of Emperor Shenzong [r. 1068–85] of the Song dynasty, there was a famous scholar by the name of Su Shi [1037–1101], courtesy name Zizhan, who also called himself Dongpo [Eastern Slope]. A native of Meishan in Meizhou, Sichuan, he made a name for himself by passing the imperial examinations on his first try and attained the rank of Academician in the Hanlin Academy. A highly gifted man, he was able to memorize a passage verbatim after a single reading and to speak as elegantly as a master of literature writes on paper. With the romantic inclinations of Li Bai and a mind sharper than that of Cao Zhi, he worked under Prime Minister Wang Anshi, who later came to be enfeoffed as the duke of Jing.[4] Wang Anshi had a high regard for Su's talent, but Su Dongpo, made presumptuous by his own cleverness, heaped scornful remarks on the prime minister.

Prime Minister Wang had written a book titled *Etymology,* in which he gave one definition to each character. About the character *po* [slope], as in the name Su Dongpo, the definition given was that *po,* consisting of the left radical "earth" and the right radical "skin," was "the skin of earth." Dongpo commented with a grin, "By the prime minister's logic, the character *hua* [slippery], consisting of the radical 'water' and the radical 'bone,' means nothing less than 'the bone of water'!"

One day, Wang Anshi further explained that the character *ni* [salamander], composed of the radicals "fish" and "son," meant "small fish," that the character *si,* composed of "horse" and "four," meant a team of four horses, and that the character *can* [silkworm] was made up of the upper radical "sky" and the lower radical "insect." He concluded that the ancients had created new characters by grouping meaningful radicals together.

At this point, Dongpo folded his hands respectfully in front of his chest and said, "There is indeed a reason why the character *jiu* [turtledove] consists of the radicals 'nine' and 'bird.'"

The prime minister trustingly asked to be enlightened.

Dongpo replied, all affability, "*The Book of Songs* says, 'On the mulberry perch chirping turtledoves,[5] / Seven of which are little fledglings.' So the seven little ones plus the mom and the dad do make nine!" (*Indeed as flippant as he was said to be!*)

Wang Anshi fell silent. Displeased by Su Shi's flippancy, Wang demoted him to the post of prefect of Huzhou. Truly,

A big mouth is the source of all trouble;
A glib tongue is to blame for all sorrows.

When his three-year term of office came to an end, Dongpo went back to the capital and found lodging in the Great State Councillor Monastery. He recalled how he had offended the prime minister years before and knew that he had only himself to blame. As the saying goes, "Before you go to see the emperor, you should first visit the prime minister." Carrying his résumé and visiting card, which he had told his attendants to prepare for him, he mounted his horse and headed for Prime Minister Wang's residence.

About a stone's throw from the Wang mansion, Dongpo dismounted and walked up to the gate. Seeing many officials standing at the gate, he raised a hand and asked, "Gentlemen, may I ask if the prime minister is in?"

The custodian stepped out and replied, "My master is taking a nap. Please sit in the custodian's room for a while." So saying, he had a servant put a recliner in the room. Dongpo sat down, leaving the door ajar.

A few moments later, a young man of about twenty years of age in a servant's big horsehair hat and a casual blue silk robe emerged from the house and strutted importantly down the steps. All the officials bowed and made way for him. After the young man had gone off in a westerly direction, Dongpo sent his servant to ask who that man was. The servant came back with the answer that the young man, named Xu, was an attendant in the prime minister's study.

Dongpo did recall, from three years before, a certain Xu Lun employed in the study, a boy who had gained much favor with the prime minister. Twenty years old now, wearing a hat befitting his age, he still looked the same as before. Dongpo said to his servant, "Well, since that's Mr. Xu, go after him quickly and ask him to come back here."

The servant ran as fast as his legs could carry him. When he caught up with the young man, he dared not call out from behind but took a few more hurried steps forward, shot past the young man, and then stopped in his tracks right there on the street, his hands respectfully at his sides. "Sir," he addressed the young man, "I am an attendant of Master Su of Huzhou Prefecture. Master Su is now in the custodian's room and wishes to have a word with you."

"Is it Master Su with a beard?" asked Xu Lun.

"None other."

Being the romantic scholar that he was, Dongpo was all geniality to everyone he met and was on quite good terms with Xu Lun, having sometimes given the young man gifts of fans with his handwriting on them. So at the name of Academician Su, Xu Lun smiled and turned back.

The attendant reached the custodian's room first and reported that Mr. Xu was coming. Upon entering the room, Xu Lun made as if to drop to his knees, but Dongpo held out his hands and stopped him. Now, this Xu Lun, being in charge of the prime minister's private study in the mansion, was someone to whom important officials from other places sent gifts and presented visiting cards when they asked to see the prime minister. So why would he want to kneel in Master Su's presence? It was because Master Su had been a regular visitor in the prime minister's mansion for so long that Xu Lun, who had been accustomed to serving him tea and waiting on him in the study, looked on him as an old master and could not very well put on airs the moment they met. (*Good analysis.*)

Out of consideration for the young man's pride, Master Su held him and said, "Mr. Xu, don't stand on ceremony with me."

"A custodian's room is no place for you," said Xu Lun. "Please go inside and have some tea in the east study." The east study was where the prime minister received students and close friends.

Xu Lun led Master Su into the east study, offered him a seat, and had a page boy serve tea.

"Master Su, I have to run an errand for my master to get some medicine at the medical bureau. I won't be able to wait on you here. What's to be done?"

"Please go ahead and do whatever you need to do."

After Xu Lun left, Dongpo looked around the room and saw that the bookshelves along the four walls were all locked and on the desk there were only a brush-pen and an ink slab. He opened the lid on top of the ink slab and found the slab to be a green one made in Duanxi [present-day Zhaoqing, Guangdong]. A splendid ink slab it was. On it, there was still some wet ink. He was about to close the lid when his eyes caught the corner of a piece of paper sticking out from underneath. Lifting the ink slab, he saw that it was a folded piece of white writing paper. He picked it up and found it to be an unfinished poem with only two lines. Titled "Ode to the Chrysanthemum," it was in the prime minister's handwriting.

Dongpo said to himself with a smile, "As the proverb says, 'A scholar who has been away for three days must be looked at in a different light.' Back in the days when I was serving in the capital, that old man was able to write thousands of words as fast as his brush-pen could go without even pausing for reflection. How things have changed in three years! Like the poet Jiang Yan [444–505], whose talent ran out in his old age, he can't even finish a poem now." After reading the two lines, he cried out, "Even these two lines are sheer nonsense!" What were these two lines?

The west wind swept through the garden last night,
Gilding the ground with petals of yellow.

Why did Dongpo say these two lines were sheer nonsense? Well, the wind of each of the four seasons has its own specific name. The wind of spring is "the gentle breeze," the wind of summer is "the southeasterly breeze," the wind of autumn is "the metal wind," and the wind of winter is "the north wind." The four names match the four seasons. The first line of the poem begins with mention of the west wind. Now, the west is represented by metal [one element of the five phases, which are metal, wood, water, fire, and earth], and the metal wind is the wind of autumn. When it starts to blow, the leaves of the *wutong* trees turn yellow, and flowers wither and fall. The second line says "Gilding the ground with petals of yellow." The "petals of yellow" are an obvious reference to chrysanthemums, which bloom in late autumn, and match the phase of fire. Defying autumn frost, the chrysanthemums survive the longest. However withered they become in the end, the petals do not fall. Isn't it a mistake to say that, swept by the wind, they are "gilding the ground"?

Quite carried away by his poetic mood, Dongpo took up the brush-pen, dipped it in the ink, and wrote two finishing lines in the same rhythm.

In autumn, flowers don't fall as in spring,
A fact for the poet to ponder.

(These two lines were actually written by Ouyang Xiu to make fun of Wang Anshi.[6] *The storyteller is transplanting them to this story and falsely attributing them to the great Su Dongpo.)*

After writing the two lines, Dongpo began to regret what he had done. "If the old man comes here to receive me, he'll see what I've written. It will be a breach of etiquette if I, a younger man, bandy words with him, face-to-face. But if I slip the sheet of paper into my sleeve and leave no trace of it, I'm afraid that when he finds it missing, Xu Lun will be in trouble." Without any idea as to the best course of action, he resignedly folded the sheet of paper as before, put the ink slab over it, closed the lid, and walked out of the study.

At the gate, he handed his résumé and visiting card to the custodian, saying, "When the prime minister comes out, tell him that Mr. Su waited for him for quite a while. Having just arrived in the capital, I haven't had time to get my documents ready. I'll come again tomorrow after I submit my documents to the morning court session." With that, he mounted his horse and returned to his lodgings.

Soon thereafter, the prime minister emerged from the mansion. Though the custodian had received instructions from Master Su, he did not bother to relay the latter's message because Master Su had not given him a gift. He just gave the prime minister Master Su's résumé and visiting card and showed him the visitors registration book. His mind preoccupied by the unfinished poem on chrysanthemums, the prime minister did not look at what he thought were some routine documents.

It so happened that, at this moment, Xu Lun came back from his errand. The prime minister had Xu take the medicine to the east study, while he himself followed. After he sat down, he lifted the ink slab and took up the poem. After one look, he asked Xu Lun, "Who has been here?"

Dropping to his knees, Xu Lun said, "Master Su of Huzhou Prefecture was here to see you."

Now recognizing Academician Su's handwriting, the prime minister thought to himself, without saying anything out loud, "That little beast Su Shi is as flippant as ever, not yet subdued by the setbacks in his career! With his limited talent and learning, how dare he make fun of me? At tomorrow morning's court session, I'll submit a memorial to the emperor and have this man stripped of all official posts!" Then a second thought struck him. "Wait! He is not really to blame, because he doesn't know that chrysanthemums in Huangzhou [in present-day Hubei Province] do shed their petals." So thinking, he had Xu Lun bring the list of post vacancies in Huguang.[7] Checking for vacancies in Huangzhou Prefecture, he found that there was only a vacancy for a vice-commissioner of military training [a nominal post with no power]. He made a mental note of this before ordering Xu Lun to post the poem on a pillar in the room.

At the court session the following morning, he told the emperor privately that Su Shi, of inadequate learning and ability, should be demoted to the position of vice-commissioner of military training in Huangzhou. All the other officials who had come to the court for reappointments readily accepted their promotions, demotions, or removals from office. Su Shi was the only one full of resentment. Even though he knew all too well that the prime minister was seeking revenge on account of the poem and abusing his power because of a personal grudge, he could not do otherwise than mouth some obligatory words of gratitude to the emperor.

Back in the dressing room of the court, he had just removed his ceremonial robe when an attendant called out, "The prime minister is leaving the court!"

Dongpo went out the door to pay his respects. The prime minister, sitting in his sedan-chair, raised a hand and said, "Join me for lunch." Dongpo dutifully accepted the offer.

Upon returning to his lodgings, he sent his attendants and his butler, who had followed him from Huzhou, back to Huzhou to escort his family to Huangzhou, where his new post was to be. A little after eleven o'clock, Dongpo, wearing a white robe and a belt with decorations made of rhinoceros horn and equipped with a visiting card and a new résumé listing his new post in Huangzhou, rode to the prime minister's mansion for lunch. Upon being notified by the custodian, the prime minister said, "Invite him in."

In the main hall, the prime minister received Dongpo as he would a student. After the order for tea was given, the prime minister said, addressing him by his courtesy name Zizhan, "Your demotion to Huangzhou was the emperor's idea. Much as I wished to help, there was nothing I could do. You didn't blame me unjustly, did you, Zizhan?" (*Those wearing officials' gauze caps do make a habit of lying.*)

"How would your humble student dream of nursing a grudge against the prime minister? I know the limits of my learning and abilities."

The prime minister said with a laugh, "You are a great talent all right, but in Huangzhou, if you have a leisurely moment or two, you will do well to further your studies and broaden your knowledge." (*Doesn't that remark make your blood boil?*)

Now, Dongpo was a man who had read tens of thousands of books and was endowed with the talent of one thousand people put together. Why would he need advice to further his studies and broaden his knowledge? What more books were there for him to read?

"I thank you, sir, for your advice," said Dongpo, inwardly more infuriated than before.

The prime minister being a frugal man, the lunch consisted of nothing more than four dishes, three cups of wine, and just enough rice to be picked up at one time with a pair of chopsticks.

When Dongpo bid him farewell, the prime minister walked him out as far as the eaves of the house and, holding his hands, said, "In my diligent studies in younger days, I contracted an illness that has come back to me in my old age. The imperial physician says that the problem is caused by excessive phlegm and internal heat. I've been taking medicine, but the medicine only alleviates the symptoms without effecting a thorough cure. Yangxian tea is my only hope for a cure.[8] Whenever tributes of Yangxian tea are offered to the court, the emperor kindly passes them on to me. I asked the imperial physician about the correct way to make the tea, and I was told that I must use water from the middle gorge of the Three Gorges of the Yangzi River in Sichuan. I have tried several times to send someone there to fetch the water, but it never worked out. The messengers might not have really made an effort. Now you, Zizhan, are a native of that region. If, in your travels to visit your parents, you could fill a jar with water from the middle gorge and send the jar to me, I will be most grateful to you for prolonging my life."

Thus instructed, Dongpo went back to the Great State Councillor Monastery. The following day, he went to the court to bid farewell and left the capital for Huangzhou, traveling by day and by night.

Having heard of Dongpo as a famous scholar and a demoted member of the Hanlin Academy, all the Huangzhou prefectural officials went quite a distance from the city gate to welcome him. An auspicious day was then chosen for his inauguration. His family arrived more than a month later.

In Huangzhou, Dongpo developed a friendship with a certain Chen Jichang, a native of Sichuan. He spent his time touring the mountains and rivers, drinking wine, and composing poems, without doing a stroke of work on military and civil affairs.

Time flew. Almost one year elapsed. After the Double Ninth Festival, a strong wind rose and lasted for several days.[9] One day, after the wind had subsided, Dongpo was sitting alone in the study when a thought struck him. "The yellow chrysanthemums that the abbot of Dinghui Monastery gave me have been planted in the backyard. Why don't I go take a look?" Before he had time to take one step, Chen Jichang came in. Overjoyed, Dongpo took him to the backyard to view the chrysanthemums. Upon reaching the chrysanthemum arbor, they saw that the ground was covered with golden chrysanthemum petals and the stems were bare, without a single petal left on them. Dongpo was aghast. For a good while, he stood transfixed in speechless amazement.

"Zizhan," said Chen Jichang, "what made you so startled when you saw the fallen chrysanthemum petals?"

"Listen to this, Jichang: I thought chrysanthemums usually wither and rot away without shedding their petals. Last year, in Prime Minister Wang's residence, I saw two lines that he had written, saying, 'The west wind swept through the garden last night, / Gilding the ground with petals of yellow.' Believing that the old man was mistaken, I finished the quatrain with two lines saying, 'In autumn, flowers don't fall as in spring, / A fact for the poet to ponder.' Well, what do you know! Chrysanthemums in Huangzhou do shed petals! So it was to make me witness this that the old man demoted me to Huangzhou!"

Chen Jichang said with a laugh, "The ancients put it well:

"Whatever you know, keep your mouth shut;
Whenever talked to, just nod your head.
If you don't even have to give a nod,
Your life will be free from worry and care."

Dongpo continued, "When I first learned about my demotion, I thought the prime minister was abusing his power to avenge himself on me because I pointed out his mistake. But as it turned out, he was right and I was wrong! Even those of true learning and insight, not to mention other people, can make mistakes. We must remember not to criticize or laugh at people too rashly. It's indeed a case of 'A fall into the pit, a gain in your wit.'" He then ordered that wine be served and sat down with Chen Jichang on the flower-strewn ground.

In the course of their drinking, the gatekeeper came to announce, "Prefect Ma is on his way here for a visit."

"Turn him away!" said Dongpo. That day, the two men drank and chatted until late in the evening.

The next day, Dongpo wrote a visiting card and went to see Prefect Ma to return the courtesy. The prefect stepped out of the house to greet him and then led him into a back hall, for prefectural yamens at that time did not have separate guest houses. After they took their seats as guest and host, tea was served. Then Dongpo related how, in the prime minister's residence the year before, he had made a mistake in a poem about chrysanthemums and thereby offended the prime minister.

With a smile, Prefect Ma said, "When I first came here, I didn't know either that chrysanthemums in Huangzhou shed petals. I didn't believe it until I saw it with my own eyes. Clearly, the prime minister is a very knowledgeable man who knows all there is to know under the sun. It was in a momentary lapse that you, Academician Su, made a mistake. It might be worth your while to go to the capital to apologize to the prime minister. His anger will surely change to delight."

"I do wish to go, but there's no good reason for making the trip."

"I have something coming up that might be of help to you, but I'll have to ask a favor of you," said the prefect.

Dongpo asked what it was.

The prefect replied, "As a rule, a local official is sent to the capital each winter solstice with a message of greetings. If you don't find this mission too trivial, it would give you a good reason for going to the capital."

"Thank you so much, sir, for being so thoughtful. Yes, I'll be glad to take on the mission."

"But I'll have to bother you with the writing of this message, Academician Su."

Dongpo agreed.

Back in his own residence after taking leave of Prefect Ma, Dongpo remembered that the prime minister had asked for water from the middle gorge of the Three Gorges. Full of resentment at the time, he had totally forgotten about the request. Now, he made up his mind to render his service so as to make amends for his insolence. (*Sensible people correct their mistakes. They know better than to persist in willful ways.*) But this was not a matter to be lightly entrusted to other people. Since his wife was ill and growing nostalgic for their native place, he thought he might as well avail himself of the prefect's kind offer, ask for leave at the same time as the mission, and escort his family back to Sichuan to get water from the gorge, thus fulfilling two obligations at the same time. Because Huangzhou and Meizhou are separated by the Yangzi River, the journey to Meizhou, his native place, would take them right through the Three Gorges. Which three?

Xiling Gorge, Wu Gorge, and Gui Gorge.

Xiling Gorge is the upper one, Wu Gorge the middle one, and Gui Gorge the lower one. Xiling Gorge, to the east of Kuizhou Prefecture [in what is now Fengjie County, Sichuan], is also called Qutang Gorge, and between its two cliffs flows the Yangzi River. With the colossal Yanyu Rock serving as a gate at the mouth of Qutang Gorge, the Three Gorges are also called the Three Gorges of Qutang.[10] Stretching for more than seven hundred li, the section of the Yangzi River that flows between the Three Gorges is flanked on both sides by continuous, undulating, overlapping chains of hills that block out the sky and the sun. The wind blows not horizontally but vertically.

Kuizhou being at the midpoint in the more than four-thousand-li journey from Huangzhou to Meizhou, Dongpo thought to himself, "If I take the family all the way to Meizhou, the round trip will be almost ten thousand li, which means the delivery of the winter solstice greetings will be delayed. Why don't I take care of official business and family duties at the same time? I can take the family to Kuizhou by land and let them go to Meizhou from there on their own while I take a boat at Kuizhou, travel down the gorges, collect some water at the middle gorge, and return to Huangzhou before I head for the Eastern Capital.[11] Wouldn't that be nice on both counts?"

Having thus drawn up his plans, he explained them to his wife, packed, and took leave of Prefect Ma. He had a tablet hung over the gate of the yamen, saying that the vice-commissioner of military training was on leave. On a chosen auspicious day, he prepared the means of transportation and assembled the servants, and the whole family started on their journey. It was an uneventful journey. It hardly needs to be said that

After Yiling, they came upon Gaotang.
Then, the footman's good news: Kuizhou was near.

After arriving in Kuizhou, Dongpo said good-bye to his wife and told his competent butler to take good care of the mistress the rest of the way. He himself hired a boat and rode downstream from Kuizhou.

Yanyu Rock, you see, stands all by itself at the mouth of the gorges, submerged in water in the summer and rising from the water again at the onset of winter. Because boatmen are not sure which way to go when the rock is submerged in water, the rock is also called the Rock of Hesitation. There is a saying that goes:

With Hesitation big as an elephant,
Do not go up the Qutang Gorges.
With Hesitation big as a horse,
Do not go down the Qutang Gorges.

Dongpo had set out after the Double Ninth Festival, and it was now late autumn, just before the onset of winter. It being a leap year with an extra eighth month and therefore another month before the end of autumn, the water was still high. Going upstream was much more time-consuming than going downstream. On his way to Kuizhou, Dongpo had chosen to travel by land instead of by boat because he had been afraid that the journey would take too long, but now that he was riding downstream, the boat glided rapidly down the river with the greatest ease. Impressed by the sight of the cliffs towering over the narrow strip of water, Dongpo waxed poetic, but his attempts at composing an "Ode to the Three Gorges" were unavailing. He sat by the table while trying to compose the poem, but, tired from successive days of travel, he ended up drifting off to sleep without leaving instructions for the boatmen to collect the water. (*Writing makes a mess of things.*)

By the time he woke up and asked where he was, they had passed the middle gorge and were at the lower gorge. "I need to collect water from the middle gorge," he said. "Turn the boat back, quick!"

The boatman said, "Sir, with the Three Gorges linked together, the water is as rapid as a waterfall, and the boat goes as fast as an arrow. If we turn the boat back, it will be going upstream, and we can make only a few li a day, however hard we try."

Dongpo reflected a long while before saying, "We can anchor here. Are there people living around here?"

"It's impossible to anchor the boat by the cliffs of the two upper gorges, but at Gui Gorge, the hills and the river are not as rough, and there's a town just a short distance from the shore."

Dongpo ordered that the boat be anchored and said to his servant, "Go up the shore and if you can find someone old and knowledgeable, bring him back here, but don't say anything that might alarm him."

Thus instructed, the servant went ashore. A short while later, he brought back an old man.

"Please accept a deep bow, sir, from a local resident," said the old man.

Dongpo said to him reassuringly, "I'm just a traveler passing by here, not some official with local jurisdiction. I just want to ask you one thing: Which of the three gorges yields the best water?"

The old man replied, "The three gorges are all linked together with no break in between. The water flows nonstop, day and night, from the upper gorge to the middle one, and then from the middle one to the lower one. It's hard to say which gorge yields the best water because the water is the same throughout."

Dongpo thought to himself, "What a one-track mind the prime minister has! Why does he have to ask for water from the middle gorge when the three gorges are linked and the water from all three is the same?" So thinking, he had his attendants buy a clean porcelain jar from the locals at the official rate. Then he himself stood at the prow and watched the boatmen fill the jar to the brim with water from the lower gorge and wrap it up with paper. After he had affixed his own signature to the jar, the boat set sail again.

Back in Huangzhou, he called on Prefect Ma, and in the evening, he drafted the memorial of Winter Solstice greetings and had it sent to the prefect's residence. Upon reading the memorial, Prefect Ma was deeply impressed by Mr. Su's immense talent. The official in charge of matters relating to memorials to the court put Su Shi's name on the memorial, and on a chosen auspicious day, a farewell dinner was given in Dongpo's honor.

Carrying the memorial and the jar of Sichuan water with him, Dongpo traveled posthaste to the Eastern Capital before the night was out and took up lodgings in the Great State Councillor Monastery. Early the next morning, he mounted his horse and, followed by an attendant carrying the jar of water, went to visit the prime minister at his residence.

The prime minister was sitting idly when he heard the custodian announce, "Master Su, commissioner of military training from of Huangzhou, requests an audience!"

With a smile, the prime minister said, "So, one year has already gone by!" He turned to the custodian and said, "Take your time on your way out and then lead him to the east study." And so the custodian went to carry out the order.

The prime minister was the first to reach the study. At the sight of the poem posted on the pillar, blurred with dust that had accumulated over the year, he took a fly-whisk from a magpie-tail jar and whisked off the dust to reveal the poem, which looked the same as before. He then sat down solemnly.

Meanwhile, the custodian dawdled for quite some time before he invited Master Su in. Hearing that he was to be led into the east study, Dongpo reddened at the memory of his correction of the prime minister's poem. Reluctantly, he entered the mansion. Upon reaching the study, he dropped to his knees and bowed to the prime minister. Raising Dongpo to his feet, the prime minister said, "We are not meeting in the main hall precisely because you can feel more relaxed here, since you must be tired from the long journey. So don't be overly concerned about etiquette." So saying, he had a page boy show Dongpo his seat.

After sitting down, Dongpo looked furtively at the poem posted on the pillar directly opposite him.

Pointing to his left with the fly-whisk, the prime minister said, "Zizhan, how time flies! It's been a year since this poem was written!"

Dongpo rose from his seat and prostrated himself on the floor.

Raising him to his feet, the prime minister asked, "Why are you doing this, Zizhan?"

"Your humble student pleads guilty!"

"Is it because you saw fallen chrysanthemum petals in Huangzhou?"

"Yes."

"But you are not to blame, Zizhan, for not having seen this kind of chrysanthemum before."

"Please bear with this humble student's lack of talent and learning."

After tea, the prime minister asked, "Did you bring water from the middle gorge of the Three Gorges as I asked you to?"

"Yes, the jar is right at the entrance to the mansion."

At the prime minister's order, two attendants carried the jar into the study. The prime minister wiped the jar with his own sleeves and opened the seal on the paper wrappings. He then had a page boy start a fire in the tea stove and boil some water in a silver teakettle. In the meantime, he put a pinch of Yangxian tea leaves in a white porcelain bowl made by Dingzhou Kiln [in what is now Quyang, Hebei]. When the water boiled and bubbles like crabs' eyes appeared, he quickly lifted the kettle and poured some water into the bowl. It was quite a while before the water turned the color of tea.

"Where did you get the water?"

"From Wu Gorge."

"The middle gorge?"

"Yes."

The prime minister laughed. "There you go again, making a fool of this old man! This water is from the lower gorge. How can you claim that it's from the middle one?"

Aghast, Dongpo repeated what the local resident had said, that the three gorges were linked together, and the water was the same throughout. "I believed what I heard and indeed collected the water from the lower gorge. How can you tell?"

"A scholar devoted to learning should not be given to rash actions. Careful research is highly necessary. Had I not been to Huangzhou and seen the chrysanthemums there, how would I dare come up with a line about their shedding petals? As for the water of the Three Gorges, I read about it in the *Supplementary Commentary on The Waterways.*[12] Water from the upper gorge is too strong; water from the lower gorge is too weak. Only water from the middle one is neither too strong nor too weak. The imperial physician, being the wise physician that he is, knows that the source of my ailment lies in my stomach and therefore advises me to use water from the middle gorge to help the medicine work better. If water from the Three Gorges is used to brew Yangxian tea, that from the upper gorge has a strong flavor, that from the lower gorge tastes bland, and that from the middle one is neither too strong nor too bland. I can tell that your water is from the lower gorge because it took a long time for the water to turn the color of tea."

Dongpo left his seat and asked for forgiveness.

"What is there to forgive?" said the prime minister. "It's because you are so brilliant that you paid no attention to those things. I'm glad that you are here, because it so happens that I have nothing to do today. I have known you for quite some time now, but I can't say I know the extent of your knowledge. (*How humiliating!*) Now I will make so bold as to give you a little test."

Dongpo said with delight, "Please go ahead."

"Not so fast!" said the prime minister. "If I give you a test all of a sudden, I might be accused of bullying a younger man. Now, you give me a test first, before I benefit from your knowledge."

"How could I dream of doing that?" said Dongpo with a bow.

"So you don't want to test me, but I can't allow myself to be presumptuous. Oh well, I'll have Xu Lun open all the bookcases in the study. All twenty-four, three shelves each, are filled with books. Just pick a book at random and read any line aloud. If I can't come up with the next line, you can call me an ignorant man."

Dongpo thought to himself, "This old man does talk big! He can hardly have memorized all these books! Even though he says so, I can't very well put him to the test." So thinking, he said, "I would never dream of doing that!"

"Well, haven't you heard the saying 'The best way to show someone respect is to follow his orders'?"

So Dongpo cunningly set about searching among the dusty books, thinking that if the prime minister had not read these books in a long time, he would have forgotten the lines. He picked a book at random and, without finding the name of the author, opened it at the middle and read a line out loud: "'How is the Delightful One?'"

Without missing a beat, the prime minister said, "'I have eaten him up.' Is that correct?"

"Yes."

Taking the book from Dongpo, the prime minister asked, "What do you make of these lines?"

Dongpo had not read the lines closely and thought, "In satires about Empress Wu Zetian, people of the Tang dynasty gave Xue Aocao the epithet 'The Delightful One.'[13] Maybe the empress sent someone to inquire after him, hence the first line. But the answer 'I have eaten him up' doesn't make sense." After reflecting a while, he thought, "I'd better not irritate the old man. One phrase admitting the truth is better than a thousand far-fetched guesses." So thinking, he said out loud, "This humble student does not know."

The prime minister said, "This is not some book of great obscurity. How can you not know? (*How humiliating!*) Here's the little story: Under the reign of Emperor Ling [108–188], toward the end of the Han dynasty, there was a fox pit tens of feet deep behind Mount Wugang in Changsha Prefecture [in present-day Hunan]. In the pit lived two nine-tail foxes that, in their long lives, had acquired the magic power of metamorphosis and often assumed the forms of beautiful women to lure male passersby into their pit for sexual pleasure. Those who failed to gratify them fully were eaten up between the two of them.

"Now, there was a man by the name of Liu Xi, who was accomplished in the art of lovemaking. When he was picking medicinal herbs in the mountains, the two evil spirits captured him, and at night, when they sought intimacy, he applied the same method one would use when tending a fire, adding or reducing fuel as the occasion demanded. The two foxes were so fully gratified that they called him The Delightful One. When the big fox was out on the mountain looking for food, the small fox kept watch on him. When the small fox went out, the big fox stayed with him. With the passing of time, the foxes relaxed their alertness, and, one day, after drinking some wine, they revealed their true forms, giving Liu Xi such a shock that his stamina began to wane.

"One day, when the big fox was out looking for food, the small fox in the pit asked for clouds and rain, but the man failed to gratify her.[14] The small fox flew into a rage and ate Liu Xi up. Upon returning to the pit, the big fox asked, thinking of Liu Xi, 'How is the Delightful One?' The small fox replied, 'I have eaten him up.' The two foxes chased each other all over the mountain. A woodchopper heard their screams, and what he witnessed came to be recorded in *The Complete History of the Last Years of the Han Dynasty*.[15] You have never heard of this story, Zizhan?"

Dongpo said in reply, "How can what little I know be compared to your vast knowledge, sir?"

"So, I have been put to the test," said the prime minister with a smile. "Now it's my turn to test you. Be sure to share your knowledge with me!"

"Please make it easy, sir."

"If I test you on other things, I'll be accused of trying to put you on the spot, but I've long heard that you are good at providing a missing line to form a matching couplet [*zuodui*].[16] (*Preposterous!*) This year is a leap year with an extra eighth month. We had the beginning of spring in the first month and it will come around again in the twelfth month, giving us a year with spring at both ends. With this as a theme, I will now write something for you to match, and for me to admire your talent." Thereupon, he had a page boy bring over a piece of paper and a brush-pen and wrote the following two lines:

One year, two springs and double eighth months;
Two years go by within the space of one.

However talented he was, Dongpo found himself unable, on the spur of the moment, to come up with another two lines to match those bizarre ones. His face went crimson in embarrassment.

The prime minister continued, "When you traveled from Huzhou to Huangzhou, did you go by Suzhou and Runzhou [present-day Zhenjiang]?"

"Yes, they do lie on the way."

"The road from the Jinchang Gate of Suzhou to Huqiu is called Hill Pond Road. The midpoint of this approximately seven-li road is called Half Pond. Runzhou, called in ancient times Iron Jar Town, borders on the Yangzi River, with three hills overlooking the city. They are Gold Hill, Silver Hill, and Jade Hill. All of these places have Buddhist temples and monasteries. Have you seen them all?"

"Yes, I have."

"Now, let me again give you a couple of lines about Suzhou and Runzhou, for you to think of lines to match."

The two lines about Suzhou are as follows:

Three and a half li, and you reach Half Pond,
Midpoint in the seven-li Hill Pond Road.

Next, the two lines about Runzhou:

Standing to the west of Iron Jar Town,
Three piles of treasure: Gold, Silver, and Jade.

Dongpo thought for a long time without being able to come up with matching lines. Seeing no other way, he apologized and took leave of his host.

Knowing full well that Dongpo had been treated somewhat unfairly, the prime minister was in fact, still appreciative of his talent. (*Deep down, this old man is not a bad sort after all.*) The following day, he submitted a memorial to Emperor Shenzong, by force of which Dongpo was reinstated as a Hanlin Academician.

In later times, someone commenting on these events said: Even a genius like Su Dongpo was humiliated three times by Wang Anshi, duke of Jing. Imagine what would happen to those less gifted than Su! Hence the following poem to caution the world:

Confucius honored Xiang as his teacher,[17]
But Wang Anshi had to torment Dongpo.
Modesty is the best human virtue;
The pursuit of knowledge knows no end.

4

In the Hall Halfway-up-the-Hill, the Stubborn One Dies of Grief

Try to prolong your life while you still can;
Seize the moments of joy when they come your way.
With heaven disposing human affairs,
Why do you have to worry yourself sick?
Relax! Think nothing of the trivial things!
Life's ups and downs are more than can be told.
The lavish Gold Valley Garden turned to dust;[1]
The once mighty Han Xin died a tragic death.[2]
Wu Zixu, the hero of Lintong fame,[3]
Was reduced to playing the flute for food.
When in luck, weeds outshine the spring flowers;
When out of luck, pure gold loses to rough iron.
You're better off if happy and carefree;
This you will know when old age sets in.
Be content with simple food and clothes
And live modestly throughout your life.

Having thus begun, let me take more time and cite four lines from a Tang dynasty poem before I launch into the story proper:

The duke of Zhou lived in fear of rumors;
Wang Mang won the hearts of his followers.
If they had died before the truth came out,
Who would have known them to be what they truly were?[4]

This quatrain says in essence that there are honest people and there are hypocrites and that one must learn to see good in those who appear to be evil and evil in those who appear to be good.

The first line of the quatrain is about the duke of Zhou, surname Ji and given name Dan, who was a younger son of King Wen of the Zhou dynasty [ca. 1027–256 B.C.E.]. A man of saintly virtue, he helped his older brother, who later became

King Wu, overthrow the Shang dynasty and found the Zhou dynasty, which was to last for eight hundred years. When King Wu fell ill, the duke wrote a prayer to heaven, asking to die in the king's place, a prayer that he hid in a golden box without anyone's knowledge. After King Wu died, the duke held the young King Cheng, King Wu's son, the crown prince, on his lap in court sessions with the feudal lords. The lord of Guan [Ji Xian] and the lord of Cai [Ji Du], both King Wu's half brothers born of concubines, harbored designs upon the throne and, jealous of the duke of Zhou, spread rumors, accusing him of bullying the young king and planning to usurp the throne before long. King Cheng did grow suspicious. The duke resigned from his post as prime minister and went to an eastern region, where he lived in fear as a recluse.

One day, during a raging storm, a clap of thunder shook open the golden box. It was only after King Cheng saw the duke's written prayer that he realized the duke's loyalty. The duke was brought back and reinstated as prime minister. The lord of Guan and the lord of Cai were executed, and the house of Zhou regained peace. If the duke of Zhou had fallen ill and died soon after the lord of Guan and the lord of Cai had started spreading rumors that accused him of harboring designs of betrayal, and if the golden box containing the prayer had remained closed and King Cheng's suspicions had never been dispelled, who would have been there to defend the duke? Wouldn't such a man of virtue have gone down in history as a villain?

The second line of the quatrain is about Wang Mang [45 B.C.E.–23 C.E.], courtesy name Jujun, an uncle of Emperor Ping [r. 1–5 C.E.] of the Western Han dynasty. He was an evil man who, emboldened by his kinship with the much favored empress, exercised enormous power as prime minister and set his sights on the throne.[5] However, afraid of opposition from the populace, he went out of his way to present the image of a modest man respectful of decorum and worthy men. He gave every appearance of acting in the name of justice and overstated his accomplishments. Throughout the land, there were four hundred eighty-seven thousand five hundred and seventy-two people who submitted memorials in eulogy of him. Knowing that he had enough popular support, he poisoned Emperor Ping, dismissed the empress dowager, ascended the imperial throne, and changed the dynastic title to Xin (New), a dynasty that lasted for eighteen years before it was overthrown by Liu Xiu [later to be Emperor Guangwu] of Nanyang, who rose in arms to restore the house of Han. Had Wang Mang died eighteen years earlier, he would very well have gone down in history as a good prime minister of impeccable integrity, and wouldn't a villain have thus passed as a good man? That is why the ancients said, "It takes time to get to know a person's heart," and also, "Only when the lid is closed on one's coffin can final judgment be passed on the person." It will never do to take someone as a gentleman on account of a few transient words of praise, nor can one condemn a man as a villain on the basis of similarly short-lived words of slander. There is a poem that bears witness:

Never heed words of praise or slander;
Right or wrong will be made known in the end.
If idle words are given credence,
The wise will cry out at the injustice.

Now I propose to tell of a prime minister in an earlier dynasty. Before his rise to power, he enjoyed a fine reputation, but once in power, he willfully committed all manner of outrages, for which he came to be showered with curses, and in the end he died with a grievance in his heart. If he had died in peaceful slumber at the height of his reputation, people would have deeply lamented such a loss to the country. A good man like this, not yet in a position commensurate with his great ability, would have left behind a good name. But by the time he was showered with curses, even death could not have saved him. He should not have lived those extra years in the first place!

Who was this prime minister? Which dynasty was it? Well, the dynasty is not too distant from us, nor is it too near. During the reign of Emperor Shenzong [r. 1068–85] of the Northern Song dynasty, there was a prime minister, a native of Linchuan [in present-day Jiangxi], by the name of Wang Anshi [1021–1086]. He was able to take in ten lines at one glance and had read ten thousand books. Famous court ministers like Wen Yanbo [1006–1083], Ouyang Xiu, Zeng Gong [1019–1083], and Han Wei all marveled at his talent.[6] He was barely twenty years old when he gained instant fame upon passing the imperial examinations on the first try. He started from the post of magistrate of Yin County in Qingyuan Prefecture, Zhejiang, where he made a name for himself by initiating good practices and eliminating harmful ones and was promoted to be prefectural notary for the administrative assistant of Yangzhou.

He often read all night through without a wink of sleep, and when the sun was high and he heard that the prefect was holding a session, he would rush over without first washing his face and rinsing his mouth. The prefect of Yangzhou at the time was Han Qi, duke of Wei. Seeing Wang Anshi's unkempt appearance, he attributed this neglect of personal hygiene to nocturnal indulgence in wine and admonished Wang to devote more time to reading. Wang thanked the prefect for his advice without uttering a word in his own defense. Later, upon learning that the man often read through the night, Mr. Han was deeply impressed and grew even more enthusiastic in his praises. (*Such a man is indeed hard to come by.*) So Wang Anshi was promoted again and became the prefect of Jiangning. His good name spread far and wide, and reached the ears of the emperor. Truly,

Through good deeds done early in his career,
He gained fame and ruined the land for years to come.

Now, Emperor Shenzong, the Son of Heaven, was an emperor who would go to any length to make the empire prosperous. Upon hearing of Wang Anshi's good repute, the emperor went out of his way to make him a Hanlin Academician in the capital. When the emperor asked him about ways to rule the land, Wang cited the examples of Yao and Shun, a reply that immensely pleased the Son of Heaven.[7] Barely two years had gone by before he was made prime minister and enfeoffed as the duke of Jing.

All in the court rejoiced over what they thought was the rebirth of Gao Yao, Kui, Yi Yin, and the duke of Zhou.[8] There was a Li Chengzhi, however, who predicted that Wang Anshi would surely wreak havoc throughout the land because, with more white than black in his eyes, he had the look of an evil man. Su Xun, in his turn, believed that Wang Anshi's slovenliness and neglect of personal hygiene, to the extent of forgetting to wash his face for months on end, bespoke a lack of the human touch and wrote an essay titled "On Recognizing Characteristics of Evil Men" in order to mock him.[9] (*One judged by a facial feature, and the other judged by general appearance. Both men were proved right. Why?*) However, these two men stood alone. Who would believe them? But let us go on with the story.

Now that he was prime minister, Wang Anshi gained the favor of Emperor Shenzong, who followed all of Wang's advice and promulgated a series of new policies. What policies were they?

> *The farmland policy, the water conservancy and irrigation policy, the crop loans policy, the local goods transportation policy, the militia policy, the corvée commutation policy, the market trading policy, the horse care policy, the land grids policy, and the guild tax policy.*[10]

Wang followed only the advice of an evil man named Lü Huiqing [1032–1111] and of his own son Wang Pang [1044–1076]. They consulted one another day and night, reprimanded and expelled those loyal to the court, and rejected remonstrations. Cries of discontent were heard throughout the country, and the occurrence of unusual natural phenomena rose in frequency. The duke of Jing, however, remained as opinionated as ever, asserting that there were three things that one would do well to ignore:

> *Natural phenomena need not be feared;*
> *Idle gossip need not be taken seriously;*
> *The ancestors' laws need not be observed.*

He was a stubborn man. Once his mind was made up, not even Buddha could talk him out of it. Hence his nickname "The Stubborn One." (*It is possible to bring evil people around to doing good deeds, but the stubborn ones do not change their ways and are, therefore, greater evils.*) Many famous court ministers, such as Wen Yanbo and Han Qi, who had sung his praises, began to regret their mistake. One after another, they submitted memorials to present their views but were invariably rejected, whereupon they handed in their resignations and left the court. Henceforth, Wang Anshi became more determined in enforcing the new policies. Numerous changes were made to the laws established by the ancestors, resulting in unemployment on a massive scale.

One day, his beloved son Wang Pang died of an ulcer. Overcome with grief, the duke of Jing summoned eminent monks from all over the land and held a forty-nine-day prayer service to ensure that the spirit of the deceased would be spared the torments of hell. The duke personally lit the incense and presented the farewell speech.

Upon completion of the forty-nine-day service, the duke was lighting incense to send off the Buddha at the fourth watch of the night when he suddenly fainted and collapsed on the prayer mat.[11] Despite the efforts of the attendants around him, he did not come to. It was at the fifth watch that he woke up as if from a dream. "How very strange!" he said. "How very strange!" The attendants raised him and helped him enter the middle door of the house. From there, his wife, Lady of Wuguo, had maidservants escort him into the bedchamber, where she asked him what had happened.

With tears in his eyes, he said, "When I was in a coma a moment ago, I was dimly aware of arriving at a place that looked like a big, imposing yamen with its gate closed. I saw our son Wang Pang in a huge cangue too heavy for him, a cangue that must have weighed a hundred catties.[12] With disheveled hair, a dirty face, and blood all over him, he stood in front of the gate and tearfully poured out his woes to me, saying, 'I'm here because the King of Hell accuses me of being the son of a highly placed man who, instead of committing himself to good deeds, stubbornly persists in his willful ways and enacts new laws like the crop loans law—laws that bring calamity to the land and the people and cause rancor to rise all the way to heaven. Your ill-starred son's career in the human world was brought to an end before yours, and I am being punished for crimes far greater than prayer services can redeem. Father, you'd better change your ways as soon as possible. Do not cling to wealth and rank.' Before he was quite finished, the gate opened, someone shouted an order, and I woke up."

His wife said, "Well, 'To believe is better than not to believe,' as the saying goes. I, too, have heard many complaints against you. Why don't you resign before your career goes downhill? One less day in office is one less day of being cursed at."

Following his wife's advice, the duke of Jing submitted about ten memorials in succession, requesting permission to resign on grounds of ill health. The emperor, not unaware of public opinion, had also grown weary of him. The request was approved, and he was made commissioner of Jiangning Prefecture.[13]

During the Song dynasty, retired prime ministers were all given posts in local governments and were paid salaries without having to do any work. The duke of Jing was most delighted to be sent to Jiangning, because Jiangning, being the ancient city of Jinling and former capital of the Six Dynasties, was an opulent place with beautiful scenery and fashionable people, a place where he could very well settle down to a comfortable life. Before departure, his wife donated all of her jewelry and other prized possessions worth thousands of pieces of gold to nunneries and monasteries, held prayer services, and burned incense to seek blessings for their son Wang Pang in the netherworld.

On a chosen day, Wang Anshi took leave of the imperial court, ready to set off on his journey. The assembly of court officials prepared farewell dinners for him, but he declined, pleading illness. In his residence, there was a clerk by the name of Jiang Ju, who was quite good at getting things done. This man he took with him, along with servants and page boys for his family.

From the Eastern Capital to Jinling, they traveled by water. The duke chose not to use a ship provided by the court but, wearing commoner's clothes, hired a small boat and drifted down the Yellow River.

Before the boat got under way, he summoned Jiang Ju, the servants, and the page boys and said to them, "I have already resigned as prime minister. Wherever we moor the boat along the way, should anyone ask about my name and rank, just say that we are travelers passing by this area. Do not, on any account, tell them the truth, because I'm afraid that if the local officials hear about it, they'll come to greet me and to see me off, or even hire guards to provide protection. That would be putting the local inhabitants to too much trouble. If my identity does leak out, I'll assume that you have given out my name for the purpose of extorting bribes from the local people, and if I do hear that you've done that, you can be sure the punishment will be heavy."

"We understand."

Jiang Ju said, "Now that you are dressed like a commoner, traveling with a hidden identity, what if we run across people who don't know better and speak ill of you?"

The duke replied, "As the saying goes, 'A prime minister's heart is big enough to pole a boat in.' Idle gossip should never be taken seriously. Kind words about me do not make me complacent. Criticisms of me do not make me angry. Just take them as a puff of wind passing by your ears. Whatever you do, don't invite trouble."

Jiang Ju passed the instructions on to the boatmen. And the journey went smoothly with nothing of note happening.

Before they knew it, they found themselves in Zhongli County more than twenty days later. In the past, the duke had an ailment caused by excessive phlegm and internal heat. So many miserable days spent in the small boat brought the ailment back. Wishing to go ashore to view the sights and the markets and take his mind off his misery, he told his butler, "We're not far from Jinling now. You take good care of the mistress and continue the journey by boat, crossing the river from Guabu and Huaiyang.[14] I'll go by land and meet you at the mouth of the river at Jinling." So Wang Anshi saw his family off, and they continued their journey by boat, while he went ashore, along with Jiang Ju, a servant, and a page boy, forming a company of four.

By boat on water, by carriage on land,
Travelers get wherever they want to go.

Jiang Ju said, "If you travel by land, sir, you will have to hire some porters. Shall I go to the county courier station, present them with the official letter from the court, and get porters for free, or do you want to hire some at your own expense?"

The duke replied, "I've already told you not to bother local authorities. Go hire some men with my money."

"In that case," said Jiang Ju, "we'll have to find a broker."

With the servant and the page boy carrying the baggage, Jiang Ju led the duke to see a broker. The host greeted them, offered them seats of honor, and asked, "Where are you going?"

"To Jiangning," said the duke. "We would like to rent a sedan-chair and three mules or horses. We'll be on our way immediately."

"Things are not the way they were before," said the broker. "You'll have to wait a while."

"Why?" asked the duke.

"It's a long story! Since the Stubborn One came to power and established new laws, people have been reduced to poverty, and many fled from here. (*This denunciation against him is the first of many more to come all along this journey.*) The few poor families who stay behind are so busy running errands for the government that no one is free for hire. Moreover, the local people have been made so poor that they can't even fill their stomachs, not to speak of having spare money to raise horses and mules. The few there are can't meet the demand. Now you sit here, while I go find some for you. If I succeed, don't rejoice. If I fail, don't complain, but whatever I find will cost twice as much as before!"

"Who is the Stubborn One?" asked Jiang Ju.

"It's Wang Anshi. They say he has more white in his eyes than black. That's the look of an evil man."

The duke lowered his eyelids and told Jiang Ju not to poke his nose into other people's affairs.

After a long while, the broker came back and said, "You can only have two sedan-chair carriers. A third one is nowhere to be found. Those two want to be paid as four, because there will be no one to relieve them. There's no horse. I managed to find only a mule and a donkey. You can come to my place tomorrow morning at the fifth watch to be picked up. If you agree, you must pay them a deposit now."

Displeased by the bitter words against him a while earlier, the duke could hardly wait to be on his way. He thought to himself, "If we go slowly, having only two men shouldn't be a problem. But we are one animal short. The only choice is to let Jiang Ju have one. The page boy and the servant can take turns riding the other one." Thereupon, he told Jiang Ju not to haggle over the price but to pay whatever the broker asked. Accordingly, Jiang Ju weighed out some silver and paid the broker.

As it was still early in the day and staying in the broker's house was too boring, the duke had the page boy follow him and went out for a stroll down the streets. Indeed, what he saw was a desolate place with few shops in business. The sight saddened him, but he kept his feelings to himself. His steps took him to a teahouse that looked clean enough. He walked in and was about to order some tea when his eyes fell upon a quatrain written on the wall. (*This is the second time.*)

The old system was judicious and sound;
For a hundred years, peace reigned in the land.
But along came the stubborn white-eyed man
To force changes that bring chaos and pain.

Written below, in lieu of the author's signature, were the words "Anonymous but indignant at the way things are."

The duke sank into silence. Losing all interest in the tea, he promptly left the place. A few hundred steps farther on, he saw a temple. "Why don't I go in to look around and while away the time?" The gate led to three halls of worship. Before he crossed the threshold to bow, he saw, posted on the vermilion wall, a piece of yellow paper with a poem written on it. (*The third time.*)

The last five emperors gave the land peace.
Why bother to bring changes here and there?
If Yao and Shun are models to follow,
Help the court's wise rule, as did Yi and Zhou![15]
He ousted old ministers of the court;
His new laws brought ruin to the people.
The Cozy Nest man, if you remember,
Once told the future by the cuckoo's cries.

During the reign of the previous emperor, Emperor Yingzong [r. 1064–67], there was a wise man by the name of Shao Yong, alias Yaofu, who was well versed in the laws of the cosmos and knew everything there was to know about heaven and earth. He called his residence "The Cozy Nest." In one of his frequent walks with friends on the Heavenly Ford Bridge in Luoyang, he heard the cries of a cuckoo. With a sigh, he said, "There will be chaos throughout the land!" When asked the meaning of that remark, he said, "If the land is to enjoy peace and order, the earth's energy should travel from the north to the south. If the land is to be torn by chaos, the earth's energy travels from the south to the north. No cuckoos have ever been seen in Luoyang before, and yet today, I heard one. This is a sign that the earth's energy is going from the south to the north. Before long, the Son of Heaven is going to appoint a southerner as prime minister. That man will abolish the laws our ancestors established, and the land will know no peace till the end of our Song dynasty." And that prophecy had now been borne out by Wang Anshi.

After silently reading the poem once, the duke asked an acolyte, "Who wrote this poem? There's no signature."

"A few days ago," replied the acolyte, "a monk came here and asked for a piece of paper on which to write a poem. Then he posted it on the wall, saying it was a criticism of a certain Stubborn One."

The duke peeled off the sheet of paper, hid it in his sleeve, and went out without a word. He returned to the broker's house, where he spent a none-too-cheerful night.

At the first crow of roosters at the fifth watch, the two porters arrived, along with a man leading a mule and a donkey. Without combing his hair and washing himself, as was his wont, the duke mounted the sedan-chair. Jiang Ju rode the donkey, and the servant and the page boy took turns riding the mule. Around noontime, after traveling about forty li, they arrived at a small town. Jiang Ju dismounted, took a step forward, and said to the prime minister, "Sir, it's time for lunch."

Because of the recurrence of the duke's ailment, his servants had brought along some lung-clearing dried cakes, tea cakes, and pills. The duke told his men, "Bring me a bowl of hot water before you go ahead and eat your lunch." The duke steeped some tea in the hot water and ate some of the dried cakes. While his men were still at lunch, he saw a lavatory by the side of a house. He asked for a piece of toilet paper and stepped inside. There, on the earthen wall, he saw an eight-line poem written in white lime (*The fourth time.*):

When in Yin County before his time had come,
He had much support in his undeserved fame.
How wise Su Xun was in detecting evil!
How accurate Li Chengzhi's predictions!
He ousted the good and monopolized power;
He bred deception and brought on chaos.
Most odious were his words "need not be,"
Words that live in infamy down the years.

After finishing what he had to do, the duke took advantage of a moment when no one was looking in his direction to remove the square shoe from his left foot and wipe the characters on the wall until they became blurred. When his men came back from lunch, he remounted the sedan-chair and resumed the journey.

Some thirty li later, they came upon a courier station. Jiang Ju said, "This government establishment looks spacious enough. Let's spend the night there."

"What did I tell you yesterday?" demanded the duke. "Wouldn't we be inviting probing questions if we take up quarters here tonight? It would be safer to go to the next village and pick a local resident's house in a quiet corner."

Another five li later, as dusk began to set in, they came upon a villager's thatched house with a bamboo fence and a firewood door left ajar. Instructed by the duke to go up to the house and ask to be put up for the night, Jiang Ju pushed open the gate and approached the door. An elderly man with a cane stepped out and asked what they wanted.

"We are travelers," replied Jiang Ju, "wishing to spend the night in your honorable house. We will pay you at the going rate."

"Please make yourselves comfortable," said the old man.

Jiang Ju led the duke into the house to meet the host. The old man offered the duke the seat of honor. Seeing that Jiang Ju and the other two stood to one side, he realized that he was looking at a man of exalted status, and so he took the three attendants into a side room. While the old man was away, making preparations for tea and supper, the duke saw an eight-line poem written in bold characters on the newly whitewashed wall. (*The fifth.*) The poem said,

> *Say not that his writings are divinely inspired;*
> *Those who see through his fallacies are few.*
> *His defense in the quail case was unjust;*[16]
> *His eating of fish-bait not without motive.*[17]
> *His evil plots have fulfilled his ambitions;*
> *His stubborn ways will give him infamy after he dies.*
> *The sight of his cangued son in the netherworld*
> *Revealed to him the truth of heavenly justice.*

The poem plunged the duke into low spirits. In a short while, the old man served supper. The servants fell to heartily. The duke also helped himself to a little bit of the food.

"Who wrote the poem on the wall?" he asked the old man.

"It was done by a traveler passing by. I don't know his name."

His head bent, the duke thought to himself, "My defense in the case of the quail and my eating the fish-bait by mistake are incidents known to the public. But my son's wearing a cangue in the netherworld is something I told only to my wife. No one else could have known about it. Why has it come up in that poem? How very strange!"

Puzzled by the poem's last two lines, which had struck a sore spot, he asked the old man, "May I ask your venerable age?"

"I'm seventy-eight."

"How many sons do you have?"

That question brought tears to the old man's eyes. "I had four sons, but they all died. There's only me and my wife living here now."

"How did all four of them die?"

"Over the last ten years, the new laws have brought us great suffering. (*The sixth time.*) My sons took on the responsibility of managing the household, but they died one after another, either in an official post or on the road. Since I'm an old man, I survived, but had I been younger, I would also be dead and gone."

Wang Anshi asked in astonishment, "What's so bad about the new laws that they did such harm to you?"

"That poem on the wall says enough. After the imperial court appointed Wang Anshi as the prime minister, he brought changes to the old system established by our ancestors, imposing heavy taxes, refusing to hear objections, covering up his mistakes, and ousting good officials while promoting evil ones. He started with the crop loans policy to oppress the peasants, and then went on to the militia policy, the corvée commutation policy, the horse care policy, the local goods transportation policy, and so on and so forth. Local officials fawned on their superiors and oppressed their subordinates. (*All the wrongdoings of such officials are summed up in that little phrase "fawned on their superiors and oppressed their subordinates."*) During the day, they plunder the people, their whips at the ready; at night, their lackeys yell from door to door, giving the people no peace even in their sleep. Every day, several tens of local men abandon their properties and head for the mountains with their wives to take refuge there. This village used to have more than a hundred households. Now only eight or nine remain. This family of sixteen has been reduced to only four!" At this point, his tears fell like rain.

The duke was also stung by a pang of grief. He asked again, "There are people who say that the new laws benefit the people, but you say not. I'd like to hear more about this."

"Wang Anshi is a stubborn man. People call him 'The Stubborn One.' He angrily denounces anyone who says anything against the new laws and promotes anyone who's for them. Those who say that the new laws benefit the people are an evil lot and a plague on the people! Let me give you as an example the militia law, whereby every family has to send one son into the unit for training and send another one to bring him daily supplies. Even though the training is said to be done once every five days, the heads of the security units don't release the men from the training grounds until they are bribed. If no bribes come their way, they just hold the young men there, saying that the young men are not yet skilled enough in the martial arts. As a result, farmwork is neglected, and people die of cold and hunger." (*He rules best who leaves the people alone, as can be deduced from what is described above.*)

Having said that, the old man asked, "Where's that Stubborn One now?"

The duke replied, tongue-in-cheek, "He's still in the court, helping the emperor rule the land."

Spitting onto the ground, the old man lashed out, "Where is justice when such an evil man is still in power? He should be executed! Why doesn't the court fill the position of prime minister with good men like Han Qi, Fu Bi [1004–1083], Sima Guang [1019–1086], Lü Hui, and Su Shi, instead of keeping such a scoundrel?"[18]

Hearing all this noise coming from the guest hall, Jiang Ju and the others came in to find out what it was all about. At these harsh words spoken by the old man,

Jiang Ju said sharply, "Please stop this nonsense. Should Prime Minister Wang hear about this, you'll be in for some harsh punishment."

Abruptly, the old man rose in anger and said, "I'm almost eighty years old. Why should I be afraid of death? If I ever see that villain, I'll cut off his head with my own hand, take out his heart and liver, and eat them. (*Bravo!*) And then, I'll have no regrets even if I end up dying in a boiling cauldron or by a sword!"

At these words, all of Wang's attendants flinched and stuck out their tongues in horror. His face turning ashen, the duke dared not venture a response. He rose and said to Jiang Ju, "The moon is as bright as day. We should be getting on with our journey." Jiang understood. He paid the old man for the meal and went about preparing the means of transportation.

When the duke waved farewell to the old man, the latter said, laughingly, "My curses against that scoundrel Wang Anshi had nothing to do with you. Why do you have to leave so soon, looking annoyed? (*Brilliant!*) Might you be related to Wang Anshi in any way?"

"No, no!" said the duke. He mounted the sedan-chair and told the men to make haste. With the attendants bringing up the rear, they pressed on, treading the moonlit roads.

Another ten li or so farther on, they came upon a grove, where stood a lonesome three-room thatched cottage. The duke said, "Now, this looks like a quiet little place where we can take a good rest." So saying, he had Jiang Ju knock at the door. When an old woman answered the door, Jiang Ju said, as before, that they were travelers passing by who had been so eager to cover more distance that they had passed the last inn without stopping. They now wished to be put up for the night and would pay her thankfully the following morning.

Pointing to the middle room, the old woman said, "That's an empty room. You can stay there, but it's too small for the sedan-chair and the animals."

"That's all right," said Jiang Ju. "I'll take care of that."

The duke stepped down from the sedan-chair and walked into the cottage. Jiang Ju had the sedan-chair put under the eaves and the mule and the donkey led into the grove. Sitting in the room, the duke saw that the old woman was in rags and her hair disheveled, but he found her mud-walled thatched cottage quite clean inside. The old woman brought over a lamp, made sleeping arrangements for the duke, and went off to her own room to retire for the night. Some characters on the wall between two windows caught the duke's eye. He lifted the lamp and saw an eight-line poem. (*The seventh time.*) The poem said,

In life, he seeks fame and shows off his power;
In death, he tries to cheat posterity.
With no good provisions for Wuguo in his will,
He has florid rhetoric for Ye Tao.
Throughout the empire, farmers flee their homes;

Curses against crop loans echo down the years.
Passing by here and witnessing the scene,
He finds his hair white with grief overnight.

The poem gave him as much pain as if ten thousand arrows were piercing his heart. In dejection, he thought, "All along the journey, I've seen poems of satire—in a teahouse, in a monastery, and even in a villager's home. Now this is an old woman who lives alone. Who could have been here to write this poem? Clearly, complaints and curses must have spread throughout the land. 'Wuguo' in the second couplet of that poem is an obvious reference to my wife, Lady of Wuguo, and Ye Tao is a friend of mine. But the meaning of these two lines is most obscure." He was about to summon the old woman for some questions when he heard snores coming from the next room. Jiang Ju and the others were already fast asleep after a tiring day.

Tossing and turning in his bed, the duke gave himself up to thought. With deep regret, he said to himself, stroking his chest and stamping his feet, "I trusted only one man, that man from Fujian. He said the new laws did the people good, and that's why I forced them through over objections from all quarters. How was I to know that people's rancor was running so deep? That man from Fujian ruined me!" Lü Huiqing was a native of Fujian, so the duke called him "that man from Fujian." Heaving sigh upon sigh, the duke lay face down on the bed, not bothering to take off his clothes, and sobbed noiselessly throughout the sleepless night, soaking both sleeves with tears.

When day broke, the old woman rose and, her hair in disarray, drove two pigs out the door with the help of a barefoot, stupid-looking maid. The maid brought out some chaff while the old woman fetched water, and then, stirring a wooden ladle in a wooden basin, the old woman called out, "Lo! Lo! Lo! The Stubborn Ones! Come over here!" The two pigs trotted over to the basin and ate from it.

Then the maid called out to the chickens, "Cluck! Cluck! Cluck! Cluck! Wang Anshi, come over here!" And the flock of chickens swarmed up to her (*Look at this!*), a scene that appalled Jiang Ju and the two servants. His heart sinking lower, the duke asked the old woman, "Why do you call the chickens and pigs these names?"

"Don't you know that Wang Anshi is the incumbent prime minister, and 'The Stubborn One' is his nickname? Since he became the prime minister, he has passed new laws to torment the people. I've been a widow for twenty years. I have no son or daughter-in-law and live with my maidservant, but even women like us two have to pay corvée commutation taxes, and yet, despite all the money we pay, we are still dragged into corvée. In my case, I grew mulberry and hemp for a living, but before the silkworms were ready, I had to borrow money against the silk. Before the hemp was put on the loom, I had to borrow against the fabric. Having failed in the mulberry and hemp business, I have no other choice but to raise pigs and chickens and wait for the government clerks and local headmen to come and collect corvée commutation taxes. I either give them the money or feed them a big meal. I myself never get to eat a piece of meat.

"So people around here hate the new laws so much that we call the pigs and chickens 'The Stubborn Ones' and 'Wang Anshi', and treat that Wang Anshi as an animal. There's nothing I can do to him in this life, but the next time around, I wish he'd be reincarnated as an animal for me to cook and eat up, and I can give vent to all this hatred pent up in me!" (*Is this also some "Idle gossip that need not be taken seriously"?*)

The duke silently shed tears without daring to say a word. His men were dumbfounded as they realized that the duke's appearance had changed. He asked for a mirror and saw in it that his hair had turned all white and his eyes were swollen. Feeling wretched, he knew that this had been caused by his grief. Recalling the line "He finds his hair white with grief overnight," he thought, "Isn't this all in my fate?" He had Jiang Ju pay the old woman and prepare for departure.

Walking up to the sedan-chair, Jiang Ju said, "Sir, your policies for the empire are excellent. It's just that those people are too ignorant and complain about you instead. We must not stay with peasants again tonight. Let's go to a government establishment to save ourselves further humiliation."

Without saying anything, the duke nodded his consent. After covering quite a distance, they came upon a courier station. Jiang Ju got down first from his donkey and helped the duke out of the sedan-chair and into the courier station, where the duke sat down. While Jiang Ju was making breakfast preparations, the duke saw two quatrains on the wall. The first one said,

Fu, Han, and Sima were the few good ones[19]
Whose advice passed his ears like puffs of wind.
In Lü Huiqing alone he placed his trust;[20]
Yet, remember who killed Yi but Fengmeng![21]

The second quatrain said,

A glib preacher of high morality,
He pushed through more new laws than one can count.
When his luck runs out, he'll know boundless grief
Brought on by accusing humans and ghosts.

The duke flew into a rage. He summoned the courier station clerks and said, "What madman wrote this, slandering government policies like this?"

An elderly clerk replied, "It's not just this station that has such a poem. These poems turn up everywhere."

"Why was that poem written?"

"Wang Anshi came up with new laws to torment the people. That's why the people hate him to the marrow of their bones. It is said that he recently resigned and has been transferred to Jiangning Prefecture. Because he will have to pass by this place on his way there, hundreds of peasants are gathered around from morning to night to wait for him."

"Are they going to greet him formally?" asked the duke.

"Why do that to an enemy?" said the clerk with a chuckle. "The peasants are waiting for him with clubs in their hands, and the moment he shows up, they'll beat him to death and eat him up."

The duke was horrified. Before the breakfast on the stove was ready, he hastened out of the courier station and mounted the sedan-chair. Jiang Ju gathered the other men, and they continued with their journey, buying dry provisions along the way whenever necessary to allay their hunger.

For the rest of the journey, the duke did not step out of the sedan-chair even once. By his orders, they pressed ahead at double speed until they arrived in Jinling, where the duke greeted his wife, Lady of Wuguo. Too ashamed to go into the city of Jiangning, he chose to live halfway up Mount Zhong and called his house "The Hall Halfway-up-the-Hill." There, he spent his days reading Buddhist scriptures and intoning Buddha's name, hoping to atone for his sins.

A most brilliant man able to memorize a passage verbatim after a single reading, he remembered every word of every poem he had encountered on the road. When he reproduced the poems and secretly showed them to Lady of Wuguo, he came to realize that it was no accident that their deceased son Wang Pang was suffering in the netherworld. From that time on, he never had a moment's relief from his depression.

When his ailment of phlegm and internal heat recurred, its violence complicated by a concentration of gas around his diaphragm, he could not take in food or drink. A year later, he was reduced to a bag of bones. He was sitting in his bed, propped up on a pillow and on the verge of death, when his wife, Lady of Wuguo, asked him tearfully, "Have you made any provisions by way of a will?"

"The feelings between husband and wife," said the duke, "are those that come from an accidental union. Think no more of me after I'm gone. Just give away all the family possessions and do good deeds far and wide."

Before he had quite finished, it was announced that a friend, Ye Tao, had arrived to inquire after his health. The duke's wife removed herself from this male presence. The duke had Ye Tao step over to his bedside and, holding Ye's hands, said to him, "Being an extremely intelligent man, you should study the Buddhist scriptures as much as you can instead of wasting your energy on useless writing that does no one any good. I have spent my whole life trying to excel in my writing, but all that effort has been in vain. Now that I'm dying, regrets are too late."

Trying to comfort him, Ye Tao said, "You are destined for a long and blissful life. Why do you say such a thing?"

The duke continued with a sigh, "Life and death are matters one can never predict. I'm afraid that I won't be able to speak when my time comes. That's why I said those words to you."

After Ye Tao took his leave, the duke suddenly recalled the second couplet of the poem he had seen in the old woman's cottage:

With no good provisions for Wuguo in his will,
He had florid rhetoric for Ye Tao.

The incident that had just occurred bore out the prophecy. Stroking his thigh, he said to himself with a prolonged sigh, "Everything is predestined. Nothing ever happens by accident! Whoever wrote that poem must have been either a ghost or a god. Otherwise, how could one foretell what was going to happen to me in the future? Being disparaged like this by ghosts and deities, how can I expect to hang on to this mortal world any longer?"

A few days later, his condition turned critical. Becoming delirious, he slapped himself across the face and cursed himself, saying, "I let the emperor down, and at the other end, I also let the people down. How will I have the nerve to face Tang Zifang and the others in the Nine Springs?"[22] The curses went on for three days in a row before he threw up liters of blood and gave up the ghost. (*To be cursed is not as good as to end up cursing himself.*)

The Tang Zifang he had mentioned was named Tang Jie, Zifang being the courtesy name, an upright official in the Song court whose remonstrations against the new laws had been ignored by Wang Anshi. Tang Jie had also vomited blood and died in the same way, although in honor rather than in disgrace.

Even now, there are farmers in mountainous villages who call their pigs "The Stubborn Ones." Popular belief in later times held that the new laws in the Xining reign period [1068–77] depleted the vitality of the Song dynasty and led to the calamities of Jingkang.[23] There is a poem in testimony:

Despite all the voices against the new laws,
He stubbornly went on with his own ways.
Had he not dealt such a blow to the land,
The Jurchens never would have crossed the river.

There is another poem lamenting the duke of Jing's misplaced talent:

What a brilliant man, that Wang Anshi!
He graced his posts with integrity and talent.
What a pity he ended up a failure!
Among scholars he should have spent his life. (A real pity that his talent was used in the wrong place.)

5

Lü Yu Returns the Silver and Brings about Family Reunion

Mao Bao freed a turtle, and he rose in rank;[1]
Song Jiao saved some ants, and he passed the exams.[2]
They all say that heaven is far away;
None sees that good deeds quietly gain you merit.

As the story goes, in the vicinity of Long Pond in Jiaxing Prefecture, Zhejiang, there lived an immensely rich man, Jin Zhong, from a family whose heads of household had for generations been addressed as "Squire." A most stingy man, he had in his life five objects of hatred. Which five?

Heaven, earth, himself, his parents, and the emperor.

He hated heaven for not making summer last long enough and for generating too much autumn wind and winter snow, which force people to spend money on clothes to keep out the cold. He hated the earth for giving life to trees that lack good sense, for if they knew better, they would all grow to ideal heights so that the trunks could serve as pillars of houses, the bigger branches as beams, and the thinner ones as rafters. Wouldn't that have saved him the expense of a carpenter? He hated himself because his stomach did not know how to take care of itself but suffered from pangs of hunger after a day without eating. He hated his parents because they left behind them many relatives and friends who had to be served tea and water free of charge when they came to visit. He hated the emperor because of the taxes imposed on land that he had inherited from his ancestors.

Apart from these five objects of hatred, he also had four wishes. Which four?

First, he wished to have Deng Tong's copper hill.[3]
Second, he wished to have Guo Kuang's gold vault.[4]
Third, he wished to have Shi Chong's treasures.[5]
Fourth, he wished to have Patriach Lü Chunyang's finger that could change stone into gold.[6]

With these four wishes and five objects of hatred, he was an insatiably greedy man who devoted all his time to the accumulation of money and grain, so much so that he literally counted the grains of rice before cooking and weighed the sticks of firewood on his scales before lighting the kitchen fire. Thus, he came to be known in the village as Cold Water Jin and Skinflint Jin.

He loathed monks most of all, because, of all kinds of people in the world, the monks are the best at gaining undue advantages. They are always at the receiving end of alms, and for a monk to donate back to the lay community is something quite unheard of. Therefore, Cold Water Jin saw monks as nails in his eye and thorns in his tongue.

In his neighborhood, there was a Fushan Temple, but in his fifty years of life, Squire Jin had never donated one cent to it. Luckily, his wife Shan-shi—who had been born on the same day, in the same month and the same year, though not in the same hour, as he had been—was a woman who followed a vegetarian diet (to his delight) and was much given to good deeds (to his chagrin). When she was past forty years of age and still without issue, she gave some of her own jewelry, worth more than twenty taels of gold, to the temple without her husband's knowledge, so that the old monk could gild the Buddha's statue and hold services to pray for children on her behalf. The Buddha was most responsive. She did indeed give birth to two lovely baby boys in succession. Because they owed their lives to the prayers at the Fushan Temple, the older boy was named Fu'er and the younger one Shan'er.

After becoming the mother of two sons, Shan-shi often donated firewood and rice to the temple, without her husband's knowledge, to support the old monk. Whenever he heard about this, Squire Jin would burst into a torrent of curses, and the couple would quarrel until both could not take it anymore. This happened quite a few times, but, being a woman with a mind of her own, the wife kept to her own ways despite the quarrels.

When husband and wife were both fifty years of age, Fu'er was nine and Shan'er, having been born close on his brother's heels, was eight. Both boys were in school, and all was well with the family. On the couple's birthday, Squire Jin left home and took refuge somewhere else so as to avoid having to entertain relatives and friends who might come to offer congratulations. (*A petty man who did not know that he should be counting his blessings.*) Again, Shan-shi put together some private savings and sent the money over to the temple for a prayer service, partly in celebration of the couple's birthday and partly as a votive offering for the boys' well-being. She had suggested this to her husband a couple of days before, but he had refused. So she had to do it on the sly.

That night, while preparing for the ceremony of lighting longevity lamps, the monks sent an acolyte to the Jin household to ask Madam Jin for a few *dou* of brown rice.[7] Shan-shi opened the granary door quietly and gave the monk three *dou* of rice. The monk left. She was in the very act of locking up the granary door when Squire Jin came home and saw her. Noticing also some grains of rice scattered about on the ground, he realized what she had been up to. He was about to cry out when he thought to himself, "Today is our birthday, a lucky day. Besides, what's gone is gone. Since I can't get it back anyway, I might as well not waste my breath." So he pretended not to have seen anything and tried to swallow his anger.

Throughout the sleepless night, he turned his mind this way and that and said to himself, "The way that confounded baldhead keeps pestering my household, he will soon be eating me out of hearth and home! Only if that wretch dies will I be free of all troubles." He fretted and fretted, but no plan came to his mind.

After daybreak, the old monk brought along a disciple and came to the Jin residence for a reply concerning the ritual, but dreading the sight of Cold Water Jin, he stopped at the door and peered in. But Mr. Jin saw him. Knitting his eyebrows, Mr. Jin struck upon an idea. He took a few pennies, left the house by a side door, and went to an herbal medicine shop downtown, where he bought some arsenic. He then headed for a pastry shop owned by a certain Wang Sanlang.

While some dough made of powdered sweet rice was being steamed on the stove, Wang Sanlang prepared a bowl of sugar filling for the rice cakes. Cold Water Jin took out eight pennies, tossed them on the counter, and said, "Take the money, Sanlang, and make four big cakes for me. Don't be sparing with the filling. Just knead the dough into cakes, and let me put in the filling myself."

Without saying a word out loud, Wang Sanlang thought to himself, "This famous Cold Water Jin, Skinflint Jin, has never spent even half a penny in my shop since I started this business some years ago. What a stroke of good luck that I'm making eight pennies out of him today! Now, this is a man who enjoys gaining petty advantages. Let him put in as much filling as he wants, so he'll come again next time." So thinking, he plucked a piece of the snow-white dough from the steamer, kneaded it with his fingers into an open-topped pouch, and handed it to Cold Water Jin, saying, "Squire Jin, it's all yours!"

Unobserved, Cold Water Jin sprinkled some arsenic powder into the pouch (*What an evil thing to do!*), added some filling, and shaped the dough into a round flat cake. He made four altogether and slipped them, nice and hot, into his sleeves.

After leaving Wang Sanlang's store, he walked leisurely back home and found the two monks drinking tea in the hall. Cheerfully, he greeted them with a bow and then went to the inner quarters of the house. He said to his wife, "The two monks must be hungry, coming so early in the morning. A neighbor treated me to some refreshments just a moment ago. The cakes looked so nice and hot that I came home with four of them in my sleeves. Why don't we serve them to the monks?" Greatly delighted by her husband's change of heart, Shan-shi took a vermilion plate, put the four cakes on it, and had a maid take it out.

At the sight of Squire Jin returning home, the monks thought they dared not stay on, let alone take refreshments, but, when the maid came out with cakes, they felt obliged not to reject these tokens of Madam's good wishes. So they put the four cakes in one sleeve and, with some polite words of thanks, took their leave and went back to their temple. Mr. Jin rejoiced in secret, but of him, more later.

Let us now turn to the Jin boys, who often went to play in the temple after class at the local school. That evening, they went to the temple again. The old monk thought to himself, "I've never had any treat to offer the Jin boys when they've been here. The four cakes Madam Jin gave me this morning are still in the cupboard, untouched. Why don't I heat them up and offer them to the boys, along with some tea?" Right away, he had his disciple take out the cakes from the cupboard, toasted them until they turned golden brown, and put them in the room with two cups of strong tea.

Having been playing for quite a while, the two boys were hungry. As soon as they saw the steaming hot cakes, they ate them up, two each. It would have been a different story if they had not eaten the cakes, but they did, and it was unmistakably a case of

A fire burning the heart and liver;
Ten thousand spears stabbing the stomach!

Immediately, the two boys started crying and complaining of stomachaches. The page boy who was with them panicked and tried to help them go back home, but the two boys collapsed in pain, unable to move a step. The old monk was also alarmed. Without knowing what had caused this, he could do no better than to have two disciples carry the boys, one on each man's back, to Squire Jin's house, with the page boy trailing behind. Upon arrival at the Jin house, the two monks turned back.

Mr. and Mrs. Jin were terrified. They immediately asked the page boy what had happened. The page boy said, "Just a moment ago, as soon as they ate some cakes at Fushan Temple, they started complaining of stomachaches. The reverend said that he had gotten the cakes from my master this morning but had saved them for the two young masters." (*The will of heaven prevails.*)

Realizing that things had gone awry, Squire Jin could not do otherwise than tell his wife about the arsenic. Horror-struck, Shan-shi poured cold water over the boys, hoping to revive them, but they were already too far gone. A moment later, blood flowed from all seven apertures in their heads.

Alas! How young they died! Goodness knows how much trouble Shan-shi had gone through before these two boys were born in answer to her prayers! And now, they had been poisoned through her own husband's evil act. Giving him a tongue-lashing would not serve any purpose. Overcome with rage and despair, she walked into her private chamber, took off her waistband, and hanged herself.

After a fit of weeping over the death of the boys, Squire Jin went into the chamber to talk with his wife and was frightened out of his wits at the sight of her body swinging from the beam. Instantly, he took ill, was confined to his bed, and died before seven days had gone by. His kinsmen, who had always resented the miserly ways of Cold Water Skinflint Jin, jumped at this heaven-sent opportunity and swarmed, old and young, to his house and looted it clean. This was how the fabulously rich Squire Jin ended his life, a victim of his own malice. There is a poem in testimony:

Who would have guessed that cakes contained poison?
Poison meant for others killed his own sons.
All actions and thoughts are known to heaven;
Divine justice never misses the mark.

The above story is about how a certain Squire Jin destroyed his family through an evil deed. Now I propose to tell of a man who saved his family through acts of kindness. Truly,

With the good and the evil side by side,
You see which side is blessed and which is doomed.
This is a warning against evil acts
And a word of advice to do good deeds.

As the story goes, outside the East Gate of Wuxi County, in Changzhou Prefecture, south of the Yangzi River, there lived a family of three brothers of modest means. The oldest brother was named Lü Yu, the second one Lü Bao, and the third one Lü Zhen. Lü Yu and Lü Bao each took a wife. The two wives, Wang-shi and Yang-shi were women of some attractiveness. Lü Zhen, being still young, remained a bachelor.

Wang-shi gave birth to a son, whom they called Xi'er. One day, when the boy was six years old, he followed some neighbors' children to watch a religious procession. That night, he did not come home. In distress, the parents posted a notice in a public place and searched the neighborhood for several days, calling out his name, but to no avail. Rather than sit gloomily at home, Lü Yu approached a rich man from whom he borrowed a few taels of silver as capital and set off for the Taichang and Jiading region, where he traded in cotton and fabric and inquired about his son as he traveled. Every year, he left in the first or second month and returned in the eighth or ninth month for replenishment of his stocks. After four years as a traveling merchant, he amassed some wealth, but his son was still nowhere to be found. With the passing of time, his hopes began to fade, but of this, for the time being, no more.

In the fifth year, Lü Yu again took leave of Wang-shi and set out on a business journey. Quite accidentally, he met in his travels a wealthy merchant who dealt in fabric. In the course of their conversation, the latter came to appreciate Lü Yu's business acumen and asked Lü Yu to go to Shanxi with him to dispose of their goods and bring back cotton flannel for sale. He promised to pay Lü Yu a commission as a token of his gratitude. Attracted by the prospect of some profit the size of a fly's head, Lü Yu accepted the offer and followed the man to Shanxi. There, they disposed of the goods but were unable to leave because the local buyers, who had been hit by crop failures for several years in succession, were too poor to pay.

Having been celibate for quite some time, Lü Yu, who was still a young man, couldn't stop himself from visiting houses of ill repute once or twice, and these visits gave him boils all over his body. He took medicine for this condition but felt too ashamed to return home. It was not until three long years had gone by that his skin healed and all the debts were collected. The fabric merchant paid him double to compensate for the delay in his departure. Lü Yu chose not to wait for the fabric merchant to wind up his business, but used the funds to do his own trading in different kinds of fabric of varying quality. He then took leave of the merchant and headed home.

One morning, he found himself in the Chenliu region, and he went to a latrine to relieve himself. There, he saw a blue cotton shoulder bag left on the frame of the latrine pit. He picked it up and found it quite heavy. When he brought it to his lodgings and opened it, what did he find but about two hundred taels of silver!

Lü Yu thought to himself, "Even though there's nothing wrong if I keep this windfall for myself, the owner will be very upset if he can't find it. In ancient times, there were men who didn't pick up gold from the ground and a man who returned the jade belts he had found to their owner.[8] I'm more than thirty years old and still without an heir. What use do I have for all this silver that belongs to someone else?"

So thinking, he hastened back to the latrine and stood there, waiting for the rightful owner to show up so that he could return the silver. He waited for a whole day without anyone coming to look for the money. The next day, he resignedly continued on his journey.

Three hundred to five hundred li farther on, he entered the Nansuzhou region. That night, in his lodgings, he struck up an idle conversation about business matters with a fellow lodger, who spoke of his own carelessness.

This is what had happened: five days earlier, upon arriving in Chenliu County at dawn, that man took off his shoulder bag and relieved himself in a latrine. At the noise of an official's entourage passing by in the street, he gave a start and got up, forgetting all about the shoulder bag, which contained two hundred taels of silver, until he undressed to go to bed that night. Because a whole day had gone by, he'd been sure that someone must have picked up the bag and walked away with it, so it would have served no purpose to turn back and look for it. There was no choice but to accept his bad luck. (*This is a merchant who takes things philosophically.*)

"What is your honorable name?" asked Lü Yu. "Where do you live?"

"My surname is Chen. I am a native of Huizhou. I run a grain shop by the Yangzho floodgate. May I ask your honorable name?"

"My surname is Lü. I'm a native of Wuxi County in Changzhou Prefecture. I'll be passing by Yangzhou on my way home. May I accompany you back and visit your home?"

Not knowing why Lü Yu had offered to do that, Mr. Chen agreed, saying, "I would like nothing better than for you to visit my humble home."

The next morning, they set out together. A couple of days later, they arrived at the floodgate of Yangzhou. Lü Yu followed Mr. Chen to his shop and went into the main hall, where they exchanged formal greetings. After Mr. Chen offered him a seat and served him tea, Lü Yu brought up the subject of his host's loss of silver in Chenliu County and asked what the shoulder bag looked like. Mr. Chen replied, "It's a dark blue bag, with the character *chen* embroidered in white thread at one end."

Knowing that this was the bag he had found, Lü Yu said, "I picked up a shoulder bag in Chenliu, one that quite fits your description. Let me show it to you. Tell me if it's yours."

At the sight of the bag, Mr. Chen said, "Yes, that's the one."

With both hands, Lü Yu respectfully returned the bag to Mr. Chen with the silver therein intact. Mr. Chen could not bring himself to accept it and offered to share the silver with Lü, fifty-fifty. Lü Yu declined.

Mr. Chen said, "If not fifty-fifty, you must at least accept a few taels as a token of my gratitude, if only to make me feel better."

Lü Yu adamantly refused.

His heart overflowing with gratitude, Mr. Chen hastened to make arrangements for a dinner in Lü Yu's honor. He thought to himself, "A good man like Lü is hard to come by. What can I do to repay him for giving me back the money? I can arrange to have my twelve-year-old daughter engaged to his son, if he has one."

In the course of their drinking, Mr. Chen asked, "How old is your son, my brother?"

Lü Yu answered, tears coursing down his cheeks in spite of himself, "I have only one son, who left home seven years ago to watch a religious procession. He never came back. Nothing has been heard of him since. My wife has borne no other child. After I go back this time, I'll search for a boy to adopt so that he can help me in my business travels. But it's hard to find the right one."

"Some years ago," said Mr. Chen, "I bought a page boy for three taels of silver from a man who came from the lower reaches of the Yangzi River. He's a well-behaved boy with fine, delicate features. Thirteen years old now, he serves my son as a companion in school. If you find him to your liking, I'll give him to you. That will be my humble way of repaying you for your kindness."

"If you would be willing to lend him to me, I'll surely pay you the full price."

"What kind of talk is this?" said Mr. Chen. "My only fear is that you may not want him. In that case, I'll have nothing to give you in return for your kindness."

Without a moment's delay, he told a shop clerk to go to the school and bring back Xi'er. Hearing that name, which was the same as that of his own son, Lü Yu grew apprehensive.

Soon, the page boy arrived. In a robe of Wuhu blue cotton, the boy did indeed have refined looks. Accustomed to school discipline, he respectfully raised his folded hands and bowed deeply in greeting. Much taken with the boy, Lü Yu looked at him intently and recognized him to be none other than his son, for the boy still had the small scar by his left eyebrow caused by a fall when he was four years old.

"When did you come to the Chen family?"

"About six or seven years ago," replied the boy after a moment of reflection.

"Where are you from originally? Who sold you here?"

"I don't quite know. I remember only that my father is called Lü the Big Brother. There were also two uncles who lived with us. My mother, named Wang, is from outside the city of Wuxi. I was abducted when I was small and sold here."

Upon hearing this, Lü Yu took the boy in his arms and cried, "My very own son! I am none other than Lü the Big Brother of Wuxi, your father! Having lost you seven years ago, I never dreamed of meeting you in this place!" Truly,

The much sought needle rose from the riverbed;
The treasure that had slipped from the palm reappeared.
At the feast, they embraced in recognition,
Though afraid that it was all but a dream.

Tears streamed down the boy's cheeks, and we need hardly say that Lü Yu was overcome with emotion. He rose and bowed in gratitude to Mr. Chen, saying, "If you hadn't taken my little son into your care, how would it have been possible for this father and son to meet?"

"My brother," said Mr. Chen, "it was your noble act of returning the silver you had found that made heaven guide you to this humble house of mine for a reunion with your son. I'm sorry for having been neglectful of your son, but I didn't know who he was."

Lü Yu had the boy bow thankfully on his knees to Mr. Chen, who insisted on returning the bow over Lü Yu's objections, and it was only with much effort that Lü Yu stopped him from getting down on his knees and accepted two salutes from him instead.

Having asked Xi'er to sit by Lü Yu's side, Mr. Chen said, "I feel honored that you, my brother, have been so kind to me. I have a twelve-year-old daughter. I'd like her to form a binding relationship with your son." (*A further indication that Mr. Chen is not a vulgar sort.*)

Impressed by Mr. Chen's sincerity, Lü Yu, rather than mouthing words of demurral, felt obliged to give his consent. That night, the father and son shared the same bed and talked the whole night through.

The next day, when Lü Yu went to bid his host farewell, the latter kept him for a grand feast in honor of the departing new son-in-law and his father. After a few rounds of wine, Mr. Chen took out twenty taels of silver and said, "Because my good son-in-law did not receive the treatment he deserved in this house, I now offer you a small gift to mark the occasion of his redemption. Please take it as an expression of my feelings as a family member. You must not turn me down."

"Being much honored by a marriage tie with your family," said Lü Yu, "I should have offered betrothal gifts, but I can't very well do this while I'm on the road. How could I possibly receive generous gifts from you instead? I would never be so presumptuous as to accept this!"

"This is a gift from me to my good son-in-law. It has nothing to do with you. If you object, I'll take it to mean that you wish to decline the betrothal."

Words failing him, Lü Yu had to accept the gift. At his order, his son left the table and bowed deeply in gratitude to Mr. Chen, but Mr. Chen raised the boy up and said, "Why thank me for such a modest gift?"

Xi'er then went to the inner quarters of the house to thank his mother-in-law. That day, they drank to their hearts' content and did not leave the feast table until evening set in. Lü Yu thought to himself, "It is by heaven's will that I got to meet my son in the midst of a mission to return some silver I had found. And now, this betrothal is like adding flowers to a piece of brocade that is already gorgeous enough. What can I do to show gratitude to heaven and earth? Since these twenty taels of silver from Mr. Chen are something I never expected would come my way, why don't I pick a nice monastery, use the silver to buy some rice, and sponsor a vegetarian dinner for the monks? That would be an act of kindness that will gain me credit, like sowing in the fields of blessings." And so, his mind was made up.

The next morning, Mr. Chen again laid out breakfast, and afterward, Lü Yu and his son packed up their luggage and gratefully took leave of Mr. Chen. Several li after their small hired boat had rowed its way out of the floodgate, there came to their ears an excited hubbub of voices from the riverbank. As it turned out, a boat was sinking, and the passengers who had fallen into the river were crying for help. Those on the shore were calling out to some small boats, asking the boatmen to go to the rescue, but the boatmen were busy clamoring for a reward.

Lü Yu thought to himself, "To save a human life is better than to build a seven-layered stupa. Rather than sponsoring a dinner for the monks, why not use the twenty taels of silver as a reward for the rescue effort? That will be a good deed here and now!" Without a moment's delay, he said to all those present at the scene, "I'm offering a reward. Go to the rescue, quick! Those who manage to save the lives of the drowning passengers will get twenty taels of silver."

Hearing that a reward of twenty taels of silver was being offered, the small boats swarmed over like so many ants. Even a few of the people on the shore who knew how to swim jumped into the water for the rescue effort. In no time, everyone who had been on that boat was brought to shore alive, whereupon Lü Yu dispersed the silver among the crowd. While those who had been saved were offering profuse thanks, one man among them, looking at Lü Yu, cried, "Older brother, where did you come from?"

Lü Yu looked in the man's direction and found him to be none other than his youngest brother Lü Zhen. Joining his palms together, Lü Yu said, "What a stroke of luck! Heaven made me save my brother's life."

He made haste to help his brother onto his own boat and gave him a dry change of clothes. Lü Zhen bowed deeply, a salutation Lü Yu returned before he summoned his son to greet his uncle. When Lü Yu recounted how he had returned the silver and met his son, Lü Zhen was all amazement.

"But why are *you* here?" asked Lü Yu.

"It's a long story. Three years after you left, rumors got around, saying that you had died of some poisonous boils in Shanxi. Second Brother investigated and confirmed the rumors. Sister-in-law put on mourning clothes, but I never believed that you had died. Recently, Second Brother began to pressure Sister-in-law to remarry, but she refuses to obey, and so I've been instructed to go to Shanxi in person to find out what really happened to you. I never expected to run into you here. And then I almost drowned. It's by the grace of heaven that you saved my life! You don't have a moment to lose. Go home quickly to put Sister-in-law's mind at ease before something happens."

Alarmed upon hearing these words, Lü Yu hurriedly bade the boatmen to continue on their way, and pressed on posthaste, like an arrow, day and night. Truly,

> *Quick as an arrow, he still chafes at the pace;*
> *Fast as a shuttle, he still grieves at the speed.*

Let us retrace our steps and go back to Wang-shi when she first heard about her husband's death. She, too, was quite doubtful as to the truth of that news, but Lü Bao's eloquence convinced her, and as was the usual practice in such cases, she changed into white mourning clothes.

Lü Bao, in fact, was harboring an evil plan. He reasoned that, with his older brother dead and gone, leaving behind a young childless widow, he could very well make a profit by talking her into remarrying and keeping the betrothal gifts for himself. He made his wife Yang-shi do the talking, but Wang-shi turned a deaf ear. In addition, with Lü Zhen also in the way, remonstrating with him day and night, his plan did not go through.

Wang-shi thought to herself, "As the saying goes, 'It's better to see once than to hear a thousand times.' Though my husband is said to have died, I don't know that for a fact because of the thousands of li that separate us." So thinking, she pleaded with her husband's younger brother Lü Zhen, saying, "It looks like you'll have to go personally to Shanxi and find out everything about this. If he has indeed died, which would be too unfortunate, please at least bring back a bone."

After Lü Zhen left, Lü Bao became more reckless in his ways. For several days in a row, he lost at gambling and could not come up with the money for repayment.

It so happened that a traveler from Jiangxi, recently widowed, was looking for a new wife. Lü Bao offered him his sister-in-law. The traveler, having learned that Lü the Big Brother's widow was a woman of some attractiveness, gladly offered thirty taels of silver. After the silver changed hands, Lü Bao said to the traveler, "My sister-in-law is a demure sort. She'll refuse to come out the door the proper way. You'll have to bring a sedan-chair quietly to my house this evening after it gets dark. The one wearing mourning white on her bun hairpiece will be my sister-in-law. You don't have to say anything. Just get her into the sedan-chair and set off in your boat under cover of night." The traveler agreed to do what he had been told.

After returning home, Lü Bao, afraid of his sister-in-law's objections, did not even breathe a word of his plans to her, but privately, he said to his wife with a meaningful gesture, "I've dumped that two-legged thing on a traveler from Jiangxi. I'm afraid that she'll make a scene, so I'll go hide somewhere. After it gets dark, urge her to get into the sedan-chair but don't tell her anything about this during the day." Without bringing up the subject of the bun hairpiece, Lü Bao turned and went away. (*This was all dictated by the will of heaven.*)

As a matter of fact, Yang-shi was on the best of terms with her sister-in-law Wang-shi. Her husband's words pained her heart, but as he had already made the decision, there was nothing she could do. She debated with herself the whole afternoon about whether or not to tell. Finally, toward evening, she said quietly to Wang-shi, "My husband has married you off to a traveler from Jiangxi. In a moment, the man will be coming to get you. My husband told me not to say anything, but the two of us are such good friends that I just can't keep you in the dark. You can go ahead and pack up any valuables you have in your room, so you won't be caught unprepared when the man comes."

Wang-shi burst into sobs and cried loudly to heaven and earth.

"It's not that I'm trying to talk you into anything," said Yang-shi, "but a young woman like you won't be able to maintain widowhood for very long. Now the water bucket has already been let down into the well, and that's the way it should be. Crying doesn't get you anywhere!"

"What kind of talk is this, Sister-in-law? Though my husband is said to be dead, I haven't seen any evidence to prove his death. I'm still waiting for Third Brother to come back with some definite news. And now you have to come after me like this!" With that, she broke into another fit of sobbing.

After much effort to calm her down on Yang-shi's part, Wang-shi stopped crying and said, "Sister-in-law, if I have to remarry, well, that would be that. But how can I go wearing a bun of mourning? Please find a black one and exchange it with mine."

Wishing to obey her husband's instructions and be nice to her sister-in-law at the same time, Yang-shi hastened to look for a black hairpiece, but, as dictated by the will of heaven, there were no old black ones to be found. Wang-shi said, "Sister-in-law, you'll be staying at home anyway. Why don't you give me your bun for now? Tomorrow morning, you can have your husband buy you another one."

"Right," said Yang-shi, whereupon she took off her bun hairpiece and handed it to Wang-shi, who removed her bun of mourning and gave it to Yang-shi. Yang-shi put on her sister-in-law's bun, and Wang-shi then changed into colored clothes.

After evening set in, the traveler from Jiangxi came rushing to the Lü house with the speed of a wind-driven rainstorm, leading a team of men carrying lanterns and torches and a much decorated sedan-chair. They brought along a set of wind and percussion instruments but discreetly held back from striking up the music. Following the secret instructions that Lü Bao had given them, they pushed open the gate and went for the woman with a bun hairpiece in mourning white. Yang-shi screamed, "I'm not the one you want!" but the men could not have cared less. They pushed her into the sedan-chair, and in the midst of music, the sedan-chair carriers raced off.

She was hustled off amid wedding music;
The wrong hairpiece led to a marriage.
To the groom, the bride poured out her sorrows;
She blamed her husband rather than heaven.

Privately, Wang-shi gave thanks to heaven and earth. She closed the gate and retired to her room.

At daybreak, a high-spirited Lü Bao came back and knocked at the gate. He gave a start upon seeing his sister-in-law open the gate. Failing to find his wife in their room and noticing the black hairpiece his sister-in-law was wearing, he grew apprehensive. "Sister-in-law," he asked, "where is my wife?"

Inwardly amused, Wang-shi replied, "Last night, some hooligans from Jiangxi took her away by force."

"What nonsense is this? And why are you not wearing your bun of mourning?"

As Wang-shi explained the exchange of hairpieces, Lü Bao smote his chest and cried out in anguish. How was he to know that his plan to sell his sister-in-law would backfire and end up in the selling of his own wife? The traveler from Jiangxi had already left in his boat, and the bulk of the thirty taels of silver had been lost in gambling the previous night. To get himself another wife in this lifetime was an impossible dream. Then he thought again, "I might as well finish off the job, now that I've already started it. Let me keep my eyes open and find another patron to whom I can sell Sister-in-law, so I'll have enough money to get another wife." (*How tightly knit the plot of this story!*) He was on the point of going out the gate when a group of five people rushed in. They were none other than his older brother Lü Yu, his younger brother Lü Zhen, his nephew Xi'er, and two porters carrying their luggage. Feeling too ashamed to show his face, Lü Bao slunk out the back gate and disappeared, destination unknown.

Wang-shi greeted her husband, and seeing her son, now quite grown up, she asked what had happened. Thereupon, Lü Yu gave a full account from beginning to end. Wang-shi also related how a man from Jiangxi had kidnapped her sister-in-law and how Lü Bao, too ashamed to show his face, had slunk out the back gate.

Lü Yu said, "Had I greedily kept those two hundred taels of silver that I had never even expected to have, how would I have been reunited with my son? Had I begrudged those twenty taels of silver and held back from rescuing some drowning people, how would I have been reunited with my brother? Had I not met my brother, how was I to know what was happening at home? It's by the will of heaven that I'm reunited with my wife and the rest of the family. As for that treacherous brother of mine who sold his wife, he brought all this upon himself. How true it is that divine retribution never misses the mark!"

Henceforth, he devoted himself to more works of charity. His family circumstances grew more and more prosperous. Later, Xi'er married Squire Chen's daughter, and the family line thrived. Many of their descendants attained high rank and fame. As the poem says,

He who returned silver got back his son;
He who tried to sell his in-law lost his own wife.
Nothing in this world works like divine will,
Which never fails to tell good from evil.

6

Yu Liang Writes Poems and Wins Recognition from the Emperor

The sun rises and sets, the moon waxes and wanes,
And the stars shine and dim in their cycles.
How can human lives not have their ups and downs?
In his youth, Zhang Liang took refuge in Xiapi;[1]
Yi Yin plowed the fields of Youxin;[2]
Lü Wang fished by Panxi Creek.[3]
Consider how Han Xin crawled between legs,[4]
How Lü Mengzheng lived in a cave,[5]
How Pei Du lodged in an old temple.[6]
When their time came, they all rose to high rank
And showed their qualities as men of worth.

In the second year of the Yuanshou reign period [121 B.C.E.], under Emperor Wudi of the Han dynasty, there was, in Chengdu Prefecture, Sichuan, a scholar named Sima Xiangru [d. 118 B.C.E.], courtesy name Changqing, who, not having anyone to turn to for help after his parents died, lived by himself in the most straitened circumstances. He was well versed in the hundred schools of thought and knew everything there was to know about the classics and the histories. Though he wandered around the country seeking knowledge and making friends, his real ambition was to attain fame and fortune. The day he left home, he wrote the following line in big, bold characters on a pier of the Bridge from Which Immortals Ascend to Heaven, located about seven li north of the city: "This man of true worth will not cross this bridge again unless in a grand four-horse carriage."

In his travels, Sima Xiangru reached the capital Luoyang in the north and the regions of Qi and Chu in the east.[7] He then entered into the service of King Xiao of Liang and made friends with men like Zou Yang and Mei Gao.[8] After the king of Liang died unexpectedly, Xiangru returned to Chengdu, pleading illness.

Wang Ji, the magistrate of Linqiong County [in modern Qionglai, Sichuan], often sent him invitations to visit. One day, Xiangru again accepted an invitation and stayed for ten days. In the course of their conversation, they got on to the subject of the wealth of Squire Zhuo Wangsan, who lived in the area in a mansion with pavilions, terraces, ponds, and belvederes. They thought it would be a most beautiful and interesting place to visit. The county magistrate thus sent a messenger to tell Squire Zhuo to be prepared for visitors.

Now, this Squire Zhuo was fabulously rich. He had hundreds of servants in his lavishly furnished mansion. On the grounds, he had a pavilion called Auspicious Fairy Pavilion, which was a riot of colors and a most pleasant place for relaxation in a garden that could hold its own with any of the famous ones in the capital.

Squire Zhuo was a widower. Determined not to marry again, he devoted himself to the cultivation of the Dao [Tao, the way]. He had only one daughter, whose name was Wenjun. Recently widowed at the age of nineteen, she was living at home with her father. She was an exceptionally intelligent girl with unusually graceful posture and was skilled in the arts of music, chess, calligraphy, and painting.

That morning, when the squire heard the announcement that the county magistrate and his friend Sima Xiangru, an eminent scholar, were there to visit and see the garden, he made haste to greet them and escorted them to Auspicious Fairy Pavilion in the back garden. After an exchange of amenities, Squire Zhuo set out wine. Deeply impressed by Xiangru's graceful bearing and his friendship with County Magistrate Wang (*Xiangru's talent did not make an impression on him.*), Squire Zhuo said, "It's not very convenient for you to take up quarters in the county yamen. Why not stay in my humble home for a few days?"

Gratefully, Xiangru sent for his page boy, who brought his luggage to Auspicious Fairy Pavilion so that he could settle in. In the twinkling of an eye, half a month went by.

Let us now turn to Zhuo Wenjun. Sitting idly in her boudoir, she heard her maid Chun'er say, "A scholar called Sima Xiangru came for a visit, and Master has kept him on as a houseguest. He now stays in Auspicious Fairy Pavilion. He's a handsome young man, and he plays the zither very well."

Her heart aflutter, Wenjun went to the east wall and peeped through the latticed window. Impressed by Xiangru's graceful appearance, she thought to herself, "This man will surely go far. I wonder if he's married. If I could have such a man for a husband, what more would I want from life? But he's so impoverished that Father will never agree to the marriage if a matchmaker approaches him. And yet, if I let him go, such a man may never come my way again."

A couple of days later, the maid Chun'er, noticing that her mistress wore a worried frown and looked as if something was on her mind, said to her, "Tonight being the fifteenth of the third month, the moon is full and shining brightly. Why don't you go into the garden to cheer yourself up?" (*Chun'er was most perceptive.*)

Without saying a word, the young lady thought to herself, "Ever since I laid eyes on that scholar, he's been so much in my thoughts day and night that I can hardly eat or sleep. My mind is made up. I may be breaking the code of behavior for women, but the well-being of my whole life is at stake." Thereupon, she packed some jewelry and other valuables and told Chun'er to set out wine and some tidbits to go with it, adding, "Yes, I'll go out with you to view the moon and cheer myself up."

After making the arrangements, Chun'er followed her mistress to the garden.

Now, let us return to Xiangru. Having long heard of Wenjun's beauty, intelligence, and musical talent, he, on his part, was thinking of trying to win her affections. On that bright moonlit night, hearing movements near the flowers' shadows, he had his page boy take a stealthy look and was told that it was the young lady, whereupon he lit some incense and started playing the zither. As Wenjun walked along, the clear notes of the zither struck her ears. She went to Auspicious Fairy Pavilion and stopped in the shadow of some flowers. This was what she heard in the notes:

> *The phoenix, yearning for its native place,*
> *Roams the four seas in search of a mate.*
> *The time not yet ripe, it has nowhere to go,*
> *But why not land in this hall this very night?*
> *Here, a lovely maiden in her chamber,*
> *So far from me, yet so close by my side.*
> *May we never part, like a pair of mandarin ducks!*
> *May we stay wing to wing, as we fly through the air!*
> *O phoenix, follow me to my nest,*
> *To roost in eternal love,*
> *Body to body, heart to heart.*
> *Let's leave in the night! Who'll be the wiser?* (So, Xiangru has made the decision for Wenjun.)
> *Let our wings take us toward the sky!*
> *But how sad if I pine all alone!*

Having heard this much, the young lady said to her maid, "The scholar's feelings *are* reciprocated. Since I'm already here tonight, I'll go up and greet him." And so, she directed her steps toward the pavilion.

At the sight of Wenjun in the moonlight, Xiangru rose with alacrity and said in greeting, "I have been picturing your beauty to myself, but I never expected that you would be here! Please forgive me for failing to meet you at a distance and bring you here."

After curtsying, Wenjun took a step forward and said, "To such an honored guest as you, the host has been less than generous. I have been worrying that you might feel lonely in this forlorn pavilion."

"Please don't trouble yourself about me. I have the zither to keep myself amused."

With a smile, Wenjun said, "You need not be evasive. Your feelings as demonstrated through the music have not been lost on me."

Xiangru fell to his knees, saying, "Now that I have had the good fortune of seeing such beauty, I can die content."

"Please rise. I am here tonight to view the moon with you over a few cups of wine."

Accordingly, Chun'er set out the wine and tidbits in the pavilion for Wenjun and Xiangru to enjoy as they sat face-to-face. Upon taking a close look at Wenjun, Xiangru saw that, indeed,

Her eyebrows as black as a kingfisher's feathers,
Her skin as fair as white snow,
Her body covered in silk and brocade,
She is neither too showy nor too meek.
The very image of the River Goddess,
A replica of Chang'e, goddess of the moon.

After a few rounds of wine, Wenjun told Chun'er to clear the table and leave them, adding, "I'll be with you soon."

"If you don't find my present position too humble," said Xiangru, "I pray that you will indulge me in the pleasures of the pillow."

With a smile, Wenjun replied, "I am determined to serve you as your wife for the rest of my life. Some momentary pleasure is not what I am after."

"What plans do you have in mind?"

"I have here some valuables that I've packed. The best thing for us to do is to leave here tonight and live somewhere else. Later, if my father misses me, we can move back and be reunited with him. Wouldn't that be nice?"

Without a moment's delay, the two stepped down from the pavilion and left the mansion through the back gate. Truly,

The sea turtle freed itself from the golden hook,
Shook its head, wagged its tail, and vanished for good.

At daybreak, Chun'er found that her mistress was absent from her chamber. A search in the pavilion also turned up nothing. She reported the matter to the old master, who went to the pavilion, but both the young lady and Xiangru were missing.

"How could a fine scholar like Xiangru be capable of such a beastly thing?" fumed Squire Zhuo. "And the little hussy! Having started your education at an early age, haven't you heard that for women, 'There's nothing they should do on their own; there's nowhere they should go unaccompanied'? Now, by eloping in defiance of your father, you are no longer my daughter!" He thought of lodging an official complaint with the yamen but abandoned the idea because a domestic scandal could not very well be made public. "We'll see whether they'll ever have the nerve to show their faces again in front of kith and kin!" he said. So he swallowed his anger and raised no fuss. Nor was any effort made to track them down.

Let us return to Xiangru and Wenjun. Now back in his home, Xiangru was troubled by thoughts of his poverty and lack of livelihood. "My wife is from a wealthy family. How was she to know that life could be so hard? But I'm glad she hasn't shown the least sign of displeasure. Quite a fine, magnanimous mind she has! She must have confidence that I, Sima Changqing, will rise in life someday."

In the midst of these none-too-happy thoughts, he found that Wenjun had drawn near to him. He said to her, "Someday, I'll have to talk with you about setting up a small business, except I have no capital."

"All my jewelry can be sold. It's quite unimaginable that my father, with all his fabulous wealth, can't help me out. The best thing to do now is to open a wineshop, with me working at the front counter. If Father hears of that, he'll surely regret what he has done."

Xiangru agreed. A house was built, and the wineshop opened for business, with Wenjun as both the server and the bookkeeper.

One day, a servant from the Zhuo residence was sent to Chengdu on some errand. As chance would have it, he walked into the very wineshop owned by Sima Xiangru for a drink. At the sight of the young mistress at the counter, he gave a start and rushed back to Linqiong to report to Squire Zhuo. With shame written all over his face, the Squire adamantly refused to acknowledge that he had such a daughter (*Squire Zhuo was right, of course.*) but did nothing more than shut his door to visitors.

After Xiangru and his wife had been selling wine for about half a year, there came one day an imperial messenger, the scroll of an imperial edict in hand, asking where to find Sima Xiangru. After receiving directions, he made his way to the wineshop and said, "The imperial court finds your prose poem titled 'Mr. Fantasy' a most splendid piece of writing, superior in style to those of the ancients.[9] The emperor said that it has an ethereal, transcendent grandeur that rises above the clouds and wished that he could spend some time with the poet. There was a Yang Deyi who said, 'This prose poem was written by Sima Changqing, who is from the same part of the country as I am. He is now living in Chengdu, without an official post.' The emperor was greatly pleased and sent me to summon you to the court without delay."

Xiangru started packing, ready to be on his way.

"Now that you are heading for fame and fortune," said Wenjun, "I'm afraid that you will forget your days in Auspicious Fairy Pavilion."

"My debt to you is greater than I've been able to repay. Why do you say this?"

"There are two kinds of scholars," said Wenjun. "There are the gentlemanly scholars who remain constant in their feelings and behavior whether rich or poor. There are also petty ones who act in a certain way when poor but forget about their humble days as soon as they find themselves rich."

"Don't worry, my lady!" said Xiangru.

The two could hardly tear themselves apart. As Xiangru was about to leave, Wenjun reminded him again, "Now that the wish you wrote on the bridge has come true, do not betray the one serving wine and washing dishes!"

Let us not follow Xiangru on his journey with the emperor's messenger but turn our attention to Squire Zhuo, who learned from a servant just back from Chang'an that Sima Xiangru had been summoned by the court upon the recommendation of Yang Deyi. He said to himself, "My daughter does have quite a prophetic vision! (*Squire Zhuo is not as unyielding as Grand Historian Jiao.*)[10] She married him because she knew that this man, endowed with both talent and looks, would surely rise to eminence. Now that I think about it, a marriage is in fact a major event in human relationships. I'd better take along Chun'er the maid and go to Chengdu for a visit before my son-in-law assumes an official post. No one will laugh at me for this fatherly thing I do. But if I go *after* he becomes an official, I'll be accused of trying to ingratiate myself with the powerful." (*It would have been even better if he had gone before the recommendation was made in favor of Sima Xiangru.*)

The next day, he took Chun'er and went posthaste to see Wenjun in Chengdu. At the sight of her father, Wenjun bowed and said, "Father, please forgive me for my lack of filial piety!"

The Squire replied, "My child, I missed you so much! Why don't we let bygones be bygones! Now, this happy news from the imperial court must be what you've been waiting for. I've brought Chun'er along today to serve you and to bring you back home permanently. I will send a servant to Chang'an to let my good son-in-law know about this."

Wenjun firmly declined the offer.

Realizing that his daughter was not to be shaken in her resolve, the Squire gave her half his wealth, built an impressive mansion right there in Chengdu, and bought fertile fields and three hundred to four hundred servants. He himself stayed with his daughter while waiting for good tidings from his son-in-law.

Let us return to Sima Xiangru, who followed the emperor's messenger to the capital, where he was granted an audience with the emperor. Upon presentation of his "Ode to the Imperial Hunting Ground," an immensely delighted emperor made him editorial director then and there and told him to go to Golden Horse Gate to await assignments.

At the time, claiming to be implementing the Wartime Troops Deployment and Transportation of Goods Act, some officials in areas bordering Sichuan and the southern regions inhabited by ethnic minorities were transporting provisions by land as well as by water, giving the minority peoples no peace. When he heard about this, the emperor flew into a rage. He summoned Xiangru for a consultation about the matter and authorized him to draft an official denunciation of culpable Sichuan officials. The emperor added, "This matter requires the attention of an envoy. And you are the only one suitable for the job."

Thereupon, Xiangru was honored with the title Imperial Corps Commander and equipped with tokens of authority including the official tablet, the emperor's sword of command, and golden badges, with full power to act first and report afterward. Xiangru voiced his gratitude, took leave of the emperor, and went on his way at top speed. Upon arriving at his destination, he began to exercise his skills of persuasion, and he restored peace to the area and to the lives of the minority peoples.

In less than half a month, the local people having resumed their tranquil ways of life, he set off in triumph for his hometown. In a matter of days, he arrived in Chengdu and was greeted by prefectural officials. When he approached the new mansion, Wenjun came out to greet him. "Scholarly pursuits do pay off," said he to Wenjun. "Today, I have fulfilled the wish that I wrote on the bridge."

"There's one more pleasant surprise for you," said Wenjun. "Your father-in-law is here to welcome you back."

"That is too much of an honor for me! Too much of an honor!" said Xiangru over and over again. When the old man emerged from the mansion to greet him, Xiangru took a step forward and saluted him. Both said words of gratitude to each other. A feast was laid out to celebrate the joyous occasion. Henceforth, Sima Xiangru became one of the richest men in Chengdu, as this poem testifies:

The full moon over the terrace in the still night;
A clear wind rustling the trees in the grove.
A wistful tune of love played on the zither,
Meant only for a truly appreciative ear.

This, then, is the story of how Sima Xiangru, a poverty-stricken scholar of Chengdu, gained instant fame and fortune because the emperor took a liking to his poetry.

I now propose to tell of a poor man of the Southern Song dynasty, also a native of Chengdu but living in Zhuojinjiang. In like fashion, he gained fame and fortune through a poem and returned to his hometown in triumph.

Yu Liang by name, courtesy name Zhongju, this man, twenty-five years of age when our story begins, had lost his parents in his youth and taken a wife, Zhangshi. Day and night, this scholar applied himself assiduously to books of history and poetry and became a veritable fountain of knowledge and learning. When the examination grounds opened in Lin'an [capital of the Southern Song dynasty, now Hangzhou], so that talented scholars throughout the land could take the spring examinations, Yu Liang packed up his zither, sword, and boxes of books and chose a day for his departure. He was invited to send-off dinners by kith and kin. He said to his wife, "This journey of mine in quest of a career as an official will take me three years at the longest and one year at the shortest. I'll come back as soon as I obtain a position, however insignificant."

Having said that, he took leave of his wife, mounted a lame donkey, and left. The days went by. He had only gone part of the way when he contracted an illness and had to look urgently for an inn, feeling quite dejected. As it turned out, the illness lasted half a month. His money and provisions exhausted, he was reduced to selling the donkey for traveling money. Afraid that he would miss the examination dates, he resignedly bought a pair of straw sandals and, his bags of books on his back, continued with his journey. Not many days passed before his feet were lacerated and dripping blood. In the midst of all this misery, he thought to himself, "When will I ever get to Hangzhou?" Looking at his feet, he composed a lyric poem to express his feelings. Set to the tune of "An Immortal's Auspicious Crane," it said,

With the spring examinations drawing near,
I'm still far, far away from the capital.
How I hate my feet, so unused to travel,
As I drag them through mud and water,
While they burn in pain from the sandals' straw.
When they are tired out from too much walking,
I comfort them with words gentle and sweet:
Make a good showing, please, and get me there.
I will reward you when I gain a post.
I will put you in official's boots
And place you in a sedan-chair
To be carried hither and thither;
I will feed you well with fragrant mutton,
For you to regain the smoothness of your skin.
I'll also look for a pair of small feet
To keep you company throughout the night.

A few days later, he arrived in Hangzhou. By the bridge in front of the examination grounds, there was a Madam Sun's Inn. Yu Liang took up lodgings there. In another few days, he completed his examinations and began to wait for the list of successful examinees to be posted.

Now, all those who sit for imperial examinations must go through many trials and tribulations. In Yu Liang's case, he had trudged more than eight thousand li to Lin'an in hopes of passing the examinations on the first try and thereby attaining instant fame. However, his time had not come. His name did not appear on the list of successful candidates. With tears in his eyes, he thought gloomily to himself, "I've traveled here over such a long distance, and now, with so little money left, how am I going to make it home?" And so he was stranded in Hangzhou.

Every day, when he walked up and down the streets, he spent whatever money he had on wine to drown his sorrows, and all too soon, he became penniless. At first, there were still a few acquaintances who looked after him. (*Those who took the trouble of looking after him at the beginning were not uninspired by the generous spirit of the ancients.*) But later, he came to be loathed, as more and more people found him a nuisance.

Every time he saw some scholars drinking in a wineshop, he would send in his card and join the group. Every day, he drank himself into a stupor, swallowing two bowls of wine on an empty stomach, and returned to the inn to rest. The innkeepers, Madam Sun, seeing him in such a state, would grumble bitterly, "Scholar, instead of paying your bills, you get drunk every day. I wonder how you could afford the wine!" Yu Liang never said anything in his own defense. Every morning, he asked the inn clerk for some hot water, washed his face, and went out the door. By writing some "long articles for prime ministers and short ones for dukes and ministers," he earned enough to buy himself a few bowls of wine. (*Nowadays, where can you even hope to exchange articles, long or short, for a drop of wine?*) After he had gotten himself dead drunk, he would return to the inn after nightfall. Things went on this way day after day.

One day, Yu Liang went to Zhong'an Bridge, where he saw a teahouse with several scholars inside. He stepped in and found a seat for himself. A waiter came up, chanted a greeting, and asked, "What kind of tea for you, scholar?"

Without saying anything out loud, Yu Liang thought to himself, "I haven't even had breakfast, and yet he asks me about tea. Without a penny on me, how am I going to pay for it?" So thinking, he said, "I'm waiting for a friend. Come again when he's here."

The waiter turned away.

Yu Liang sat down right by the door, hoping in vain to find an acquaintance among the passersby. Feeling melancholy, he suddenly saw a man holding a sign that said "Divine foresight," whereupon he said to himself, "So, this is a fortune-teller. Let me ask him to tell my fortune." At Yu Liang's request, the man stepped into the teahouse and sat down. After obtaining Yu Liang's date of birth—complete with the hour, day, month, and year—the man started working.

Seeing the two, the waiter said, "So, his friend is here." He walked up and asked, "What kind of tea for you scholars?"

Yu Liang said, "Bring us two cups of spiced tea."

After tea, the man said, "Scholar, you are in great luck! Within three days, you will encounter a most eminent man and gain unspeakably great fame and fortune."

Having heard these words, Yu Liang thought to himself, "As wretched as I am, when will I ever gain fame and fortune? I don't even have money for the tea." Seeing his chance, he rose and said, "If I really gain fame and fortune, sir, I will surely pay you in gratitude." With that, he headed for the door.

"Scholar, you have to pay for the tea!" said the waiter.

"I sat here for only a moment, and you had to come over and serve tea. How would I have any money to pay for it? That gentleman says I'll gain fame and fortune any time now, so I'll pay you back when I've struck it rich!" With that, Yu Liang again turned to go.

"Scholar!" cried the fortune-teller. "You haven't paid me for telling your fortune!"

"Sorry! I'll pay you most gratefully when I do gain fame and fortune."

"I'm new in this business," said the fortune-teller. "What a miserable beginning!"

"I'm not any luckier!" said the waiter. "I served the tea for nothing!" With that, they went their separate ways.

Yu Liang continued his freeloading and drank a few more bowls of wine on his empty stomach. At nightfall, he stumbled in an inebriated state back to Madam Sun's Inn and lay down in a stupor. Upon seeing him, Madam Sun exploded, "What a shameless man this scholar is! Instead of paying me what you owe, you spend your money getting drunk day in and day out. You say that you were treated to the wine as a guest, but how do you manage to get invitations every day?"

"What business is it of yours if I get drunk? Whether I get invitations or not is none of your business either!"

"If you clear out of here tomorrow, I'll gladly cancel all your bills."

Under the influence of wine, Yu Liang ranted, "If you want me to go, give me five strings of cash, and I'll be gone tomorrow."

Madam Sun burst into laughter. "I've never seen such a patron! You've been staying here for free all this time, and now you turn around and demand money from me. What a horrible man! Where's your scholar's sense of decency?"

At these words, Yu Liang snapped back, "I have the aspirations of Han Xin, but you lack the kindness of the woman washing clothes.[11] I'm a learned scholar, and I may have failed the exams this time, but I'll make it the next time. That's only to be expected. What's the big deal even if you support me until the next examination comes around?" (*He does have a point there. How can one not follow his logic?*) Exhilarated by the wine, he started banging the tables and pounding the stools, getting so carried away that what he had begun half-heartedly turned into a big scene. Seeing the man acting like a crazy drunkard, Madam Sun dared not provoke him further. She closed the door and went to her own room.

This wild outburst exhausted Yu Liang. He collapsed onto his bed and drifted off to sleep. (*A veritable scene of boredom.*) When he woke up from the wine-induced sleep at the fifth watch of the night, he remembered what he had done and felt ashamed. He thought of leaving without saying good-bye to the innkeeper, but there was no place for him to go.

While he was debating with himself as to how to get out of this scrape, Madam Sun was consulting her son, Sun Xiao'er. They saw nothing for it but to offer Yu Liang two strings of cash along with an apology and beg him to vacate the premises. They would thank their lucky stars as long as he agreed to leave quietly.

Yu Liang wanted to reject the offer, but being penniless, he could do no better than swallow his pride and take the two strings of cash. With a few words of gratitude, he went on his way, thinking to himself, "It's eight thousand li from Lin'an to Chengdu. These two strings of cash will buy me only a few meals. How am I going to get enough money to make it to Chengdu?"

After leaving Madam Sun's Inn, he wandered around in the neighborhood without running into any acquaintances. He walked until it was well past the usual mealtime. Stung by the pangs of hunger and feeling morose, he decided to buy some wine and food with his two strings of cash and, with his stomach full, throw himself into West Lake. If he had to become a ghost, at least he would not be a hungry one.

Right away, he headed straight for West Lake. After passing through Yongjin Gate and arriving at the shore of the lake, he saw a tall building with a large sign.

Written in vermilion on the sign were the bold characters "Hall of Bounty and Bliss." There came to his ears the melodious notes of wind instruments amid drum music that rose to the skies. He stopped in his tracks to look. There, standing on both sides of the door with their hands folded across their chests were two men wearing square hats, purple robes, silk shoes, and white stockings. "Please come in and take a seat!" they said to Yu Liang.

At this invitation, Yu Liang joyfully stepped inside. He went all the way upstairs and sat down in a private booth near the railing with a nice view of the lake. A waiter on duty came up to him and asked, after chanting a greeting, "Scholar, how much wine shall I serve you?"

"I'm waiting for a friend. You can put two pairs of chopsticks and two plates on the table for now and come back later."

Thus instructed, the waiter laid before Yu Liang wine cups, a wine ladle, spoons, chopsticks, plates, and saucers—all of silver. Without saying anything out loud, Yu Liang thought to himself, "What a place of luxury! And yet I'm in such a wretched state! What good can those two strings of cash do?"

A moment later, the waiter appeared again. "Scholar, how much wine do you want? Shall I bring it to you now?"

"It looks like that friend of mine is not coming after all. Bring me two vessels of wine anyway."

The waiter took the order and asked again, "Scholar, what do you want to go with the wine?"

"Bring me whatever you see fit."

Taking Yu Liang to be a rich patron, the waiter brought as many plates of fresh fruit, delicacies, and seafood as he could carry and laid out a fine spread, with every kind of food imaginable. He filled a silver wine jar with two vessels of wine and placed on the table a ladle for Yu's use.

The waiter heated one serving of wine after another, and Yu Liang drank all by himself from morning till late afternoon until nothing was left on the table. His hand stroking the carved railings, his eyes resting on the shining surface of the lake, he felt his heart torn with grief. He summoned the waiter and said, "May I borrow a brush-pen and an ink slab?"

"Scholar," said the waiter, "in borrowing a brush-pen and an ink slab, are you thinking of writing a poem? Please don't spoil our whitewashed walls. (*Those who spoil whitewashed walls be cursed!*) We have tablets for writing down poems. If you write on the wall, I'll lose a day's wages."

"In that case, bring me a poem tablet along with the brush-pen and ink slab."

In the twinkling of an eye, the waiter laid a poem tablet, a brush-pen, and an ink slab on the table.

"You may withdraw now," said Yu Liang. "Don't come again until I call you." Immediately, the waiter withdrew.

Yu Liang pulled the partition door shut and put a stool against it, saying to himself, "I'm going to make myself famous in this wineshop and make my name known to posterity. (*What a miserable wretch! He wishes for nothing more than to make himself famous in a wineshop!*) Writing on the tablet is not going to serve my purpose." Then another thought struck him. "With only two strings of cash, how am I going to pay for all the wine and food that I've had? I might just as well write the poem, push the windows open, and jump into the lake. If I'm going to be a ghost, I'd better be one with a full stomach." Then and there, he rubbed the ink stick against the ink slab until the ink was the right thickness. After dipping the brush-pen in the ink, he dusted a stretch of the wall and wrote on it a lyric poem to the tune of "Immortal at the Magpie Bridge":

I left in late fall, arrived in late spring;
Now, on my way home, it's again late fall.
Looking west from the Hall of Bounty and Bliss,
I see eight thousand li from here to home.
Endless are the blue hills, white clouds, and green waters,
But few ever live beyond seventy.
Given the allotted spans of life,
How long can one ever aspire to live?

With the poem finished, he added at the end, "By Yu Liang, scholar of Chengdu, Sichuan."

As he lay down the pen, tears coursed down his cheeks before he knew it. He thought, "What's the point of going on living? I'd be better off dead, so as not to suffer anymore from all this poverty and misery!" Then and there, he pushed open the windows above the railings and was on the verge of jumping into the lake when a thought struck him: "The water is quite a distance away. What if I don't die but just end up breaking a foot or a leg?" (*He's not ready to die, after all.*)

He hit on a plan. He took off his old, worn waistband, threw it over the beam in the private booth, and made a slipknot in it. With a sigh, he prepared to stick his head into the knot, but, as coincidence would have it, the waiter, wondering why he had not been called for quite some time, went to the booth. Finding the door closed, he dared not knock but peeped through an aperture in the window. What did he see but Yu Liang at the point of sticking his head through the knot yet unable to bring himself to do it? With a violent start, the waiter frantically turned to the door, pushed it open, rushed in, and, in one sweep of his arms, held Yu Liang tight. "Scholar," said he, "what are you doing? If you kill yourself, this wineshop will be implicated!"

Hearing the commotion, the manager, chefs, waiters, and handymen hurried up the stairs, raising quite a clamor. There for all to see was Yu Liang, less than totally inebriated but raving and ranting, apparently under the influence of wine. At the sight of the wall now covered with characters, each the size of a teacup, the waiter cried out in anguish, "Woe is me! I can forget about today's wages!" He continued, "Scholar, please pay for the wine and food before you go."

"Why?" shot back Yu Liang. "Go ahead and beat me to death if you want the money!"

"Scholar, be reasonable. You owe me five taels of silver in total for the wine and the food."

"Five taels of silver, you said? I'll gladly offer you my life, but silver I have none! I was passing by this place when your two men in purple stopped me and invited me in for a drink upstairs. I have no money. Let me die!"

So saying, he made as if to jump out the window. Horrified, the waiter held him fast. Some onlookers gave this advice: "Why don't we just accept our bad luck and let him go back to wherever he lives? If we end up with a death on our hands, we'll have a lot of explaining to do."

Someone asked Yu Liang, "Scholar, where do you live?"

"I'm staying at Madam Sun's Inn by the bridge near the examination grounds. I'm a famous scholar from Chengdu Prefecture in Sichuan, here for the imperial examinations. (*The audacity!*) If I fall in some river on my way back, I won't let you off easy!"

"It won't reflect well on us if he really dies," said the crowd. Accepting their bad luck, they had two men accompany him back to his lodgings, so as to make sure that he reached his destination, lest he bring a lawsuit against them. And so, two waiters helped Yu Liang down the stairs.

The day was already drawing to a close by the time they started off. The two men supported him all the way until they arrived at Madam Sun's Inn, only to find the door closed. They propped Yu Liang against the wall by the door and knocked. Thinking some guests had arrived, those inside quickly answered the door. As soon as they saw the door opening, the waiters let go of Yu Liang and raced off, leaving him staggering and swaying every which way, looking as if he was about to fall. Madam Sun took a lamp and was aghast to see by its light that it was none other than Yu Liang. Resignedly, she had her son Sun Xiao'er help Yu Liang into his room to retire for the night.

"Yesterday, he raised hell in my inn," said Madam Sun bitterly, "and got two strings of cash from me for doing nothing. He said he was going back home, but now I see that he spent the money on wine!"

As he was supposed to be drunk, Yu Liang had to let her carry on and dared not make a sound. (*Poor thing.*) Truly,

Without dignity, he looked crestfallen;
With no money, he had to bite his tongue.

But our story forks at this point. Let me now tell of Emperor Gaozong [r. 1127–62] of the Southern Song dynasty. Having passed his throne to Xiaozong [r. 1163–89]

and making himself Imperial Patriarch, he took up residence in the Hall of Virtue and Longevity. Emperor Xiaozong proved to be a most filial son, gingerly fulfilling the Imperial Patriarch's every desire, lest he find anything contrary to his wishes. Every morning, Emperor Xiaozong went to pay his respects to his father. The Imperial Patriarch not only toured the scenic sites with his son but also, not infrequently in his leisurely life in the Hall of Virtue and Longevity, sought the company of eunuchs in his tours of West Lake. In order not to disturb the people, he made a habit of going incognito.

One day, the Imperial Patriarch went to Lingyin Monastery and sat idly in Cold Fountain Pavilion. How do we know about the charms of Cold Fountain Pavilion? There is a quatrain by Zhang Yu that describes the place:

Hills upon hills surround the royal canopy;
Towers that touch the clouds serve as homes to monks.
No human sound heard all day along the railings;
My feet in the cold spring, I count the falling petals.

While the Imperial Patriarch was sitting and looking at the spring, the abbot of the monastery ordered that tea be served. An acolyte, holding a tray high above his head, fell to his knees. Turning his royal eyes upon the man, the Imperial Patriarch was impressed by his imposing physique and polite manners. In his royal voice, he said, "We do not believe you have the looks of an acolyte. Tell us the truth. Who are you really?"

With tears falling thick and fast, the acolyte said respectfully, "Your subject's name is Li Zhi, formerly prefect of Nanjian. I offended the inspector and, as a result, was convicted of accepting bribes on the basis of some trumped-up charges. Deprived of all official posts, I was reduced to such poverty that I had nothing to live on. The abbot of this monastery is my uncle, so I am here working as an acolyte in exchange for some porridge to keep me alive." (*To be so poor as to have to make a living in a monastery after dismissal from office bespeaks his spotless record as an incorrupt official. How unjust for the inspector to charge him of bribery!*)

Saddened by these words, the Imperial Patriarch said, "After we return to the palace, we shall tell the emperor about this."

It so happened that upon his return to the palace that night, Emperor Xiaozong sent a eunuch to the Hall of Virtue and Longevity to inquire after the Imperial Patriarch's health. The Imperial Patriarch accordingly told the eunuch to convey to the emperor a message about the case of Li Zhi, the former prefect of Nanjian, asking that Li be reinstated.

A few days later, the Imperial Patriarch visited Lingyin Monastery again, and the same acolyte served tea.

"Has the emperor reinstated you?" asked the Imperial Patriarch.

"Not yet," replied the acolyte with a kowtow.

The Imperial Patriarch looked embarrassed.

The next day, while in Jujing Garden with his wife at the respectful invitation of Emperor Xiaozong, the Imperial Patriarch kept his lips tight, saying not a single word, giving not a single smile, and wearing a sullen look on his face. Emperor Xiaozong said, "I do wish that such nice and balmy weather would cheer you up, sire."

His father held his silence.

The empress dowager said, "Our boy invited us for this excursion with the best of intentions. There's surely no reason for you to sulk like this."

With a sigh, the Imperial Patriarch replied, "As the saying goes, 'An old tree invites the wind; an old person invites contempt.' Now that I am an old man, nobody takes my words seriously."

Emperor Xiaozong was aghast. Having no idea what had led to this remark, he kowtowed and begged for forgiveness.

His father continued, "The other day, I put in a good word for Li Zhi, the former prefect of Nanjian, but you brushed it aside. Yesterday, when I saw him again in the monastery, I was embarrassed to death!"

"I told the prime minister about this the very day after I received you message, sire. The prime minister said, 'Li Zhi was a notorious bribe taker and should not be reinstated.' But since you care so much about this case, I'll do something about it tomorrow. It's really a trivial matter. But now, please drink to your heart's content."

Only then did the Imperial Patriarch's expression soften. Regaining his cheerful mood, he drank until he was tipsy.

The next day, Emperor Xiaozong again instructed the prime minister to reinstate Li Zhi, but again, the prime minister refused. Emperor Xiaozong said, "This is the Imperial Patriarch's idea. Yesterday, he had such an outburst of anger that I wished I could have disappeared through some crack in the floor. Even if that man is guilty of plotting a rebellion, he has to be set free." Consequently, Li Zhi was reinstated as prefect, and we shall speak no more of this.

Now, let us return to Yu Liang. The night Yu Liang was brought back to Madam Sun's Inn, the Imperial Patriarch had a dream in which he was touring West Lake when, in the midst of the myriad fine rays of light, there arose two tall black columns. He woke up with a start. The next morning, he summoned an interpreter of dreams and gave a full description of the dream. The dream interpreter said, "There must be a worthy man who is stranded in this place, unable to go home. When he was touring West Lake, his bitter sighs rose to heaven in breaths of rancor and appeared in Your Majesty's dream. This is an omen that, as of today, the imperial court will gain the services of a worthy man. Whether this portends good or ill, it is not for me to say."

Greatly delighted, the Imperial Patriarch paid the dream interpreter and went into his room, where he changed into a scholar's robe. Taking with him a few eunuchs, all dressed like scholars, he walked leisurely out into the streets. Their steps took them to the Hall of Bounty and Bliss, where they saw two men in purple at the entrance, inviting people in. Readily, the Imperial Patriarch and his retinue entered the wineshop and mounted the stairs to the second floor.

That day, it so happened that all the booths on the second floor were occupied, except the one where Yu Liang had attempted suicide the night before. Pushing aside the curtain, the Imperial Patriarch was on the point of stepping in when the waiter said, "Scholar, don't go in! That booth is unlucky! My master is going to fumigate it with vinegar today.[12] The booth won't be ready for you until after it's been treated."

"Why is this booth unlucky?" asked the Imperial Patriarch.

"Scholar, that's a long story. Yesterday, a scholar from Chengdu in Sichuan came here. He was stranded in this town after failing the examinations. Well, in this very booth, all by himself, he had wine and food worth five taels of silver and got himself dead drunk. At around dusk, he said he had no money to pay for the wine and food, and he made a terrible scene, trying to kill himself and all that. We were afraid of getting involved in some legal trouble, so we had no choice but to have two of our men escort him back as far as Madam Sun's Inn by Examination Grounds Bridge, where he lives. That's why I said this booth is unlucky. Don't use it until it's been treated with vinegar."

After hearing these words, the Imperial Patriarch said, "That's all right. We are learned scholars and have no fear of such things." So saying, he and his attendants all sat down. Raising his head, he saw the wall covered with characters, each the size of a teacup. Upon reading, he found it to be a lyric poem to the tune of "Immortal at the Magpie Bridge." When he reached the end, he came upon the line "By Yu Liang, scholar of Chengdu, Sichuan." Inwardly rejoicing, the Imperial Patriarch thought to himself, "So, this must be the worthy man in my dream because the poem does have a bitter tone."

"Who wrote this poem?" he asked the waiter.

"Scholar, it was written by none other than the scholar who made a terrible scene here last evening."

"Where is he staying?"

"At Madam Sun's Inn by Examination Grounds Bridge."

The Imperial Patriarch had some wine and food, paid the bill and returned to the palace. In the meantime, he had the eunuchs issue an imperial edict ordering the local yamen officials to go to Madam Sun's Inn and bring Yu Liang, scholar from Chengdu, to him posthaste.

When relaying the edict, the eunuchs said only that Yu Liang was to be summoned by the Imperial Patriarch without specifying the reason. Knowing nothing about what had led to this edict, the official charged with the mission sped on horseback with his men to Madam Sun's Inn. Upon arriving, they threw a rope around Madam Sun and, still breathless from their frantic riding, cried out, "Yu Liang! Yu Liang!"

Thinking that Yu Liang must have lodged a complaint against her with the yamen, Madam Sun was seized with fear, and her face drained of all color. (*An honest woman she was.*) She fell on both knees and began kowtowing nonstop.

"Easy, woman!" said the official. "Yu Liang, scholar from Sichuan, is wanted by the emperor. Is he or is he not in this inn?"

It was only then that Madam Sun mustered enough courage to reply, "Sir, there was indeed a Scholar Yu here, but early this morning he left for his hometown. My son went to see him off but hasn't come back yet. Yu Liang wrote a poem on the wall before leaving. If you don't believe me, you can dismount and come see it."

And so, the official went into the house and saw that, there, written on the wall, was indeed a poem, with the ink still wet. Set also to the tune of "Immortal at the Magpie Bridge," it read,

In the pink rain of apricot blossoms,
Among the snowflakes of white pear petals,
I face with shame the road that leads to home.
The Spring Fairy on a return journey,
Willow catkins fly, flowers strew the ground.

Ten thousand books I have learned by heart;
All history lies at the tip of my pen,
But a scholar's career is not my fate.
Rush not! There are other ways to rise to the clouds.
In my straw sandals, I now return.

What had happened was that Madam Sun, finding Yu Liang in a drunken stupor again the previous night, had yelled at him throughout the night. At the fifth watch, afraid that he would again try to stay on, she woke her son Xiao'er and had him escort Yu Liang out the door. Before his departure, Yu Liang wrote that poem on the wall. Sun Xiao'er had not yet returned from his mission.

After reading the poem, the official had his men copy it down before jumping back onto his horse. He gave Madam Sun an extra horse so she could ride with them and pressed ahead in a northerly direction. On the road, they ran head-on into Sun Xiao'er. The official let go of Madam Sun but grabbed Sun Xiao'er, asking, "Where is Yu Liang?"

Trembling with fear, Sun Xiao'er replied, "Scholar Yu is reluctant to go on because he has no traveling money. He's now sitting in the dumpling shop by the North Gate."

Straightaway, the official raced off to the North Gate, taking Sun Xiao'er along as a guide. Lo and behold, there was Yu Liang, eating dumplings from a bowl he was holding in his hands. At the emissary's cry of "Yu Liang, hark the imperial edict!" he gave a violent start. Hastily putting down the bowl, he stepped out the door and dropped to his knees.

"Yu Liang is hereby ordered to repair to the Hall of Virtue and Longevity for an audience with the Imperial Patriarch," said the emissary, reading the edict.

Before Yu Liang could figure out what it was all about, he was hustled onto a horse and led all the way to the Hall of Virtue and Longevity, where everyone dismounted and went to the reception office to await instructions. The local official kowtowed at the palace entrance, announcing, "Scholar Yu Liang is here!" At an order from the Imperial Patriarch, Yu Liang was allowed to borrow a purple robe and enter the palace.

Wearing a purple robe, a waistband, a gauze cap, and a pair of black boots, Yu Liang proceeded to the flight of steps leading to the throne and, prostrating himself on the ground, performed the necessary ritual of homage to the Imperial Patriarch. "Did you write the poem to the tune of 'Immortal at the Magpie Bridge' in the Hall of Bounty and Bliss?" asked the Imperial Patriarch.

"I wrote it in an inebriated state. Never did I expect that the Imperial Patriarch would lay eyes on it."

"You undertook such a long journey to this place. That you, with your talent, failed the examinations was the fault of the examination supervisor. Do not be resentful."

"To be poor or to be rich is a matter of heavenly will. I would never dream of being resentful."

"With your great talent, you are more than equal to any official post in any locality. Take the purple robe you are wearing as a gift from me. I will have the emperor appoint you to an important post. What do you say to that?"

Yu Liang kowtowed, saying gratefully, "What virtues and ability do I have to deserve such kindness?"

"Now, write a poem or a lyric poem[13] for me right here, and make it better than the one the emissary copied from the wall of the wineshop."

To Yu Liang's request for a topic, the Imperial Patriarch replied, "Just write about your encounter with us."

Thus ordered, Yu Liang took the four treasures of the scholar's study[14] that the palace attendants held out to him and, with never a moment's hesitation, wrote a lyric poem to the tune of "Over the Dragon Gate":

I crossed the Qinguan Pass, risking my life,
And trudged along the Yangzi River
Over a rugged ten thousand li,
Until here I am in Qiantang.
Failing to gain fame, unable to return,
I ended up living off my neighbors.

What ill luck! What a hard life!
My art in poetry and writing quite useless, till
A little poem of mine caught the emperor's eye.
And now, with a purple robe bestowed on me,
To my hometown I return,
Resplendent in honor and glory.

The Imperial Patriarch found the poem delightful. "If it's your wish to return to your hometown in glory, we shall grant it." Then and there, wielding his royal brush-pen, he wrote six lines:

Yu Liang of Chengdu,
Fine poet and scholar.
His talent unrecognized,
He lamented his ill fate.
Hereby granted a high post,
In glory he returns home.

The Imperial Patriarch then ordered that the eunuchs convey the message to the emperor and bring Yu Liang into the latter's presence. Now, Emperor Xiaozong had just nearly missed provoking an outburst of rage from his father over the case of Li Zhi, prefect of Nanjian. How could he fail to give this matter proper attention? (*The timing happened to be just right.*) He thought that since his father wanted the scholar from Chengdu to return to his hometown in glory, he would very likely be contradicting his father's wish if he assigned Yu Liang somewhere else. Thereupon, he wrote, "Yu Liang is hereby appointed prefect of Chengdu and granted a thousand taels of silver to cover his traveling expenses." (*Emperor Xiaozong was indeed a filial son* [*xiao* means "filial piety"].)

The next day, Yu Liang, in his purple robe and golden waistband, was brought into the court, where he thanked the emperor for his imperial bounty and then went to the Hall of Virtue and Longevity to offer his thanks to the Imperial Patriarch. With the silver bestowed upon him by the emperor, he engaged servants and saddled horses and gave Madam Sun a hundred taels of silver as a reward.

How he returned home in style amid a grand procession is of no concern to us here, but on that very day, Emperor Xiaozong went in person to the Hall of Virtue and Longevity to thank his father for having brought him a worthy man. The Imperial Patriarch replied, "Issue an edict and let it be known throughout the land that in future, scholars sitting for imperial civil service examinations must first pass examinations at the local level before coming to the capital for the last round of examinations in the palace."[15]

That is how local-level examinations came into being. The practice is still alive and well unto this day, and this is the story that is passed down in history to explain its origin.

Sima of old had Yang Deyi to thank;
Yu Liang of today chanced upon the emperor.
If all talents are recognized in the end,
Why worry, when it's only a matter of time?

7

Chen Kechang Becomes an Immortal during the Dragon Boat Festival

Fame and fortune he was not meant to have;
His life a lamp flickering in a draft.
Not much chance, either, with life as a monk,
For a luckless monk he turned out to be.

The story goes that during the Shaoxing reign period [1131–62] of Emperor Gaozong of the great Song dynasty, there lived, in Yueqing County, Wenzhou Prefecture, a scholar named Chen Yi, courtesy name Kechang. Twenty-four years of age at the time our story begins, he was a young man of refined looks and keen intelligence. There was no book that he did not read, and no history with which he was not familiar.

During the Shaoxing reign period, he sat three times for the imperial civil service examinations, but all three times he failed. He went to a fortune-teller by Zhong'an Bridge in Lin'an Prefecture [Lin'an being the capital, where the examinations were held] to find out what lay in store for him. The fortune-teller said, "You were born under the wrong star. You are not meant to be an official. Your only choice is to become a Buddhist monk."

Ever since childhood, Scholar Chen had heard his mother say that when he was born, she dreamed of a gilded arhat heading for her belly. Mortified by the fortune-teller's words now that his prospects of fame and fortune looked dim, he went back to his inn to retire for the night. Early the next morning, he rose, paid for his lodging, and, with a hired hand carrying his luggage, went straight to Lingyin Monastery to become a monk under Abbot Iron Ox Yin, who was well versed in all the classics. The abbot's ten acolytes, named after the ten Heavenly Stems, were all brilliant students, and Chen Kechang took the position of second acolyte in this succession.[1]

When the fourth day of the fifth month was drawing near,[2] in the eleventh year of the Shaoxing reign period [1141], and *zongzi*[3] were being prepared in the mansion of Prince Wu Yi, Emperor Gaozong's maternal uncle,[4] the prince gave an order to the butler, saying, "Tomorrow, I'll be going to Lingyin Monastery to take some donations to the monks. Get some vegetarian food ready for me." Thus instructed, the butler proceeded to make arrangements for money and all the miscellaneous items that would be needed.

After breakfast the next morning, the prince checked all the items and mounted his sedan-chair. He took along the butler, a few administrative assistants, his personal guards, and a number of low-ranking military officers. They went through Qiantang Gate, past Shihan Bridge and the Big Buddha Head, and proceeded toward Lingyin Monastery on West Hill. Having received a visiting card in advance, the abbot had the monks strike the chimes and beat the drums to welcome the prince. After the prince was led into the main hall and invited to light incense, he was ushered into the abbot's cell, where he sat down. Following the abbot's lead, the monks saluted the prince and served him tea, after which they withdrew and stood against the wall in two rows, one on the left, one on the right.

The prince said, "On every fifth day of the fifth month, I come to make donations to the monastery and bring you *zongzi.* Today is no exception."

Some young attendants carried in food offerings to the Buddha and then went to all the monks' rooms, distributing *zongzi* from the large trays they held on their palms.

While walking leisurely along the corridors, the prince saw a quatrain written on the wall:

In the state of Qi was born Lord Mengchang;
During the Jin lived that powerful Zhen'e.
Only I was born under the wrong star;
Let me call the fortune-tellers to account!

After reading it, the prince commented, "This poem has a bitter tone. I wonder who wrote it?" He returned to the abbot's cell where the abbot had set out dinner, and asked, "Abbot, who in your monastery writes good poems?"

"Your Excellency," replied the abbot, "of the many monks in this monastery, the ten acolytes named after the ten Heavenly Stems are all capable of writing poetry."

"Summon them for me."

"Only two are in the monastery. The other eight are out in the villages."

Thereupon, the first two acolytes, Heavenly Stems Number One and Number Two, were brought before the prince. Addressing himself to the first acolyte, the prince said, "Compose a poem for me."

The acolyte asked for a topic. The prince designated *zongzi* as the topic, and so the acolyte produced this poem:

With four sharp corners and a string around its waist,
It dances in the boiling water in the pot.
Should it bump into the Monk of Tang,[5]
He will surely strip it naked.

The prince burst into laughter. "Good!" he said, "but it lacks literary grace."

Next, he ordered the second acolyte to make a poem. The acolyte saluted the prince and asked for a topic. He was also given the topic of *zongzi.* His poem went:

Fragrant zongzi *are offered yearly to Qu Yuan;*[6]
Today, with the monks, they fulfill their happy fate.
Of the array set out in every hall,
Which ones will go first in moments of life and death?

An immensely delighted prince exclaimed, "Good poem!" He asked the acolyte, "Did you write the poem on the wall of the corridor?"

"Yes, sir, it was written by me."

"Since you wrote it, explain it to me."

"In the state of Qi, there was a Lord Mengchang [d. 297 B.C.E.] who supported three thousand retainers in his household. He was born around noon on the fifth day of the fifth month. In the state of Jin, there was a general named Wang Zhen'e, who was also born around noon on the fifth day of the fifth month. My humble self was born in the same hour on the same day of the same month, and yet I suffer from such poverty. That is why I wrote those four lines lamenting my fate. (*The principles of fortune-telling work in most subtle ways. Cases abound of people who are far apart in wealth and status sharing the same eight characters of the astrological chart.*[7] *It is the same with physiognomy.*)

"Where are you from?" asked the prince.

"I am a native of Yueqing County in Wenzhou Prefecture. My surname is Chen, given name Yi, and courtesy name Kechang."

Impressed by the acolyte's clear enunciation and air of distinction, the prince decided to do something for him. That very day, he sent a guard to the Bureau of Religion in Lin'an to request an ordainment certificate for Chen Yi. The prince then had Chen Yi take the tonsure and, using Chen's courtesy name Kechang as his ordained name, pronounced Chen his protégé. After evening set in, the prince returned home, and there we shall leave him.

Time flew like an arrow. Quite unnoticeably, one year went by. On the fifth day of the fifth month, the prince again paid a visit to Lingyin Monastery to make a donation of food. The abbot led Kechang and other monks in welcoming the prince into the abbot's cell, where a vegetarian dinner was set out in his honor, as was the usual practice.

After sitting down, the prince called Kechang to him and said, "Compose a lyric poem for me, and make it the story of your life." Kechang saluted the prince and recited a lyric poem he composed on the spot to the tune of "Deva-like Barbarian":

"The day of my birth is the bane of my life,
But today's bliss makes up for all past woes.

The Double Fifth comes around once a year,
A day of bounty that monks eagerly await.

"For two years now, my lord, in his kindness,
Has shown me much gracious favor.
In quiet and peaceful seclusion
Shall this monk live out the rest of his life."

A greatly delighted prince did not return home until he was quite inebriated. He brought Kechang with him and presented the monk to his wife, a twice-titled lady, saying, "This monk, Chen Yi, a native of Wenzhou, forsook the world and joined the Buddhist order after failing the exams three times. He was serving in Lingyin Monastery as an acolyte when I found out that he was a good poet and had him take the tonsure and become a monk and my protégé. His ordained name is Kechang. A year has passed since then. I've brought him home so he may see you."

His wife was most pleased. All the other members of the household were also much taken with Kechang's intelligence and guilelessness. While they were untying the strings that bound the *zongzi,* the prince and his wife gave one to Kechang and asked for another lyric poem set to the tune of "Deva-like Barbarian," this time on the subject of *zongzi.*

Kechang saluted them, asked for paper and a brush-pen, and wrote the following:

The sweet rice all wrapped into nice shapes,
Colorful threads all twisted into strings,
In the wine cups float calamus leaves—
All signs that the fifth month of the year is here.

In this setting, my lord, in his kindness,
Shows me much gracious favor.
When is the best time to tour the mountains?
When hollyhocks and wormwood begin to bloom.

The prince was delighted beyond measure. He ordered that Sister Fresh Lotus be brought in to sing what Kechang had just written.

The girl called Fresh Lotus had long eyebrows, narrow eyes, a fair complexion, red lips, and a light and airy gait. Ivory clappers in hand, she stood before the dinner table and started singing in her sweet voice. After an enthusiastic ovation from the audience, the prince told Kechang to write a lyric poem on the girl, again to the tune of "Deva-like Barbarian." (*It is already quite unusual for a monk to join female company at dinner. And now, to have him dedicate a poem to a girl called Fresh Lotus is nothing short of encouraging debauchery.*) Without a moment's hesitation, Kechang wrote:

Born with a narrow waist and filled with grace,
She sings the lyrics in her dulcet voice.

The clear and sublime notes of the song
Send specks of dust floating around.

At the feast, my lord in his kindness,
Favors me with the presence of beauty.
To admire the lotus in its freshness,
There is not a moment to lose!

The prince was all the more delighted. It was evening before the feast came to an end, and Kechang was released back to the monastery.

On the fifth day of the fifth month of the following year, the prince was about to go to Lingyin Monastery to treat the monks again when a pouring rain began. Instead of going himself, the prince told a senior servant, "You go ahead and distribute the food among the monks, and then bring Kechang over for a visit."

Thus instructed, the senior servant went to the monastery and said to the abbot, "The prince wants me to bring Kechang to see him."

The abbot replied, "Kechang has been afflicted with a heart ailment for the last few days and hasn't left his room. (*A twist in the plot.*) Let's go and ask him."

Thereupon, the servant and the abbot went to Kechang's room and found him lying in bed. "Please tell the prince," said Kechang to the servant, "that this humble monk cannot go because of a heart condition. Please give this letter to my benefactor, the prince."

So the servant went back with the letter. When the prince asked why Kechang had not come, the servant replied, "My master, Kechang cannot come because of a heart ailment, but he gave me a letter that he sealed with his own hands."

The prince broke the seal and saw that it was another lyric poem to the tune of "Deva-like Barbarian":

Last year, we drank calamus wine together;
This year, I'm confined to the monk's cell.
The journey to happiness never goes smoothly,
And the way things are can hardly be changed!

My lord, in his kindness to me,
Knows the pain in my heart.
How I wish to admire the fresh lotus,
But when will I ever recover?

Immediately the prince ordered that Fresh Lotus be brought in to sing the lyrics, but a female attendant appeared and said, "Master, Fresh Lotus doesn't look quite herself these days. With her breasts swollen and her belly protruding, she can't very well appear in public."

The prince flew into a rage and ordered that Fresh Lotus be sent to his fifth wife for questioning. Fresh Lotus confessed, "I had an affair with Kechang and got pregnant."

When the Fifth Lady reported this to the prince, he exploded, saying, "That bald donkey did write about 'admiring the fresh lotus' each time in his lyrics. So, it's not some heart condition he has, but lovesickness! It's out of a guilty conscience that he doesn't dare show his face around here! Get someone to tell officers at the Lin'an prefectural yamen to arrest Monk Kechang!"

When officers from Lin'an Prefecture went to Lingyin Monastery to apprehend Kechang, the abbot set out the obligatory wine and food and gave them some money. As the proverb says, "Expect no leniency from the laws, for they are as merciless as a red-hot furnace!"

Realizing that he was not going to be excused for his illness, Kechang dragged himself out of bed, followed the officers to the prefectural yamen, and knelt down in the courtroom. As the prefectural magistrate called the court to order,

> *Boom, boom went the drums;*
> *Officers lined up on both sides.*
> *King Yama was to try the cases;*[8]
> *The God of Mount Tai was to snatch away the souls.*[9]

Kechang having thus been brought into the court, the magistrate began the interrogation, saying, "Being a monk and a much favored protégé of the prince's, how could you have done such an evil thing? Confess!"

"I am not guilty," replied Kechang.

Turning a deaf ear to Kechang's protestations of innocence, the magistrate said to his men, "Give him a good thrashing!" And so they did. They threw him on the ground and beat him until his skin split, his flesh tore, and his blood flowed.

"I did have an illicit affair with Fresh Lotus in a moment of weakness," said Kechang. "I do confess that the charges are true."

Fresh Lotus, also summoned for interrogation, stuck to her story. Consequently, the Lin'an prefectural yamen presented the confessions of Kechang and Fresh Lotus to the prince. The prince wanted to have Kechang put to death, but out of his high regard for the monk's literary talent, he could not bring himself to give the order. (*To have such scruples means that the prince is still a good man—scruples that spared Kechang from an unjust death.*) Instead, Kechang was put in prison.

In the meantime, Abbot Yin thought to himself, "Kechang is a monk of moral rectitude. He spends all his time reading the scriptures in front of the Buddha's image without ever taking a step outside the monastery gate. Even when he's called to the prince's residence, he returns promptly enough and has never stayed there overnight. How could he have had any illicit affairs? (*The yamen officials' failure to conduct careful investigations has resulted in injustice for goodness knows how many innocent people.*) There must be something wrong here." He hurried to Chuanfa

Monastery in the city and persuaded Abbot Gao Dahui to follow him to the prince's residence to beg for mercy on Kechang's behalf.

The prince came out to the reception hall and offered seats to the two abbots. While waiting for tea to be served, the prince spoke up, "How impertinent Kechang is! I had such high regard for him, and look what a filthy thing he did!"

The two abbots dropped to their knees and said over and over again, "We would not dream of defending him in his guilt, but please forgive him a little, considering how you, sir, have had such affection for him, however little he deserves it."

The prince told the two abbots to go back to their monasteries, adding, "Tomorrow, I'll have the Lin'an prefectural yamen give him a lighter sentence."

Abbot Yin said, "Your Highness, the truth will out in due course."

Displeased at these words, the prince withdrew to the interior of the house and did not reemerge. The two abbots, after waiting in vain for him to reappear, also left the hall and went out of the mansion. Abbot Gao said, "The prince must be angry because of what you said about the truth coming out in due course. He is not one to admit having made a mistake. (*Refusal to admit to a mistake is a major mistake in itself, and highly placed people who commit evil deeds are mostly guilty of it.*) That's why he refused to come out again."

"Kechang is a man of moral rectitude," said Abbot Yin. "He spends his time reading the scriptures in front of the Buddha's image and never steps outside the monastery gate without a good reason. Even when he was called to the prince's mansion, he always returned soon enough and never spent a night there. How could he have had any illicit affairs? That's why I said, 'The truth will out in due course.' He must have been unjustly accused."

Abbot Gao said, "As the saying goes, 'The poor are no match for the rich; the lowly do not fight the highly placed.' How could a monk dare fight a prince? This is just another case of injustice carried over from a previous life. Let's see if he gets a lighter sentence before we decide on the next thing to do." With that, they went their separate ways, each to his own monastery, and of this, no more.

The next day, the prince sent a letter to the Lin'an prefectural yamen with the order that Kechang and Fresh Lotus be given light sentences. The magistrate reported to the prince, "The sentencing should be postponed until after Fresh Lotus gives birth," but the prince ordered that the sentences be given without delay. The prefectural yamen had no choice but to revoke Kechang's ordainment papers, give him a hundred thrashings with the rod, and send him back to Lingyin Monastery, where he was to be dismissed from service and returned home to resume life as a commoner with corvée duties. Fresh Lotus was given eighty thrashings with the rod and sent back to Qiantang County before being returned to her parents and ordered to give back to the prince the one thousand strings of cash he had paid for her.

Now, Abbot Yin brought Kechang back to the monastery, and all the monks advised the abbot not to keep Kechang there because he would be a disgrace to the monastery. The abbot said to them, "There's something fishy about this matter.

The truth will come out in due course." The abbot ordered that a thatched hut be set up at the back of the hill where Kechang could stay until his wounds had healed and he was ready to return home.

In the meantime, the prince sent Fresh Lotus back to her parents, demanding a refund of the one thousand strings of cash he had paid for her. Fresh Lotus's parents said to her, "We have no money. If you have private savings, you can use them to pay the prince back."

"There *is* someone willing to pay for me," said Fresh Lotus.

Her father lashed out, "What a cheap hussy! The person you carried on with is but a penniless monk whose ordainment papers have been revoked. How could *he* have the money to pay the prince on your behalf?"

"Too bad I wronged that monk! (*So, the truth does come out in due course.*) I had an affair with the prince's butler, Qian Yuan. Seeing that I was pregnant, he was afraid of a scandal and said to me, 'When you confess to the prince, just say that you did it with Monk Kechang. The prince is fond of Kechang and will surely let you off. I'll take care of you and pay for everything you need.' With that promise, I can very well go ahead and ask him for money and for repayment of the one thousand strings of cash. He is the one who sullied my body. How can he go back on his word? If he denies everything, well, I have nothing to lose anyway. You can take me to the prince. I'll tell him everything, and Monk Kechang's name can be cleared, too."

Having heard these words, her parents went to the prince's residence and asked to see Butler Qian. At their account of what their daughter had told them, Butler Qian flared up and growled, "You old bums! You old fools! Don't you have any sense of decency? Your daughter carried on with some monk, and the yamen has already settled the case, and yet you're trying to shift the blame to me with this pack of lies! If you can't come up with the money for your daughter's redemption, you could have put it nicely, saying you are too poor to afford the payment. I might have helped you out of pity with a couple of strings of cash. But as it is, how am I going to face the world if your lies are overheard by other people?" (*It just so happens that the evil ones know best how to deny what they did.*) After this outburst, he turned away.

Swallowing the insult, Mr. Zhang returned home and told his daughter about it. With gushing tears, Fresh Lotus said, "Don't worry, father and mother. We'll let him have it tomorrow!"

The next day, Fresh Lotus followed her parents to the prince's residence, where they loudly cried out their grievances. The prince promptly ordered that those making the noise be brought in. Seeing that they were none other than Fresh Lotus's parents, the prince said severely, "Your daughter committed a heinous crime. What grievances could you have to call out at my door?"

Falling to his knees, Mr. Zhang said, "Your Highness, my accursed daughter did do an evil thing, but she wronged a man. Please make sure that justice is done!"

"Whom did she wrong?" asked the prince.

"I don't know," replied Mr. Zhang, "but you can easily find out if you question the little hussy."

"Where is that cheap hussy?" asked the prince.

"She's waiting at the gate."

The prince had Fresh Lotus brought in for thorough questioning. Once inside the hall, she dropped to her knees.

"You wanton woman," said the prince, "a fine thing you did! Now tell me, whom did you wrong?"

"Your Highness, I wronged Monk Kechang by naming him."

"Why did you wrong him? If you tell the truth, I'll be lenient with you."

"I did have an illicit affair, but it had nothing to do with Kechang."

"Why didn't you say so earlier?"

"Butler Qian Yuan is the one who seduced me. When I found out I was pregnant, he became afraid of being exposed. He told me, 'If this comes out, be sure not to mention me on any account! Just say that you had an affair with Monk Kechang. The prince is fond of Kechang and will surely let you off.'"

The prince lashed out, "You cheap hussy! How could you have done as he said and ruined that monk's life!"

Fresh Lotus continued, "Qian Yuan said, 'If you are acquitted, I'll support your whole family, old and young. If you have to pay for your redemption, I'll take care of that, too.' After I was sent home and Your Highness demanded the money, I had no choice but to turn to him for help. So my father approached him, only to be beaten up by him and accused of trying to incriminate the innocent. Now that I have come out with the truth, I shall have no regrets if I die this moment in front of Your Highness."

"When he promised to support you and your whole family," said the prince, "did he give you anything, as a token of his good faith?" (*Good question, but when false accusations were made against Kechang, why did he readily believe the story without asking for evidence?*)

"Your Highness, when Qian Yuan promised to support me, I was afraid that he might not make good on his word, so I took one of his vermilion badges of duty as evidence."

The prince fumed with anger. Stamping his feet, he roared, "You slut! What a thing you did, accusing Monk Kechang so unjustly!"

Straightaway, he sent a messenger to Lin'an Prefecture and had Qian Yuan brought under guard to the prefectural yamen for interrogation. Under torture, Qian Yuan confessed. A hundred days later, he was given eighty thrashings of the rod on his back and sent to Shamen Island to work as prison labor under surveillance.[10] Fresh Lotus, sent back home, was forgiven the money for her redemption. Then, a messenger was sent to Lingyin Monastery to bring Monk Kechang to the prince.

In the meantime, Kechang had recovered from his wounds in the thatched hut.

When the fifth day of the fifth month rolled around, he took up a brush-pen, a piece of paper, and some ink, and wrote a poem, "On Departing from This World":

Born into this world on the Double Fifth,
Ordained as a monk on the Double Fifth,
Accused of a crime on the Double Fifth,
Departed this life on the Double Fifth.
I owe that one a debt from a previous life.
Had I denied the charge at the time,
I would have made the other one suffer.
The truth now made known to all,
I'd fain return from whence I came. (With the poem "On Departing from This World," the story thus comes to an end.)
A note written at noon on the Double Fifth
Ends all strife that wagging tongues lead to.
With the Double Fifth Dragon Festival
Goes all strife that wagging tongues lead to.

After writing the poem, Kechang walked to a spring by the thatched hut, removed his clothes, washed himself clean, put the clothes on again, and entered the hut, where he assumed a lotus position and willed himself to death in meditation.

Upon hearing the news from a monk, the abbot had Kechang's body put in a wooden coffin that he had prepared for himself and had it carried to the top of the hill. The abbot was about to light the cremation fire when a senior servant from the prince's mansion came for Kechang. The abbot said to the servant, "Tell the prince that Kechang has passed into nirvana. I was about to light the cremation fire when you came on behalf of the prince. So I will stop and wait for the prince's instructions."

The servant said, "The truth is now known. Kechang had nothing to do with that case. Because he was wronged, the prince told me to come and get him, but now that he has passed away, let me tell the prince. He will surely come here in person for the cremation ceremony." Hurriedly the servant went back, reported the matter to the prince, and showed him the poem. The prince was astounded.

The next day, the prince and his wife went to Lingyin Monastery for the cremation ceremony. The assembly of monks led them to the back of the hill, where the prince and his wife personally lit the incense. After the prince sat down, Abbot Yin led the monks in reading the scriptures, after which the abbot took up a torch and intoned:

"He left behind zongzi *in Qu Yuan's honor*
And dragon boats in their merry races.
The green silk ties are now all cut,
Not to be used to form bonds in his next life.

"To the respectful memory of Monk Kechang: On the Double Fifth, a lucky day, who bathed in perfumed water? The *zongzi,* however expensively wrapped in gold, are gone, as are the calamus leaves, although as pure as jade. You, who know all there is to know about the Lotus Sutra and all the scriptures of Mahayana, bore a wrongful insult yet never touched Fresh Lotus. Now that the truth is out, the occasion calls for a joyful song. Today being the fifth day of the fifth month, why head for the west in such haste?[11] Life being nothing but emptiness, why lament one's bitter fate? This monk of the hills is here now to give you the flame of brightness, to see, by the light of the *samadhi* fire, what your true nature would be.[12] (*Abbot Yin's words are well said.*) Yi!

While singing 'Deva-like Barbarian,'
He returned to the Tusita Heaven."[13]

In the midst of the flames, Kechang emerged for all to see. With a salute of gratitude to the prince and his wife, the abbot, and the assembled monks, he said, "I have repaid a debt that I incurred in a previous life and am now bidding farewell to the mortal world, to go to the land of the immortals. I am, in fact, one of the five hundred arhats. I am the one named Always Happy." (*A nice name for an arhat.*)

Truly,

Has Heaven ever been hard of hearing?
Good and evil will be found out in the end.
All are exhorted to perform good deeds,
To practice virtues and accrue credit.

8

Artisan Cui's Love Is Cursed in Life and in Death

A fine mist shrouds the scenic sunlit hills;
The warm day sees returning wild geese rise from the sand.
The eastern suburbs delight the eyes with budding flowers;
The southern footpaths are faintly green with tender grass.

Before crows build their nests in the willows by the shore,
My quest for flowers leads me to a mountain cottage.
Around the edge of the fields, red plum petals fall,
But apricot branches remain bare of red blossoms.

The above lyric poem to the tune of "Partridge Sky," which describes a scene in early spring, is not as well written as the following "Ode to Mid-spring":

I spend my days midst courtesans and drunken dreams,
Unaware that outside the city, another spring is at its height.
The first apricot blossoms spin down in sprinkles;
The willow twigs sway softly in the gentle breeze.

Afloat in a pleasure boat, astride a piebald horse,
I enjoy the greenness by the bridge outside the gate.
This is a fairyland not meant for mortal beings.
Behind which beaded portiere in the house is she?

The above lyric poem describing mid-spring scenery is, in its turn, not as well written as the poem by Lady Huang[1] titled "Ode to Late Spring":

The charms of spring are as mellow as wine;
Swallows' songs filter through curtains from time to time.
Fragrant willow catkins float over the small bridge;
Red peach blossoms fall by the mountain temple.

The orioles grow old, the butterflies flit about;
Spring departs, to one's profound sorrow.
The morning rain wets the grass before the terrace;
The dawn wind spreads pear blossoms all over the ground.

None of the above three poems is as well written as the one by Wang Anshi, duke of Jing.[2] Watching wind-scattered flower petals spinning to the ground, he concluded that it was the east wind that precipitated spring's departure. His poem says,

The wind on a spring day sometimes is blissful;
The wind on a spring day sometimes does mischief.
Without the spring wind, flowers do not bloom,
But after they bloom, the wind blows them away!

Su Dongpo[3] said, "It's not the east wind but the spring rain that sends off the spring." His poem says,

Before the rain, tender pistils are in full view;
After the rain, the leaves are stripped of all flowers.
The bees and butterflies cross over my walls.
Could spring have moved on to my neighbor's yard?

Qin Shaoyou[4] said, "Neither the wind nor the rain is to blame. It's the willow catkins that send spring away." His poem says,

Willow catkins of the third month lightly scatter;
They dance in the sky as they send spring away.
Fickle and heartless in their caprice,
One flies to the east, one to the west.

Shao Yaofu[5] said, "The willow catkins have nothing to do with it. The butterfly is the culprit." (*People of the Song and Yuan dynasties are better than we are at making such idle comments.*) His poem says,

In the third month, the flowers are in bloom;
Busily, the butterflies flit to and fro.
Taking the delights of spring to the end of the world,
They add to the sorrows of the traveler on the road.

Zeng of the Grand Secretariat and the Privy Military Council[6] said, "The butterflies have nothing to do with it. It's the orioles' songs that send spring on its way." His poem says,

The flowers in full bloom, at the height of their charm,
What could have saddened them one spring night?
The orioles' songs send the spring on its way;
In a trice, the gardens are swept of all flowers.

Zhu Xizhen[7] said, "The orioles have nothing to do with it. The cuckoo is the culprit." His poem says,

The cuckoo's cries send spring on its way,
The drops of blood still fresh around its beak.[8]
The day is long in the quiet and empty courtyard,
Giving one fears of the coming of dusk!

Su Xiaoxiao[9] said, "None of these is to blame. It's the swallows that carry spring away in their beaks." There is, in testimony, her lyric poem to the tune of "Butterflies Lingering over Flowers":

I live by the Qiantang River, where
Flowers bloom and fall, year in and year out.
The swallows carry spring away in their beaks;
Flurries of "plum rain" beat on the window screens.[10]

A horn comb atilt halfway in my cloudlike hair,
I click the sandalwood clappers and sing "The Gold Threads."
The song over, I find the rosy clouds all gone;
I wake up to see the moon at the southern shore.[11]

Wang Yansou[12] said, "This has nothing to do with the wind, the rain, the willow catkins, the butterflies, the orioles, the cuckoos, and the swallows. The fact of the matter is, the ninety-day spring season must come to an end, hence the departure of spring." He once wrote a poem that reads,

Blame neither the wind nor the rain;
Spring departs with no help from wind or rain.
Red blossoms fading, the plums are green and small;
The yellow gone from their beaks, the young swallows fly.
As the cuckoos cry, the flowers wither away;
As the silkworms feed, the mulberry leaves vanish. (Good lines for a poem.)
How sad that spring is gone and nowhere to be found,
Disappointing the angler in his straw rain cape.

Storyteller, why all this citing of poems on the demise of spring? Well, in the Shaoxing reign period [1131–62], there lived in the provisional capital Lin'an [present-day Hangzhou] a man who was a native of Yan'an Prefecture in Yanzhou west of the Tong Pass [in present-day Shanxi Province]. He was, in fact, prince of Xian'an and lord of three commanderies.[13] One day, afraid that spring would soon be over, he took many of his family members on a spring outing. (*What a roundabout way of starting a story!*) On their way back late in the afternoon, they came to the Carriage Bridge inside Qiantang Gate. The sedan-chair carrying the prince approached the bridge after those of the family members had crossed, and at this moment, a man in a picture-mounting shop called out, "My child, come out and look at the prince!"

At the sight of the girl who came out, the prince said to the officer marching next to the window of his sedan-chair, "I've been trying to find a girl like the one over there, and now here she is. Be sure to bring her to my place tomorrow."

Thus ordered, the officer set out on his mission. What kind of person was the one who had come out to look at the prince? Truly,

The dust of traffic never settles,
But the bonds of love sooner or later break off.

By Carriage Bridge stood a house with a signboard on which was written "The Qu Family Shop: We Mount Paintings and Calligraphy Old and New." In the shop was an old man with his daughter. What did the girl look like?

Her cloudlike hair arranged like cicada wings,
Her lightly painted eyebrows the color of spring hills,
Her lips like a red cherry,
Her teeth two rows of white jade,
Her dainty feet curved like tiny bows,
Her voice trilling sweetly like that of an oriole.

So she was the one who had stepped out to look at the prince. The officer sat down in the teahouse across the street. When the old woman of the teahouse brought him tea, he said, "Granny, please go to the mounting shop across the street and invite Master Qu over. I'd like to talk with him." The woman did as she was told. After saluting each other, the two men sat down. "What can I do for you, sir?" asked Artisan Qu.

"Oh, nothing in particular. I just wanted to chat. The girl who just came out to look at the prince—is she your daughter?"

"Yes. There are only three of us in the family."

"How old is your daughter?"

"Eighteen."

"Are you going to marry her off or have her serve some official?"

"Being as poor as I am, how could I come up with the money to marry her off? When the time comes, there'll be nothing for it but to offer her up to some official."

"What skills does she have?"

Artisan Qu's reply as to her skills has as testimony the following lyric poem set to the tune of "Enticing Eyes":

In her secluded room, as the days grow,
She embroiders on silk and brocade.
Though not a life-giving goddess of spring,
She makes flowers with her needles.
With tilting stems, tender leaves, buds, and pistils,
Her flowers lack only a sweet fragrance;

If placed in the depths of the garden,
They attract bees and butterflies galore.

So this girl was skilled in the art of embroidery. The officer said, "Just a moment ago, the prince saw from his sedan-chair that your daughter was wearing an embroidered apron around her waist. It so happens that we need someone who is good at embroidery in the royal household. Why don't you offer her to the prince?"

Mr. Qu went home and told his wife about this. The next day, he drew up a statement declaring his intention of offering his daughter to the prince and took her to the prince's residence. The latter paid the price and named her Xiuxiu the Maid.

Some days later, the prince received a flower-patterned embroidered warrior's robe from the imperial court. Then and there, Xiuxiu took up her embroidery needles and produced another warrior's robe with identical patterns.

Delighted, the prince said, "His Majesty gave me this nice robe, but what can I give him in return? And it must be something out of the ordinary, too." From his treasury, he picked out a piece of translucent mutton-fat jade. Without losing one moment, he summoned his personal jade carvers and asked them, "What can you make out of this piece of jade?"

One of the carvers replied, "I'd say a pair of wine cups,"

"It would be a waste to make wine cups out of such a fine piece of jade," said the prince.

Another carver suggested, "Being pointed at the top and round at the bottom, it can be made into a *muhurta* doll."[14]

"But *muhurta* dolls are of no use except on the Double Seventh Festival when girls pray for better skills in sewing," said the prince.

Among the carvers was a twenty-five-year-old youth, Cui Ning by name. A native of Jiankang [present-day Nanjing] in Shengzhou, he had been in the prince's service for a number of years. With his hands respectfully folded across his chest, he stepped forward and said to the prince, "Your Highness, a piece that is pointed at the top and round at the bottom is not fit for anything else but a statue of the bodhisattva Guanyin of the Southern Sea."

"Good!" exclaimed the prince. "That's exactly what I've been thinking!" Then and there, he ordered that Cui Ning start on the carving.

In less than two months, the jade bodhisattva was completed. The prince promptly submitted a memorial and presented the jade statue to the emperor, to the latter's great joy. As for Cui Ning, having thus won the prince's good graces, he received a raise in his salary and provisions.

The days went by, and spring rolled around again. On his way back from a spring excursion, Artisan Cui stepped into a wineshop by Qiantang Gate. He had just downed a few cups of wine with three or four acquaintances when a commotion in the streets became audible. Swiftly, he pushed open the window and heard people beneath shouting amid all the noise, "There's a fire at Well Pavilion Bridge!" Leaving the table in haste, he rushed down the stairs, and this is what he saw:

What started out like a glowing firefly
Brightened into the glare of lamp flames.
With a thousand candles ablaze
And ten times more braziers afire,
The Fire God pushed over the heavenly furnace;
The celestial guards set whole mountains aflame.
Had this been the beacon on Mount Li,
Baosi must be looking as charming as could be.[15]
Had this been the fire in the Red Cliff battle,
It must be Zhou Yu masterminding it all.[16]
The Wutong god held on to the fire gourd;[17]
Song Wuji hastened on his fire-red donkey.[18]
With no candle drippings, no fuel added,
The smoke swirled up and the flames burned high.

At the sight, Cui cried out in alarm, "That's not far from the prince's mansion!" And he dashed off in that direction.

By the time he arrived, he found the mansion quiet and deserted, with everything removed and everybody gone. There being no one in sight, Cui walked down the left corridor, which was lit as bright as day by the flames. As he did so, a woman emerged from the hall and staggered into the corridor, muttering something to herself. When she bumped into Cui Ning, he recognized her to be Xiuxiu the Maid. He took a few steps back, bowed, and mumbled a greeting. As a matter of fact, the prince had once said to Cui Ning, "After Xiuxiu has served out her term, I'll marry her to you." Everyone present at the time had chimed in, "What a fine couple they'll make!" More than once, Cui Ning had thanked the prince for this promise. Being a bachelor, Cui Ning was quite taken with the idea. Xiuxiu, impressed by the young man, also looked forward to the marriage.

And now, as she bumped into Cui Ning in the corridor while a fire was raging, carrying in her hand a kerchief full of jewelry and other valuables, she said, "Master Cui, I came out too late. The other maids have run off in all directions. No one stopped to take care of others. Now you'll have to take me to a safe place." Whereupon, the two left the mansion and walked along the riverbank until they came to Limestone Bridge.

"Master Cui, my feet hurt. I can't walk another step."

Pointing ahead, Cui Ning said, "My place is right there, just a few steps ahead. You can rest there."

So they went to Cui Ning's house. After sitting down, Xiuxiu said, "I'm hungry, Master Cui. Please buy me some refreshments. After such a shock, I'd also appreciate a cup of wine." Right away, Cui Ning went out to buy some wine. After a few drinks, it was truly a case of

> *Three cups of green bamboo leaves down the throat,*
> *Two pink peach blossoms on the cheeks.*

As the saying goes, "Spring breathes life into flowers; wine brings lust in its wake." Xiuxiu said, "Do you remember how, when we were looking at the moon on the balcony one night, you were promised to me in marriage? And you kept on thanking the prince. Remember?"

With his hands respectfully folded in front of his chest, Cui Ning made a vague sound. (*This detail shows that Cui Ning is a cautious man.*)

Xiuxiu continued, "At the time, everyone cheered, 'What a fine couple they'll make!' How could you have forgotten?"

Cui Ning again made a vague sound.

Xiuxiu continued, "Rather than waiting for that to happen, why don't we become husband and wife this very night? What do you say to that?"

"I wouldn't dare," replied Cui Ning.

"You wouldn't dare? Then I'll scream and ruin you. Why did you bring me to your home in the first place? I'll report you to the prince tomorrow!"

"Young lady, if you want to be my wife, that's fine with me, but there's one thing. We can't live in this place anymore. Let's take advantage of all the commotion and get out of here tonight. That's the only way to go about it."

Xiuxiu said, "Since we're going to be husband and wife, I'll do whatever you say." And so, they became husband and wife that very night. (*Failure to follow through with his resolve was to be the death of Cui Ning.*)

They left after the fourth watch of the night, each carrying some gold, silver, and other valuables. They traveled by day and rested by night, eating and drinking when necessary, and thus wended their way to Quzhou.

Cui Ning said, "Here is an intersection of five roads. Which one shall we take? We might just as well take the road to Xinzhou, where I have a few acquaintances. With my skills as a jade carver, we may be able to settle down there." So they took the road that led to Xinzhou.

After they had been there a few days, Cui Ning said, "There are a lot of travelers between here and the capital. If word gets out that we two are living here, the prince will surely send men to hunt us down. So this isn't a safe place. I say we leave Xinzhou for somewhere else."

The couple again set out on a journey, heading, this time for Tanzhou. Some days later, they arrived in Tanzhou, finally far enough from the capital. There, they acquired a house and put up a signboard that said "Artisan Cui, Jade Carver from the Capital."

"We are now more than two thousand li from the capital," Cui Ning said to

Xiuxiu. "I don't think we're in any danger. Let's forget all our worries and settle down as a regular wedded couple."

In Tanzhou, there lived a number of officials who had retired from the imperial court. Impressed because Cui Ning was a jade carver from the capital, they gave him enough work to keep him occupied every day. Secretly, Cui Ning made inquiries about happenings in the prince's establishment. Someone who had been to the capital told him that a maidservant had disappeared during the fire of that night. A reward had been announced for her return, but after several days of searching, her whereabouts remained a mystery. No one knew that she had followed Cui Ning and was now living in Tanzhou.

Time flew like an arrow. The sun and the moon shot back and forth like a shuttle. More than one year went by. One day, Cui Ning's shop had just opened for business when two men in black robes, looking like yamen runners, stepped in, sat down, and told him, "Our master has heard about an Artisan Cui from the capital and wishes to invite him over to do a job."

After leaving some instructions with his wife, Cui Ning followed the two men to Xiangtan County. They brought him to their master's residence and the official gave Cui Ning some jade to work on.

On his way home, Cui Ning saw coming in his direction, a man who wore a bamboo hat, a cotton shirt with a lined collar of white satin, blue and white leggings tying up his trousers, and a pair of hemp sandals on his feet. The man was carrying a load across his shoulders and gave Cui Ning a look as he passed. Cui Ning did not quite see the man's face, but the man recognized Cui Ning. Taking big strides, he turned back and followed Cui Ning. Truly,

Whose child banged the side of the boat
And made the frightened mandarin ducks fly apart?

Who was this man? Let me tell you in the next session.

Bamboo-trellised morning glories fill the streets;
Moonlight filters through the fence of my thatched hut.
In the finely glazed cup, crude home-brewed wine;
On the white jade plate, salt-preserved plums.

Grieve not! Be of good cheer!
A lifetime of achievements deserves a smile!
Within three thousand li, there is no friend
For the one who once led a hundred thousand men.

The above lyric poem to the tune of "Partridge Sky" was written by a General Liu, a native of Xiongwu County, Qinzhou Prefecture, west of the Tong Pass.[19] After the big battle at Shunchang, he retired to Xiangtan County, Tanzhou Prefecture, in Hunan.[20] Albeit a famous commander, he attached no importance to money and lived in poverty. On his frequent visits to the village wineshop, people who did not know who he was yelled at him. He said, "A million Jurchen invaders did not intimidate me, and yet today, I find myself humiliated by these people!" So he wrote the above lyric poem, and the poem came to be circulated in the capital.

Prince Yang of He, commander of the imperial guards at the time, felt distraught upon reading the poem.[21] "So, General Liu lives in such loneliness and poverty!" Then and there, he ordered the treasurer to have some money sent to General Liu. Cui Ning's former master, the prince of Xian'an, had heard about Liu's straitened circumstances and also sent a messenger with an offer of money. It was this messenger, passing by Tanzhou, who ran into Cui Ning on his way back from Xiangtan. He followed Cui Ning all the way home. (*Another roundabout way of getting to the point.*)

At the sight of Xiuxiu sitting behind the counter, the messenger confronted them, saying, "I haven't seen you in a long time, Master Cui! So you live here! But why is Xiuxiu the Maid here, too? The prince sent me to Tanzhou to deliver a letter. Fancy meeting you two here! So Xiuxiu the Maid is now your wife. That's just as well."

Realizing that the man had guessed the situation, Cui Ning and his wife were frightened out of their wits.

Who was that man? Well, he was a guard in the prince's establishment and had been in the prince's service since childhood. It was on account of his honesty that he had been charged with delivering money to General Liu. Guo Li by name, he was called Guard Guo. At this point, the couple invited him to stay and offered him wine, saying to him, "When you go back, please don't say anything about this to the prince!"

"How would the prince ever know that the two of you are here?" said Guard Guo. "Don't I have better things to do? Why should I say anything?"

He thanked them, bade them farewell, and returned to the prince's establishment, where he presented the prince with the letter of reply. Then, looking the prince in the face, he said, "When I passed by Tanzhou on my way back, I ran into two people living there."

"Who are they?" asked the prince.

"Xiuxiu the Maid and Artisan Cui. They treated me to wine and food and told me not to tell you about them." (*As an honest man, Guo Li does nothing wrong in volunteering the truth, but he should not have promised Cui Ning that he would not tell the prince. That is dishonest.*)

Immediately, the prince said, "A fine thing they did! But how did they end up there?"

"I don't know the details. I only saw that they were living there and taking orders for work under a shop sign."

The prince had a messenger deliver instructions to the Lin'an prefectural yamen. An inspector was dispatched to Tanzhou right away, along with some runners and money for traveling expenses. After delivering the official documents to the

Tanzhou prefectural yamen, they set out to find Cui Ning and Xiuxiu in a manner not unlike

> *Black eagles hunting young swallows,*
> *Fierce tigers preying on little lambs.*

Within two months, the two captives were brought to the prince's establishment. When informed of their arrival, the prince called his tribunal to order.

Now, in his battles against the Tartars, the prince had wielded in his left hand a sword called "Small Green" and in his right hand one called "Big Green". Goodness knows how many Tartars had been cut down by these two swords, which were now hanging in their sheaths on the wall. As the prince ascended to his seat, everyone called out in salutation, and the couple were brought in and made to kneel down. Furiously, the prince took Small Green from the peg on the wall with his left hand and unsheathed it with one swipe of his right hand. Sword in hand, he opened his eyes wide as he had done when slaying the Tartars and gnashed his teeth so hard that the sound was loud and clear.

Horrified, the prince's wife said to him from behind the screen, "Your Highness, this is the capital of the empire, not the frontier. If they are guilty, you need only send them under guard to the Lin'an prefectural yamen for justice to be done. How can you kill people just like that?"

Hearing this, the prince said, "It was an outrage that these two lowlifes escaped in the first place. Now that they've been brought back, why can't I kill them, as angry as I am? But since you intervene on their behalf, let Xiuxiu be taken to the back garden and Cui Ning sent under guard to the prefectural yamen for sentencing and punishment." He then ordered that meed, in the form of money and wine, be given to those who had brought back the captives. (*Even to this day, the archaic word "meed" is used in the Wu region to refer to rewards for service.*)

After being brought under guard to the Lin'an prefectural yamen, Cui Ning gave a detailed confession, starting from the beginning. "On the night of the fire, I went to the mansion and found that everything had been carried off. Xiuxiu the Maid came out from the corridor and grabbed me, saying, 'Why do you put your hand on my breast? If you don't do what I say, I'll ruin you!' She wanted me to escape with her. I saw that there was nothing for it but to do as she said. And that is the truth."

The Lin'an yamen submitted the confession to the prince, who, being of a frank and straightforward nature, said, "In that case, I'll let Cui Ning off easy. But he shouldn't have run away. So he shall be beaten and banished to Jiankang Prefecture [present-day Nanjing]."

Right away, Cui Ning was taken under guard out of the mansion and to the road. After leaving the North Gate and reaching Gooseneck Point, he saw behind him a sedan-chair carried by two men and heard a voice calling, "Master Cui, wait for me!" Cui Ning recognized the voice of Xiuxiu and wondered why she had come after him. Being, as it were, a bird wounded by an arrow, he dared not bring any more trouble upon himself. He hung his head and kept walking. Soon the sedan-chair caught up with him. After it was put down, who should step out but Xiuxiu!

"Master Cui," said she, "now that you're going to Jiankang, what is to become of me?"

"Indeed, what is there to do?" asked Cui Ning.

Xiuxiu replied, "After you were taken to the yamen for trial, I was taken into the back garden, where they gave me thirty thrashings with a bamboo stick and threw me out. I learned that you were on your way to Jiankang, and so I rushed over, hoping to catch up with you and join you."

"That's good," said Cui Ning. (*There he goes again, not knowing what's good for him.*)

They traveled by boat for the rest of the journey, and when they arrived at Jiankang, the guard escorting them turned back. Had he been the gossipy kind, the couple would have been in for some trouble again, but the guard knew that the prince, with his fiery temper, would never relent once he found himself provoked. Besides, not being a member of the prince's household, why should he meddle in other people's affairs? Also, throughout the journey, Cui Ning had generously treated him to wine and food. So, after returning, the guard said only nice things and made no mention of what could have done Cui Ning harm. (*Good detail, like the fine stitches of a good piece of needlework.*)

So Cui Ning and his wife took up residence in Jiankang. Now that his case had been closed, he was no longer afraid of being spotted by old acquaintances. As before, he opened a jade carving shop.

One day, his wife said, "The two of us are living comfortably here, but my parents have been through a lot since you and I fled to Tanzhou. The day I was seized and taken to the prince, they tried to kill themselves. How about sending someone to the capital to bring them here so that they can live with us?"

"That would be nice indeed," Cui Ning agreed, whereupon he sent a man to the capital to fetch his in-laws.

Equipped with the address, names, and other relevant information given to him by Cui Ning, the man made his way to Lin'an and found the house. He checked with a neighbor, who said, pointing to the house, "That's the house all right." The man walked up to the door, only to find the two panels locked and bolted with a bamboo pole. He asked the neighbors, "Where have the old couple gone?"

"You may well ask! They have a daughter as pretty as a flower, whom they sent to live in a wonderland of a place. But instead of enjoying her good fortune, the girl eloped with some jade carver. Some time ago, they were caught and brought back from Tanzhou in Hunan. The man was taken to the Lin'an prefectural yamen for trial, and the girl was taken into the prince's back garden. After hearing about what had happened to their daughter, the old couple tried to kill themselves. They haven't been heard from since then. What we see is only the closed door."

At these words, the man started back to Jiankang, but one day, while he was still on his way, Cui Ning was sitting in his house when he heard someone outside saying, "You are looking for Master Cui's house? It's right here." Cui Ning had his wife go outside to see who it was, and who should be there but her parents, old Mr. and Mrs. Qu! So happy were they to see one another that they embraced in joy.

The man who had been sent to bring back the old couple did not return until the following day. He gave an account of what had happened and added, "I didn't find them and made the trip for nothing, not knowing that they were already here."

The old couple said, "We are really sorry to have put you to so much trouble. We didn't know that you live in Jiankang now, so we asked all around until we finally found ourselves here." The four began to live under the same roof, and there we shall leave them for now.

Let us turn to the emperor, who went one day to a side hall to view the collection of treasures. As he picked up a jade statue of the bodhisattva, his hand slipped and knocked a jade bell off the statue. Immediately, he asked an attendant, "How can it be fixed?"

The attendant examined the statue front and back and commented, "What a nice jade statue! Too bad the bell fell off!" Then he saw a few characters carved on the bottom: Made by Cui Ning. "That's easy," he said, "Since we have the name of the artisan, we need only summon him here and have him fix it."

A decree was duly sent to the prince, ordering him to bring Cui Ning the jade carver to the imperial court. In reply, the prince said, "Cui Ning has committed a crime and is now living in Jiankang Prefecture." Right away, an envoy was sent to Jiankang to get Cui Ning.

After arriving in the capital and depositing his luggage at an inn, Cui Ning was called into the emperor's presence. The emperor handed him the jade bodhisattva and told him to take it home and fix it with care. Cui Ning thanked the emperor and went to find a piece of jade of the same kind. He then carved it into a bell, affixed it to the statue, and returned the statue to the emperor. The emperor thereupon ordered that an exception be made, allowing Cui Ning to live in the capital as a jade carver under the patronage of the imperial court.

Cui Ning said to himself, "Now that I've won favor from the emperor, I can hold my head up again. I'm going to find a house by the Qinghu River and open a jade carving shop there. What do I have to fear now if I'm seen?".

And, as coincidence would have it, less than three days after the shop was open for business, who should step in but Guard Guo! At the sight of Cui Ning, he said, "Congratulations, Master Cui! So you're living here now!" Raising his head, he saw that behind the counter stood Master Cui's wife. Quite shaken by the sight, Guard Guo turned and took to his heels.

Xiuxiu said to her husband, "Stop that man for me. I have a few questions for him." Truly,

One who does nothing to raise a frown
Has no enemy in the whole wide world.

Straightaway, Jade Carver Cui gave chase and grabbed the man. Shaking his head, Guard Guo mumbled to himself over and over again, "How very strange! How very strange!" But he could not do otherwise than follow Cui Ning back.

After he sat down in Cui Ning's home, Xiuxiu greeted him and said, "Guard Guo, the last time I saw you, I served you wine with the best intentions, but you told the prince about us and ruined our happy situation. Now that we've won favor from the emperor, you may very well go ahead and report on us again for all we care."

Unable to come up with a response, Guard Guo said only, "I am sorry!"

With that, he took leave of the couple and returned to the prince's residence. To the prince, he said, "I saw a ghost!" (*There he goes again, shooting off his big mouth.*)

"What's wrong with this man?" said the prince.

"Your Highness, I saw a ghost!"

"What ghost?"

"I was just passing by the Qinghu River when I saw Cui Ning's jade carving shop. Behind the counter stood a woman. And she was none other than Xiuxiu the Maid!"

The prince snapped impatiently, "What nonsense is this? I had Xiuxiu beaten to death and buried in the back garden. You must have seen it, too. How could she have been there in the shop? (*Nice plot.*) Are you trying to make fun of me?"

"How would I ever dare to make fun of Your Highness? She stopped me some moments ago and talked to me. If Your Highness doesn't believe what I say, I can write you a military pledge."[22]

"If she's really still alive, yes, write me the pledge!"

That ill-starred man did draw up a military pledge. The prince put it away and summoned two sedan-chair carriers on duty to bring over a sedan-chair, adding to Guo Li, "Get me that woman. If she's really still alive, I'll cut her down with my sword. If not, you will be put to the sword in her place!" Thereupon, Guo Li and the two sedan-chair carriers set out to get Xiuxiu. Truly,

Two ears of wheat grow from the same stalk;
The farmer finds them hard to tell apart.

Guo Li, a native of the region west of the Tong Pass, was a simpleminded man. Little did he know that a military pledge was not something to be given so lightly. Upon arrival at Cui Ning's house, the three men found Xiuxiu sitting behind the counter. She had no inkling that Guard Guo, coming in such haste, was here to get her on a military pledge.

"Young woman," said Guard Guo, "we are here to arrest you by order of the prince."

"In that case," said Xiuxiu, "wait for a while. I need to do my toilette before joining you." So saying, she disappeared into the interior of the house and changed her clothes before reemerging to mount the sedan-chair. After she bid farewell to her husband and left him with a few words of instruction, the two sedan-chair carriers carried her all the way to the prince's mansion.

Guo Li went in first. He chanted a greeting to the prince, who was waiting in the main hall, and said, "Xiuxiu the Maid has been brought here."

"Bring her in!" said the prince.

Guo Li went out and said, "Young woman, the prince wants you to come in." But when he lifted the curtain of the sedan-chair, he felt as if a bucketful of water had been poured all over him. He stood there, mouth agape, for there was no Xiuxiu to be seen. (*Guo Li the busybody is to suffer consequences of his own making.*) When asked, the two sedan-chair carriers said, "We have no idea what happened. We saw her get into the sedan-chair, we carried her all the way here; and we never moved from this spot."

Shouting his way into the hall, Guo Li said, "Your Highness, she's indeed a ghost!"

"This is too much!" said the prince. Calling forth his men, he ordered, "Seize this man! Bring me the pledge he wrote, and let me put him to the sword!" With that, he turned to take his "Small Green" from the wall.

In all his life serving the prince, there had been more than ten opportunities for Guo Li to earn a promotion, but because he was quite an uncouth fellow, he never rose above the rank of guard. In panic, he said, "I have the two sedan-chair carriers as witnesses. Please call them in and ask them."

Right away, the carriers were summoned into the hall. "We did see her mount the chair," they said. "But she disappeared after we arrived here."

Hearing the same story, the prince thought, "Could she really be a ghost? I need only question Cui Ning." Accordingly, Cui Ning was brought into the prince's presence. At Cui Ning's account of the whole thing from start to finish, the prince concluded, "Cui Ning had no hand in this. Let him go." Cui Ning bowed and went off. In a rush of anger, the prince ordered that Guo Li be given fifty strokes of the rod on his back.

Having heard that his wife was a ghost, Cui Ning went home to question his parents-in-law. The old couple looked at each other in dismay and then walked out the door and threw themselves with a splash into the Qinghu River. Cui Ning lost no time in calling for help, but a search turned up no corpses.

Here's what had happened: Upon hearing that Xiuxiu had been beaten to death, her parents threw themselves into the river and drowned. So these two were also ghosts. A dejected Cui Ning returned home, and who should be sitting on the bed in his chamber but his wife! Cui Ning said, "Sister, please spare my life!"

"All because of you, I was beaten to death at the prince's orders and buried in the back garden. How hateful that busybody Guard Guo! Now I've had my revenge. The prince has ordered fifty strokes of the rod on his back. (*Busybodies who are likely to incur hatred, take warning!*) Now that everybody knows I'm a ghost, I can't live here anymore." As she rose to go, she grabbed Cui Ning with both hands. With a cry, he fell to the ground. When neighbors came in for a look, they saw that—

The pulses of both his wrists had stopped,
His life gone back under the yellow earth.

So Cui Ning was also dragged along to make a group of four ghosts. A later poet put it well:

The prince of Xian'an couldn't curb his rage;
Guard Guo couldn't help shooting off his mouth.
Xiuxiu couldn't bear to part from her man;
Cui Ning couldn't break free from his ghost of a wife.

9

"Li the Banished Immortal" Writes in Drunkenness to Impress the Barbarians

How enviable Li the Banished Immortal!
Between cups of wine, he poured out poem after poem.
In talent, he outshone scholars of the day;
In writing style, he surpassed worthy men of old.
His letter to the barbarians inspired awe;
His lines praising Consort Yang graced the zither strings.
Say not that the gifted poet is no more;
The bright moon still hangs over the Caishi Cliffs.[1]

The story goes that during the reign of Emperor Xuanzong [712–55] of the Tang dynasty, there lived a gifted poet, Li Bai [also spelled Li Po or Li Bo] by name, courtesy name Taibai, who was a ninth-generation descendant of Emperor Li Hao of Western Liang[2] and a native of Jinzhou, Sichuan. Before giving birth to him, his mother dreamed that the star Taibai [the god of the planet Venus] had fallen into her abdomen. Hence, Bai for his given name and Taibai for his courtesy name. He turned out to be a comely boy with an air of refinement that was quite out of this world. At age ten, he was already well versed in history and the classics, and words that flowed from his mouth had the literary grace of well-composed essays. All and sundry praised him for his remarkable talent, saying that he was a reincarnated immortal from heaven, hence the nickname "Li the Banished Immortal." There is, in testimony, a poem Du Fu[3] wrote for him:

In days gone by, there was that free spirit
Called "Immortal Banished from Heaven,"
Whose pen summoned the winds and rain,
Whose poems moved ghosts and deities to tears.
From oblivion, he rose to sudden fame,
And his name began to spread far and wide.
His talent now widely recognized,
His name goes down in history, unrivaled.

Li Bai, who called himself the "Blue-Lotus Recluse," had a lifelong passion for drinking. His ambition was not to have a career as an official but to ramble around all the four seas and famous mountains and taste all kinds of good wine that could be found in the land. After climbing Mount Emei, he took up residence in the Yunmeng Marshes. After that, he went to live as a hermit at Bamboo Creek on Mount Zulai, where he drank to his heart's content day in and day out with Kong Chaofu and four other men. They called themselves "The Six Men of Leisure of Bamboo Creek." When he heard about the superior quality of the Wucheng wine of Huzhou, Li Bai readily undertook the long journey to Huzhou, where he went on drinking bouts in wineshops, totally oblivious of people around him.

One day, Mr. Jiaye, the deputy magistrate, was passing by a wineshop when he heard Li Bai's wild singing. He sent an attendant to find out who the man was. Without missing a beat, Li Bai came up with a quatrain by way of reply:

"Blue Lotus Layman, Banished Immortal,
For thirty years, in wineshops have I taken shelter.
The magistrate of Huzhou need not ask;
A Vimalakirti born again am I."[4]

Much taken aback, Magistrate Jiaye asked, "Might he be Li of Sichuan, the Banished Immortal? I have long heard of his fame." Thereupon, he asked to see Li Bai. He kept Li Bai for ten days, during which time much wine was consumed. At their parting, he showered gifts upon Li Bai and said, "With your talent, gaining a career as an official would be as easy for you as picking up a blade of grass. Why don't you travel to Chang'an to sit for the examinations?"

Li Bai replied, "With the imperial court in such a confused state, there's no fairness to speak of. Those who pull strings and pay bribes left and right are given high honors in the exams. Those who don't resort to such means get nowhere, even if they are as virtuous as Confucius and Mencius or as talented as Chao Cuo and Dong Zhongshu[5] (*Such have been the ways of the world for all too long. How lamentable!*) It's precisely to avoid being bullied by stupid examiners that I've been indulging myself in the pleasures of poetry and wine."

"What you say may all be very true," replied the magistrate, "but who hasn't heard of your name? Once you're in Chang'an, there will surely be someone to recommend you for a position."

Li Bai followed his advice and traveled to Chang'an.

One day, he was touring the Heavenly Palace when he ran into Hanlin Academician He Zhizhang.[6] After learning each other's names, each expressed admiration for the other's talent, whereupon He Zhizhang invited Li Bai to a wineshop. There, he took off the ornament on his official's cap and exchanged it for wine to share with Li Bai. By night, still unwilling to part from Li Bai, he took Li to his house for the night, and, there, they pledged brotherhood. (*In some old novels, Li*

Bai is said to be a son of He Zhizhang's by one of his maidservants. And now, this account debunks that falsehood.)

The next day, Li Bai moved his luggage into Academician He's residence, where host and guest talked about poetry every day over cups of wine and enjoyed each other's company.

Time sped by. Before they knew it, the date of the examinations drew near. Academician He said, "The chief examiner appointed by the Imperial Secretariat this spring is Grand Preceptor Yang Guozhong, Consort Yang's older brother, and the supervisor is Grand Commandant Gao Lishi. Both are of the greedy sort. If you have nothing with which to bribe them, you, my good brother, won't ever get to see the emperor, however learned you are. Being an acquaintance of both of them, I'll write them a letter and put in a few words for you. They may do something for you out of their regard for me."

However proud Li Bai was, he found it hard to reject the Academician's kind offer under the circumstances. Thereupon, Academician He wrote the letter and had it delivered to Grand Preceptor Yang and Grand Commandant Gao Lishi.

Upon reading the letter, the two men said with sardonic smiles, "So, Academician He has kept Li Bai's bribes for himself and has written this worthless letter to ask for a favor, free of charge. On the day of the exams, whatever the circumstances, let's flunk that man Li Bai the moment we see his name on the exam paper!"

On the third day of the third month, the Grand Secretariat opened wide its doors for talented men from all over the empire to sit for the examinations. Li Bai, in an exuberance of brilliant imagination, composed his essay with never a pause of his brush-pen and was the first to hand in the paper. Seeing the name Li Bai on the paper, Yang Guozhong wrote sloppily, without even a single glance at the essay itself, "Such a student is only good for helping me grind an ink stick to make ink." Gao Lishi, in his turn, wrote, "This man is not even good enough for making ink. He's only good enough for taking boots off my feet and putting socks on them." By their order, Li Bai was pushed out of the examination grounds. Truly,

> *Scholars would rather please the examiners*
> *Than gain excellence in their writing.*

His examination paper having been thus unjustly rejected by the examiners, Li Bai returned to Academician He's residence in a blazing rage, swearing to himself, "If I ever rise to power in future, I won't rest until I make Yang Guozhong grind ink for me and Guo Lishi take off my boots."

Academician He tried to placate him, saying, "Calm down for now. Stay here with me until the next examination three years from now under different examiners. You'll surely make it."

Day in and day out, the two of them spent their time drinking wine and composing poems. The days stretched to months, and quite unnoticeably, the months stretched to a year.

Suddenly, one day, an envoy from a foreign country arrived to deliver a message. The imperial court urgently summoned Academician He to greet the foreign envoy, who was then escorted to an inn. The next day, the official greeter of the court received the letter from the envoy. The Hanlin Academicians whom Emperor Xuanzong had summoned opened the letter but found themselves unable to decipher even one word. Prostrating themselves on the floor, they said, "This letter is written in an alien script completely unknown to these Academicians of little learning."

Hearing this, the Son of Heaven told Yang Guozhong, Examiner of the Imperial Secretariat, to read the letter. When he unfolded the letter, Yang Guozhong's eyes stared like those of a blind man, recognizing none of the words. The Son of Heaven asked the whole assembly of civilian and military officials, but none of them could read the letter. None knew whether it boded ill or well. In a towering rage, the Son of Heaven lashed out at the court ministers, "What use is there in having such a multitude of civilian and military officials when none of you knows enough to relieve us of vexation! If this letter cannot be read, how shall we respond to it? What shall be done with this envoy? We shall end up being laughed at by his country, which will then bully us and raise an army to cross our borders. What is to be done then? We give you three days. If no one can read this letter, all of you will be paid no more salaries. If no one can do this in six days, all of you will lose your posts, and in nine days, all of you will be convicted of a crime. We shall select worthier men than you to work for the empire."

The assembly of officials found themselves speechless at this imperial decree. No one dared venture a word again, which upset the Son of Heaven even more.

Upon returning home after the court session, Academician He related to Li Bai what had happened at court. Smiling ever so slightly in a sarcastic way, Li Bai said, "Too bad I failed last year's exams and missed the opportunity to help the Son of Heaven." (*Goodness knows how many loyal and useful men have been consigned to oblivion by the imperial examinations!*)

Academician He gave a start and said, "So, I take it that you, my good brother, with your versatile learning, are able to read that foreign language. I will surely report this to the emperor."

During the next day's court session, He Zhizhang approached the throne and said, "Your Majesty, I have a houseguest, a scholar called Li Bai, who is a man of versatile learning. He is the only one able to translate the letter."

The emperor gave his assent to He's proposal and sent a messenger to Academician He's residence to summon Li Bai.

"I am but a commoner from afar, with neither talent nor learning," said Li Bai to the messenger. "With so many learned scholars serving in the court, why bother asking me, a crude commoner? I dare not comply with the decree for fear of giving offense to the noble officials."

The last phrase was a veiled reference to Yang Guozhong and Gao Lishi. The messenger duly reported back to the emperor, who then asked He Zhizhang, "What does Li Bai mean by not complying with the imperial decree?"

He Zhizhang replied, "To my knowledge, Li Bai's literary talent is unrivaled throughout the land, and his learning is also truly astounding. But in last year's examinations, his paper was unjustly rejected by the examiners, and he was pushed out of the examination grounds in humiliation. So he is now too ashamed to come to the court in commoner's clothes. If Your Majesty will be so kind as to send a court minister to him, he will surely comply."

"We shall do as you say," said Emperor Xuanzong, "and make Li Bai a *jinshi.* He will come here in proper attire, complete with a purple robe, a golden waistband, a gauze cap, and an ivory tablet in hand. We shall trouble you with the mission. Do not refuse us."

Equipped with the imperial decree, He Zhizhang returned home and had Li Bai spread the scroll and read it for himself. He then conveyed to Li Bai in detail the emperor's sincere wishes for enlisting the services of worthy men. Having donned the robe bestowed upon him by the emperor, Li Bai made thankful obeisances in the direction of the palace gate. Then, he mounted a horse and followed Academician He to the court, where Emperor Xuanzong had been waiting on his throne for him. Li Bai prostrated himself at the foot of the steps leading to the throne and chanted words of gratitude three times before he rose to stand, his head bowed.

At the sight of Li Bai, the emperor was as delighted as a poor man who acquires some treasure, as a dark room that is given light, as a hungry man who finds food, and as a drought-ravaged place that sees clouds. Moving his royal lips, he said in his august voice, "There is a letter from a foreign country that no one is able to read. So we have summoned you, to relieve us of this vexation."

With a bow, Li Bai said, "I am but a man of little learning. My examination paper was rejected by the Grand Preceptor, and I was pushed out of the examination grounds by Grand Commandant Gao. Why does Your Majesty not have the examiners translate the letter? Why keep the foreign envoy here day after day? How can I, a failure at the examinations, ever hope to please Your Majesty when I have failed to please the examiners?"

The Son of Heaven said, "We know who you are. Do not turn us down!" So saying, he ordered that an attendant present Li Bai with the letter. Li Bai read it, and, a slight, sardonic smile hovering on his lips, he translated the letter into Chinese, right there in the emperor's presence, and the words fell trippingly from his tongue like a stream of water. The letter said:

From the kodu[7] *of Parhae [Bohai, in modern Chinese]*[8] *to the house of Tang:*

"Since you occupied Koguryo, thus bringing your border close to that of my country, your troops have repeatedly violated our border, actions that must have been authorized by you. Finding such encroachments more than we can bear, we

have therefore sent an envoy with the proposal that the one hundred and seventy-six walled towns of Koguryo be ceded to my country. In return, we have the following gracious gifts for you: tigers of the Taibai Mountains [now the Changbai mountains], kunbu herbs of Nanhai [in present-day Korea], drums of Shancheng, deer of Fuyu [present-day Songyuan in China's Jilin Province], hogs from Moji, horses of Shuaibin [in present-day Russia], the cotton of Wozhou [in present-day Korea], the carp of Meituo Lake [now Xingkai Lake, in China's Heilongjiang Province], plums of Jiudu, and pears of Leyou—all of which are to be shared with you. If you refuse our offer, we shall resort to force to see who will come out the winner."

Having heard the translation of the letter, the assembly of officials stared at one another in amazement, saying, one and all, "Extraordinary!"

The Son of Heaven was displeased. He reflected for a long while before asking the civilian and military officials standing in rows on both sides of the throne, "Now that a foreign country is trying to occupy Koguryo by force, what plans do you have to meet the challenge?"

The civilian and military officials stood as still as if they were statues made of mud and wood. None ventured to say a word, but He Zhizhang spoke up. "When Emperor Taizong led three expeditions against Koguryo, goodness knows how many lives were lost, but victory remained as elusive as ever and the imperial treasury was depleted. By a stroke of good luck sent from Heaven, General Yon Kaesomun died. His son Namsaeng, in fighting his brothers for power, served as our guide.[9] (*A detailed description of the Korea incident.*) It was not until Emperor Gaozong had the elderly generals Li Ji and Xue Rengui lead a mighty million-strong army in a hundred battles, big and small, that the war was won. After enjoying so many years of peace, the empire has no competent commanders or soldiers at its disposal. Should hostilities be resumed, there is no guarantee that we will win. And who knows how long the miseries of war will last? I wish Your Majesty would lend your divine wisdom to the consideration of this matter!"

"If things are as you say, what reply should we give?" asked the emperor.

"Your Majesty can ask Li Bai," suggested He Zhizhang. "He will surely come up with some nicely crafted language."

Thereupon, the emperor put the question to Li Bai. And this was Li Bai's reply: "Your Majesty does not need to worry over this matter. Tomorrow, if the foreign envoy is called to the court, I shall write a reply in their language, using insulting words to shame their *kodu* into humble submission."

"What is a *kodu*?" asked the Son of Heaven.

Li Bai explained, "In the Parhae custom, their ruler is called *kodu,* in the same way a Uighur ruler is called *khan,* a Tibetan chief *btsanpo* (*In this case, the character* pu [in *btsanpo*] *is pronounced "po"*), the six Wuman [in present-day Yunnan Province and the southwestern areas of Sichuan Province] tribal chiefs *zhao,* and the Walaing [in present-day Java, Indonesia] woman chief *ximo.* Each tribe has its own customs."

Immensely delighted at Li Bai's fluent answer, the emperor granted him the title Hanlin Academician that very day. A feast was then set out in the Palace of Golden Bells, music was struck up, and court ladies served wine while colorfully clad maidens passed the cups. The emperor said, "Mr. Li, you may drink to your heart's content. Never mind the rules of etiquette." Li Bai drank as much as he could, and before he knew it, his body had gone limp under the effects of the wine. The emperor ordered that court attendants help him to the side of the hall and put him up for the night.

At the fifth watch the next morning, the emperor opened the court session.

> *The whip ordering silence cracked three times;*
> *The officials lined up in two neat rows.*

Li Bai had not quite wakened from his wine-induced sleep when the court attendants urged him to present himself at the court. After the salutations were completed, the emperor called forth Li Bai but, seeing his wine-sodden eyes and the tipsy look on his face, turned to a court attendant and said, "Have the imperial chef make some sour fish chowder to sober him up."

Soon, the attendant came back with a golden tray on which was a bowl of fish chowder. Seeing that the soup was too hot, the emperor picked up the ivory chopsticks with his royal hand and stirred the soup for quite some time to cool it down before handing the bowl over to Academician Li. (*Another one of those emperors who cherished talent.*) Li Bai dropped to his knees and ate the soup. Immediately, he felt much better. Witnessing the emperor's kindness to Li Bai, all those present were astonished at this disregard of rank but also delighted that the imperial court had obtained the services of a worthy man—all except Yang Guozhong and Gao Lishi, who wore sullen looks on their faces.

By the emperor's order, the foreign envoy was summoned to court, where he went through the usual salutations. In a purple robe and a gauze cap, looking as ethereal as an immortal rising above the clouds, Li Bai stood by the post on the left side of the hall. Holding in his hand the letter the envoy had delivered, he read it aloud in the original language with never a mispronounced word, much to the envoy's amazement. Li Bai then added, "His Majesty the emperor, in his boundless magnanimity, chooses to overlook the breach of etiquette committed by your insignificant country. Now listen quietly to His Majesty's reply."

In trepidation, the envoy fell to his knees at the foot of the steps. The emperor ordered that a bejeweled couch be placed by the side of the throne. After an ink slab made of white Yutian jade, a rabbit-hair brush-pen with an ivory shaft, a fragrant ink stick, and five-colored stationery paper with golden flower patterns were duly laid out, the emperor called Li Bai to the couch and told him to sit on a brocade-covered mat and draft the imperial letter of reply. (*None but this man deserves such honors.*)

"My boots being not clean enough for me to approach Your Majesty," said Li Bai, "I beg for Your Majesty's permission to take them off and tie up my socks before I mount the steps."

The emperor granted his request, saying to a junior court attendant, "Take off Academician Li's boots."

Li Bai spoke up again, "I have another request, but I dare not say it unless Your Majesty forgives me my presumptuousness."

"Whatever you say, however presumptuous, will be forgiven," said the emperor.

"I sat for the imperial examinations in spring last year," began Li Bai, "but I was failed by Grand Preceptor Yang, and Grand Commandant Gao had me driven from the examination grounds. As these two gentlemen are the masters of ceremony today and I feel a lack of inspiration, I beg that Your Majesty have Yang Guozhong hold the ink slab and grind the ink stick for me and Gao Lishi take off my shoes and tie up my socks so that I may find inspiration and do justice to my mission of drafting the imperial reply on behalf of Your Majesty."

In his eagerness to enlist the services of a worthy man, the emperor did not wish to turn him down and resignedly ordered Yang Guozhong to hold the ink slab and Gao Lishi to take off Li Bai's boots. Privately, the two men knew that this was all because they had humiliated Li Bai at the examinations with their remarks that such a student was only good for grinding ink sticks and taking off boots for them. And now he was taking advantage of the emperor's momentary partiality to him to settle an old score. Out of necessity more than choice, they complied with the emperor's order. It was truly a case of "choking with silent fury," as the idiom goes. In the words of a proverb,

Never create enemies for yourself,
For a feud, once started, will know no end.
Bully others, and you shall be bullied;
Malign others, and you shall be maligned.

At this point, an exalted Li Bai went up to the couch, his socks sagging at the heels, and sat down on the brocade mat. Having ground the ink stick until the ink achieved the right texture, Yang Guozhong stood to one side, ink slab in hand. Given such a difference in rank, how could Academician Li be seated while Grand Preceptor Yang had to stand? Well, that was because the Son of Heaven had granted an exception for Li Bai, who was writing on behalf of the emperor, and Grand Preceptor Yang, who had been ordered to make the ink, had to stand to one side because he had not been given permission to sit.

Li Bai stroked his beard with one swipe of his left hand and with his right hand picked up the brush-pen made of Zhongshan rabbit hair. He began writing on the floral-patterned stationery with never a pause. In a moment, the letter to strike terror into the barbarians' hearts was finished. The scroll, in neat penmanship with never a misplaced stroke, was spread out on the emperor's desk. Much to the emperor's amazement, it was written in the same foreign language used in the letter delivered by the envoy, not a word of which was comprehensible to the emperor. As the letter was passed among the assembly of officials, everyone was awestruck. At the emperor's bidding, Li Bai started reading it aloud, right there by the emperor's throne:

> *"From the great emperor of the great Tang dynasty to the* kodu *of Parhae:*
>
> *"Just as eggs cannot be used to fight stones, snakes do not fight dragons. This dynasty, in conformity with its mandate from heaven, has since its beginning years pacified all the four seas with its army of valiant commanders, well-trained soldiers, and superior weaponry. The Turk* khan *Jili was captured because of his breach of treaty obligations. Sron btsan sgambo of Tibet was granted a title because of his kind gift of a golden goose to the emperor. The kingdom of Silla offered tributes of brocade; India offered a parrot that talked; Persia offered a snake capable of capturing mice; the Eastern Roman Empire presented us with a dog that could pull horses. A white parrot came from Walaing, a giant luminous pearl from Vietnam, a prized horse from Guligan [a region north of Lake Baikal], superior vinegar from Nepal. All these tributes were offered for the sake of peace and security in recognition of the might and the benevolence of this empire.* (What a long list!) *However, against Koguryo, which rose in rebellion, the Son of Heaven dispatched punitive expeditions and wiped out overnight the nine-hundred-year-old kingdom. That serves as a lesson for those who attempt to resist the powerful and go against the will of heaven.*
>
> *"Being a vassal state of Koguryo, your tiny state is no bigger than a county in China, with less than one ten-thousandth of China's troops and grain storage. If the angry little mantis tries to stop a chariot, if the fighting goose gets carried away with arrogance, the imperial army shall sweep over your land and leave it awash with blood. Your king will fall a prisoner like Jili; your country will go the way of Koguryo. While the emperor, in his boundless magnanimity, is still willing to forgive your insolence, you will do well to show remorse and assiduously acquit yourself of the duties of annual tributes so as not to court self-destruction and become an object of ridicule to other foreign states. Be advised to think thrice before any action is taken!"*

The emperor was most pleased. He told Li Bai to read the letter again to the envoy and affixed the imperial seal to the letter. Commandant Gao had to put Li Bai's boots back on before Li Bai went down the steps and ordered the envoy to listen to the imperial reply. When Li Bai reread the letter of reply in his resonant voice, the envoy's face turned the color of mud. Without venturing a word, the envoy made repeated prostrations, called out three times "Ten thousand years to the emperor!" and bid the emperor farewell. On his way out, in a subdued voice, he asked Academician He, who saw him as far as the city gate, "Who was the man who read the imperial letter of reply?"

"That was Li Bai, a Hanlin Academician."

"How highly placed can an Academician be to have the Grand Preceptor hold the ink slab for him and the Grand Commandant take off his boots?"

"Grand preceptors, court ministers, grand marshals, and the emperor's favorite courtiers—however highly placed they may be—belong to this mortal world. But Academician Li is an immortal being that heaven has sent down to assist the dynasty. Where can he find an equal?" (*He certainly knows how to praise.*)

With a nod, the envoy bid Academician He adieu and returned to his own country, where he related everything to his king. Much startled after reading the letter, the king consulted his men and concluded that they were no match for a dynasty blessed with the support of an immortal. The king wrote a letter of surrender, promising to pay yearly tributes to the Tang dynasty, but that is a story for another time.

To continue with this story of ours, the Son of Heaven was about to grant Li Bai an important post out of his high regard for him when Li Bai said, "I have no wish for an official post. My wish is to serve Your Majesty while living a leisurely and carefree life, much in the same way as did Dongfang Shuo of the Han dynasty."[10]

"Since you have no wish to assume a post," said the emperor, "you may pick any gold, silver, jade, and other prized possessions of ours that are to your liking."

"Gold and jade do not interest me either," said Li Bai. "I will be content to follow Your Majesty in your travels and drink three thousand vessels of fine wine every day!"

Realizing that Li Bai was a man above worldly considerations, the emperor could not bring himself to exert any pressure on him. Henceforth, every so often, the emperor would grant him a seat at feast tables, keep him for the night in the Palace of Golden Bells, and seek his opinion on affairs of the empire. The emperor's kindness to him grew deeper with each passing day.

One day, Li Bai was touring the Avenue of Eternal Peace on horseback when he heard the sound of drums and gongs. Then, a tumbrel surrounded by a team of executioners came into view. He stopped in his tracks and, upon inquiry, found out that the prisoner was a military officer convicted of incompetence, being brought under guard from Bingzhou to the East Marketplace for execution. The prisoner in the tumbrel was a handsome man of powerful physique. When asked his name, he replied in a ringing voice, "I am Guo Ziyi."[11]

Impressed by his distinguished bearing, which bespoke a future career as a pillar of the empire, Li Bai sharply ordered the executioners to come to a halt, adding, "Wait until I come back from a trip to the palace to make a plea for clemency."

Recognizing him to be Academician Li, the Banished Immortal, to whom the emperor had served fish chowder, the executioners readily obliged. Turning his horse back, Li Bai raced off to the palace, knocked at the palace gate, and requested an audience with the emperor, from whom he obtained a decree of pardon. Upon returning to the East Marketplace, Li Bai read the decree aloud, unlocked the tumbrel, and released Guo Ziyi, bidding him to render meritorious service in atonement for the crime of which he had been convicted. In thanking Li Bai for saving his life, Guo Ziyi said, "I will not fail to repay you for your kindness someday." But of this, no more need be said.

In those days, the most prized flowers in the palace gardens were what we now call "tree peonies," known in the Tang dynasty as wood peonies, which were sent from Yangzhou as tribute. There were in the palace gardens four kinds in four colors.

Which four? *Bright red, deep purple, light red, and pure white.*

Emperor Xuanzong had some transplanted in front of the Eaglewood Pavilion for Consort Yang to enjoy and engaged a group of singers and dancers for some entertainment. The emperor said, "In the company of the Imperial Consort amid prized flowers, we need fresh melodies for the fresh flowers." He ordered that Li Guinian, head of the singing and dancing group, call Academician Li into the palace.

A court attendant said, "Academician Li is in a wineshop in the Chang'an marketplace." And so, forsaking any other possible route, Li Guinian headed straight for the Chang'an marketplace. There came to his ears from a multi-story wineshop a man's voice singing the following lyrics:

Three cups send you off to the thoroughfare;
One liter makes you blend with nature.
The pleasures derived from wine
Are not to be shared with the sober.

"Who else could it be but Academician Li?" said Li Guinian. In big strides, he mounted the stairs, and whom did he see but Li Bai, sitting all by himself at a small table, on which was a vase with a sprig of flowering peach. Pouring himself cup after cup in front of the flowers, he had already drunk himself into a stupor, but his hand still held on tightly to the giant wine jar. Guinian walked up to him and said, "His Majesty wants you, sir, to go to the Eaglewood Pavilion. You have no time to lose!"

The mention of His Majesty so shocked the other patrons that they stood up to look. Totally oblivious to their curious stares, Li Bai opened his wine-sodden eyes and replied to Guinian by quoting a line by Tao Yuanming: "Be gone, and let me drift into wine-rapt sleep."[12]

With that, he drifted off to sleep. Li Guinian, quite the man of action, motioned through the window to his attendants downstairs, and up came seven or eight of them. Without further ado, they busily hustled Academician Li out the door and put him on the horse, holding him steady from left and right, and off they went, with Li Guinian bringing up the rear on his horse.

At the Five Phoenixes Tower, they ran into the court attendant sent by the emperor to hurry them along. Instructed by the emperor to let Li Bai enter the palace grounds without dismounting the horse, Li Guinian, instead of helping Li Bai get off his horse, joined the court attendant in leading Li Bai all the way into the private sections of the palace grounds. After passing Xingqing Pond, they arrived at the Eaglewood Pavilion.

At the sight of Li Bai asleep on the horse with his eyes tightly closed, the Son of Heaven ordered that court attendants spread a purple woolen carpet outside the pavilion and carry Li Bai off the horse so that he could lie down and rest. When approaching Li Bai for a closer look, the emperor noticed a trickle of saliva at a corner of the Academician's mouth. With his royal sleeve, the emperor wiped off the saliva. (*What a true admirer of talent!*)

Consort Yang said, "I have heard that a splash of cold water on the face can dispel the effects of wine." Accordingly, a court attendant was told to bring water from Xingqing Pond. A court lady then held some water in her mouth and squirted it in a fine sprinkle onto Li Bai's face.

With a start, Li Bai woke up from his dreams. At the sight of the emperor, he was seized with alarm and prostrated himself, saying, "I deserve ten thousand deaths! Your Majesty, please forgive this wine-nurtured free spirit!"

With his royal hands, the emperor raised Li Bai to his feet and said, "We called you because we need new lyric poems today when viewing some prized flowers in the company of the Imperial Consort. Write us three lyric poems to the tune of 'Pure Serene Music.'"

Promptly, Li Guinian brought over stationery in gold-traced floral patterns. With a single flourish of the brush-pen, the wine-inspired Li Bai produced three poems. The first one said,

Her clothes seen in clouds, her face in flowers;
A beauty in the spring breeze by the dewy rails.
If not a goddess atop the Jewel Mountains,
She must be from the Jasper Terrace by the moon.

The second one said,

The red sprig's fragrance frozen by the dew,
Her charm outshines the Clouds and Rain Fairy.[13]
Who in the Han palace matched her beauty?
Not even Zhao Feiyan in all her finery![14]

The third one said,

A beauty amidst the flowers, what a sight!
For the smiling sovereign's eyes, what a delight!
All regrets gone in the gentle spring breeze,
Against the railings of the pavilion she leans.

After reading the poems, the emperor was effusive in his praise. "Doesn't this genius put many a Hanlin Academician to shame?" said he. Immediately, he had Li Guinian sing out the lyrics while the ensemble of singers struck up their music to the accompaniment of a jade flute played by the emperor himself. The singing over, Consort Yang held her embroidered shawl and made bows of gratitude.

"Don't thank me," said the emperor. "Direct your thanks to Academician Li!"

Holding a bejeweled glass cup in her hand, Consort Yang filled it with wine made of grapes from Western Liang and handed it to a court lady so that she might offer it to Academician Li. The emperor then granted Li Bai the privilege of touring the length and width of his private gardens, followed by court attendants plying him with fine wine. Henceforth, Li Bai received frequent summonses to join the emperor at his private dinners. Even Consort Yang grew to be fondly respectful of him.

Gao Lishi still nursed a bitter grudge against Li Bai for having made him take off his boots, but there was nothing he could do about it. One day, he came upon the Imperial Consort, who was leaning against the railings and reciting in admiration the three lyric poems to the tune of "Pure Serene Music." After first looking in every direction to make sure that no one was around, he said, "I thought Your Ladyship would be deeply offended by those poems of Li Bai's. Why does Your Ladyship seem to enjoy them?"

"What is there to be offended about?" asked Consort Yang.

"It's the line 'Not even Zhao Feiyan in all her finery,'" said Gao Lishi. "Zhao Feiyan was the wife of Emperor Cheng of the Western Han dynasty. In one of the paintings of our day, there is a warrior with a golden plate in his hand. On the plate is a woman dancing with flowing sleeves. That woman is Zhao Feiyan, a woman with a lithe and narrow waist and a light and airy gait, as fragile as a blossoming sprig held in the hand. She was, beyond all comparison, Emperor Cheng's most favored woman. But in fact, Feiyan had an adulterous relationship with Yan Chifeng [an attendant in the palace] and used to hide him in a double wall. During one of Emperor Cheng's visits, the emperor heard a man coughing from behind the curtains, and a search was made. Chifeng was found and executed. Thanks to her younger sister Hede's frantic efforts to intercede on her behalf, the emperor stopped short of deposing her but banned her from entering the empress's quarters in the palace for the rest of her life. Now Li Bai is comparing Your Ladyship to Feiyan. How can Your Ladyship ignore such vicious slander?"

The fact of the matter was that Consort Yang was having an adulterous relationship with An Lushan the Tartar, whom she had claimed as her adopted son. An Lushan's constant visits to her private chambers and the true nature of their relationship were known to everyone in the palace except Emperor Xuanzong. The connection Gao Lishi made with Feiyan struck her right on her sore spot.

Out of spite, she began to complain to the emperor against Li Bai, saying that he was a wild drunkard disrespectful of the throne. Seeing that Consort Yang was displeased with Li Bai, the emperor stopped calling him to private dinners and keeping him in the palace overnight. Having guessed that Gao Lishi's malice must have caused the emperor's estrangement from him, Li Bai repeatedly asked for permission to leave, requests that the emperor denied. Henceforth, Li Bai abandoned himself to wine with even greater gusto, making friends at the wine table with He Zhizhang, Li Shizhi, Wang Jin of Ruyang, Cui Zongzhi, Su Jin, Zhang Xu, and Jiao Sui. The eight men came to be called by contemporaries "The Eight Immortals of Wine."

Meanwhile, Emperor Xuanzong was, deep down, still as appreciative of Li Bai as before. He distanced himself a little from Li Bai only because of Consort Yang's displeasure. Observing that Li Bai had no wish to stay on at the court but repeatedly asked for permission to leave, he said to Li Bai, "Since you have nobler interests to pursue, we will let you go for now but will call you back soon. However, with your impressive record of distinguished service to the court, how can we let you go empty-handed? Every need that you have shall be gratified."

Li Bai replied, "I have no wish other than to have enough money to buy myself some wine to get drunk on every day."

Thereupon, the emperor gave Li Bai a gold badge on which he wrote, "By imperial order, Li Bai, the Carefree Academician and Blithe-spirited Scholar (*What novel official titles!*), shall be paid, upon demand, five hundred strings of cash by the county and a thousand strings of cash by the prefecture to defray his wineshop bills. Any military or civilian official, soldier, or commoner who shows him disrespect shall be punished for disobeying an imperial decree." The emperor also granted him a thousand taels of gold, a brocade robe with a jade belt, a fine horse with a gold saddle, and twenty attendants. As Li Bai kowtowed in gratitude, the Son of Heaven added two gold flowers and three cups of wine, after which Li Bai mounted the horse and left the court.

The assembly of officials were all given leave to take along some wine and see him off. An unbroken line of wine vessels stretched from the Avenue of Eternal Peace all the way to the Farewell Pavilion ten li away. Only Grand Preceptor Yang and Grand Commandant Gao did not show up because of their grudge against him. His seven friends of the wine table, including Academician He, accompanied him for a distance of a hundred li and stayed with him for three days before bidding him farewell.

In the collection of Li Bai's poems, there is one titled "To My Good Friends upon Leaving the Palace for the Mountains." In brief, the poem says,

Favored by imperial grace,
I rose to sudden fame as in a dream.
Once I leave the palace gate,
I drift like withered fleabane grass.
In leisure, I shall intone Dongwu poems;[15]

The poems may end, but my feelings will linger.
With these lines, I thank my good friends;
In my boat, I search for fellow anglers.

Wearing his brocade robe and gauze hat, Li Bai mounted his horse and set out on his journey, presenting himself as "Gentleman of the Brocade Robe" all along the way. And, sure enough, his wineshop bills were duly paid from local government treasuries.

In a matter of days, he was back in Jinzhou and reunited with his wife Xu-shi. Having heard of Academician Li's return, the local officials all came to greet him. Not a day passed without his drinking himself into a stupor. The days and the months went by, and quite unnoticeably, half a year elapsed.

One day, Li Bai told his wife that he was going out on a sightseeing trip. Dressed like a scholar, with the emperor's gold badge hidden on him, he brought along a page boy and, riding a strong donkey, went wherever his whim took him. All along the way, his wine bills were paid out of county and prefectural treasuries in accordance with the imperial decree on the badge.

One day, he found himself in Huayin County. Hearing that the county magistrate was a greedy man who had brought much affliction to the people, Li Bai devised a plan to punish him.

When he arrived at the county yamen, he told his page boy to go away. All by himself, he sat facing backward on his donkey and rode around the yamen gate three times.

While attending to business in the main hall, the magistrate saw Li Bai and said over and over again, "What an insult! What an insult! How dare that man make fun of an official whom he should respect as he does his parents!"

Straightaway, he had runners bring Li Bai into the hall for questioning. Li Bai pretended to be slightly tipsy with wine and ignored all the questions. The magistrate ordered that a prison guard take him to prison and, on the next day, after the effects of the wine wore off, have him write a confession before judgment of his case. Accordingly, the prison guard led Li Bai into the prison. At the sight of the prison officer, Li Bai broke into such hearty laughter that his beard shook. The officer said, "Is this man a lunatic?"

"Not at all," replied Li Bai.

"If not, then write a good confession for me. Who are you? Why did you ride facing backward on the donkey to make fun of the magistrate?"

"If you want me to write a confession, bring me paper and pen."

When the prison guard brought paper and a brush-pen and set them on the table, Li Bai pulled the prison officer aside, saying, "You step aside so that I can write!"

The officer said with a chuckle, "Let's see what this lunatic will come up with!"

And this is what Li Bai wrote:

This confession is written by Li Bai, a native of Jinzhou. By the age of twenty, I was already a master of prose, moving ghosts and gods to tears with a flourish of my pen. In Chang'an, I was named one of the Eight Immortals; by the Bamboo Creek, I was called one of the Six Carefree Souls. My letter of warning to the barbarians spread my fame to the far ends of the world. A constant companion of the emperor, I took the Hall of Golden Bells in the palace as my bedchamber. The royal hand has stirred my soup to cool it down for me; the royal sleeve has wiped the drool away from my mouth. Grand Commandant Gao has helped me take off my boots; Grand Preceptor Yang has helped me grind the ink stick. The Son of Heaven allowed me to ride a horse through the palace grounds. Why can't the Huayin County magistrate let me enter on a donkey's back? Read my gold badge, and you shall know who I am!

Upon finishing, he handed the paper to the prison officer. Frightened out of his wits, the officer bent low in obeisance and said, "Your Highness the Academician, please forgive me in your magnanimity. I had to follow my superior's orders."

Li Bai said, "I have no quarrel with you. Just put this question to your magistrate for me: I am here with a gold badge bearing an imperial decree. What crime have I committed to deserve this detention?"

The officer bowed in gratitude. With all the speed he could muster, he went to the magistrate and presented the confession to him, adding that Li Bai had in his possession a gold badge bearing an imperial decree. As stunned as a child hearing a thunderbolt for the first time, the magistrate wished there was a hole somewhere for him to disappear into, but he could not do otherwise than go with the prison officer to see Academician Li. He pleaded plaintively with deep bows, "This humble official failed to recognize in you a person as important as the great Mount Tai. Please forgive me for the offense!"

All the other officials of the local yamen, hearing about the matter, rushed to the scene to plead on the magistrate's behalf. At their invitation, Li Bai sat down in the seat of honor in the main hall. After they had finished their salutary obeisances, Li Bai took out the gold badge and showed it to them. On the badge was written: "Any military and civilian official, soldier, and commoner who shows him disrespect shall be punished for disobeying an imperial decree."

"Now, do you know what punishment such an offense carries?" demanded Li Bai.

The assembly of officials said in unison, with lowered heads, "We deserve to die ten thousand deaths."

Amused by the sight of a group of officials pleading piteously for clemency, Li Bai said, "Aren't you all paid by the imperial court? How can you so greedily fleece the people? You'll be forgiven only if you mend your ways."

With hands respectfully folded across their chests, the officials voiced their readiness to do as Li Bai bade and to never revert to their old ways. A grand feast was laid out in the hall in honor of the Academician. The wining and dining lasted for three days. Henceforth, the magistrate turned over a new leaf and became an exemplary official.

When the story spread around to other counties, speculation arose that Academician Li was on a secret court-assigned mission to inspect the work of local governments. Consequently, all the corrupt and merciless officials changed their ways. (*He brought benefit to the people with his playful ways, something only talented men can do.*)

Li Bai toured the regions of Zhao, Wei, Yan, Jin, Qi, Liang, Wu, and Chu, enjoying the scenic mountains, rivers, and lakes and indulging in the pleasures of poetry and wine.

Later, when An Lushan rose in rebellion, Emperor Minghuang fled to Sichuan and, on the way there, had Yang Guozhong executed and Consort Yang strangled in a Buddhist temple. In all this upheaval, Li Bai sought the tranquillity of the Lushan Mountains and took up residence there as a hermit. Prince Ling of Yong, commander of the southeast region, harbored designs on the throne and, having heard of Li Bai's great talent, forced him down from the mountains. The prince offered Li Bai a post in his illegitimate regime. Li Bai turned down the offer and ended up a detainee in Prince Ling's establishment. Soon thereafter, Emperor Suzong succeeded to the throne at Lingwu [in present-day Ningxia Autonomous Region]. Honored as the new grand commandant, Guo Ziyi recovered Chang'an and Luoyang.

At reports of Prince Ling of Yong's rebellious intentions, Emperor Suzong dispatched Guo Ziyi on an expedition against the prince. It was not until the prince's troops were routed that Li Bai found himself free. He took flight, but upon reaching the mouth of the Xunyang River, he was captured by sentinels and brought as a rebel before Grand Commandant Guo. Recognizing him to be Academician Li, Guo Ziyi sharply ordered the guards to step aside. With his own hands, he freed Li Bai from the ropes, sat the latter in the seat of honor, and said with a deep bow, "If you, my savior, had not saved my life years ago at the East Marketplace of Chang'an, I wouldn't be here today!" At once, he ordered that wine be served to help Li Bai get over his shock. Before the night was out, he submitted to the emperor a memorial in which he defended Li Bai and, recalling Li Bai's letter of warning to the barbarians, recommended that his talent be put to good use. Now, this was a man who repaid a kindness. Truly,

> *Two leaves of duckweed meet in the ocean;*
> *You never know whose path you're bound to cross.*

By now, Yang Guozhong was dead and Gao Lishi had been banished to a remote place. Emperor Xuanzong returned to the capital from Sichuan as the Imperial Patriarch and recommended the extraordinary talent of Li Bai to the new emperor Suzong. Thereupon Emperor Suzong conferred upon Li Bai the post of remonstrance official, which Li Bai declined, lamenting that life as an official required too much commitment to fit his carefree style of life.

After bidding Guo Ziyi farewell, he toured Lake Dongting in Yueyang by boat. He passed Jinling and moored the boat by the Caishi Cliffs. That night, the moon shone as brightly as day. Li Bai was merrily drinking by the river when he heard clear notes of music drawing nearer and nearer, audible to none but him. Suddenly, a windstorm sprang up. From the sprouting waves leaped a whale several tens of feet in length. There appeared in front of Li Bai two celestial youths holding official tablets who said to him, "The Lord on High invites you to return to your rightful position among the constellations." All the boatmen fainted from the shock. When they came to a moment later, what did they see but Li Bai riding on the back of the whale, wafting toward the sky, following the lead of the music!

The next day, they reported what they had seen to Li Yangbing, magistrate of Dangtu County, and Li Yangbing duly reported their account to the court. By the emperor's order, a temple in honor of Li Bai, the Banished Immortal, was erected on top of Mount Caishi, where memorial services were henceforth held twice a year, in spring and in autumn.

In the Taipingxingguo reign period [976–83] of the Song dynasty, a scholar was passing the Caishi Cliffs one moonlit night when he saw, coming from the west, a boat with a brocade sail. At the bow was a white placard on which was written "Poet of Poets." The scholar intoned two lines:

"Who on the river claims to be 'Poet of Poets'?
Let them be shown, the poems as good as jewels!"

Someone in the boat added two lines to make it a quatrain:

"I make no poems in the still of the night,
Lest the stars fall into the cold river in awe."

Agape with astonishment, the scholar was about to approach the boat when it moved away to moor by the bank. Then, a man wearing a purple robe and a gauze hat wafted with the floating lightness of an immortal from the boat and into the temple of Li Bai, the Banished Immortal. The scholar followed him into the temple but, finding no trace of a human being, came to realize that the man who had completed his poem was none other than Li Bai himself. To this day, Li Bai is still revered as an unrivaled "wine god" and "poet of poets."

His talent shown in the letter of warning,
The emperor served him soup—what an honor!
Astride a whale's back, he rose to heaven,
Leaving sorrows behind on the Caishi Cliffs.

10

Secretary Qian Leaves Poems on the Swallow Tower

The charming sights and sounds of spring are gone,
But the Swallow Tower stands to this day.
Could spring orchids fade from dreams of love?
Memories of the beauty's frowns last a lifetime,
With few dancers left, the zhe *cannot start afresh;*[1]
Of the twin lotus flowers, only one blossoms.
No beauties are spared burial in the yellow soil,
But their stories never cease to be told.

The story goes that for one hundred and ninety-three years after the founding of the great Tang dynasty by Emperor Taizong, until Emperor Xianzong, the twelfth Tang emperor, ascended the throne, peace reigned throughout the land. Weapons collected dust, and instruments of corporal punishment lay idle. There was a certain Zhang Jianfeng, secretary of the minister of rites, who asked the emperor for permission to retire from his long career and spend the rest of his days in his native town, so as to make way for the advancement of worthier people. Emperor Xianzong said to him, "You are hardly past your prime. How can you be talking about retirement? If you really want to seek a quiet life free of complications, we shall make you commander of counties like Qingzhou and Xuzhou."

Jianfeng replied, "However untalented I am, I shall surely do my best to be worthy of Your Majesty's kindness to me." Thereupon, Jianfeng, to his immense delight, was made military commander of Wuning District.[2]

Being much drawn to talented men and given to hospitality, Zhang Jianfeng, in his new position, selected many men of ability to enter into his service. As for the singing and dancing girls for his private entertainment, he recruited only those with some claim to learning and proper decorum.

In Wuning, there was a courtesan named Guan Panpan, a beauty matchless in the Xuzhou region. Behold:

Singing with a sweet, clear voice,
She danced with light, airy steps.
She played her zither with a refreshing tone

And her flute with ethereal beauty.
In music, she followed old melodies;
In chess, she created new strategies.
In poetry, she sought nuanced refinement;
In painting, she captured life's best moments.

Although he had heard of her unrivaled talent and beauty, Jianfeng, being new in his post, had not yet found time to call for her services at the dinner table.

One day, there arrived in Xuzhou an old friend of Jianfeng's, a man named Bai Juyi, courtesy name Letian, who was a secretary in the Imperial Secretariat.[3] He was passing through Xuzhou on his way from Chang'an to Yanzhou and Yuncheng to deliver an imperial decree. Delighted by this visit of a guest from afar, Jianfeng set out wine in his residence in honor of Bai Juyi. Behold:

The tasseled curtains are drawn;
The red shades are lowered.
Wisps of smoke rise from the duck-shaped incense burner;
Fragrant wine sparkles in jade cups filled to the brim.
The fruit juices are as sweet as nectar;
The food is as delicious as ambrosia.
Bedecked in jewels and fine silks, the beauties
Stand in two rows in all their finery.
The orchestra, in crisp notes,
Strikes up sweet and fresh music.
Brocade carpets are spread out for the dancers;
Rosewood clappers are beaten to the song's rhythm.

After several rounds of wine and two food courses, the singing came to a halt, and the sleeves of the dancers stopped waving. There emerged in front of the feast table a courtesan holding a *pipa* [four-stringed lute] in her arms. After tuning the instrument, she began playing solo, her dainty fingers gently tapping, pressing, and plucking at the strings. A delicate fragrance dispelled the effects of the wine, and the refined notes of the music dissolved all worries. In a short while, she stopped playing and stepped to one side, her *pipa* in her arms.

Charmed by the sweet music, Jiangfeng and Bai Juyi took a good look at the player and saw that, with rosy cheeks and bright, sparkling eyes, she had a far more refined and natural air than her peers. Turning their eyes to the other courtesans, Jiangfeng and Bai Juyi found them all as unworthy as dirt. They called the *pipa* player forth and asked, "What is your name?"

The *pipa* aslant in her arms, the courtesan took a few delicate, mincing steps forward and replied, "My humble name is Guan Panpan."

Beside himself with joy, Jianfeng said to Bai Juyi with a laugh, "What greater pleasure does the whole city of Xuzhou have to offer?"

Bai Juyi rejoined, "So, what I've heard in the capital about this beauty is no fiction!"

"It is indeed as you say," said Jianfeng. "You will not begrudge composing a poem in her honor?"

"I'm afraid only that my clumsy lines will be an insult to her beauty."

Guan Panpan put down the *pipa* and said, shielding her face with her sleeves, "With my uncomely looks, I would not dream of winning a jewel of a poem in my name, but if you, sir, do not find it beneath your dignity to write on such a lowly subject, your immortal poem will lend me some glory after I am gone, however insignificant I am."

Impressed by her eloquence, Bai Juyi intoned a quatrain:

> *"The phoenix plucks at the bejeweled zither,*
> *With ribbons behind the sandalwood grooves.*
> *In soft breezes, as if tipsy with wine,*
> *The wind flutters the peony on the branch."*

With a bow, Panpan said gratefully to Bai Juyi, "Should I be so fortunate as to have my name go down to posterity, I have you, sir, to thank for the honor."

The host and the guest went merrily on with their drinking and did not part company until quite inebriated. The next day, Bai Juyi continued his journey east.

Henceforth, Jianfeng showered his favor exclusively on Panpan. He picked a lot near his establishment and had a tower built for her, which he named "The Swallow Tower." In moments of leisure after official business was done, he would go there discreetly, unaccompanied, for a few drinks with Panpan. They toasted each other with jade cups and played musical instruments together. Holding each other in tender embrace, they shared the same quilt of love. By the gauze window, they intoned poems on flowers and the moon. Pouring out words of love in her exquisite boudoir, they pledged vows with pine trees as witnesses. Amid joyful songs and music, their love knew no bounds.

But rosy clouds disperse all too quickly, and the bright full moon wanes all too soon. Jianfeng became ill. Panpan engaged a physician, but the medicine did not work, nor did the oracles bode well. His illness grew worse, and he died. His children and grandchildren escorted his coffin to the burial ground, leaving Panpan alone in the Swallow Tower.

Her clothes and her quilts lost their fragrance, and her musical instruments gathered dust. The silent vermilion doors remained closed, and the quiet green curtains stayed drawn. Lighting an incense stick, Panpan pointed to heaven and pledged an oath: "With no other means to repay the secretary of rites' kindness to me, I shall enter the Buddhist order as a tonsured nun, read the scriptures, and pray for his well-being in the netherworld. I vow never to marry for the rest of my life." (*Such chastity is truly hard to come by.*)

Henceforth, she lived all alone behind closed doors and did not show her face again in public for ten years in a row. Some of the restless men in the neighborhood wrote surreptitious notes to her out of admiration for her talent and beauty as well as pity for her forlornness. To their attempts at sounding her out, she replied in poems, which came to total more than three hundred. They were later compiled in a volume titled *The Swallow Tower Collection,* which circulated in a woodblock edition.

One day, the autumn wind sent summer away, and the jadelike drops of dew grew chilly. Formations of migrating wild geese spread across the sky, and the chirps of crickets echoed through the grass. In the loneliness of her courtyard, which served as a frame for the autumn scene, Panpan heaved a deep sigh as she stood leaning against the balustrade. "My poems," said she to herself, "tell of nothing but my sorrows. I wonder if my feelings are understood by others." She reflected for a long while, and then a sudden thought struck her: "Mr. Bai of the Hanlin Academy should be able to understand me. Let me send him some poems so as to express my true feelings and let him know that I shall not betray Mr. Zhang's kindness to me." Then and there, she wrote three quatrains, which she sealed up and gave to an old servant for him to deliver to Mr. Bai in the capital.

Bai Juyi opened the seal and saw that the first one said:

Doleful mists hover over the pines by his grave;
She of the Swallow Tower mourns him in silence.
Since his hat and swords were buried, the songs stopped;
Ten years have gone by as beauty fades.

The second one said:

Behold! The wild geese return from Yueyang;
The swallows escort the new season here.
In no mood for the zither and the flute,
I let them gather dust amid the spiderwebs.

The third one said:

In the lamp's last flicker over the morning frost,
She who sleeps alone rises from the conjugal bed.
Goodness knows how deep the nightly longings;
How long the night that stretches to the ends of the earth![4]

After reading the poems, Bai Juyi sighed in admiration for quite a while. Who would have expected a courtesan to have observed the virtue of chastity so scrupulously? He could not very well ignore the poems and send no reply. So he wrote three poems in response in commendation of her goodwill and had the old servant carry them back to Panpan posthaste.

Upon opening the seal, Panpan saw that the first poem said:

The color of the silk robes fades away;
Each look at them brings tears to the eyes.
"The Rainbow Feathers" no longer put to the dance,
How many years will they stay folded in the trunks?

The second one said:

A friend arriving today from Luoyang
Has visited Secretary Zhang's grave.
The white poplars have grown into mighty pillars
To keep beauty from turning to dust.

The third one said:

With moonlight over the shades and the frosty yard,
She dusts the bed, the quilt cold, the fragrance gone.
The autumn night rain over the Swallow Tower
Drips without end, so it seems to her.

After reading the poems out loud, Panpan pondered them for a long while and concluded that no precious object of art could ever match their beauty. Smiling, she said to her maid, "These are poems that truly lay my heart bare."

She was about to put them away in her small suitcase when her eyes chanced to rest upon several lines of small characters in pale ink at the bottom of the paper. Spread out again, the scroll revealed another poem:

He spent a fortune on the beauty,
Fresh as a flower in bloom.
After all the pains taken training her to sing and dance,
He dies, and she chooses not to follow.

After she read this poem, Panpan's brow furrowed in grief. Her face awash with tears, she sobbed to her maid, "When the secretary died, I did want to hang myself so I could follow him, but I was afraid that if a concubine died with him, he would be spoken of as a lecherous man and his good name would be tarnished. Mr. Bai wrote this satirical poem without knowing how miserable I am trying to keep myself alive from day to day. If I don't kill myself, slanderous words will never cease." (*Such things happen all too often. Panpan's case is presented here not only to seek sympathy for her alone.*)

She then wrote a poem in response:

My brows knit in grief, I live all alone,
My body like a dry twig after spring is gone.
Mr. Bai knows not the misery in my heart
But scorns me for not following the one who has gone.

Having finished writing, she threw her brush-pen to the floor and, covering her face with her hands, let out a prolonged sigh.

A considerable while later, she wiped away her tears and said to the maid, "The only way I can repay the secretary for his kindness is to throw myself from the tower to show my sincerity." With that, she rolled up her sleeves with her delicate hands and leaned her soft body against the carved balustrades, ready to pay her debt of gratitude rather than hang onto a miserable life. Looking down from the tower, she was about to jump when the maid frantically tugged at her clothes, pleading, "Don't kill yourself like that!"

"With no one to appreciate my good faith, what else can I do but die?"

The maid continued trying to talk her out of the idea, saying, "However good your intentions are in killing yourself to repay a debt of gratitude, how would smashing your body into pieces help my deceased master in any way? Also, who is to take care of your aged mother?"

Panpan thought for a moment before saying, "Since I can't die, I'll chant the scriptures and pray for his well-being in the netherworld."

From then on, Panpan sustained herself on one vegetarian meal a day and spent her days burning incense and chanting the Buddhist scriptures in her seat. Even the neighbors did not get to see her. Gradually, she began to leave her hair uncombed and her eyebrows unpainted. Her musical instruments lay idle, and she loathed the sight of the pillows and quilts embroidered with love birds and phoenixes. Her unpowdered and unrouged face looked like a fading plum blossom on Mount Yu at the end of spring.[5] Her waist was like the withered willows on the Sui Dyke after autumn is gone. At the sight of blooming flowers and the full moon, she was consumed with nostalgia and grief. Her sleeping and eating habits disrupted, she came down with an illness that confined her to bed for more than a month until she died. Her aged mother picked an auspicious day and buried her behind the Swallow Tower.

Within twenty years after Panpan's death, Zhang Jianfeng's descendants were dispersed and the family fortunes declined. The Swallow Tower where Panpan had lived became government property. (*How pitiable! Even more tragic than the story of Gongsun Hong's "East Hall" being reduced to a stable.*[6]) Because of the property's topographical features and its proximity to the county park, it was converted into a garden for the exclusive use of the commanders of the county.

The stars moved in the heavens; frost came and went. The years that went by witnessed the demise of the Tang dynasty and the rise and fall of the Five Dynasties. Toward the end of the Xiande reign period [954–60] of the Later Zhou dynasty, the Sage from Tianshui [Zhao Kuangyin, the first emperor of the Song dynasty] followed the dictates of destiny and rose to power. He cleaned up the imperial court and revived the rituals and the laws. Wherever he turned his eyes, the miasma of evil vanished. Wherever he directed a finger, the air was purified.

By the time the second emperor of the dynasty came to the throne, no dogs needed to bark in warning throughout the land.

In the Imperial Secretariat, there was a secretary named Qian Yi, courtesy name Xibai, who was a descendant of Qian Liu, king of Wu and Yue, and a fine poet and a master of prose.[7] Since he had long worked in the Grand Secretariat, he wished to be given a post in the provinces. Taking advantage of an opportunity to submit a memorial to the emperor on another matter, he wrote, "Never having rendered the least bit of useful service in all my years in this position, I plead that I be given a small county where I may put to use what little ability I have."

The emperor replied, "The Qing-Lu area in Shandong is a place with fertile land inhabited by kind-hearted people. You may take the post of the commander of Pengmen." He then conferred upon Secretary Qian the title Regional Commander of Wuning District. Qian thanked the emperor for the decree.

As soon as he arrived at his new post, he set about publicizing the emperor's policies, cleaned up the rules and regulations, visited the local people in their homes to learn about their grievances, and reviewed prison cases in which injustices had been done. Treating the people better than he treated himself, he personally took part in the tilling of the land to promote farming. Lenient and benevolent, he resorted only to gentle exhortations to make the delinquent change their ways. All and sundry applied themselves assiduously to their work and fulfilled every obligation, and all official business was conducted prudently, fairly, and without corruption.

More than a month into his administration, the Clear and Bright Festival rolled around. As it was a holiday and he had no business to attend to, he took a leisurely walk on the east terrace. With nothing better to do on such a fine day, he summoned a servant and had the latter guide him on a tour of the park. Behold:

A glorious sunny day!
A charming scene of spring!
The fresh peach blossoms wear a deep blush;
The tender willows bend their narrow waists.
The quiet pavilions and the elegant terraces
Stand embowered among thick foliage.
The small painted pleasure boat
Lies safely moored by the bank of the lake.
Enchanted by the spring, the orioles sing;
Playing with sunlight, the butterflies flit about.

Qian Xibai's leisurely steps took him deep into the flower beds. While he was walking around and admiring the riot of colors, he suddenly caught sight of a magnificent railed tower that stood on a high point, soaring into the sky. Xibai lifted his head and saw that under the painted beams hung a placard inscribed with the characters "The Swallow Tower." (*If a woman could have such loyalty in her, imagine what a man could do!*) Xibai said to himself, "This was where Zhang Jianfeng lived with his beloved Panpan. Who would have thought that the site still remains after so many years!" Adjusting his clothes, he mounted the stairs, and saw:

The painted rafters nestling in the clouds;
The carved beams rising to the sky.
One sweeping glance takes in all the land below;
You see distant objects as clearly as your palm.
To keep out the wind, the curtains are hung high;
To block the sun, the shades are let down low.
One step forward brings you closer to the clouds;
One look tells you how vast the universe is.

Leaning against the balustrade, Xibai heaved a deep sigh and said, "In days gone by, Mr. Zhang used to entertain guests with wine and singing and dancing. With his death, all the joviality came to an end, just as clouds eventually disperse and rain eventually lets up. This is nothing to lament, for it has always been so. But what *is* remarkable is the fact that a courtesan like Panpan was willing to die in repayment of Jiangfeng's kindness. A worthy gentleman could not have done more. How could Bai Juyi have scorned her for not having killed herself when Jianfeng died? How tragic that nothing has been written about her chastity in observing widowhood for more than ten years. Since I know the whole story, Panpan in her grave will surely think ill of me if I fail to make her virtues widely known." (*To everyone who has as much compassion as he had, I wish to* [illegible].)

Right away, Xibai called a servant to prepare the ink for him, and, after dipping his brush-pen in the ink, he wrote a long poem to an ancient melody on a white screen. The poem said:

How long can human lives last?
Time flies by all too quickly!
With the wine cups full, why not make merry?
Empty fame after death—what good does it do?
Prefect Zhang, an extraordinary man;[8]
Planted peaches and plums in the spring wind
To preserve the good times in memory.
But, alas, the beauty perished, like water gone.
She valued honor more than her own life
And chose death to repay her debt of gratitude.
Her three hundred poems that conveyed her feelings
Vie with the classics in pleasing the ear.
On the tower that soars to the heavens,

The curtains are let down to lock up the swallows.
Her enchanting soul nowhere to be found,
I search through the balustrades, but in vain!

After finishing the poem, Xibai read it aloud several times. All of a sudden, a soothing breeze sprang up, bringing with it an extraordinary fragrance. Xibai gave a start. It was not the fragrance of flowers. And where could it have come from?

He was full of misgivings when he heard footsteps from behind the white screen. Xibai walked around the screen to take a peek, and there he saw a woman with hair as thick as a cloud, eyebrows plucked into the shape of a crescent moon, skin as fair as glistening snow, a face that would put the most prized flower to shame, a light but steady gait on feet as dainty as golden lotuses, and a waist as lithe as a thin bundle of silk. At the sight of Xibai, she colored deeply. In haste, she grabbed the door and tried to hide herself behind it. Even plum blossoms amid shining white snow were no match for her charms. (*While alive, she shunned even her neighbors. After death, how would she readily show her face to a stranger? If she had to, she would do so only to someone who truly understood her heart.*)

In astonishment, Xibai asked for her name. Emerging from behind the door, she stepped forward, shielding her face with her sleeves, and said with a greeting, "I am the gardener's daughter. I was in the tower amusing myself on this festival day when you, sir, made your appearance. Hurriedly, I hid my ugly self here. But then, I heard your poem in the ancient style in memory of Panpan. As delighted as if acquiring some prized jewelry, I came out quietly to listen behind the screen, and that, in detail, is how I came into your presence, sir."

Impressed by her comeliness and refined speech, Xibai found himself overwhelmed by a joy greater than he could express in words. Flirtatiously, he said, "Judging from what you said, I take it you have much knowledge of poetry. What do you think of the poem I just wrote?"

"Though of humble origin, I take great delight in poetry. The poem I just heard is so admirable that even the rancor of someone under the Nine Springs would melt away in an instant."[9]

These words added further to Xibai's delight. "With you such a beauty and me such a gifted poet, the two of us truly make an ideal couple. Would you be similarly inclined, by any chance?"

The woman's face fell. Covering her face with her sleeves, she said, "I am glad that you, sir, have not done anything to tarnish my chastity. I have here a poem in gratitude for your kindness." So saying, she took out of a sleeve a scroll of colored stationery and presented it to Xibai, who spread it out and saw on it a poem that said,

The tower long empty since I was gone,
Mr. Bai's words sadden my heart to this day.

But for your magnificent lines,
Who would comfort the one in the Nine Springs?

After reading the poem, Xibai said to her, "Someone capable of such poems is no daughter of a gardener. Who are you?"

"If you read the poem closely, you should be able to figure out who I am. Why do you have to press for an answer?"

Unable to control his desire, Xibai took a step forward and pulled at her clothes, but all of a sudden, he heard the wind-blown bamboos knock against his window. He woke up with a start and, finding that his head was resting on a pillow by the window of his study, realized that it had been but an amorous dream.

The lingering smoke from the incense burner and the shortened shadows of flowers in the quiet courtyard told him that it was already high noon. Pushing away the pillow, he rose to a sitting position, thinking to himself, "The woman I saw in the dream must have been Guan Panpan. How vivid it was! This was truly a good dream the likes of which have never been heard of in all history." Heaving sigh upon sigh, he said, "I should write a poem to record what happened." Then and there, he wrote a lyric poem to the tune of "Butterflies Lingering over Flowers":

Sleeping through noon on a lazy spring day,
I dreamed of the land of the immortals,
Where I encountered a fairy maiden.
Full of charms, she said little, her brows knit in grief.
On colored paper, she left me wonderful lines.
Before she could pour out her heart,
The wind-blown bamboo knocked against the window.
Startled, I looked back, only to find her gone.
Sadly, the offer of love failed to make her stay.
In grief, I gaze at the road that leads to romance.

Before the ink was dry, he heard someone singing sweetly and clapping hands in time outside the window. Listening closely to the clear notes that penetrated the window, he realized that it was his lyrics being sung. Much taken aback, he said, "How can anyone be singing what I have just written down?"

As he opened the window to look, his eyes came to rest upon a woman wearing an emerald headdress, pearl earrings, a jade pendant hanging from the waist, and a silk skirt, walking in the direction of the misty green bamboo grove by the dark mass of Taihu rockery. Her feet in their embroidered shoes kicked up no dust. Her clothes fluttered, blown by the wind, lending more grace to her bearing. Staring more intently, Xibai watched her disappear through the willows and flowers. As he marveled at what he had witnessed, a great sadness stole over him.

Later, Xibai rose to be the secretary of a ministry. With his deep concern for the military and compassion for the people, he came to be much loved and respected among the populace. He died of old age, unafflicted by illness, but that is a story for another time. Truly,

A good poem mourning the beauty
Led him in a dream to meet her smiling chaste soul.
What happened to the learned and famous
Came to be recorded as tales for commoners.

11

A Shirt Reunites Magistrate Su with His Family

The morning tide gone, the evening tide comes;
Sixty times in one month, they flow back and forth.
The days go by, the mornings and the nights;
Hangzhou grows older, hastened by the tides.

This quatrain was written by Bai Juyi[1] of the Tang dynasty when he was watching the tides by the Qiantang River in Hangzhou. The story goes that in Hangzhou Prefecture, there lived a talented scholar by the name of Li Hong, courtesy name Jingzhi, who was able to write beautifully in the most exquisite diction and elegant style. He sat for the imperial civil service examinations three times, but, his destined time having not yet come, all three times he failed. In late autumn after his third failure, he decided, with a heavy heart, to cross the Qiantang River and pay a visit to a friend in Yanzhou. He had his page boy pack up his book bags and other personal belongings, rented a boat, and set out on the journey. When the boat had passed beyond the mouth of the river, he pushed open the mat shade and saw a spectacular afternoon autumn river scene. A poem by Su Dongpo[2] of the Song dynasty, to the tune of "River Goddess," bears witness:

The rain has just let up by the Phoenix Hill,
The water clean, the wind fresh, the sunset clouds bright.
A lotus, still lovely though past its bloom,
Attracts two white egrets, struck with its charm.

Suddenly, one hears sad zither notes on the river;
The mist and clouds disperse to unveil the river goddess
I wish to go up and talk once the music is gone,
Yet, no humans are seen, only green peak after green peak.

Mr. Li was admiring the scenery when his eyes came to rest upon a small pavilion at the mouth of the river. It bore a placard with the inscription "Pavilion by the Autumn River."

"Every day, there are visitors touring the pavilion," said the boatman. "But it's so quiet today."

Mr. Li thought to himself, "A man as luckless as I am had better see it when there's no one around." So he cried out to the boatman, "Please get me to that pavilion."

Thus instructed, the boatman rowed to one side of the pavilion, laid down the oars, and tied up the ropes. Mr. Li went ashore and stepped into the pavilion. He pushed open the windows on all four sides and leaned against the railings for a look out. He saw the hills along the river stretching to the horizon where the water and the sky merged in one color. In delight, Mr. Li had the page boy wipe the table and the chairs clean and light some incense of superior quality. He then laid his zither across the table and played a few strains. When he finished playing, he raised his eyes and saw on the wall many scribbles done by different hands. In one place, a few lines written in large characters in a mixture of the regular and cursive styles caught his eye. He rose for a closer look and saw that it was a lyric poem to the tune of "Moon over the West River," listing the evils of wine, lust, money, and *qi* [anger, life force, breath, etc.]:

Wine is the flame that burns the body;
Lust is a sword that cuts away the flesh.
Money brings envy and leads to trouble,
And qi *is dynamite without the smoke.*

If one is to compare these four evils,
None falls short of the other three.
The best approach for self-cultivation
Is to stay away from all four of them.

After reading the poem, Mr. Li commented with a laugh, "This is not quite true. Wine, lust, money, and *qi* are indispensable for life in this world. Without wine, sacrificial ceremonies and feasts would be lacking in formality. Without lust, married couples produce no offspring. Without money, the Son of Heaven and the populace would all live in deprivation. Without *qi,* officials of integrity and righteous men of courage will lose all fighting spirit. Why don't I also write a lyric poem as a commentary to this one?"

Then and there, he ground the ink until it was nice and thick, dipped his brush-pen well into the ink, and wrote next to the first poem another lyric poem also to the tune of "Moon over the West River" and in the same mixture of regular and cursive styles:

Three cups of wine settle ten thousand disputes;
One drunken moment dispels a thousand sorrows.
Union of yin and yang—what a happy event!
A life of abstinence ends the family line.

Money, a wonder that nurtures the family;
Qi, *a source of vitality to life.*

Such good qualities are taken as foes,
How wrong and how absurd such assertions!

Upon finishing, Mr. Li threw his brush-pen down on the table. Noticing that the incense had not yet burned out, he was about to sit down and play the zither some more when a gust of wind sprang up from under the painted eaves.

It brings together the leaves of grass in the yard;
It sends floating duckweeds drifting apart;
It roars with the voice of a thousand trees.
But how does it look? No one ever sees.

At this point, Mr. Li unwittingly drifted into a trance. He bent his head over the table and went to sleep. While he was in this drowsy state, the clinking of jade pendants came to his ears, and an extraordinary fragrance assailed his nostrils. There came in from outside four beautiful maidens, one in yellow, one in red, one in white, and one in black. All bowed deeply in greeting to Mr. Li. Feeling as if in a dream, Mr. Li asked, "Who are the four of you? Why are you here?"

The four maidens replied affably, "We four are sisters. We are immortals roaming the human world. The other day, a poet touring this place wrote a poem to the tune of 'Moon over the West River.' It insults us with such abominable words that we were overcome with shame. But you, sir, kindly wrote another 'Moon over the West River' to redress the injustice done to us. We are here to thank you."

Realizing that he was in the presence of the spirits representing wine, lust, money and *qi,* Li said without the least fear, "Please tell me your names, my four gentle sisters."

The four maidens each came up with one line of a poem. The one in yellow began,

"Du Kang gave me life to bring joy to the world."[3]

The one in red said,

"I have charms that inspire fervent love."

The one in white said,

"Life, death, poverty, and wealth are all in my hands."

The one in black said,

"I am what fills the whole universe."

So, the maiden in yellow represented wine; the maiden in red, lust; the one in white, money; and the one in black, *qi.* Now that their identities were known, Li beckoned to them with a slight movement of his hand: "Now listen to my comments, all four of you.

> *"Of all that please the palate, wine comes first;*
> *To youthful beauty, lust adds greater charm.*
> *Wealth stored in thousands of trunks brings honor and rank;*
> *A sage is one who regulates* qi *best."*

Immensely pleased, the four maidens bowed in gratitude, saying, "We are much obliged to you for your comments and praises. Now, please choose from the four of us sisters one who is flawless, to serve you in bed in repayment for your kindness."

Waving his hand in a gesture of refusal, Li said over and over, "This won't do! This won't do! I have my eyes on high honors in the civil service examinations. I have no interest whatsoever in wildflowers in the open fields. Say no more, lest my integrity be compromised."

The four maidens laughed. "You've got it wrong, sir. We are no 'wayside willows or flowers,' so to speak, but river goddesses of the Wu Mountains.[4] Sima Xiangru of the Han dynasty, a scholar of the finest caliber, eloped with Zhuo Wenjun.[5] Li Jing, the duke of Wei, who helped found the Tang dynasty, eloped with Hongfo.[6] Both men have become romantic figures of whom much is told. Throughout the years, no scornful words have ever been uttered about them. Moreover, if you miss the opportunity for such a nice rendezvous, it is unlikely ever to come your way again. Please think thrice before you make up your mind."

Mr. Li being, after all, in the prime of his youth, his desires were aroused. But still unable to make up his mind, he changed his tune and said, "Since you show me such kindness, may I ask who among you is flawless? I'll be glad to take her."

Before he had quite finished what he was saying, the wine maiden in yellow quickly took a step forward to say, "Sir, I am flawless."

"How do I know that?"

"Listen to this poem to the tune of 'Moon over the West River':

> *"I help mighty heroes gain more courage;*
> *I lend gifted poets more inspiration.*
> *The gods made the brew to dispel sorrows,*
> *To enjoy better the moon, snow, winds, and flowers."*

She added, "Listen to another important thing:

> *"Lust leads to illness;*
> *Wine only turns you heady.*
> *The Eight Immortals, tipsy in Purple Cloud Land,*[7]
> *Envy not the princes and the dukes."*

Laughing heartily, Li said, "I like that line 'The Eight Immortals, tipsy in Purple Cloud Land.' Yes, I'll take you."

Hardly had he finished saying that when Lust, the one in red, came forward. Her willowlike eyebrows arched with rage, her starry eyes wide open, she said, "Don't listen to that cheap hussy. Let me ask that slut something: If you had just said good things about wine, well and good. Why did you have to speak ill of others while praising yourself and assert that lust leads to illness? Don't tell me that the illness of a three- or four-year-old child is also caused by lust? You compliment yourself on your good qualities, but what about your flaws?

"Emperor Ping died from poisoned wine;[8]
Li Bai drowned himself, a drunken man.[9]
Stay away from that ruthless liquid!
It boggles your mind after a drop too much!"

Mr. Li said, "That's right. Wine has toppled kingdoms and killed all too many ancients. I wouldn't presume to take you."

At this point, lo and behold, the one in red approached, walking seductively. "I am flawless," said she. "I also have a 'Moon over the West River' in testimony:

"The love birds—what an enviable couple!
Twin lotus blossoms—what a lovely pair!
Even birds and flowers can be seized with desire.
How can humans be deprived of love?

"Gentlemen fancy pretty women;
Beauties love talented scholars.
A union in the red gauze canopy is
More precious than a thousand pieces of gold."

Li said pensively, "'More precious than a thousand pieces of gold.' How true!"

He was about to take the Lust maiden when the one in white flew into a rage. "You whore!" she cursed. "How can you say that's 'More precious than a thousand pieces of gold'? Am I to understand that I am inferior to you? Let me list some of the harm you do:

"Weisheng was drowned while holding onto the bridge;[10]
Xishi of Wu had a sad story to tell.[11]
A weakness for women leads to calamity;
Even predestined good marriages can go awry."

Li said, "It is true that lust caused the death of Weisheng and the end of Fuchai's kingdom. It's not any better than wine. Now go away! Be gone!" He turned to the one in white and asked, "What have you got to say for yourself?"

The one in white stepped forward and said,

"I hold all the powers of heaven, earth, and humans;
Riches, rank, and honor, I have them all.
To practice charity and compassion,
Empty hands hardly ever suffice.

"With me comes respect from everyone;
Without me, there is nothing but contempt.
Do not fight to vent your qi *[anger];*
Ask me, and you'll know what lies in store for you."

Nodding his head, Li said, "You do have a point. What commands respect in this world is wealth. If I were a rich man, to win honor in the examinations would have been as easy as turning over a hand." (*It has always been like this. How lamentable!*)

He was about to take her joyfully when who but the one in black should say with a scowl on her powdered face and anger in her starry eyes, "Why did you say 'Do not fight to vent your *qi*'? How can life on earth do without *qi?* In fact, as far as wealth is concerned,

"Heroes those with riches and power may be,
But those not so destined work hard to no avail.
Wealth brought death to Shi Chong of old;[12]
Deng Tong's copper hill offered him no help."[13]

Li shook his head and kept silent while thinking to himself, "Shi Chong was ruined by wealth, and Deng Tong's copper hill failed to save him from starvation. What good does wealth do, indeed?" Whereupon he asked the *qi* maiden, "That was all very well said, but how do you conduct yourself in the world as a rule?"

The maiden in black replied, "Well, this is how I conduct myself:

"After the primal chaos came yin and yang.
When static, qi *is vitality;*
When let loose, it becomes the wind
That breathes life into all beings.

"In humans who measure six feet in height,
It flows up and down the three-inch throat.
Wealth, wine, and lust, none can do without qi.
In its absence, what is there to enjoy?"

Before Li could say a word in response, the wine, lust, and money maidens said in unison, "Don't listen to her! How is it possible that the three of us cannot do without her? Let us enumerate some of her offenses:

"Xiang Yu killed himself by the Wu River;[14]
The brilliant Zhou Yu died in his prime.[15]
All too many valiant warriors
Breathed their last in moments of qi *[anger].*

"You must not keep her!"

In weighing his choices, Li thought to himself, "My goodness! None of the four is without flaws." He then said aloud, "My four good sisters, I wouldn't presume to keep you, because my quilt is too thin and too humble for you. Please go back."

At this point, the four maidens started reproaching one another. One said, "The gentleman was about to take me. Why did you have to stop him?" Another one said, "I am the one he loves. Why did you push me aside?" Bitter words soon led to blows.

Wine cursed Lust for sapping one's energy;
Lust cursed Wine for leading to trouble;
Wealth cursed Qi *for ruining human health;*
Qi *cursed Wealth for corrupting the mind.*
They fought till Wine's hair was all disheveled,
Till Lust's well-combed bun went awry,
Till Wealth screamed, her fists pounding her chest,
And Qi *collapsed onto the ground.*
Their loose hair came down over their faces,
Their phoenix shoes flew off their gold lotus feet.

As the four maidens fell in a tangle, Li thought to himself, "All this fighting is for my sake." He was about to step forward to say some pacifying words when the *qi* maiden gave him a push. "Step aside, sir," said she, "and let me beat those three cheap hussies to death!"

As Li gave a violent start, his sleeves brushed against the zither strings. The loud twang woke him up. Rubbing eyes still heavy with sleep, he looked around, but not even a trace of the four maidens could be found. Giving his thigh a stroke, he said to himself with a deep sigh, "They appeared in my dreams because they had been too much in my thoughts. As was revealed in the dream, all four have their flaws. Why did I have to write that poem in their praise? Should readers of later generations be led by my poem into excessive indulgence in wine, lust, money, and *qi,* I'll be held accountable as an instigator of crime. But now, I can't very well change what I've already written, even though I do have bad things to say about them. Well, well, let me add another quatrain and exhort moderation."

After his first poem to "Moon over the West River" on the whitewashed wall, he wrote another poem with a flourish of his brush-pen:

A master drinks but does not get drunk;
A hero admires women but shuns lust.
Stay away from ill-gotten wealth;
Forgive, curb your qi *[anger], and all will be well.*

In the above story, wine, lust, money, and *qi* are equally undesirable. But a closer examination tells us that because there are those who find no enjoyment in wine and those who easily contain their *qi,* money and lust are the greater evils. But then again, the avaricious and lustful ones are more than likely to have a weakness for wine and have anger to vent, thus subsuming wine and *qi* under wealth and lust.

I propose now to tell an extraordinary story in which money and lust lead to a grievous tragedy. The sorrows and the subsequent joys, the partings and the subsequent reunions are the stuff of a wonderful story. Truly, the story

Frightens the treacherous out of their wits
And breaks the hearts of the kind and righteous.

The story goes that in the Yongle reign period [1403–24] at the beginning of this [Ming] dynasty, two brothers lived in Zhuozhou, in the northern district directly under the jurisdiction of the imperial court. The older one was called Su Yun [Cloud] and the younger one Su Yu [Rain]. Their father having died a long time ago, they had only their mother Zhang-shi with them.

Su Yun, a hardworking student since a tender age, was a most accomplished scholar. At the age of twenty-four, he passed the imperial examinations upon the first try. After winning second honors at the palace examinations, he was assigned the post of magistrate of Orchid Creek County, Jinhua Prefecture, Zhejiang. Su Yun thereupon returned home and stayed for several months before the time came for him to choose an auspicious day and leave for his post. He said to his wife, Zheng-shi, "Having passed the examinations so early in my life, I am determined to be a good official in my very first post. Water from the Orchid Creek will be the only thing I take from the local people during my stay there. Everything else that I will need, I shall take with me from home. So, take good stock of all our family possessions, leave one third for Mother's subsistence, and let me take the rest to my post."

That day, he respectfully took leave of his aged mother and gave his brother Su Yu this advice, "Take good care of mother. If I don't give offense to the locals and am able to complete my three-year term and pass the first performance appraisal, I'll see you again upon expiration of the term."[16] (*Too bad such a potentially good official did not get to assume greater responsibilities.*) With these remarks, sad tears rolled down his cheeks.

"My brother," said Su Yu, "your assumption of an official post should be a joyous occasion. I'll take care of the household. Don't worry. You have a bright future ahead of you. Take good care of yourself!"

Su Yu accompanied him some distance farther before bidding him farewell. With the help of Su Sheng the servant and his wife, Su Yun and his wife Zheng-shi embarked on their journey. When they came upon a place called the Zhang Family Bay, Su Sheng said to his master, "We need to go by water from here. If we can find some government-owned boat that happens to be going our way on its return journey, that would be most convenient for you, sir."

"All right," said Magistrate Su.

Now, it was established practice that cargo boats on their return journeys, fully laden with goods belonging to either the boat owners or others, find an official and transport him for free, so that the cargo, now under that official's name, would be exempt from taxes and tolls for the duration of the journey. And, on the official's part, instead of having to pay for the ride, he would receive a gift of several tens of taels of silver as a token of gratitude for his presence in the boat. Being an honest man, Magistrate Su knew nothing about such tricks. He was content enough upon hearing that he did not have to pay. The expectation of compensation did not even enter his mind. As for Su Sheng, he was beside himself with joy over the four to five taels of silver he had received as a tip. At his urging, Magistrate Su and his family boarded a government-owned boat.

They went downstream all the way, crossed the Yellow River, went past Guangling of Yangzhou, and approached Yizhen. Since the boat was old and overloaded, it began to leak, to the panic of everyone aboard. Magistrate Su called out for the boat to pull in toward the shore. Before long, his family members and all the baggage were transported ashore. Because of this move, alas, Magistrate Su's whole family came to grief. This bore out two lines of ancient origin that say,

One who fails to hide things well invites thieves;
She who overly bedecks herself invites lust.

Now, on Upper Five Dams Street in Yizhen County, there lived a man called Xu Neng. A smuggler by profession, he had long been transporting people up and down the river in a big passenger boat owned by Secretary Wang of Shandong, to whom he paid an annual fee for renting the boat. He had under him a group of sailors, all unsavory characters, named Zhao Three, Runny Nose Weng, Sharp Tongue Yang, Skinflint Fan, and Beardie Shen. Together with Yao Da the servant, this group of men, whenever they set their eyes on something valuable, would quietly move the boat to a deserted place in the middle of the night, kill the passenger, and take his possessions. After more than ten years in this business, Xu Neng had accumulated quite some wealth, and his group of men also lived a comfortable life with bountiful supplies of food and clothing. This is truly a case of "To be rich is not to be good. To be good is not to be rich."

But, you may well ask, why would Xu Neng, a native of Yizhen County, be operating on a boat that belonged to Secretary Wang of Shandong? What's more, with all the wealth he had gathered as a smuggler, couldn't he afford to buy a boat for himself? Well, here's the reason: When Secretary Wang first assumed his post in Nanjing, he took a young concubine from Yangzhou. Later, the young woman's parents relocated to Yizhen, but Secretary Wang still often sent them money. However, Yizhen being too far away, Secretary Wang decided to give them a boat instead, so that they could make a living by leasing the boat out. It was that boat, displaying Secretary Wang's banner, that came to be engaged by Xu Neng the first time it was put into the water. Being in the smuggling business, Xu Neng could not very well use his own boat. With Secretary Wang's title and influence, his operations never came under suspicion and had remained undiscovered so far. (*Wealthy families, be sure to* . . . [illegible]*!*)

Because something was destined to happen to Magistrate Su that day, Xu Neng's boat happened to be lying idle. Xu Neng was walking along the shore, looking for a client, when he heard that a government boat was leaking. Rushing over for a look, he saw quite a few trunks and cases being carried ashore, a sight that stirred his greed. And, to top it all off, he saw stepping onto the shore a beautiful young woman of the freshest looks. Xu Neng being a greedy and lecherous sort, his lust got the better of him, making his heart itch and his eyes blaze with fire. At the sight of Su Sheng carrying the baggage, he assumed that Su was a servant and, making his way through the crowd, tugged at Su Sheng's clothes from behind. (*Described like a picture.*) As Su Sheng turned around, Xu Neng flashed him an ingratiating smile and asked, "Where is your master going? Is he changing boats here?"

"My master has just won a *jinshi* degree and is on his way to take up his post as magistrate of Orchid Creek County. But the boat is leaking, so he has to go on shore for now to look for a good boat so as not to end up at some inn."

Pointing at the river, Xu Neng said, "That boat there displaying the banner of Secretary Wang of Shandong is my boat. It's been newly renovated and is clean and sturdy. We ply the river in this area all the time, and the boatmen are all quite capable. If you get off the boat tonight, we'll make some offerings to the gods tomorrow morning to pray for their blessing. If the wind is favorable, we'll be able to get there in just a couple of days."

Delighted, Su Sheng relayed the message to his master. Magistrate Su had Su Sheng go to look at the boat first. Then and there, an agreement was made on the fee. Xu Neng also agreed not to take on any more passengers out of respect for the magistrate's family. Right away, half the fee was measured out on a scale, with the balance due upon arrival.

After Magistrate Su's family and the baggage were all aboard, Xu Neng hurriedly went to gather his gang of depraved cohorts. Zhao Three and some others showed up, with only Weng and Fan missing. Having bought some items of offering for the gods, Xu Neng was about to start the boat when a man jumped from the shore onto the boat, saying, "Let me help you!" (*Important twist of the plot.*)

Xu Neng froze at the sight of this man and stared vacantly for quite a while before he came to himself again. Xu Neng [Able] you see, had a younger brother named Xu Yong [Useful]. The brothers were called by the gang "Big Brother Xu" and "Second Brother Xu." As the saying goes, "By nature, there are some who are good and some who are evil." Xu Neng had chosen to be a smuggler, but Xu Yong was, on the contrary, much given to good deeds. Whenever Xu Yong was on board, he would thwart Xu Neng's shenanigans eight or nine times out of ten. That was why Xu Neng had kept this journey a secret from his brother, who, however, was very much alert. After hearing that a young magistrate had changed to his brother's boat on the way to assume an official post and witnessing his brother assembling those wolves and tigers of men without telling him a word about it, he grew suspicious and joined them with an offer of help. Afraid that Xu Yong would ruin his otherwise surefire plan, Xu Neng was none too happy. Truly, they were like

> *The Jing and Wei Rivers, one clear, one muddy;*[17]
> *The* xun *and* you *herbs, one sweet, one smelly.*

Now, Magistrate Su was about to have the boat get under way when he saw that last man rushing onto the boat. He felt a little apprehensive (*How wrong of him to be apprehensive in this case!*), but then he thought the man might have been a passenger. To Su Sheng he said, "Go ask who that man is who just came on board."

Su Sheng did as he was told and came back to report, "The man who just came is named Xu Yong, brother of the head boatman Xu Neng."

"So, they are family," thought Magistrate Su.

That day, the boat started on its way. Several li farther on, Xu Neng moored the boat by the shore, saying, "We don't have a favorable wind yet. Let's share among us the wine offerings to the gods."

In the course of the drinking, Xu Neng went ashore, pretending he had to relieve himself. He motioned to his brother Xu Yong to follow him and said, "As far as I can judge from Magistrate Su's heavy baggage, he should be worth no less than a thousand pieces of gold, and there's only one servant following him. This good opportunity is not to be missed. Do not stop me."

"My brother," said Xu Yong, "You must not do this! If he were leaving office laden with ill-gotten treasures that he most probably gained through corruption, it wouldn't matter if you took them. (*Xu Yong deserves a seat in the Hall of Loyalty and Justice.*[18]) But as it is, he is on his way to take up his first post. What he has with him is but a few taels of silver for travel expenses. How can there be a thousand pieces of gold? Also, for such a young man to be a *jinshi,* he must be the incarnation of a star in heaven. If you do him harm, heaven will not forgive you. You'll surely regret it in the future."

"The money doesn't matter very much," rejoined Xu Neng, "but what a beautiful wife he has! Since my wife just died, I need a replacement to take good care of the household, and she is a godsend! You must not ruin this marriage bond!"

Xu Yong shot back, "It's always been said that 'The status of a husband-to-be must match that of the woman.' Being an official's wife, she must have come from an official's family herself. To break up the well-matched couple and force her to marry you won't make yours a harmonious marriage. This can never be done!"

From the stem of the boat, Zhao Three saw the two brothers whispering to each other. Wondering what they were talking about, he went ashore with one jump. At the sight of Zhao Three, Xu Yong slowly walked away.

"What were you and Second Brother talking about?" asked Zhao San.

Xu Neng whispered everything into his ear. "Since Second Brother doesn't agree," said Zhao Three, "then don't tell him anything more. You need only me to do the job for you. (*Alas! Good men stand alone, whereas bad men get plenty of help.*) Tonight, this and this need to be done."[19]

Overjoyed, Xu Neng said, "You are not called 'Sharp Knife Zhao' for nothing." As a matter of fact, Zhao Three was a brutal man who would often say, boasting about his prowess, "I am a sharp knife that cuts clean, leaving no skin and bone on the edge." Hence his nickname "Sharp Knife Zhao."

By now, the drinking had come to an end, and everyone retired for the night. The hour being late, Magistrate Su and his wife also went to bed.

At about the first watch of the night, the magistrate heard movements about the boat and the sound of ropes being prepared to set sail. He had Su Sheng ask the boatman what was happening, and this was the reply Su Sheng got: "Sailing in the river depends entirely on a favorable wind. If we take advantage of the all-night wind, we should be in Nanjing tomorrow morning. Now you all sleep tight and ask nothing. I'll take care of everything." Being a northerner with little knowledge about sailing, Magistrate Su stopped asking.

Xu Neng had punted the bow of the boat away from the shore and was pleased that the wind was going in the other direction, just as he had been hoping. He unfurled the sail to its fullest and directed the boat back into Huangtian Lake, which was a totally deserted place. Once in the middle of the lake, where the water stretched as far as the eye could see in every direction, Yao Da cast the steel anchor, Sharp Tongue Yang stood guard at the door of the cabin, Beardie Shen positioned himself at the helm, and Zhao Three, carrying a sword, headed for the cabin, with Xu Neng following behind, armed with an ax. Xu Yong was the only one who was not notified.

Now, Su Sheng was sleeping on the floor by the cabin door. Hearing the door being pushed open, he poked his head out from under the quilt to take a look. Aiming well at his target, Zhao Three swung his sword right into Su Sheng's neck. Su Sheng managed to cry out, "Burglar!" before he was cut dead by a second swing of the sword. The body was dragged out of the cabin and dumped into the water. Su Sheng's wife, sleeping in her clothes, groped her way out upon hearing the commotion and was cut down by Xu Neng's ax. Yao Da lit a torch that brightened up the entire cabin. In panic, Magistrate Su knelt down on both knees, crying, "Chief! I don't want the least bit of my baggage. Just spare our lives!"

"No!" said Xu Neng. He raised his ax and was about to bring it down on Su's head when a man held him around the waist, yelling, "You can't do this!" It was like

A convict getting a pardon in late fall,[20]
A gravely sick man being saved by a fairy!

Who, you may ask, was this man? He was none other than Xu Neng's very own brother, Xu Yong. Hearing movements on board, he knew the men were up to no good, and so he entered the cabin. Now he held his brother around the waist and pulled him aside to prevent him from striking. Xu Neng said, "My brother, now that I'm already riding on the back of a tiger, so to speak, I can't very well let go."

Xu Yong reasoned, "He just won the degree of *jinshi* and has not worked even one day as an official. Robbing him of his property, his wife, and his children, killing his servants, and taking his life as well, that's going too far."

"My brother," said Xu Neng, "I can do what you say in every other thing except this one. To spare his life is to leave a source of trouble. Our own lives will be in danger. Let me go!"

But Xu Yong tightened his clasp. "My brother, if you can't let him go, why don't you just throw him into the lake so that he can at least keep his body whole?"

"All right, I'll do as you say."

"Throw down your ax before I let go of you." (*Every detail shows what a cautious man Xu Yong is.*) Sure enough, Xu Neng threw down his ax, and Xu Yong let go of him.

To Magistrate Su, Xu Neng said, "I spare you the ax, but I can't set you free." He bound the magistrate with coir ropes and threw him, with a splash, like a wonton into the lake.

To all appearances, Magistrate Su had no chance of survival. His wife Zhengshi gave a mournful cry and tried to jump into the water, but how could Xu Neng let her do that? Closing the cabin door, he turned the boat around, unfurled the sail to its fullest, and went back. Now, sails were useful both up and down the rivers and lakes, except when going dead against a strong wind. It being but fifty li from Yizhen to Zhaobo Lake, they found themselves back at Five Dams at dawn.

Back home now, Xu Neng hired a sedan-chair and made Granny Zhu, his housekeeper, help the young woman into it. The young woman wept all the way as the sedan-chair carriers took her straight to Xu Neng's home. Xu Neng told Granny Zhu, "Now you try to calm her down and say to her, 'Things being the way they are, there's nothing you can do but obey. Don't be so miserable. Tonight, if you give in, you'll be rich the rest of your life. Wouldn't that be better than living with that pauper of an official?' If you bring her around, you'll get a handsome reward."

Thus instructed, Granny Zhu took the young woman to her room. Xu Neng, in the meantime, ordered that all the trunks and boxes in the boat be carried to shore. After they were opened and examined, they were divided into six equal portions. For the occasion, a pig was slaughtered and some paper horses were burned as a sacrifice to the gods. Runny Nose Weng and Skinflint Fan were also invited over for a celebration feast.

Xu Yong was in a great deal of anguish. He knew his evil brother would surely force himself on Magistrate Su's wife by nightfall. If she refused to submit, her life would be in danger, but if she gave in, wouldn't her name be tarnished? Even though he was seated at the feast table, he felt as if he were on pins and needles.

The group of men went on drinking wine and eating meat to their hearts' content until deep into the night. An idea suddenly occurred to Xu Yong. He filled a big bowl with about a catty of warm wine and, bowl in hand, went to kneel at Xu Neng's feet. (*Xu Yong is indeed most useful.*) In alarm, Xu Neng raised him to his feet and said, "Why are you doing this, my brother?"

"You must have been angry with me because I contradicted you earlier tonight in the boat. If you are not angry, please drink up the wine."

Xu Neng may have been a robber, but he at least had a good relationship with his brother. Afraid that Xu Yong might get suspicious, he drank up the wine in one gulp. (*Brothers who fall out with each other are thus worse than robbers.*)

Seeing Xu Yong offering wine, the other men all rose and said, holding wine cups, "With Big Brother Xu taking on a new wife, let each of us offer him a drink in celebration of this festive occasion!" By this time, Xu Neng was already more than half inebriated and tried to turn them down, but the men said, "Second Brother Xu is your brother all right, but what about those of us with different surnames? Aren't we your brothers as well?"

Succumbing to the pressure, Xu Neng had no choice but to accept a drink from each one and soon drank himself into a stupor. Seeing that his brother had fallen asleep in a chair, Xu Yong took a lantern and, giving the excuse of having to relieve himself, went out the main gate and headed straight for the back door, only to find it locked. He then jumped over the fence wall, got into the house, broke open the lock on the back door, hid his lantern, and, passing the kitchen where two maids were heating more wine, headed directly for the chamber.

He found the door of the chamber ajar, and the voices within were quite audible. Xu Yong's ears pricked up. (*A meticulous man.*) It was Granny Zhu trying to talk Lady Zheng, Magistrate Su's wife, into marriage. Goodness knows how hard she had been trying, but Lady Zheng still would not listen and kept weeping. Granny Zhu said, "Since you are so determined not to give in, why didn't you kill yourself when you were on the boat? Now that you are already here, you can't very well find a hole in the ground to crawl into!"

Lady Zheng replied between sobs, "Mother, it's not that I fear death and want to hang onto life. The fact is, I am nine months pregnant. I don't mind if I die, but my death will mean an end to my husband's family line."

"Madam, let's suppose you do give birth to a child. Who will take care of it for you? I am just a woman. I can't do what Cheng Ying and Gongsun Chujiu did."[21]

Upon hearing this remark, Xu Yong kicked the door open with a swift movement of his foot. Lady Zheng was shocked out of her senses. Even Granny Zhu was unnerved. Xu Yong said, "Don't panic. I'm here to save you. My brother is quite drunk. I'll take this chance and lead you out the back door. Then you run for your life. If ever we should meet again, remember I had no hand in all of this."

Lady Zheng kowtowed in gratitude. Having talked with her for quite a while, Granny Zhu felt deeply for the young woman and offered to flee with her, as a companion.

Xu Yong took out ten taels of silver and gave them to Granny Zhu as travel money. He led the two women out the back door and escorted them to a major thoroughfare. "Take care!" said he, and with that, he went his own way. It was like

> *A phoenix flying from the smashed jade cage,*
> *A dragon freed from a broken gold lock.*

With nowhere to go in the darkness of the night, Granny Zhu and Lady Zheng thought it best to pick their way only through places that looked quiet and deserted. After they had walked for about fifteen to sixteen li on their small bound feet, even though Madam Su, in her state of fright, did not mind her foot-ache, Granny Zhu could not move another step. There being no other choice, they supported each other and covered another ten li or more, but daybreak still did not come. After so much walking, Granny Zhu succumbed to an attack of asthma, an old ailment of hers. "Madam," she said, "it's not that I'm a person who doesn't finish what I've started. It's just that I can't move another step. I don't want to be a burden to you. Luckily, day will be breaking soon. You go ahead and find shelter for yourself. I know this area well. Don't worry about me."

"In this time of misery, there's nothing I can do but part company with you. However, when you meet people, don't say a word about me!"

"Go ahead, Madam. I won't do anything to harm you."

Lady Zheng had hardly turned around than Granny Zhu heaved a sigh and thought to herself, "With no place to go, I might as well put an end to my life while my name is still good and clean." Seeing a public well by the roadside, she took off her worn old shoes and threw herself into the well and died. (*The gauze-washing maiden has one more follower.*[22])

A teary Lady Zheng saw nothing for it but to press on with her journey. After covering another ten li, making it more than thirty li altogether, she began to feel the spasms of unbearable abdominal pain. By the first faint light of dawn, she saw a thatch cottage by the roadside with its door still shut. She knocked at the door, hoping to rest in the cottage. As the door was opened, she raised her eyes, and what she saw added to her alarm. "I've come to the wrong place," she thought to herself. "It's a monk! I've heard that monks in the south are the worst. (*Not necessarily.*) I fled from a robber only to run into a monk. What back luck! Oh well, I'm as good as dead anyway, by whatever means. Why don't I go in first and then see what happens?"

Impressed by Lady Zheng's looks and clothes, which bespoke a woman of the upper class, the monk respectfully led her into a lounge before asking her name. Only then did Lady Zheng realize that the person she was talking to was a nun. In relief, Lady Zheng told her about the robbery at Huangtian Lake. The old nun said, "You may stay here for a few days, madam, but I don't dare to keep you long, because if the robbers get word of this, both of us will be in trouble." Before the nun had quite finished her sentence, Lady Zheng began having abdominal spasms again, each one worse than the one before.

Having joined the Buddhist order after spending a good part of her life in the mundane world, the nun, now more than fifty years of age, was not unaware of some of the ways of the world. "Madam," she asked, "might you be having labor pains?"

"To be frank with you, I am nine months pregnant. I did too much frantic walking last night, and now I'm afraid I *am* having labor pains."

"Now, don't take amiss what I'm going to say, madam. This is a sacred Buddhist nunnery. It must not be sullied by childbirth. Please go somewhere else. I can't keep you here."

With tears flowing from her eyes, Lady Zheng begged plaintively, "Reverend Mother, mercy is the guiding principle of the Buddhist order. Where can I go for help if this nunnery doesn't keep me? The Su family must have done many evil deeds in a previous generation to deserve such misfortune. I'd be better off dead!"

The old nun softened. "Oh well, there is a lavatory behind the nunnery. If you have nowhere else to go, you may go there and come back into the nunnery after you give birth."

Resignedly, Lady Zheng went to the lavatory behind the nunnery, her hands over her belly. A lavatory though it was, luckily the pit had a cover, and it was tolerably clean. Barely had she stepped inside than a series of spasms set in, and the baby was born.

Hearing the baby's cries, the old nun rushed over for a look. "I'm so glad you're all right, madam. But there's one thing: I can't keep both mother and son. If you leave the baby here, I'll have someone take care of him for you, but you can't stay. If you want to stay, you'll have to give the little boy up. Otherwise, people will get suspicious if they hear a baby crying in a nunnery. If this whole thing is found out, there'll be trouble."

Turning her thoughts this way and that, Lady Zheng found it hard to come to a decision. "I have an idea," she said. She took off a silk blouse that she was wearing next to her skin and wrapped the baby up in it. Then, she took a gold hairpin from her hair and laid it on the baby's chest. Looking up to heaven, she prayed on her knees: "If my husband Su Yun is meant to have a child to continue the family line, please take pity on me, oh Heaven, and send a good person to adopt my baby." With that, she handed the baby to the nun to have him placed at a crossroads.

Chanting "Amitabha," the nun took the baby. She walked for about half a li and left the baby at the foot of a willow tree in a place called Big Willow Village.

> *It was another Qi by the roadside,*[23]
> *Another Yi born in a hollow tree.*[24]

The nun returned and reported to Lady Zheng, who almost died from grief. How the nun tried to console her need not be described here. The nun washed her hands and chanted a section of the sutra on childbirth before serving Lady Zheng liquids and attending to her other needs. Lady Zheng gave up all her jewelry to pay for living in the nunnery. When a full month had elapsed, she entered the nunnery as a nun and spent her days paying homage to Buddha and reading the scriptures. Several months later, out of fear that trouble might arise in the local area, the nun took Lady Zheng to Mercy Lake Nunnery in Dangtu County, where she clandestinely took up residence, never stepping outside the door, but of this, we shall speak no further.

Let us return to Xu Neng, who, in a drunken stupor, fell asleep in the chair and did not wake up until the fifth watch of the night. In the meantime, with the host in such a besotted condition, the other men had dispersed. When he awoke, Xu Neng remembered Madam Su and walked into the chamber, only to find her gone. Even Granny Zhu was nowhere to be seen. He called the maids for questioning, but they were unable to give him an answer, their eyes unblinking and mouths agape. Then, noticing that the back door was wide open, he realized Madam Su had escaped. Even though he had no idea where she could have gone, he felt bound to give chase. Guessing that she must have taken a northerly rather than southerly direction, he headed north, wending his way through quiet, secluded places.

As heaven willed it, he took exactly the same route that Madam Su had taken. Coming upon the well, he saw a pair of woman's shoes, which he recognized as Granny Zhu's because they had belonged to his deceased wife. "Could it be that they ran all the way here just to drown themselves in this place?" he wondered. Peering through the railings of the well, he saw nothing but a black hole. "Well, never mind," he thought to himself, "let me walk some more."

Another ten or so li later, he came to Big Willow Village but still could find no trace of the women. He was on the point of turning back when he heard a baby crying. He took a step forward and saw that at the foot of the big willow tree lay a comely baby with a gold hairpin on its bosom. Wondering who could have left the baby, he said to himself, "I'm going on forty and am still childless. Does this mean that heaven, in all its fairness, has given me an heir?" (*Heaven is indeed fair.*) As soon as he picked the baby up, it stopped crying. Wildly overjoyed, Xu Neng abandoned all thoughts of giving chase and turned back, the baby in his arms.

After arriving home, he recalled that Yao Da's wife had been nursing a baby daughter who died before she was one month old and she could therefore serve as a wet nurse. He gave the hairpin to Yao Da's wife as a reward and told her to nurse the baby with good care. "After he grows up, I'll take care of you," he promised. Of this, no more need be said. There is a poem in testimony:

Plant a rose, and it will grow thorns to prick you;
Nurse a tiger cub, and it will kill you.
Those who know little of heaven's power
Sow the seeds of trouble and watch them grow.

Let us follow another thread of the story and return to Magistrate Su at the moment when the robbers dropped him into Huangtian Lake. As an ancient saying goes, "Life and death are preordained by fate."

If one is meant to die, a thousand opportunities to live will not help. But Magistrate Su was meant to enjoy heaven's bounty later in life. He sank and rose in the water until he was carried by the current to Xiangshui Floodgate. It so happened that a boat belonging to a traveling merchant from Huizhou was moored by the floodgate. Mr. Tao, the traveling merchant, was relieving himself when he felt that there was something underneath the boat. At his bidding, a boatman retrieved the object with his pole and found it to be a man all trussed up. Shocked at the sight and wondering if the man was dead or alive, Mr. Tao was about to have him dropped back into the water when something quite extraordinary happened. Still alive despite having soaked in the water for a good part of the night, Magistrate Su said, "Help! Help!"

Seeing that the man was alive, Mr. Tao hastened to untie the ropes. After feeding him some ginger soup to bring him back to full consciousness, Mr. Tao asked him what had happened, whereupon Magistrate Su gave a detailed account of how some boatmen working for Secretary Wang of Shandong had robbed him, adding that he intended to file a lawsuit. Being a law-abiding man who minded only his own business, Mr. Tao was a little vexed at the mention of a lawsuit against Secretary Wang of Shandong because he was afraid of being involved. Observing the change in Mr. Tao's expression, Magistrate Su changed his tone, afraid that Tao would not keep him. "Now that I'm out of all travel money and my papers are gone, I have nowhere to go. If I could have a place to stay, I'll think of what to do next."

"Don't blame me for speaking out of turn," said Mr. Tao, "but if you are going to file some lawsuit, I don't think I should meddle in your affairs. But if you just want a place to stay, there is a school in my humble village. Should you be willing, you may very well stay there for some time."

"Thank you so much! So much!"

Mr. Tao took out some dry clothes for Magistrate Su and then brought him home. The village, although called Village of Three Households, was actually inhabited by fourteen or fifteen families, each with children in school. By order of Mr. Tao, the village leader, the families took turns providing for the schoolmaster, who taught only at home, never taking a step outside his door. Dear audience, remember well that Magistrate Su now began to teach in the village. Truly,

Before working in the public service,
He first taught the basics of the classics.

Let us turn now to old Madam Su in her home. Missing her son Su Yun, she said to her younger son Su Yu, "It's been three years since your older brother left for his post, but nothing has been heard from him. Now, for your brother's sake, won't you make a trip to Orchid Creek where he is? You can then bring me back a message so as to put my worries to rest."

Thus instructed, Su Yu packed and set out on his journey. He went by land, stopping to rest along the way, as well as by water, in a boat. Before many days had passed, he arrived at Orchid Creek. Being a simpleminded farmer who knew little about social decorum, he headed straight for the county yamen. As the magistrate had already dismissed the day's session, he went around to the magistrate's private quarters and knocked at the door.

With alacrity, the janitor stopped him and demanded to know who he was. Su Yu replied, "I am a member of the magistrate's family. Announce me, quick!"

"You've certainly got some spirit in you, sir," said the janitor. "Since you are a relative, please give me your name so that I can announce you."

"I am Magistrate Su's brother by flesh and blood, and I've come all the way from our native town Zhuozhou."

Spitting in contempt, the janitor cursed, "Go to hell! The Magistrate's surname is Gao. He's a native of Jiangxi. You are trying to match horses' mouths with cows' heads!"

The commotion drew the attention of a few idle officers who were hanging around in a back hall nearby. They came over to join the fun, yelling, "That lowlife from nowhere, beat him and drive him out!"

To Su Yu's words defending himself, they turned a deaf ear. All the yelling and tugging and pulling caught the attention of Magistrate Gao. Emerging from his residential quarters, he asked what it was all about. Hearing that the magistrate was before him, Su Yu opened his eyes wide but saw that it was not his brother. In panic, he dropped to his knees and said, "My humble name is Su Yu, a native of Zhuozhou in the northern district directly under the jurisdiction of the imperial court. My older brother Su Yun was appointed three years ago to be the magistrate of this county, but nothing has been heard from him since he left home to take up his post. My mother is still eagerly waiting for news and has sent me here despite the thousand-li distance. I did not expect to see Your Honor. Since Your Honor is the incumbent magistrate, you must know what has happened to your predecessor, my brother."

Magistrate Gao quickly raised him to his feet, bowed to him with clasped hands, and showed him a seat before saying, "Your brother never came to take up the post. The Ministry of Personnel thought he had died of some illness and assigned the vacant post to my humble self. But since even you have had no news of him, his boat must have capsized, or he must have run into robbers. If he had died of an illness during the journey, how could no other traveling companions, not even one, have returned home?"

At these words, Su Yu burst into tears, saying, "Mother is still waiting for him to return home in glory. Who would have guessed that he had died? And it was a mysterious death, too! Now what am I going to tell Mother?"

Watching him, Magistrate Gao was overcome with sympathy for the misfortunes of a fellow official. He said, trying to console Su Yu, "Now that things have already come to this, please calm down. Stay with me for a couple of months while I have messengers search for clues of your brother's whereabouts. You can stay until they return. I'll take care of all their traveling expenses."

So saying, he told an attendant to take out ten taels of silver from the treasury and offer it to Su Yu for his travel expenses. An officer escorted the younger Mr. Su to the temple of the city god, where he took up residence. However kindly Mr. Gao treated him, he was still so distraught that he wept from morning to night. Half a month later, he suddenly caught an illness. Medicine failed to work, and he died.

He did not meet his brother in life
But bid his mother farewell in death.

Magistrate Gao bought a coffin and attended the funeral himself. When the coffin was placed in the temple, he told the monks to keep a good watch over it, but of this, no more.

To pick up another thread of our story, after carrying home the baby he had found, Xu Neng made Yao Da's wife the wet nurse and raised the child as his own. As the proverb says, "Worry not about your children's growth but about their education."

When the boy grew into an exceptionally brilliant six-year-old, he was given the name Xu Jizu [Continue the Ancestral Line] and went to school. By the age of thirteen, he was already well versed in the classics. He passed the examinations at the local level and became a government-supported student. At fifteen, he became a *juren* and left home for the next round of examinations in the capital.[25]

While passing by Zhuozhou, he felt tired and dismounted his horse for a rest. Catching sight of an old woman drawing water from a well with a porcelain jar, her face like an autumn leaf, her hair like silvery threads, he walked up to her and, with a bow, asked for some clear water to allay his thirst. (*Good detail.*) With her age-blurred eyes, she saw a pleasant, refined-looking young man and invited him for tea at her home. Xu Jizu said, "But Granny, your house might be too far from here."

"It's only ten steps away," said the old woman.

Thereupon, Xu Jizu got off his horse and followed her to her home. The house looked as if it had seen its days of glory, but it was now quite dilapidated. A fire had reduced the rooms at the back to nothing but heaps of rubble. Only three rooms were left, partitioned by earthen walls. The room on the left was the old woman's bedroom; the one on the right was a storage room for some miscellaneous items that were sadly in disrepair. The one in the middle was empty except for two spiritual tablets set to one side bearing the inscriptions "Older Son Su Yun" and "Younger Son Su Yu."

In a side room, an old maidservant was making a fire. The old woman made the young man sit down in the middle room. She herself also sat to keep him company before ordering the maidservant to bring out a cup of hot tea on a tray.

"Young man, please have some tea," said the old woman. As the old woman fixed her eyes on the young man, her tears fell thick and fast. Surprised, Xu Jizu asked why she was crying.

"As I am a seventy-eight-year-old woman, I hope you will not take my words amiss if I speak out of turn."

"Please go ahead and say whatever you have on your mind. I won't take anything amiss."

"What is your name? How old are you?"

Xu Jizu gave his name, adding, "I am fifteen years old. By a stroke of good luck, I passed the civil service exams at the provincial level and am on my way to the capital for the next round of exams."

The old woman bent her fingers and counted to herself, the tears never ceasing to flow down her cheeks. Without knowing why, Xu Jizu also felt upset. "Granny," he said, "you must be thinking of something very sad to be crying like that."

"Well, I had two sons. Fifteen years ago, the older one, Su Yun, was appointed as a *jinshi* to be magistrate of Orchid Creek County. He went with his wife to take up the post and has never been heard from since. I sent my second son, Su Yu, to the county where his brother had been assigned, and he never came back either. Later, I heard rumors that my older son had been killed by some robbers along the river and that my younger son had died at Orchid Creek. I was heartbroken. And then, my neighbor's house caught fire, and the fire spread to my house. Now, my maidservant and I have to make do with these rooms while waiting for death to come. When I saw you some moments ago, I was struck by your resemblance to Su Yun. And you happen to be fifteen. That's what saddened me so much. But it's getting late now. If you don't object to these humble circumstances, please stay here tonight and let me serve you a simple meal." With these words, she broke down in tears again.

Being of a kindly nature easily moved to compassion, Xu Jizu felt pity for the old woman. Unable to bring himself to take leave of her, he agreed to stay. The old woman slaughtered a chicken and cooked a meal for Xu Jizu. They talked until it was sometime between the second and third watch of the night before the young man was made to sleep in the middle room.

The old woman rose the next morning and served him breakfast. Before reluctantly letting him go, she took from a well-worn trunk a silk shirt that looked as if it had never been unfolded. "I made this shirt myself," she said. "I made two of them of the same pattern—one in man's style, the other in woman's style. My daughter-in-law was wearing the other one when she left. As for this one, some burned lamp wick fell on it when I was folding it and burned a hole in the collar. I thought that was a bad omen, so I didn't give it to my now deceased son and have kept it here all this time. Now that you make me feel as if I am looking at my own son, I'd like to give this shirt to you. If you still remember this old woman by the time you return home in glory after passing next spring's examinations, please do me a favor: Send someone to Orchid Creek County to find out what happened to Su Yun and Su Yu and let me know about it. I'll be able to find peace then even in death." With that, she burst into loud sobs. (*How sad!*) Xu Jizu, also, for no apparent reason, shed some tears in spite of himself. After watching Xu Jizu mount his horse, the old woman wept her way back into the house. Xu Jizu was also stricken with grief.

In the capital, he passed the examinations, won the *jinshi* degree with second-grade honors, and was given the post of a secretary in the Imperial Secretariat. All the officials of the court, whatever their positions in the hierarchy, showed him much respect, impressed as they were by his maturity in spite of his youth and his skillfulness in handling matters. Some learned, upon inquiry, that he was not betrothed and offered to betroth their daughters to him, even if they had to sustain a financial loss for it. But Xu Jizu firmly declined all such offers because he had not consulted his father.

In his second year in the capital, he was made an imperial inspector so as to fill a vacancy on an urgent basis and was sent to Nanjing to review criminal cases. This was an opportunity for him to return home and get married. He had just had his nineteenth birthday.

Being now the father of a court-appointed official, Xu Neng threw his weight around in the neighborhood, all puffed up with pride. As a poet of olden times put it:

With a scornful eye, I watch the crabs run wild.
For how much longer is the insolence to last?

Let us return to Lady Zheng. Nineteen years had gone by since she had taken up residence in Mercy Lake Nunnery, and in all these years, she had never taken a step outside the gate. One day, she looked into a mirror and saw that her face was not what it had been. Tears rolled down her cheeks. She thought to herself, "The death of my husband remains unavenged, nor do I have any idea if my child is dead or alive. Even if someone had picked him up and raised him, I have no way of knowing that person's identity and place of residence. Now that I am so emaciated, and in a nun's clothes, I don't think anyone would recognize me. Moreover, I feel uneasy for having lived off the nunnery all these years without doing anything in return for the trouble I gave them. Let me take a trip to Yizhen to beg for alms, partly to help support the nunnery, partly to inquire about my son along the way. As it's often said, 'Even duckweeds floating apart on the ocean will get to meet someday.' If, by heaven's compassion, the baby was picked up and raised by a family living nearby, I may even get to see him. If so, I'll tell him about the circumstances of his birth and have him seek revenge, and thus take a load off my mind." Then and there, she consulted the old nun, and with everything agreed upon, she left the nunnery, an alms bowl in hand.

She begged her way to Dangtu County, where she found the streets colorfully decorated for the arrival of Imperial Censor Xu. As she approached a house, which happened to be that of the local headman, she was rejected and told by a member of the household, "This family is too busy preparing to greet the imperial censor. Come here for alms some other day."

At the next house, a woman stood idly by the door watching the decorations being put up. When she saw the middle-aged refined-looking nun begging unsuccessfully for alms, she called her over. Hearing someone call her, Lady Zheng went over and exchanged a greeting with the woman, who then invited her into the main hall, served her a vegetarian meal, and asked about her background. Thinking that the woman could not have been a member of some criminal gang, Lady Zheng said to herself, "If I go on keeping my secret, I'll never find out anything." Thereupon she gave a detailed account of the tragedy that had occurred nineteen years ago.

Little did she know that her account had been overheard by the woman's father, who was hiding behind the screen. His indignation aroused by the story, he emerged and addressed the nun. "With such an injustice done to you, why don't you file a complaint with the visiting imperial censor?"

"Being a woman, I never learned to read, so I can't write a complaint."

"If you want to," said the man, "I can help you write it." (*This is a case in which sticking one's nose into others' affairs is a good thing to do.*) He went out to buy a sheet of tissue paper three feet and three inches long and, after coming back, wrote the following:

> *From the plaintiff, Zheng-shi, age forty-two, a native of Zhuozhou in the district directly under the jurisdiction of the court:*
>
> *My husband Su Yun, a* jinshi *appointed as magistrate of Orchid Creek County, Zhejiang, took me on a journey years ago to assume his post. When we passed Yizhen, the boat leaked because of excessive weight. The boatman Xu Neng, an old hand at robbery, in collaboration with other members of his gang, stole my husband's money in the middle of the journey, killed him, and tried to take advantage of me. Fortunately, I escaped and took refuge in a nunnery. Nineteen years have elapsed, but the injustice remains unavenged. As Robber Xu is a current resident on Five Dams Street, please bring him to justice. If this is done, I shall be eternally grateful, in life and in death.*

Zheng-shi took the paper and left, with thanks. When she arrived at the pavilion of reception for new officials, Censor Xu was in the boat cabin exchanging greetings with Commander Zhou of the Ningtai Circuit. As the bow of the boat was quiet and unguarded, Zheng-shi, unaware of proper decorum, tottered onto the boat. When the boatman rushed over to stop her, she began to cry out her grievances.

Inspector Xu, who was predestined to meet her at this time, found her voice especially heartrending. He had a guard take in the letter of complaint, which he and Commander Zhou then read together. It would have been another story had he not read it, but as he did, he became so frightened that his face turned the color of earth. Dismissing all attendants, he privately sought Commander Zhou's advice, saying, "The man accused by this woman is none other than my father. If I reject this letter of complaint, I'm afraid she might go to some other yamen."

Commander Zhou roared with laughter. "Mr. Inspector," he said, "you're too young to know how to deal with contingencies. This is by no means a difficult situation. You can have your guard take the woman to your court tomorrow for questioning. That woman can be beaten to death right there in the court. Wouldn't that stop all future troubles? ([Illegible] *the human heart.*)

Inspector Xu rose and said, "Thank you for your advice." He took leave of Commander Zhou and told his guard to take the complainant to his court the next morning for a face-to-face questioning. He then went back to his court to retire for the night. But he stayed awake the whole night through, thinking, "My father has indeed been a robber for many years. The woman's story just might be true. To beat her to death in addition to the robbery and killing would be to add injustice to injustice. But if she is not to be beaten to death, I'll be in for big trouble." (*Valid point.*)

Suddenly he remembered that the old woman he had met in Zhuozhou three years ago had told him that her son Su Yun had been killed by some robbers. "So, this must be what the complaint is all about." He continued thinking to himself, "Goodness knows how much karmic sin my father has committed in his life as a robber. How could he have accumulated any merit in the netherworld for his son to pass the imperial examinations? I remember that in school when I was small, schoolmates often laughed at me, saying that I was not my parents' flesh and blood. I wonder where I came from? Only Yao Da, my nurse's husband, knows the truth." Hitting on a plan, he wrote a letter home, saying, "I am too busy with work to come back home, but I shall meet Father, my uncles, and others at my yamen in Nanjing. As I need someone to help me in my journey, please send Yao Da to Caishi Station, Dangtu. Please do not fail me."

The next day, as soon as the yamen gate was opened, he gave the letter to a courier, instructing him to deliver the letter to Five Dams Street, Yizhen, into his father's hands. Upon seeing Zheng-shi, who had been brought into the yamen by a guard, Xu Jizu could not help but feel saddened. After the first few standard questions, he asked, "Don't you have a son? Why do you have to file this complaint yourself?" Thereupon, a tearful Zheng-shi gave a detailed account of how she had given birth to a baby in a nunnery, wrapped up the baby and a golden hairpin in a silk shirt, and left the baby in Big Willow Village.

Unable to come to a decision, Xu Jizu told Zheng-shi, "You may go back to the nunnery and stay until I call you. I must first hunt down the robbers and verify the facts." Zheng-shi bowed her thanks and left. Xu Jizu also left the yamen and went to Caishi Station, where he stayed at an inn until Yao Da, husband of his wet nurse, arrived.

Nothing of note happened on the day Yao Da arrived. After evening had set in, he called Yao Da to his room and, after some nice words to put Yao Da at ease, asked, "Who is my birth father?"

"The old master," replied Yao Da.

However often Xu Jizu pressed the question, Yao Da held his ground. Mr. Xu Junior flared up. "I know all the facts. I was adopted. If you tell the truth, I will spare you from the sword, considering what I owe your wife for having nursed me. But if you don't come out with the truth, I'll have you beaten to death!"

"The old master is indeed your birth father. I wouldn't dare lie."

"Don't tell me that you know nothing about the violence done to Magistrate Su on Huangtian Lake!"

Yao Da still prevaricated.

In a towering rage, Inspector Xu took out a form for the punishment of convicts and wrote on it Yao Da's name as well as the remark, "This man is to be given a hundred strokes. Report his death ex post facto." The form was to be delivered to the Dangtu County yamen.

Witnessing the signing of the form, Yao Da panicked. With a series of kowtows, he said, "I will tell the truth, but, Master, please don't let on about any of this to the old master."

"I'll take care of everything. You have nothing to fear!"

Thereupon, Yao Da gave a detailed account of how Magistrate Su had been robbed, how Madam Su had been made Xu Neng's wife, and how the baby had been picked up at the foot of the big willow tree and given to his wife for wet-nursing.

Inspector Xu asked further, "There was a silk shirt wrapped around the baby and also a gold hairpin. Are those things still there?"

"The shirt has bloodstains that can't be washed off, but both the shirt and the gold hairpin are still there."

Now that he had learned the truth, Inspector Xu said, "This is to be a secret between you and me. Tomorrow morning, I'll send you home. Take the hairpin and the shirt and go posthaste to the Nanjing yamen to see me before the night is out."

Thus instructed, Yao Da went his way. The next morning, Mr. Xu told his subordinates, "Prepare some silver as travel money and bring the nun Zheng from the Mercy Lake Nunnery to the capital to see me." At the same time, he ordered that his journey to Nanjing for his post commence right away. Truly,

> *As a young* jinshi, *he enjoyed great fame.*
> *As an inspector, his name inspired awe.*

In the meantime, Magistrate Su Yun, while teaching in the Village of Three Households, thought of what had happened nineteen years ago. Day and night, he brooded over the fact that he had no way of communicating with his aged mother at home and that he knew nothing about whether his pregnant wife Zheng-shi was dead or alive. He told Mr. Tao about his worries, adding that he wished to go to Yizhen to look them up and make inquiries. Mr. Tao tried desperately to talk him into accepting his fate rather than looking for trouble.

But while all the families in the neighborhood were out on the day of the Clear and Bright Festival, paying their respects at their ancestors' graves, Su Yun left a letter of gratitude for Mr. Tao at the school, packed his writing implements, and set out on his journey. All along the way, he supported himself by selling his writing services.

When he came upon the temple to Emperor Lie in Changzhou one night, he took up lodging there.[26] That night, he dreamed he was praying and drawing a bamboo divination slip in the brightly lit temple. The divination said,

Safe by land but disastrous by water,
Fierce winds blow apart the autumn leaves in the woods.
To know when the family reunites,
Go no farther than the yamen of Jinling.

When he awoke at the fifth watch of the night, he still remembered every word in these four lines. In trying to explain these lines, he said to himself, "It was on a lake that the robbery happened, and after I was rescued, I've kept to the mountains all these years. This bears out the meaning of the first line 'Safe by land but disastrous by water.' 'Fierce winds blow apart the autumn leaves in the woods' is a reference to my family being broken up. Can it be that the family will one day reunite? Jinling being another name for Nanjing, where the imperial inspector's yamen is located, I shouldn't go to Yizhen but instead to the imperial inspector's yamen in Nanjing to file a complaint. I may find vindication there."

At daybreak, he rose, prayed to the gods, and picked two bamboo slips, which served as means of divination. "If I should be going to Nanjing, please give me a sign," he prayed. He threw the two slips on the floor three times, and sure enough, all three times, both slips fell smooth side up. Delighted, Mr. Su went out the temple gate and headed straight for Nanjing. Once there, he wrote a letter of complaint and filed it with the local inspector's yamen. The complaint read:

From the plaintiff, Su Yun, a jinshi *and a native of Zhuozhou in the district directly under the jurisdiction of the court:*

Upon receiving my first assignment to the post of magistrate of Orchid Creek County, I took my family and set out on the journey to assume the post. All my misfortunes began when my boat started to leak upon reaching Yizhen. I changed to the boat that belonged to Secretary Wang of Shandong, little knowing that the boatmen Xu Neng, Xu Yong, and others were in fact robbers who operated on the rivers and lakes. In the middle of the night, they moved the boat to a deserted place, tied me up, and threw me into the water. Luckily, I was rescued and have been teaching for a living, but all of my belongings are gone, and I have no idea if my wife and servants are dead or alive. Any incumbent powerful official who supports robbers should be eliminated by divine justice.

The local inspector, Mr. Lin, happened to be a *jinshi* who had gained his degree in the same year that Mr. Su had. In great sympathy, he immediately notified the governor and inspector of Shandong to apprehend the robbers Xu Neng, Xu Yong, and others through Secretary Wang. No sooner had he sent out the notification than Xu Jizu, the visiting imperial inspector, came to call on him. In their conversation, Inspector Lin brought up the subject by chance. Xu Jizu made a mental note of that remark and, when leaving the yamen after bidding farewell to Inspector Lin, called the messenger and said, "Summon an officer of the local yamen to my court to receive my instructions."

After Inspector Xu returned to his yamen, an officer from the local yamen came in response to the messenger's order. With a kowtow, he said, "What instructions do you have for me, sir?"

Mr. Xu said, "I have learned something about the robbers on Secretary Wang's boat. I will award you two taels of silver to use toward your travel expenses. Don't do anything for a couple of days and then come here when I call for you. I guarantee that you'll be able to capture those robbers with their loot without having to make a special trip to Shandong." The officer took the order and left.

A moment later, the arrival of Master Xu Senior was announced. In trepidation, Inspector Xu went to greet him, determined to exercise proper decorum to the fullest extent out of gratitude for his upbringing, because gratitude and grievance should be kept distinct and separate. Then and there, he sent subordinates to the riverside to bring the gang of robbers to court. It so happened that when Xu Neng and Xu Yong were about to set out on their journey, the other members of the gang—Zhao Three, Runny Nose Weng, Sharp Tongue Yang, Skinflint Fan, and Beardie Shen—equipped with lavish gifts for Inspector Xu, came to join them as nonconsaguineous uncles to congratulate Master Xu Junior on his new post. They were, indeed, sent by heaven to meet their death.

Yao Da was the first to step into the yamen and offer his kowtows. Inspector Xu then invited Master Xu Senior and his uncle into the yamen, where carpets were laid out for the occasion. Inspector Xu prostrated himself on the ground in homage to Xu Neng, who readily accepted the honor, but when Inspector Xu turned to Xu Yong, the latter vigorously declined the honor, insisting that the inspector only bow from the waist rather than fall on his knees. Zhao Three and the others had always treated Xu Jizu as a junior in the Xu household, but now, with the young man in such an exalted position, things were quite different. With Zhao Three and the others calling him "Your Honorable Inspector" and Xu Jizu calling them "my dear uncles," the host and the guests greeted each other and sat down to a feast.

After night fell, Xu Jizu secretly summoned Yao Da to his study and asked him to produce the gold hairpin and blood-stained silk shirt. True enough, the pattern on the fabric was the same as that of the shirt given to him by the old woman of Zhuozhou. He thought to himself, "The old lady also commented that I looked exactly like her son. Clearly, she is my grandmother, and the nun of Mercy Lake Nunnery is my own mother. Even more happily, my father is far from being dead. He's the very person who has filed a complaint at the yamen. Now is the time for a family reunion."

The next day, a fine feast was laid out in the back hall in honor of Xu Neng and the other six men. Much wine was consumed to the accompaniment of loud music. Claiming that he had official business to attend to, Inspector Xu left the hall alone to assemble fifty to sixty able-bodied militiamen. When the preparations had been completed, he said to them, "Wait for a signal from me. As soon as you see me wave a fan, all of you will go into the back hall to arrest the seven robbers." He then turned to the officer from the local inspector's yamen and said, "Bring Mr. Su, the one making the complaint, to meet me at the yamen gate."

A moment later, Mr. Su showed up. He was about to drop to his knees at the sight of Inspector Xu when the latter held him with both hands and stopped him from doing so. Inspector Xu then asked Mr. Su some questions, both of them standing upright. After Mr. Su's tearful replies, Inspector Xu said, "Cheer up, sir. Please go to the back hall. Many of your acquaintances are there. See if you can recognize them."

Thus, Mr. Su went into the back hall. Partly because Mr. Su was now dressed in the blue robe and small hat of a commoner, partly because many years had gone by, and partly because Mr. Su's appearance was not in the least expected, Xu Neng and the others failed to recognize him, whereas Mr. Su, who had never forgetten the event, still remembered the men's faces. He took a good look at them and was so startled that he withdrew from the hall and said to Inspector Xu, "These men are none other than the robbers I ran into on the boat. Why are they here?"

Instead of replying, Inspector Xu waved his fan. About fifty to sixty officers swarmed in and tied up all seven men. "Jizu, my son," yelled Xu Neng, "come and save me!"

"You cursed robber," Inspector Xu cried out, "who is your son? Do you recognize Magistrate Su from nineteen years ago?"

Xu Neng swung on Xu Yong and said furiously, "You refused to listen to me at the time and insisted that his body be kept intact. Now it's too late to have regrets!"

Yao Da was called forth to bear testimony. None of the men had anything to say. Inspector Xu told the officers, "Put all eight men in jail for now. Tomorrow, I will have documents ready and have them sent to the local inspector's yamen."

After giving the proper instructions, Inspector Xu ordered the gate closed before he invited Mr. Su into the back hall again. Wondering why the gang of robbers had been apprehended right at the feast table, Mr. Su was about to ask before expressing his thanks when Inspector Xu placed a chair in a south-facing position and asked Mr. Su to sit in that seat of honor. As he dropped to his knees, his head bent low, Mr. Su rushed to hold him and said, "Your Honor and I have never met before. Why do me such honor?"

Inspector Xu replied, "I am your unworthy son. But, never having heard anything about you, Father, I have failed to perform my filial duties. Please forgive me for my failure as a son!"

Mr. Su said, "Your Honor is quite mistaken! I don't have a son."

"But I *am* your own son. If you don't believe me, I'll show you the silk shirt as proof." So saying, Inspector Xu produced the silk shirt given to him by the old woman of Zhuozhou and handed it to Mr. Su.

Recognizing the hole burned in the collar by the lamp wick, Mr. Su said, "This shirt was made by my old mother. How did it get here?"

"There's more," said the inspector and produced the blood-stained silk shirt and the gold hairpin.

Mr. Su examined the objects and recognized the hairpin. "This is my wife's hairpin," he said. "Why is it also here?"

It was after Inspector Xu gave a detailed account of his encounter with his grandmother at Zhuozhou, the nun's complaint at Caishi Station, and Yao Da's confession that Mr. Su came to know the truth. Father and son fell upon each other's shoulders and broke down in tears. As coincidence would have it, while father and son were thus reunited, the drum at the yamen gate was struck, and the announcement came that the nun from Mercy Lake Nunnery had arrived as requested.

"Invite her into the back hall," said Inspector Xu promptly.

After a separation of nineteen years, Mr. Su and his wife were now reunited in this place. Mr. Su had the young man bow to his mother, and then husband, wife, and son hugged one another in a flood of tears brought on by the memory of the painful experience. (*Good reunion.*) The back hall was then cleaned up for another celebration feast. Truly,

The old tree bursts into new leaves again;
The clouds disperse to let the moon shine through.

The next morning, officials of the five commanderies, the six departments of personnel, revenue, rites, war, punishments, and public works, the six bureaus and the imperial inspectors of Nanjing as well as officials from the prefectural and county yamen, having heard about Mr. Xu's reunion with his parents, all came to offer their congratulations. The local inspector returned Mr. Su's letter of complaint to Inspector Xu so that he could conduct the trial himself.

Inspector Xu took leave of the assembly of officials and told his men to arm themselves with big rods and wait on one side of the hall. The robbers were summoned from jail and, in foot chains and handcuffs, dropped to their knees at the foot of the steps leading to the dais. Having grown up in the Xu household, Inspector Xu knew all too well that this evil gang had killed and committed robbery more than once. There was no need for interrogation. Among the gang members, Xu Yong was the only one who had often raised objections and offered words of remonstration. Moreover, Mr. Su and his wife, both feeling indebted to him for what he had done to save their lives, urged their son over and over again to pardon him. (*When have good people ever gone unrewarded?*)

With one stroke of his brush-pen, Inspector Xu pardoned Xu Yong and ordered him out of the yamen. Xu Yong bowed his thanks and left. Secretary Wang of Shandong being unrelated to the case, no action against him was deemed necessary. The two ringleaders, Xu Neng and Zhao Three, were each given eighty strokes. Sharp Tongue Yang and Beardie Shen were given sixty strokes each for their part in the crimes. Because Yao Da's wife had, after all, been Inspector Xu's wet nurse, Yao Da, although also a willing accomplice on the boat, was given only forty strokes, as were Runny Nose Weng and Skinflint Fan. Whatever the number of strokes, they were all beaten so hard that the skin split, the flesh tore, and the blood flowed. Unable to hold out any longer, Yao Da cried out in pain, "Your Honor promised to save me from the sword. How could you have gone back on your word?" Whereupon Inspector Xu reduced his number of strokes to thirty. After the beating was finished, he ordered that the men be sent back to prison.

Inspector Xu then withdrew to the back hall, where he asked for his father's permission and wrote a memorial to the emperor in which he gave an account of these happenings and announced that his name would be changed to Su Tai [Bliss], taking the character *tai* from the idiom "Out of the depth of misfortune comes bliss." Next, he requested that the criminals be executed before autumn and that their property be registered and confiscated and diverted for use in national defense at the borders. He ended the memorial by saying, "My father Su Yun, a *jinshi,* rendered unable to assume a single official post, has lost interest in a public career after nineteen years of suffering. My grandmother, in her eighties, has been living alone in our native town, but I do not know if she is still alive or not. I, at nineteen years of age, stand a poor chance of continuing the family line if I remain unmarried. I therefore request a short leave to follow my father to Zhuozhou and contract a marriage."

The memorial sent, Xu Jizu changed his name to Su Tai. With his new name written on visiting cards, he called at every yamen in Nanjing. He also paid a grateful visit to Mr. Lin, the local inspector, presenting a card that referred to himself as the son of Mr. Lin Senior's friend who had passed the examinations the same year that Mr. Lin Senior had.

Recalling his grandmother's words, he wrote an order for inquiries to be made at Orchid Creek County as to Su Yu's whereabouts. Reports came back saying that Second Master Su had indeed been there fifteen years before but had died of illness and that his coffin, bought by County Magistrate Gao, was for the time being in the temple of the city god. The Su father and son shed bitter tears and, taking along some travel money, went to Orchid Creek and hired a boat to carry Second Master Su's coffin back to Zhuozhou to be buried in the ancestral burial ground.

Soon, the emperor granted all the requests presented in the memorial. Moreover, Su Yun was appointed an imperial inspector, and the father and son were given permission to return to their native town. The Ministry of Justice invited the Su father and son to go to the execution ground to witness the execution of the criminals. Su Tai had, in advance, told prison wardens to have Yao Da hanged so as to spare him the sword and keep his body intact. Xu Neng said with a sigh, "Although I didn't get to have Madam Su as my wife, I have no regrets in death after three years of life as the father of an official." The criminals looked at each other in despair and stuck out their necks for the swords to be brought down. (*It is not in the nature of evildoers to repent.*) Behold:

Amid the thundering beats of the drum,
Amid the deafening clanging of the gong,
The overseer stood like King Yama of hell,
The executioners like yakshas, *one and all.*[27]
The wealth obtained by their swords and axes
Now all gone, as was everything else.
The awe they had inspired on the rivers and lakes
Now all vanished into thin air.
In the Palace of Darkness,
They trembled at the sight of the demons.
In the World of Light,
All rejoiced over the criminals' deaths.

Before the inspector's memorial had been sent, an order was given to officials of Yangzhou Prefecture and Yizhen County to drive out the families of the six criminals and seal their houses. Their mountains of gold and treasure were confiscated by the government. That the children cried and the families were broken up and reduced to poverty goes without saying. Yao Da's widow, Inspector Su's former wet nurse, was the only one who went to Nanjing, sobbing every step of the way, to ask to see His Honor the inspector. Now, Inspector Su was still grateful to her for having nursed him. Moreover, the wife and children of the executed should not be held accountable for the crimes committed. However, he could not very well keep her for fear of upsetting his mother, so he gave her fifty taels of silver with which to live out the rest of her life in comfort and told her to take up residence wherever she chose.

There being no other business to attend to in Nanjing, Mr. Su Senior took leave of his friend Inspector Lin, and Inspector Su said farewell to the local officials. With two placards raised high in front, one bearing the inscription "Visiting parents by imperial order" and the other "Returning to hometown by imperial grace for matrimonial purposes," the grand procession marched south, complete with flying banners and loud drum-and-wind music. After passing Yangzhou, they came to Yizhen, a place that evoked painful memories for Mr. Su Senior. Lady Zheng again related to her son how Granny Zhu had thrown herself into a well and how indebted she was to the old nun at the nunnery. The inspector sent a local headman to make inquiries in the vicinity of the well. The local inhabitants said that nineteen years ago, a corpse had indeed floated to the surface of the water. After it was retrieved, no one came forward to claim it. Three days later, the local people resignedly collected some money, bought a coffin for the corpse, and buried it in a spot to the left of the well, within an arrow's shot of it.

After hearing this report from the headman, the inspector ordered that some sacrificial offerings, paper money and imitation ingots of silver, be prepared so a messenger could conduct a memorial service by the well. He also gave a hundred taels of silver to the old nun and another ten taels of silver with which to hold a Buddhist service for the souls of Second Master Su, Granny Zhu, and Su Sheng and his wife. This is a case of returning justice for injustice and repaying kindness with kindness. The Su father and son attended the service, where they picked incense sticks and paid homage to Buddha. And so, all that needed to be done was done.

In a matter of days, they found themselves in Linqing, Shandong, and stopped for a rest at the first courier station they saw at the ferry. Their arrival caught the attention of a noted personality in the area. Named Wang Gui, he was a retired first-grade secretary of a ministry, the very owner of the boat rented out to Xu Neng. When Xu Neng's crimes were exposed, the local inspector sent for the gang, causing quite a stir in the whole county of Yizhen, Secretary Wang's young concubine and other family members moved to the secretary's residence in Shandong to stay out of trouble. Later, upon learning from inquiries that Inspector Su had determined that the Wang family was not part of the conspiracy, since the boat flying his flag had been on loan, old Secretary Wang was filled with gratitude. Now that the inspector's procession was here, he went out to the ferry to welcome them. As he greeted the Su father and son, he uttered profuse words of thanks. At the feast table he laid out in honor of the visitors, he asked, "May I ask whose daughter the inspector is going to marry?"

"My son has not yet made a choice," replied Su Yun.

"My youngest daughter," said Secretary Wang, "is a talented and beautiful sixteen-year-old. If the inspector is not disdainful of this old man, I would be glad to form a marriage alliance between the two families." (*A wonderful twist in the plot. This is, again, a case of an act of kindness being repaid with an act of kindness. From the fear of being implicated in the case to a marriage alliance, what more could he ask?*)

Mr. Su Senior's demurral notwithstanding, the marriage proposal was accepted. The Su family took up temporary residence at Linqing and chose auspicious days for the betrothal and wedding ceremonies. There is a poem that bears witness:

A red thread had been tied to their feet.[28]
Why bother hitting the peacock in the eye?[29]

The secretary's boat, how hateful it had been!
The secretary's now an in-law, who would have guessed!

On the third day after the wedding, Mr. Su Junior wished to continue his journey. To Secretary Wang's pleas for them to stay, Mr. Su Senior said, "After so many years of separation from my old mother, without knowing whether she was dead or alive, I can't wait to go back." Secretary Wang could not very well keep him any longer. Seven days later, he engaged horse carriages, loaded them with a lavish dowry, and saw his daughter off as she set out with her husband to return to his native place after having made a name for himself.

Nothing of note occurred along the journey. Upon arrival at their home in Zhuozhou, they rejoiced to find the old lady still in good health. Seeing that her son and daughter-in-law were both past their prime, she was distraught with grief, but at the sight of her grandson, whom she recognized as the very young man she had met years before while fetching water, her sadness turned to boundless joy. She had grieved over the loss of her sons, but she now had a grandson. What was left of the burned house being too small to accommodate the two generations of *jinshi* and their many servants, they found temporary lodging at the yamen instead. As construction of the inspector's residence began, the prefectural and county yamens sent men to help. Within a matter of days, the house was completed.

Su Yun stayed at home and supported his mother, who lived to be more than ninety years old. Su Tai rose in the echelon of officialdom until he became chief inspector of the Upper Inspectorate. Of the two sons born to his wife, Lady Wang, the younger one became Su Yu's adoptive son. (*There are no ties left loose.*) Both sons passed the imperial civil service examinations. To this day, stories are still being told in the villages about how County Magistrate Su found vindication for his suffering. A later poet had this to say:

The moon dim, the wind strong, the waves spouting high,
The robbers on Huangtian Lake wreaked havoc.
Divine justice prevails in the end.
Has any evil man ever lived long?

12

A Double Mirror Brings Fan the Loach and His Wife Together Again

Curtains are raised on West Water Tower
Midst singing of a new tune with doggerel lyrics.
About romantic nights and youthful dreams,
Sing no more!
Just finish the wine while you live and breathe!

Tomorrow when we board the boat again,
Tonight will be but a memory.
Fellow travelers stranded in a distant land,
Grieve no more!
How far does the crescent moon shine?

The last line of the above lyric poem is taken from a folk song popular in the Wu region. This is how the song goes:

How far does the crescent moon shine?
It finds some households joyful, some in sorrow,
Some married couples sharing the same bed,
Some families scattered throughout the land.

Originating in the Jianyan reign period [1127–31] during the Southern Song dynasty, the above song captures the miseries of families separated in those troubled times. Back in the Xuanhe reign period [1119–25], government affairs were at sixes and sevens with evil men in power. This situation lasted into the Jingkang reign period [1126–27], when the Jurchens ravaged the capital, captured Emperors Huizong and Qinzong, and carried them off to the north. After Prince Kang crossed the river on a clay horse,[1] he abandoned Bianjing [also called the Eastern Capital],[2] contented himself with exercising control over only one part of the empire, and changed the reign title to Jianyan. At the time, residents of the Eastern Capital and surrounding areas, out of fear for the Jurchen troops, followed the emperor [Emperor Gaozong, formerly prince of Kang] in a massive migration to the south. Goodness knows how many families were torn apart amid the flames of war as they fled helter-skelter from the pursuing Jurchen cavalry! All too many fathers and sons, husbands and wives never saw each other again for the rest of their lives. But there were also a few cases in which separated families were reunited, and the stories went around from mouth to mouth. Truly,

The Fengcheng swords joined together again;[3]
The shattered dewdrops on lotus leaves merged anew.
Fate dictates everything under the sun;
Nothing is free of the will of heaven.

The story goes that there lived in Chenzhou a man called Xu Xin, who had been learning martial arts from an early age. His wife Cui-shi was a woman quite fair to look upon. They had enough means to live a comfortable life. But then, the invading Jurchen troops came and carried the two emperors off to the north. Xu Xin and Cui-shi consulted each other and concluded that this was not a safe place for a permanent home, whereupon they packed up what valuables they could carry into two bundles, and, each carrying one bundle over a shoulder, they followed the crowd of refugees and pressed onward day and night.

When they reached Yucheng, they heard earthshaking cries behind them. They thought that the Jurchens had caught up with them, but as it turned out, the cries came from defeated Song troops in flight. The Song army had been lax for so long in its preparedness against war that the soldiers had thrown all discipline to the winds. When ordered to fight the enemy, they trembled with fear and took to their heels, one and all, without ever bothering to engage the enemy, but when they encountered civilians, they turned ferocious, committing robbery left and right and seizing children by force. (*This is what becomes of an army after years of prolonged peace.*)

Although reasonably skilled in martial arts, Xu Xin by himself stood no chance of prevailing against the swarming troops in flight, and so he ran for all he was worth. Surrounded by wails of grief, he turned back to look, but his wife was nowhere to be seen. It being impossible to search amid all the chaos, there was nothing for it but to push ahead. After walking for several days, he heaved a sigh of resignation and gave up all hope of finding her.

Hungry and thirsty when he came upon Suiyang, he stopped at a village inn to buy some food and wine. As it turned out, in this time of war, the inn was not what it had once been. There was no wine to be had, and what was offered in the way of food was nothing but some coarse stuff, served only after it was paid for, to forestall attempts to snatch it away.

Xu Xin was counting out the money when, all of a sudden, he heard a woman sobbing. As the saying goes, "Better not let things get to your heart. If they do, they'll give you no peace of mind." He stopped counting the money and rushed out of the inn for a look. There, he saw a woman, thinly clad, with disheveled hair, sitting on the ground outside. She was not his wife but was of about the same age and bore a physical resemblance to his wife as well. Xu Xin's compassion was aroused. In empathy, he thought, "This woman must have been through a lot, too." So he stepped forward and asked her who she was.

The woman replied, "My maiden name is Wang, my given name Jinnu. I am a native of Zhengzhou. I became separated from my husband when we were fleeing from the fighting, and then, all alone, I was seized by the soldiers and ended up here after walking for two days and a night. Because I couldn't move another step on account of my swollen feet, the scoundrels stripped me of my warmer clothes and dumped me here, cold and hungry, with no one to turn to for help. I'd be better off dead. That's why I'm crying."

"I lost my wife in the commotion. You and I are in the same boat, so to speak. Luckily, I still have some traveling money. You'd better stay a few days in this inn for a good rest. I'll go out to make inquiries as to my wife's whereabouts, and while I'm at it, I'll also ask about your husband. How does that sound to you?" (*Nice words.*)

The woman stopped crying and said thankfully, "That would be nice."

Xu Xin untied his bundle and took out a few pieces of clothing for the woman to wear. After they had something to eat, he rented half a wing for their lodging. Every day, with much attentiveness, he brought her tea and food, and she was very grateful for the kindness. The search for a lost spouse being most probably quite a hopeless undertaking, the two of them, one without a wife and the other without a husband, could hardly refrain from doing what human beings would do when two warm bodies are thus brought together by the will of heaven.

A few days later, since the woman's feet had stopped aching, they set out for Jiankang as husband and wife. This happened at a time when Emperor Gaozong's court, having moved south and assumed the reign title of Jianyan, was putting up notices recruiting men for the army. Xu Xin enlisted as a low-ranking officer and took up residence in the city of Jiankang.

The days and the months flew by. Before they knew it, it was the third year of the Jianyan reign period. One late afternoon, they were on their way back from visiting relatives outside the city when, his wife being thirsty, Xu Xin took her to a teahouse for some tea. A man who had been sitting in the teahouse rose at the sight of the woman entering and stood by one side, his eyes furtively fixed on her. The woman, her eyes lowered, did not notice anything, but Xu Xin grew apprehensive. A few moments later, the tea finished, the couple paid the bill and departed, but the man followed them at a distance. When they reached home, the man stood still at the gate, reluctant to leave. Xu Xin flared up. "Who are you?" he snapped. "How can you steal glances at someone else's wife?"

Apologetically, the man said, his hands respectfully folded across his chest, "Please do not be angry, my honorable brother. I have a question for you."

His anger not yet subsided, Xu Xin said curtly, "Whatever you have to say, out with it!"

"If you don't mind, may I ask you to come out and talk? I have something to tell you, but if you're going to yell at me, I won't dare say a thing."

As the man requested, Xu Xin followed him to a secluded alley. The man was about to say something but held himself back, looking quite ill at ease. Xu Xin said, "I am an easygoing man. Feel free to say to me whatever you have to say." (*If he were to speak his mind to someone less easygoing, wouldn't he be bringing humiliation upon himself?*)

Only then did the man make so bold as to ask, "Who is the woman with you?"

"She's my wife."

"How many years have you been married?"

"Three years."

"Is she from Zhengzhou? Is she called Wang Jinnu?"

Xu Xin gave a start. "How did you know that?"

"She was my wife," said the man. "We were separated in the war. Who would have guessed that she would be with you!"

Feeling quite uneasy upon hearing these words, Xu Xin told the man everything about how he had lost his own wife at Yucheng and how he had met this woman at the inn in Suiyang. "At the time, I very much pitied her in her helplessness. I had no idea she was your wife. What's to be done now?"

"Don't worry," said the man. "I have remarried. My former marriage need not be mentioned again. But I didn't even get to say a word of good-bye to her in all that chaos. If I could see her for a moment and tell her what I've been through, I'll have no regrets when I die." (*How sad!*)

"Real men treat each other with an open heart," said Xu Xin, also overcome by sadness. "There's nothing one real man can't do for another. Come to our house tomorrow. Since you have remarried, bring your new wife along. Let's claim some kinship, so that the neighbors won't think anything is amiss."

The man happily bowed his thanks. Before they parted company, Xu Xin asked for his name. The man replied, "I am Lie Junqing of Zhengzhou."

That night, Xu Xin told Wang Jinnu what had happened. Recalling her former husband's love, she shed many a surreptitious tear throughout a wakeful night.

After daybreak, they had hardly finished washing their faces and rinsing their teeth when Lie Junqing and his wife arrived. As Xu Xin went out to greet the guests, both he and Lie's wife were stunned and burst into loud wails of grief, for it turned out that she was none other than Xu Xin's former wife Cui-shi.

After losing sight of her husband and looking for him in vain, she had followed an old woman to Jiankang and rented a room using her jewelry. When three months had gone by without any news from Cui-shi's husband, the old woman volunteered to be a matchmaker and married Cui-shi off to Lie Junqing, insisting that it would not be possible to maintain widowhood for the rest of her life.

Who could have predicted that the two couples would meet in such a chance encounter by the will of heaven? They fell on the shoulders of their former spouses and wept. Then and there, Xu Xin and Lie Junqing pledged brotherhood in an eight-bow ceremony. Wine was set out. After evening fell, the wives were returned to their former husbands to resume the old marriage ties. (*How remarkable!*) Henceforth, the two families visited each other back and forth in a never-ending stream. There is a poem in evidence:

> *The husbands changed wives; the wives changed husbands.*
> *All this shuffling around—how senseless!*
> *And so they met by the will of heaven*
> *And reunited in joy by the lamp.*

The above story, titled "The Exchange of Spouses," took place in the third year of the Jianyan period in the city of Jiankang.

At about the same time, there unfolded another story, about a broken mirror being made whole again. The plot is not as extraordinary as the previous one, but as far as marital fidelity is concerned, this story is far superior in moral terms. Truly,

> *Stories in simple words circulate more widely;*
> *Stories that teach morals touch the heart more deeply.*

The story goes that in the fourth year of the Jianyan reign period during the Southern Song dynasty, to the west of Tong Pass, there lived an official called Lü Zhongyi, who had just been assigned the post of tax commissioner of Fuzhou. At that time, the Min region [present-day Fujian Province] was at the height of its prosperity. Zhongyi took his family there, partly because Fuzhou, located by the mountains and the sea, was a rich metropolis in the southeastern region and partly to get away from the war-ravaged central plains. They set out on their journey in that year, and in the spring, their route led them past Jianzhou. According to *The Atlas,* "Jianzhou, with its green waters and red mountains, is a famous scenic spot in the eastern Min region." But, just as was said by an ancient poet's two lines:

> *Luoyang being a sea of flowers in spring,*
> *I picked the wrong season for a visit.*

Since time immemorial, war and famine have gone together. As the Jurchens crossed the Yangzi River, they left in their wake nothing but devastation throughout the Liang-Zhe region [present-day Zhejiang Province, Shanghai, and the southern part of Jiangsu Province]. The Min region, though spared the flames of war, was in the throes of a lean year by the will of heaven. In Jianzhou, where our story takes place, a picul of rice cost a thousand in cash, and the people could hardly survive the famine.[4] But the government still aggressively collected taxes to support the much needed army in spite of the fact that people were living in dire poverty. As the proverb goes, "Even the cleverest housewife cannot cook gruel without rice." Pushed by the relentless officials to come up with the money and grain that they did not have, the local people could not take the hard life any longer. In twos and threes, they fled into the mountains and formed gangs of bandits. (*Now is the time for competent officials to rise to the occasion and handle such situations properly.*) As the saying goes, "A snake without a head goes nowhere." Sure enough, a certain Fan Ruwei [d. 1132] appeared on the scene as a ringleader. He spoke words of justice and offered the people the help they so desperately needed. Outlaws in the region flocked to him, and soon, he had under his command more than a hundred thousand men much given to the usual acts of such gangs:

Setting fires when the wind is high;
Taking lives on moonless nights,
Starving together on foodless days,
Sharing meat when it comes their way.

Unable to fend them off, government troops were beaten in one battle after another. Fan Ruwei took the city of Jianzhou and, calling himself the Supreme Commander, sent his men in all directions to loot and rob. All the men in his clan were given phony titles as commanders of all levels.

Among his relatives was a nephew called Fan Xizhou, twenty-three years of age and known for his remarkable swimming skills, which he had acquired at an early age. For his ability to stay underwater for three to four days and nights in a row, he gained the nickname "Fan the Loach." He had been forced by Fan Ruwei to give up his unsuccessful pursuit of a scholarly career and take up banditry. The fact was, any clan member who refused to join Fan Ruwei would be beheaded in a public place. To save his skin, Xizhou felt obliged to submit. Even though he was a member of a gang of bandits, he took every opportunity to help people and refrained from acts of robbery and looting. Scorning his faint-heartedness, his fellow bandits changed his nickname to "Fan the Blind Loach," for they thought him a man capable of nothing. (*Among the good, there are evil ones. Among the evil, there are good ones. "Blind Loach" is a case in point.*)

Now, Lü Zhongyi had a daughter whose pet name was Shunge. At sixteen years of age, she was as pretty as she was sweet and gentle in temperament. She was with her parents on their journey to Fuzhou when, as they neared Jianzhou, they ran into a group of Fan Ruwei's bandits. All their possessions were taken away, and parents and daughter were driven apart. It being impossible to find his lost daughter, Lü Zhongyi sighed for some time but then continued his journey to take up his post.

Let us turn our attention to Shunge. With her small feet, she could hardly cover much distance and ended up a captive of the bandits. When they brought the sobbing girl to Jianzhou, Fan Xizhou saw her on the road and took pity on her. He asked about her family background, and Shunge told him that she was from an official's family, whereupon Xizhou sharply ordered the men to go away, untied the ropes that bound her, and led her to his home, where he comforted her with kind words. In all sincerity, he said, "I'm not some rebellious bandit. I'm here because my clansman forced me to join him. Should the imperial court offer us amnesty someday, I'll become a law-abiding subject as before. If you are not disdainful of my lowly station and agree to marry me, that will be a blessing that will last me through three incarnations."

Shunge did not wish to comply, but having fallen into bandits' hands, she resignedly gave her consent. The next day, Xizhou reported the matter to Fan Ruwei, the ringleader, much to the latter's joy. Xizhou then escorted Shunge to the ringleader's residence and chose an auspicious day for the betrothal. Xizhou offered as betrothal gift a prized family heirloom—a shining two-leafed folding mirror. It bore the inscription "love birds" on the inside and was called "The Precious Love Birds Mirror." All the members of the Fan clan were invited to the wedding.

He a descendant of landed gentry;
She an offspring of a distinguished clan.
He a learned man with refined manners;
She a woman of a warm, gentle nature.
Though among bandits, he kept his lofty bearing;
Though a captive, she maintained her dignified air.
That day, the outlaws were the honored guests;
That night, the beauty was wedded to a good man.

Henceforth, the husband and wife lived in harmony in full respect of each other.

As the ancient proverb says, "A water jar that stays by the well breaks by the well." Fan Ruwei was able to commit heinous crimes only because the imperial army was engaged elsewhere, but Zhang Jun, Yue Fei, Zhang Jun, Zhang Rong, Wu Jie, Wu Ling, and other famous generals repelled the Jurchens' attacks, and the empire began to regain peace.[5] Emperor Gaozong made Lin'an [present-day Hangzhou] his capital and changed the reign title to Shaoxing [1131–62].

That winter, Emperor Gaozong ordered Han Shizhong, later enfeoffed as Prince of Qi, to lead a mighty army a hundred thousand strong on a punitive expedition against the bandits.[6] Fan Ruwei, certainly no match for Prince Han, could do no better than close the city gates and try to hold his position against the oncoming army. Prince Han had fortifications erected all around the city and laid siege to it.

It so happened that Prince Han and Lü Zhongyi were old friends from their days in the Eastern Capital. Now that he was leading troops against the bandits, Han thought that Lü, being the tax commissioner of Fuzhou, must be familiar with the customs and sentiments of the people of the Min region. In those times, army commanders on expeditions carried blank letters of appointment so that they could, on their own authority, appoint to office any competent qualified person they found in the local area. Accordingly, Han made Lü Zhongyi a deputy commander, to be stationed with him by the Jianzhou city walls to direct the siege against the city.

Within the city walls, wails of grief were heard day and night. Several times, Fan Ruwei tried to fight his way out, but each time he was pushed back by the government troops. In such a desperate situation, Shunge said to her husband, "I've heard the saying 'A loyal minister does not serve a second sovereign; a chaste woman does not serve a second husband.' When I was captured by the bandits, I swore to take my own life. When you were so kind as to save me, I became your wife and committed myself to you. With a mighty army laying siege, the city will surely fall. And when the city falls, you, a member of the ringleader's clan, will not be spared. I'd rather die before you than witness your death." (*This is a woman with vision and moral fortitude.*) So saying, she drew out a sharp sword from the head of the bed and tried to cut her own throat, but with alacrity, Xizhou put his arms around her and snatched away the sword.

Trying to calm her down, he said, "I became a member of the gang against my will, but there being no way for me to exonerate myself now, fine jade and common stone will perish together, and I leave everything to fate. But you are the daughter of an official, and you were captured and brought here by force. You're not guilty in any way. Supreme Commander Han's men, officers as well as soldiers, are all northerners, just as you are. As you both speak the same dialect, they'll surely be kind to you. You might even meet an old friend or kinsman who will send your father a message, and you'll be reunited with your family. There *is* hope for you. Nothing is more precious than life. How can you think of dying needlessly in this place?"

"If I do indeed survive," said Shunge, "I vow never to remarry. But if I fall a captive again, I'd rather die by the sword than lose my chastity."

"With this solemn vow, I'll be able to die without regrets," said Xizhou. "If by any chance I should slip through the net, so to speak, and manage to live, I also vow never to remarry out of gratitude to your devotion."

"Let's each take one half of the Precious Love Birds Mirror, the betrothal gift from you, and hold on to it. Some day, the mirror will be made whole again, just as we will be reunited." With that, husband and wife shed many a tear.

This happened in the twelfth month of the first year of the Shaoxing reign period [1131].

In the first month of the following year, the city of Jianzhou fell under Han's assault. In desperation, Fan Ruwei set a fire and burned himself to death. Prince Han had a yellow imperial flag raised to offer amnesty to all of Fan's followers except members of his clan, half of whom had died in the chaos. The other half were captured by government troops and sent to Lin'an. ([Illegible.]) At this ominous turn of events, Shunge thought Xizhou must have died. In panic, she rushed into an abandoned house, took off her silk kerchief, and put her neck through the noose. Truly,

She would rather die early but chaste
Than live and lose her virtue.

But her allotted span of life was not meant to expire at this time. It so happened that Deputy Commander Lü Zhongyi was passing by, followed by his troops, and he caught sight of the body hanging from the ceiling of a dilapidated house.

Without a moment's delay, he had a soldier take the woman down. When he went for a closer look, he found the woman to be none other than his very own daughter Shunge. She returned to life from the brink of death, but it was a long while before she was able to speak. Father and daughter now reunited, both were overcome by mixed emotions of joy and sorrow. Shunge told of how she had been captured by the bandits and how Fan Xizhou had saved her and married her. Her father was struck speechless.

Now, having brought peace back to Jianzhou and pacified the local people, Supreme Commander Han returned to Lin'an with Lü Zhongyi to report the victory to the emperor. How the Son of Heaven rewarded them for their accomplishments need not be described here.

One day, Lü consulted his wife, saying that it would not do for their daughter to remain single while so young. He and his wife both urged Shunge to remarry, but Shunge firmly refused, citing the vows she had exchanged with her husband. Mr. Lü exploded: "It was out of necessity rather than choice that you, of such a good family, married a bandit. Now that he has died by the grace of heaven, you are free. Why think about him any more?" (*He does have a point.*)

Tearfully, Shunge said, "Mr. Fan was a scholar and a gentleman. He was forced into banditry by his kinsman against his will. He may have been among bandits, but he did good deeds whenever he could and stayed away from anything that is against the law of heaven. If heaven is judicious, he will surely be saved from the jaws of death. (*She will be proved right.*) Even duckweeds that float apart in the ocean might get together again. But until that happens, I'll gladly join the Daoist order and serve you and mother at home. I'll die without complaints even if I stay a widow until the end of my life. If you insist that I remarry, I'd just as soon kill myself to keep my name as a chaste woman untarnished." Impressed by her eloquence, Mr. Lü gave up trying to pressure her.

Time shot by like an arrow. Quite unnoticeably, it was the twelfth year of the Shaoxing reign period. Mr. Lü had risen steadily in the official echelon to become regional commander in chief, leading a regiment stationed in Fengzhou [in present-day Guangdong Province].

One day, the commander of Guangzhou sent Major He Chengxin to deliver an official document to Lü's headquarters in Fengzhou. Lü invited him into the hall and asked him about the local situation in Guangzhou. Their conversation lasted quite a while before the man took his leave. Shunge watched furtively from behind the curtain that separated the front and back sections of the hall. (*To peep from behind a curtain is better than to peep from behind a wall or a window. An inadvertent act that will prove to be consequential.*) When Mr. Lü came back to the living quarters of the yamen, she asked, "Who was that man delivering documents?"

"He Chengxin, a major from Guangzhou."

"How very strange!" exclaimed Shunge. "He walks and talks just like my husband Fan Xizhou of Jianzhou."

Mr. Lü laughed. "After Jianzhou fell, none of the Fan clan members was spared. There are only cases of people who were killed by mistake. Have you ever heard of anyone who survives by mistake? That man from Guangzhou is Mr. He, and he's a court-appointed officer, too. He has absolutely nothing to do with that Fan of yours. You are fantasizing. Wouldn't the maids laugh at you if they heard about this?"

Thus ridiculed by her father, Shunge felt so ashamed that she dared not utter another word. Truly,

The love between the husband and the wife
Pitted the father against the daughter.

Six months later, He Chengxin again came to Mr. Lü's yamen to deliver military documents. Again, Shunge watched skeptically from behind the curtain. She then said to her father, "Having forsaken the mundane world and joined the Daoist order, I hardly have any passionate feelings left in me. But that Mr. He whom I watched carefully is truly the very image of my husband. Could you take him into the back hall and gradually sound him out over some wine and food? My husband has a nickname, 'The Loach.' Years ago in the siege of Jianzhou, knowing the city was going to fall, he gave me half of a double-leafed love birds mirror as a keepsake. If you call him by his nickname and test him with this mirror, you'll find out the truth."

Mr. Lü promised to do as she said. The next day, when He Chengxin came again to the yamen to get the letter of reply, Mr. Lü invited him into the back hall and set out some wine and food in his honor. In the course of the drinking, Lü asked about Chengxin's native place and his family background. Chengxin became evasive, looking as if ashamed. Lü said, "Isn't 'The Loach' your nickname? This old man knows everything. You can tell me! No harm will be done to you!"

Chengxin asked Lü to dismiss the servants and, dropping on his knees, said, "I've committed an offense punishable by death!"

Lü raised him to his feet and said, "You don't have to do this!"

It was then that Chengxin made a clean breast of his past. "I am a native of Jianzhou. My surname is Fan. In the fourth year of the Jianyan reign period, my kinsman Fan Ruwei incited the starving people to rebel and made the city his stronghold. I joined them against my will. When the government troops stormed the city, all members of the ringleader's clan were killed, but I was saved by some people because of my frequent acts of kindness. (*Had he not been given to acts of kindness, what would have happened to him?*) So I changed my name to He Chengxin and enlisted in the army through the amnesty.

"In the fifth year of the Shaoxing reign period, I was assigned to Yue Fei's regiment. I followed him in the expedition against Yang Yao of Dongting Lake.[7] Yue Fei's men, being all northwesterners, were not accustomed to battles on water. (*The Loach is by no means blind.*) But I am a southerner. I learned to swim at an early age and can stay underwater for three days and nights in a row. That's why I'm called 'Fan the Loach.' General Yue himself picked me to be in his vanguard. In each battle, I was always in the forefront. After Yang Yao's rebellion was put down, Yue Fei reported my merits to the court, and I was assigned a military post, from which I have risen to be a major in Guangzhou. In all these ten years, I have never let on about any of this to other people, but now that you are asking, I dare not keep anything from you."

"What is your wife's surname? Is she your first wife or second?"

"When I was with the bandits, I came across a girl from an official's family and took her as my wife. When the city was stormed the follow year, we took flight separately. We had vowed that any one who survived would never remarry. Later, I went to Xinzhou and found my old mother, who now lives with me. There's just the two of us, plus a maidservant who does the cooking. I have not remarried."

Lü asked again, "Did you and your wife give each other a keepsake when you exchanged vows?"

Chengxin replied, "There was a double-leafed love birds mirror, which is one mirror when put together and two mirrors when taken apart. Each of us took one part of it."

"Do you still have your part of it?"

"I carry it with me day and night without ever parting with it."

"May I see it?"

Chengxin lifted his clothes and took from his brocade waistband an embroidered purse in which lay the mirror. Lü looked at it and took the other half of the mirror from his own sleeve. He put the two halves together and found them to be a perfect match.

Seeing the mirrors joined as one, Chengxin burst into sobs in spite of himself. Moved by his profound feelings, Lü said, with tears flowing unbeknownst to himself, "Your wife is my daughter. She is now in this house."

So saying, he led Chengxin into the main hall to meet his daughter. The couple burst into loud wails of grief. Lü comforted them with soothing words and had a celebration feast prepared. He kept Chengxin in his residence for the night. A few days later, Lü gave his official letter of reply for his son-in-law to deliver back to Guangzhou, telling his daughter to follow Chengxin and take up residence in Guangzhou.

A year later, with his term of office expiring, Chengxin took his wife Shunge to Lin'an. As they were passing by Fengzhou, they paid a visit to Lü to bid him farewell. Having prepared in advance a lavish dowry worth a thousand taels of gold, Lü dispatched guards to escort the couple to Lin'an.

Now, believing that what had happened such a long time ago was not likely to be scrutinized and feeling that the Fan family line should not be broken, Mr. Lü wrote an appeal to the Ministry of Rites (*The right thing to do.*), by whose permission Chengxin's former surname, but not his former given name, was then restored and his new name became Fan Chengxin. Later, he rose in rank until he became governor of the Huai region and lived happily with his wife to a ripe old age. The Precious Love Birds Mirror became a family heirloom that was passed down from generation to generation.

In later times, it was said that Fan the Loach's escape from the jaws of death and his reunion with his wife were the workings of heaven, a reward for his good deeds of saving many lives and leading a clean life although surrounded by bandits. There is a poem in testimony:

Like birds that flew apart for ten long years,
They rejoined, as did the Love Birds in the Mirror.
By no means was it a chance happening,
But a divine reward for his good deeds.

13

Judge Bao Solves a Case through a Ghost That Appeared Thrice

Gan Luo achieved fame young, and Ziya late;[1]
Peng Zu lived long, and Yan Hui died early;[2]
Fan Dan was penniless, and Shi Chong rich;[3]
It is all a matter of time and fate.

The story goes that during the reign period of Yuanyou [1086–93] in the Song dynasty, there was, in the imperial court, a chamberlain for ceremonies by the name of Chen Ya. After a failed attempt to impeach Zhang Zihou,[4] Chen Ya was demoted to pacification commissioner of the Jiangdong Circuit and concurrently magistrate of Jiankang [present-day Nanjing].

One day, he was feasting with his assembly of officials in the Riverside Pavilion when he heard someone cry outside, "I can tell your fortune even without knowing the five phases and the eight characters in your horoscope!"[5]

"Who has the temerity to make such a claim?" said the magistrate.

Those officials who had seen the man before replied, "This is Bian'gu, fortune-teller from Jinjing."

"Bring him over to me."

And so the man was brought to the pavilion. There, for all to see, was

A man in rags with a brimless and tattered hat,
A frosty beard, sightless eyes, and stooping shoulders.

Carrying his walking cane, Bian'gu entered the pavilion and, with a deep bow, groped for a place to sit before he sank down on a step. The magistrate said in anger, "Being a blind man unable to read the classics, how can you think so highly of yourself that you speak so lightly of the five phases?"

Bian'gu replied, "I can foresee changes by listening to the clicking of bamboo tablets and predict life or death by listening to the sound of footsteps."

"How accurate are you?" Even as the magistrate spoke, a painted boat was seen coming downstream, its oars creaking. The magistrate asked Bian'gu what he could make of it. Bian'gu rejoined, "The creaking of the oars sounds sad. That boat must be carrying some high official's coffin."

The magistrate sent someone to make an inquiry. Sure enough, the boat was carrying a coffin in which lay the body of Director Li of Linjiang District [in present-day Jiangxi Province], who had died at his post, on its way to Director Li's hometown. Agape with astonishment, the magistrate exclaimed, "Even if Dongfang Shuo[6] were reborn, he couldn't be as good as you are." He gave the fortune-teller ten jars of wine and ten taels of silver before sending him away.

This is a man able to tell things by the sound of oars. Now, let me tell of another fortune-teller, Li Jie by name, who was a native of Kaifeng, the Eastern Capital. He traveled to Fengfu County, Yanzhou Prefecture, and opened a fortune-telling shop in front of the county yamen. Under a Tai'e sword[7] covered with gilded paper, he hung up a sign that said "Death to all those with little learning but too much readiness to echo the views of others." And he was indeed most accurate in his applications of the yin and yang theories in his divinations.

Well-versed in the Book of Changes *of Zhou,*
Knowing all methods of divinations,
He read signs in all patterns in heaven,
And was a master of feng shui on earth.
Knowing all there was to know about the stars,
He told fortunes with divine accuracy.
Conversant with every law of destiny,
He never missed the mark in his prophecies.

He had just hung up the signboard when a man walked into the shop. How did he look? He had

A bag on his back, a cap on his head,
A black double-collar shirt with a silk waistband,
A clean pair of shoes and socks on his feet,
And a scroll of writings in his sleeve.

After exchanging a greeting with the fortune-teller, the man gave the date and the hour of his birth, and the astrological chart was drawn. But, quickly, the fortune-teller announced, "No, I can't do this for you."

The man, Sun Wen by name, was chief clerk at the Fengfu County yamen. He asked, "Why won't you tell my fortune?"

"Your Honor, this is too difficult a job for me."

"What do you mean?"

"Stay away from wine, and stop covering up for anyone."

"I haven't been drinking, nor am I covering up for anyone."

"Give me the date and the hour of your birth again, in case there was a mistake."

The chief clerk repeated the information. The fortune-teller set to work again and then said, "Sir, you'd better give up."

"I don't mind hearing whatever you've come up with."

"It doesn't look good." So saying, the fortune-teller wrote a quatrain that said,

This is the day the white tiger arrives,[8]
Bringing with it sorrow and misery.
Before one o'clock tomorrow morning,
All the kith and kin will be in mourning.

The chief clerk read it and asked, "What does all this mean?"

"I won't keep anything from you, sir, but you are going to die."

"In what year am I going to die?"

"This very year."

"Which month?"

"This very month."

"On which day?"

"This very day."

"At what hour?"

"Around midnight tonight, at the third quarter of the third watch."

"If I do indeed die tonight, you'll be off the hook, but if I don't, I'll settle the score with you tomorrow at the county court."

"If you don't die tonight, sir, come again tomorrow and cut off my head with this sword, which is meant for all those who have little learning but are much too ready to echo others' views."

At these words, the chief clerk fumed with rage. With one swipe, he grabbed the fortune-teller and threw him out of the shop. How did this end for the fortune-teller?

For all his knowledge of human affairs,
He brought upon himself sorrows galore.

From the county yamen emerged several officers, who blocked Chief Clerk Sun's way and asked what the commotion was all about. Sun complained, "What an unreasonable man! I asked him to tell my fortune. I did this just for fun, but he said that I was going to die at the third quarter of the third watch tonight. I am a perfectly healthy man. How am I going to drop dead this very night just like that? I'm taking him to the county yamen to have the court settle the matter."

Someone in the crowd said, "If you believe in fortune-telling, you'll end up selling your house. If you make a living telling fortunes, you do nothing but make up stories." The crowd pacified Sun and sent him on his way.

Turning back, they scolded the fortune-teller, saying, "Mr. Li, now that you've offended this well-known chief clerk, you won't be able to keep your business here. It's always easier to tell if someone is going to be poor and lowly than to say how long someone is going to live. You are not King Yama's father or a brother of the Judge of the Dead. How can you be so sure about the exact hour of someone's death? You'd better use some ambiguous words."

"If I say only things that please people, I'll be sacrificing accuracy. And yet, when I speak the truth, I give offense. Oh well, as the saying goes, 'If this place doesn't tolerate me, there will be places that do!'" (*Cynical words.*) With a sigh, he picked up his things and moved his business elsewhere.

Now, even though Sun had been calmed by the crowd, he still felt uneasy. After disposing of his official business for the day, he returned home in dejection. Noticing his knitted brows and worried look, his wife asked, "Is there anything troubling you? Is some work at the yamen baffling you?"

"No. Don't ask."

"Were you punished in any way by the magistrate today?" she pressed.

"No."

"Did you fight with someone then?"

"No. It's just that I went to a fortune-teller in front of the county yamen, and he said that I would die around midnight tonight at the third quarter of the third watch."

His wife bristled at these words. Her willow-shaped eyebrows raised high, her starry eyes opened wide, she said, "For a perfectly healthy man to die this very night! How preposterous! Why didn't you take him to the county court?"

"I did try, but the onlookers stopped me."

"Husband, you just stay at home. Am I not usually the one who goes forward and pleads to the magistrate on your behalf when the need arises? (*Women who enjoy going forward into the limelight are to be feared.*) Now this time, let me go find that fortune-teller and say to him, 'My husband doesn't owe the government or anyone any money, nor is he driven to desperation by some lawsuit. How can you say he's going to drop dead tonight?'"

"Don't go. After I live through tonight, I'll deal with him tomorrow myself. That'll be better than having a woman take care of this."

Evening fell. The chief clerk said, "Give me a few cups of wine. I want to stay awake the whole night through." Several cups later, he got quite drunk before he knew it, and, his eyes glazed with wine, he dozed off on his folding chair.

His wife said, "Husband, how can you go to sleep?" She called out for Ying'er the maid. "Come here," said she, "and shake Father to wake him up."

Ying'er came over, shook him, and called his name but to no avail. "Ying'er," said the wife, "let's carry him to the bedroom." If this storyteller had been born in the same year as the chief clerk and grown up with him shoulder to shoulder, I would have put my arms around his waist and dragged him back to where he had been. He should have stayed awake throughout the night, sipping his wine. The last thing he should have done was go to bed to sleep. But as it was, he died that very night, a death more tragic than that of Li Cunxiao [d. 894], as described in

The History of the Five Dynasties, and of Pen Yue [d. 196], as described in *The History of the Han.* Indeed,

> *The cicada feels first the autumn winds,*
> *And he had a foreboding of his death.*

With the husband already in bed, the wife told Ying'er to put out the kitchen fire, adding, "Did you hear Father say that a fortune-teller told him today that he was going to die at midnight tonight?"

"Yes, Mother, I did indeed. What nonsense!"

"Ying'er, let's do some sewing and stay awake tonight to see if that's really going to happen. If not, we'll deal with that fortune-teller tomorrow. Don't go to sleep!"

"I wouldn't dare!" said Ying'er. But before the words were quite out of her mouth, she started drifting off to sleep.

"Ying'er! I told you not to sleep, but you are already dozing off!"

"I am not!" But even as she spoke, she fell asleep again.

Her mistress woke her up and asked, "What time is it now?"

At this moment, Ying'er heard the county yamen's night-watch drum striking the third quarter of the third watch.

"Ying'er!" exclaimed Mrs. Sun. "Don't sleep! This is the moment!"

But Ying'er fell asleep again, this time giving no response. All of a sudden, Mrs. Sun heard her husband jump out of bed, and then, the middle door of the house made a noise. Hurriedly, she woke up Ying'er, and by the time a lamp had been lit, they heard the outer gate opening. Carrying the lamp, the two gave chase, and what did they see but a man in white walking out with a hand over his face and throwing himself with a splash into the Fengfu County river. Indeed,

> *When life comes to be filled with pain,*
> *To the east wind one give oneself away.*

The river was a tributary of the Yellow River, and it was quite impossible to retrieve the body in the rapid currents. Mrs. Sun and the maid stood by the river and burst out crying, "Chief Clerk! Why did you have to throw yourself into the river? Who is going to support the two of us now?"

They started shouting for the neighbors to come out. Mrs. Diao from up the street, Mrs. Mao from down the street, Mrs. Gao and Bao from across the street, all rushed over.

At Mrs. Sun's account of what had happened, Mrs. Diao said, "How very strange!"

Mrs. Mao said, "I saw him return home in his black shirt, carrying documents. I even exchanged greetings with him." Mrs. Gao said, "That's right, so did I!" Mrs. Bao had this to say, "My husband went to the county yamen on some business in the morning and saw the chief clerk grabbing the fortune-teller. He told me about it when he came home. Who would have thought that he would really die!"

And then Mrs. Diao put in, "Oh, Mr. Sun, how could you have died without even a word to us neighbors!" With these words, tears dropped from her eyes. Mrs. Mao commented again, "How sad! Especially when you think of all the kindnesses he did!" She also burst into tears. (*Nice description of a bunch of garrulous old women.*) Mrs. Bao wailed, "Mr. Sun, when shall we ever get to see you again?"

Losing no time, the local headman reported the matter to the authorities, and, as would be expected in such a case, Mrs. Sun had some sutras chanted in memory of the deceased.

With the snap of a finger, three months sped by. One day, Mrs. Sun and Ying'er were sitting at home when two women, flushed red with wine, came in the door, one carrying a bottle of wine and the other holding two paper flowers. Raising the cotton portiere, they stepped in, saying, "Yes, this is the place."

Mrs. Sun looked up and saw that they were matchmakers with surnames that could not have been any other than the common Zhang and Li. Mrs. Sun said, "Long time no see, grannies!"

The matchmakers said, "Sorry to disturb you, ma'am! We didn't hear about it earlier, so please forgive us for not sending any incense or paper money. How long has it been since your husband died?"

"I just observed the hundredth day of his death the day before yesterday."

"How time flies! So it's been more than one hundred days. What a nice man he was. Whenever I greeted him, he always greeted me back. Since he's been gone for so long, you must be very lonely. Why don't we make a match for you?"

The widow rejoined, "Where can I ever find a man as good as he was?" (*Good men often don't know what happens right under their noses, and the chief clerk was one of them.*)

The matchmakers said, "But that's not all that difficult! We do have a good candidate for you."

"Stop it! How can there possibly be anyone like my deceased husband?"

The two matchmakers had some tea and left, but a few days later, they came back for a second attempt. The widow said, "Don't come again with any of your marriage proposals unless you can meet all three of my conditions. Otherwise, don't bring up this subject ever again. I'd rather live out my days as a widow." So she listed her three conditions, and as a consequence, the two lovers, whose love bond dated back five hundred years, came to be punished according to the law of the land. Truly,

> *The case of the deer baffled the Qin prime minister;*[9]
> *The dream about butterflies confused Zhuangzi.*[10]

"What three conditions?"

"First, my deceased husband's surname was Sun, and Sun must also be the surname of whomever you propose. Second, my deceased husband was the number one chief clerk in Fengfu County. Your man must have the same post. Third, I'm not leaving this house. He has to move in." (*Clever words.*)

At these demands, the two matchmakers said, "Hooray! So you want to marry a man with the surname of Sun, with the same job as your deceased husband, and who will move into your house. Well, other conditions might be harder to meet, but these three things are no problem! Let me tell you, ma'am, your deceased husband, being the number one chief clerk of Fengfu County, was called Big Chief Clerk Sun. The man we have in mind for you used to be the number two chief clerk of the county. Now that Big Sun is dead, number two has become number one. He is known as Young Chief Clerk Sun. And he's willing to move in. Now what do you say?"

"This is too much of a coincidence to be true!" exclaimed the woman. (*Clever words!*)

Matchmaker Zhang said, "I am seventy-two years old. If I fabricated anything, may I change into seventy-two dogs to eat shit at your house!"

"If it's indeed as you say," said the woman, "please go ahead and make the proposal to him. I wonder if there's a predestined marriage bond between him and me."

"Today being an auspicious day," said Matchmaker Zhang, "write us a note on some lucky red paper."

"I don't have such stationery at home," said the widow.

"I've got some with me," said Matchmaker Li. So saying, she produced from her apron a sheet of floral-patterned paper. Truly,

Egrets are not seen till the snow melts away;
Parrots in willows are not noticed till they talk.

Then and there, the widow had Ying'er bring over a brush-pen and an ink slab. The note thus drawn up was taken away by the matchmakers. As was expected, betrothal gifts were offered, and messages traveled back and forth. Before two months were out, Young Chief Clerk Sun had moved in, and a nice, loving couple the two turned out to be.

The days went by. One evening, the couple, in an inebriated state, told Ying'er to make some soup to sober them up. While she was trying to make the kitchen fire, Ying'er said aloud resentfully, "If the old chief clerk were alive, I'd have gone to bed by now. But these two make me work!" Noticing that one end of the fire tube was blocked and would not burn, she bent down to knock it against the foot of the stove. She had knocked just a few times when the stove gradually rose until it was more than a foot up in the air. A man appeared, pushing up the stove with his head, his neck framed by the railings of a well, his long hair coming loose, his tongue hanging low, his eyes dripping blood. (*First apparition.*) He cried, "Ying'er! Help your father!'

Ying'er was so frightened that with a loud scream, she collapsed on the ground, her face sallow, her eyes glazed over, her lips purple, her fingernails turning blue.

We do not know what was happening to her internal organs, but her limbs had all gone limp. Truly,

> *Weak as the waning moon at the fifth watch,*
> *Feeble as the spent oil lamp before dawn.*

The couple rushed over to bring Ying'er her back to consciousness. After feeding her with some "soul-pacifying" liquid, they asked, "What did you see that made you faint?"

Ying'er said to the woman, "I was making a fire when the stove gradually went up in air, and I saw the deceased chief clerk, his neck framed by the railings of a well, his eyes dripping blood, his hair hanging loose. He called my name, and I was so scared I fell to the ground."

At this account, the woman slapped Ying'er on the face and said, "A fine maid you are! You could have just said that you're too lazy to make the soup. You didn't have to come up with such tricks, faking death and all! Well, no more work for you now. Put out the fire and go to sleep." And Ying'er did as she was told.

Back in their own room, the woman whispered to her husband, "Second Brother, that girl saw something. We can't keep her any longer. Let's send her away."

"But where?"

"I have an idea."

After breakfast the next morning, Young Sun went off to the yamen for work. The woman called Ying'er over and said to her, "Ying'er, you've been with me for seven or eight years now, and I like you a lot. But you're not working as hard as when the other chief clerk was alive. Is it because you are thinking of marriage? If so, let me make a match for you."

"How could I dream of marrying? But who are you marrying me off to?"

The man Mrs. Sun had in mind was to be the cause of vindication for the deceased Big Sun. Truly,

> *Cicadas in the trees aren't heard till the wind dies;*
> *The moon outside isn't seen till the lamp goes out.*

To pick up our story, Ying'er was married off, without having any say in the matter, to a fellow called Wang Xing, nicknamed Wang the Wino, a drinker and a gambler. Less than three months into the marriage, he had used up all of Ying'er's dowry.

One day, in a drunken state, the man came home and yelled at Ying'er, "You cheap slut! How can you watch me live in such misery without going to your master and mistress to borrow a few hundred in cash?"

Unable to bear such abuse, Ying'er put on a skirt, tied it up around her waist, and walked all the way to Young Sun's house. At the sight of Ying'er, the woman said, "Ying'er, you are a married woman now. What could you have to say to me?"

"To be honest with you, this is a bad marriage for me. My husband drinks and gambles, and in less than three months, he has spent all my dowry. There's nothing for it now but to ask you for a loan of a few hundred cash to tide us over."

"Ying'er," said the woman, "being married to the wrong man is your problem. Now, here's one tael of silver for you, but don't come here again." Ying'er accepted the silver and thankfully took her leave.

But the money was gone in a matter of four or five days.

One evening, an inebriated Wang Xing walked up to Ying'er and said, "You worthless slut! Why don't you go again and get something from your mistress when you see me in such misery?"

"The last time I went, I was given a good talking-to for that one tael of silver. How can you tell me to go again?"

"You cheap slut! If you don't go, I'll break your leg!"

Unable to fend off the stream of curses, Ying'er could not do otherwise than go to Sun's house before the night was out, but upon reaching the house, she found the gate closed. She thought of knocking but checked herself for fear of being scolded. In a quandary, she saw nothing for it but to turn back. After passing two or three houses, she heard a man say, "Ying'er, I have something for you." Now, this man makes me fear for Mrs. Sun and Young Sun! Truly,

A turtle in water—black amid blue;
A crane on a pine branch—white amid green.[11]

Ying'er turned around to look at the man, and there he stood, under the eaves of a house, wearing a cap, a red robe, and a waistband with a horn clasp and carrying a scroll of documents in his arms. In a subdued voice, he continued, "Ying'er, I'm the dead chief clerk. I can't tell you where I live now, but hold out your hand, I've got something for you."

Ying'er held out her hand. The moment something was placed in it, the man disappeared. Ying'er saw that in her hand was a package of loose silver. She returned home, and at her knock, Wang Xing said from within, "Sister, what took you so long at your mistress's house?"

"Let me tell you what happened. I went there to borrow some rice, but their gate was closed. I didn't dare to knock for fear that she might get angry. When I turned back, I saw the deceased chief clerk standing under the eaves of a house, wearing a cap, a red robe, and a horn waistband, and he gave me a package of silver. Here it is."

"You slut! What nonsense is this! You have some more explaining to do about that package of silver, but get inside first."

Ying'er went in. "Sister," said Wang Xing, "I remember what you said before about seeing the dead man by the stove. There must be something fishy about all this. I said those things a moment ago because I was afraid that the neighbors might hear you. Put the silver away for now. Let's wait until tomorrow morning to go to the county yamen to press charges against them." Truly,

Flowers wither when given too much care;
Willows flourish when left unattended.

The next morning, Wang Xing thought to himself, "Hold it! I can't press charges for two reasons. First, he is the number one chief clerk in the county. How could I ever dare make an enemy of him? Second, there's no hard evidence. Even these loose pieces of silver would be confiscated, and it would be a lawsuit without a suspect. I'd better redeem a few pieces of clothing from the pawnshop, buy a couple of boxes of sweets for Mr. Sun with the money, and pay him a visit." His mind thus made up, he went out and bought two boxes of sweets.

After dressing up neatly, the couple went to Sun's house. At the sight of the neatly dressed couple bearing boxes of gifts, Mrs. Sun asked, "Where did you get the money?"

Wang Xing replied, "I earned two taels of silver drawing up a paper for the chief clerk. So I'm bringing some gifts for you. I've given up drinking and gambling."

"Wang Xing," said Mrs. Sun, "you may go home now, but I'd like to keep your wife here for a couple of days."

After Wang Xing was gone, the woman said to Ying'er, "I need to travel to Eastern Peak Temple to offer some incense. Go with me tomorrow."

Nothing of note occurred that night. The next morning, after washing up, the chief clerk went to the yamen, whereas his wife, after locking up the gate, set out with Ying'er on their journey. After burning some incense in the main hall of Eastern Peak Temple, they went to offer more incense in the corridor. When they were passing the Shrine of Retribution, Ying'er's skirt belt came loose. While Ying'er was busy tying up her belt, Mrs. Sun went ahead on her own. Suddenly, a statue of a judge wearing a cap, a red robe, and a horn waistband called out from inside the shrine, "Ying'er, I am the deceased chief clerk! (*Third apparition.*) Redress the wrong done to me! I've got something here for you."

Ying'er took the object and said, looking at it, "How very strange for a mud statue to talk! Why did he give me this?" Truly, this is something

Unheard of since the beginning of the universe
And hardly ever seen from time immemorial.

Hastily Ying'er hid the object in her bosom and did not dare to reveal anything about this to Mrs. Sun. After offering incense, they went their separate ways.

Upon hearing Ying'er's account of what had happened, Wang Xing asked to see the object and found it to be a scroll of paper bearing the following inscription:

The big daughter's child, the small daughter's child,
The former sowed for the latter to reap.
To know what happened at the third watch of the night,
Remove the fire and drain the water underneath.
In the second or third month of next year,
Ju Si will come to solve this riddle.

Unable to make head or tail of it, Wang Xing told Ying'er, "Don't let anyone else know about this. It looks like something's going to happen in the second or third month of next year."

In the time it took to snap a finger, the second month of the new year rolled around. A new county magistrate came to replace the old one. A native of the town of Jindou in Luzhou, he was called Bao Zheng [999–1062], the very Judge Bao who came to be so celebrated in stories of our day. Later known as Academician Bao after he rose to that post in the Longtu Pavilion Imperial Academy, he was, at the time this story took place, a county magistrate serving in his first official post. From an early age, he had been known for his intelligence and integrity. While serving as a county magistrate, he manifested a deep understanding of hidden human feelings and solved cases that would have baffled others.

On the third night after taking up office, before he began to attend to official business, he had a dream in which he was seated in a hall with a couplet posted on the wall:

To know what happened at the third watch of the night,
Remove the fire and drain the water underneath.

The next morning, Magistrate Bao called a court session and asked all the clerks on duty to explain these two lines, but no one was able to come up with an answer. He then asked for a blank placard and had none other than Young Sun copy the couplet onto it in the regular style of calligraphy. The magistrate then added with his vermilion brush-pen: "A reward of ten taels of silver will be offered to anyone able to solve this riddle." The placard was hung on the gate of the county yamen, and soon a large crowd of county employees and commoners had gathered, all attracted by the reward offer and jostling one another for a better view.

Wang Xing was buying some date cakes near the county yamen when he heard that the magistrate had hung out a placard bearing a couplet that no one could interpret. He went to take a look. When he saw two lines that he had seen on the scroll from the judge at the Shrine of Retribution, he was quite shocked. "If I go and tell the truth," he thought, "that new county magistrate is so unpredictable that I'm afraid I might give him offense. But if I don't say anything, no one else will ever know what is behind these two lines."

After returning home with the date cakes, he told his wife about this. Ying'er said, "The dead chief clerk has appeared three times, telling me to redress the wrong done to him. We also got a package of silver from him without having done anything to earn it. If we don't go to the authorities, I'm afraid the ghosts and gods will be after us."

Wang Xing remained undecided. Once again, he headed for the county yamen and there ran into a neighbor, a county clerk named Pei. Knowing Clerk Pei to be a wise man, Wang Xing pulled him into a secluded alley and consulted with him. "Should I or should I not come forward?"

"Where's that scroll from the Shrine of Retribution?" asked Pei.

"It's hidden in my wife's clothes trunk."

"First, let me go to the yamen to report the matter on your behalf. In the meantime, go back to get that scroll and bring it to the yamen. When the magistrate calls you, you can present it as evidence."

So Wang Xing went back home. Clerk Pei went into the yamen and waited until Magistrate Bao dismissed the court session. Observing that Young Sun was not around, Pei approached the magistrate and, falling to his knees, said, "Your Honor, my neighbor Wang Xing is the only one who knows the story behind the couplet on the placard. He says that he received at the Shrine of Retribution in Eastern Peak Temple a scroll of paper on which were written these two lines and a lot more."

"Where is this man Wang Xing?" asked the magistrate.

"He has gone back home to get the scroll."

Magistrate Bao sent an officer to bring Wang Xing to court posthaste.

Meanwhile, Wang Xing, back at home, opened his wife's trunk and took out the scroll. As soon as he spread it out for a look, he let out a cry of dismay. It was now a blank piece of paper without the slightest trace of a character. Losing all courage to go to the county yamen, he stayed indoors in trepidation. But the officer dispatched by the county magistrate arrived. How could Wang Xing resist the fiery zeal of a county administration in its first term of office? Resignedly, he took the blank paper and followed the officer to the yamen and straight into the inner hall.

Magistrate Bao dismissed his attendants, keeping only Clerk Pei by his side, and asked Wang Xing, "Mr. Pei said that you received a scroll of paper from Eastern Peak Temple. Show it to me."

With one kowtow after another, Wang Xing said, "My wife made an incense-offering trip to Eastern Peak Temple last year. While she was passing the Shrine of Retribution, a god gave her a scroll of paper. It contained, among other lines, the very couplet inscribed on Your Honor's placard. I put the scroll in a trunk, but when I went just some moments ago to take it out, I found it to be blank. It is here now. Everything I said is true."

Magistrate Bao took the scroll. After one look, he asked, "Do you remember what was written on it?"

"Yes, I do." Right away, Wang Xing started reciting the lines.

After taking down every word on a piece of paper, Magistrate Bao perused the lines for a while before he said, "Wang Xing, let me ask you, what did that deity say to your wife when he gave her the scroll?"

"He told her to redress the wrong done to him."

The magistrate flew into a rage. "You are lying! How can a deity have grievances that need to be redressed by humans? And he begs your wife, of all people, to help him? (*Exactly so.*) Whom are you trying to fool with such nonsense?"

Wang Xing hastened to reply with another kowtow, "Your Honor, there is an explanation for this."

"Then tell me! And be specific! I'll have a reward for you if what you say makes sense. If not, you'll be the first one to be put under the rod!"

"My wife Ying'er used to be a maid serving Big Chief Clerk Sun of this county. A fortune-teller predicted that he was going to die at the third quarter of the third watch that very night, and so he did. His widow married Young Chief Clerk Sun, her current husband, and married Ying'er off to me. The first time the deceased chief clerk appeared to my wife was in the kitchen of the Sun house. With the railings of a well around his neck, his hair coming down loose, his tongue hanging out, and his eyes dripping blood, he cried, 'Ying'er, help your father!' The second time was at the gate of the Sun house one night. This time he wore a cap, a red robe, and a horn waistband. He gave my wife a package of loose silver. The third time was in Eastern Peak Temple, where he appeared as a judge of the Shrine of Retribution and gave my wife this scroll, telling her to redress the wrong done to him. The judge looked exactly like Big Sun, my wife's deceased master." (*Clear exposition.*)

At this account, Magistrate Bao burst into a peal of laughter. "So that's what happened!" By his order, his men apprehended the Sun couple and brought them to court.

"A fine thing the two of you did!" he said to the couple.

Young Sun retorted, "I didn't do anything wrong!"

Magistrate Bao launched into an explication of the inscription given by the judge at the Shrine of Retribution. "As for the first line, 'The big daughter's child, the small daughter's child,' well, 'a daughter's child' is a 'grandchild,' which is the character *sun,* a surname that is obviously shared by the two chief clerks, the big one and the small one. As for the line 'The former sowed for the latter to reap,' 'to reap' means to have something to live on, a reference to the fact that you, at no expense to yourself, took his wife and enjoy his family property. As for the third and fourth lines 'To know what happened at the third watch of the night / Remove the fire and drain the water underneath,' Big Sun died at midnight, and to find out the cause of his death, one would have to drain the water under the fire. Ying'er saw her master by the kitchen stove, his hair coming down loose, his tongue hanging out, his eyes dripping blood. These are signs of death by strangulation. There were the railings of a well around his neck. A well is the source of water. The kitchen stove is the source of fire. As for 'the water underneath,' there must be a well under your kitchen stove, and the dead body must be inside the well. 'The second or third month of next year' is now. As for the line 'Ju Si will come to solve this riddle,' well, the characters *ju* [sentence] and *si* [the sixth of the twelve Earthly Branches], when put together, make the character *bao,* which means that I, Bao Zheng, would be here to serve as the judge and solve the riddle to redress the wrong done to him." (*Well explained.*)

He then ordered his men and Wang Xing to take Young Sun under guard to his own kitchen and, whatever the circumstances, bring back the dead body. Somewhat skeptical, the men went to Sun's house. When they removed the stove, a stone slab underneath came into view. When the slab was pried open, they saw that there was indeed a well. They hired some laborers to drain the well. A man and a bamboo basket were let down into the well, and sure enough, the man came up with a dead body. The men gathered around for a look and found that the face appeared as if still alive. Some of the men recognized it as the face of Big Sun. Around his neck there was indeed a piece of silk with which he had been strangled. Young Sun was so frightened that he was struck dumb, his face turning the color of mud. The others were also appalled.

What had happened was that the younger Sun had once almost frozen to death in the snow. Big Sun saw him and, taking pity on the fine-looking young man, brought him back to life and later taught him to read and write. Little did he expect that his wife would carry on an affair with the young man. On the day that the older Sun came home after having his fortune told, the younger Sun happened to have sneaked into his house. Hearing that the older Sun was to die at around midnight, the younger man took the opportunity to get him drunk and then strangled him and threw him into the well. The younger Sun then walked toward the river, covering his face with his hand, and threw a rock into the water, making a loud splash, to make people believe that the older Sun had thrown himself into the river. The kitchen stove was then moved to cover the well. Later, the couple got married through the services of the matchmakers.

The officers reported the matter to Magistrate Bao. The Sun couple confessed without being put under the rod and were sentenced to death as repayment for Big Sun's life. Keeping his promise to an insignificant villager, Magistrate Bao gave Wang Xing the reward of ten taels of silver. Wang Xing, in his turn, gave Clerk Pei three taels as a token of his gratitude, but that need not be gone into here.

Having solved the case in the first few days of his term of office, Magistrate Bao became a well-known figure, and his name spread throughout the land. Even today, stories about how he solved his cases among mortal beings in daytime and among ghosts at night still circulate far and wide, as testified by the following poem:

The lines contained a most baffling riddle;
Judge Bao's verdict amazed ghosts and deities.
Let it be known to those guilty of crimes:
Never assume that heaven does not know.

14

A Mangy Priest Exorcises a Den of Ghosts

The apricot blossoms, washed by the rain,
Fade and fall, their petals the color of rouge,
Their fragrance flowing with the river.
The dear one is farther away, but love lingers.
One leaves in sorrow, the other gazes
And waits in vain in the shadow of the wall.
Who will be picking the green plums?
Where is the gold-saddled horse going?
Green willows still line the road to the south.

In a moment, the clouds and rain are gone;[1]
The tender feelings—easily they come and go.
The swallows chatter away,
Spreading news about the one afar.
The vows of everlasting love—
When will we meet face-to-face again?
Only then would the mind know any peace.
But now, there is little else to be done
Than to bear the overwhelming weight of grief.

The above lyric poem to the tune of "The Charms of Niannu" was written by a scholar named Shen Wenshu[2] while he was in the provincial capital for the civil service examinations. It is in fact a cento, with lines written by poets of earlier times. How do we know this? Well, let me start from the beginning.

The first line, "The apricot blossoms, washed by the rain," is based on a line from Chen Zigao's poem, "Cold Food Festival,"[3] to the tune of "A Visit at the Golden Gate":

When the thin willow twigs turn green,
Cold food is set under the trees.
Chirping orioles midst lonely flowers,
Jade terraces wet with spring grass,
I lean on the incense burner, idle and tired.

With whom can I share what weighs on my mind?
With joss sticks all around the windows and walls,
I watch the rain-washed apricot blossoms.

The second line, "Fade and fall, their petals the color of rouge," comes from a line in Li Yi'an's[4] lyric poem, "Late Spring," to the tune of "The Official Ranks":

The color of rouge, the petals fade and fall;
Spring returns: willow catkins fly, bamboo shoots grow.
In solitude, I watch the small garden,
A patch of tender green.
I climbed a hill and looked out, but in vain;
How sad that the traveler has tarried!
In a fond dream, at yonder stream by the wall,
I see my loved one's eyes in the waves.

The third line, "Their fragrance flowing with the river," comes from the lyric poem "Spring Rain," by a certain Li-shi of Yan'an, to the tune of "Sand of Silk-washing Stream":

The roses droop low under the raindrops;
The butterflies flit lovingly midst the flowers,
Whose fragrance flows with the river as young swallows sing.
I grieve on the southern bank,[5] but spring is less caring
Than the mirror that told Dongyang of his gaunt looks.[6]
Tonight, the moon lingers over the roof.

As for the fourth line "The dear one is farther away, but love lingers," there is a lyric poem titled "Spring," by the Precious Moon Chan Master,[7] to the tune of "Budding Tips of Willow Branches":

Love lingers as the dear one is farther away,
Leaving me with the sorrow of parting.
The rain washed away the chill in the air;
The wind sends wafts of gentle aroma;
Spring dwells in the blossoms of the pear trees.

The one at the oar travels throughout the land.
Waking from his wine-induced sleep,
He sees the sun setting midst flying crows.
A swing in the yard, a rouged face atop the wall,
Whose imposing mansion might this be?

The fifth and sixth lines, "One leaves in sorrow, the other gazes / And waits in vain in the shadow of the wall," originate in the poem "Clear and Bright Festival," by Ouyang Yongshu,[8] to the tune of "A Bushel of Pearls":

Spring fills the heart with sadness;
After Clear and Bright come orioles and flowers.[9]
I urge you not to head for the path of sorrow,
Where perfumed wheels crush the green grass again.

As the moon and the wind give way to dawn,
One waits in vain in the shadow of the wall.
The other leaves, how deep the sorrow!
The sudden spring chill withers the buds ere they bloom.

The seventh line, "Who will be picking the green plums?" is from Chao Wujiu's[10] lyric poem "Spring" to the tune of "The Sad Qingshang Tune":

The wind sways and shakes, the rain blurs and blinds,
The twigs too weak to bear the weight of the blossoms.
The spring clothes too thin for the feeble body,
I recall the days when you and I picked green plums.

When shall we share these dreamlike memories?
How sad that my hair is too thin for hairpins now!
Topped by twilight clouds, the mountain pass blocks the way;
The swallows come, but they bring me no news of you.

The eighth and ninth lines, "Where is the gold-saddled horse going? Green willows still line the road to the south," are from Liu Qiqing's[11] lyric poem "Spring" to the tune of "Pure and Serene Music":

Overcast one moment, sunny the next;
The pale sun sets off the contours of the clouds.
What fragrant path seeks the gold-saddled horse?
Green willows still line the quiet road to the south.

My last vestiges of tender feelings,
Alas, are too old to have much meaning.
The frosty hairs plucked from my temples
Do not grow back like the green grass of spring.

The tenth line, "In a moment, the clouds and rain are gone," is taken from Yan Shuyuan's[12] lyric poem "Spring" to the tune of "The Beautiful Lady Yu":

The flying petals drift toward the ones they love;
The branch is not where they prefer to stay.
Sadly, the morning wind blows them apart,
Into the river east, past the house of pleasure.

In a moment, the loathsome clouds and rain are gone;
Idly she leans against the balustrade,

Shedding tears that wet the rosy cheeks.
Alas! The beauty shares the flowers' fate.

The eleventh line, "The tender feelings—easily they come and go," is from Lady Wei's[13] lyric poem "Spring" to the tune of "Raising the Beaded Curtain":

You came, I remember, before spring was late;
Hand in hand, we plucked flowers whose dew soaked our sleeves.
Secretly we prayed to the flowers for love;
Both tried to be the first to find twin blossoms.

The tender feelings were betrayed, but why?
Easily they come and go—who can share my grief?
My tears wet the crab-apple blossoms;
The god of spring gave me orders in vain.

As for the twelfth line, "The swallows chatter away," there is a lyric poem about spring by Kang Boke[14] to the tune of "Magnolia Blossoms, Abbreviated":

The willow catkins are all blown away;
The clouds hang over the green; the wind is still.
The curtains are down; the flying swallows chatter.

Her room quiet, her morning toilette not yet done,
She laments that his return had been but a dream,
And teardrops stain her gold-threaded dress.

The thirteenth line, "Spreading news about the one afar," comes from Qin Shaoyou's[15] lyric poem "Spring" to the tune of "Touring the Palace at Night":

Why is the god of spring gone again?
The deserted courtyard is strewn with
Fallen flowers and willow catkins.
The swallows twitter and chirrup in my ears
But bring me no news about the one afar.
The melancholy deepens at the thought
Of the one at the far end of the earth.
In dreams, the pangs of love come back again,
Midst a drizzle that lasted through the night.
Adding to the grief, the cries of cuckoos![16]

The fourteenth and fifteenth lines, "The vows of everlasting love— / When will we meet face-to-face again?" come from Huang Luzhi's[17] lyric poem about spring to the tune of "Pounding White Silk":

The plum blossoms fade and wither;
The willows sway and spill gold.

The gentle rain and soft breeze clear the dusty road.
The vows of everlasting love—who will listen?
When will we meet face-to-face again!

The sixteenth line, "Only then would the mind know any peace," is from Zhou Meicheng's[18] lyric poem about spring to the tune of "Drops of Gold":

The plum blossoms herald the advent of spring;
The willows bud; the grass turns green.
All too soon, my temples turn the color of frost.
How I lament the passage of time!

In her boudoir, a toast to the one far away,
With knit eyebrows and sad thoughts of spring.
To meet over a distance of a thousand li,
Only then would the mind know any peace.

The seventeenth and eighteenth lines, "But now, there is little else to be done / Than to bear the overwhelming weight of grief," borrow from Ouyang Yongshu's lyric poem to the tune of "Butterflies Lingering over Flowers":

The curtains keep out the chilly east wind;
Plum blossoms in the snow herald the spring.
There is little else to be done
Than to bear the gut-wrenching pangs of longing
And the overwhelming weight of grief.

With the golden stove lit for a perfumed bath,
Gloomily I take up the golden scissors
And make paper-cuts of exquisite patterns.
Under an embroidered quilt, I at last fall sweetly asleep,
("Sweet sleep" can well serve as a name for a boudoir.)
Unaware that dawn has lit up the window screens.

The Shen Wenshu quoted above was a scholar, and now, let me tell of another scholar whose trip to Lin'an to sit for the civil service examinations provided material for a most remarkable story more than ten episodes in length.

Storyteller, what is the name of that scholar? Well, in the tenth year of the Shaoxing reign period [1131–62], a scholar named Wu Hong left his home village in the Weiwu commandery of Fuzhou and went to Lin'an to seek fame and fortune through the examinations, hoping to

Take first honor on the first try,
And gain the highest office in ten years.

But he failed in the examinations, his time not having come yet. In low spirits, Scholar Wu felt too ashamed to return home, nor for that matter did he have enough money to travel. Seeing no alternative, he managed to open a small school at the foot of what is now Prefecture Bridge. In this way, he intended to make a living while he waited for another chance to seek fame and fortune at the next examination, in spring in three years' time. And so, month after month, he kept company with little boys and girls.

In the snap of a finger, more than a year went by. Thanks to the neighborhood residents who sent their children to his school, he had put aside a tidy sum of money.

One day, he was teaching in the schoolroom when the bell by the blue-cloth portiere rang, and in walked a woman. Schoolmaster Wu recognized her as Granny Wang, a former neighbor and a matchmaker by profession who had moved away about half a year ago.

Schoolmaster Wu bowed with folded hands and said, "I haven't seen you for a long time, granny. Where do you live now?"

"I thought Schoolmaster Wu had forgotten all about me! I now live by the city gate of Qiantang."

"What is your venerable age?" asked the teacher.

"This old woman is seventy-five. And how about you in your blooming youth?"

"Twenty-two."

"For a twenty-two-year-old, you look like you're over thirty. You must be working too hard every day! In my humble opinion, you really can't do without a wife to keep you company."

"Well, I have indeed been asking around, but there's just no one suitable."

"As the saying goes, 'Those not predestined for each other will never get to meet.' Let me tell you, I have a good match for you. She has a thousand strings of cash for a dowry, and she'll bring a maidservant with her. A real beauty she is, too, and she's able to play all sorts of musical instruments, write, and do accounting. What's more, she's from a prominent official's family. Her only wish is to marry a scholar. Now, what do you say?"

Imagine his joy at this blessing from heaven! Wreathed in smiles, he said, "How nice it would be if there really were such a person! But where is the young lady?"

"Let me tell you, Mr. Wu. Goodness knows how many marriage proposal letters this young lady has received in the two months since she left the establishment of the deputy prefect, the third son of Grand Preceptor Qin.[19] There have been letters from officials in the three departments,[20] the six ministries,[21] and the Privy Military Council, from runners for the various palace bureaus, and from merchants and shopowners, but they are either too highly placed or too lowly for her. She said, 'I wish to marry none but a scholar.' Having lost both parents, she has only a maidservant, Jin'er, with her. Because she plays all kinds of musical instruments, she's called 'Li the Music Lady' by all and sundry in the establishment. She's now staying with a former neighbor at White Wild Goose Pond."

While they were talking, a woman was seen passing the door as a gust of wind blew up the portiere. Granny Wang said, "Schoolmaster Wu, did you see the woman passing by? You are indeed destined to have Li the Music Lady for your wife!" She rushed out the door and overtook the woman, who was none other than Madam Chen, called Godmother Chen, with whom Li the Music Lady was staying. Granny Wang brought her in to exchange greetings with Schoolmaster Wu.

"Godmother," said Granny Wang, "has match been made yet for the young lady at your house?"

"No," replied Godmother Chen. "It's not that there are no good candidates. It's just that she's so stubborn. She insists on marrying a scholar, but it's not something that works out all that easily."

"I have a good candidate here," said Granny Wang. "But I don't know if Godmother and the young lady would be willing to accept him."

"Whom do you have in mind for my child?"

Pointing at Wu, Granny Wang said, "This very gentleman here. What do you say?"

"You must be joking. How wonderful if she could be married to this gentleman!"

Too excited to teach the rest of the day, Wu dismissed the children early. After they left, chanting farewell, the schoolmaster locked the door and went out with the two women for a drink, which he felt he owed them. After three cups, Granny Wang stood up and said, "If the schoolmaster accepts this match, I'll have to ask Godmother for a betrothal letter."

"I have one right here." So saying, Godmother Chen produced one from her undergarment.

"Godmother," said Granny Wang, "as the saying goes, 'One doesn't tell lies to honest people, just as one doesn't swim on dry land.' Set a date to bring the young lady and her maid Jin'er to the wineshop by Mei Family Bridge so that the schoolmaster and I can go and size her up."

Godmother agreed. She and Granny Wang thanked Wu and took their leave. After paying the wine bill, Wu returned home.

Let us skip over trivialities and come to the big day. Schoolmaster Wu changed into new clothes, dismissed his pupils, and walked all the way to the wineshop by Mei Family Bridge. Granny Wang met him on the way when he was still a good distance from the wineshop, and, together, the two entered the wineshop and went upstairs. After Godmother Chen greeted them, the schoolmaster asked, "Where is the young lady?"

"My child and Jin'er are sitting in the east room."

The teacher wet the paper window with the tip of his tongue and made a hole through which he took a peek. With a cheer, he exclaimed, forgetting himself, "These two are not human!"

How could they not be? Well, as a matter of fact, he was so struck with their beauty that he thought the young lady was the bodhisattva Guanyin, and Jin'er a jade maiden serving the Jade Emperor. How do we know their beauty was out of this world? This was how Li the Music Lady looked:

Her eyes were sparkling pools of water;
Her cheeks the color of blushing flowers.
Her cloudlike hair shaped like cicada wings;
Her eyebrows, two lines of distant spring hills.
Her red lips like a cherry;
Her white teeth, two rows of jade chips.
Her manner naturally graceful,
She stood out among her peers,
Like the Weaving Maiden from the Jade Terrace,
Like Chang'e from the Moon Palace.

He then looked at Jin'er the maid, and this was what he saw:

Her eyes limpid and lovely;
Her hair done up high and a sight to see.
Her eyebrows the shape of crescent moons;
Her face a pink peach blossom.
Her manner like a bud before opening;
Her skin soft and fragrant.
Embroidered shoes on her golden lotus feet;
A small gold hairpin in her shell-shaped bun.
A green plum in youthful love;[22]
A red apricot blossom over the fence.

After meeting his intended that day and sticking a hairpin in her hair, Teacher Wu sent over the obligatory betrothal gifts and a goose, and documents were exchanged.[23]

In a matter of days, the young lady moved in as teacher Wu's wife. Each found in the other a perfect companion:

A pair of phoenixes up in the clouds;
Loving mandarin ducks in water.
They vowed never to part in this world
And formed ties of love for future lives.

One day, as it happened to be the midpoint in the lunar month, the pupils arrived early for a ritual to pay homage to Confucius. Schoolmaster Wu said to his wife, "Sister, I'll have to get up first and go to the ceremony." As he passed the kitchen stove, he saw Jin'er the maid. Lo and behold! Her hair was hanging loose down her back, her eyes were slanting upward, and her neck was stained with blood. With a loud cry, the schoolmaster fell to the ground.

Immediately, his wife rushed over and brought him back to consciousness. Jin'er also came and helped him to his feet. His wife asked, "Husband, what did you see?"

Being a responsible head of a household, he was prudent with his words, and he could not very well describe the state in which he had found Jin'er. Believing that his eyes had deceived him, he lied, "Sister, I didn't put on enough clothes after I got up, so I suddenly felt dizzy at a cold draft and collapsed." Hastily, Jin'er fed him some soup with a soothing effect, and, soon, the excitement was over, but not Wu's misgivings.

Not to encumber our story with unnecessary details, let us tell of what happened on the day of the Clear and Bright Festival. It being a holiday, there was no school. Wu told his wife that he was going to take a walk. After changing clothes, off he went. When he passed by Ten Thousand Pines Ridge, he stepped into what is now Cleansing Mercy Temple and looked around. On his way out, he saw a man chanting a greeting to him. He quickly returned the greeting. The man was a waiter in the wineshop opposite the temple. He said, "A gentleman in the wineshop told me to invite you over, sir!"

As Wu followed the waiter into the wineshop, he saw that the gentleman was none other than Administrative Assistant Wang Qi, better known as Third Master Wang Qi. After an exchange of greetings, Wang Qi said, "I didn't dare call you when I saw you a moment ago. That's why I asked the waiter to invite you over."

"Where are you off to, Third Master?"

Wang Qi thought to himself, "Schoolmaster Wu is newly married. Let me play a prank on him." Aloud, he said, "Shall we go together to visit my family graves? The grave watcher came over earlier and said, 'The peach trees are in bloom, and the homemade wine is ready.' Let's go and have a few drinks, shall we?"

"All right," said the teacher.

The two men left the wineshop and headed for Su Causeway, where they saw lots of people on spring outings. Truly,

Crowds milling around; horse carriages lining up.
Soft breezes fan the scenery;
The bright sun lends it greater luster.
The orioles chirp among green willows;
The butterflies play amid prized flowers.
The music of wind and string instruments—
From which hall do the strains come?
Jovial chitchat and laughter
Arise from spring towers and summer pavilions.
Perfumed carriages and jade-reined horses compete;
Fair-faced men loudly kick their gold stirrups;
Women in red watch from behind the curtains.

At South New Road Crossing, they hired a boat and sailed up to Mao Family Pier, where they went ashore and wended their way past Jade Spring and Dragon Well. Wang Qi's family graves lay at the foot of Camel Ridge of West Hill, and a fine tall hill it was! After climbing up the hill, they began descending and covered another li before they reached the graves. They were greeted by Zhang An the grave watcher, and Wang Qi told him to bring some wine and refreshments. He and Schoolmaster Wu then went to sit in a small garden nearby. They drank the home-made wine until they were quite inebriated. By this time, evening had set in.

The red orb has sunk in the west;
The jade hare has risen in the east.
The beauty returns to her room, candle in hand;
The fisherman goes home from the river
To sell the fish along the bamboo paths;
The herdboy rides a calf to the village of flowers.

As it was getting quite late, Wu wished to go. Wang Qi said, "Have another drink. I'll go with you. We'll cross Camel Ridge and spend the night in some brothel on Nine-Li Pine Road."

Without saying anything out loud, Wu thought to himself, "I'm a newly married man. How can I make my wife wait for me at home while I fool around and stay out all night? But at the same time, even if I start on the way home right now, by the time I get to Qiantang Gate, it will be closed for the night." Resignedly, he followed Wang Qi up Camel Ridge, helped by Wang's supporting hand.

As coincidence would have it, when they gained the top of the ridge, clouds gathered in the northeast, a fog rose from the southwest, and a heavy rain came down with the force of the surging currents of the Silver River [Milky Way] and the raging waves of the vast ocean. A fine rainstorm it was! Finding no shelter around them, they plodded ahead in the rain for several tens of steps before they saw a small gateway with a bamboo arch over it. Wang Qisan said, "Let's go there for shelter." Actually, what they were about to do would not bring them shelter from the rain but,

Like pigs and sheep on their way to the butcher's,
With each step they went nearer to their deaths.

When they reached the gate, they saw that it led to an unguarded cemetery. Behind that gate lay no houses of any kind. The two men sat down on a rock slope to wait out the rain before continuing their journey. Amid the downpour, a man who looked like a prison warden jumped over the bamboo fence into the cemetery and walked to a grave mound, shouting, "Zhu Xiaosi, you are needed. It's your turn to get out today."

A voice called out from within the mound, "Coming, Grandpa!" In a moment, the grave mound split open. A man jumped out and was led away by the prison warden. When Wu and Wang saw this, they hunched their backs over their bent knees, and their legs shook violently in spite of themselves.

As soon as the rain let up, they pushed on, sloshing though the slippery mud, their fearful hearts throbbing like those of frightened young deer and their feet as weak as those of a rooster defeated in a cockfight. They would not even take so much as one quick look back, as if afraid a mighty army was pursuing them.

When they gained the top of the ridge, they strained their ears to listen and heard, echoing throughout the empty valley, the beating of a rod coming from the woods. Soon, the prison warden came into view, chasing the man who had jumped out of the grave mound. At the sight, Schoolmaster Wu and Wang Qi turned on their heels and ran. They caught sight of a dilapidated temple to the mountain god on one side of the ridge, entered, and quickly shut both sides of the double door. Throwing their whole weight against it, they dared not even breathe or fart. They heard a voice crying, "You're beating me to death!" Another voice said, "You monster! You promised me a favor but failed to deliver. How can I not beat you?"

Wang Qi whispered to Schoolmaster Wu, "Listen! It's the prison warden and the man from the grave!" As they cowered in fear, trembling all over, Wu complained to Wang, "Didn't you have anything better to do than to bring me here for such misery? My wife at home must be worried sick!"

Before these words were quite out of his mouth, a knock was heard at the door. "Open up!" came the demand.

"Who's there?" they asked. When the reply came, they listened intently and realized it was a woman. "Third Master Wang Qi! A fine thing you did, taking my husband here for the night and making me go on this search for him all this way! Jin'er, let's force the door open and get your master out."

Recognizing the voice as none other than that of his wife, Wu thought to himself, "It's my wife and Jin'er, but how did they know Mr. Wang and I were here? Could they also be ghosts?" Neither of the two men dared make a sound.

"If you don't open up, I'll have to squeeze myself in through a crack!"

At these words, the wine that the two men had drunk earlier in the day turned into cold sweat seeping out through their pores. Another voice said, "Ma'am, I don't want to speak out of turn, but it might be better if you go back home now. Tomorrow my master will surely come home by himself."

"You're right, Jin'er. Let's go now before we do anything more." Then she called out, "Third Master Wang Qi, I'm going home now. Be sure to escort my husband home tomorrow."

Neither men dared utter a word in reply. The woman and Jin'er left after having spoken those words.

"Schoolmaster Wu, your wife and her maid Jin'er are both ghosts. This is no place for humans. Let's get out of here!"

After opening the temple door, they saw that it was about the fifth watch of the night before dawn, still too early to see people moving about. A little more than one li before they reached the foot of the ridge on their way down, they saw two people emerge from the woods. The first was Godmother Chen, and the second was Granny Wang. "Schoolmaster Wu," they called out, "we've been waiting for you for a long time. Where have you been with Third Master Wang Qi?"

At the sight of these two, Wu and Wang said, "So they are ghosts, too. Let's get out of here!"

With the speed of river deer and stags, with the agility of apes and falcons, they fled down the ridge, followed by the two women moving at their own leisurely pace.

"We haven't had anything to eat throughout this hectic night. We're starved. How I wish we could run into a real human being to offset the bad luck that's been dogging us."

They had hardly said this than they saw, at the foot of the ridge, a house that looked like a wineshop, with a pine tree branch hanging at the door by way of a sign. "This is most probably a place that sells home-brewed wine," said Wang. "Let's have a cup or two to fortify ourselves and hide from the two old hags." So they ran into the wineshop, where they saw a man wearing

A green turban the color of cow's gall bladder,
A red waistband the color of pig's liver,
A pair of old pants, and a pair of straw sandals.

"How much for the wine?" asked Wang Qi.

The man answered, "I haven't prepared water to heat up the wine."

"Just give us a bowl of cold wine, then!" said Wu, but the man fell silent, without breathing.

"This wineshop owner is so weird," said Wang Qi. "He must be a ghost, too! Let's go!" Before he had quite finished speaking, a gust of wind sprang up in the wineshop.

It is neither the roar of a tiger
Nor the bellow of a dragon.
Not the kind to make willows die and flowers bloom,
But one that hides demons on hills and in waters.
It whips up the soil by the gate of hell;
It stirs up dust at the door of the underworld.

When the wind died down, the two men found themselves standing on top of a grave mound, with neither the wine seller nor the wineshop anywhere in sight. Frightened out of their wits, they raced all the way to Nine-Li Pine Wineshop, where they took a boat and headed straight for Qiantang Gate. After going ashore, Wang Qi went home, whereas Wu made for Granny Wang's house by Qiantang Gate, only to find the door padlocked. Upon inquiry, the neighbors told him, "Granny Wang has been dead for more than five months now." Wu stood there stupefied, eyes wide open, mouth agape, without the least idea of what to do. He left Qiantang Gate and went past what is now the Jingling Palace examination grounds, Mei Family Bridge, and White Wild Goose Pond until he arrived at Godmother Chen's house, by whose door, sealed as it was with two bamboo sticks laid crosswise, hung a lamp bearing the insignia of the local government. On the door was written: "The human heart may be as hard as steel, but the law of the land is the furnace." Upon inquiry, he was told, "Godmother Chen has been dead for more than a year."

After leaving White Wild Goose Pond, he returned home by Prefecture Bridge, only to find his own house also padlocked. He asked the neighbors, "Where did my wife and the maid go?"

The neighbors told him, "After you left home yesterday, your wife said to us, 'I'm taking Jin'er with me to visit my godmother.' And they haven't come back yet."

Schoolmaster Wu was still staring speechlessly at the neighbors when a mangy Daoist priest came into view. Fixing his eyes on Wu, he said, "I can see that you've been much plagued by evil spirits. Let me do an exorcism for you, to forestall future trouble."

Right away, Wu invited the priest inside and had incense, candles, and holy water prepared. Muttering incantations, the priest began his exorcism. As he cried out, "Quick!" a celestial warrior appeared.

A yellow silk band around his forehead,
A brocade belt around his waist,
A black embroidered robe,
Close-fitting gold armor,
A flashing sword hanging by his side,
Lion-patterned boots on his feet,
He moves about both in heaven and in hell.
If a dragon makes mischief,
He dives to the seabed to capture it.
If an evil spirit makes trouble,
He enters its cave to ferret it out.
Among the celestial warriors,
He is the one guarding magic charms;
Before the Lord on High, he's a divine general.

The celestial general chanted a greeting and asked, "Where does the sage want me to go?"

"Bring me all the evil sprits that are wreaking havoc in Wu Hong's home and on Camel Ridge!" Thus instructed, the celestial general conjured up a gust of wind right there in Wu's house.

Formless, shadowless, it pierces one's bosom,
It blows open the peach blossoms of early spring,

It sweeps withered leaves on the ground,
It enters mountains and expels white clouds.

When the wind was gone, the ghosts that had been wreaking havoc were brought into the presence of the priest. Schoolmaster Wu's wife, Li the Music Lady, had been the concubine of Grand Preceptor Qin's third son, who had died in childbirth. Jin'er the maid had slit her own throat after being beaten by Mr. Qin Junior's wife, who was jealous of her beauty. So she, too, was a ghost and had died by her own hand. Granny Wang had died of schistosomiasis. Godmother Chen had drowned in White Wild Goose Pond while washing clothes. Zhu Xiaosi, the ghost that had jumped out of a grave on Camel Ridge at the call of the prison warden, was a grave watcher who had died of consumption. The owner of the wineshop at the foot of the ridge had died of typhoid fever.

Having now established all the facts, the priest took a gourd from his waist. To human eyes, it was a gourd, but to a ghost, it was a representation of hell. As the priest conjured up his magic, the ghosts covered their heads with their hands and scurried off like frightened mice, but they were all caught and put into the gourd. Turning to Schoolmaster Wu, the priest said, "Take it and bury it at the foot of Camel Ridge." Then, the mangy priest tossed his cane into the air. When the cane turned into a red-crowned crane, the priest rose in the air and onto the crane's back, ready to fly away.

Wu dropped to his knees and said with a bow, "With the eyes of a human, I, Wu Hong, did not know that you were an immortal. I wish to follow you and enter the Daoist order. Please redeem me and take me as your disciple!"

The priest said, "I am Sage Gan from heaven. You used to be one of my disciples responsible for picking medicinal herbs. But you had not rid yourself of all the desires of a mortal human being and regretted having left the mundane world, hence your downfall. As punishment, you were destined to be a poor Confucian scholar in this life, to experience ghostly antics to the full and to be a victim of lust. But now that you've seen the truth, you may renounce the mundane world and enter the Daoist order. I shall come to redeem you after another twelve-year cycle." With this, he vanished in a refreshing puff of wind.

Henceforth, Schoolmaster Wu renounced the mundane world and became a traveling Daoist. Twelve years later, he met Sage Gan in the Zhongnan Mountains and went away with him. There is a poem that says,

If the heart were set against the mundane,
No evil spirits would dare draw near.
If the heart could tell right from wrong,
All ghosts on West Hill would have been set free.

15

Clerk Jin Rewards Xiutong with a Pretty Maidservant

A gain may turn out to be a loss;
A misfortune can be a blessing in disguise.
What lies in the future no one can tell;
Just do the right things to repay heaven's kindness.

Our story takes place in the prefecture of Suzhou. Within the city gates there stands a Xuandu Temple, built in the Later Liang dynasty. The line "A thousand peach trees in Xuandu Temple," written by Prefect Liu Yuxi [772–842] of the Tang dynasty, is a reference to this very temple, which is also called Xuanmiao Temple.[1] Situated in the heart of the city of Suzhou, it is a famous landmark covering a large area, a magnificent building complete with a hall devoted to the Three Pure Ones and one devoted to Yama, King of the Ten Halls of Hell. Priests wearing yellow caps and serving in the various halls numbered in the hundreds. There was in the temple a North Pole Zhenwu Hall,[2] more commonly known as the Hall of the Patriarch. Priests who served in this hall were all successors of the Zhengyi sect of Daoism, good at drawing magic figures, deploying celestial warriors to exorcise evil spirits, and predicting the ups and downs in people's lives.

Let me now tell of one of these priests, with the laic surname Zhang before he joined the Daoist order. His fondness for a pet sparrow earned him the nickname Sparrow Zhang. He was an eccentric man. His love of meat and wine was nothing out of the ordinary, but he had an unusual passion for one thing. What was it?

It barks at the moon in deserted villages
And runs with the wind on wintry days of snow.
As for how the character for it is written,
Move to the right the dot in the character tai.

In short, he had a passion for dog meat. The dog slaughterer treated him as his biggest patron. Whenever a big dog was slaughtered, the butcher invariably asked him over to eat the meat. At the height of his enjoyment, Sparrow Zhang would hand the butcher all the money he had received as donations, without ever bothering to ask for the bill. (*That's why those mundane mortal beings who like to eat and keep their money at the same time will never achieve immortality.*) When asked to draw magic figures to exorcise evil spirits that haunt people, he would, if he was in the midst of eating dog meat, dip his chopsticks in the gravy and draw a magic figure to be posted on the front gate of the household that had asked for help. Wherever such magic figures were posted, local residents would see celestial warriors on patrol at night, and the evil spirits' doings would immediately come to an end.

There was a rich man, Jiao, who, out of gratitude to heaven and earth for a lucrative pawnshop business over the years, wished to build an altar and hold a prayer service to offer his thanks. The Daoist priest he asked to officiate at the service, Priest Zhou of Qingzhen Temple, praised Sparrow Zhang's efficacy. Mr. Jiao, who also admired Sparrow Zhang, had his shop manager deliver an invitation. The Jiao household had a watchdog. Sparrow Zhang had long had his eye on that dog of goodly size. Now that the very owner of the dog had invited Sparrow Zhang to his home, the monk said, "If you want me to come, you'll have to slaughter that dog. Only when its meat is cooked tender and wine is nicely warmed up will I come to your house."

At the shop manager's report, Mr. Jiao saw nothing for it but to give his consent, knowing that Sparrow Zhang was an eccentric man. As was told, wine was heated and dog meat was cooked tender, and sure enough, Sparrow Zhang showed up at the door. The host led him to the main hall and requested his service. Well lined with images of deities along the walls, the hall was brightly lit with candles, and the assembly of priests had already made incense offerings to the gods. Sparrow Zhang strode in jauntily and, dispensing with the obligatory bow to the images of the gods and greetings to the priests, shouted, "Bring me the tender dog meat and be quick about it! And make sure the wine is warm!"

Mr. Jiao said to himself, "Let's wait and see what he does after he eats and drinks." Right away, large plates of dog meat and large flasks of wine were set before Sparrow Zhang. Heartily he ate and drank until there was no bone left on the plates nor a drop of wine in the flasks. Now quite full with the meat and the wine, he said, "Thanks!" Contentedly, he lay down on a prayer mat without even bothering to wipe his mouth clean and immediately began to snore like thunder. He slept from late afternoon all the way to the small hours of the next morning. The priests found him still asleep after they had finished the prayer service, but they dared not disturb him. Mr. Jiao lost his patience and grumbled that it was all Priest Zhou's fault. An ashamed Priest Zhou dared not say a word in defense of himself. He thought, "Sparrow Zhang often sleeps for two or three days at a stretch when he's the worse for liquor. I wonder when he'll wake up this time." Resignedly, he burned the petition to the gods, offered words of thanks to the celestial warriors, and cleaned up the hall.

At about the fifth watch, the priests were about to take their leave after being treated to wine and food, when, lo and behold, Sparrow Zhang jumped up from the prayer mat and, spinning himself around, screamed, "Ten days! Ten days! Five days! Five days!"

Believing he had gone quite mad, Mr. Jiao and the priests gathered around him to watch. Priest Zhou, being braver than the rest, went up to Sparrow Zhang, held him tight, and woke him up while he was still screaming, "Five days! Five days!"

Priest Zhou asked him what he was talking about. Instead of answering, he asked, "Who wrote that petition?"

"This humble priest did," replied Priest Zhou.

"You missed one character and got two characters wrong."

Mr. Jiao intervened, "I read the petition aloud several times and found no mistakes. How can you say such a thing?"

With a rustle, Sparrow Zhang produced from his sleeve a scroll of yellow paper and said "Isn't this the petition?"

Appalled at the sight, everyone present said, "The petition has been burned. How could it have ended up in his sleeve, without so much as a crumpled corner?" Upon giving it another careful reading, they realized that one character was indeed missing from the list of deities' names invoked, but still, none was able to locate the wrong characters. Pointing to one couplet in the petition, Sparrow Zhang read aloud,

> *"Suffering losses and hardships,*
> *He doubled his riches.*
> *Enduring trials and tribulations,*
> *He attained but modest wealth.*

"The character for 'suffering' here, as in 'suffering a loss' [literally, "to eat losses"] is wrong. You used the one that means 'to stutter' [*chi* in modern Chinese], whereas you should have used the one that means 'to eat.' The one you used should be pronounced 'ge.' The character for 'enduring' [*nai*] is also wrong. The character you wrote is a homophone that is the name of a kind of apple, not the one that means 'endure.' How can you throw in an apple in this context? Are you assuming that the Lord on High is illiterate and are therefore trying to cheat him? If the Lord gets angry, there isn't much I can do to help."

With the petition right before them, Mr. Jiao and the priests could not reject the evidence of their eyes. In unison, they begged, "May we write another petition and build another prayer altar from scratch?"

"No use!" said Sparrow Zhang, "No use! A few wrong characters is nothing major, but because you sent this petition, the Lord on High checked your file in the Heavenly Registry and found that, ever since you started your business, you have been ruthless in your pursuit of wealth. You pay cheaply for pawned objects but charge steeply for redemptions. You pay out in low-quality silver but take in pure silver of the finest quality. You replace nice pieces of pawned jewelry and keep them for yourself. (*All the heartless rich, be warned!*) You also disallow redemption for valuable objects when their term expires, falsely claiming that they have been sold. It's through such exploitation of the poor that you amassed your wealth. And yet, your petition is full of self-praise, without a word of repentance for your trespasses.

"The Thunder Department has already been ordered to burn your house this very day and destroy all of your possessions. Out of gratitude for your dog meat, I begged for a ten-day grace period, but the Lord on High denied my request. I kept on pleading and finally got the Lord to grant a five-day grace period. You can put up a notice to say, 'In the next five days, pay no interest for redemption of pawned items.' It may be impracticable for you to return to your clients all the money you got by cheating them out of their jewelry and other pawned items, but you can still perform some good works like paying for the building of bridges and the repair of roads. Such good deeds will surely alleviate the anger of the Lord on High. He may even revoke his order to the Thunder Department for all I know."

At the beginning, Mr. Jiao felt inclined to follow the advice, but at the words that the Lord on High "may even revoke his order to the Thunder Department," a suspicion entered his mind: "Might this crazy priest be using this as an excuse to make me give away my money and possessions? The Thunder Department can't be as flexible as that!" Moreover, being in charge of a business, he had a quick head for calculating capital and profits. How was he to let go easily of his money? Outwardly, he voiced his agreement, but inwardly, he thought otherwise.

After Sparrow Zhang and the assembly of priests took their leave, Mr. Jiao did nothing about his promise. Five days later, a fire broke out in his warehouse. The flames consumed everything from the front to the back of the house. The next day, customers flocked to the shop to demand the return of their pawned items, but Mr. Jiao refused to pay compensation for their losses. After a series of lawsuits, Rich Man Jiao sold everything he had, including his land, and was reduced to abject poverty. Those who knew that Sparrow Zhang had predicted a thunder-induced fire henceforth held him in even greater awe.

After he had spent more than fifty years altogether in the Xuandu Temple, Sparrow Zhang took a trip across Qiantang River one day. As the boat was struggling against the wind, he summoned celestial warriors to tow the boat, and the boat started to speed ahead as if flying through air. But his roars of laughter so enraged the celestial warriors that they killed him.

Later, in a divination exercise in a Huizhou merchant's home, when a T-shaped wooden rod was placed in a tray filled with sand, the following characters, by Sparrow Zhang's hand, appeared in the sand: "I, Grand Marshal Gou in heaven, was not killed but was invited back to heaven by the celestial warriors upon expiration of my predestined bond with the mortal world." Having heard that Zhenwu Hall was most responsive to prayers, the Huizhou merchant donated a thousand pieces of gold and had a rock hill built in front of the hall to add to the grandeur of the view. A delight to the eye though the rock hill was, it destroyed the *fengshui.* Henceforth, no priest of this hall ever attained the Dao. As the poem says,

A thunder fire burned the pawnshop warehouse,
Bearing out the words of the soothsayer.
Sparrow Zhang of Xuande Temple
Was not without divine powers.

Why all this talk about Sparrow Zhang? Well, there was a man whose blind faith in magic and celestial warriors almost led to the loss of human lives. The man, Jin Man by name, was also a native of Kunshan County in Suzhou Prefecture. Having failed in his studies earlier in his life, he bought himself a government post as a clerk in the county revenue office. Being a clever man with modest ways in his dealings with people, he got along very well with his colleagues. In less than three months as a clerk, he had won the hearts of all in the yamen, high and low. He also went out of his way to befriend the janitors, inviting them to have wine from time to time and giving them small gifts, so that they might put in a good word for him with the county magistrate. Whenever they were detained by the magistrate until late at night and beaten for dereliction of duty, he put them up at his home overnight and kept them entertained, to their deep gratitude. Though the janitors were not able to ask the magistrate for favors for Jin Man, they did everything they could for him.

The middle of the fifth month drew near, which, as Clerk Jin knew, was the time for the personnel office to draw lots to fill the post of treasurer, a sinecure that he coveted. In the old days, the treasurer was appointed by the county magistrate. Everyone coveted this lucrative post, which rotated every two seasons, and contested the magistrate's choice each time. An appeal was made to higher authorities, requesting a public lot-drawing session using a list of candidates from all the six offices. These candidates had to be independently well-off and honest and have clean records. Petitions were also sent to higher authorities, asking to exclude those who were new to their posts as well as those whose terms of office would soon expire. And yet, because power rested with the office of personnel, those who were on good terms with personnel officers sent over gifts and managed to get themselves nominated, irrespective of considerations such as length of service, financial background, etc. This is a case of good rules ending in abuse.

Now, Jin Man thought to himself, "I may be a newcomer, but Clerk Liu of the personnel office is a good friend of mine. Why don't I give him some gifts? And let me spare no cost! He'll surely put my name on the list for lot-drawing. And yet, if I am picked, all this scheming will of course have been worthwhile, but if not, won't I have thrown away money for nothing and be ridiculed into the bargain? I wish I could come up with a surefire plan!"

Suddenly he recalled Wang Wenying, a janitor who had been serving in the yamen for some years and quite an insightful man at that. Why not consult him? He walked out of the yamen, and, as coincidence would have it, at the very gate, he ran into Wang Wenying.

"Uncle Jin," said Wang, "where are you rushing off to?"

"My good brother, I was on my way to look for you!"

"To do me a favor?"

"Well, let's sit down and talk."

They entered a nearby wineshop and sat down. While drinking, Jin Man told Wang Wenying about his wish to land the post of treasurer.

"As long as the personnel office puts your name on the list, I'll make sure that your name is picked in the lot-drawing."

"I'll take care of the personnel office, but the lot-drawing has to be done in public. How can you be so sure?"

Wang Wenying whispered in his ear, "What's so difficult about that? I only need to do this and that. . . ."

Much delighted, Jin Man was profuse in his thanks. "If this works out, I'll surely have a handsome thank-you gift for you."

After some more drinking, they rose, paid their bill, and left.

Back in the yamen, Jin Man had dinner prepared after some shopping around and invited Liu Yun, clerk of the personnel office, to whom he expressed his wish. Liu Yun consented. Jin Man took out five taels of silver and, handing it to Liu, said, "This is a small gift, just for you to buy some sweets. After this thing works out, I'll give you five taels more."

With affected demureness, Liu Yun said, "Aren't we brothers? Why stand on such ceremony with me?"

"You can be direct with me," said Jin Man. "If you don't object to the paltriness of the sum, I'll take that to be a great kindness."

"In that case," said Liu Yun, "I'll keep it for now and get something done." So saying, he slipped the silver up his sleeve. Fruit and some food were laid out. They toasted each other back and forth and did not part company until late at night.

The next day, a clerk got wind of this and, gathering together some other clerks, said to Liu Yun, "Mr. Jin is a newcomer who's been here for less than half a year. It's too early for him to want to be treasurer. This will never do. It is up to you whether to pick him or not, but the lot-drawing has to be conducted in public. I'm afraid this thing won't make you look too good either. Don't blame me when that happens!"

"You don't have to yell like that," rejoined Liu Yun. "Be reasonable. He's a nice, popular man who has done absolutely nothing that can be faulted. Even if his name is put on the list of candidates, how likely is it that he will be picked? This is a promise I'm only too glad to give him. If you report the matter, you'll be ruining our friendship with him. People will say we are a bunch of false-hearted crooks."

"In fighting for fame and fortune," said one man, "who cares about friendship or false-heartedness?"

"Hey!" said Liu Yun, "Don't fight with *people.* Fight only your fate. It will be a good thing if you end up being picked. If not, what you said should have been left unsaid. You could have saved your breath."

A few older and wiser men among the crowd, convinced by Liu Yun's logic, commented, "Old Liu, you do have a point, but isn't he overeager? Even if he does land the treasurer's post, he won't know until his term is over if it's a good thing for him or not. So what's the big deal? Whether he gets the job or not isn't worth fighting about. Let's all go our separate ways and tend to our own business." (*Words of the older and wiser.*) Thereupon, the crowd dispersed.

Having heard that there was gossip about him, Jin Man was afraid that his chance might be ruined. Again, he went out to borrow money. Then, he had an eminent literati scholar of the county write to the county magistrate, describing him as a "mature and sensible man of independent means, to whom important tasks can well be entrusted." This was a broad hint to the magistrate, short of saying in so many words that Jin should be entrusted with the treasury.

Let us skip trivialities and come to the day of the lot-drawing. Liu Yun made a list of candidates and showed it to the magistrate. He next had the staff of the magistrate's study write the names on small slips of paper and then showed the slips to the magistrate. Finally, he assigned a janitor to mix the slips of paper together and call the candidates to come up one by one to draw lots. The janitor assigned to roll up the slips of paper and pass them along was none other than Wang Ying, who had already played his tricks. Jin Man picked up the first slip of paper that came to his hand, spread it open, and found it to be the right one.

You may very well ask, how could there be any tricks when the lot-drawing was done in public? Well, the fact of the matter was, when making the list, Liu Yun had followed the ranking order of the six offices of the county yamen: the offices of personnel, revenue, rites, war, justice, and public works. Among the candidates from the office of personnel, some had already served as treasurers, and some were soon leaving office. With these men ruled out, Jin Man, as a senior clerk in the office of revenue, became the first one on the list. When rolling up the slips of paper, Wang Wenying made a secret mark. Jin Man being the first one to go forward and do the picking, wasn't this whole thing as easy as turning over a hand? None of those present had any inkling of what was afoot. Truly,

However righteous the authorities,
The subordinates get to play their tricks.

Upon witnessing Jin Man drawing the right lot, the assembled officials all fell to their knees and entreated the magistrate, "He is too new in his post to be a treasurer. Moreover, for such an important post involving money and grains, we are supposed to write a letter of acknowledgment to higher authorities. If Jin Man becomes the treasurer, we can't very well rush into such an acknowledgment."

"If he is new," said the magistrate, "his name should not have appeared on the list in the first place."

"It was Liu Yun of the personnel office who accepted his bribe and maneuvered to get his name on the list."

"If this is the case, why didn't you report the matter to me earlier? The fact that you waited until he picked the right lot shows all too clearly that you are saying this out of jealousy."

Now that the county magistrate had taken Jin Man's side, no one dared utter another word of objection for fear of a rebuff. The magistrate was only too glad to be doing a favor for a fellow official. Moreover, since the lot-drawing was a public event, no objection could be justified. However jealous they were, there was nothing the clerks could do. Yielding to a great deal of persuasion, Jin Man prepared a wine feast in their honor and engaged a theatrical troupe for the occasion. Only then did they agree to write the letter of acknowledgment of Jin Man's assumption of the post.

The handover of the treasury took place on the first day of the sixth month. Jin Man thanked Liu Yun with the additional five taels of silver he had promised and treated as his benefactors the janitors whose tricks had gotten him his new position. They became even closer than before.

Though he was now in charge of the treasury, there was no tax to collect because, as it was the busy farming season, everything other than farming had ground to a halt. Then, the lack of rain in the seventh and eighth months caused a drought in the autumn. Even though it was not the worst famine ever, the situation was severe enough. Villagers flocked to the county seat to ask for emergency relief. The county magistrate had to go on tours of inspection without knowing what more he could do. In a few months' time, the county treasury was barely able to cover all the expenses.

Time flew. Quite unnoticeably, it was already the eleventh month of the year. The Imperial Bureau of Astronomy, predicting a lunar eclipse on the fifteenth day of the month, issued throughout the land a directive for the populace to hold prayer services. The prefecture relayed the directive to subordinate counties. That very night, the county magistrate assembled local officials, monks, and scholars in the county yamen for a prayer service. According to established practice, it was the treasurer's job to make preparations for a feast in the back hall of the yamen in honor of all those present. With no one to help him, Jin Man paid the kitchen staff to prepare the feast, but he himself dared not leave the treasury. He asked Liu Yun and other janitors to keep an eye on the wine vessels and take care of everything related to the feast. The guests made a few perfunctory bows by way of fulfilling their obligations and then proceeded to the back hall for the feast. The monks were kept in the front hall to play percussion and string instruments. The service lasted until the fourth watch of the night. The dishes had scarcely been cleared away than an announcement came that the new inspector was ready to take up his post. Losing no time, the county magistrate took a boat to the prefectural seat to extend his welcome. Jin Man was kept so busy, first with the feast and then with making arrangements for the boat, that he did not get so much as a wink of sleep the whole night through.

After daybreak, an inventory made of the treasury found four ingots of silver missing. Jin Man thought to himself, "I never left the treasury yesterday. Who could have played some magical trick and stolen them? Maybe they are still around somewhere." A thorough search turned up nothing. Then he panicked. "What bad luck!" he cried in anguish. "How am I going to pay back these two hundred taels of silver? If I don't pay them back, there will be a lawsuit and a scandal. Oh, what am I going to do?"

So saying, he started another search, almost turning the storage house upside down, but not even a shadow of an ingot was seen. He cowered in fear, without the least idea of what to do. By this time, news of the lost treasury silver had spread, and inquiries came pouring in. He had to explain the situation until his mouth ran dry and his tongue fell to pieces. Those who had objected to his assumption of the treasurer's post were overjoyed. With relish, they indulged in sarcastic comments along with many a grimace. Truly,

All gloated over his misfortune;
None gave a helping hand or shared his grief!

Five or six days later, after the county magistrate had returned, escorting the inspector to the county yamen, Jin Man had no choice but to report the loss to the magistrate. Before the magistrate so much as opened his mouth, the clerks standing by spoke up, one after another, "The treasury is his responsibility. Instead of making up for the missing amount out of his own pocket, he tells the magistrate about the loss. He can't be thinking of having the magistrate pay for it?"

Vexed that Jin Man, whom he had defended at the lot-drawing session, had been remiss in his duty, the magistrate said sharply to him, "The treasury is your responsibility. How could any silver be missing when no outsiders have been allowed in? You must have spent the money in some gambling house or brothel, and now you come to me with your lies. I'll spare you from a thrashing today. Pay back the entire amount within ten days. Otherwise, you'll be in for some disciplinary action."

A dejected Jin Man left the county yamen and consulted officers responsible for making arrests. He invited all the officers and their aides to a wineshop for a few drinks. "It is not for my own sake," said he, "that I am asking this favor of all of you today. An ordinary family is not likely to have as many as four ingots of silver. Also, since large ingots are more unwieldy than loose silver, the thief is bound to be exposed. Please do the best you can. I'll offer twenty taels of silver as a reward to anyone who can solve the case and find the culprit as well as the silver."

The officers replied in unison, "We'll try."

One day stretched to three, and three days to nine. All too quickly, the ten days allowed went by. The officers were treated to one feast after another, but to no avail.

The county magistrate summoned Jin Man to his court. "Have you recovered the silver?" he asked.

"I have been on the case with the officers, but no trace has been found."

"I gave you ten days to make the repayment. I'm not going to wait until you solve the case!" He ordered his men, "Take him down for a thrashing!"

With one kowtow after another, Jin Man pleaded for mercy. "I am willing to pay, but please give me another ten days so that I have enough time to sell off my household effects." The magistrate granted him the ten days.

Jin Man had never embezzled when he was treasurer. And now, out of the blue, he had to scrape together two hundred taels of silver, which would be quite an effort for him. Even if he sold all the jewelry and clothes in the house, he still would not come up with enough money. He had a young maidservant named Golden Apricot who, at fifteen years of age, was quite fair to look upon. She had

A well-shaped nose, a charming face,
White teeth, red lips, trim eyebrows, lovely eyes,
Black, cloudlike hair that hung down to the floor,
Fingers slender and pointed, skin smooth and glossy,
Verily a sweet budding flower,
A peach blossom before full bloom.

Mr. Jin loved this girl as he did his own daughter and was hoping to offer her in a couple of years as a concubine or a maidservant to some rich young man in exchange for a hundred or so taels of silver. To dispose of her at this moment of crisis for less than she was worth would be too much of a pity.

Turning his thoughts this way and that, he found himself with no better alternative than to mortgage his house, for which he got two hundred taels of silver. He had the silver cast into four ingots and, after having them weighed in the presence of witnesses in the magistrate's court, put them under seal in the treasury warehouse. After being told to be more careful in the future, Clerk Jin gloomily locked up the treasury door and returned to his official residence. Sitting by the door all alone, he brooded over what had happened, growing more and more furious as he did so. The whole thing had cost him so much money, and all for what? Why all this bad luck?

He was still in this somber mood when Xiutong, a page boy in his household, entered from outside in a half-inebriated state. The young man recoiled a few steps at the sight of his master. Mr. Jin lashed out, "You stupid ass! How could you have been merrily drinking when your master is so miserable? Where did you get the extra money for wine when I don't have a penny?"

"I've been feeling low these last couple of days, seeing how unhappy you are, Father. I often hear people say that wine can drown all sorrows. As I happen to have saved a few mace of silver, I went to buy some wine to take my mind off all this. If you don't have money for wine, Father, I've left enough at the wineshop for another flask. I'll go get it for you."

Jin Man snapped, "Who wants anything from you?" As a matter of fact, it was the custom in Suzhou to address all government clerks as "Uncle." Xiutong, now in his twenties, had been sold to the Jin family at the age of nine and, having grown up in the Jin household as an adopted son, called Jin Man "Father." It was out of filial piety that he offered to drown Jin's sorrows with wine. But human hearts are different. His offer, contrary to what he had expected, aroused his master's suspicion and almost led to his death. Indeed,

When the old turtle's meat won't cook tender,
Innocent mulberries are cut down to feed the fire.

After Xiutong went into the house, Clerk Jin was suddenly struck by a thought: "How could outsiders have come in and stolen anything when I was wide awake all through the night? Only Xiutong came in a few times to fetch and carry. Could he have committed the theft? But this boy has been following me around ever since he was a child. He's been such a help to me, and I've never had any reason to suspect him of theft. How could he have suddenly become a thief?" Then he thought again, "This boy drinks. All those who steal start out of a love for drinking and gambling. He could very well have incurred a large wine bill but has no means of paying for it, and at the sight of large ingots of silver there for the taking, how could he not be tempted? Otherwise, where could he have gotten so much money to spend on wine?" (*Vivid description of the twists and turns of his thoughts.*) Then again, another thought struck him: "No, it's not him. If he were the thief, he would have taken just a few pieces of loose silver. He wouldn't have had the audacity to take large ingots. Even if he had, where could he have gotten them off his hands? He couldn't very well leave them in a banking house and withdraw from the account every time he needs money, because that would have attracted attention. Even if he did do that, he could only deposit one ingot and leave the other three at home. Let me search his bed tonight, and everything will come to light." But again, he thought otherwise: "That isn't the way to go, either. Had he indeed stolen so much silver, he would have deposited them with his parents instead of keeping them with him. If my search turns up nothing, I'll be held up to ridicule, and if he's not the culprit, I'll have wronged him and broken his heart. Oh, yes, I have it! They say there's a Priest Mo in the city who has the power to summon celestial warriors to solve cases and get at the truth. He's now living in Jade Peak Temple. Why don't I invite him over and have him solve my problem?" (*This story was written for the express purpose of debunking the myth about the magic power of Daoist priests.*)

The next day, Jin Man rose early and instructed Xiutong to buy some candles, paper horses, and fruit, wine, and meat to offer to celestial warriors in gratitude, while he himself made his way to Jade Peak Temple to invite Priest Mo.

Now, among Clerk Jin's former neighbors was an idler named Ji the Seventh, who happened to catch sight of Xiutong walking sulkily down the street, laden with purchases. When Ji asked Xiutong what was bothering him, Xiutong replied, "How laughable! My father must be under some evil star to be thinking of doing such an absurd thing! He has already paid for the loss of two hundred taels of silver out of his own pocket. Shouldn't he have just accepted his bad luck and let the matter drop? But he listened to some stupid advice and is hiring some kind of priest to summon celestial warriors. After fooling around and gorging himself on the food and wine today, that swine of a priest will surely also ask for payment tomorrow. As the saying goes, 'Three jars of wine are gone before anything is done.' Paying for the loss was no easy job, and now he's adding interest to the capital. What a senseless thing to do! Mr. Ji, do you think there can be any real immortals among those priests? Why, *I* am the one who can use the good wine and meat, so as to do my father better service! To think of wasting all the good stuff on that swine of a priest! Will he even say one word of thanks?"

At this point, Clerk Jin was seen returning from his trip to Jade Peak Temple. At the sight of his master, Xiutong turned away. Jin Man exchanged greetings with Ji the Seventh and asked him, "What were you and Xiutong talking about?"

Not one to believe in celestial warriors, Ji repeated Xiutong's words, adding, "That young man is not without good sense."

Jin Man fell silent as he reflected on what he had heard. Ji the Seventh did not think more of what he had said, little knowing that he had added to Jin Man's suspicions. (*Nothing would not arouse his suspicions.*)

The master's suspicious mind
Jeopardized the young man's life.

Clerk Jin said good-bye to Ji the Seventh and returned to the county yamen. What he had just heard filled his mind with apprehension. "If he were not guilty, he wouldn't have objected to having celestial warriors on the case. And he bad-mouthed the priest, too!" Without saying anything out loud, he was assailed by suspicions.

In a short while, Priest Mo arrived and had an altar laid out. Trying to induce a celestial warrior to possess a little schoolboy from next door, Priest Mo put on an act, bowing to the constellations, chanting incantations, and drawing magic figures. The little boy started moving his limbs and assumed the posture of someone holding a sword, saying in a voice too sonorous to belong to a little boy, "I, General Deng, have stepped down from the altar."

Believing that a celestial warrior had indeed descended from heaven, Jin Man made one kowtow after another and implored the warrior, in all earnestness, to bring the thief to justice.

The celestial warrior said, shaking his head, "I am not supposed to reveal anything." Jin Man fell to kowtowing again and begged the warrior to reveal the thief's name. Priest Mo laid out another spiritual tablet and ordered in a harsh voice,

"Ghosts and deities have nothing to hide;
Retributions are all in the open.
To every question, an answer!
For every answer, quick action!"

With Jin Man kowtowing nonstop, the celestial warrior said, "Dismiss everyone else present, and I will tell you." The hall was at this point filled with yamen employees and family members of the clerks, all gathered there to watch the spectacle of Priest Mo summoning celestial warriors on behalf of Jin Man. With courteous words, Jin Man asked them to leave. Only Xiutong stayed behind in case his services were needed. The celestial warrior exclaimed, "This hall is not yet cleared of all those who have no business here!" Thereupon, Priest Mo said to Clerk Jin, "Send Xiutong away as well."

The celestial warrior told Jin Man to hold out his hand. Jin Man fell to his knees and stretched out his left hand. The celestial warrior dipped a finger in wine and wrote the two characters *xiutong* in Jin Man's palm. "Remember this!" he thundered.

Jin Man gave a violent start. This tallied with his own suspicions. Yet, not being absolutely sure, he kowtowed again and prayed silently, "I've been supporting Xiutong for more than ten years. He has never stolen anything. If he is indeed the culprit this time, I'll surely put him under strict interrogation, but this is no trivial matter. I pray the celestial general to give the matter more consideration and refrain from following a human's train of thought."

Again, the celestial warrior dipped a finger in wine and wrote the characters *xiutong* on the table. With the same finger, he then traced the same two characters in the air. Jin Man was now fully convinced. Not a doubt remained in his mind. Right away, Priest Mo drew a magic figure to end the session. Just as quickly, the little boy fell backward. After he was helped up, he gradually regained consciousness and, when asked, professed to know nothing about what had happened.

Jin Man gave the priest the sacrificial offerings he had prepared for the celestial warrior. Under the pretext of escorting the priest out, he went posthaste to the police officers. The sheriff, known as Second Brother Zhang, asked for an explanation. Mr. Jin gave him the whole account of what Xiutong had said and how the celestial warrior had written Xiutong's name three times. Even the sheriff was more than half convinced, but unwilling to shoulder responsibility for a case he had not sought, he declined, saying, "No charge has been made officially. Torture is hardly in order in this case."

Being a man familiar with the ways of the yamen, how could Jin Man not understand what was expected of him? He said, "I'll take all responsibility for this matter. I won't implicate any of you. If you apply torture and force him to produce the stolen silver, I will give you twenty taels of silver, not a mace less."

Sheriff Zhang gave in and, along with his brother, known as Fourth Brother Zhang, and an assistant, followed Clerk Jin home. It being about the first watch of the night, Xiutong had put the hall in order, eaten his supper, and, lantern in hand, was on his way out of the yamen to meet his master. He was barely outside the gate when he ran into three or four officers, who threw a hemp rope around his neck. Without allowing him one word of explanation, they dragged him all the way to a courier post in a deserted place in the suburbs. Before Xiutong could open his mouth, an officer slapped him hard on the shoulder with a steel ruler, roaring, "A fine thing you did!"

Xiutong cried out in pain, "What did I do?"

"Where are the four ingots of silver you stole from the treasury? To whom did you give them? Your master has already learned the whole truth of the matter and has handed you over to us. Now, out with the truth, if you want to be spared the pain!"

Xiutong burst into loud wails, calling on heaven and earth to be his witnesses. There is an ancient saying:

Those in the right speak with force;
Those wrongly accused raise their voices.

The fact was, Xiutong was not guilty. Throughout the torture, he kept his teeth clenched and refused to admit any wrongdoing, despite the unbearable pain. *The Laws of the Great Ming Dynasty* had an article that prohibited unauthorized torture during the interrogation of suspects. If the interrogation led to the arrest of the real criminal, the interrogators could claim credit. If the suspect refused to confess and had to be released, the suspect could sue the interrogators and charge them with framing an innocent person. The punishment for this crime was equal to the punishment for whatever crime the suspect had been accused of. After hanging Xiutong up, thrashing him, and applying finger squeezers without getting a confession, the officers began to panic. They consulted one another and decided to resort to the two remaining tools of torture—the "king of hell" hoop, which, when tightened across the forehead, could make the eyeballs pop out about an inch, and the iron-knee pants, a pair of rods filled with pieces of crushed stone that caused excruciating pain when the rods were tightened over the knees. These were the cruelest instruments of torture.

With the hoop across his forehead, Xiutong went through several rounds of fainting and reviving. At last, in a moment of haziness, he admitted to the theft, but as soon as he woke up, he reverted to his protests of innocence. When the officers applied the iron-knee pants, Xiutong found the pain more than he could bear. In desperation, he said, "I stole the silver ingots in a moment of greed and hid them under the bed of my brother-in-law, Li Da. I have not touched them since then."

The officers carried Xiutong on a door plank to Sheriff Zhang's home and fed him porridge to help him recover. After the much awaited daybreak came, they went to Jin to make their report. By this time, Xiutong was on the verge of death, unable to walk or even crawl.

Clerk Jin hired a boat and joined the officers on a trip to Li Da's home to search for the silver. Li Da lived in the countryside, not far from Xiutong's parents' home. When the officers arrived, Li Da was not at home. Xiutong's older sister was so frightened that her face turned the color of earth. Not knowing what the commotion was all about, she opened the back door and fled to her parents' home. The officers entered the bedchamber and moved the bed, only to find the ground firm and solid with no signs of having been dug. They knew immediately that Xiutong had made up the confession, but Jin Man still insisted on digging with hoes. After they had dug more than one foot deep into the ground without finding anything, they said, "We'll have to turn this place upside down." They rummaged through the chests and trunks and searched throughout the house, but there was no trace of a silver ingot to be seen.

Jin Man could do nothing more than return with the officers to question Xiutong personally. With tears pouring like rain, Xiutong replied, "I did not do it, but you put me to such horrible torture to make me confess that I couldn't take it anymore. And yet, I couldn't bring myself to name other people, so I had to say *I* did it and made up all that nonsense about hiding the silver under my brother-in-law's bed. Father has supported me ever since I was nine years old. Being now in my twenties, I have never ever done the least wrong in the household. A few days ago, it made my heart ache to see Father repay the treasury out of his own pocket. I felt worse when I saw how Father believed in a charlatan priest and spent money on a ritual to summon celestial warriors. I never thought Father would suspect me. The only thing I owe Father now is death. I have nothing further to say." (*What sad words!*) This said, he fainted. After the officers' cries brought him back to consciousness, he sobbed unceasingly. Jin also felt wretched.

In a little while, Xiutong's parents and his brother-in-law Li Da arrived. At the sight of Xiutong lying on a door plank, breathing his last and with bruises all over him, they burst into tears and ran to the county yamen to cry out their grievances.

The county magistrate happened to be in session. After listening to the complaints, he immediately sent for Jin Man and said to him, "You lost some silver of the treasury through your own carelessness. How could you have colluded with the arresting officers and murdered an innocent man through unauthorized torture?"

Jin Man replied, "Having depleted my own resources to pay back the treasury, I of course had to investigate and get to the bottom of the matter. I engaged a Priest Mo known for his skill in summoning celestial warriors. A celestial warrior descended from the altar and wrote Xiutong's name three times. Xiutong himself also had said things that sounded suspicious to me. That's why I believed the celestial warrior. Apart from this servant of mine, I have no other suspects. I did this out of necessity rather than choice. I didn't mean to hurt him."

The county magistrate knew that repaying the missing silver had cost Jin dearly, but with the case unsolved and pressed by Xiutong's parents' constant complaints, he was at a loss as to what to do. It being already the eighteenth day of the last month of the year, he said, "There are too many things to be done before the end of the year. Let us wait until after the tenth day of the new year before I take over the case and find the real culprit."

Everybody present had no choice but to leave. Jin Man returned home with a guilty conscience, afraid that Xiutong would die. He asked Xiutong's parents to stay at his residence to take care of their son. He also sent for a physician and provided Xiutong with large portions of wine and meat every day, but Xiutong's parents still wept endlessly and kept up a constant stream of complaints. Truly,

A green dragon and a white tiger[3]
Bring either joy or woe, when together.

Let us turn our attention to the officers, who, panicking when they heard that the county magistrate had sided with Xiutong's parents, consulted one another, saying, "We put that fellow through such severe torture without getting a confession from him. He'll surely stick to his story when he's tried at the county court. And if he does refuse to confess, we'll be in for punishment because we put him through unauthorized torture." They set up an image of the city god in the treasury and, with candles lit and incense burning, prayed to the image every day. At night, they slept in the treasury with Jin and prayed together for a response from the city god. Clerk Jin could hardly avoid spending some money on the officers.

On New Year's eve, the county magistrate took careful stock of the inventory and entrusted matters of the treasury to a new treasurer. Jin Man was relieved of all his duties, but with the case of the theft still unsolved, he and Sheriff Zhang asked the new treasurer to let Second Brother Zhang sleep in the treasury. Being a native of the county and a good friend of Jin's, the new treasurer readily gave his consent. That night, Jin Man prepared some incense, paper, and sacrificial beef, lamb, and pork and brought them to the warehouse to offer to the city god. The ritual over, he offered the food and wine to the new treasurer and Second Brother Zhang. After three cups, the new treasurer said that he had to attend to some domestic affairs and asked Jin Man to take care of things for him. Since it was New Year's eve, Jin Man thought it better not to insist that he stay. After checking the seals and locks on the cabinets, the new treasurer gave Jin Man the key to the warehouse and left with a word of thanks.

A few more cups later, Jin Man also rose and said to Second Brother Zhang, "It being New Year's eve, and tomorrow New Year's Day, please drink as much as you want and have an inspiring dream, but I have to ask to be excused." So saying, he closed the warehouse door after him, locked it, and went home, carrying the key with him. Thus locked in the warehouse, Second Brother said to himself with a sigh, "On such a festive occasion, no married couple stays apart, except luckless me, guarding the warehouse for them!"

Feeling melancholy, he served himself one cup of wine after another, and before he knew it, he had drunk himself into a stupor. Without even bothering to take off his clothes, he lay down and fell asleep.

At the fourth watch of the night, he saw in his dream a divine being kicking him with a booted foot, saying, "The silver is there, in a gourd that Chen Dashou put on top of the cabinet."

Waking up with a start, Sheriff Zhang hastily clambered to his feet and groped across the top of the warehouse cabinets, but no gourd was found. "Do divine beings also play tricks on people? Or is it just my nerves?"

Soon he drifted off to sleep again, only to dream again. This time, the deity said, "The silver is right there in the gourd. Why don't you take it?"

Sheriff Zhang woke up again in alarm. Sitting on the bed, he listened to the strikes of the night-watch drum. He then rose and pushed open the window to let in the first faint light of dawn. He looked back at the cabinets, top to bottom, but saw nothing placed on top. He was about to report the matter to Jin when he remembered that the door was locked from the outside. He saw nothing for it but to go back to sleep.

A few moments later, there came into his hearing the clamor of voices as well as drum music. It was the county magistrate, accompanied by an assembly of subordinates, on his way to the Confucian temple to offer incense in celebration of the new year. When it got lighter, the new treasurer opened the door and came in to get red paper and the seal, Jin Man having already returned the key to him. Impatient with the waiting, Sheriff Zhang put on his hat and rushed out of the warehouse.

By this time, the county magistrate had returned to the yamen and, with the assembled officials taking their assigned places, was ready to call the court to order. Jin Man, neatly attired in an official's costume, stood respectfully among the other officials, at the service of the magistrate. Sheriff Zhang walked up to him, pulled him to one side, and told him about his dreams. "This extraordinary thing happened twice in a row," he added. "That's why I rushed over here to report to you. You may want to check if there's a man called Chen Dashou in this county." Having said that, Sheriff Zhang returned home, and there we shall leave him.

After paying his respects to the county magistrate, Jin Man kowtowed four times to the image of the city god in the treasury warehouse before he returned for lunch. Instead of going out to pay New Year calls, he stayed in the county yamen, searching the registry books for Chen Dashou's name, but after three days of searching intensively through all current and former employees—including clerks, scribes, officers, janitors, prison wardens, and night watchmen—no Chen Dashou was found. Having missed all the usual festive feasts on account of these three days of futile work, he was so upset that, his face flushed with anger, he went to reproach Sheriff Zhang for lying to him. Sheriff Zhang retorted, "I did have those dreams, unless the divine being was playing tricks on me."

Jin Man recalled what had happened a few days ago with the celestial warrior who lied even after taking the trouble to descend the altar. Compared with that, how trustworthy could a few words said in a dream be? So Jin Man put the matter out of his thoughts.

Two days later, on the fifth day of the first month of the new year, it was the custom of the Suzhou region for every household to make sacrificial offerings to the god of wealth. No business was to be done on that day until after the sacrificial meal was eaten. Jin Man was at home, eating the sacrificial meal, when Lu You'en, an old janitor of the yamen, came to pay a New Year call. "Uncle Jin," he called out, "Happy New Year! Let me share your sacrificial meal!"

"Brother," said Jin. "I couldn't very well invite you over for just another sacrificial meal, but I'm so glad you are here! Please have a few drinks with me!" Right away, he told his wife to heat up a jar of wine and set out whatever food they had in the house in the way of fish and pork and started toasting Mr. Lu.

In the course of their conversation, Lu said, "Uncle Jin, how is the case of the theft coming along?"

Jin shook his head and said, "I don't have a clue!"

"As they say, 'To get a thief, ask the police.' Offer the police officers a handsome reward, and they'll get the thief for you, even if the thief is on wings."

"I did offer them twenty taels of silver. Too bad they're not competent enough to claim the money from me."

"If someone has found the thief and offers you the information, will you still be willing to part with the twenty taels of silver?"

"Why would I not be?"

"Uncle Jin, if you really give me the twenty taels, I will produce the thief."

"My good brother, if you really can do that, you'll be helping me close the file on this case and let Xiutong off the hook. My good brother, you'd better be an eyewitness. I'm not going to put up with more riddles!"

"How would I dare say anything if I wasn't an eyewitness?"

With alacrity, Mr. Jin took off his hat, from which he drew out a gold ear pick weighing one eighth of a mace. He handed it to Lu You'en, saying, "This little thing will serve as a token. If you can really produce the evidence, even if I'm left with only twenty taels of silver, I'll give it all to you, not to speak of more if I have any."

"I shouldn't demand anything from you, but as today is the fifth day of the month, I deserve a little windfall."

Lu You'en being a janitor senior enough to wear an official hat, he inserted the ear pick in his hairnet and said, "Uncle Jin, please close the door and let me tell you the whole story."

Jin Man closed the door, and the two men sat down, face-to-face, for a long talk. Truly,

> *You've worn out iron shoes on a long, fruitless search,*
> *And now you hit upon it without a stroke of work.*

It so happened that Lu You'en had an eighteen-year-old next-door neighbor, Hu Mei by name, who was also a janitor and was living with his widowed brother-in-law by the name of Lu Zhigao. Hu Mei's good looks attracted much amorous attention, but he had been a well-behaved young man kept in line by his older sister after the death of his parents. However, after his sister's death, he had no good example to follow in the person of his brother-in-law and strayed into a life of gambling, drinking, and womanizing.

One day in the last third of the previous month, while Lu You'en was out, his wife heard the sound of hammering next door. She did not think it out of the ordinary the first time she heard it, but afterward, every time Lu You'en was out, she heard the neighbor's door being bolted and then loud hammering. As soon as Lu returned home, the noise stopped.

On New Year's eve, the husband and wife were drinking when she brought up the subject, wondering what the neighbors could have been up to. Lu grew suspicious. After New Year's Day, he stayed at home the following two days as well and listened with ear cocked, but all was quiet. On the fourth day of the new year, he left the house, pretending to be going out to pay a New Year call on a relative. Instead, he stopped at a distance from the house. After the neighbor's door was bolted, he sneaked back home. Sure enough, he heard the sound of hammering coming from the other side of the wall. Peeping through a crack in the wall, he saw Hu Mei and Lu Zhigao squatting on the floor, Hu Mei holding a large ingot of silver and Lu Zhigao chiseling the edge off the ingot with an ax.

When he ran into them that evening, Lu asked, "What is it that you're chopping away at?"

Hu Mei reddened but didn't say anything. Lu Zhigao replied, "We have a good bar of iron, a family heirloom, that we are trying to fashion into a kitchen knife."

Lu thought to himself, "What else can it be but the famous lost silver? How else could the likes of these two be in possession of such an ingot of silver?"

He kept the knowledge to himself that night and went to report to Jin the next day, expecting him to be at home making offerings to the god of wealth.

After listening to his account, Jin Man went with Lu to look for Second Brother Zhang but failed to find him at home. That night, he kept Lu You'en in his house.

The next day, the sixth day of the month, they rose bright and early and went again to Second Brother Zhang's home. This time, they got him, and along with Fourth Brother, the company headed for Hu Mei's house, only to find the door locked with no one inside. Lu You'en called for his wife and asked her what had happened. She said, "Yesterday I heard them talking about hiring a boat to Hangzhou to make incense offerings. Both of them left this morning just a short while ago. Even if the boat has set out, it shouldn't have gotten far."

The four men raced off. They had just gained Four Horse Bridge when they saw Wang Liu'er, a boatman, buying wine and rice by the bridge. The yamen employees often hired his small pleasure boat and were therefore on quite good terms with him. "Mr. Jin," said Wang Liu'er, "how early you got up today!"

"Liu'er," said Jin, "where are you going, buying wine and rice so early in the morning?"

"I have patrons going to Hangzhou on business for a month or two."

"Who are they?" asked Jin Man, patting Liu'er on the shoulder.

Wang Liu'er whispered in his ear, "It's Janitor Hu and his relative Lu."

"Are they in the boat at this moment?"

"Lu is, but Hu is still on shore getting a prostitute."

At these words, Sheriff Zhang threw his hemp rope over Wang Liu and held him tight. "What did I do wrong?" protested Wang Liu'er.

Jin Man replied, "This has nothing to do with you. You just lead us to the boat. You'll be set free soon enough."

Depositing the wine and rice in the shop, Liu'er led the four men down the bridge, their eight hands ready to catch the thieves. Truly,

For those who tend to go astray,
Regrets always come too late.

Lu Zhigao was leaning against the railing in the boat, looking forward to having some fun with the prostitute Hu Mei was supposed to bring back, but his heart gave a jump when he caught sight of Jin with Wang Liu'er in tow, a rope around his neck. Feeling that something was wrong, he leaped ashore, leaving his bedding and personal effects behind, and ran as fast as his legs could carry him. Wang Liu'er said, pointing at him, "That man wearing a white cap of mourning is Lu."

The four men gave chase, crying, "Stop the thief who stole from the treasury!" Lu Zhigao panicked and slipped. The men were immediately upon him. Throwing a rope around his neck, they asked, "Where's Hu Mei?"

"He's with the prostitute Ugly Sister Liu."

The men made Lu Zhigao lead the way to Ugly Sister Liu's house, but Hu Mei, having heard the hue and cry, was so frightened that without saying anything to the prostitute, he had taken to his heels, destination unknown. The men had to take Ugly Sister Liu along with Lu Zhigao to Second Brother Zhang's home.

A search of Lu's body turned up nothing, but in his stocking was found the remains of an ingot of silver, its two protruding ends as well as the edging all chiseled off. When Second Brother Zhang threatened to take him to a courier station in a deserted place outside the city for torture, Lu Zhigao said, "Spare me the torture. I confess. In the eleventh month of last year, Hu Mei and I gambled ourselves into more debt than we could ever pay back. Hu Mei said to me, 'There are a lot of silver ingots in the county treasury, sitting there and doing nothing.' I told him to bring a few home for our use. On the fifteenth night of the month, when there was a lunar eclipse, he stole four ingots, two for each of us. We didn't dare allow them to be seen in public, so we had to chip off small pieces. There's another ingot hidden at home in a rice bucket covered up with some tattered clothes. The other two are with Hu Mei."

"But that night, I didn't sleep even a wink," said Jin Man. "How did he manage to steal them? What a neat job he did!"

"He entered the warehouse several times without being able to do anything because you were sitting there, but your page boy happened to knock over some sesame oil when he was getting a candle from a cabinet inside, and you went to take a look. That was when Hu Mei made his move."

Having obtained a confession, the men gave up the idea of torturing Lu. When Xiutong, who was recovering in Second Brother Zhang's home, still incapable of movement, heard that the real thief had been identified and the silver found, he cursed through clenched teeth, "That goddamn scoundrel! He stole the silver but brought *me* all this suffering! There's no one to do right by me anyway, so let me bite off a piece of his flesh and feel vindicated!" He struggled to get up from his straw bed, but, alas, any movement was far beyond him. The men all tried to pacify him and calmed him down. As rage turned to grief, he broke into sobs.

Feeling apologetic, Clerk Jin found himself also in tears. He hastened to have Xiutong carried to his residence to be nursed back to health, whereas he himself went with the men to Hu Mei's house and unlocked the door to conduct a house search. They turned over the rice bucket, and a silver ingot with the edging chipped off rolled out with the rice.

That day, the men brought Lu Zhigao to the county yamen and reported the matter to the county magistrate, who, after having the silver examined, realized that this time, they had the right man. By his order, Lu Zhigao was given fifty strokes of the rod. His confession was put on file, and he was scheduled to be sentenced together with Hu Mei when the latter was caught. A wanted circular was issued ordering the arrest of Hu Mei. As for Wang Liu'er the boatman and Ugly Sister Liu, they were released on bail because they were not involved in the case nor had they taken any share of the stolen silver. The two confiscated ingots of silver should, by rights, be returned to the treasury, but since Jin Man had already repaid the treasury by mortgaging his property, the ingots were given to him in accord with the relevant rules. (*A good magistrate.*) No one in the Kunshan region was not impressed by the fairness of this ruling. Indeed,

With good rulers at the imperial court,
Heaven gives its blessings to the land.
With good officials in the government,
People live in peace and contentment.

Now, Jin took the edgeless ingots to a silversmith's shop on his way home and had them broken into loose pieces of silver. In keeping with his promise, he gave sixteen taels of it to Lu You'en. To Second Brother Zhang, he gave ten taels, promising more if Hu Mei was captured. The next day, Jin Man waited until the county magistrate entered the court and bowed thankfully to the latter. Out of compassion for Jin Man, the magistrate hated Hu Mei with great intensity. He announced a reward of ten taels of silver and ordered the police to hunt down the man within a set deadline.

Half a year later, Fourth Brother Zhang was in Shuanglin of Huzhou on some business when, passing by Gate Lou of Suzhou on his boat, he suddenly caught sight of Hu Mei walking by Gate Lou pond. Without losing one moment, Fourth Brother Zhang pulled the boat over to the bank and went ashore, shouting, "Brother Hu, slow down!" Turning around to look, Hu Mei recognized Zhang as an officer from the yamen. He took to his heels and dived into a tofu shop. Before the old tofu seller could cry out, Hu Mei took out a big ingot of silver, white as snow, shining as if polished by a waterstone, and, throwing it on the straw lid of a wine jar, said, "Let me hide here. If I can pass tonight safely, I'll share the silver with you, half and half."

Coveting the silver, the old man quickly took it and motioned Hu Mei to a hiding place. By the time Fourth Brother Zhang reached the corner, Hu Mei was already out of sight. A meddlesome idler pointed at the tofu shop. When Fourth Brother Zhang stepped into the shop and asked for Hu Mei, the old man insisted that no such man was there. Fourth Brother Zhang looked all around the room, and, sure enough, no Hu Mei was to be seen. Zhang took out a piece of silver weighing about three to four mace and gave it to the old man, saying, "That young fellow is a janitor employed by Kunshan County. He's a fugitive wanted by the county magistrate for stealing from the county treasury. If you know what's good for you, bring him out, and this silver will be yours to buy some goodies with. If you hide him, I'll report you to the magistrate, and you'll be charged with abetting a criminal."

The old man was so frightened that he dared not take the offer of silver but pointed upward with his hand. What do you suppose he pointed at?

Beneath the ceiling but above the floor,
A good hiding place, if undisclosed.

The old man and his wife occupied only one room, which doubled as a workshop for making tofu and white wine. Left with no space in which to sleep, they had put up a wooden frame for a makeshift bed. To reach the bed, they had to climb up a short ladder behind which stood a cabinet. Hu Mei was hiding there quite safely when Fourth Brother Zhang, with one swipe of his hand, dragged him down and trussed him up with hemp rope. "You swine! Where did you hide the silver?" said Zhang.

Trembling all over, Hu Mei replied, "I spent one ingot. The other one is on the lid of the wine jar."

Not daring to conceal anything any longer, the old man took the silver from the wine jar. Fourth Brother Zhang asked the old man, "What's your name?"

The old man was too afraid to answer. A man nearby answered, "He's Chen Dashou."

Fourth Brother Zhang nodded and placed the three or four mace of silver he had promised on the old man's counter. With Hu Mei in tow, he took a boat and returned to Kunshan County before the night was out. Truly,

> *Do nothing that would trouble the conscience;*
> *The wicked will get their fill of torment!*

By this time, Lu Zhigao had died of illness in prison, which greatly saddened the county magistrate. Moreover, many clerks who were buddies with Hu Mei approached Jin Man to ask for leniency for the young man. Head Janitor Wang Wenying succumbed to their pleas and also came to put in a good word for Hu Mei with Jin Man. Remembering the favor Wang Wenying had done him at the lot-drawing session, Jin Man acquiesced, ostensibly to please the many petitioners. To the county magistrate he said, "Though Hu Mei did the stealing, it was, in fact, his brother-in-law who gave him the idea. Moreover, the stolen silver is not a significant amount. Please be lenient in your settlement of the case."

Placing the entire responsibility for the crime on the dead man alone, the county magistrate sentenced Hu Mei to nothing more than thirty thrashings of the rod as a warning against abetting a criminal act. The one ingot left was also given to Jin Man, who, in his turn, gave ten taels of silver to Fourth Brother Zhang as a reward.

Zhang's account of what had happened at the old man's tofu shop startled everyone, because it evoked memories of Second Brother Zhang's dream of the year before in which a city god told him that Chen Dashou had put the silver in a gourd on top of a cabinet. The word for "gourd" being *hulu*—*hu* as in Hu Mei, *lu* as in Lu Zhigao—"Chen Dashou" being the name of the old man, and Hu Mei being found on top of a shop cabinet, the divine being's statement was borne out to the last word. Indeed,

> *An evil deed done in the dark*
> *Is seen as clear as lightning by the gods.*

A few days later, pigs and sheep were carried to the city god temple to be offered as gifts of thanks.

Jin Man felt bad about having wronged Xiutong who, a most honest and loyal man with no complaints even when on the verge of death, had gone through so much suffering for no misdemeanor other than a weakness for wine. Jin Man showed his gratitude by changing the young man's name to Jin Xiu and, in giving the young man his own surname, treating Xiutong as his son. He also betrothed his beautiful maidservant Golden Apricot to the young man and held the wedding after Xiutong regained his health. Jin Xiu's parents were also greatly delighted. Later, as Jin Man did not have a son of his own, Jin Xiu inherited the family property. Jin Junior also attained a post in the yamen and came to be known as "Little Clerk Jin." After passing the three triennial examinations required for incumbent government clerical employees, he rose to be a registrar in the Surveillance Bureau.

A poet of later times had this to say in lament over the wrong inflicted on Jin Xiu:

Use none whom you suspect; suspect none whom you use;
Turn a deaf ear to idle gossip!
Believe only what you see with your own eyes!
Too many injustices have been done!

16

The Young Lady Gives the Young Man a Gift of Money

Who says the world will run short of stories to tell?
The ups and downs of life all vanish in the end.
However free you claim your life to be,
You're no match for the swan geese above the clouds.
Before you know it, the eyebrows turn snowy;
In a trice, the color in the cheeks fades away.
Sad and forlorn, I cast a look around;
The bleak evening woods stir in the mournful wind.

The above eight-line poem was written by Wang Chuhou of Huayang County, Chengdu Prefecture, in Xichuan, lamenting a few white hairs he saw in the mirror when he was approaching sixty. All beings in this world progress from youth to the prime of life to old age. No one is exempt from this eternal law of nature. Other things may go from white to black, but hair and beards go the other way around, from black to white.

A certain Prefect Liu, who was in the habit of wearing flowers in his hair, composed a lyric poem to the tune of "The Tower with the Wine Pavilion" at the sight of his graying hair in the mirror:

A carefree man with a love for the charms of spring,
I revel in the beauty of flower-lined paths.
The years go by, but the heart remains young;
The flowers sit heavy all over my hat,
Over temples that are frosty white, alas!
Some advise dyeing, some counsel plucking,
But dyeing and plucking, to what avail?
I once feared a death before my time,
But here I still am, past the prime of my life.
I'll keep the white to adorn my last years.

Now I propose to tell of a rich man more than sixty years of age who lived in Kaifeng Prefecture in Bianzhou [or Bianjing], the Eastern Capital. His hair was all snowy white, but instead of reconciling himself to his age, he indulged in the pleasures of the flesh until he dissipated all his family fortune and almost ended up a ghost in an alien land. What was the name of this man and what did he do? Truly,

The dust of traffic will never settle;
The bonds of love easily fade away.

The story goes that on Jieshen Street in Bianzhou, the Eastern Capital, there was a general store owned by a Squire Zhang Shilian, a childless man in his sixties, living alone after his wife had passed away. With personal wealth amounting to a hundred thousand strings of cash, he employed two managers to take care of his shop. Suddenly one day, Squire Zhang said to the two men, sighing and pounding his chest, "Why would a childless old man like me need all this money?"

The two men replied, "Why don't you get yourself a new wife so as to have a child, be it a boy or a girl, to continue your family line?"

Delighted, Squire Zhang immediately sent for Matchmakers Zhang and Li. Now, about those matchmakers:

Their eloquence matches up couples;
Their words tie up the marriage knot.
They tend to solitary phoenixes;
They take care of all who sleep alone.
With tricks, they drag over the Jade Maiden;
With sweet words, they seize the Golden Boy by the waist.[1]
They make the Weaving Maiden sick with longing;[2]
They urge Chang'e the Moon Goddess to leave the moon.

Squire Zhang said, "Being childless, I would like to ask you a favor: Please find me a wife."

Without saying anything out loud, Matchmaker Zhang thought to herself, "He's so old and rickety. There's no way I can find him a wife. But what shall I say in reply?"

Nudging Matchmaker Zhang, Matchmaker Li said, "That will be easy to do!"

As they turned to go, Squire Zhang stopped them, saying, "I have three conditions." It was these three conditions that made him

A poor wretch who could have had a good life;
A ghost in a strange land with no grave for his bones.

"What three conditions?" asked the matchmakers.

"Listen! First, she must have better than average looks. Second, she must be from a family of the same class as mine. Third, since I have a hundred thousand strings of cash, she must bring over a dowry of equal value."

Laughing inwardly, the two matchmakers replied, without meaning what they said, "These three conditions can be easily met." With that, they took leave of Squire Zhang.

On their way back, Matchmaker Zhang said to Li, "If we do pull off this match, we'll make about a hundred strings of cash, but his conditions are much too unreasonable. Wouldn't those who meet all three conditions be better off with a young man than this ancient one? Does he think his beard is white because it's coated with white sugar?"

"But I do have someone in mind," said Matchmaker Li. "It just so happens that she does have better than average looks and is from the same class as he is."

"Which family is she from?"

"I'm talking about Pacification Commissioner Wang's concubine," said Matchmaker Li. "When she was first married to Commissioner Wang, she was made much of, but later, she lost his favor over a misspoken word, and so Mr. Wang is offering her to anyone of decent status. Her dowry won't be less than several tens of thousands in cash. The only thing is, she's too young."

Matchmaker Zhang said, "Being too young is better than being too old. Squire Zhang will be only too pleased with this match, but the girl will surely be none too happy. Let's take ten to twenty years off Mr. Zhang's age when we speak to her, so that the age disparity won't be too much of a problem."

"Tomorrow is a lucky day," said Matchmaker Li. "Let's first go to Mr. Zhang to set the amount of the betrothal gifts before we go to Mr. Wang. I'm sure we'll pull this off on the first try." That night, they parted and went their separate ways home, and nothing of note happened until the next day.

After meeting at an appointed place the next day, the two matchmakers went to see Mr. Zhang. "Mr. Zhang, we've found someone who meets all three of your conditions. Such a coincidence is rare, you know! First, she is as pretty as can be. Second, she is from Pacification Commissioner Wang's establishment, and his is a well-known name! Third, she has a dowry worth a hundred thousand strings of cash. We're only afraid that you'll think she's too young for you."

"How old is she?" asked Squire Zhang.

"She's thirty to forty years younger than you are, sir," replied Matchmaker Zhang.

Beaming with smiles, Zhang said, "Well, I'm counting on you to make this match!"

Let us skip trivialities and come to the point at which both parties gave their consent. As was the usual practice, betrothal gifts were sent to the bride, the bridegroom went to the bride's home to greet her, and bridal candles were lit for the wedding ceremony.

The next morning, when it was time to pay homage to the ancestors' tablets at the family altar, Squire Zhang appeared in a purple silk robe, a new cap, new shoes, and new socks. The young lady wore a wide-sleeved crimson gown of gold lamé in floral patterns and a similar gold-lamé kerchief over her face. She had

Eyebrows shaped like the crescent moon,
Cheeks rosy as the peach blossoms of spring.
Her posture lovely as a secluded flower;
Her fair and tender skin lustrous as jade.

She had more grace than could be told,
And more charm than could be painted.
A cloud over the Wu Mountains,
A fairy on Penglai Island.

Looking her over from head to foot, Squire Zhang cheered inwardly, but when the young lady's kerchief was lifted, she secretly cried out in anguish at the sight of his frosty hair and eyebrows. The day after the wedding ceremony found Squire Zhang gleeful but the young lady dejected.

More than a month later, a man came and said with a bow, "Today being Squire Zhang's birthday, this unworthy priest is here to present you, sir, with a prayer."

It so happened that Squire Zhang was in the habit of offering a Daoist prayer on the first and the fifteenth day of every month as well as on his birthday. When the young lady spread open the prayer scroll for a look, the tears began to roll down her cheeks as she read that the Squire was already more than sixty years old. Filled with resentment against the two matchmakers, she moaned to herself, "They've ruined me!"

As for Squire Zhang, with the passage of the days, he had more of the following than ever before (*He overtaxed himself.*):

More pain in his back, more tears in his eyes, more deafness in his ears, and more mucus in his nose.

One day, he said to his young wife, "I'm going out on some minor business. You'll have to put up with the loneliness."

The young woman forced herself to say, "Come home early." But after he left, she thought to herself, "With my looks and lavish dowry, how come I ended up with a white-haired old man for a husband?"

She was in the midst of these gloomy thoughts when her maid, who had come with her from the Wang establishment, suggested, "Madam, why don't you cheer yourself up and go to the door to watch the goings-on in the street?"

At this suggestion, the young lady followed the maid out for a look. The front of the residence was occupied by Zhang's small general store, which had cabinets all along the walls and a purple-silk-rimmed portiere that separated it from the interior of the house. As the maid let down the portiere from its hooks, the two store clerks, a Mr. Li Qing of about fifty years of age and a Mr. Zhang Sheng, about thirty, asked, "Why are you doing this?"

"The mistress is here to see what's going on outside," replied the maidservant.

Bowing low, the two managers greeted the mistress from the other side of the portiere. The young lady, her red lips opening slightly and revealing her pearly teeth, said a few words that caused Zhang Sheng enough troubles to

Fill a vast desert and the deepest sea
And weigh heavier than Mount Tai and Mount Hua.

The young woman first addressed Clerk Li. "How many years have you been with Squire Zhang?"

"I am Li Qing. I've been working here for more than thirty years."

"Does the Squire treat you well?"

"Every expense of mine is paid for by the Squire's grace." (*So, Manager Li is well taken care of.*)

She then turned to Clerk Zhang, who replied, "I am Zhang Sheng. My now deceased father came here to work more than twenty years ago. I was with him, and it's been more than ten years since I myself began serving the master."

"Does the Squire take good care of you?" asked the young lady.

"The Squire kindly pays for all the expenses incurred by my family."

"Please wait a moment," said she, whereupon she turned back and disappeared into the house. A few moments later, she reemerged and handed a packet to Clerk Li, who respectfully took it, covering his hand with his sleeve, and thanked her with a bow. She then said to Clerk Zhang, "I can't very well give him something while neglecting you. This may not be worth much, but it may come in handy." Clerk Zhang took the packet in the same way as Li had and thanked her with a bow.

From behind the portiere, the young lady continued watching events on the street for a while before she went back into the interior of the house. The two clerks returned to the front of the store and tended to business. As a matter of fact, Li had received ten silver coins, whereas Zhang had been given ten gold coins, but at the time, neither had any idea what the other had received. That evening, as the sky darkened, there, for all to see, were

Strands of fog merging over the wilderness,
Birds returning to their nests in the woods,
Ladies going to their rooms, candles in hand,
Wayfarers finding lodging at roadside inns,
Fishermen, laden with fish, walking down bamboo-lined paths,
Herdboys on buffaloes returning to the village.

That evening, the two clerks balanced the books, submitted them to Squire Zhang, and affixed their signatures to the accounts of the day, which listed sales, purchases, and amounts payable. The two men usually rotated night duty in the shop, and it so happened that Clerk Zhang was the one on duty that very night. Near the door was a small room, lit by a lamp. After sitting idly for some time, Zhang was preparing for bed when suddenly he heard a knock at the door. "Who is it?" he asked.

"I'll tell you as soon as you open the door. Hurry!" As Zhang opened the door, someone slipped in and dived behind the lamp. Finding the visitor to be a woman, Zhang gave a start and hastened to say, "Young lady, why are you here at this hour of the night?"

The woman said, "I came not for myself but for the one who gave you a gift earlier today."

"It was the young mistress who gave me ten gold coins. So she sent you to take the money back?"

"No. You may not know that Mr. Li got only silver. And now I have another thing for you from the young mistress." She took a package of clothes from her back and opened it, saying, "These are a few pieces of clothing for you. There are also some women's clothes for your mother." She put the clothes down and took leave of him, but before she was quite out the door, she turned back to add, "I forgot an important thing." So saying, she took out a fifty-tael ingot of silver from her sleeve and put it down before she went off. That night, Zhang Sheng found himself a much richer man for no reason that he could figure out.

After a sleepless night, he rose bright and early the next morning and went about taking care of the day's business. Upon Li's arrival, he handed the business over to him and returned home, where he showed his mother the clothes and the money.

"Where did you get them?" his mother demanded, whereupon Zhang gave her a full account of what had happened the day before. Upon hearing these words, the old lady said, "My son, what does the young mistress mean by giving you all this gold and clothes and silver? I'm now in my sixties and have only you since your father's death. If you get into trouble, to whom shall I turn for support? Don't go to the store tomorrow." (*What a wise mother!*) Being a decent man and a filial son, Zhang followed his mother's advice and did not go back to work.

Finding him absent from the shop, Squire Zhang sent for him with the question, "Why doesn't Mr. Zhang show up for work?" To which the old lady replied, "My son can't come because he has caught a cold and is not feeling well these days, but please tell the master that he'll be back as soon as he has recovered."

Another few days later, anxious over his continued absence, Li went personally to his house, saying loudly, "Why doesn't Mr. Zhang come to work? I have no one to help me in the shop!" The old lady insisted that he was not feeling well, adding that his conditions had, in fact, worsened in the last couple of days. Li left. Over and over again, Squire Zhang sent for him, but each time, Clerk Zhang's mother said that he had not yet recovered. Wondering why he still would not show up, Squire Zhang said, taking a guess, "He must have found another job," but in fact, all this time, Zhang Sheng was at home.

Time flew. The sun and the moon shuttled back and forth, and within the time it takes to snap a finger, Zhang had stayed home for more than a month. As the saying goes, "Those who sit idle and do nothing can eat away a mountain of fortune." The young mistress had been generous, but he dared not redeem the large ingot of silver nor could he very well sell the clothes. Without income, his resources began to dwindle with the passing days and months. He said to his mother, "You told me not to go back to Squire Zhang, but without a job, how am I going to pay for our daily expenses?"

Upon hearing these words, the old lady pointed at a beam in the ceiling, saying, "Don't you see what's up there, my son?"

Zhang took a look and saw a package hanging from the beam. As he took it down, his mother said, "This was how your deceased father supported you while you were growing up." He opened the paper wrappings to reveal a wicker basket. The old lady continued, "You can very well do what he did and make a living as a traveling peddler of miscellaneous household items."

It being the day of the Lantern Festival, Zhang said, "Tonight, there will be a lantern show at Duan Gate. I'd like to go and see the lanterns."

"My son, you haven't been to that street for quite some time. You'll only be inviting trouble if you pass by Squire Zhang's door on your way to see the lanterns at Duan Gate."

"People are all going out to see the lanterns. They say it's a great lantern show this year. I'll be back soon enough. I won't go past Squire Zhang's door."

"All right, you may go, but you must not go alone. You'll have to go with a friend."

"I'll go with Second Brother Wang."

"All right, if you go together. But first, don't drink! Second, be sure to go and come back *together!*"

Thus instructed, Zhang went with Second Brother Wang to see the lanterns by Duan Gate. They came upon a bustling scene where wine from the emperor as well as money were being distributed to a swarming crowd. Second Brother Wang suggested, "We can't very well see much of the lanterns in this spot. We are not big and strong enough to fight off all the pushes and shoves. Why don't we go to another place where there's also a lantern hill?"

"Where's that?" asked Zhang.

"Don't you know? Commissioner Wang has also put up a lantern hill, though a smaller one, and those lanterns are lit up tonight, too."

The two men wended their way to the Wang residence but found as much hustle and bustle there as at Duan Gate. By the gate of the Wang residence, Zhang Sheng lost sight of Second Brother Wang. He cried out in desperation, "How am I going to face my mother? She told me before I left to come back with him. And now he's nowhere to be seen! If I go home first, she won't be worried, but if she sees Second Brother Wang first, she'll worry about me." Forgetting all about the lanterns, he paced around by himself, and then, he suddenly recalled, "My former master Squire Zhang lives right ahead. Every Lantern Festival night, he would close up shop and put on lots of lanterns. Maybe he hasn't taken them down yet." So he proceeded to Squire Zhang's house. (*Casting his mother's admonition to the winds.*)

To his astonishment, he found the squire's door sealed with two bamboo poles laid crosswise. Above the poles was a poster visible by the light of a pig bladder lamp nailed to the door through a leather pad. Appalled at the sight, Zhang stood there stupefied, eyes wide open, mouth agape, not knowing what to do. He then took a step forward and began to read: "The police bureau of Kaifeng Prefecture has found Zhang Shilian guilty of. . . . " At the words "guilty of," he wondered what wrongs Squire Zhang could have committed.

At this point, he caught sight of a man under the lamp. The man yelled, "How dare you poke around in this place!" Startled, Zhang took to his heels. The man chased him with big strides, shouting, "Who goes there? How dare you come here! Why read the poster at this time of the night?" Zhang was so frightened that he ran all the faster to the corner of the lane, where he turned and headed home.

It was about the second watch of the night with a lambent moon shining in the sky. As he was pressing ahead, a man ran after him, calling, "Mr. Zhang, you are being invited!" Looking around, Zhang saw that the man was a waiter in a wineshop. He thought, "It must be Second Brother Wang waiting for me at the corner to have a few drinks with him before going home. That's just as well."

He followed the waiter to the wineshop, where they climbed up the stairs and stopped in front of a private booth. The waiter said, "Right here." Lifting the portiere, Clerk Zhang saw a shabbily dressed woman with disheveled hair. Truly,

Her hair tousled, she thought only of her past glory;
Tears flowing, she recalled her wealth of yesteryear.
The moon was obscured by the autumn clouds;
The peony was buried under the earth.

The woman exclaimed, "Mr. Zhang, I am the one who invited you here." Zhang took a look at the woman. Although he thought she looked familiar, he could not quite place her.

"Mr. Zhang, why don't you recognize me? I'm your former master's wife."

"Oh, but why are you here, madam?"

"It's a long story."

"How did you end up in such a state?"

"I shouldn't have listened to the matchmakers and married Squire Zhang. He has been accused of counterfeiting silver and was tied up and taken under guard to the police bureau. Nothing has been heard from him since. His possessions and many real estate holdings have been sealed and confiscated by the government. I am left all alone, with nowhere to go. You are my only hope. Please keep me in your home for a while, for old time's sake."

"This can't be done! First, my mother is very strict. Second, as the saying goes, 'To avoid suspicions, don't bend to pull your shoes in a melon field nor reach to adjust your cap under a plum tree.' For you to stay in my home is quite out of the question!"

The young lady said, "You must be thinking of the proverb 'It's easier to have a snake come than to make it go.' You're afraid that if I stay long, the expenses will be high. Let me show you this." So saying, she took something out from her bosom.

The temple hidden in the hills is not known
Until one hears its bells strike.
The village by the water is not seen
Until the boat moors at the shore.

What the young lady took out was a string of one hundred and eight shining pearls, each the size of a water lily seed, of the kind that foreign merchants shipped inland from the coast. Zhang exclaimed, "I've never seen anything like this before!"

"The government has confiscated all my dowry except these pearls, which I had hidden away. If you're willing to take me, you can sell off the pearls one by one and get more than enough for daily expenses." These words made Zhang

Eager to go home before the sun sets
And afraid that the horse goes too slowly.
Romance, wine, and overnight wealth,
Who does not fall under their spell?

So Zhang said, "Madam, if you want to live in my house, you'll have to get permission from my mother."

"I'll go with you. While you talk to her, I'll wait across the street."

Back at home, Zhang acquainted his mother with everything that had happened. Upon hearing of the young lady's misfortunes, the softhearted old lady cried out, "How sad! How sad! Where is the young lady now?"

"She's waiting across the street."

"Bring her in!"

After an exchange of greetings, the young woman repeated in detail what she had told Zhang, adding, "With no relatives to turn to, I've come expressly to see you, madam. Please let me stay."

At these words, the old lady said, "You're welcome to stay for a few days, but since we're too poor to be good hosts, you may consider going to some other relative later on."

At this point, the young lady took out her string of pearls and handed it to Zhang's mother, who looked at it by lamplight and repeated her invitation to the young woman to stay.

"Let's cut one pearl off the string in a couple of days," suggested the young lady, "and then sell it so as to open a small general store. A basket can be hung by the door as a store sign."

"With this treasure in the house," said Zhang, "we can get a pretty sum of money any time we sell a pearl or two. We also have that fifty-tael ingot of silver intact. That alone should be enough for us to purchase the goods we need."

So Zhang opened a store, continuing Squire Zhang's line of business. He came to be called Squire Zhang Junior by all and sundry. (*Personal integrity and social status don't matter. Whoever has money rises to the top. How lamentable!*) Time and again, the young lady tried to seduce Zhang, but Zhang remained unperturbed, his heart as hard as steel. He treated her consistently as a mistress of the household with never a slip in proper decorum.

As the Clear and Bright Festival rolled around,

Wisps of smoke rose to the clear and bright sky;
Paper coins of mourning fluttered in the wind.
Songs and laughter echoed through the meadows;
On apricot blossoms, rain one moment, sunshine the next.
Birds chirped on the crab-apple branches;
A drunken traveler slept by the willow-lined dyke.
The beauties frolicked on the swings in the yards,
Flying through the air like brightly clad fairies.

All the residents of the city turned out to tour Golden Bright Pond, Squire Zhang Junior among them. On his way back in the evening, he was about to go through Wansheng Gate when he heard a voice behind him calling, "Zhang Sheng!" He thought to himself, "Everybody calls me Squire Zhang Junior now. Who could be calling me Zhang Sheng?" As he turned around to look, whom did he see but Squire Zhang, his former master! Noticing the convict's tattoo on his face, his disheveled hair, and unkempt appearance, Zhang Sheng immediately invited him into a wineshop and sat down with him in a discreet private booth.

"My master," said Zhang Sheng, "why are you in such a state?"

"I shouldn't have married that woman from Commissioner Wang's house! On the last New Year's Day, she was watching the street from behind the portiere when she saw a page boy from the Wang establishment passing by, carrying a box. She stopped him and asked for news from the Wang establishment. The page boy replied, 'There's been nothing else exciting, but the other day, Commissioner Wang couldn't find his string of one hundred and eight pearls. All the servants in the household were blamed." As she heard this, the color on her face came and went. Soon after the boy left, about twenty to thirty men came to my house, carried off all her dowry and my possessions, and took me to the police bureau, where they demanded that I hand over the string of pearls. Having never laid eyes on it, I said I didn't have it. They beat me black and blue and threw me in jail. The woman had enough sense of honor to hang herself in her room. (*The young lady had brought trouble to too many people to be spared a violent end.*) But the mystery being still unsolved, the court convicted me instead. To this day, I still have no idea where that string of pearls is."

At these words, Zhang Sheng thought to himself, "Both the young lady and the pearls are in my house, and many pearls have already been sold." He became quite frightened and plied Squire Zhang with wine and food before they parted company.

On the way home, Zhang Sheng thought to himself, "How very strange!" Upon arriving home and seeing the young lady, Zhang Sheng recoiled a step and said, "Madam, please spare my life!"

"Why do you say such a thing?" asked the young lady.

After Zhang repeated what he had heard from the squire, the young lady exclaimed, "What a wild story! Look! Don't you see that I'm dressed in real clothes with seams and stitches? Don't you hear me speaking with a real voice, now louder than before? Knowing that I'm in your house, he said those things on purpose, to make you drive me away."

"Yes, you do have a point there," conceded Zhang.

A few days later, a voice from outside the house was heard crying, "Squire Zhang Junior has a visitor!"

Emerging from the house to greet the visitor, Zhang Sheng found the latter to be none other than Squire Zhang. Zhang Sheng thought to himself, "Let me get her out, and we'll know if she's a ghost or not." (*Having done nothing wrong, Zhang Sheng has nothing to fear.*) Forthwith he instructed a maidservant to invite the young lady out. The maidservant went in, but the young lady was nowhere to be found.

Realizing now that she was indeed a ghost, Zhang Sheng felt obliged to tell Squire Zhang everything he knew. When asked the whereabouts of the string of pearls, Zhang Sheng went into the house and reemerged with the string.

Squire Zhang had Zhang Sheng accompany him to Commissioner Wang's establishment, to report the matter and return the pearls and to pay in cash for the few pearls missing from the string. Commissioner Wang pardoned Squire Zhang and gave him back his property. After resuming his business, Squire Zhang engaged priests from Tianqing Temple to perform a memorial service for the young lady, who had been enamored of Zhang Sheng while alive and had sought him out after her death. Luckily, Zhang Sheng had remained unshaken in his resolve not to have an illicit relationship with her. As a result, he stayed out of harm's way and avoided being implicated in the case.

Now, in this day and age, all too many people fall victim to the temptations of money and lust. There may not be a Zhang Sheng in ten thousand men. There is a poem that says in praise of him:

Who loves not money and pleasures of the flesh?
But a man of virtue is hard to corrupt.
If only our youth were all like Clerk Zhang,
No humans and ghosts could ever do them harm.

17

The Luckless Scholar Rises Suddenly in Life

Mengzheng had once chafed in his humble cave,[1]
Maichen had been a peddler to support his studies.[2]
Great men are scorned when they're down on their luck;
Praises come only when they rise in life.

The red sun can be overcast at times;
The Yellow River flows clear at places.
Trust not the clouds that float before your eyes,
But plant your feet on ground solid and firm.

The above lyric poem to the tune of "Moon over the West River" basically makes the point that the timing of the ups and downs in one's life is predestined. Therefore, one must not be boastful of one's talents in a moment of glory, nor should one lose heart in a moment of failure.

In the Ganlu reign period of the Tang dynasty,[3] there was a Prime Minister Wang Ya, who, having attained the highest grade in officialdom with power over all the other court officials, lived in unspeakable luxury. He had as many as a thousand servants; his daily food expenses ran to ten thousand in cash. His kitchen being adjacent to a Buddhist monastery, the water that was dumped into the ditch after washing pots and pans flowed out the other end into the monastery.

One day, an old monk was on his way out of the monastery when he caught sight of white spots in the ditch water, some as big as flakes of snow, some as small as pulverized jade. Upon taking a closer look, he saw that they were grains of cooked white rice of the highest quality, flowing out into the ditch after the pots and pans were washed in Prime Minister Wang's kitchen. Joining his palms, the abbot said, "Amitabha! What a sin!" Then and there, he intoned a poem:

"Farmers plow in spring and weed in summer;
Into every seedling goes much hard work.
Husked and chaffed, like jade being polished,
The grains cook into fragrant, silvery rice.
Thrice a day, they nourish the idle rich,

> *While one mouthful can save a poor man's life.*
> *Alas! Here they lie, dumped into the ditch,*
> *While, sadly, those in need go hungry!"*

After intoning the poem, the abbot had some acolytes dredge up the grains of rice from the ditch with bamboo strainers, rinse them in the clean water of the river, spread them out on big bamboo trays, let them dry under the sun, and store them in a porcelain vat. Now you may well ask when the vat would ever be filled up. Well, it was filled to the brim in less than three or four months. Within two years, more than six big vats were filled with rice from the ditch.

As for Prime Minister Wang Ya, he thought his wealth and luxurious lifestyle were to last through thousands of generations, but who would have expected that extreme joy brought sorrow in its wake!

One fine day, he gave offense to the imperial court. His entire family stood accused. With the fate of the family yet unknown, the retainers went their separate ways, the servants and page boys took flight, and the grain barns and storage houses were all seized forcefully by enemies of the Wang family. Prime Minister Wang and his closest relatives, all twenty-three of them, found themselves with no food. As they wailed and wept in starvation, their cries reached the monastery and pained the abbot's heart.

The Wang establishment was connected to the monastery by a wall through which a hole could be dug, and the abbot soaked the dried grains of rice in large jars until they became soft, steamed them, and offered them to the Wangs. Prime Minister Wang found the rice delicious. (*Rice already thrown away is not supposed to be eaten, but in this case, heaven makes him repent.*) He sent a maidservant to the old monk to ask how someone who had renounced the world had come to have such fine rice. The monk replied, "This is by no means the usual fare for this poor monk. What I offered came with dishwater from your kitchen into the ditch. I find it too wasteful to throw away whatever can be used again, so I had the rice rinsed in clean water, dried in the sun, and put aside for the poor for a rainy day. Little did I expect that it would ever be offered to your distinguished family in a time of need. Now, doesn't this bear out the saying 'Every bite, every drink, is determined by fate'?"

At these words, Prime Minister Wang Ya said with a sigh, "How could I not come down in the world when I was so wasteful of the products of nature? Nothing could have prevented the misfortune that has befallen me." That night, he took poison and died.

How could he have foreseen such an end when he was at the height of his wealth and power? Truly, the poor and humble aspire to wealth and power, but the rich and mighty are beset with pitfalls. When their good fortune changes to calamity, they have only themselves to blame. The poor and humble of today can hardly foresee a future life of wealth and power. Similarly, the rich and mighty of today can hardly believe that misfortune will befall them later in life.

I now propose to tell a story of misery turning to joy. Dear audience, there may be among you a Han Xin suffering the humiliation of crawling between someone's legs, or a Su Qin snubbed by his wife.[4] After listening to this story of mine, go back home and live your life with your head held high. Do not lose heart while you wait for your turn to rise in life. There is a quatrain that says,

The wind-swept dead autumn grass will grow back in spring;
The lowliest worm will crawl its way out of the mud.
Don't laugh at a tiger yet half painted;
Add fangs and claws and it will strike terror into one's heart.

During the Tianshun reign period [1457–64] in this dynasty, there lived an official in Jiangle County, Yanping Prefecture, in Fujian. Ma Wanqun by name, he held the post of supervising secretary in the Bureau of Personnel. Later, for his criticisms of Wang Zhen the eunuch, who abused power and jeopardized national interests, he was deprived of his post and reduced to the status of a commoner.

His wife had died early, leaving him one son called Ma Ren, courtesy name Decheng. He started schooling at twelve years of age. A brilliant and well-learned young man he turned out to be. Like Yan Ziyuan, he could draw inferences about ten cases from knowledge about one instance, and like Yu Shinan, he had learned by heart enough books to fill five carriages.[5] Truly, throughout the land, his writings were second to none, and his reputation had no equal. It goes without saying that Secretary Ma cherished him as he did fine gold and beautiful jade. Partly because he was the beloved son of a highly placed official and partly because, with his outstanding talent, he would rise considerably sooner or later, the sons of the rich in the area vied with one another in currying favor with him, with two among them outdoing all the others. Truly,

In cold weather, they sent him warmth;
Lest he be bored, they brought him fun.
On outings, they called him "Brother,"
Paying his bills at every turn.
He had only to mention a certain wineshop,
And they would take him there for three cups.
He had only to praise a certain courtesan,
And they would engage her for him for a month.
Their hands on his buttocks, holding his fart,
They said the sweet smell passed on to their hands.
Whenever he spit, they would rush
To wipe out the phlegm with their feet.
They smirked, they flattered, they bowed, and they scraped;
They stopped short only of offering a wife or a son. (Good description.)

One of the two was called Huang Sheng, nicknamed "Huang the Sickly Man." The other was called Gu Xiang, nicknamed "Sky-rising Firecracker." Generations earlier, the two well-off clans had produced scholar-officials. Both men were illiterate but still claimed to have had some education. They showed as much veneration to Ma Decheng as they would to a Buddha in the hope of keeping the relationship after he rose to fame and fortune. Being the honorable gentleman that he was, Ma Decheng reciprocated their acts of kindness according to decorum and, impressed by their attentiveness, accepted their friendship. Huang Sheng even betrothed his younger sister Liuying to Decheng, who, hearing that Liuying was as talented as she was beautiful, could not have been more delighted. However, he had taken a vow much earlier in his life

Not to marry until winning honor
In the imperial examinations.

Impressed by this wise decision, Secretary Ma let him have his way. Therefore, now in his twenties, he remained a bachelor.

The year came around in which the provincial examinations were to be held. One day, Huang Sheng and Gu Xiang took Ma Decheng to a bookshop to buy books. Next to the bookshop was a fortune-teller's shop with a sign that read,

To know what lies in your future,
Ask Zhang, the master who never errs.

Ma Decheng commented, "If the man never errs, I suppose he'll be honest and tell the truth, whatever it is." His shopping done, he went next door and said to Mr. Zhang, folding his hands in a bow, "Would you please tell my fortune?"

The fortune-teller asked for the eight characters of his horoscope,[6] studied the relationship of mutual production and mutual conquest among the five phases and the arrangements of the five planets,[7] and said, "Only if you, sir, promise not to take amiss what I'm going to say will I dare to tell you the truth."

"A gentleman wants to know only about the misfortunes in his fate, rather than the blessings," said Ma Decheng. "There's no need to hide anything from me."

However, Huang Sheng and Gu Xiang, standing at his side, were afraid that the fortune-teller would foolishly blurt out something offensive to Ma. (*Good characterization all along.*) "Go over the horoscope carefully, sir," said Huang Sheng to the fortune-teller. "Don't say anything lightly!"

"You are talking about a distinguished man of this county," admonished Gu Xiang. "He needs to know only if he'll be among the top five in the exam, or if he'll win first honors."

The fortune-teller said, "May I just tell what I see? According to your eight characters, sir, you must have been born into an eminent official's family, with your father in a powerful position."

Huang and Gu clapped their hands in glee. "Ha, ha! How accurate!" they said.

The fortune-teller continued, "You were born under the two stars of learning, which means you are blessed with outstanding literary talent."

The two men again burst into hearty laughter. "What a good fortune-teller! How accurate! How accurate!"

"However, at twenty-two years of age, you will have some bad luck. You will suffer a major blow that will not only break up your family but also take some lives. If you manage to live past the age of thirty-one, you will be in for fifty years of booming prosperity. But I'm not sure that you can jump over this ten-foot-wide ditch."

Huang Sheng broke into a stream of curses, "What a lot of garbage! How can this ever be?"

Gu Xiang raised a fist, saying, "Let's beat up this guy, and smash his mouth!"

Ma Decheng stopped them with both hands, saying, "Fortune-telling is a difficult art. Let's just say that he doesn't know what he's doing, and that will be the end of it. Why all this fuss?"

Huang and Gu went on swearing at the fortune-teller, but Ma managed, as best he could, to calm them down. The fortune-teller, eager to be left in peace, did not ask for payment for his service. Truly,

Everyone loves those who flatter;
All detest those who tell the truth.

Even Ma Decheng himself thought that, for him, fame and fortune were within easy reach. Though he did not bitterly resent the fortune-teller, he did not believe what he had been told. But as it turned out, although he thought he had done well on the three sessions of the examinations, his name was not on the list of successful candidates.

From the age of fifteen until he was twenty-one, he sat for the examinations three times and failed each time. He was still young, but the repeated failures frustrated him. Another year went by. He was now twenty-two.

A protégé of Secretary Ma's wrote a memorial to the emperor, requesting impeachment of Wang Zhen. Suspecting that Secretary Ma was behind the move, Wang Zhen secretly ordered some of his trusted men at court to dig up records of misdemeanors in Ma's past. Thus, Ma came to be accused of embezzling ten thousand taels of silver while serving at an earlier post, and the case was to be handled by the local yamen. In fact, Ma was not a corrupt official. The news gave him such a shock that he choked and fell ill. A few days later, he passed away.

A grief-stricken Ma Decheng wished with every fiber of his being to hold a proper burial service in fulfillment of his filial duties, but local officials, trying to please their superiors, pressed him to repay the ten thousand taels of silver. He had no choice but to sell off family property. All items registered on government tax books were sold off at prices determined by local officials. The proceeds from the sales went into government coffers. There was, however, a small manor, bought after the major purchases, that had not been taxed and was therefore unknown to the government. Taking Gu Xiang to be the good friend that he had been in better times, Ma Decheng claimed that the small manor was the Gu family's property and pleaded with Gu Xiang to acknowledge it as such for the time being. He also entrusted to Huang Sheng some antiques and books worth hundreds of taels of silver.

Now the local officials, finding that the proceeds from the sale of all of Secretary Ma's real estate were still short of the target, continued probing for more possibilities. (*By probing for more, they are trying to curry favor with their superiors. Those of integrity will never stoop so low.*)

In the meantime, Ma Decheng had taken up lodging in a hut by his father's grave. Suddenly, one day, a messenger sent by Gu Xiang came to say, "The government has learned about that manor of yours. It's no use trying to lie about it anymore."

At his wits' end, Ma Decheng had no choice but to yield it to the government. Later, he learned that it was Gu Xiang who had informed the authorities, partly to avoid being implicated and partly to win a smile from the local officials. Aware of how treacherous people could be, Ma Decheng dismissed it all with a laugh.

More than a year later, he went to Huang Sheng's home to claim the items he had entrusted to his friend, but however many times he went, he was denied admission into the house. Finally, a letter was sent to him. He opened the envelope, only to find that instead of a personal letter, it was a list of expenses, stating that on a certain day of a certain month, a certain amount of silver was spent for a certain purpose, and so the list went on. It also specified which expenses should have been partly paid by Ma and which ones entirely by him. More such bills followed. The estimated value of the antiques and books was then deducted as payment. Thus, nothing was left to be returned to Ma Decheng.

Flying into a rage, Decheng tore the bills into strips in the presence of the messenger, crying furiously, "I don't want to see such a dog and a pig of a man ever again!"

Henceforth, the subject of the betrothal was never brought up again. Huang Sheng was only too anxious to sever all ties with Ma, and what Ma had said could not have suited him better. This bears out the lines by Mr. Feng of the Western Han dynasty:

> *A rise, a fall, a moment of life and death,*
> *Such are the times that put friendship to the test.*

Living as he now was in a hut by his father's grave during the mourning period, dressed in rags, his daily subsistence uncertain, Decheng thought to himself, "My father helped other people when he was alive, but now that I am the poor and needy one, there's no one to offer me a helping hand."

Old Wang, the grave-watcher, urged him to sell the trees around the grave. He refused. Old Wang then pointed to a few big cypress trees by the roadside and suggested, "These trees are not around the grave. There's no harm in selling them."

Decheng agreed. After the price had been settled, he had one of the cypress trees felled, only to find it a worthless, worm-eaten hollow tree. A second tree was cut down, but it was just as hollow. With a sigh, Decheng said, "Such is my fate!" With that, he gave up the attempt. The two trees could be sold only as cheap firewood, and the money lasted for not more than two days.

There remained with him one last servant, a twelve-year-old page boy born of servants in the Ma household. Upon Ma's request, with Old Wang as a middleman, the boy was sold for five taels of silver. But after going to the new master, the boy began urinating in his bed every night. The master returned him to Old Wang and demanded the five taels of silver back. (*Those who drop stones on someone who has fallen into a well are no better than worms in graveyard trees or the urine of a little boy.*) Left with no alternative, Decheng sold the boy again to the same man for two taels less. How very strange! This time, the boy did not urinate at night. It was obviously a twist of fate meant to make Ma poorer by two taels of silver, but of this, no more need be said.

Time flew by with the speed of an arrow. Soon, the mourning period came to an end. Reduced to extreme poverty, Decheng had no one to turn to for help. But he recalled that he had an uncle who was the deputy prefect of Hangzhou, Zhejiang, and that the magistrate of Deqing County, Huzhou, was a former protégé of his father's. He thought he might just as well try his luck with these two men and see if one of them would be willing to take him. Right away, he put together a few miscellaneous housewares and asked Old Wang to sell them off for travel money. Carrying a parcel containing his washed and starched but worn-out clothes, he took a boat to Hangzhou. When he inquired, he was told that his uncle had died of illness only ten days before. He then went to see the magistrate of Deqing County, but the magistrate was in the middle of a dispute with his superiors over a financial matter, and, angrily claiming that he was returning to his hometown and pleading illness, he closed his doors to visitors. Truly,

When your time comes, good luck falls in your lap;[8]
When your time goes, bad luck follows on your heels.[9]

Decheng's hopes in both cases were dashed. Recalling many other officials in Nanjing who were his father's acquaintances, having passed the examinations in the same year as his father had, Decheng again took a boat to Jingkou [modern-day Zhenjiang]. He was about to cross the river when he was told that a strong westerly wind that had been blowing for the last few days made it impossible for boats heading west to move an inch. He saw nothing for it but to walk via Jurong in the direction of Nanjing, a city guarded by the gates of Shence, Jinchuan, Yifeng, Huanyuan, Qingliang, Shicheng, Sanshan, Jubao, Tongji, Hongwu, Zhaoyang, and Taiping.

Ma Decheng entered the city through Tongji Gate and stayed at an inn for the night. The next morning, he went to the various bureaus to make inquiries and learned that of the many officials who had known his father, some had been promoted, some had transferred out of Nanjing, some had died, and some had come to grief. Having met no one he had hoped to see, he returned to his lodgings with none of the cheerfulness he had felt when he left.

Time went by, and before he knew it, more than six months had passed. All his means were exhausted. If his was not exactly the case of Wu Zix begging for food at Wu Gate, he was at least as desperate as Lü Mengzheng trying to live off a monastery.[10]

One day, he was at Great Gratitude Repayment Monastery, trying to get a meal from the monks, when he ran into an acquaintance from his hometown. Upon asking for news from his hometown, he was told that the chief examiner was in their region to supervise the examinations of that year, but the local education officials, who had not received any gifts from him when his mourning period expired, had not written on his behalf a new application for candidacy or a statement of intention to travel. Nor had anyone expected his journey to be so prolonged. With no communication possible, he had already been disqualified as a candidate for the examinations. ([Illegible.]) Being a thousand li away from his hometown, there was nothing he could do to plead his case. Truly,

An all-night rain wrecks a hut already leaking;
A headwind thwarts a boat already slow.

At this news, Decheng heaved one deep sigh after another. Too ashamed to return home, he thought of finding a place to teach for a living before deciding on the next thing to do. But, alas, the ordinary man of the world lacks a discerning eye. Hearing of the reduced circumstances of the young man from another part of the land, everyone assumed he was a good-for-nothing. However refined and talented he was, none believed in him. None wanted his services. Some time later, the monks also began to loathe him. Their verbal insolence need not be repeated here.

Luckily, heaven always leaves a door open. There was a Grain Commissioner Zhao who wanted to hire an educated man to join him in escorting a shipment of grain to Beijing, partly to keep him company and partly to write documents for him. Hearing that Commissioner Zhao was consulting the abbot of Great Gratitude Repayment Monastery about a candidate, Decheng thought to himself, "If I could take this chance and go to Beijing, wouldn't that work out nicely in more ways than one?" Thereupon, he asked the monks for a recommendation. Those worldly monks who could not wait for the pauper to get out of their sight, sang his praises to the commissioner, adding that he would ask for very little by way of remuneration. As a military official, what else did Zhao care for besides keeping down expenses? So at Zhao's invitation, Decheng handed in his visiting card and met the commissioner at the monastery.

On a chosen day, Zhao invited Decheng onto his boat to start the journey. Decheng was as eloquent as could be, and the two got along quite well.

When they reached the mouth of the Yellow River several days later, Decheng was on shore, relieving himself, when he suddenly heard a tremendous blast as terrifying as if the skies had collapsed and the earth had cracked open. Hastily, he rose to take a look. With a start, he saw that the river levees had given way. The boats of grain Zhao was escorting had been washed away and scattered in all directions by the raging waves that surged as far as the eye could see. Feeling all alone in the world with no one to turn to for help, Decheng burst into cries of despair, his face turned toward the sky. "If heaven is so determined to have me die," he lamented, "I might as well do so!"

He was about to throw himself into the river when an old man stopped him. The old man asked him who he was. After hearing his account, the old man said in pity, "How can a handsome young man like you not be destined to rise in life someday? You are not very far from Beijing now. You won't need a lot of money. I have with me three taels of silver that I have no use for. Please take them."

So saying, he started groping in his sleeve, but he found nothing. "How very strange!" he exclaimed over and over again. Upon closer inspection, he found a small hole in his sleeve. He had left home early that day, and along the way, some thief must have cut his sleeve and stolen his silver. The old man commented with a sigh, "As the ancients say, 'The day you win sympathy and support is the day your luck begins.' But what happened today tells me that even with sympathy and support, you still need heavenly will. It's not that I begrudge my money, but you are just not in luck. I would gladly invite you to my humble home, but it's too far from here." Instead, he took Decheng to a friend of his who lived in the center of the town and borrowed five mace of silver, which he then gave to Decheng as a gift. (*What a kind old gentleman! Just as kind as the washerwoman of Huaiyin.*[11])

Deeply grateful, Decheng felt obliged to accept the money and took his leave with profuse words of thanks. Since five mace of silver was not going to get him much farther along on his journey, he thought of an idea. He used the money to buy a brush-pen and some paper so that he could sell his writing services along the way. Decheng was accomplished in the arts of writing as well as calligraphy, but since his time had not yet come, he had not won appreciation from scholars and connoisseurs. People in village shops buying sheets of calligraphy to use as wallpaper could not tell good penmanship from bad and were quite unwilling to pay good money for it.

And so, in a half-starved state, never knowing where his next meal was coming from, Decheng made his way to the city of Beijing and betook himself to an inn, where he asked the innkeeper for a directory of officials living in the city. In the listing, he found two of his father's close friends who had passed the examinations in the same year as his father. One was Deputy Secretary You of the Ministry of War, and the other, a Mr. Cao, was deputy director of the Court of Imperial Entertainments.

Right away, Decheng made two visiting cards and went first to see Director

Cao. The young man's shabbiness displeased Mr. Cao. Moreover, knowing of the feud between Wang Zhen and the Ma family, Mr. Cao dared not make any commitment. He gave the young man a small gift and dismissed him.

Next, Decheng went to see Secretary You, but he did not turn out to be much of a friend either. Not giving Decheng anything by way of a gift, he wrote a letter recommending him to Commander Lu on the frontier. Impressed by the title on the envelope, the innkeeper felt confident in Decheng's eventual rise to fame and fortune and lent him five taels of silver for his journey.

However, it turned out in a way they never could have expected. Because the Mongol tribes were wreaking havoc in the north, kidnapping people and taking animals, Commander Lu was taken under guard to Beijing to face charges of failing to keep the situation under control. Even Secretary You himself was stripped of his official rank and had to return to his hometown.

So, having accomplished nothing in these three to four months of life on the frontier, he went back to the old inn in the capital. The innkeeper could not bring himself to demand repayment of the five taels of silver on top of the bills for room and board. Instead, he made a virtue of necessity and let Decheng stay on. (*What a good man, the innkeeper!*)

Then an idea occurred to him. In a nearby lane, there was a Commander Liu who was looking for a tutor from the south to teach his eight-year-old son. The innkeeper recommended Decheng. Commander Liu was delighted and settled with the innkeeper on a salary of twenty taels of silver. The innkeeper kept a part of the salary for himself and wrote off the amount Decheng owed.

Acting the part of a generous employer, Commander Liu gave Decheng a set of new clothes by way of welcoming him to the establishment. Henceforth, Decheng found himself well supplied with the necessities of life. He devoted what free time he had left after class to reviewing the classics and histories and doing his writing exercises.

However, barely had three months gone by than his pupil came down with chickenpox. The physician's prescriptions did not work, and the boy died twelve days later. Overcome with grief at the loss of his only son, Commander Liu heard these unkind remarks from some spiteful people: "Ma Decheng is nothing short of bad luck itself. Wherever he goes, misfortune follows suit. (*A valid point.*) Director Zhao hired him, only to lose all the grain shipments in his charge. Secretary You recommended him, only to be stripped of his official rank. He's a scholar who brings bad luck, certainly not someone to keep around." So instead of attributing the boy's death to fate, the commander blamed the tutor for bringing his son bad luck.

As the story got around, Decheng came to be known in the capital as the "Luckless Scholar." Wherever the Luckless Scholar went, all doors along the street closed, one after another. Those who ran into him in the morning were dogged by bad luck the rest of the day. Those in business suffered a loss; visitors missed the ones they came to see; those filing lawsuits lost their cases; those demanding repayment of debts were either beaten up or yelled at. Even a pupil would be slapped on the palm by the teacher. Hence, Decheng was made out to be quite a monster. (*A great man reduced to such dire circumstances. Poor thing!*) Those who ran into him on a narrow path would spit onto the ground and say, "Good luck be with me!" before moving on. How tragic that Ma Decheng, a learned scholar from a respectable family, now found himself down on his luck, without even adequate food and housing!

At the time, there was a Mr. Wu in the mid-Zhejiang region, a student at the National University, who, being quite an upright and straightforward man, did not believe what he had heard about the Luckless Scholar. He went out of his way to invite the latter home so as to sound him out about his knowledge, and a cordial host Mr. Wu turned out to be. But before the mats they were sitting on got warm, Wu suddenly received a letter from his hometown, saying that his aged father had died of an illness. Staggering from the shock, he bid his guest adieu but recommended him to a fellow townsman, Mr. Lü, minister of ceremonies.

Accordingly, Mr. Lü invited Decheng home and treated him to a fine meal, but barely had they raised their chopsticks than the kitchen caught fire, and the whole family fled in fright. Decheng, too weak from hunger to run as fast as the others, was caught by the local headman, who accused him of causing the fire and brought him to the authorities. Without being given an opportunity to explain, he was thrown into jail. Fortunately, Minister Lü was a man of high morals. He went to much expense and got Decheng acquitted.

From that time on, the Luckless Scholar took on greater notoriety. With no one willing to extend a helping hand, he eked out a living as before, by selling his calligraphy,

Writing scrolls of birthday greetings for art sellers
And auspicious couplets for Spring Festivals.

At night, he often lodged in Patriarch Temple, Lord Guan Temple, and Five Manifestations Temple. Sometimes he also wrote prayers for Daoist priests in exchange for a few pennies to keep himself alive.

Let us pick up another thread of the story and come to Huang Sheng, Huang the Sickly Man. For a time after Ma Decheng's departure, he still feared Ma's possible return. Then, during Ma's continued absence after the chief examiner disqualified him, Huang heard that Ma had followed Director Zhao to Beijing to escort a shipment of grain and had drowned when the levees gave way to the surging waters of the Yellow River. The news put his mind at ease.

Morning and night, he pressed his younger sister Liuying to marry some other man, but she vowed that she would rather die than marry any man other than the one already betrothed to her. In the examinations at the provincial level toward the end of the Tianshun reign period, Huang Sheng bribed those in key positions and bought himself the degree of *juren.* Sycophants coming to offer congratulations filled up his house, blocking the doors and the windows. Hearing that he had a sister of marriageable age but still unbetrothed, suitors swarmed to his house day in and day out. Liuying's resolve was as firm as ever, and there was nothing Huang Sheng could do about it. At the end of winter, he packed for a journey to Beijing for the palace examinations.

Having read Huang Sheng's name on the list of successful candidates who had passed the provincial level of the examinations, Ma Decheng thought that Huang Sheng would surely go to Beijing. With bitter memories coming back to him, he felt too ashamed of his present circumstances and decided to leave Beijing so as to avoid seeing Huang Sheng.

As a matter of fact, all the fame and success had turned Huang Sheng's head. Had he gained fame through his learning, he would have taken everything in stride and not made too much of it, but as his *juren* degree had been bought with money, he literally danced with joy, for it was indeed a case of a petty rogue stepping into the shoes of a gentleman. With fifty taels of silver, he bought an official travel permit and, once in Beijing, took up lodging in a fancy inn. Instead of reviewing the classics and the histories, he spent the days in the street of ill repute and wallowed in pleasure in the prostitutes' quarters. As the saying goes, "Extreme joy begets sorrow." His dissolute life gave him boils all over his body. As the day of the examinations drew near, he offered a hundred taels of silver to a physician, hoping for a rapid recovery. The physician applied strong doses of calomel, and within several days, Huang Sheng's skin regained its smoothness. He went through the examinations perfunctorily and returned home.

In less than half a year, the boils came back with a vengeance, this time beyond cure. He died, leaving no brothers or children. As the relatives pounced on his property, his wife Wang-shi had no idea what to do. It was Liuying who made arrangements for the funeral, dealt with the relatives, and supervised matters relating to inheritance among kith and kin in accordance with the family lineage books. All this she did by herself, much to the satisfaction of all and sundry. No one raised any complaints. Liuying herself also got one portion of the property worth several thousands taels of gold. ([Illegible.])

Recalling the rumor about her fiancé having drowned, she spent goodness knows how much money, sending people to find out if it was true or not. Someone from Beijing said that Ma Chengde was still alive and that, stranded in Beijing, he was called the "Luckless Scholar." Being a truly worthy woman and one of action, Liuying put together some luggage and, equipped with much silver, hired a boat and traveled with her maidservants all the way to Beijing to look for her fiancé. (*What a worthy person!*) Through inquiries, she learned that Ma Decheng was copying the Lotus Sutra in Great Compassion Hall of Longxing Monastery in Zhending Prefecture and sent Wang An, an old house servant, to greet her husband, along with a hundred taels of silver, several suits of new clothes, and a sealed letter she had written herself. To Wang An she gave these instructions: "I'm going to pay the National University to get Master Ma into it. So your job is to invite him over so that he can study here in preparation for the examinations. Now, go with all speed."

Upon arrival in Longxing Monastery, Wang An saw the abbot and asked, "Where, may I ask, is Master Ma from Fujian?"

The abbot replied, "I have here only a Luckless Scholar. There's no 'Master' Ma here."

"Well, that's him! Please let me see him."

The monk led Wang An to Great Compassion Hall and said, pointing, "That's the Luckless Scholar copying the sutra at the desk."

Wang An had seen Ma Decheng a few times at home and did not fail to recognize him, however shabbily he was dressed. Promptly, he fell to his knees and started kowtowing. Ma Decheng, in this lowest moment of his life, found this reverence all too unexpected. Unable to recall who this man was, Decheng quickly raised him to his feet and asked, "Who might you be?"

"I am a servant in the Huang household of Jiangle County, here to greet you, sir, by the young mistress's orders. Here's the young mistress's letter for you."

"Whom did your young mistress marry?"

"She remains unmarried to this day. She has vowed never to marry another man. My master passed away recently. The young lady is now in Beijing to see you and to pay your way into the National University. She also asks you to leave this place as soon as possible."

At that moment, Decheng opened the envelope and saw a poem inside:

Why does he of my heart linger afar?
He should know that a career is at hand.
The wind and clouds help the roc soar high;[12]
The flutes attract the phoenix to the roof.

After reading the lines, Decheng smiled slightly. As Wang An presented the clothes and silver and asked when he was going to leave the monastery, Decheng said, "I am certainly well aware of the young lady's good intentions, but I have said before, 'Not to marry until winning honor / In the imperial examinations.' Being such a poor man, I've been neglecting my studies. Since the young lady is fortunate enough to have money to spare, she may use it to pay for items like lamp oil for my use. I will not presume to see her until after I pass the examinations next autumn." (*What a man of honor!*)

Wang An did not press him but asked for a letter of reply. Using what remained of a silk scroll on which he had been copying the sutra, he wrote a quatrain by way of a reply:

Travel-worn, I'm tired of a life on the road;
The servant's face was a delight to see.

The Moon Goddess has a date to pick the flowers;
Let not the flute notes leave the phoenix tower.

Decheng put the poem in an envelope and handed it to Wang An, who then returned to Beijing posthaste to report back to Liuying. After reading the poem, she heaved sigh upon sigh.

That year [1049], Emperor Tianshun was captured by the Mongols at Tumubao, in consequence of which the empress dowager asked Prince Cheng to act as regent. The reign title was changed to Jingtai. All the property of the evil minister Wang Zhen was confiscated. Those who had suffered retaliation because of their attempts to impeach Wang Zhen all received promotions for themselves and titles for their offspring.

After hearing this news in her temporary lodging, Miss Huang sent Wang An to Longxing Monastery to report to Ma Decheng, who, though still an unpaying guest at the monastery, was living in changed circumstances, with books piling up on his desk and an ample supply of nice clothes and good food. Now aware that he was a Mr. Ma or a Master Ma, the monks, one and all, showed him much respect and admiration. He was thirty-two years old, the year that, just as Mr. Zhang, the never-erring fortune-teller, had predicted, was to mark the beginning of the lucky part of his life. Indeed,

Everything in life is determined by fate;
Nothing follows the dictates of human will.

Decheng was reviewing his lessons in the monastery when Wang An arrived with the news. He packed up his belongings, took leave of the abbot, and went to Beijing, where he took up lodging in a different inn. Miss Huang sent over two servants and a constant supply of items for his daily needs.

Decheng wrote a memorial to the court, stating that his father Ma Wanqun, former court official, had been made to suffer because of his blunt criticism of Wang Zhen. He did this partly to rehabilitate his father and partly out of consideration for his own future. The regent responded by reinstating Ma Wanqun, giving him a three-grade promotion, and restoring Ma Decheng's status as a scholar candidate for the imperial examinations. All of the confiscated estate and property were to be returned by the local officials. Decheng dispatched a servant to inform Miss Huang of what had happened, and she in turn had Wang An send silver to Decheng so that he could pay his way into the National University.

The following spring, Decheng won first place in the examinations at the university level. In autumn, he won first honors in the provincial-level examinations. There, in his own lodgings, he had a feast laid out in celebration of his and Miss Huang's wedding. The following Spring, he won tenth place in the examinations on the Five Classics and second place in the last round of the palace examination and was admitted into the Imperial Academy.

He wrote another memorial to the court, this time requesting permission to return to his hometown and pay homage at his father's grave. He also intended to tell his deceased father about the imperial favors by burning a letter written on yellow paper to him. The request was granted.

In glory, the couple returned to their hometown. They were greeted well before they reached the city gate by an assembly of officials from the county and prefectural yamens. The confiscated estate and property were returned to them at government price, strictly in accordance with the account books and not even one penny short. Those friends who had shunned Decheng now swarmed to his door. Only Gu Xiang felt so ashamed that he moved to another county. Mr. Zhang, the never-erring fortune-teller, went to offer congratulations upon hearing that Young Master Ma had returned after winning honors at the examinations. He left with a handsome reward from Decheng.

Later, Decheng rose to be secretary of the Ministries of Rites, War, and Justice. Liuying was enfeoffed as Lady of the First Order. Both of their sons won the *jinshi* degree in the civil service examinations, and the family line never ran short of officials. To this day, in Yanping Prefecture, unsuccessful scholars are still being compared to the Luckless Scholar. A later poet had this to say:

Shunned by all during ten years of distress,
He rose to fame and fortune overnight.
The right flowers will bloom in the right season.
Why fish uselessly for a needle in the sea?

18

A Former Protégé Repays His Patron unto the Third Generation

Buy an ox and learn to till the fields;
Build a thatched hut by the spring in the woods.
Without much time remaining in this life,
Why not spend a few years in the hills?
Wealth and rank are but an illusion;
Only poems and wine bring true bliss.
The price of everything is on the rise;
But worthless is the talent of the old.

The above eight lines are truly words of the wise, but I take issue with the last line "But worthless is the talent of the old." Generally speaking, the timing of one's rise in life, whether early or late, is predetermined by fate. Those who achieve fame and fortune early in life may not, after all, retain what they have for the rest of their lives. Those who get there late in life may not be any less successful. The young must not be conceited, nor should the old give up hope. Even the terms "old" and "young" are relative.

For example, Gan Luo became prime minister at the age of twelve but died at thirteen.[1] Thus, he had reached the age of hoary hair, loose teeth, stooped shoulders, and a bent back when he was twelve. Without much time left in his life, he no longer qualified as a youth. There is also the case of Jiang Taigong,[2] who, at eighty years of age, was fishing at the Wei River when he was accosted by King Wen of Zhou. He was invited onto the king's carriage and addressed respectfully as "Master". After King Wen died and King Wu took the throne, Jiang became his military adviser. He helped King Wu conquer King Zhou of Shang and found the Zhou dynasty that was to last for eight hundred years. After he was granted the territory of the state of Qi, he had his son Duke Ding rule Qi while he himself remained in the Zhou dynasty court as the prime minister until he passed away at the age of 120. How could you have foreseen the long and prosperous career for which an eighty-year-old fisherman was destined? Now, in his case, at eighty years of age, he was like a young man just reaching the stage when his hair should be tied up under a cap, when he should get married and make his first attempt at the lowest level of the imperial examinations. At that point, an old man he was not.

The ordinary men of the world judge a man only by his status at the moment, with never a thought of future possibilities. Like the shortsighted ignoramuses they are, they dance attendance on rich young men but give the cold shoulder to older men whose talents have not won recognition. Think of the farmers; they grow rice for early as well as late harvesting. It is hard to say which rice yields a better crop. Consider what the ancients used to say:

Peach and plum blossoms in the east garden,
First to bloom and first to wither;
Pine trees by the ravines, slow in their growth,
Last the longest in their verdant splendor.

But enough of this chatter. Let me now tell a story that takes place in the Zhengtong reign period [1436–49] of this dynasty.

In Xing'an County, Guilin Prefecture, Guangxi, there lived a scholar by the name of Xianyu Tong, courtesy name Datong. At eight years of age, he was given the title Child Prodigy upon recommendation. At eleven, he started formal education in a government school and skipped two grades to become a student supported by government stipend. So profound was his erudition that he thought nothing of men like Dong Zhongshu and Sima Xiangru.[3] Truly, he had learned ten thousand books by heart, his brush-pen mighty enough to wipe out an army one thousand strong. So high was his opinion of himself that he turned up his nose at men like Feng Jing [1021–1094] and Shang Luo [1414–1486] who had won first honors at three successive levels of the examinations. Truly, he rode the wind and the clouds, and his ambition soared to the stars.

As it happened, however, for all his literary talent, his was an unhappy lot. Despite his ambitions, fate was against him. Year after year, he sat for the civil service examinations, and year after year, he failed. By age thirty, he had enough seniority to be assigned a minor government post if he were recommended to the National University, but with his high aspirations, he would not stoop to gaining a career in that way. In weighing his choices, he thought that however poor he was, he at least had some money from his school—a few taels of silver per year for his tuition. Should he leave the school and go to the National University, he not only would be cutting himself off from this source of income but would incur extra expenses as well. Moreover, he stood a greater chance of passing the examinations at the provincial level than at the National University. It therefore would not make sense for him to change the status quo.

After Xiangu made his thoughts known during a casual conversation with friends, the scholar next in line on the waiting list approached him and asked that he yield his place in exchange for several tens of taels of silver. Xianyu Tong was pleased by the deal. After doing it once as a personal favor, he did it a second time and then made it an established practice. Since everyone fought to be first on the roster of candidates to be recommended to the National University, he yielded his right eight times after he reached the age of thirty. When he was forty-six, he was still a student at the same school. Some laughed at him, some pitied him, and some gave him words of advice. To the laughs he turned a deaf ear, and the pity he rejected out of hand, but to those who gave him words of advice, he would retort hotly, "You advise me to wait my turn for appointment as a National University student because you think I'm too old ever to pass the civil service examinations, but you may not know that first honors in the exams are meant for those who are older and more mature. Liang Hao [963–1004] won that honor at eighty-two years of age. He was a credit to all men who proudly apply themselves to their studies.

"Had I been willing to settle for less, I would have accepted the National University option when I was thirty years old. Had I curried favor with the powerful, I would have at least landed the post of a county magistrate. Had I sought personal gain against the dictates of my conscience, I would have been a rich and successful man by now. But this is an empire built upon the system of civil service examinations. If Confucius had not won some academic honor, who would have acknowledged his learning and scholarship? Suppose a young man in some remote village roughly memorizes a few trite essays in preparation for the examinations, happens to meet a brainless examiner who capriciously praises his essays at random, and ends up being awarded a *jinshi* degree without even knowing what's happening. Admirers will still honor him as a patron and a teacher and treasure the opportunity to talk with him. Would anyone dare to put him, now an official, through another examination?

"And there's more. Even among officials, inequalities abound. Those with *jinshi* degrees are as invulnerable as if made of copper and iron, able to do everything their own way with no one daring to protest. Those assigned to their posts as National University students go about their jobs as cautiously as if crossing a narrow bridge with a load of eggs in their hands. Even so, their superiors are still constantly on their backs. When complaints against officials are reviewed, if the official under investigation is a *jinshi,* however corrupt and cruel he is accused of being, his case will be handled with exceptional leniency. The fact of the matter is, there is this fear that corrupt and cruel officials will be wiped off the face of the earth. (*This is certainly a comment that will infuriate the corrupt and the cruel.*) The sentencing will go like this: 'This subject of the emperor may have violated the code of conduct for officials, but he is either a newcomer or too young and can well be expected to turn over a new leaf and mend his ways in the future. Therefore, he is hereby demoted for his impetuous style of work or his lack of competence.' Within a few years' time, he'll be working his way up again. If he bribes higher-ups with whatever silver he can scrape together, he'll just be transferred at the same rank to a different locality, and that will be that. But when it comes to officials who got their posts as National

University students, the slightest misdemeanor will be magnified ten times. If nothing can be done to an influential *jinshi* official under investigation, then, however incorrupt and virtuous you are, you'll be the luckless scapegoat.

"With so many inequalities, my conclusion is that those without *jinshi* degrees had better not aspire to be officials. I'd rather be an untitled scholar all my life so that when I call out my grievances before King Yama of hell after I die, I may be compensated in my next life. So why should I stoop low and accept a minor post and suffer humiliation day after day?" Then he intoned a poem,

"Ranking has always been unfair;
Degrees weigh more than personal merits.
The madman of Chu despaired of saving the land;[4]
The king of She loved dragons, but only fake ones.[5]

"If not meant to pass the examinations,
I'd rather die an untitled scholar.
To wear out an iron ink slab—how heroic!
Didn't Lord Pingjin's rise in life come late?"

In the Han dynasty, there was a Lord Pingjin, named Gongsun Hong, who began studying *The Spring and Autumn Annals* at the age of fifty and won first place in the examinations when he was sixty. Later, he rose to be a prime minister and an enfeoffed lord. Xianyu Tong passed the imperial examinations at the age of sixty-one, an event that was believed to have been forecast in the above poem. But more of this later.

Now, let us come back to the time when Xianyu Tong intoned the above eight-line poem. Henceforth, his determination grew firmer. However, his time had not come yet. By the age of fifty, "Su Qin remained his old self."[6] His status had not changed. A few years later, he began to do badly even on minor examinations. Every time the imperial examinations were held, he was invariably the first one to show up at the examination grounds, an object of widespread scorn and contempt. In the sixth year of the Tianshun reign period [1454–67], a fifty-seven-year-old Xianyu Tong, graying at the temples, still found himself among young men in tireless discussions about literature and the arts. The youngsters looked upon him either as some kind of freak who should be given a wide berth or as a laughingstock to be ridiculed, but of this, no more need be said.

I shall now tell of a certain Kuai Yushi, courtesy name Shunzhi, magistrate of Xing'an County and a native of Xianju County, Taizhou Prefecture, in Zhejiang. Having passed the imperial examinations at an early age, he was held in high esteem. He delighted in discussions about literature and the arts, ancient and modern. He had, however, one idée fixe: he loved the young and despised the old and refused to treat them equally. He rewarded handsome youths liberally but insulted the old, whom he dismissed as worthless, addressing them sarcastically as "Honorable Seniors."

The year of which we speak being a year for civil service examinations at the local level, the county held a screening examination by order of the grand examiner. Without opening the seals at the corners of the examination papers where the examinees' names were entered, County Magistrate Kuai read all the examination papers submitted by scholars over the length and breadth of the county. Fully confident in his own good judgment and fair-mindedness, he picked out the best paper without bothering to find out anything as to the identity of the candidate. Proudly, he said to the assembly of scholars gathered before him, "I have graded all the papers, the best of which, with the graceful style typical of the Wu and Yue region south of the Yangzi River, will surely win honors at the imperial examination. None of the scholars throughout this county can measure up to this one."

The scholars stood with hands respectfully folded in front of their chests, waiting for that scholar's name to be revealed, in much the same way as the assembly of generals waited for Liu Bang, emperor of Han, to name the commander in chief.[7] When the seal on the paper was broken and the name was called out, there, for all to see, emerged a man, threading his way through the crowd. How did the man look?

Short and fat, with as much white hair as black,
His cap in shreds, his blue gown in tatters.
Everyone went up for a good close look:
Why! Isn't this the king of hell without the crown?
Undeserving praises give him none;
"Honorable Senior" comes easily to the tongue.
Do not envy him, do not lament your fate;
At worst, your turn will come in hoary old age.
Do nothing, take no pains;
You'll win first place when you are old enough.

The one who had placed first in the screening examination was none other than the fifty-seven-year-old freak and laughingstock Xianyu Tong. All the scholars present burst into hearty laughter. "'Honorable Senior' Xianyu Tong receives his appointment to office again!"

Magistrate Kuai colored deeply, at a loss for words. In a careless moment, he had picked the wrong man for the honor, but since he was in public, how could he change his decision? Checking his fury, he hastily opened all the examination papers. Fortunately, apart from the one who had won first honors, all who passed the screening examination were handsome young men, something that gave him a little comfort in his vexation. After announcing the results of the examination, Mr. Kuai returned to his yamen in dejection, but of this, no more need be said.

In his youth, Xianyu Tong had enjoyed fame, but after so many years of frustration, even though he had not given up all hope, he had felt

As lonesome as Qu Yuan by the marshes,[8]
As ashamed as Su Qin of Luoyang.

Now, much heartened by this unexpected honor, he went on to sit for the examinations at the circuit level. It was thanks more to his being the number one successful candidate at the county level than to the quality of his writing that he was allowed to sit for the examinations at the provincial level.

Merrily, he traveled to the provincial capital. The other candidates were all in their rooms, studying the classics in preparation for the last two sessions of the examinations while he, being well learned enough, spent his days roaming up and down the streets. Those who saw him guessed, "This old gentleman must be accompanying a son or a grandson to the examinations. Not being in the game, he *is* taking it easy!" Had they known he was a candidate for the examinations, they surely would have exploded with mirth.

Time flew by. In a trice, the seventh day of the eighth month rolled around. On the streets, a celebration with a great fanfare of drums and wind instruments welcomed the examiners into the examination grounds. Watching the spectacle, Xianyu Tong saw Mr. Kuai of Xing'an County being honored as the examiner for the section on *The Book of Rites.* Xianyu Tong thought to himself, "It so happens that I'll be in Mr. Kuai's section. Being the one who granted me first place in the screening examination, he must have liked my style. Now that my path crosses his, the odds are eight or nine out of ten that I'll make it!"

Little did he know that Mr. Kuai thought otherwise. His line of reasoning ran like this: "If I pick a young man with a long career ahead of him, I, as his onetime examiner, can count on his loyalty in the future. I have no use for those old ones." Pursuing these thoughts, he said to himself again, "I shouldn't have been so careless at the screening examination and picked that Honorable Senior Xianyu. What a fool I made of myself in front of all those people! If I pick this man again, won't I be laughed at again? When grading the papers this time, I'll disregard those that are written neatly throughout the three sessions because those will surely be the work of well-learned scholars advanced in years. I'll pick only those papers that lack a confident tone, that have jumbled grammar, that bungle the meter of the verses, and that offer faltering arguments in answering essay questions about state policies and muddleheaded judgments of legal cases, for those will be the work of young beginners. They may not be learned enough, but I can afford to allow them one or two more chances to pass the examinations, and that way, I'll be able to rid myself of that pest Xianyu Tong."

His mind thus made up, he went through the papers in the way he had prescribed for himself and picked a few that, though written in a disorderly fashion, were not without merit. He transmitted the papers, with bold, conspicuous markings showing his approval, to the chief examiner, who duly gave his endorsement.

On the twenty-eighth day of the eighth month, in the Hall of Ultimate Fairness and in the company of the examiners of all sections, the chief examiner opened the seals over the candidates' names on the examination papers and copied the names of successful candidates onto announcement posters. The candidate who had won first place in the section on *The Book of Rites* turned out to be Xianyu Tong, student from Xing'an County, Guilin Prefecture. The fifty-seven-year-old freak and laughingstock was again in luck.

Mr. Kuai was flabbergasted. Observing the scowl on Mr. Kuai's face, the chief examiner asked for an explanation. Mr. Kuai replied, "That Xianyu Tong is too old to be on the honor roll. Young students will complain. He should be replaced."

Pointing to the board hanging on the wall, the chief examiner said, "This very hall being the Hall of Ultimate Fairness, how can we discriminate on the basis of age? Since ancient times, it's always been the older and more experienced people who win the highest academic honors. If anything, we'll be giving a boost to the morale of all those who are devoted to learning."

Refusing to have Xianyu replaced, the chief examiner gave him fifth place. There was nothing Mr. Kuai could do about it. Truly,

You may try and try again,
But you can't change what's in your fate.
A young man he had meant to pick,
But the old freak won out, as before.

Determined to reject Honorable Senior Xianyu, Mr. Kuai had picked only inferior papers. Being a fine scholar, Xianyu Tong should not have done so poorly. How could he have ended up winning Mr. Kuai's favor?

The fact of the matter was that after telling himself on the seventh day of the eighth month that he stood a good chance with Mr. Kuai as the examiner for his section, he returned to his lodging and had a few cups too many of unheated wine, which upset his stomach and gave him diarrhea. But he still dragged himself to the examination grounds, where he worked out his draft in his mind during bouts of diarrhea until he had no more than one or two wisps of breath left in him. It was in such a state that he managed to finish the essay for the first session of the examinations. The second and third sessions went by in the same way. Not even one tenth of his talent found its way into his essays. (*Even one tenth would have worked against him.*) He thought he did not have the slightest chance of passing the examinations, little knowing that Mr. Kuai was not looking for quality. That was how he ended up with such high honors. Because he was destined for bliss after the misery of his life had run its course, the reversal in his fortunes occurred at the same time that the examination standards were turned upside down. In the whole of Xing'an County, he was the only one who was granted the degree of *juren.*

The district yamen held a celebration banquet in honor of the examiners and the successful candidates who had received *juren* degrees. The banquet over, the new *juren* degree holders asked one another their ages, and he ranked first. Each section examiner was delighted to get to know the *juren* who had taken the examination in his section. Only Mr. Kuai was in low spirits. Xianyu Tong, on his part, was overflowing with gratitude to Mr. Kuai for having twice recognized his talent, but the more deferential and attentive Xianyu was, the more he upset Mr. Kuai.

At the national level of the examinations in the capital, everything was done in strict accordance with the rules. No favors could be extended to anyone. Xianyu took these examinations when he was fifty-eight; a year after he had become a *juren,* but he failed. He went to see Mr. Kuai, who said only that he would advise Xianyu to accept an official post and stop taking the examinations. But having been an untitled scholar for the last forty-odd years without accepting a post as a National University student, how was he to stop now and be content with a post as a mere *juren* only one year after passing the provincial examinations?

He returned home and continued his studies with greater gusto than before. Every time local scholars had a literary gathering, he did not fail to show up to make his contribution, bringing his rice paper, ink stick, brush-pen, and ink slab. However much the others made fun of him, laughed at him, yelled at him, or loathed him, he did not pay the least attention. After making his contribution, he read all the writings of the other scholars and returned home in high spirits. This grew into a habit.

Time passed quickly. Quite unnoticeably, another three years elapsed in the twinkling of an eye, and the national examinations rolled around again. That year, Xianyu Tong was sixty-one years old but still as hale and hearty as ever.

While he was in Beijing for his second attempt at the national examinations, he dreamed that he had made it onto the list of successful candidates and won first honors, but instead of *The Book of Rites, The Book of Songs* appeared under his name. As he was a learned scholar, there was no classic he did not know well. In his eagerness to achieve fame and fortune, he thought it prudent to believe in the dream and changed his examination topic to *The Book of Songs.*

Well, coincidences will happen. County Magistrate Kuai, being an upright and incorrupt official, received a promotion. He went to Beijing, where he was granted the post of supervising secretary in the Bureau of Rites. The same year, he was further appointed to be a section examiner for the national examinations. Completely unaware of Xianyu Tong's change of subject, Mr. Kuai thought to himself, "My plans went wrong twice, and both times that Honorable Senior Xianyu ended up winning first place. Now, this time around, he's even older. Should he place first in the section on *The Book of Rites,* I'll never be able to live down the embarrassment. I'd better change from *The Book of Rites* to *The Book of Songs,* so that Honorable Senior Xianyu's success or failure will have nothing to do with me."

Once in the examiners' chamber behind the portiere, he asked to read the papers from *The Book of Poems* section. He then thought, "There must be more than one man like Honorable Senior Xianyu in this world. If I reject him only to pick another old man, wouldn't I be running from the thunder god only to be hit by lightning, as the saying goes? (*He who runs away from the old is stuck with the old. Could it be that heaven is giving Mr. Kuai a lesson out of its love for him?*) I know what to do. Old scholars must all be well versed in *The Book of Songs,* whereas youngsters, concentrating on the Four Books, may not know *The Book of Songs* well enough.[9] Let me skip over those papers that show solid knowledge of the four topics and pick those that are not without evidence of talent and do not stray from the topic, because such papers must be the work of young men."

He read the papers and transmitted them to his superiors. When it came time to publicize the results, he saw that the best paper from the section on *The Book of Songs* was tenth on the list of all successful candidates. When the seal over the examinee's name was broken, there, for all to see, was the name of Xianyu Tong, student from Xing'an County, Guilin Prefecture, none other than that sixty-one-year-old freak and laughingstock! Kuai Yushi was so appalled that his eyes popped wide open, his jaw dropped, and he looked more dead than alive.

Had he known that wealth and rank are in one's lot,
He would have regretted his futile plots.

Then Mr. Kuai thought, "Even though there's no lack of people sharing the same surnames and given names, there can't be a second Xianyu Tong in Xing'an County, Guilin Prefecture.[10] And yet, he has always concentrated on *The Book of Rites.* I wonder why he switched to *The Book of Songs.* How very strange!"

When Xianyu paid Mr. Kuai a courtesy call, Mr. Kuai asked for an explanation of the switch, whereupon Xianyu told of his dream. Heaving sigh upon sigh, Mr. Kuai said, "You are truly destined to gain the *jinshi* degree!" Henceforth, a bond developed between Mr. Kuai the mentor and Xianyu Tong the student.

At the palace examinations, Xianyu Tong came out at the top of the second class and was appointed an administrative aide in the Department of Justice. That this old man, in spite of having won his first success in the imperial examinations, was put in a post of little importance made many people feel that he was being unfairly treated, but he himself remained as cheerful as ever.

Now, Kuai Yushi, when making his usual frank remonstrations regarding the work of the Bureau of Rites, offended Grand Academician Liu Ji with one of his memorials. Liu Ji had Mr. Kuai locked up in the Ministry of Justice detention house on some false charges. Many of the officials in that ministry, eager to ingratiate themselves with Liu Ji, wanted to have Mr. Kuai put to death. Fortunately, by the grace of heaven, Xianyu Tong was in the same ministry. It was thanks to Xianyu's determined efforts in pleading his case and taking care of him that Mr. Kuai did not suffer too much. Xianyu also sought help from other officials who had passed the examinations in the same year, and, together, they pleaded to various government offices for leniency on Mr. Kuai's behalf. Upon receiving a lighter sentence than he had anticipated, Mr. Kuai thought to himself, "As the poem goes, 'Flowers wither when given too much care / willows flourish when left unattended.' If I had not let that old man pass the exams, I wouldn't be alive today." (*A debt of gratitude has been repaid.*)

He went to Honorable Senior Xianyu's home to express his gratitude. Xianyu Tong said, "Three times you granted me academic honor in your kindness. What little I have done for you is not enough to repay even one ten thousandth of the debt of gratitude I owe you!"

That day, the mentor and the student drank to their hearts' content before they parted company. Henceforth, wherever Mr. Kuai was, whether in his hometown or in the place of his post, Xianyu would have someone take his greetings to Mr. Kuai once or twice every year as a token of his devotion, however meager his pay.

As time went by, Xianyu Tong was transferred from one post to another within the ministry. Before he knew it, six years had elapsed, and he was due for a promotion to the rank of prefect. As he was held in high regard in the capital for his competence, his integrity, and the experience that came with his age, the Ministry of Personnel was determined to find him a good post, but he could not care less.

It so happened that a letter arrived from Xianju County, saying that Mr. Kuai's son, Kuai Jinggong, was involved in a fight with the wealthy Cha family over the border of the two families' graveyards and that the Cha family had charged Mr. Kuai Junior with beating to death a page boy missing from the Cha establishment and had reported the alleged murder to the authorities. Unable to counter the charges, Kuai Jinggong fled to his father in Yunnan. His disappearance aroused the local authorities' suspicions. As the case involved a human life, the authorities dispatched a large team of officers to track down the fugitive. Even a few family members were taken into custody, to the shock of the entire household.

Xianyu Tong, having learned upon inquiry that the post of prefect in Taizhou was vacant, asked to be appointed to that position. The Ministry of Personnel was aware that the post of Taizhou prefect was not an enviable one, but since Xianyu Tong had volunteered, why not comply with his wishes? Thus, Xianyu Tong was promoted to be prefect of Taizhou Prefecture.

Within three days following Xianyu Tong's assumption of his post, the Cha family learned that the new prefect was Mr. Kuai's protégé. Since he had requested the post in order to solve the dispute, the family thought he would surely take the defendant's side. So they started vicious rumors about him in the yamen, rumors to which Xianyu Tong turned a deaf ear. Nor did he listen to the grievances of members of the Kuai clan.

In the meantime, he secretly sent officers to track down the page boy who was missing from the Cha establishment and told them not to fail in their mission. A little more than two months later, the page boy was captured in Hangzhou. Prefect Xianyu held a court trial and found that the page boy had fled for private reasons that had nothing whatsoever to do with the Kuai family. The page boy was then returned to the Cha establishment to be dealt with by the Chas. The detained members of the Kuai clan were all released.

On an appointed day, Xianyu went in person to inspect the border between the two families' graveyards. With the page boy found, the Chas knew that they did not have a case. Afraid that the court's judgment would be unfavorable to them, they implored those with clout to put in a good word for them with the prefect. At the same time, they sent a messenger to the Kuai residence to say that they were willing to yield on the matter of the border and negotiate peace. The Kuais, for their part, had no intention of maintaining a feud now that the case had been solved. Prefect Xianyu approved the truce. The Cha family paid a small penalty, and the matter was reported to higher authorities. Both families were satisfied. Truly,

With a sharp eye in the court of judgment,
No foul deeds go undetected.

Prefect Xianyu sent a messenger to deliver a letter to Yunnan Prefecture, to Mr. Kuai, his mentor. A delighted Mr. Kuai thought to himself, "As the saying goes, 'Plant a thistle, and you get thorns. Plant pear and plum trees, and you enjoy the shade.' If I had not let that old man pass the exams, my family would have been ruined." (*A repayment of a debt of gratitude extends to the second generation.*) He wrote a letter stating his sincere gratitude and had his son Kuai Jinggong deliver it to Xianyu Tong's residence.

Xianyu Tong said, "This humble old man was a loser abandoned by the world. It was my honorable mentor who saw me for what I am and let me succeed in the examinations. What I fear most is to leave this world before repaying his immense kindness. My brother, the unjust charges against you should, by rights, have been overturned. What I did was nothing more than fanning the flames when the wind was favorable. This is not nearly enough to repay you for your kindness to me in the examinations." Mr. Kuai Junior being in charge of the household affairs, Xianyu advised him to apply himself to his studies behind closed doors. Nothing of note occurred for a time after that.

His reputation having soared in his three-year term of office as prefect of Taizhou, Xianyu Tong was promoted to be commander of Huizhou and Nanjing, and then, after a series of promotions, he rose to be investigation commissioner of Henan. In all these posts, he served with great assiduity. While in his eighties, and still more energetic than younger men, he received another promotion and became governor of Zhejiang. He thought to himself, "Though my success as a scholar came late in life after much frustration, yet, since I passed the examinations at the age of sixty-one, my career has been plain sailing, without ever running into a storm. Now that I've been appointed to be a governor, I've truly come as far as I can. Having always reminded myself to be an upright, clean, and hardworking official worthy of the trust of the imperial court, I should retire before my career goes downhill.

However, I have not yet paid in full my debt of gratitude to Mr. Kuai for having recognized my ability three times. This new post being in the very region where my mentor lives, I may be able to do something for him."

On a chosen day, he left to take up his post. The splendor of the sending-off and welcoming ceremonies and the fanfare that accompanied his journey need not be described here. In a matter of days, he arrived at the provincial seat of Zhejiang.

By this time, Mr. Kuai had risen to the level of assistant provincial administration commissioner, but he was living at home in retirement, incapacitated by an eye ailment. He heard that Honorable Senior Xianyu was to be the governor of the province and went to visit him in Hangzhou, taking along his twelve-year-old grandson. Though he was Xianyu's mentor, he was more than twenty years younger than Xianyu. But now that he had retired and was afflicted with an eye ailment, he looked frail and forlorn, whereas the eighty-odd-year-old Mr. Xianyu, at the height of his career, looked as if he were still in the prime of his life. It can thus be seen that the timing of one's rise in life is not all that important. Mr. Kuai heaved many a sigh. Truly,

Pines and cypresses, envy not peaches and plums;
Cherish your branches that defy severe winters.

After assuming his post, Xianyu Tong was just about to send someone to convey his greetings to Mr. Kuai when he heard the announcement that Assistant Commissioner Kuai was already at his door. Beside himself with joy, he rushed out to greet Mr. Kuai. In such haste was he that he did not even bother to check if he had his shoes on right. He invited Mr. Kuai all the way into his private quarters, and the two men exchanged greetings, one as a teacher, the other as a student. Mr. Kuai said to his twelve-year-old grandson, "Greet His Honor."

"Who is this young man to you?"

"You saved my life," began Mr. Kuai in response, "and you proved my son innocent when he was in trouble. The infinity of your kindness can be matched only by the sky and the earth. And now, the star of happiness is again shining over this province. Being old and sick, I don't have many days left in this world. My son failed as a scholar, and I have only my grandson here, named Kuai Wu, who is quite talented. I brought him along to ask for your help."

"At my age," said Xianyu, "I shouldn't be holding any more official posts. I came in all brazenness because I haven't paid in full my debt of gratitude to you. Now that you have deigned to ask me to take care of your grandson, I'm only too glad to have a chance to repay my debt. I propose that your grandson stay with me and study the same lessons as my grandchildren do. I wonder if you, my mentor, would worry too much if he stays here?"

"If you would be kind enough to teach the boy, I'll be able to find peace even in death," said Mr. Kuai.

Thereupon, two page boys were assigned to serve Kuai Wu in his studies in the governor's mansion. Mr. Kuai took leave of his host and went his way.

With his exceptionally sharp intelligence, Kuai Wu made daily progress in his studies. That very autumn when the grand examiner came for a visit, Mr. Xianyu strongly recommended that Kuai Wu be made a stipend student as a designated Child Prodigy but remain in Xianyu's residence for continued studies. Three years later, with Kuai Wu's studies completed, Xianyu said, "This young man is ready for the civil service examinations, and my debt of gratitude to my mentor can now be paid off." He gave Kuai Wu three hundred taels of silver from his salary with which to buy writing implements and escorted the boy all the way to Xianju County in Taizhou, only to be told that Mr. Kuai had died of illness three days before. After paying a tearful homage to the deceased, Mr. Xianyu asked, "What words did my mentor leave before he passed away?"

Mr. Kuai's son Kuai Jinggong replied, "My deceased father's last words were that he, having unfortunately passed the examinations too early in his youth, favored the young against the old. It was by accident that he came to know Your Honor. Goodness knows how many young men of varying degrees of worthiness and status he promoted, but none of them did anything for him in return. You are the only one who never stopped taking care of him. Older men should never be neglected, never ever in generations to come!" (*Words said with deep emotion.*)

Mr. Xianyu burst into hearty laughter. "Three times I tried to repay my debt of gratitude to my mentor precisely for the purpose of letting the world know that helping older men is not an unworthy cause. It will never do to favor the young against the old." With that, he took his leave and returned to his yamen, where he wrote a memorial requesting permission to retire.

His request granted, he returned to his home village and lived a leisurely life in the woods. What time he had left after teaching his grandchildren he spent with the older men in the village, drinking and writing poems. Eight years later, his oldest grandson Xianyu Han placed high in the provincial examinations and went to the capital for the national examinations. There, he ran into Kuai Wu from Xianju County, who was also there for the examinations after having passed the provincial examinations. With family connections going back two generations and having studied together in childhood, the two young men shared the same room for their studies. When the results of the examinations were announced, they learned that they both had been awarded the *jinshi* degree, an event both families celebrated with joy.

Xianyu Tong's career lasted for a total of twenty-three years, starting with his success at the local examinations at the age of fifty-seven and at the national examinations at sixty-one. After retiring to his home village with enough glory and wealth to last for three generations, he witnessed his grandson's academic success and lived to be ninety-seven years old. His good fortune, though late in coming, lasted for a full forty years. To this day, people in Zhejiang persevere in their studies up to the age of sixty or seventy, and, among them, there is no lack of scholars who gain fame and fortune late in life. A later poet had this to say,

> *Why work your fingers to the bone for wealth and rank?*
> *Heaven decides the timing of your rise in life.*
> *Why not be more like peaches of immortality?*
> *A life of three thousand years is by no means long.*

19

With a White Falcon, Young Master Cui Brings an Evil Spirit upon Himself

For her sake, he cut the court sessions short;
None dared offer more advice to the throne.
She greeted him in the Fairyland Hall;
She enjoyed lychee in Calyx Tower.
The battle drums drowned the music of dance;
The beauties fled, the men in armor charged.
He let long-standing peace be turned to war;
He failed the founder of the house of Tang.

The above poem is about the seventh emperor of the Tang dynasty, posthumously titled Emperor Xuanzong [r. 712–56]. As an old legend has it, there is, in the sky, a star called variously the Darkening [*xuan,* as in Emperor Xuanzong] Star, the Gold Star [Venus], the *shen* star, the *changgeng* star, the *taibai* star, and the Enlightening Star. Ordinary folks who do not know the proper name for it call it the Morning Star. It rises in the sky before the eastern sky has brightened. When daybreak draws near, it gradually dims. The process of going from bright to dark is captured by the character *xuan* [as in Emperor Xuanzong].

When Yao Chong [650–721] and Song Jing [663–737] were serving as prime ministers in Emperor Xuanzong's court, rice and wheat cost only three or four mace of silver a bushel. A traveler on a one-thousand-li journey did not need to worry about running short of food. But after Prime Ministers Yao and Song died and were replaced by Yang Guozhong [d. 756] and Li Linfu [d. 752], Emperor Xuanzong began to be afflicted with a weakness for four things: lust, hunting, wine accompanied by singing and dancing, and fancy buildings.

Emperor Xuanzong had a most beloved consort named Yang Taizhen, who, in her turn, had a clandestine love relationship with a Tartar named An Lushan. Even though he weighed three hundred and sixty catties, An Lushan could catch a flying swallow while he was seated, walk as fast as a galloping horse, and, while dancing the Tartars' dance, spin round and round with the speed of wind. Emperor Xuanzong liked him for being valiant and robust and showered favors upon him. Thus, the man honored the emperor as his father and Consort Yang as his mother. The latter shaved

Lushan's head, powdered his face and nose, painted his eyebrows, wrapped him in brocade and colored silk, and had him carried around the inner quarters of the palace grounds by palace maids of strong physique. This began as a practical joke, but the intimacy led to an illicit sexual relationship between Consort Yang and An Lushan.

One day, Lushan was sporting with Consort Yang in her chamber when a palace maid came to announce, "The emperor is here!" Being a man of exceptional agility, Lushan jumped over the wall and disappeared. In all haste, Consort Yang, with disheveled hair, rushed out to greet the emperor, but in her confusion, she mistakenly called the emperor "My love" instead of "Your Majesty." Emperor Xuanzong turned back right away and ordered Gao Lishi [684–762] and Gao Gui, officers in charge of internal affairs of the palace residential quarters, to send Consort Yang back to her home to reflect on her misdemeanor. Consort Yang asked to see the emperor, but her request was denied. In tears, she left the palace.

Now, three days without Consort Yang left the emperor in a miserable state. He found no taste in his food, and no peace in his sleep. Having learned what was on the emperor's mind, Gao Lishi remarked, "The consort gave offense to Your Majesty only because she was confused in her speech after a daytime nap. After reflecting on her misdemeanor for three days, she should be quite remorseful. Why does Your Majesty not summon her back?" (*What a bootlicker, that Gao Lishi!*)

The emperor told Gao Gui to go and see what Consort Yang was doing at home. Thus ordered, Gao Gui went to Preceptor Yang's residence. After seeing the consort, he reported to the emperor in these words, "Her Ladyship looked miserable. She does not even bother to comb her hair or take a bath. The moment she saw me, she asked how the emperor was, her tears falling like rain. She then took a mirror, let her hair down, and with a pair of Bingzhou scissors,[1] cut off a lock, tied it up with a five-colored string, sealed it with her own hands, and told me to bring it to Your Majesty. Her Ladyship said tearfully, 'Everything I have, I got from His Majesty. Only my body, my hair, and my skin are given to me by my parents. I am sending this lock of hair as a token of my gratitude to His Majesty and also as a reminder of the vow he took at Eaglewood Pavilion at midnight on the Double Seventh.'"

It was a fact that at midnight on a Double Seventh Festival,[2] Emperor Xuanzong had taken a vow with Consort Yang in Eaglewood Pavilion to share the same quilt and pillow with her, lifetime after lifetime. After he had heard Gao Gui's report and opened the package containing the lock of hair, Emperor Xuanzong was overcome with grief. Right away, he ordered that Gao Lishi bring Consort Yang back to the palace in a perfumed carriage. Henceforth, he lavished even more favors upon her.

At that time, tributary gifts poured in from all directions: The Xixia [Tangut] offered moon-shaped pipa (four-stringed lutes,) Vietnam offered jade flutes, Xiliang brought grape wine, and Silla offered a white falcon. The grape wine was served to the emperor, who gave the *pipa* to Zheng Guanyin, the jade flute to Prince Ning, his younger brother,[3] and the white falcon to Prime Minister Cui. (*What a roundabout way of introducing the falcon!*)

Later, Academician Li Bai, in his poem in praise of the peonies of Eaglewood Pavilion, compared Consort Yang to Zhao Feiyan.[4] Detecting the veiled satire in the poem, Gao Lishi reported against Li Bai, and following Consort Yang's tearful complaint to the emperor, Li Bai was demoted. Prime Minister Cui, being an old friend of Li Bai's, was implicated and demoted by imperial order to prefect of Zhongshan in Dingzhou, Hebei. Truly,

When the old turtle's meat won't cook tender,
Innocent mulberries are cut down to feed the fire.

So Prime Minister Cui went to Zhongshan Prefecture, Dingzhou. He was greeted, still some distance from his destination, by an assembly of local officials and led all the way to the prefectural yamen, where the usual handover formalities were observed. After he took up the post, his administration proved to be, not surprisingly, as clean as water, as fair and untilted as a well-balanced scale, as straight as a tightly pulled cord, and as perceptive in solving cases as a shining mirror. In less than a month, his governance had made such a difference in people's morals that nothing lost on the road would be pocketed by any pedestrian walking by. What I shall be relating next happened one early spring during the Tianbao reign period [742–56].

Spring! Spring!
The willows tender, the flowers fresh,
The plum blossoms fall on the carpet of grass.
The northern orioles warble, the southern swallows chirp;
The horses neigh on the suburban paths;
The carriage wheels run on rustic roads.
The sun thaws the ice and turns the water green,
The wind mild, the rain gentle, the mist soft.
Grand feasts are set out in fancy halls;
Flower viewers fill the much bedecked town.

Prime Minister Cui had a son called Cui Ya, about twenty years of age, a handsome young man much given to hunting. Inspired by the charms of spring, he said to his father in the hall, taking a step forward with his hands respectfully folded across his chest, "Father, I would like to request a one-day leave for a hunting trip in the country. Would you approve?"

"If you go, be sure to come back soon."

"As you say, Father. But I have another request."

"What is it?"

"I wish to borrow the white Silla falcon that the emperor gave you."

"All right, but take good care of it. Don't lose it. It's a tribute from Silla that the emperor gave me, and the only one of its kind in the world. Be sure not to lose it! Should the emperor want it back, where do you suppose I could find another one like it?"

"I'm taking it out just to show it off to admirers and bring honor to our prefecture."

"Come back soon, and don't drink too much," admonished the father.

Mr. Cui Junior had a professional birdman to take care of the borrowed falcon, and indeed, where could another like it be found? His horse now brought before him, he mounted the saddle that was much adorned with gold and silver and set out on his journey.

If this storyteller had been born in the same year and had grown up shoulder to shoulder with him, I would have stopped him from going. He should never have taken this white falcon out. As it was, however, the trip led to a most strange adventure, so strange that the likes of it had never been heard of since time immemorial. There is a poem in testimony:

He has a weakness for hunting and women;
A little indulgence does little harm.
He takes out the falcon in the morning
And returns at dusk, smelling of perfume.

With his love for hunting, Young Master Cui was much delighted with the falcon he had borrowed that day and placed it under the care of the birdman. Equipped with slingshots with horn handles polished with waterstone and crossbows made of ebony and accompanied by eagles with round eyes, ironlike talons, and hook-shaped beaks as well as dogs with floppy ears, narrow waists, and long muzzles, the hunting team marched into the country. They rode over creeks lined with peach trees, crossed groves of plum trees and poplars, forded streams amid green meadows, and passed villages ablaze with apricot blossoms and banner-flying wineshops behind green portieres hanging from the eaves of thatched roofs. Truly,

The weather neither warm nor cold,
The houses half urban, half rural.

About twenty to thirty li farther on, they felt tired and stopped by a wineshop. Young Master Cui dismounted from his horse and went into the wineshop, asking, "Any good wine? Give me some to reward my men with."

A waiter came out to greet the patrons. How did the man look? He was

Eight feet tall, with a leopard head, a swallow's chin,
Round eyes, and a bristling beard,
A Zhang Fei with his fearsome roar at Changban Bridge,[5]
A veritable Wang Yanzhang of Yuanshui Town.[6]

Cui was startled at the sight of the man. "How can a human being look so evil?" he asked himself.

Having chanted a greeting to the guests, the waiter stood to one side. Cui said, "I need some good wine to reward my men."

The waiter brought a jar of wine from within. One of Cui's attendants put on the table a wine cup that they had brought with them, filled it with the wine, and offered it to the young master.

Wine! Wine!
Friends! Tarry not till it's too late!
Before meals and after tea,
It's a must in the breeze and under the moon.
Li Bai drank a hundred liters a time,[7]
Liu Ling needed ten just to sober up.[8]
One sip gives a young man's cheeks the color of peach
And makes a girl's eyebrows droop like willow leaves.

Cui was alarmed to see that the wine was unusually red. "How can it be so brightly red?" he wondered. He sneaked up behind the waiter, followed him to the inner quarters of the shop, lifted the cover of the wine vat, and looked into it. That one little look so frightened Cui that

His three souls escaped from the top of his head;
His seven spirits fled from the soles of his feet.

What he saw was a vat full of bloody water with grains of rice soaking in it. He went out and, telling his men to stay away from the wine, gave the waiter three taels of silver in payment of the bill. (*In stories of the Song dynasty, bills and tips all too easily ran into several taels of silver and several strings of cash. Why so much? Because stories were often presented to the imperial court, and the figures had to be inflated out of fear that the court might cut wages. The reader must bear this in mind.*) The waiter took the money with a chant of thanks. Cui mounted his horse and left the wineshop.

After a li or two, they came to a hill. They had left behind the city's inner and outer gates, passed the suburbs and rural areas, and were now deep into the wilderness. Half a day later, they found themselves at the foot of Mount Heng, or North Mountain, where a small peak caught their attention with its imposing look.

Mountains! Mountains!
Steep or rolling, of all shades of green and blue.
Clouds float by the mouths of the caves,
Over murmuring creeks in the ravines.
The verdure spreads over a thousand hills,
Stretching as far as the eye can see.
The cloud-shrouded peak should still be there;
In our spiked shoes let us climb our way up.
The Bamboo Grove Seven were surely likable,
But the Mount Shang Four certainly were not idle.[9]

Young Master Cui was about to start climbing up when he raised his head and saw at the foot of the hill two wooden columns bearing a board on which a few lines were inscribed. He stopped his horse and read the inscription.

"This is a terror of a place!" he exclaimed. Reining in his horse, he cried, "Let's turn back!" When the rest of his company drew near, he pointed at the board, and those who were literate read the inscription aloud: "This hill, leading to Mount Heng, or the North Mountain, is named Ding Hill. There is a road up and down this hill, but, it being infested with spirits, ghosts, and demons, wayfarers are hereby admonished not to avail themselves of it. Take instead the footpath around the base of the hill. Do not attempt to climb over it. Be advised."

"Now what should we do?"

"We'll have to turn back," said Cui.

He was about to start back when a birdman with an eagle perched on his arm stepped forward and said, "Master, I'm from these parts. I know that up there in the mountains, there is so much to see, and there are all kinds of rare and precious birds and animals, too. Since you're on a hunting trip, how can you not climb this hill? The footpath is on flat land. How are you going to see birds and animals along the footpath? It would be a shame if the white falcon from Silla and this eagle on my arm can't be put to use. And the same goes for the small eagles, hunting dogs, slingshots, and crossbows." (*That sycophant can read his young master's mind.*)

"You do have a point," said Cui. "Now, listen, all of you! Those who catch animals alive and take them back to my house will each be rewarded with three taels of silver and a few cups of wine before going home. Those who take back dead animals will each be rewarded with one tael of silver and several cups of wine before going home. Those who get no bird or animal get no money or wine."

The men chanted their consent. Cui whipped his horse and led the way up the hill. His men followed. Strange to say, there were no birds or animals in sight, but only some rustling sounds in the grass. Cui looked with the left and right pupils of his all-seeing eyes and gave a cheer. From the grass emerged a red rabbit. As the men moved forward, Cui exclaimed, "Five taels of silver for anyone who catches that red rabbit!"

Behind Cui's horse stood the man with the white Silla falcon on his arm. "Why don't you give chase?" said Cui.

"Sir, you didn't order me to, so I didn't dare," replied the man, who was doing nothing.

"Go now, on the double!"

Thus ordered, the man freed the white falcon to hunt down the red rabbit. The falcon flew with the speed of an arrow, heading straight for the rabbit. With the falcon hot in pursuit, the rabbit ran into a patch of taller grass. The rabbit now lost from sight, the white falcon winged its way over the top of the hill. "Bring the white falcon back for me!" shouted Cui, while he rode ahead around the hill.

About halfway up the hill, he came upon a pine forest.

Pines! Pines!
How majestic! What deep shades!
They last down the years through the winters.
They reach into the sky from the hills;
They twist in the shape of canopies;
They wind like crouching dragons.
The heavy foliage rustles in the wind;
The thriving branches cast shadows of the moon.
They keep gentlemen's morals in all four seasons;
They are honored as Grand Masters of the Fifth Grade.[10]

Cui rode ahead, holding in his hand a slingshot with a horn handle that had been polished with waterstone. When he saw the white falcon flying into the pine forest, he gave chase.

Behind the forest was a steep cliff with no path leading up. The white falcon had a small bell on its neck. At the sound of a bell jingling from the top of the cliff, Cui raised his head and gave a start. "Never have I seen such a strange thing before!" he said to himself. At the top of the cliff, under a big tree, sat a skeleton about ten feet tall, wearing

An official's cap adorned with a gold cicada,
Glittering gold armor over a brocade gown,
A headband the color of lychee shells,
And a pair of shoes of parrot green.

The skeleton had the white falcon perched on his left hand and was fiddling with the falcon's bell with a finger on his right hand while making playful clucking sounds with his tongue. (*What a picture of joy!*)

"How very strange!" said Cui to himself. "I have to claim it, but there's no path for me to go up." He had no choice but to remain where he was. To the skeleton, he said loudly in an imploring tone, "Honorable god, forgive my ignorance of who you are, but that white falcon from Silla is mine. Would you please return it to me?"

The skeleton took no notice of him. Cui repeated his supplication between five to seven times and made seven or eight deep bows. (*What a fearless man!*) None of his men had made it into the forest yet. As the skeleton continued to ignore him, Cui found his patience wearing thin. He raised the slingshot in his hand, pulled it with all his might, and took good aim at his target. *Bang* went the pellet. When he looked closely again, the skeleton had disappeared, and so had the white falcon.

Cui rode out of the forest, only to find that his men were nowhere in sight. He turned and looked back, and there was the forest, with green grass spreading all around it. He slowly started to move away as he noticed the sky beginning to darken.

Feeling the pangs of hunger, he dismounted and led his horse by the reins. He approached the end of the mountain path and saw that the hour was in fact still early.

The red sun was sinking in the west;
The ravens and magpies crowed in the woods.
The fishermen, but not the travelers, stopped for the day;
Plumes of kitchen smoke curled above the villages.
In the quiet mountain temple,
A silver lamp shone before the Buddha statue.
With the moon ascending the eastern sky,
The lonely village wineshop took in its banner.
The woodchopper returned, treading ancient footpaths,
Crossing creeks, listening to the apes and tigers.
The lady of the house stood waiting,
Leaning against the gate.

All alone, Cui led his horse along a road that was not the one he had taken earlier. Under the starlight, he made out a few thatched huts in the distance. "Thank goodness!" said he to himself. "If there are people living here, I'll be all right." As he drew near, he saw that the huts were part of a farmstead.

Farmstead! Farmstead!
By the dike and the hill, blue-tiled roof, whitewashed walls.
Mulberry and hemp leaves blocked out the sun;
Elms and willows stood in straight rows.
Pheasants' cries echoed through the bamboo groves;
Wild dogs' barks rang through the farmstead houses.
Light wisps of smoke rose from the thatched roofs;
A floating mist shrouded the fields of crops.
With grain to spare, chickens and dogs well-fed,
And free from corvée, the people thrived and prospered.

Cui tied his horse to a willow tree in front of the farmstead and knocked at the gate, saying aloud, "I am a wayfarer passing by your house. I have lost my bearings and wish to stay here overnight before making my way home tomorrow." No answer came from within. He continued, "I am the son of Prefect Cui of Zhongshan, former prime minister. I lost my bearings because my white falcon from Silla disappeared, and I hope to stay here for the night."

He knocked two or three times before a voice from inside said, "Coming! Coming!" With a slip-slop of shoes, a man walked out to open the gate. One look was enough to make Mr. Cui cry out in anguish, for the man was none other than the waiter at the village inn where Cui had stopped earlier.

"Why, it's you!" said Cui.

"Sir, this is the residence of my master," said the waiter. "Let me go inside to announce you. I'll be right back."

A few moments later, there emerged from the house a girl in red escorted by several maidservants.

Wu Daozi, the master of painting,[11]
Would have failed to capture her charm.
Kuai Wentong, however glib a talker,[12]
Could not have found words to describe her grace.

Without daring to raise his head, Cui said, "Madam, I, Cui Ya, have lost my bearings and would like to stay here overnight. After I return home tomorrow, my father, the prime minister, will surely reward you."

"I've been waiting for you for a long time," said the young lady. "And now, here you are, finally doing me the honor. Please enter this humble house."

"How would I dare go straight in like this?"

But she insisted despite his demurrals. At last, he gave a chant of consent and followed her in. They entered a room brightly lit with candles, and maidservants brought in tea. Cui asked the young woman, "May I venture to ask what place this is? And what is your surname, young lady?"

At these questions, the young woman opened her ruby lips slightly, revealing two rows of small gems of teeth, and said something that made Cui think, "How very strange!"

The tea over and the cups and saucers taken away, Cui said to himself, "I am hungry, and yet they serve nothing but tea!" He was in the midst of these thoughts when the young lady ordered that wine be set out. In a trice, the maidservants moved a small table over and soon laid out a fine spread.

The much bedecked hall was ablaze with lights;
On the feast table, an array of
Wondrous cups and vessels of gold and jade.
In the pearl compotes, exotic fruits;
On the jade plates, the finest delicacies.
By the coral table stood fair maidens
Holding colorful wine goblets
And pouring nectar into precious cups.

His hands respectfully folded in front of him, Cui stepped forward and said, "I would not dream of accepting the wine that you so kindly offer."

"Please go ahead and take just a sip. This is also the residence of a highly placed official."

"May I ask which official's establishment this is?"

"There's no need to ask. You'll know soon enough."

"My parents at home are waiting for me to return. Please give me directions, so that I can be on my way as soon as possible."

"All right. My family being related by marriage to some leading families of the land and you being the prime minister's son, we are a perfect match as far as family background is concerned. I have seen my father rejecting on my behalf one marriage proposal after another. Who would have known that I was to meet my destined one here?"

These words frightened Cui all the more. He did not dare to contradict her and mumbled something noncommittal. One cup of wine led to another. After several rounds, he pleaded, "Please give me directions, and let me go back."

"All right, I'll tell my father to escort you home tomorrow."

"As the saying goes, 'A man and a woman should not share the same meal table.' As another ancient proverb says about not arousing suspicion, 'Don't bend to pull on your shoes in a melon field / Don't reach to adjust your hat under a plum tree.' I'm deeply afraid of giving your father offense."

"That's all right. Even if we don't become husband and wife, I'd still wait until tomorrow to escort you back."

The young man was in a half-drunken torpor when he heard a man speaking and a horse neighing outside. A maidservant announced, "The commander is here."

"My father's here. Please wait for a while." Moving her lotuslike feet, she went off.

"How can there be a military commander in this place?" Cui wondered. On tiptoe, he followed her and saw her turn a corner into a room, where a voice could be heard. Hiding himself in a dark spot, Cui wet the window paper with the tip of his tongue, and what he saw gave him such a shock that he broke into a cold sweat and stood there incapable of movement. "I am as good as dead!" he thought. "I've been running around the whole night, only to end up in his home!"

What he had seen through the window was that in the room, which was lined on both sides with vermilion chairs, a ten-foot-tall skeleton sat in the seat of honor. It was the very one that Cui had hit with his slingshot earlier in the day. Now let us watch what happened next.

The girl chanted a greeting to her father and asked, "Father, are you all right?"

The skeleton replied, "My child, you may very well ask! After I went out earlier in the day, I saw a snow-white falcon. I was so impressed that I caught it and put it on my hand. Then a man aimed a slingshot at me from the foot of the hill and hit me right in one eye. How it hurt! I asked the local mountain god and was told that it was the son of Prime Minister Cui. If I ever get my hands on that bastard, I'll tie him up to a big column, cut open his chest, and gouge his heart out. With a wine cup in my left hand and his heart in my right hand, I'll down one cup with each bite of the heart and savor my revenge."

The words were still ringing in the air when a man emerged from behind the screen. It was none other than the waiter of the village inn. The commander said, "Doggy, did you hear what I said?"

"Yes, I did. That was outrageous! That Cui paid for wine in my shop earlier today. I didn't know he hurt the commander's eye!"

The girl said, "He must have hurt you by mistake, Father. Please forgive him."

The man who was called Doggy said, "Sister, don't blame me for shooting off my mouth, but Mr. Cui Junior was just drinking with you in the hall."

The girl pleaded with her father, "I was drinking with him because I have a marriage bond with him that goes back five hundred years. Please forgive him for my sake!" But the commander went on ranting and raving, and the daughter kept trying to calm him down.

Cui, hearing all this from the other side of the window, said to himself, "I'd better get out of here right now! What am I waiting for?" He made his way out of the hall, opened the gate, jumped on his horse, and gave it a stroke of the whip. The horse galloped blindly ahead in its fright, its hooves flying through the air.

After being on the run for the rest of the night without knowing where he was heading, Cui finally saw, by the light of dawn, that Mount Ding was behind him. "Thank goodness," he said, but the words were hardly out of his mouth when more than ten men charged out of the woods and, with a mighty shout, encircled him. "Woe is me!" he lamented, "I just escaped from the dragon pond, only to plunge right into the tiger's lair!"

Upon taking a closer look, however, he saw that the men were his followers. "You scared me!" said he.

The men asked him, "Where were you all night? If we hadn't found you today, we'd have been in big trouble!" After hearing his account of what had happened, they all rejoiced, their hands on their foreheads, saying, "How lucky that you're alive! We didn't dare go back last night and waited in the woods until now. The white falcon had flown to a tree at the back of the woods, and we've just got it down."

The keeper of the eagle said, "Young master, I'm from these parts, so I know the hills here are full of rare birds and animals. We should be doing some more hunting. Too bad the white falcon from Silla is not doing anything."

"There he goes again!" snapped Mr. Cui Junior.

The men escorted Cui back home and, upon arrival, dispersed to claim their rewards, whereas Cui went into the hall, where he chanted a greeting to his parents.

"Where were you all night? Your mother was worried sick," said the prime minister.

"A most extraordinary thing happened to me last night," said Cui, and he repeated the account he had told his followers.

The prime minister grew impatient. "What a tall tale from a fanciful youngster! Now, this is your punishment: Stay in your study! An attendant will be watching you, to make sure you don't leave the room."

In resignation, the young man went into the study.

Time sped by like an arrow. The sun and the moon shot back and forth like a shuttle, and in the snap of a finger, three months went by. It was summer now.

Summer! Summer!
The rains are abundant, the pavilions spacious,
The silk fan light, the fragrant air breezy.
Let down your hair, loosen your clothes,
And play a game or two of horse chess.[13] (The game of horse chess originated in the Jingkang reign period [1126]. It was not yet in existence in the Tang dynasty.)
Fragrant incense in the ancient tripod;
Famous paintings on the screen walls.
A nice breeze down the bamboo trail;
Tiled roofs among the two rows of green pines.
Nothing better to have than this: plums and melons
And salted fish over a cup of wine.

Mr. Cui Junior did not step outside the study for three months. One day, it was so hot that he left the study and went to a cool spot in the back garden. After sitting down, he said to himself, "For three months I didn't dare take a step out the study door. How nice it is to be enjoying the cool air here!" As the night drum struck two, behold! The moon rose in the east.

Moon! Moon!
It never pauses for a rest
But rises at night in the east
And sets at dawn in the west.
In shape more often crescent than round,
It shines best at midnight and midautumn.
Its lambent light the color of cold frost,
Its bright gleam sparkles like shining snow.
Its rays through the windows on windy nights
Break the hearts of those missing their loved ones.

By the light of the moon, Mr. Cui Junior took a leisurely walk around the garden. Suddenly, he noticed a black cloud rise into the sky and then part in the middle to reveal a fancy carriage with a driver and a woman passenger. The driver turned out to be none other than the waiter called Doggy. The woman, clad in dark red, was, as Cui saw by the moonlight, the very same young woman who had kept him for wine at the farmstead. She alighted from the carriage and said, "Young Master, the other day, I was full of good intentions when I asked you to stay. Why did you leave without saying good-bye?"

"If I had stayed, someone would have held my heart in his left hand, to make it go with the wine in his right hand! Please spare my life, young lady!"

"Don't be afraid," said the girl. "I am neither a human being nor a ghost. I am a fairy from the upper world. I have a marriage bond with you going back five hundred years. I'm now here to enjoy conjugal pleasures with you."

With that, she bade the waiter drive away in the carriage and leave her behind. In a moment of weakness, Cui was captivated by her charm.

Lust! Lust!
Hard to be rid of, easy to be lured.
It lurks in the boudoir and on willow-lined paths,
Aiding petty rogues, ruining gentlemen's morals.
The King of Chen's talent did him no service;[14]
King Zhou's mighty strength was rendered useless.[15]
The killer with the painless knife
Is the very one in front of your face.
Her lovely eyes are in fact sparkling waves
That drown the good as well as the foolish.

After the two had spent several days in the study, the attendant on guard duty commented, "I wonder why the young master forbids us to go into his study."

That very night, he caught sight of a seductive-looking woman and reported what he had seen to the housekeeper and the master. Carried away with rage, the prime minister stormed into the study, armed with a sword. The young man felt obliged to chant a greeting to his father.

"My son," said the father, "I told you to do your studies here. How could you have brought in some woman from the neighborhood? Should the imperial court get word of this, I will be blamed for having spoiled you rotten, and your own future career will be jeopardized!" (*He does think far ahead.*)

The son said only, "Father, I have done no such thing."

Before the father could ask further, a girl emerged from behind the screen and chanted a greeting. All the more enraged, the prime minister took a step forward and swung the sword in his hand, shouting, "Here it goes!"

Everything would have been all right had he not used his sword, for of the sharp sword in his hand, only the handle remained. Astounded, the prime minister recoiled three steps, at a loss as to what to do. The girl said, "Don't be angry, sir! I have a five-hundred-year marriage bond with your son. As husband and wife, we will soon become immortals together."

Without any idea what to do next, the prime minister went to consult his wife. He hired an exorcist, but there was no hope of capturing the girl.

The prime minister was fretting and fuming when the janitor came to him, saying, "Sir, there is a Luo Gongshi, the new director of the Law Section, who asked to see you. I told him that the prime minister is not seeing visitors. He asked why, so I told him about the matter. Director Luo said that in this area, there *is* someone who can do the exorcism. The man has achieved immortality through cultivating his spirit. His name is Luo Gongyuan, Director Luo's older brother."

Right away, the prime minister asked to see him. After tea was served, Mr. Cui Senior asked where Sage Luo lived.

Having obtained detailed information, Cui wrote a letter to Luo Gongyuan, asking him to go down the mountain to the Cui residence, and so he did. Much impressed by Sage Luo's unusual appearance (*In Song dynasty novels, all acts of exorcism were invariably attributed to Sage Luo because of his fame.*), the prime minister led him to the study to see the woman.

Sage Luo advised her, "Let Young Master Cui Junior go, as a favor to me." But the woman turned a deaf ear. After trying a few more times in vain to convince her, Sage Luo began his conjury. An eerie gust of wind suddenly sprang up.

Wind! Wind!
It blows bits of green and red to north, south, east, and west.
In spring, it pushes open the willow buds;
In autumn, it withers the parasol leaves.
It chills wealthy homes behind vermilion doors;
It freezes rundown huts in humble alleys.
It shakes the earth with the force of drumbeats;
It makes the sky vibrate with thunderbolts.
It sweeps the universe clean of dust;
It brings out the sun and expels darkness.

After the wind died down, the sage summoned two Daoist youths down to earth; one held a demon-subduing rope, and the other carried a black staff. As Sage Luo ordered that the woman be seized, she cried, "Doggy!" And from midair, Doggy leaped onto the ground, his fists raised in anger, ready to do battle. But evil is no match for righteousness. With the rope, the two Daoist youths bound up Doggy and then the girl in red.

"Show your true selves!" they ordered sharply. Doggy changed into a tiger, and the girl in red changed into a red rabbit.

The skeleton used to be a commander in Jin times and after his death had been buried on Mount Ding. Over the years, it matured into a havoc-wreaking demon. Thus, Sage Luo subdued the three evil spirits and saved the life of Mr. Cui Junior. From that time onward to this day, the Mount Ding region has never known any trouble. This story has been variously called "The White Falcon from Silla" or "The Three Evil Spirits of Mount Ding." There is a poem that bears testimony:

A tiger, a rabbit, a living skeleton,
Banded together to wreak havoc on the hills.
Ever since the sage subdued the demons,
Wayfarers on the road have had nothing to fear.

20

The Golden Eel Brings Calamity to Officer Ji (Formerly titled "The Story of the Golden Eel")

The days go by in wine-induced dreams;
While spring is not yet gone, I climb the hills.
Passing the monks' bamboo yard, I stop to chat
And gain another half day of leisure.

As the story goes, during the reign of Emperor Huizong [1101–25] of the Song dynasty, there lived a man called Ji An, who was an officer in the Privy Military Council. He lived with his wife. One hot day when he was off duty, he took up a fishing rod and went to Gold and Bright Pond, for lack of a better way to spend his time. A whole day went by without a single fish taking the bait. His patience running out, he was about to put away the fishing rod and return home when he felt the rod sinking into the water. As he pulled it up, heavy with his catch, he gave a cheer, not knowing what he was in for. "Even money can't buy this anywhere!" said he. He placed the catch in the creel, put away his fishing rod, and started for home.

As he walked, he heard a voice crying, "Ji An!" He looked back, but there was no one to be seen. He pressed on, and the voice said again, "Ji An! I am the god of Gold and Bright Pond. If you let me go, I will make sure that you enjoy more wealth and honor than can ever be described. But if you kill me, I will make you and your whole family die violent deaths." (*Why not just let it go instead of killing it?*)

Ji An listened intently and realized that the voice came from his own creel. "How very strange!" he muttered to himself. Nothing of note happened the rest of the way.

Upon arriving home, he had barely put down his fishing rod and creel than his wife said, "Husband, go quickly to the yamen. The sheriff sent for you twice. I don't know what it's about, but he said you must go to see him as soon as you come back."

"It's my day off today. What can he want of me?"

Before he had quite finished, a messenger came again. "Officer Ji! The sheriff is waiting for you."

In haste, Ji An changed clothes, followed the messenger, and attended to official business. His job done, he returned home, took off his formal robe, and asked to be served supper. When his eyes fell upon a dish that his wife had put before him, he gave a start and cried out in anguish, "I'm as good as dead!"

His wife responded in alarm, "Why say such a thing for no good reason?"

The husband told her what had happened on his fishing trip earlier in the day. "A golden eel said to me, 'I am the god of Gold and Bright Pond. If you let me go, I will make sure that you enjoy more wealth and honor than can ever be described. But if you kill me, I will make you and your whole family die violent deaths.' Why did you have to kill it? We're going to die for this!"

At these words, his wife spit and retorted, "What you said is nothing but a fart! How can an eel talk? There was nothing to go with the rice, so I cooked it for supper. Nothing will happen. If you don't eat it, I will."

Ji An remained in low spirits. When night came, he and his wife undressed and went to bed. Noticing his distressed look, the wife tried hard to cheer him up. And that very night, she got pregnant. (*The golden eel's reincarnation.*) Her brows and eyelids began to look bloated, her belly protruded, and her breasts swelled.

Soon, ten months had gone by, and she had reached full term. She engaged a midwife, went into labor, and gave birth to a girl. Truly,

> *Wildflowers, never planted, come up every year;*
> *Worries, though rootless, grow daily to haunt the mind.*

Ji An and his wife were delighted beyond measure. They named the girl Qingnu.

Time flew by like an arrow. In the twinkling of an eye, Qingnu was sixteen years old. She had a good figure and a sharp mind and acquired many skills. Her parents loved her as much as their own lives.

In the turbulent year of the Jingkang reign period [1126], the Ji family of three put together their valuables and some personal belongings and fled with the parcels to the prefectural seat. Upon hearing that the emperor had taken up temporary residence in Hangzhou, and that a multitude of officials were following suit, Ji An also made his way there. After several days of traveling, the family came to the city and found lodging. Ji An sought out officials whom he knew from his old post and was kept in the local yamen as an officer, but of this, no more need be said. He asked someone to find a house for him.

One day, sometime after the family moved into the house, Ji An looked at his wife and said, "Now that I don't have a job anymore, I'm thinking of starting a small business, because if we sit idle, we'll eat away all our savings."

His wife agreed. "I've been thinking about the same thing. As far as I can see, there's little we can do except to run a wineshop, so that when you're at work, Qingnu and I can take care of it."

"Exactly what I've been thinking, too."

The decision thus made, Ji An went about making preparations. The next day, he interviewed a measurer of wine, named Zhou De, the third son of his family; he was not a native of Lin'an but had been working in the city ever since he had been orphaned in childhood. With the preparations complete, the wineshop opened on a chosen auspicious day. Zhou San [the third one] was positioned at the entrance selling refreshments and making tea. At night, he slept in Ji An's house. In Ji An's absence, the mother and the daughter took care of the shop. Zhou San proved to be a hardworking man who never loafed on the job.

Several months went by quickly. One day, Ji An said to his wife, "I have something to say to you. Don't get mad at me."

"Whatever you want to say, just go ahead and say it."

"These last few days, I've noticed that our daughter is not carrying herself like a girl anymore."

"I never let her out of the house. She can't have done anything wrong. It's just that she's now a grown woman."

"You're not noticing things! I saw her and Zhou San making eyes at each other." ([Illegible.]) Nothing further was said about the matter that day.

One day, when Ji An was not at home, the mother called Qingnu over and said to her, "My child, I have something to say to you. Don't hide anything from me."

"There's nothing to hide," said Qingnu.

"I've noticed recently that you look quite out of shape. Tell me the truth."

Qingnu prevaricated. Observing her incoherence and consternation, her stuttering and the coming and going of color on her face (*There should be no more doubt by now.*), the mother said, "There must be something wrong!" She seized Qingnu and examined her body, and then gave a mournful shriek and slapped the girl across the face. (*What good would a few slaps do?*) "Who did this to you?" she demanded.

The slap was too much for Qingnu. She sobbed out, "There *is* something between Zhou San and me."

At this confession, the mother stomped her feet and cried out in dismay, but she dared not make too much of a commotion. "Now what's to be done? Your father will blame me for not keeping an eye on the goings-on in this house and letting such a scandal happen!"

Not knowing what had occurred inside the house, Zhou San carried on with his job, selling wine at the door. In the evening, Ji An returned home and took a rest. After supper, his wife said, "I have something to tell you. Just as you suspected, our girl has been deflowered by that brute Zhou San."

Had Ji An not been told of this, everything would have been all right, but as it was, a smoldering rage burned in his heart, and he was seized with an urge to beat that Zhou San. (*What good does beating do?*) His wife stopped him, saying, "Let's talk about this first. Don't you know that beating him up isn't something a family of our status should do?"

"I was hoping that hussy would marry a decent official," said Ji An. "And now look at what happened! Let's kill her, as if we'd never had her!" The mother did her best to calm him down. About two hours later, when his anger had subsided somewhat, he asked, "Now what's to be done?"

Quite unruffled, his wife told him of her plan. Indeed,

Cicadas are the first ones to feel the autumn wind;
Death comes to those who least expect to die.

"There's only one way to avoid a scandal," said she.

"Go on," urged Ji An.

"Since that brute Zhou San is working for us, why not take him on as a live-in son-in-law?" (*Not a bad idea. His future betrayal will all be the golden eel's doing, not something that could have been prevented by human efforts.*)

Storyteller, you may well say, had they not married their daughter to Zhou San but instead braved the derision of acquaintances and driven the lovers apart, there would have been no story to tell.

Well, as it happened, Ji An agreed with his wife. "That's a good idea," he said. That very day, he dismissed Zhou San from his service.

On his way out, Zhou thought to himself, "I saw the mother slap Qingnu earlier in the day, and now that Officer Ji is home for the evening, I'm sent on my way. Could it be that I've been found out? If this leaks out, they'll surely take me to the authorities. What's to be done?" And so he fretted. Truly,

A crow and a magpie when together[1]
Bring either joy or woe for all one knows.

Not to encumber our story with trivialities, let us come to the point when Officer Ji sent a matchmaker to Zhou San to make the marriage proposal. The betrothal gifts were sent, the preliminaries gone through, and the wedding took place on a chosen day, but of this, we shall speak no further.

Soon, more than a year had elapsed since Zhou San had become a live-in son-in-law. A loving young couple he and Qingnu were. With their hearts secretly set on moving out, they shirked their duties, rising late and retiring early. Unable to put up with the way that brute Zhou San swaggered around, looking for trouble, Ji An found himself constantly at loggerheads with his son-in-law. Consulting his wife, he said, "Why don't we sue him and put an end to the marriage? (*Letting them move out should have sufficed. Divorce is not a good way out.*) We didn't do anything earlier because we were afraid of being laughed at. This time, we'll just put the blame on him."

Thereupon, they set a trap, caught him in some wrongdoing, and raised a big fuss, resorting to a lawsuit that ended in a divorce, despite the neighbors' exhortations to the contrary. Resignedly, Zhou San left the Ji household to make a living on his own. Qingnu dared not say anything but seethed with inward resentment, more willing to die than live.

About half a year after the divorce, a matchmaker came to see Mrs. Ji. After an exchange of greetings, the matchmaker sat down and said, "I'm here because I heard that you're looking for a match for your daughter."

"If you have a good candidate in mind, please do us this favor," said Ji An.

"The one I have in mind is a court-appointed officer serving with the palace guards. His name is Qi Qing."

Believing this to be a predestined match, Ji An gave his consent. Then and there, he prepared a letter of betrothal and treated the matchmaker to a few cups of wine. His wife said, "Please do the best you can, Granny. We'll show you our gratitude when this match is pulled off."

After the matchmaker left, with thanks, the husband and wife said, "It's not a bad deal. First, he's a court-appointed officer. Second, he may be some years older, but he's wiser and more discreet. Third, once our daughter is married to an official, that brute Zhou San won't dare to come back and make trouble." The husband added, "I know that man Qi Qing. He's a nice man."

Soon enough, the match was made. After the many premarital formalities were completed, the wedding took place.

However, Qingnu and Qi Qing did not get along. No wonder there is the saying, "In young lovers is found mutual passion." Qi Qing was too old to capture Qingnu's heart. All day long, the couple bickered and fought. Not a day went by in peace and quiet. Finding such behavior too unseemly, the parents again wanted a divorce on their daughter's behalf. (*Parents should not make everything their own business as far as children are concerned. Officer Ji is too meddlesome.*) They pulled some strings, and the officials concerned accepted their complaint and granted a divorce, all as personal favors. Qi Qing, who had little influence in local official circles, was expelled from the house. In moments of drunkenness, he would go up to Officer Ji's door and unleash volleys of curses. (*He brought this on himself.*)

Suddenly, one day, he said something that led to a situation in which "Mr. Li gets drunk when it is Mr. Zhang drinking," and "Blood spurts from the mulberry tree when the ax hacks into the willow tree." Truly,

He could have enjoyed the comfort of his nest,
But a note came from a visitor in the hall,
Most likely a note to bring him fame and wealth.
He should have left it unopened by the bed.

Every time a drunken Qi Qing came to swear at the Jis' door, they dared not talk back. In the beginning, the neighbors tried to calm Qi Qing, but later, his all too frequent drunken outbursts became routine, and they stopped doing anything about him. One day, Qi Qing swore, pointing at Officer Ji, "Believe me, I'm going to kill that dog of a man!" With that remark, which the neighbors all heard, he departed. (*One can't be too cautious about what one says.*)

Meanwhile, Qingnu remained at home. Another half year went by. One day, an old woman came in for a chat. Could she be a matchmaker? After an exchange of greetings, tea was served. The tea consumed, the woman said, "I have something to say to you, but I'm afraid Officer Ji might get angry with me."

"Go ahead and tell us," said Ji An and his wife.

"Your daughter having had two marriages that didn't work out, why don't you offer her to a good, decent official? Three to five years later, she'll still be young enough for another match."

At these words, Ji An thought to himself, "That's just as well. For one thing, there have been two scandals. For another, I've gone to quite some expense. But I wonder what kind of man it is this time." Aloud, he asked, "What good candidate do you have in mind for my child, Granny?"

"There's an official who has his eye on your daughter and asked me to make the proposal. He's now resting at home. He came to my house for wine and saw your daughter. He is the assistant magistrate of Gaoyou District, here on some business, without a female companion. He wants to bring your daughter back to his home in Gaoyou later on. Would you be willing?"

After consulting each other, Ji An and his wife said, "We're not going to let you down. Please take care of this for us."

That very day, the matter was settled, a day was chosen, and documents were drawn up. Qingnu bade farewell to her parents and went to serve that official. Alas, she was to become a ghost stranded in an alien land, never to see her parents again. Indeed,

Heaven makes not a sound in reply.
Where to find one's bearings in the vast land?
What matters, in fact,
Is not the distance but the human heart.

That official was the assistant magistrate of Gaoyou District, Li Ziyou by name, whose wife and children were at home in Gaoyou while he was on business in Lin'an. After acquiring Qingnu, he treated her like his own wife, spending each day as if it were a day of festival and satisfying her every whim for clothes and food. A few months later, Li Ziyou received a letter from home, urging him to return lest he spend too much money in the capital. He completed his business in a matter of days, packed up his belongings, bought some gifts, and promptly started for home in a hired boat. All along the way, he indulged his weakness for sex and wine, resentfully putting off the day of his return.

When he finally reached his hometown, officers on duty met him at some distance from his house. At home, his wife came out to greet him. Returning her greeting, he said only, "It hasn't been an easy job for you, taking care of the household."

He then had Qingnu enter the hall to greet his wife. Qingnu walked in, her head lowered, and was about to kowtow when the wife said, "That's not necessary, but who is this woman?"

"I'm not going to hide anything from you," said Li Ziyou. "I had no one to serve me in the capital, so I picked a woman at random just to keep me company. Now I'm bringing her home to serve you."

Looking at Qingnu, the wife snapped, "A good time you had with my husband! What did you come here for?"

"This happens to be my situation. Madam, please consider the fact that I have left my parents and my hometown."

The wife summoned two maidservants and ordered them, "Take the headdress off that cheap hussy. Take off her clothes, too, and give her some coarse clothes to wear instead. Take off her shoes and let down her hair. As punishment, she is to help out in the kitchen, fetching water, making the fire, and cooking meals."

Crying out in despair, Qingnu pleaded tearfully with the wife, "For the sake of my parents, please send me back home if you don't want me. I'll gladly return the money paid for me."

"Going home—that's too good for you! You've had your full share of happiness, and now it's your turn to suffer and do some hard work in the kitchen."

Qingnu looked at Li Ziyou and said, "You brought me here, only to land me in such a situation! You have to plead my case with the lady."

"You've seen what a temper she has," he said. "Even the great Judge Bao wouldn't be able to do anything in this case. There's nothing you can do for now, because my very life will be at stake. Let me wait until she calms down before I talk to her on your behalf." (*What a man of spirit!*)

Right away, Qingnu was taken into the kitchen. Li said to his wife, "If you don't want her, you need only give her back to the go-between and get the money back. Why are you so carried away with anger?"

"What an act you are putting on, talking like that!" retorted his wife.

Henceforth, Qingnu worked in the kitchen as a punishment. One month went by.

One evening, Mr. Li went to the kitchen, where, in the darkness, he heard someone call him. Recognizing Qingnu's voice, he walked up to her. They held onto each other, stifling their sobs lest they be heard.

"I shouldn't have brought you here, to let you suffer like this!" he lamented.

"This is all your doing. When will it ever end?"

He thought for a while before replying, "I do have a plan to get you out of here. The best thing is for me to plead with her to send you back to the go-between and get back the money. But in fact, I'll find a secret place for you to live. I'll have someone send money to you, and I myself will visit you from time to time. What do you say to that?"

"That would be wonderful, if it works out. That will mean my spell of bad luck is over."

That very night, Li commented to his wife, "Qingnu has suffered enough. If you don't want her, just send her back to the go-between and get the money back." His wife agreed, without knowing what was behind his suggestion.

Li had a trusted attendant, Zhang Bin, take care of the matter. Qingnu was thus put up in a government-owned house a couple of blocks away from the Li residence. Li's wife was the only one in the dark. Every so often, Li came in and, after a few cups of wine, couldn't help engaging Qingnu in some indecent sport. (*The root of trouble.*)

Li had a most adorable seven-year-old boy called Folang. Sometimes Folang came over from the Li residence to play with Qingnu. Li warned him, "My child, don't tell Mommy about this. This girl here is your older sister." The boy promised not to tell.

One day, Folang showed up and walked straight in, only to see Zhang Bin and Qingnu sitting shoulder to shoulder and drinking. Folang said, "I'm going to tell Daddy."

In a rush to separate themselves, Zhang Bin scurried away and hid while Qingnu gathered the boy in her arms, sat him on her lap, and said, "Now, don't you go around telling lies. I was here drinking alone, waiting for you to come and share the candies."

But Folang kept saying, "I'll tell Daddy what you and Officer Zhang were up to." (*The little boy is to be a victim of his own smartness.*)

When she heard this, Qingnu thought to herself, "If you tell, what's to become of Zhang Bin and me?" Knitting her brows, she thought hard and hit upon an idea. "Far better that you suffer instead of me. I can't help it, but this day next year will be the first anniversary of your death!" (*One death.*) She grabbed a kerchief, held Folang tight with it, pinned him down on the bed, and strangled him. (*What an evil woman!*) In less time than it took to eat half a bowl of rice, the little boy's soul returned to the netherworld. Truly,

The raging wind and fire of the moment
Swept all tranquillity out of the heart.

In a moment of rage, she strangled the little boy.

She was wondering what to do next when Zhang Bin emerged from hiding. "That little swine wanted to tell my husband," said she. "In a moment of panic, I strangled him."

Zhang Bin cried out in anguish. "Sister, I have my old mother to take care of. Now what am I going to do?"

"What a thing to say! Wasn't it you who told me to kill him? (*What an evil woman!*) So you have a mother. Well, I have parents, too. Now that things have come to this, why don't the two of us pack up our things and go to live with my parents? You wouldn't object?"

Left with no other choice, Zhang Bin had to comply. The two took their parcels and fled the scene. (*Since they were going to flee anyway, they could have done so without killing Folang. Mr. Li would not have dared give chase. Wouldn't they have got what they wanted? What a stupid woman!*)

As was to be expected, Folang's disappearance prompted a search. When the boy's body was discovered in Qingnu's bed, and Qingnu and Zhang Bin were nowhere to be seen, the matter was reported to the authorities, who then offered a reward for the arrest of the fugitives. But of this, no more for the time being.

When they reached Zhenjiang, Zhang Bin came down with an illness, preoccupied as he was with thoughts of his mother and what he had gotten himself into. They stopped at an inn so he could recuperate. As the days wore on, the valuables and clothing they had brought with them all went to pay for their daily expenses. He lamented, "There isn't a penny left. What's to be done?" As the tears rolled down his cheeks, he added, "A ghost in an alien land I will be!"

"Don't worry," Qingnu assured him. "I have money."

"Where is it?"

"I have talent. I sing well. I have nothing to feel shy about here. Why don't I buy a gong and go out to sing in the wineshops of this area? Wouldn't the money, however little, come in handy?"

"You're from a decent family. How can you stoop so low?"

"There's no other choice. I only wish you'd recover, so we can go back to my parents in Lin'an." Henceforth, Qingnu made the rounds in the wineshops of Zhenjiang.

Let us pick up another thread of the story and turn our attention to Zhou San. After the divorce, he could not find a job, nor did he have any luck when he went back to his hometown to seek help from relatives. His clothes, stained by sweat in the summer, were tattered by the time autumn set in. Upon his return to Lin'an, he went past Officer Ji's door. At the sight of Ji An standing by the door in the misty rain of late autumn, Zhou San chanted a greeting. Recognizing Zhou San, Ji An felt awkward about asking why he had come.

"I was passing by. Greetings to you, my father-in-law."

Moved to compassion by the sight of Zhou San's ragged clothes, Ji An said, "Come in and have a cup of wine before you go."

Everything would have been all right had he not invited that brute in. He should never have offered him wine. (*Storytellers make judgments based only on the success or failure of the characters.*) But as it was, Officer Ji

> *Died a death most tragic,*
> *Met an end most grievous.*

To resume our story, as Ji An led Zhou San into the house, Mrs. Ji grumbled, "Why did you have to bring him in? You had nothing better to do?"

Zhou San chanted a greeting to his former mother-in-law and said, "It's been a long time since I saw you last. After the divorce, I fell ill and couldn't find a job.

I went all the way to my hometown to ask my relatives for help but didn't get any. Is Sister well?"

"You may well ask!" said Ji An. "Since you left, she hasn't been able to find another match. She's now with an official. She'll stay in his household for about two to three years before she does anything else." He then had his wife heat some wine and serve it to Zhou San. There being nothing to talk about, after the wine was finished, Zhou San thankfully took his leave.

Night had come on and there was a light drizzle. Zhou San thought to himself, "How nice of him to ask me in for some wine! They are not really to blame. I brought all this trouble upon myself." As he walked along, he continued thinking, "Now what am I going to do? Autumn will soon be over. How am I going to survive the winter?" It has been said since time immemorial that ideas come to men in desperate situations. Zhou San suddenly came up with an idea. "Why don't I sneak into Officer Ji's house in the dead of night and take a few things for the winter. That old couple go to bed early, and they probably haven't taken any precautions against me."

Zhou San turned back to Ji An's street. It was a quiet street without much activity. He waited a while before he maneuvered the door open and sneaked into the house. Having shut the door after him, he listened intently and heard Mrs. Ji's voice, saying, "Did you close the door? I heard some noise from the front door."

Officer Ji replied, "I did bolt it nice and tight."

"It's raining. There might be a thief lurking about. Get up and go for a look, so that we can breathe easier."

Officer Ji got up to take a look. Hearing the movements, Zhou San groaned, "Woe is me! What if he catches me?"

He went to the kitchen stove and groped around for a knife. Knife in hand, he stood in the darkness, waiting.

Little knowing what was in store for him, Ji emerged from his room. Zhou San waited until Ji An passed him and then aimed a blow at the back of Ji's head. So strong was the blow that Ji fell to the ground with a thump, and his soul returned to the netherworld. (*Two deaths.*) Zhou San said to himself, "Now there's still that old woman left. Let me bump her off as well." Without uttering a sound, he approached the bed, lifted the bed curtain, and killed Mrs. Ji. (*Three deaths.*) He lit the lamp and spent the better part of the night frantically searching throughout the house for valuables and putting what he found into a parcel. He then hung the parcel on his back, shut the door behind him, wended his way in a northerly direction, and went out the northern city gate. (*The golden eel has had its revenge. What follows is an account of the death of the reincarnated golden eel.*)

It was broad daylight by now. The neighbors all opened their doors. Only Officer Ji's house remained quiet. The neighbors wondered, "Are they still sound asleep?" They called at the door, but no answer came. When they tried to push the door open, it yielded readily. There, for all to see, was Officer Ji's corpse on the floor. The neighbors called out for Mrs. Ji, but there was still no answer. They entered the bedchamber and found her blood-soaked body on the bed, with all the trunks and cases open. They concluded, "This must have been the work of that brute Qi Qing who has come here every day, drunk, to shout threats about killing. And now, he's really done it!"

Without a moment's delay, the matter was reported to the local sheriff, who immediately set out to arrest Qi Qing. Qi Qing, who knew nothing about what had occurred, was trussed up with rope and, hustled along by the neighbors, taken under guard to the Lin'an prefectural yamen.

At the report of a murder case, the prefect immediately opened a court session. To Qi Qing he said, "As an appointed official, how could you have dared to kill and rob? And in the capital city, too!"

At first, Qi Qing tried to defend himself, but with the neighbors screaming accusations against him, nothing he said was of any avail. (*There is no lack of similar miscarriages of justice. A closer inspection is imperative.*) The verdict was reported to the imperial court. Qi Qing, an appointed official, was found guilty of the crime of murder for money, and in the capital of the empire at that. He was duly taken under guard to the marketplace for execution. Behold:

The ax went down with a whiff of air;
The corpse fell, the street awash with blood.

An unjust death it was. (*Four lives gone.*) If the story had ended here, with Zhou San still at large after taking two lives, there would have been no divine justice. But the fact is, heaven never misses the mark. It is only a matter of time.

But the story goes on. Zhou San proceeded to Zhenjiang and took up lodging at an inn. With nothing to do, he went out for a walk. As he was feeling a little hungry, he began to look for a place to buy some wine, and his eyes happened to rest upon a wineshop with a banner that bore these lines:

Our wine brewed for spring, summer, autumn, and winter
Intoxicates travelers from east, west, north, and south.

Zhou San stepped inside and was greeted by a waiter. His order for wine taken, plates of food were laid out on the table. He had just downed two cups of wine when a woman with a small gong on her head entered his booth and chanted a greeting. When he looked up, both were astounded, for the woman was none other than Qingnu.

"Sister, why are you here?" asked Zhou San. He offered her a seat and asked the waiter for another wine cup before continuing, "Your parents said that you had been sold off to an official. But why are you in such a state?"

When Qingnu heard this, her tears came thick and fast. Listen:

Her voice as sweet as the oriole's warbles,
As clear as clicking pearls falling from a string.

She said, "After the divorce, I wasn't able to find a good match. I was then sold to the assistant magistrate of Gaoyou District. I was brought to his house, but his wife was so jealous of me that she punished me by putting me in the kitchen to do things like making the fire, carrying water, and cooking meals. I can't tell you in a few words all the hardships I've been through."

"But how did you end up in here?"

"I'll be honest with you. I had an affair with one of my husband's attendants, and my husband's little boy happened to see us together. He said he was going to tell his daddy about us, so I strangled him. Not knowing what to do, we fled that place and ended up here because that fellow fell ill and has to rest at the inn. Since we ran out of money, I decided to make some. What a stroke of luck for me to run into you! After you finish the wine, come with me to my place."

"To be with that man of yours? Not a chance!"

"Don't worry! I know what to do."

Bringing Zhou San home was to cause the death of one more victim. There is a poem in testimony:

A reunion at sunset in her chamber;
A night of joy after a hundred years of longing.
The crickets flapped their wings outside the window;
The passion went in pursuit of the morning wind.

So the two of them went to the inn where Qingnu and Zhang Bin were staying. Qingnu and Zhou San felt so attached to each other that Qingnu, who used to take care of Zhang Bin, buying medicine and cooking porridge for him, abandoned her duties and spent all her time with Zhou San. With his meals few and far between, and the two flirting openly in his presence, Zhang Bin went from bad to worse. One short breath, and he died.

Things were working out so perfectly for them that Zhou San moved in, and he and Qingnu began to live as husband and wife. First, though, as could scarcely be avoided, they bought a coffin and had the body laid in it and cremated.

"I need to talk to you," said Zhang San one day. "Don't go out to sing anymore. I'll think of some other way to make a living."

"The way you put it! I did it because I had no choice."

Henceforth, their love for each other was like that between

Phoenixes riding faint clouds in the sky,
Love birds gliding in the water of the pond.
A night filled with pleasure goes by all too quickly;
Moments of loneliness stretch all too long.

One day, Qingnu said, "I haven't heard anything from my parents since I left home. What do you say about going back to the capital to ask for help from them? 'Even the most ferocious tiger doesn't eat its cubs,' as the saying goes."

"Well, that's not a bad idea, but we can't go back."

"Why?"

Zhou San was about to tell her but he restrained himself. If he had not told, everything would have been all right. He should never have come out with the truth, for he was only courting his own death, like a moth flying into a flame. Truly,

Even the leaves of flowers harbor thorns.
How can human hearts not contain venom?

As Qingnu insisted on being told the truth, Zhou San said, "All right, I'll level with you. The fact is, I killed both your parents and ended up here after fleeing the scene. How can I go back?"

At these words, Qingnu burst into wails of grief. Seizing Zhang San, she screamed, "Why did you have to kill my parents?"

Zhang San retorted, "Stop it! Granted I shouldn't have killed your parents, but you shouldn't have killed the little boy and Zhang Bin either. We are even. Both of us have committed capital crimes."

Qingnu fell silent, full of thought and unable to come up with a reply.

Several months passed quickly. All of a sudden, Zhou San took ill and was confined to bed. Their means exhausted, Qingnu said, looking at Zhou San, "We are out of firewood and rice. What's to be done? Don't get mad at me, but as the song says, 'What I had on my mind still is with me.' I'll go out and sing, as before, until you get better."

Zhou San saw nothing for it but to give his consent. After she began going out to work, he would say nothing when she brought back a few strings of cash at the end of the day but would burst out in curses on a bad day when she brought back nothing. "You must have used the money to help out some man who struck your fancy!" Nor would he allow any explanation. Consequently, on bad days, Qingnu had to borrow a few strings of cash from the wineshops she frequented, show them to Zhou San, and then return them to the wineshops as soon as she made enough money.

One day, in the depth of winter, a snowstorm came on. Qingnu was leaning against the railings of a belvedere when she saw three or four men coming upstairs for some wine. She said to herself, "In such a big snowstorm, I won't be able to make much, and that brute will surely yell at me again if I go back tonight without bringing him anything. What good luck that a few patrons are coming! I'll go up to them and sing something."

As she lifted the portiere of their booth, her eyes met those of the patrons, and she let out a cry of dismay, for who should be there but a guard employed by the assistant magistrate of Gaoyou!

"Qingnu!" cried the guard. "A fine thing you did! So here's where you live now!" Qingnu was speechless with fright. This is what had happened. The assistant magistrate had reported the matter to the authorities, and after learning that Qingnu was somewhere in Zhenjiang, he dispatched a guard to go to Zhenjiang with a few officers from the yamen to track her down. "Where is Zhang Bin?" demanded the guard.

"He died of an illness," replied Qingnu. "I'm now staying at an inn with my former husband Zhou San, who killed my parents in Lin'an. We ran into each other in this place and are now living together." ([Illegible.])

Forgetting about their wine, the men tied up Qingnu then and there. Next, they went to the inn, dragged Zhou San out of bed, and tied him up as well. They brought the two to the prefectural yamen for investigation and settlement. Both pleaded guilty. The report to the imperial court contained these words: "Qi Qing died unjustly. His case shall be dealt with separately. Zhou San, who should not have killed his parents-in-law for money, and Qingnu, who should not have taken two lives because of her adulterous affairs, are to be taken under guard to the marketplace for execution." (*Six lives gone.*) Behold:

The poster listing the crimes leads the way;
The clubs and the cudgels bring up the rear.
The procession passes through the alleys,
But will it ever return?
With eyes wide open, they learn only now
That retribution from heaven is near at hand.

Truly,

Even a modicum of Confucian morals
Will keep one away from Xiao He's criminal code.[2]

As shown in the case of this couple, people are ruled by the laws of the land but are also watched, unseen, by the ghosts and the gods. Indeed,

All deeds, good and evil, are repaid in the end,
But the requitals may come early, or late.

According to comments from people of later generations, the golden eel caught by Officer Ji did indeed say, in the bamboo creel, "If you kill me, I will make you and your whole family die violent deaths," but Ji and his wife should have been the only ones involved. Why were Zhou San, Zhang Bin, Qi Qing, and others also implicated? Well, they also must have been predestined to die, so they were caught up in the same case, with the golden eel serving as a trigger. Even if the golden eel's claim to be the god of Gold and Bright Pond was unsubstantiated, it should have been evident that the eel represented a sinister omen of disasters to come. Since Ji An *was* aware that there was something extraordinary about the eel, he should not have brought it home to be killed. In most cases, no harm should be done to creatures that show signs of being out of the ordinary. There is a poem in evidence:

Li, who saved a red snake, got a beautiful wife;[3]
Sun, who cured a dragon, received a wondrous book.[4]
Do not harm extraordinary creatures;
Retribution, good or bad, never misses the mark.

21

Emperor Taizu Escorts Jingniang on a One-Thousand-Li Journey

The moon hare and the sun crow speed along;[1]
A hundred years leave only faint memories.
Wealth and rank through the dynasties are but a dream;
The reigns of monarchs last as long as a chess game.
Yu established the Nine Regions, followed by Tang;[2]
Qin annexed the six states, succeeded by Han.
A hundred years' time is all too short
For the pursuit of joy night and day.

During the last years of the Song dynasty, under the house of Zhao, there lived on Stone Chamber Mountain east of the Yellow River a hermit who did not reveal his true name but called himself "the Old Man of Stone." Those who knew him said he was a man of talent and bold spirit, who proposed strategems to the military during the invasion of the Mongols and, when his proposals were ignored, raised an army of volunteers and won back several prefectures and counties from the Mongols. Later, seeing that the situation was deteriorating and knowing the game was as good as lost, he fled to Stone Chamber Mountain under a concealed identity, named himself after the mountain, and lived a secluded, self-sufficient farmer's life. He regarded any talk of an official's career as a disgrace, but discussions about the rise and fall of dynasties never tired him.

One day, two Confucian scholars, one old and one young, who lived on a nearby mountain were taking a leisurely walk on Stone Chamber when they encountered the hermit. As their conversation turned to the founding of the Han, Tang, and Song dynasties, the hermit asked, "In what ways is the Song dynasty superior to the Han and the Tang?"

One of the scholars replied, "In giving more importance to civilian than to military affairs."

The other said, "Under the different emperors of the Song, no court minister was put to death."

The hermit burst into hearty laughter. "Both of you gentlemen have got it wrong," said he. "The Han court frequently launched expeditions against alien tribes in all four directions. Confucian scholars accused it of militarism, but the barbarians were terrified and called the empire 'the Mighty Han.' What remained of its might sufficed for Emperor Wu of Wei to subjugate the Huns.[3] In the early Tang, the militia system worked well, but later, powerful regional commanders began to defy the imperial court. Still, they were kept in check through an intricate balance of power, and their military might did render service to the court in the final analysis. As for the Song dynasty, after the Chanyuan peace treaty, it dared not resort to military force and preferred to offer annual tributes rather than repell the invaders.[4] This led to the rise of the Jurchens and the Mongols and the Song's demise. Such were the dire consequences of promoting civilian rather than military causes.

"That no court ministers were put to death may attest to the benevolence of the court, but the evil ministers who betrayed national interests were protected as well, receiving undeserved advancement instead of suffering the consequences for their treachery. Throughout the Song dynasty, the power of the imperial court was in the hands of evil ministers. (*Good analysis.*) Toward the end of the dynasty, Han Tuozhou's head was presented to the Jin court, and Jia Sidao had to be struck dead in a lavatory.[5] But wasn't all this too late? How can you say the Song is superior to the Han and the Tang?"

"So in your view," said the two scholars, "in what way was the Song superior?"

"The Song may not be equal to the Han and the Tang in those respects, but it was superior in one thing: its emperors were not prone to lust."

"How is that so?"

"Emperor Gaozu of Han was enamored of Consort Qi; Emperor Taizong of Tang had an incestuous relationship with his sister-in-law. Empress Lü-shi and Empress Wu-shi wreaked havoc on the land.[6] Empress Zhao Feiyan and Lady Yang Yuhuan brought disgrace to the imperial consorts' quarters in the palace.[7] As for the emperors of the Song dynasty, granted that some were the pleasure-loving sort, but none was obsessed with lust, and Empresses Gao, Cao, Xiang, and Meng were therefore all women of great virtue.[8] This is where the Song is far superior to the Han and the Tang."

The two scholars, fully convinced, voiced their admiration before they bade the hermit adieu. Indeed,

To know the truth about past and present,
Ask only the insightful and the wise.

It was, in fact, thanks to the admonitions of the first Song emperor, Emperor Taizu, that later emperors of the dynasty, as was said above, were not prone to lust. From the time he assumed the throne, he began the morning court sessions early and retired late in the evening, seldom sparing time for female company. Even before his rise to power, he was a man of iron will, honest and upright, who never strayed into moral turpitude. The story about his escorting Jingniang on a thousand-li journey suffices to illustrate this point. Truly,

His high morals transcended all time;
His honorable spirit rose to heaven.
The true ruler of the eight hundred commanderies,
He showed himself a hero with his one cudgel.

There is a quatrain that describes the chaos of the Five Dynasties period:

The Houses of Zhu, Li, Shi, Liu, and Guo
Of the dynasties Liang, Tang, Jin, Han, Zhou,
All the fifteen emperors,
Brought havoc to the land for fifty years.

These five dynasties [907–60] were headed by regional hegemons who never joined forces with one another. In those years, the empire was divided and the people lacked a leader who would stay in power for any prolonged period of time. By the late Zhou, though the Five Dynasties period was drawing to an end, there remained five kingdoms and three regions. Which five kingdoms?

Zhou under Guo Wei [r. 951–53], Northern Han under Liu Chong [r. 951–54], Southern Tang under Li Jing [r. 943–61], Shu under Meng Chang [r. 935–65], and Southern Han under Liu Sheng [r. 943–57].

Which three regions?

Wuyue under Qian Zuo [r. 942–47], Jingnan under Gao Baorong [r. 949–60], and Hunan under Zhou Xingfeng [unidentified].

Despite the existence of the five kingdoms and the three regions, the Zhou dynasty, after the Liang, the Tang, the Jin, and the Han, proclaimed itself the orthodox dynasty. Zhao Kuangyin, later to be Emperor Taizu, founder of the Song dynasty, served as the marshal of the Zhou palace guards. With the Chen Bridge mutiny, he became emperor of the new Song dynasty, which replaced the Zhou and unified the land.[9]

Before his rise to power, he was called Zhao Dalang or Young Master Zhao, being the son of Zhao Hongyin, defense commissioner of Yuezhou in the service of the Later Han dynasty. Zhao Kuangyin had a ruddy complexion and eyes like morning stars as well as the prowess to do battle with ten thousand men and enough lofty spirit to fill the four seas. He had a propensity for befriending men of heroic mettle in other parts of the land and giving free rein to his chivalrous spirit. Wherever he was, when he saw injustice being done, he would fight for the wronged side, his sword at the ready. He was nothing short of the king of busybodies and the master of troublemakers.

In the city of Bianjing [present-day Kaifeng, Henan], he went on a rampage in the imperial theater and garden. Having thus made himself an enemy of the last

Later Han emperor, he fled the capital and roamed the land. In Guanxi, he killed Dong Da of the toll bridge and took possession of a prized horse named Red Unicorn. In Huangzhou, he killed Song Hu; in Suzhou, he finished off Li Ziying with three blows of his cudgel and slew Li Hanchao, prince of Luzhou, as well as Li's entire family.

When he came to Taiyuan, he met his uncle, Zhao Jingqing, a Daoist priest at Clear Oil Temple, who kept him at the temple. It so happened that he fell ill at this time and was confined to his bed for as long as three months. After he recovered, his uncle kept him company day and night, admonishing him to rest and not to walk about outside the temple.

One day, Jingqing had to go out on an errand. He said to the young man, "My nephew, sit patiently here. You must not tire yourself out when you're just beginning to recover!"

With Jingqing gone, the young man found it hard to sit around doing nothing. He thought to himself, "If I can't go out and see the neighborhood, I can at least take a walk inside the temple. There shouldn't be any harm in doing that." So he closed the door behind him and went on a tour of the many halls of the temple. He started with the Hall of the Three Pure Ones and from there proceeded to the east and west corridors with their seventy-two shrines before turning to Eastern Hill Hall and Jianing Hall. He heaved a sigh of admiration. Indeed,

In the golden censer burned a thousand-year flame;
In the jade lamp shone an eternal light.

Walking past Panorama Tower and Jade Emperor Hall, Young Master Zhao gave one admiring cheer after another at the magnificence and grandeur of the buildings. What an impressive temple it was! There was more to admire than his eyes could take in. Then, in the quiet, secluded area around Netherworld Hall, he saw, opposite the Hall of Posterity, a tightly closed door and above it the inscription "Demon Subjugation Hall." He looked around for a while and was about to turn back when, suddenly, he heard the sound of a woman sobbing. He listened intently and determined that the sound was coming from within that very hall. "How very strange!" he said to himself. "How can there be a woman hidden in a priests' residence? There must be some secret goings-on here. Let me get a key from an acolyte and find out what this is all about, or I won't be able to put my mind at ease."

He returned to his room and asked an acolyte for the key to Demon Subjugation Hall. The acolyte said, "The key is in the care of His Reverence himself. This matter is so important that no unauthorized persons are allowed into the hall."

Young Master Zhao thought to himself, "As the saying goes, 'Believe not even the most honest; beware of those with evil hearts.' So, my uncle is not a decent sort! He told me over and over again to sit tight and not move around, and this is what he's up to! How can a priest do such a thing? I'm going to break into that hall. What do I have to fear?"

He was about to go when he saw his uncle Zhao Jingqing coming back. In anger, the young man stepped forward and, without even addressing Jingqing as "Uncle," said curtly, "A fine thing you did as a priest!"

Without the least idea of what his nephew was talking about, Jingqing asked, "What did I do?"

"Who is the person you locked up in Demon Subjugation Hall?"

Now realizing what his nephew was referring to, Jingqing waved his hands and replied, "My good nephew, don't be meddlesome."

The young man boiled with rage. (*Worthless people meddle. Heroes empathize.*) He cried out at the top of his voice, "A priest who has renounced the world is supposed to be free from the dust of the mortal world. Why is there a woman weeping behind these locked doors? You must have done something dishonorable. You have your conscience to answer to. If you come out with the truth, we can still talk it over, but if you choose to lie, I certainly won't be on your side!"

At these harsh words, Jingqing said, "My good nephew, you do me an injustice!"

"Doing you justice or not is beside the point," retorted the young man. "Just tell me, is there a woman in that hall?"

"Yes."

"Now you're talking!"

Well aware of his nephew's fiery temper, Jingqing dared not tell him the whole story but instead chose his words carefully. "There is indeed a woman in the hall, but the whole thing has nothing to do with the priests of this temple."

"Being the head of the temple, you should know what goes on in this place, even if someone else did something bad and brought that woman here."

"My good nephew, please don't be angry. The woman was kidnapped, I know not where, by two notorious bandits, who then deposited her here and told us to keep watch over her, saying that if anything should happen to her, not even a blade of grass would be left in this temple. I didn't tell you about it before because you hadn't yet recovered from your illness."

"Where are the bandits?"

"Somewhere else for now."

Not convinced, Young Master Zhao said, "What nonsense! Now open the door of that hall for me, call the woman out, and be quick about it! Let me question her." With that, he rushed forward, his iron cudgel in hand.

Knowing his nephew's temper all too well, Jingqing thought it better not to stop him. Hurriedly, he took the key and hastened to Demon Subjugation Hall. While Jingqing was opening the lock, the woman inside heard it turning. She thought the bandits were back and started crying even more loudly. Unconcerned with proper etiquette, Young Master Zhao rushed in ahead of his uncle, entering the hall in one stride as soon as the door was opened. The woman had hidden behind the statue of a deity, cowering in fear. When he drew near, he put down his cudgel and looked at her. A truly beautiful woman she was,

Her brows shaped like the rolling hills of spring;
Her eyes sparkling like pools of autumn water.
In grief and despair, she looked like Xishi when ill;[10]
In tears and sobs, like Consort Yang cutting her hair.[11]
With a lute, she could have been Lady Ming[12]
Before crossing the frontier pass.
With a reed pipe, she could have been Cai Yan,[13]
Who was forced to live among the Tartars.
Her grace and charm, endowed by heaven,
Could hardly be captured by the paintbrush.

Young Master Zhao assured her, "Young lady, I am not a bad sort. Don't be afraid. Tell me, where do you live? Who kidnapped you? If you are being unjustly treated, let me help you."

Only then did the woman wipe her tears away with her sleeves and bow deeply, a courtesy which Zhao returned.

"What is your honorable surname?" asked the woman.

Jingqing replied for him, "This is Young Master Zhao from Bianjing."

"Young Master, let me tell you what happened." Before she had quite started, the tears began to trickle down her cheeks. It turned out that her surname was also Zhao. Jingniang by given name, she lived in Xiaoxiang Village, Xieliang County, in Puzhou Prefecture. Now seventeen years of age, she had been traveling with her father to make votive offerings at Northern Mountain[14] in Yangqu County when they ran into two bandits, Chang Guang'er, nicknamed "Flying in the Sky," and Zhou Jin, nicknamed "Rolling on the Ground." Their lust aroused by Jingniang's beauty, the bandits let her father go but took her to a temple of the local deity. Both wanted her as a wife, and neither was willing to yield to the other. After two to three days of talk, afraid of ruining their friendship, they deposited Jingniang at Demon Subjugation Hall in Clear Oil Temple. After telling the priests to watch over and take good care of her, they departed to look for another attractive woman to abduct, so that each could have a wife. The wedding ceremonies were to be held on the same day, and the two women would be the mistresses of the bandits' lair. The two bandits had been gone for a month and still had not returned. The priests were too afraid of them not to do their bidding.

It was only after this account that Young Master Zhao said to Jingqing, "I have been very rude, Uncle, and almost gave you offense. Since Jingniang is from a decent family and was abducted by bandits, who will save her if I don't?" He turned to Jingniang and said, "Cheer up, young lady. I'll take care of everything. I'll make sure that you go back home to your parents."

"It's so kind of you to offer to save me from the tiger's jaws, but my hometown is a thousand li away. How can a woman like me make the journey all alone?"

"If I save someone, I might as well do a thorough job of it. Let me escort you home, whatever the distance." (*Who else would be willing to do this?*)

Jingniang said with a thankful bow, "If so, you'll be the father of my rebirth."

"My good nephew," Jingqing intervened, "this can't be done. Those bandits are so powerful that even the authorities haven't been able to hunt them down. If you take the young lady away, I as her guardian will surely be held responsible. What am I going to say when they come back to claim her? You'll be getting me into trouble as well!"

The young man laughed. "Courage gets you everywhere in the world; timidity doesn't get you even one step from where you are. All my life, I have never failed to fight for a just cause whenever I saw one, nor am I afraid of anyone, even if I'm up against ten thousand men. Those bandits may be powerful, but can they compare with the prince of Luzhou? If they have ears, they should have heard my name. But since you priests are afraid of getting into trouble, let me leave a mark here, so that you'll know what to say to the bandits."

So saying, he swung his iron cudgel high, turned his body sideways, and brought the cudgel down with all his might upon the latticed vermilion door of the hall. With a crash, the lattice strips fell to the ground. Another blow, and the four leaves of the door crumbled into pieces, scattering every which way. (*As easy as that!*) Trembling in fear, Jingniang retreated to a far-off corner. Jingqing, his face drained of all color, cried over and over again, "What a sin! What a sin!"

"If the bandits come back," said Young Master Zhao, "just say that Mr. Zhao smashed the door and took the woman by force. Every injustice has its perpetrator; every debt has its creditor. If they want me, tell them to look for me in Puzhou."

"Puzhou is a thousand li from here, and the road to Puzhou is swarming with bandits. It's difficult enough to go by yourself. How much more so when you're encumbered by a woman! You'd better think thrice before you do anything!"

The young man laughed. "In the Three Kingdoms period toward the end of the Han dynasty, Guan Yunchang[15] escorted his two sisters-in-law on a thousand-li journey, crossing five passes and slaying six generals before arriving in Gucheng for a reunion with Liu Bei. Now, that was the act of a worthy man. If I can't even do something for one young lady, what kind of a man am I? If those two bandits and I are to meet on a narrow road, as enemies are bound to do, it will mean death for both of them."

"That may very well be so," said Jingqing, "but there's another thing. In the old days, men and women did not sit on the same mat and share their food utensils. Your offer to escort the young lady a thousand li was made out of the best intentions and a most generous spirit, but other people don't know this. A young man and a young woman traveling together will give rise to suspicions and gossip. Your good intentions will be misconstrued, and your heroic name will be tarnished." (*It must be out of fear of the bandits that Jingqing is trying to stop him from going.*)

With a hearty laugh, the young man replied, "Don't take my words amiss, Uncle, but you priests like putting on a show. You think in one way and act in another. As for us rough fellows, as long as we don't do anything against our consciences, we don't mind what people say." (*Words of a worthy man.*)

Finding him determined to go, Jingqing asked, "So, when are you leaving, my good nephew?"

"Tomorrow morning."

"I'm afraid you're not well enough to undertake the journey, my good nephew."

"That's all right."

Jingqing had an acolyte set out wine for a farewell dinner. At the dinner table, Young Master Zhao said to Jingniang, "Young lady, my uncle was just saying that people may gossip about our traveling together. Let me pledge brotherhood to you right here at this table. My surname is Zhao, and so is yours. ([Illegible]. *In such a ritual in ancient times, the surname did not even have to enter the picture.*) Our ancestors must have belonged to the same clan five hundred years ago. From now on, let's just address each other as brother and sister."

"But how could I dream of claiming a connection with someone so far above my station in life?" asked the young woman.

"If you are going to travel together," put in Jingqing, "this will be the best thing to do." So saying, he had the acolyte bring over a prayer mat.

Jingniang said to her savior, "Please accept this kowtow from your little sister." Young Master Zhao stood by one side and bowed in return. Jingniang then kowtowed to Jingqing, addressing him as "Uncle."

During the course of the dinner, Jingqing related the many heroic deeds of his nephew, to the immense delight of Jingniang. That night, the drinking lasted until after the first watch of the night. Jingqing yielded his own bedchamber to the young woman and joined his nephew in an outer room.

When the roosters crowed at the fifth watch, Jingqing rose, made breakfast, and prepared some dry provisions and beef jerky for his nephew and Jingniang to take on the road.

Young Master Zhao got Red Unicorn ready and tied up the baggage on the horse's back. He then cautioned Jingniang with these words: "Sister, you must dress like a village girl. Do not put on makeup and fancy clothes, so as not to attract undue attention." With breakfast over, the young man dressed as a traveler and Jingniang made herself up as a village girl, wearing a common snow cap that came down to her eyebrows.

The two travelers bade Jingqing farewell. As he escorted them out the door, a thought suddenly struck him. "My good nephew," he said, "you can't leave today. We still need to talk."

What was it that Jingqing wanted to talk about? Truly,

A magpie needs feathers to fly afar;
A tiger fangs and claws to make its way.

Jingqing said, "Two persons can't ride on one horse. How can the young lady keep up with you, with her small bound feet? Wouldn't that slow down the journey? Wouldn't it be better to take your time and find a carriage first?"

"Yes, I've been thinking about that for some time now," said Young Master Zhao. "It's too much trouble to tend to a carriage. I'll let Sister ride the horse. I'll be glad to cover the one thousand li on foot. I won't complain." (*Who else would be willing to do this?*)

"I am ever so obliged to you, my savior, for escorting me over such a great distance. I only regret that I'm not a man and don't know how to hold a horsewhip, put my feet in the stirrups, and ride. How could I dream of taking your horse? This is an order I'll never obey."

"A woman needs an animal to ride on. My feet are not small. Walking suits me fine."

Her pleas rejected by Young Master Zhao, she had no choice but to mount the horse. After strapping on his sword at his waist and taking up his iron cudgel, the young man bowed to his uncle and bade him farewell.

"My good nephew," said Jingqing, "be careful along the way! You may run into those two bandits. Take good care! When you strike, do a clean job of it, so no one at this temple will be implicated."

"Of course, of course," promised Young Master Zhao. With that, he gave Red Unicorn a slap on the rump, shouting, "Now go!" Off went the horse, with the young man striding along behind.

On the road, they ate and drank when necessary, resting by night and traveling by day. Soon enough, they found themselves in Jiexiu County, Fenzhou. Red Unicorn, a prized horse with the speed of wind and lightning, could well have covered in half a day the three hundred li from Clear Oil Temple to Fenzhou, but Zhao kept a tight rein on it, partly because he was afraid he would not be able to keep pace on foot, and partly because Jingniang, being a woman, was not used to riding a galloping horse. Moreover, because the road was infested with bandits, they had to start late and retire early, and so they made only one hundred li a day.

One day, they came to a place called Yellow Thatch Inn at the foot of a small hill. There had been a village, but it was now deserted in the chaos of those troubled times. All that remained was a tiny inn. The sun was about to set and they could see nothing before them but a vast expanse of wilderness, so Zhao said to Jingniang, "Let's stay here and leave tomorrow morning."

"As you wish."

The innkeeper took their luggage while Jingniang dismounted and removed her snow cap. As soon as he caught a glimpse of her, the innkeeper's tongue hung out as much as three inches. While trying unsuccessfully to draw it back, he thought to himself, "How can there be such a beautiful woman?"

The innkeeper led the horse to the back of the house and tied it. In the meantime, Young Master Zhao escorted Jingniang inside and sat down. When the innkeeper showed up again, gawking at Jingniang, Zhao asked, "Is there something you want to say, innkeeper?"

"How is this young lady related to you, sir?"

"She's my younger sister."

"Sir, don't blame me for speaking out of turn, but you shouldn't be bringing such a beauty with you on a journey through all these mountains and rivers!"

"Why not?"

"Fifteen li from here, there's a Mount Jie, a large region with very few inhabitants but throngs of bandits. If they hear about her, you'll have to surrender her to them to be the wife of the bandit chieftain. Not only will you get nothing in return, you'll have to offer a gift as well!"

In a rage, Zhao thundered, "How dare this miserable dog scare patrons with such lies!" He took one swing, and his fist landed on the innkeeper's face. Spitting blood, the man scurried off into the street, a hand over his face.

As the innkeeper's wife shouted angrily from the kitchen, Jingniang said to Zhao, "My kind brother, you were a little too impatient."

"Judging by the atrocious things that brute said, I don't think he's a decent sort. I did that to let him know what kind of a person he's dealing with!"

"But if we're going to stay here for the night, we shouldn't make an enemy of him."

"What's there to fear from him?"

Jingniang went to the kitchen to greet the innkeeper's wife. Only after Jingniang had said many soothing words to placate her (*Jingniang is by no means of the common run.*) did the woman calm down and start a fire to make supper.

Jingniang returned to her room. It was still light, and the lamp in the room had not yet been lit. Young Master Zhao was seated, talking with Jingniang, when he saw a man sneak up to the door and peek inside.

"Who dares to spy on us?" he snapped.

"I'm here to chat with the innkeeper. It has nothing to do with you, sir." With that, the man went to the kitchen, where he talked with the innkeeper's wife in a subdued voice for quite a while before he left.

While keeping a watchful eye on the man, Zhao was gripped with suspicion. After the lamps were lit, the innkeeper still had not returned. The innkeeper's wife brought supper to Zhao and Jingniang. When they had finished, Zhao told Jingniang to close the door and go to sleep, whereas he, saying he needed to relieve himself, took up his sword and cudgel and went out for a walk around the house.

At about the second watch of the night, he heard Red Unicorn neighing and kicking in the thatched shed at the back of the house. It was near the end of the tenth month, and the rising moon shone brightly. Young Master Zhao tiptoed ahead to see what was happening. The horse had just kicked a man to the ground. Noticing someone approaching, the man scrambled to his feet and took to his heels. Zhao realized that the man must be a horse thief and gave chase.

Before he knew it, he had covered several li. After making a turn at Liushui Bridge, he lost sight of the man, but his eyes fell upon a small, brightly lit hut on the other side of the bridge. Suspecting that the man had hidden himself there, he walked into the hut. Inside, he saw a hoary old man sitting solemnly on an earthen bed, chanting scriptures. What did he look like?

His eyes foggy, his beard frosty,
His eyebrows flowing like willow catkins,
His face glowing like pink peach blossoms.
He must be the mountain god, if not the Gold Star.

Seeing Young Master Zhao enter the room, the old man stood up with alacrity and bowed in greeting. Zhao returned the greeting and then asked, "What scripture were you chanting, sir?"

"The scripture is *The Heavenly Emperor Saving a Suffering World.*"

"What good will come of chanting the scripture?"

"With the empire falling apart, I wish to ask for blessings for a new emperor to appear soon to clear away all the flames and dust of war and put an end to the people's misery."

These words delighted Zhao, for they matched his own innermost thoughts. He spoke up again. "This being a bandit-infested area, do you, sir, happen to know anything about the bandits?"

"Might Your Excellency be the traveler with a woman on horseback, now staying at the inn with a thatched roof at the foot of the hill?"

"Yes."

"You are lucky to have met me. Otherwise, Your Excellency would have been in for a shock."

When Zhao asked to know more, the old man invited him to take the seat of honor, sat down to one side, and unhurriedly gave the following account: "Two new bandits appeared in the Jieshan area recently. They gathered together some followers and plundered the Fenzhou and Luzhou region. One of them is called Zhang Guang'er, nickname Flying in the Sky, and the other is called Zhou Jin, nickname Rolling on the Ground. About half a month ago, they abducted a woman from goodness knows where. They got into a fight over which of them would have her for a wife and left her somewhere while they went in search of another woman, so that each would have a wife. They instructed innkeepers all along the road to report immediately to them for a handsome reward whenever they saw a woman of beauty.

"Earlier this evening, when you, sir, arrived, the innkeeper went to report to Zhou Jin, who then sent Wildfire Yao Wang to check things out. Yao Wang reported back in these words: 'Not only is the woman a beauty, but she also rides a fine horse, and there's only one man with her. So there's nothing to fear.' There is a Chen Ming, nickname Swift of Foot, who is the fastest walker there is. He is able to cover three hundred li in one day. The bandits sent him over to steal the horse while the rest of them lie in wait in the red pine forest down the road. They'll ambush you when you pass by at the fifth watch at dawn. Be prepared."

"I see. But how did you, sir, come to know all this?"

"I've been living here for so long that I know everything that goes on around here. But when you see the bandits, don't mention me on any account."

Zhao thanked him for the warning, picked up his cudgel, and walked back the way he had come. The door of the inn was ajar, so he turned sideways and sidled in.

In the meantime, the innkeeper, who had come back to help Chen Ming steal the horse, was talking with his wife over some wine that she had heated up for him. As soon as he saw Young Master Zhao enter, he ducked behind a lamp.

Zhao had thought of a plan. He had Jingniang ask for some wine. So the innkeeper's wife took an empty flask and went to the wine vat by the door to ladle out the wine. While she was not looking, Zhao struck her head from behind. Down she fell, and the wine flask tumbled to one side. Hearing his wife's screams, the innkeeper rushed out of his room, sword in hand, but in his haste, he was no match for the one who was waiting for him, calm and at ease. With a swing of the cudgel, the innkeeper was also struck down. Another two blows, and both husband and wife were dead.

In alarm, Jingniang tried to revive them, but to no avail. When she asked Zhao why he had to kill them, he repeated what the old man had told him. Turning pale, Jingniang said in panic, "What's to be done if the rest of the journey is going to be just as dangerous?"

"But you have me with you. Don't worry, my good sister." So saying, Zhao bolted the main door and went to the kitchen to warm some wine. After getting himself half drunk, he fed the horse and padded the horse bells to stifle the sound. When the parcels were all nicely bound in place, he dragged the two corpses onto the pile of firewood in the kitchen, ignited the pile, and set fire to the front and back doors as well. He waited until the flames leaped high before helping Jingniang up onto the horse and starting on their way.

By this time, the eastern sky had brightened. When they passed Liushui Bridge, he tried to find the old man to ask for directions, but the house where the latter had chanted scriptures was nowhere to be seen. Instead, Zhao saw a three-foot-high earthen wall surrounding a tiny temple, on one side of which sat the statue of the local deity. It dawned on Zhao at this moment that it was this local god who had given him advice the night before.

"He called me 'Your Excellency,'" thought Zhao, "and he dared not take the seat of honor in my presence. I must be someone out of the ordinary. Should I amount to something someday, I'll surely give him a title."

Zhao urged his horse on, and after they had covered several li, there came into view a forest of pine trees that looked like a fiery red cloud.

"Slow down, Sister! That must be the red pine forest ahead!" As he spoke, a man emerged out of the bushes and charged at him with an iron pitchfork. With the composure of a master, Zhao caught the pitchfork with his iron cudgel. The man retreated while continuing to fight, meaning to lead Zhao into the woods. Zhao was so enraged that he held his cudgel high with both hands and, shouting "There!" struck off half the man's head. The man turned out to be none other than Wildfire Yao Wang. Zhao then told Jingniang to hold the horse and added, "I'm going into the woods to make short work of that gang of bandits. And then I'll come back and we can go on with our journey."

"Be careful, Brother!"

Zhao strode ahead. Truly,

A hundred spirits aided the Son of Heaven;
In all directions, the mighty warrior inspired awe.

In the meantime, Zhou Jin "Rolling on the Ground" and forty to fifty of his men were stationed in the red pine forest. When he heard footsteps approaching from outside the forest, Zhou Jin thought it was Yao Wang coming back to report. Holding his spear, he emerged from the woods, only to run right into Young Master Zhao, who, knowing this must be one of the bandits, struck at him without bothering to say a word. Zhou Jin fought back with his spear. After about twenty rounds, the men in the woods, realizing that Zhou Jin must have run into the enemy, beat the gong and hurried out to form a circle around the two.

"Come on, those who think you're good enough to take me on!" shouted Zhao. His iron cudgel whirled up and down in the air like a golden dragon shrouding his body and a jade python winding around him. The bandits who were struck by the cudgel flipped and spun like so many wind-blown autumn leaves; those who got near him fell like the dropping petals of flowers, tumbling to the ground every which way. Zhou Jin began to panic. His movements became confused, and he fell at one blow from Zhao. His followers gave a cry and ran pell-mell into the wilderness. With another strike, Zhao finished off Zhou Jin.

When he turned around, however, Jingniang was nowhere to be seen. In alarm, he searched all around, but five or six of Zhou Jin's men had taken her, and the group was already clear of the woods. With all the speed he could muster, Zhao caught up with them. "Where do you think you're going, you scoundrels?" he roared.

Seeing him running toward them, the men dispersed in all directions, abandoning Jingniang, "My good sister," said Zhao, "it must have been quite a shock for you!"

"Two of the men recognized me because they had accompanied their chiefs to Clear Oil Temple. They said, 'Chief Zhou is fighting it out with that traveler. Our chief will surely win, so we're taking you to Chief Zhang first.'"

"I've already finished off that brute Zhou Jin. I wonder where Zhang Guang'er is."

"I hope you won't run into him," said Jingniang.

Zhao urged the horse on. About forty li farther on, they came to a town. Feeling the pangs of hunger, he held the reins and brought the horse to a halt, meaning to help Jingniang down and go into a restaurant. Observing, however, that the waiters were too busy laying out dinner to pay them the least attention, he grew suspicious. But with Jingniang by his side, he did not want to get into trouble and led the horse past the restaurant.

Only closed doors met his eyes, one house after another. Even a small house at the end of the road had its door shut. Intrigued, he knocked at the door, but no one answered. He walked around the house, tied the horse to a tree, and gently tapped on the back door. An old woman opened the door and looked out, fright written on her face. Zhao quickly stepped in and, bowing to the old woman, said, "Madam, don't be afraid. I am a traveler with a female relative. If we could use your kitchen, we'll be on our way again as soon as we finish eating."

In consternation, the old woman warned. "Hurry!" After Jingniang went in, the old woman closed the door.

"Over at the restaurant, they are laying out a feast. What mighty official are they expecting?" asked Zhao.

Waving her hands, the old woman said, "Don't ask about what doesn't concern you." (*The old lady was of the same mind-set as the priest Zhao Jingqing.*)

"What could be so terrifying about all this? Please enlighten this traveler from afar!"

"Well, today, Master Flying in the Sky will be passing through. We villagers have pooled our money to pay for a feast in his honor so that he'll leave us in peace. My son has also been called to help out in the restaurant."

Upon hearing this explanation, Zhao thought, "So, that's what it is. Now that I've started the job, I might as well make a clean sweep and wipe out the root of trouble for Clear Oil Temple."

Aloud, he said, "Madam, this is my younger sister. We're stopping by this place on our way to South Mountain to make a votive offering. I don't want her to be frightened by the bandits. Could you do her a favor and hide her in your home until after the chief has left? I'll surely have much to offer you by way of thanks."

"What a pretty girl!" exclaimed the old woman. "Yes, it will be all right for her to stay with me for a while, but please don't cause trouble, sir."

"Being a man, I know how to take care of myself. I'm going to find out how things are."

"Be careful!" cautioned the old woman. "I have some steamed buns here. I'll boil some water for you to drink with the buns when you come back, but I'm afraid I won't be able to serve a regular meal."

Zhao picked up his cudgel and went out by the back door. He was about to mount his horse to meet the bandits when a thought suddenly struck him: "I said in the temple that I would be undertaking a thousand-li journey on foot. If I go on horseback out of fear of the bandits, what kind of a man am I?" Thereupon, he strode out onto the street.

Having come up with a plan, he made his way back to the restaurant and shouted in a swaggering manner, "The chief will be here soon. I'm his advance man. Have you got the dinner ready?"

"Yes, we have."

"Well, set out a table for me first."

As they were used to the bandits' abuses, no one dared to verify whether the man was indeed the person he presented himself to be. On the contrary, hoping that he would put in a good word with the chief on their behalf, they brought him generous portions of fish, meat, warmed wine, and steaming hot rice. Zhao fell to heartily. When he was quite full, a commotion arose outside. Someone announced, "The chief is here. Set out the incense altar, quick!"

Cool and collected, Zhao took up his cudgel and went outside. He saw more than twenty spears, swords, clubs, and cudgels held high in the air as the advance party marched along. Upon reaching the restaurant, the men all dropped to their knees. Zhang Guang'er "Flying in the Sky" was riding a big horse, followed closely by Chen Ming "Swift of Foot," armed with a whip. Bringing up the rear were thirty to fifty bandits and about ten carriages.

You may well ask, of the two bandit ringleaders, why was Zhang Guang'er the one with all the pomp and show? Well, the bandits had no fixed rules of etiquette when they were on the move. Zhou Jin having heard that he had to deal with only one male traveler naturally underestimated his foe. As for Zhang Guang'er, he was away on a looting expedition when Chen Ming "Swift of Foot" reported to him, "Second Chief has acquired a beautiful woman and invites you to meet him at Jieshan." Hence the impressive procession that passed through villages and towns.

Hidden behind the north wall, Zhao had a good view of the approaching procession. When Zhang Guang'er's horse drew near, Zhao shouted, "Watch out for my cudgel, scoundrel!"

With that, he leaped through the crowd and pounded like an eagle swooping down from midair. In less time than it takes to describe, the horse jumped forward in alarm, and a mighty blow of the cudgel broke one of its front legs. The horse collapsed in pain. An agile man, Zhang Guang'er quickly jumped down from the horse. From behind him, Chen Ming emerged with a club, ready to do battle with Zhao, but one blow of Zhao's cudgel knocked him down. Brandishing a sword in each hand, Zhang Guang'er charged at Zhao, who ran to an open space and assumed a martial stance. After more than ten rounds, Zhang Guang'er aimed a blow at Zhao, but Zhao swung his cudgel up and hit Zhang on the fingers. The sword dropped from Zhang's right hand, and he felt his left hand losing strength as well, so he turned on his heels and ran.

Zhao roared, "Isn't your nickname Flying in the Sky? I'll see to it that you don't rise to the sky today!" He stepped forward and smashed Zhang's head from behind. How tragic that two mighty bandits perished on the same day. Indeed,

> *Their three spirits flew in the sky;*
> *Their seven souls rolled on the ground.*

The rest of the men were about to flee when Zhao yelled, "I am Zhao Dalang from Bianjing. My quarrel is only with the bandits Zhang Guang'er and Zhou Jin. Now that both of them are dead, I have nothing against any of you. (*Spoken like a magnanimous sovereign.*)

Throwing down their spears and swords, the men all dropped to their knees and said, "We've never seen anyone as heroic as you. We'll gladly serve you as our chief."

With a hearty guffaw, Zhao said, "I don't even care for positions in the imperial court. Why would I settle for life as a bandit?" Catching sight of Chen Ming among the men, he called him forward and asked, "Are you the one who came last night to steal the horse?"

Chen Ming kowtowed in acknowledgment of his trespass. Zhao said, "Come with me. I'll treat all of you to dinner." Thereupon, the men followed him to the restaurant.

To the owner of the restaurant, Zhao said, "I've rid you of two sources of evil today. These are all good men. Feed them well with the food you have prepared. I'll deal with them afterward. As for the table reserved for Zhang Guang'er, save it for me. I need it for a purpose." The innkeeper dared not do otherwise but obey.

With dinner over, Zhao summoned Chen Ming, saying, "I heard you can walk three hundred li a day. How could you, such an able man, have allowed yourself to serve bandits? Now I've got a job for you. Will you do it?"

"Sir, I'll do anything you say, whatever the risk."

"I am here because I fled Bianjing after smashing up the imperial garden and theater. May I trouble you to go to Bianjing to find out for me how things stand now? In half a month, wait for me at Priest Zhao's place in Clear Oil Temple, Taiyuan Prefecture. Do not fail me!" He borrowed a brush-pen and an ink slab, wrote a letter to his uncle Zhao Jingqing, and handed the letter to Chen Ming.

He then divided the bandits' carriages and money into three portions. One share was for the town's inhabitants, as compensation for the harassment they had suffered. (*Well done! The best part of the division.*) He told the townspeople to take the bandits' corpses and weapons to the authorities to claim the rewards. He gave the second share to the bandits, telling them to divide it among themselves to pay for food and clothing so that they could return to their home villages and lead honest lives. The third share was divided into two halves; one went to Chen Ming for his travel expenses, and the other went to the temple to pay for repairs to the door and windows of Demon Subjugation Hall. Everyone present was impressed with the fairness of the distribution and gave him their thanks.

Zhao then had the innkeeper take the food on the table that had been reserved for Zhang Guang'er and carry all of it to the old woman's house. Her son also came to exchange greetings with Zhao and Jingniang. The old woman was given an account of how the two bandits had been eliminated. Everyone was overjoyed. To Jingniang, Zhao said, "Your unworthy brother has never once treated you to anything throughout the journey. Today, let me 'present the Buddha with borrowed flowers,' so to speak, and serve you wine to help you recover from the shock." How Jingniang thanked him profusely need not be described here.

That night, Zhao took ten taels of silver from his bag and gave it to the old woman as payment for providing lodging.

Reflecting on the young man's kindness to her, Jingniang said to herself, "In the old days, even a courtesan like Hongfo got to pick her own hero.[16] Now, I have nothing with which to repay his kindness. As for my marital future, to what other person but this hero shall I commit myself?" (*Right!*) Thinking it would be too embarrassing to recommend herself yet wondering how that straightforward man was to guess her mind if she said nothing, she turned her thoughts this way and that throughout a wakeful night. Before she knew it, the night watch drum had struck five, and the roosters were crowing.

Zhao rose and saddled the horse for the day's journey. Feeling dejected, Jingniang thought of an idea. As they proceeded, she complained of unbearable stomachaches and said time and again that she had to relieve herself, asking the young man to help her mount and dismount the horse, each time leaning against him, holding his neck, and cradling his shoulders, using her charms in every possible way. At night, claiming to be cold one moment and too hot the next, she had him add and then remove a layer of bedding, trying to arouse him with the soft warmth and fragrance of her body. Being an upright man, Zhao did his utmost to tend to her without ever entertaining an undue thought. (*What an iron-hearted honorable man! How respectable!*)

After three or four more days on the road, they came upon Quwo, about three hundred li from Puzhou. That night, they took up lodging in a deserted village. Without saying anything aloud, Jingniang debated with herself about what to do now that she was almost home. If she continued to be too bashful to broach the subject, the opportunity would be lost forever once she arrived at home, and regrets would be too late. Dusk fell. In the silence that shrouded the neighborhood, Jingniang stayed up tearfully by the feeble flame of the lamp, heaving deep sighs.

"My good sister," said Zhao, "what is bothering you?"

"I have something hidden in the depths of my heart, but I'm afraid it would be too presumptuous of me to bring it up. Please don't take offense, my savior!"

"What is there to hide between brother and sister? Go ahead and tell me."

"Having been brought up in a secluded boudoir, I had never ventured out of the house before taking that trip with my father to offer incense. And then I was abducted by bandits and locked up in Clear Oil Temple. Luckily for me, the bandits went away. My life was thus prolonged for a few days, and I got to meet you, my savior. Had the bandits tried to violate me, I would have preferred to die rather than submit. (*She never said this before.*) You have so kindly delivered me from the sea of misery, escorted me a thousand li on foot, and taken revenge on my behalf, putting an end to their threat once and for all. Your kindness to me is like that of a parent of my rebirth. I'll never be able to repay you. If you don't find me too ugly, I'd be glad to serve you as your wife, so that I can pay off a tiny fraction of my debt to you! Would you agree to that?"

With a hearty laugh, Zhao said, "My good sister, you've got it all wrong! We met by chance, just like two patches of duckweed meeting in the water. I took those risks for you out of sympathy, not desire for your beauty. Moreover, since we have the same surname and call each other 'brother' and 'sister,' we can hardly marry each other, for that would be a breach of proper human relationships. I am a Liuxia Hui, impervious to feminine beauty.[17] How could you imitate that wanton Wumenzi in violation of proper etiquette?[18] Stop this wild talk! People will laugh!"

With shame written all over her face, Jingniang fell silent. After quite a while, she spoke up again, "Please don't take amiss what I'm going to say now. I'm not a wanton sort. It's just that I gained a new life because of your kindness. I have nothing else with which to repay you except this very body. I wouldn't dream of being your wedded wife. I'll die content if only I could be your maidservant for one day."

The young man was enraged. "I've been a man of honor all my life. I've never done anything evil. Why do you take me for a petty, treacherous man who expects repayment for service and seeks to gain from a supposedly altruistic act? If you keep having such wicked thoughts, I'll have to leave right away and stop sticking my nose into other people's affairs. Don't blame me for abandoning you midway."

At this indignant outburst, Jingniang bowed deeply and said, "Now I do see what lies deep in your heart. You are superior even to Liuxia Hui and the man of Lu.[19] I am but a woman. Please forgive me for my limited understanding."

His anger subsiding, Zhao explained, "My good sister, it's not that I'm a stubborn, inflexible man, but I offered to escort you over a thousand li out of a sense of honor. If I'd had designs on you, wouldn't I be like the two bandits? My sincere offer of help would turn out to be a hypocritical show in the end, for which I'd be ridiculed by all worthy men."

"These are wise words indeed. If I can't repay your kindness in this life, I will surely do so in my next."

Their conversation lasted until dawn. Truly,

The flowers fall into the water, seeking love,
But the water does not love them in return.

Henceforth, Jingniang held Young Master Zhao in even greater esteem, and he in turn had greater compassion for her. Nothing of note happened for the rest of the journey.

Soon, they arrived at Puzhou. Even though she was a native of Xiaoxiang Village, she did not know the way there, and Zhao had to ask for directions along the way. The scenes of her native place saddened Jingniang as she rode along.

In the meantime, Squire Zhao and his wife, of Xiaoxiang Village, had been shedding many a tear every day for more than two months over the loss of their daughter Jingniang. All of a sudden, a tenant came to report that Jingniang was coming home on a horse, followed by a big, ruddy-complexioned man with a cudgel. "Oh no!" exclaimed Squire Zhao. "The bandit is here to demand a dowry!"

"How could there be just one bandit?" Mrs. Zhao wondered. "Let's have our son Zhao Wen go and find out what is happening."

Zhao Wen commented, "Does a tiger ever return its prey? How could my sister be returned by her kidnapper? It can't be my sister. It must be someone who looks like her."

Even as he spoke, Jingniang stepped into the main hall of the house. At the sight of their daughter, the parents fell upon her and, embracing her, burst into tears. After crying their fill, they asked her how she had managed to return home. Thereupon, Jingniang explained that she had been locked up by the bandits in Clear Oil Temple, but, fortunately for her, Young Master Zhao, passing by, had learned about the injustice and broken into the hall to rescue her, pledged brotherhood with her and escorted her on foot over a thousand li, and eliminated the two bandits along the journey. "My savior is here. He should be treated with proper respect."

Immediately, Squire Zhao rushed out of the hall and greeted Young Master Zhao with a thankful bow. "If it were not for you, mighty hero," said he, "my daughter would still be at the mercy of the bandits, and we would never have been reunited with her." He then bade his wife and daughter bow their thanks to the young man and summoned his son to greet the savior. A pig was slaughtered, and a grand feast was laid out in the young man's honor.

Privately, Zhao Wen said to his father, "As the saying goes, 'Good news never leaves the house, but bad news travels a thousand li.' My sister's abduction was an unfortunate event for the entire family, but now that she's back with that ruddy-faced man, I suspect there's something between them, for, as another saying goes, 'Who'd be willing to rise early if not for self-interest?' Why else would he have taken the trouble to escort her over such a distance? Considering everything she has gone through, she's not likely to get a decent marriage proposal. It would be better to have that man as a live-in son-in-law, which would prevent tongues from wagging. Wouldn't that be nice on both accounts?"

At this suggestion, Squire Zhao, being an old man without a mind of his own and apt to lean in whatever direction the wind was blowing, had his wife put the idea to Jingniang. "Since that young man has escorted you over a thousand li," said the mother to her daughter, "you must have yielded yourself to him. Your brother has just suggested to us that we take him on as a live-in son-in-law. What do you say to that?"

"Mr. Zhao is a most honorable and selfless man. After pledging brotherhood with me, he's behaved like a true brother with never a flirtatious word. I hope only that you and father will allow him to stay for about ten or fifteen days, just to show our gratitude. Don't ever bring up this matter again."

The mother repeated these words to Squire Zhao, but he did not think much of them.

A short while later, when the dinner table had been set out, Squire Zhao offered the seat of honor to Young Master Zhao, whereas the old couple themselves sat opposite him, with Zhao Wen on his right and Jingniang on his left. After several rounds of wine, Squire Zhao spoke up, "This old man has some words to offer: My entire family is grateful to you for giving my daughter a new lease on life, but we have nothing to repay you with. Fortunately, she is as yet unbetrothed. Let me offer her to you as a wife. Please do not turn me down."

At these words, Young Master Zhao blazed with rage. "You old fool!" he lashed out. "I came here out of a sense of loyalty and honor, only to be subjected to such an insult! If I were a lecherous man, I would have made her my wife somewhere along the road. Why would I have escorted her all the way here? I shouldn't have wasted my goodwill on people who can't tell good from bad!" With that, he pushed over the table and headed straight for the door.

Squire Zhao and his wife trembled with fear, nor did the son dare make a move, seeing what a violent temper Zhao had. Only Jingniang, feeling very ill at ease, rushed over and, grabbing Zhao's sleeve, pleaded, "My savior, for my sake, please don't be angry!"

Far from yielding, he freed himself from her grip and ran all the way to the willow tree, where he untied Red Unicorn, leaped into the saddle, and galloped away as if on wings. In tears, Jingniang collapsed to the ground.

After taking her to her room, the parents turned to their son and scolded him. Ashamed and angry, Zhao Wen left the house in a huff. His wife, greatly displeased upon hearing that her parents-in-law had scolded her husband on account of her sister-in-law, said maliciously to the girl in a feigned gesture of consolation, "Sister-in-law, parting may be sorrowful, but how heartless of him to leave so abruptly after such a long journey with you! (*A woman so full of malice naturally ends up with a swine of a husband.*) If he were a man of honor, he would have accepted the marriage offer. But with your youth and beauty, you'll surely get another good match. You have nothing to worry about on that score!"

Tears flowing, Jingniang was at a loss for words. She thought, "Because I was born under the wrong star, I was kidnapped by bandits. Luckily, a hero rescued me, and I hoped to commit the rest of my life to him. And yet, not only did things not work out but I've even come under suspicion. My own parents, brother, and sister-in-law don't believe me. What can I expect from other people? Instead of repaying my savior's kindness, I ended up tarnishing his good name. It's all my fault that a good deed has gone awry. (*Words worthy of a great hero.*) With such a sorry fate, I should have died at Clear Oil Temple. That would have spared me all this gossip and made things a lot simpler. Regrets are too late now, but one has to die anyway, in whatever way. Let me show them that I am a chaste woman."

When night came at last and her parents were fast asleep, she took up a brush-pen and wrote a quatrain on the wall. Then, taking a pinch of earth as a substitute for incense, she bowed four times toward an imaginary Young Master Zhao somewhere up in the air and, using a white silk handkerchief, hanged herself from a beam in the ceiling. (*Poor thing!*)

How sad that a girl worth her weight in gold
Faded away into the realm of dreams!

Wondering why their daughter did not make an appearance after they got up the next morning, the parents went to her room. There, they found her body hanging from a beam. In shock, they burst into loud wails of grief. They saw on the wall a poem that said:

Heaven gave me a fair face but a sorry fate,
To suffer from insults and tyranny.
With death I repay my debt of kindness;
Heaven and earth know how blameless we both are!

After Mrs. Zhao took down her daughter's body, her son and daughter-in-law arrived on the scene. Realizing from the poem that his daughter was as innocent and pure as untainted ice and jade, Squire Zhang gave his son a severe tongue-lashing before setting about buying a coffin and picking a lot for burial, but of this, no more.

In the meantime, Young Master Zhao, riding Red Unicorn, arrived before the night was out in Taiyuan, where he met with Priest Zhao and was told that Chen Ming "Swift of Foot" had been there for three days. He also learned that the last emperor of the Later Han had died, yielding the throne to Lord Guo, who had changed the name of the dynasty to Zhou and was recruiting worthy men from all over the land.[20] Young Master Zhao was overjoyed.

After staying in the temple for a few days, he took leave of Priest Zhao and returned with Chen Ming to Bianjing, where he joined the army as a petty officer. From then on, he followed Emperor Shizong on expeditions north and south and rose, on the basis of his meritorious service, to be chief of the imperial guards.[21] Later, he accepted the offer of the Zhou emperor and became Emperor Taizu of the Song dynasty. Chen Ming, a loyal follower, was made a regional commander.

After ascending the throne, Emperor Taizu wiped out the Northern Han dynasty. Recalling his brotherly affection for Jingniang, he sent a messenger to Jieliang County, in Puzhou, to seek her out and was given a copy of the quatrain as a response, much to his chagrin. He bestowed on Jingniang the posthumous title Lady Zhenyi [Chaste and Righteous] and had a shrine built for her in Xiaoxiang Village. The local deity of Liushui Bridge near Yellow Thatch Inn was given the title Deity of the Taiyuan Region. Ever since the temple dedicated to him was built on a chosen lot, it has never been short of worshipers. The story began to circulate under the title "Young Master Zhao, the Smasher of Clear Oil Temple, Escorted Jingniang Over a Thousand Li." A later poet had this to say in praise of him:

Untempted by beauty, undaunted by bandits,
He escorted her on foot for a thousand li.
In the chaotic years of Lü of Han and Wu of Tang,[22]
None measured up to Zhao Dalang the hero.

22

Young Mr. Song Reunites with His Family by Means of a Tattered Felt Hat

Seek not a marriage that is against your fate.
Marriages are predestined; you need not fret.
However high the waves may roll,
Your boat midstream will safely stay its course.

In the Zhengde reign period [1506–21], there lived, in the main street of Kunshan, Suzhou Prefecture, a man named Song Dun, a descendant of a long line of officials. He and his wife, Lu-shi, lived off rent from some inherited land, without seeking other means of livelihood. Over forty years of age now, they still had no issue, male or female.

One day, Song Dun said to his wife, "You know what's been said since ancient times, 'Raise children to provide for old age, just as you store up grain against a rainy day.' Both of us are over forty now and still have no children. At the speed time flies, our hair will be turning white in the twinkling of an eye. Who's going to take care of our funerals?" With these words, the tears started to flow from his eyes.

His wife replied, "The Song family has been doing good for generations and has never been guilty of any evil deed. Moreover, you are the only son. Surely heaven will not end your family line. Some people have children at a later age than others. Even if we had borne and reared one, we would have lost him somewhere along the way if we are not destined to have children. Wouldn't our pains have been for nothing? Wouldn't we have suffered the grief of bereavement unnecessarily?"

"Right you are," Song Dun nodded. He had barely wiped his eyes dry when he heard a cough in the sitting room near the door. A man said loudly, "Is Yufeng [Jade Peak] at home?

It was the custom in Suzhou for people from families rich as well as humble to call each other by their sobriquets, and "Yufeng" was Song Dun's. Song pricked up his ears, and the second time the question was asked, he recognized the voice of Liu Shunquan, also known as Liu Youcai, who had a family shipping business of long standing. He had a large boat and made quite a handsome profit transporting goods to various provinces. All of his considerable family wealth came from the business. The boat itself, made entirely of fragrant *nanmu* wood, was worth hundreds of taels of silver. There was no lack of people in this line of work in the region south of the Yangzi River.

Liu Youcai being Song Dun's best friend, Song hurried out into the sitting room as soon as he recognized Liu's voice. Without having to stand on ceremony with each other, they dispensed with the customary bows, and only greeted each other with hands folded across their chests. They then took their seats and were served tea, but these details need not be gone into here.

Song Dun said, "How did you manage to get some free time today, Shunquan?"

"I'm here for one purpose, to borrow something from you, Yufeng."

"Doesn't your great ship have everything? Why would you need to borrow anything from this humble house?"

"I won't trouble you with anything else, but this is something I know you have and can spare. That's why I made so bold as to come and ask this favor."

"If I do have it, I certainly won't be stingy."

Slowly and deliberately, Liu Youcai named what he wanted to borrow. Truly,

It holds no royal decree when carried on one's back;[1]
It is not a vest when hung in front from the neck.
Sewn in fine stitches in light yellow cloth,
It is held by clean hands at prayer services.

It holds money offerings for the dead;
It adds to the solemnity when prayers are said.
It has followed its owners to hills and temples;
It bears the aroma of incense.

The fact of the matter was that Song Dun and his wife, who were having difficulty conceiving, had been burning incense and offering prayers in temple after temple. They had made themselves yellow cloth wrappers and yellow cloth bags to hold paper horses and paper coins. After each pilgrimage, they piously hung the yellow cloth wrappers and bags in the Buddhist shrine at home.

Liu Youcai was forty-six, five years older than Song Dun. His wife Xu-shi was also childless. They heard that a salt merchant from Huizhou, eager to pray for a son, had recently built a temple to the goddess of Chenzhou outside Chang Gate in the city of Suzhou. The temple came to be filled at all times with people offering incense and prayers. Liu Youcai wished to take advantage of a business trip to Maple Bridge in Suzhou to go and offer incense there as well. As he had not prepared cloth wrappers and bags, he was there to borrow one each from Song.

Upon hearing the purpose of Liu's visit, Song Dun sank into thoughtfulness. When Song remained silent, Liu Youcai said, "You won't begrudge our using them, will you? If we somehow ruin one of them, we'll give you back two."

"What kind of talk is this?" exclaimed Song Dun. "There's just one thing. Since the goddess of the temple is so responsive to prayers, I'd like to go with you in your boat. When are you leaving?"

"Right now."

"My wife has another pair of cloth wrapper and bag. So we'll bring along two pairs, one for each couple."

"How nice!"

Song Dun went to the interior of the house and told his wife, to her delight, about his wish to go on an incense-offering trip to Suzhou. From the wall above their Buddhist shrine, Song Dun took down two pairs of cloth wrappers and bags, one for himself and one for Liu Youcai.

Liu said, "I'll go first and wait for you in the boat. Please come quickly. The boat will be waiting under Daban Bridge by North Gate. If you don't mind the lack of ceremony, we'll just eat some prepared vegetarian food along the way. You need not bring rice."

Song Dun agreed. Hurriedly, he packed some joss sticks, candles, paper horses, paper coins, and ingots made of tinfoil paper. After putting on a brand-new white Huzhou silk robe, he hastened to North Gate and boarded the boat. With a favorable wind, they covered the seventy-li distance in less than half a day. They moored their boat by Maple Bridge, and nothing of note happened at night. There is a poem in evidence:

The moon sets, the crows cry, and frost fills the sky;
Sadly I sleep midst maples and fishing boat lights.
Beyond the Suzhou walls, from Cold Mountain Temple,
Echoes of the midnight bells reach my boat.

The next morning, they rose before dawn. After washing, they ate some vegetarian food, rinsed their mouths, and washed their hands. Carrying on their shoulders the yellow cloth wrappers filled with paper coins and the yellow cloth bags laden with paper horses and prayer sheets, they walked up to the temple of the goddess of Chenzhou.

By this time, the sky had begun to brighten. The gate of the temple was open, but since the door of the main hall was still closed, the two friends toured the covered corridors. They were commenting with admiration on the architecture, every bit as magnificent as they had expected, when the door of the hall creaked open, and an acolyte emerged to invite them in. There being as yet no other worshipers, the candelabra were still unfilled. The acolyte took down a glazed oil lamp, lit the candles, and asked them for their prayer sheets. After the prayers had been offered, the incense burned, and the obeisances completed, each gave the acolyte several tens of coins as a token of his gratitude. Then, Liu and Song burned the paper coins and left the temple. Again, Liu Youcai invited Song Dun to join him on his boat, but Song Dun declined, whereupon Liu returned the cloth wrapper and bag he had borrowed, and, with words of thanks, they bade each other farewell.

Liu Youcai went in the direction of Maple Bridge to meet some clients. It being still early in the day, Song Dun decided to go to Lou Gate to take a boat home. He was about to leave when he heard a moan coming from a corner of the wall. Upon drawing near, he saw a low hut made of reed mats by the side of the temple wall. In the hut lay an old monk who, looking deathly ill, gave no response when addressed. Saddened, Song Dun could not take his eyes off the monk. A man walked up to Song and remarked, "Traveler, what's the use of staring at him like that? Why don't you do a good deed before you go?"

"What good deed can I do?" asked Song Dun.

"This monk is from Shaanxi. He's seventy-eight years old. He says that he's been a vegetarian all his life and spends every day reading the Diamond Sutra. Three years ago, he came here to ask for alms for building a temple, but, there being no donors, he put up this reed-mat hut and lodged here, chanting the scriptures all the time with never a stop. In this neighborhood, there is a restaurant that serves vegetarian food. He went there every morning for his one meal of the day and ate nothing after that. Whatever money and rice he received from people who felt sorry for him, he offered to the restaurant as payment for his meals and never kept even a penny for himself. Recently, he became ill and hasn't eaten anything for half a month. Two days ago, when he was still capable of speech, we asked him, 'Wouldn't it be better just to go instead of living on and suffering such pain?' He replied, 'My destined one has not come yet. I'll have to wait another two days.' This morning, he lost his ability to speak. He'll be dying any time now. If you pity him, you'd be doing a good deed by purchasing a modest, thin coffin and paying for his cremation. He said his destined one had not yet come. Who knows? Maybe you are the one he's expecting!"

Song Dun thought to himself, "Since I'm here today to pray for a son, I might as well do a good deed before I return home. Heaven will know about it." Aloud, he asked, "Is there an undertaker around here?"

"Chen Sanlang, who lives down the lane, is an undertaker," the man replied.

"Could I trouble you to take me there?"

The man led him to the undertaker's shop, where they found Chen Sanlang giving instructions to a carpenter who was sawing planks of wood. The man said, "Sanlang, I brought you a patron."

Turning to Song Dun, Chen Sanlang said, "If you wish to look at different kinds of wood, I have inside some planks made of two-ply genuine Wuyuan [in Jiangxi Province] wood, but if you want a ready-made coffin, you can take your pick from the ones we've got here."

"I'll take a ready-made one."

Pointing to a coffin, Chen Sanlang said, "This is the finest one. Three taels of silver, even."

Before Song Dun could start bargaining, the man accompanying him spoke up. "This is a traveler, here to buy a coffin for that old monk in the reed-mat hut.

Half of the merit for doing this good deed goes to you. So don't ask for more than it's worth."

"Since it's for a good deed," conceded Chen Sanlang, "I won't presume to ask for too much. Give me one tael and six mace. That's what it cost me. I can't do with any less."

"Fair enough." So saying, Song Dun recalled that he had a piece of silver worth five to six mace in one corner of his waistband, plus a little less than one hundred in copper cash left over from paying for the incense. But that would still be less than half the price asked for. "I have an idea," he thought. "Liu Shunquan's boat is not far from Maple Bridge." Aloud, he said to Chen Sanlang, "The price is fine. It's just that I'll have to borrow some money from a friend. I'll be right back." (*A vivid scene in a tightly woven plot.*)

Chen Sanlang said, "All right, as you wish."

But the man with Song Dun bristled. "You wanted to do good," said he, "and yet you try to slip away. If you don't have the money, why bother to come here and look around?"

Before he had quite finished, they heard passersby saying how sad it was that the old monk, whose intoning of the scriptures had been heard about half a month before, had died that very morning. Truly,

> *Everything is done with the three inches of breath;*
> *All is gone once the last breath goes out.*

The man said, "Didn't you hear, traveler? The old monk is dead. He's waiting in the netherworld for you to take care of his burial!"

Song Dun thought to himself, "I'm determined to take this coffin, but if I go to Maple Bridge and don't find Liu Shunquan on the boat, I can't very well sit around and wait for him to come back. As the saying goes, 'Goods set at the same price are not picky about buyers.' Should another patron be willing to pay more for the coffin, I'll lose it and let the monk down. Oh well!" (*So, the one of Yanling who gave his sword to a deceased friend must also have done so only for the prosperity of his own descendants.*[2])

He took out the piece of silver, the only one he had, and asked for a scale. Upon learning the actual weight of the piece, he let out a cry of surprise, for it weighed over seven mace, more than it looked. After giving it to Chen Sanlang, he took off his brand-new, white Huzhou silk robe and said, "This robe is worth more than one tael of silver. If you think it's worth less, please consider it a pawn. I'll come back to redeem it. But if you think it's acceptable, please take it."

"If I may be so bold," said Chen Sanlang. "It's not that I haggle. Please understand." So saying, he took the silver as well as the robe.

Song Dun pulled a silver hairpin, worth about two mace, from hair-bun and gave it to the man who was with him, saying, "Please exchange this hairpin for some copper coins to pay for funeral expenses."

At this point, onlookers in the shop commented, "What a kind-hearted man! Now that he has paid the bulk of the expenses, we locals should pitch in and take care of the rest." So saying, they went off to scrape together some money.

Song Dun returned to the hut and saw that the old monk had indeed passed away. Before he knew it, tears fell from his eyes, as if he were looking at his own kith and kin. (*So, there is indeed a predestined bond, and family ties do exist!*) For some inexplicable reason, he felt sick at heart. Finding the sight too painful, he turned away with tears in his eyes and continued on his journey. Upon reaching Lou Gate, he realized he had missed the last passenger boat, whereupon he hired a small boat and arrived at home before the night was out.

Wondering why her husband had returned so late, wearing no robe and with a forlorn expression on his face, Mrs. Song supposed he must have been involved in some dispute and quickly walked up to ask what was wrong. Shaking his head, Song Dun said, "It's a long story!" With that, he headed straight for the Buddhist shrine, hung up the two pairs of cloth wrappers and bags, and kowtowed to the Buddha's image.

It was not until he had entered his own chamber and been served tea that he began to tell her about his encounter with the old monk. "You did the right thing," said his wife, without a word of reproach. Her kindness cheered him up.

That night, the couple slept all the way through the fifth watch, when each had a dream. Song Dun saw the old monk coming to thank him with a bow, saying, "My benefactor, you were destined to be childless, and your life span was to end at this point. However, due to your compassionate nature, the Lord on High has ordered that your life span be extended for six years. In addition, this old monk has a predestined bond with you. I will gladly reincarnate into your home and be your son, out of my gratitude to you for buying my coffin." Lu-shi, on her part, dreamed of a gilded arhat walking into the room. She woke herself as well as her husband with her screams. As they listened to their accounts of these dreams, they heaved sigh upon sigh, unsure whether to believe them or not. Truly,

Plant melons, and you get melons;
Plant beans, and you get beans.
Let all be advised to do good works,
For as you sow, so will you reap.

That night, Lu-shi became pregnant. When she had carried the baby to full term, in ten months' time, she gave birth to a son, who was given the name Song Jin, nickname Jinlang [Golden Boy], because of his mother's dream of a gilded arhat. The couple's joy goes without saying.

At the same time, Liu Youcai's wife gave birth to a daughter, to whom the couple gave the pet name Yichun. As the boy and the girl grew up, the two families were urged to form a marriage alliance. Liu Youcai was willing, but Song Dun looked down upon Liu's status as a ship proprietor and not a member of some distinguished clan of long standing. But he said nothing, and kept his disapproval to himself.

When Song Jin was six years old, Song Dun was afflicted with an illness from which he never recovered. His death bore out the saying "The prosperity of the household depends on the well-being of the master." Even ten women couldn't make up for the loss of a man.

After Song Dun's death, Lu-shi took over the management of the household, but, what with one bad crop after another and government authorities collecting more taxes from the widow and the fatherless child, Lu-shi could not hold out any longer. She had no choice but to sell the family's landed estates little by little and move into a rented house. In the beginning, she exaggerated her poverty, but after living off her savings for a little less than ten years, the poverty became real. She, too, fell ill and died.

After the funeral, Song Jin, with nothing left but his bare hands, was expelled from the house by the landlord and had no one to turn to for help. Luckily, he had, as a child, learned to write and calculate. It so happened that a provincial graduate, Mr. Fan, of the same area, having just been appointed magistrate of Jiangshan County, Quzhou Prefecture, Zhejiang, was looking for a clerk who could write and do arithmetic. Song Jin was recommended to him, and Mr. Fan sent for him. Pleased at the sight of this good-looking boy, he tested him on his skills and found him to be truly proficient in writing and the use of the abacus in multiplication and division. That very day, Mr. Fan decided to keep him in the study, had him change into a new suit of clothes, and shared the same table with him at dinner—such were the favors showered upon him.

On a chosen auspicious day, Magistrate Fan and Song Jin embarked on a government boat on their journey to the magistrate's post. Truly,

The drums urged the boat to be on its way;
Gentle breezes filled out the brocade sails.

However poor and lowly now, Song Jin was, after all, from a distinguished old family. Even though he was a mere retainer in the service of Magistrate Fan, he would not stoop to the level of the other servants or let them take liberties with him, and the servants resented this boy for his airs. As the journey by water from Kunshan was to end in Hangzhou, from whence they were to travel by land, the servants offered this advice to their master: "That little brute Song Jin needs to be subdued while serving you as a clerk. He knows absolutely nothing about good manners. You, sir, treat him too generously, letting him sit and eat with you. In the boat, he can get away with such behavior, but when traveling on land, you must consider proper decorum when lodging at an inn. As we see it, it wouldn't be right unless you have him draw up a statement of indentured service to you, so that after you assume office, he won't dare to make trouble in the yamen." (*It takes someone with a mind of his own and a clear head to make a wise judgment when presented with such seemingly flawless logic.*)

Mr. Fan, who was an easily influenced man without a mind of his own, followed their advice. He called Song Jin to his cabin and ordered him to write a statement of indentured service. How could Song Jin ever consent to such a thing? When his many harsh words of command came to naught, Mr. Fan flew into a rage and roared, "Take off his clothes and throw him out of the boat!"

Pulling and tugging the boy, the servants stripped him of all his clothes, down to the shirt next to his skin, and drove him out onto the shore. Song Jin was so mortified that he was unable to get a word out for quite some time. Witnessing the assembly of attendants helping the magistrate start the journey on land, with sedan-chairs and horses and all, Song Jin, with tears standing in his eyes, felt obliged to remove himself from the scene. Penniless as he was, and with hunger getting the better of him, he could hardly avoid imitating the two ancients:

Prime Minister Wu playing a flute by Wu Gate,[3]
King Han being fed by the washer woman.[4]

He begged for food on the streets by day and slept in old temples at night. But being from a clan of long standing, Song Jin retained some of his pride after all, even though he was down on his luck. He refused to grovel as shamelessly as the average street beggar. He took whatever he was given and starved when nothing came his way, never knowing where his next meal was to come from. In time, he grew sallow and emaciated, a mere shadow of his former comely self. Truly,

The storm-ravaged flowers fade and lose their red;
The frost-laden grass withers, its green all gone.

It being late autumn, the blustery wind brought a sudden rainstorm. Song Jin was stranded, hungry and cold, with little food or clothes, in the Temple of Lord Guan in Beixinguan. The rain lasted from mid-morning to early afternoon. Tightening his belt, Song Jin stepped out the temple gate. Before he had gone far, he ran head-on into a man who, after a good look, he realized was his father Song Dun's best friend Liu Youcai, sobriquet Shunquan. Feeling too ashamed to greet someone from his hometown, he lowered his head and kept walking, his eyes fixed on the ground. But Liu Youcai had already recognized him. Grabbing the young man from behind with one swipe of his hand, Liu cried out, "Aren't you Young Master Song? Why are you reduced to such a state?"

With tears streaming from his eyes, Song Jin said, his hands folded respectfully in front of him, "Being in such rags, I dare not greet you in the proper way, but I'm much obliged to you, Uncle, for asking."

He then proceeded to give an account of Magistrate Fan's abuse, to which Mr. Liu responded, "You know what they say, 'Compassion dwells in every heart.' If you could help me out on my boat, I'll make sure you don't go hungry and cold."

Down on his knees, Song Jin said, "If you would be so kind as to keep me, Uncle, you'll be as dear to me as a parent of my rebirth."

Right away, Mr. Liu led Song Jin to the riverside. Liu boarded his boat first and told his wife about the matter. "Wouldn't this be nice in more than one way?" she asked, whereupon Mr. Liu went to the bow of the boat and waved to Young Master Song, signaling him to come on board. He then took off his old robe and put it on Song Jin before leading the young man to the stern to greet his wife, Xu-shi. His daughter Yichun also greeted the young man. After Song Jin went back to the bow, Mr. Liu said, "Offer some rice to Young Master Song."

"Rice I do have, but it's cold," said Mrs. Liu.

"There's some hot tea in the pot," said Yichun. She then filled a clay jar with boiling-hot tea. Mrs. Liu gave Song Jin the cold rice along with some pickled vegetables she had taken from the kitchen cupboard and said, "Young Master Song, our business is run from our boat, which doesn't have the comforts of home. Please make do with whatever I can offer!"

Song Jin accepted the food. Noticing that it had started to drizzle, Mr. Liu cried out to his daughter, "There's an old felt hat by the rudder at the back. Bring it over for Young Master Song."

As she picked up the hat, Yichun noticed that the seam on one side was split. Being swift of hand, she took a needle and thread from her hair and sewed up the hat before tossing it onto the mat. "Here's the hat for you," said she. Song Jin put on the old felt hat and poured the hot tea over the cold rice and ate it. After telling him to tidy up the cabins and sweep the boat clean, Mr. Liu went ashore to greet clients. He returned late, and the night went by without further ado.

Upon rising the next morning, Mr. Liu saw Song Jin sitting idly at the bow of the boat. He thought, "He's just starting out. Let's not spoil him." Aloud, he said harshly, "You there! You owe everything you eat and wear to this family. If you have time to spare, do something useful like making some cord and rope. How can you just sit there without doing anything?"

With alacrity, Song Jin replied, "I'll do whatever you want me to do. I would never dream of disobeying you."

Thereupon Mr. Liu gave him a sheaf of hemp and taught him how to make rope with it. Truly,

When the eaves of his host's house are so low,
How would he dare not to bend his head down?

Henceforth, Song Jin went about his duties carefully, working hard from morning to night with never an idle moment. Being proficient in writing and arithmetic, he doubled as a bookkeeper, recording all transactions without the slightest error. Other shipowners came to ask for his help with the abacus and bookkeeping. All the clients held him in high regard and praised him for his brilliance in spite of his youth. Impressed by his conscientiousness and useful service, Mr. and Mrs. Liu began to see him in a favorable light and provided him with good food and clothing. They presented him to clients as their nephew. Song Jin was also content with the arrangement. His health improved, and his emaciated form began to fill out, to the delight of Liu's business associates.

Time flew by like an arrow. Quite unnoticeably, two years went by. One day, Mr. Liu thought to himself, "I'm getting on in years. With only one daughter, I need a good son-in-law to provide for me in my old age. Young Master Song would suit us perfectly. I wonder what Mother has in mind."

That night, when he and his wife were half tipsy with wine, Mr. Liu pointed aside to Yichun and said to his wife, "Now that Yichun is of marriageable age, what are we going to do about her future?"

"This is an important matter that concerns our livelihood in our old age," said his wife. "Why don't you do something?"

"I have in fact been thinking about it constantly. It's just that a good candidate is hard to come by. Someone as capable and handsome as Young Master Song is one in a thousand."

"Then why not take him in as our son-in-law?"

"What are you talking about?" Mr. Liu pretended to object. "He has no family to fall back on. He works for me and doesn't have a penny to his name. How can we commit our daughter to him?"

"Young Master Song is from an official's family," countered his wife. "Plus, he's the son of an old friend. There *was* a marriage proposal when his father was alive. How could you have forgotten? He may be down on his luck, but look at him! Such a handsome young man able to write and calculate won't be a disgrace to his in-laws, and the two of us could have someone to support us in our old age."

"Mother," said Mr. Liu, "are you quite determined?"

"Why wouldn't I be?"

"So much the better," said Mr. Liu.

As a matter of fact, Liu Youcai was a henpecked husband. He had set his mind on Song Jin a long time ago but was afraid that his wife would object. Now that she had agreed so readily, he was delighted beyond measure. Then and there, he called for Song Jin and, with his wife present, offered the marriage proposal. Song Jin demurred at first, but, touched by the couple's sincerity and relieved that he was not expected to spend one penny, he gave in to Mr. Liu. Mr. Liu then went to see a fortune-teller, who picked an auspicious day for the wedding. After reporting back to Mrs. Liu, he brought his boat back to Kunshan. There, he had Young Master Song tie up his hair in a bun at the top of his head to mark his coming of age and had a silk gown made for him. Decked out in new clothes, a new hat, and new shoes and socks, Song Jin looked all the more striking:

He might not have Cao Zhi's literary talent,[5]
But he was every bit as handsome as Pan An.[6]

For her part, Mrs. Liu went about preparing clothes and jewelry for her daughter. On the chosen auspicious day, the couple invited relatives from both clans to a grand feast to celebrate Song Jin's new status as a live-in son-in-law. The next day, the relatives offered their presents, and the feasting lasted three days. I shall skip over details about the young couple's love for each other after the wedding, but henceforth, the shipping business grew more and more prosperous day by day.

Time flew like an arrow. All too quickly, a year and two months had gone by. When her pregnancy reached full term, Yichun gave birth to a daughter, whom the young couple cherished like a piece of gold and took turns holding in their arms. However, hardly had the baby girl passed her first birthday than she caught smallpox and, failing to respond to medicine, died twelve days later. Song Jin cried so bitterly over the loss of his beloved daughter that his excessive grief wore him down, and he fell victim to consumption. His temperature went down in the early morning but rose to a fever at night, and he ate and drank less and less. Soon, his bones stood out in his emaciated body, and his movements were slow and painstaking.

In the beginning, Mr. and Mrs. Liu hoped for his recovery, and they engaged doctors and asked for divinations on his behalf. But as the illness dragged on for more than a year and got worse instead of better, with Song Jin looking more like a ghost than a human and unable to write or do arithmetic, the Liu couple began to see him as a thorn in their flesh. They could hardly wait for him to die, and yet he hung on to life. Overcome with regret, they busily blamed each other. They had counted on this son-in-law to support them in their old age, but the miserable wretch, now more dead than alive, was like a rotting dying snake twining itself around them. Unable to shake him off, what were they going to do about their daughter? She was still in the bloom of youth, and her future was being ruined. They needed a plan to get that cursed wretch out of the way so that they could take on another son-in-law. Only then would they feel content.

After much consultation with each other, they drew up a plan but did not tell their daughter. Claiming that they had to pick up a shipment of goods from north of the river, the Lius took Song Jin on the trip up river. When they came to Five Creeks, Chizhou [present-day Guichi in Anhui], they brought the boat to a deserted place where all that met their eyes were forlorn hills, a vast expanse of water, and a stretch of uninhabited land with no sign of human life. Against a slightly unfavorable wind, Mr. Liu maneuvered the boat toward the sandy shore and deliberately ran it aground. He then told Song Jin to go into the water and push the boat. Song Jin's movements being slow, Mr. Liu burst into a torrent of curses. "What a sick dog! If you're too weak to push, why don't you go on shore and chop some firewood so as to save me some money?"

Feeling ashamed, Song Jin took up an ax and dragged himself ashore to chop firewood. In Song Jin's absence, Mr. Liu punted the boat away with all his might and turned it back the way it had come. At full sail, the boat glided downstream.

What did he care about his son-in-law's plight?
To his delight, the cursed wretch was out of sight.

In the meantime, Song Jin's steps took him into the depth of the woods. Although the supply of wood was abundant, wielding the ax was far beyond the little strength he had left. He could do no more than pick up fallen branches from the ground, cut some withered twigs from the bushes, and pull out dried-up vines. He tied them into two big bundles, but they were too heavy to carry on his back. Then, an idea came to him. He took another withered vine, and bound the two bundles together with part of it, leaving the rest dangling. He then held the end of the vine and tugged on the bundles, much as a herdboy leads a water buffalo by a rope. After walking like this for a while, he remembered that he had left his ax on the ground, so he turned back, retrieved it, and stuck it in with the firewood. Slowly, he dragged the bundles all the way to the spot where the boat had been moored, but the boat was not there. All he saw was a boundless stretch of mist-shrouded water and sandy islets.

He walked along the river, looking around as he went, but no trace of the boat was to be found. By the time the red sun began to sink below the horizon, he realized that his father-in-law had abandoned him. He was left with no way out, no road to heaven or gate into the earth. Feeling a stab of pain in his heart, he broke into violent sobs, weeping until he choked and collapsed in a swoon. When he regained consciousness a considerable time later, he caught sight of an old monk, coming from goodness knows where.

Knocking his cane against the ground, the monk asked, "Where are your companions, sir? This is no place to stay!"

In haste, Song Jin rose and told the monk his name, adding, "My father-in-law Mr. Liu tricked me into coming to this place. And now, all alone by my poor self, I have nowhere to go. Please help me, Your Reverence, and save my humble life."

"My thatched hut is not far from here. You may stay with me tonight and decide what to do tomorrow."

His heart swelling with gratitude, Song Jin followed the old monk. After about a li, a thatched hut did indeed come into view. The old monk struck fire from stones and made porridge for Song Jin. After Song Jin had eaten, the monk asked, "What grudge does your father-in-law have against you? I'd like to hear more."

Thereupon, Song Jin gave him a full account of how he had been accepted as a live-in son-in-law and had fallen ill.

"Do you hate your father-in-law?"

"He was kind enough to have taken me in when I was a beggar, and then he married his daughter to me. His abandonment of me during my critical illness is attributable only to my own sorry fate. How can I blame anyone for that?"

"These are indeed the words of a kind-hearted man," observed the monk. "Your illness was brought on by grief. Medicine will not work. You'll regain health only if you rest in peace and quiet. Do you read the Buddhist scriptures at all?"

"No, I've never done that."

The monk took out a scroll of scripture from a sleeve and gave it to Song Jin, saying, "This is the Diamond Sutra. You will gain an understanding of the Buddha through the heart. Let me teach you how to read the scriptures. If you read them aloud once a day, all improper thoughts will go away, as will your illness, and you'll add years to your life. This will be much to your gain, in more ways than you could ever count!"

As a reincarnation of the old monk in front of the temple to the Chenzhou goddess, Song Jin had, in his previous life, spent much of his time chanting this very book of scripture. (*This old monk must have assumed the same form after reincarnation. Recalling that it was a gilded arhat who found reincarnation in Song Jin, I don't think Song Jin is related to this old monk in any way.*) The fact that he could recite the lines fluently after hearing it only once testified to his unsevered ties with his previous life.

Joining the old monk in meditation, Song Jin sat and chanted the scriptures with his eyes closed. As dawn approached, he dozed off without realizing it. When he woke up, he found himself sitting on a deserted grassy slope. The old monk and the thatched hut were nowhere in sight, but the sutra was in his bosom. He opened the volume and found he was able to chant the lines. Much surprised, he rinsed his mouth with water from the pond and intoned the scriptures from beginning to end. All his worries vanished, and his ailing body forthwith regained its health and strength. By this time, he realized that a holy monk had manifested himself in order to save him, in fulfillment of a predestined bond. Song Jin made obeisances toward the sky, giving thanks for the gods' blessings. However, like a duckweed in the ocean, he still had nowhere to go. As he moved ahead aimlessly, he began to feel the pangs of hunger. Seeing something that looked like a house on a wooded hill farther down the road, he could not resist doing what he had done before and walked up to beg for food. These adventures were to deliver Young Master Song from peril and lead him on to fortune. Truly,

What looked like a dead end opens up a new path;
Where the stream seems to dry up is found a new source.

Drawing near to the hill, Song Jin saw no signs of human habitation, but there were spears, swords, dagger-axes, and halberds planted on the ground throughout the woods. He grew apprehensive but mustered enough courage to go forward. There was a dilapidated temple to a local deity, in which he saw eight large chests, all tightly sealed and covered with pine needles and straw. He thought to himself, "These must have been hidden here by robbers. The weapons are but a ruse. These being ill-gotten goods, it wouldn't be wrong to take them." An idea came to his mind. He broke off some pine branches and drove them into the soil as he walked back toward the river so as to mark out the trail.

As his life was predestined to begin changing for the better at this time, Song Jin saw a big boat moored by the shore. Its rudder had been damaged by the countercurrents and was being repaired. Feigning panic, he said to the people on the boat, "I am Qian Jin from Shaanxi. (*Song Jin was a native of Shaanxi in his previous life, and again, it was the predestined bond that led to this coincidence.*) I was passing by this place with my uncle on a business trip to Huguang when we ran into a group of bandits. They killed my uncle. I told them I was but a page boy, and a very sick one at that, accompanying my master on the trip, so they spared me. The ringleader had one of his men stay with me in the local god's temple to watch over the loot, while he went to find other people to rob. Luckily, the man who stayed with me died last night after being bitten by a poisonous snake. That's how I freed myself and came here. Would you please give me a ride?"

The people in the boat were not quite convinced. Song Jin continued, "There are eight huge chests in the temple. They all belong to my family. The temple is not far from here. Please go on shore and carry them to the boat. You can keep one chest as a token of my gratitude. Please be quick about it. If the bandits come back, not only will you get nothing but there will surely be big trouble, too."

All of the men in the boat, who had left home on a quest for wealth, readily volunteered to go for the eight chests of goods. In no time, they put together a team of sixteen able-bodied young men. Carrying eight sets of ropes and poles, they followed Song Jin to the temple. Sure enough, there, for all to see, were eight huge chests, and enormously heavy they proved to be. With two men to each chest, all eight chests got off the ground. Song Jin picked up the spears and swords that were scattered all over the woods and hid them deep in the grass.

By the time the eight chests were brought onto the boat, the rudder had been fixed. The helmsman asked Song Jin, "Where would you like to go, sir?"

"To Nanjing to visit my relatives."

"We're heading for Guazhou. How nice that Nanjing happens to lie along the way!" said the helmsman.

Immediately, the boat set sail. It traveled more than fifty li before stopping so that the men could take a rest. Dancing attendance on the rich traveler from Shaanxi, the men collected some silver and bought wine and meat in his honor, to help him get over his shock as well as to offer him congratulations.

The next day, a high westerly wind sprang up. With the sails unfurled, the boat arrived in Guazhou in a matter of days and cast anchor. Nanjing being only about ten li by water from Guazhou, Song Jin hired a ferryboat and had seven of the heavier trunks brought down, leaving one as a gift for the men, as he had promised. How the men opened the chest and divided the contents need not be described here.

Upon reaching the mouth of Dragon River, Song Jin took up lodging in an inn and had an ironsmith make keys for the chests. He opened them and found that they were filled to the brim with gold, jade, and other valuables. In fact, the bandits had been hoarding their treasure for many years. These things had by no means been taken from one household in one act of robbery. Song Jin sold off the contents of one chest at the marketplace and made several thousand taels of silver. Afraid that the innkeeper might grow suspicious, he moved into the city, where he bought some household servants and began living in grand style, wearing silk and satin and eating the finest foods. Of the items in the remaining six chests, he kept only the choicest and sold off the rest, fetching no less than tens of thousands of taels of silver. With the money, he bought a big mansion by Yifeng Gate in Nanjing, remodeled the halls, gardens, and pavilions, and beautified the whole place with furniture of the most luxurious kind. He opened a pawnshop by the front gate and acquired several farmsteads, enough page boys for several tens of rooms, and ten capable butlers. For servants to answer to his personal needs, he engaged four fine-looking boys. (*He refrained from keeping female personal servants and concubines out of his regard for Yichun. He was too much her soul mate to ever betray her.*)

To all and sundry throughout the city, he was known as Squire Qian, who never left his gold-filled residence without a grand horse-and-carriage procession. As the ancients say, "A change in one's station in life changes one's demeanor; a change in living conditions changes one's physical constitution." Song Jin's newly acquired wealth brought him good health. His skin became smooth, and his face glowed. Not the least bit of his former haggardness and shabbiness remained. Truly,

When your lucky star shines, you glow in high spirits;
When autumn comes, the moon shines with greater luster.

Let us pick up another thread of the story and come back to Liu Youcai. After tricking his son-in-law into going ashore, he turned the boat back and, to his and Mrs. Liu's secret delight, sailed downstream in a favorable wind, covering a hundred li in no time.

Yichun, who had no inkling of what had happened, had brewed some herb medicine soup for her husband. Believing he was on the boat, she called out for him to come out and drink it, but when she got no response, she thought he must have fallen asleep on board. She was about to go over and get him when her mother wrested the medicine bowl from her hand, dumped its contents into the river, and snapped, "Don't you know that the wretch isn't here any more? Why do you still think about him?"

"But where can he be?"

"Because his illness doesn't go away, your father is afraid that it will spread to other people, and so, some moments ago, he tricked your husband into going ashore to chop some firewood and then turned the boat around and came back."

In one quick move, Yichun held her mother fast and began to wail at the top of her voice. "Give me back my husband!" she cried.

Mr. Liu came over at the sound of the wails. Trying to calm his daughter down, he said, "My child, listen to me. For a woman, to be married to the wrong husband is the curse of her life. That miserable wretch is about to die anyway. Since the predestined bond is going to be dissolved, why not get out of it sooner, while you are still young? I'll pick another husband for you, a good one, to live with you for the rest of your life. Put this one out of your mind now!"

"What a thing you did, Father! This is a most atrocious violation of the will of heaven! It was at the initiative of you and Mother that I married him. As husband and wife, we are bound together in life and in death. How can I back out of the commitment? Even if he is to die of his illness, he should die in peace. How could you have had the heart to abandon him in that deserted place? If he is to die today because of me, I will not go on living by myself. If you have any pity for me, turn the boat around this instant and bring him back. Otherwise, people will ridicule and condemn you."

"But that wretch probably went to some village to beg for food once he found the boat gone," countered Mr. Liu. "What's the good of looking for him? Moreover, we've already gone a hundred li downstream on a favorable wind. As they say, 'Better stay put than move.' I advise you to give him up."

Seeing that her father would not do as she asked, Yichun burst into loud sobs and went to the side of the boat, ready to jump overboard. Luckily, Mrs. Liu was quick enough and held her back just in time. Yichun vowed to kill herself and cried bitterly as though she would never stop. Little had her parents expected her to be so stubborn. At their wits' end, they kept watch on her the whole night, and when morning came, they resigned themselves to heading back upstream. Going against the wind as well as the current, they covered less than half the distance in a day. The night was again unrestful, with Yichun weeping and sobbing all the while. They did not arrive at the spot where the boat had moored until late afternoon three days later.

Yichun went ashore to search personally for her husband, but all she saw were two untidy bundles of firewood and an ax lying on the sandy beach. Recognizing the ax as belonging to the family, she was sure that the firewood had been gathered by her husband. With physical evidence at hand but the person gone, she became all the more aggrieved, and instead of giving up, she insisted on pushing farther ahead. Her father was obliged to follow.

After walking for quite some time without seeing any signs of human presence among the dark shadows of the trees and the hills, Mr. Liu urged Yichun to return to the boat. Another tearful night went by.

Before dawn on the fourth day, she again made her father go ashore with her to continue with the search but saw nothing other than the expanse of wilderness. Left with no other choice, she wept her way back to the boat, thinking to herself, "Where is he to beg for food in such a deserted wilderness? Moreover, he's been sick for so long that he doesn't have the strength to walk far. The fact that the ax lies abandoned on the beach means that he must have thrown himself into the river and drowned." After another burst of sobs, she again tried to jump into the water, but her father held her back.

"You, my parents, gave me my body, but you have no control over my heart. I'm determined to die anyway. Why don't you let me die earlier, so that I may even get to see my husband?

Pained by their daughter's agony, the old couple cried out, "Child, this is all our fault. What a thing we did in a moment of folly! But since it's already been done, regrets are too late. Both of us are getting on in years. Have pity on us! You are our only child. If you die, our days will also be numbered. Please forgive us, and take it easy. Father will put up notices in towns and marketplaces along the river. If Song Jin isn't dead, he'll see the notices and come back to you. If there's no news in three months' time, you can have the best memorial service you want. Father will pay for it, whatever the cost."

It was only at this point that Yichun stopped crying. Gratefully, she said, "If so, I'll be able to die content."

Then and there, Mr. Liu wrote notices announcing his son-in-law's disappearance and posted them in conspicuous spots on walls in towns and marketplaces along the river.

Three months went by without any news of Song Jin. Yichun said, "So, my husband must have indeed died." Promptly, she set about preparing her mourning headdress and hemp clothes. In mourning white from head to foot, she had a spiritual tablet set up for the memorial ceremony and engaged nine monks for a prayer service that lasted three days and nights. She also donated her jewelry in order to ask for blessings for her deceased husband. Out of their boundless love for their daughter, Mr. and Mrs. Liu did not dare raise the slightest objection. During the fanfare, which lasted quite a few days, Yichun wept from dawn to dusk. People on neighboring boats, one and all, sighed with emotion upon hearing her. All of the clients who had gotten to know the family well lamented the fate of Young Master Song and pitied Miss Liu. Yichun wept for six whole months before she calmed down.

To his wife, Mr. Liu said, "Our daughter hasn't been crying these last few days, which means she's beginning to put the whole thing behind her. This would be a good time to advise her to marry. The two of us old folks can't very well cling to a widow of a daughter the rest of our lives, can we? Who will take care of us if something happens to us?"

"Good point, old man," said Mrs. Liu. "But I'm not sure if our daughter will listen. Let's talk her into it gradually."

More than a month later, on the twenty-fourth day of the twelfth month, Mr. Liu returned by boat to Kunshan from a business trip for the New Year's celebrations. After having drunk at a relative's home until he was tipsy, he approached his daughter, under the emboldening influence of the wine, and said, "The new year being upon us, why don't you take off your mourning clothes?"

"The mourning for my husband is to last for the rest of my life. How can I take off the mourning outfit?"

His eyes opening wide, Mr. Liu roared, "Lifelong mourning, indeed! Your father is the one who decides when you may wear mourning and when you may not!"

Alarmed by the old man's harsh tone, Mrs. Liu rushed over to make peace. "Let's wait until the year's gone. We'll offer some porridge on New Year's eve and remove the spiritual tablet before we talk about putting an end to the mourning."

Yichun was distressed that the conversation had taken a wrong turn and sobbed, "The two of you brought about my husband's death and now you forbid me to wear mourning for him, all because you want to make me marry someone else. But how could I ever lose my chastity and betray my husband? I would rather die a widow in mourning than live without it."

Mr. Liu was about to throw another fit when his wife stopped him with a sharp reproof. Pressing a hand against the back of his neck, she pushed him back to his cabin and told him to go to sleep. As before, Yichun wept throughout the night.

On the thirtieth day of the month, which was also New Year's eve, she poured libations for her husband and wept some more. Her mother calmed her, and the family of three sat down together for dinner. Displeased that she touched neither meat nor wine, Mr. and Mrs. Liu commented, "My child, we know you're determined not to take off your mourning clothes, but how can meat or fish harm you in any way? A young person of your age must not let the vital energies be weakened."

"I am one to die soon. These being the last days of my life, this bowl of rice with vegetables is one bowl too many. Meat is out of the question."

"Well, if you're determined not to touch meat," said her mother, "how about a cup of wine, which is made of rice? It will help you feel better."

"How can even one drop of wine get to the Nine Springs in the netherworld? With the dead in my thoughts, I'll never be able to swallow any wine." With that, she began sobbing again and went away to sleep, leaving even her rice and vegetables untouched. Realizing that their daughter was not to be shaken in her resolve, Mr. and Mrs. Liu gave up further attempts to change her mind. A later poet had this to say in praise of Yichun's chastity:

Stories abound about chaste women, past and present,
But a boat woman could not have read the classics.
Vowing never to waver in her firm resolve,
She is worthy of her predecessor Gongjiang.[7]

Our story forks at this point. Let us turn our attention to Song Jin, who had been living in Nanjing for one year and eight months. Now as prosperous a man as could be, he had a butler take care of the establishment while he himself, equipped with three thousand taels of silver and accompanied by four servants and two fine-looking page boys, journeyed by hired boat to Kunshan to seek out the Liu family.

The neighbors told him, "The Lius left for Yichen three days ago." Thereupon, Song Jin bought some bales of fabric with some of the silver and wended his way to Yizhen, where he did some trading with a well-known client. The next day, he found the Liu family's boat at the mouth of the river. From a distance, he saw his wife at the bow, wearing white clothes of mourning. Realizing that she was still observing mourning for him and had not remarried, he was overcome with emotion.

After returning to his lodgings, he said to his landlord Mr. Wang, "On a boat on the river, there is a very beautiful woman in mourning. I've learned that the boat belongs to Liu Shunquan of Kunshan and that the woman is his daughter. I have been a widower for two years and would like this woman to be my wife." So saying, he took out ten taels of silver from a sleeve, handed the silver to Mr. Wang, and continued, "This meager amount is just for you to buy some wine. Please be my matchmaker. If you work things out, I'll thank you with some handsome gifts. As for wedding gifts, I begrudge nothing, not even a thousand pieces of silver."

Pleased with the silver, Mr. Wang went straight to the boat and invited Mr. Liu to a wineshop, where he ordered a fine spread and asked Mr. Liu to take the seat of honor. In alarm, Mr. Liu said, "Why treat a boatman so sumptuously? There must be a reason for you to do so."

"Have three cups of wine before I make so bold as to say what I have to say."

Mr. Liu grew all the more apprehensive. "If you don't say it right now, I won't dare sit down."

And so Mr. Wang said, "Well, there's a traveler in my inn, a Squire Qian, from Shaanxi. He's a very rich man, and he's been a widower for the last two years. He's impressed by your daughter's beauty and wants to have her for his wife. He asked me to be the matchmaker and offers a thousand pieces of silver as a wedding gift. Please don't turn me down."

"Wouldn't it be nice for a boatman's daughter to marry a rich man? But my daughter is determined to stay a widow. The moment we bring up the subject of remarrying, she threatens to kill herself. So I wouldn't presume to comply with your wish or accept your great kindness."

He was about to stand up when Mr. Wang held him fast, and said, "This dinner is Squire Qian's idea. He asked me to represent him as the host. Since the bill has already been paid, it won't do to have all the food go to waste. Even if things don't work out, having dinner can't do any harm."

Mr. Liu had to oblige. In the course of the drinking, Mr. Wang brought up the subject again, "Squire Qian's proposal is made out of the deepest sincerity. Please think about it after you go back to your boat."

Still haunted by the horror he had experienced each time his daughter tried to throw herself into the river, Mr. Liu kept shaking his head and never changed his line. When dinner was over, they went their separate ways.

Mr. Wang returned home and relayed Mr. Liu's response to the squire. Realizing how firmly determined his wife was to observe widowhood, Song Jin said to Mr.

Wang, "Oh well, the match is off then, but I want to hire his boat to carry some goods up the river for sale. He can hardly turn me down again."

"Boats are supposed, by rights, to transport passengers," replied Mr. Wang. "Needless to say, he'll surely agree."

Right away, Mr. Wang went to tell Mr. Liu about the offer to hire his boat. Mr. Liu indeed gave his consent, whereupon Song Jin had his servants carry his personal belongings on board, leaving the commercial goods to be loaded the following day. With Song Jin wearing a brocade robe and a marten hat and followed by two comely boys in green velvet robes carrying an incense burner and a jade *ruyi* rod with a cloud-shaped handle,[8] Mr. and Mrs. Liu failed to recognize him and greeted him as Squire Qian from Shaanxi. However, husbands and wives are, after all, closer to each other than to anyone else, and Yichun, who was peeping out from the stern, gave a start. Although not yet convinced that it was her husband, she thought to herself, "The resemblance is quite striking."

While she was watching, Squire Qian went on board. No sooner had he boarded than he said in the direction of the rudder, "I'm hungry. I want a bowl of rice. If it's cold, give me some hot tea to pour over it."

Yichun grew apprehensive. To a page boy, Squire Qian snapped, "You there! You owe everything you eat and wear to this family. If you have time to spare, do something useful, like making cords and ropes. How can you just sit there without doing anything?" (*How wonderful that he should be repeating these lines in this context.*) This all too clearly, was what Mr. Liu had said to him when he, Young Master Song, first got onto the boat years before. Yichun was all the more apprehensive.

In a short while, Mr. Liu personally served Squire Qian tea. The squire said, "Please lend me the tattered felt hat on your rudder." Being the stupid man that he was, Mr. Liu detected nothing unusual in that remark and went straight to his daughter to ask for the tattered felt hat. As she handed it to her father, Yichun intoned a quatrain in a subdued voice:

> *"However tattered the felt hat may be,*
> *It was sewn up by my very own hands.*
> *But the one wearing the hat*
> *Looks different from before."*

Quietly, Squire Qian listened to these lines from behind the rudder and understood. The hat now in his hands, he also came up with four lines:

> *"The mortal, reborn as a fairy,*
> *Is recognized by none from his past.*
> *He may have returned in wealth and splendor,*
> *But he forgets not the old tattered hat."*

That night, Yichun said to her parents, "That Squire Qian in the cabin must be none other than Song Jin. Otherwise, how could he have known that we have this tattered old hat on board? Also, he does look and talk like my husband. You must sound him out carefully."

Mr. Liu burst out laughing. "Silly girl! That miserable sick wretch has gone from this world, flesh and bones and all! Even if he didn't die, he must be begging for food somewhere far away. How could he have come into such enormous wealth?"

"You blamed us for trying to talk you into taking off your mourning clothes and remarrying, and threatened at every turn to jump into the river," put in Mrs. Liu. "Yet now you're so impressed by this traveler's wealth that you are quick to claim him as your husband. If you say he's the man but he denies it, how embarrassing that would be!"

With shame written all over her face, Yichun dared not speak up again. Mr. Liu motioned his wife to a quiet corner and said to her, "Mother, don't say such things. Marriages are made in heaven. The other day, Mr. Wang the innkeeper invited me to a wineshop for a cup of wine, saying that Squire Qian from Shaanxi would gladly offer a thousand pieces of silver as a wedding gift for our daughter. But knowing her stubbornness, I turned him down. Now that she herself is having second thoughts, why not grab the chance and marry her off to Squire Qian? That way, you and I can live well for the rest of our lives."

"You're right, old man. That Squire Qian may already have something in mind in coming over to hire our boat. Why don't you sound him out tomorrow?"

"I know what to do," said Mr. Liu.

The next morning, Squire Qian rose, washed, and combed his hair. He then went to the bow of the boat and toyed with the tattered hat with his hands. Mr. Liu spoke up. "Squire," he said, "what's there to see in this old hat?"

"I like the stitches on it. Such stitches must have been made by someone with remarkable sewing skills."

"Oh, it's just the work of my daughter. What's so remarkable about it? Well, the other day, when Mr. Wang the innkeeper was relaying a message from you, he mentioned one thing, but I don't know if it's true."

Squire Qian asked purposely, "What did he say?"

"He said you've been a widower for two years and that you wish to have my daughter for wife."

"Would you be willing, sir?"

"I am more than willing, but it's too bad that this daughter of mine is so determined to remain a widow that she has vowed never to marry again. So I dare not promise lightly."

"How did your son-in-law die?"

"Unfortunately, he came down with consumption, and that year he went ashore to chop some firewood and never came back. I did't realize he was not on board and so I turned the boat around and went back. And then I put up posters for him and waited for news for three months, but nothing came of it. Most likely he had thrown himself into the river and drowned." (*Quite logical.*)

"No, your son-in-law did not die," said the squire. "He met a god. Not only did he regain his health, but he has also come into possession of enormous wealth. If you would like to see your son-in-law, please call your daughter forward."

At this point, Yichun, who had been listening intently to one side, started crying out loud. Furiously, she said, "How heartless you are, Mr. Qian! I've been in full mourning for you for three years. Goodness knows how much I've suffered! And yet, you still haven't come out with the truth. What are you waiting for?"

Song Jin, for his part, also broke down in tears. "Wife! Step over here and let me look at you!" Husband and wife fell upon each other's shoulders and wept their hearts out.

"Mother!" exclaimed Mr. Liu. "He's not some Squire Qian, that's for sure! There's nothing for us to do but go and ask for forgiveness." So saying, they stepped into the cabin and made one bow after another as though they would never stop.

"You don't have to do this, my parents-in-law," said Song Jin. "But next time I complain of some illness, don't trick me again." The old man and the old woman were overcome with shame.

Yichun took off her mourning clothes and tossed the spiritual tablet into the water. Song Jin summoned his servants to kowtow to their mistress. Mr. and Mrs. Liu had a chicken slaughtered and wine set out in honor of their son-in-law. It was a feast to welcome him home and to celebrate the reunion. After they took their seats at the table, Mr. Liu mentioned that his daughter had abstained from meat and wine. With sad tears rolling down his cheeks, Song Jin personally served his wife and advised her to resume her normal diet. To his parents-in-law, he said, "You deliberately tricked me, hoping for my death. By rights, I should sever all ties with people who bore me such malice. It's entirely for your daughter's sake that I accept this dinner against my better judgment."

"But," put in Yichun, "had you not been tricked, how could you have made such a fortune? What's more, Father and Mother treated you well before. You should remember only the kindnesses you have received and not think hard thoughts of people."

"All right, I'll do as my good wife says. (*None measures up to her as a good wife.*) Now that I've already acquired much land and property in Nanjing, wouldn't it be nice if you, my parents-in-law, could give up your business and follow me there to share my prosperity?"

Mr. and Mrs. Liu said their thanks over and over again. That night passed without further ado.

The next day, upon hearing what had happened, Mr. Wang the innkeeper went to the boat to offer his congratulations, and another day was spent wining and dining. Song Jin had three of his servants stay with Mr. Wang to take care of the bales of fabric and the bills, while he himself went by boat to his establishment in Nanjing. He stayed there for three days before going with his wife to Kunshan, their native town, to pay respects to his deceased parents at the family grave. They also sent generous gifts to members of their clans.

By this time, Magistrate Fan had returned to Kunshan to live in retirement. Hearing that Young Master Song had returned, a rich man, he took refuge in the countryside, afraid that it would be too awkward should he run into him on the street. He kept away from the town for more than a month.

After he had completed his business in his hometown, Song Jin went back to Nanjing, where the whole family's joy and delight in their lives of peace and comfort hardly need detailed description here.

In the meantime, Yichun noticed that Song Jin went every morning without fail to the Buddhist prayer hall to pay homage to the Buddha and intone the scriptures and asked him why he did so. Thereupon, Song Jin told her about the effectiveness of the Diamond Sutra, which the old monk had taught him, in curing illnesses and prolonging life. Yichun also embraced the Buddhist faith and had her husband teach her the scriptures. They intoned the scriptures together and maintained their youthful vigor until an advanced age. (*What a good idea to end the story by coming back to the sutra.*) Both of them lived into their nineties and died without ailments.

Their descendants became the richest people in Nanjing, some of whom also distinguished themselves in the imperial civil service examinations. A later poet had this to say,

Old Man Liu failed to carry through with a good deed;
Young Master Song's woes turned out to be a bliss.
The scriptures drove away all misfortunes;
The tattered hat saw the family reunite.

23

Mr. Le Junior Searches for His Wife at the Risk of His Life (Also titled "A Story of Joy and Harmony")

From Sea Gate, the roaring waves surge with fury;[1]
It's Zixu's aggrieved soul, the boatmen say.[2]
The whitecaps blot out the sky midst peals of thunder;
The silvery peaks race like horses on land.
They rise and ebb on preordained days of the month,
At hours set by the laws of the universe.
Where are the sites of the war of Wu against Yue?
A fisherman's song rings through the village at dusk.

The above lines are a description of the extraordinary tides of the Qiantang River in Hangzhou—tides that have never deviated from their cycle. Since ancient times, no one has been able to figure out the causes of their rising and falling. It has always been said that there are four wonders in the empire. They are

> *The changing of the thunder drums in Leizhou, the buried treasures of Guangde, the mirages of Dengzhou, and the tides of the Qiantang River.*[3]

The first three wonders occur only once a year, but the Qiantang tides rise and fall twice every day. The river used to be called the Rakshasa River because the perilous, wind-blown, surging waves all too often capsize boats.[4] The mountains that flank the river used to be called the Hu [Tiger] Forest because they are infested with tigers and leopards. Later, the name was changed from Hu Forest to Wu Forest because the name of Emperor Gaozu's grandfather happened to contain the character *hu* and the character therefore was regarded as taboo. The region came to be called the Ninghai [Pacifying the Sea] County in the hope of pacifying the rapid, surging tides that often wreaked havoc among the local residents.

Later, toward the end of the Tang dynasty and the beginning of the Five Dynasties, a baby son was born to a Mr. Qian Kuan, a native of Lin'an living at the foot of Mount Jing. At the time of the baby's birth, the room was suffused with red light. The neighbors thought the house was on fire and rushed over to help put it out, only to find that a baby boy with inch-long dark hair on the soles of his feet had been born to the family. Believing the child to be a monster, the parents wanted to kill him, but the maternal grandmother stopped them and kept the baby. Hence his nickname Poliu [Kept by Granny].

The baby grew up to be a handsome, intelligent, and courageous man and stood more than seven feet tall. He was named Qian Liu, courtesy name Jumei. In his youth, he was a good-for-nothing ruffian, going about town smuggling goods and doing all sorts of mischief. When he was wanted by the police, he fled to Abbot Faji on Mount Jing for protection. That night, Faji heard a temple deity say, "King Qian of Wusu is here tonight. Do not let him come to harm." Realizing that this was no ordinary man, Faji dared not keep him but wrote a letter recommending Qian Liu to An Shou, prefect of Suzhou, who took him on as a guard. And so, Qian Liu took up residence in the horse stable in the prefect's establishment.

On a sweltering summer night, the prefect rose from bed and took a walk to the backyard. He approached the horse stable and saw Qian Liu asleep there. He was about to sit down when, lo and behold, two imps emerged from a dry well behind the main hall and began to tease Qian Liu. At this point, a god in gold armor appeared and sharply ordered the imps to go away, saying, "This is the king of Wusu. Behave yourselves!" Much startled, the prefect hastened back into the house, marveling at what he had witnessed. Henceforth, he treated Qian Liu with much kindness.

Later, for his role in repressing the rebellion led by Huang Chao, Qian Liu was promoted by Emperor Xizong to be a regional military commander.[5] Some time later, he put down a rebellion by Dong Chang, for which Emperor Zhaozong granted him the title King of Wu and Yue.[6] King Qian made Hangzhou the capital and brought peace and stability to the kingdom, but he was often grieved by the raging waves of the Yangzi River that threatened the narrow confines of the city.

One day, a local official acquired a golden carp. It was more than three feet long and had bright, sparkling eyes. The chef planned to cook it for the king's dinner, but King Qian could not bear the thought of killing such a vigorous-looking fish. He ordered that it be kept in a pond.

That night, an old man appeared to him in a dream. Wearing a tall hat and a broad waistband, the distinguished-looking old man said, "In a moment of drunkenness, my unworthy little son changed himself into a golden carp so he could play by the riverbank. He was then caught and offered to Your Highness's kitchen. I am much obliged to Your Highness for having spared his life. I am here to implore Your Highness to have him put back into the river as an act of compassion. I will surely repay you handsomely."

King Qian consented, and the Dragon King withdrew. When he woke with a start, King Qian realized he had been dreaming. Next morning, when he held his court session, he ordered his attendants to retrieve the fish from the pond and have it put back into the river.

That very night, the Dragon King again appeared to him in a dream, saying gratefully, "I cannot thank Your Highness enough for giving my son a new life. In my palace, I have stored some very exotic treasures, such as luminous pearls and jade disks more than a foot in diameter. Your Highness can have as many of them as you want."

King Qian responded, "I have no desire for treasures. But in my kingdom, which measures less than a thousand li but happens to lie right by the great Yangzi River, my people all too often fall victim to the daily ravages of the surging tides. My wish is for you to lend us a portion of your domain so as to enlarge my kingdom." (*Spoken like a sovereign.*)

"That is easily done," said the Dragon King. "Yes, you may borrow it, but when should I expect to have it back?"

"You may have it back after five hundred kalpas."[7]

"Tomorrow," said the Dragon King, "have twelve iron posts cast, each measuring twelve feet. Your Highness must board a boat. I'll have shrimp and fish gather on the surface of the water. Put an iron post wherever Your Highness sees them. The water will gradually subside of its own accord, and the sand will harden into flat land. Your Highness may then build a stone dike along the bank to mark out your enlarged territory." With that, the Dragon King vanished, and King Qian woke with a start.

The next day, King Qian ordered twelve iron posts made and rode out on a boat to check the surface of the water himself. Sure enough, he saw twelve spots where fish and shrimp had gathered. Hardly had the iron posts been lowered into the water at his order than the water subsided. He went ashore and watched the sand harden quickly into flat land that stretched from Mount Fuyang all the way to Mount Zhou at Sea Gate.

Exultantly, King Qian ordered stonemasons to build a dike by chiseling rocks from the hills into slates and then piling up the slates and running wooden stakes through them. Since this was a time-consuming process, he commanded, "Soldiers and civilians who have new or old stone slates to offer shall be rewarded with a full boatload of rice for each boatload of slates they bring." Consequently, boats came from all directions, carrying so many stone slates to exchange for rice that after construction was completed, there were stone slates left over. That was how the river came to be called Qiantang [Qian's Dike] River.

Later, when Emperor Gaozong of the Song dynasty moved his court to the south, he established his capital at Qiantang but changed the name to Lin'an Prefecture [present-day Hangzhou], calling it his temporary place of residence. The population in the city began to grow, and a wholesome ethos and good customs came into being.

Every year, on the eighteenth day of the eighth month, when the tides were at their highest, all residents of the town, regardless of class, turned out in droves to amuse themselves at the dike. Those natives who were good at swimming repeatedly submerged themselves in the water and reemerged again, each holding ten banners above water level, in a game called "playing with the tides." An amazing sight it was. There were also some poor swimmers who tried to imitate the feat but ended up being engulfed in the waves and drowned. When the matter was brought to the attention of the prefect of Lin'an, he had notices put up banning the practice, but, despite the many times his order was repeated, the custom of playing with the tides continued to be observed. A poem titled "Watching the Tides," by Academician Su Dongpo,[8] bears witness:

Men of Wu grow up playing with the waves,
Lightheartedly putting their lives at risk.
Had the East Sea God known what the king wanted,
He would have turned the water into farmland.

As the story goes, in Lin'an Prefecture during the Southern Song dynasty, there lived a man called Le Meishan, descendant of a distinguished family of long standing. Due to recent straitened circumstances, he relocated from Anping Lane of Xianfu Ward, where seven generations of his forefathers had lived as eminent officials, to a house outside of Qiantang Gate, where he opened a general store. All and sundry called him "Uncle Le" out of respect for his family background.

His wife, An-shi, bore him only one son, whom they called Le He [Happy, Harmonious]. He was a fine-looking boy with well-formed eyebrows and bright eyes and was quick and clever by nature. In his childhood, he was placed in the care of his maternal uncle, An Sanlao, on Yongqing Lane. There, he took lessons from Mr. Xi, a low-ranking civil official who lived next door. Mr. Xi had a daughter with the pet name of Xi Shunniang [Joyous, Congenial]. Being one year younger than Le He, she took her lessons with him. Classmates said in jest, "Your two names combined read 'happy, joyous, harmonious, congenial.' Doesn't that mean you are a couple made in heaven?" With their growing consciousness of the ways of the world, the young boy and girl were pleased by these playful words and privately pledged to be husband and wife. This was said in a moment of jocularity, but it turned out to be a prophecy that was meant to be fulfilled in the future. Truly,

Marriage bonds are determined in previous lifetimes
At the immortals' annual peach parties.

They stopped seeing each other when, at age twelve, Le He returned to his parents' home, and Shunniang, who was eleven years old in the same year, went back to the depths of her boudoir to learn needlework. Young as he was, Le He was more mature than his years, for he constantly recalled Shunniang's kindnesses to him and could not bear to put her out of his thoughts.

Three years went by. With the Clear and Bright Festival drawing near,[9] An Sanlao took his nephew along on a trip to the family cemetery, and on their way back, they took a tour of West Lake.

According to a Lin'an custom, all tourists on pleasure boats—whether with friends or family, whether male or female—were free to sit wherever they liked, to enjoy the hilly scenery over cups of wine. An Sanlao led his nephew onto a boat and had barely taken a seat at a table when they saw a group of women boarding the boat at the bow. Upon taking a closer look, they realized that the newcomers were Mr. An's neighbors, Mrs. Xi and her daughter, along with a maid and a maidservant. An Sanlao quickly bowed in greeting and had his nephew step forward to greet them as well. Now fourteen years old, Shunniang was prettier than before. Not having seen her in three years, Le He was as happy as if he had come upon some highly prized treasure. Even though they sat at different tables, they kept exchanging glances, well aware of the love between them and resentful of the many watchful eyes that prevented them from talking to each other.

When the boat got to Mid-lake Pavilion, An Sanlao and all the other men went to the pavilion for a walk, but Le He stayed behind in the cabin, pleading a stomachache. He moved closer to Mrs. Xi, ostensibly to strike up a conversation with her but, in fact, to be nearer to Shunniang. Whenever Mrs. Xi was not looking, the two exchanged meaningful glances. In a short while, the men returned to the boat, and Le He and Shunniang sat apart. At dusk, they all went their separate ways, and An Sanlao escorted his nephew home. His thoughts still on Shunniang, Le He wrote a poem:

The tender petals not yet in full bloom,
They need not bees and butterflies to fall in love.
Should we join as a couple years from now,
We'll tour West Lake daily midst the joy of wine.

After writing the poem on stationery paper adorned with peach blossom prints, he folded the paper into the shape of two overlapping diamonds, slipped it into his sleeve, and without telling anyone, went to Yongqing Lane. There, he waited at the door of the house where the Xi family lived, on the chance that he might encounter Shunniang. But there was no way he could communicate with her. He went several times, without success.

Hearing that the God of Tides was most responsive to prayers, he secretly bought some incense, candles, and fruit for sacrificial purposes and prayed in the Temple of the God of Tides, "Please make Xi Shunniang and me a married couple in this life." The obeisances over, he began burning paper in the incense burner. All of a sudden, the piece of folded paper fell out of his sleeve, and a gust of wind blew it into the flames. With alacrity, he retrieved it from the fire, but only the character "couple" [lü] remained legible. Le He looked at it and thought to himself, "That this character, which means 'a married couple,' survived the fire must be a good omen." His heart exulted. At this point, he saw an old man with unearthly refined looks sitting inside a stone monument pavilion. Wearing clothes and a hat of the simple style of olden times, he held a round fan on which was written "Marriages are predestined."

Le He stepped forward and bowed. "May I ask your honorable name, Grandfather?"

"This old man's surname is Shi [Stone]" was the reply.

"Can you make predictions in matters of matrimony?"

"Yes, I certainly can."

"My name is Le He. Could you please do me a favor and tell me where the red thread of marriage will lead me?"[10]

The old man replied with a smile, "You're not yet even twenty. Why are you already thinking of this?"

"Well, when Emperor Wudi of Han was a little boy, the queen mother held him on her knees and asked him, 'Would you want to have Ajiao as your wife?' He replied, 'If I can have Ajiao, I'll keep her in a house of gold.' So, you see, love knows no age."

The old man asked him for the hour, the day, the month, and the year of his birth and then, after calculating a while on his fingers, said, "The one destined for you is someone you already know."

Encouraged by this prediction, Le He said, "To be frank, sir, I do have in mind someone I already know. I wonder how the marriage destiny will work itself out."

The old man led him to an octagonal well and told him he could find out by looking into the well. With his hands on the railings, Le He looked into the well. Behold: In the well were huge waves rolling over what looked like thousands of acres of land and, underneath the water, as clear as a mirror, stood a beautiful girl about sixteen or seventeen years old, wearing a purple silk blouse and an apricot yellow skirt. A graceful and lovely girl she was. Looking closer, Le He recognized her to be none other than Shunniang. In his state of happy astonishment, he was pushed from behind by the old man and fell right onto the girl. Uttering a loud cry, he awoke with a start and realized that it had been a dream, but still, he reached for one of the columns in the pavilion and put his arms around it. Indeed,

While the yellow millet was cooking,[11]
He reached fairyland in his dream.

Now wide awake, Le He directed his attention to the stone monument in the pavilion. He saw that it was dedicated to a Shi [Stone] Gui of the Tang dynasty who had donated money for the dike for water control and, after death, was granted the title King of Tides and assumed god status. Le He thought to himself, "So, that Mr. Shi of my dream is none other than the King of Tides. The odds are nine to one that I'll get to marry her."

Upon returning home, he asked his mother to have a matchmaker approach Xi Shunniang's mother with a marriage proposal. Being a woman without much sense, Mrs. Le urged her husband to take action. Mr. Le said, "Husband and wife should be well matched in status. Even though our clan has produced officials for seven generations in a row, we've fallen on hard times and have to make a living as business brokers. The Xi family is so rich and distinguished that the parents will get plenty of marriage proposals for the girl. Why would they ever stoop to a match with our family? If we have a matchmaker approach them, we'll only be inviting ridicule."

His father having rejected the idea, Le He asked his mother to seek help from his maternal uncle, but An Sanlao's response was the same as Mr. Le's. Grievously disappointed, Le He sighed to himself throughout a wakeful night.

The next morning, he covered a tablet with a piece of paper on which he had written "In honor of my dear wife Xi Shunniang." At every meal, three times a day, he ate facing the tablet. At night, he put the tablet by his bedside and gently called her name three times before going to sleep. On every Clear and Bright Festival on the third day of the third month, the Double Ninth Festival on the ninth day of the ninth month, the Dragon Boat Festival on the fifth day of the fifth month, and the Festival of Playing with the Tide in the eighth month, he would, without exception, comb his hair well, wash, dress up, and and make his way through the crowds on the chance that he might see Shunniang, should she also be on an outing to the same places. Those business associates of the Le family who had marriageable daughters, seeing that Young Master Le was now of a suitable age, came forward with propositions. Several times, Mr. and Mrs. Le were quite ready to accept the offers, but each time, Le He firmly turned them down. He vowed not to give up his hopes until Xi Shunniang married first.

As coincidence would have it, while Le He was under a vow not to marry, Shunniang was not favored by the heavenly bliss of marriage either. Not quite a match for candidates of higher status, but unwilling to stoop lower than her own, she remained unbetrothed.

Time flew by like an arrow. Three years elapsed in the twinkling of an eye, and we now find Le He at eighteen years of age and Shunniang at seventeen, both unmarried.

His talent and her beauty make a perfect match,
But is there a marriage bond between them?
Luckily, both remain yet unbetrothed,
Waiting for the magpies to come and form a bridge.[12]

Our story forks at this point. At the time, China was on good terms with its neighbors to the north. In the year of which we speak, Gao Jingshan, an envoy from the Jin state, undertook a friendly visit to China. As Gao Jingshan was quite a scholar, the imperial court appointed Academician Fan of the Hanlin Academy to escort him.

The Mid-autumn Festival was over, and the Tide Festival rolled around. On the eighteenth day of the eighth month, when the tide was at its highest, a sumptuous feast was set out in the extravagantly embellished Zhejiang Pavilion, located outside of the city by the river. The feast was in honor of the Jin envoy, who had been invited to watch the tides. Quite a few Chinese officials had also been invited to help entertain the guest of honor. A navy warship under the command of the military commissioner sailed up and down the river, setting off multicolored fireworks. The leading rich families of the city erected colorful tents for more than thirty li along the riverbank, and the surface of the water glittered like brocade. Hundreds of local people went into the water, treading the waves and vying with one another in performing feats on water, including dances on lumber logs and puppet shows. Behold:

Slapping against the banks and tossing boats,
The waves sweep in from Sea Gate,
Their thunderous roars reaching the sky.
On earth, a Milky Way; from heaven, spring thunders.
From afar, they look like silk scarves flying through the air
And sound like a mighty army galloping.
Brave swimmers bob up and down on the white waves;
Agile fishermen ply their boats in mid-river.
Indeed, the endless green waves roll along;
Their snowy spray reaches high into the clouds.

Gao Jingshan, the envoy of Jin, was so thrilled that his hair stood on end. He heaved one sigh of amazement after another at such a spectacular sight. Academician Fan suggested, "Why don't you write a poem for us on viewing such a sight?" So saying, he ordered that the four treasures of the scholar's study be brought over.[13] After many demurrals, Gao Jingshan composed a lyric poem to the tune of "The Charms of Niannu":

Wave upon wave of clouds stretch for a thousand li;
The world has never seen a sight so majestic,
A sight unknown except in the Southeast.
Green waters merge with clouds at the horizon;
A sudden roar of thunder shakes the earth.
Ten thousand horses gallop toward the sky,
Flocks of geese flutter to the ground,
Kicking up spray and mist that spout high.
Men of the Wu region, brave souls they are,
Treading the waves in games of competition.
Flags and banners dot the scene;
Music from Wu, wind instruments from Chu,
Play forth together with Tartar pipes.
Blessed with such people, such rivers and hills,
This is a land where demons have no chance.
This city, where the emperor resides,

Enjoys the five blessings from the stars,
So brightly lit by the blazing flames.
In speechless awe, I lean against the railings
And wait for the lambent moon to rise in the sky.

Upon finishing, Gao Jingshan was showered with praise from everyone present, but Academician Fan commented, "A nicely written poem, except for one flaw: The lines 'Ten thousand horses gallop toward the sky; / Flocks of geese flutter to the ground' do not do full justice to the tides. In fact, the tides can well be likened to jade dragons." Right away, the Academician composed a lyric poem to the tune of "Prelude to Water Music":

Looking far out at the islet down below,
One marvels at the vastness of the universe.
The water meets the sky at the far horizon;
One ripplet swells into ten thousand li of waves.
Majestically they surge ahead,
Like jade dragons playing with the water,
Going under the waves one moment and out the next.
Snowy whitecaps spout high under the clouds;
The spray sparkles like beaded crystal portieres.

Engulfing the choppy waves of the sea
Whisking off the Fairy Mountain midst the waters,
They churn up the torrents of the oceans.
The heavenly stars have come down to earth,
Adding splendor to both sides of the river.
Where, may I ask, can Wu Zixu be found?[14]
The duke of Bowang's raft—when will it be back?[15]
The Milky Way, all too narrow,
Flows down to the human world.

Upon reading Academician Fan's poem, Gao Jingshan exclaimed in delight, "What a wonderful poem! They are indeed more like jade dragons playing with water than ten thousand galloping horses."

Now, let us leave the officials at their wining and dining and turn our attention to the residents, rich and poor, of Lin'an. At the news that entertainment of every description was being presented that day in honor of an envoy from the north who was a guest of the imperial court, all the people in town turned out to watch. Le He, having learned upon inquiry that the entire Xi family was going to watch the tide, dressed himself up early the next morning and went to the mouth of the Qiantang River, where he searched diligently for Xi Shunniang, without success. Then he betook himself to a spot called variously "Panorama" and "Spin-around"—

"Spin-around" because one sees the tide wherever one turns. With the passage of time, "Spin-around" was corrupted and became "Fish-around." This is a spot where the tides are at their fiercest. There has been no lack of people who slipped and were swallowed up by the surging water, and, at the same time, there were others wringing their clothes under Xiapu Bridge. There is a lyric poem to the tune of "Immortal at the River" that ridicules tide watchers:

Since ancient times, there has been no place like Qiantang;
In groups, in crowds, the tide watchers jostle their way
To the riverside before the Mid-autumn Festival.
On the sandy beach, they look far out for the tide;
Before they know it, the waves burst as high as the sky.

Their caps all wet, they try wringing their clothes dry.
By Xiapu Bridge, a veritable scene of hell:
Crowds of ghosts, naked, with hair hanging loose.
Back in the city, their clothes dried over a fire,
They ask when the tide will rise again.

After searching in vain for Shunniang at Spin-around, Le He turned back, keeping an eye out for her as he went. Being nimble of limb, he threaded his way through huge crowds around makeshift tents, looking around with each step. Quite some time later, he caught sight of a woman walking into a crowd around one of the tents. Le He recognized her to be a maidservant of the Xi family. He followed closely behind her and did indeed find the Xi family sitting together, drinking wine and enjoying themselves. He dared not get too close, nor could he bear the thought of staying too far from Shunniang, so he leaned against the tent and fixed his eyes on her. How he wanted to walk up to her, hold her in his arms, and say a few tender words! The girl, who was looking around, her head raised, recognized Young Master Le from afar. Pity swelled in her heart as she watched him pace nervously back and forth. But with her parents never more than an inch away wherever she went, meeting him face-to-face was out of the question. (*An awkward moment.*) Truly,

The secret in their hearts
They shared in wordless passion.

While Le He and Xi Shunniang were gazing despairingly at each other, a sudden cry was heard: "The tide is here!" The voices were still in the air when, with an earth-splitting roar, waves tens of feet high came sweeping in, as this poem testifies:

The soaring silver mountains roll forward;
Rising from the ground, they fly through the air.
It must be the soul of Wu Zixu,
Showing its divine power even to this day.

Choppier than in years past, the waves broke against the higher ground of the bank, tore open the brocade sheets, and knocked down the tents. With a cry, the crowd recoiled, but Shunniang, her mind entirely on Young Master Le, did not know what she was doing and took a few steps forward instead. Losing her foothold, she disappeared into the waves. (*Had the King of Tides not intervened, the devoted lovers would have perished for the sake of love.*)

How sad that the well-protected girl
Now floats along with the currents!

Alert to the danger, Le He had run to higher ground before the tide could get him and, his thoughts still on Shunniang, cried out toward the tent, "Get away from the water!"

Suddenly, to his great alarm, he saw Shunniang fall into the water. In less time than it takes to narrate, the very moment Shunniang fell, Le He followed her into the water, first with his eyes and then with his feet. With a splash, he jumped into the water and was also caught in the current, for he was no swimmer. He did this out of love and at the risk of his life.

Witnessing their daughter's fall, Mr. and Mrs. Xi cried out frantically, "Help! Help! A reward for whoever saves my daughter!" Wearing a purple blouse and an apricot yellow skirt, Shunniang was easy to see. (*The very clothes he had dreamed about in the Temple of the King of Tides.*) Lured by the promise of a reward, many a young man who could swim as easily as walking on land readily came forward, parting the waves in search of a girl in a purple blouse and an apricot yellow skirt.

After throwing himself into the water, Le He sank all the way to the bottom of the river, but instead of being overwhelmed by the water, he felt he had experienced all of this in his dream. Presently, he found himself in the Temple of the King of Tides, which was ablaze with candlelight and fragrant with swirling wisps of incense. Le He prostrated himself on the floor. To his prayers that Shunniang be saved from drowning, the King of Tides replied, "Xi Shunniang is here with me. Let me deliver her to you." That said, an attendant escorted Shunniang out from behind the curtains. Le He bowed his thanks to the King of Tides and led Shunniang out of the temple. Such was their joy that speech was quite beyond them. Holding each other tightly in a face-to-face embrace, they rose, after some ups and downs, to the surface of the water.

At the sight of a purple blouse and an apricot yellow skirt emerging from the waves, the many swimmers rushed to the rescue. They retrieved from the water not one body but two. Four or five men carried them to shore holding each by the head and feet and said to Mr. Xi, "Luckily, we saved your son-in-law, too."

When Mr. and Mrs. Xi, the maidservants, and the nurse drew closer, they saw the two, thinly clad in the warm weather of the eighth month, face to face, chest to chest, shoulder to shoulder, thighs to thighs, in an embrace so tight that no one could pull them apart. However hard those around tried to wake them, they gave no response. But the bodies were still slightly warm, looking neither dead nor alive. Mr. and Mrs. Xi were so panic stricken that they had not the slightest idea what to do, and those members of the Xi clan who were at the scene collapsed in a heap, weeping. The onlookers, contending for a better view, commented that they had never seen anything so remarkable.

In the meantime, Le Meishan was at home when someone came to tell him that his son had been swallowed up by the waves while watching the tide of Fish-around. Frightened, Mr. Le Senior dragged himself to Spin-around, stumbling every step of the way. There, he heard that a man and a woman had been retrieved from the water and that the woman was Mr. Xi's daughter. Pushing through the crowd, Mr. Le reached the bodies and recognized his son Le He. "My child! My very own!" he cried. Bursting into loud sobs, he said, "My child! You couldn't have the one you loved, but who would have known that you would be reunited with her only after death!"

Mr. Xi asked him why he said such things. At Mr. Le's account of how, three years before, his son had stubbornly asked him to present a marriage proposal to the Xi family and then had vowed not to marry before Shunniang did, Mr. and Mrs. Xi said with displeasure, "With seven generations of officials in your family history, yours is a distinguished family of long standing. What's more, the two of them studied together when they were children. Why didn't you tell us earlier what you said just now? Let's try to revive them. If they come to, we'll be only too glad to marry our daughter to your son."

And so, Mr. and Mrs. Xi tried to wake their daughter, and Mr. Le tried to revive his son. After about an hour, the two youngsters gradually opened their eyes and began to breathe, but their four arms remained locked as firmly as before. Mr. Le Senior said, "My son, wake up! Mr. Xi has promised to marry Shunniang to you."

Before he had quite finished, Le He opened his eyes wide. "My father-in-law, you must not go back on your word!" So saying, he jumped up and bowed his thanks to Mr. and Mrs. Xi. Miss Xi also came to. The young couple looked as spirited as ever, nor did they need to spit out any water as those rescued from drowning usually do. Mr. Xi and Uncle Le were delighted beyond measure. (*This was all the work of the playful King of Tides.*) The two families had the young couple change into dry clothes and hired small sedan-chairs to carry them home.

The next day, Mr. Xi took the initiative and sent a matchmaker to the Le family with the message that he would be glad to have Le He as a live-in son-in-law. The matchmaker was none other than An Sanlao. The Le family readily agreed to all the terms.

On a chosen auspicious day, the Xi family sent over some lavish gifts, and amid the festive music of flutes and drums, a wedding procession escorted Le He to the Xi residence for the ceremony. The young couple's love for each other hardly needs more description here. One month later, Le He and Shunniang went to the Temple of the King of Tides to make sacrificial offerings as a token of their gratitude.

Impressed by Le He's intelligence, Mr. Xi engaged a celebrated scholar to tutor him at home. Later, Le He passed the imperial civil service examinations at all levels. To this day, storytellers in Lin'an still use the four-character phrase "happy, joyous, harmonious, congenial" to describe blissful marriages. There is a poem in witness:

His love for her grew with the years—
A love that moved the King of Tides.
When love reaches the deepest depths,
Storms of life and death can do it no harm.

24

Yutangchun Reunites with Her Husband in Her Distress (A different version of the traditional story "Young Master Wang's Assiduous Application of Himself")

In his youth, he toured the houses of pleasure;
At first sight, he lost his heart to Yutangchun.
All his heaps of gold went down the drain;
She shed bitter tears of grief in vain.

The jewelry taken, the page boys and horse gone,
She was thrown into Hongtong Prison.
Only when the inspector redressed her wrongs
Did they join in blissful, enduring marriage.

Our story takes place during the Zhengde reign period [1506–22]. There was a man named Wang Qiong, courtesy name Sizhu, who was a native of Jinling, Nanjing. After passing the imperial civil service examinations as a *jinshi,* he rose through a series of promotions to be secretary of the Ministry of Rites. But because he wrote a memorial to the imperial court to demand impeachment of the power-abusing eunuch Liu Jin, the emperor ordered him to return to his native place, Nanjing. Not daring to remain in Beijing a moment longer, he packed and got the horses and carriages ready for his family. Before he set off on the journey, he thought to himself, "I don't have time to collect the small loans I made to others out of my salary." Since his oldest son was occupied as a secretariat drafter in Nanjing and his second son was in the midst of the imperial examinations at the provincial level, he decided, after much hesitation, to summon his third son Jinglong, courtesy name Shunqing [to Beijing].

At seventeen years of age, the third young master had fresh features and a graceful deportment. He was able to read ten lines at a glance and write essays as fast as his brush pen could go. A dashing young scholar he was. Mr. Wang Senior loved this son as he did the breath of his life and treasured him as he would a precious pearl in his palm.

As we were saying, Mr. Wang Senior summoned him and gave him these instructions: "I want you to stay here and continue with your studies while waiting for Wang Ding [a servant] to collect the debts. Return home as soon as the money is in, so that your mother and I won't worry. All the account books here I leave to you." He then called for Wang Ding and said to him, "You stay here with Third Young Master. He will be continuing with his studies while you collect the debts. Do not lure him into any wrongdoing. (*If Wang Ding is trustworthy, the third son need not stay. If Wang Ding is not trustworthy, how can he be expected to keep the young master from wrongdoings?*) If I find out about any mischief, you'll have much to answer for!"

Wang Ding said with a kowtow, "I would never dream of disobeying."

The next day, Wang Ding and the young master saw Mr. Wang Senior off on his journey before they returned to Beijing and moved to a temporary residence. Obeying his father's orders, the young master kept up his studies at his lodging while Wang Ding went about collecting debts. Before they knew it, three months had gone by, and Wang Ding had recovered all the debts, which came to thirty thousand taels of silver. Upon checking the amount collected against the amount recorded in the account books, the young master did not find the least discrepancy. He told Wang Ding to choose a day for departure, adding, "Wang Ding, now that our business is done, let's go out into the streets and have some fun before our departure tomorrow."

So Wang Ding locked the rooms and told the landlord to keep an eye on their draft animals. "Don't you worry!" said the landlord. "I'll take care of everything." Thereupon, the two ventured out to enjoy the sights and sounds of the capital. Behold:

What a heaving mass of humanity,
Speaking in the accents of all regions of the land!
What a clatter the horse carriages make,
Transporting officials of all the bureaus!
Traders deal in goods from all parts of the empire;
Idlers enjoy the bliss of those peaceful times.
The lanes and alleys are paved with brocade;
The houses echo with wine-induced singing.

The young master was delighted beyond measure. Watching five or seven rich-looking young men merrily drinking, with stringed instruments in hand, he commented, "Wang Ding, what an exciting place this is!"

"Third Master," rejoined Wang Ding, "if you think this is exciting, you haven't seen anything yet!" (*What a troublemaker Wang Ding is!*) They wended their way to Donghua Gate, where the young master found himself dazzled by the sight of golden phoenixes and dragons carved on the gate and the columns.

"Third Master, do you like it?"

"Yes! This is wonderful!"

Farther down the street, he asked Wang Ding, "What's this place called?"

"This is the Forbidden City."

The young master looked inside and was impressed by the glittering red lanterns and auspicious air. He looked a while longer. Indeed, in terms of wealth and luxury, none exceeds the emperor. He sighed in admiration. After leaving Donghua Gate, they walked on and, a while later, came upon an establishment at the entrance of which stood several well-dressed women.

"Wang Ding," said the young master, "what is this place?"

"This is a restaurant."

They went in. The young master took a seat and noticed that gathered around the tables, drinking, were five to seven groups of men, and one group included two girls even prettier than the ones who were standing out front. While he was staring at them, a waiter brought wine. "Where are these girls from?" he asked the waiter.

"They are Cuixiang and Cuihong. These girls are in Yichengjin's service." (*This waiter is another busybody.*)

"Pretty girls!" exclaimed Third Master.

"Well, if these two are pretty," said the waiter, "then you should see Third Sister, usually called Yutangchun, of the same house. Now that's a fine one to look at! But the madam asks too high a price for her, so she hasn't taken any clients yet."

The young master made a mental note of what he had just heard and had Wang Ding pay the bill. After going downstairs, he said, "Wang Ding, let's take a walk to the courtesans' quarters."

"No, no, Third Master! What if your father learns about this?"

"One quick look can't do any harm." And so, they walked to the entrance of the courtesans' quarters, which were registered with the Office of Music. Indeed,

The streets are lined with flowers and willows
Amid ornate houses and vermilion buildings.
Music wafts from behind every door;
Rouge and powder are applied to every face.
Wealthy young men purchase laughter with gold;
Coquettish women beckon with their red sleeves.
As a fragrant mist spreads across the sky,
Singing voices rise above the halls.
Even moralists find themselves bewitched;
Even the best monks break their vows.

In a daze, the young master wondered which door was Yichengjin's. At this moment, a young melon peddler named Jin'ge drew near. The young master asked him, "Which house is Yichengjin's?"

"So you want to have some fun, sir? I can take you there," offered Jin'ge.

"My young master is no patron of prostitutes," Wang Ding snapped. "Don't take him for that kind of man."

"But I do wish to visit," insisted the young master.

Promptly Jin'ge went to announce the visitor to the madam, who rushed out to greet the patron and invited him in for tea, an act of courtesy that frightened Wang Ding. "Third Master," he urged, "let's get out of here!"

Hearing this, the madam asked, "Who might this be?"

"He's my servant."

"Big Brother," said the madam, "please also come in for a cup of tea. Don't be a killjoy!"

"Just don't pay any attention to him," said the young master. (*Wang Ding* is *a killjoy. He makes his master lose face.*) With that remark, he followed the madam into the house.

"Third Master!" cried out Wang Ding. "Don't go in there! If your father finds out about this, I'll say I had no part in it!" And so he rattled on from behind. Turning a deaf ear to him, the young master marched straight in and sat down. The madam had a maid serve him tea, and after he drank it up, she asked, "What is your honorable surname?"

"My surname is Wang. My father is the secretary of the Ministry of Rites."

With a bow, the madam said, "I didn't know you were from such a distinguished family. Please forgive me for not showing you proper respect."

"That's all right. Don't take it to heart. I'm here because I've long heard of your daughter Yutangchun's fame and would like to see her."[1]

"Yesterday, someone offered a hundred taels of silver to be her first patron, but I turned him down," said the madam.

"But a hundred taels is too little! I don't want to sound boastful, but apart from the emperor, my father is the richest man in the land. Even my grandfather was a vice-minister."

Secretly filled with delight at these words, the madam sent Cuihong the maid to escort Third Sister out to greet the honored guest. A short while later, Cuihong returned to say, "Third Sister is feeling indisposed and asks that she be excused."

The madam rose and said affably, "This little daughter of mine has been quite pampered since childhood. Let me go to get her myself."

Wang Ding was dismayed. "It's all right if she doesn't come out. Don't bother to go and get her!"

Ignoring him, the madam went to the girl's room and called out, "Third Sister, my child! Your time has come! Secretary Wang's son is here expressly to see you!"

Yutangchun kept her head lowered and said nothing in response. Exasperated, the madam cried, "My child, Mr. Wang is a handsome young man of only sixteen or seventeen, with deeply lined pockets. If you hang on to this patron, you'll not only build a nice reputation for yourself but also have enough money to last a lifetime."

Upon hearing these words, Sister Yu began to make herself up, so as to be ready to go and greet Young Master Wang. Before she left the room, the madam added, "My child, serve him well. Don't be negligent in any way."

"All right," said Sister Yu.

The young master found Yutangchun to be truly beautiful:

She has dark clouds for hair, crescent moons for eyebrows;
Her skin is like the snow, her cheeks the rosy dawn;
Half-hidden in her sleeves, dainty bamboo-shoot hands;
Underneath her skirt, tiny gold-lotus feet.
An unassuming beauty with little makeup,
Her charm needs no help from rouge and powder.
None of the famed courtesans of the house
Could in any way measure up to her.

Stealing a glance at the young master, Sister Yu was secretly delighted to see that he was a well-dressed young man with refined features, a fair complexion, red lips, and a graceful bearing. After she bowed to the young master, the madam said, "This is no place for a distinguished guest. Let's go to the study for a little talk."

And so the young man let her take him into the study, which was, not surprisingly, an exquisitely furnished room, with bright windows, clean tables, antique paintings, and incense burners. But Mr. Wang Junior was in no mood for admiring the furnishings. His heart was set on Sister Yu. To move matters along, the madam made the girl sit down by the young man's shoulder. She then ordered maids to set out wine. At the mention of wine, Wang Ding grew all the more alarmed. Over and over again, he urged Third Master to leave the place. Throwing the maids a significant look, the madam said, "Invite this gentleman to another room for a cup of wine." (*Wise move.*)

"Brother," said Cuixiang and Cuihong to Wang Ding, "let's go to another room for a cup of wine to celebrate the occasion."

Over Wang Ding's objections, the two maids dragged him off. With sweet words, they plied him with one cup of wine after another. In the beginning, he complied grudgingly, but then, in the growing excitement, he threw all caution to the winds and gave himself up to the pleasures of the moment. In the course of the revelry, word came that Wang Ding was wanted by the young master. Wang Ding rushed to the study, where he saw a fine spread on the dinner table and a band of musicians provided by the house. Amid strains of music, the young master was drinking to his heart's content. When Wang Ding drew near him, he whispered into the servant's ear, "Go back to our lodging, take out two hundred taels of silver, four bolts of silk, and twenty taels of loose silver and bring them back here."

"Why do you need so much silver, Third Master?"

"That's none of your business."

Resignedly, Wang Ding went back to their lodging, opened a leather trunk, and took out four shoe-shaped ingots of silver weighing fifty taels each plus some silk fabric and loose silver. Upon returning to the courtesans' quarters, he announced to his master, "Third Master, what you asked for is all here."

Without even looking at what Wang Ding had brought, the young master ordered that everything be given to the madam. Then he said to her, "The silver and the fabric are a gift for your daughter, to mark the occasion of our first acquaintance. The twenty taels of loose silver are for you to use as tips and for miscellaneous purposes."

Wang Ding had thought that the young master needed all the silver so that he could bring the girl home as his wife. When he heard that it was simply to mark the occasion of their first acquaintance, he was so horrified that his tongue hung out three inches from his mouth. As for the madam, at the sight of the lavish gifts, she had the maids move over an empty table on which Wang Ding could put them down. After a few moments of feigned hesitation, the madam said to Sister Yu, "My child, give Young Master Wang a bow of thanks." She then added, turning to the young man, "Today, I still call you Young Master Wang, but soon enough, you'll be known as Brother-in-law Wang!" After ordering the maids to take the gifts to the interior of the house, the madam said, "There's some more wine set out in my girl's room for the young master to enjoy."

Hand in hand, the young man and Sister Yu went to the latter's boudoir, where a small table, shielded by a folding screen, was laid out with fruit and delicacies. The young master took the seat of honor, and the madam played the *xianzi* [a three-stringed plucked instrument] while Yutangchun sang and plied him with wine, sending him into such raptures that his bones itched and his soul was transported with ecstasy. (*This is the first day his amorous desires are stirred.*)

The hour being late, Wang Ding grew anxious when the young master showed no signs of wishing to leave. By the madam's orders, the maids refused to relay to the young master his repeated pleas that they be on their way, nor did the women allow Wang Ding to enter the inner quarters. And thus he waited the whole evening. Cuihong offered to accommodate him for the night, but he refused and went back alone to his lodging. The young master kept on drinking until the second watch of the night. Yutangchun attended devotedly to his needs. She helped him take off his clothes and get into bed, where they indulged in sexual pleasures the whole night through, and there we shall leave them.

At daybreak, the madam had the kitchen staff set out wine and boil some hot water while she went into the boudoir with a reward in mind. "Brother-in-law Wang," she called out, "congratulations!"

The maids and page boys also went in to kowtow. Thereupon, the young master told Wang Ding who had returned early in the morning to escort the young master back to their lodging, to reward each one with a tael of silver. Cuixiang and Cuihong each also got a suit of clothes worth three taels of silver. Wang Ding was visibly displeased by such largesse. The young man thought to himself, "What a pain in the neck that flunky is! Why should I be begging him for money? I'd better have the leather trunk carried to this place so that I can do whatever I like with it."

The sight of the leather trunk further increased the madam's obsequiousness. Truly, every day was spent like a festival day, and quite unnoticeably, more than a month slipped by. With designs on more of Mr. Wang's money, the madam set out a grand feast, complete with music and theatrical performances, exclusively in honor of Third Master and Sister Yu. Raising her cup of wine, the madam offered a toast to the young patron, saying, " Brother-in-law Wang, now that my daughter and you have become husband and wife in an everlasting union, I'll be counting on you to help us with our household expenses."

Afraid of incurring the madam's displeasure, Third Master parted with his silver as if it were so much dung and dirt, paying all the debts the madam falsely claimed she owed, ordering jewelry, silverware, and clothes, renovating the house, and building a "Hundred Flowers Hall" for Yutangchun's private use. In short, he granted every request the madam made of him. Truly,

Wine does not intoxicate;
Men themselves fall ready prey.
Beauty does not infatuate;
Men themselves fall willing captive.

At his wits' end, Wang Ding the servant repeatedly begged Third Master to go back to their lodging. In the beginning, Third Master fobbed him off with some evasive answer, but later, as the pressure grew, he turned the tables on Wang Ding and gave him a good tongue-lashing. Wang Ding saw nothing for it but to ask Sister Yu to intervene. Knowing all too well how unscrupulous the madam was, Sister Yu tried to talk some sense into the young man, saying, "As the proverb says, 'Whoever remains a saint after a thousand days? How long does a flower keep its color?' As soon as your money runs out, she'll turn against you. By then, don't expect mercy from her!" (*How unusual for someone in Sister Yu's position to say these words! Her devotion to him stems from gratitude for his determination to stay with her.*) Still well-stocked with silver at the time, Third Master turned a deaf ear to her admonitions.

Wang Ding thought to himself, "He doesn't even listen to his beloved one, let alone me! Just imagine what will happen if his father finds out about this! I'd better go home and report it to the old master. Whatever he decides to do, I won't be held accountable." (*Good move, but too late.*) To Third Master, Wang Ding said, "As I'm useless in Beijing, I'd better go home."

Third Master loathed Wang Ding for his meddlesomeness and couldn't wait to get rid of him. "Wang Ding, if you're going, let me give you ten taels of silver for your traveling expenses. Just tell Father that I haven't finished with business and that I sent you to pay my respects to him."

Sister Yu and the madam also gave Wang Ding five taels of silver each. Wang Ding bowed his farewell to Third Master and took himself off. Truly,

Each sweeps the snow from his own doorstep
And ignores the frost on his neighbor's roof.

Wallowing in the pleasures of wine and sex, Third Master stayed on with never a thought of returning home.

Time flew by like an arrow. Quite unnoticeably, one year went by. The procurer and his wife the madam never ceased fleecing the young master, asking him to pay for the initiation of new girls, for birthday parties and wedding celebrations, for purchasing maidservants, and even for preparing the procurer's future grave site. At last, Third Master's resources ran out. As soon as he saw that Mr. Wang had been reduced to a penniless pauper, the procurer's usual obsequiousness disappeared, and he turned his back on the young man. Two weeks later, a terrible racket broke out, led by the madam, who barked at Sister Yu, "You know what they say, 'The rich visit the brothels; the poor go to the poorhouses.' Mr. Wang has no money now. Why is he still hanging on here? Have you ever heard of a brothel supporting a paragon of virtue who maintains her loyalty to a miserable penniless wretch?"

Sister Yu treated these words like a puff of wind passing her ear. One day, while Third Master was out, a maidservant reported his absence to the madam, who then summoned Yutangchun downstairs and said to her, "Let me ask you something. When are you going to send that lowlife packing?"

Offended by the hostile tone, Sister Yu turned and went back upstairs. The madam followed closely on her heels, saying, "You slave! Are you trying to cut me dead?"

Sister Yu shot back, "Don't you have any sense of decency? Mr. Wang spent thirty thousand taels of silver in this house. Had it not been for him, we would have been in debt here, there, and everywhere. How else could you ever have gotten where you are?"

In a transport of rage, the madam charged at her, head first, screaming, "Third One is beating up her mother!"

Upon hearing her cries, the procurer stormed up the stairs, a whip in hand. Without bothering to find out what had truly happened, he threw Sister Yu to the ground and flogged her until her hair came loose, and blood and tears flowed together.

In the meantime, Third Master was outside Wu Gate chatting with a friend. Suddenly, his face flushed red, and a shiver ran through him. Feeling apprehensive, he took leave of his friend. When he reached Hundred Flowers Hall and saw Yutangchun, he felt as if he had been stabbed with a knife. He rushed over and began stroking her, asking what had happened. Sister Yu opened her eyes. At the sight of Third Master, she said with forced cheerfulness, "This is a family matter. It doesn't concern you." (*Poor thing.*)

"My love, you were beaten because of me. How can you say this doesn't concern me? I'm leaving tomorrow so that you won't have to suffer so much!"

"My brother, I did advise you to go, but you didn't listen. And now, how are you going to make the three-thousand-li journey without any money? How am I going to set my mind at rest? (*Money is less important than her peace of mind over his well-being.*) If you can't return home and will have to lead a vagrant life anyway, you're better off swallowing the insults and staying here for a few more days."

At these words, Third Master choked and collapsed. Sister Yu went over and held him in her arms, saying, "Brother, don't go downstairs any more. Let's wait and see what they are going to do about us."

Third Master lamented, "If I go home, I'll hardly be able to face my parents, my brother, and my sister-in-law, but if I stay, the procurer's vicious words will be too much for me to take. I can't bear the thought of leaving you, and yet, with me here, they'll go on beating you."

"Brother, never mind about their beating me. You and I became husband and wife at such an early age, you can't abandon me and leave me here alone!"

Evening set in as they talked, but the maidservants had stopped bringing lamps up to them. Seeing Third Master so griefstricken, Sister Yu pushed him to the bed to retire for the night. Heaving sigh after sigh, Third Master said to Sister Yu, "I'd better go, so that you can take on some rich clients and be spared more bullying."

"Brother, whatever the procurer and the madam do to me, don't leave me. If you're here, I'll go on living. If you go, I'll have to die."

The two of them wept until daybreak. After they got up, no one brought them anything, not even a bowl of water. Sister Yu called out to the maidservants, "Bring a cup of tea for your brother-in-law."

Upon hearing this, the madam shouted at the top of her voice, "The temerity of that slave! She's in for some more flogging! Let Third One come and get it herself!"

None of the maidservants dared go forward. Sister Yu saw nothing for it but to go downstairs to the kitchen herself, where she filled a bowl with rice and tearfully brought it upstairs.

"Brother," said she, "here's your bowl of rice."

The young master was about to start eating when he again heard curses from downstairs. He put the rice away, but Sister Yu insisted that he eat something. He had just taken a mouthful when the procuress screamed again from down below, "Third One, you slave, listen up! Have you ever heard of a clever housewife who could cook a meal without rice?"

The implication of these words certainly was not lost on Third Master, but he could do no more than swallow the humiliation. Truly,

High spirits come with a well-lined pocket;
Empty hands bring one nothing but shame.

Despite the procurer's annoyance with Sister Yu, he could not very well beat her again, because if she was injured in any way, she could hardly be a source of income for the house. But at the same time, if he spared her from beating, she would be glued to that Wang the Third, who, with a mind quite befuddled by wine and sex, was very likely to commit suicide. And if Secretary Wang should send for his son, they wouldn't be able to produce even a clay statue of the young man, complete and dry, at a moment's notice. So, turning his thoughts this way and that, he was not able to come up with a plan. The madam spoke up, "I have a wonderful idea that will make him clear out of here. Tomorrow being your sister's birthday, we can do thus and thus. This is known as the trick to 'shake the man off.'"

"All right," the procurer agreed.

At the madam's bidding, a maid went upstairs and asked if Brother-in-law had eaten. Then the madam herself went up. "Please don't take offense at what happened earlier. That was a family matter that doesn't concern Brother-in-law." Wine was laid out as before. In the course of the drinking, the madam said with an ingratiating smile, "Third Sister, tomorrow is your aunt's birthday. Please let Brother-in-law Wang know about this, so that he can go with us to offer her a birthday present."

Sister Yu prepared the present that very night. Early the next morning, the madam called out, "Brother-in-law Wang, get up! Let's go while it's still cool! We need to send the birthday present to the aunt's house!"

Everyone at the house set out on the journey. They had gone about half a li when the madam feigned alarm, saying, "Brother-in-law Wang, I forgot to lock the gate. Please go back and lock it." The unsuspecting young man did as he was told, but of him, more later.

At this point, the procurer appeared out of a small lane and called, "Third Sister, you dropped a hairpin!" Sister Yu fell for the trick and turned around to look. In the meantime, the procurer gave the animal she was riding two cracks of his whip, and it galloped with all speed out of the city gate.

After locking the gate, Third Master hastily continued on his way, but instead of seeing Sister Yu, he ran into a group of men. He asked them with a bow, "Did you see a group of people? Where did they go?"

These men were by no means of the decent sort. In fact, they were bandits. Observing that Third Master was quite well dressed, they came up with a wicked plan. "They were going in a westerly direction toward the reed pond," they told him.

"Thank you all," said Third Master and started for the reed pond. Having tricked Third Master to go in that direction, the bandits hurried to get there before he did. And there they lay in ambush. When Third Master drew near, they jumped up with a shout and pounced on him. After stripping off his clothes and his hat, they trussed him up with ropes and threw him to the ground. Incapable of moving even a hand or a foot, Third Master lay there half-conscious until daybreak, thinking only of Yutangchun. "Sister," he moaned, "where are you? You have no idea what I'm going through!"

We shall leave the young master in his distress and come back to the procurer and the madam who had abducted Sister Yu. After covering a hundred and twenty li in a single day, they took up lodging at a wayside inn. Well aware by now that she had been tricked, Sister Yu wept as she went along, her thoughts on nothing but Third Master.

In the meantime, Third Master was still lying amid the reeds, crying out for help. Some local residents passing by saw him and untied the ropes. "Where are you from?" they asked.

Being completely naked, he was too ashamed to say he was from a distinguished family, or to admit he was a patron of the courtesan Yutangchun. Tearfully, he said, "Gentlemen, I'm a native of Henan, here on a trip for my small business. Unfortunately, I ran into some bandits, who stripped me of my clothes, and I don't have even one penny left."

The villagers gave the young man a few pieces of clothing and a hat. Thankfully, he rose and put on the rags and the tattered hat. With Sister Yu nowhere in sight and not a penny in his pocket, he made his way back to Beijing, walking under the eaves of the houses and keeping his head down. From morning to night, he had nothing to eat or drink, not even a drop of water. His eyes had turned yellow with hunger by nighttime, and when he tried to find lodging, no one wanted to put him up. A man said to him, "The way you look, who'd be willing to take you? But you might try the night patrol office. If they happen to need a night watchman, you'll be able to make a living if you work hard enough."

To the patrol office Third Master went. It just so happened that a local headman was there, looking for someone to strike the hours of the night. Third Master stepped forward and cried, "Uncle, let me strike the first watch of the night!"

The headman asked, "What's your name?"

"Wang the Third."

"I'll let you strike the second watch. If you miss the time, you'll get a beating instead of money."

Being a young man unaccustomed to discipline, he overslept and missed the watch he was supposed to strike. The headman was furious. "Wang the Third!" he bellowed. "Your lazy bones are not meant for a nice job like this! Now get out of my sight this instant!"

At his wits' end, the young master was reduced to seeking shelter in a poorhouse. Truly,

From a house of pleasure to a house for the poor,
How these circumstances are worlds apart!

Now back to the procurer and the madam. "We've been away for a month now," they said, conferring with each other. "That Wang the Third must have gone back to his hometown. Let's go home."

So they packed up and returned to the courtesans' quarters. But Sister Yu missed the young master so much that she could barely force herself to sleep and eat. The madam went upstairs and tried hard to change her mind, saying, "My child, that man Wang the Third is with his family now. Why do you still think about him? Goodness knows how many rich young men there are in Beijing, and yet you think only of him and refuse to see other patrons. Now, you know what kind of woman you're dealing with. You'd better come to your senses. I'm not going to have talks like this with you anymore." That said, the madam took herself off.

Her tears falling like rain, Sister Yu could think only of Wang Shunqing struggling to survive without having even a penny. "Wherever you are," she addressed him in her imagination, "you should have dropped me a message, so that I, Su San, wouldn't have to worry so much. Oh, when will I ever see you again?"

Let us leave Sister Yu in her room, thinking of the young master, and return to the latter, who was living a beggar's life in the poorhouse in Beijing. There was in the city a Mr. Wang, a very skilled silversmith, who had made some wine vessels for Secretary Wang as well as items of jewelry for Sister Yu's madam. One day, walking past the poorhouse, he suddenly caught sight of the young master. Appalled, he stepped forward and grabbed the young man, exclaiming, "Third Master, why are you in such a state?"

Third Master told him the whole story, whereupon Silversmith Wang said, "Brothel procurers have always been known for their ruthlessness. Third Master, come with me to my humble home. You can share our simple food and stay with us for a few days until your father sends for you."

Joyfully, Third Master followed Silversmith Wang home. Honoring him as Secretary Wang's son, the silversmith treated him royally, and the better part of a month thus went by. (*Such a* [illegible] *person can hardly be done without.*)

The silversmith's small-minded wife, however, suspected her husband of lying because no one from Secretary Wang's family had as yet shown up to claim the third son. While her husband was out one day, she set her bitter tongue to work. "We have our own family to take care of," she said. "Where are we supposed to find the food to feed an extra mouth? Out of the goodness of our hearts, we offered him room and board for a few days, but one should be sensible. He can't very well expect us to support him until he dies of old age."

This insult was too much for Third Master. Keeping his head down, he left the house, walking under the eaves, and began to wander aimlessly. When his steps took him past Lord Guan's temple, he suddenly recalled that the saintly Guan Yu was said to be most responsive to prayers.[2] Why not pray to him? Into the temple he went. On his knees before Guan Yu's statue, he poured out an account of the treachery of the procurer and his wife. (*Silly! Silly*) After much praying, he finally rose and idly examined the walls on which were painted scenes from stories about the Three Kingdoms period.

In the meantime, out on the street by the temple gate, a young lad was crying, "Beijing melon seeds! One penny a box! Gaoyou duck eggs! Half a penny each!" Who was this lad? He was none other than Jin'ge, peddler of melon seeds. (*It was Lord Guan, in his divine power, who sent Jin'ge along!*) "What a bad time for business!" Jin'ge thought to himself. "When Third Master was in the courtesans' quarters, he would buy my melon seeds for two hundred cash at a time, and I made more than enough to feed my parents. But ever since he went home, nobody has been buying from me. (*A tribute to that spendthrift.*) I haven't sold anything the last couple of days. How am I to survive? Well, let me take a rest in the temple before moving on."

So thinking, Jin'ge stepped into the temple, put his tray on the altar, fell to his knees, and started kowtowing. Third Master recognized him but, too ashamed to greet him, sank down in one corner by the threshold, his hands covering his face. Jin'ge rose after finishing his kowtows and also sat down on the threshold. (*The plot thickens.*) Thinking that the lad must have left the temple by now, Third Master lowered his hands, only to be recognized by Jin'ge.

"Third Master!" the boy exclaimed. "Why are you in this place?"

Tearfully, a shamefaced Third Master told him what had happened.

"Don't cry, Third Master. Let me treat you to a meal."

"I've eaten."

"You haven't seen Third Sister-in-law these last couple of days?"

"No. In fact, I haven't seen her for a long time. Jin'ge, could you do me a favor? Please go to the courtesans' quarters and quietly tell Third Sister-in-law how poor I am now. And then come back here and let me know her reaction."

Jin'ge promised to do as he'd been told. He picked up his tray and made for the street, but Third Master added, "When you're there, be sure to watch for her reaction before you say anything. If she misses me, you can tell her about my situation. If she doesn't really care about me, don't tell her anything but just come back and let me know what she says. I say this because those who live in that place treat the rich and the poor differently." (*He has learned his lesson, though belatedly.*)

"I know," said Jin'ge.

After taking leave of Third Master, Jin'ge went to the courtesans' quarters and stood under Sister Yu's window. Sister Yu was there, resting her lovely chin on one hand and wiping away her tears with a handkerchief while crying over and over again, "Wang Shunqing, my brother! Where are you?"

Jin'ge thought to himself, "So, she does miss Third Master!" He gave a cough. Hearing the cough, Sister Yu asked, "Who is it outside?"

Jin'ge went up the stairs and said, "It's me, here to offer you some melon seeds."

Tearfully, Sister Yu replied, "Jin'ge, I don't have the stomach for even the choicest mutton and the best wine, let alone melon seeds!"

"Third Sister-in-law, why have you lost weight?"

Sister Yu ignored the question.

"Apart from Third Master, what other person do you miss? Tell me, and I'll get him for you."

"Ever since Third Master left, he has never been absent from my thoughts. How can I think about anyone else? But I do recall the story about some people in the old days."

"Who are they?"

"In the old days, there was a girl called Li Yaxian.[3] A man called Zheng Yuanhe spent all his money on her and was reduced to singing 'The Lotus Petals Fall,' a beggar's song, as a hired mourner. Later, he changed his ways and took up his studies. After he passed the examinations on the first try, Li Yaxian became a celebrated name in the courtesans' circle. I often imagine myself to be Li Yaxian, hoping that Third Master will go the way of Zheng Yuanhe."

Jin'ge did not say anything out loud but thought to himself, "Wang the Third is going the way of Zheng Yuanhe all right. He may not actually be singing as a hired mourner, but he's not doing much better in a poorhouse." In a low voice, he said, "Third Sister-in-law, Third Master has taken up lodging in a temple and wants me to ask you secretly to give him money for a trip to Nanjing."

Sister Yu gave a start. "Jin'ge, you must be joking."

"Third Sister-in-law, if you don't believe me, follow me to the temple and see for yourself."

"How far is it from here to the temple?"

"About three li."

"I wouldn't dare to go. But what more did Third Master say?"

"Just that he had no money. He didn't say much else."

"Go tell Third Master to wait for me in the temple on the fifteenth day of the month."

Jin'ge went back to the temple to report to Third Master. He then took the latter to Silversmith Wang's home. "If he doesn't keep you," he said to Third Master, "you can always come to my home." Luckily, Silversmith Wang returned at this point and kept the young master in his house, and there we shall leave them.

In the meantime, the madam said to Sister Yu, "You've been refusing to eat the last couple of days. Are you still obsessed with that Wang the Third? Well, you may miss him, but he doesn't miss you. What a foolish girl you are! I'll find you someone better than him, and it will be a new experience for you, too."

"Mother, there's one thing that bothers me."

"What is it?"

"Back when I was taking all that money from Wang the Third, in one of our conversations at night, I made a vow to the city god. So I must redeem my vow and take some offerings to the city god before I accept another patron."

"When do you want to go?"

"Let's make it the fifteenth."

Merrily, the madam went about preparing the necessary incense, candles, and paper horses. When the fifteenth day of the month rolled around, she awakened a maidservant before dawn, saying, "Go heat up some water so your sister can wash her face."

Her mind also preoccupied with this event, Sister Yu rose and did her toilette. After putting together her private savings and pieces of jewelry, she made straight for the temple of the city god, with the maid carrying the paper horses. The sky had not yet brightened when she arrived at the temple. Third Master was nowhere in sight, but he was in fact hiding in the eastern corridor. Seeing her first, he coughed once. Sister Yu knew it was him and told the maid to burn the paper horses, adding, "You go ahead first. I want to look at the statues of the gods and the king of hell in the corridors on both sides."

Having disposed of the maid, Sister Yu turned toward the eastern corridor to look for Third Master. At the sight of her, he reddened with shame, "Wang Shunqing my brother," she exclaimed, "why are you in such a state?" They fell on each other's shoulders and wept. Sister Yu gave him her two hundred taels of silver as well as the other articles she had brought and told him to buy clothes, hats, and a mule and return to the courtesans' quarters. "Just say that you have only recently come from Nanjing. Be sure to do as I say." With that, they took tearful leave of each other.

The madam was beside herself with joy upon seeing Sister Yu returning to the quarters. "My child," said she, "so you have redeemed your vow?"

"Yes. Not only that, I also made a new vow."

"What's the new vow, my child?"

"That if ever I receive that Wang the Third again, this whole family will die off, and the entire household will be burned by heavenly fire." (*A good vow.*)

"Well, you're certainly overstating it, my child."

Let us leave the madam in her rapture and come back to Third Master, who returned to Silversmith Wang's home and gave him the two hundred taels of silver and other valuable items. The silversmith went joyfully to the marketplace and bought the young master a suit of clothes made of patterned silk, a pair of black boots with thick, white soles, a pair of woolen socks, a tile-shaped hat, a blue silk ribbon, a genuine Sichuan fan, a leather trunk, and a mule and a horse. After these items were duly purchased, the silversmith set to wrapping bricks and tiles in pieces of cloth so they would pass as pieces of silver. They were then put into the leather trunk.

The packing done and his personal toilette finished, the young master hired two page boys to accompany him on his journey. He was about to depart when Silversmith Wang said, "Wait, Third Master! Let me offer you a farewell cup of wine."

"Oh, don't go to such trouble. I'm much indebted to you for your kindness. Someday, I'll come back to repay this debt of gratitude." So saying, he mounted the horse and rode off.

Laying a trap, he rode into the lane;
Madam could hardly resist the decoy.
Applaud Sister Yu's constancy in love;
What true heroines women can be!

Now, having taken leave of the silversmith and his wife, the young master sallied forth to the courtesans' quarters, where several young musicians were chatting at the gate. Startled by Third Master's pomp and show, a far cry from the wretched state in which they had last seen him, they went with all speed to alert the madam.

At their report, the madam was at a loss for words for a good while. "What am I going to do about this?" she thought. "Third Sister had indeed said he was from a distinguished official's family, with more gold and silver than they could count. I didn't believe her and kicked him out. And now he's coming back, loaded with money. How terrifying!" Turning her thoughts this way and that, she decided to brazen it out. Stepping outside, she called out, "Brother-in-law, where did you just come from?" So saying, she reached out and held his horse by the reins.

The young master dismounted, chanted a greeting, and made as if to leave again, saying, "My men are all waiting for me in the boat."

With an ingratiating smile, the madam said, "Brother-in-law, how heartless you are! As they say, even if the temple is run down and the monks are ugly, due respect should still be paid to the Buddha's statue. If you have to go, shouldn't you see Yutangchun first?"

"Well, those few taels of silver that I spent here were such a pittance that I'm not going to give them a second thought. In that leather trunk of mine, I have fifty thousand taels of silver. And I've also got several boats filled with goods and tens of employees under Wang Ding's supervision."

The madam tightened her grip on the horse's reins.

Afraid of losing his advantage, the young master decided to play into the madam's hands. He passed through the gate and sat down. The madam quickly ordered the kitchen staff to set out a welcome feast. As soon as he finished his tea, he rose as if to go, but as he did, he deliberately dropped two ingots of silver, both of fine quality and weighing five taels each. He picked them up and slipped them up his sleeve.

"When I arrived at my sister-in-law's house," said the madam, "I asked about you before I even took a cup of wine. I was told that you had headed for the east, but you were nowhere to be found. We searched for you for more than a month before returning here."

Seeing his chance, the young master said, "You do have a kind heart. What happened was that I also failed to find you anywhere in sight. But Wang Ding came for me, so I followed him home. However, Sister Yu is still on my mind. That's why I came all this way in such haste."

The madam promptly ordered a maid to take the news to Yutangchun. The maid giggled all the way up the stairs.

Sister Yu, knowing all too well that the young master was there, said with calculated innocence, "What are you giggling about, girl?"

"Brother-in-law Wang is back!"

Feigning surprise, Sister Yu said, "You're trying to fool me!" and refused to go down. In alarm, the madam rushed upstairs, only to find Sister Yu lying in bed, facing the wall.

"My darling!" cried the woman. "Don't you know that Brother-in-law Wang is here?"

Sister Yu remained silent and turned a deaf ear to the madam's question, which was repeated four or five times. The madam would have liked to give Sister Yu a tongue-lashing but held back, for she had a use for the girl. Pulling over a chair, she sank down on it and heaved a deep sigh. Quite aware of the madam's movements, Sister Yu purposely turned around, rose from bed, and dropped to her knees, pleading, "Mother, please don't beat me!"

Hastily, the madam pulled her up and said, "My child! Listen! Brother-in-law Wang is back! He has brought along fifty thousand taels of silver, of fine quality, too. And he has boats laden with goods, and tens of employees. It's a much grander show than before! You must go greet him and serve him well."

"But I have made a new vow. I won't see him."

"My child! Just pretend that the vow was made in jest." With one swipe of her hand, she grabbed Sister Yu and dragged her along, crying out halfway down the stairs, "Brother-in-law Wang! Third Sister is here!"

At the sight of Sister Yu, Third Master clasped his hands in a gesture of greeting, icy and aloof, with none of his usual attentiveness. The madam had the maidservants set out a table, and, with a deep bow, she poured a cup of wine and offered it to Wang, saying, "Just put all the blame on me. (*Lightly said!*) But for the sake of Third Sister, please don't go to any other place. People will laugh."

With a slight, sardonic smile, Third Master said, "Mother, I am the one to blame." The madam busily plied him with wine, and he downed a few cups before rising as if to go, saying, "Sorry to have bothered you." With alacrity, the maidservant Cuihong grabbed him and cried, "Sister Yu, please give Brother-in-law a smile!"

"Brother-in-law Wang," ejaculated the madam, "you are being unreasonable!" To the maid, she said, "You, bolt the door. Don't let him out!" Then she had the young man's baggage carried to Sister Yu's quarters. Another feast was laid out downstairs, complete with an orchestra playing soft music. The madam continued to dance attendance on the young master as the feast progressed. About an hour later, she said, "I have to go. I'll leave you, husband and wife, to have a little talk between yourselves."

Her departure could not have suited the couple better. Hand in hand, Third Master and Sister Yu ascended the stairs. It was like

Having sweet rains after a long drought;
Meeting an old friend in an alien land.

They spent the whole night talking. It was indeed a case of "In happiness, the night slips by all too quickly; in loneliness, the night never comes to an end." Before they knew it, it was already the fourth watch of the night. The young master rose from bed and said, "Sister, I have to go!"

"Brother, how I wish to keep you for a few more days, but no matter how long I keep you, even for a thousand days, we will have to part. Now, go home quickly and have no more amorous adventures. Once you are back with your parents, you should study hard. If you make a name for yourself, you'll be able to hold up your head."

Neither of them could bear to part with the other. Sister Yu said, "Brother, what I dread most is that once you're home, you'll get yourself a wife, start a family, and forget all about me."

"What *I* dread most is that *you* will take on another patron here in Beijing. There won't be any point in my coming again then."

"Why don't you make a vow to the gods?" suggested Sister Yu.

Both knelt down. The young master said, "I pledge that if ever I marry another woman in Nanjing, I should die of illness at the height of summer."

"I, Su San," said Sister Yu, "pledge that if ever I take on another patron, I should be locked up under a long cangue and a steel padlock till the end of time."

That said, they took apart a double-mirror, and each kept one half as a token. Sister Yu said, "Now that you are going home empty-handed after squandering thirty thousand taels of silver, you should take along some jewelry and other valuable items." (*Travel money should suffice. Why would he need jewelry and other items?*)

"But what are you going to do when the procurer and the madam find out about this?"

"Don't worry. I know what to do." After putting these valuables together, Sister Yu gently opened the door and saw the young master out.

At daybreak, the madam rose and ordered a maid to heat some water for the couple to wash their faces and prepare some water for them to rinse their mouths. "When your Brother-in-law wakes up," she said to the maid, "carry the water upstairs, and also ask him what he wants to eat, so that I know what to prepare. But don't disturb him if he's still asleep."

So the maid went upstairs, only to find the ornaments in the room missing and the jewelry box empty and discarded. Lifting the bed curtain, she found half of the bed unoccupied. She ran down the stairs, crying out, "Mother! The whole thing is off!"

"Slave!" snapped the madam. "What's all this excitement about? You'll be waking up Brother-in-law!"

"What Brother-in-law? He's gone! And goodness knows where! My sister is sleeping, facing the wall."

In consternation, the madam looked for the page boys and groom and found them gone, too. She hastened upstairs and was delighted to see the leather trunk still there, but, upon opening it, she found nothing but bricks and tiles. "Slave!" she yelled at Sister Yu. "Where is that Wang the Third? I'll have to beat you to death! So he's gone off with all the money and valuables!"

"You know the new vow I made. I certainly did not lead him in here."

"The two of you talked the whole night through. You must know where he's gone."

As the procurer went to get his whip, Sister Yu wrapped her head with a kerchief and said, "Let me go find Wang the Third and return him to you."

So saying, she hurried down the stairs and into the street. Afraid that she was trying to get away, the madam and the musicians gave chase. There, on the street, Sister Yu cried out at the top of her voice, "Murder! Murder for money!" (*A stroke of brilliance!*)

As the local headmen arrived, the madam said to Sister Yu, "You slave! He stole as much of my gold, silver, and jewelry as he could carry. How can you make a scene like this!"

"Let her be!" put in the procurer. "We'll settle this within the family when we go back home."

"Now stop trying to sound nice!" retorted Sister Yu. "What do you mean—go back home? Where's my home? Let's settle this in the court of the Ministry of Justice! Mr. Wang is from a most distinguished family. What use could he have for those worthless trinkets of yours? Now, have some sense. What profession can be lowlier and more base than owning a brothel? What valuable jewelry can you have? What grand social functions do you attend that you need to show them off? Secretary Wang's son spent thirty thousand taels of silver in this house, and yet, as everyone knows, the moment he left, you began to bully me. Yesterday, you were so impressed by his money that you tricked him into the house and cheated him of his things, and who knows what you did to him! Everyone here is my witness."

The madam was speechless, but the procurer said, "*You* put Wang the Third up to the theft, and now you turn around and accuse us!"

Ready to risk everything, Sister Yu let out a stream of curses. "You filthy procurers! Murderers! You murdered Mr. Wang for his money, and yet you try to talk your way out of it! You opened up his trunk and took out all the silver. If you say you didn't murder Mr. Wang, I'd like to know who did!"

"He had no silver!" the madam protested. "The trunk was filled with bricks and tiles to trick us!"

"You said yourself that he had brought fifty thousand taels of silver. And now you deny that?" As the quarrel went on, the onlookers, knowing that Third Master had indeed spent thirty thousand taels of silver in that place but not quite believing the murder story, tried to intervene and calm them down.

Addressing the crowd, Sister Yu said, "Since you all advise me not to bring charges to the authorities, I may drop the idea, but let me at least give these two a lecture, just to let off a little steam."

"All right, go ahead!" the onlookers encouraged her. And so, Sister Yu unleashed a torrent of angry words:

"You, the procurer, are a dog that's always hungry, however much you are fed. You, the procuress, are a bottomless pit, never content, however much you are paid. You never go by the rules when conducting business but only scheme to pluck patrons clean. Your servileness is just a dragnet for catching your prey; everything you say is a trap to ensnare your victims. You care nothing for others but think only of your own family wealth. You bought me with eight hundred cash, but goodness knows how much more money you've made with me. My father Zhou Yanheng was a highly respected man in Datong. What is the punishment for the crime of buying girls from decent families and forcing them into a life of filth? A trader in human beings should be banished. If you can get away with abducting people from decent families, you certainly won't when it comes to murdering for money. Of the ten thousand evil things you and other members of your family have done, I've mentioned only two or three."

The onlookers intervened, saying, "Sister Yu, you've gone on long enough."

"You've been at it for so long that you should be going back now," said the madam.

"If you want me back," said Sister Yu, "you'll have to write a statement for me."

"What kind of statement?" asked the crowd.

"To say that you bought me wrongfully from a decent family and forced me into prostitution and that you have murdered for money."

Why would the procurer ever agree to write such a statement? Sister Yu again cried out her grievances. The onlookers commented, "It's true that brothels often do buy decent girls and force them into prostitution, but the charge of murder can hardly be substantiated. They won't admit to that. We suggest that they write you a statement of redemption." (*They certainly know how to solve a problem, and a fair and square solution it is.*)

The procurer still turned a deaf ear. The onlookers turned to him and remarked, "Let's forget about the other things. Those thirty thousand taels from Mr. Wang alone are enough to buy three hundred girls. Sister Yu's heart has turned against you anyway. Why don't you just let her go?"

The crowd went into a wineshop, where they asked for a sheet of paper. With one person dictating and one person drafting, they drew up a statement and asked the procurer and the procuress to sign it. "If the statement is not fair," announced Sister Yu, "I'm going to tear it up."

"It is quite fair to you," the crowd assured her. The statement read as follows:

> *This is to testify that I, Su Huai, owner of a registered entertainment house, and my wife Yichenjin bought Yutangchun, daughter of Mr. Zhou Yanheng of Datong Prefecture, for eight hundred cash, hoping that she would support us in our old age by serving patrons. However, this girl rejects a life of prostitution.*

At this point, Sister Yu said, "That last line is a good one. Add also that you took thirty thousand taels of silver from Patron Mr. Wang as redemption money."

"Third Sister!" exclaimed the procurer. "Why don't you show some fairness? Much of that money has gone for daily expenses over the last year. That money shouldn't count!"

"All right, write up twenty thousand, then," the onlookers suggested. The statement went on to say,

> *Mr. Wang Shunqing from Nanjing, who is in love with her, offered twenty thousand taels of silver, which, as decided by all the witnesses present, shall be used to redeem Yutangchun. Henceforth, she is free to marry, and we hereby dissociate ourselves from her.*
>
> *Signed on the __th day of the __th month of the __th year of the Zhengde reign period by Su Huai, owner of a registered entertainment house, and wife Yichenjin*

The witnesses, of whom there were more than ten, affixed their signatures first, and then Su Huai reluctantly did the same. Yichenjin drew a cross by way of a signature. After putting away the statement, Sister Yu spoke up again. "Gentlemen! There's another thing that I have to make clear in advance."

"What is it now?" asked the onlookers.

"Mr. Wang built the Hundred Flowers Hall for me. The new maidservants were also bought with Mr. Wang's money. I need two of them as personal attendants. Supplies of rice, flour, firewood, vegetables, and other food items should be duly provided to me. No skimping will be allowed. I'll stay there under these conditions until I marry."

"All right, it will be as you say," said the onlookers. Sister Yu thankfully took leave of all present and returned to her quarters. The procurer stayed behind and treated the witnesses to a meal and some wine before the crowd dispersed. Truly,

> *Zhou Yu's clever plan—how it was shattered!*
> *He lost both the lady and the battle.*[4]

Now let us continue with our story: Traveling by day and resting by night, Mr. Wang Junior arrived a few days later in Jinling and got off his horse in front of the Wang residence. At the sight of the young master, a much startled Wang Ding came forward and took over the reins of the horse. Once inside the house, Third Master sat down as Wang Ding and his family gave the young man their greetings.

"Is my father well?" asked Third Master.

"Yes, he's well," replied Wang Ding.

"How are my two uncles, my brothers-in-law, and my sisters?"

"They're all fine."

"Have you ever heard my father mention me? What's he going to do with me?"

Instead of answering, Wang Ding heaved a deep sigh and looked up at the sky outside.

Third Master understood the implied message. "So, you'd rather not say anything, which means my father wants to have me beaten to death."

"Third Master! Your father has disowned you. Don't even try to see him. Just go pay a quiet visit to your mother, sisters, brothers, and sisters-in-law, ask for some traveling money, and go seek shelter somewhere else!"

"Who have been my father's close friends these last couple of years? I can have them put in a word for me."

"No one would ever dare to do that, except your sisters and brothers-in-law, but even they can only do it in passing. They don't dare to be direct with him."

"Wang Ding, go bring my brothers-in-law over. I want to talk with them about this."

Wang Ding left right away on his errand and brought back Mr. Liu and Mr. He. After an exchange of greetings, Liu and He said, "Third Brother, wait here while we try to talk with Father. We'll send for you if the talk goes well. But if he refuses to listen to us, we'll just send you a message that you should run for your life."

That said, the two men went straight to Secretary Wang at his quarters. After they had seated themselves and finished their tea, Mr. Wang Senior asked Mr. He, "How are things on your farmstead?"

"Oh, everything's fine!"

Mr. Wang turned to Mr. Liu. "How are you getting along in your studies?"

"I'm sorry. I've been so occupied these days that I've been ignoring my studies."

Mr. Wang said with a smile, "You know what they say, 'Read ten thousand books before you can write inspired lines.' What's most important for a scholar? As another saying goes, 'A family without a student is a family without an official.' Remember to keep at your studies and not waste time."

Mr. Liu humbly thanked him for the admonition.

"When did you have that wall put up?" asked Mr. He. "I haven't seen it before."

Mr. Wang replied, smiling, "With me getting on in years, I'm afraid that my two sons will fight over what little I own. So I had that wall put up to divide the estate into two portions in advance."

The two men laughed. "Why do you divide the family property into two portions when there should in fact be three? After Third Master comes back, where's he going to stay?" (*A good way to raise the subject.*)

These words irritated Mr. Wang. "This old man has only two sons," he said. "How can there be a third one?"

The two sons-in-law cried out, "Sir, why don't you love Wang Jinglong as one of your own? Actually, it was all your fault, letting him collect debts in Beijing without sending anyone to bring him back. Beijing being such a dissolute place, even an experienced man of the world would be tempted, let alone a sixteen- or seventeen-year-old like Third Brother." So saying, the two men tearfully dropped to their knees.

"That swine! He'll come to no good end! He may well have died goodness knows where. Never ever bring his name up again!"

At this point, the two daughters arrived on the scene. Everyone except the father knew that Third Master was back at home.

"With all of you suddenly showing up without an invitation, there must be something afoot," said Mr. Wang.

As the servants set about laying out wine at Mr. Wang's bidding, He Jing'an said with a slight bow, "Last night, your daughter had a dream in which she saw her brother Wang Jinglong. He was in rags and cried out for her to save his life. She had this dream at the third watch of the night, and for the rest of the night until daybreak, she kept crying, pounding the bed, thumping the pillow, and blaming me for not going to bring him back home. So I came here today to ask for news about Third Brother."

Liu Xinzhai had this to say, "With Third Brother in Beijing, my wife and I can find no peace day and night. Now let me and my brother-in-law put together some traveling money and go tomorrow to Beijing to bring him back."

With tears standing in his eyes, Mr. Wang said, "My good sons-in-law, I have two other sons at home. Why can't I do without him?"

The two sons-in-law headed for the door. Mr. Wang stepped forward and grabbed them. "Why are you leaving, my good sons- in-law?"

"Please let us go. If you treat your own son like this, just imagine what you will do to us sons-in-law!"

All those present, old and young, burst into loud wails, and the two older sons and the two sons-in-law dropped to their knees in supplication. As Mrs. Wang broke down in sobs at the back of the room, Mr. Wang was also moved to tears. (*With so many allies, Third Master needn't worry that his father will not accept him.*)

At this point, Wang Ding rushed out of the hall to the room where Third Master was waiting. "Third Master! Your father is crying for you. Go quickly to see him before he loses his temper again!"

With Wang Ding pushing him from behind, Third Master entered the main hall and knelt down. "Father! Your unworthy son Wang Jinglong is back."

Dabbing at his teary eyes, Mr. Wang Senior said, "That shameless swine has died goodness knows where. This man is surely one of the many loafers on the streets of Beijing. Because there happens to be a resemblance, he must be an imposter who's here to swindle me out of my money. Get the servants to march him off to the Bureau of Justice and let him have it!"

The young master turned around and headed for the door. The two older sisters rushed to the door and stopped him, saying, "You little devil! Where do you think you're going?"

"My sisters, please get out of my way and let me run for my life!"

Without loosening their grip, the two sisters pushed him back and made him drop to both knees. Pointing at him, the sisters said, "You little devil! Mother is heartbroken because of you, and all of us in the family have cried until we can barely see. Everyone here has missed you!"

In the midst of the heartrending sobs, Mr. Wang Senior sharply ordered everyone to stop. "If I do as my sons-in-law say and accept this swine, how shall I punish him?"

"Try to calm down a little before you do it," someone suggested.

Mr. Wang Senior shook his head. His wife suggested, "Let *me* beat him."

"How many strokes are you going to give him?"

"As many as you say," was the general response.

"In that case, do as I say and don't try to stop me. Give him one hundred strokes!"

The two elder sisters fell to their knees. "We would not dream of objecting to Father's orders, but let us take the beating on his behalf."

The two elder brothers took twenty strokes each, and the two sisters also took twenty strokes each. Mr. Wang Senior said, "Now it's his turn to take the remaining twenty strokes."

The sisters interceded again, "Let his brothers-in-law take the twenty strokes for him. He's so bony and sallow. Where can the rod land? Let him gain some weight and put some flesh on his bones before beating him." (*What a wonderful scene! More filled to the brim with human kindness than even "The Story of Zheng Yuanhe."*[5])

Mr. Wang Senior said laughingly, "That's a good point. The swine doesn't even have the slightest bit of decency and conscience left in him. What's the use of beating him anyway? Let me ask you something. As the saying goes, 'Without a means of livelihood, heaps of gold will vanish in a flash.' I no longer hold an official post and therefore have no income. How are you going to make a living? If you want to set up a business, I have no money to put up as capital."

The two brothers-in-law asked, "How much silver has he left?" They then turned to Third Brother. "How much silver do you have left?"

Wang Ding carried the leather trunk over and opened it, revealing an abundance of gold and silver jewelry and other ornaments. Mr. Wang Senior flew into a rage. "You cursed swine! Where did you steal these things? Write a statement of confession for the police this minute! Don't you dare tarnish this family's good name!"

Third Master cried at the top of his voice, "Father! Don't be so angry! Listen to your unworthy son!" He then gave a detailed account of how he had first met Yutangchun, how he had later been cheated out of all his money by the madam, how Silversmith Wang had kindly taken him in and given him a home, and how Jin'ge had brought him messages from Yutangchun. "She gave me her own silver for my journey home. These jewelry and ornaments are all gifts from her."

Mr. Wang Senior again lashed out, "Shameless dog! You spent thirty thousand taels of silver and then turned around and accepted money from a whore! How shameful!"

"I didn't force her. She gave all this to me of her own free will."

"All right, I'll let the matter drop. For the sake of your brothers-in-law, I'll give you a farmstead. You can make a living as a farmer."

Third Master said nothing. Angrily, Mr. Wang Senior demanded, "Wang Jinglong, what do you mean by your silence?"

"Farming is not for me."

"Not for you indeed! So, go ahead and whore around in the brothels as before!"

"I want to study."

His father said jeeringly, "With your dissolute ways, with a heart as wild as that of a monkey or a horse, how can you be talking about studying?"

"This time, I am determined to apply myself."

"If you knew studying was a worthy pursuit, why did you do all those outrageous things?"

At this point, He Jing'an stood up and remarked, "Having gone through so many hardships, Third Brother is now determined to turn over a new leaf. I believe he will truly apply himself to his studies."

"All right, as you say," conceded the father. "I'll send him off to the study. He'll be attended by two page boys." Then and there he summoned two page boys and told them to escort Third Master to the study.

The two sons-in-law spoke up again. "We haven't seen Third Brother for a very long time. Please allow him to have a few drinks with us."

"My good sons-in-law, that's no way to bring up the young. Don't ever spoil them."

"How right you are!" they chanted.

And so, the father and the sons-in-law and everyone else fell to drinking. They did not part company until they were quite inebriated. The reunion between father and son was indeed like

> *The moon shining again from behind the clouds;*
> *Flowers blooming again in spring after the frost.*

Sitting quietly alone in the study, the young master swept his eyes over the shelves of books, the hills of brush-pens, and the sea of ink slabs. "Books, o books!" he sighed. "I haven't seen you for so long that I feel quite a stranger to you. But if I leave you alone, how am I going to pass the examinations and make something of myself? And I would be letting Sister Yu down. And yet, if I do take you up, my heart is indeed as wild as that of a monkey or a horse, and quite untamable." After a few moments of reflection, he took a book and read for a while, but his thoughts were all on Yutangchun. Suddenly, an odor came to his nostrils, and a sound came to his ears. He asked a page boy, "What's this smell in the books? What sound do you hear?"

"Third Master, I smell and hear nothing."

"Nothing? Ah, so what I smell is the scent of face powder. What I hear is the music of the zither." *(One with a heart as wild as that of a monkey or a horse can never amount to anything. There is hope for the prodigal son only if he changes his ways. What he needs is a hard push.)* Then a thought struck him: "What words of admonition did Sister Yu give me? She told me to apply myself diligently in my studies. Now I'm certainly not applying myself. I miss her so much that I can scarcely sit still or go to sleep. I have no appetite for food and tea, nor any interest in combing my hair and bathing. I feel as if I'm in a trance. What am I going to do?" So thinking, he walked out the door, and, as he did so, his eyes came to rest upon a vertical couplet on both sides of the door frame:

Ten years of painstaking study by the window
Bring overnight fame that spreads far and wide.

He thought to himself, "Grandfather is the author of this couplet. He passed the exams and rose through the official ranks until he became a vice-minister. Father did his studies in this room and rose to be secretary of a ministry. I should also be doing my studies here, attach myself to the flying dragons and the phoenixes, so to speak, and carry out my forefathers' behests." Then he caught sight of another couplet of the frame of the inner door:

Without taking the greatest pains,
One can never rise above the ranks.

He hurried back into the study. As his eyes fell upon a book titled *The Secrets of Love* and another one titled *Spring Scenes in the Bedchamber,* he told himself, "It was those two books that led me astray. Let me feed them to the flames. Let me also put away my half of the mirror and the broken hairpin." And so he made a firm resolve to apply himself assiduously to his studies.

One day, there being no fire in the study, the page boy went out to get fuel. From his seat, Mr. Wang Senior called to him. The boy fell to his knees, and Mr. Wang asked, "Has Third Master been studying hard?"

"In the beginning, Third Master didn't study at all but just let his thoughts run wild, and he was so thin that he looked like a bag of bones. But in the last six months, he's been at the books from morning to night, going to bed at the third watch of the night and rising at the fifth watch. He doesn't comb his hair and wash until after breakfast. Even when he's eating, he keeps his eyes on the books."

"What a liar! Let me go and see for myself!"

The page boy called out, "Third Master! The old master's here!"

Calm and collected, the young master greeted his father. Mr. Wang Senior was inwardly pleased at the young man's poised manner, which bespoke a learned mind. The father sat down facing the son. After the son bowed in homage, the father asked, "Have you read the books I assigned you? How many of the essay questions I assigned you have you answered?"

"Father, in addition to having read all the books you assigned and answered all the essay questions you gave me, I have also been reading books on other schools of thought as well as history."

"Show me some of your writings."

Accordingly, the young man produced some of his essays. Mr. Wang Senior was quite impressed, finding each essay better than the last. "Jinglong!" he exclaimed, "you are ready for the civil service exams!"

"With so little learning, what chance do I have of passing at the provincial level?"

"There's no lack of people who succeed at the first attempt, and many more who make it the second time around. Why don't you go and see what it's like? You may make it in the next round of exams." Thereupon, the father wrote a letter to the Bureau of Education, which then gave the young man permission to take part in the examinations.

On the ninth day of the eighth month, after the first session of the examinations was over, he reproduced from memory what he had written and showed it to his father, who said with delight, "Each one of these seven essays stands a good chance of passing!" After the second and third sessions were over, his father again inspected what he had written from memory, and predicted exultantly, "You'll not only pass, but pass with high honors."

Let us follow another thread of the story and turn our attention to Sister Yu, who, ever since her return to Hundred Flowers Hall, had not taken even one step down the stairs. One day, feeling listless and tired, she said to a maid, "Bring me the chessboard. Let's play a game of chess."

"But I don't know how."

"Do you know how to play horse chess?"

"No."

Sister Yu flung the chessboard and the horse chess board onto the floor. Noticing tears in Sister Yu's eyes, the maid quickly brought over some food, saying, "Sister, you haven't eaten anything since last evening. Please take some refreshments." Sister Yu took a piece and broke it in half. She took a bite of one half and held out the other half, as if to give it to the young master. While the maid was wondering whether she should accept it or not, Sister Yu looked up sharply and realized that it was not the young master. The piece of food fell from her outstretched hand onto the floor.

The maid quickly brought over a bowl of soup, saying, "Rice is too dry. Have some soup!" Sister Yu had scarcely swallowed one mouthful of the soup than she put the bowl down, tears gushing out of her eyes as from a fountain. "What's that noise outside?" she asked.

The maid replied, "Today is the Mid-autumn Festival. Everybody is out to see the moon and play music. Even Sisters Cuixiang and Cuihong are accepting patrons!"

At these words, Sister Yu said to herself, "So, Brother has been gone for a year now." She had the maid bring her a mirror. After taking one look at herself, she gave a violent start. "What! I didn't know I look so emaciated!" she exclaimed.

Tossing the mirror onto the bed, she heaved sigh after sigh. She then went to the door and said to the maid, "Bring me a chair. I want to sit here for a while." After sitting for quite some time, watching the bright moon rise high in the sky and listening to the night watch drum of the drum tower, she said to the maid,

"Bring me some joss sticks and candles. Today is the fifteenth day of the eighth month, the day your brother-in-law takes all three sessions of the exams. I want to burn incense and ask for blessings for him." She went downstairs and knelt down in the courtyard, praying, "Gods of heaven and earth, on this fifteenth day of the eighth month, please let my brother Wang Jinglong win first place in the exams and let his name be known throughout the four seas." With that, she bowed deeply four times. There is a poem that bears witness:

She burned incense to the moon and prayed to heaven.
When could she ever voice her grievances?
If Young Master Wang wins honor in the exams,
Her bond with him would not have been in vain.

Now, in the West Tower, there was a patron named Shen Hong, who was from Hongtong County, Pingyang Prefecture, in Shanxi. Carrying tens of thousands of taels of silver with him, he was in Beijing for his horse-trading business but had come to the courtesans' quarters because of Yutangchun's fame. Impressed by his well-lined pocket, the madam dressed up Cuixiang and passed her off as Sister Yu, but, after a few days with her, Shen Hong learned that he had been given the wrong girl and had since been pestering the madam for a visit with the real Yutangchun.

That night, when Sister Yu's maid Little Cuihong went downstairs to get a fire so that Sister Yu could burn incense, the urge to speak up got the better of her. She blurted out, "Brother-in-law Shen! I know you've been thinking about Sister Yu every day. She's downstairs now in the courtyard, burning incense. Let me take you there so that you can see her without anyone else knowing about it."

Shen Hong bribed Sister Yu's maid with three mace of silver and followed her stealthily downstairs. In the bright moonlight, he got a clear view of Sister Yu. After she finished with her prayers, he walked up to her and chanted a greeting. In alarm, Sister Yu asked, "Who are you?"

"I am Shen Hong from Shanxi. I'm here with tens of thousands in silver for my horse-trading business. I have long heard of your fame but no chance to see you until this moment. Seeing you is like seeing the blue sky shining through the clouds and the fog. Would you be kind enough to follow me to my quarters in the West Tower?"

In anger, Sister Yu said, "You are a total stranger to me. What do you mean by bragging about your wealth in the middle of the night? Are you trying to make trouble?"

Shen Hong pleaded, "I am just as worthy a person as Third Master Wang, and just as wealthy. How is he better than me in any way?" With that, he stepped forward to hug Sister Yu, but she spit in his face and rushed up the stairs. Closing the door behind her, she lashed out at her maid, "How could you have let that wild dog in? The audacity!"

Thus rejected, Shen Hong went off. After reflecting on the matter, Sister Yu concluded that it must have been the work of Cuixiang and Cuihong. "Little sluts!" she started up again. "Cheap girls! Couldn't you be happy enough with a rich patron and not drag me into it?" After a volley of curses, she burst into loud cries of grief. "If Brother Wang were here, no lowlife like that would have dared take such liberties with me!" In her anger and misery, she let her thoughts grow more and more bitter. Truly,

The loved one is gone, never to return;
The disgusting ones come, uninvited.

Let us turn our attention to Third Master Wang, who, after finishing the examinations at the provincial level in Nanjing, found himself quite idle. Not a day went by without his thinking about Sister Yu. (*What a loyal lover!*) Nanjing had its own courtesans' quarters, but he kept his distance from them.

On the twenty-ninth day of the month, the day scheduled for the posting of the results of the examinations, his mind was preoccupied only with Sister Yu. He did not fall asleep until after the third watch was struck and was then woken up from his dream by loud exclamations of congratulations from outside, "Wang Jinglong won fourth place in the examinations!" He rose promptly, washed himself, combed his hair, and, amid a jostling throng, mounted a horse, with a flourish of the whip, to go to the government-sponsored celebration feast. His parents, his brother and sister-in-law, and his brothers-in-law and sisters were beside themselves with joy and held grand celebration feasts for days on end. The young master thanked the chief examiner, bade the education superintendent farewell, paid his respects to the Wang family ancestors' graves, and got his documents ready. To his parents, he announced, "I wish to go to Beijing as soon as possible, so as to find a quiet place to stay and study for a few months to get ready for the palace exams."

The parents knew all too well that he wanted to be with Yutangchun, but now that he had passed the provincial examinations, they felt obliged to let him have his way. (*Snobbery begins at home, and wealth and high status are the ruin of domestic discipline.*) Mr. Wang Senior summoned the two older sons and asked them, "How much money does Jinglong need to go to Beijing for the palace exams and to pay for sweeping the graves yesterday?"

"A little more than three hundred taels of silver should be enough," replied the oldest brother.

"That's only enough for gifts," said the father. "Add another one or two hundred taels."

"Father," put in Second Brother, "he doesn't need that much."

"What do you know? He needs money to socialize with my many friends and students in Beijing. What's more, with enough money, he can concentrate more on his studies."

Jinglong was then told to pack up for his journey and to find two or three close friends who had also passed the provincial examinations to serve as travel companions. A servant of the family was sent to a fortune-teller named Mr. Zhang so as to pick an auspicious day. The young master could hardly wait to be in Beijing. He found a few traveling companions, hired a boat, and took leave of his parents, brothers, and sisters-in-law. His two brothers-in-law invited some friends and family to escort him as far as a wayside pavilion ten li from the city to offer him toasts of farewell. Hardly had he boarded the boat than he started dancing about, quite forgetting himself in his excitement. Those who were there to see him off little knew that his mind was filled, to the exclusion of everything else, with thoughts of Third Sister Yutangchun. In a few days, he arrived in Jining Prefecture. How he left the boat and continued the journey by land need not be described here.

To pick up another thread of our story, ever since seeing Sister Yu that night of the Mid-autumn Festival, Shen Hong missed her so much that he cared nothing for sleep and food. "My two good sisters!" he entreated Cuixiang and Cuihong. "That one, my nemesis, has all but taken my last breath and completely turned my head. Please take pity on a lonely man in a strange place. Talk to Sister Yu and make her agree to see me, if only for one time. Even after I get to the Nine Springs,[6] I'll remember you for your kindness in giving me a new lease on life!" That said, he fell on both knees.

The maids said, "Brother-in-law Shen! Please rise. We don't dare to tell her that. Didn't you see how she yelled at us on the night of the Mid-autumn Festival? Wait until the madam is here and ask *her* to help you out."

"My two good sisters! Please invite the madam here for me!"

Cuixiang said, "Kneel down and kowtow to me a hundred and twenty times."

Shen Hong dropped to his knees with alacrity and started busily kowtowing to the maid. (*Poor thing, that Shen Hong! A veritable Zheng Heng of* The Story of the West Chamber.) Promptly, Cuixiang went to report Shen Hong's words to the madam, who then took herself to the West Tower and said to Shen Hong, "Brother-in-law Shen, what do you want me to do?"

"It's just that I have no way of getting Yutangchun. If you could help me do this, I'd be willing to repay you with my life, not to mention gold and silver!"

At these words, the madam thought to herself, "If I make him a promise but Third One turns me down, what am I going to do? And yet, if I say no to him, how am I going to get any money from him?"

Noticing the madam's hesitation, Shen Hong turned his eyes to Cuihong, who gave him a meaningful look and headed downstairs. (*Cuihong can very well succeed the madam in this business.*) Shen Hong followed her. She offered this advice, "You know what they say, 'The girls love a good-looking face; the madam loves the sight of cash.' As long as you can use money to persuade her to help you, she'll surely put her mind to the job. She's a big spender and doesn't care for small sums of money."

"How much would be enough?"

At this point, Cuixiang put in, "You'd better not be stingy! Nothing less than one thousand taels will do."

Shen Hong was, after all, fated to meet his doom. As if possessed by some evil spirit, he followed Cuixiang's suggestion and took out a thousand taels of silver. "Madam!" he called out, "I've got money for you!"

"All right, I'll accept the money for now," said the madam, "but you've got to be patient. Let me slowly convince her."

Bowing thankfully, Shen Hong said, "I'll be waiting eagerly to hear from you." Truly,

He engaged the master strategist
To entrap Yutangchun the courtesan.

Now, since the names of successful candidates at the examinations in all thirteen provinces had been posted on the wall by Wu Gate, Silversmith Wang suggested to Jin'ge the peddler, "Let's go check if Third Master has passed the exams!" They went to Wu Gate and saw on the Nanjing area list that the examinee with the highest honors was one who specialized in *The Book of History* and that the fourth name from the top was Wang Jinglong.

"Jin'ge!" exclaimed the silversmith. "How nice! Third Master has won fourth place!"

"You'd better be sure!" admonished Jin'ge. "I thought you couldn't read."

"What a bully you are! Are you saying that I, who have gotten as far as *Mencius* in my studies, don't even know these three characters? Well, you go ahead and grab anyone you see and have them read the name for you." (*A good student does not need to go as far as* Mencius *to find enlightenment.*)

Jin'ge was overjoyed. He and Silversmith Wang bought a copy of the descriptive listing of all successful candidates at the provincial level and went to the courtesans' quarters to report to Yutangchun. "Third Master has made it!"

Sister Yu had the maids bring the listing to her. She spread it out and saw written on it the words "Fourth place: Wang Jinglong, scholar from Yingtian Prefecture, specializing in *The Book of Rites.*"

Sister Yu went out through the gate and had the maids set out an altar where she could burn incense in gratitude to heaven and earth. Upon rising after completing this homage, she first thanked the silversmith and then turned around to thank Jin'ge.

The procurer and the procuress were frightened out of their wits. The procurer said to the madam, "Wang the Third has passed the exams and will be in Beijing any time now. If he reclaims Yutangchun without paying a penny, won't we be losing both the girl and the money? The girl being so devoted to him, she won't have a good word for us, that's for sure. And what if she stirs up trouble and has him take revenge on us for what happened in the past? What are we going to do?"

The madam said, "Well, the one who strikes first gains the upper hand."

"How do we strike?"

"We've already taken a thousand taels of silver from Mr. Shen. Let's ask for another thousand from him and consider her sold at a cheap price."

"What if the girl refuses?"

"Tomorrow, let's slaughter a pig and a lamb and buy enough paper coins for one altar. We'll just say that we're going to Eastern Mountain Temple for a fair, to burn the paper coins and take a vow that everybody in the household will give up this business once and for all. That girl, Third One, will surely want to join us on the trip to the temple as soon as she hears about giving up this business. We'll have Mr. Shen prepare a sedan-chair and carry her off to Shanxi, his hometown. When young Mr. Wang shows up and fails to see his lover, he'll put her out of his mind. (*True lovers miss each other more the longer they stay apart. This is something procuresses can never understand.*)

"What a brilliant idea!" exclaimed the procurer. Right away, they went for a secret consultation with Shen Hong and got another thousand taels of silver from him.

The next morning, the maids reported to Sister Yu, "We've slaughtered a pig and a lamb. The whole family's going to Eastern Mountain Temple."

"Why?" asked Sister Yu.

"I heard Mother say, 'Now that Brother-in-law Wang has passed the exams, he'll probably come to Beijing to take revenge against us. Let's take a vow today that everyone in the household will give up the business.'"

"Is that true?" asked Sister Yu.

"Of course it's true! Even Brother-in-law Shen left yesterday. No more patrons will be accepted from now on."

"In that case," said Sister Yu, "tell Mother that I'll join you on the trip to the temple to offer incense."

"Third Sister,'" said the madam, "if you want to go, finish with your toilette quickly. I'll call a sedan-chair for you."

Her toilette done, Sister Yu went out the gate with the madam. Seeing four men carrying an empty sedan-chair, the madam asked, "Is this sedan-chair for hire?"

"Yes."

"How much do you charge to go from here to Eastern Mountain Temple?"

"One mace of silver for a round trip."

"How about half of a mace?"

"That little detail is easily taken care of. Please get into the sedan-chair, madam."

"No, it's not for me, but for my daughter."

So Sister Yu mounted the sedan-chair. Instead of heading for the temple, the carriers hurried off in the direction of the West Gate. After they had gone several li, at a high point where there was a turn in the road, Sister Yu looked back and saw none other than Shen Hong following behind on a mule! (*What a hateful sight!*)

"You dogs!" she cried at the top of her voice. "Where do you think you're taking me?"

"Where?" said Shen Hong. "To my home in Shanxi! I've paid two thousand taels of silver for you, you know."

Amid loud wails, Sister Yu poured out a ceaseless stream of curses while the sedan-chair carriers strode along with the speed of the wind. As the day drew to a close, Shen Hong found an inn, where he ordered fine food and wine in anticipation of the joys of the bridal chamber. As it turned out, Sister Yu burst into bitter curses as soon as he addressed her and slapped him as soon as he tried to touch her. Afraid of making a scene in public, Shen Hong thought to himself, "She's like a turtle trapped in a jar. She won't be able to break free. Let me wait for a couple of days. Once she's in my house, she'll have to submit." So, changing his tone, he began to cajole her with sweet talk and held back from any move that she would find offensive. How Sister Yu wept day after day needs no description here.

In the meantime, Young Master Wang arrived in Beijing. After depositing his baggage at an inn, he took two servants and went straight to Silversmith Wang's home to inquire about Yutangchun. The silversmith asked him to sit down, saying, "I have some wine here. Let's drink three cups to celebrate your coming before I tell you everything."

So saying, the silversmith brought wine and served it to Third Master, who, finding it hard to turn him down, drank three cups in a row before he spoke up again. "So, Sister Yu doesn't know I'm coming?"

"Take it easy, Third Master. Have another three cups."

"That's enough. No more, please."

"It's been a long time since I saw you last, Third Master. Please drink some more. Don't stand on ceremony with me."

Young Master downed another few cups. "Have you seen Sister Yu these last few days?" he asked.

"Don't ask about this yet, Third Master. Drink another three cups!"

Growing suspicious, the young man stood up and said, "Whatever it is, tell me all about it. Don't keep me in the dark. I can't stand it." But the silversmith kept forcing more wine on him. It so happened that Jin'ge passed by the door. Learning that the young master was inside, he entered and offered his congratulations with a kowtow.

"How has Third Aunt been these last few days?" asked Third Master.

Lacking the caution of a grown-up, Jin'ge blurted out, "She's been sold."

Third Master was quick to ask, "To whom?"

Silversmith Wang gave Jin'ge a look that made him keep his mouth shut. But as the determined young master continued to bombard them with questions, the two knew that they could not keep the truth from him any longer. "Yes, she's been sold," they conceded.

"When?"

"About a month ago," replied Silversmith Wang.

At these words, the young master collapsed onto the ground. Quickly the silversmith and the boy helped him up. Third Master asked Jin'ge, "Who bought her?"

"A Shen Hong of Shanxi."

"Why was Third Aunt willing to go?"

Thereupon, Jin'ge told him the whole story. "The madam pretended to be giving up the business. She said they were going to Eastern Mountain Temple to offer a sacrificial pig and a sheep, and so she coaxed Third Aunt into going along to burn incense. But in fact she had made a secret arrangement with Shen Hong. Hired sedan-chair carriers took her off to goodness knows where."

"So, the procurer stole my Yutangchun and sold her! I'll make them pay for this!" Telling Jin'ge to follow him, the young master led his servants to the courtesans' quarters. As soon as he appeared at the gate, the procurer, being swift of eye, dodged and hid himself. "Where's Sister Yu?" the young master demanded of the maids. No one dared to venture an answer. Furious, the young man found the madam in a room, grabbed her with one swift movement of his hand and had his servants beat her, but Jin'ge stopped him with some placating words. As he walked through Hundred Flowers Hall, the young master found that the sight of the brocade and silk curtains and the luxurious decor made him so much angrier that he had the trunks and cases all smashed up. In a blind rage, he yelled at the maids, "Who is the man who married Sister Yu? Tell me the truth, and I'll spare you from a beating."

"She went to offer incense and ended up being sold without her knowledge."

His eyes brimming over with tears, the young master said, "Tell me, you wretched girl. Is she a wife or a concubine?"

"That man already has a wife."

At these words, his rage flared up again. "Those filthy, treacherous procurers!" he cursed.

A maid commented, "Well, she's married now. Why do you still care so much about her?"

Tears flowing from his eyes, the young man was about to reply when suddenly a messenger came to announce that he had visitors at his inn. Jin'ge said, "Come, come, don't feel so bad. Third Aunt is not here. She doesn't know anything about your grief. Some friends of yours are at the inn to see you. They'll all come over here if they know you're in a brothel." Afraid that his friends would laugh at him, the young man promptly rose and returned to the inn.

In low spirits, he was in no mood for taking the next level of the examinations and decided to pack up and go home. When they heard of this, his friends came to offer advice. Calling him by his courtesy name, they said, "Shunqing, your career is so much more important than a prostitute. How can you give up your career prospects because of a prostitute?"

"Let me tell you, it was actually Yutangchun who encouraged me to study hard. How can I give her up so easily after she has gone through all these hardships for my sake?"

"Shunqing," his friends said. "If you win honors in the exams, maybe you'll be assigned a post in that region. You can easily see her then! (*A prophecy that would later turn out to be true.*) If you return home and fall ill from all the fretting and agonizing, you'll only make your parents worried and your friends contemptuous. What good will you get out of that?"

Third Master reflected on these words and realized they were quite true. If he should have the good luck to be assigned to Shanxi, that would fulfill his greatest desire in life. So those words of advice woke him up. When the day of the examinations came around, he took all three sessions, and, sure enough, he won eighth place in the second category of successful candidates and was assigned to the Ministry of Justice as an intern.

Three months later, he was made the judge of Zhending Prefecture, whereupon he dispatched a horse carriage to his parents to invite them and his brothers and sisters-in-law to visit. His parents turned down his invitation, saying in reply, "Be hardworking, cautious, fair, and honest in discharging your duties as an official. Considering that you are still a bachelor at your age, we have betrothed Commander Liu's daughter to you. Soon, we'll be sending her to your duty station for the wedding ceremony." With his heart set on Yutangchun, the young man found little joy in the news about marriage. Truly,

He treated a wayside willow as a wife
And a domestic hen as a wild duck.

Now, let us turn our attention to Shen Hong. His wife, Pi-shi, was quite an attractive woman. Even though she was in her thirties, she was more captivating than a sixteen-year-old. She had always resented her husband's uncouth and unromantic ways. Moreover, since her husband was away traveling more often than he was at home, Pi-shi, the lustful woman, found it difficult to withstand her desires. Next door there lived a man named Zhao Ang, a former student of the Imperial College and quite a libertine. His wife had died recently. Though of the genteel class, he had bought his way into the Imperial College and was in fact reduced to straitened circumstances.

One day, Pi-shi was viewing the flowers in the backyard when she ran into Zhao Ang. Both being on the lookout for an affair, they were attracted to each other. Zhao Ang asked around and learned that Granny Wang, a go-between by profession, who lived at the mouth of the lane, knew the Shen family well and, with her glib tongue, was most adept at making matches and pairing off lovers. So, with twenty taels of silver, he bribed Granny Wang into pulling the strings for him. Granny Wang was not unaware of Pi-shi's reputation as a woman of easy virtue. And now, with both the man and the woman taking a fancy to each other, it took but a word from Granny Wang to establish the liaison and start a secret relationship.

With only a wall and a ladder between them, they did things that could not very well have been done in the open. Partly out of desire for Pi-shi's charms and partly because he had designs on her money (*These are indeed the facts.*), Zhao Ang did his best to please the woman in bed. As for her, being quite infatuated with him, she granted his every request, all too ready to hand over to him everything she owned in the house. Within a year, all her boxes and trunks were empty. Each time he took money, he always claimed that it was just a loan to tide him over an emergency, but in truth, he never returned a single penny.

Worried about how to answer her husband's questions upon his return, Pi-shi said to Zhao Ang one night that she wished they could elope. Zhao Ang replied, "I'm not some homeless bachelor. How can I leave just like that? Even if I do, I can hardly escape the reach of the law. The only solution is to murder Shen Hong so that we can be lawfully wedded husband and wife. Wouldn't that be nice on all accounts?" Pi-shi nodded without saying anything.

Now, Zhao Ang started making inquiries about Shen Hong and learned that he was on his way home, bringing with him a concubine called Yutangchun, a former prostitute. He reported the news promptly to Pi-shi, not without adding some inflammatory words to make Pi-shi's blood boil. Between bitter curses, Pi-shi lamented, "Now what's to be said to him?"

Zhao Ang offered this advice, "As soon as he steps into the house, you start yelling at him. Make a big scene and tell him to take that whore to live in a separate room, so that you can be in control. I've got here some arsenic that I asked Granny Wang to buy for me. When you get a chance, put it in some food and serve it to them. If they both die, well and good; if one dies, it will be just as good!"

"He likes spicy hot noodles," said Pi-shi.

"Just the kind of food to put the poison in."

Having worked out the scheme, they waited for Shen Hong's return.

In a matter of days, Shen Hong arrived in his hometown. Telling the servant and Sister Yu to stay outside for the moment, he went into the house to greet Pi-shi. With an ingratiating smile, he said, "Don't get mad at me, Sister, for what I've done."

"You've got yourself a concubine?"

"Yes, that's it."

In a rage, Pi-shi lashed out at him, "I've been living like a widow for all these months and years while you enjoyed yourself, whoring around, and now, you even bring a whore back home, totally ignoring a wife's feelings. If you want to keep that slut, you go ahead and take the west wing of the house and leave me alone. I wasn't born to such a happy lot that I deserve a bow from that whore, so don't even let her get near me." (*Convincingly realistic.*) After this indignant outburst, she started wailing, pounding the tables and chairs, and keeping up a stream of curses against "the procurer" and "that whore."

Unable to calm her down, Shen Hong thought to himself, "Let me humor her for the time being and stay in the west wing for a couple of days. That, in fact, is just as well, for I can enjoy myself more. After her anger dies down, I'll have Yutangchun kowtow to her."

He thought his wife was only jealous. Little did he know that she was having an affair, and, afraid that he would go into the bedchamber and find her dowry gone, she was taking this opportunity to drive him out. Indeed,

One goes east, one goes west;
Both with plans known only to themselves.

But of this, we shall speak no further.

As for Yutangchun, having vowed loyalty to Mr. Wang, how could she ever compromise her chastity and yield to Shen Hong? All the time, she was thinking to herself, "When I get to that disgusting thing's home, I'll tearfully complain to his wife and beg her to do right by me so as to preserve my chastity. Then I'll write to Third Master and have him come to redeem me with two thousand taels of silver. Wouldn't that be nice?"

But upon arriving at Shen Hong's home, she learned, much to her alarm and chagrin, that Mrs. Shen refused to see her and had ordered her and Shen Hong to take up quarters in the west wing. So much for her plan. Shen Hong made arrangements for bedding in the west chamber, helped Su San [Yutangchun][7] settle in, and then went to play the companion at Pi-shi's dinner table. To Pi-shi, who repeatedly demanded that he get out of her sight, he said, "But if I really go to the west wing, I'm afraid I'll make you angry."

"My temper gets short only when you try to stay around me. It will improve as soon as you get out of my sight."

"My apologies," said Shen Hong. Sheepishly chanting a good-bye, he left the room and headed straight for the west wing. In the meantime, Sister Yu had taken advantage of his absence to throw his bedding out into the hallway, close the door of the bedchamber, and retire for the night. However hard Shen Hong knocked at the door, she turned a deaf ear. It so happened that Pi-shi sent a maid, Little Xiaming, to the west wing to see if Shen Hong had gone to sleep. As he had always been sweet on this maid, he pulled her up into his makeshift bed and perfunctorily fulfilled his amorous desires with her. After it was over, Little Xiaming went her way. Feeling tired, Shen Hong fell asleep and did not wake up until daybreak.

Meanwhile, Pi-shi had been waiting in vain throughout the night for Zhao Ang. As her husband was also unavailable, having fallen asleep after Little Xiaming's departure, she kept tossing and turning in her bed, unable to so much as close her eyes all night long.

At the first light of dawn, she rose and began making noodles. After the noodles were cooked, she put them in two bowls. She sprinkled some arsenic in the noodles, quite unobserved, poured spicy hot sauce over them, and called out to Little Xiaming, "Send the noodles over to the west wing for the master."

Little Xiaming carryied the bowls over to the west wing and called out, "Master! See how Mistress cares about you! She's made some spicy hot noodles for you!"

Seeing two bowls, Shen Hong said, "My child, send one bowl to Second Mistress."

When she heard Little Xiaming's knocks, Sister Yu called out from her bed, "What is it?"

"Second Mistress, please rise and have some noodles."

"I don't want any."

"Your Second Mistress hasn't had enough sleep, I believe," put in Shen Hong. "Don't disturb her." So he quickly ate up both bowls of noodles.

After Little Xiaming left with the bowls, Shen Hong felt a sharp pain in his stomach. "Oh no! I'm going to die! I'm going to die!" Sister Yu thought he was pretending, but noticing the gradual change in tone, she opened the door and looked in, only to find him dead, with blood flowing from all nine apertures. Alarmed, she screamed, "Help!"

In a trice, footsteps were heard, and Pi-shi showed up. Before Sister Yu had a chance to speak, Pi-shi's face hardened. Purposefully, she said, "How could a perfectly healthy man have died so suddenly? You little whore, you must have killed him so that you can go off and marry again."

Sister Yu said, "The maid sent over some noodles for me, but I didn't want any. I didn't even open the door. Who would have known that he ate it and died with a stomachache! There must have been something suspicious in the noodles."

"What rubbish!" Pi-shi snapped. "If there was something suspicious in the noodles, it must have been your doing, you little whore. Otherwise, how did you know that the noodles could not be touched and therefore refused to eat them? You said you didn't even open the door, but aren't you standing outside the door this very moment? If you didn't murder him, who did?!" With that, she burst into loud wails, calling her husband "the sky of protection over the family." The servants in the household, male and female, grew frantic. Pi-shi used a white cotton kerchief three feet long to drag Sister Yu all the way to the county magistrate's yamen, where she called out her grievances.

It so happened that the magistrate, a Mr. Wang, was holding a court session, and the women were summoned inside for questioning. Pi-shi said, in stating her case, "I am Pi-shi, and my husband was Shen Hong. On a business trip to Beijing, he bought that whore Yutangchun to be a concubine with a thousand taels of gold. That whore hated my husband for his ugliness and secretly put poison in his spicy hot noodles. My husband died as soon as he ate them. Your Honor, please make her pay with her life!"

After listening to this statement, Magistrate Wang turned to Sister Yu, "Yutangchun, what do you have to say?"

"Your Honor, I am a native of Datong Prefecture in the district under the direct jurisdiction of the imperial court. In a year of drought, my father sold me to a brothel owned by a Su family. Three years later, Shen Hong saw me and brought me to his home as a concubine. Out of jealousy, Pi-shi secretly put poison in the noodles and murdered her husband. But then she turns around and brazenly accuses me."

Thereupon, the magistrate exclaimed, "Pi-shi! You must have harbored a grudge against your husband for turning his back on you and getting himself another woman, and so you poisoned him. You may very well have done it."

"Your Honor! I was married to my husband in my early youth. How could I have brought myself to do such a ruthless thing? That concubine Su-shi is a sinful woman with her heart set on other men. It is all too clear that she's the one who poisoned him to death, so that she can marry another man. Please do right by me, Your Honor!"

To Su-shi, the magistrate said, "Step forward. In my judgment, since you're a prostitute, you're interested only in dashing young men and were so dissatisfied with your husband's ugliness that you poisoned him to death. That, I believe, is what happened." He ordered the lictors, "Apply the ankle-squeezers to Su-shi!"

"Your Honor!" Sister Yu protested. "I may have lived in a brothel, but how could I have done such a horrible thing to Shen Hong, who never did me the least bit of harm! If I did have evil intentions, why didn't I murder him at some point along the journey? Once in his home, would he have allowed me any chance for foul play? Pi-shi drove away her husband last night and forbade him to enter the room, and she made the noodles this morning. I had nothing to do with the whole thing."

Seeing that there was some truth in what both women said, Magistrate Wang had lictors put them both in jail for the time being, adding, "I'll have detectives look further into the matter." And so, the women were put into the South Jail, and there we shall leave them for now.

From the jail, Pi-shi sent a secret message to Zhao Ang, asking him to come up quickly with bribes. Using silver that belonged to the Shen family, Zhao Ang gave the officer of the Bureau of Punishment a hundred taels, the scribe eighty taels, the file keeper fifty, the janitor fifty, the two groups of lictors sixty, and the prison wardens twenty each. Having thus bribed high and low, he put a thousand taels of silver in a jar, sealed it, and presented it as a jar of wine to Magistrate Wang. The magistrate accepted it.

Early the next morning, after he opened his court session, the magistrate ordered the lictors to bring the two women forward. A few moments later, they made their appearance and knelt down in the courtroom. The magistrate declared, "Last night, I had a dream in which Shen Hong said to me, 'I was poisoned by Su-shi. Pi-shi had nothing to do with this.'"

Yutangchun was about to protest when the magistrate forestalled her by yelling angrily, "Human beings don't have fur or scales to protect them and can be beaten to make them confess!" He ordered the lictors sharply, "Apply the ankle-squeezers and beat her. Then ask if she will confess. If she won't, just beat her to death."

Breaking down under torture, Sister Yu said, "I'll confess."

"Put down the instruments of punishment," ordered the magistrate.

The lictors brought a brush-pen to Sister Yu so she could sign her confession.

The magistrate announced, "My judgment is that Pi-shi shall be bailed out and Yutangchun sent to prison." Thereupon, the lictors took Sister Yu, shackled at the hands and chained at the feet, to the South Jail. The prison wardens, who had all taken bribes from Mr. Zhao, humiliated her in every way they could think of. As soon as their superiors gave them the go-ahead, they were going to submit a written indictment and finish her off. Indeed, they laid traps

To capture the tiger and the dragon,
To finish off the lamenting phoenix.

Fortunately, there was in the Bureau of Justice a clerk named Liu Zhiren who was a fair-minded, selfless man. He had long been aware of the adulterous relationship between Pi-shi and Zhao Ang and knew that Granny Wang was the go-between. A few days before the case came up, he had run into Granny Wang, who was buying arsenic in a medicinal herb store, saying she needed it to kill mice. A slight suspicion crept into Liu Zhiren's mind at the time. And now, a man was dead, and Scholar Zhao was bribing high and low in the yamen, being all too generous with Shen's money, so that Su-shi ended up a convict awaiting execution. Where, he wondered, was divine justice? After hesitating for some time, he said to himself, "Let me visit her in the jail."

He arrived at a moment when the prison wardens were pressing Sister Yu for bribes. After ordering them sharply to go away, Liu Zhiren comforted her with gentle words and asked if any wrong had been done to her. Tearfully, she recounted what had happened. Seeing that the coast was clear, Liu Zhiren told her what he knew about the affair between Scholar Zhao and Pi-shi as well as his encounter with Granny Wang in the herbal shop, adding, "Now, you wait here patiently. I'll tell you when to go and raise a protest. In the meantime, I'll take care of your daily meals." Over and over again, Sister Yu bowed her thanks. Now that Liu Zhiren had taken the matter into his hands, the wardens dared not say anything. Of this, no more for the time being.

Let us now come to Young Master Wang, who, in his new post in Zhending Prefecture, was fostering good causes and doing away with what had been plaguing the people. The local officials held him in respect, and the populace rejoiced. As before, however, Yutangchun was never absent from his thoughts, not even for a brief moment.

One day, he was again feeling gloomy when a servant came to announce, "Her Old Ladyship has sent the bride over." Accordingly, the young master greeted the new arrivals and let them in. At the sight of the bride, he thought to himself, "She's not unattractive, but she has none of Yutangchun's charm."

As he downed the groom's wine at the wedding banquet, marking the beginning of the marriage, Yutangchun suddenly came again to his mind. "I had hoped to be with you always, even unto hoary old age," he thought to himself. "Who would have known that you'd be married off to a Shen Hong, yielding to another the title granted by the emperor?" Physically, he was with his wife Liu-shi, but his mind was still with Sister Yu. In his misery, he came down with a fever that very night. Recalling how both he and Sister Yu, when bidding each other farewell, had vowed not to marry another, he began to hallucinate and saw Sister Yu by his side as soon as he closed his eyes. Liu-shi had prayers said for him everywhere, officials from the prefectural and county yamens came to wish him recovery, and famous physicians were engaged for diagnosis and treatment. It was not until a month later that he recovered.

In the more than one year of his term of office, he built such a good name for himself that he was recommended to take a post in the capital, as the Ministry of Personnel was in the process of conducting an appraisal of all officials throughout the land. After the roll call in the ministry was over, the young master returned to his inn, burned some incense, and prayed to heaven and earth that he be reassigned to Shanxi so that he could make inquiries about Yutangchun. A moment later, an announcement came, saying that he had been appointed inspector of Shanxi. Raising both hands to his forehead in a gesture of jubilation, he said, "So, my dearest wish in life has been granted." The next day, equipped with his official seal and documents, he took leave of the court and rode posthaste to the seat of Shanxi Province. Without delay, he issued an order and went to Pingyang Prefecture for the first stop on his tour of inspection.

As he sat examining the files in the office of the inspectorate of Pingyang Prefecture, he came upon a severe sentence passed on a certain Yutangchun with the surname Su. He was appalled but felt sure there must be something questionable about the case. Calling for the clerks, he said, "I need the most competent one among you to go on a secret inspection tour with me. Don't tell anyone else about this."

Right away, he changed into a blue robe and a white cap and, following the clerk he'd chosen, left the inspectorate, quite unobserved. He then hired two mules and headed for Hongtong County. The young man driving the mules said, by way of making conversation, "Why are you two gentlemen going to Hongtong County?"

The young master replied, "To get a concubine. Do you know any matchmakers?"

"What? You're getting a concubine, too? A rich man in our county died precisely because he got one for himself!" (*What a good way to introduce a story!*)

"How did he die?" asked Mr. Wang.

"Well, that rich man was called Shen Hong. The concubine is called Yutangchun. He had brought her home from the capital. His wife Pi-shi was having an adulterous relationship with their neighbor Zhao Ang. They were afraid that the husband would find out about this after his return, so they poisoned him to death. And then, they turned around and delivered Yutangchun to the county authorities. They bribed the yamen and had Yutangchun beaten until she confessed. Now she's in prison under a death sentence. If it hadn't been for the help of a clerk, she would have died."

"Are you saying that Yutangchun has already died in prison?"

"No, no."

"If I want a concubine, which matchmaker would you recommend?"

"Let me take you to Granny Wang. She's best as a go-between."

"How do you know that?"

"She's the go-between for Zhao Ang and Pi-shi."

"All right, let's go to her then."

The young driver led Mr. Wang straight into Granny Wang's home. "Godmother!" he called out. "I brought you a visitor who wants a concubine. He can use your services!"

"Thank you," said the woman. "I'll thank you properly when I get the money." The young man went off.

After conversing with Granny Wang in the evening, Mr. Wang concluded from her glib talk that she was nothing short of a procuress with many years of experience. At daybreak, he went to check Zhao's front and back doors and found that the house, being just a wall away from Shen Hong's, was most conveniently located for clandestine activities. He then went back, ate his breakfast, and, when settling the bill with Granny Wang, said, "I didn't bring any betrothal gifts. Let me take care of this after I return from a trip to the provincial seat."

He left Granny Wang's house, hired a mule, and rode posthaste to the provincial seat. By evening, he had arrived in the office of the inspectorate. The next morning, he issued urgent orders and went to Hongtong County, where, after being greeted respectfully by the assembly of county officials, he ordered a review of cases. Thereupon, Magistrate Wang returned to the county yamen and summoned the clerks of the Bureau of Justice to review the files. All documents necessary for the trial the following day were drawn up before the night was out, but of this, we shall speak no further.

In the meantime, Liu Zhiren had written an appeal on behalf of Sister Yu and concealed it on his person. Early the next morning, as Magistrate Wang sat in front of the prison door, prisoners involved in cases that were to be reviewed were escorted out. Wearing chains and a cangue, her face awash with tears, Sister Yu followed the lictors all the way to the inspectorate and waited for the gate to open. After the police chief reported to the inspector that everything was ready for the court session to start, orders were issued for the prisoners to be escorted under guard into the court chamber. Young Master Wang called on Su-shi as the first case for retrial.

Protesting that she was being unjustly punished, Sister Yu took her written appeal from her bosom. Lifting his head, the young master felt a stab of grief as he saw the state to which Sister Yu had been reduced. He had an attendant bring the paper to him and, after reading it, asked, "So, was Shen Hong your first husband? For how many years had you taken on patrons?"

"Your Honor, my first patron was a young gentleman from Nanjing, the third son of the secretary of the Ministry of Rites."

Afraid that she might reveal his identity and cause a scandal, he stopped her, saying curtly, "That's enough! I'm interested only in the murder case. Say nothing irrelevant."

"Your Honor, about the murder, you need only ask Pi-shi."

The young master had Pi-shi give her story, after which Sister Yu also stated her case. The young master said to a judge named Liu, "I've heard that you are a fair-minded, honest, and capable judge who never bends the law to serve personal interests. While I was here in Hongtong County, before my inspection duties have really started, I learned about this case in which Pi-shi poisoned her husband and falsely accused Su-shi. Please review it carefully for me." (*It's a good thing he gives these instructions. Otherwise, the judge would have been afraid of hurting the county magistrate's feelings.*) At this, the inspector withdrew from the court.

Judge Liu went back to the court and called the session to order. "Su-shi," he thundered. "You murdered your husband. Why?"

"I'm not guilty!" cried out Sister Yu. "It was all too clearly the work of Pi-shi, Granny Wang, and Scholar Zhao. They banded together and poisoned the man to death. The greedy county magistrate forced a confession from me. But now I wish to appeal even if it costs me my life. Please do right by me, Your Honor!"

Judge Liu had lictors bring up Pi-shi and asked her, "Is it true that you have an adulterous relationship with Zhao Ang?"

Pi-shi denied it. Right away, Judge Liu summoned Zhao Ang and Granny Wang to be questioned in Pi-shi's presence. They were subjected to a round of physical punishment, but none admitted any wrongdoing.

To Little Xiaming, Judge Liu said, "Being the one who delivered the noodles to your master, you must have known the truth." And he ordered the ankle-squeezer applied to her.

"Your Honor! I'll confess!" said Little Xiaming "It was my mistress who put the noodles into the bowls and told me to serve them to the master. So I carried the bowls to the west wing. The master told my new mistress to eat with him, but she kept her door closed and refused to get up, saying, 'I don't want any.' So the master ate the noodles by himself, and he died on the spot, bleeding from the nose and the mouth."

Judge Liu then pressed her on the adulterous relationship between Pi-shi and Zhao Ang. She also came up with the truth.

"This girl is a false witness bribed by Su-shi," interjected Zhao Ang.

After a few moments of reflection, Judge Liu decided to have everyone involved in the case taken to jail. He then called for a clerk and said to him, "Those brazen lowlifes are not going to confess. Now I've come up with an idea. Put a big wardrobe on the red lacquer steps and drill some holes in it. You will take along some paper and a pen and hide in the wardrobe. Don't let on about any of this to anyone. I'll then summon them for more questioning. If they still refuse to confess, I'll have them locked up somewhere near the wardrobe. And your job is to be sure to write down whatever they say to one another."

Thus instructed, the clerk had a big wardrobe placed on the steps and hid himself in it, after which Judge Liu had the lictors bring in Pi-shi and the others for another interrogation. "Are you going to confess or not?" he asked.

Zhao Ang, Pi-shi, and Granny Wang pleaded in unison, saying, "We have nothing to confess even if you beat us to death."

Enraged, Judge Liu gave these instructions to the lictors, "You go ahead and eat your meal. After you come back, torture these lowlifes. In the meantime, lock up the four of them, including Little Xiaming, in four separate places around the steps and make sure they don't even whisper to each other." Accordingly, the lictors locked up each one near a corner of the wardrobe and went their own separate ways.

Pi-shi raised her head and, seeing no one around, began to lash out at Little Xiaming: "You worthless wretch! Why did you have to shoot your mouth off like that? If you give any more such testimony, I'll beat you to death when we get home."

"I wouldn't have told if I could stand the pain of the ankle-squeezer."

"Sister Pi!" exclaimed Granny Wang. "I, too, can't put up with the pain of the thrashings anymore. When Judge Liu comes out again, I'm going to tell!"

"My good godmother!" said Zhao Ang. "What have I ever done to hurt you? If we aren't found guilty, I'll be nice to you in every way I can think of and treat you as my own mother."

"I'm not going to be fooled by you again. Imagine! Treating me as your own mother after I get you out of this mess, indeed! Well, you promised me two piculs of wheat, but you still owe me about eight pints. You promised me one picul of rice, but what I got was nothing but chaff. Of the promised two suits of clothes, you delivered only a blue cotton skirt. And I haven't seen the nice house you said would be mine. Why should I be put to torture and suffer for the evil things you did?" (*Earlier in the story, there was but a brief mention of Granny Wang's doings as a go-between, and this is the place to fill in the details.*)

"My godmother!" added Pi-shi. "If we get out of this mess, I'll never forget my debt of gratitude to you. If we stick to our story and manage to make it through today, we'll be off the hook."

The clerk hidden in the wardrobe wrote down everything that had been said. When the court session resumed, Judge Liu ordered the wardrobe to be opened and out stepped the clerk, to the consternation of one and all. So frightened were they that their legs gave way under them. Judge Liu read what the clerk had recorded. Before he could give orders for more torture, the three accused volunteered their confessions. Zhao Ang made a written statement recounting the entire background of the case, and when all three signatures were affixed to it, the paper was submitted to the judge. After he read it, Judge Liu asked Su-shi, "Did you grow up in a brothel or were you brought up in a decent family?"

Su-shi supplied a full account of how she had been bought from a decent family by Su Huai and placed in a brothel, how she had met the son of Secretary Wang, who was her first patron, how he had squandered thirty thousand taels of silver, how he had been ousted by the procuress, and how she had been cheated and sold as a concubine to Shen Hong with whom she had never shared a bed, even after they began the journey to Hongtong. Presuming that the said Mr. Wang was none other than the inspector, Judge Liu took up his brush-pen and wrote the following verdict:

Pi-shi is to die from a thousand cuts;
Decapitation will be Zhao Ang's lot.
Woman Wang helped in the crime with the poison;
As a warning, Xiaming shall be beaten.
The corrupt and cruel Magistrate Wang
Shall be removed from his post.
The yamen will recover the bribes; expect no mercy!
Su Huai, for making prostitutes of decent girls,
Deserves to be banished.
Yichenjin shall stand for three months in a cangue. (Good settlement of the case.)

After drawing up the document to be submitted to his superiors, Judge Liu ordered that Pi-shi and the others be taken back to jail. The next day, they were sent under guard to the inspectorate, with Judge Liu himself leading the way, holding the documents in his hand. The inspector approved of his judgment and invited the judge for tea in a back room. "What are you going to do with Su-shi?" asked Wang.

Judge Liu replied, "I'm going to send her back to her native place. She'll be free to marry."

Inspector Wang dismissed the attendants and confided to Judge Liu the vow he had taken years before, adding, "If you could quietly have someone escort her to Silversmith Wang in Beijing, where she may stay temporarily, I will be most grateful."

Judge Liu did as he was told, but we need not go into the details. In the meantime, by order of Young Master Wang, runners from the yamen went to Beijing to bring Su Huai and Yichenjin to justice. Su Huai had already died. When Yichenjin was taken to the inspectorate, she recognized the inspector and called out, "Brother-in-law Wang!" The inspector sharply ordered that she be given sixty heavy strokes and put in a big cangue weighing a hundred catties. In less than half a month, she gave up the ghost. Indeed,

Ten thousand taels of gold can't prolong one's life;
One fine day, she's reduced to a heap of ashes.

When his one-year term of office expired, Mr. Wang returned to the capital. After reporting to the court, he went to see Silversmith Wang and ask for news. The silversmith told him, "She's living in Dingyin Lane, with Jin'ge taking care of her." Immediately the young master headed for Dingyin Lane. Upon seeing each other, the young master and Sister Yu broke into loud cries of grief. The young master had learned about Sister Yu's chastity, and Sister Yu knew that Inspector Wang was none other than Third Master Wang, so both showered each other with words of gratitude.

The young master said, "My parents arranged a marriage for me to Liu-shi, a very kind person. She knows about you and will never be jealous."

That night, they drank together and slept together, as inseparable as lacquer and glue. The next day, Silversmith Wang and Jin'ge came to kowtow and offer their congratulations. The young master thanked them for their help and also gave these instructions: With Su Huai and his wife dead and gone, all of Su Huai's family belongings that had been purchased with Yutangchun's money were to be turned over to Silversmith Wang and Jin'ge, as compensation for their kindness. He then wrote a memorial requesting permission to go on leave, left the court, and rode on horseback with Yutangchun back to Nanjing.

Upon their arrival at the gate of the Wang residence, the janitor went quickly to announce to the master, "The young master's here!" Mr. Wang Senior was overjoyed. After entering the main hall, where an incense altar had been laid out, the young master made bows of gratitude to heaven and earth and to his parents, his brothers and sisters-in-law, and his two brothers-in-law and sisters. He then took Yutangchun to greet everyone. Upon entering the bedchamber, Sister Yu said to Liu-shi, "Madam, please accept a bow from this humble one."

"Sister," protested Liu-shi, "how can you say such a thing? You are actually the first wife. I came later."

"You, madam, are from a distinguished official's family, whereas I was but a courtesan from a humble background."

The young master was delighted beyond measure. That very day, the question of the two women's status was settled, with Liu-shi as the wife and Sister Yu as the concubine. The two women addressed each other as "Sister," and harmony reigned throughout the household.

To Wang Ding the servant, the young master said, "Wang Ding, you advised me time and again in Beijing to change my ways. You were absolutely right. I'll suggest to father that he make you the chief butler." He also rewarded Wang Ding with a hundred taels of silver.

Later, Third Master Wang Jinglong rose to be an imperial inspector and was blessed with sons born to both his wife and his concubine. And the family line thrives even to this day. There is a poem that says in praise:

The story of Zheng Yuanhe is well known;
Third Master's romance makes the news.
Of all those wallowing in the world of love,
Few have attained wealth and rank, both husband and wife.

25

Squire Gui Repents at the Last Moment

No friendship measures up to that among ancients;
No spring dreams and autumn clouds are to be trusted.
Expect no help from false friends when in need;
Expect no solicitude from polite greetings.
Of old, Chen and Lei were inseparable;[1]
In poverty, life, and death, Guan and Bao remained friends.[2]
People of today scorn such fidelity;
Only pine trees make staunch friends on wintry days.

In the Dashun reign period of the Yuan dynasty,[3] there lived in Wuqu Lane in Suzhou Prefecture south of the Yangzi River an elderly man named Shi Ji, courtesy name Jinren. His father, Shi Jian, courtesy name Gongming, was a prudent, kindly, and honest man who ran his household thriftily, never failing to put every penny to good use. Already in his fifties when Shi Ji was born, he cherished this son as if the child were made of gold.

At eight years of age, the boy was sent to the school of a Scholar Zhi in the neighborhood. Impressed by his brilliance, Mr. Zhi made him share a desk with his own son, Zhi De, who was about the same age. Among the many pupils of varying ages in the school, these two boys distinguished themselves by their intelligence and diligence and made rapid progress day by day in their studies. Later, when Schoolmaster Zhi died of an illness, Shi Ji invited Zhi De to live at his home at no charge for room and board, with the permission of his father. They compared notes in their studies, and loving friends they were indeed.

Soon afterward, they attended government-sponsored schools and, together, sat for the civil service examinations. Zhi De passed the examinations and became a government official, whereas Shi Ji failed time and again. Consequently, he began to spend money freely, making friends, helping the poor and the widowed, wishing to make a name for himself as a man with a generous and bold spirit.

His father Shi Jian, being a frugal, albeit rich, man prone to keeping every drop of excrement as if it were a piece of gold, agonized over the young man's lavishness. Afraid that his son would fritter away all the family possessions and fall into poverty after his death, he secretly buried much gold and silver in the cellar and several other spots. Keeping the knowledge to himself, he planned to pass the money on to his son only upon his death. This is, in fact, a common practice among rich parents. Truly,

> *In a fat year, think ahead to a lean one,*
> *Or you'll miss the blessed days, come a rainy one.*

If Mr. Shi Senior had been afflicted with frequent headaches or stomachaches and felt indisposed every other day, he would have prepared for his death, now that he was advanced in years. Even if, being otherwise quite healthy, he had been bedridden for just half a month or ten days, with his son attending to him day and night, he would have told his son about his secret. However, as it was, he was still the picture of good health in his nineties with an appetite heartier than average and a step as springy as if he had wings. All too unexpectedly, he died in his sleep early one morning. It was a painless, blissful death, but he did not leave a last will and testament. There is a proverb that puts it well:

> *Everything is done with the three inches of breath;*
> *All is gone once the last breath goes out.*

Shi Ji, always eager to do the right thing, spared no expense with the funeral and burial ceremonies.

Shi Ji was now more than forty years of age but yet without a son. After the three-year mourning period was over, his wife, Yan-shi, urged him to take on a concubine, but he turned a deaf ear to the advice. He began to intone the "White-Robed Bodhisattva Sutra," made copies of it, and freely gave out alms. To the gods, he pledged: "If a son is born to me, I will donate three hundred taels of silver to renovate a temple." A year later, Yan-shi found herself pregnant, and sure enough, a son was born.

While shaving the baby's head three days after his birth, the husband and wife brought up the subject of fulfilling the pledge, whereupon they named the boy Shi Huan [Fulfill a Votive]. When the baby was one month old, a feast was laid out to mark the occasion. Then, after a talk with his wife, Shi Ji took three hundred taels of silver and went to Water Moon Bodhisattva Temple at Tiger Hill to make offerings of incense. He was on the point of asking the abbot about the renovation project when he suddenly heard the sound of weeping coming from below. Upon listening closely, he found the sobs heartrending. Down the steps he went until he came to the rocks by Sword Pond known as Thousand People Rocks and saw that by the pond sat a man looking into the water and sobbing uncontrollably.

Shi Ji stepped forward and recognized the man to be Gui Fuwu, who, in his childhood, had lived on the same street as the Shi family and had also gone to Schoolmaster Zhi's class. After attending the school for a year or so, Gui Fuwu's parents took the family to Xukou to till the land, and Fuwu left the school. Shi Ji and Fuwu had met a few times afterward but not in the last ten years or so. Shi Ji had never expected to run into Fuwu like this. In surprise, he accosted Fuwu, had him rise to his feet, exchanged greetings with him, and asked what had happened to him. Gui Fuwu just kept weeping, unable to get a word out. His heart aching at the sight, Shi Ji pulled him into the main hall of the temple and asked, "My brother, what is it that pains you? If you let me know, I may be able to help you."

In the beginning, Gui Fuwu refused to tell, but after much pressing, he unburdened himself. "I had an inherited house and a hundred *mu* of land. By tilling the fields and growing our own food, we were quite self-sufficient. Unfortunately, I believed some wrongheaded opinions about merchants making more money than farmers do. So I mortgaged off what little land I had to Grand Councilor Li for three hundred taels of silver, which I used to purchase cotton yarn to be sold in Yanjing. But, as it turned out, luck ran against me. After several trips back and forth, I ended up losing all the profits along with the capital. Mr. Li has been after me like a wolf or a tiger, trying to get back his money plus the exorbitant interest. I've lost all my land, my house, my property, even my wife and two sons to him. But even so, I haven't paid back everything I owe him. He's now demanding that I press my relatives for money so as to make up the full amount. In desperation, I escaped under the cover of night. I've been crying because, with nowhere to go, I was about to throw myself into the ravine."

His heart going out to Fuwu, Shi Ji said, "Don't worry, my brother. I brought three hundred taels of silver for the temple, but let me give them to you instead, so that you can reclaim your family. What do you say?" (*This kind deed is better than renovating temples.*)

With a start, Gui Fuwu said, "You must be joking."

"Why should I try to fool you when you're not asking me for anything?" replied Shi with a hearty laugh. "I may not know you very well, but we did go to school together for a time in our childhood. Now, in our Suzhou region, morals are so low that one mouths empty words of comfort to friends in trouble, without offering even a penny's worth of a gift. In worse cases, one feigns sympathy while actually gloating over others' misfortunes. I find such people most repugnant. (*Mr. Shi is most probably not a native of the Suzhou region.*[4]) Moreover, what you are going through also involves your wife and son. I had wanted a son for so long, and now that I am blessed with a son, who's only one month old, I pray that Buddha will protect him as he grows up. How could I have the heart to see you give up your son and bring shame to your family? These words are truly from the bottom of my heart." So saying, he opened his trunk and took out three hundred taels of silver, which he offered with both hands to Mr. Gui.

Thinking it presumptuous to take the silver right away, Mr. Gui said, "Please let me draw up a receipt, so that when my circumstances improve, I can repay you for your kindness in helping me out for old times' sake."

"I'm giving this to you out of sympathy. Why would I expect to be repaid? Please go home quickly. Your wife must be worried about you."

Beside himself with joy over this stroke of good fortune, which was beyond even his wildest dreams, Mr. Gui took the silver and instinctively sank to his knees. Shi Ji swiftly raised him to his feet. Tearfully, Mr. Gui said, "You've given my entire family a new lease on life. You are no less than a parent who has given us rebirth. In three days, we'll come to see you and offer our thanks." Turning to the image of the bodhisattva, he kowtowed and made this pledge: "Mr. Shi has saved my life, and I shall repay him for his act of kindness. If it can't be done in this life, let me serve him in my next life as a dog or a horse." And he went merrily down the mountain. A later poet had this to say in praise of Mr. Shi's act of kindness:

Against friendship and compassion for the poor,
The three hundred taels were as worthless as dust.
Let me ask the high and mighty of our day:
Would you likewise care for a childhood classmate?

To the abbot of the temple, Mr. Shi said, "An emergency came up that demanded the three hundred taels I had brought for the renovation of the temple. I'll give you the money tomorrow."

"One day doesn't make any difference," the abbot assured him.

Upon returning home, Shi Ji recounted what had happened to his wife Yanshi. She did not take it amiss. (*Good woman.*) The next day, he put together another three hundred taels of silver and had them sent over to the Water Moon Bodhisattva Temple in fulfillment of his pledge.

On the third day, Gui showed up at Shi Ji's door with his eldest son, twelve-year-old Gui Gao, to offer his gratitude.

Pleased beyond measure at the sight of father and son together, Shi Ji entertained them with great hospitality, treating them to wine and food and asking them to stay longer. In the course of the conversation, he casually brought up the subject of Gui's debt, to which Gui Fuwu responded, "Thanks to your generosity, the capital has been paid back in full, but the land and estate are gone to pay off the interest. The family is all we've got." With that, his tears flowed thick and fast.

"But what are you going to live on?" asked Shi Ji.

"With nothing left to live on, we have to move to another county to work for a living. Being genteel folks from a family of long standing, we would be ashamed to be seen fallen to such a lowly status in our home village."

"Well, as they say, to help people out, you must go all the way. Outside of Xu Gate, I have a mulberry and date orchard on ten *mu* of land and a thatched cottage of several rooms. With diligent work, the orchard should yield enough for subsistence. If you don't object to the tediousness of such a life, would you be willing to stay there for the time being?"

"If we are able to stay there, we won't end up as hungry ghosts in some alien land! But I haven't even repaid the previous debt of gratitude. I'll feel too uneasy if I accept another favor. Now, I have two sons. The older one is twelve years old, and the younger one is eleven. Please choose the son you prefer and keep him as a servant, so that he can at least render some small service to you. He could have served in the establishment of some highly placed official anyway."

"You and I being friends, your son is my son. How can you say a thing like that?" Then and there, he had a page boy bring over a lunar almanac and picked an auspicious day for Gui Fuwu's son to move into the household. He also had a message sent to the old servant guarding the orchard, instructing him to clean up the rooms and prepare to hand over management of the orchard to the Gui family. Mr. Gui had his son Gui Gao make a bow of gratitude to his benefactor. As Gui Gao kowtowed, Mr. Shi tried to return the courtesy, but Mr. Gui Senior stopped him. Resignedly, Shi accepted the homage. Mr. Gui Senior chanted his words of good-bye seven or eight times and, with profuse thanks, departed with his son.

On the day scheduled for moving, the Shi family sent over cakes, rice, and money. It was truly a case of

A helping hand appearing out of midair
To rescue the ones caught in the cosmic net.

A few days later, Mr. Gui filled four gift boxes with the usual fare of fresh fruit, fat chickens, and large fish and asked his wife, Sister Sun, to go by sedan-chair to the Shi household to offer their thanks. Yan-shi, Mr. Shi's wife, had the dinner table set and kept her for a meal. Sister Sun was a woman with a clever tongue, best at vicious gossip and fawning flattery. On their first meeting, Yan-shi took an instant liking to her and found her as endearing as a sister. There was another remarkable thing: Even Yan-shi's little baby son, not yet a year old, liked Auntie Sun so much upon first sight that he clung to her, wanting to be carried in her arms. (*He's indeed predestined to be her son-in-law.*)

"To be honest with you, Sister," said Sister Sun, "I'm pregnant. So I can't hold your baby." Indeed, according to a popular belief, if a pregnant woman held a child in her arms, that child would get sick in the stomach and bowels and have greenish stool. The sickness would last until after the woman gave birth.

"How many months along are you?" asked Yan-shi.

"Five full months."

Counting on her fingers, Yan-shi remarked, "So, you got pregnant in the twelfth month of last year, which means you should be giving birth in the ninth month of this year. You already have two sons. If it's a girl this time, I say our two families should form a marriage alliance!"

"You are too kind! I'm only afraid that my family is not worthy enough for you!" And so the conversation went. They did not part company until evening set in.

Upon returning home, Sister Sun repeated Yan-shi's words to her husband. In exultation, both husband and wife wished for a daughter so that they could form a marriage alliance that would provide them with lifelong support.

Time flew by like an arrow. Soon, it was the beginning of the ninth month, and sure enough, Sister Sun gave birth to a daughter. The Shi family sent over firewood and rice. In addition, Yan-shi had a maidservant go over to convey her good wishes. The two families treated each other as cordially as if they were already relatives, but of this, no more need be said for the time being.

Now, in the mulberry and date orchard, there stood a gingko tree with a trunk that measured about ten arm spans around. It was said that the God of Five Blessings and Saintly Virtues dwelled on top of it. On the first day of the first month every year, the gardener would make offerings of wine and burn paper coins under the tree, an old custom of which Gui Fuwu was aware. He was indeed destined for an upturn in his life, for, as he was burning the paper coins, he suddenly caught sight of a white mouse. It went around the tree once and then dived under the tree and disappeared. Gui took a closer look and found the white mouse peeping out from a cup-size hole under the roots of the tree.

Gui told his wife about it, wondering aloud if the mouse was the manifestation of that god. Sister Sun said, "As they say, when the birds are thin, their feathers grow longer, and when people are poor, their wits grow short. I've often heard that a golden snake represents gold, and a white mouse represents silver, but I've never heard of a god assuming the shape of a mouse. Maybe there's money buried under the tree, and heaven, in its compassion for us in our poverty, made a white mouse appear to you. Why don't you go tomorrow to Blind Man Tong's house by Xu Gate and have him do a divination for us? Ask him if the star of wealth will be shining on us."

Being an obedient husband, Gui Fuwu rose bright and early the next morning and went to Blind Man Tong's house for a divination. (*Biggest mistake.*) And he was told that the star of wealth was indeed shining fully upon him.

After consulting with each other, the couple bought a pig's head to offer as a sacrifice to the god of buried treasures. In the stillness of the night, the two of them, each wielding a hoe, dug deep into the hole under the roots of the tree. When they reached a depth of about three feet, they came upon a small square tile, under which stood three porcelain jars. There was a layer of rice, all rotten now, at the top of each jar, and after they scraped aside the rice, they saw that the jars were filled with silver. The popular belief was that ingots of silver buried in the earth would somehow wander off by themselves unless covered by a layer of rice.

With a cry of joy, the husband and wife set to removing all the silver with their bare hands. After emptying the porcelain jars, the couple left them where they were, put the tile back on, and spread the soil over it as before. Upon returning to their room, they found that the silver amounted to about fifteen hundred taels. Gui wanted to give the Shi family three hundred taels as repayment for the amount Shi had given them and keep the balance for future use.

"That won't do," objected Sister Sun.

"Why not?"

"The Shi family knows us to be poor. That's why we came here in the first place.

What if they ask how we came by the three hundred taels? They'd get suspicious. If they learn that the silver was dug out from under the gingko tree, they'll say that the family inheritance buried in the yard rightfully belongs to them. And what if they claim that the silver amounts to three or four thousand taels? You're in no position to argue. And so, even if we hand over the entire amount to them, they'll still say it's not enough. Our good intentions will be misconstrued, and that will only make things worse." (*Specious reasoning. A vicious, fearsome tongue.*)

"So what does my good wife think?"

"These ten *mu* of land and the few mulberry and date trees won't be enough to see us through our old age. Now that heaven has bestowed such a windfall on us, why don't we secretly buy some property in another town, gradually shake ourselves free of this place, and start living as a family of independent means? If we can repay our debt of gratitude to them by then, that will be better for both families." (*An idea that's not all that bad if they really will repay the debt of gratitude.*)

"Just as the proverb says, 'Smart women are worthier than men.' Your point is well taken. I have some distant relatives living in Huiji. We haven't heard from each other for a long time because of my poverty. If we go there with a thousand taels of silver, I'm sure we won't be snubbed. We can buy some fertile land and decent property there and go over every year to collect rent. With the interest we can make from loans, I guarantee we'll be fabulously rich in several years."

Their minds thus made up, Gui Fuwu and Sister Sun took a trip to the middle Zhejiang region the following spring, ostensibly to visit relatives, but in fact, they bought land and property and engaged a rental agent. Once every year, they traveled there to settle the accounts. Upon returning, they changed back into their worn, old clothes and hid all signs that might betray their wealth. (*Schemers capable of becoming moneybags.*) After five years had gone by in this fashion, Gui had amassed quite a large fortune in Huiji County, Shaoxing Prefecture, including his own house. The Shis were the only ones kept in the dark.

One day, the children of both families came down with chicken pox at the same time. Shi Ji engaged a physician. After his own son had been seen, Shi had the physician go to attend to Gui's daughter, whom he treated as his very own daughter-in-law. To everyone's joy, the children recovered.

In the neighborhood, there lived an old man, Li, with the sobriquet Meixuan, who was a close friend of the Shi family. At his suggestion, some friends and neighbors put together some money and held a celebration feast for Mr. Shi, a feast that Mr. Gui also attended. When Shi Ji again brought up the subject of the betrothal, Li Meixuan volunteered to be the matchmaker, an offer that received hearty cheers. Gui was ready to accept the offer, but, upon returning home and discussing the matter with his wife Sister Sun, he was told: "You know the old saying, 'Those with kind hearts should not command the troops; those with high moral standards should not manage financial matters.' Shi is a good man, all right, but good men don't get rich. He has come down in the world. His means are not what they were. (*Valid point.*) Since all our possessions are in Huiji, we can find a local family there with a higher social position, and we'll get to keep our landed property, too."

"You're right. But he's so full of goodwill. What excuse can we use to turn him down?"

"Just say that we're too lowly to claim the connection. If he insists, you can say that the children are still too young. The betrothal can wait until they've grown up. What's the hurry?"

The ancients put it well, "Greed makes a snake try to swallow an elephant." In their down-and-out days, a marriage alliance with a family of higher standing was more than anything they could have asked for, but now, having struck it rich thanks to some unearthed treasure, they turned around and began to pick and choose.

Once on shore and out of danger,
They forget their struggle in the water.

Being a straightforward man, Shi Ji assumed Mr. Gui had declined as a gesture of genuine modesty. Never did the slightest suspicion cross his mind.

Time went by quickly. Another three years elapsed. Suddenly, Shi Ji came down with an illness. He failed to respond to treatment and passed away. We shall skip over the details of the funeral and burial and come to the point at which Gui Fuwu's wife urged her husband to take advantage of the opportunity and set themselves free. Carrying a chicken and a jar of wine, the couple went to the Shi household to offer their condolences.

Gui took the lead and bowed to the spiritual tablet of the deceased, while Sister Sun stayed behind and said to Yan-shi, "Not a day goes by that my unworthy husband is not mindful of his benefactor's kindness toward him. Now that the benefactor is gone and my husband hasn't rendered him any service, we dare not go on occupying your estate. We will have to move and try to make a living elsewhere. We're here today to bid you farewell."

"Sister, how can you say such a thing? Though my husband is gone, I am still here to make decisions! In my loneliness, I need your company. How can you be so hardhearted as to leave me at a time like this?"

"I do hate to part with you, but as we're not related to you in any way, we shouldn't be here, occupying the estate of a widow, because people will talk. After your son grows up, we'll have to return everything to him anyway. We might as well be sensible before it's too late, so that what started well will end well and fulfill the deceased benefactor's kind wishes." (*What she says does make sense.*)

Yan-shi's pleas for her to stay were to no avail, and they bade each other a tearful farewell. And so, the Gui family moved to Huiji. Like birds released from a cage, they were gone forever, never to return.

As for the Shi family, Shi Ji had been so generous in performing charitable works that the family fortunes had dwindled away. And now, the funeral costs left the family in debt. Yan-shi was a kind-hearted woman but not very good at getting things done. She found it too hard to take care of a fatherless child and manage the household at the same time, and so, she began to sell off the family's land. Within five or six years, the family resources were completely exhausted. The family had nothing left with which to eke out a living, and all the servants and page boys ran away.

As the proverb says, "With heaven looking after the virtuous, they find rescue when things get desperate." It so happened that at this time, there appeared on the scene a man named Zhi De, who had just come back to his hometown from his station of official post. A former schoolmate of Shi Ji's, he had passed the civil service examinations on his first attempt and was assigned to a post in another part of the country. Later, he rose to be vice-commissioner of Sichuan. It being the Zhizheng reign period [1341–68] under Emperor Shun of the Yuan dynasty, when evil men were in power, wreaking havoc in the imperial court, Zhi De had no wish to remain in office. He resigned and returned to his hometown.

Pained by news of Shi Ji's death and the family's reduced circumstances, he paid the Shi family a visit to offer his condolences. The son, Shi Huan, went out to greet the visitor. Although young, he fully observed proper decorum in every way. To Mr. Zhi's question as to whether he had been betrothed, Shi Huan said, "As my deceased father's few possessions are gone, and my mother's subsistence is in jeopardy, my betrothal is not something we can afford to take care of at this time."

With tears trickling down his cheeks, Mr. Zhi said, "Your deceased father was a most compassionate man who readily shared other people's sorrows and joys. With such good people in the world, divine justice, if it still exists, will make sure that their descendants thrive. (*Evil men may carry the day for a while, but gentlemen believe in divine justice.*) I may have been a schoolmate of your father's, but I'm ashamed to say that I failed to share his worries and sufferings from my post far away. Indeed, I have betrayed him! I have a beloved thirteen-year-old daughter, about the same age as you. I'd like to have a matchmaker make a marriage proposal to your mother. Please give this message to your mother first, and do not turn me down!"

Shi Huan bowed his thanks with a few words of demurral.

The next day, Mr. Zhi sent gift-bearing servants to accompany a matchmaker, who proposed that Shi Huan move into the Zhi household as a live-in son-in-law. Grateful for his kindness, Yan-shi gave her consent. On a chosen day, Shi Huan joined the Zhi household and honored Mr. and Mrs Zhi as his parents-in-law. A good teacher was engaged as his private tutor at home. Worrying about Yan-shi's lack of daily necessities, Mr. Zhi had firewood and rice sent over to her and made sure that the young man visited her once every ten days. Yan-shi and her son were grateful beyond measure. People of later times commented that in a world where marriage pledges were easily broken by those contemptuous of the poor, Mr. Zhi stood out as a man of integrity by marrying his beloved daughter well beneath her station in life to the son of a deceased poor friend. This was indeed a case of

Looking upon money as dung and dirt,
But upon kindness and justice as precious gold.

But the story goes on. Being an honest official committed to opposing corruption, Mr. Zhi had accumulated little savings even though he had served several consecutive terms of office. The added expense of supporting Shi Huan and Yan-shi further strained his budget. Quite by accident, he heard that Gui Fuwu had made his fortune after leaving the mulberry and date orchard for Huiji County and, with much fertile land and a grand mansion, he had wealth numbering in the tens of thousands of strings of cash. Now renamed Gui Qian, he was called Squire Gui by all and sundry.

Well aware of past events, Mr. Zhi suggested to his son-in-law after hearing the news, "Gui Fuwu benefited greatly from your family's kindness. Repayment of his debt alone, not to speak of other expenses, should amount to three hundred taels of silver. The fact that he has made his fortune but hasn't come to offer help must mean that he doesn't know your family has fallen on hard times. If you, my good son-in-law, were to go to Huiji and ask him for help, he'd surely be generous with you. You are quite entitled to whatever he'll offer you. I believe that he and his wife will be only too happy to see you. Why don't you talk with your mother about it?" (*He's using his own mind, that of a gentleman, to read the mind of a villain.*)

During a visit to his mother, Shi Huan told her about this. Yan-shi said, "If the Guis have indeed made their fortune, they will certainly not turn their backs on us. But you were too young at the time to know the details. Gui's wife, Sister Sun, and I were as close as sisters. Let me go with you, so that if the man of the house is away, I can talk with her in an inner room."

Shi Huan duly reported the conversation to Mr. Zhi, who then gave them money for travel expenses and wrote a letter to Gui Qian, reminding him of their days in the same school and asking him to take good care of Mrs. Shi and her son. Without a moment's delay, he rented a boat for them, and they set off on their journey to Huiji County in Shaoxing.

"Where does Squire Gui Qian live?" they asked.

Someone gave them directions: "He lives in the first tall sprawling mansion you'll see on the main street within West Gate."

Shi Huan and his mother took up lodging at an inn outside West Gate. The next day, Yan-shi stayed at the inn while Shi Huan, bearing Mr. Zhi's letter and his own visiting card, which specified his status as the son of a friend, went into the city, to Gui Qian's residence. An impressive sight the mansion was:

A tall gate leads to an imposing mansion;
Flowers and trees embellish the courtyard;
Tables and chairs in neat rows in the halls.
On a tile path and stone steps three feet high,
Servants come and go, tending to house and land;

Humble farmers approach to pay debts and rents.
He who dug up silver from the orchard
Is now a leading figure in Huiji.

Finding the Gui family residence so impressive, Young Master Shi was inwardly delighted, for he thought he had come to the right people for help. The janitor asked who he was, took his visiting card and letter, and led him to a room opposite the main hall by the inner gate. From where he was seated, he could see that the inscription "Be Thankful for the Bounty" on the board hanging high up on the wall was by the famous calligrapher Yang Tieya.

For a considerable time after the visiting card was delivered to the inner quarters of the house, there was no sign of anything astir. After waiting for approximately four hours, he heard the inner gate open and footsteps coming out of the main chamber. Believing that he would be seeing the master of the house, Shi Huan adjusted his clothes and his cap, crossed the threshold, and stood expectantly, but quite some time passed with no sign of anyone coming his way. He moved toward the inner gate for a furtive look. Lo and behold, there stood Gui Qian in all his finery in the middle of the courtyard, surrounded by more than ten attendants. Pointing to the east one moment and to the west the next, Gui was giving orders to the men. As soon as one group left, another group came in, some to receive orders, some to report to the master, and never had they any lack of things to say! The servants did not disperse for about another two hours. (*A vivid description of the man's superciliousness.*)

At the janitor's announcement of a visitor, the squire asked, "Where is he?"

"In the room opposite the main hall."

Gui Qian did not instruct the janitor to invite the guest in but paced out the inner gate, taking his time in doing so, and headed for the room where Shi Huan was waiting. Shi Huan, his back bent respectfully, stepped forward and bowed in greeting. Casting a glance at him, Gui Qian asked, feigning nonrecognition, "Who might you be?"

"I am Shi Huan of Changzhou, my deceased father being the one with the courtesy name Jinren. The friendship between our two families goes back many years, but I have been negligent in sending over my greetings. So here I am, to pay my respects. Please take the seat of honor, Uncle, and accept a bow from me."

Dispensing with the usual exchange of amenities, Gui Qian said, "You don't have to do this! You don't have to do this!" After offering Shi Huan a seat and having tea served, Gui instructed a page boy to prepare a meal for the guest, much to Shi Huan's inner delight.

"My mother sends her greetings to Aunt. She's now at an inn and sent me over first to let you know about our visit."

Considering how kindly he had been treated in the old days, Gui should have said, "Since your mother is here, please ask her to come and meet my wife." But, as it was, he hemmed and hawed without saying anything in direct response to Shi's remarks.

In a short while, the page boy came back to report that lunch was ready. Gui ordered that it be set in the room where they were sitting. Two sets of dishes were laid out on the only table in the room, one for the supposed guest of honor, one for the host. Declining the seat of honor, Shi Huan pulled his chair to one side, and Gui Qian did not offer to correct the position.

"How old are you?" asked Gui Qian.

"When you, Uncle, departed for this place, I was only eight. My mother is still grateful for the condolences that you kindly offered. And now, six years have passed since then. My family has fallen on hard times, but Uncle, your fortune has been on the rise day by day. What a sharp contrast! And how enviable your prosperity!"

Gui Qian nodded without a word. After three rounds of wine, Shi Huan said, "I don't have much of a capacity for wine, and my mother is waiting for me back at the inn, so I'd better not drink too much."

Without taking the cue, Gui Qian said, "Well, since you're not going to drink much, let rice be served!" Nor did he bring up the old friendship or ask how the Shi family was faring, even after the meal was over.

Unable to restrain himself any longer, Shi Huan felt he had no choice but to hint at the purpose of his visit. "In my childhood, while sitting beside my now deceased father, I used to hear him say that of all his schoolmates, you, Uncle, were the closest to him. Even then, he predicted that Uncle Gui would surely experience a spectacular rise later on in life. My mother also often speaks highly of Aunt Sun's virtues and kindness. Luckily, when you, Uncle, were staying temporarily in my humble family's orchard, my parents did not fail to be generous with you. Otherwise, I would not have had the temerity to come here."

His eyes lowered, Gui Qian kept waving his hand without saying a word in reply. (*One keeps pushing closer; the other keeps fending him off.*)

Shi Huan went on, "I trust that Uncle still remembers how my father met you at the Water Moon Bodhisattva Temple in Huqiu?"

Afraid that Shi Huan would go on, Gui Qian stopped him short by saying, "I know the purpose of your visit. You need not say another word. (*Fending off step by step the other party's advances.*) People might hear you, and what an embarrassment that would be for me!" With that, he rose to his feet.

Shi Huan saw nothing for it but to take his leave. "Let me bid you good-bye for now, Uncle. I'll come again another day." Gui Qian saw him out the gate before starting back, his hand raised high in a polite gesture. Truly,

> *What I give is much needed rain of early spring;*
> *What I get is icy frost, even in summer.*

In the meantime, Yan-shi was waiting expectantly at the inn, saying to herself, "The Gui family will surely send servants to escort me to their home." Wondering why it was taking so long, she leaned against the door and looked out. All she saw was her son returning, looking dejected.

At his account of Gui's attitude and what he had said, Yan-shi was reduced to tears. "Gui Fuwu," she said bitterly, "how can you not remember the day when you were about to throw yourself into Sword Pond?"

Before she could launch into the details, her son hastened to forestall her, saying, "At this moment when we need help, please don't say things that will only hurt feelings. Since he knows the purpose of our visit, he'll surely come up with something. Didn't he swear before the bodhisattva he would repay the debt of gratitude even if he had to serve my father as a dog or a horse in another life? Surely he won't go back on his own words. Let me go again tomorrow and see what he'll do." With a sigh, Yan-shi stifled her anger, and the night passed without further ado.

The next day, Shi Huan rose early, betook himself again to the Gui residence, and asked to see the master of the house.

As it turned out, after seeing Young Mr. Shi, Gui Qian did think of sending some handsome gifts to the young man and his mother before they returned home, but his wife, Sister Sun, firmly stopped him from doing so, saying, "To help the poor is a lifelong job, to be yelled at by them is a one-time thing. If we let that bastard have something from our home, he'll hang on to us, like grass that keeps on growing from its roots and roses that bloom every month. Even if they once did something good for us, they did the same for everybody. We were not the only recipients of their generosity. Out of a thousand people who took the medicine, why should we alone pay back the money? Why should we be the unlucky ones? If there is divine justice, those who go out of their way to perform good deeds should enjoy wealth and good fortune for thousands of years. How could such people ever be reduced to such a state? In this world of ours, it's the hardhearted who get all the good deals. To help the poor is to let your money go down the drain. You'll end up a poor man yourself." (*Vicious words, but spoken with emotion that is not entirely unjustifiable.*)

"You're right, my good wife. But the mother and the son have already made this trip. Plus, they brought along a letter from my old schoolmate Mr. Zhi. How can we turn them away?"

"How do you know that the letter from that man Zhi isn't forged? When we were living in Suzhou, no official named Zhi offered us any help, and now, he is quick to write us a letter! (*Those who did help are not treated any better.*) Since he's so full of compassion for the poor and the widowed, why doesn't he reach into his own pocket? Even ten thousand such letters don't mean a thing! Go and tell the janitor to ignore that down-and-out wretch if he shows up again. Let him wait until all his hopes are dashed before we throw him some travel money. If new vinegar doesn't taste strong enough, it will lose all its pungency when water is added to it. So if he's given no reason to hope in the first place, he'll stop pestering us." For Gui Qian, this speech had the effect of

Adding malice to his already evil heart,
Making more vicious his already devious mind.

Shi Huan was made to wait a considerable time at the gate. Giving all sorts of excuses, the janitor refused to announce him. When Shi Huan reminded him, he pretended not to have heard and walked away. Smarting with the humiliation, the young man furiously rolled up his sleeves and, his face flushed crimson, yelled at the top of his voice, "I did not come here without a good reason. Spring winds expect summer rains to follow. When we were rich, we had people coming to us for help, and we never turned our backs on them like this!"

He was still carrying on when a well-dressed young man approached the gate from outside. "To whom do we owe this tirade?" asked he.

Seeing a stranger before him, Shi Huan straightened his clothes and said, stepping forward, "I am from Suzhou. My name is Shi—"

Before he had finished, the newcomer hastened to bow, saying, "So we are old acquaintances. We haven't seen each other for so long that we don't recognize each other anymore. Yesterday, my father was talking about the purpose of your visit. He's doing something about it. Why be so impatient and work yourself into such an angry state? This is not something hard to do. Let me talk to my father. You'll get an answer tomorrow."

Only at this moment did Shi Huan realize that the young man was none other than Gui Gao, the elder son of the Gui family. His pleasantness made Shi Huan regret having lashed out as he had. However, before he could say anything, the young man went through the gate and into the house without so much as a word of good-bye. The rudeness made Shi Huan flare up again, but hoping for an answer the following day, he could think of nothing else but to return to the inn, his eyes brimming with tears.

At his account of what had happened, his mother Yan-shi counseled, "Having traveled hundreds of li to seek help, we, mother and son, would do well to keep our tempers and be courteous at all times. Let's not get argumentative and stir up their anger." (*Before, it was the son pacifying his mother, and now it's the mother trying to pacify her son, all because of the hardships of seeking assistance. Pitiable! Pitiable!*)

The next morning, Yan-shi again reminded her son, "Now, this time when you go, be courteous. Don't ask for too much either, not more than the three hundred we lent them in the beginning. That will be enough for our needs."

Thus instructed, Shi Huan went to the Gui residence again. He stood politely at the gate, holding his breath and keeping his head bowed. The servants and page boys streamed in and out, but the janitor he had seen the day before was not there. After waiting in vain for a long time, the young man grabbed an older servant and said, "I am Shi Huan from Suzhou. I have been waiting for two days to see Squire Gui. Would you please announce my visit?"

"The squire is still asleep after his drinking of last night," replied the servant.

"I wouldn't dream of disturbing him but will be content if I can see the young master. I'm not self-invited. I made an appointment with him yesterday."

"The young master left by boat at the fifth watch this morning to collect rent for the east farmstead."

"The second young master will do."

"The second young master is studying in class, and he never concerns himself with such things anyway."

While speaking, the servant heard someone call him and rushed off. Shi Huan fumed with rage. He was about to explode but then thought that he shouldn't give too much weight to a lackey's words because what he had said about the master might not be true. Resignedly, he swallowed his anger and continued to wait.

A moment later, the inner gate swung wide open, and Gui Qian rode out from the courtyard on a horse. Shi Huan bowed respectfully in the direction of the horse, an act of courtesy that Gui Qian did not reciprocate. Pointing with his horsewhip at the young man, he said, "Granted, you came a long distance to seek help, but I didn't hold you up for ten days to half a month, did I? Why did you have to lose your temper and use foul language? I did mean to be generous with you, but now I can't do that anymore." (*He turns the tables and puts the blame on the other party.*) Turning to a servant, he ordered, "Give Mr. Shi two ingots of silver in a gift box and send him away." To Shi Huan, he added, "I give you these two ingots of silver out of my regard for your deceased father. For you, with your youthful arrogance, I wouldn't have spared a penny. Now that you've got your traveling money, be off without delay!" Before Shi Huan could get a word out, Gui Qian flourished his whip and rode off with the speed of the wind. Truly,

The tongue in the viper's mouth,
The sting on the scorpion's tail,
Neither are venomous enough
To match the poison in the ingrate's heart.

The two ingots of silver being only twenty taels, the young man would have impulsively thrown them to the ground out of scorn. But, partly because the master of the house was already gone and partly because he had come with only enough money for the journey here but not for the return trip, he saw no alternative but to be reconciled to the situation.

Back at the inn, with tears in his eyes, he told his mother what had happened. Mother and son broke down into sobs at the sight of the two ingots of silver. Granny Wang, the innkeeper, asked them why they were crying their hearts out, whereupon Yan-shi gave her a tearful account of the whole story.

Granny Wang addressed them in the following words: "Please don't worry, madam. I know Sister Sun well. I often visit her. She's the kindest woman there is, and a perfect hostess, too. If her husband goes around treating former benefactors badly, she doesn't know it! (*Nice twist.*) Since you and Sister Sun are such good friends, let me send a message to her and tell her that you are at my inn. She'll surely invite you." Yan-shi restrained her tears and thankfully accepted Granny Wang's offer.

The next day, Granny Wang went to tell Sister Sun what she thought was happy news. Sister Sun said, "Granny, don't believe her. When my husband was having a bad time in business, he did indeed borrow some small items from them, but he has paid back the capital and the interest in full. She doesn't know how to manage her money and frittered away what was a large family fortune, and now she comes here to demand money from us. Out of the goodness of his heart, my husband treated her son to a meal and gave them twenty taels of silver, for old times' sake. Another man would not have been so kind. And yet she turns around and accuses us of refusing to pay off our debt. Granny Wang, I'm not going to quibble with her over whether I'm in debt or not. Just let her show me the receipt for the loan. Whatever amount the receipt says, a hundred or a thousand, I'll gladly pay it in full."

"Right! Right!" said Granny Wang. As she hurriedly turned away, Sister Sun called her back. She ordered that a maidservant wrap up and seal a packet containing one tael of silver along with a kerchief and said to Granny Wang, "Please take these things to Mrs. Shi as a small token of my regard for her, but tell her not to come again by any account, because I'm afraid our feelings will be hurt if she believes we shortchanged her."

These words made Granny Wang doubt Yan-shi's innocence. Back at home, she extolled the virtues of Sister Sun to Yan-shi and delivered the gift, adding, "If she hasn't paid the old debt in full, she wants you, madam, to send over the receipt of the loan so that she can repay the capital and the interest to the last penny."

Yan-shi said no receipt had ever been drawn up, which Granny Wang found quite unbelievable, for three hundred taels was to her a mind-boggling amount, as momentous as a high mountain and the vast sea.

After a miserable night, Yan-shi and her son paid their bill at dawn and set off on their return journey to Suzhou. Truly,

The spirits sink when there's nothing to celebrate;
Loneliness sets in when one's down on one's luck.

What with her grievances against the Gui family and physical exhaustion from the travel, Yan-shi fell ill as soon as she arrived home. Her illness lasted three months. Shi Huan engaged physicians as well as fortune-tellers, but nothing worked, and she died. With no money for burial clothes and a coffin, the son had to permanently sell off his rights to the ancestral family property to a Young Master Niu in the same county. The young master's father, Commander Niu, had long served under Vice-Prime Minister Li and had gotten rich by acting as the middleman in briberies. Emboldened by his father's power, Young Master Niu bullied people wherever he went. He had in his employ a certain Guo the Sly One, whose job was to seek out widows and fatherless children and buy their land and property at half price.

Shi Huan being as young as he was, and his father-in-law Mr. Zhi being a kind-hearted country gentleman who thought it was undignified to bother about even his own family's affairs, let alone those of his son-in-law, Young Master Shi fell into Niu's trap in his eagerness to sell. The estate, which was worth thousands of taels of silver, was appraised by Guo the Sly One at only four hundred taels. Of this amount, Guo was willing to pay only one hundred as down payment, promising to pay the balance after the premises were vacated. Planning to relocate after the funeral, which was to cost much more than a mere hundred taels, Shi Huan repeatedly asked for a larger down payment but could secure a promise for only forty more taels. Shi Huan barely managed to pay for the burial and the grave and then found he had little money left. While he was trying without success to look for housing, messages from Young Master Niu poured in like flakes of snow, urging him to vacate the premises.

Mr. Zhi could not stand any more of this and went to see Young Master Niu to put in a good word for his son-in-law. He went quite a few times in a row, but each time, he was denied a reception. Mr. Zhi thought to himself, "Let me wait for him to pay a return call." But Niu adopted the strategy Yang Huo used when trying to visit Confucius and paid his return call only when he knew Mr. Zhi was not home.[6] Upon returning and learning of Niu's visit, Mr. Zhi hastened to the Niu residence, only to be told, as before, that Niu was not home. Angrily, Mr. Zhi said to his son-in-law, "Let's not go begging for help from such unreasonable boors. My good son-in-law, why don't you just stay with me for a while until you find a place of your own? We can then talk about your moving out, and we can take our time doing it."

Shi Huan decided to follow his father-in-law's advice and to move his furniture and other belongings to the Zhi residence. He started by removing the furnishings in his grandfather's bedchamber and taking them to the Zhi residence for repairs. As he was doing so, he found in the ceiling a small, well-sealed box. He opened it and saw nothing else but an account book in which were written reminders of various locations where silver was buried. At the end was a line that read "In the handwriting of ninety-year-old Gongming [Shi Jian's courtesy name]." Shi Huan was overcome with joy. He put the account book in his sleeve, told the servants to stop removing things from the room, and went to Mr. Zhi's house for a consultation.

Upon reading the account book, Mr. Zhi said, "In that case, there's no need for you to move." He then went with his son-in-law to check the left post by the window railing of Grandfather Shi's bedchamber and found two thousand taels of silver, just as described in the account book. They offered 140 taels to redeem the estate deeds, but Young Master Niu turned a deaf ear, insisting that the sale was already finalized. Mr. Zhi sought high and low for help from Niu's relatives, beseeching them to put in a good word for Shi Huan. Young Master Niu then demanded twice the amount, assuming that Shi could not come up with the money. To his surprise, a full 280 taels were measured out on the scale, as Shi Huan was now a man with a well-stocked coffer. Left with no excuse, Young Master Niu could do nothing else but take the silver, but, claiming that he could not find the deeds on the spur of the moment, he said he needed a day to return them. Shi Huan believed his story, and as soon as Shi Huan let him go, Young Master Niu filed a complaint with the prefectural yamen, charging Shi with breach of contract. Luckily, Prefect Chen was an upright man without selfish motives. Knowing all too well what kind of person Young Master Niu was, and convinced that Mr. Zhi's account on behalf of his son-in-law was true, he ruled that Niu was entitled only to the original 140 taels plus 14 taels as penalty for breach of contract on Shi's part. The balance of 126 taels was to go toward the repair of schoolrooms. The deeds were to be returned to Young Master Shi and Guo Diao'er was to be beaten with the rod as punishment for his role as an abettor. (*Good judgments.*)

Enraged by the humiliation, Young Master Niu wrote a letter to his father and had a servant dispatch it to the capital. In it, he falsely accused the three generations of the Shi family of nonexistent crimes and asked his father to have Vice Prime Minister Li use his influence to make local officials arrest Shi Huan so as to vent Young Master Niu's spleen. But in fact, however hard humans may scheme, divine justice will catch up with them. Truly,

He drags another into the water
But fails to drown him;
He lights a fire against the wind
And burns himself first.

At the time, the empire was under the misrule of Emperor Shun of the Yuan dynasty. With the Red Turban rebels looting and wreaking havoc across the land, the imperial court ordered Military Affairs Commissioner Yao Yao to go on a punitive expedition against the rebels. Vice Prime Minister Li, heavily bribed by the Red Turbans, advocated amnesty. When his secret dealings with the rebels came to light, he was charged as an accomplice and thrown into prison. All of his adherents, with Commander Niu heading the list, were to be punished for their involvement, and all members of the Niu family were to be executed. Soon, the emperor issued an edict to that effect. Upon learning the horrible news, a Niu household employee ran back to report to the Niu residence posthaste. In a panic, Young Master Niu packed up his valuables and fled to the sea with his wife and concubine, only to run into stragglers from the rebel Fang Guozhen's troops.[7] They forcibly took the women and the money and killed him with a sword. This was retribution for his evil deeds.

After Shi Huan hit upon the pile of silver, he redeemed the estate and started a life of comfort. Then he began digging in the various locations described in the account book, and sure enough, he came upon tens of thousands of taels of silver, not even one penny short of the recorded amounts. The only amount missing was the fifteen hundred taels that were supposedly buried under the gingko tree in the mulberry and date orchard. Only three empty jars were found in that spot. Thinking that some divine beings might have taken them, he gave no thought to the matter. Not a shadow of a suspicion entered his mind that this could have anything to do with Mr. Gui. Henceforth, he bought land everywhere, and with Mr. Zhi as his manager, he became immensely wealthy. Upon completing the period of mourning for his father, he married, but this is of no concern to us here.

To pick up another thread of the story, Squire Gui was having a difficult time being a rich man in Huiji, meeting corvée obligations on his plentiful land as well as extortionary demands from the local yamen. Among his neighbors was a Mr. You, nicknamed Funny Man You, who was a middleman of sorts by profession and frequented the residences of powerful officials in the capital.

One day, Squire Gui consulted this man about his plight. The man suggested, "Why don't you buy yourself an official title? You'll not only bring glory to your own name but also be exempted from corvée. Wouldn't that be nice on both counts?"

"I wonder how much it costs," said Squire Gui. "Would you help me do it?"

"Well, I'm quite experienced in this line of work," boasted Mr. You. "I'm the one who got titles for Commander Xu and Commander Wei of Wu County, Jiangsu. Now they are wallowing in wealth and richly paid by the government. If you want to do it, I will gladly offer you my services. The cost ranges from two thousand on the lower end to three thousand at most."

Taken in by these words, Mr. Gui gave Mr. You fifty taels of silver as a preliminary payment and, taking along more than three thousand taels, made the trip to the capital with Mr. You on a chosen day. All along the way, Mr. You cajoled Gui with sweet words. Believing the man to be sincere, Mr. Gui pledged brotherhood with him. As soon as they arrived in the capital, Gui all too readily handed over the three thousand taels of silver, leaving them at Mr. You's disposal.

An official's cap was all he wanted,
Even if he had to empty his pocket.

About half a year later, Mr. You came to offer congratulations, "My brother, congratulations! You'll get to be a highly placed official any time now! But the prime minister is so greedy that all fees have increased ten-fold. Your three thousand taels are not enough. Anything less than five thousand won't do."

Afraid that the three thousand he had already paid would go to waste, Gui Qian had Mr. You borrow two thousand from one of his influential acquaintances. He then kept half of it for himself and gave one thousand to Mr. You.

Another two or three months passed. Suddenly, four lictors came one day to announce that the newly appointed commander wished to talk with the squire. Wondering if it was just a low-ranking official, Gui Qian asked, "What is the commander's surname?"

"You'll know when you get there. We're not supposed to say anything here."

Gui Qian hastily straightened his clothes and followed the four lictors to an impressive yamen. The commander, looking very important, was sitting in the tribunal, wearing a black gauze official's cap, an official's robe, and a belt. Two of the lictors stayed with Gui Qian while the other two went in to announce his arrival. Soon, he heard his name called in the hall. Having never visited a yamen before, he found himself in a state of great trepidation, his heart thumping violently. An officer led him to the hall and sharply ordered him to kneel and make obeisance. Without returning his courtesy, the commander said, all cool and collected, "I already made use of your contribution the other day. Now that I am an official by a stroke of luck, I will surely return the money to you someday." (*How does that compare with the way you treated Shi Huan?*) But, being new in my post, I am in need of funds. To my knowledge, you still have a thousand. You may lend it to me now. I'll return it to you along with the rest." That said, he ordered the four lictors, "Take him to his lodging and get the money. If he disobeys, bring him back to me for punishment. I won't go easy on him!"

Pressed by the lictors, Gui Qian had no choice but to hand the silver over to them, choking with silent fury. Soon thereafter, the creditor came to Gui Qian with a receipt demanding repayment of the debt because they saw that Gui Qian had no prospect of an official title. Gui, resigned, sent a messenger home, had some property sold off, and used the proceeds of the sale to repay the two thousand taels plus interest. Chafing at the injustice and frustrated that he had no one to turn to for vindication, he thought of returning home but felt too ashamed to do so. When he saw Funny Man You sitting majestically in a canopied carriage with many attendants all around him, his eyes grew bloodshot and his heart burned with rage. Furiously, he said, "It's either him or me!"

He went to a blacksmith's shop and had a sharp knife made for him. Hiding the knife in his bosom, he said to himself, "When that man You goes to the court session tomorrow morning at the fifth strike of the watch drum, I'll stab him to death. Even if I have to pay with my life for it, I'll at least be avenged!"

The truth is, once you set your heart on doing something, you will know no peace of mind. Thinking about this big job, he stayed awake all night. Mistaking the moonlight shining on the windows for the first light of dawn, he scrambled out of bed, but when he heard the watchtower drum strike only three times, he sat down and waited for the day to break. About another two hours passed. Unable to calm himself, he picked up his knife and ran with the speed of the wind to the house of Funny Man You, only to find the door still closed. At this point, he stumbled and fell. Without knowing what he was doing, he crawled into an opening by the door. In the opening, which was brightly lit by candles, there was an old man sitting by a table. Recognizing the old man to be none other than Shi Ji, he was overcome with shame. It was too late to dodge, as he had already been seen by Mr. Shi, so he thought of bowing but found himself unable to rise, his hands still down on the ground. Resigned, he crawled toward Mr. Shi, raised his head as high as the latter's knees, and said, wagging his tail, "I can never forget the kindness you showed me. When your son came from afar to see me the other day, I failed to offer him generous assistance, not because I'm an ingrate, but because I happened to be short of funds at the time. I'll surely pay your family back in future."

Mr. Shi said sharply, "What a horrible beast, barking nonstop like that!"

Wondering dejectedly why Mr. Shi would not listen to him, Gui suddenly saw Shi Huan coming outside. With an obsequious smile, he held a corner of Shi Huan's clothes in his mouth and begged to be forgiven for his rude treatment of the young man.

"What's this beast up to?" With that, Shi Huan kicked him aside.

Not daring to say anything in his own defense, Gui walked ahead, keeping his head down. Before he knew it, he found himself in the kitchen, where he saw Shi Huan's mother, Yan-shi, sitting in a chair, ladling out meat soup. Excited by the aroma of meat, Gui kept jumping up and down before he finally squatted on his heels, kowtowed, and said plaintively, "Your son was too impatient last time and refused to wait a little longer, and that led to your passing away. Please don't hold this against me anymore and kindly give me a piece of meat."

Madam Yan called a maid and ordered, "Drive this thing away," whereupon the maid picked up a stove poker. Alarmed, Gui ran to the backyard, where he saw his wife, Sister Sun, his two sons Gui Gao and Gui Qiao, and his young daughter Qiongzhi, all huddled together. Upon taking a closer look, he saw they were all in the shape of dogs. He looked down at himself and was appalled to find that he was also a dog. Tearfully, he asked his wife, "Why have we been reduced to such a state?"

"Don't you remember what you said in the hall of the Water Moon Bodhisattva Temple? You said, 'If I can't repay him in this life, let me serve him in my next life as a dog or a horse.' Vows are given the utmost importance in the netherworld. What is there to say about this retribution for our betrayal of Mr. Shi's kindness?"

Gui grumbled, "Way back when we dug up the silver in the mulberry and date orchard, I wanted to pay off our debt to the Shi family. It was all because I listened to an evil woman like you that I took the money against my conscience. When the mother and son came to ask for help, I again wanted to be generous with them, but you did everything you could to stop me. It was you who brought all this misery on me."

His wife retorted, "Don't you know the saying, 'A man should not listen to a woman'? My words are but the words of a woman. Why did you have to do everything I said?" (*Good point!*)

The two sons stepped forward to mediate, saying, "Why don't you two let bygones be bygones? Otherwise, you'll only hurt each other's feelings. We're hungry. Looking for food is more important than anything else."

Thereupon, the husband, wife, and two sons all huddled together and went to the backyard. While they were walking around the fishpond, their eyes chanced upon some human excrement. Even though they were aware of the filth, they were so starved that they did not find the smell repugnant.

At the sight of his wife and two sons gathered around and eating excrement, Gui Qian drooled in spite of himself and tentatively licked at it with his tongue. The taste turned out to be delicious. While he was fretting that there was too little of it, he saw a child coming to the edge of the pond to empty his bowels and went to wait off to one side. After the child went away, leaving some excrement behind, he tried to take a bite but missed, and it fell into the pond, much to his disappointment. (*This is retribution in a dream.*)

All of a sudden, a chef was heard transmitting the master's order, "Pick a fat dog and cook it." The next thing he knew, his older son was tied up with a rope and taken away.

In the midst of his son's heartbreaking screams, he woke up with a start, perspiring all over. It had been but a dream. He was still in his lodging, and it was already broad daylight. Recalling his dream, he stared blankly into the air for a considerable while, thinking, "I betrayed the Shi family, and now, that man You betrays me in the same way. Heaven gave me that dream to warn me not to be demanding with others but easy on myself." With a sigh, he tossed his knife into the river, packed his belongings, and set off posthaste for home, to consult with his wife about how to repay his debt of gratitude to the Shi mother and son.

A dream of the strangest kind
Woke up the one with an ungrateful heart.

That strange dream threw Squire Gui into such a frenzy that he rushed all the way home from the capital, but, when he arrived at the gate, he found the house looking quite deserted, with not a single soul in sight. As he entered the main hall, his eyes fell upon two coffins against the left wall. Two tablets bearing the names of Gui Gao, the older son, and Gui Qiao, the younger son, stood on the altar table set up in front. He was appalled. Could his eyes be playing tricks on him? Rubbing his eyes with both hands, he looked more closely and cried out, "Woe is me!"

Upon hearing his cries, three or four maids and servants ran out from the inner quarters of the house. At the sight of their master, they said, "The very person we need is here! The mistress is critically ill. She's expecting you."

Scared out of his wits, Squire Gui staggered to his wife's bedchamber, where their daughter and two daughters-in-law were gathered, sobbing away. When they saw the squire, they called out, "Father-in-law!" "Father!" Without bothering to observe proper etiquette, they screamed frantically, "Come quickly and look at her!"

No sooner had Gui Qian managed to call out, "Wife!" than Sister Sun said, leaning against the pillow and staring at him with eyes that suddenly slanted upward toward the temples, "Father, why have you come back so late?"

Realizing that she was delirious, Gui Qian shouted, "Wake up! Look at me here!" The daughter and daughters-in-law also took up his cries.

Sister Sun opened her eyes and said tearfully, "Father, I am your oldest son Gui

Gao. I was beaten to death by Commissioner Moqi. How I suffered!" In alarm, Gui Qian asked for details, and the woman continued between sobs, "I won't go over with you what you've done in the past, but the King of Hell has ruled that, because our family betrayed the Shi family's kindness and since father once vowed to repay their kindness as a dog or a horse in another life, my brother, my mother, and I will be reincarnated tomorrow in the Shi household as three puppies from the same litter. The two male ones will be my brother and I, and the female one with a tumor on her back will be Mother. You, Father, still have some time to go before your allotted life span expires, so you will die in the eighth month of next year and be reincarnated in the Shi family as a dog, in fulfillment of your vow. Only my sister will be spared this misfortune, because she is destined to be Shi Huan's wife."

These words bore out what the squire had seen in his dreams. Feeling his hair stand on end, he was about to ask further when his wife breathed her last. In deep sorrow, the family set about making arrangements for the funeral.

To Squire Gui's questions about the causes of the two sons' deaths and his wife's illness, the daughter replied, "After you left for the capital, Second Brother took up whoring and gambling, squandering so much money every day that gradually, unknown to us, he wrote off much of our family estate to Commissioner Moqi for only half the money it was worth. About a month ago, he died of consumption. Big Brother, not knowing anything about the land sale, was on his way to East Farmstead to collect rent when he ran into Commissioner Moqi's servants. He got into an argument with them and was beaten so badly that he coughed up blood right there on the spot. He died a few days after he was carried back home. Mother was already feeling none too happy because she had learned about Father's unfortunate experience in the capital. With the deaths of my two brothers one right after the other, she was overwhelmed with grief and, while waiting in vain for your return, felt so dejected that she began to run a fever. Three days ago, an ulcer broke out on her back, and she went into a coma. Every physician who came said her case was beyond cure. By the grace of heaven, you returned in time to send Mother off on her way to the otherworld."

These words pained Gui Qian like stabs of a knife. He engaged monks for a prayer service that lasted nine days and nine nights so as to redeem the dead and spare their souls from misery. The servants were so tired after days of nonstop exertion that when they weren't paying attention, the mansion caught fire and burned to the ground. The three coffins also were reduced to ashes. Not even a plank of wood survived. Gui Qian, his two daughters-in-law, and his daughter were spared but were left with no possessions other than what they had on their backs. They cried out to heaven, earth, and their ancestors and wept until their eyes grew bloodshot, their throats went hoarse, and they fainted over and over again. Truly,

Things he did before
Came back to haunt him.

As the proverb says, "A thin camel may still be as strong as an elephant." Though virtually homeless, Squire Gui still had some landed property, which he sold for some gold and silver. Out of consideration for his two daughters-in-law, who he thought were too young to observe widowhood, he sent them to their respective parents and gave them freedom to remarry. Of the page boys and maids, he gave away some, sold off a few, and kept only his own personal servants and two maid-servants for his daughter.

He went to Suzhou on a hired boat, with the intention of fulfilling the promised marriage alliance with Shi Huan and offering some gifts to the Shi family. "Shi Huan being as poor as he is," he thought to himself, "he's surely still a bachelor, but I wonder where he may have drifted to. Let me make some inquiries when I arrive at the Shi family's old residence, and I'll know soon enough."

Upon arriving at Wuqu Lane, Gui Qian disembarked and went ashore. At the sight of the brand-new gate at the Shi residence, which looked more imposing than it had years ago, he said to himself, his heart full of misgiving, "I wonder who bought this house from them. Whoever bought it certainly did a fine job of renovation!" ([Illegible] *good.*) He asked a neighbor, "Where is Young Master Shi who used to live here?"

"He still lives here, right in this mansion!"

"How has the family been doing the last few years?"

The neighbor recounted to him how Shi Huan's mother had died and the intended sale of the house had led to the discovery of buried treasure, adding, "How nice it is that Mr. Shi is now married to Vice-Commissioner Zhi's daughter! She's both talented and virtuous and good at managing the household as well. The couple get along perfectly, and with the family circumstances improving day by day, they're doing much better than the Old Master ever did in his time."

These words filled Gui Qian with feelings of mixed joy, alarm, shame, and regret. He had been thinking of marrying his daughter to Shi Huan, but the young man already had a wife. If he withdrew his offer, he most likely could not find another way to redeem himself. If he expressed condolences for Shi's deceased mother, he was afraid he would be rejected. But if he did not do so, he would have no excuse to see the young man. After deliberating for a considerable time, he turned away and found lodging by Chang Gate.

He then sought out an acquaintance, Li Meixuan, and asked him to convey a message to Shi, stating his wish to offer his daughter to Shi as a concubine. Meixuan said, "This thing is not to be done rashly. Let me take you to see the young master first before bringing up the matter."

The next day, Mr. Li and Gui Qian paid a visit to the Shi residence. Mr. Li went in first and gave an account of the Gui family's misfortunes as well as Gui's remorse and his wish to see Shi Huan. Shi Huan refused to see Gui, but Mr. Li pleaded hard on Gui's behalf. Considering the fact that Mr. Li was his father's friend, Shi Huan gave in to his pleas and reluctantly agreed to see Gui Qian.

With shame written all over his face and his clothes dripping with sweat, Gui Qian made obeisance and asked for forgiveness.

"What brought you here?" asked Shi Huan.

Mr. Li answered for Gui, "Partly to pay respects to your deceased parents and partly to ask for your forgiveness."

With a sardonic smile, Shi Huan replied, "I wouldn't dream of troubling him like this!"

Mr. Li continued, "As the ancients say, 'Do not reject those who are not remiss in civility.' Mr. Gui is paying this visit out of the best intentions. Do not reject him out of hand."

Much against his will, Shi Huan had a servant open the ancestral hall so Gui Qian could lay out sacrificial offerings to Shi Huan's deceased mother. Hardly had Gui Qian completed the ceremony than three black dogs dashed out from the interior of the house and, gathering around him, grasped his clothes with their mouths and barked at him, as if they wanted to say something. One of the dogs did indeed have a lump on its back, and so, it was the reincarnation of Sister Yu. The other two were his sons. Recalling what his wife had said on her deathbed about reincarnation and retribution, words that had turned out to be prophetic, he broke down in a fit of sobs and collapsed to the floor.

Knowing nothing about the reincarnations, Shi Huan was moved by Gui's grief, attributing it to remorse for the wrongs he had done. After the ritual was over, Shi Huan, in a softer tone, invited Gui to stay for dinner. Believing that Young Master Shi had put past grievances behind him, Gui Qian brought up the subject of the betrothal promised years before.

Shi Huan's face hardened. He went to the inner quarters of the house and did not reappear. Gui Qian returned to his lodging and told his daughter about his strange encounter with the three dogs. The father and daughter were filled with grief.

Had they known they would become dogs,
They would have behaved more like humans.

The next day, Gui Qian dragged Mr. Li along for another visit, but Shi Huan refused to see them, pleading illness. They went four times but were denied reception each time. (*Hadn't Mr. Gui done the same thing to Shi?*) Left with no choice, Gui Qian invited Mr. Li to his lodging and told him about his dream and what his wife had said on her sickbed. He then called for his daughter, introduced her to the guest, and added, pointing to her, "This girl's betrothal with Shi has been in place ever since she had the chicken pox, and how I regret it now! But I wouldn't dare try to contradict what has been determined by fate. What's more, as I've lost my wife and both sons and am homeless, I'm only asking for a chance for my daughter to be a maid and me a servant, so that we can devote ourselves to serving the Shi family for the rest of our lives and not have to do so as dogs." With that, he broke down in tears.

Out of sympathy for him, Mr. Li talked with Shi Huan again and tried his best to persuade the young man to change his mind. Shi Huan said in reply, "When I was poor, my father-in-law did me a great kindness in offering his daughter to me to be my wife. After we got married, I've been much indebted to my wife for her management of the household. How can I betray her and take another woman? Moreover, my mother died with grievances against him in her heart. So he's my enemy! With what shall I comfort my mother when I see her under the Nine Springs? Do not bring this matter up ever again!"

Mr. Li retorted, "Since your father-in-law is a scholar from an old genteel family, your wife must be well versed in *The Guidelines for Women in the Home.* So if you present her with the facts, she'll surely understand. Moreover, Miss Gui is most virtuous and filial. Yesterday, after she heard the extraordinary account of the three dogs in the ancestral hall, she wept the whole night through, wishing she could redeem her mother's sins. If you accept her, she'll be a big help to your wife. Your parents under the Nine Springs will surely be pleased when they learn of this. The ancients easily forgave one another their old grievances and never drove people to desperation. Please consult your father-in-law on this matter."

Shi Huan was about to say something again by way of refusal when Vice-Commissioner Zhi emerged from inside, saying, "My good son-in-law, do not reject the proposal out of hand like this. I have heard everything. This is reason to rejoice! My daughter has already consented gladly, so would Mr. Li be so kind as to serve as matchmaker?"

Even as he spoke, Zhi-shi, Shi Huan's wife, sent out a few maids and waiting women with some valuables that she had put together to offer as betrothal gifts. Mr. Li conveyed the message to the other side and, with mutual consent, a day was chosen for the wedding. When ill-using the Shi family in the past, Mr. Gui had refused to acknowledge the betrothal. Little did he know then that his daughter would end up being a concubine rather than a wife. True, the girl may have been born under the wrong star, but this was also an act of heavenly retribution for Mr. Gui's treachery, and it was a retribution in good time, too, while he was still alive. Indeed,

Zhou Yu's clever plan—how it was shattered!
He lost both—the lady and the battle![8]

Miss Gui being of a gentle nature, Zhi-shi took quite a liking to her, and wife and concubine got along very well. With all the money still left to him, Gui Qian built three halls for Buddhist worship, where he kept the three dogs, observed the dietary laws, and paid homage to Buddha every day. Miss Gui burned incense every night in penitence for the sins of her mother and brothers. After more than a year had gone by in this fashion, her mother and brothers appeared before her in a dream one night to bid her farewell, saying, "Thanks to the grace of Buddha, we have been absolved of our sins." Early next morning, her father came to tell her that the three dogs had died in the course of the night. Miss Gui exchanged her jewelry for a burial lot. The grave site for the three dogs still exists to this day outside Chang Gate. By observing Buddhist dietary laws in repentance for his sins, Gui Qian remained free of illness to a ripe old age.

With his wife and concubine taking care of household affairs, Shi Huan concentrated on his studies and won a high place in the imperial civil service examinations at the provincial level. Gui Qian accompanied him to the capital for the next level of the examinations.

This happened at a time when Funny Man You had just been impeached by officials of the Remonstration Bureau on charges of seeking bribes as a commander of the imperial army, a violation of the laws of the land. On his way to the Bureau of Justice for interrogation, he ran into Gui Qian. Overcome with grief and shame, he prostrated himself and confessed that he had cheated Gui in years past. His wife, following behind, also kowtowed to Mr. Gui and asked for help. Moved to compassion, Gui Qian gave them what little money he had with him. Mr. You said thankfully, "It's too late in this life, but let me repay you in my next life and serve you as a dog or a horse." With a sigh, Mr. Gui went his way. Later, he heard that Mr. You, unable to withstand torture, had died in prison. This further strengthened Gui Qian's belief in the never-failing principle of divine retribution. Firmly, he set his heart on practicing Buddhist virtues.

That very year, Shi Huan passed the civil service examinations and obtained an official post. His wife and concubine followed him to his duty station and later gave birth to two sons each. Gui Qian was well provided for by the Shi family, with whom he lived out the rest of his days. The Shi and Zhi clans prospered and multiplied and came to be leading clans of the East Wu region of our day. Truly,

For his repentance, Gui Qian was free of illness;
For Shi Ji's good deeds, the family line prospered.
To all and sundry, this word of advice:
Heaven blesses not the ungrateful man!

26

Scholar Tang Gains a Wife after One Smile (Originally titled "Scholar Tang's Remarkable Romance")

Roosters crow at the fourth strike of the night-watch drum;
The moon descends following the rise of the sun.
Autumn and winter bring spring and summer;
Boats and carts go one way and then another.
The mirror shows the aging of the face;
The world witnesses the ups and downs of life.
To get away for a moment of peace,
A flask of wine and an exquisite meal.

The above eight lines were written by a talented scholar of the Wu region. Tang Yin [1470–1523] by name, courtesy name Bohu, he had a sharp mind that was unrivaled anywhere on earth and knew everything there was to know under the sun.[1] A master in all the arts of calligraphy, painting, and music, he was also prodigiously gifted in the writing of prose and verse, which he invariably did with one flourish of his brushpen. He was most unconventional in his social behavior and held the material world in disdain. Born in Su County, he later took up residence in Wuqu Street in the city of Suzhou.

After he passed the imperial examinations at the county level and became a *xiucai,* he wrote more than ten poems on flowers and the moon, using a parallel rhythmic style, with each line containing the words "flowers" and "the moon." For example, "Flowers greeting the moon cast shadows on the sky / I return home to flowers bathed in moonlight" and "The moon peeks at flowers through cracks in the clouds / Flowers sleep in moonlight deep in the night." These lines won much praise.

Cao Feng, the local prefect, was so impressed by Tang Yin's poems that, at the next provincial-level civil service examinations, he recommended that Tang Yin be admitted to the exam without taking the screening examination on account of his talent. The examiner, Fang Zhi by name and a native of Yin County, was most ill-disposed toward literary compositions in ancient styles. ([Illegible.]) Upon hearing that Tang Yin was a man with a high opinion of his own talent and did not feel bound by conventional decorum, the examiner had a good mind to single him out for punishment. Thanks to Prefect Cao, who defended Tang to the best of his ability, no calamity befell Tang, but he was barred from the examinations. It was not until the exams had already started that, owing to the desperate pleas of Prefect Cao, he was granted permission to take the examinations, as the very last person on the add-on list of unscreened candidates. As it turned out, he came out first.

For the next level of the examinations, Tang Bohu traveled to the capital, where he built a name for himself as a man of literary talent. The lords and ministers set their dignity aside and took pride in making his acquaintance.

It so happened that the chief examiner, Imperial Tutor Mr. Cheng, who was known to have sold examination questions for personal gain, was on the lookout for a celebrated and talented scholar to put at the top of the list of successful candidates, so as to prevent tongues from wagging and silence his detractors. (*Public opinion, however, is most just.*) Much delighted upon making Tang Yin's acquaintance, he promised to let him win top honors.

Being a straightforward man by nature, Bohu boasted to his drinking companions, "This year, I'll place first in the exams, and that's for sure!"

Imperial Tutor Cheng's shady dealings were no secret to the public and Tang Bohu's talent was an object of jealousy, so rumors of the examiner's unfairness began to float around. When officials charged with remonstrating with the emperor got wind of this,[2] they wrote a memorial to the emperor, who then ruled that Imperial Tutor Cheng be barred from grading the papers and had Cheng and Tang Yin both thrown into jail for interrogation and demotion.

As a result, Tang Bohu was sent back to his hometown. He abandoned all interest in making his way in the world through the examinations and indulged his love for poetry and wine. He came to be called by all and sundry "Provincial Graduate with the Highest Honor." Those who obtained his writings in verse or prose, pieces of calligraphy, or paintings treasured them, even if they were done on small scraps of paper, as they would priceless objects of art. Painting being his forte, he used it as the means to express the joy, anger, grief, and exultation in his heart. (*What better way to relieve himself of boredom!*) Every time he finished a painting, buyers fought to outbid one another. There is in testimony a quatrain on his outlook of life:

Daoist alchemy or Buddhist meditation,
Trading or farming—all these pursuits, not for me.
I paint and sell my art in moments of leisure
And keep my hands off ill-gotten money.

Now, in Suzhou, there are six city gates—the gates of Feng, Pan, Xu, Chang, Lou, and Qi. Of these, Chang Gate saw the most hustle and bustle of the city and the most congested traffic. Truly,

Well-dressed visitors swarm up and down the towers;
Goods worth millions travel across the waters.

Markets stay open late into the night;
Dialects from all over echo in the air.

One day, Tang Bohu was riding in a pleasure boat past Chang Gate when quite a number of men with a penchant for literature and the arts approached him out of admiration for his fame and spread out their folding fans for him to write or paint on them. So he wielded his brush-pen in the ink-and-wash style of painting and wrote a few quatrains. As word got around, more and more people came over. In irritation, Tang Bohu told his page boy to bring him a large flask of wine and positioned himself by his cabin window to enjoy the wine all by himself. Suddenly, he saw a painted boat passing by. Amid the glittering array of jewelry in the cabin, he noticed a young maid dressed in green, with beautiful features and a graceful deportment. With her head outside the cabin window, she was looking at Bohu and trying to hide her smile behind her hand. (*She is a good judge of men.*) In a trice, the boat overtook Bohu's. As if in a trance, Bohu asked the boatman, "Do you happen to know who owns that boat?"

"It belongs to Academician Hua of Wuxi."

Wishing to follow the boat closely, Bohu called out for a small skiff, but none was to be had. He felt as if he had lost something precious and was about to have his page boy go out to find a boat when he saw one rowing out of the city in his direction. Without caring in the least whether on not there was a passenger in it, he waved and shouted until a man emerged from the cabin, walked to the bow, and said loudly, "Bohu, where are you going? Why all this rush?"

Upon a closer look, Tang Bohu recognized his good friend Wang Yayi. "I need to pay a return visit to a friend from afar. That's why I'm in such a rush. Where are you off to, my brother?"

"I'm going with two relatives to Mount Mao to offer incense.[3] We'll be staying there for a few days."

"I've also been meaning to go to Mount Mao and offer incense but haven't been able to find a companion. Now, I can go with you."

"If you want to join me, go home quickly and pack. I'll moor the boat here and wait for you."

"I'm ready to go now. Why should I go home first?"

"But don't you need to prepare some incense and candles?"

"I'll buy them over there!" So Tang sent his page boy home, and without so much as a word of good-bye for those who were still waiting for his poems and paintings, he jumped into Wang Yayi's boat.

After greeting Wang's friends in the cabin, he shouted, "Let's get under way!" Knowing this was Tang, Provincial Graduate with the Highest Honor, the boatman dared not ignore him but hastened to punt and row. Some moments later, they came in sight of the painted boat. Tang Bohu told the boatman to follow the big boat. No one had any idea why he wanted to do so, but all felt obliged to humor him.

The next day, they arrived in Wuxi, the painted boat having preceded them and rowed its way into the city. Tang said, "Once in Wuxi, only the uncultured would fail to fetch water from Hui Mountain Spring." So saying, he asked the boatman to go to Hui Mountain to get some water and return to the mooring spot before they continued the journey the next day, adding, "We'll take a walk in the city and come back to the boat in good time."

Thus instructed, the boatman set off on his errand. Tang Bohu, Wang Yayi, and a couple of the other passengers went ashore and onto the city streets. Amid the hustle and bustle, Tang abandoned his friends and commenced a one-man search for the painted boat. But as he was unfamiliar with the layout of the city, he wandered around for quite a while without seeing a trace of the boat. Eventually, he found himself on a major thoroughfare. Upon hearing cries to clear the street, he stopped in his tracks and saw a curtained sedan-chair led by about ten valets coming from an easterly direction. Following the sedan-chair was a procession of maidservants.

As the ancients put it, "Those with a predestined bond will meet, however great the distance between them." Among the maidservants, he spotted the very girl in green whom he had seen when passing by Chang Gate. Joyfully he followed the procession at a distance until it stopped at the gate of a big mansion and was ushered in by some female servants who had come out to greet it. Upon inquiries of passers-by, he learned that this was the establishment of Academician Hua and that the person in the sedan-chair was the Academician's wife. Having acquired this information, he asked for directions out of the city.

By a happy coincidence, the boatman had also just arrived with the spring water. Soon, Wang Yayi and the others came back, too. They asked Tang Bohu, "Where were you? We looked for you everywhere!"

"I don't know what happened," replied Tang, "but somehow I got pushed away from you in the jostling crowd, and without knowing my way around, I had a hard time getting back here." Of what truly had happened, he said not a word.

At midnight, he broke into frenzied cries, as if he were under an evil spell in a nightmare. His friends all woke up in alarm. To their questions, he replied, "In my dream just a moment ago, a god in gold armor hit me with a golden rod, scolding me for not being devout enough in my incense-offering trip. I kowtowed to him and asked for forgiveness, promising to observe a vegetarian diet for one month before I go to the temple alone to apologize. At daybreak, you can continue on your way, but I'll have to be excused."

Yayi and the others believed his story. At dawn, a small boat heading for Suzhou happened to appear, so Tang Bohu took leave of his friends and leaped into it. Some moments later, he told the boatman to turn back, saying that he had left something behind. He produced a few pennies from his sleeve, paid the boatman, and stepped ashore in high spirits.

Into a restaurant he went. There, he bought some worn, old clothes and a tattered hat and changed into them, making himself look like a pauper. He then proceeded to a pawnshop run by the Hua establishment and, claiming he had some items to pawn, asked to see the manager. In all humility, he said to the manager, "My name is Kang Xuan, a native of Wu County. Being a good calligrapher, I used to run my own school, but recently my wife died (*A story spun on the spur of the moment.*) and I lost my school. Left on my own and without a means of support, I would like to serve as something of a scribe in a rich man's establishment. I wonder if your master is in need of my services? If so, I would be ever so grateful!" From his sleeve, he pulled out a scroll bearing several lines of his calligraphy in small script.

Impressed by the well-shaped and graceful characters, the manager replied, "Let me report to the master tonight. Come back tomorrow for a reply."

That very evening, the manager did indeed show the sample of Tang's calligraphy to the Academician, who said in praise, "Beautiful! Certainly not the work of some run-of-the-mill calligrapher. Bring him to me tomorrow."

The next morning, Tang Bohu arrived at the pawnshop again. The manager then led him into the presence of the Academician. Observing Tang's refined manners, the Academician asked him his name and where he lived. He also asked, "How much education have you had?"

"I've sat for the examinations several times in my youth without ever having had a chance for formal education, but I do remember the classics."

"Which books of the classics?"

Though he specialized in *The Book of History,* Tang Bohu was in fact well versed in all five classics but, knowing that the Academician specialized in *The Book of Changes,* he said, "*The Book of Changes.*"

Much delighted, the Academician said, "I already have enough people doing calligraphy work for me in the study, but I could use you as my son's study companion."

When the Academician queried him as to wages, Tang replied, "I wouldn't dare demand wages. Some clothes will suffice. Later, should the master be pleased with my service, I'll be content if I'm given a good wife."

Even more pleased, the Academician had the manager find a few pieces of clothing for Tang in the pawnshop and changed his name to Hua An. Hua An was then conducted into the study, where he greeted the young master. When the young master gave him some script to copy, he made corrections freely whenever he came upon an infelicitous choice of words. Much surprised by the stylistic improvements, the young master said, "So, you are quite an educated man. When did you abandon your studies?"

Hua An replied, "I've never been remiss in my studies. It's just that poverty has reduced me to such a state."

A delighted young master asked him to revise his daily homework. With never a pause, Hua An made corrections that veritably changed iron into gold.

Sometimes when the young master had difficulties understanding the essay questions, Hua An explained things to him. When the young master found himself baffled, Hua An wrote the essays on his behalf. The young master's mentor, struck by the rapid progress, praised the young man to his father in glowing terms. The Academician asked for a sample of his son's recent writing and, after reading it, said, shaking his head, "This is beyond my son. This is either copied from somewhere, or the work of a hired ghostwriter."

When summoned for questioning, the young master dared not hide the truth. "Hua An revised it," he admitted. ([Illegible].)

Astounded, the Academician summoned Hua An and gave him a topic on which to write an essay on the spot. Without a moment's hesitation, Hua An wrote the essay as fast as his brush-pen could go. When he had finished, he held it out in his hands for the Academician to examine, and the latter noticed that Hua An's wrist was as smooth as jade and there was an extra thumb on his left hand. Upon reading the essay, the Academician found the diction so refined, the argument so well developed, and the calligraphy so graceful that he commented, "If you can write like this in the contemporary style, you must be proficient in the traditional style as well!" Thereupon, he decided to keep Hua An in the study to take charge of all his correspondence. Henceforth, all letters going out of the Hua establishment were penned by Hua An according to oral instructions from the Academician. Whatever the length or complexity of the letters, the Academician never saw a need to add or delete one character.

As he rose higher and higher in the Academician's favor and received more rewards than any other employee in the establishment, Hua An often bought wine and food to share with the page boys on duty in the study, to their immense joy. Quietly, he asked around about the girl in green and found out that her name was Qiuxiang [Autumn Fragrance]. But, being Lady Hua's personal maid, she was never out of her mistress's presence. Unable to come up with a plan, he wrote a lyric poem to the tune of "Song of an Oriole," lamenting the imminent demise of spring:

The wind and the rain send spring on its way;
The cuckoos grieve; the flowers fly around.
The yard overgrown with moss, the red gate is closed.
With the forlorn lampwick burning low,
I lie sideways on my woebegone quilt,
All by my lonely self, my face awash with tears.
When shall I return to my much-missed one?
My spring dreams vanish to the end of the sky.

One day, the Academician went by chance to Hua An's room and saw the poem on the wall. Knowing it must be the work of Hua An, he praised it with enthusiasm. As for the melancholy tone of the poem, he assumed that Tang, a man still in the prime of his life, must be heartbroken over the death of his wife. The

Academician little knew that the poem had been written with someone else in mind.

The manager of the pawnshop happened to die of illness at this time, and the Academician had Hua An take over the shop. After more than a month, upon finding Hua An to be meticulous in his work with never a slightest error in the account books, the Academician had a mind to make him manager. However, as it would be awkward to entrust a bachelor with an important responsibility, the Academician consulted his wife and engaged a matchmaker to find a wife for Hua An.

Hua An gave the matchmaker three taels of silver and asked her to convey this message to Lady Hua: "Hua An is profoundly grateful to the master and the mistress for the promotion as well as the offer to find him a wife. But he's afraid that girls from ordinary families outside the establishment won't be able to adapt to the house rules here, so he's hoping to marry one of your maids." The matchmaker duly conveyed the message to Lady Hua, who then spoke to the Academician.

"That would be even better for both parties," said the Academician. "There's one thing, though. He said when he first came here that he was willing to forgo wages and wished only for a good wife. Now that he's become so useful to me, I'm afraid he might pursue other ambitions if the girl we offer him is not to his liking. We'd better summon him to the main hall and let him take his pick among the many maids we'll present to him." (*That could not have suited Bohu better.*) Lady Hua nodded in agreement.

That very night, with Lady Hua sitting in the brightly lit main hall, more than twenty maids, all dressed up in finery, stood on both sides of her, not unlike the fairy maidens gathered around the Queen Mother of Fairyland by the Jasper Pool. At Lady Hua's order, Hua An entered the hall and greeted her with a bow.

Lady Hua announced, "The master wants to offer you a wife as a reward for your faithful service. You may take your pick among these maids." This said, she had an old housekeeper hold a candle so that Hua An could take a good look at the girls. By the light of the candle, Hua An inspected all the candidates and found most to be pretty, but the girl in green was not there. He stepped to one side of the hall and stood still in silence.

Lady Hua addressed the old housekeeper, "Go ask Hua An which one he likes. He can have whomever he fancies."

Hua An remained silent. Displeased, Lady Hua raised her voice, "Hua An! Are the pupils of your eyes not large enough to see all these maids of mine? Don't tell me none is to your liking!"

"Madam, I can never repay your immense kindness in offering me a wife and allowing me to choose her myself. Such kindness has never been known since time immemorial. I'll never be able to repay you. But Your Ladyship's personal maids are not all here yet. Since you are already doing me such a kindness, may I be granted the privilege of seeing all of them?"

Lady Hua replied with a smile, "So you suspect me of being stingy? All right, bring the four girls in my chamber and show them to him, just to make him happy."

These four girls were Chunmei [Spring Charm], Xiaqing [Summer Limpidity], Qiuxiang [Autumn Fragrance], and Dongrui [Winter Fortune]. Each had her own responsibilities: Chunmei was in charge of Her Ladyship's jewelry and cosmetics, Xiaqing's job was to tend to the incense burner and tea stove, Qiuxiang's responsibilities were to prepare clothes for all four seasons, and Dongrui took care of wine, fruit, and food. Acting on Lady Hua's orders, the old housekeeper summoned the four girls. Having been given no time to change, the four emerged in their daily casual wear, Qiuxiang still in green. The old housekeeper conducted them into the main hall and made them stand behind Her Ladyship. The hall was lit as bright as day, and Hua An easily saw the girl in all her grace and charm, just as he remembered her. Before he had a chance to speak, the housekeeper asked tactfully, "So, does any one of them strike your fancy?"

Knowing all too well that her name was Qiuxiang, Hua An said, pointing a finger, without daring to blurt out the name, "If I could but have that young lady in green, I shall have nothing more to wish for throughout the rest of my life."

Casting a glance at Qiuxiang over her shoulder, Lady Hua smiled ever so slightly and told Hua An to leave.

Back in the pawnshop, Hua An was filled with feelings of mixed joy and fear—joy because the opportunity could not have been better, and fear because she was not yet his and anything could still go wrong. As his eyes happened to rest upon the glorious moon, shining as bright as day, he paced up and down and intoned a poem:

"Listless, I pace around in the deepening night;
Birds perch on green willows in the windless air.
With no one to share what weighs on my mind,
I tell it to the blue sky and the lambent moon."

The next day, Lady Hua recounted what had happened to the Academician. A room was cleaned and decorated, complete with bed curtains and all other furnishings imaginable. Eager to please the new manager, the servants and page boys of the entire establishment scurried around, fetching and carrying, until the bridal chamber looked like a piece of ornate embroidery.

On a chosen auspicious day, with the Academician and his wife officiating at the wedding ceremony, Hua An and Qiuxiang made their bows in the main hall before proceeding to the bridal chamber, led by a drum orchestra, for the consummation of their marriage. Let us spare the audience the details of the fulfillment of their love but come to the point where, at midnight, Qiuxiang said to Hua An, "I think I must have seen you before, but where?"

"Think hard, young lady!" replied Hua An.

A few days later, Qiuxiang suddenly asked Hua An, "Was it you I saw in the pleasure boat by Chang Gate some time ago?"

Smiling, Hua An said yes.

"If that was indeed you, you're by no means of lowly status. Why do you degrade yourself by accepting employment in this place?"

"I saw you smile by your cabin window, and the memory of that smile stayed with me so vividly that I did all this scheming and plotting, just to be with you."

"I saw you drinking all by yourself at the cabin window, totally oblivious of those young men around you begging you to write and paint on their white fans. I smiled because I could see that you are not of the common run." (*A good judge of character.*)

"As a woman who recognizes a man of worth from among the uncultured masses, you're as remarkable as Hong Fo and Zhuo Wenjun."[4]

"But after that encounter, I believe we met once again on South Gate Street, didn't we?"

Hua An said laughingly, "What sharp eyes you have! Yes, that is quite true, quite true."

"If you're not as lowly as you make yourself out to be, who *are* you? Tell me your real name."

"I am Tang of Suzhou, Provincial Graduate with the Highest Honor. My wish has been fulfilled because I have with you a predestined bond that's long enough to last three lifetimes. Now that you know who I am, I can't stay here any longer. Would you be willing to follow me so that we can live out the rest of our lives together?"

"Since you didn't hesitate to degrade your noble self for my sake, how can I not do what you want me to do?"

The next day, Hua An copied details of all pawnshop transactions into an account book. In another notebook, he listed all the articles of clothing, jewelry, and furnishings in the bridal chamber. Next, he made a record of all the gifts he had received. Without taking a fraction of a penny's worth of anything, he locked the three documents in a book box and left the key in the lock. Then, he wrote a poem on the wall:

I was on my way to Huayang Cave[5]
When the beauty stopped me right in my tracks.
Hoping for a quiet life with Hong Fo,[6]
Humbly I entered the service of Zhu Jia.[7]
Whoever would scoff at this happy event?
Sheepishly I take my leave, quite ashamed.
Should the master wish to know who I am,
In Kang Xuan is found my name.

That very evening, he hired a small boat and moored it by the riverbank. In the quiet of the evening, he locked his door, got into the boat with Qiuxiang, and set off posthaste for Suzhou.

At daybreak, a servant noticed the lock on Hua An's door and ran to report the matter to the Academician, who ordered the door to be opened. When all the furnishings were found intact and account books containing detailed entries were discovered in the book box, the Academician was plunged into thought, wondering what could have led to this. Raising his head, he saw the eight lines on the wall and, after reading them, thought to himself, "Surely Kang Xuan isn't his name." But why, he wondered, would the man want to stay in his house for so long? If he had evil designs, why did he leave without taking a penny? Why was Qiuxiang willing to elope with him, and where could they be now? "Losing this maid is not important to me," he thought, "but I want to get to the bottom of this." Thereupon, he had servants summon the police. He wrote a note offering a reward for the capture of Kang Xuan and Qiuxiang and had posters put up everywhere. After more than a year had gone by without the slightest clue, the Academician put the matter aside.

One day, the Academician went to Suzhou to visit a friend. A page boy employed by the Academician was passing by Chang Gate and saw a scholar who bore a strong resemblance to Hua An sitting in a bookstore reading a book. The scholar's left hand also had an extra thumb. The Academician did not believe the page boy's report and told the boy to go back for a closer look and find out the man's name. So the boy went back. Upon entering the bookstore, he found the scholar in conversation with another man of a similar age. As soon as they left the store and walked down the steps, the sharp-witted page boy followed stealthily behind, and saw that the two men made for Tongzi Gate, where they embarked on a boat, followed by four or five servants. Viewed from behind, the scholar was the very image of Hua An, but the page boy dared not make a move that would be construed as presumptuous.

He returned to the bookstore and asked the storekeeper, "Who was the man reading here some moments ago?"

"That was Tang Bohu, Provincial Graduate with the Highest Honor. He's just been invited by Mr. Wen Hengshan[8] to have a drink on his boat."

"So the man with him is Mr. Wen?"

"No, that's Zhu Zhishan,[9] another celebrity."

The page boy made a mental note of the names and reported back to Academician Hua. The Academician was astounded. "I've long heard of Tang Bohu and his unconventional behavior," he thought to himself. "Can Hua An be the same man? Let me pay him a visit tomorrow, and I'll find out the truth."

The next day, he wrote up a visiting card and went to Wuqu Street to visit Tang. With alacrity, Tang went out to greet him, and they sat down as host and guest. Taking a good look at Tang, the Academician thought him to be indeed the very image of Hua An. When Tang offered a cup of tea, the Academician noticed that his host's hands were as white as jade, and there was an extra thumb on his left hand. He had a good mind to ask but found it hard to frame the words.

When they had finished their tea, Tang Bohu invited the Academician into the study. Unwilling to leave with the question in his mind unanswered, the Academician followed his host into the study. There, he burst into praises for the tasteful furnishings. Soon, wine was brought in. When they were well into their drinking, the Academician spoke up. "In your county, there is a man called Kang Xuan. He had no luck with the examinations but is quite a fine scholar. Do you, sir, happen to know him?"

Tang mumbled something noncommittal. The Academician continued, "Last year, he entered into service in my household and had his name changed to Hua An. He started out as a study companion for my son and then took charge of affairs in my study. Later, he rose to be the manager of my small pawnshop. He was a bachelor, so I let him choose a wife from among the maids of the household, and he picked Qiuxiang. Several days after the wedding, the couple slipped away without taking anything from the house. I wonder why they did that. I sent investigators to your county, but they failed to locate this man. Have you, sir, heard anything about him?"

Tang again mumbled something unintelligible. His patience wearing thin at the man's evasiveness, the Academician continued, "That man bears a strong resemblance to you. He even has an extra thumb on his left hand, just as you do. I marvel at the coincidence."

Tang again gave a vague sound. Soon, he rose, excused himself for a short absence, and went to the inner quarters of the house. While he was away, the Academician flipped through the books on the desk. He came upon a scroll bearing an eight-line poem, read it, and found it to be the very same poem written on the wall of Hua An's room. When Tang Bohu returned, the Academician asked, holding the poem, "This eight-line poem was written by Hua An, and in his own handwriting, too. How did it get here? There must be a reason behind this. Please tell me the truth and solve this mystery for me."

"Let me tell you everything in a while."

Feeling even more vexed, the Academician countered, "I'll stay if you will enlighten me. Otherwise, I must take my leave."

"The story can be easily told," said Tang. "Please have a few more cups of my watery wine, sir."

After the Academician did so, Tang Bohu plied him with more, using an oversize wine vessel. Half tipsy, the Academician said, "I've had more than enough. I shouldn't keep drinking. All I'm asking with such determination is simply that you shed light on this mystery that preys on my mind. Nothing more."

"Please stay just a little longer for a simple supper," pleaded Tang.

With supper over, tea was served. As evening began to set in, a page boy entered with lit candles. All the more disconcerted, the Academician felt obliged to rise and take his leave.

"Please don't go yet, sir. Your question will be duly answered." So saying, Tang had a page boy lead the way, bearing candles, while he and the Academician followed, until they entered the brightly illuminated back hall. As a shout announced the arrival of the bride, a young lady appeared, supported by two maids, her dainty feet moving gracefully, her lovely face covered with stringed beads hanging from her headdress.

Alarmed, the Academician tried to avoid the encounter, but Tang Bohu grabbed his sleeve and explained, "This is my wife. You need not try to remove yourself from this female presence because, being a venerable elder from the bride's family, you, sir, should by rights accept bows of greeting from her."

The maids having spread out a carpet, the young bride prostrated herself. Before the Academician could return the courtesy, eager as he was to do so, Tang Bohu held him fast and stopped him. The Academician responded to the young lady's prostrations, which she repeated four times, bowing slightly from the waist two times, feeling quite embarrassed. The greetings over, Tang led the young lady to the Academician and said with a smile, "Please take a good look, sir. You said that I bear a strong resemblance to Hua An. Perhaps you will find that this girl resembles Qiuxiang?"

The Academician looked closely at her and broke into hearty laughter. He hastened to bow and offer his apologies.

"No, I should be the one offering apologies," said Tang, whereupon the two men returned to the study. Tang Bohu ordered that tableware be laid out anew and the wine cups washed clean for another round of drinking, In the course of the drinking, the Academician inquired about the details, and Tang replied with an account of how he and Qiuxiang had first seen each other on their boats by Chang Gate. As both men roared with laughter, rubbing their hands, the Academician said, "I won't presume to salute you as an official, but at least, I should observe the decorum of a father to a son-in-law."

Tang replied, "If we are to formally celebrate our relationship as son-in-law and father-in-law, I'm afraid that I'll be putting you to the expense of a dowry!" Again, they erupted into laughter. That night, they did not part company until they had thoroughly enjoyed themselves.

After returning to his boat, the Academician took out the scroll of poem from his sleeve and laid it on the desk. Pondering the meaning of the lines, he said to himself, "As for the first couplet, the first line 'I was on my way to Huayang Cave' refers to the intended trip to offer incense at Mount Mao. 'When the beauty stopped me right in my tracks' says that the journey was abandoned for the sake of Qiuxiang, whom he encountered halfway. The second couplet, 'Hoping for a quiet life with Hong Fo / Humbly I entered the service of Zhu Jia' means that he had plans to elope from the time he first entered my service, stooping below his station in life.

The third couplet 'Whoever would scoff at this happy event? / Sheepishly I take my leave, quite ashamed' is clear enough in meaning. As for the last couplet, 'Should the master wish to know who I am, / In Kang Xuan is found my name,' the character *kang* has the same upper radical as the character *tang,* and the character *xuan* has the same upper radical as the character *yin.* I would never have been able to take that hint and figure out the name Tang Yin. He may have acted like a love-crazed man, but the fact that he left the clothes and jewelry behind shows that he fully deserves his fame as a romantically inclined man of worth with a profound sense of decency and decorum."

Upon returning home, he related the story to his wife, to her utter astonishment. They prepared a generous dowry worth thousands of taels of silver and had the old housekeeper escort the gift-bearing procession to Tang's residence. Henceforth, being related through marriage, the two families kept up an endless stream of visits to each other. To this day, this romantic story is still circulating in the Wu region. There is a most well-written song by Tang Bohu stating his philosophy of life. It says:

Reflecting on my life while sitting by the incense,
I murmur to myself, voicing my thoughts.
Do I wish to do harm to others?
Have I evil thoughts that find their way to my mouth?
To speak from the heart is the beginning
Of filial piety, loyalty, and faith.
Lapses in virtues of a lesser nature
Do little harm to overall conduct.
A flower stem on my head, a wine cup in hand,
I listen to songs and watch the dances.
Eating and sex are human nature, the ancients said,
But people of today regard them as a disgrace.
With a gap between the heart and the mouth,
Divine will is flouted all too often.
To cover up vice with moralistic talk
Is but fruitless labor to no avail.
Sit still, and take this advice from me:
All human beings go through birth and death.
He who faces the King of Hell with a clear conscience
Is truly a man of dignity and honor.

27

Fake Immortals Throw Guanghua Temple into an Uproar

Those trying to attain immortality,
First take a lesson in morality:
Eternal life is nothing but a myth;
An immortal is he who has
Good health, few worldly desires,
And a pure heart open and frank.

As the story goes, in the Song dynasty, there stood a Baoshan Temple by Puji Bridge in Hangzhou. Built in the Jiatai reign period [1201–05], it was also called Huaguang Temple and was dedicated to the Five Gods of Wuxian.[1] Which five?

First, the god of judiciousness, benevolence, and kindness;
Second, the god of wisdom, righteousness, and harmony;
Third, the god of integrity, sapience, and responsiveness;
Fourth, the god of probity, love, and largesse;
Fifth, the god of morality, trust, and joy.

These five deities corresponding to the five phases are 'most responsive to prayers.[2] Some say they are none other than the Five Gods of Wutong, but that is not true.[3]

In the first year of the Shaoding reign period [1228–34], Prime Minister Zheng Qingzhi had the temple renovated and expanded until it looked absolutely magnificent. During the wars of the Yuan dynasty, the priests fled and went their separate ways, the walls of the temple crumbled, and the houses of the local inhabitants around the temple also fell into decay. In the first years of the Zhizheng reign period [1341–68], priests solicited donations for repairs to the temple and worship services resumed, but of this, no more need be said.

Let us now concentrate our attention on a scholar named Wei Yu, who pursued his studies with his cousin Fu Daoqin in a small two-storied house in the vicinity of the temple. Mr. Wei was seventeen years of age and had the graceful deportment, gentle manners, and soft speech of a virgin. At every literary gathering that he attended, his peers would make fun of him, calling him "Lady Wei." His cheeks burning with the humiliation, he decided never to be seen at social functions again. He shut himself up on the second floor of the house and devoted himself to his studies, with Mr. Fu his only companion day in and day out.

One day, Mr. Fu went home to take care of his sick mother, leaving Mr. Wei alone at his studies. At about the second watch of the night, a knock was heard at the door. Thinking it was his cousin, he opened the door and saw a gentleman wearing a silk hat and a yellow robe with blue sleeves and carrying a horse-tail whisk in his hand. With his graceful bearing and elegant beard flowing in a soft, fragrant breeze, he had the air of an immortal flying over the clouds. Behind him stood a young, refined-looking Daoist acolyte holding a vermilion box in his hands.

The gentleman spoke up. "I am Lü Dongbin,[4] also known as Chunyang [Pure Yang], and I am passing this place in my wanderings across the four seas. From up in the air, I heard your voice ringing clear when you were reading your text aloud. With your diligence, you will surely succeed in the civil service examinations. Moreover, you are fated to be an immortal. (*Resorting to flattery because mortal beings have a weakness for it.*) As I have a predestined bond with you, it is my duty to deliver you from this world. That's why I pay you this visit, knowing you now live by yourself."

These words came as such a pleasant surprise to Wei that he promptly sank to his knees and bowed. Then, after inviting the immortal to sit facing south in the seat of honor, he sat down by one side. Lü Dongbin had the acolyte bring over a box and lay its contents on the table. Soon, the table was covered with fresh exotic fruits and delicacies from the mountains and the seas, the aromas of which assailed the nostrils. There also stood gold wine cups and a white jade flask less than three inches tall from which flowed an unending stream of wine the color of amber and with the taste of the finest cream. Dongbin said, "This spread of food and wine is for the consumption of immortals. You are allowed to enjoy it because you have a predestined bond with the world of the immortals."

By this time, Wei was in a trance, feeling as if he were in a fairyland. In the course of the drinking, Dongbin said, "This remarkable encounter tonight is an occasion that calls for poems." Wei was eager to see a poem by an immortal and laid out the four treasures of the scholar's study on the table.[5] Without pausing to reflect, Dongbin picked up the brush-pen and wrote four poems.

The first one said:

The Yellow Crane Tower emits a divine aura;
At the Peach Feast, the immortals enjoy the nectar.
Their swords shining across the sea in the autumn sun,
They ride the clouds every dusk to the Lord's abode.

The second one said:

Clouds and mist float around the tall towers;
I take a nap up in a fairyland.
The sky and the earth grow old as I sleep;
I wake up to a world beyond recognition.

The third one said:

A gold pill gives one immortality;
Few can ever fathom the mystery.
As night falls, the strains of celestial music
Mark the hour for immortals to ride the cranes.

The fourth one said:

The swords across the sky, the moon over the sea,
In an instant, I travel across the land.
The magic peaches ripen three thousand times,
While in the mortal world, nine hundred years go by.

At the sight of the lively calligraphic flourishes, Wei was profuse in his praise.

Dongbin said, "With your outstanding talent, why don't you improvise a poem? I'll see how soon you'll be fulfilling your destiny as an immortal."

Wei composed two quatrains. The first one said:

Over the jade trees tower the twelve peaks;
I spend this life climbing the ladder to the sky.
In the clean air of the cosmos, free of dust,
Draped in rosy clouds, to the Big Dipper I bow.

The second one said:

With the moon shining in the faraway sky,
I find myself in Feiyin Pavilion.[6]
In the moonlit quietness of the night,
The crane takes me all the way to a fairyland.

After reading the poems, Dongbin said, smiling at Wei, "So you have your heart set on fairyland. An immortal you are indeed meant to be. Back in the Western Han dynasty, General Huo Qubing [140–117 B.C.E.] was praying in a temple when the god of the temple appeared to him in the shape of a woman and asked to be his wife. Qubing was enraged and left in a huff. Later, he became critically ill and sent a follower to the temple to plead for help. The god said, 'Since General Huo has such a feeble constitution, I meant to build up his health with the essence of the *yin* element in the universe, but the general, in his ignorance, rejected my offer, believing it to be motivated by lust. There's no hope that he'll recover from his illness now.' Soon thereafter, the general died. So, the immortals have different means at their disposal for delivering mortal beings, means that are quite beyond mortal knowledge. Only those predestined to be immortals are free of doubt. (*What a clever tongue!*) I have another poem for you."

Meeting you tonight in this jade tower,
The self-invited guest toasts you by the lamp.
The flowing nectar glistens like crystal;
The inspired poems travel to Mount Wu.[7]
Bid farewell to this world of mortals;
Fulfill your destiny and rise to the sky.
With that day approaching soon enough,
You'll roam, a free soul, among the white clouds.

Wei read the poem, understood the message, and wrote a quatrain in response:

The fairyland is free of earthly desires;
The Way allows no worldly thoughts.
The Rear Court should be bare of trees and flowers;[8]
Envy not the lecherous Emperor Suiyang.[9]

After this exchange, the two felt ever more well disposed toward each other. To the acolyte, Dongbin said, "You may go. I'm staying here overnight." Turning to Wei, he said, "If you could meet with me for ten days and nights, I will surely give you such energy and agility of mind that you'll be able to memorize a ten-thousand-word essay every day." Wei believed him.

When they were quite tipsy with wine, Dongbin went to bed first. After Wei lay down by his side, fully clothed, Dongbin said, "It is only through physical contact that a mortal being receives divine energy. If you sleep fully clothed like this, I won't be of use to you at all." Thereupon, he held Wei in his arms, undid Wei's clothes, and made the young man share his pillow. He then started caressing Wei until he got quite carried away with his act of debauchery. In order to benefit from his divine energy, Wei put up with him.

At the first crowing of the roosters, Dongbin said to Wei, "You are not to divulge this celestial secret to anyone. I have to take my leave now, while it's still dark. Let's meet again tonight." So saying, he pushed open a window and was gone.

Mouth agape in astonishment, Wei was convinced that the visitor was a genuine immortal. He picked up the wine vessels and examined them and found them to be truly made of gold and jade, exquisitely carved and lovely in design. The fragrance from the pillow and the bed still lingered in the air, plunging Wei into dreamy thoughtfulness.

When evening set in, Dongbin appeared again to spend the night with Wei, and more than ten nights thereafter went by in like fashion. The two grew more and more fond of each other and came to hate the thought of parting.

One evening, in the midst of drinking, Dongbin said to Wei, "Yesterday, on her way back from an immortals' fair, He Xiangu learned about what's been happening between you and me.[10] She's in a tearing rage and wants to report me to the Jade Emperor and have the two of us punished. It was only after my repeated pleas that her anger subsided. She was intrigued by my description of your good looks and wants to see you. So, when she does come one of these evenings, you must watch your every move and beg for mercy. I will, of course, also put in a good word for you along the way. If she takes a liking to you, she might even join in the fun. This will never leak out if we can get her on our side, and some divine *yin* vitality from her will also do you good."

Wei's heart exulted. The next day, he busily prepared fine wine and exquisite refreshments and then waited for evening to fall.

Happily for him, Fu Daoqin continued to be absent day after day, leaving him alone on the second floor of the house. Having waited until the night was deep and all was quiet, Wei lit some incense of good quality, laid out the wine and refreshments, made himself up, and waited, dressed in all his finery, for the two immortals to appear.

Lo and behold! Dongbin came into view, leading into the house the female immortal He Xiangu, whose radiant beauty and elegance threw Wei into such raptures that he fell involuntarily to his knees at her feet. Pleased by Wei's good looks, which lived up to the descriptions she had been given, she feigned anger and snapped, "A fine thing the two of you did, violating the rules of the divine realm! This is hardly the behavior of someone who's supposedly pursuing his studies and wants to join the Daoist order, too!" But those sharp words of rebuke were not spoken without a trace of delight. While Wei kowtowed, begging for forgiveness, Dongbin pleaded for mercy, choosing his words carefully.

"Since both of you seem to be repentant," said Xiangu, "I'll forgive you this time." With that, she rose as if to go. Wei begged her to stay, saying, "I have prepared some coarse food of this mortal world for you as a small token of my respect."

Dongbin also urged insistently, "Don't reject the offer of a few well-intended cups of wine. If you go, won't you, an immortal, be hurting human feelings?"

Unable to resist the pressure, Xiangu resignedly sat down.

While they were drinking, Donbgin said to Xiangu, "Mr. Wei writes good poems. We can't let this joyous occasion go by without a poem."

"All right," agreed Xiangu. "You are of a more senior rank, so you may begin with the first couplet."

Dongbin did not bother with the polite pretense of declining.

In the daily pleasure of the cup I wallow
And make merry with fellow immortals. (Dongbin)
With close friends I spend a delightful night,
By the green pond with gold lotus flowers. (Xiangu)

Lucky the man who feels the warmth of the skirt;
A phoenix descends on the human world. (Wei)
Waste not time over the peach blossom creek;
This is the night for the pleasures of the bed! (Dongbin)

Upon reading the lines, Xiangu burst out indignantly, "How dare you two flirt with me?"

Wei promptly kowtowed in apology, while Dongbin gave her these words of advice, "There is as much passion in heaven as on earth. Don't we immortals have stories about the goddess of the Luo River giving a lover her girdle pendant as a keepsake, and the Divine Maiden playing games of clouds and rain?[11] In the mortal world, beautiful women and talented men rarely meet, but this Mr. Wei, who is destined to be an immortal anyway, is actually one of us. Why draw such a line between us and them? Aren't you following the narrow-minded and opinionated ways of the mortal world?"

At these words, Xiangu lowered her head and quietly played with her skirt belt. Dongbin continued, "Now that an understanding has been reached, Wei Yu may bow his thanks to Xiangu for her condescension."

Wei promptly dropped to his knees and bowed. Affably, Xiangu raised him to his feet and the company of three sat down for more drinking. They did not leave the table until they had enjoyed themselves to the full. That night, the three slept together. Wei snuggled up to Xiangu first, and Dongbin's advances followed. With *yin* and *yang* intermingling, they made merry with one another the whole night through.

Xiangu said, "What a remarkable predestined bond has put us together! Let's make another poem, right here against the pillow." Xiangu took the lead in intoning the following poem:

"Eyes dazzled by the light and the mist,
To the passionate the reluctant yields." (Xiangu)
"The willow branches dance in the spring wind;
Rain-washed peach blossoms bob up and down on the waves." (Wei)
"Doubt not your bond with the immortals,
Fulfill your destiny with the joyful union." (Xiangu)
"Touring the universe in fragrant dreams,
I mount the yellow crane, late after a night's sleep." (Dongbin)

At the roosters' first crows, the two immortals rose to leave. Hating to see them go, Wei entreated them to stay a while longer and asked them to come again that evening. Xiangu said bashfully, "If you're cautious and don't breathe a word of this to anyone, I'll come here often."

Henceforth, at least one of the two immortals came every evening. Sometimes they came together. Even though Wei's cousin Fu lived in the same house, he was totally unaware of the activities taking place on the other side of the wall, for the visitors used the window for their comings and goings.

About half a year went by in this fashion, and Wei gradually became emaciated and sallow, a shadow of his former self. His appetite declined, and he felt his spirits rise at night but sink in the daytime. Noticing his sleepiness, Mr. Fu asked what was ailing him, but Wei firmly refused to answer. Fu felt he had no choice but to inform Wei's father.

Mr. Wei Senior went for a visit and was flabbergasted. He took out a mirror so that his son could see himself. The young man was astounded to realize what a bag of bones he had become, yet he turned a deaf ear when his father advised him to return home and seek treatment. So Mr. Wei Senior engaged a physician to go to the young man's study, feel his pulse and diagnose the ailment, and prescribe medicine for a cure.

That very night, the two immortals appeared again. Wei recounted how his father wanted him to move back home after observing his haggard look, and Dongbin said, "For you, a mortal being, to gain eternal life, you need to cast off your old physical form, which means that the flesh of your body must be completely worn away before you find yourself in an immortal's form. This change cannot be detected by the naked eye of a mortal being."

This was enough to convince Wei. He even refused to take the medicine. A few days later, there was not much breath left in him. In panic, Mr. Wei Senior brought his bedding to his son's study and kept him company overnight. At midnight, he noticed the young man talking deliriously, his face turned toward the other side of the bed. Mr. Wei Senior's efforts to wake him were to no avail. Even Fu Daoqin came in from the next room to take a look.

"What are you afraid of, my two venerable teachers?" exclaimed Wei. "Don't go!" So saying, he reached out for them, but his hands landed on none other than his father!

With tears flowing, Mr. Wei Senior cried, "My son! You're more dead than alive now, and still you hold back the truth! Who are the two venerable teachers? They must be evil demons."

"They're two immortals, here to deliver me. They're not evil demons."

Observing that his son was gravely ill, Mr. Wei Senior hired a small sedan-chair and, disregarding the young man's wishes, ordered that he be carried home for recuperation. The young man said, "They gave me some gold cups and a white jade flask. I put them in the bookcase. I want to take them with me." When the bookcase was opened, there for all to see were cups made of yellow mud and a flask made of white mud.

"My son, you should realize now that they are not immortals but evil demons!"

At this point, Wei Junior panicked and came up with a full account of how he had met Lü Dongbin in the temple and Xiangu had appeared on the scene. Mr. Wei Senior was aghast. After asking his wife to get a clean room ready for their son and prepare to attend to the young man in his sickbed, he went out to find a Daoist priest who could perform an exorcism.

Before he had gone many steps, he ran into a Daoist priest coming straight toward him, shaking an announcement bell. The priest greeted him with folded hands, and Mr. Wei hastened to return the courtesy, saying, "Your Reverence, where, may I ask, are you going?"

"I am a disciple of Master Zhang Sanfeng of Mount Wudang in Huguang.[12] My surname is Pei, my Daoist name Shouzheng. My job is to save the people of the land with the Five Thunders method that I have learned. I greeted you, sir, because I noticed an evil aura hovering over your residence."

These words impressed Mr. Wei. He immediately invited the priest into the house and offered a seat reserved for an honored guest. After tea was served, Mr. Wei told Priest Pei what had happened to his son.

"Where is your son now?" asked the priest, whereupon Mr. Wei conducted him to the young man's room. Upon first laying eyes on the son, the priest said to Mr. Wei, "Your son has been bewitched by two evil spirits—one female, one male. Another ten days like this, and he'll be gone."

In terror, Mr. Wei got down on his knees and begged, "Your Reverence, please have compassion and save my unworthy son! I will never forget your kindness!"

"I will capture the evil spirits for you this very night."

"That would be wonderful! If you need anything, please let me know, and I'll get it for you."

"I need cooked meat for sacrifice, wine, fruit, paper horses for the Five Thunders method, incense, candles, cinnabar, and some yellow paper." After giving these instructions, he added, "I'm taking leave of you now. I'll be back in the evening."

When he was seeing Priest Pei out, Mr. Wei said, "Be sure to come this evening."

"Of course," promised Priest Pei, and he began walking down the street, shaking his announcement bell, as before.

Without a moment's delay, Mr. Wei set about preparing the required items. Soon, everything was ready for Priest Pei's exorcism. And the priest did return in the evening. Mr. Wei greeted him and said, "All the things you requested are ready, but where do you want to put them?"

"In your son's room."

Thereupon, two tables were carried in, the sacrificial meats and other items were laid out, and incense sticks were lit. Priest Pei put on his Daoist cap, donned his robe, and, sword in hand, began moving around the floor along the imagined outline of the Big Dipper, chanting incantations and drawing magic figures with cinnabar. He was about to burn a magic figure when he noticed that it was dripping with water and therefore not flammable.

"Vermin!" he thundered. "Don't you try to get smart with me!" With that, he tossed his sword into the air, but the evil spirits caught the sword and fixed it there in the middle of the room. Nothing the priest did would budge it the least bit.

Terrified, Priest Pei went through his entire repertoire of magic tricks, but none worked.

Eyeing the priest, Mr. Wei Senior asked, "Where's Your Reverence's cap?"

"I didn't take it off. Why is it gone? How very strange!" Immediately he sent someone to look for it. It was found floating on the surface of some night soil outside the door. Though the cap was retrieved, it had such a foul stench that it could not be worn. Priest Pei conceded, "These evil spirits are too powerful for me. I'm no match for them. You'll have to find someone else."

Despite his disappointment, Mr. Wei Senior felt obliged to have the priest distribute the sacrificial items to onlookers and to offer him some wine and food. As it was already well into the night, he put the priest up for the night. Both were in low spirits.

In a side room, a dejected Priest Pei took off his clothes, ready to go to sleep, but when he was about to close his eyes, he saw three or four muscular men clad in yellow lowering onto him a stone slab weighing forty to fifty catties. They were saying, "This is to thank you for the nice job you did, you scoundrel of a priest!"

Choking and unable to move at all under the weight, Priest Pei cried out in consternation, "There are evil spirits around! Help! Help!"

It so happened that Mr. Wei Senior and some household staff were still at work, putting the house back in order. They heard the priest crying for help and went to his room, carrying lamps and candles in their hands. Finding him motionless under a stone slab, two or three men rushed forward, moved the stone, and helped him up. They then fed him warm ginger soup. When it grew light in the east, Priest Pei woke up. After washing and combing his hair, he ate some porridge for breakfast, took leave of Mr. Wei, and went his way. But of him, no more. Thus left to their own devices, Mr. Wei and his wife could do no more than shed tears, and indeed, their cheeks were never dry even for a moment.

The next day, Cousin Fu Daoqin came to visit Wei Junior. Mr. Wei Senior told him about Priest Pei being defeated by demon spirits the night before. "What's to be done?" asked Mr. Wei Junior.

Fu answered, "The Huaguang Buddha of this very temple is most responsive to prayers. Since the evil spirits did their work in this temple, let's prepare some sacrificial items, write up a prayer sheet, and burn it. I'm sure the gods will prevail over the demons. Your son may yet have a chance."

Fu told his friend Li Lin and others about the matter. Since all were well disposed toward Wei, they vied with one another in offering money and preparing sacrificial items, incense, candles, paper horses, wine, and fruit and laid them out on the altar. Together with Mr. Wei Senior, they made obeisances to the deity. Mr. Wei Senior then read aloud the following prayer:

"Your divine righteous spirit permeates the mountains and rivers, rewarding the good and punishing the evil with never an error in judgment; your might extends

across the universe, dispensing woe and weal with unfailing fairness. Wei Yu, who studies in this temple, has unfortunately been seduced by evil spirits. Male and female intermingling, they make merry in the same bed night after night; yin *and* yang *intermixing, they give themselves up to the pleasures of the flesh day after day. To indulge in fornication, they lawlessly sneak over walls. In their illicit union, they shamelessly commit debauchery. The first one, in his lasciviousness, pretends to be Lü Dongbin. The second one, in her lechery, presents herself as He Xiangu. As a consequence, Mr. Wei Junior grows haggard in appearance and confused of mind, with never a moment of soberness. His will has dissolved; his ardor for life is gone. Whether they are demons of the moon or the flowers, please destroy them once and for all. Whether they are the spirits of mountain beasts or water monsters, please exterminate them so that they never appear again. We, Li Lin and others, pray that* yang *and* yin *be restored to their proper standing, that the land prosper, and that the populace thrive."*

With the prayer read and the paper burned, the service came to an end. In the ensuing discussion about the doings of Lü Dongbin and He Xiangu, Li Lin said, "In Zhongqing Lane, there's a newly built temple dedicated to the real Lü Dongbin. Let's go there together tomorrow morning to offer some incense and report the matter. If the real Lü Dongbin hears us from the divine realm, he will surely be enraged." The suggestion won general approval.

On the morrow, the ten men all gathered in front of Patriarch Lü Dongbin's image. With incense burning, they made their obeisances and said their prayers. Upon returning, they told Mr. Wei Senior about it. That very night, Wei Junior began to feel better, much to Mr. Wei Senior's joy, although his strength was yet to be regained.

A few days later, Mr. Wei Senior went to Huaguang Temple, bringing along sacrificial items partly for votive offerings and partly to pray for blessings. Having heard of his intentions, his friends joined him on the trip. After the prayers were said and the papers burned, Mr. Wei Senior strode up to the altar, his eyes tightly closed. He sat down firmly and solemnly by the altar and exclaimed, "Wei Zeyou, I, God of Wuxian, saved your son's life."

Realizing that Bodhisattva Huaguang was speaking through Wei Zeyou, all those present stepped forward to pay homage. They asked, "Exactly what demons were molesting Wei Yu? How are you, God of Wuxian, going to save him? And when will he recover fully from his illness?"

The following speech was heard from Mr. Wei Senior's lips: "Those two demons are age-old turtle spirits, one male and the other female. After establishing the fact that they are addicted to victimizing young boys and girls, I sent one of my subordinates to capture them, but the two demons possess such great magical powers that they outmaneuvered my subordinate. So I went myself to get them. Still claiming that they were Lü Dongbin and He Xiangu, they refused to surrender and put up resistance. After a hundred rounds of battle without a winner, the real Lü Dongbin and He Xiangu, who happened to have learned about the matter, reported on it to the Jade Emperor, who then dispatched celestial warriors to earth. In the presence of the real immortals, the impostors naturally found themselves overpowered. They fled to the Mengzi Tributary of the Black River. Using my fiery wheels, I set their hiding place on fire and forced them out for more fighting. The honorable Lü Dongbin tossed his sword into the air and finished off the male turtle. The female one was driven under the ice of the North Sea to suffer for eternity, with no possibility of redemption.

"When Lü Dongbin, He Xiangu, and I reported back to the Lord on High, he ordered us to punish your son for his gullibility, but I said, 'He's just a young student under their spell, and his parents and friends are all praying in repentance on his behalf. Moreover, this young man is destined for success in the civil service examinations. Please forgive him.' It was then that the Lord on High agreed not to punish him.

"My sleeve got torn in battle. Look! I cut off the part of the male turtle's shell that covered his belly and buried it under the peach tree in the backyard. If you want your son to recover quickly, you may cook the shell in water until the soup thickens into a jelly and make your son take it with wine. He'll get well."

That said, Mr. Wei Senior collapsed onto the floor. When he was raised to his feet and roused, he was unable to answer any questions about the bodhisattva's possession of his body. Shocked upon hearing what had happened, Mr. Wei Senior lifted the curtain and saw that, sure enough, there was a tear in the sleeve of the god's image.

When the surface soil was dug up under the peach tree in the backyard, there, for all to see, lay a piece of turtle shell. About three feet in length, it still had some blood and flesh on it. Mr. Wei Senior retrieved it, cooked it in water, and fed his son the jelly three times a day along with some wine. By the time the jelly was gone, the young man had fully regained his health.

Father and son went to Huaguang Temple, where they made sacrificial offerings and donned the god's statue in a new robe. They then went to the Temple of Lü Dongbin to offer incense. Later, Wei Yu did indeed win honor in the imperial civil service examinations. There is a poem in testimony:

The real and the fake, the difference lies in the heart.
Why would immortals ever stoop to vice?
Humans who withstand evil temptations
Find the divine realm right before their eyes.

28

Madam White Is Kept Forever under Thunder Peak Tower

Hill beyond green hill, tower beyond tower,
When will songs and dances by West Lake ever cease?
Enchanted by the warm breezes,
The sightseers take Hangzhou for Bianzhou.[1]

Our story takes place by beautiful West Lake amid green hills and clear waters. In the Xianhe reign period [326–34] during the Jin dynasty, when a raging mountain flood swept past West Gate, an ox was suddenly seen in the water, glittering all over with the color of gold. The ox then followed the receding flood all the way to North Hill, where it became lost to view, destination unknown. The event caused quite a stir throughout the city of Hangzhou, for the residents believed that the ox was an apparition of some deity. Thus, a temple was built and named Jinniu [Golden Ox] Temple. At West Gate, now called Yongjin [Golden Flood] Gate, a temple dedicated to General Jinhua [Golden Splendor] still stands.

At the time, a foreign monk with the Buddhist name Hunshouluo commented when viewing the hills of Wulin County on one of his wandering journeys: "A little peak in front of Spirit Vulture Hill [Grdhrakuta] has suddenly disappeared. So, here's where it has flown to." Reacting to the disbelief these words generated among his audience, he continued, "As far as I remember, that little peak is called Spirit Vulture Peak. It has a cave in which lives a white ape. Let me try to call the ape out by way of proof." And indeed, a white ape emerged in response to his calls.

At the foot of the hill was a pavilion, now called Cold Fountain Pavilion. In the middle of West Lake stands a solitary hill. When the poet Lin Hejing[2] was living as a hermit on that hill, he had stones and earth carried over and a walkway built between Broken Bridge to the east and Sunset Peak to the west. The walkway thus came to be called Solitary Hill Road. During the Tang dynasty, Prefect Bai Juyi[3] also had a causeway built, reaching from Green Screen Hills to the south and Sunset Peak to the north, and it came to be called the Bai Causeway. The two roads were often damaged by mountain floods, and money had to be withdrawn from government coffers each time to pay for repairs. Then, during the Song dynasty, Su Dongpo,[4] who was prefect of Hangzhou, bought timber and stones, hired laborers, and had the two water-damaged roads repaired and reinforced. Railings on the six bridges were painted vermilion and peach, and willow trees were planted all along the causeway. In the balmy days of spring, the scenery is most picturesque. Later, it came to be known as the Su Causeway. Two stone bridges were built by Solitary Hill Road to part the flow of the water. The one to the east is called Broken Bridge and the one to the west Xiling Bridge. Truly,

Three hundred temples half hidden in the hills;
Two tall peaks locked in faint, fluffy clouds.

But, storyteller, you may well object, why talk only about the scenery of West Lake, men of immortal fame, and sites of historic interest? Well, let me now launch into the story proper and tell of a dashing young man who, because of his encounter with two women while touring West Lake, caused quite a sensation throughout the romance-filled streets of the region's cities and towns, providing material for a love story from the writer's pen. Now what was the young man's name? What manner of women did he encounter? What did he do to cause a sensation? There is a poem in testimony:

In the dismal rain of the Qingming season,[5]
The wayfarer on the road is stricken with grief.
"Where, pray, might I find a wineshop?"
The herdboy points to Apricot Village afar.

The story goes that in the Shaoxing reign period [1132–62], after Emperor Gaozong of Song moved to the south, there lived, in Black Pearl Lane by the Reward the Troops Bridge in Lin'an Prefecture, Hangzhou, a certain Li Ren. He served as a petty official in the treasury of the Southern Song court while doubling as bursar for a Marshal Shao. His wife had a younger brother, Xu Xuan, who was the oldest son of the family. Xu's father used to own an herbal medicine store, but both parents had died when Xu Xuan was still a boy. Now twenty-two years old, Xu Xuan worked as an assistant in an herb store owned by a distant uncle, Squire Li. The store was situated at the corner of Officials Street.

One day, Xu Xuan was attending to his business in the store when a monk appeared at the door and said after a greeting, "This poor monk is from Baoshu Pagoda Monastery. I sent some steamed buns and twisted rolls to your house the other day. Now that the Clear and Bright Festival is drawing near, I hope that you, Master Xiaoyi [Oldest Son], will come to our monastery to offer incense in memory of your ancestors. Please do remember to come."

"I'll surely be there," promised Xu Xuan. The monk took his leave.

In the evening, Xu Xuan returned to his brother-in-law's house. Being a bachelor, he lived with his older sister's family. That evening, he told his sister, "A monk from Baoshu Monastery came today and asked me to go and burn sacrificial straw baskets.[6] So I'll make the trip tomorrow to honor our ancestors."

He rose bright and early the next morning and bought some paper horses, candles, sutra streamers, and strings of paper coins. Afterwards he ate breakfast, changed into new clothes, socks, and shoes, wrapped the baskets and offerings in a piece of cloth, and went to Squire Li's house on Officials Street. When Squire Li asked where he was off to, Xu Xuan replied, "I'm going to Baoshu Pagoda to offer incense in memory of my ancestors. Please give me a day's leave, Uncle."

"All right, but come back as soon as possible."

Xu Xuan left the store. He took Peaceful Longevity Lane and Flower Market Street, crossed Well Pavilion Bridge, went through Qiantang Gate behind Clear River Street, crossed Stone Box Bridge, and passed the Monument to the Release of Captured Living Creatures.

Once he arrived at the monastery, he sought out the monk who had brought him steamed buns and made his confession. He then burned the baskets containing the paper offerings and went up to the main hall to watch the monks recite the scriptures. After a vegetarian meal, he bade the monk good-bye and left to take a leisurely walk around.

He crossed West Peace Bridge and Solitary Hill Road and went to the Temple of the Four Sages, meaning to continue on to Lin Hejing's grave and Six Ones Spring. But all of a sudden, clouds gathered in the northwestern sky, and a fog closed in from the southeast. The drizzle that followed soon grew into a steady rain. As it happened to be around the Clear and Bright Festival, the Lord of Heaven, in observance of the laws of nature, lent a determined insistence to the rain so as to speed the growth of flowers. Seeing that the ground outside was wet, Xu Xuan took off his new socks and shoes and stepped out of the temple to look for a boat. There being none in sight, he wasn't sure what to do, when suddenly, he was overjoyed to see an old man rowing a boat in his direction. A closer look revealed the boatman to be Grandpa Zhang. "Grandpa Zhang," cried Xu Xuan, "please take me on board!"

At the cry, the old man looked around and saw that it was Master Xiaoyi. Rowing his boat toward the shore, he said, "Master Xiaoyi, so you're caught in the rain! How far do you want me to take you?"

"I'll get off at Golden Flood Gate."

The old man helped him into the boat and rowed away from the bank toward Harvest Joy Tower. Before they had gone more than a hundred feet, they heard a cry from the shore, "Grandpa, would you give us a ride, please?"

Xu Xuan turned to look and saw a woman wearing a white silk blouse, a fine flaxen skirt, and white hairpins in her jet-black hair, which was arranged in a chignon covered in mourning white. By her side stood her maid, dressed all in green. Her hair was fastened in two knots, each tied with a bright red string and adorned with a piece of jewelry. She was carrying a package in her hand. Both appeared eager to get on the boat.

Old Man Zhang remarked to Xu Xuan, "As the saying goes, 'When there's a wind blowing, you need do nothing to keep the fire going.' Since we don't have to do anything extra, why don't we take them on board?"

"Have them come down, then," said Xu Xuan. (*The beginning of all the troubles to come.*)

So the old man drew the boat up to the shore, and the woman and her maid stepped on board. At the sight of Xu Xuan, the woman flashed a smile, revealing dainty white teeth between red lips, and dropped a curtsy. Xu Xuan rose with alacrity and returned the greeting. After the woman and the maid were seated in the cabin, the woman kept casting significant glances at Xu Xuan, who found his desires stirring, despite his prudishness, at the sight of such an enchanting beauty accompanied by the flower of a maid. (*It so happens that prudish ones tend to be the easiest to catch.*)

"May I ask your name, sir?" said the woman.

"I am Xu Xuan, the oldest son in the family."

"Where do you live?"

"I live in Black Pearl Lane by Reward the Troops Bridge and work in an herbal medicine store."

Now that the woman had asked her questions, Xu Xuan thought it was his turn. Rising from his seat, he inquired, "May I ask your name, madam? And where do you live?"

"I am the younger sister of Officer White [Bai] of the imperial guards. My husband, Zhang, has unfortunately passed away and is buried here on Thunder Peak. The Clear and Bright Festival being near, I took my maid to sweep his grave and make some offerings today. We were on our way back when we got caught in the rain. If you hadn't taken us in, we would have been in quite a sorry state."

After they had chatted for a while, the boat approached the shore. The woman said, "I left home in such haste that I didn't bring enough travel money. Could you please lend me some money so that I may pay the boatman? I'll surely pay you back." (*An excuse for continuing the association.*)

"As you wish, madam, but don't worry about such a trivial amount," Xu Xuan assured her.

After the boatman was paid, the rain came down even harder. As Xu Xuan helped her go ashore, the woman said, "My house is at the entrance to Double Tea Lane by Arrow Bridge. If it's not beneath you, please follow me to my humble home for tea, so that I can repay the money."

"Oh, don't worry about such a trifle. It's getting late now. I'll come for a visit another time," said Xu Xuan. And so, the woman and her maid took leave of him.

Xu Xuan then went through Golden Flood Gate and wended his way under the eaves of the houses to Three Bridges Street, where Squire Li's brother's herb store was located. Xu Xuan walked up and saw the younger Squire Li at the door.

"Brother Xiaoyi," said Li, "where are you going at this late hour?"

"I went to Baoshu Pagoda on an incense-offering trip and got caught in the rain. Could you lend me an umbrella?

"Old Chen!" cried out Li. "Get Master Xiaoyi an umbrella!"

Soon, Old Chen emerged with an umbrella. Opening it, he said, "Master Xiaoyi, this umbrella is the work of Honest Shu by Character Eight Bridge on Clear Lake, and a fine umbrella it is, with its eighty-four ribs and purple bamboo handle. It's not torn anywhere, either. So don't ruin it! Be sure to take good care of it!" (*Remarks quite unexpected. A comic touch.*)

"Of course, don't worry," said Xu Xuan as he took the umbrella. After some words of thanks to Squire Li, he left, heading in the direction of Sheep Dike. As he approached Rear Market Street, he heard someone call, "Master Xiaoyi!" Turning to look, he saw a woman standing under the eaves of the small teahouse at the entrance to Shen's Well Street, the very Madam White who had been his companion on the boat.

"Why are you here, madam?"

"With the rain pouring like that, my shoes became wet, so I had Little Green go home to fetch an umbrella and my galoshes. Now that it's getting dark, may I share your umbrella for part of the way?"

So they walked as far as the dike, sharing one umbrella. "Now where do you want to go, madam?"

"To Arrow Bridge after crossing that bridge."

"Well, I'm heading for Reward the Troops Bridge, which is quite close by. You might just as well take the umbrella. I'll come to get it tomorrow." (*Volunteering to continue the relationship and inviting trouble. There's no one more tender, affectionate, and* [illegible] *than Madam White.*)

"You're too kind. Thank you so much," said Madam White.

Keeping under the eaves, Xu Xuan walked on in the rain. Upon arriving, he ran into Wang An, his brother-in-law's servant, who had just returned after looking vainly for him to deliver his galoshes and umbrella.

Xu Xuan ate supper at home and spent a wakeful night, tossing and turning, thinking about the woman. When he finally fell asleep, the events of the day reappeared in a dream, stirring up amorous passion. At the rooster's crow, he woke up and realized that it had all been but a dream. Truly,

His heart as wild as a fast-running ape or horse,
His amorous desires kept him awake till dawn.

When it grew light at last, he rose, washed, did his hair, ate breakfast, and went to the store. With his mind in a fluster, he could hardly concentrate on his job. In the early afternoon, he thought to himself, "How am I going to get the umbrella back and return it without having to tell a lie?" Addressing the older Squire Li, who was sitting by the counter, he said, "My brother-in-law wants me to go home earlier than usual today to deliver a present for him. May I take the rest of the afternoon off?"

"All right, go ahead. Come in earlier tomorrow!"

After chanting his good-bye, Xu Xuan headed straight for Double Tea Lane by Arrow Bridge and asked for directions to Madam White's house, but no one knew where it was. He was wondering what to do when Little Green, Madam White's maid, appeared, coming from an easterly direction.

"Sister!" exclaimed Xu Xuan. "Where exactly do you live? I've come to get my umbrella."

"Follow me, sir."

And so he did. A few moments later, she announced, "Here we are!"

He saw that the house was two-storied with a double door flanked by four long, latticed windows, two to a side. A finely woven vermilion curtain hung in the middle of the door. The main hall was lined with twelve black lacquer armchairs and decorated with four landscape paintings by famous artists of olden times. Opposite the house stood the mansion of Prince Xiu, father of Emperor Xiaozong of Song.

Disappearing behind the curtain, the maid said, "Please come in and take a seat, sir!"

Xu Xuan followed her to the inner section of the house. Little Green then whispered, "Ma'am, Master Xiaoyi is here!"

"Invite him in for tea," said Madam White from inside.

Xu Xuan had not made up his mind what to do, but Little Green kept urging him to go in, and so he did. There came into view four veiled latticed windows. When the blue cotton portiere was raised, he saw a small parlor with a table on which stood a pot of bearded calamus. Two paintings of beautiful women hung on either side, and on the central wall was a picture of a deity. On another table was a bronze vase in the shape of an incense burner.

Madam White stepped forward and said with a deep bow, "I'm much indebted to you, Master Xiaoyi, for having taken such good care of us upon our first encounter yesterday. How can I ever thank you enough?"

"Oh, it's hardly worth mentioning."

"Please sit and have some tea," said Madam White. After they finished the tea, she continued, "Let me serve you some wine as a token of my gratitude."

Before Xu Xuan could decline the offer, Little Green had laid out a fine spread of vegetables and fruits.

"I thank you, madam, for your hospitality, but I really shouldn't be imposing on you like this." After drinking a few cups of wine, he rose and said, "It's getting late. As I have quite a long way to go, I beg to take leave of you now."

"A relative of mine borrowed your umbrella from me last night," said Madam White. "Please have a few more cups while I try to have it sent back."

"It's getting late. I really must be going."

"Just one more cup!"

"But I've had enough. I'm much obliged!"

"If you insist on leaving now, please be good enough to come back tomorrow for the umbrella." (*Trying again to continue the relationship. Another twist in the plot.*) There was nothing Xu Xuan could do but take leave of her and return home.

The next day, after working in the store for a little while, he got away again on some excuse and went to Madam White's house to reclaim his umbrella. Again, she kept him for wine.

"Please give me back my umbrella," said Xu Xuan. "I don't want to impose on you like this."

"But since the wine is ready, please take just one little cup," the woman insisted. Xu Xuan felt he had no choice but to sit down. Madam White filled a cup, handed it to Xu Xuan, and said, her cherry-red lips moving, her pearly teeth glistening, her voice sweet and coquettish, her face radiant with joy, "My respects to you, sir. As they say, 'To an honest person, be honest.' The fact is, my husband has died. Judging from your kindness to me the first time we met, I believe that I must have a predestined marriage bond with you and that the feeling is mutual. Wouldn't it be nice if you could find a matchmaker and we two who are made for each other can join in blissful marriage?"

These words set Xu Xuan to thinking. "That would indeed be a good match. To have such a wife wouldn't be a bad deal at all. I am more than willing, but there's one matter to consider. Working during the day for Squire Li and lodging at night at my brother-in-law's house, I have saved a little money, but it's just enough for my own clothes. How can I afford to have a family?"

As he sat there, pensively silent, Madam White asked, "Why don't you answer me?"

"I'm very honored, but the fact of the matter is, I don't have the means to comply with your wish."

"That problem is easily solved," replied Madam White. "I have money to spare. You needn't worry on that score." To Little Green, she said, "Go up and get an ingot of silver for me."

Holding on to the railing, Little Green went up and down the stairs and handed a package to Madam White. "Master Xiaoyi," said the woman, "Take this. When in need, come here again for more." So saying, she gave the package to Xu Xuan with her own hands. Xu Xuan opened the package and saw inside fifty taels of snow-white silver. He put it in his sleeve and rose to go. Little Green returned his umbrella to him. Umbrella in hand, Xu Xuan took his leave, went straight home, and hid the silver. The night passed without further ado.

In the morning, he rose and went to Officials Street to return the umbrella to Squire Li. With some loose pieces of silver, he bought a fat and juicy roast goose, fresh fish, lean meat, a young chicken, fruit, and a jar of wine and carried them home. He gave everything to the housekeeper and the maids for them to take care of.

His brother-in-law, Officer Li, happened to be at home that day, and Xu Xuan invited him and his sister to sit down around the dinner table with the fine spread on it. Much taken aback at the invitation, Officer Li said to himself, "Why is he going to so much expense today? I've never seen him with a wine cup. Something's wrong here!"

The three sat down in order of seniority. After a few rounds of wine, Officer Li said, "My honored brother-in-law, why are you going to so much expense when there's nothing special happening?"

"I'm much obliged to you, Brother-in-law, but please don't make fun of me. This is really not worth mentioning. I am very grateful to you and Sister for taking care of me all these years. But, as they say, one guest should not impose himself on two hosts. I'm a grown man now and should make sure I'll have support in my old age. I've had a marriage offer. Could you, my brother-in-law and sister, please make the necessary arrangements on my behalf so that I can settle down once and for all?"

At these words, his brother-in-law and sister thought to themselves, "This is a man who hardly ever parts with a penny. And now, with what little he has spent, he expects us to get a wife for him?" Exchanging glances, the husband and wife refrained from answering. After the meal was over, Xu Xuan went back to work.

A couple of days later, Xu Xuan wondered, "Why does Sister still keep silent about the matter?" He asked his sister, "Have you consulted Brother-in-law-about what I said the other day?"

"No."

"Why not?"

"Well, unlike other things, this isn't something that should be done in a rush. Also, your brother-in-law's been looking worried the last couple of days, so I haven't dared ask him, so as to avoid adding another burden to his mind."

"Sister, why are you dragging your feet? What's so difficult about it? You're ignoring me only because you're afraid I'll be making a demand on my brother-in-law's pocket!" With that, he rose, went to his bedroom, opened his trunk, and took out Madam White's silver. Handing the ingot to his sister, he said, "Now, no more excuses. I need Brother-in-law to make the arrangements for me."

"So, you've saved up quite a tidy sum all these years while working for Uncle! No wonder you are talking about getting married! You go along now and leave the money here with me."

When Officer Li returned, Xu Xuan's sister told him, "Husband, you know why my brother is talking about marrying? The fact is, he has saved up quite a tidy sum for himself and has offered some to me. It looks like we'll have to take care of this matchmaking business."

"So that's what it is!" exclaimed Officer Li. "Well, it's a good thing he has some private savings. Show me the money." Promptly, his wife handed the silver to him. He turned the ingot over and over in his hand, examining the characters engraved on it. "We're in trouble!" he burst out in alarm. "This means death for the whole family!"

Seized with fear, his wife asked, "What can be so terrible?"

"A few days ago, fifty large ingots of silver disappeared from Marshal Shao's treasury. The seal and lock on the door are intact, and there is no underground tunnel that leads to it. And now, Lin'an Prefecture has been given the urgent task of hunting down the thief, but there's no clue whatsoever. Goodness knows how many people have been implicated! Bulletins have been posted, complete with the serial numbers of the missing ingots. The bulletin says, 'Whoever captures the thief and finds the silver shall receive a reward of fifty taels. Anyone who withholds information or gives shelter to the thief shall be duly punished, and all members of his family shall be banished to remote regions.' Now, the serial number on this ingot is exactly the same as the one in the bulletin, which means that the silver comes from Marshal Shao's treasury, and there's a big hue and cry after it! Indeed, 'In a spreading fire, you can't afford to take care of all your relatives.' If this theft is discovered, I won't be able to talk my way out of trouble. I don't care whether he stole it or borrowed it, but it's far better to have him punished than to be implicated myself. I'll have to take the silver to the authorities, so as to protect my family." His wife was so stunned at these words that her jaw dropped and she stared at him, her eyes unblinking.

And so, off he went to the prefectural yamen to surrender the ingot of silver. His report deprived the prefect of a whole night's sleep.

The next day, He Li, the arrest officer, was summoned posthaste. Taking a few assistants and a team of lictors keen of eye and swift of movement, Officer He Li went straight to Squire Li's store on Officials Street to apprehend the thief Xu Xuan. At the store counter, the men gave a shout and bound Xu Xuan with rope. Beating a drum and a gong along the way, they took him to the yamen of Lin'an Prefecture, where Prefect Han happened to be holding court. Xu Xuan was taken to the middle of the hall and made to kneel down.

"Beat him!" roared the prefect.

"Hold the torture for now, Your Honor," protested Xu Xuan. "First, let me know the charge against me."

Furiously the magistrate thundered, "What does a thief have to say for himself when the evidence is there? How dare you try to claim innocence! Fifty of the largest ingots of silver have disappeared from Marshal Shao's treasury, with the seal and lock intact. Officer Li has brought in one of the ingots, and the other forty-nine ingots must be in your possession. If you are able to steal without touching the seal, you must be a sorcerer as well as a thief! All right, hold the beating for now, but bring me some animal blood!"[7]

Now realizing what this was all about, Xu Xuan shouted at the top of his voice, "I'm not a sorcerer! Let me explain!"

"All right, go ahead and tell me where you got the silver."

Thereupon, Xu Xuan gave a detailed account of how he had lent his umbrella and had gotten it back.

"What manner of woman is Madam White?" the prefect demanded. "And where does she live?"

"She says she's the younger sister of Officer White of the imperial guards. She lives in the black house on the slope opposite Prince Xiu's mansion at the entrance to Double Tea Lane by Arrow Bridge."

Right away, the prefect ordered Arrest Officer He Li to escort Xu Xuan to Double Tea Lane to apprehend the woman and bring her to court.

Thus ordered, He Li and his men hurried to the black house opposite Prince Xiu's mansion on Double Tea Lane. When they got there, all they saw were four windows looking out onto the street, a big double door, a heap of garbage on the steps leading up to the door, and a bamboo pole across the door. The men stood astounded. Then they set out to a search for some neighbors and came back from one end of the street with a Mr. Qiu Da, a maker of artificial flowers, and from the other end of the street a Mr. Sun, a cobbler. The latter was so overwhelmed by the shock that he had a rupture and collapsed to the ground. Other neighbors came over and told the officers, "There isn't any Madam White around here. About five or six years ago, an Inspector Mao who used to lived there died in an epidemic, as did all other members of his family. Since then, because ghosts have often been seen coming out of the house in broad daylight to buy things, no one has dared to live in it. A few days ago, a madman was seen standing in front of the door chanting greetings."

By He Li's order, the bamboo pole barring the door was removed. As the door opened, a gust of foul-smelling wind sprang up from the deserted interior of the house. Astounded, the men staggered back, while Xu Xuan stood speechless.

Among the constables was a stout-hearted Mr. Wang, the second son in his family, better known as Wino Wang the Second because of his weakness for wine. "Follow me!" shouted Wino Wang the Second as he led the men in.

The walls, the parlor, and the table and chairs were all there as Xu Xuan had described them. When they came to the staircase, Wino Wang was made to go up first, and the rest of the men followed. They found the upper floor covered with a layer of dust three inches thick. Continuing on to a bedchamber, they pushed open the door and saw that, on a canopied bed surrounded by trunks and cases, sat a woman in white, as pretty as a flower and as fair as jade. Lacking the courage to step forward, the men said, "Are you, madam, a goddess or a ghost? We are ordered by the prefect of Lin'an to summon you to court to bear out Xu Xuan's testimony." The woman did not move.

"It won't do if none of us dares to go forward!" exclaimed Wino Wang. "Bring me a jar of wine. She can't hurt me after I drink, and I'll be able to take her to the prefect."

Two or three men promptly hurried downstairs and came back with a jar of wine. Wang the Second broke the seal over the mouth of the jar and drank up the wine. "She can't hurt me now!" With that, he hurled the empty jar at the bed curtains. It would have been a different story had he not done so, but as he did, they heard an earsplitting crack, like a bolt out of the blue. Everyone collapsed to the floor in shock. By the time they scrambled to their feet to look around, the woman had vanished. All they saw was a heap of glittering silver. Moving closer for a better view, they exclaimed, "Good!" They counted forty-nine ingots in all.

"Oh well, at least we can take the silver to the prefect," they said, and they returned to the Lin'an prefectural yamen carrying the silver.

At He Li's report, the prefect concluded, "This must have been the work of a demon spirit. Very well, then, the neighbors are innocent and can go home." He then dispatched a messenger to take the fifty ingots of silver to Marshal Shao along with a report containing detailed explanations. Xu Xuan was charged with "having committed an improper act" and was given a few thrashings of the rod. Though spared the disgrace of a facial tattoo, he was sentenced to hard labor in a Suzhou Prefecture prison camp until his term expired.

Feeling guilty for having informed on Xu Xuan, Officer Li gave Marshal Shao's fifty-taels reward to Xu Xuan for use on his journey. The squire wrote two letters on behalf of Xu Xuan, one addressed to Warden Fan and the other to Mr. Wang, the owner of an inn by Lucky Bridge. After a violent fit of sobbing, Xu Xuan bade farewell to his brother-in-law and his sister and was put into a cangue. Escorted by two guards, he left Hangzhou and embarked on a boat at East New Bridge.

In a matter of days, the party arrived in Suzhou. The first thing Xu Xuan did upon arrival was to present the letters to Warden Fan and Mr. Wang. On his behalf, Mr. Wang bribed high and low throughout the yamen. The two guards were then sent on to the Suzhou prefectural yamen to deliver the official documents as well as the convicted man. Once they got a return message, they went back. Warden Fan and Mr. Wang managed to get Xu Xuan released on bail. After settling down in a room on the upper floor of Mr. Wang's inn, Xu Xuan gloomily wrote a poem on the wall:

Alone in a tower, I look toward home;
Sadly, I watch the setting sun by the window.
A man of honesty throughout my life,
I was doomed when I met the bewitching one.
Where could the one in white have gone?
And where could the one in green be now?
Here, in Suzhou, away from kith and kin,
I'm overwhelmed with nostalgia for home.

Only when there is a lot to say will the story be a long one, but at this point in our narration, there being little to tell, let us skip over the more than six months that flitted by like an arrow amid the busy risings and settings of the sun and the moon. During all this time, Xu Xuan continued to stay with Mr. Wang. Now, toward the end of the ninth month, Mr. Wang was standing idly at the door of his inn, watching the goings-on in the street, when he saw, coming from afar, a sedan-chair with a maidservant walking by its side.

"Might this be Mr. Wang's inn?" asked the maid upon drawing near.

Mr. Wang hastened to reply with a bow. "Yes. Are you looking for someone?"

"We're looking for Master Xiaoyi from Lin'an."

"Just a moment. Let me have him come out."

The sedan-chair parked in front of the door, while Mr. Wang went inside and inside and cried out, "Brother Xiaoyi! You have visitors!"

Xu Xuan hurried out to the door with the innkeeper. Who should be there but Madam White in the sedan-chair, attended by Little Green!

"Oh, you'll be the death of me yet!" burst out Xu Xuan. "You stole silver from an official's treasury and got me into goodness knows how much trouble, and there's no one who can right the wrong done to me. Now that I've come to such a pass, why do you have to run after me like this? I'm ashamed to death!"

"Don't blame me, Master Xiaoyi," pleaded Madam White. "I'm here today to explain. Let me go in first." So saying, she had Little Green take the luggage and got down from the sedan-chair.

"Since you're an evil spirit, you cannot come in," announced Xu Xuan. With that, he blocked the door and refused to let her enter.

With a deep curtsy to the innkeeper, Madam White said, "I'm not trying to hide anything. You, sir, can see that I am not an evil spirit. Look at the seams in my clothes and the shadow I cast in the sun. Unfortunately for me, my husband died and left me a victim of such abuses! Whatever was done was my husband's doing. I had nothing to do with it. I came all this way just to explain to you because I was afraid you might bear a grudge against me. After I've said what I came to say, I'll happily take my leave."

"Please go in and be seated while you talk," said Mr. Wang.

"Yes, let's go inside and speak to the mistress of the house," said Madam White, whereupon the onlookers who had gathered at the door went their separate ways.

Once inside, Xu Xuan addressed the innkeeper and his wife. "I've been punished by the law because of her theft. I wonder what she has to say for herself, rushing all the way here like this."

"I gave you the silver my deceased husband left behind out of the best intentions," explained Madam White. "I had no idea how he had come by it."

"But when the officers went to arrest you, why was there so much garbage at the door? And why is it that we heard one loud bang behind the bed curtain and then you disappeared?"

"When I heard that you had been arrested because of the silver, I was afraid you might name me. How embarrassing it would be if I were brought to the authorities and had to show my face in public! So I saw nothing for it but to seek refuge in my aunt's house by Splendid Treasure Temple. Then I arranged to have garbage piled up at the door and silver placed on the bed. I also asked the neighbors to lie on my behalf."

"So you got away free and left me behind to be caught up by the law!"

"I put the silver on the bed because I thought that would close the case. How was I to know that so many things would happen? After learning your whereabouts, I brought some money and came all this way by boat to look you up. And now that everything has been explained, I'm leaving. You and I are not predestined to be husband and wife after all!"

"Madam," put in Mr. Wang, "you can't leave like this after such a long journey. Stay here for a few days before you decide what to do next."

Little Green urged, "Since the host is offering to keep you, why don't you stay here for a couple of days, madam? You did once promise to marry Master Xiaoyi."

Without missing a beat, Madam White said, "How humiliating! I can't be as unwanted and eager to be married off as that! I came only to set the record straight." (*Calculatedly going the other way, to throw off suspicions.*)

"Since you promised to marry him," said Mr. Wang, "why do you have to go? Stay!" And he dismissed the sedan-chair carrier, but of this, no more.

Several days later, Madam White having done her best to win Mrs. Wang's heart, the old lady persuaded Mr. Wang to use his powers of persuasion on Xu Xuan and make the match. The eleventh day of the eleventh month was then chosen for the wedding ceremony, to mark the beginning of a long and blissful marriage.

In the twinkling of an eye, the auspicious day rolled around. Madam White took out some silver and asked Mr. Wang to prepare the wedding feast. After the bride and the groom made their wedding bows in the main hall and partook of the wedding feast, they retired to the curtained bed in their bedchamber. Madam White used such charms on Xu Xuan that he was thrown into as much ecstasy as if he had met a divine being. How he wished he could have known her earlier! They were still sporting joyfully when the roosters crowed three times and the eastern sky began to brighten. Truly,

In joy, the night goes by all too quickly;
In loneliness, the hours drag on, and dawn never comes.

Henceforth, the two spent all their time in delirious pleasure at Mr. Wang's inn, as inseparable as fish and water. The days grew to months. Soon, six months had slipped by, bringing in the balmy days and blooming flowers of spring. Noticing the hustle and bustle in the streets, Xu Xuan asked his host, "Why is everybody out on the street? What's all this excitement about?"

"Today being the fifteenth day of the second month, men and women are going out to see the image of the Reclining Buddha," explained Mr. Wang. "Why don't you also go to Chengtian Monastery for some fun?"

"Right! I'll go, but let me tell my wife about it first." So Xu Xuan went upstairs and said to his wife, "Since today is the fifteenth day of the second month, there are lots of men and women out to see the Reclining Buddha. I want to go and take a look, too, but I'll be back soon enough. If anyone asks for me, just say I'm not at home. Don't go out to be seen in public."

"But what's there to see? What's so bad about just staying at home?" protested Madam White. "Why do you have to go?"

"I'll just go and have a little fun. I'll be back soon. No harm can come of it."

So saying, Xu Xuan left the inn. In the company of a few acquaintances, he went to the monastery to see the Reclining Buddha. After touring all the halls along the corridors, he was on his way out when he saw a priest wearing a Daoist robe, a casual head wrap, a yellow silk waistband, and a pair of hemp shoes sitting in front of the monastery gate, selling medicine and distributing charms and holy water. Xu Xuan stopped to watch.

"This poor priest is from the Zhongnan Mountains," announced the priest. "I dispense charms and holy water everywhere I go in my travels, to cure diseases and dispel disasters. Those afflicted with ailments, please come forward." Espying a column of black vapor over Xu Xuan's head, the priest immediately concluded that this man was being haunted by an evil spirit. "You there!" he called out. "An evil spirit has been haunting you for some time now, and it's doing you no little harm! Let me give you two charms to save your life. One is for you to burn at the third watch of the night, and the other is to put in your hair."

Xu Xuan took the charms with a deep bow, thinking to himself, "I do have the feeling that she's most probably an evil spirit. So it's true." Thankfully, he took leave of the priest and returned to the inn.

At night, while Madam White and Little Green were asleep, Xu Xuan rose and said to himself, "It should be the third watch of the night by now."

With that, he put one of the two charms in his hair and was about to burn the other when Madam White spoke up with a sigh, "Brother Xiaoyi, we've been husband and wife for quite some time now, and yet, instead of having faith in me, you believed some stranger and try to burn a charm in the middle of the night to exorcise me! Well, go ahead and burn it!" So saying, she grabbed the charm and burned it up. Nothing happened.

"Are you convinced now?" asked Madam White. "Imagine accusing me of being an evil spirit!"

"It wasn't my idea," protested Xu Xuan. "A mendicant priest in front of Reclining Buddha Monastery said that you are."

"All right, let me go with you tomorrow and see what manner of priest he is."

The next morning, Madam White rose bright and early. After she had completed her toilette, put on her jewelry and her white outfit, and instructed Little Green to take care of things in their rooms on the second floor of the inn, husband and wife made their way to Reclining Buddha Monastery. There, they saw a crowd gathered around the priest, who was distributing charms and holy water. Her bewitching eyes wide open, Madam White walked up to the priest and shouted at the top of her voice, "How dare you, a priest, tell my husband that I am an evil spirit and write up a charm to subdue me!"

The priest shot back, "With my Five Thunders heaven-centered orthodox method, I can make any demon reveal its true shape as soon as it swallows my charm."

"In the presence of everyone here, why don't you make me eat one of those charms of yours?" challenged Madam White. Accordingly, the priest drew a charm and gave it to Madam White, who took it and swallowed it up. The onlookers watched intently, but nothing happened.

They commented, "How can you accuse such a nice lady of being an evil spirit?" And they went on berating the priest while he stood there stupefied, fear written all over his face.

Madam White addressed the crowd, "You all witnessed how he failed to trap me. Now, let me try something on him that I learned as a child. Watch!" As she murmured something quite incomprehensible, the priest huddled up and rose in the air as if clutched by an invisible hand. The onlookers stood aghast. Xu Xuan was dumbfounded.

"If it were not for my respect for all of you," said Madam White, "I would keep him up there in the air for a year." She blew a puff of air, and the priest came down to the ground. How he wished his parents had given him two wings at birth! As he raced off, the crowd dispersed.

Needless to say, the husband and wife went back home together. With Madam White paying for the daily expenses, theirs was truly a harmonious conjugal life in which:

The husband sings, the wife follows;
The mornings delightful, the nights joyous.

Time flew by like a darting arrow. Again, the eighth day of the fourth month, Sakyamuni's birthday, rolled around. On the streets, people were seen taking donations from door to door and carrying cypress shrines to the monasteries where statues of Buddha would be washed. To Mr. Wang, Xu Xuan commented, "The customs here are the same as in Hangzhou."

At this point, a young neighbor called Iron Head remarked, "Brother Xiaoyi, there's a Buddhist gathering at Chengtian Monastery today. Why don't you go and take a look?"

Xu Xuan went inside and told Madam White about it. "What's there to see?" said she. "Don't go!"

"It'll just be a harmless little trip to kill some time," insisted Xu Xuan.

"If you're determined to go, let me dress you up. Your clothes are too old and ugly." So saying, she had Little Green bring over a few fashionable pieces of clothing, which turned out to fit him so well that they seemed to have been tailor-made for him. They included a black hat with a pair of white jade rings dangling at the back, a blue silk robe, and a pair of black boots. Carrying in his hand an exquisite folding silk fan bearing gold-traced portraits of women and adorned with a coral pendant, Xu Xuan looked the very picture of elegance from head to foot. In a voice as sweet as that of an oriole, the woman admonished him, "Come back early, husband! Don't make me worry about you!"

Accompanied by Iron Head, Xu Xuan went to Chengtian Monastery to watch the Buddhist gathering. Everyone who saw him gave a cheer, for he was a marvel to the eye. A man was heard saying, "Last night, some jewelry and other valuables worth four to five thousand strings of cash disappeared from Squire Zhou's pawnshop. They reported the case to the authorities, along with a list of the missing items. The search is on, but the thief hasn't been found yet."

Xu Xuan heard these words, but not seeing their significance, he continued to tour the monastery with Iron Head amid the jostling crowds of men and women who had come to offer incense. Then he told himself, "She wants me to be home early, so I'd better go." But, when he turned around, he didn't see Iron Head anywhere. As he went out the gate alone, he ran into a group of five or six men who looked like yamen lictors, with identification badges hanging at their waists. Upon taking one look at Xu Xuan, one of the men commented to the others, "What this man wears and holds in his hand look like you know what."

Another lictor, who happened to know Xu Xuan, accosted him, saying, "Master Xiaoyi, would you please show me your fan?"

An unsuspecting Xu Xuan handed the fan to him.

"Look!" the man exclaimed, "the pendant of this fan exactly fits the descriptions on the list!"

All shouting "Get him!" the men threw a rope over Xu Xuan and tied him up, much like

Black vultures chasing a baby swallow;
Hungry tigers devouring a lamb.

"This is a mistake," protested Xu Xuan. "I'm innocent!"

"Whether you are or not, we shall see when we get to Squire Zhou's house in front of the prefect's tribunal! They lost jewelry and other valuables worth five thousand strings of cash, a pair of white jade rings, and an exquisite folding fan with a coral pendant. How can you protest your innocence, with the actual stolen objects right here on you? And a reckless fellow you are, too, coming out into the open and showing them off from head to foot! What do you take us for?"

Xu Xuan was petrified. It was quite a while before he was able to speak. "So that's what happened," he said. "Yes, yes, there is indeed a thief."

"You can tell that to the Suzhou prefectural yamen," said the men.

The next day, the prefect called the court to order, and Xu Xuan was led into his presence. "Where are the valuables that you stole from Squire Zhou's treasury?" the prefect began. "Out with the truth, or you'll be put under the rod!"

"Your Honor, please do right by me! These clothes and everything else I'm wearing were given to me by my wife, Madam White. I have no idea where they're from, and that is the truth, as Your Honor will surely see in your wisdom!"

"Where is your wife?" thundered the prefect.

"She's on the upper floor of Mr. Wang's inn by Lucky Bridge."

Right away, the prefect ordered Arrest Officer Yuan Ziming to escort Xu Xuan there and bring the woman to court posthaste.

Stunned by the sight of Arrest Officer Yuan Ziming, the innkeeper, Mr. Wang, asked, "What is this all about?"

"Is Madam White upstairs?" asked Xu Xuan.

"Soon after you and Iron Head left for Chengtian Monastery, she said to me, 'My husband is off to the monastery for some fun. He told Little Green and me to take care of things upstairs, but he's been gone for so long that we're going to the monastery to look for him. Could you please keep an eye on our rooms?' And so they left. They did not return that night, and they haven't shown up so far. I thought you had all three gone to visit some relatives."

By order of the officers, Mr. Wang searched for Madam White throughout the house, back and front, but without success, whereupon Yuan Ziming brought Mr. Wang to see the prefect.

"Where is Madam White?" asked the prefect.

Mr. Wang gave a detailed account of what he knew and added, "Madam White must be an evil spirit."

After further questioning, the prefect announced, "Put Xu Xuan in jail for now!"

Through bribery, Mr. Wang managed to have himself released on bail to wait for a settlement of the case.

Now, Squire Zhou was sitting idly in the teahouse opposite his house when a servant came to report, "The jewelry and the valuables have all been found! They're right there in the treasury, in a trunk that used to be empty."

Upon hearing this, Squire Zhou rushed home and saw that the items were indeed there, with only the cap, the jade rings, the fan, and the pendant still missing. "All too clearly, they've wronged Xu Xuan, an innocent man," said he to himself, "and that's not right." Secretly, he approached the officials in charge of the case and pleaded with them to charge Xu Xuan for a minor offense only.

Now, Officer Li, who had been sent on a mission by Marshal Shao, went to Suzhou and took up lodging at Mr. Wang's inn. Upon hearing Mr. Wang's account of how Xu Xuan had first come to him and then been charged with a crime, Officer Li thought to himself, "Now I can't very well stand by and do nothing. He's a member of the family, after all." So he felt obliged to seek help from acquaintances and pay bribes high and low. (*Good for him, Officer Li!*) Finally, the prefect settled Xu Xuan's case after a thorough interrogation, attributing the offense squarely to Madam White and convicting Xu Xuan only on the charge of "failure to report the presence of an evil spirit to the authorities." He was given a hundred lashings and sentenced to a labor camp in Zhenjiang Prefecture, three hundred and sixty li away.

"Going to Zhenjiang is not bad," remarked Officer Li. "I have a sworn uncle, Li Keyong, who owns a medicinal herb store there by Needle Bridge. I'll write a letter for you to present to him." Left with no other choice, Xu Xuan borrowed travel money from his brother-in-law, took grateful leave of Mr. Wang and his brother-in-law, bought wine and a meal for the two yamen guards, and packed his belongings for the journey. Mr. Wang and his brother-in-law accompanied Xu Xuan for some distance before they returned home separately.

On the road, Xu Xuan and the guards ate and drank when necessary, traveling by day and resting at night. In a matter of days, they arrived in Zhenjiang. Xu Xuan's first priority was to seek out Li Keyong, so he found his way to the herb store by Needle Bridge, where he saw an assistant at the door, tending to his business. As Squire Li emerged from inside, the two guards and Xu Xuan hastened to chant their greetings. "I am a relative of Officer Li of Hangzhou," said Xu Xuan. "I have a letter from him."

The assistant took the letter and handed it to Squire Li, who opened and read it. "So, you are Xu Xuan, I presume?" asked the old gentleman.

"Yes, I am."

Li Keyong ordered that a meal be served to the three men. He then had a clerk take them to the prefectural yamen, where they delivered the official documents and paid to have Xu Xuan released on bail. The guards returned to Suzhou with the yamen's letter of reply, while Xu Xuan followed the clerk back to Squire Li's house, where Xu Xuan thanked Li Keyong and paid his respects to Mrs. Li. Li Keyong said to her, having read Officer Li's letter, "Xu Xuan used to work in a medicinal herb store." Thereupon, he hired him to work in his store. At night, Xu Xuan slept on the upper floor of Mr. Wang's tofu store on Fifth Lane. Li Keyong came to be impressed by Xu Xuan's meticulous work.

The store already had two managers, a Manager Zhang and a Manager Zhao. The latter was by nature an honest and law-abiding man, whereas the former was a crafty and treacherous one who took advantage of his seniority to bully younger men. Displeased by the arrival of a newcomer because he feared his services might no longer be needed, he thought up an evil plan to give vent to his jealousy.

One day, Li Keyong paid a visit to the store and asked, "How's the newcomer doing?"

Manager Zhang thought to himself, "Here he falls into my trap!" Aloud, he said, "He's all right, except for one thing."

"What one thing?"

"He's interested only in the bigger transactions and turns away clients who don't bring much profit. That's why he's not popular among our clients. I've tried several times to talk some sense into him, but he just won't listen."

"I can easily take care of that," said old Squire Li. "Let me talk to him. He'll surely listen to me." (*The whole story is a fabrication.*)

Having overheard the conversation, Manager Zhao said privately to Manager

Zhang, "We should all be nice to one another. Since Xu Xuan is a newcomer, you and I should by rights be taking good care of him. If he does anything wrong, we should tell him face-to-face rather than criticize him behind his back. If he hears about this, he'll say we're jealous." (*Manager Zhang* [illegible.])

"What does a young man like you know?" snapped Manager Zhang.

The hour being late, they went back to their respective lodgings.

Later, Manager Zhao went to Xu Xuan's place and offered him this advice, "Manager Zhang spoke ill of you to the squire out of jealousy, so you should be more careful. In future, just remember to treat clients alike, regardless of the volume of the sales."

"It's so kind of you to give me this advice," said Xu Xuan gratefully. "Let's go for a drink!"

The two men went to a wineshop and took their seats. After the waiter set out the dishes they had ordered, they drank a few cups of wine.

"The old squire is a straightforward man who can't stand being contradicted, so you'd do well to humor him and be patient in your work," admonished Zhao.

"Many thanks for your kindness! How can I ever thank you enough?" exclaimed Xu Xuan.

After another couple of drinks, Zhao said, noticing that it was quite dark, "It's late. We'd better go before the roads are too dark for walking. We'll meet again some other time."

Xu Xuan paid the bill, and they went their separate ways. Feeling the influence of the wine, Xu Xuan was afraid that he might inadvertently bump into people and chose to make his way home under the eaves of the houses along the street. As he was walking, a window above him opened, and down onto his head came a stream of ashes from charcoal used to heat irons. He stopped in his tracks and cursed, "What swine did that? Don't you have eyes? What a thing to do!"

A woman hurried downstairs and apologized, "Please don't get angry, sir! It was my fault for being so careless. Please don't take it amiss!"

In his half-drunken state, Xu Xuan raised his eyes and saw that the woman was none other than Madam White. Rage seized him. With the flames of fury leaping three thousand feet high, he burst out, "You foul evil spirit! A fine mess you got me into! I've been punished twice by the law because of you!" As the saying goes, he who harbors no indignation is no gentleman; he who is free of venom is not destined for greatness. Truly,

Iron boots are worn out in the hunt for her;
But here she is; you need not have searched.

"Why do you always appear wherever I am? If you are not an evil spirit, I don't know what is!" So saying, Xu Xuan lunged forward and held Madam White in a firm grip. "Do you want to settle this in or out of court?"

"Husband," Madam White said with a placating smile, "as they say, husband

and wife for one night, tender lovers for a hundred nights. I have a long story to tell you. Listen to me. The clothes were left behind by my deceased husband. It was out of my deep love for you that I asked you to put them on. How could you repay my kindness with such hostility and turn me into an enemy?"

"But why did you disappear when I came back that day to look for you? Mr. Wang said that you and Little Green went to the monastery to look for me. And how is it you manage to be here now?"

"I did go to the monastery, where I heard that you had been captured and taken away. I had Little Green make inquiries, but she wasn't able to find out anything more. We thought that you must have escaped. I was afraid they would be after me next, so I had Little Green hire a boat and we hurried to my uncle's home in Jiankang Prefecture. I arrived here only yesterday. I know that I got you in trouble with the law twice, and I wondered how I would ever have the nerve to face you! Scolding me won't serve any purpose now. But since we were a loving wedded couple, we can't very well end the relationship just like that, can we? After all, you and I had vowed to live the rest of our lives together in a love as eternal as Mount Tai and the East Sea. For the sake of old times, could you take me to your lodging? Wouldn't it be nice if you and I could grow old together until the end of our days?"

Upon hearing these honeyed words, Xu Xuan felt his anger turn to joy. He lapsed into silence, but lust took possession of him, and thoughts of being with her began to stir in him. Instead of returning to his lodging, he spent the night with Madam White at her place upstairs.

The next day, upon returning to Mr. Wang's inn on Fifth Lane, he announced to Mr. Wang, "My wife and maid have come from Suzhou." After explaining further, he added, "I'd like to have them move in here and join me."

"How nice! You needn't have asked!" exclaimed Mr. Wang.

That very day, Madam White and Little Green moved into Mr. Wang's inn and took up lodging on the upper floor. The following day, they held a tea party for the neighbors, and the day after that, the neighbors reciprocated in Xu Xuan's honor. The feast over, the neighbors dispersed and went their separate ways, but of this, no more need be said.

On the fourth day, Xu Xuan rose early and, after combing his hair and washing, said to Madam White, "I'm going to see the neighbors and thank them and then go to work. You and Little Green just stay where you are and keep an eye on the place. Don't, on any account, go out the door!" After this admonition, he went to the store to tend to the business, and henceforth, he left early for work and came home late in the evening.

Time flashed by, and the sun and moon shot back and forth like a busy shuttle on a loom. Another month went by.

One day, Xu Xuan asked Madam White if she could visit his employer Squire Li and the Squire's wife and family. Madam White said, "Since you're working for him, it's only right that I go to see him, so that there will be more mutual visits in the future."

The next day, a hired sedan-chair was brought to the house for Madam White. With Mr. Wang carrying gift boxes on a pole over his shoulder and Little Green bringing up the rear, they went to Squire Li's house. Madam White got out of the sedan-chair, went into the house, and asked to see the squire. Li Keyong emerged with alacrity from the interior of the house to greet her. Madam White curtsied deeply and bowed twice to Mr. Li and then twice to Mrs. Li before presenting herself to the other women of the family.

Now, this Li Keyong, albeit advanced in years, was a lustful man. At the sight of Madam White's ravishing beauty, truly,

His three souls took leave of his body;
His seven spirits gave him the slip.

The squire gazed raptly at Madam White. As dinner was served in honor of the guests, Mrs. Li commented to her husband, "What a nice young woman! She's not only beautiful but also gentle, courteous, meek, and well behaved."

"Hangzhou women are indeed pretty," the squire remarked. After the meal, Madam White thanked the hosts and returned home.

Li Keyong thought to himself, "What must I do to spend a night with that woman?" As he knitted his brows, he hit on a plan. "My birthday is coming up on the thirteenth day of the sixth month. I can take my own sweet time and make her fall into my trap that day!"

Time flew by. Soon after the Dragon Boat Festival was over, the sixth month began. The squire said to his wife, "Mother, the thirteenth being my birthday, let's set out a feast and invite relatives and friends for an entire day of fun. It will be a joyous day to remember for the rest of my life."

That very day, invitations were sent to relatives, neighbors, friends, and assistants of Squire Li's store. The next day, all the invited guests came to offer gifts of candles, noodles, and handkerchiefs. On the thirteenth, the [male] guests attended the feast, which was an all day affair. On the following day, the women came to offer their congratulations. About twenty women arrived, including Madam White, who was extravagantly arrayed in a blue blouse woven with golden thread, and a scarlet gauze skirt and her hair glittered with hairpins of silver, gold, pearl, and jade. Taking Little Green with her, she went inside to offer birthday wishes to Squire Li and pay her respects to the hostess.

A feast was laid out in the east hall. In point of fact, Li Keyong was a miser who, if he were to eat a flea, would save a hind leg for later. It was out of his lust for Madam White's beauty and for the purpose of trapping her that he set this grand feast. (*Feminine beauty can change a miser's ways.* [illegible.]) The wine cups were passed around the feast table, and in the midst of the drinking, Madam White rose to go to the lavatory. Squire Li had already instructed his most trusted maidservant to lead Madam White to a secluded room behind the house should she need to relieve herself. Having thus drawn up his plans, he hid himself there in anticipation. Truly,

He need not scale walls or crawl into holes
But steals the fragrant jade, risk-free.

So when Madam White rose to relieve herself, the maidservant led her to the secluded room behind the house as instructed. After the maidservant left, the squire, finding it hard to suppress his lustful longings and yet afraid to go straight in, peeked through a crack in the door. Everything would have been all right had he not taken that peek, but he did, and the sight that met his eyes gave him such a shock that he turned on his heels and ran. As soon as he gained the rear section of the house, he collapsed on his back.

Dead or alive, no one could be sure,
But his limbs were not moving at all.

What the squire had seen was no pretty woman but a coiled-up white snake, its body as thick as a water bucket and its eyes as large as lanterns, emitting a myriad of golden rays. (*The evil spirit is showing its true shape at last, but by choosing this moment to do so, it scares off Squire Li. How remarkable that an evil spirit should also know the importance of chastity!*)

Scared half to death, he turned on his heels and ran, but stumbled and fell. When the maidservants helped him up, they saw that his face was green and his lips were white. Terrified, a store assistant fed him pills to pacify his spirits. When he came to, his wife and the guests who had joined the crowd around him asked, "What happened to frighten you like that?"

Instead of telling the truth, Squire Li replied, "I got up too early this morning, and I've been working too hard these last few days. All this brought on a headache so bad that I passed out." After he was taken to his own room to lie down in bed, the guests resumed their seats at the table and drank a few more cups of wine before thankfully taking their leave when the feast came to an end.

Back at home, Madam White gave herself up to thinking, for she was afraid that Squire Li would tell Xu Xuan her true form the next day when they met in the store. An idea came to her. While she was taking off her clothes, she heaved a sigh.

"Why are you sighing? Didn't you have fun at the feast?"

"Husband, you won't believe this! Squire Li was in fact using the birthday celebrations to cover up his evil designs. When I went to the lavatory, I had no idea that he was already hiding there. He tried to force himself on me, tugging at my skirt and pants. I almost screamed but was afraid to alarm all the people there. So I knocked him down. He was too ashamed to admit the truth and told them that he had fainted. Curse my luck! If only I could get back at him!"

"Since he didn't have his way with you in the end, we'll just have to put up with it because he's my employer. We have no other choice. Just don't accept his next invitation, and that will be it."

"What? How are you going to face the world if you don't take my side and do something about it?"

"Well, my brother-in-law wrote to him on my behalf asking for his help, and he was kind enough to take me on as a manager of his store. What do you want me to do now?"

"What kind of man are you? He took liberties with me, and you'll continue working for him?"

"But where do you want me to go? How am I going to make a living?"

"A store manager is a lowly position. It would be better if we could have an herb store of our own."

"It's all very well for you to say, but where's the money?"

"You needn't worry. That can be easily taken care of. I'll give you some silver tomorrow so you can rent a house first, and we'll go from there."

As the saying goes, "What's true today was true in olden times, and what was true in olden times is true today." Everywhere, there are, and have always been, people who go out of their way to help others. Living next door to them was a man called Jiang He, who, throughout his life, was given to altruistic deeds. The next day, equipped with Madam White's silver, Xu Xuan asked Jiang He to rent a house by the Zhenjiang ferry pier and buy a set of drawered cabinets in which he could gradually lay up a stock of medicinal herbs. By the tenth month of the year, with all the necessary preparations completed, a day was chosen for the opening of the store, and Xu Xuan quit his job. Troubled by an uneasy conscience, Squire Li knew better than to call him back.

After he opened the store, Xu Xuan found to his surprise that his business prospered day by day and was yielding substantial profits. He was selling medicinal herbs at the door one day when a monk approached with a register of alms, saying, "I'm a monk from Golden Hill Monastery. The seventh day of the seventh month is the birthday of Yinglie the Dragon King. I humbly ask you to offer incense and make donations at the monastery for the occasion."

"You don't have to record my name in your book, but I have here a piece of fine fragrant wood[8] that you can burn as incense." So saying, Xu Xuan opened a cabinet, took out the wood, and handed it to the monk. The monk accepted the piece of wood, saying, "Please be at the monastery on that day!" With a bow, he left.

Having witnessed the scene, Madam White remarked, "How foolish of you to give that lousy bald one such a good piece of wood. He's only going to buy wine and meat with it!"

"I gave it to him in good faith. If he squanders it, that's his problem." (*Both are right.*)

All too quickly, it was again the seventh day of the seventh month. Xu Xuan opened up the shop and saw that the street was a scene of bustling traffic. Jiang

He, who was helping out, suggested, "Master Xiaoyi, since you made a donation the other day, why don't you take a trip to the monastery today just for fun?"

"Let me get my things in order and then we can go together. Wait for me a little while."

"All right, I'll go with you."

Xu Xuan hastily put things in order and went to the interior of the house, where he said to Madam White, "I'm going to Golden Hill Monastery to burn some incense. You take care of the house."

Madam White replied, "As the saying goes, 'One never goes to the temple without a reason.' Now, what's your reason for going?"

"First, I've never been there, so I want to see it. Second, having given a donation the other day, I'd like to offer some incense."

"If you're so determined to go, I can't stop you, but you have to promise me three things."

"What three things?"

"First, don't go into the abbot's cell. Second, don't talk with the monks. Third, come back as soon as possible. If you don't, I'll have to come and get you."

"Fair enough. I'll do as you say." He changed into clean clothes, shoes, and stockings and slipped his incense box into his sleeve. Then, together with Jiang He, he walked to the riverside, got on a boat, and went to Golden Hill Monastery.

They started their tour from Dragon King Hall, where they burned incense. Afterward, they took a leisurely walk around the monastery. Xu Xuan followed the crowd and was approaching the door of the abbot's cell when he suddenly recalled his wife's admonition. "My wife warned me not to enter the abbot's cell," he said. He stopped in his tracks and stayed outside.

"It's all right," said Jiang He. "She's at home, so she won't know. Just tell her you didn't go in." (*What a liar!*) With that, they went in, took a look around, and came out.

Sitting in the center seat in the cell was a monk of great moral integrity. With finely marked eyebrows, bright eyes, a round head, and a monk's robe, he did indeed possess the looks of a truly great master. At the sight of Xu Xuan passing by, he called out to his attendant, "Bring me that young man, quick!"

The attendant looked around, but unable to recall the young man's features as he stared at the masses of people before him, he said to the abbot, "I have no idea where he's gone."

At these words, the abbot picked up his cane and left the cell to search on his own. He didn't see Xu Xuan anywhere and went outside, where a crowd was waiting for the stormy waves to subside before embarking on the boats. But the tempest rose higher. Amid laments of "This is no time to go," there, for all to see, came a boat speeding toward them as if on wings.

Xu Xuan commented to Jiang He, "This big storm has stranded all of us here. How can that boat go so fast?" Even as he spoke, the boat drew near. Two women, one in white and one in green, were seen coming to shore. What was Xu Xuan's astonishment when, upon a closer look, he found them to be Madam White and Little Green!

As they gained the shore, Madam White called out, "Why didn't you come back earlier? Get on the boat, quick!"

Xu Xuan was about to board when a voice was heard shouting from behind, "What is that foul beast doing here?"

As Xu Xuan turned around, he heard voices saying, "Abbot Fahai is here!"

"You foul beast!" continued the abbot. "This old monk is here to make sure you won't dare come again and do harm to people!"

At the sight of the monk, Madam White rowed the boat away from the shore. Then, she and Little Green tipped the boat over and disappeared into the water.

Xu Xuan bowed to the abbot, saying, "Your Reverence, please save this worthless life of mine!"

"How did you meet that woman?" asked the abbot, whereupon Xu Xuan recounted all that had happened.

After listening to his story, the abbot said, "That woman is an evil spirit. Now, go back to Hangzhou as soon as possible. If she comes to pester you again, you can find me at Clear Mercy Monastery south of the lake. Let me give you a quatrain:

"An evil spirit in the shape of a woman,
Her voice rings sweet by West Lake.
Unsuspecting, you fell into her trap;
When in distress, come to me south of the lake."

Thankfully, Xu Xuan took leave of Abbot Fahai and embarked on a ferry boat with Jiang He. After crossing the river, he went ashore and returned home, but Madam White and Little Green were not there. Now convinced that they were evil spirits, he had Jiang He spend the night with him to keep him company. He felt so miserable that he did not sleep a wink throughout the night. The next morning, he rose early and had Jiang He take care of the house while he went to Li Keyong's house by Needle Bridge and told the squire everything that had happened.

Squire Li said, "On that day during my birthday celebrations, I ran into her accidentally when she went to the lavatory and saw her in her true beastly form. I was scared to death, but I didn't dare tell you about it. Now that things have come to this, why don't you move into my house while you decide what to do next?"

Xu Xuan thanked Squire Li and moved in. Quite unnoticeably, two months slipped by.

One day, he was standing by the door when he saw the local headman going from door to door, soliciting donations of incense, flowers, lanterns, and candles to celebrate the imperial court's amnesty. Emperor Gaozong had designated his heir apparent, who was later to be Emperor Xiaozong, and an amnesty was granted to mark the occasion. Except those convicted of homicide, all prisoners throughout the land were released and allowed to return home. Jubilantly, Xu Xuan intoned a poem:

"The emperor be praised for this act of mercy!
The freed convict gains a new lease on life.
I am not fated to die in an alien land
But will resume my life in my hometown.
My ill-starred meeting with the demon brought me woe;
I never dreamed that I'd be cleared of all charges.
On my return, I shall fill the house with incense
To thank the cosmos for a life reborn."

After intoning the poem, he asked Squire Li to present gifts of money to those high and low throughout the yamen. He then had an audience with the prefect and was given a pass that guaranteed safe passage to his hometown. He offered his thanks to the neighbors, Squire Li's wife and other members of the Li family, old and young, as well as the two managers. Carrying with him some local products that the ever helpful Jiang He had bought for him at his request, he made his way back to Hangzhou.

As he bowed four times to his brother-in-law Officer Li and his sister, his brother-in-law said in irritation, "How arrogant you can be! Twice I wrote letters of recommendation on your behalf, but you never even bothered to write and tell me that you were married at Squire Li's place. What a false-hearted scoundrel you are!"

"But I'm not married."

"Two days ago, a woman who claimed to be your wife came here with her maid, saying that you couldn't be found anywhere after your trip to Golden Hill Monastery on the seventh day of the seventh month. After learning that you were returning to Hangzhou, they came here and have been waiting for you for two days." So saying, the brother-in-law had a servant summon the woman and the maid. Who should appear but Madam White and Little Green! Xu Xuan was flabbergasted. Not wishing to give a detailed explanation to his brother-in-law and sister, he listened resignedly to a harsh lecture, after which Officer Li told him to retire with Madam White to a room assigned to them.

Seeing that it was now getting dark, Xu Xuan grew afraid of Madam White. Nervously, he fell to his knees, facing her but not daring to go near her, and pleaded, "Please spare my life, whoever you are, goddess or evil spirit!"

"What are you doing, Brother Xiaoyi?" said Madam White. "In all our married years, I've never done you any wrong. Why are you saying such absurd things?"

"Since I've known you, you've twice gotten me in trouble with the law. I went to Zhenjiang Prefecture, and you came after me. The other day, I was just a little late returning from a trip to Golden Hill Monastery, and you had to run after me with Little Green. When you jumped into the river at the sight of the abbot, I thought you had died. What a surprise when you turned up again here, and before I arrived, too! Please have mercy!"

Her fiendish eyes wide open, Madam White said, "Brother Xiaoyi, I did everything out of the best of intentions, little knowing that I would turn out to be the cause of such resentment! We were a loving couple, sharing the same pillow and the same quilt, and yet you had to believe some vicious gossip meant to sow dissension between us. Let me tell you something frankly. If you do as I say, everybody will be happy and every grudge forgotten. But if you betray me, I'll drench the whole town in a bloodbath and toss everyone from wave to wave in the river until all die violent deaths."

Xu Xuan trembled with fear and was speechless for quite a while, neither did he dare take a step forward. Then Little Green spoke in a pacifying tone, "Madam loves you because of your Hangzhou native's good looks and your deep affection for her. Now listen to me and make up with her. Have no more suspicions."

Thus under pressure from both of them, Xu Xuan cried out, "Woe is me!"

Upon hearing the cry, his sister, who was enjoying the cool air in the courtyard, rushed to their door. Believing it to be just another conjugal fight, she dragged Xu Xuan out of the room, whereupon Madam White closed the door and went to sleep alone.

When Xu Xuan was giving his sister a detailed account of everything that had happened, his brother-in-law returned from the courtyard. The sister told him, "They just had a fight. I wonder if she has gone to sleep or not. Could you go take a look?"

Accordingly, Officer Li went up to Madam White's room, but since the lamp had gone out, there was only a faint glimmer inside. So, he wetted the window paper with his tongue and looked in through the hole. Everything would have been all right had he not looked, but since he did, he saw a python with a body as thick as a water bucket sleeping in the bed, its head resting against the skylight so it could take in fresh air. Its shining white scales made the room as light as day. (*Judging from the case of Empress Wu, how do we know that this white snake is not a beautiful woman? Who is to say that a white snake can't change into a beautiful woman?*) In shock, he turned on his heels and fled.

Back in his own room, instead of telling anyone what he had seen, he said, "She's gone to bed. There isn't a sound." But Xu Xuan still hid himself in his sister's room, not daring to show his face, nor did his brother-in-law question him. The night passed without further ado.

The next day, Officer Li took Xu Xuan outside to a secluded spot and asked, "Where did you get this wife of yours? Tell me the truth! Don't hide anything from me! Last night, I saw with my own eyes that she is a big white snake. I didn't say anything at the time because I didn't want to frighten your sister."

Upon learning the entire story, Officer Li said, "In that case, let's go to Mr. Dai, the snake charmer in front of White Horse Temple. He's good at catching snakes."

The two men proceeded to White Horse Temple and saw Mr. Dai standing right there by the gate. "Greetings to you, sir!" they called out.

"What can I do for you?"

"There's a big python in our house," said Xu Xuan. "Could you please go and catch it?"

"Where is your house?"

"It's Officer Li's house on Black Pearl Lane by Reward the Troops Bridge." Taking out a tael of silver, Xu Xuan added, "Please take this for now. We'll have more to offer you by way of thanks after the snake is caught."

Mr. Dai took the silver and said, "You can go home now, gentlemen. I'll come right away." So Officer Li and Xu Xuan returned home by themselves.

Armed with a bottle of medicated wine,[9] Mr. Dai headed straight for Black Pearl Lane and asked for directions to Officer Li's house. Upon being told that it was the very two-storied house up ahead, he went to the door, lifted the portiere, and coughed, but no one came to answer. He kept knocking on the door until a young woman emerged. "Which family are you looking for?" she asked.

"Is this Officer Li's home?"

"Yes."

"I heard that there's a big snake in the house. Two gentlemen just came to ask me to catch it for them."

"How can there be a snake in our house? You're quite mistaken."

"The gentlemen gave me one tael of silver, saying that they'll have a handsome reward for me after the snake is caught."

"But there is no snake," insisted Madam White. "Don't believe the nonsense they told you."

"Why would they play tricks on me?"

Her repeated attempts to drive him away were futile, and Madam White grew impatient. "Do you really know how to catch snakes? I'm afraid you won't be able to get this one!"

"We've had seven or eight generations of snake charmers in our family. Why wouldn't I be able to get this particular snake?"

"You may very well say so," retorted Madam White, "but I'm afraid you'll want to get out of here as soon as you see it!"

"I won't! If I do, I'll let you fine me one ingot of silver."

"Follow me, then."

When they got to the courtyard, the woman turned a corner and disappeared into the house. Bottle of wine in hand, Mr. Dai stood in the empty courtyard. Soon, a chilly wind sprang up. As it blew past, a python with a body as thick as a water bucket thrust fiercely at him. Truly,

The human means no harm to the tiger;
The tiger is bent on harming the human.

A terrified Mr. Dai fell backward, smashing his bottle of medicated wine. The python lunged forward as if to bite him, its blood-red mouth wide open, showing its snow-white fangs. He scrambled desperately to his feet and, regretting that his parents had not endowed him with two extra legs, ran all the way across the bridge in one breath. There, he bumped into Officer Li and Xu Xuan.

Xu Xuan asked, "How did it go?"

"Let me tell you what happened." After recounting the event, he took out the tael of silver and returned it to Officer Li, adding, "Had I not been blessed with these two legs of mine, I would have died. Now, you gentlemen save this for someone else." With that, he scurried off.

"Brother-in-law, what are we going to do now?" asked Xu Xuan.

"Well, we know for sure that she's an evil spirit. Now, Zhang Cheng of Red Hill Town owes me a thousand strings of cash. You go there, wait patiently, and rent a room. With you out of its sight, that monster will surely leave."

Xu Xuan saw no alternative but to agree. Upon arriving at home with his brother-in-law, he found the house quiet with nothing astir. Officer Li wrote a letter and put it in an envelope, along with the receipt of the loan, for Xu Xuan to take with him to Red Hill Town.

At this point, Madam White called Xu Xuan to her room. "The audacity!" she said. "Hiring a snake charmer to get me! If you are good to me, I'll be as kind as a Buddha to you. Otherwise, I'll have to make the entire population of the town suffer and die violent deaths!"

Shaking with fright, Xu Xuan dared not utter a word. In low spirits, he took the envelope and went to Red Hill Town, where he found Zhang Cheng. When he tried to take the loan receipt out of his sleeve, he realized it was gone. With a cry of anguish, he turned back, looking for it along the way, but without success. Dejected, he found himself in front of Clear Mercy Monastery, which suddenly reminded him that Abbot Fahai of Golden Hill Monastery had told him that if that evil spirit followed him to Hangzhou to pester him again, he could find the monk at Clear Mercy Monastery. He thought to himself, "Now is the time to do that. What am I waiting for?" Without a moment's delay, he entered the monastery and asked the head monk, "Your Reverence, is Abbot Fahai here?"

"No, he's not here."

These words made him feel even more miserable. He turned around and proceeded to Long Bridge. Stopping at the foot of the bridge, he said to himself, "As the proverb goes, 'When down and out, one falls easy victim to the devil.' Why would I want to hang on to life?" Gazing at the clear water, he prepared to jump into the lake. Truly,

> *If King Yama wants you at the third watch,*[10]
> *He won't let you live till the fourth watch.*

He was about to throw himself into the water when he heard a voice behind him calling out, "Why would a grown man want to kill himself? Don't you know that ten thousand deaths can be easily written off as only five thousand when you count them in pairs? Don't you see the worthlessness of death? Why don't you ask for my help when you find yourself in trouble?"

Xu Xuan turned around and whom did he see but Abbot Fahai! His cassock and alms bowl on his back, his cane in his hand, he had indeed just arrived. Xu Xuan was not destined to die at this hour after all, for if the abbot had tarried for as long as it takes to eat a bowl of rice, Xu Xuan would have perished. At the sight of the abbot, he bowed deeply, saying, "Please save my life!"

"Where is that cursed beast?"

Xu Xuan told him what had happened, adding, "She's after me again. Please save me, Your Reverence."

The abbot produced an alms bowl from his sleeve and handed it to Xu Xuan, saying, "After you get home, don't let her know you're back, and place the bowl firmly over her head. Press it down hard. Don't panic. You may go home now."

Xu Xuan thankfully took leave of the abbot and returned home. There, he saw Madam White, seated and muttering to herself, "I wonder who poisoned my husband's mind against me. I'll have it out with him when I find out!"

Now, just as a person with a plan waits for the right moment to pounce on the unsuspecting party, Xu Xuan sneaked up on Madam White from behind and put the bowl over her head. As he applied all his weight on the bowl, the woman disappeared, but he kept pushing the bowl down without ever letting up. A voice from inside the bowl pleaded, "How can you be so heartless after we have lived together as husband and wife for all these years? Release the bowl just a little bit!"

Xu Xuan was wondering what to do when he heard the announcement, "There's a monk here who says he's come to subdue an evil spirit."

Xu Xuan immediately asked Officer Li to invite the abbot into the house. "Please save me!" pleaded Xu Xuan.

After muttering goodness knows what words to himself, the abbot gently lifted the bowl, and there for all to see was Madam White, reduced to a length of only seven or eight inches, looking like a puppet, her eyes tightly closed and her body huddled up on the floor. The abbot shouted, "What are you? How dare you pester human beings? Tell me everything!"

"Abbot, I am a python. In a raging storm of wind and rain one day, I went to West Lake to find shelter and joined Little Green there. And then, something unanticipated happened. I met Xu Xuan. Unable to control my desires, I violated the heavenly rules, but I never took a life. Please have mercy on me, Abbot!" (*One can hardly find her equal anywhere!*)

"And what exactly is Little Green?" the abbot persisted.

"She's a carp from the pond under the third bridge in West Lake. She acquired immortality after a thousand years of spiritual cultivation. I met her quite by accident and made her my companion. She hasn't had any fun, not even for one day. Please have pity on her, Abbot!" (*In such a desperate situation, she still remembers to put in a good word for Little Green. A truly kind evil spirit she is!*)

"I'll spare your lives, considering the thousand years of spiritual cultivation that you have undertaken. Now show your true selves!"

Madam White refused. In a rage, the abbot intoned an incantation and shouted, "Guardian of the Buddha-truth [*lokapala*]! Where might you be? Get me the carp, and make it and the white snake show their true forms so that I may render judgment on them!"

In a trice, a fierce wind sprang up in the yard. After the wind had swept past, a carp more than ten feet long fell from mid-air with a heavy thud. It bounced on the ground a few times before shrinking into a small carp one foot in length. By this time, Madam White had also been reduced to her true form as a three-foot-long white snake, staring at Xu Xuan, its head raised high. The abbot put the snake and the carp in the bowl, sealed it with a piece of cloth torn from his cassock, and took it to Thunder Peak Monastery. He laid the bowl on the ground in front of the monastery and ordered men to transport bricks and stones to the site to build a pagoda. Later, Xu Xuan sought donations and with the money thus raised made it into a magnificent seven-story pagoda. For tens of thousands of years, the white snake and the carp were not to be freed from that spot.

Let us retrace our steps and come back to the moment when the abbot laid the bowl on the ground. He intoned the following quatrain:

"When West Lake is drained of its water,
When all the rivers and the lakes run dry,
When Thunder Peak Pagoda falls down,
Only then may the white snake see the light of day."

Abbot Fahai then intoned another eight lines as a warning to posterity:

"Be advised! Do not abandon yourselves to lust;
Those who do will be held under its spell.
Evil eschews the pure in heart;
Bane visits not the virtuous.
Consider how Xu Xuan, a victim to his lust,
Found himself in trouble with the law.
Had it not been for this old monk's succor,
The white snake would have swallowed him whole."

After the abbot finished intoning this poem, the crowd dispersed, but Xu Xuan stayed behind to ask to join the Buddhist order. Honoring the abbot as his mentor, he took the tonsure right there by Thunder Peak Pagoda and became a monk.

After several years of spiritual cultivation, he willed his death while sitting in his seat one evening. The assembly of monks in the monastery bought a monk's coffin for him, had his body cremated, and built a tower for his ashes as a monument to his eternal memory. Before he died, he also wrote a poem by way of an admonition to posterity:

The abbot delivered me from the mortal world;
The iron tree burst into spring blossoms.
The wheel of life and death goes round and round;
Reincarnation occurs life after life.
The phenomenal world is elusive,
The formless, in fact, is not lacking in form.
The Form is the Void; the Void is the Form;
Yet the two should be clearly set apart.

29

Zhang Hao Meets Yingying at Lingering Fragrance Pavilion

I read books old and new in moments of leisure;
Unlike grass or trees, humans are born with feelings.
Of all intriguing stories of romance,
None matches that about Zhang Hao and Li Ying.

Our story took place in Luoyang, where there lived a gifted young man, Zhang Hao by name, courtesy name Juyuan. Endowed since his earliest years with unusually refined looks, he had delicate features, a graceful deportment, and a cultured style of conversation. He was also a brilliant scholar. Left with an inheritance worth tens of thousands of taels of silver from his grandfather, he was widely known throughout the region for his immense wealth. Some local leading families, coveting his status, sent matchmakers every day with marriage proposals, which he sternly rejected. People said to him, "You are twenty now. Why don't you want to marry some nice girl from a good family?"

To such words he retorted, "A lifelong marriage must be a flawless one. (*Valid point.*) I may not be a talented scholar, but I am an admirer of beauty. If I can't have a wife of ravishing beauty, I'd rather be a bachelor all my life. My wish is more likely to be fulfilled if I pass the civil service examinations." For this reason, he remained unbetrothed at the age of twenty.

A man of expensive tastes, he lived in a spacious mansion with walkways connecting the many halls, in splendor the match of royal residences. But the mansion still was not big enough for him. To its north, he had another garden built. It contained:

Pavilions in which to enjoy the moon and breezes,
A dock, a creek, flanked by apricot and peach trees.
The towers rise into the blue sky;
The gazebos stand at the edge of clear waters.
Spanning the ponds, connecting the curving banks,
Fly crescent-shaped, rainbow bridges.

Vermilion balustrades and carved railings
Over ornamental rocks in the forms of clouds.
The exotic flowers a riot of colors;
The greenhouses embowered by bamboo groves.
Fowl from alien lands flutter about;
Fruit trees worthy of the royal garden thrive here.
The footpaths are overgrown with green lotus leaves;
Weeping willows shroud the amusement grounds.

In his leisure time, Zhang Hao often entertained relatives and friends in the new garden. As was the custom in Luoyang, when spring came around, flowers and trees were pruned and clipped and pavilions and verandas swept clean for the enjoyment of visitors in gardens of all sizes. The rich as well as the poor vied with one another to show off their gardens.

In Haolü Lane lived a celebrated scholar, Liao Shanfu, of exemplary moral conduct and scholarship, who was a dear friend of Zhang Hao's. Proud of his new garden, aglow with thriving flowers and trees, Zhang Hao invited Shanfu to take a leisurely walk on the grounds. Upon reaching Lingering Fragrance Pavilion, they sat down. (*Good name for a pavilion.*) It was the height of spring, with the peach and plum trees flowering and the soft white and bright red peonies in full bloom all around the pavilion.

Zhang Hao suggested to Shanfu, "On such a glorious spring day, nothing but poems and wine can make the happiness complete. Luckily, we have no mundane chores to perform today, so let's drink a few cups and come up with a poem each in praise of the scenery around us. Even though my humble garden is not worthy of your poetic talent, a few lines from you will lend it everlasting glory."

"At your service," said Shanfu.

Delighted, Zhang Hao had his page boy bring wine and writing implements for his guest. After three rounds of wine, Shanfu was about to have Zhang Hao designate a title for the poem when he saw an oriole rise into air from the flowers around a pavilion some distance away, fluttering its wings in alarm. "Why would a sweet-voiced oriole be so alarmed?" Shanfu wondered aloud.

"Perhaps some sightseers are stealing flowers. Let's go and find out."

They left the pavilion and, bending low, tiptoed along a flower-lined path in search of the intruders. As they rounded a Lake Tai rock that adorned the pond, they saw, leaning against the railing in front of the peonies, a girl about fifteen years of age accompanied by a young maid. Behold:

Her eyebrows the shape of the crescent moon;
Her face a ripe peach in spring.
With the charm of a bud not yet in bloom,
She had soft skin that glowed like jade.
Her lotuslike feet in embroidered shoes;

Her two topknots adorned with gold hairpins.
Flaunting her beauty to the god of spring,
She smiled at the peonies, leaning on the railing.

The sight of the girl threw Zhang Hao into such raptures that he could scarcely contain himself. Afraid that she would recoil in fright, he led Shanfu back into the shadow of the flowers and studied her for a long time, marveling at her unmatched beauty. To Shanfu he commented, "Such a beauty can't belong to this mortal world. She must be a fairy of the flowers and the moon!"

"How could a fairy be seen in broad daylight? There's no lack of beauties in this world. It's just that people who are not destined for each other don't meet."

"I have known a precious lot of women," claimed Zhang Hao, "but such beauty is hard to come by. If I could have her for a wife, I'd ask for nothing more the rest of my life. Please, think of a way to make this match for me as soon as possible. I'll be as indebted to you as I am to my parents."

"With your talent and family status, forming a marriage alliance should be as easy as turning over a hand. Why go to all this trouble?"

"That's no way to talk. If I don't marry the right woman, I'd rather be celibate to the end of my life. Now that I've seen the right one, I can hardly wait another moment! It takes months and years for a match to go through the usual channels. Wouldn't I be like a fish dying in a fish store?" (*Mr. Dengtu*[1] *was a lecherous man, but this one is a true admirer of feminine beauty.*)

"Lack of conjugal harmony is what one should worry about. But if that's not a concern, why begrudge the length of time leading up to the marriage? You need to find out about her background before you do anything."

Overcome by his amorous desires, Zhang Hao adjusted his cap and clothes, stepped forward, and bowed. The young woman returned the greeting with a curtsy.

"Which distinguished family are you from?" asked Zhang Hao. "Why are you here?"

Affably, she replied, "I'm a neighbor, from the house east of yours. Today, everyone in my family, old and young, went to a family gathering. I'm the only one who stayed behind. Having heard about your blooming peonies, I slipped through the doors, along with my maid, to take a look at them."

Only then did Zhang Hao realize that she was his childhood playmate Yingying, daughter of Mr. Li. He continued, "This humble garden of mine is not much of a sight to see. Luckily, I have a small dining hall. What would you say to my setting out food and wine and playing host to a neighbor?"

"I did intend to see you on this visit, but I wouldn't dare accept the honor of being treated to wine. I wish only to say something to you without breaking any rules."

With his hands folded respectfully across his chest, Zhang Hao said, "I'm all ears."

"I have admired your fine qualities ever since childhood, but, my parents being strict observers of established codes of behavior, I've never had a chance to meet you. Now, as you are a bachelor and I'm still unbetrothed, why don't we get married, as long as you don't find me too ugly? I shall perform my wifely duties around the house, stand in line to offer sacrifices to the ancestors, serve my parents-in-law, promote harmonious relations between the two clans, and avoid the seven offenses that constitute grounds for divorce. Such have been my wishes all along. I hope you won't find them objectionable." (*This is a girl with a mind of her own.*)

Overjoyed upon hearing these words, Zhang Hao said, "If I could spend the rest of my life with a beauty like you, what more would I need to ask for? But I wonder if there is indeed a predestined bond between us."

"If both hearts are set firmly on the other, that means a predestined bond does exist. If you agree, I would like to ask for a token of our commitment. I'll keep it with me as a reminder of our meeting today."

In his haste to produce something by way of a token, Zhang Hao took off his embroidered purple silk waistband and said to her, "Please keep this until the match is settled."

The young woman took off her silk scarf and gave it to Zhang Hao, saying, "Please write a poem on the scarf, so that it will serve as a token."

Delighted, Zhang Hao had a page boy bring over the writing implements. After indicating a peony bud behind the railing as the inspiration for his poem, he wrote a quatrain on the silk scarf:

On a dewy stem by Lingering Fragrance,
It stands in all its demure charm and grace.
The prized flower deserves a master poet;
The dashing scholar offers it a poem.

Delighted upon reading the poem, the young woman said, scarf in hand, "What an exquisite poem! And there's much unsaid between the lines, too. You are really a talented poet! Please keep this a secret by all means. Do not tell anyone anything. If you don't forget what has been said today, you will surely be visited by happiness in the future. Now, I have to go because I'm afraid my parents may have returned." With that, she turned and, with tiny, delicate steps, slowly went off with her maid.

Under the influence of the wine he had drunk with Shanfu, Zhang Hao found his amorous yearnings hard to contain. He said to himself, "If I don't run after her now, I may never have another chance. How can I let her go? If I could make love with her on the soft grass in the shadow of the flowers, I'd have no regrets, even if I were to die."

Striding after her, he caught up with her and pulled her into his arms. Loath to be parted from the one she loved, the young lady could not bring herself to break free from his embrace. Before she could speak up and shyly ask to be released, a voice suddenly was heard from behind, "To meet like this already violates decorum, and what you're about to do is absolutely out of the question! If you listen to my advice, I guarantee you a lifelong blissful marriage."

Zhang Hao and the young woman turned around and saw that it was Shanfu. After the young woman left, Shanfu admonished Zhang Hao in these words: "One who has studied the classics should know what constitutes proper behavior and avoid doing anything that might arouse suspicions. Now, being a scholar well versed in the Confucian classics, how can you debase yourself like that? If you had delayed the girl and her parents returned home before she did, they would surely have interrogated her as to her whereabouts, and you would have been implicated. It will never do to compromise one's lifelong integrity by indulging in momentary pleasure. Please think well before you do anything that might cause you regret later in life." (*The older are wiser, after all.*)

Crestfallen, Zhang Hao returned, against his will, to Lingering Fragrance Pavilion. There, he and Shanfu drank until they were quite tipsy before they parted company.

Henceforth, Zhang Hao took no joy in singing and drinking. To the moon, he heaved deep sighs. To the flowers, he shed furtive tears. All too soon, the colors of spring began to fade.

One day, Zhang Hao was pacing pensively alone in his study, fretting that there was no one to listen to his sad story, when in came Huiji, the old nun from the Zhang family's private shrine. After greeting her, Zhang Hao asked, "What brought Your Reverence here?"

"I'm here to deliver a message."

"A message from whom?"

The nun sat down near him and said, "It's Yingying of the Li family, your neighbor to the east of the house. Time and again, she has asked me to convey her sentiments to you."

Alarmed, Zhang Hao said, "That can't be true, Your Reverence!"

"Why try to conceal it? Listen, Mrs. Li has been my disciple for more than twenty years. Actually, everyone in the Li family, old and young, is a Buddhist. Earlier today, I was there intoning the scriptures for Mrs. Li when I learned that her daughter Yinging was ill. When I advised Yingying to take medicine more frequently, she dismissed her maidservants and whispered to me, 'My illness is not something medicine can cure.' (*Truly a woman with a mind of her own.*) When I pressed her, she told me about the encounter with you in your garden and produced the silk scarf bearing the poem that she said had been written by you. She then asked me to convey her sentiments to you and tell you not to forget her, so that another meeting might be worked out in the future. All this she confided to me. Why deny it?"

"I have no wish to deny the facts. It's just that the neighbors will laugh at me if the story spreads around. Now that Your Reverence knows all about it, what do you suggest I do?"

The nun continued, "As soon as I learned about this, I raised the subject of Yingying's marriage with her parents. (*It is not unseemly for a nun to offer services as a matchmaker.*) Their answer was, 'Our daughter is still too young to be managing a household.' Judging from their tone, I believe that the subject is not to be brought up for another two to three years. And it also depends on whether or not there's a predestined bond between you two." With that, she rose and added, "As I have other engagements, I can't stay for a good talk, but if there are any messages you want me to deliver for you, just let me know." And so they bid each other farewell. Henceforth, the nun served as a courier, delivering clandestine love letters between the boudoir and the study.

Time sped by. In a trice, one year had elapsed. As Zhang Hao leaned against the railing and gazed upon the scattering peach and pear blossoms and the withered peonies in the days after the Clear and Bright Festival, his thoughts dwelled sadly upon his loved one. Long he tarried, reminiscing about this time the previous year when he had met her by the flowers. And now, the flowers were blooming again, but she was nowhere to be seen. After much thought, he decided to pick some flowers and send them to Yingying by way of the nun, so that she could share the joy with him. So he summoned Huiji the nun and said to her, "I picked some flowers today. Could you do me a favor and take them to Mrs. Li? Just say that they are a gift from you. If you see Yingying, please give her my regards. Last year, when the flowers were blossoming, I met her by the western railing. And now, the flowers have bloomed again, but we are so far apart. Words cannot convey my longing for her. I only wish we could see each other often, like the flowers and leaves that are able to stay together year after year."

"This is easily done," promised Huiji. "Wait here for me. I'll be back soon." So saying, she left with the bouquet.

Upon her return, Zhang Hao stepped forward and asked eagerly, "Well?"

Taking out a daintily folded letter written on flower-patterned stationery, the nun said, "This is from Yingying to you. Be sure not to let anyone else see it!" With that, she went off.

Zhang Hao opened the seal. The letter said:

From Yingying, with respect:

It has been a year since we met last, but not a day has gone by without my thinking of you. At my request, my nurse raised the subject of my marriage to my parents, but they are firmly against the idea. We must not be hasty but wait for the right opportunity to arise. My only wish is that you will not forget me. As for me, I shall never fail you! If I can't marry you, I vow never to marry. Ask Huiji, and she will tell you what else is on my mind. Last evening, a feast was laid out by the flowers, but I was torn with grief among the jovial company. I wrote a little lyric poem to give some expression to my feelings. Upon reading it, you will gain an idea of my feelings. Please destroy the letter after reading it. Be sure not to let anyone else see it!

Amid all the mirth by the riot of colors,
Grief and misery still hang heavy.
Longing for my love, I stare at the moonlight
And shed many a tear on the flowers.

The vows exchanged, all wishes known,
Yet we find ourselves far apart.
The phoenix still without a mate finds
Most painful a clear night with a round moon.

After reading it, Zhang Hao knit his brows and heaved a deep sigh. "How true is the saying 'The road to happiness never runs smooth,'" he lamented. He spread the stationery out on the table and then held it in his hands as if he would never let it go. With his heart full of grief, he burst into tears. Afraid that other members of the household might become suspicious and ask for explanations, he bent over the table and covered his face with his arms to muffle his sobs.

After a considerable time, he raised his head and looked around to find that the window had darkened and dusk had set in. Recalling the line "Ask Huiji, and she will tell you what else is on my mind," he thought that rather than sitting gloomily all alone, it would relieve his sadness somewhat if he paid Huiji a visit and heard what she had to say. He walked slowly out of the house.

By the time he passed the Li house, the doors on the streets had all closed in the gathering darkness. He was so overwhelmed with longing for Yingying that he stopped in his tracks and said, pointing at the door of the Li house, "How am I ever going to enter this house without wings?"

He was pacing around when he suddenly noticed a side door standing ajar and no one anywhere in sight. He rejoiced to himself, "Heaven is giving me this opportunity to fulfill my wish. Rather than seek help from Huiji, I might just as well slip into the house and find out where Yingying is."

His love for Yingying made him throw all concerns about decorum to the winds. He tiptoed to the main hall of the house and from there stealthily turned down a winding corridor. Looking all around him, he saw:

A courtyard quiet, dark, and deep;
Except for the wind chimes, there was not a sound;
In the darkness, the fireflies flew about.
As the night deepened, the lamp flickered in the wind;
In the growing darkness, the shadows of flowers
Moved with the moon across the terrace steps.

Her boudoir must be behind that hill of a screen,
Farther away than the distant Wushan Mountains.[2]

Zhang Hao stood there alone for quite some time, not knowing which way to turn. Suddenly, he realized the folly of his actions. If he were caught, he thought, what would happen next? Undoubtedly punishment and misery for himself, and disgrace for his ancestors. He decided he should be cautious and devise a better plan. However, since the side door had already been closed by this time, he had to go back to the corridor. He was looking for a way out when he heard a voice singing softly in one of the rooms. Who could be singing in this secluded place at this time of the night? He hid in the shadows, turned sideways, and strained his ears to listen. It was a lyric poem to the tune of "Xingxiangzi":

After the rain, the wind dies down, the colors fade;
The swallows' nests dot the remaining boughs,
The late sun shines on the willow catkins,
The partridges' chirps evoke the grief of parting.

The tryst to no avail, my best years gone to waste,
My silk clothes fade in color, and all for what?
At the pavilion, by the red peonies,
The feelings, the sorrows—who would ever care?

As he listened, he saw in his mind's eye a young oriole singing in the foliage of green willows and a colorful phoenix chirping on the leafy bough of a parasol tree. The silence of the night intensified the beauty of the melody. Reflecting on the lyrics, Zhang Hao concluded that the author must be Yingying, for who else would refer to their rendezvous at Lingering Fragrance Pavilion? If he could see her, if only once, he could leave this world with no regrets. He was about to tap on the window and ask a few questions when he heard a voice speaking in a reproachful tone: "A gentleman does not take a wife without a matchmaker; a decent woman does not marry without a good reason. Now, with the woman singing inside and the man trespassing outside, both are guilty of indecent conduct that violates the code of proper human behavior. Any yamen official would use you as an example with which to warn all potential sinners of the flesh."

Horrified, Zhang Hao stepped backward but lost his footing and fell down the flight of steps. He opened his eyes a long time later and found he was waking up from a nap, his head on his elbow, which rested on the table next to the window of his study. It was late afternoon. "What a strange dream!" he said to himself. "Why was it so real? Could it be that we are destined to meet after all, hence this good omen?"

He was in this perturbed state of mind when Huiji the nun appeared again. When he questioned her as to the purpose of her visit, she replied, "In my haste to deliver the letter, I forgot to tell you one thing. Yingying wants me to tell you that behind her house is your eastern wall, which measures only a few feet high. On the twentieth day after the summer solstice, her whole family will be away for the night attending a wedding in the clan, but Yingying will plead illness and stay at home. She wants you to wait for her by the wall that evening. She'll climb over the wall to meet you. Remember this well!" With that, Huiji departed, leaving him more jubilant than words can describe.

He counted off the days on his fingers, and the appointed day finally arrived. He had curtains put up and wine utensils and art objects laid out in Lingering Fragrance Pavilion, and when the day came to an end, he sent all the servants away except for one young maidservant. After closing the garden gate from the outside, he propped a ladder against the wall and waited with bated breath.

Soon, the westering sun sank below the branches of the weeping willow, and the shadow of the night cast its shroud over the flowers. The Big Dipper's handle pointed to the south, and the first drumbeats of the night echoed through the air. "Could Huiji have been playing a trick on me?" Zhang Hao wondered, but before he could quite finish his thought, a powdered and rouged face appeared over the top of the low wall. He raised his eyes and saw that it was none other than Yingying. (*What a reversal of roles for Yingying to be the one scaling the wall!*[3]) Quickly, he climbed up the ladder and helped her down, supporting her by an arm. Hand in hand, they went to the pavilion, where they sat side by side in the bright candlelight. All the more delighted upon examining her face closely, he said, "I never expected that you would indeed come here!"

"Wasn't I on the point of committing myself to the act of the boudoir the other day?" she replied. "Why would I play a trick on you?"

"Are you willing to drink a little bit of wine to celebrate our rendezvous tonight?"

"I'm afraid I won't be able to hold the wine. I don't want to incur my parents' anger tomorrow."

"Well, if you won't have wine, how about taking a little rest?"

Giggling, she leaned bashfully against Zhang Hao's chest but gave no answer, whereupon he took off her belt and clothes and brought her to the bed behind the curtains. Behold:

By the flickering flames of the red candles,
On the sweet-smelling mattress,
Behind the gold-traced and embroidered screen,
Shielded by the gauze bed curtains,
They joined their pillows, side by side,
Like a pair of mandarin ducks on water.
They spread out their fragrant quilts, side by side,
Like the cocoons of two spring silkworms.
The raptures of a game of clouds and rain
Might just be too much for the narrow waist!

Before long, they had broken into a sweat. They clung to each other, panting for breath, their joy greater than the bliss experienced by the King of Chu in his dream encounter with the Divine Maiden and by Liu and Ruan in the Cave of Peach Blossoms.[4]

A few moments later, Yingying said to Zhang Hao, "The night is deep. I have to go."

Zhang Hao dared not try to keep her. As they straightened their clothes and got out of bed, he said to her, "We'll meet again. Please keep me in your heart!"

"Last year when we met by chance, you made a poem for me, and now that we've shared the same bed, don't you have a few lines to give me? Can it be that my humble self is not worthy of your talent?"

"What a thing to say!" Zhang Hao said with a grateful laugh. "Now, here's a poem dedicated to you:

"The lovely dream about Huaxu is but hearsay;[5]
The gift of jade by the river is but fiction.[6]
So much happened in the night by the east window!
Han the incense stealer pales in comparison."[7]

Poem in hand, Yingying announced to him, "All of me henceforth belongs to you. I'm glad we were able to be together this time." Hand in hand, they left the pavilion. After threading their way through the willows and flowers, they came to the wall, and Zhang Hao helped Yingying mount the ladder.

From then on, they managed to communicate with each other frequently, but the opportunity for another rendezvous did not present itself. Some days later, Huiji came to say, "Yingying wants to tell you that her father has been transferred to Heshuo. The whole family is leaving tomorrow. She hopes that you will not forget her. Upon her return, she'll bring up the subject of marriage." After Huiji departed, Zhang Hao's spirits sank. With each day as long as a year to him, two miserable years went by.

One day, Zhang Hao's uncle sent for him and gave him these words of admonition: "As they say, of all offenses against filial piety, the lack of male issue is the worst. You are approaching thirty but are still unbetrothed. I'm not saying that you are already the end of the family line, but you simply must get a wife. Now, there's a rich Sun family that comes from a long line of officials. They have a daughter of marriageable age who has received a fine education at home since childhood and is well trained in the feminine virtues. I wish to make this match for you. If you lose this chance, you won't receive another offer from a family as distinguished as the Suns!"

Zhang Hao had always been afraid of his uncle's hot temper and dared not contradict him, nor did he have the courage to bring up the name of Li Yingying. (*Women are better than men. Zhang Hao and Li Yingying serve as but one example.*) Consequently, a matchmaker was sought to present the marriage proposal to the

Sun family. But before the chosen day for the wedding ceremony arrived, Yingying's father returned when his term of duty expired. Hardly forgetting his love for Yingying, Zhang Hao sent Huiji the nun to Yingying with this message: "It's not that I betrayed you, but my uncle drove me to it. This betrothal with Miss Sun is truly against my wishes. My heart is torn by grief!"

Yingying said to the nun, "I do believe this was the work of his uncle. I'll come up with a way to work things out."

"Be sure you know what you are doing!" admonished Huiji before she took her leave.

Yingying said to her parents, "Your daughter has committed a sin and brought disgrace to the family name. I have something to say before I ask permission to die."

In horror, her parents asked, "What could possibly have happened to drive you to such desperation?"

"Ever since childhood, I have admired Zhang Hao, who lives in the house west of ours, for his talent. I have secretly committed the rest of my life to him. I asked my nurse to talk to you about marriage, but Father rejected the proposal then and there. I just heard today that Zhang Hao will be married to a Miss Sun. Now where am I, an abandoned woman, to end up? Having already lost my chastity, I cannot marry another man. Since this wish of mine is to be denied, I have to take my own life, and do it gladly, too." (*The parents* [illegible].)

The panic-stricken parents said, "We do regret not having chosen a good husband earlier for you, our only daughter. Had we known this, we could have talked about it. But now that Zhang Hao is already betrothed, what can be done?"

"If you betroth me to him, I'll think of a way to make everything work out."

"We'll consider anything, as long as the marriage can be accomplished," said her father.

"If so, please allow me to appeal to the yamen." So saying, Yingying took a piece of paper and wrote an appeal. She then changed her clothes and went directly to the court of appeals in Henan Prefecture.

While he was working at his desk, Judge Chen noticed a woman advancing toward him with a scroll in her hand. He put down his brush-pen and asked, "What complaint do you have?"

Falling on her knees, Yingying said, "In my audacity, I have a complaint to submit to Your Honor."

The judge had an attendant take the scroll and spread it out to read:

This is a complaint from plaintiff Miss Li:

It is said, 'Women should not marry without going through the proper matchmaking procedures.' This may be most wise, but it may not always hold true. For example, in the olden days, Zhuo Wenjun, out of her love for Sima Xiangru,[8] *and Jia Wu, out of her admiration for Han Shou,*[9] *both eloped with their lovers, and yet no one has ever accused them of not availing themselves of matchmaking services, because the men they chose earned their places in history with their great accomplishments, and their examples can be freely followed without fear of being accused of debauchery. Last year, out of admiration for the literary talent of Zhang Hao, my next-door neighbor, I secretly committed the rest of my life to him. An agreement once made should not be reversed. But Zhang Hao has suddenly breached the agreement, leaving me crying out in anguish to heaven and earth, wishing for vindication. I have heard that the law has strict codes for enforcing justice and that the rules of decorum follow the dictates of human sensibilities. If Your Honor does not make the right ruling, to whom should this forlorn abandoned woman turn for help ever again for the rest of my life? At the risk of offending Your Honor, I plead that Your Honor judge in my favor out of compassion!*

After reading the complaint, Judge Chen asked Yingying, "You said you had a secret agreement with Zhang Hao, but do you have any evidence of it?"

Yingying produced from her bosom the silk scarf bearing Zhang Hao's poem and another poem written by Zhang Hao on flower-patterned stationery. Accordingly, Judge Chen ordered that Zhang Hao be brought to court. As the judge lashed out at Zhang Hao for planning to marry Miss Sun when he was already betrothed, Zhang Hao hastened to defend himself, saying that he had not meant to do so but that his uncle had driven him to it. The judge asked Yingying, "What is your opinion?"

"With his literary talent, Zhang Hao will truly make an ideal husband. Should I marry him, I will assiduously perform my wifely duties out of gratitude for Your Honor's great kindness."

"I am not going to tear apart a talented young scholar and a beautiful maiden who are meant for each other by heaven's will. Let me make this match for you." (*Good judge.*) At the end of the letter of complaint, he wrote his judgment:

An encounter by the flowers
Led to a betrothal.
To bring it to an end
Is to betray their everlasting devotion.
Human sensibilities favor loyalty;
The codes of law dispense justice.
The first betrothal prevails;
The second one is hereby nullified.

Having done so, the judge announced to Zhang Hao, "My judgment is for you to be married to Miss Li."

Overjoyed, the couple bowed to the judge and thanked him for his kindness. They married and lived happily ever after. Their two sons both won high honors on the imperial civil service examinations. This story is known as "Zhang Hao Meets Yingying at Lingering Fragrance Pavilion."

Cui Yingying of old had Zhang to save the day,[10]
Zhang of today is delivered by Li Yingying.
Of these two eternal stories of romance,
The latter outshines the former.

30

Wu Qing Meets Ai'ai by Golden Bright Pond

Zhu Wen encounters Liu Qian by the lamp;[1]
Han Shihou meets his deceased wife's ghost at Mount Yan.[2]
Even death does not part them;
Love, the deepest of all emotions.

The story goes that in the Zhonghe reign period [881–84] of the great Tang dynasty, there lived in Boling a talented and dashing scholar named Cui Hu who had no equal in ability or in appearance. As the date of the spring imperial civil service examinations approached, he collected his zither, sword, and books and went to Chang'an to sit for the examinations. He secured lodging at an inn and then went for a walk in the suburbs south of the city to see the sights of late spring. Partly because of his vigorous walking and partly because of the warm weather, Cui Hu felt his mouth and throat dry, his lips parched, and his nose burning. While he searched for a mountain brook at which to alleviate his thirst, he came upon a place with

Fiery peach blossoms among misty green willows,
Bamboo fences, thatched huts, yellow mud walls, white gates,
A veritable haven of peace, with
A dog bark or two, an oriole chirp here and there.

Cui Hu went up to a door and knocked, meaning to ask for a drink of water, but he stood there for a considerable time without anyone showing up. As he was wondering what to do, he heard laughter from behind the door. Quick of eye, he peeked through a crack in the door and saw that the laughter came from a girl about sixteen years old. As she emerged to answer the door, Cui Hu felt his mouth and throat even drier, his lips more parched, and his nose burning worse than before. With his hands folded respectfully across his chest, he hastened forward and said, "Please accept a greeting from me, young lady."

Coyly, the girl dropped a curtsy and asked, "What can I do for you, sir, honored as I am by your visit to this humble hut?"

"I am Cui Hu from Boling. I'm thirsty and short of breath from all the walking I've been doing and came just to ask for a drink of water."

Upon hearing these words, the girl rushed into the house without a word and returned bearing a porcelain jar, half filled with tea, in her soft and delicately shaped hands. Cui accepted the jar and took a sip. What a cooling effect it had on his body! Now totally refreshed, he thanked her and continued on his way to the examinations, for his mind was filled with desire for rank and title. However, not being in luck at this time of his life, he failed the examinations and hurriedly left Chang'an for home.

All too quickly, another year elapsed. It was again time for the examinations, and Cui Hu set out once more for the capital to sit for the examinations. Recalling the girl he had met a year ago, he pushed the examinations to the back of his mind and hastened to the south of the city, looking all around as he went, afraid that he might miss the girl's house. Before long, he found himself at the right door. As before, the peach blossoms were in bloom amid the green willow trees, and he heard the same dog barks and oriole chirps. Wondering why there was no trace of a human being around as he approached the door, he again peeked through a crack in the door but saw no one inside. After pacing up and down for a good while, he stopped to write the following quatrain on the white wooden door:

This very day last year by this door,
Peach blossoms were in bloom against her blushing cheeks.
But where, pray, is she now, while the peach blossoms
Are still there, smiling in the spring breezes?

After writing the poem, he left, but the next day, still unable to calm his mind, he went back to the house for another look. All of a sudden, the door opened with a creak, and out came an old man with

Hoary eyebrows, thin beard and hair,
A white cloth robe, and a mottled bamboo cane.
He could well be one of the four Shang hermits[3]
Or the one who angled at Pan Creek.[4]

The old man asked, "Might you be Cui Hu?"

"Please accept a bow from me, sir. Yes, I am Cui Hu, but how did you know?"

"You are killing my daughter. How could I not know?"

His face turning the color of mud, Cui Hu said in horror, "I have never even set foot in your house. How can you say such a thing?"

"Last year, my daughter was at home alone when you came to ask for a drink of water. After you were gone, she fell into a trance as if drunk and was confined to bed. Yesterday, she suddenly said, 'This very day last year I met Mr. Cui. I believe he'll be here again today.' (*A meeting of minds.*) She walked to the door and stayed at this spot for the longest time, watching for you in vain. When she turned around, she looked up and saw the poem on the door. With a long drawn-out cry, she collapsed to the ground. I helped her to her room, where she lay unconscious throughout the night. This morning, she suddenly opened her eyes and said, 'Mr. Cui is here. Please go and greet him, Father.' And sure enough, here you are. Isn't this something predestined to happen? Please come inside and see."

But as soon as Cui entered the house, a sob was heard and, as it turned out, the girl was dead.

The old man shrieked, "You owe me my daughter's life!"

Overcome by shock and grief, Cui walked to the bed and sat down next to the girl's head. Gently, he moved her head onto his outstretched legs and, kissing her cheeks, said, "Young lady, Cui Hu is here." (*Good physician.*) In a trice, the girl's three souls and seven spirits returned to her body, and she rose to walk.

Overjoyed beyond measure, the old man offered a dowry and had Cui Hu stay on as a live-in son-in-law. Later, Cui Hu rose considerably in life and became an official. The husband and wife live happily to the end of their days. Indeed,

> *The moon wanes but waxes again;*
> *The mirror comes apart but joins again.*
> *The flowers fall but bloom again;*
> *Humans die but come back to life again.*

Why did I tell this story? Because it is about a resurrection from death. Now, what follows is a story about a passionate but luckless girl who met a young profligate. Her love unrequited, she died needlessly and, if anything, helped to bring about the wedding of the man and another girl. Truly,

> *Those with predestined bonds will meet,*
> *However far apart they are.*
> *Those without will miss each other,*
> *Face-to-face though they may be.*

Now, the young man whom our girl met was the only son of Squire Wu Zixu of Kaifeng Prefecture, eastern capital of the Song dynasty. Squire Wu, an honest man, loved his only son Wu Qing to the point of foolhardiness, so much so that he forbade the boy to go out the door, not even for one day. However, the son turned out to be a profligate bent on making friends and embarking on amorous adventures.

One day, two friends of his, Zhao Yingzhi and his younger brother Zhao Maozhi, came to visit. Being sons of Prince and Regional Commander Zhao and therefore descendants of the royal family, they were prodigal spendthrifts. When their arrival was announced, Young Master Wu went out to greet them. After they had taken their seats as host and guests and tea was served, Young Master Wu asked, "To what do I owe this visit?"

"It being the season of the Clear and Bright Festival, Golden Bright Pond is swarming with sightseers, male and female. Would you be willing to go there with us?"

Delighted, Wu said, "Since you do not disdain my lowly status, I'll surely be happy to oblige." Accordingly, he had a page boy carry a load of wine and food utensils and prepare three horses for the outing. And so, they followed the many twists and turns in the road and wended their way to Golden Bright Pond. I present the poem by Academician Tao Gu[5] to provide a description of the pond:

Amid drunken singing from the ten thousand seats,
A mist rises to shroud the pond like a curtain.
The clouds hide the palace in the sky;
The sun shines on the multicolored universe.
The painted bridge over the waves comes from heaven;
Sightseers by the shore walk in the mirror.
The emperor joins the dragon-boat feast
Amid cheers carried by the flower-scented wind.

As the threesome toured the lake, they saw:

Peach blossoms as bright as brocade,
Green willows as hazy as mist.
Among flowers, butterflies flit in pairs;
On tree branches, orioles perch in twos.
Young men and women swarm to the site;
Sightseers descend in an endless stream.

Stopping for a round of drink in a quiet spot, Young Master Wu commented, "What a glorious day! Too bad we don't have a nice girl to serve us wine."

The Zhao brothers said, "We've had enough to drink. How about taking a leisurely walk to watch the sightseers? Wouldn't that be better than sitting here with nothing to do?"

Hand in hand, the three set off, but before they had gone more than a few steps, a whiff of fragrant wind swept past, assailing their nostrils with an aroma that could not have been anything else but musk mixed with the scent of rouge and powder. As Young Master Wu moved in the direction of the fragrance's source, he saw a group of women as delightful to the eye as a cluster of brightly colored flowers vying to outshine one another in beauty. Among them was a girl in an apricot yellow blouse, no more than fifteen or sixteen years of age. How did she look?

Her eyes two pools of autumn water;
Her brows the shape of rolling verdant hills.
Her hair done up like a cloud;
Her feet dainty as lotus petals.
Her unrouged lips as red as cherries;
Her waist as narrow as a willow twig.
The sweetness of her body not easily judged,
Her charm and grace were evident from afar.

At the sight, Young Master Wu melted all over with desire. He was about to approach the young lady when the Zhao brothers pulled him back, saying, "You can't take liberties with a girl from a decent family! Besides, there are too many eyes and ears around. You'll only get yourself into trouble." (*The argument of moralists. Quite useful.*)

Wu did not object, but he felt as if his soul had been snatched away. The young lady went away with her group, and Young Master Wu parted company with the Zhao brothers and returned home. As he lay awake the whole night through, he said to himself, "What a beauty she is! I should have asked for her address and her name. If I can find out what they are, I'll have a matchmaker propose to her. I may have a chance."

The next day, preoccupied with thoughts about the young woman, he changed into nicer clothes and asked the Zhao brothers to go with him to Golden Bright Pond again in search of the young lady he had seen the day before.

It's the same old path to the balcony,[6]
But where's the one in the rain from the other day?

Young Master Wu searched in vain among the sightseers for the young lady of yesterday. To a dejected Young Master Wu, Elder Brother Zhao remarked, "As far as I can tell, you are in none too good a mood because you've been let down in your quest for romance. Well, there's no lack of young wineshop waitresses in this area. Let's take you to them. If you see a girl who strikes your fancy, go ahead and drink three cups and count that as a romantic experience of sorts. What do you say?"

"I never pay attention to those faded flowers and withered willows. They are all past the prime of their lives."

"But in the fifth house from the northern end of this street, there's an exquisite little wineshop," put in Second Brother Zhao. "And in that wineshop, the one who measures out the wine is a very attractive girl. She's only about sixteen, and she doesn't come out to the front of the shop very often."

That information cheered up Young Master Wu. "Take me there!" he said.

The three young men went up the street and saw that there was indeed a small wineshop with well-spaced flowers and bamboos growing in front of the door and cups and plates displayed in neat rows inside. "This is it!" exclaimed Second Brother Zhao, pointing a finger. They entered and found the house dead quiet.

"Anybody here?" they called out.

In a trice, an imperceptible movement disturbed the air, and a fifteen- or sixteen-year-old girl emerged in all her charm and coquettishness, pretty as a flower and romantically inclined by nature. At the sight of the girl, the three young men bowed deeply and, as if coordinating their movements, bent their three heads toward the ground, folded their six arms across their chests, and chanted, "Greetings to you, young lady!"

Overcome by irrepressible passion at the sight of the three young men, the flirtatious girl found it hard to take her feet back to the interior of the house. Instead, she sat shoulder to shoulder with the young men and called out for Ying'er to serve wine. What a good time they thought they were going to have, these four, whose ages added together totaled less than one hundred! (*One should never fail to observe decorum.*) But they had barely raised their first cups of wine when they heard the clip-clop of a donkey's hooves and the rumble-tumble of carriage wheels. The girl's parents had returned from the family's ancestral grave. Bitterly let down, the three young men returned home.

As time went by, the colors of spring faded and the scenic spots attracted hardly any sightseers, but thoughts of the lovely one kept recurring in dreams. In the twinkling of an eye, another year elapsed. As if by prior agreement, the three young men again set out on a trip to the same wineshop. They arrived a short time later and found the shop bleak and unattended. After resting, the three were just about to make inquiries when the elderly couple they had seen last year came out.

"Greetings to you, sir," the three young men said. "A flask of wine, please." Then they continued, "Sir, when we were here last year, there was a young lady serving at the counter, measuring out wine, but we don't see her today."

At these words, the old man burst into tears. "I am Lu Rong. The girl you saw was my daughter Ai'ai. This very day last year, while we were out paying our respects at the family's ancestral grave, three frivolous young men came and drank wine with her. They went away when they saw us coming back, and I have no idea what happened between them. My wife and I said a few reproachful words to our girl—nothing harsh—but, being of a sensitive nature, she became sulky and refused to eat or drink. She died a few days later. The little mound behind the house is her grave." At this point, the tears trickled down his cheeks again.

The three young men were dumbstruck. They didn't dare to ask anything more, but hastened to pay the bill. On their way back, riding their horses in a straight line, they kept looking back at the shop, their gowns stained with tears, their hearts heavy with grief. Truly,

In the depths of the now silent night,
The moon shines on the ponds and terraces.
The tranquillity remains undisturbed
Till sunrise, when unforeseen events come to pass.

As they were traveling, they became vaguely aware of the presence of a woman. She wore a white head-wrap and a red vest and walked with shaky, hesitant steps. Casting a coy glance at the three young men, she chanted a greeting in a subdued voice. The young men, feeling as if they were in a trance, didn't know what to do. She could have been a ghost, but her clothes were properly sewed, and she was casting a shadow on the ground. They could have been dreaming, but a pinch caused a twinge of pain.

The woman spoke. "You know who I am. I am the one you met last year by

Golden Bright Pond. When you were in my home earlier today, my parents lied to you in saying that I was dead. That grave is nothing but a mound of earth piled up to deceive you. I believe it is our predestined bond that makes our paths cross. I've moved to a small house on a secluded lane in the city. It's quite a nice place. If you don't think it's beneath your dignity, would you be kind enough to follow me there?"

The three young men dismounted and followed her. In an instant they found themselves at the door of a house. When they stepped in, this was what they saw:

A garden connected to the small house,
A curtain for concealing amorous games.
The low eaves cast shadows on the red shade;
The deep boudoir had its brocade canopy drawn.
The feeble light blurred the bodies' contours;
The gaudy colors matched the fiery passion.

As soon as they were upstairs, Ai'ai called out, "Ying'er! Serve wine to wish the three gentlemen joy!" In no time, they set to drinking to their hearts' content. There was nothing the girl was not good at. She sang a song in a coquettish tone, performed a passionate dance in a suggestive way, played a heady tune on the zither, and chanted most sweetly a salute to the three young men, addressing them as "Your Highnesses." The Zhao brothers departed after having their fill of wine, but Young Master Wu stayed behind. He turned toward the girl, put his arm around her soft shoulders, held her to him by her narrow waist, squeezed her delicate hands, and, his eyes heavy with wine, had his way with her in all his eagerness, as if they were in a bedchamber. Truly,

Her blouse taken off, the embroidered quilt spread out;
Her chest a plum blossom against the snow;
Her tiny feet the shape of crescent moons.
The peach blossom bud could hardly withstand
The advances of the amorous butterfly.
The flower pistils were too tender
For the thrusts of the brutal bee;
In each other's arms, they sweated and panted.

At daybreak, they rose, washed, and combed their hair. With breakfast over, they still had much to say to each other, hating the thought of parting. Young Master Wu lit some incense and made a vow, biting his own arms until they bled. Ai'ai covered her face and went merrily to the interior of the house. Young Master Wu returned home in low spirits.

"Son," said his parents upon seeing him, "where did you spend the night? You made us lose a whole night's sleep. Such nightmares we had!"

"Father, Mother, it was because those two friends of mine, who are members of the royal family, wanted me to stay overnight, so I had to do as they wished."

At the mention of the royal family members, who had visited their son before, the parents relented. No suspicion crossed their minds. Little did they know that their son was conducting a romance that was hard for him to explain. There is a poem in testimony:

The thistles cleared away, a tower appeared
In which songs and music came to reign.
By farewell time, the merrymaking at an end,
The rampant thistles took over again.

Young Master Wu and Ai'ai became a most loving couple, and this was only natural, for he was a tender bamboo shoot and she a blooming flower in the best season of the year. Truly,

The beauty is in the spring of her life;
The dashing young man in the prime of his life.

His heart filled with passion for the girl, the young man would not let two days go by without spending a night with her. However, there was one remarkable thing about these visits: The moment he saw her, he felt more vigorous and handsome than usual, but as soon as he got home, he appeared sallow and haggard. As time wore on, he began to look more like a ghost than a human. He lost his appetite, nor would he take any medicine.

His parents were alarmed at his condition. There being a deep bond between father and son, the father, casting aside all scruples about friendship and connections with royalty, invited the Zhao brothers to visit and addressed them in the following words: "I'd like to know where you took my son some time ago and what mischief he got himself into. He's critically ill now. If he recovers, I won't say a word against you, but if something happens to him, I'll have to press charges against you at court. Don't blame me if it comes to that."

Upon hearing these words, the brothers whispered to each other, "We may be members of the royal family, but the law is the law. At best, well-behaving descendants of the royal family are assigned to official posts just as commoners are, but when something happens, we aren't spared in the least. If this old man does press charges against us, we'll be in for some trouble." More loudly, they replied, "Sir, your son's illness has nothing to do with us." Thereupon, they gave an account of their encounter with the flirtatious pretty girl at the wineshop by Golden Bright Pond.

The old man was appalled. "So, my son is involved with a ghost! What do you think we can do to save him?"

"There is a Daoist sage, Huangfu, who is equipped with magic figures and a sword that subdues demons. The only course of action now would be to have him exorcise that evil ghost and thus ensure your son's well-being."

Bowing thankfully, the old man said, "Then I'll count on your help." So the two brothers immediately set out to accomplish the mission. Truly,

A green dragon and a white tiger[7]
Bring either joy or woe, when together.

The Zhao brothers took to the road. After a long journey, they came to a mountain, where they saw amid the white clouds a temple with a thatched roof.

A yellow thatched roof,
A white stone wall.
Cranes fly among the pine trees;
Turtles bask in the sun by a small pond.
Green willows and plants flank the path;
Black apes and white cranes greet guests at the gate.

Soon after they had stopped at the gate, a Daoist acolyte emerged from the temple, saying, "Are you two gentlemen here to seek my master's help to save a human life?"

"Yes! Please announce us to your master."

"My master takes only cases involving the demon of lust. Why? Because lust gives life but also takes life away. In the Daoist belief, giving life is of central importance, but killing is the number one taboo."

"We are here precisely to ask your master to subdue a demon of lust and save a human being from death."

Without a moment's delay, the acolyte went back inside and soon returned with Sage Huangfu. The acolyte having already explained the situation, the sage said readily, "I will go," and followed the Zhao brothers all the way to Squire Wu's house.

He had hardly reached the door when he commented, "This house is wrapped in a demonic aura, but there is still a breath of life."

At this point, Young Master Wu happened to come to the door. In alarm, the sage exclaimed, "This is a serious case! The odds are nine to one that you're going to die. There's only one way to save you."

The panic-stricken old couple came to plead on their knees, saying, "Please be so kind as to use your magic and save everyone in our family."

"Do as I say," ordered the sage. "Go quickly in a westerly direction and take shelter somewhere a good three to four hundred li away. Nevertheless, wherever you go, you'll surely find the ghost already there. If she's not gone after a hundred and twenty days, your life, Young Squire Wu, will be beyond salvation."

The young man agreed to this course of action. After being treated to a vegetarian meal, Sage Huangfu bade his hosts farewell and departed. Squire Wu Senior quickly ordered servants to pack for his son to go to Luoyang, the Western Capital in Henan Prefecture, to get him out of harm's way. Truly,

Those who have read The Record of Previous Lives
Know that men have no control over life and death.

The young master asked the two Zhao brothers to accompany him. All along the way, whether climbing mountains or crossing bridges over ravines, whether in quiet spots or places bustling with activity, whether with company or not, every time the young master ate, the girl was by his side, serving him, and every time he went to bed, she stayed with him and helped him undress. When he went to the lavatory, she held his clothes for him. There was no way he could get away from her, anywhere, anytime.

Before they realized it, they had been in Luoyang for quite a few days. Suddenly, one day, he counted up on his fingers and realized that it was exactly one hundred and twenty days since he had left home. What was to be done? The Zhao brothers and the servants escorted him to a wineshop to cheer him up, but in their worry and fear, they could barely refrain from weeping. And yet, afraid that the young master would see their tears, they quickly wiped them away.

The young master was perplexed and had not the least idea of what to do. He was leaning against the railing, his head down, when Sage Huangfu approached on a donkey. Upon seeing him, one of the Zhao brothers rushed down the stairs and fell to his knees right there on the street. He caught the sage by his clothes, imploring him to help. Young Master Wu and everyone in his entourage got down on their knees in supplication.

Right there in the wineshop, the sage set up an altar, lit some incense, and walked along the imagined outline of the Big Dipper, all the while muttering an incantation. When the ritual was over, the sage handed a sword to Wu, saying, "You are supposed to die today. Now take this sword. In the late afternoon, close your door tightly. At sundown, you'll surely hear a knock at the door. Don't ask who it is. Just use this sword to quickly cut down the person outside. If you're lucky, you'll kill the demon and you'll live. If luck goes against you and you kill an innocent person, you'll have to die, but you were going to die anyway. And now, at least you have a chance." After giving these words of instruction, the sage rode off on his donkey.

Sword in hand, the young master waited eagerly for the afternoon to draw to a close. He shut the door, and evening began to set in. A knock came on the door. Quietly, he pulled the door open and brought down the sword. He felt something fall to the ground at his strike. Startled but delighted, he called out, his heart pumping violently, "Bring me a lamp!" A lamp was soon brought to him. Even the innkeeper joined the crowd to look. It would have been all right if they had not looked, but as they did, all those present stood aghast.

The eight pieces of his skull opened up,
And half a bucket of ice and snow poured in.

The innkeeper recognized the corpse as that of Ashou, a fifteen-year-old page boy who had served at the inn. He had gone out to the street to use the lavatory and, finding himself locked out upon his return, had knocked on the door and been cut down. The commotion at the inn drew the attention of the local headman. Upon arriving at the scene, he saw that he had a case of homicide on his hands and had Young Master Wu as well as the Zhao brothers tied up.

The next morning, the suspects were taken under guard to Henan Prefecture. When told there had been a homicide, prefectural magistrate read the complaint and sent the suspects to the inspector for questioning. There, the young master recounted how Sage Huangfu had instructed him to cut down the demon.

"How absurd!" snapped the inspector. "How can a story like that explain away the death of the page boy, a flesh-and-blood human being?"

He then ordered that torture be applied. As the young master's followers had bribed people left and right at the yamen, a prison warden declared, "Wu Qing, who has not yet recovered from a prolonged illness, is too weak to withstand torture, and the two members of the royal clan are involved only in a minor way." The chief prison warden, pushing the boat with the current, so to speak, ordered that Wu Qing be detained for the time being, to be tried again after his recovery. The two Zhao brothers were set free on bail. At the same time, the local headman was ordered to have the corpse placed in a coffin to await a forensic examination in court. The demon-subduing sword, being the weapon used in the homicide, was put away in the yamen storehouse.

Let us turn our attention to Young Master Wu in his prison cell that night. He said to himself with a tearful sigh, "Since I'm the only child, my parents have never left my side since my earliest years, never dreaming that I would die in an alien place! If I'm meant to die at this time, why let me die away from my hometown?" Then he continued, addressing himself to the young lady, "I never anticipated that our love in this life would turn into rancor after death! You are the one who brought me into all this suffering, separating me from my parents and leaving me to die without even a proper burial place. How wretched I am! Oh, the misery of it all!" After lamenting for a good part of the night, he drifted into sleep.

In a dream, he saw Ai'ai, pretty as a flower and full of tenderness, walking up to him flirtatiously. Dropping a deep curtsy, she said, "Young Master, please don't hold it against me. When I died, the Goddess of the Universe, who happened to be passing in the sky, took pity on me because I died without being guilty of any wrongdoing and taught me the secrets of keeping my corpse alive. That was how I preserved my human form and was able to move around in the world of mortals. Out of gratitude to you for still thinking about me the second year after we met, I shamelessly offered myself to you. We are indeed predestined to be husband and wife for one hundred and twenty days, but now that the bond is completed, I should be leaving you.

"The other night, I came to say good-bye, little expecting that you would wish me harm and cut me down with a sword. Your misery in prison tonight is repayment of that debt to me. As for Ashou the page boy, he's in the ancient cemetery outside East Gate. If you can get the authorities to do a forensic examination, you'll be exonerated. I've obtained two Jade Snow pills from Goddess Shangyuan.[8] Take one, and you'll be free of all illnesses and regain your vital forces. The other one is for you to keep. It will bring you a good marriage as repayment of the debt of gratitude I owe you for our 120 days as husband and wife." (*Truly a young woman of tender feelings.*)

Thereupon, she produced two pills the size of chickpeas. Of a bright red color, they looked like two beads of fire. Putting one pill in the young master's sleeve and the other in his mouth, she said, "Off I go now. After you return home, be sure to visit my deserted grave, just for old times' sake."

Young Master Wu was about to ask for more details when suddenly the chime of bells came to his ears, and he woke up with a start. A most unusual fragrance filled his mouth, and his stomach burned as if a ball of fire was rolling around in it. He broke into a heavy sweat. When daybreak finally came, the sweating stopped, and all of a sudden, he felt his old healthy self again. Groping in his sleeve, he found one pill, just like the one he had seen in his dream.

The young master told the authorities what the female ghost had said about the whereabouts of Ashou the page boy and requested that a forensic examination be made so as to uncover the truth, but he kept the rest of the dream to himself. After obtaining permission from the prefectural magistrate, the prison warden had the coffin opened. Inside, there was nothing but an old broom. A search party went to the ancient cemetery outside East Gate and found Ashou the page boy in a broken stone coffin, as if in a wine-induced sleep. After being wakened with some ginger soup forced down his throat, he professed total ignorance as to how he had ended up in this place. The prison warden brought the boy and the broom to the magistrate and summoned the innkeeper to make an identification. It was definitely Ashou.

Only then did it become known that this had all been the work of the female ghost. The magistrate had everyone driven out of the court. Knowing how ineffective his demon-subduing sword had turned out to be, Sage Huangfu betook himself to the mountains to seek perfection of his skills. The Zhao brothers went to greet Young Master Wu and bring him home, showering words of congratulations upon him. The innkeeper also came, to ask for forgiveness. The three young men took leave of the innkeeper and, followed by the servants, set out merrily on their journey back to Kaifeng Prefecture.

About fifty li from the city, they came upon a large town and stopped at a wineshop for lunch. On the gate of an imposing mansion, they saw a poster seeking the services of a physician. It said:

"The beloved daughter of this family is critically ill with an affliction that none has been able to name. Any skilled physician with a cure will be rewarded with a hundred thousand in cash plus red silk, lamb, and wine. There will be absolutely no retraction of this offer."

After reading the poster, Young Master Wu asked a waiter at the inn, "What family lives next door? What kind of illness is it? Is it really something no one recognizes?"

"This place is Chu Manor. Squire Chu's family lives next door. Old Squire Chu has a sixteen-year-old daughter who's as pretty as a flower and as fair as jade. They've had no lack of marriage proposals, but the old squire is not one to give his consent lightly. Less than a month ago, the girl suddenly came down with an illness. She became delirious and refused to eat or drink. One physician after another wrote prescriptions for her, but she got worse instead of better. What a pity there's no qualified candidate fortunate enough to inherit the vast family fortune, and she's such a rare girl, too! How sad! It looks as if she's going to die any time now. The parents are weeping day and night, praying to the gods, paying homage to the Buddha's images, and doing good deeds. Goodness knows how much they've spent."

Concealing his delight, Young Master Wu said, "Second Brother, would you do me a favor? Please serve as my matchmaker. I want this young lady to be my wife."

The waiter replied, "The odds are nine to one that she's going to die. If you want to propose, at least wait until she recovers from her illness."

"I know how to cure such illnesses of the mind. I'll forgo all rewards. As long as the family agrees to a betrothal, I guarantee that the illness will be gone the moment I take on the case."

"Please sit, sir. Let me convey your message to them."

In a trice, the waiter brought Mr. Chu into the wineshop. After exchanging greetings with the three young men, Mr. Chu asked, "Which gentleman is the physician?"

Raising their hands, the Zhao brothers said, "Young Master Wu here is the physician."

"If you cure my daughter, I promise that I will not hold back the least fraction of a penny from the amount of reward announced in the poster."

"My name is Wu Qing. I live with my parents on Main Street within the city gate. I'm reasonably well off, so the reward doesn't mean anything to me. But, being yet unbetrothed at the age of twenty and a longtime admirer of the beauty and virtues of your daughter, I will offer my services as a physician only if you agree to marry your daughter to me."

The Zhao brothers praised Young Master Wu profusely, testifying to his family's exalted status and immense wealth and extolling his virtues as an honest man. As there was nothing he would not do for the love of his daughter, Mr. Chu readily accepted the offer. "If you can indeed cure my daughter, I will not fail to send the modest dowry to your house and marry my daughter to you."

To the Zhao brothers, Wu Qing said, "Please be my matchmakers and make sure that they don't break off the engagement."

"Why would I ever dream of breaking it off?" protested Mr. Chu.

Mr. Chu promptly invited the three young men into the house and treated them to dinner. In his eagerness, Wu Qing said to the old squire, "Please take me to your daughter's room. I'll see what ails her and write a prescription." Mr. Chu obliged. There being a predestined bond between Young Master Wu and the girl, she came out of her delirious state the moment he came through the door. Purposefully, he said he wanted to feel her pulse, so the nurse lifted the bed curtain just enough for the girl to stretch out an arm. With a tinkling sound of golden bracelets, a hand as delicately shaped as one sculpted out of jade or ice appeared. Truly,

Before her lovely face could be seen,
His eyes fell on her jade-smooth wrist.

After feeling the pulse in both wrists, he said with feigned seriousness, "Evil spirits have taken possession of the patient. I am the only one who can cure her."

So saying, he produced the remaining Jade Snow pill and made the girl swallow it with water freshly drawn from the well. Immediately, she felt relieved, and all her symptoms were gone. Mr. Chu's heart overflowed with gratitude. Later that day, the three young men were treated to a sumptuous dinner in the Chu manor, and they drank to their hearts' content. Mr. Chu then put them up in the study for the night. The next morning, after breakfast, the Zhao brothers said, "After putting you to so much trouble, we should be on our way, but don't go back on your word about the marriage."

"My daughter owes her life to him. Why would I ever betray such a benefactor and fail to do as you say?"

At these words, Young Master bowed thankfully to his future father-in-law. Mr. Chu presented them with a prodigious amount of gifts as a token of his high regard, but the three young men declined all of the offerings, took their leave, and went home.

Squire Wu Senior's joy at his son's return in good health need not be described here. When the Zhao brothers told him about the marriage, Squire Wu Senior was delighted beyond measure. Naturally, a day was chosen for the wedding. When all the six preliminaries had been completed,[9] Mr. Chu escorted his daughter to the Wu establishment for the wedding, bringing along a dowry worth a thousand taels of gold. By the light of the wedding candles, Young Squire Wu took a look at his bride and gave a start, for she resembled the very beauty in an apricot yellow blouse whom he had seen by Golden Bright Pond.

About half a month later, when the husband and wife had gotten to know each other better, Young Master Wu asked his wife the question he had on his mind. She replied that she had indeed been in the city last year to visit relatives two days before the Clear and Bright Festival, wearing an apricot yellow blouse, and that she had toured Golden Bright Pond. Truly, if there is a wish, heaven will never fail to grant it. Miss Chu's pet name happened to be Ai'ai as well.

One day, Young Master Wu told the Zhao brothers about this, much to their amazement. "So, you owe this marriage to Miss Lu," they commented. "You mustn't forget what she did for you."

That very day, Young Master Wu went to Mr. Lu's wineshop north of Golden Bright Pond. He gave the Lu couple an account of what had happened to their daughter and, offering lavish gifts, honored them as his parents-in-law. He then asked them to dig up the grave so that he could see the corpse, adding that he would buy a new coffin for the reburial. Being of a lowly status, Mr. Lu was only too happy to be connected with a rich squire. After a fortune-teller had chosen an auspicious day, the young master performed a ritual complete with sacrificial offerings of wine and all three animals before the grave was opened and the coffin uncovered.[10] Ai'ai's corpse had a complexion as fresh as if she were alive, and the fragrance from the body permeated the air. This, he realized, was the result of her having perfected the art in retaining her human form. After some emotional sighs of admiration, Young Master Wu commenced the reburial ceremony and engaged celebrated monks for a prayer service that lasted seven days and nights. On the last night of the service, Ai'ai appeared to him in a dream to offer her thanks, and that was the last he saw of her.

Young Master Wu and Chu Ai'ai remained a devoted couple to the end of their lives. He also took care of the burial rites of Mr. and Mrs. Lu, such was the extent of his kindness. There is a poem in testimony:

He met two beauties by Golden Bright Pond;
In life and death, he fulfilled the predestined bonds.
If all lovers were as devoted,
From the flames of fire would emerge golden lotuses.

31

Zhao Chun'er Restores Prosperity to the Cao Farmstead

Last night, a singing girl in the next room
Stirred the traveler's thoughts with her pipa.[1]
Not that women are the only friends to make,
But the world has always lacked good men.

These four lines are in praise of women. It has always been said since ancient times: "Worthy women are superior to men. " No woman is lowlier than a prostitute, and yet, even a good many prostitutes stand out as women of great merit. There was Lady Liang, who saw Han Shizhong's estimable qualities before he rose from a humble foot soldier to become a general.[1] When he was leading forces in battle against Jin Wuzhu, the fourth son of the Jurchen king, Lady Liang rewarded the soldiers with her jewelry and, by beating the battle drum to bolster the soldiers' morale, helped put the Jurchens to rout. Later, Han Shizhong, granted the title Prince of Qi, retired to West Lake, where he lived out the rest of his life with her. Another example is Li Yaxian, a celebrated courtesan in Chang'an. One of her clients, a Zheng Yuanhe, used up all his money and was reduced to living in a poorhouse. One snowy day, he was singing the beggars' song "Lotus Petals Fall" when Li Yaxian heard him and, upon recognizing his voice, took him into her house. She gave him an embroidered jacket to keep him warm and urged him to study, going as far as to injure her own eyes because their beauty distracted him from his studies. Later, on his first attempt at taking the imperial civil service examinations, Zheng won first honors as a *zhuangyuan,* and Li Yaxian also received titles until she became a Lady of the First Rank. These are two examples of worthy prostitutes who,

Compared with commonplace men,
Should replace their headdresses with men's hats.

Let me now tell of another prostitute who may not be as remarkable as Li Yaxian and Lady Liang but who endured all manner of hardships and helped her husband establish a career and attain a measure of success. She was also truly one in a thousand.

As the story goes, outside the city gate of Yangzhou Prefecture, there was a Cao

Farmstead headed by the wealthy but widowed Mr. Cao Senior. His only son, Cao Kecheng, was a handsome youth, quick and clever in everything except studying and managing his finances. As the proverb says, "An only son gets all the love." Being a beloved only son from a rich family, he was spoiled rotten. Moreover, he was addressed by all and sundry outside family circles as "Young Master" after he had been admitted early on as a paying student at the National College, which only added to his impudence. He did little but frequent houses of ill repute, drinking with the prostitutes and squandering money on amorous adventures. His high spirits and extravagance earned him the nickname "Cao the Featherbrain." Knowing his lavish spending habits but unable to keep him under control, his father cut off his allowance. Consequently, he used family property as collateral with which to borrow money left and right without his father being any the wiser.

Now, a prodigal son who resorts to borrowing is inevitably shortchanged in the following ways: First, the silver is usually of poor quality and therefore is worth less. A heartless lender might even palm off goods in kind to make the full amount. Second, the interest is as high as it can possibly be. Third, with compound interest, even though the loan does not have to be repaid in a year or ten months but only renewed, the substantial principal plus the heavy interest will add up to more than the borrower can ever repay, whatever the worth of his family property. Fourth, middlemen take deductions for their services. A middleman, considering himself half a creditor, presses aggressively for repayment of the loan, flaunting his connections with creditors like a fox walking in the company of a tiger. Fifth, when drawing up the contract, the lender picks the best landed estate to serve as the pledge. Once the documents are signed, the property cannot be sold to another client. By the time it is sold, the lender will try to reduce the price. If the sale should result in a profit of a few taels of silver for the borrower and the borrower tries to claim it, the lender will drag his feet and play fast and loose, refusing to yield the money readily.

In most cases, these five disadvantages lead to bankruptcy. The head of the household hangs on tightly to what he believes are the key family possessions, little knowing that the lion's share has gone to line someone else's pocket. Of all his possessions, he is able to enjoy less than half. He would do well to focus on life here and now rather than care about what will happen after his death. If you have a prodigal son who is going to wipe out the family wealth anyway, you may as well watch him do it before you die so that you won't be left in suspense!

Knowing your heir to be an unworthy sort,
You try to keep him under lock and key.
Your children will draw up plans for themselves
Why slave for them as if you were a horse or an ox?

Let me not encumber this story with any more of these idle comments but come to tell of Zhao Chun'er, daughter of Madam Zhao, and a courtesan well known in the region. As lovely as a flower and the moon, as fair as jade and a lustrous pearl, she accepted only clients of immense wealth, whether merchants or otherwise, and made liberal amounts of money out of them. She struck Cao Kecheng's fancy the moment he laid eyes upon her. He stayed with her for a whole month, spending lavishly. They grew to be as inseparable as lacquer and glue. Both were willing to marry each other and took an oath by lamplight before images of the gods. However, with his father still the head of the family, Cao Kecheng dared not bring her into the house as a concubine. Aware of his free-spending generosity, the courtesan asked that he redeem her with money.

In the parlance of brothels, clients who are given virgins are called "first-timers." Those who redeem the girls from the procuress and free them from her control are called "redeemers". When redeemers want to stay in the brothel overnight, other clients must yield to them, be it for five or ten nights at a stretch and free of charge, too. If a redeemer wants to take a girl for a wife, no extra money is demanded of him. With so much to be gained from an act of redemption, Cao Kecheng announced his intention to redeem Chun'er, but the madam demanded five hundred taels of silver, to be paid in full, and not the slightest fraction of a tael less. Kecheng sought help everywhere without success.

Suddenly, one day, he heard that his father had hired a silversmith to forge many shoe-shaped ingots of silver, none of which had been put to use. He began poking around and found out that all the ingots were hidden in the curtained double wall behind the bed in his father's bedchamber. He waited until the coast was clear, slipped quietly into the room, and stole a few. Afraid that his father would check the ingots, he had fake ones made. Having replaced each stolen ingot with a fake one filled with lead, he redeemed Chun'er with much ostentatious display and bought her clothes and jewelry aplenty. Henceforth, whenever he felt the need, he replaced the real ingots with fake ones and put the silver at Chun'er's disposal. She had a free hand with the money and there was never a question asked. Truly, it was a case of "Easy come, easy go." As the days wore on, the silver flowed out in a steady stream, and the young man never bothered to keep track of the amounts. Chun'er thought his lavish spending was well within his family's means, little knowing how he had come by all the silver.

One day, Mr. Cao Senior fell critically ill. He called Kecheng and his daughter-in-law to his bedside and uttered these words of admonition: "My son, you are in your thirties now. You are not a young man any more. As they say, 'A prodigal son, once returned, knows best how to be frugal.' Now, stop visiting brothels and settle down to a quiet domestic life. In addition to the family property, I also have some money put aside. Since you don't have to share it with a brother, there should be enough for you and your wife to enjoy." Pointing toward the back of the bed, he continued, "Lift the curtain, and you'll see a double wall. Hidden there are one hundred shoe-shaped ingots of silver, five thousand taels in all. This is my life's savings. I never told you about it before because of your dissolute ways. But now, I give it to both of you so that you can buy some property and pass it on to your children and grandchildren. Don't squander everything again!"

To his daughter-in-law, he said, "My daughter-in-law, a marriage lasts forever. Don't treat him with contempt. Give him sound advice and manage the household together, with one heart and one mind. If you do, I'll rest content under the Nine Springs."

Soon after saying these words, he passed away. Kecheng shed many a tear.

After the necessary arrangements for the burial were made, he wondered how much real silver was still left inside the double wall. Right away, he removed the ingots and spread them out on the floor to count. Of the one hundred ingots, ninety-nine were fake ones filled with lead. Only one was real. Of the 5,000 taels of high-quality silver, 4,950 were gone. He suddenly realized that if he had known all this would be his sooner or later, he could have taken his time spending it. Now, with virtually nothing to pay for the cost of burial rites, not to speak of the debts he had run up, he was overcome with such remorse that he burst out wailing over the fake ingots of silver.

Trying to pacify him, his wife said, "I forgive your past dissolute ways. But now, with so much silver here, why are you crying like this instead of doing the things you're supposed to be doing?"

At this point, Kecheng came clean about what he had done on the sly, replacing the real ingots with fake ones. His wife, whose words of admonition had always fallen on deaf ears, was already ill from the vexation, and in this moment of bereavement, knowledge of the fake silver only added to her despair. In an instant, her hands and feet went cold. She had to be escorted back to her room and helped onto her bed. A few days later, she died. Truly,

The wicked things he had done in the past
All came back to haunt him at the same time.

The double bereavement left Kecheng aching with grief, and he had to struggle to keep himself alive. After the forty-nine-day mourning period was over, the pack of creditors descended upon him, demanding repayment. The ancestral estates of the Cao Farmstead ended up in the hands of new owners. What with the sale of the house and the demanding funeral schedule, Kecheng could find no shelter but the hut beside the grave, and there, alone and forlorn, we shall leave him.

In the meantime, Zhao Chun'er, worried about Kecheng's prolonged absence, heard about the deaths of his father and his wife, who had died of her shock over the fake silver. But Chun'er dared not go and offer condolences for fear of setting gossipy tongues wagging. Later, upon learning that he had sold all the family's landed property and was reduced to living in a hut by the grave, she was so saddened that she wrote a letter inviting him to stay with her. Kecheng at first was too ashamed to accept the offer, but in spite of his repeated refusals, Chun'er persisted. He eventually went to her, swallowing his shame.

When she saw him, Chun'er fell on his shoulders and wept, saying, "Everything I have is yours. Luckily, I've still got some money that I can use to help you. Why didn't you tell me you were in trouble?" She had wine set out for him and kept him there for the night.

The next morning, she gave him a hundred taels of silver, telling him to go home and begin living a frugal life, adding, "When the money runs out, come to me again."

As soon as he laid hands on the silver, Kecheng forgot all about his wretched circumstances and was so enraptured by Chun'er that he refused to get out of bed. When he did, he went out to buy wine and meat and shared them with his good-for-nothing friends of the old days. Chun'er felt she couldn't very well stop him the first time, but the second time it happened, she counseled him with these well-chosen words, "To have such good-for-nothings as friends is not at all to your advantage. They are the ones who brought your family to ruin. You mustn't associate with them again. My advice is for you to go back, if you know what's good for you. I'll have more to talk about with you after your three-year mourning period expires."

She repeated her words of advice several times, but Kecheng remained the same impoverished moneybags. Suspecting that Chun'er looked down on him, he left her place in a huff. Feeling uneasy, Chun'er secretly made inquiries about him and was told that although he did not seek the company of other women, he was living as just extravagantly as before. Chun'er thought to herself, "He has not suffered enough to realize how hard life can be. Let him go through more."

Some days later, Kecheng's money ran out. Despite not knowing where his next meal was coming from, he refused to swallow his pride and seek help from Chun'er, nor was Chun'er inclined to invite him over, however much she missed him. Yet, she guessed that he must be in desperate straits and had some firewood, rice, and such things sent to him. However, these small favors were not enough to lift him out of poverty.

Now, Kecheng had some relatives and friends who, unable to help him themselves, were quite offended when they saw packages from Zhao Chun'er being delivered to him now and then. To Kecheng they said viciously, "You spent thousands of taels of silver in the Zhao establishment. You even redeemed that girl, Chun'er. Now look at how far you've fallen, but she's still living well. Why don't you file a complaint against her with the authorities? Any amount you can get from the redemption money will be better than nothing."

"Whatever I did before, I did willingly. We were lovers. If I turn against her now, my friends will laugh at me."

Some busybody with a loose tongue repeated these words to Chun'er, who then said to herself with an imperceptible nod, "So he's all right, deep down." Then again, she thought, "As they say, 'No one remains a saint after a thousand days; no flower stays in bloom after a hundred days.' If someone prods him again, he may yet change his mind." After much hesitation, she sent for Kecheng and addressed him in these words: "Didn't I promise to marry you? That wasn't something I said in jest. But you're still in mourning, so I'm afraid of what people will say. Also, knowing the difficulties you're going through, I think it would be better if I can make some more money before we marry, so we'd have something to live on in future. Don't let idle gossip ruin our love as husband and wife."

"Others may not have nice things to say," responded Kecheng, "but I know what to do. Don't you have any doubts about me!" He stayed for a couple of nights and then left, laden with gifts.

Time flew like an arrow. Quite unnoticeably, the three-year mourning period came to an end. Bringing along sacrificial items, joss sticks, candles, and paper coins, Chun'er went to the Cao family grave to pay her respects, after which she gave Kecheng three strings of cash so that he could hold a prayer service for the removal of his father's spiritual tablet. Kecheng was overjoyed. After the prayer service, he went to thank Chun'er, who then invited him to stay for some wine. During the course of their drinking, Kecheng brought up the subject of marriage.

Chun'er said, "It's not that I'm unwilling. I'm just afraid you may want another wife and put her above me!"

"In my wretched circumstances? What a thing to say!" protested Kecheng.

"You may be saying this now, but in the future, when things get better, you'll seek a good match through the proper channels. Won't that be quite a disappointment for me?"

Thereupon, Kecheng took a vow, calling upon heaven as a witness.

"Since you're so determined," said Chun'er, "there's nothing more for me to say. But a wedding ceremony can hardly be held in a hut next to a grave."

"To the left of the grave, there's an empty house for sale. The asking price is only fifty taels of silver. Wouldn't it be nice if we could buy it?"

So Chun'er scraped together fifty taels of silver and gave the money to Kecheng so that he could make the purchase. With some loose pieces of silver, she had him fix the rooms and buy furniture. On the chosen auspicious day, she filled several trunks with her valuables and personal belongings and, accompanied by Green Leaf, her chambermaid, hired a boat and went with all speed to Cao's house for the wedding ceremony, quite unobserved by god or ghost.

She bade farewell to a dissolute life
And became a lawfully wedded wife.

With the ceremony over, Chun'er consulted Kecheng on their means of livelihood. She said, "Since you grew up wallowing in wealth, you don't know how to run a business. So I think the most practical way is to rent a few *mu* of land to farm."

Boastfully, Kecheng said, "But all these adversities have made me a wiser man. I'm no longer one who can be easily cheated."

Chun'er put together three hundred taels of silver and gave them to Kecheng, a man addicted to a life without discipline. Wondering how he should invest this money, he consulted fortune-tellers in the city. While thus loitering around, he ran into his good-for-nothing friends again. Upon learning that he had taken Chun'er as his wife and was in possession of a tidy sum, they set to work, trying to cheat him out of his money, offering him deals that carried interest and deals that didn't, some with more interest and some with less, some at fifty percent interest and some at one hundred percent interest. Soon enough, they had relieved him of all his silver.

He returned empty-handed and asked Chun'er for more. With tears of exasperation, she said, "You know what the proverb says, 'It's better to prepare for a lean year in a fat one than to miss the good times when you're down and out.' It was your wastefulness that brought you to this pass. And my money is not unlimited. One penny spent is one penny fewer."

In the beginning, Chun'er hardened her heart and refused to do anything more for Kecheng. But as time wore on, her wifely feelings gained the upper hand. Unable to watch him suffer, she had no choice but to withdraw money, a little at a time, to pay for firewood, rice, and other necessities. With each withdrawal, her savings dwindled, and she made a great many withdrawals. Kecheng was somewhat grateful at first, but as the days and months passed, he began to take things for granted. Believing that she was still sitting on sizable savings, he began to accuse her of refusing to give him all that she had. Day in and day out, he made violent scenes and demanded to see the money. Worn out by the harassment, Chun'er succumbed to a fit of temper, gave him the keys to the trunks, and said, "These things will be yours sooner or later anyway, so take them all and stop thinking about them! From now on, I'll make a living by weaving, together with Green Leaf. I won't need you to support me. Just don't bother me anymore!" From that very day, Chun'er went on a vegetarian diet and wove at the loom from morning till night to support herself.

For a short time, Kecheng felt contrite, but then, delight with his material possessions got the better of him. He thought to himself, "Let me make more money with them and buy some landed property, both to regain my family's past wealth and to salvage my pride in front of my wife." But these plans remained thoughts that were never put into action. As the proverb says, "Food that goes into your mouth is money that goes out of your hand." One penny spent is one penny fewer. When a person sits idle, he eats away a mountain of a fortune.

In less than a year, Kecheng was broke again. As he had nothing else to sell, he sold Green Leaf the maid, without his wife's knowledge. The loss of her companion at the weaving loom so exasperated Chun'er that she gave him a good talking-to and, while she was at it, brought up old grievances as well. Knowing he was in the wrong, Kecheng was overcome with remorse, and the tears flowed from his eyes.

Some time later, he again found himself starving. He said to Chun'er, "As I see it, weaving, which is what you do from morning till night, is not a bad way to make a living. Now, you don't have a companion, and I don't have anything to keep myself busy, so why don't you teach me how to weave? That will fill my bowl with rice."

Amused but infuriated at the same time, Chun'er burst into angry words. "Surely

I'm not expecting a perfectly healthy man like you to support your wife, but don't tell me there's no other way for an able-bodied man to make a living!"

"Well said, well said, my good wife. As the proverb goes, 'A thin bird is long on feathers; a poor man is short on wits.' Tell me the best way to make a living. I'll do whatever you say."

"You're an educated man. They need a schoolteacher in the village, and the hut next to the graveyard is vacant. Why don't you gather a few village children into a class? The tuition will be enough for you to live on."

"As they say, 'Wise women are superior to men.' Your idea makes perfect sense."

Right away, he consulted the more venerable elders of the village and recruited about ten children. Teaching and supervising their calligraphy practice bored him, but he saw no alternative. With the passage of time, he grew used to the plain living, subsisting on inferior tea and simple fare, with never a thought of seeking what lay beyond his reach. Moreover, every so often, Chun'er would lecture him, reminding him of what had led to the current state of affairs. Each time she did so, Kecheng dared not say a single word in retort. Memories of the past invariably brought tears to his eyes. Consider how, in the old days, he had squandered the family's spectacular wealth! But even without the family fortune, Chun'er's contributions alone should have been enough to live on, with proper planning. Regrets were too late now.

Fifteen years went by in this fashion. One day, on a trip to town, Kecheng ran into an acquaintance. The man was wearing an official's robe embroidered with the legendary *xiezhi*,[3] a silver belt, a black gauze cap, and a pair of black shoes and was riding in a canopied sedan-chair followed by a great procession of servants. The man recognized Cao Kecheng and stepped out of the sedan-chair to greet him. Since it was too late to try to get away, Kecheng had to stop right there on the street and exchange greetings.

Yin Sheng—for such was the man's name—was a native of Tongzhou, which was in the same prefecture as Kechang's hometown, and had been a fellow student at the National University. The two had been selected at the same time to serve as interns at official posts. Yin Sheng had just recently been appointed registrar of the surveillance commission of Zhejiang and was on his way to his new duty station. A jovial procession it was.

After bidding Yin Sheng farewell, Kecheng gloomily went home and said to his wife, "All my possessions are gone except one: my title as a student of the National University. Today, I ran into Yin Sheng of Tongzhou. He was on his way to Zhejiang to take up his post as head of the bureaus of military affairs, civil administration, and justice. How impressive! We were both selected at the same time to serve as interns, so I should be up for an assignment as well, but where am I going to get the money for a trip to the capital?"

"Don't you start dreaming! How can someone who doesn't even have enough to eat think of becoming an official!"

A few days later, envious of Yin's glory, Kecheng abruptly brought up the subject again. Chun'er asked, "How much do you need for an assignment?"

"The larger the capital, the higher the interest. These days, even those who pass the imperial examinations, not to mention those selected from the National University, use money to secure their posts. The more money you spend, the better your assignment, and therefore, the more money you make. If you are willing to offer more bribes, you'll be reappointed for another term or two. If you spend too little, you'll be given some unenviable post and, a couple of years later, promoted to some prince's mansion where the position doesn't carry any power. You won't even get back what you invested in your studies at the National University."

"How much do you need for a good post?"

"A thousand taels of silver."

"A hundred taels is hard to get, let alone a thousand! Teaching is at least a steady source of income."

With tears in his eyes, Kecheng had no other choice but to go back to teaching in the hut beside the graveyard. Truly,

Ashamed that he brought no honor to his ancestors,
He went back in sorrow to face his students.

One midnight, Chun'er awoke to find Kecheng sitting up in bed, his clothes draped around his shoulders, weeping as if he would never stop. When she asked why he was weeping, he explained, "I just had a dream in which I was assigned an official post in the Chaozhou Prefecture of Guangdong. (*It's a good thing he still has some ambition in him.*) I was sitting in the main hall, accepting obeisances from the clerks. I had just raised my teacup when a tall, thin clerk with a sparse yellowish beard approached me with documents in his hands. Inadvertently, he knocked over my teacup and wet my sleeve. At this point, I woke up with a start and realized that it had been a dream. It made me think that, as poor as I am, there's no hope of my ever putting on an official's robe. Disgrace is the only thing I have to offer to my ancestors and my offspring. That's why I'm shedding these bitter tears."

"Having grown up in a rich family of distinction, don't you have a couple of kind-hearted relatives from whom to borrow money for the trip? If you do indeed land a post, you'll surely be able to pay them back."

"I've always been such a prodigal son that all the relatives rejected me out of contempt for my unworthiness. And now, when I'm in such a sorry state, who would be willing to help? All my pleas will be in vain. And even if someone agrees to give me a loan, what shall I offer as a pledge?"

"But this time, the loan is for a trip to seek an official post, not for some frivolous purpose as in the past. Maybe they will help. You never know."

"You do have a point, my good wife."

Accordingly, he called on his relatives the very next day, but he was refused admission by some and told in other cases that the masters were not home. Even those who did see him either responded only with a sardonic smile to his request or declined because they did not have the money. There were also some who, out of consideration for the humiliation he must have suffered in having to ask for a loan, offered small gifts in the form of money or rice. Bitterly disappointed, he returned home and reported to Chun'er.

Had he known how hard it was to borrow,
He would not have thrown away his fortune.

At his wit's end, Kecheng wept and wept unceasingly. Chun'er remarked, "What's the use of crying? You cry when there's no money, but the moment you lay your hands on some silver, you start squandering it in grand style!"

"When I'm reduced to such a state, even my wife doesn't trust me, much less other people!" After another outburst of sobbing, he said, "I'd be better off dead! I'm sorry to have to let you down after you've given me fifteen years of your life, but I can't concern myself about that now!"

He was looking for a way to kill himself when Chun'er stepped up and said in a placating tone, "You know the saying: 'If objects change once throughout their useful lives, humans change a thousand times until they die.' Heaven never seals off all the exits. Why do you treat life so lightly?"

"Even mole crickets and ants love life, not to mention human beings. It's just that it would be better for a useless man like me to be dead so as not to sponge off you for the rest of my life."

"There's no rush yet. If you can truly turn over a new leaf and keep your feet on the ground, I have an idea."

Kecheng quickly fell to his knees and pleaded, "Mother! What idea do you have? Please save me, quick!"

"Before I married, I pledged sisterhood with eighteen friends. I've never visited them, but for your sake, my sweet foe, I'll swallow my pride and go to see them and ask for favors. If one sister offers ten taels, that amount from all eighteen will add up to 180 taels of silver."

"Please go right away!"

"But I need eighteen sets of gifts, because it will be my first visit to them."

"Eighteen sets of gifts! I can't come up with even one!"

"If you had only spared me one or two pieces of jewelry, that would have come in handy now." Kecheng began sobbing again. Chun'er continued, "You did have your day, didn't you? And now the tears come down in torrents! Why don't you go get the papers required for a government appointment? You'll need them in the capital. Once you have the papers, I'll muster up the nerve to approach my sisters. Without the papers, won't all my efforts be pointless?"

"I swear not to return home without the papers!" With this boast, Kecheng sallied out into the street, saying to himself, "To get the papers, I need money now, so that I can deal with the prefectural and county yamen." But he couldn't very well nag his wife for money again, so he had no choice but to venture forth to the homes of his pupils and borrow from them. What an uphill struggle it was, collecting a few pennies here and a few pennies there! If he had not been reduced to such poverty over the last fifteen years, he would have turned up his nose at such a paltry amount, which was in fact less than what he would have given as a tip. How times had changed!

Having scraped together about one tael of silver, he betook himself to the Jiangdu County yamen to ask for his appointment papers. In the yamen, there was a Vice Director Zhu, who was a most kindly man and an old acquaintance of Kecheng's. Aware that Kecheng had come down in the world, Mr. Zhu collected from various officials and put together a loan on Kecheng's behalf. He had a receipt drawn up, pledging that Kecheng would repay the loan with interest as soon as he obtained a post. Merrily, Kecheng turned homeward, carrying the documents in his bosom. All along the way, he prayed to heaven, earth, and his ancestors that his wife would take the trip to borrow money and that she would not be turned down.

He walked into the house and saw his wife sitting in her chamber as before, working at the loom. This sad scene frightened him. He thought that she might have gone on her mission but failed. The tears gushed out before he realized it, but he dared not make a fuss. With the documents in his bosom, he stood outside the chamber door and called gently, "My good wife!" (*What a vivid scene for a painting as well as for the stage!*)

Chun'er heard him and asked, even as her hands continued moving on the hempen threads, "Have you got the papers?"

Kecheng stepped into the room, took out the papers from his bosom, and laid them on the table, saying, "Thanks to your lucky star, here they are."

Chun'er rose, read the papers, and thought to herself, "This idiot is certainly coming along!" Looking Kecheng in the face, she said, "So you really want to be an official? But I doubt I have the good fortune to be called a lady!"

"What kind of talk is that? If I ever amount to anything, it will be thanks to your support and guidance. But were you able to get a loan?"

"I visited them all. They'll send the money as soon as you settle on a date of departure."

Kecheng did not have the courage to ask how much money she was talking about, but he scurried off to a fortune-teller and picked an auspicious day. He reported back to Chun'er, and she said, "Go borrow a hoe from a neighbor." When he promptly brought in the hoe, Chun'er moved the basket containing her hempen threads and said, pointing at the ground, "When I married you, I buried an official's gauze cap for you in this very spot."

Kecheng thought to himself, "Wouldn't a buried gauze cap have disintegrated by now? But I'd better not contradict her and first see what I dig up." After swinging the hoe up and down a few times with all his strength, he heard a clang and was startled to see that an object had come up with the soil. He picked it up and saw that it was a small porcelain jar. Inside were some loose pieces of silver and several silver wine utensils.

Chun'er told him to take the contents of the jar into the city and have the silver melted and recast, so it could be weighed for its actual worth. Kecheng did as she'd said and had it made into ingots, which came to 167 taels. Upon returning home, radiant with smiles, he handed the ingots to his wife with both hands. Chun'er, well aware of the exact figure, had just been testing him. Pleased at his honesty, down to the last fraction of a tael, she told him to get the hoe again. She had him remove her small stool from the very spot where she had sat weaving for the past fifteen years and dig into the ground. As he dug, a large porcelain jar was exposed to view. It contained gold and silver that could not have weighed less than a thousand taels. What had happened was this: after observing Kecheng's extravagant style of living, Chun'er planned ahead and quietly buried all the treasure she had saved and then sat at the very spot for fifteen years, working at her loom day in and day out without ever breathing one word about the secret. A truly worthy character among women! (*Being such a useful person, Chun'er well deserves to be a lady.*)

At the sight of so much wealth, Kecheng was all tears. Chun'er asked, "What makes you grieve so?"

Kecheng replied, "My good wife, you've been working so hard for the last fifteen years, eating nothing but vegetables and dressing only in coarse cloth. Who would have guessed that you had taken such painstaking precautions! It is Cao Kecheng, my unworthy self, who has brought you all this suffering! Now, my good wife, please accept a bow from me!" With that, he sank to his knees.

Chun'er quickly raised him up and said, "Now that our days of misery have come to an end and a happy life begins, let's enjoy ourselves!"

"As we have more than enough for travel expenses, I can't leave you all by yourself at home while I go to the capital to wait for an appointment. It would be far better if you joined me, and I'd have the benefit of your advice, too, if need be."

"That's a good idea. If I stay behind, I'll worry too much," said Chun'er. Right away, the husband and wife packed up their belongings, engaged a couple of servants, hired a boat, and started for Beijing. Truly,

> *When one's luck runs out, even gold glitters no more;*
> *When one's time comes, even iron takes on luster.*

Once in the capital, Kecheng found lodging in an inn and submitted his documents to the Ministry of Personnel. With a liberal supply of silver at his disposal, he succeeded in receiving his very first appointment, as deputy magistrate of Tong'an County, Fujian. Later, he rose to be prefect of Quanzhou in the same province. His wife assisted him in the performance of his duties, and his fame spread far and wide. Owing to his generous bribes as well as his competence, he was promoted to assistant prefect of Chaozhou Prefecture in Guangdong.

While the prefect was away in the capital for reappointment, there happened to be vacancies for the posts of vice prefect and prefectural judge. Kecheng's superior believed in his ability and handed over the prefect's official seal of authority to him. On a chosen day, Kecheng mounted the prefect's seat and opened his court session for the business of the day. After the clerks had paid their respects to him, a valet brought him tea. He had barely raised his hand when an official approached to offer him documents and, in doing so, knocked over the teacup and spilled tea all over his sleeve. Kecheng was about to flare up when he noticed that the official had a tall, lean figure and a sparse yellow beard. All of a sudden, he recalled his dream of some years back in which he had seen the very man who now stood before him. He came to realize that one's career and future were dictated not by chance but by the will of heaven. In a panic, the official kowtowed in apology, but Kecheng consoled him with kind words, showing not the slightest trace of irritation. All those present were impressed by his magnanimity. That very day, after the court session adjourned, he told his wife about seeing the man before in his dream. Chun'er was also aghast.

"That dream," said she, "means that your career as an official should end with this term of office. In the old days, when you were teaching village children in the hut by the family grave, you did not have enough clothes to cover your body, or enough food to fill your stomach. Now, having served three terms of office and attained the sixth rank, you, with your background as a student of the National University, have risen as high as you can. As they often say, 'Be content, and you shall not be humiliated.' You would do well to retire at the height of your career to enjoy a life of leisure in the hills and among the woods." Kecheng nodded in agreement.

So, after only three days in his new office, he resigned, pleading illness. As there was no one else to whom they could entrust the prefectural seal, his superiors declined his request. Much against his will, Kecheng continued to perform his duties as a prefect for half a year until the new prefect arrived. After he handed over the seal, he again submitted his letter of resignation the very next day. Impressed by his sincerity, his superiors agreed to let him go. Thousands of local inhabitants who wanted him to stay went out into the street to block his carriage. To one and all, he offered words of consolation.

Kecheng and Chun'er returned in glory to their hometown. Having accumulated thousands of taels of silver during his three terms of office, Kecheng was able to buy back the family's landed estate. The Cao Farmstead regained its former splendor and achieved impressive status as an ex-official's residence. Granted, all this was made possible because Cao Kecheng mended his ways, but it was Zhao Chun'er's support that sustained him. A later poet had this to say in praise of her:

Her beauty reduced him to poverty,
But the beauty helped him regain his fortune.
Such women being all too few throughout the ages,
Be advised: lust not for beauty nonetheless!

32

Du Shiniang Sinks Her Jewel Box in Anger

With the Mongols wiped out, the new capital was born
Midst the grandeur of dragon- and phoenix-shaped hills.
On its east, the vast sea joins the sky;
On its west, the Taihang Mountains stretch afar.
The frontiers well guarded by the nine garrisons,
The emperor revered by all countries,
Peace reigns throughout the blissful land;
The empire shines forever with the sun.

This is a poem in praise of the magnificence of Yanjing, capital of this dynasty. The city is so situated that it is protected by an impregnable mountain pass to the north and is poised for a descent on the central plains to the south. It is indeed a richly endowed and indestructible city, destined to last for ten thousand years.

The dynasty began when Emperor Taizu of the Hongwu reign period [1368–98] wiped out the Mongols and founded the capital in Jinling, which became Nanjing, or the Southern Capital. Later, Emperor Chengzu of the Yongle reign period [1403–24] raised an army from Beiping, put down a rebellion, and moved the capital to Yanjing, which became Beijing, or the Northern Capital. This move transformed the desolate region into a world of opulence and prosperity. After the Yongle reign, the throne passed through nine successions to Emperor Shenzong of the Wanli reign period [1573–1620], the eleventh emperor of this dynasty. With sharp intelligence, an impressive bearing, and a virtuous nature, and richly blessed by fate, he ascended the throne at the age of ten. During the forty-eight years of his reign, he had one invasion repelled and two rebellions suppressed. Which ones? An invasion of Korea by the Japanese *kanpaku* Hideyoshi[1] and two rebellions by Bo Chen'en of Xixia and Yang Yinglong of Bozhou, both local officials of non-Han origin.[2] They were all wiped out, one after another. In awe, foreign nations vied with one another in coming from afar to offer tributes. Truly,

Divine blessings on one brought joy to all;
The four seas tranquil, the empire at peace.

Our story begins with the twentieth year of the Wanli reign period [1592], when the *kanpaku* of Japan invaded Korea. In response to an emergency appeal for help from the king of Korea, our Heavenly Court dispatched troops across the sea to go to his aid. With the endorsement of the emperor, the Ministry of Revenue announced that the National University would be open, for the time being, to any student who could offer tribute, to make up for the shortfall in army provisions. Now, status as a tribute student at the National University had the following advantages: the opportunity to study, eligibility for the imperial civil service examinations and a greater chance of passing them, and, when all's said and done, a none-too-shabby career. Therefore, the sons of officials and rich families gave up attempts to sit for the examinations even at the preliminary level, and once a precedent was set, they all followed suit and bought their way into the National University. The number of tribute students increased to more than a thousand on each campus of the university in the two capitals.[3]

Among the new tribute students was a certain Li Jia, courtesy name Ganxian. A native of Shaoxing Prefecture, Zhejiang, he was the oldest of the three sons of a Provincial Commissioner Li. He started his formal education at an early age but had not yet achieved success at the examinations. He took advantage of the new practice and was admitted to the National University in Beijing. While in the capital, he toured the courtesans' quarters with a fellow student from his hometown, Liu Yuchun, and, there, he met a celebrated courtesan by the name of Du Mei. Being tenth in seniority among the courtesans of the house, she was called by all and sundry Du Shiniang [Tenth Girl].

Her body full of grace and charm,
Her skin soft and fragrant,
Her brows the color and shape of distant hills,
Her eyes as limpid as autumn water,
Her cheeks as lovely as lotus petals,
She was the very image of Zhuo Wenjun.[4]
Her lips the shape of a cherry,
She was a veritable Fan Su.[5]
How sad that such a piece of flawless jade
Has fallen by misfortune into the world of lust!

Now age nineteen, Du Shiniang had lost her virginity when she was thirteen. In those seven years, she had taken on goodness knows how many young men from rich and noble families, who were, one and all, so enamored of her that they were ready to throw away their family fortunes for her sake. There came into circulation among the courtesans' quarters a four-line song that says,

With Du Shiniang at the dining table,
Those who hardly drink drain a thousand cups.

He who gets to see Du Mei the beauty
Turns up his nose at a thousand powdered faces.

Now, young Mr. Li was a romantically inclined young man who had never before encountered a real beauty. Acquaintance with Du Shiniang threw him into such ecstasy that he lavished on her all the love he had in him. With his handsome face, gentle temperament, free-spending habits, and eager attentiveness, he won her heart, and the two grew deeply attached to each other. Having observed the madam's greed and treachery, Shiniang had long wished to leave the brothel and get married, and now, impressed by Li Jia's kindly disposition and his devotion to her, she was quite inclined to marry him. However, Li stood in such fear of his father that he dared not commit himself. Even so, their love deepened. They gave themselves up to pleasure from morning till night, spending as much time together as if they were a lawfully wedded couple and swearing eternal love and fidelity. Truly,

Their love was deeper than the sea,
Their devotion higher than the mountains.

Now, as Madam Du's girl was thus occupied with Li Jia, other patrons with well-lined pockets were denied access to the one whose reputation had drawn them to the establishment. When Li spent extravagantly in the beginning, the madam wore an ingratiating smile, humbly bent her shoulders, and busily danced attendance on him. With the sun and the moon exchanging places day after day, all too quickly, more than a year went by. Li's funds began to run out. As his payments dwindled, much against his wishes, the madam began to give him the cold shoulder. Provincial Commissioner Li, having heard about his son's involvement with a house of ill repute, wrote the young man one letter after another, demanding that he return home, but Li Junior was so enamored of Shiniang's beauty that he postponed his return again and again. Reports of his father's outbursts at home only added to his fear of returning.

The ancients said, "Friendship based on profit falls apart when the money runs out." But since Du Shiniang's feelings for the young man were genuine, the less he had in his pocket, the more passionate her love became. Time and again, the madam urged Shiniang to put Li Jia out, and when her words fell on deaf ears, she turned on the young man herself, hurling insults at him, in attempts to provoke him into leaving. But, being of a gentle nature, he grew even meeker in his responses. (*A good-for-nothing with no pride in him!*) In exasperation, the madam screamed at Shiniang day after day, saying, "In this line of business, we depend on our patrons for a living, sending the old ones out the front door and greeting the new ones at the back. The more activity there is in the house, the higher our pile of money. With that Li Jia making a nuisance of himself here for more than a year now, old patrons are not coming, not to speak of new ones! The way he scares away every soul with any money to offer, he's a veritable incarnation of Zhong Kui![6] Now look at this house! There may still be breath left in us, but there's certainly no kitchen fire going. How low have we sunk because of him!"

Unable to put up with such abuse, Du Shiniang shot back, "Mr. Li didn't come with empty hands. He's been quite generous."

"How times have changed! Just tell him to spare a little money so I can buy firewood and rice to keep the two of you alive. (*The madam does have a point.*) In other houses like ours, the girls are like money-growing trees. They're living in luxury, while I have to be the unlucky one, feeding a white tiger that keeps money out of the house![7] From the moment the door is opened every morning, I busy myself preparing the seven necessities of life [firewood, rice, cooking oil, salt, soy sauce, vinegar, and tea] for the household. Now, where am I supposed to get food and clothes to support that pauper of yours, you little hussy? You tell that pauper, if he's still a man, why doesn't he scrape together a few taels of silver and take you away from here? I'd be happy to get myself another girl."

"Mother, do you mean it?"

Knowing that it was impossible for the penniless Li Jia, who had pawned everything he owned, to come up with any money, the madam said, "I never lie. Of course I mean it."

"Mother, how much do you want from him?"

"If it were anyone else, I'd ask for a thousand taels of silver. But in the case of that penniless wretch, I'll be merciful and ask for only three hundred taels, so that I can find a replacement for you. But there's one condition: he has to pay me in three days. When he gives me the money, I'll give him his girl. He may be a gentleman, but if he can't pay up in three days, whatever the circumstances, I'll beat him and kick him out. When it comes to that, don't hold me to blame!"

Shiniang pleaded, "He doesn't have money with him because he's away from home, although he should be able to raise three hundred taels. But three days is not enough. Could you make it ten days?"

The madam thought to herself, "That miserable wretch has nothing left now but his bare hands. Even if I allow him a hundred days, he won't be able to do anything. Without the money, he won't dare show his face around here again, however cheeky he may be. And by that time, the girl should have no objection to starting over again." Aloud, she promised, "For your sake, I'll allow him ten days. But if I don't see the money on the tenth day, don't blame me for anything I do!"

"If he can't come up with anything on the tenth day, I don't think he'll ever have the nerve to come here again. But if he does deliver the money, you, Mother, wouldn't back out of the deal, would you?"

"I'm already fifty-one years old, and I follow the Buddhist diet ten days out of the month. Why would I even dream of lying? If you don't trust me, let's clap our hands on the deal. If ever I should back out of it, let me become a pig or a dog!"

The sea is not to be measured in scoops;
How laughable the evil crone!
Knowing the student to be penniless,
She demands payment to smash the girl's hopes.

That night, with their heads against the pillow, Shiniang consulted Li Jia about her marital future. He said, "It's not that I'm disinclined, but it takes at least a thousand taels to get your name deleted from the courtesans' registry book. My pocket being as empty as it is, what can I do?"

"I've talked with Mother. She asks only for three hundred taels, but they have to be paid in ten days. Your own means may be exhausted, but don't you have relatives and friends in the capital you can borrow from? (*Poverty is a test of compassion.*) If you can raise the amount, I'll be yours, and we won't have to bear the old witch's abuses any longer!"

"All my relatives and friends have forsaken me because I refuse to leave this place. Tomorrow, I'll go and tell them I'm packing for the journey home and have come to say good-bye. And then I'll ask for travel money. I may even be able to collect the whole amount." (*If, by a stroke of luck, he does manage to get the money, what next? He still doesn't have a plan for the future. I fail to see what Shiniang sees in this good-for-nothing Li Jia.*)

The next morning, Li rose, washed, combed his hair, and took leave of Shiniang. "Be sure to come back soon," she admonished. "I'll be waiting for good news."

"Don't worry," said he. He left the house and called on friends and relatives. They were delighted to hear that he was there to bid them farewell before starting his journey home. Then he mentioned his lack of funds and asked for a loan. As the proverb puts it, "Talk of money drives friends away." His relatives ignored his request, and not without reason, for they saw him as a dissolute prodigal who had been away from home, wallowing in vice in a brothel for more than a year, while his father was fuming with rage. And now, all of a sudden, he claimed he was going home, but who could be sure he was telling the truth? Should it be but a trick so he could use the supposed travel money to pay the brothel again, his father would surely misconstrue their good intentions when he heard of it. If his father was going to blame them anyway, they'd be well advised not to get involved in the first place. Without exception, everyone said, "I happen to be short of money at this moment. I'm really sorry I'm not able to help you out." No one was generous enough to part with so much as ten or twenty taels.

Li ran around for three days straight without raising the slightest fraction of a tael. He did not dare tell Shiniang the truth and put her off with evasive answers. When the fourth day also failed to bring him any hope, he felt too ashamed to return to her. (*Just as the madam had predicted.*) But, having made the Du house his home, he had no other place to stay. He had no choice but to ask Liu Yuchun, the fellow student from his hometown, to put him up for the night. Concerned by the miserable look on Li's face, Liu Yuchun asked what was wrong, whereupon Li told Liu all about Du Shiniang's offer of marriage.

Yuchun shook his head and said, "I doubt it, I doubt it. Du Mei is the number one courtesan. If she wants to get out of the business and marry, the madam would ask for no less than ten pecks of pearls and betrothal gifts worth a thousand taels of silver. Why is she asking for only three hundred taels? My guess is that the madam resents the fact that you are keeping her girl without paying anything. This is her way of driving you out. As for the girl, having known you for so long, she can't very well tell you to leave outright, for fear of hurting your feelings. Knowing all too well that you're penniless, she purposely sets the price at three hundred taels as a favor to you and gives you ten days to come up with the money. If you can't deliver, you can't show up at her door any more. If you do, she'll ridicule you and laugh at you and make you feel too humiliated to stay on. Brothels often use this trick to drive out unwanted clients. Now think carefully. Don't be fooled. In my humble opinion, the best thing to do is to make a clean break with them as soon as possible."

Li lapsed into silence, unable to make up his mind. After a good while, Yuchun continued, "Don't make a wrong move. If you do decide to go back home, the travel expenses won't amount to much. There will surely be people willing to help you out. But if you ask for three hundred taels, you're not likely to get it even in ten months, let alone ten days. You know how the world is today. Who will bother to care about other people's troubles? The brothel is deliberately making things difficult for you because they are sure you won't be able to get a loan."

"Right you are, my good brother." Even as he mouthed these words of agreement, Li could not bear the thought of parting with Shiniang. Again, he set about begging for loans here and there, though he did stop going back to the brothel at night. For three days in a row, he stayed with Tribute Student Liu. Six days passed.

Deeply worried by Li's continued absence, Du Shiniang had Si'er, a page boy, go out to look for him, and it so happened that Si'er ran into Li on a main street. "Brother-in-law Li!" called out Si'er. "Mistress is expecting you at home!"

Feeling ashamed, Li answered, "I'm too busy today. I'll come tomorrow."

Determined not to fail Shiniang, Si'er grabbed him and, holding him tightly, said, "Mistress told me to look for you. You must come with me!"

His heart longing for Shiniang, Li submitted and followed Si'er. When he saw Shiniang, he could think of nothing to say.

"How are you coming along in what you set out to do?" asked she. As tears flowed down his cheeks, she continued, "Can there be so little human kindness that you haven't been able to put together three hundred taels?"

Tearfully, Li intoned a couplet, "'It's easier to catch a tiger in the hills / Than to open your mouth and beg for favors.' I've been running around for six days and haven't gotten even one cent. I felt so ashamed to come back to you with empty hands that I stayed away these last few days. It was only because you sent for me that I came in all humiliation. It's not that I haven't tried, but such are the ways of the world."

"Don't let Madam know about any of this. Why don't you stay here tonight? I need to talk to you about something."

Shiniang prepared food and wine, and she and Li enjoyed a hearty meal before they went to bed.

When she awoke in the middle of the night, Shiniang asked him, "So are you truly unable to come up with even a cent? What's to be done about my marital future?"

The young man continued to shed tears, unable to speak.

Gradually, it began to grow light, and the fifth watch struck. Shiniang said, "I've hidden one hundred and fifty taels of loose silver inside my mattress. This is my private savings. Take it. So that's half of the three hundred taels. Now that you only need the other half, you may stand a better chance. There are only four days left. You've got no time to lose." So saying, she rose and gave the mattress to Li.

Beside himself with joy, Li had a page boy carry the mattress for him and follow him all the way to Liu Yuchun's place. There, he told Liu all that had happened during the night. The mattress was then torn open to reveal pieces of loose silver all wrapped up in the padding. They weighed exactly one hundred and fifty taels. Yuchun was astounded. "So, she does mean it! In that case, her sincerity must not be betrayed. Let me try to raise the money for you."

"If this turns out well for us, I'll never forget your kindness."

So Liu Yuchun kept Li Jia at his place, while he went everywhere to borrow money. In two days, he raised one hundred and fifty taels. Handing the money to Li, he said, "I went into debt on your behalf, not for your sake, but because of Du Shiniang's devotion to you."

With the three hundred taels in his possession, Li Jia rejoiced at this heaven-sent good fortune. All smiles, he went merrily to see Shiniang, one day before the ten-day limit was to expire.

"You didn't have a cent the other day," said Shiniang. "How did you come by these one hundred and fifty taels?"

After listening to Li's account of what Tribute Student Liu had done, Shiniang said, her hand raised to her forehead in a gesture of great delight, "So Mr. Liu is the one who has gotten us what we want."

Happy beyond measure, they spent the night together in the house.

The next morning, Shiniang rose bright and early and said to Li Jia, "As soon as the silver is delivered, I'll be free to go with you, but we need to arrange for transportation. Yesterday, I borrowed twenty taels of silver from my sisters. Take them to pay for our travel expenses."

This news was most welcome because Li had been worrying about the lack of travel funds but had not dared to bring up the subject. While they were talking, the madam knocked on the door. "My girl Mei," she called out. "It's the tenth day today!"

Upon hearing this, Li opened the door and said invitingly, "Thank you for coming here, Mother. I was just going to ask you over." With that, he laid the three hundred taels of silver on the table.

The madam, who had not expected him to produce any money, was dumbstruck. Her face hardened, and she looked as if she was going to back out of the deal. Shiniang said, "In the eight years I've been living here, I've made thousands of taels of silver for you. Today is the happy day I leave and get married, and you have given me your word. The three hundred taels are all here, not a fraction of a tael less, nor have we exceeded the ten-day limit. If you go back on your promise, Mr. Li will walk out with the money, and I will immediately kill myself. If that happens, you will lose both me and the money, and regrets will be too late."

Not knowing what to say in reply, the madam fell silent. After much thinking, she resignedly took up a scale and weighed out the silver. "Since things have come to this," said she, "I guess I won't be able to keep you. But if you must go, be off this very instant. Don't even think of taking any of the jewelry and clothes you wear every day." With that, she pushed the two of them out, asked for a padlock, and locked the door.

It was the ninth lunar month of the year, and the weather was growing chilly. Since she had just risen from bed, Shiniang had not yet dressed and groomed herself. In her old clothes, she bowed twice in the madam's direction. Li also bowed. That done, they left the madam's house as husband and wife.

The carp broke free from the golden hook;
Flicking its tail, shaking its head, it's gone for good.

Li told Shiniang to stop for a moment, adding, "I'll get a small sedan-chair for you. Let's go first to Mr. Liu's place before deciding on the next thing to do."

"My sisters have always been very kind to me. I ought to say good-bye to them. Moreover, they loaned me money for travel expenses, and I can't leave without saying thanks." Accompanied by Li, she went to bid her sisters a thankful farewell.

Of the sisters, Xie Yuelang and Xu Susu lived nearest to the Du house and were Shiniang's most intimate friends, so Shiniang went to Xie Yuelang's house first. Surprised to see Shiniang with her hair unadorned and her clothes old and worn, Yuelang asked her what had happened. Shiniang told Yuelang the whole story and introduced Li Jia to her. Pointing at Yuelang, Shiniang said, "This is the sister who helped us out with travel money. You should thank her." Accordingly, Li Jia gave her one bow after another.

Yuelang let Shiniang do her toilette and, in the meantime invited Xu Susu to come over for a reunion. After Shiniang had finished, the two beauties Xie and Xu offered her their kingfisher-feather hair ornaments, gold bracelets, jade hairpins, earrings inlaid with jewels, a brocade blouse, a floral-pattern skirt, a phoenix belt, and a pair of embroidered shoes. With Du Shiniang now aglow in all her splendor, a farewell celebration feast was laid out. When the feast was over, Yuelang offered her own bedchamber to Li Jia and Du Mei for the night.

The next day, another feast, a grand one, was set out, to which all the courtesans of the quarters were invited. Everyone who had warm feelings for Shiniang came to toast and congratulate the couple. The guests played musical instruments, sang, and danced, offering the best of their talents for the joyous occasion, and the drinking and merrymaking lasted until midnight. When Shiniang offered words of thanks, they replied, "Now that you, the very best of us, are going away with your husband, we might never see you again. Let us know when you're going to set out on your journey, and we'll come to see you off."

Yuelang said, "When the date is decided, I'll surely let all of you know. But Sister Shiniang's journey with her husband will be long and arduous and one that they can ill afford. We sisters are duty bound to do something so that she won't have anything to worry about."

The sisters all agreed to the proposal before dispersing. That night, Li and Shiniang again stayed in Yuelang's room.

At the fifth strike of the night drum, Shiniang said to Li, "Where shall we settle down after leaving this place? Do you have any definite ideas?" (*These things should have been worked out before they left the brothel. Why wait until this moment?*)

Li said, "My father, as angry as he is, will surely raise hell if he knows I'm returning home married to a courtesan, and that will make things even worse for you. I've been racking my brains over the matter but haven't come up with a surefire plan."

"The natural bond between father and son can't be broken. But if this is not yet the right time to approach him, why don't we take up temporary residence in a scenic city like Suzhou or Hangzhou? That way, you can go back to your hometown and ask relatives and friends to mediate on your behalf and pacify your father. Only then can you take me to your parents. That would be better for both sides." (*Yes, that is indeed a felicitous solution.*)

"Well said," Li agree.

The next morning, Li and Shiniang took leave of Xie Yuelang and set out for Tribute Student Liu's place, where they were to stay for a while and pack for their journey. As soon as she saw Liu Yuchun, Du Shiniang fell to her knees and made obeisance. Thanking him for his help in bringing about the marriage, she said, "My husband and I will surely return your kindness."

Yuchun promptly bowed in return and said, "You, madam, are indeed an exceptional woman, who does not let poverty stand in the way of your love. I did nothing more than fan the fire when the wind was favorable. Such a trivial thing is hardly worth mentioning."

The three spent the day at the wine table. On the morrow, they chose an auspicious day for the couple's departure and hired sedan-chairs and horses. Shiniang then had a page boy dispatch a letter to Xie Yuelang, thanking her and bidding her farewell.

As the hour of their departure drew near, there came a stream of sedan-chairs. It was Xie Yuelang and Xu Susu leading all the sisters to see them off. Yuelang addressed Shiniang in the following words: "We cannot bear the thought of letting you follow your husband on a thousand-li journey with an empty purse. We have put together a modest gift. Please accept it. It may come in handy on your long journey." So saying, she had a servant give Shiniang a gold-traced jewel box locked so securely that there was no clue as to its contents. Shiniang neither opened it nor declined the gift but busied herself in saying thanks.

A short while later, the sedan-chairs and horses were ready, and the footmen urged them to be on their way. Tribute Student Liu offered three cups of farewell wine and, along with the beauties, escorted the couple as far as Chongwen Gate, where everyone tearfully said farewell. Truly,

They knew not when they would meet again
At this sad moment of farewell.

To continue with our story, Li Jia and Du Shiniang proceeded to the Lu River, where they were to board a boat. There happened to be a government courier boat returning to Guazhou, so they negotiated the fare and paid for the cabin. Once on board, Li found that he had already spent the last cent in his pocket. Now you may wonder, didn't Du Shiniang give him twenty taels of silver? They couldn't all be gone, could they? Well, having spent all his money in the brothel until he was in rags, Li could hardly resist the temptation of redeeming a few articles of clothing from the pawnshop once he laid his hands on some silver. He had also bought bedding, and the remainder of the silver was just enough to pay for the sedan-chairs and horses.

Noticing his woebegone look, Shiniang said, "Don't worry. My sisters' gift should be of some use."

With that, she took out the key and opened the box.

Li was standing beside her, but he felt too ashamed to look into the box. All he saw was a red silk purse, which Shiniang took out. She threw the purse on the table and said, "Won't you open it and see what's inside?"

When he picked it up, Li thought it was quite heavy. He opened it and found it was filled with pieces of silver amounting to fifty taels. Shiniang locked the box again without mentioning what else it contained. Instead, she said to him, "Thanks to the kindness of my sisters, we have not only enough money for this journey but also some to spare for our stay south of the river."

At this pleasant surprise, Li said, "If it were not for you, I would have been stranded in an alien land and died without even a burial place. I'll never forget your kindness to me."

Henceforth, every time past events came up in conversation, Li would shed tears of gratitude and Shiniang would go out of her way to console him with soothing words. And nothing else of note occurred as they continued their journey.

In a few days, they came to Guazhou. After the courier boat had anchored by the shore, Li hired a passenger boat, transferred their luggage to it, and arranged to set sail early the next morning. It was the middle of the eleventh month of the year, and the moon was as bright as sparkling water.

Sitting at the bow with Shiniang by his side, Li said, "Ever since we left the capital, we've been cooped up in a cabin with other people all around us and never had a chance for a good talk. Now, with a boat to ourselves, we can finally disregard all scruples. (*This is not yet the right time for endearments. Small wonder that the relationship was not fated to last long.*) Since we've left the north and are approaching the south side of the Yangzi River, let's drink to our hearts' content to shake off the gloom of the last few days. What do you say?"

"I was thinking along the same lines, because I, too, miss having a good talk and a good laugh. Your bringing this up shows that we are truly of the same mind."

Li fetched wine utensils, spread out a rug on the bow, and sat down shoulder to shoulder with Shiniang. They began passing the cups back and forth. When well warmed with wine, he said to Shiniang, wine vessel in hand, "Your voice is the very best in the courtesans' quarters. When I first met you, my soul took flight every time I heard you sing. With all the troubles we've gone through, we've been in such low spirits that I haven't heard your divine singing in a long time. Now, with the moon shining brightly on the clear water and no one around us in the depths of the night, would you be willing to sing for me?"

Shiniang was so carried away that she cleared her throat and, beating time with her fan, started singing. (*She, too, lacks prudence.*) Set to the tune of "Small Red Peaches," the song was about a scholar offering wine to the moon, from the play *Moon Pavilion,* by Shi Junmei of the Yuan dynasty.[8] Truly,

Her voice rose into the sky and stopped the clouds,
Dived down into the deep spring and brought out the fish.

Now, in another boat, there was a young man called Sun Fu, courtesy name Shanlai, a native of Xin'an, Huizhou, who was from a fabulously rich family that had been in the salt business in Yangzhou for generations. He was twenty years of age and also a tribute student at the National University in Nanjing. A licentious and frivolous man, he frequented houses of ill repute and was a master in matters relating to the pleasures of the flesh.

As coincidence would have it, his boat was also anchored at the Guazhou ferry that night. Drinking alone and feeling bored, he suddenly heard a clear voice singing so beautifully that metaphors of phoenix songs were not enough to capture its beauty. He stood up in the bow and listened for a good while before deciding that its source was the very next boat. He was about to pay a visit when the singing stopped, whereupon he told a servant to slip out and ask the boatman who the singer was. When he was told that the boat had been hired by a Mr. Li but nothing was known about the singer, Sun Fu thought to himself, "Obviously, the singer is not from a decent family. How shall I get to see her?" These thoughts kept him awake throughout the night.

When the fifth watch of the night finally came, he heard a windstorm spring up on the river. By dawn, the sky was overcast with ominous clouds, and flakes of snow whirled frantically in the air. How do we know this? There is a poem in testimony:

Trees vanish into the clouds from hill to hill;
All footprints disappear from path to path.
An old man with a straw hat sits in a small boat,
Fishing all alone on a river clad in snow.

Since he was stuck in the snowstorm and unable to continue with his journey anyway, Sun Fu ordered his boatman to move closer to Li's boat. Sun Fu put on his sable hat and fox-fur coat and pushed open the window as if to watch the snow. At this very moment, Shiniang, having finished her toilette, raised the short curtain of the cabin window with her delicate hands and emptied her basin into the river. As she did so, Sun Fu caught a partial glimpse of her face. Just as he had thought, the woman was a ravishing beauty. He was thrown into such raptures that he kept his eyes fixed upon the same spot, waiting for her to appear again, but to no avail. After reflecting a good while, he leaned against his window and intoned aloud two lines from the poem "Plum Blossoms," by Academician Gao Qi.[9] (*Shi Junmei's song and Academician Gao's poem are the ruin of Du Shiniang's life. Outrageous! Outrageous!*):

"On the snow-clad hill sleeps the hermit;
In the moonlit woods walks the beauty."

Upon hearing someone intoning a poem in a neighboring boat, Li Jia craned his neck out the cabin window to look. With that one glimpse, he fell victim to Sun Fu's scheme. Sun's very purpose in chanting the poem was to entice Li to show his face so that he could take the chance to strike up a conversation. With alacrity, he raised his hands in greeting and asked, "What is your honorable name?"

After saying his name and where he was from, Li directed the same question to Sun Fu, who readily answered. After some small talk about the National University, they gradually warmed to each other. Sun Fu said, "To be stranded here in the snowstorm is a god-sent opportunity for me to have the honor of meeting you, my honorable brother. As there's little to do on the boat, I'd like to invite you to go ashore and have a drink or two in a wineshop, so that I may have the benefit of your conversation. I hope you won't turn me down."

"I've just met you as a total stranger! How can I put you to such trouble?"

"What kind of talk is this? As they say, 'All men within the four seas are brothers.'" With that, Sun Fu had his boatman put down the gangplank, and his page boy held out an umbrella for Mr. Li to cross over to his boat. After an exchange of greetings at the bow, Sun asked Li to precede him as they went ashore.

Before they had gone many paces, a wineshop came into view. They went upstairs, chose a clean table by the window, and sat down. After the waiter laid out a fine spread of wine and food on the table, Sun Fu raised his cup and plied Li with wine. While they were drinking and viewing the snowy scenery, their conversation, polite and innocuous enough at first, gradually turned to houses of ill fame. Being frequenters of such places, they found that they shared the same tastes and, in the excitement of the conversation, became the closest of friends.

Sun Fu dismissed the waiters and said in a subdued voice, "Who is the girl who was singing so beautifully last night in your boat?"

In his eagerness to show off his connoisseurship, Li Jia told him the truth (*His imprudence made him unable to keep a secret.*): "That's Du Shiniang, a celebrated courtesan in Beijing."

"But why does a courtesan now belong to you alone?"

Thereupon, Li acquainted him with all the details of the first time he'd met Du Shiniang, how they had fallen in love, her desire to marry him, and how he had borrowed money to redeem her.

Sun Fu said, "To take a beautiful woman home is a happy event, to be sure, but I wonder if your family will accept her?"

"I'm not worried so much about my wife as about my father. He's very strict. I need to think well before I approach him."

Seeing his chance, Sun Fu pressed further, "If your father refuses to take her in, where are you going to put her? Have you worked out any plans with her?"

With a frown, Li replied, "I have indeed talked about it with her."

"So, your beloved one must have come up with a wonderful idea," said Sun Fu lightheartedly.

"Well, she wants to take up temporary residence in Suzhou and Hangzhou to enjoy the hills and the waters. I'll return home first and ask relatives and friends to put in a good word for me with my father. When my father comes around, I'll take her home. What do you think?"

After reflecting for a good while, Sun Fu assumed a concerned expression and said, "I'm afraid you might take amiss any advice coming from someone you've only just met."

"I do need your advice. Please don't hesitate."

"As an important official in the region, your father must be firmly against improper love affairs. Since he's already scolded you for frequenting places of ill repute, he's not likely to let you marry a loose woman. As for your relatives and friends, who among them would not try to play up to your father? Your pleas to them will surely be rejected. Even if there's someone who doesn't know better and puts in a good word on your behalf with your father, that person will change his tune as soon as he finds out what your father thinks. On the one hand, you'll sow discord in the clan; on the other, you'll disappoint your beloved one. And to enjoy the hills and the waters is not a viable, long-term solution either. What if you run out of money? Wouldn't you find yourself in a dilemma?" (*Rogues like him do have a way with words.*)

Knowing all too well that the bulk of his fifty taels of silver was already gone, Li nodded in agreement when Sun Fu got to that last part.

Sun Fu continued, "I have something more to say, and it's from the bottom of my heart, but you may not want to hear it."

"You are too kind. Please say whatever you want to say."

"Well, I'd better shut up, because as the proverb goes, 'An outsider shouldn't come between those near and dear to each other.'"

"Please go ahead. It's quite all right!"

"Well, as the ancients said, 'Women are as fickle as water.' Prostitutes are much more so. Those who feel true love are greatly outnumbered by those who don't. Since she was celebrated among the courtesans' quarters, she must have lovers everywhere. She may have an old flame south of the Yangzi River and is using you to take her there, so as to be reunited with him."

"I don't think that's the case."

"Even if it's not, young men south of the river are known for their ways with women. If you let her live by herself, you can't say for sure that a man won't climb over the wall or sneak in through some hole, so to speak. And yet, if you take her home, you'll only add to your father's anger. I don't have a good plan for you, but the natural bond between father and son should never be broken for any reason. If you turn against your father and abandon your family because of a prostitute, you'll be considered a debauched and wayward person by all and sundry. In due course, you will be forsaken by your wife, brothers, and friends. How will you be able to justify your existence on earth and under the sky? You'll have to do some solid thinking now!" (*Had these words not been said with an ulterior motive, they would have been good advice.*)

Li was so dismayed upon hearing these words that he moved his seat closer to Sun and asked, "So, what's your advice?"

Sun Fu replied, "I do have an idea. It will be very much in your favor, but I'm afraid you might be too deeply infatuated with her to follow my advice. In that case, wouldn't I have wasted my breath?"

"If you really have a plan to help me rejoin my family, you'll be nothing less than my savior. Why are you afraid to speak?"

"You've been away from home for more than a year. Your father is angry, and your wife is estranged from you. If I were you, I'd hardly be able to eat or sleep. Your father is angry with you because your philandering ways and lavish spending habits have made him afraid that you will surely squander everything once you come into your inheritance. By returning empty-handed now, you'll only make him angrier. (*A stab at Li's heart.*) If you give up your woman and do the right thing under the circumstances, I'll offer you a thousand taels of silver for her. You may present the thousand taels to your father and say that you have been teaching in the capital and saved every possible cent. He will surely believe you. Henceforth, you'll enjoy domestic peace with never a harsh word said against you. In a trice, your woes will be changed to bliss. Please think carefully. I say all this not because I covet the woman's beauty but because I wish to help you in any small way I can."

Li Jia being a man without a mind of his own and in mortal fear of his father, Sun Fu's words struck a deep chord in his heart and dispelled all his worries. He rose and said with a bow, "You have made me see the light. But I can't very well break my ties with her after she has followed me this far on such a long journey. Please let me consult her first. I'll report back to you if she agrees."

"Put it gently to her. If she's really devoted to you, she won't have the heart to cut the ties between you and your father and will surely help you return home." (*Another attempt to poison Li's mind.*)

They continued drinking a while longer. The wind subsided, and the snow stopped when dusk set in. Sun Fu had his servant settle the bill, and, hand in hand, they returned to their boats. Truly,

Never disclose everything on your mind;
Never pour out all of your heart.

In the meantime, Du Shiniang had laid out wine and fruit in anticipation of a good time with Li and, after waiting for him in vain throughout the day, was sitting by the light of the lamp when he stepped onto the boat. Shiniang rose to greet him, noticing that he looked preoccupied and slightly irritated. She filled a cup with warm wine and offered it to him with some soothing words, but he shook his head in refusal and went to bed without speaking. None too pleased, Shiniang put away the cups and plates and helped him take off his clothes and lie down against the pillow. "What did you hear today that makes you so upset?"

Li sighed but didn't utter a word. Shiniang repeated the question three or four times but found he had fallen asleep. Full of misgivings, she sat down at the head of the bed, unable to sleep. At midnight, Li woke up with another sigh.

"What is it that you find so hard to say? Why so many sighs?" asked Shiniang.

Gathering the quilt around him, Li sat up and, after several futile attempts to speak, began to weep. Shiniang held him to her bosom and said gently, "It's been two years since I fell in love with you. We've gone through all kinds of difficulties together to get where we are. Along the thousands of li we've covered on our journey, you never felt sad, but now that we're on the point of crossing the Yangzi River to start a happy life, why are you suddenly looking so miserable? There must be a reason behind this. Husband and wife are supposed to share life and death. You can tell me whatever's on your mind. Don't hide anything from me."

Yielding to her insistence, he said, with tears in his eyes, "When I was penniless and stranded away from home, you, in your kindness, chose to be with me. No favor can be greater than that. But I've been giving the matter a lot of thought. You see, my father, being an important official in the region, is a man who clings to conventions, and he's a very rigid and demanding person, too. I'm afraid he'll be so angry that he'll drive us out of the house. If so, when will our itinerant life ever come to an end? Our love will not last, and the bond between father and son will be destroyed. Earlier today, a friend, Mr. Sun from Xin'an, invited me to drink with him and discussed this with me. My heart aches as if it's been stabbed with a knife!"

Alarmed, Shiniang asked, "So, what are you going to do?"

"Since I'm the one involved, I don't see the situation as clearly as an onlooker would. Mr. Sun has come up with a good plan for me, but you may not go along with it."

"Who's this Mr. Sun? If his idea is as good as you say, why wouldn't I go along with it?"

"He's Sun Fu, a salt merchant from Xin'an and a dashing young man. He heard you sing last night. That's why he asked about you. I told him your background as well as the reason for our not going home. He offered me a thousand taels of silver if you would marry him, so that I'll have something to give my parents and you'll have a husband. But the thought of leaving you makes me want to cry." With that, his tears fell like rain.

Shiniang withdrew her hands from him. With a scornful laugh, she said, "What a great hero, the fellow who designed this plan for you! You get your one thousand taels of silver, I get a man, and both of us will be spared the tribulations of life on the road. What a perfect plan—what began as an affair of passion now ends in proper decorum! All right, where's the money?"

Holding back his tears, Li answered, "The money's still with him because I didn't have your consent."

"Go give him my consent first thing tomorrow morning. Don't miss the chance! But a thousand taels of silver being quite a handsome amount of money, they must be weighed out and handed to you before I step over to the other boat. Don't let that brute of a merchant take advantage of you."

The night drum struck the fourth watch. Shiniang rose, lit the lamp, and began her toilette. "Today," said she, "I'm sending off the old and greeting the new. This is a special occasion!" She applied powder, rouge, and fragrant hair oil with great care and put on hair ornaments and an embroidered gown. There she stood in all her radiance, her perfume sweetening the air, her beauty dazzling to behold.

By the time she had finished her toilette, the sky was beginning to brighten. A page boy sent by Sun Fu stood at the bow of the boat, waiting for a reply. Glancing quickly at Li, Shiniang saw a faint glow of joy on his face. She urged him to go quickly and give his reply and reminded him to have the silver weighed out as soon as possible. (*If he really could not bear the thought of leaving her, he would have acted otherwise.*)

So Li Jia went to Sun Fu's boat and replied in the affirmative. Sun Fu said, "Weighing out the silver is not a problem, but I need her jewel box as a pledge."

Li reported back to Shiniang, who said, pointing at her gold-traced jewel box, "Take it."

A jubilant Sun Fu immediately sent the thousand taels of silver to Li's boat. Shiniang personally inspected them and found them to be of standard purity and not the slightest fraction of a mace short in weight. With one hand holding on to the side of the boat, she beckoned to Sun Fu with the other, a sight that sent him into raptures. Then she said, revealing pearly white teeth between her ruby lips, "May I have the jewel box back for just a moment? Mr. Li's travel permit is in it. I must return it to him."

Believing that he had already caught Shiniang in his trap, Sun Fu had his page boy put the jewel box on the bow. Shiniang took out her key and unlocked it to reveal a stack of small drawers. At Shiniang's bidding, Li drew out the first drawer. Lo and behold, it was filled with pieces of expensive jewelry worth hundreds of taels of silver. She picked them up and tossed them into the river, to the astonishment of Li Jia, Sun Fu, and everyone else on the two boats.

She then told Li to pull out another drawer, which was seen to contain jade flutes and golden pipes. Yet another drawer was filled with jade and gold objects of art worth thousands of taels of silver. Shiniang tossed them all into the water in full view of the wall of spectators now gathered on the shore. "What a pity!" they exclaimed in unison, wondering what on earth could have made this woman do such a thing.

The last drawer was pulled out to reveal a small box. When it was opened, there, for all to see, was a large handful of luminous pearls as well as emeralds, cat's-eyes, and other precious objects, the likes of which none had ever seen and the value of which none could determine. Amid thunderous cheers from the onlookers, Shiniang was about to throw them into the river when Li Jia, overcome with bitter remorse, flung his arms around her and broke into wails of grief. When Sun Fu came over to try to calm her, Shiniang pushed Li aside and unleashed an explosion of furious words on Sun Fu. "Mr. Li and I went through a lot together before we got here. But you cajoled him with clever words out of lecherous motives and destroyed a marriage of love in one day. You are my worst enemy. If my spirit survives my death, I'll certainly bring a complaint against you to the gods. As for the pleasures of the pillow, you don't have a ghost of a chance!"

Turning to Li Jia, she went on, "In my years as a courtesan, I put away some private savings to support myself in the future. After we met, you and I took many a vow of lifelong love and fidelity. Before we left the capital, I had my sisters give me what were in fact my own possessions. The treasures hidden in the jewel box were worth no less than ten thousand taels of silver. I meant to add some grandeur to your return, so that your parents might act out of compassion and accept me as a member of the family. With the remainder of my life committed to you, I would have had no regrets in life and in death. Little did I know that you trusted me so little that you followed some evil advice and abandoned me before the journey was even completed. You have betrayed my devotion to you. I opened the box and showed its contents in public so that you'll know that a mere thousand taels of silver are of little importance to me. I am not unlike a jewel box that contains precious jade, but you have eyes that fail to recognize value. Alas, I was not born under a lucky star. Having just freed myself from the tribulations of a courtesan's life, I find myself abandoned again. All those present will testify, by the evidence of their eyes and ears, that I have not failed you in any way. It's you who have betrayed me!"

There was not a dry eye among the onlookers, all of whom cursed Li for being the fickle ingrate that he was. Ashamed and exasperated, Li shed tears of remorse and was about to apologize to Shiniang when she threw herself into the middle of the current, the jewel box in her arms. The horrified onlookers cried out for her rescue, but with a heavy mist hanging over the raging waves, not the slightest trace of her could be seen. How tragic that a celebrated courtesan as pretty as a flower and as fair as jade fell prey to the fish of the river!

Her three souls returned to the Water Palace,
Her seven spirits wafted to the underworld.

Gnashing their teeth and raising their fists, the crowd swarmed menacingly toward Li Jia and Sun Fu. In fear, Li and Sun called for their boats to get under way and fled in different directions. For Li Jia, Sun Fu's thousand taels of silver were a constant reminder of Shiniang, and he was haunted day and night by guilt and shame. His depression worsened into mental derangement, from which he never recovered. For his part, Sun Fu had sustained such a shock that he fell ill and, while confined in his bed, saw Du Shiniang at his side. She gave him tongue-lashings day and night for more than a month until he gave up the ghost. His death was generally explained as retribution for what had happened on the river.

In the meantime, Liu Yuchun finished his studies at the National University in the capital, packed up his belongings, and started his journey home by boat. When he reached the town of Guabu, he stopped and was washing his face by the side of the boat when his brass basin fell into the water. He sought out a fisherman to retrieve it, but what came up was a small box.

Yuchun opened it and saw that it was filled with bright pearls and other priceless jewelry. He gave the fisherman a handsome reward and kept the box by his bed so that he could examine the contents and admire them at his leisure. That very night, he dreamed he saw a woman approaching him, treading upon the waves of the river. He looked closely at her and recognized her to be Du Shiniang.

When she had drawn near, she curtsied and told him about Li's act of treachery, adding, "You generously helped me out with one hundred and fifty taels. I meant to repay you for your kindness after I settled down. Little did I expect that things would not turn out that way, but I haven't forgotten my debt of gratitude to you. This morning, I gave you that little box by way of the fisherman as a small token of my gratitude. I shall never see you again." At this point, Yuchun woke up with a start and realized that Shiniang had died. For days on end, he heaved one sigh after another.

In later times, when commenting on the account we have given above, people had this to say: Sun Fu, in scheming to gain a beauty and lightly throwing away a thousand taels of silver, was by no means a decent sort; Li Jia, in failing to appreciate Du Shiniang's devotion, was nothing but an imbecile on whom it was not worth wasting one's breath. But Shiniang was a true heroine of all time. She could very well have found a worthy husband and had a blissful marriage, and yet, she picked Li, whose character she misjudged. As a result, a bright pearl, a piece of fine jade, was thrown in front of a blind man. How tragic that love turned to hate and went into the flowing river! There is a poem that says in lament,

Those who don't know what love is, hold your tongue!
"Love" is a word too deep to understand.
If its meaning can be grasped in full,
Feel no shame when you're called a lover.

33

Qiao Yanjie's Concubine Ruins the Family

Affairs of the world are too numerous to tell;
Wise men keep themselves out of harm's way.
Those who ruin the state and the family
Are men with a weakness for the other sex.

Our story begins during the first year of the Mingdao reign period [1032], under Emperor Renzong of the great Song dynasty, in Ninghai, Zhejiang, known in our day as Hangzhou. In the vicinity of the Guanyin nunnery, to the north of Zhong'an Bridge in the city, there lived a merchant, a native of Qiantang, who was called Qiao Jun, courtesy name Yanjie. He had lost his parents in his childhood. He was a lustful and debauched man with a powerful physique. He and his wife were both forty years of age and had no sons. They only had a daughter, Yuxiu, who was eighteen years old. This family of three had a servant called Sai'er.

With capital most likely ranging from thirty thousand to fifty thousand strings of cash, Qiao Yanjie traveled regularly to the towns of Chang'an [in Haining County, Zhejiang Province] and Chongde [in present-day Tongxiang County, Zhejiang] to buy silk and then to Dongjing, the Eastern Capital, where he exchanged it for dates, walnuts, and other miscellaneous items. He then brought these goods back to his hometown to sell. He was thus absent from home six months out of the year. He had Sai'er open a wineshop in front of his house and hired a brewer, called Hong San, to make wine. His wife, Gao-shi, was in charge of all the money that went in and out of the house and the shop everyday, but of this, no more need be said.

In the spring of the second year of the Mingdao reign period [1033], Qiao Jun, having disposed of his silk in the Eastern Capital and bought walnuts, dates, and other items, was on his way home when his boat made a stop upon reaching the Shangxin River in Nanjing. By the time the boat was ready to continue on its way, a windstorm had sprung up, and the boat could not set sail. For three days in a row, the wind was too strong for the boat to leave. All of a sudden, Qiao Jun caught a glimpse of a beautiful woman in the boat next to his, her skin as white as snow and hair done up like a black cloud. Quite smitten, he asked the other boatman, "Who is your client? Why is he bringing his family on his travels?"

The boatman replied, "Inspector Zhou of Jiankang Prefecture has died of an illness. His family is now in my boat, escorting his coffin back to Shandong. The young woman is the inspector's concubine. But why do you ask, sir?"

"Boatman, do this for me," said Qiao Jun. "Go and ask the inspector's widow if she would be willing to give up the concubine. I would be glad to offer a handsome betrothal gift and take her as my concubine. If you can accomplish this for me, I'll give you five taels of silver by way of thanks."

So the boatman went down into the cabin to deliver the message. After a brief exchange of words, the woman became Qiao Jun's concubine. As a consequence,

Everyone in the family perished;
All the family wealth was wiped out.

To retrace our steps, the boatman went down into the cabin and asked, "Madam, would you be willing to marry off that young woman?"

"Do you have a good candidate in mind? If someone is willing to take her, I'll agree. A betrothal gift of only a thousand strings of cash will do."

"There's a date merchant on the next boat who wants a concubine. He sent me over to talk with you."

The lady agreed. The boatman went back to Qiao Jun and said, "The lady is willing to give the concubine to you for a betrothal gift of a thousand strings of cash."

Immensely delighted, Qiao Jun opened his trunk, took out a thousand strings of cash, and had the boatman deliver them to Madam Zhou. She accepted the money and instructed the boatman to invite Qiao Jun over to exchange greetings. Qiao Jun changed his clothes and crossed to the neighboring boat to see Madam Zhou.

After asking him about his hometown and what his name was, the old lady had the concubine come out and said to her, "With the master gone and my son a difficult person to get along with, I have decided to marry you to this gentleman as his concubine. You may go to Mr. Qiao's boat now. Ninghai is a busy and prosperous town, a nice place in which to enjoy life's pleasures. Be sure to serve Mr. Qiao well, and remember not to put on airs!"

The young woman and Qiao Jun took leave of Madam Zhou, who then had a trunk of clothes and various items delivered to the other boat as a gift to the concubine. After rewarding the boatman with the promised five taels of silver, Qiao Jun asked the young woman, his heart overflowing with joy, "What is your name?"

"My name is Chunxiang [Spring Fragrance]. I'm twenty-five years old."

That very night, Qiao Jun shared a bed on the boat with Chunxiang.

The next day, the weather cleared. The wind died down, and the waves became smooth. All boats, big and small, commenced their journeys.

After five or six days, Qiao Jun arrived at Beixinguan [near Hangzhou], moored the boat, and went ashore. He hired a sedan-chair for Chunxiang, and he followed behind, through Wulin Gate and all the way to his house.

After Chunxiang descended from the sedan-chair, he dismissed the carriers and led her into the house. But only after he first told his wife, Gao-shi, about the matter did he take Chunxiang to see her. Gao-shi flared up at the sight of Chunxiang. Turning to her husband, she said, "Since you've already brought this woman here, there's precious little I can do to turn her away. But you have to promise me two things before I agree to let you have her."

"What two things, pray?"

Gao-shi's demands deprived Qiao Jun of a home he could call his own. Truly,

Never listen to a woman's advice;
A split household violates social customs.
Ignore your wife's words and take the high road
But how many men have such good sense?

Gao-shi continued, "Since you've already brought the woman home, anything I say now is too late. But I do have one request, which is that the two of you go live somewhere else. I won't have her in this house." (*The source of all troubles to come.*)

At these words, Qiao Jun said, "That is easily done. I'll just rent a separate house where I can live with her."

Gao-shi went on, "As of today, I'll have nothing to do with you. All the money, jewelry, clothes, and other items of the household will be for the exclusive use of me and my daughter. Don't come and ask for anything. As for government taxes and duties as well as household chores, just have the maidservant take care of them. Don't bother me with these things. Now, will you do as I say?"

Qiao Jun fell silent, thinking to himself, "If I don't, she'll make things difficult for me. Well, well, so be it!" He said aloud, "All right, you shall have your way in everything."

Gao-shi gave no response.

The next morning, Qiao Jun rose early and had his merchandise and personal effects carried from the boat to the house. Then he had someone rent a separate house for him. The house was right in front of the mint opposite what is now the civil service examination grounds. On a chosen auspicious day, Qiao Jun took Zhou-shi, for this was how Chunxiang came to be called, along with all the furniture and household goods that they would need, to the new place. Henceforth, he returned home to his wife only once every two or three days.

Time went by with the speed of an arrow, and the days and months passed as quickly as the weaver's shuttle. Before they knew it, more than half a year had gone by. With the money he charged his clients plus his private savings, Qiao Jun now had enough capital for another business trip. Having collected all the silk he needed, he bought firewood, rice, and other household necessities and admonished Zhou-shi with these words: "Be patient. I'm going away on a trip, but it's only for two months at most. If some emergency comes up, go tell my wife."

He then went home and said to Gao-shi, "I'm leaving tomorrow on a trip, but

I'll be back in two months at most. If something happens, please take care of Zhou-shi, for my sake!"

His daughter said, "Be sure to come back early, Father!"

After saying good-bye to his wife and daughter, he went back to his new place to pack up, for he was to start his journey the very next morning. It was the ninth month of the year. He left the house, boarded a boat, and was on his way.

Two months went by. Day after day, Zhou-shi stood expectantly at the door, waiting in vain for his return. Soon, winter set in, and a cold winter it was.

One evening, the sky became overcast with dark clouds and snowflakes came swirling down in a storm that lasted throughout the night and into the next day. Gao-shi began to wonder why her husband would choose not to return when winter had already begun. She thought that Zhou-shi must be feeling cold and wanted to do something for her, but as Sai'er the maid was confined to bed with an illness, she had Hong San, the hired winemaker, send firewood, rice, charcoal, and money to Zhou-shi. (*Since she was so kindly disposed toward the young woman, why not take her into the house and be one family?*)

Zhou-shi was weeping at home behind closed doors at the sight of the heavy snow when she heard a knock at the door. Thinking it must be her husband, she eagerly opened it, only to see Hong San, carrying a load. She asked, "Have the mistress and the young lady been well?"

"The mistress is worried that you don't have much money left because the master hasn't returned. So she sent me to bring you firewood, rice, and money."

"Give the mistress and the young lady a few deep bows for me when you go back," said Zhou-shi.

Hong San went away. At around noon the next day, another knock came at the door. Zhou-shi wondered who could be there in such heavy snow. As a consequence of this visit, Zhou-shi was never to be united with Qiao Jun again. Truly,

While one sits peacefully at home behind closed doors,
Disaster strikes right down from heaven.

To return to our story: While the snowstorm gathered force outside, Zhou-shi was sitting by the fire when she heard a knock at the door. She opened the door and saw a man in worn-out clothes and a tattered cap. "Sister," he said, "is Qiao Jun at home?"

"He left on a trip in the ninth month and hasn't returned yet."

"I'm the local headman," said the man. "I'm here to order Qiao Jun to go to Haining for ten days of corvée service on the dike project. He will rest for twenty days and then go back to work for another ten days. But since he's away, let me find someone else to do it for him. You'll just have to pay the man." (*Zhou-shi should have sent him on to the mistress.*)

"In that case," said Zhou-shi, "please go ahead and find someone. I'll pay for the service."

The local headman went off. After lunch the next day, he brought a young man of about twenty years of age to Zhou-shi. "This young man," said the headman, "is a native of Shanghai County.[1] He's called Dong Xiao'er. He lost his parents very early on and makes a living doing odd jobs for people. You need only pay him three hundred to five hundred strings of cash per year, plus some winter and summer clothes. Without a man in the house, you'll need his services."

Zhou-shi said, delighted, "I do need help around the house. He looks like a nice, well-behaved man. The wages will be as you say." She thanked the headman and kept Xiao'er at home.

On the following day, the headman came with the order for corvée service in Haining. Provided with money by Zhou-shi, Xiao'er left with the headman. Ten days later, he came back and did odd jobs around the house, attending to the incense and sweeping the floor, doing everything with the utmost care.

In the meantime, Qiao Jun, while selling silk in the Eastern Capital, got involved with a celebrated courtesan named Shen Ruilian and spent lavishly on her. So enamored he was of this woman that he stayed on with her, indulging in all manner of pleasures, and completely forgetting about his wife and concubine. Little did he know that the housemaid, Sai'er, had died after more than two months of illness. Gao-shi had Hong San buy a coffin, which was then carried out of the city to the crematorium. Being a chaste woman, Gao-shi went about her work selling wine by the front door without ever a wild thought. (*True saints don't watch only their own behavior. How much does Gao-shi accomplish by preserving her chastity alone?*)

As it turned out, after Dong Xiao'er came to live in her house, Zhou-shi took a fancy to the young man. Sometimes, when he returned from a corvée assignment, she would serve him hot soup and hot meals. There being no man in the house, Xiao'er applied himself diligently to his work. Zhou-shi tried to lead him on with significant glances. Although he felt attracted, he did not dare to do anything. (*With the flames of passion burning nearby, even if the pile of dry wood does not ignite right away, a scandal is in the making.*)

On New Year's eve, Zhou-shi had Xiao'er go out to buy wine, fruit, fish, and meat for the occasion. In the evening, she told him to bolt the front gate while she heated a flask of wine on the stove and filled a plate with slices of meat. She then set out the dishes on the table in front of her bed, had a fire going in a brazier, and lit a lamp. As Xiao'er tended to the kitchen fire, she called out softly, "Xiao'er, come to my room. I have some treats for you." Xiao'er never should have set foot in that room, for he was to die without even a burial place. Indeed,

Households cannot be run without servants,
But here, along comes an evil one.
A sordid affair it turned out to be,
With the husband completely in the dark.

Zhou-shi summoned Xiao'er to her bed and said to him, "Come here, Xiao'er! Let's have a couple of drinks. You may sleep here in my room tonight."

"I wouldn't dare!" Xiao'er protested.

"What a slave you are!" While thus cursing him a few times, she put her arms around him and made him sit shoulder to shoulder with her on the bed. She then pulled him close to her bosom, untied her girdle, and had him fondle her white breasts, which were as soft and smooth as dumplings made of glutinous rice. Enraptured, Xiao'er held her face in his hands and stuck his tongue into her mouth. After they had thus enjoyed each other to their hearts' content, Zhou-shi poured the wine. They drank one cup, crisscrossing their arms, and shared five or six more cups in the same manner.

"If you sleep outside, I'll be in here alone, suffering from the cold. You'll miss a great deal of fun if you turn me down."

Dropping to his knees, Xiao'er said, "You are so kind! I've had my heart set on you for quite some time now. I just never dared say anything. I'll never be able to repay you for such kindness, not even in death!"

At this point, they took off their clothes and belts and became man and wife. Of their amorous sport throughout the night, we shall speak no more.

At the crack of dawn, Xiao'er rose first, boiled water, washed the dishes, and prepared breakfast. When everything was done, Zhou-shi rose, did her toilette, and ate breakfast. Truly,

Both are in the bloom of youth,
Well matched in passion and lust.

Henceforth they lived like husband and wife. All the neighbors knew what was afoot, but none wanted to be meddlesome.

In the meantime, Gao-shi was taking care of the wineshop herself because she had no one to help. One day, she overheard a casual comment about Zhou-shi and Xiao'er having an affair. She could not quite believe what she had heard but could not dismiss it out of hand either. (*Never employ a person you can't trust.*) So she had Hong San relay the following message to Zhou-shi: "Move back into the house so we can cut down on expenses." (*Too late.*)

Upon hearing these words from Hong San, Zhou-shi fell silent. Finally, she forced herself to say, "The mistress is most kind. I'll move back this very evening, along with all the furniture."

After Hong San had gone to transmit her reply, Zhou-shi called Xiao-er in for a discussion. "The mistress wants me to move back. I can't very well disobey her, but what's to be done about you?"

"Well, she doesn't have anyone to help her out around the house either. I'll be glad to work for her, delivering wine and doing other chores. There's one thing though: we won't be able to indulge ourselves as we do here. Or we may have to go our separate ways as of today." With that, they fell into each other's arms and cried.

Zhou-shi said, "Don't worry. I'll go ahead and pack. You can carry the load to the mistress's house. Then I'll ask her for permission to keep you there, so that we can still enjoy ourselves when no one's around. (*Shameless!*) Let's wait for my husband to return before deciding what to do next."

Relieved upon hearing these words, Xiao'er said happily, "Take good care of yourself!" The packing was done that afternoon, and Xiao'er went first, carrying the load of trunks and cases. When dusk finally came, Hong San took a lantern and went to get Zhou-shi. She locked the gate with a padlock and set out for the mistress's house with Xiao'er. Truly,

> *A moth darting into a flame courts death;*
> *A bat hurtling against a pole will not live.*

So Xiao'er and Zhou-shi went into the house and greeted Gao-shi.

"Why do you have to bring Xiao'er with you?" asked Gao-shi. "You'd better dismiss him."

"You have no one to do chores around the house, ma'am," replied Zhou-shi. "Wouldn't it be better if you kept him and had him run errands for you? You can always dismiss him after the master comes home."

Being a virtuous woman with an unblemished reputation, Gao-shi thought to herself, "Even if he stays, nothing can go wrong with me keeping a watchful eye on him."

So she let Xiao'er stay on as a handyman who did everything from attending to the shop to acquiring wine jars.

All too quickly, another few months went by. Despite her attachment to Xiao'er, Zhou-shi was unable to consort with him as much as she had before, when she was in her own house. One day, encouraged by Gao-shi's praise of Xiao'er's industriousness and good behavior, Zhou-shi suggested, "Why don't you take him on as a son-in-law? Wouldn't that be quite convenient?"

Rage seized Gao-shi. "You cheap hussy!" she snapped. "How can you think of lowering our family like that? A hired worker for my daughter, indeed!" (*It's high time she kicked Xiao'er out of the house.*)

Zhou-shi dared not say another word. Silently, she endured more verbal abuse from Gao-shi for a good three to four days. Being an upright and straightforward person, Gao-shi did not have the slightest suspicion that Zhou-shi had made the suggestion in order to continue her adultery with Xiao'er. Had she thought of that, she could have just put Xiao'er out and escaped being beaten to death along with her daughter while they were in prison later on, and the Qiao family would not have been wiped out.

Now, let us turn our attention to Xiao'er, who joined the mistress's household in the third month of the year. As the ancients put it, "A hired hand the first year, master of the house the second year, and patriarch the third year." More than a year later, it turned out, quite unexpectedly, that during Qiao Jun's prolonged absence, Xiao'er had gained ready access to the various rooms of the house and won Gao-shi's trust in many matters. (*Why trust him so much when he's suspected of wrongdoing?*) Thus, he put on the airs of a veritable Master Qiao and began to bully Hong San. Whenever he laid eyes on Yuxiu, Gao-shi's daughter, he enticed her with flirtatious words. Soon, he was able to have his way with Yuxiu. Zhou-shi knew what was happening. Gao-shi was the only one who was kept in the dark.

Another month went by. It was now the middle of the sixth month, and Yuxiu was bathing in her room in the extreme heat of the season when Gao-shi walked in. Much taken aback by the sight of her daughter's swollen breasts, she summoned her after the girl had put on her clothes and asked, "Who did this to your body? Look at these swollen breasts! I won't punish you if you tell me the truth."

Seeing that she would not be able to lie her way out of this, Yuxiu told the truth. "Xiao'er seduced me."

Gao-shi stamped her feet and gave a mournful shriek. "So, that wench has allied herself with him to ruin my little girl. Oh, what's to be done?" She could not very well say anything in public for fear that her daughter's marital future would be jeopardized if the story became known. Knitting her eyebrows, she plunged into thought. A good while later, she came up with a plan. The only way to keep this a secret was to murder that swine. (*Even firing him at this moment would have been unwise. Killing him is the height of stupidity. It's because she loves her daughter too much.*)

Quite unnoticeably, two more months passed. When the Mid-autumn Festival came around in the eighth month of the year, Ga-oshi had Xiao'er buy fish, meat, and fruit and set out a family feast. That evening, Gao-shi, Zhou-shi, and Yuxiu went to the backyard to view the moon, and Hong San and Xiao'er were told to eat by themselves off to one side. At midnight, Gao-shi called for Xiao'er and offered him two big bowls of wine as a reward. He did not dare to decline the offer and drank up both bowls. Soon, he was overcome by the wine and collapsed. Hong San, who had also been given some wine, went to sleep by himself in the brewery room. In his drunken state, Xiao'er fell victim to Gao-shi's plan, and, that very night,

> *Hell gained another murdered soul;*
> *The mortal world lost one young man.*

Gao-shi sent her daughter off to sleep and then addressed Zhou-shi in the following words: "My mind has been so full of the family's business that I knew nothing of your adultery with that swine. Now, you have conspired with him and made him seduce my daughter. What shall I say to the master when he comes home? I'm a woman of spotless reputation, but with you in the house, the family's good name has been tarnished. What's to be done? There's no other choice but for you and me to kill that beast. This will be unknown to god or ghost. When my husband comes back, you and my daughter will both be spared a scandal. Now go find a rope for me!"

At first, Zhou-shi refused, but Gao-shi lashed out, "Slut! It was because of your adultery that my daughter became involved. Don't tell me you're still in love with him!"

Wilting under Gao-shi's scolding, Zhou-shi gave up and went to her room. She returned and handed Gao-shi a hempen rope. Gao-shi put the rope around Xiao'er's neck and tightened it. Being a woman, she did not have the strength to finish him off quickly but spent two hours pulling on the rope without succeeding. As Xiao'er screamed, an exasperated Gao-shi, lacking a tool at hand, had Zhou-shi go to the stove and bring her an ax used for woodchopping. She swung it against Xiao'er's forehead. One blow dashed out his brains, and he died.

Gao-shi said to Zhou-shi, "He's dead all right, but we have to get rid of the body before the night is out."

"Let's wake up Hong San," Zhou-shi suggested, "and have him carry the body to New Bridge River, tie a big rock to it, and dump it in. The body will rot at the bottom of the river, unknown to god or ghost."

Gao-shi was greatly pleased. She went to the brewery room, woke Hong San, and brought him to the backyard. At the sight of the body, Hong San said, "It's a good thing this pain in the neck has been done away with. If he's still here by the time the master comes back, there will be quite a scene."

"Before it grows light, carry the corpse to New Bridge River," said Zhou-shi to Hong San. "Then tie a big rock to it and dump the body into the river. If anyone asks about him tomorrow, just say that Xiao'er stole our jewelry and valuables and slipped away in the night. He had no friends. So nothing will happen."

At about the fifth watch of the night, with Gao-shi lighting the way with a lamp, Hong San carried the corpse on his back to the riverside. He lifted a big rock, tied it to the body, and tossed the rock and the body into the middle of the river. Right away, the rock sank to the bottom of ten feet of water, taking the corpse with it. Believing that no shred of evidence would ever be found, Hong San returned home and quietly bolted the gate. Gao-shi and Zhou-shi went back to their own rooms and retired for the night.

Gao-shi may have been a woman with a spotless record, but she lacked good sense and did the wrong thing. Upon learning the facts, she should have expelled Xiao'er and left the matter at that. On no account should she have strangled him, because she was later to be accused of murder and beaten to death in prison. The family line was to be cut off. By then, regrets were too late!

Now, to continue with our story. Hong San slept until daybreak, when he rose and opened the wineshop for business. Gao-shi went about selling wine, as usual. Yuxiu noticed Xiao'er's absence but dared not ask about him. Zhou-shi, talking to herself, murmured purposefully, "That swine Xiao'er stole my jewelry and fled during the night." Yuxiu kept to her room and refrained from asking any questions, nor did the neighbors care whether Xiao'er was there or not. With Xiao'er's murder weighing on her conscience, Gao-shi became dejected, afraid at all times of the day that the murder would come to light. Truly,

If you want the respect of others, study hard.
If what you might do can't be made known, don't do it.

Our story forks at this point. By Clear Lake Dam, outside Wulin Gate, there was a shoemaker called Chen Wen. He and his wife, Cheng Wuniang, supported themselves by making shoes and boots. One day, at the beginning of the tenth month, he quarreled with his wife. In a huff, he went to buy leather at the leather market by Full Bridge, on the other side of the gate. He didn't return that day, nor the day after. On the afternoon of the second day, Cheng Wuniang began to fear for him. Another night passed, and her husband still did not show up.

After fretting alone at home for almost a month without any idea of his whereabouts, Cheng Wuniang went to town to make inquiries, as is only to be expected. She headed straight for the leather market and asked around, only to be told, "We didn't see your husband here buying leather about a month ago. Perhaps he dropped dead somewhere."

Some busybody asked, "What clothes was he wearing when he left home?"

"A two-tiered cap shaped like the character *wan* and a sleeveless, sheathlike blue silk gown. A month ago, he said he was going to the leather market to buy leather, but I haven't heard anything from him since then. I wonder where he could be."

"Why don't you ask around in the city?"

Cheng Wuniang thanked them all and went off to the city, where she asked everyone she saw about her husband. A whole day went by without any news.

Two days later, after eating breakfast, she went back into the city to continue her inquiries. Of all places in the city, she found herself on New Bridge. Indeed, coincidences do happen. At this point, she saw a crowd gathered on the shore. Someone was shouting, "A dead body in a blue gown has floated up under the bridge!"

Upon hearing this, Cheng Wuniang rushed to the shore and pushed through the crowd. There, floating on the river for all to see, was a corpse in a blue gown, looking at such a distance not unlike her husband. Cheng-shi wailed, "Husband! Why did you have to drown like this?" The bystanders were astounded. Plaintively, Cheng-shi asked, "Which of you gentlemen would be kind enough to pull the body to the shore so that I can see for sure if it's my husband? I'll offer a reward of fifty strings of cash."

Among the onlookers was a local ruffian known as Wino Wang who spent his time loafing on the streets, searching for people who might need his services in stirring up trouble, and looking for opportunities to gamble and cheat people out of their money. He was the kind of rogue whom decent people kept at arm's length. His ears pricked up at the mention of a reward, and he said, "Young lady, I'll do it!"

Wuniang stopped weeping. "I'd be ever so grateful to you, sir!"

Seeing a boat passing by, Wino Wang jumped on it and called out, "Stop, boatman! I'll help the young lady drag the corpse to shore."

And so Wino Wang brought the body ashore. He recognized the dead man to be Dong Xiao'er of the Qiao family, but he kept the knowledge to himself and told Cheng-shi to take a good look. (*Adultery is not punishable by death. So there was no justification for Dong Xiao'er's murder.*) This was going to lead to the violent deaths of Gao-shi and the other members of her household. Truly,

> *He found his way to every scene of excitement*
> *To extort money, to make a profit.*
> *A claim for the wrong corpse in this case*
> *Led to events that had tragic results.*

Wino Wang punted the boat toward the store with a bamboo pole. Cheng-shi looked at the face, but it was so bloated that it was unrecognizable. The clothes, however, she thought were his. Bursting into loud wails of grief, she entreated Wino Wang, "Please go with me to buy a coffin before I decide what to do next."

So Wino Wang followed her to Undertaker Li's shop, where she bought a coffin and hired two men to retrieve the body from the water. After the body had been placed in the coffin, Cheng-shi left the coffin by the riverside for the time being because, at the time of this story, there were very few people living near New Bridge, only some boats going back and forth.

As promised, Cheng-shi rewarded Wino Wang with fifty strings of cash. With the money in his possession, he went straight to Gao-shi's wineshop and, posing as a patron, said to her, "Why did you people beat Dong Xiao'er to death and throw the body into New Bridge River? The body has floated up. (*How can he be so sure that the man was beaten to death? It's because the scandal is by no means a secret.*) And the funniest thing happened: A woman appeared out of nowhere and claimed the body to be that of her husband. What a mistake! She has bought a coffin for the body and will be burying it soon enough."

"Wino Wang!" Gao-shi shot back. "What nonsense is this? Our Xiao'er is on the run after he stole some jewelry and clothing, and I wasn't able to have him caught. What a story you made up!"

"Ma'am, don't try to talk your way out of this! You can fool others, but not me! Now, cough up some money, and I'll let that woman go on believing it's her husband. If you refuse, I'll report you to the authorities, and you'll be tried for murder!"

Gao-shi burst into an explosion of bitter words: "You low-life swine, you deserve death by a thousand cuts! You good-for-nothing beggar, here to blackmail me because my husband is away!" (*Gao-shi's willfulness is the bane of her life.*)

At this torrent of abuse, Wino Wang went off in a huff. A woman capable of killing is, after all, not on high moral ground. Had she placated him with some money, nothing would have happened. She should never have given Wino Wang such a tongue-lashing. That swine went to the office of the commissioner of Ninghai, District and cried out, "Injustice!"

The commissioner, who was processing documents in the main hall, had his men bring Wino Wang to him and asked, "What injustice?"

On his knees, Wino Wang said, "I am Wang Qing, a native of Qiantang County, here today to report a murder. I have a neighbor, Qiao Jun, who is away on business. He has a wife, Gao-shi, a concubine, Zhou-shi, and a daughter, Yuxiu. There was an adulterous affair going on in the house involving Dong Xiao'er, a hired hand. And then, for some reason, Dong Xiao'er was murdered, and his body was dumped into New Bridge River. It has just come to the surface. I went to tell Gao-shi about it, and she yelled at me in the most vicious language. They also have another hired laborer in their wineshop, called Hong San, who must have been in on it, too. I'm here to report the murder because I feel that justice should be served. Please consider this case with all your wisdom!"

The commissioner had the clerk record Wang Qing's deposition and sent two officers, equipped with an arrest warrant, and Wang Qing to bring the three women and Hong San to court without delay. They headed straight for Gao-shi's home, and the officers arrested Gao-shi, Zhou-shi, Yuxiu, and Hong San. They then closed the gate and padlocked it. Once in the commissioner's court, the suspects all fell to their knees.

The commissioner, named Huang Zhengda [Righteousness], a native of Caizhou, was a mean-spirited man much given to applying torture. He asked Gao-shi, "Where's that Dong Xiao'er who works for you?"

Gao-shi replied, "Xiao'er stole my things and has fled no one knows where."

"If you want to know the facts, Your Honor," said Wino Wang, "just ask Hong San, and everything will be clear."

Thereupon, the commissioner had Hong San thrown to the floor and given fifty strokes on the legs with the rod. Blood flowed across the floor. Unable to withstand the pain any longer, Hong San confessed: "Dong Xiao'er had an adulterous affair with Zhou-shi before they moved back to the house. Later, he seduced Yuxiu. When Gao-shi learned of this, she was afraid of what her husband would say about such a disgrace to the family name when he returned.

"On the fifteenth day of the eighth month of this year, when viewing the moon on the night of the Mid-autumn Festival, she told me to have a few cups of wine with Xiao'er a little distance away from family members. We both got drunk. Afraid of doing something foolish under the influence of the wine, I went to the brewery room to sleep. At about the fifth watch of the night, Gao-shi and Zhou-shi came to my door and told me to go to the backyard, which I did, and there, I saw Xiao'er's corpse lying on the ground. I was told to carry the body to the river and dump it. I asked Gao-shi why this had happened. She told me and said, 'Those two colluded to seduce my daughter. What am I going to do when my husband comes back? I did this because there was nothing else I could do. I couldn't drive him out, nor could I reveal the truth. I had no choice but to strangle him with a hempen rope.'

"Being a straightforward man, I said, 'That fellow *was* a crook. It's a good thing this pain in the neck has been done away with.' So I carried the body on my back all the way to the river by New Bridge, tied a large rock to him to make him sink to the bottom, and dumped him into the water. Everything I have said is true."

The commissioner found the confession clear enough and told Hong San to affix his signature to the deposition. Now, Hong San's confession scared the two women out of their wits. Yuxiu, too, was so frightened that she trembled all over. When the commissioner ordered his men to bring the three women to him to make their confessions, Yuxiu felt obliged to tell the truth. "It all started with the adulterous affair between Zhou-shi and Xiao'er. After my mother, Gao-shi, made them move back home, he began to take liberties with me, but I rejected his advances. He tried again, I rejected him again, but he forcibly carried me off to the backyard, where he had his way with me. On the fifteenth day of the eighth month, while viewing the moon over cups of wine and fruit, my mother told me to leave the party first and retire to my own room for the night. I knew nothing about Xiao'er's death."

The commissioner turned to Zhou-shi. "You had an adulterous affair with Xiao'er. Why would you want to ruin that girl? Out with the truth now, if you don't want to be put to torture!"

Tears gushing, Zhou-shi gave up and admitted the truth. The commissioner then turned to Gao-shi. "Why did you have to murder Xiao'er?"

Realizing that she was not going to be able to talk her way out of this, Gao-shi confessed everything. All the accused were taken under guard to jail. The commissioner placed the depositions on file. The next day, he dispatched a county marshal leading a team of officers, who took Gao-shi and the others to New Bridge River to examine the corpse. That very day, the news spread throughout the town and beyond. Untold numbers of men and women swarmed over to watch the spectacle. Truly,

Good news stays behind closed doors;
Scandals travel a thousand li.

To get back to our story, the county marshal marched the group to New Bridge, opened the coffin, and removed the body for an examination. Afterward, the body was returned to the coffin, and the county marshal marched the group back to report to the commissioner. The corpse's forehead had been smashed by an ax, and marks of the hempen rope were still evident. At the commissioner's order, Gao-shi and the other four were given twenty strokes each, fainting and reviving several times. (*No distinction is made between the principal offender and the accessories. What a brainless commissioner!*) Gao-shi was then put in a long cangue, and Zhou-shi, Yuxiu, and Hong San were locked up in iron chains. All were taken under guard to prison. Wino Wang stayed behind to render service to the court.

In the meantime, the shoemaker's wife had realized her mistake and no longer went around crying out her grievances. The memory of what had happened still made her shiver with fear. For a time, she dared not even show her face in public, but of her, no more.

Let us return to the jail. Refusing all offers of food and water, Yuxiu died on the second day of her imprisonment. Two days later, Zhou-shi also died. Hong San fell gravely ill. The prison warden reported his illness, and the commissioner sent over a physician, but Hong San died anyway, leaving Gao-shi all by herself. Her body a swollen, aching mass of welts and bruises from the beating, she did not eat or drink anything except medicinal soup. The medicine failed to work, and she also died. How tragic that all four died in jail in less than half a month! Upon receiving the prison warden's report, the prefect consulted with lesser officials about his course of action. Since Qiao Jun had been away from home for a long time, his wife and concubine were rightfully the ones who should pay their lives for the crime of premeditated murder.

All those involved in the murder being dead and gone, a memorial was written to the imperial court to ask for a settlement of the case. Some days later, the imperial decree came. The scroll containing the decree was spread out and read aloud. It said, "As those involved in the act of murder have perished, all possessions of the Qiao household are to be confiscated. There being no kith and kin to reclaim Dong Xiao'er's corpse, let it be cremated." Right away, the commissioner dispatched officers to Qiao Jun's house. They forced open the front gate and confiscated all the valuables. (*What crime did Qiao Jun commit to be thus deprived of his possessions?*) Dong Xiao'er's corpse was then cremated, but of this, we shall speak no further.

Throughout this time, Qiao Jun had been living in Shen Ruilian's quarters in the Eastern Capital, totally ignorant of what was happening at his own home. Being destined for a decline in his fortunes, he found himself penniless at the end of two years. The madam often said bitterly, "My girl is so infatuated with you that she doesn't accept other clients, and that simply won't do! If you have money, don't begrudge it. If you don't have money, why don't you get out of here and let my girl get back to work? Surely, you don't want our whole family to die of hunger!"

Qiao Jun was a man accustomed to spending freely. Now reduced to poverty and humiliated by the madam's repeated attempts to oust him, he found the tears gushing from his eyes. He would have returned home but had no money for traveling expenses. At the sight of his tears, Shen Ruilian also began to cry. "Mr. Qiao!" she said. "I'm so sorry I've brought you to this pass! I have a little private savings. Take some for your trip back home. If you really care for me, you can withdraw some money when you get home and then come back again."

Qiao Jun was immensely pleased. That very night, he packed his old clothes into a bundle. Courtesan Shen gave him three hundred strings of cash, which he also placed in the bundle. After bidding the madam farewell and taking tearful leave of Shen Ruilian, he set off on his journey, the bundle on his back and a staff in his hand.

Qiao Jun reached Beixinguan by boat in a few days. The hour being late, he made his way to the home of a boat owner, an acquaintance of his, where he could stay for the night and enter the city the next day.

Much taken aback at the sight of Qiao Jun, the boat owner said, "Mr. Qiao, where have you been all this time? Why didn't you come back earlier? Your concubine Zhou-shi had an affair with a hired worker, so your wife moved them back to the house, and the fellow then had an affair with your daughter. I heard that, out of jealousy or whatever other reason, your wife murdered the worker, and Hong San the winemaker tossed the corpse into New Bridge River. Two months later, the corpse rose to the surface, and someone reported them to the commissioner, who then had your wife, concubine, daughter, and Hong San arrested. They confessed under torture and were thrown into jail. All four died because of the ill treatment they received there, after which the imperial court issued a decree and confiscated all your family possessions. Now where are you going to live?"

At these words, Qiao Jun felt as if

The eight bones of his skull opened up;
Half a bucketful of ice and snow poured in.

In short, Qiao Jun was dumbfounded. For a considerable while, speech was beyond him. His host set out wine and food for him, but he had no appetite. Two streams of tears kept flowing from his eyes as uncontrollably as rain. As he sobbed mournfully, he thought, "I never imagined I would end up without a home to call my own. What am I going to do?"

After tossing and turning throughout the night, he rose before dawn, took leave of the boat owner, and raced off to Wulin Gate, his bundle on his back. He stopped at the door of an antiques shop owned by Mr. Wang, staring across the street at the empty lot where his house had stood, for it had been torn down. Mr. Wang just happened to open the door at that moment. Qiao Jun put down his bundle and stepped forward with a bow, saying, "Mr. Wang, I never expected to return home to such a mess."

"Mr. Qiao, where have you been all this time?"

"I wasn't able to come back because all my money was gone. I didn't know what had happened at home."

Mr. Wang invited Qiao Jun inside, offered him a seat, and said, "Now, let this old man tell you what happened in your home after you left." He recounted everything up to the murder and then continued, "Then, along came a foolish woman, the wife of a bootmaker, who claimed that the corpse was her husband, who, she said, had died away from home. But that swine Wino Wang went to the authorities and had your wife, concubine, daughter, and Hong San brought to court. There, they were beaten so badly that they died in jail. All your family possessions have been confiscated and placed in government coffers. Now, where will you go?"

Weeping copiously, Qiao Jun took leave of Mr. Wang. With nowhere to go either north or south, he heaved a sigh and said to himself, "Oh well, being in my forties now, with no children, with all my possessions taken and both my wife and concubine dead and gone, to whom can I turn for help?" He went straight to the second bridge on West Lake, threw himself into the clear water, and drowned. How tragic the fate of Qiao Jun and his whole family!

Let us come now to Wino Wang. That very afternoon after Qiao Jun died, Wino Wang was loafing by West Lake with other bums like himself when they sat down by the very same second bridge of the lake and tried to scrape together some money for a bowl of wine. "Big Brother Wang," said the others to Wino Wang, "please go and buy the wine for us, since you know how to get a good deal."

Lo and behold, as soon as Wang had the money, he tossed it into West Lake. His eyes popping wide, he yelled, "Wang Qing! Dong Xiao'er deserved to die because he had seduced another man's wife and daughter. What business was that of yours? You put me, Qiao Jun, through such misery just because your blackmail attempt didn't work! All four members of my family died and don't even have a proper burial place, Now, pay me back for all those lives!" (*An act of retribution is indispensable.*)

Realizing that Qiao Jun was speaking through Wino Wang, all those who had witnessed the scene kowtowed and asked for mercy for Wino Wang. Before their very eyes, Wang Qing slapped himself on the face more than a hundred times, heaping curses upon himself as he did so. He then jumped into the lake and drowned.

As the story went around, people commented that although Qiao Jun may have been a lustful man, he had done no harm to anyone. Having died so tragically, how could he, under the Nine Springs, let Wang Qing off lightly? Demanding Wino Wang's life in return was nothing less than an act of divine justice. A later poet had this to say:

Qiao Jun's lust ruined the whole family;
Wino Wang's malice led to his own death.
Lust brings ruin to family and state, but
No one is ever hurt by scholarly pursuits.

34

Wang Jiaoluan's One Hundred Years of Sorrow

In heaven, the crow flies and the hare runs;[1]
On earth, the days and the months rush by.
Bustling theaters of old now overgrown with weeds;
Rights, wrongs, rises, falls—all change places in a trice.

Be sure to seek peace amid noisy surroundings;
Do not fall victim to your own cleverness.
Stay free of lust and greed,
And no harm will ever come your way.

Our story takes place in Changle Village, Yugan County, Raozhou Prefecture, Jiangxi, where there lived a certain Zhang Yi, a man of humble circumstances. On a trip to the county seat to sell some miscellaneous goods, he stopped one night at an inn outside the city gate, but it was already full. There was, however, a vacant room, all locked up, adjacent to the inn.

"Why don't you give me that room?" Zhang Yi asked the innkeeper.

"That room is haunted. I dare not let any patron stay in it."

"Even if it is, I'm not afraid.

The innkeepr resignedly opened the padlock and handed Zhang Yi a lamp and a broom.

Once inside, Zhang Yi put the lamp down in a safe place and picked the lampwick until the flame was nice and bright. In the room, there was a rickety old bed covered with dust. He swept it clean, spread his bedding on it, and went out for some wine and food. As soon as he returned, he took off his clothes and went to bed. In a dream, a beautiful woman, elegantly dressed, approached him to offer her services. It was an offer he accepted. When he awoke, the woman was still by his side. He asked who she was, and she replied, "I live in a nearby house. My husband is away on a trip, and I found it hard to sleep by myself. So I came here to seek your company. Don't tell anyone about this. Just keep the knowledge to yourself." Zhang did not ask any more questions.

At daybreak, the woman departed but she came again at night to resume the joys of the night before. Three nights went by in like fashion.

Seeing that Mr. Zhang was still alive and well, the innkeeper casually remarked that the room used to be haunted by a woman who had hanged herself there. He added that all was evidently well again. Zhang Yi made a mental note of what he had heard but said nothing.

At night fall, when the woman appeared again, Zhang Yi said, "Earlier today, the innkeeper told me that a woman had hanged herself in this very room. Might it be you?"

"Yes, it's me," she replied without a hint of shame or evasiveness. "But I won't hurt you. Don't be afraid."

"I'd like to hear more," said Zhang Yi.

"I was a prostitute. My surname is Mu. Since I was twenty-second in seniority at the brothel, they called me 'Sister Twenty-two.' I was very fond of a patron from Yugan called Yang Chuan, who promised to marry me and take me to his hometown. I gave him a hundred taels of silver from my private savings to help him out, but he left and never returned. I felt so miserable that three years after his departure, I hanged myself because the madam kept such a close watch on me that I had no chance to escape. The madam sold this room, which ended up being part of the inn. But my soul, which did not perish, still lives here, where I lived before my death. Yang Chuan comes from the same place as you do. Do you happen to know him?"

"Yes, I do."

"Is he still around?"

"He moved last year to the South Gate of Raozhou, where he married and opened a shop, and business is good."

The woman sighed with emotion for a considerable while, and relapsed into silence.

Two days later, when Zhang Yi wanted to return home, the woman said, "May I follow you wherever you go?"

"Yes, by all means."

"Please make a small wooden tablet, inscribe on it 'To the memory of Sister Twenty-two,' and put it in your trunk. I'll come whenever you take out the tablet and call my name."

Zhang Yi agreed. The woman continued, "I have fifty taels of silver buried under this bed. No one knows about it. You may have them."

Zhang Yi dug under the bed, and to his great joy, there was indeed a jar filled with silver. The night passed without ado.

The next day, Zhang Yi prepared the tablet, put it in his trunk, took leave of the innkeeper, and set out on his journey home. Upon arrival, he told his wife about what had happened. She was displeased at first, but at the sight of the fifty taels of silver, she relented. Zhang Yi then placed the tablet to the memory of Sister Twenty-two by the eastern wall. When his wife playfully called out her name, she did indeed emerge in broad daylight and saluted Mrs. Zhang. (*Ghosts that assume human shape in broad daylight do so on the strength of male sperm.*) Mrs. Zhang was quite startled, but later became accustomed to the ghost and began to take her for granted. At night, Sister Twenty-two shared the bed with Zhang Yi and his wife, yet the couple never felt crowded.

More than ten days later, the woman said, "I have some old debts to settle in the city. Could you go with me to collect them?"

Zhang Yi readily agreed, coveting her money. Right away, he hired a boat and set out but not without first placing the tablet in the cabin. All along the way, the woman was at his side day and night, making no attempt to remove herself from the presence of other people. Some days later, they found themselves at the South Gate of Raozhou. The woman said, "I'm going to Yang Chuan's house to collect the debts." Before Zhang Yi could ask a question, she was already ashore.

He followed her and saw her disappear into a shop. Upon inquiry, he was told that it was Yang Chuan's house. Zhang waited a long time in vain for her to reemerge. Suddenly, a commotion broke out inside the house, and, a few moments later, the earth shook with wails of grief. A clerk in the shop answered Zhang Yi's question by saying, "My master Yang Chuan, who had always enjoyed the best of health, suddenly fell violently ill and died, with blood flowing from all his nine apertures."

Knowing all too well that it must have been the work of Sister Twenty-two, Zhang Yi quietly stepped onto the boat and called out in front of the memorial tablet, but however hard he tried, the woman did not appear again. He now realized that the debt to which she had referred was Yang Chuan's debt of betrayal. There is a poem that laments:

The ingrate Wang Kui was rightly punished;[2]
The heartless Li Yi also came to grief.[3]
Consider again the case of Yang Chuan;
Heaven never blesses scoundrels like these.

In the above story, although Sister Twenty-two was avenged in the end, it was the work of a ghost, hardly a dependable redresser of wrongs. Let me now tell a story called "Wang Jiaoluan's One Hundred Years of Sorrow," in which the aggrieved is vindicated in a better way.

The story takes place not in the Tang dynasty, nor the Song dynasty, but in the first year of the Tianshun reign period [1457] of this dynasty [Ming]. When garrison troops from various regions were redeployed to Guangxi to put down a rebellion by the Miao people, Wang Zhong, commander of the Lin'an region, was impeached because his contingent of Zhejiang soldiers had arrived late. He was thus demoted to battalion commander of the Nanyang region in Henan and reported immediately for duty, with his family in tow.

Wang Zhong was in his sixties and had only one son, Wang Biao, quite a valiant warrior, whom the military commissioner kept in his service. Wang Zhong also had two daughters. The older one, Jiaoluan, was eighteen years old, and the younger one, Jiaofeng, was sixteen years old. Jiaofeng had been raised from an early age by her maternal grandparents and was betrothed to her cousin. Jiaoluan, however, was still unbetrothed. Wang Zhong's wife, Zhou-shi, who had married him after the death of his first wife, had an older sister, Mrs. Cao, a widow who was living in poverty before Zhou-shi invited her to live in the Wang house as a companion to Jiaoluan. She came to be called "Auntie Cao" by those in the household.

Since an early age, Jiaoluan was well versed in the classics and the histories and gifted in literary composition. The parents being too cautious in selecting a husband for this beloved daughter, she remained unbetrothed at the marriageable age of fifteen. Every so often, she would heave a sigh to the wind and share her melancholy with the moon. Only Auntie Cao, who was very close to her, knew what was weighing on her mind and was aware of what her parents were not.

One day, with the Clear and Bright Festival drawing near, Jiaoluan was playing on the swing in the back garden with Auntie Cao and the maid Mingxia when, in the midst of the merriment, she saw a handsome young man in a purple robe and a cap in the Tang style standing by a gap in wall. He was craning his neck for a better view and giving one cheer after another. Mortified, Jiaoluan pushed Auntie Cao along and scurried back to her chamber, her face flaming red. The maid followed them into the house.

With the garden quite deserted, the young man scaled the wall and neared the swing, where a fragrance lingered. He was deep in thought when his eye caught something in the grass. He picked it up and saw that it was a three-foot-long embroidered silk kerchief. (*The source of all trouble to come.*) He was as delighted as if he had found a piece of treasure. At the sound of footsteps coming from the direction of the house, he climbed over the wall again to stand, as before, by the gap in the wall. It was the maid, coming to look for the kerchief. Noticing the look on the maid's face, weary after much searching, the young man said affably, "Young lady! Someone has picked up the kerchief. You are not going to find it!"

Raising her eyes the maid saw that it was a young man who looked like a scholar. She stepped forward and said with a curtsy, "You must be the one who picked it up, sir. Would you please give it back to me? I'll be ever so grateful."

"Whose kerchief is it?"

"It belongs to my mistress."

"Since it's your mistress's, I'm not going to give it back unless she asks for it herself."

"Where do you live, sir?"

"My name is Zhou Tingzhang. I'm a native of Wujiang County, Suzhou Prefecture. My father is the local education commissioner, and I've come to live with him in the house on the other side of this wall."

As a matter of fact, the commander's mansion and the education commissioner's mansion were parts of the same compound, the former being the eastern wing, and the latter the western wing. Beyond the garden lay a patch of unused land that belonged to the education commissioner.

The maid said, "I didn't know that you were a next-door neighbor, sir. I apologize for not having shown you proper respect. I'll report back to my mistress about your request."

"May I ask your mistress's name and your name?"

"My mistress is Jiaoluan, beloved daughter of the old master. I am her chambermaid, Mingxia."

"I'll give the kerchief back to you if you'll present a little poem of mine to your mistress," said Tingzhang.

Mingxia did not like the idea of delivering poems, but in order to get back the kerchief, she gave her consent.

"Please wait," said Tingzhang, turning away. A few moments later, he returned with a piece of peach-blossom-patterned stationery paper folded into a double square. Mingxia took the poem and asked, "But where's the kerchief?"

Tingzhang said with a chuckle, "The kerchief is nothing less than a treasure, hard to come by. How can you expect me to return it just like that? I'll give it back only after you show her the poem and bring me her response."

Resignedly, Mingxia departed.

An ordinary silk kerchief
Led to a song of eternal sorrow.

Now, let us come to Jiaoluan. In spite of her embarrassment upon seeing the handsome youth, her passion was aroused. She thought to herself, "What a dashing young man! If I could marry him, I won't have lived in vain, however brilliant I am." All of a sudden, she saw Mingxia enter her room in a huff. "You found the kerchief?" she asked.

"The strangest thing happened!" said Mingxia. "It was picked up by Young Master Zhou of the west wing, the very one in purple who cheered by the gap in the wall."

"Get it from him, and that will be that."

"As if I didn't try! But he has to agree to return it first!"

"Why didn't he give it back to you?"

"This is what he said: 'My name is Zhou Tingzhang. I'm a native of Wujiang County, Suzhou Prefecture. My father is the local education commissioner, and I've come to live with him in the house on the other side of this wall.' And he said since it's your kerchief, you have to ask for it yourself."

"So, what did you say?"

"I told him I would report back to you about his request. Then he said he had a little poem for me to present to you and would give back the kerchief only after I brought him your response." So saying, Mingxia handed the stationery to the young lady. Joy stirred in Jiaoluan at the sight of the folded double square. She opened it and saw written inside a quatrain:

The silk from the beauty, with its sweet scent,
Is sent by heaven to the admirer.
Tenderly I send over words of love,
Words that will lead me to the bridal chamber.

If Jiaoluan had known better, she would have forgotten about the kerchief, burned the poem, and told the maid never to deliver letters again, and all would have been well. However, partly because she had reached puberty still unbetrothed and yearned for love and partly because she did not want her literary talent to go to waste, she wrote an eight-line poem on a sheet of fine stationery:

This piece of flawless precious jade
Was born in a noble house.
In peace, I look at the moon with my family;
In leisure, I view the flowers, all alone.
The green wutong tree admits only the phoenix;
The verdant bamboo grove allows no ravens.
A word to the forlorn soul in an alien land:
Let not confused thoughts weigh on your mind.

Bearing the poem, Mingxia went to the back garden, where Tingzhang was already waiting by the gap in the wall. Mingxia said, "My mistress has a poem for you in reply. Now you can give me back the kerchief."

Tingzhang read the poem and was so impressed by Jiaoluan's talent that he decided to win her over. "Please wait, young lady," he said to the maid. "Let me write a reply." He returned to his study and wrote a quatrain:

By a predestined bond, I live nearby,
A wretched, forlorn soul in an alien land.
With the pair of phoenixes in the same tree,
Flute notes echo through the sky all night long.

Mingxia snapped, "I'm not going to deliver another poem if you keep the kerchief!"

Pulling a gold hairpin out of his sleeve, Tingzhang said, "This is a small gift for you as a token of my respect. Please give my warm regards to your young mistress."

Mingxia liked the gold hairpin so much that she again acted as messenger. After reading the poem, Jiaoluan sank into gloomy silence.

"Is there anything in the poem that you find offensive?" asked Mingxia.

"It's full of flirtatious improprieties. What a frivolous scholar!"

"With your great talent, couldn't you write a poem to scold him and put a stop to his advances?"

"Young men tend to be short tempered. I don't need to use harsh words. I'll just give him a nice piece of advice." (*So, Jiaoluan already has her heart set on the young man.*) On another piece of fine stationery paper, she wrote eight more lines:

There he stands, amid the green in the yard;
What tender words—those relayed by the maid!
Bent on stealing the piece of fragrant jade,
Eager to stir up the clouds and rain.[4]
Red cassia is not meant for one too young;
Bed curtains do not yield to morning gusts.
Be advised: dream not of the balcony;
Study hard, and join the Academy!

And thus the letters went back and forth in an endless stream, growing warmer in tone as Mingxia's feet busily trod the path in the back garden while Tingzhang kept his eyes glued to the gap in the wall. There were too many poems to be cited in full here.

When the Dragon Boat Festival came around, Commander Wang held a family feast in the garden pavilion. From his place at the gap in the wall, Tingzhang gathered that the young mistress was in the garden, but he had no excuse for seeing her, nor was the maid Mingxia free to deliver a message.

Feeling dejected, he suddenly ran into Sun Jiu, a footman. Sun Jiu was also a skilled carpenter and had long served both the commander and the education commissioner. Tingzhang sealed up one of his poems, gave Sun Jiu a tip of two hundred in cash, and asked him to deliver the poem to Sister Mingxia in the commander's wing of the compound. Faithful to the task entrusted to him, Sun Jiu waited until the next morning before he saw an opportunity to deliver the poem. Mingxia then passed it to her young mistress, who opened the seal and saw that the line preceding the poem read: "Having looked for you in the garden in vain during the Dragon Boat Festival, I send you the following quatrain, which I intoned on the spur of the moment:

Weave colorful threads into lovers' knots;
Fill both cups with dogwood wine.
With the loved one hidden by river fog,
The sunflower seeks the sun, but in vain.

The poem was followed by the line "Respectfully, Zhou Tingzhang of Pine Hill [another name for Wujiang County, Jiangsu]." Jiaoluan put the poem on her table and went to do her toilette. In the meantime, before she had time to write a reply, Auntie Cao suddenly walked in. Astounded upon reading the poem, she said, "So, there's a love affair going on without a matchmaker's blessing! Why hide this from me?"

Shyly, Jiaoluan replied, "There have been letters going back and forth, but that's the full extent of the relationship. I wouldn't dare hide anything from you, Auntie."

"Young Mr. Zhou being a scholar from south of the Yangzi River and of a matching family background, why don't we tell him to find a matchmaker and fulfill this marriage bond? Wouldn't that be nice?"

"Agreed!" said Jiaoluan with a nod. After her toilette was finished, she wrote the following eight lines by way of a reply:

Sequestered in the boudoir for eighteen years,
With no sweet air allowed through the curtains,
I live in comfort, but who knows my pain?
I sleep through the cold spring in my brocade bed.
How I fear the sound of the cuckoos!
How I worry that butterflies will haunt my dreams!
If he with tender feelings so wishes,
Through a medium shall word be sent.

After he received the message, Tingzhang sought the help of a Scholar Zhao, falsely claiming that it was the wish of his father, Commissioner Zhou, that Zhao present the marriage proposal to Commander Wang. Commander Wang was indeed impressed with Mr. Zhou Junior's talent and looks, but Jiaoluan was his much beloved daughter, and one with literary talent at that. Being advanced in years, he was highly dependent on his daughter's services in writing his official correspondences and could hardly entertain the thought of letting her follow a husband to some distant place. So he hesitated and withheld his consent. (*Foreshadowing "Song of Eternal Sorrow" at the end.*)

Bitterly stung by the news, Tingzhang wrote the following letter to Jiaoluan:

Respectfully from Tingzhang, your friend from Pine Hill:

Ever since I laid eyes on your beauty, my heart has not known a moment of peace. As marriage bonds are predestined, I shall have no other while I live. The matchmaker brought me a message earlier today, saying that no consent has been given. Watching your inaccessible boudoir from afar, I feel like Emperor Xuanzong of the Tang dynasty longing in vain for Chang'e the moon goddess after his legendary visit to the moon palace. Yearning to visit your garden, I feel like the Herdboy aching for the Weaving Maiden on the other side of the Milky Way.[5] Should this misery last for days and months, I will surely die in some gutter before my allotted span of life expires. If I cannot fulfill the bond in this life, I shall have no rest even after I die. I have composed the following clumsy poem in the profound hope of winning your sympathy:

Without a happy union to anticipate,
The priceless season of spring goes to waste.
In gloom, I drink three cups of wine by the window;
In sorrow, I play the zither for the flowers.
I feel better leaning against the window

But lament in bed amid dead silence.
Forlorn moon, dull and dim—
Would you kindly convey my feelings?

After reading the letter, Jiaoluan wrote a reply:

Respectfully from Jiaoluan, beloved daughter of the commander:

In the moon-viewing pavilion, facing lotus flowers that adorn the water, near curtains fluffy with willow catkins, I listen languidly to the cuckoo cries borne on the east wind and spend the long days embroidering lovebirds by the window where orioles sing. When I was feeling drowsy, your poem suddenly fell upon my table. I opened and read it, which only added to my boundless sorrow. Regrettably, I am blessed in looks but not in fate, much to the chagrin of the loving and talented scholar. Every letter that I receive deepens my pain; every poem that arrives accentuates my loneliness. Do not scale the east wall and pluck the flowers, but set your eyes on the star of learning and win academic honors. If a match does not present itself at the moment, wait until one emerges from the books. I seal my deep feelings in this letter. Make no inquiries of its deliverer. What follows is my response to your fine poem, for you to read with a forgiving heart:

The autumn moon and spring flowers are sentient,
Well aware of their priceless worth.
Through the latticed window, I caught a glimpse of Han;[6]
By the east wall, I heard the lute meant for Cui's ears.[7]
All foolish thoughts have vanished into thin air;
In dreams I intone my better poems.
In this life, let us just brother and sister be
And wait till our next lives to fulfill the bond.

After reading the letter, Tingzhang was filled with admiration. When he came to the penultimate line "In this life, let us just brother and sister be," an idea suddenly came to him. "Zhang Gong and Shen Chun had acknowledged their lovers in public as sisters.[8] Jiaoluan's mother and I share the same surname. Why don't I honor her as my aunt? In that way, the two families will see much of each other, and that means I'll have my chance!"

So, saying that the west wing of the compound was too cramped and noisy, he asked for permission to do his studies in the commander's back garden. When Commissioner Zhou raised the matter with Commander Wang, the latter agreed, adding, "Since we're neighbors, he's very welcome to join us at our meals, so as to save us the trouble of delivering the food to him."

Grateful beyond measure, Mr. Zhou Senior told his son about the commander's offer. Tingzhang said, "It's very kind of Mr. Wang to say so, but I really shouldn't impose on him without being related to the family in any way. I'm thinking of preparing a gift and honoring Mrs. Wang as my aunt. With the two families thus linked, my actions will be fully legitimate."

Being a muddleheaded person content with gaining small advantages (*Petty acquisitiveness is the cause of muddleheadedness*), Commissioner Zhou said, "Have it your way." Thereupon, Tingzhang asked someone to notify Mr. Wang and his wife.

Consequently, an auspicious day was chosen, gifts of colorful silk and other items were prepared, a visiting card was written presenting the young man as a nephew, and Tingzhang went next door, all humility, to claim kinship. And a cordial scene it was. Being a military officer, Mr. Wang enjoyed flattery. (*Who says civilian officials do not succumb to flattery?*) So he invited the visitor into the main hall and introduced him to the lady of the house. Auntie Cao became his aunt, and Jiaoluan his cousin. When the greetings were over, Mr. Wang had a feast set out in the back hall to celebrate the occasion. With everyone now seated at the same table as one family, Tingzhang and Jiaoluan were secretly overjoyed. How they conveyed their love through meaningful glances need not be described here. The feast did not come to an end until everyone had fully enjoyed the occasion.

Their marital future yet unknown,
They're taking action on their own.

The next day, Mr. Wang readied a room in which his nephew Zhou Tingzhang could study and had the young man brought to the room, but not without first locking the back door that led to the women's quarters so as to keep the women away from the garden. The staff employed in the front section of the house took care of Tingzhang's daily needs. Though Tingzhang and Jiaoluan were in the same house, communication became, if anything, more difficult. Despite her unflinching determination to keep her chastity, Jiaoluan's amorous desires had been aroused. Moreover, their proximity and the significant looks they exchanged at the dinner table made their separation during the rest of the day even more unbearable.

Jiaoluan's depression led to illness. Her temperature was low in the morning but rose to a feverish high late in the afternoon, and she forsook all food and beverage. Mr. Wang engaged physicians and fortune-tellers, but nothing worked. Time and again, Tingzhang went to the main hall to inquire about her health, and Mr. Wang accepted his regards without ever inviting him into the girl's chamber. But Tingzhang came up with a plan. He said, lying through his teeth, "When I was growing up south of the Yangzi River, I learned the theories of medicine. If I could feel my cousin's pulse, I'd be able to make a diagnosis."

After informing his wife and having Mingxia the maid tell Jiaoluan, Mr. Wang led the young man in. Sitting at the bedside, Tingzhou caressed the young lady's wrist for a considerable while, pretending to be feeling her pulse. (*This fellow, in his devious, clever way, does know how to take advantage of Mr. Wang's stupidity.*) With both parents present, Tingzhang couldn't exchange a word with the girl other than to tell her to take care of herself. Once out of the chamber, he said to Mr.

Wang, "My cousin's illness is caused by depression. If she could take frequent walks in some open space with female companionship and thus take her mind off things, she would be all right again without the aid of medicine."

Mr. Wang respected and trusted the young man so much that not the slightest suspicion entered his mind. "The only open space in this establishment is the garden," said he.

Purposefully, Tingzhang replied, "If my cousin is to take frequent walks in the garden, I'm afraid I will be in her way. I'll have to return home."

"Being brother and sister, why stand on ceremony?" asked Mr. Wang.

That very day, Mr. Wang ordered the back door to be unlocked and the key entrusted to Auntie Cao, who was to keep Jiaoluan amused as best she could. Mingxia was to attend to her young mistress's needs and never leave her for a moment. Mr. Wang thought the arrangement flawless.

To return to Jiaoluan: Since her illness was a result of her longing for young Mr. Zhou, she was overjoyed that he had managed to caress her wrist. In addition, the two people allowed to accompany her on her walks in the garden and attend to her needs were her confidantes. Immediately, her illness was half gone.

Every time she went to the garden, Tingzhang was there to see her and be with her, walking or sitting. Sometimes she also stopped by his study for tea. Gradually, they cast all caution to the winds and began to touch each other, shoulder to shoulder, back to back.

On one occasion, when the coast was clear, Tingzhang pleaded with Jiaoluan for permission to see her boudoir. Casting a glance at Auntie Cao, Jiaoluan replied in a subdued voice, "My aunt has the key. You'll have to ask her." Tingzhang got her point.

The next day, he came with two bolts of fine silk from the Wu region and a pair of gold bracelets and asked Mingxia to present them as gifts to Auntie Cao.

"I wonder why Mr. Zhou is so generous," Auntie Cao remarked to her niece.

"An impetuous young man is prone to committing improprieties. He wants you, Auntie, to look the other way."

"I know what's going on between you two but you can go ahead and see each other. I'll never say a word to anyone." So saying, she gave the key to Mingxia. Exultantly, Jiaoluan wrote a quatrain and sent it to Tingzhang. It said,

Quietly I send word to the talented one;
Act not rashly with others present.
Tonight the boudoir will be free of lock and key;
In the shadow of the moon and flowers, she comes.

The poem threw Tingzhang into raptures. When dusk set in and the watch drum had struck, Tingzhang tiptoed into the inner section of the house and sidled through the gate that had been left ajar. He had a vague memory of the route from his last venture into the boudoir to feel Jiaoluan's pulse and inched his way forward until he saw Mingxia the maid standing in a pool of light by the door. Hardly had he stepped into the chamber and exchanged a greeting with Jiaoluan than he tried to embrace her, but she pushed him away. As she did so, she told Mingxia to bring in Auntie Cao and have her sit with them. Bitterly disappointed, Tingzhang protested and accused her of breaking her word. In his chagrin, tears came to his eyes.

Jiaoluan said, "I am a chaste woman, and you are not some lecherous rake either. We have fallen in love because we are each attracted to the other's talent and looks. Since I have privately promised myself to you, I will surely stay loyal to you till the end. If you ever abandon me, you will be betraying my devotion. We must vow to the gods that we will live out our lives together. Without a proper ceremony, I would rather die than comply."

At this point, Auntie Cao arrived. She thanked Tingzhang for his gift, whereupon Tingzhang asked her to serve as matchmaker. When he took the marriage vow, he poured out a stream of curses against himself should he be remiss in his devotion. (*In fact, people prone to taking violent oaths hold the gods in contempt.*)

"My dear children," said Auntie Cao, "if you want me to be the matchmaker, draw up four copies of a marriage contract. One copy is to be burned as an offering to heaven and earth and the gods. One is to be kept by me as proof of my services as matchmaker. The two of you will keep one each, to serve as proof in the case of a reunion after a separation. Should the wife betray the husband, she shall die from a thunderbolt. Should the husband betray the wife, he shall die under myriad arrows. Whoever betrays the other will be tormented in the netherworld and will never be delivered."

Delighted by Auntie Cao's impassioned speech, Tingzhang and Jiaoluan put their marriage vows on paper. They bowed, first to heaven and earth, and then to Auntie Cao. Auntie Cao set out fresh fruit and mellow wine and offered toasts of congratulations. The three sat together, drinking wine until the third strike of the night watch. After Auntie Cao left, the young couple went to bed, hand in hand. The joys of their union can well be imagined.

At the fifth watch, Jiaoluan urged Tingzhang to get up and leave, saying, "Now that I have given myself to you, you must not betray me. Nothing escapes the eyes of the gods. Whenever I see an opportunity, I will send Mingxia to bring you over. Do not, on any account, come here on a whim, so as not to give rise to gossip."

Tingzhang agreed with every word but was loath to leave. Quickly, Jiaoluan told Mingxia to escort him as far as the garden gate. Later that day, Jiaoluan wrote him two poems:

The first one said:

What joy, what delight, what a blissful night!
The bed curtains warm, the words tender,
The two bodies joined, the passion at its height
In a raging storm of clouds and rain.

On the pillow, the soft chirp of the phoenix;
By the window, the shadow of flowers and the moon.
In the morning, a peek at the pillows of love;
On the quilt, dots of fallen red petals.

The second one said:

The quilt rolling in red waves of passion,
Shyly I embraced the loved one for the first time.
With the moon at its roundest, the flowers in full bloom,
The clouds dispersed, and the rain let up.
Conjugal love, a gift from heaven,
Has released feelings of all descriptions.
I send you these lines on this mid-month night,
Without having to watch the Herdboy star.[9]

Tingzhang wrote some lines back.

Soon, Jiaoluan had fully regained her health. As the gate was no longer padlocked, every three or five days she dispatched Mingxia to bring Tingzhang over.

As they were so often together, their love for each other grew more profound.

About half a year went by in like fashion. Commissioner Zhou's term of office expired, and he was promoted to be magistrate of Emei County, in Sichuan. Loathing the thought of leaving Jiaoluan, Tingzhang refused to go with his father, pleading illness and anxiety about the hardships of the journey. In addition, with his studies not yet completed and his teacher and classmates being congenial company, he simply had to stay behind and pursue further studies. (*How can a disobedient son be a good husband?*) Being a doting father, Commissioner Zhou never failed to grant every one of his son's wishes.

On the day of the commissioner's departure, Tingzhang saw his father off as far as the city gate before returning. Grateful to Tingzhang for his decision to stay, Jiaoluan asked him to come over later that very day, and their union was doubly tender. Things went on this way for another six months and more, during which time they wrote more poems for each other than can be recorded here.

One day, Tingzhang was reading the official newspapers when he came upon a story about his father, saying that Magistrate Zhou, unaccustomed to the climate of Emei, had returned to his hometown for reasons of health. Tingzhang had been separated from his parents for so long that he did wish to visit them but could not bear the thought of leaving his beloved Jiaoluan. Facing such a difficult choice, he became visibly depressed.

Upon learning the cause of his low spirits, Jiaoluan set out wine and gave him these words of advice: "Conjugal love may be as deep as the sea, but the love between father and son is vaster than the sky. If you neglect your higher obligations for the sake of romantic love, you will not only be remiss in your duties as a son but will also make me remiss in my duties as a wife."

Auntie Cao also said, "Meeting on the sly in this way is by no means like a proper marriage. You might just as well return to your hometown and visit your parents. During your stay with them, bring up the subject of marriage so as to fulfill your marriage vow as soon as possible and relieve your mind of a burden."

While Tingzhang was still debating with himself, Jiaoluan told Auntie Cao to inform her father about the young man's wish to return home. (*Jiaoluan is by no means any less proud of spirit than Jiang of Qi. Too bad that Mr. Zhou is no Prince of Jin.*[10])

That day being the day of the Dragon Boat Festival, Mr. Wang set out a farewell feast in Tingzhang's honor and gave him lavish gifts. Tingzhang's sense of duty won out over his less worthy inclinations, and he resignedly set about packing his belongings. That night, Jiaoluan served wine in her chamber and, in the presence of Auntie Cao, asked Tingzhang to reaffirm his vows and set a date for the wedding. They had so much to tell each other that they talked throughout the whole wakeful night. Before they parted company, she asked for his address.

"Why do you ask?" said Tingzhang.

"If you don't come back soon enough, I'll write to you."

Tingzhang requested a brush-pen and wrote the following quatrain:

> *Missing my parents, I travel a thousand li*
> *Back to Wujiang, the seventeenth township of Suzhou.*
> *Ask for Double Ripple Point in South Hemp,*
> *Where Grain Overseer Wu lives by Yanling Bridge.*

Tingzhang explained, "My mother is of the famous Wu clan, descended from the local Grain Overseer Wu. Zhou is the surname of my father, who married into the Wu clan. You won't have much use for this address because I'll miss you so much that a day will be as long as a year, and so I'll surely come back in half a year, or at most a whole year, with a letter from my parents proposing marriage. I will never allow my beauty to wait for me in anxiety." They fell on each other's shoulders and burst into sobs.

When daybreak drew near, Jiaoluan escorted Tingzhang out of the garden. The following is an eight-line poem that they composed together:

> *However deeply in love the two may be,*
> *One has to leave for his parents.* (by Tingzhang)
> *Henceforth, who will wait for the moon in the garden?*
> *Who will be in the mood for chess in the boudoir?* (by Jiaoluan)
> *I fear that absence will make hearts grow distant;*
> *I care not if my luck does not match my talent.* (by Tingzhang)

My head lowered, I keep my thoughts to myself;
Holding back my farewell tears, I trim my brows. (by Jiaoluan)

At the first light of dawn, the horse and the saddle were made ready. Mr. Wang set out wine in the main hall, where his wife and daughter were also present, to bid the young man farewell. As Tingzhang was bowing, Jiaoluan, on the verge of sad tears, quietly returned to her own room. There, she wrote a poem on black-traced stationery and gave it to Mingxia, who then slipped it into Tingzhang's hands when she was helping him mount the horse. In the saddle, Tingzhang opened the letter and read,

Hand in hand, shoulder to shoulder,
We part company sadly in tears.
Before your horse has gone past the willows,
My heart has flown to the white clouds afar.
One is as chaste as Gongjiang;[11]
The other as filial as Min Jian.[12]
Come back as soon as your wish is fulfilled,
For the sake of the one pining in the boudoir.

His tears flowing after he had read the poem, Tingzhang was overcome with emotion as the sights of the journey all reminded him of his loved one. To do him justice, he did not forget about Jiaoluan right away.

Let us not encumber our story with unnecessary details but tell of Tingzhang's arrival at the family mansion in Wujiang some days later. As he greeted his parents, the entire household rejoiced, for his father had arranged his marriage with the daughter of Prefect Wei, who lived in the same neighborhood, and his father was about to have him escorted back home for the wedding ceremony. After an initial show of reluctance, Tingzhang accepted the offer once he learned of Miss Wei's unparalleled beauty as well as the lavish dowry and Prefect Wei's immense wealth. His greed and lust made him forget about the vows he had taken.

Half a year later, Wei-shi crossed the threshold of the Zhou family as a bride. As happy as a fish in water in his loving new marriage, Tingzhang no longer remembered the existence of someone by the name of Wang Jiaoluan.

Enamored of the new love, he forgot
The one awaiting his return.

Jiaoluan had urged Tingzhang to go to his parents out of a sense of wifely duty, but after he was gone, she sorely missed him. Her days were spent in misery, her evenings in loneliness. Beside the lamp, she had none but her own shadow for a companion. Behind the bed curtains, she had no one to share her thoughts. Her sorrows were deepest when spring flowers were in bloom and when the autumn moon shone brightly. A year passed painfully without a word from Tingzhang.

Suddenly, one day, Mingxia came to inquire, "Do you want to send Brother-in-law Zhou a letter?"

"Is there a messenger?" asked Jiaoluan.

"Sun Jiu was saying just a moment ago that there's a government courier from the Lin'an District, where Hangzhou is located. Wujiang being on the way to Lin'an, he can very well deliver a letter on his return trip."

"In that case, tell Sun Jiu to make sure that the courier doesn't leave too soon." Right away, Jiaoluan wrote a letter, expressing her feelings for the one far away and reminding him to come to Nanyang as soon as possible so that they could return together to his hometown and fulfill their marriage vow. Let us skip the letter and cite only one of the ten poems attached to it:

Nothing has been heard from you since we parted;
Between us, there's only the lambent moon to share.
For your parents' sake, you left this compound;
Do not be detained by the pleasures of the South.
In the Immortals' Hall, I seek divination;
At the Moon Pavilion, I have my fortune told.
Would that you looked into your heart
And shared with me the joys of conjugal life!

On the envelope, she wrote another eight lines:

To the Wu house please deliver this note,
An imposing mansion, a source of pride.
The father, the education commissioner,
Among the ancestors, the Grain Overseer.
Be sure of the location of the house;
Do not confuse South Hemp with North Hemp.
Ask for directions as you find your way there
In which village stands Yanling Bridge?

She tipped the messenger with two silver hairpins.

Seven months elapsed without a reply. When New Year's Day drew near, Jiaoluan learned that a traveler named Zhang would soon be leaving the neighborhood to purchase merchandise in Suzhou. She took out a pair of gold flower-shaped hairpins and again had Sun Jiu ask the traveler to deliver a letter. The letter contained the same message as before. The following is one of the ten poems attached to it:

Spring brought new life to everything on earth,
But the one in the boudoir is lost in sorrow.
The east wind blows, and my loved one floats with it;
The moon waxes full, but I'm not made whole.
Worn down with sorrow, my hair turns hoary;

I seek a messenger, a blue bird in the sky.
To whom can I pour out my heart?
To the talented one I send this note.

On the envelope, she wrote a quatrain:

Near Suzhou lies Wujiang, where stands
The house of Grain Overseer Wu of South Hemp.
Please look for the place with care
And convey my questions to the talented one.

Being a sincere and responsible man, Mr. Zhang, the traveling merchant, went to Wujiang to deliver the letter personally after he had concluded his business in Suzhou. He was asking for directions on Long Bridge when Zhou Tingzhang happened to pass by. Hearing a voice with a He'nan accent asking about Grain Overseer Wu of South Hemp, he knew it must be a messenger bearing a letter from Jiaoluan. Afraid that the messenger would go to his home and find out about his new marriage, he stepped forward with a salute. After introducing himself, he invited the messenger to a wineshop for a few drinks. There, he opened the letter, read it, and, with a brush-pen and a piece of paper borrowed from the shop-owner, hastily wrote a reply saying that he had to postpone the wedding because his father was recovering from an illness and needed his services. He added that he would soon see her again and told her not to worry. At the end of the letter, he wrote "Written on the road in haste with a borrowed brush-pen. Please accept my apologies."

Mr. Zhang took the letter. Some days later, he returned to Nanyang and sent it via Sun Jiu to Jiaoluan. She opened the letter and read it. Even though no wedding date was given, the letter was, for her, a painted cake that allayed her hunger and an imaginary cluster of plums that quenched her thirst.

Three to four months passed without another word from Tingzhang. Jiaoluan said to Auntie Cao, "He must have been lying to me!"

"But his written oath is here, and heaven is a witness. He can't be courting death, can he?"

Suddenly, one day, word came that a messenger had arrived from Lin'an with the news that Jiaoluan's younger sister, Jiaofeng, had given birth. The glad tidings plunged Jiaoluan into melancholy over her own status, as compared with her sister's. But she was glad that, at least, someone could deliver a letter for her again. So she wrote another letter, the third one. There were another ten poems attached to it. The last poem said,

To the gifted one I say, seize the day!
How much more time remains for our wedded life?
Daughter of a Wang, son of a Zhou,
One of military background, one civilian.
To the blue bird I entrust all three letters

As I languish in grief in the depths of my room,
My feelings deeper than the letters can convey,
My thoughts painfully torn between the two places.

On the envelope, she wrote four lines:

To Wujiang please deliver this letter,
To Wu of South Hemp, Grain Overseer.
Take your time as you ask your way;
Pause for a rest when you reach Yanling Bridge.

Henceforth, Jiaoluan neglected her meals and spent her nights sleepless. She grew emaciated, and as her tears furtively flowed, her gloominess made her ill. Her parents offered to select a husband for her, but she turned a deaf ear, saying that she would rather devote the rest of her life to Buddhism and adopt a vegetarian diet.

Auntie Cao tried to talk her out of the idea. "Mr. Zhou is not likely to come back," she said. "While you're young, don't jeopardize your prospects by holding yourself to a minor promise."

Jiaoluan countered, "A person who breaks promises is nothing short of a beast. I'd rather have him betray me than betray the gods myself."

Time sped by. Quite unnoticeably, three years passed. Jiaoluan said to Auntie Cao, "I heard that he has married again, but I don't know if it's true. Three years' absence means that he must have had a change of heart. And yet, I won't give up hope without some kind of confirmation."

"Why not give Sun Jiu a generous sum of travel money and ask him to go to Wujiang? If Young Master Zhou's status hasn't changed, wouldn't it be nice if Sun Jiu could stay there for a while and then come back with him?"

"That's exactly what I've been thinking. Could you also write a few lines, Auntie, to urge Sun Jiu to be on the road as soon as possible?"

Right away, Jiaoluan wrote a poem in the ancient style, an excerpt of which appears below:

During a Clear and Bright Festival,
We met by chance and became friends.
We intoned poems to the wind and the moon,
Our trysts arousing youthful passion.
Breaking the gold chains that lock the mansion,
We toured the sights, hand in hand, shoulder to shoulder.
With our hair, we tied the knot of life and death,
Exchanging vows of love and constancy.
When the grass turned green under vast white clouds,
The gifted one left me for his parents.
Suddenly, my rosy cheeks lost their color;

Sadly, I listened for wild geese, the mail bearers.
You may not have left for war on a chariot
Like my father and brother, but it was sadder.
With heartrending sobs, we repeated our vows,
Holding each other by the hand and clothes.
Now that we've become a devoted pair,
Do not fall prey to the beauties of the South.
Since you left, my brows have stayed knitted,
My rouge and powder untouched, my hair like a broom.
With thoughts of my husband heavy on my mind,
With whom do I share the joys of snow, moon, wind, and flowers?
How tragic that in the full bloom of our youth,
We dream in vain of plum blossoms and butterflies.
The wind and moon give me little pleasure;
On the forlorn pillow, my soul writhes in pain.
One night, I dreamed that you married again;
The next day I found myself aged and in decay.
I would that the vows had traveled like thunderbolts
To the goddess of the ninth layer of heaven!
You returned to your hometown, not the netherworld.
Why is it so hard to see your face?
Your feelings are fake; mine are genuine.
Here again is a letter that lays out my heart.
Pity the one whose beauty puts flowers to shame;
In my lonely boudoir, my thoughts weigh me down.

In her letter, Auntie Cao also emphasized how her niece missed her loved one and wished to see him again. The two letters were put into the same envelope, on which was written:

To the mansion of the great one,
Grain Overseer of South Hemp town.
There's no need to stop the boat and ask around,
For it is the first house by Yanling Bridge.

Bearing the letters, Sun Jiu traveled by day and rested by night and made his way to Yanling Bridge in Wujiang. Afraid that he might deliver the letters into the wrong hands, he waited until he could see Zhou Tingzhang face to face. At the sight of Sun Jiu, Tingzhang reddened deeply. Without so much as a word of greeting for the visitor, he took the envelope, slipped it into his sleeve, and went into the house. Before long, a page boy emerged to announce, "My young master has been married for two years to the daughter of Commissioner Wei. Nanyang being so far from here, he's not able to go there again. Instead of writing a reply, which is hardly possible, he asks you to convey an oral message. This silk kerchief, a token of his first meeting with Sister Jiaoluan, and this copy of the marriage contract are for you to take back and return to her so that she will give up all hope. My young master wished to keep you for a meal, but he's afraid his father would question him and hold him to blame. Here are five mace of silver to cover your travel expenses. You need not come again."

Enraged by these words, Sun Jiu threw the silver to the ground. (*Good man!*) As he walked out through the gate, he cursed, "Such a heartless man is worse than a beast! You betrayed the poor girl's love! No blessings for you from heaven!" With that, he departed, crying his heart out as he went along. (*Just like Nan Jiyun crying his way back to Suiyang after a failed attempt at seeking help.*[13]) Old Man Sun poured out the whole story to every pedestrian who asked him why he was weeping. Henceforth, Zhou Tingzhang's notoriety as a heartless man spread throughout the Wujiang region. His name came to be held in contempt by all decent folks. Truly,

Those who do nothing that troubles the conscience
Should have no enemies in the world.

Let us get on with our story. Upon returning to Nanyang, Sun Jiu broke down in sobs at the sight of Mingxia the maid. "Was it a difficult journey for you?" she asked. "Or has Young Master Zhou died?"

Sun Jiu kept shaking his head. A considerable while later, he pulled himself together and told her the whole story, adding, "Instead of writing a reply, he just gave me back the silk kerchief and marriage contract to make our young lady give up all hope. I can't see her." So saying, he wiped away his tears and went off with a sigh.

Mingxia did not dare to hide anything and repeated Sun Jiu's words to her mistress. At the sight of the kerchief, Jiaoluan knew that Sun Jiu was not lying. Her heart filled with rage and her face flushed with anger, she called Auntie Cao to her room and told her what had happened. To Auntie Cao's soothing words, she turned a deaf ear.

She cried for three whole days and nights, examining the kerchief again and again. She thought of suicide but said to herself, "Being a beloved daughter of a distinguished official, endowed with beauty and talent, if I die quietly, won't I be letting that cruel man off too lightly?" Thereupon, she composed thirty-two short poems to serve as a suicide note and a long one titled "Song of Eternal Sorrow." The following is one of the thirty-two poems:

I lean against the door, my mind lost in thought.
Alas! The union didn't last through a smile.
Tender love brought the advent of spring;
Sorrow floats down the river like withered flowers.
I counted on the return of spring,

Only to know now that all is empty!
Back at the railings overwhelmed by emotion,
I languish in grief and hold the east wind to blame.

We shall skip the rest of the poems and quote only from "Song of Eternal Sorrow":

"Song of Eternal Sorrow," for whom is it written?
The very idea leaves me sickened.
Brooding day and night—when will this ever end?
Let me pour out my grief on paper.
My family used to live in Lin'an,
In imperial good graces for services rendered.
For an error in a military campaign,
Father was demoted to Nanyang.
In the depths of my boudoir I was raised,
Never taking a step beyond the middle court.
At eighteen, disaster struck out of the blue:
With my maid I took a walk to the garden.
Hardly had I descended from the swing
Than a stranger's voice rang out from a corner.
Shyly, I returned to my chamber,
Where I searched frantically for my kerchief.
Little knowing you had it in your hands,
I sent the maid to look for it, but in vain.
A poem you wrote on the kerchief
Plunged me into prolonged lovesickness.
Because you claimed kinship with my clan,
We were able to exchange letters of love.
Afraid that our love would appear improper,
We took the vow of marriage and devotion.
Yet unsatisfied with tender vows alone,
We made Auntie Cao a witness.
To heaven we offered the marriage contract,
Placing our future under heaven's dictate.
After two years of a life sweet as honey,
You fell ill with longing for home.
Pained by the sight of your misery,
I urged you to leave for home
But warned you against the pleasure quarters
During your stay in Suzhou,
And to return soon after seeing your parents,
For the forlorn one would be anxiously waiting.

With these words, I saw you off,
Leaving you free to choose the new over the old.
Who would have thought that you were never to return?
I'd rather die than be weighed down by thoughts of you.
More than once I heard reports of your new marriage;
I tried but failed to believe they were true.
Through Sun Jiu's trip to your hometown,
I learned for certain of your new married status.
Filled with bitterness against the heartless one,
I find the marriage bond hard to sever.
Betraying the love of one so close,
What joy can you find in any romance?
Whether my grief is fleeting or endless,
Every trunk and case is filled with my poems.
Five thousand sheets of paper have been covered with words;
Three hundred brush-pens have lost their hair.
The fair one in the boudoir, now gaunt and weak,
Has nothing but memories of happier times.
In vain did I seek advice from fortune-tellers;
To no avail did I consult The Book of Changes.
As my mind reviews all that has happened,
I see that I've never been unworthy of you.
Had I known that love is a floating cloud,
I would not have offered it to you.
The orioles and the swallows fly in pairs;
I'm the only one without company.
Jiaofeng, my sister, younger by two years,
Is now the mother of a three-year-old.
In shame, I end this life, all too lightly,
My lonesome heart filled with pain while you rejoice. (The sorrows of an abandoned one.)
Where, I ask, is the vow of yesteryear?
Three feet above your head dwell the gods of heaven.
With one south of the Yangzi and the other north,
Between us stand more than a thousand li of mountains.
If I found myself with wings this very instant,
I would fly to Wujiang to be with you.
Our erstwhile trysts were known only to sky and earth,
But henceforth the story will be on every lip.
The beauty hidden behind the imposing doors
Was fated to smile and fall into your trap.
I leave this world, embittered by your foul deed;

Heaven should never have brought me into being.
Henceforth, expect no reply
To letters written to the deceased one.
How sad that the general has raised in vain
A daughter lovely as a flower.
Because of my taste for music and books,
I go to an early grave after a brief romance.
The ten-foot-long white kerchief hangs from the beam,
My soul takes flight before my very eyes.
As reports of Jiaoluan's death spread,
The Wangs in Lin'an will be the joke of the town.
To my shame, I am no well-bred lady,
For I easily surrendered my chastity.
To the Nine Springs I go, all my debts to you paid;
Once there, I will not let you off lightly.
At one time, you smothered me with love;
My rancor now is as deep as the sea.
Full of the best intentions on my part,
I knew not that your heart is like that of a beast!
Here is that silk kerchief of mine,
Which I'm dutifully sending along to you,
An article that, alas, brought me love and death;
The killing forgivable, the betrayal not.
All I have to say I've laid down here;
Today marks the end of all my sorrows.
For the sake of our one-time romance,
Kindly read these words from Wang Jiaoluan.

After finishing the letter, she called for Sun Jiu and again asked him to deliver it, but Sun Jiu flatly refused, his jaw set, his eyes blazing with anger. While Jiaoluan was worrying over the lack of a messenger, her father fell ill from excessive phlegm and internal heat and told her to take care of his official correspondence. When she came upon an order to hunt down a deserter who was under her father's command but a native of Wujiang County, she had an idea. She took out the poems Tingzhang had written in reply to hers and put them into a cloth slipcase along with the suicidal poems, "Song of Eternal Sorrow," and the two copies of the marriage contract. She then added the slipcase to the package of official documents and wrote on the cover "From Commander Wang of Nanyang Commandery, to be opened by the magistrate of Wujiang County, Suzhou Prefecture." (*This is not only to make Tingzhang's actions known to the public but also to do justice to her literary talent.*) The official courier was then sent on his way, and Commander Wang was none the wiser.

That very night, Jiaoluan took a bath, changed her clothes, and, after telling

Mingxia to go and brew some tea, closed her door. Standing on a stool, she threw a piece of white silk over the beam, took out the silk kerchief that Tingzhang had returned to her, tied one end of it around her throat, and knotted the other end fast to the white silk. With a kick at the stool, her feet dangled in air. All too quickly, her three souls and seven spirits took flight from her body. She was twenty-one years old.

The kerchief, a witness from beginning to end,
An object that brought her both joy and death!

When Mingxia returned with the tea and found that the door remained tightly closed despite all her knocking and pounding, she rushed off in alarm to report to Auntie Cao. Mrs. Wang and Auntie Cao maneuvered the door open, and the sight that met their eyes gave them the shock of their lives. Commander Wang also arrived at the chamber. The whole family burst into wails of grief, not knowing what could have led to this tragedy. A coffin was duly bought and a funeral held, but of this, no more.

Now, Magistrate Que of Wujiang received the package from Nanyang Commandery, opened it, and was fascinated by what he read, for this was something unheard-of from time immemorial. It so happened that Judge Zhao of the prefectural yamen had just arrived in the county, accompanied by Mr. Fan, of the inspectorate. Magistrate Que and Judge Zhao won high honors in the imperial examinations in the same year and therefore knew each other. When Magistrate Que told Judge Zhao about this, the judge read the papers, and he in his turn informed Mr. Fan of this most remarkable story. Mr. Fan perused the poems and the marriage contract. He was greatly impressed by Jiaoluan's literary talent and detested Zhou Tingzhang for his heartlessness. He ordered that Judge Zhao quietly seek this man out.

The very next day, Tingzhang was brought to court, and Mr. Fan personally conducted the interrogation. Tingzhang started out by denying all the accusations, but later, when the marriage contract was produced as evidence, he dared not say another word. By Mr. Fan's order, he was given fifty heavy strokes and thrown into jail. A written order was then sent to Nanyang Commandery to ascertain if Jiaoluan had indeed, hanged herself. In a few days, a reply came, saying that Jiaoluan was dead, whereupon Mr. Fan had Zhou Tingzhang taken from prison to the hall of the inspectorate.

"The first indictment against you is for the crime of taking liberties with an official's daughter." So began Mr. Fan's severe lecture. "The second indictment: abandoning your wife and marrying another woman. The third indictment: causing a death through fornication. Your marriage contract contains the phrase 'Should the husband betray the wife, he shall die under myriad arrows.' Lacking arrows to shoot at you, I'm going to have you beaten to death with bamboo rods, as a warning to all heartless men."

With that, he ordered the officers in attendance to apply their bamboo rods to the young man. Accompanied by rhythmic shouts counting out the strokes, the rods went up and down, splashing drops of blood and bits of flesh. The young man died in a trice, causing jubilation throughout the whole town.

When word reached Commissioner Zhou, he was so mortified that he dropped dead on the spot. Miss Wei, Tingzhang's wife, later remarried. The greed for her money and the lust for her beauty had led to the betrayal of a previous marriage vow, but what good did it do? There is a poem that laments:

Husband and wife one night, lovers a hundred nights;
What is in store for the unfaithful?
If you say the heartless go unpunished,
Kindly read "Song of Eternal Sorrow"!

35

Prefect Kuang Solves the Case of the Dead Baby

Spring flowers and the autumn moon inspire romance;
All too soon, the rosy-cheeked find their hair turning white.
Compared to the pines and cypresses,
How many human hearts can withstand wintry cold?

These four lines talk in general about how spring flowers and the autumn moon torment the human heart, inspiring poems by young scholars lamenting autumn and by beautiful maidens bemoaning spring. More often than not, their poems are veiled expressions of lovesickness, and their eyes speak of passion. Lovers trysting under the moon among the flowers seek instant fulfillment of their desires, with no regard for lifelong reputations. But of these cases of mutual attraction, with each repaying the other a debt from a previous life, we shall speak no further.

There are also cases in which the man is willing but the woman remains unmoved, or the woman is so inclined but the man is impervious. Even though feelings are not reciprocated, the devotion of the one party remains steadfast. Consider how even a clay statue of a god in a deserted temple becomes responsive to incense and prayers offered morning and evening, day after day. Those who are predestined to have but a short-lived bond will unite but eventually separate. Those predestined for a long-lasting one will warm toward each other with the passage of time. Of these situations, which also occur in the world of love, we shall speak no more either.

Now, there is yet another kind of situation in which both the man and the woman are free of amorous thoughts, their determination as firm as the purest gold, their hearts as unflinching as the hardest rock. And yet, without the slightest justification, someone conspires and sets a trap for them. In a moment of weakness, they lose their moral integrity and fall victim to the wicked schemes, to their belated regret.

Abbot Yutong of the Song dynasty, who had practiced Buddhism for fifty years, was such a victim. He incurred the anger of a Prefect Liu Xuanjiao, who sent a prostitute named Red Lotus to seduce him. Disguised as a widow, she asked to be put up for the night in the temple and, tempting him in every possible way, nullified all the credit he had gained through the mortification of his flesh.[1] Such sexual encounters are the result of a momentary weakness of will. Let me now tell of a story about a widow who is seduced into losing her chastity, to make a pair with the story about Abbot Yutong. Truly,

Those not cleansed of desires, seek not the Dao;
Those immersed in passion, practice not the Chan [Zen].

Our story takes place during the Xuande reign period [1426–36], in Yizhen County, Yangzhou Prefecture, in the district under the direct jurisdiction of Nanjing. There lived in that county a man named Qiu Yuanji, a commoner, but quite well-off. His wife, Shao-shi, was a woman of outstanding beauty and moral rectitude. They were a loving couple, yet without issue in their sixth year of married life. All too unexpectedly, Yuanji fell ill and died. The twenty-three-year-old Shao-shi, in her extreme grief, was determined to maintain widowhood for the rest of her life.

Soon, the three years of mourning came to an end. Considering her youth and the many years of life ahead of her, her parents advised her to remarry. Her husband's uncle, Qiu Dasheng, also sent his wife over a few times to try tactfully to change Shao-shi's mind, but, her heart as firm as iron and rock, she turned a deaf ear and said, "To my late husband under the Nine Springs, I vow that if I ever serve another family and marry another man, I shall die by either the knife or the rope."

Who would ever venture another word to such a determined woman? The ancients said, "Only those who can swallow three gallons of vinegar can endure the hardships of widowhood." Widowhood is by no means easy to maintain. In fact, Shao-shi would have fared better in the long term by marrying another man, for even if she lost her status as a woman of the very best caliber by doing so, she would still have been in the middle range instead of ending up in disgrace, as she did later. Truly,

Stand on firm ground in everything you do;
Seek not empty fame for vanity's sake.

Shao-shi's bold words evoked different reactions. Depending on their intellect and moral character, people either praised her profusely or were doubtful and kept their watchful eyes open. But Shao-shi was indeed firm in her determination to remain chaste. She retired further into the inner quarters of the house, with only one maid, called Xiugu, to keep her company and assist her with her livelihood of sewing, and one ten-year-old page boy, called Degui, to guard the middle door leading to her rooms and take care of firewood, water, and other necessary purchases. All male servants twenty years of age or older were dismissed. With no casual visitors in the yard, a quiet solemnity prevailed throughout the household. After several years had passed in this way, everyone was impressed. None failed to admire Madam Shao for being mature beyond her years and maintaining discipline in the household.

Time flew like an arrow. All too soon, the tenth anniversary of her husband's death came around. Wishing to hold a prayer service in his memory, Shao-shi had

Degui invite her husband's uncle, Qiu Dasheng, to come over for a consultation. It was thus decided that the prayer service would be held by monks from all the seven classes and last for three days and nights.[2] "Being a widow," said Shao-shi, "I'll have to rely on you, Uncle, to officiate at the service." Desheng agreed.

Let us pick up another thread of our story and tell of a man called Zhi Zhu, who had recently moved into the neighborhood. He was a ruffian, certainly not the kind of person who minds his own business. Instead of trying to make an honest living, he spent his time idling on the streets of the neighborhood, poking his nose into other people's affairs. Not believing what he had heard about the young widow Madam Shao's unparalleled beauty and chastity, he loitered at the gate of her house at all times of the day and observed that indeed no one went in or came out of the house except the page boy Degui on his errands. So Zhi Zhu made his acquaintance and gradually became friendly with him. In the midst of a conversation, he asked Degui, "I heard that the mistress of the house is quite a beauty. Is that true?"

Having grown up in a household run according to the strictest rules of propriety, Degui knew nothing about the ways of the world and replied in his artless way, "Yes, that is true."

"Does she ever come out to the gate to watch the street?"

Waving a hand in denial, Degui said, "No, she never even goes beyond the middle door, let alone out to watch the streets! What a thing to say!"

One day, Degui was buying vegetarian food when Zhi Zhu ran into him. "Why do you need so many vegetarian supplies?" he asked.

"The mistress needs them for a tenth anniversary prayer service in memory of the master."

"When is it going to be?"

"It starts tomorrow and will last for three days and nights. It's a lot of work."

Making a mental note of the information, Zhi Zhu thought, "Since it's a prayer service in memory of her husband, she'll surely come out to burn incense. I'll steal a look and judge for myself if she's pretty and if she really has the appearance of a chaste widow."

The next day, the monks engaged by Qiu Dasheng—monks well-trained in the practice of mortifying their flesh—set up a statue of the Buddha in the main hall and piously struck the cymbals, beat the drums, and recited the sutra as penitence for human sins. Qiu Dasheng made frequent obeisances to the Buddha. Shao-shi also came out to the hall to burn joss sticks, but she did this only once during the day and once in the evening and went back inside as soon as she had finished.

Taking advantage of the bustle in the hall, Zhi Zhu slipped in several times to catch a glimpse of her, but he failed each time. Again through Degui, he found out that she came out to offer incense during the day only at lunchtime. So on the third day, at about that time, Zhi Zhu again slipped into the house and hid behind the partition door. He saw the monks in their cassocks playing musical instruments and intoning the name of the Buddha in front of the Buddha's statue while the acolytes busily replenished the joss sticks and candles. Being the only member of the household present, Degui ran back and forth answering calls for assistance. He certainly had no time to take care of what was happening outside the hall. Even Qiu Dasheng and some relatives were fully occupied, their eyes glued to the monks with the cymbals and drums. Who would bother to check for intruders?

In a short while, Shao-shi came out to offer incense. Zhi Zhu looked his fill. It is often said, "A woman in mourning white / Is a pleasure for the eyes." In her mourning white, Shao-shi appeared twice as fresh and refined as usual. Truly, she was none other than

The goddess Chang'e from the moon,
The fairy of Guye, as pure as snow.[3]

Zhi Zhu melted with desire at the sight of such beauty. After he returned home, his mind was still filled with thoughts of her.

With the conclusion of the prayer service that night and the departure of the monks at dawn, Shao-shi no longer ventured beyond the middle door. At his wits' end, Zhi Zhu thought to himself, "Let me work on that simpleton Degui first."

On the fifth day of the fifth month, the Dragon Boat Festival, Zhi Zhu tried to drag Degui to his home, promising the page boy a cup of *xionghuang* wine.[4] Degui said, "I don't drink. If I get red in the face, I'm afraid the mistress is going to give me a hard time!" (*Had it not been for Zhi Zhu's wickedness, Shao-shi would have kept her good name and Degui would have been a blameless servant. The workings of an evil man—how fearsome!*)

Zhi Zhu said, "All right, if you don't drink, at least have some sweet-rice dumplings!"

So Degui followed Zhi Zhu home. Zhi Zhu had his wife unwrap a plateful of pyramid-shaped sweet-rice dumplings, a saucer of sugar, a bowl of pork, and a bowl of fresh fish. With two pairs of chopsticks and two wine cups laid out on the table, Zhi Zhu picked up the wine flask and began to fill the cups.

Degui objected, saying, "I already told you I don't drink. Don't pour any for me!"

"Just one cup to celebrate the festival. This wine is so weak. It won't affect you at all."

Thus pressed, Degui obliged him. Zhi Zhu urged again, "Now, a nice young man like you shouldn't have only one cup. Make it two!"

Unable to fend him off, Degui downed another cup. Zhi Zhu also helped himself and, while gossiping about the goings-on in the neighborhood, filled another cup for Degui.

"I'm getting all red in the face! I'm drunk! I really must not take another drop."

"Since your face is flushed anyway, staying a little longer won't do you any more harm. Another cup, and I'll stop pressing you."

Three cups of wine in all did Degui drink. As he had been brought up in the Qiu household under Madam Shao's strict rules, he had never tasted wine, and these three cups turned his brain topsy-turvy. Taking advantage of his drunken excitability, Zhi Zhu said under his breath, "Brother Degui, I have something to ask you."

"Fire away!"

"Your mistress has been a widow for so long that she must be itching for a love affair. Surely she'd like it if she could get a man to sleep with her? All widows are hungry for men. It's just not easy for them to meet one. Now, how about taking me into the house and letting me give her a little test? If it works out, I'll have a nice reward for you."

"What kind of talk is this? Aren't you ashamed of yourself? My mistress is spotlessly chaste and guards her door most closely. During the day, no man is allowed past the middle door. Every evening, she and the maid check every corner with a lamp, and she doesn't go to bed until every door is locked. Even if I take you into the house, where are you going to hide? Her maid never leaves her side. She doesn't even allow a word of idle gossip. You and your fancy ideas!"

"So, does she check your room?"

"Of course she does."

"Brother Degui, how old are you?"

"Seventeen."

"Men are sexually mature by sixteen. Since you're seventeen now, aren't you interested in women?"

"What if I am? There's nothing I can do about it."

"With such a beauty around you at all times, don't tell me you don't feel a thing!"

"The way you talk! She's the mistress and beats me or yells at me every so often. She terrifies me. And you have to tease me like that!"

"If you refuse to take me there, let me teach you something so that you can get her for yourself."

Waving a hand in refusal, Degui said, "I can't do that. I just can't. I'm not bold enough anyway."

"Never mind whether my little trick works or not. Just use it to test her. If you succeed, don't ever forget that I did you a favor."

Partly because he was exhilarated by the wine and partly because he had reached that age, Zhi Zhu's words made Degui yearn for an adventure. (*That's why Confucius stayed away from women.*) He said, "So tell me, how shall I test her?"

"Remember not to close your door when you go to sleep. Leave it open. The weather being hot in this the fifth month of the year, just lie on your back, naked, with that thing of yours standing up nice and hard. When she comes to check your door, pretend to be fast asleep. She'll surely be aroused when she sees you that way. After a couple of times, her desires will get the better of her and make her come to you. (*What a horrible man!*)

"What if she doesn't?"

"Even if this plan doesn't work, she can't blame you. So you've got nothing to lose and everything to gain."

"All right, I'll do as you say. If it works, I'll surely repay you." Before long, the effects of the wine wore off. Degui left to put the plan into action that very night. Truly,

An evil plot was hatched by the lamplight
To tempt the woman in her resolve.

Considering the strictness of Shao-shi's household rules, she should have replaced Degui with a much younger boy now that he was seventeen and old enough to arouse suspicions. That would have been the best solution. But Degui had been running errands for her ever since he was a child, and, moreover, he was simple-minded and honest. Shao-shi herself had maintained no other than the purest thoughts, and so, she put things off.

That night, Shao-shi and her maid Xiugu were checking the various doors with a lamp when they came upon Degui lying on his back, completely naked. "That brute!" Shao-shi lashed out. "He leaves the door open while sleeping naked. How disgraceful!" So saying, she instructed Xiugu to close the door for him.

If Shao-shi had known better, she would have summoned Degui the next day and given him a lecture or even a thrashing for his indecorous behavior of the night before. Degui would not have dared to do the same thing again. However, as it was, she said nothing, for after living a celibate life for so long, the all-too-rare sighting of that object had been enough to add a dozen years to her life.

Degui felt emboldened. The next evening, he did the same thing. Shao-shi and the maid checked his door as before, and upon seeing him in that condition, Shao-shi again burst out, "That dog! He doesn't even cover himself with a quilt like a decent human being!" She had Xiugu the maid draw his quilt up gently without waking him. This was the moment when she first felt her desires stirring, but Xiugu's presence was an obstacle.

On the third day, Degui was out on an errand when he ran into Zhi Zhu, who asked if he had been following the plan. Being as simpleminded as he was, Degui related what had happened the previous two nights.

"If she had the maid pull up your quilt without waking you up, she must already have taken a fancy to you. Something will surely happen tonight, and you'll like it."

That night, Degui again left his door open and waited in his bed, feigning sleep. With her heart set on him, Shao-shi did her rounds alone that night, without Xiugu. She walked all the way up to Degui's bed, holding her lamp, and saw him lying on his back naked, with that member of his as erect as a spear. Aflame with desire, she took off her underwear and climbed onto the bed. Quietly, lest she wake him, she mounted him and sat astride. All of a sudden, Degui grasped her tightly and rolled over for a game of clouds and rain:

She has long abstained from the pleasure;
He is experiencing the joy for the first time.
She will not lightly let go of an old friend;
He longs for more after his first taste of sweetness.
She, in her hunger, overlooks his uncouthness;
He, thus emboldened, fears the mistress no more.
Indeed, a lowly weed, a common vine,
Is climbing the trellis of a prized flower.
How sad that the unblemished ice and snow
Have melted in the spring and are flowing eastward.
Her good name of ten years' standing has vanished;
Once besmirched, it can never be made clean again.

After it was over, Shao-shi said to Degui, "In one night, I lost to you the chastity that I had worked hard to preserve for ten years. I must have owed you a debt in a previous life. Now, keep your mouth shut and don't let on about this to anyone. I'll take good care of you."

"Why would I ever dream of disobeying you, madam?"

Henceforth, under the pretext of checking the doors, Shao-shi never missed a night of joy with Degui before retiring to her room. Afraid that Xiugu might become aware of what was afoot, she contrived an opportunity for Degui to have his way with Xiugu as well. Deliberately, Shao-shi scolded Xiugu but then asked the maid to introduce Degui to her. By doing so, she sealed Xiugu's lips, blocking a potential source of gossip. Like water flowing in the same river, they shared their secrets, hiding nothing from each other.

Grateful to Zhi Zhu for his advice, Degui often asked Shao-shi for things and offered them to Zhi Zhu, although he dared not comply with Zhi's request to be introduced to the mistress for fear of incurring her anger. Again and again, Zhi Zhu pressed for an answer, but Degui put him off each time.

Shao-shi and Degui lived like husband and wife for a few months, but their affair was destined to be exposed. In her six years of married life, Shao-shi had not borne a child, but she found herself pregnant after the few months of the affair. Afraid that her swollen breasts and protruding belly would attract attention, she gave Degui money and told him to secretly buy some medicine for abortion so that she could be rid of the illegitimate fetus and forestall a scandal. Degui, in his ignorance of the ways of the world, had no idea what kind of medicine would serve this purpose. Also, since he appreciated Zhi Zhu's advice, he honored Zhi as his benefactor and held nothing back from him. For these reasons, he consulted the man about this most confidential matter.

Zhi Zhu, depraved rogue that he was, was seething with resentment of Degui because the page boy refused to take him to Shao-shi. When Degui sought his advice, he saw his chance and said, lying through his teeth, "I know an herbalist who has the best medicine for this. Let me get some for you."

From a medicinal store, he bought four packages of herbs used for settling the fetus and gave them to Degui.

Shao-shi took all the medicine, one package after another, but nothing happened. She told Degui to go to another store for better medicine. Again, Degui turned to Zhi Zhu for help. "Why isn't the medicine working?" he asked.

"An abortion attempt is a one-time thing. If you fail once, you're not supposed to try again. What's more, the medicine from that store, and that store alone, is the best of its kind. It failed to work only because the fetus has already settled firmly. If she tries more aggressive medicine, I'm afraid her life will be in danger."

Degui repeated these words to Shao-shi, who took them to be true.

When the pregnancy was almost full term, Zhi Zhu, knowing that Shao-shi would be giving birth soon, sought out Degui and said to him, "I'm mixing up some tonic for myself and need a newborn baby. Now, your mistress will be giving birth soon. Since she won't be keeping the child anyway, why don't you give me the baby, be it a boy or a girl? Since you owe me a lot, that will be a nice way to pay me back, and it doesn't cost you a penny! You need only keep it a secret from your mistress."

Degui agreed.

Sure enough, a few days later, a baby boy was born. Shao-shi drowned the baby, wrapped it in a rush bag, and told Degui to bury it in some secret place. Degui agreed to do so, but instead of burying it, he gave it secretly to Zhi Zhu. After putting the dead baby away, Zhi Zhu seized Degui and shouted at the top of his voice, "Since your mistress is the widow of Qiu Yuanji, who died years ago, how did she manage to have this baby? I'll have to report this to the authorities."

Degui hastened to cover Zhi Zhu's mouth and said, "I looked up to you as a benefactor and asked for your advice about everything. How can you suddenly turn against me like this?"

Zhi Zhu's face hardened. "A fine thing you did! You raped your employer, a crime punishable by the death of a thousand cuts! You think it's enough just to call me a benefactor? You know that kindness should be repaid with kindness, but what have you ever done for me? If you want me to be quiet, get me a hundred taels of silver from your mistress, and I'll cover up the evil thing she has done and spread nice words about her. Otherwise, I won't stop, and I have the dead baby to show as evidence. You can very well try to defend yourself in court, but even the mistress won't be able to live down the shame. I'll be waiting here for an answer. Begone now, and come back quickly!"

Degui was so upset that he burst into tears. After he returned home, knowing that he would not be able to hide anything from Shao-shi, he felt he had no choice but to tell her what Zhi Zhu had said.

Shao-shi said reproachfully, "Of all things, how could you have given *that* away as a gift? Now you've ruined me!" And her tears began to flow.

Degui retorted, "I wouldn't have given it to just anyone, but he was my benefactor. I couldn't turn him down."

"What kind of benefactor?"

"It was he who taught me to lie naked on my back to lead you on. If it hadn't been for him, we wouldn't have come to love each other. When he said he needed a newborn baby for some medicine of his, how could I not offer it to him? How was I to know that he didn't mean well?"

"What a stupid thing you did! It was in a moment of weakness that I fell into that swine's trap. Regrets are too late now. If I don't redeem the baby with silver, he'll surely report to the authorities, and it will be too late to do anything then."

She had no alternative but to take out forty taels of silver and have Degui try to redeem the baby's body from that brute and bury it secretly, so as to forestall all possible trouble. Being as simpleminded as he was, Degui handed the forty taels of silver to Zhi Zhu with both hands, saying, "This is all the silver. Now, give me back the baby."

Zhi Zhu's greed was not satisfied by the silver, and he said to himself, "This woman has looks and a deep pocket as well. If I could take this opportunity and put both the woman and her money under my control, wouldn't that be nice?"

To Degui, he said aloud, "I was joking when I demanded silver. You took me too seriously. But since you brought it, I feel obliged to take it. I've already buried the baby. Why don't you propose to the mistress that I live with her? If she agrees, I'll run the house for her, and no one will dare to bully her. Wouldn't that be good for everyone? Otherwise, I'll dig up the baby and report you to the authorities. You have five days to reply."

Degui had no choice but to return home and relay the message to Shao-shi. "That brute can fart to his heart's content for all I care!" she burst out. Degui dared not bring up the matter again.

In the meantime, Zhi Zhu preserved the baby with lime, put it back into the rush bag, and hid it in a secret place. Five days went by without a word from Degui. He waited for another five days, making it ten days in all. Believing that the woman should have recuperated by now, he went to the Qiu house and waited at the gate until Degui came out. "So, did she say yes?" asked he.

"No, no!" Degui shook his head.

Without bothering to ask further, Zhi Zhu thrust his way in. Degui dared not stop him but instead went to the street corner some distance off to keep watch on the house.

Noticing someone entering the inner quarters of the house, Shao-shi lashed out, "A house has a front part and an inner part, and there are rules to be followed. Who are you to barge in like this?"

"My name is Zhi Zhu, Brother Degui's benefactor."

Realizing the man's identity, Shao-shi said, "If you're looking for Degui, keep to the front part of the house. This is no place for you."

"I've long admired you, madam, like a hungry and thirsty man. However unworthy I am, I don't think I'm beneath Brother Degui in any way. Why do you reject me outright?"

Irritated by the ugly turn the conversation was taking, Shao-shi turned to go, but Zhi Zhu caught up with her and, holding her in both arms, said, "Your illegitimate child is at my place. If you don't do as I say, I'll report you to the authorities."

Shao-shi was outraged beyond measure. Looking for a way to extricate herself, she came up with an excuse, saying, "I'm afraid that people will notice things in the daytime. When night comes, I'll have Degui bring you here."

"A promise is a promise," said Zhi Zhu. "Don't you ever break it!" So saying, he let go of her. Before he had gone many paces, he looked back over his shoulder and added, "And I'm not afraid even if you do!" With that, he left.

Shao-shi was so mortified that she couldn't utter a word for a considerable time. With tears streaming down her cheeks, she pushed open the door to her bedchamber and sat down on a stool. Many and varied were the thoughts that passed through her mind, but she found only herself to blame. It was in order to gain a good reputation that she had refused to remarry, and now, having caused such a scandal, how could she ever bring herself to face the world? Then she thought, "I vowed publicly that if I ever served another family and married another man, I should die by either the sword or the rope. Now, if I give up this life to apologize to my deceased husband under the Nine Springs, won't that be a neat end to all the troubles?"

Seeing her mistress in tears, Xiugu dared not step forward to calm her. Instead, she waited by the middle door for Degui to come home.

Only when he saw from the street that Zhi Zhu was safely out of sight, did Degui return. Seeing Xiugu, he asked, "Where's the mistress?"

Xiugu replied, pointing a finger, "She's inside," whereupon Degui pushed open the door to look for his mistress.

Now, let us go back a little in time to the moment when Shao-shi picked up a small knife from the head of the bed with which to cut her own throat. But when her hand failed her, she burst into tears and laid the knife on the table. From her waist, she took a sash about eight feet in length, threw it over the beam, tied it into a noose, and was about to slip her neck through it when she was overcome with grief and broke down in uncontrollable sobbing.

Suddenly, the sight of Degui coming through the door triggered this thought in her mind, "Here's the swine who laid a trap for me in the first place and ruined my good name forever!" What followed happened in less time than it takes to tell. The very moment that thought occurred to her, she picked up the knife, her eyes blazing with anger at the sight of her foe, and swung at Degui with the speed of the wind. Her blinding anger added force to the blow, and she split Degui's head in two. He died instantly, his blood flowing across the floor. In a panic, she slipped her neck into the noose and kicked away the stool. Her body swung to and fro at the end of the sash.

Two more aggrieved souls in the netherworld,
One fewer pretty widow among the living.

The proverb says, "Gambling leads to robbery; lust to murder." In this case, lust claimed two lives.

But, to get on with our story. As a rule, Xiugu would make herself scarce whenever Degui entered the room, afraid that she would be in the way. But this time, the prolonged silence made her apprehensive, and she went up for a look. At the sight of one body hanging in the air and the other lying on the floor, she collapsed in fright. After she had pulled herself together, she shut the door and ran to the home of Qiu Dasheng, Shao-shi's uncle-in-law. Alarmed, Qiu Dasheng relayed the news to Shao-shi's parents. Together, they went to the Qiu house, closed the gate, and asked Xiugu what she knew about the deaths. The fact of the matter was that Xiugu did not know Zhi Zhu, nor had she any inkling of Shao-shi being blackmailed for forty taels of silver over the dead baby. So she told them only about the affair between Shao-shi and Degui, adding, "I have no idea why they are both dead." Regardless of the many times she was asked, she repeated the same things.

With shame written all over their faces upon hearing about the scandal, Shao-shi's parents returned home, wishing to have no part in handling the matter. Qiu Dasheng had no alternative but to take Xiugu to the county yamen to report the case.

After a coroner's examination determined that Degui had died from a knife blow and Shao-shi from hanging, the county magistrate put Xiugu through a questioning session and concluded, "Shao-shi's illicit liaison with Degui has been established beyond a doubt. Because the relationship of mistress to servant had been invalidated, Degui must have given Shao-shi verbal offense, and she killed him accidentally in a moment of anger. Then she panicked and hanged herself. And that is the whole truth." By the magistrate's orders, Qiu Dasheng took care of the funeral. Xiugu, who had known about the affair, was given a thrashing and sold by the yamen.

Let us retrace our steps and come back to the day when Zhi Zhu returned home after his failed attempt at seducing Shao-shi. He was still planning to go back at night, as promised, when news came about the deaths. He was so shocked that he dared not venture out his door for quite a long time.

But one day, upon rising early in the morning, he happened to come upon the rush bag containing the dead baby preserved in lime. He picked the bag up, went out, and dropped it into the river. Right after doing that, he ran into an acquaintance called Bao Jiu, a foreman at Yizhen Floodgate.

Bao Jiu accosted Zhi Zhu. "Brother Zhi," he said, "what did you just throw away?"

"A few pieces of salted beef. I wrapped them up for a trip, but they've gone bad. Brother Jiu, if you're not busy these days, come to my home for a few drinks."

"I'm busy today. Prefect Kuang Zhong of Suzhou is traveling back to his post, and his boat will be arriving any time now.[5] So I have to gather together some people to serve him."

"In that case, I'll see you some other day." With that, Zhi Zhu went on his way.

Now, Kuang Zhong was known to the people under his jurisdiction as "Blue Sky Kuang" for the fairness and judiciousness he had shown in the one year he had been the prefect of Suzhou. He had risen to the post from a clerical position through the recommendation of Hu Ying, Minister of Rites. At the moment of which we speak, he was returning to his post from his hometown, where he had been observing a period of filial mourning. The mourning period was not yet over, but he had received orders by imperial decree to return to his post with all speed at government expense.

He was reading a book in the cabin as his boat approached Yizhen Floodgate. Suddenly, he heard a baby crying in the river. Assuming that it must be a baby on the verge of drowning, he sent someone to take a look, only to be told that there was nothing to be seen. This happened twice. Prefect Kuang heard the cries, but when he asked his men, they all said that they could hear nothing. "Most extraordinary!" exclaimed Prefect Kuang. He pushed open the cabin window to look with his own eyes and saw a small rush bag floating on the water. He had a boatman retrieve it and open it.

"It's a baby," said the boatman.

"Is it alive or dead?"

"It's covered in lime and looks as if it's been dead for quite some time."

The prefect thought, "How could a dead baby cry? A dead baby might well have been discarded. Why preserve it in lime? There must be something behind all this."

Thereupon, he had the boatman place the baby and the rush bag at the bow of the boat, saying, "Report to me confidentially if anyone has any information. I'm offering handsome rewards." The boatman did as he'd been instructed.

Recognizing the rush bag to be the one Zhi Zhu had tossed into the river, Bao Jiu the foreman wondered to himself, "Didn't he say it was a bag of beef that had gone bad? But why does it have a baby in it?" Consequently, he stepped into the cabin and said to Prefect Kuang, "I have no information about the baby, but I know the man who threw the baby into the river. His name is Zhi Zhu."

"If we get the man, we'll know the story," said Prefect Kuang. So he sent men to bring Zhi Zhu quietly to him, and at the same time, he invited the magistrate of Yizhen County to conduct a joint investigation. This done, he went to the office of the Investigation Bureau to preside over the court, carrying the dead baby with him.

By the time the county magistrate arrived, Zhi Zhu had already been brought in under guard. Prefect Kuang took the seat of honor, with the magistrate sitting to his left. Since Yizhen County was not within his jurisdiction, the prefect thought it prudent not to act arbitrarily but let the county magistrate handle it. However, knowing that Prefect Kuang bore a mandate from the emperor himself and was an eccentric person at that, the county magistrate did not dare assume the dominant role. After much demurring on both sides, Prefect Kuang felt obliged to start the interrogation. "Zhi Zhu," he called out, "how did you come by the baby preserved in lime?"

Zhi Zhu was about to deny any knowledge of the case when he noticed Bao Jiu standing by, ready to bear witness. He changed his tune and said, "I happened to see that dirty bag by the road and thought it quite an eyesore, so I tossed it into the river. I know nothing about how it got there."

Turning to Bao Jiu, Prefect Kuang asked, "Did you see him pick it up by the roadside?"

"I didn't see him until he was in the act of throwing the bag into the water. I asked him what it was, and he said it was some beef that had gone bad."

Prefect Kuang flared up. "If he chose to lie, he must have something to hide." Sharply, he ordered his men to select heavy bamboo rods and give the man twenty strokes before continuing with the interrogation. Prefect Kuang's rods were no ordinary sort, and twenty strokes with his rods did more damage than forty strokes with other rods. Zhi Zhu's skin ripped open and his blood spurted out, but he still refused to confess. Prefect Kuang then ordered that the ankle squeezers be applied. Prefect Kuang's ankle squeezers being no ordinary sort either, Zhi Zhu withstood the pain the first time but collapsed the second time. He confessed. "The dead baby belonged to Shao-shi the widow. It was the illegitimate child of the widow and her servant, Degui. Degui asked me to bury it for him, which I did, but a dog dragged it out. And so I threw it into the river."

Upon hearing this very different version of the story, Prefect Kuang pressed further, "If you were willing to do this for him, you must have been in collusion with the family."

"No. I was just friends with Degui."

"If he wanted to bury it, he must have wanted it to decompose. Why did he preserve it with lime?"

Unable to come up with an answer, Zhi Zhu kowtowed and said, "Your Honor, in fact, it was I who preserved the baby in lime. Knowing Shao-shi to be quite well-off, I wanted to keep the baby's body to demand a few taels of silver from her. But since Shao-shi and Degui both died and there was no money to be had, I threw it into the river."

"So, did the woman and the servant indeed die?" asked the prefect.

The county magistrate rose from his seat and replied with a slight bow, "Yes, they did. I personally conducted the examination."

"How did they die?"

The magistrate explained, "The servant's head had been split open by a knife. The woman hanged herself. I have also learned the details of the case: The two had carried on an illicit affair for a long time, and the class distinction between mistress and servant had long been ignored. The servant must have said something offensive that angered the woman and prompted her to attack him with a knife. After she inadvertently killed him, she panicked and hanged herself. These are all the facts of the case."

Prefect Kuang grew apprehensive and thought to himself, "The two being as close as they were, a mere verbal offense would not have provoked her to kill him. The dead baby's crying must mean there's more to be learned." He asked, "Were there other members of Shao-shi's household?"

"There was a maidservant called Xiugu," replied the magistrate. "She's been sold by the yamen."

"In that case, she must still be in this area," concluded the prefect. "Could the county magistrate please have her brought here? We'll be able to learn the truth from her."

The county magistrate promptly dispatched officers to bring Xiugu to court. Before long, Xiugu was brought in. Her deposition showed no discrepancy with the magistrate's statement of the case.

After thinking for a while, Prefect Kuang left his seat and, pointing to Zhi Zhu, asked Xiugu, "Do you recognize this man?"

Xiugu took a close look and replied, "I don't know his name, but I do recognize his face."

"That makes sense," said the prefect. "Being familiar with Degui, he must have followed Degui to the house. Tell the truth. I'll have the finger squeezers applied to you if you deviate the slightest bit from the truth!"

"I truly had never seen him in the house until the last day, when he forced his way through the middle door into the inner quarters of the house and tried to take liberties with my mistress. My mistress drove him away. When Degui came back after that, my mistress was crying. Then Degui went into her room, and soon afterward, both died."

Prefect Kuang shouted angrily at Zhi Zhu, "Villain! If you were not in collusion with Degui, how would you have dared to barge into the house? You are responsible for the two deaths!" To his men, he ordered, "Apply the ankle squeezers again!"

Dazed by the torture, Zhi Zhu unthinkingly offered a detailed account of how he had taught Degui tricks to seduce Shao-shi, coaxed Degui into giving him the dead baby, blackmailed Shao-shi, and forced Degui to introduce him to Shao-shi so he could share the sexual favors. He went on to describe how he had burst into the interior of the house, held Shao-shi in his arms, and demanded sexual favors and how she had tricked him into letting her go. He concluded by saying, "But I know nothing of what led to the deaths."

Prefect Kuang said, "Now, you're telling the truth." He ordered that the squeezers be withdrawn and that the clerk record the deposition. The county magistrate, sitting on one side, was overcome with shame upon realizing his own inferiority in wisdom and ability. Prefect Kuang picked up a brush-pen and wrote the following verdict:

> This court finds Zhi Zhu to be a depraved criminal. After his lecherous desires were aroused by a stolen look at the widow's beauty, he took advantage of the servant's gullibility and used clever words to persuade him to lie naked with his door open. The medicine to settle the fetus and possession of the dead baby were parts of his evil design, to which the widow fell victim. After his attempts at seeking sexual favors failed, he demanded money, which he later found to be unsatisfactory, and consequently reverted to his plan to obtain sexual favors. In the aftermath of a moment of weakness, Shao-shi was reduced to denial and self-deception. Several times, Zhi Zhu attempted blackmail and trespassed in her house. She turned her hatred for Zhi Zhu against Degui and changed a lover into an enemy. After killing Degui, she took her own life, her shame too great to be expiated by her death. With the mistress and servant both dead, Xiugu the maid was put to the rod, and there the case closed, with the culprit still at large. But it so happened that Bao Jiu caught Zhi Zhu in the act, and the dead baby cried. Since heaven guided the investigation of the case, the crime is not to be tolerated. The culprit is hereby given the death sentence and shall yield to the yamen all the money he has received through extortion in this case.

Prefect Kuang read his verdict aloud. Even Zhi Zhu accepted its fairness. After Prefect Kuang reported the case to his superiors, there was none who did not praise him for his remarkable ability. As the story circulated among the populace, all and sundry called him a reincarnation of Judge Bao.[6] This story has come to be titled "How Prefect Kuang Solves the Case of the Dead Baby." There is a poem that bears witness:

The pretty widow's desires were aroused;
The stupid servant's joys were followed by death.
That brute Zhi was as evil as a demon;
Prefect Kuang was as wise as a god.

36

The King of the Honey Locust Grove Assumes Human Shape (Originally titled "County Magistrate Zhao Burns the Honey Locust Grove")

Those who have gained wealth and rank seek wisdom;
Confucius deserved a title even in his youth.
People of our times know not heavenly designs
But fret and worry needlessly through wakeful nights.

Our story takes place during the Han dynasty. In Chengdu Prefecture, in Xichuan,[1] there lived an official named Luan Ba, who had been quite devoted to the arts of Daoism since youth. After attaining the rank of Gentleman of the Interior, he was assigned the post of prefect of Yuzhang [in present-day Jiangxi Province]. On a chosen day, he started out to assume his post. A few days later, at about the midpoint of his journey, he was met by officials who had come from far and near to greet him. Upon his arrival in Yuzhang, the seal of office was offered to him in a hand-over ceremony.

In the city of Yuzhang, there was a temple called the Lu Mountains Temple, and a fine temple it was. Behold:

Embowered in spreading dark green pines,
Overhung by ancient dragon-shaped junipers,
Topped by green tiles rising to the skies,
Guarded by a red gate aglow in the sun.
Its grandeur keeps the mighty river in check;
Its power controls the people's weal or woe.
The new board bears inscriptions in the ancient style;
Two rows of locust trees line the courtyard.

This was a temple most responsive to prayers. A god hidden behind a curtain would converse with supplicants and cast down winecups from midair. All the county residents had been there to ask for blessings. Prayers were so effective that a wind over the river could be parted to blow the sails of boats going in different directions.

After arriving in the county, Prefect Luan went to the local temples to offer incense. When he arrived at the Lu Mountains Temple and was greeted by the temple keeper, he said, "I heard that this temple, with a god that talks to people, is most responsive to prayers. I would like to see for myself and ask for blessings."

After making an incense offering, the prefect sank down on his knees and said, "I, Luan Ba, having just arrived in this county, am here to offer incense. Please favor me with a response in your divine compassion." He repeated the request several times but heard no response from behind the curtain. Growing impatient, the prefect said, "This must be a demon who's afraid of me because I have the power to raise thunderstorms to punish evil ones. That's why there's no response." So saying, he lifted the curtain and saw that, strangely enough, the image of the god had disappeared. As a matter of fact, that god was an evil being, afraid of coming out into the open in Prefect Luan's presence.

The prefect remarked, "So, this is but an evil spirit posing as a deity in order to prey on the populace." Right away, he instructed his men to demolish the temple. Thinking that he could not very well let the demon roam around the land, helping itself to sacrificial offerings and deceiving unsuspecting people, the prefect sought information on the demon's whereabouts from the local deities.

It so happened that the demon had taken refuge in Qi Prefecture in the shape of a scholar with a bearing graceful beyond compare and a literary talent second to none. The prefect of Qi married a daughter to him. After locating the demon, Prefect Luan submitted a memorial to his superiors asking permission to be relieved of his official duties. He then headed straight for Qi Prefecture on a demon-catching mission and paid the prefect a visit. The prefect of Qi summoned his son-in-law, but the young man refused to come out.

"Your son-in-law," said Prefect Luan, "is no human being but a demon who tried to pass itself off as a god in the city of Yuzhang. Because I gave orders to hunt it down, it fled all the way here. I can easily make it come out."

He asked for a brush-pen and an ink slab and wrote a magic figure, which he blew into the air. As if directed by a hand, the magic figure flew right into the chamber of the prefect's daughter. The scholar said to his wife, "I'll die if I go!" The next moment, with the magic figure between his lips, he walked right up to Prefect Luan.

"Old demon!" Prefect Luan roared. "Show your true form!"

In an instant, the scholar changed into an old fox. As it kowtowed, begging that its life be spared, Prefect Luan said, "For your crimes against innocent people, you shall be executed in accordance with heavenly laws." At a sharp order from Prefect Luan, a sword swung down, and the head of the fox rolled on the ground. Peace was thus restored to the region.

Storyteller, why tell us about how a Prefect Luan subdued a demon? Well, that is to prepare you for a story about an official who, out of the blue, became entangled in a most extraordinary adventure soon after assuming his new post and, as a result, almost lost his life. Here is the story.

In the Xuanhe reign period [1119–25], during the great Song dynasty, a man named Zhao Zaili, a native of the Eastern Capital, was appointed to the post of magistrate of Xinhui County, Guangzhou. We know from the following poem what a nice place Guangzhou was:

The rarest timber is used as firewood;
Lychee bushes grow around the fences.
The boats engage in trade with foreigners;
The waters transport travelers back and forth.
The ground warm, with no winter snow;
The weather balmy, with flowers in all four seasons.
How enviable—the Guangzhou region,
With amber and precious shells galore!

To resume. Zhao Zaili bid farewell to his mother and his wife and set out on the journey, followed by a few servants. Some days later, he arrived at the county seat, where the various officials offered him congratulations. On the first day, he visited the temples to offer incense. On the second day, the official seal was handed over to him, and on the third day, he began conducting official business. Behold:

Rat-a-tat go the drums;
In two rows stand the lictors.
King Yama sits to judge cases of life and death;[2]
On East Peak is set the soul-snatching platform.

The magistrate had just called the court to order when he suddenly sneezed. Everyone else in the hall also sneezed. A clerk said to the magistrate, "It's not that we imitated you, sir, but nine li from here is a temple called the Temple of the Honey Locust King, in front of which stand two honey locust trees. Since no one dares to touch the pods that the trees have borne for many years, the pods have been eaten by worms and reduced to powder. Previous county magistrates always went to the temple to offer incense before taking up official business, but since Your Honor hasn't done so, the Honey Locust King has blown the powder to this hall in a show of his supernatural power. It was the honey locust pod powder that induced everyone to sneeze." (*Most bizarre.*)

"How very strange!" exclaimed the magistrate. Right away, he set off for the temple to offer incense. Upon reaching the temple, he dismounted his horse and was escorted into the hall by the temple abbot. When the ceremony was over, the magistrate raised the curtain to see what the god looked like:

A cap adorned with a gold moth,
A war robe in a floral pattern;
A belt of Lantian jade around the middle,[3]
Tight embroidered green shoes on his feet.

Where the face should be, there was only a skull
With two hands stretching from the eye hollows:
The left one holding a halberd,
The right one making a Buddhist sign.

The magistrate was dumbfounded. He asked the temple keeper, "What sacrifices are offered in spring and autumn?"

The temple keeper replied, "A seven-year-old boy is offered in each spring sacrificial ceremony, and a girl in autumn. In both cases, the local headmen collect money and buy the children from poor families ahead of time. At the ceremony, the child is tied to a post, with arms behind the back, and is then cut open so the Honey Locust King may eat the heart over a cup of wine."

Ablaze with indignation, the magistrate ordered his men to arrest the temple keeper and send him to jail to await sentencing. "This being my very first term of office in my career as an official and both a father and a mother to the people under my jurisdiction, how can I allow such wanton killings to take place?" (*Bravo!*) Straightaway, he had his men smash the mud statue of the deity and burn the temple to the ground. (*Good!*) As his attendants helped him mount his horse, a voice rang out, "The king is here! The king is here!"

The magistrate asked his men what manner of king it was and was told that it was the Honey Locust King. The magistrate looked for himself and saw a demon king approaching, riding a horse with an ornate silver saddle and with red gauze lanterns leading the way. His eyes were like painted balls, his mouth protruded a few inches, and his outfit was exactly the same as that of the statue he had seen in the temple. The magistrate ordered that a bow and arrows be brought to him. As the arrow shot through the air, the sky darkened and the sun went out amid peals of thunder and a hundred golden flashes of lightning. A strong wind sprang up, blowing sand and stone through the air. The Honey Locust King vanished.

The magistrate was helped back to the county yamen, where he resumed his official duties the next day. The local elders submitted a memorial requesting that the Temple of the Honey Locust King be rebuilt. The memorial so upset the magistrate that he drove the elders out of his presence.

It is said that Guangzhou is a place plagued with miasma and many perils:

Tell of scenes south of the Nanling mountains,
And you send a chill down the spine:
Giant elephants move in hordes;
Pythons slither around in pairs.
Poisonous birds hide in withered trees;
Venomous water bugs lurk in ferries.
Wild apes' cries are heard here and there,
Stirring up longing for one's home far away.

After burning the Temple of the Honey Locust King, Magistrate Zhao did not encounter any more misfortune. Under his governance, no one coveted and pocketed belongings that were lost on the road, the streets were so peaceful and crime free that no dogs were heard barking at night, and farmers had one bumper harvest after another.

Time flew like an arrow. Quite unnoticeably, three years went by, and a new magistrate arrived on the scene. Magistrate Zhao returned to the Eastern Capital, followed by his attendants. After some days on the road, they came upon a government courier station called Peak Station, two thousand li from Xinhui County, in Guangzhou. The magistrate went in and was given accommodations for the night. The servants chanted good night to him and retired to their quarters.

When Magistrate Zhao woke up the next morning, his trunks and clothing were nowhere to be seen. He called for his attendants, but no one answered. He called for the courier station staff and heard no response. Wrapping himself in the quilt, he rose and opened his door to look outside, and no man or horse was to be seen. Nor was there a person anywhere around the house. In alarm, he rushed out and opened the front gate. He saw only

A deserted place shunned by travelers,
Frequented by none but the clouds.

"Where could they all have gone?" he wondered. "Could this be the work of robbers?" Still clutching the quilt around himself, he ran down the hill as swiftly as if he had wings on his feet. Several li later, not having come upon even one house, he heaved a deep sigh and thought, "Oh well, in life I am a native of the Xiang River region; in death, I'll be a ghost on the road." Then he saw a thatched hut some way off. "What a shame I didn't see it earlier!" he exclaimed. He walked up to the hut and saw an old man. "Greetings to you, sir!" said the magistrate. "My name is Zhao Zaili. Please help me!"

At the sight of a man with a quilt around his shoulders, the old man remarked, "Why are you in such a state?"

"Sir, I was the magistrate of Xinhui County, Guangzhou. I am here because I lodged last night at Peak Station, and this morning, my attendants and luggage have all disappeared."

"How extraordinary!" exclaimed the old man. He then kindly invited the magistrate into the hut, gave him some old clothes to wear, and treated him to wine and food. After five or six days, he put together some money and urged the magistrate to take it for his journey back to the Eastern Capital. The magistrate left with many a word of thanks.

Resting by night and traveling by day, he arrived some days later in the Eastern Capital. He walked up to the teahouse across from his home and asked the old waitress, "Do you recognize me?"

The old woman replied, "No, sir."

"I am Magistrate Zhao from the house across the street. I took up lodging in a courier station called Peak Station, but when I woke up the following morning, my men and my luggage had all disappeared. Luckily, an old man in a hut gave me clothes and travel money. And then I came back here after several days' traveling."

"You are quite mistaken, sir. Magistrate Zhao of the house across the street has been back home for two months."

"Then that one is an impostor. I am the real Magistrate Zhao."

"But how can there be two magistrates?"

"Could you please have my mother come over here?"

The old woman studied him carefully and found that he looked exactly like the man who had returned earlier. She had no choice but to walk over to the Zhao house, where she found a Magistrate Zhao sitting. As she bowed in greeting, she noticed that he was the very image of the man outside. She entered the interior part of the house and said to Mrs. Zhao, "There's another magistrate outside. He just arrived."

"Nonsense!" said Mrs. Zhao. "I have only one son. How can there be two magistrates?"

"Well, go and see for yourself."

Accordingly, Mrs. Zhao went across the street.

"Mother!" cried Zhao Zaili. "Don't you recognize me?"

"This man is talking nonsense!" said the old lady. "I have only one son. And now another one pops up!"

"I am your real son! I stayed for one night at Peak Station, and in the morning, my attendants and my luggage had all vanished."

As he continued with his account of how he had made his way home, a crowd gathered around them, forming a tight circle. As Zhao Zaili kept a firm hold on his mother, refusing to let go, the old woman from the teahouse suggested, "There must be a birthmark somewhere."

"There is indeed a red birthmark on the lower part of my son's back," said Mrs. Zhao.

He took off his upper garment, and sure enough, the red birthmark was exposed to view. The crowd burst into cheers. "The one who returned first is an impostor!" they cried. (*He who tries to pass himself off as someone else should at least make sure that the resemblance is strong enough. Don't end up looking like nothing but an impostor, as is so often the case nowadays.*)

The Magistrate Zhao who was sitting in the house across the street asked the janitor what all the commotion was about. The janitor replied, "There's another magistrate coming back."

"The temerity! I'm here, so how can there be another Magistrate Zhao?" By the time he stepped out of the gate, the crowd of spectators was beginning to disperse. "Mother," said the false magistrate, "who's that fellow? How dare he grab you like that?"

"He's my real son. He's got a red birthmark."

The man also took off his upper garment as the onlookers cheered. On his back, for all to see, there was also a red birthmark. "Most extraordinary!" exclaimed the onlookers.

The man took Zhao Zaili to the Kaifeng prefectural yamen, where the prefect's court happened to be in session. The Magistrate Zhao who had returned first strutted with great pomp and solemnity into the hall, sporting his official robe and belt, sat down in the seat of the guest of honor, and struck up a conversation with the prefect, who readily believed that he was talking to the real Magistrate Zhao. (*Those who strike up conversations in such a manner tend to be impostors, but few would be suspicious of them.*) For Zhao Zaili, the prefect had nothing but the harshest words, threatening time and again to subject him to torture. Fully confident of his own innocence, Zhao Zaili spoke out in a ringing voice, giving an account of what had occurred at Peak Station.

The prefect found it hard to come up with a verdict. Suddenly, an idea struck him. "Whoever bears the official appointment letter is the real Magistrate Zhao." To Zhao Zaili, he said, "If you are not an impostor, where's your letter of appointment?" (*Hadn't his attendants and his luggage all vanished? Isn't it ridiculous to ask him for a letter of appointment? It's been said that in Suzhou, when a local headman reported that a headless corpse had been found in the river, the county magistrate asked if there was any wound on the body, showing as much sense as the prefect in our story.*)

"It disappeared at Peak Station, along with my other things."

The prefect instructed that the false Magistrate Zhao be brought forward. "Mr. Magistrate," said the prefect, "do you still have your letter of appointment?"

"Yes," replied the impostor, whereupon he sent his men to Mrs. Zhao, and the document was duly brought back to court.

"Zhao Zaili," the prefect bellowed, "if you are the real magistrate as you claim to be, why is *your* letter of appointment with *him?*"

"Your Honor," said Zhao Zaili, "I lost it at Peak Station. Why don't you ask him in which year he passed the examinations? Who was the chief examiner? What were the essay questions? How did he get to be magistrate of Xinhui County?"

"He's got a point," thought the prefect. He then put all these questions to the imposter, who had ready answers for every one of them and never deviated in the slightest from the information Zhao Zaili had provided. (*Nothing baffles him.*) The prefect found a verdict even more elusive.

After returning home, the impostor put together some lavish gifts and had them sent over to the Justice Bureau. (*Wrong thing to do.*) As the ancients put it, "In public, even the gift of a needle is frowned upon; in private, gift-laden horse carriages freely come and go." Since the director of the Justice Bureau had been bribed by the fake magistrate, the real magistrate was expelled from Kaifeng prefecture and exiled to Fengfu County, in Yanzhou. With his package of clothing and his umbrella, Zhao Zaili set out on the road, escorted by two lictors.

They covered three hundred to four hundred li in a few days. When they came to the foot of Blue Rock Hill, with no sign of human habitation anywhere in sight, the lictors said to Zhao Zaili, "Mister, we'd like to have a word with you. After you get to the prison, you'll do nothing but carry loads of soil and water. You won't survive the backbreaking labor anyway, so why don't you kill yourself here and now? Don't blame us; we're only obeying orders. We really can't do otherwise. We need to get an official reply from the local authorities, but you'll have to die first, so that we can get back to the capital as soon as possible."

At these words, Zhao Zaili burst into cries of woe. "All right! All right!" he said. "I'll lodge a complaint against you in the netherworld!" Trembling all over, he closed his eyes, anticipating the blows of the rods.

Raising their rods high, the lictors chanted, "Have a good journey to the netherworld!"

They were on the point of bringing their rods down when a voice rang out behind them. "Stop!" (*Goodness knows how few grown men would be willing to save someone from danger out of the goodness of their hearts! They don't even measure up to a six- or seven-year-old boy!*)

The lictors were so frightened that they dropped their rods. They looked around and saw walking toward them a six- or seven-year-old boy wearing a plain gauze cap, a green shirt, a jade waistband, and a clean pair of shoes and socks. When they questioned him as to his identity, he replied, "I am not a mortal being."

The two lictors were awestruck. As they busily muttered in humble tones, the boy said, "He is the real Magistrate Zhao. How can you beat him to death? Here's a piece of silver for you. Take good care of him all the rest of the way to Fengfu County. If something happens to him, you two can forget about getting back home." With a gust of wind, the boy disappeared from view.

To Magistrate Zhao, the two men said, "Don't hold us to blame! We didn't know you were the real one. If you ever return to the Eastern Capital, please don't bring up our names."

They proceeded to the Fengfu County prison and handed him over to the warden. After the lictors told the warden about what had happened on their journey, he arranged to have Magistrate Zhao tutor his two children in the study instead of assigning him to heavy manual labor. Still, for someone who had enjoyed the power of an official, Zhao Zaili found his new duties as tutor too boring and the days passing too slowly.

One year went by at last, and spring came around again. As Zhao Zaili walked in the back garden to pass the time, the sight of the early spring flowers, the budding willows, and the chirping, dancing birds saddened him. After serving a term as an official, he no longer attached any value to rank and title. What grieved him was the separation from his flesh and blood. Even his mother and his wife had failed to recognize him. What sin had he committed in a previous life to deserve this tragic retribution? Why should he be condemned to such a hand-to-mouth existence in this place without any hope of ever lifting himself from misery? As tears of sorrow fell from his eyes, he suddenly saw a pond. He thought, "I'd better throw myself into the pond and file a complaint against that impostor in the netherworld."

He sighed and was on the point of jumping into the water when he heard a cry, "Don't jump!" Turning around, he saw again the child in a plain gauze cap, a green shirt, a jade waistband, and a clean pair of shoes and socks. "Magistrate," the boy said, "Granny wants you to go on the third day of the third month to the left corridor of East Peak Temple to see the Patron Goddess of Children. She'll give you something that you can take to the Eastern Capital and use to vindicate yourself."

With a thankful bow, Magistrate Zhao said, "Honorable god, who is the man impersonating me in the Eastern Capital?"

"It's the Honey Locust King of Guangzhou," replied the child. With that, he departed in a gust of wind.

When the third day of the third month came at last, Zhao Zaili bid farewell to the warden and headed in the direction of East Peak Temple to offer incense. He arrived at the temple and went to the left corridor. There, he bowed repeatedly to the statue of the Patron Goddess of Children and offered his prayers. As he made his way out of the temple, he heard a voice calling, "Magistrate Zhao!" Turning around, he saw a little boy wearing a checkered cotton vest, with his hair tied up in three knots. "Granny wishes to see you," said the child.

Zhao followed the little boy across a field and, about half a li later, came to a house with a green tile roof and carved beams, behind a red gate with golden nails. In the main hall sat an old lady with snowy eyebrows and a hair bun that looked like a ball of silk. Three or four children around her cried out, "The benefactor is here!"

Why did they call Magistrate Zhao "benefactor"? Well, back when he was a magistrate in Guangzhou, he saved the lives of two children each year, which meant quite a few lives during his three-year term of office. Hence that form of address. (*Even little children know that kindness should be repaid with kindness. Ingrates of the world, follow their example!*)

The magistrate paid homage to the old lady from his position below the dais. She invited him to climb the steps and said, "Please take a seat. Wine will be served." After several cups of wine, she said, "The one in possession of your house and family in the Eastern Capital is the Honey Locust King. This is by no means anything that a court of law can settle. I am helping you because of what you have done for little boys and girls." (*So she is none other than the Patron Goddess of Children.*) Turning to the third child, she said, "Give me the box." The child produced a box wrapped in a piece of yellow cloth. The old lady removed a gold hairpin from her hair and instructed the magistrate in these words: "Go to the end of the large pond at the foot of this hill, where you'll see a big tree. Knock the gold hairpin against the tree three times, and a yaksha will emerge from the water's surface.[4] Just say you're sent by the Patron Goddess of Children, and the yaksha will lead you to the Dragon King's palace. There, they'll put something from the palace treasury into this box. You may then go to the Eastern Capital and subdue that Honey Locust King."

After bowing gratefully to the old lady, the magistrate left the temple and walked downhill to the big tree by the pond at the foot of the hill. As soon as he had knocked the hairpin against the tree three times, a gust of wind sprang up, and a yaksha appeared on the surface of the water, asking, "Who is this?"

"By the order of the Patron Goddess of Children, I'm here to see the Dragon King."

The yaksha dived down, and reemerged a short while later, and told Zhao Zaili to close his eyes. As soon as he did, his ears were filled with the sound of wind and rain. When the yaksha told him to open his eyes, he saw

Auspicious clouds above the palace roof;
A translucent mist over the walkways.

When the yaksha told him to produce the box, he untied the yellow wrapping and handed the box to the yaksha, who then took off the lid, walked to one corner of the hall, and called out, "You evil thing! Come here!"

Lo and behold, an object that resembled a dragon, but without horns and a tiger, but with scales, got into the box! The yaksha put the lid back on, wrapped the box in a piece of yellow cloth, gave it back to the magistrate, and told him to keep a close watch over it and carry it all the way to the Eastern Capital, where he was to use it to subdue the Honey Locust King. As before, the yaksha told him to close his eyes and led him out of the water.

After leaving East Peak Temple, the magistrate headed for Fengfu county. Along the way, he thought to himself, "Should I ask for the prison warden's permission? But surely, he wouldn't let a convict under his supervision go off like that. And if he makes me stay, I won't be able to do what I'm supposed to do. I'd better keep going."

He crossed through Fengfu County and took a boat, traveling up Bian River, past bustling and prosperous towns, all the way to Kaifeng, the Eastern Capital. He cried out his grievances in front of the prefectural yamen: "I am the real Magistrate Zhao, now in exile in Fengfu County, in Yanzhou. The one living with my wife is not a human being but a demon, the Honey Locust King of Xinhui County, Guangzhou!"

As a crowd began to gather around him, lictors appeared and pushed him into the yamen, all the way to the steps of the dais in the main hall. The prefect said sharply, "How dare a convicted felon accuse me of a wrong judgment!"

Magistrate Zhao respond, "On my very first day at my post as magistrate of

Xinhui County, in Guangzhou, I was tending to official business when I suddenly sneezed, followed by everyone else in the hall. A clerk remarked that nine li away, there was a temple of the Honey Locust King, in front of which stood two honey locust trees. The worms had reduced the pods to powder, and no one dared touch them. Because I had not been to the temple to make incense offerings, the king demonstrated his magic power and blew the powder to induce sneezes. Right away, I mounted my horse and went to the temple to offer incense. The statue of the deity looked most grotesque, with two hands stretching out from the eye sockets. When I asked what kind of sacrificial offerings were made in spring and autumn, the temple keeper replied that a seven-year-old boy was the spring sacrifice, and a small girl was the autumn sacrifice. They were tied to the main column, hands behind their backs, and their hearts were gouged out for the king's enjoyment.

"The very next moment, I sent the temple keeper to jail to await indictment and had the deity's statue smashed and burned down. On the way back to my office, I heard the cry 'The king is here!' Red gauze lanterns were lighting his way. I shot an arrow at him, and nothing untoward happened thereafter.

"After my three-year term of office came to an end, I went back to the capital, lodging in a roadside inn along the way. When I rose the next morning, my attendants had disappeared, all thirty-odd of them. My clothing, including my cap, had also vanished. I had no choice but to gather the quilt around myself and venture out into the country. Luckily, an old man gave me clothes and travel money so that I could make my way to the Eastern Capital. I little expected that Your Honor would exile me to Fengfu County.

"On a trip to East Peak Temple, I encountered the Patron Goddess of Children and was given an object, which now lies in this box. This object can subdue the Honey Locust King. Please summon that fake magistrate. If I can't subdue him, I'll be reconciled to my sentence."

"Open that box first," said the prefect, "and see what it is."

Zhao Zaili countered, "No, this can't be done. If the box is opened, I'm afraid an innocent life will be taken."

Consequently, the prefect had Zhao Zaili taken to one side while they waited for the fake magistrate to be brought to court. Once the impostor arrived and sat down, the prefect said, "There is a complaint against you, saying that you are not a human being but some Honey Locust King of Xinhui County, Guangzhou."

The fake magistrate retorted, coloring, "Who says so?"

"The Patron Goddess of Children said so to the real Magistrate Zhao in East Peak Temple."

The impostor panicked and hastily rose to go. At this point, the real Magistrate Zhao, who was standing at the bottom of the steps, untied the yellow parcel and took off the lid without waiting for the prefect to give the order. In an instant, a blinding rainstorm sprang up, one in which you could not even see your outstretched hand. A moment later, the clouds dispersed, the wind died down, and the fake magistrate had disappeared.

Trembling all over with fear, the prefect saw no option but to report the matter to Emperor Huizong, who then issued three decrees: First, the prefect was to be removed from his post. Second, after reclaiming his family, Magistrate Zhao was to resume his old rank. Third, no idols of deities were to be worshiped in the Guangzhou region.

When Magistrate Zhao arrived at home, his mother and his wife burst into loud sobs. "How was I to know that you were my real son?" said his mother. (*Once an impostor comes on the scene, the mother fails to recognize her own son, the wife knows not her own husband, and the servants turn their backs on the master. Such is the harm that impersonation can do.*)

When summoned to answer queries, the attendants, more than thirty altogether, replied, "At about the fifth watch of the night, we were told to prepare the horses for departure from the inn. How were we to know that he was an impostor!"

As they all gathered around to offer their congratulations, they asked what in the box had subjugated the Honey Locust King. Magistrate Zhao said, "I don't know any more than you do. Had it not been for the Patron Goddess of Children, my entire clan would have perished at the hands of that Honey Locust King. I need to go to East Peak Temple to offer some incense in thanks."

On a chosen day, he took his mother, his wife, and some servants on a boat trip down the Bian River to Fengfu County, in Yanzhou. There, they offered thanks to the prison warden, who, knowing that this was the real Magistrate Zhao, danced attendance on him. They stayed for two or three days and then made their way up the hill to East Peak Temple. After entering the temple gate, the magistrate went directly to the left corridor, where he offered thanks to the statue of the Patron Goddess of Children. When the incense was burned, he bade a thankful farewell to the goddess and went out the door. His mother and his wife having preceded him down the hill, Magistrate Zhao was walking at a leisurely pace with two servants when he saw an old lady with a complexion as fair as jade sitting on a craggy rock. "Zhao Zaili," she called out, "congratulations!"

Magistrate Zhao took a step forward and recognized her to be none other than the Patron Goddess of Children. He quickly bowed in gratitude. The old lady said, "I know about your prayers this morning. The thing in the box is a fox spirit from East Peak. The Honey Locust King being a rat spirit, the fox is its natural enemy. You may want to write a memorial to the emperor requesting that wide publicity be given to the power of Daoism." With that, she disappeared in a gust of wind, to the astonishment of Magistrate Zhao. After descending the hill, he told his mother and his wife about the incident, his heart filled with gratitude.

Upon arriving in the Eastern Capital, he reported the matter to Emperor Huizong, a believer in Daoism. With Daoism enjoying much popularity at the time, the emperor decreed that temples dedicated to the Patron Goddess of Children be built in all prefectures and counties. Some of these temples remain to this day. As the poem says,

The world favors the fake rather than the real;
Belief in the fake brings ruin to the real.
If everyone could tell the false from the real,
None will need to appeal to the gods.

37

Wan Xiuniang Takes Revenge through Toy Pavilions

Spring flowers in bloom appeal to lovers;
Moonless windy nights appeal to warriors.
The three-inch-long tongues of the eloquent
Delight in commenting on the affairs of the world.

As the story has it, in Xiangyang Prefecture, Shandong, known in Tang times as the East Circuit South of the Mountain, there lived in the center of the city a squire called by all and sundry Squire Wan, or Third Squire Wan because he was the third son of the family. He owned a tea shop, which was located on one side of his house, and a teahouse, located on the other. He employed a waiter, now more than twenty years old, with the surname Tao and the nickname Iron Monk, who had been born in the house to a maidservant and had worked in the teahouse ever since he began wearing his hair in knots as children do. On the day of which we speak, after the teahouse had closed for the day, Squire Wan peeked out from behind the cotton portiere and saw Iron Monk Tao pick up about forty-five in cash. "Let me see what he does with the money," thought Squire Wan.

In the parlance of the local teahouse waiters, stolen money is expressed in terms of a "trip." "A trip today to Yuhang County" means having stolen forty-five in cash, because Yuhang is forty-five li away. "A trip to Pingjiang Prefecture" means three hundred and sixty in cash. "A trip all the way to Chengdu Prefecture in Xichuan" means a lot more money.[1] As Squire Wan said to himself, "Let me see what he does with the money," Iron Monk Tao shot swift, eagle-like glances around and, believing there were no peeping eyes behind the portiere, slipped the money into his bosom. Unhurriedly, Squire Wan raised the portiere, stepped out, and sat down on a stool by the counter. With one hand, Iron Monk Tao patted his own bosom in a gesture understood as a "self search," took off his waistband, and, holding his cloth bag by two corners, shook it in midair. Then, patting his belly and his sides, he seemed to be saying, "Watch this well, Squire Wan! I didn't steal your money!"

Squire Wan told Tao to approach him and said, "I saw you pick up forty to fifty in cash just a moment ago. You looked at the portiere and slipped the money into your bosom. Now, tell me the truth. The amount of money doesn't matter, but what a deceitful thing you did, taking the cloth bag and shaking it in midair and all! Where did you hide the money? Tell me, and I'll forgive you. If you don't, I'll take you to the authorities."

His thumb aimed at his heart, Iron Monk Tao said, "Squire, I'm not hiding anything from you. There are indeed forty to fifty in cash hidden somewhere." Pointing upward, he continued, "It is all on a piece of iron inside the hanging lamp."

Squire Wan climbed up on a stool and saw that, sure enough, there was a pile of forty to fifty in cash in the lamp. Squire Wan stepped down, reseated himself on the stool, and again made Iron Monk Tao approach him.

"How many years have you been in this house?"

"As a child, I helped my father wash the teacups and wipe the saucers in this house. After Father died about fourteen or fifteen years ago, you, sir, kindly kept me and have supported me all these years."

"You steal fifty in cash from me a day. That comes to five hundred in ten days, one string plus five hundred in a month, eighteen strings in a year. In these fifteen years, you've stolen two hundred and seventy strings altogether. I'm not going to deliver you to the authorities, but you are fired!" (*The calculations of a miser.* [Illegible.])

He dismissed Iron Monk Tao immediately. The young man took leave of the squire, packed, and left the teahouse.

Iron Monk Tao found himself without a means of support, having not even a pair of clappers with which to beat time so that he could sing a beggar's songs. In less than ten days, he had used up whatever little money he had in his parcel. Because Squire Wan had warned all the teahouses in Xiangyang Prefecture about him, he could not find a job. (*A heartless person is beyond cure.*) It was autumn, the bleakness of which is captured by the following ancient poem:

The lotuses wither away;
The parasol trees have shed all leaves.
A drizzling rain fills the air with a fine mist,
Urging the advent of winter.
Crickets chirp amid the wilted grass;
Wild geese descend onto flat stretches of sand.
Those who are not drifting from place to place
Know not the misery of it all.

While the autumn winds alternated with autumn rain, Iron Monk Tao remained jobless. He had thought that he could always find a job at any other teahouse. Little did he know that the squire had alerted all the teahouses against him and thus deprived him of his livelihood. The only two shirts on his back—one made of raw silk, the other of yellow grass—gradually deteriorated.[2] As I recall, there is a lyric poem titled "Partridge Sky," by a gentleman of Jiankang Prefecture:

Yellow grass clothes are least fit for late fall;
Sadly frayed at the shoulders, tattered at the sleeves,
The collar thin, the color gone, the sleeves torn,
They can hardly ward off the ceaseless autumn wind.

Barely covered in these rags, I frown,
Afraid of seeing old acquaintances.
Softly, the neighbor woman asked me,
"May I have your clothes to make shoes with?"

As he watched his yellow grass shirt curl up in the screeching wind, he made his way again to the home of Mr. Zhou, the local head of the profession, thinking to himself, "What a vicious man Squire Wan is! Granted that I took thirty to fifty in cash from him, he could have just fired me and stopped at that. As they say, 'No cat doesn't steal food.' He didn't have to warn all the teahouses in Xiangyang Prefecture against me. (*So, now he knows why he can't find a job.*) And now, I have nowhere to go to make a living. What am I going to do in the autumn and the winter? What am I going to live on?"

He was in the midst of these thoughts when he saw a man enter Mr. Zhou's house, asking, "Mr. Zhou, I'd like to borrow a carrying pole from you."

"Why do you want a carrying pole?" asked Mr. Zhou.

The man replied, "Squire Wan's daughter, Wan Xiuniang, is coming home today because her husband has died. I need a pole so I can carry her luggage."

Iron Monk Tao said to himself, "Had I not been driven out, I surely would have gone with him to help carry the luggage and made a hundred or so in cash." The more he thought about it, the more he resented the squire. He continued, "I'll go out of the city and watch her homecoming procession. If I meet her on the road, I'll tell her about the whole thing. She may be able to change her father's mind. Then I can go around again and look for a job." (*The Iron Monk started out meaning well. He's not the kind of man whose services are to be rejected out of hand.*)

So thinking, he stepped out of the door and walked all by himself to a place called Wulitou. In his shabby clothes, he was dragging his feet along when a voice behind him cried out, "Iron Monk! I have something to say to you!" Turning around, he saw:

A man with awe-inspiring looks,
A demon king poised to wreck the earth's axis;
A man with a majestic bearing,
One to subdue the yaksha by heaven's gate.[3]

Iron Monk Tao chanted out a greeting and said, "So, it's the Master! What do you want to talk to me about?"

"I went to your teahouse several times for tea, but I didn't see you."

"That's because Squire Wan acted most unreasonably and drove me out quite a few days ago. Since then, he's done something even worse: He told all the teahouses in Xiangyang not to employ me. Now, look, Master! I'm all in rags. The autumn wind has started to blow, and I have no idea where my next meal is coming from. I'll die of hunger either this autumn or the coming winter."

"Where are you going now?"

"I heard earlier today that Squire Wan's daughter Wan Xiuniang is coming back this evening because her husband has died. She'll be bringing all her belongings, worth tens of thousands of strings of cash. I'm going to stop her and ask her for help."

As the Master heard these words, the following lines came to mind:

It's easier to capture a tiger in the hills
Than to bring oneself to ask for help.

"A true man doesn't ask for help," said he. "Better to help yourself than to ask other people for help." Pointing into the distance, he said to Iron Monk Tao, "Let's go there. This is no place to talk. Follow me."

The two men left the main thoroughfare of Wulitou and took a small path that led to a hut in a secluded spot.

In front of it, a path trodden by robbers;
Behind it, a hill where murders take place.
Seen from afar, it has a dark and frightening air;
A closer look sends chills down one's spine.
By no means the house of a kind host,
It harbors men who kill and burn.

The door was closed, so the Master did not go up to it but took hold of a brick on the ground and tossed it onto the roof. In an instant, the door was unbarred and opened, and out came a strongly built man with a square jaw, a big mouth, and six characters tattooed on his face. For whatever reason, the man was called by all and sundry Big Characters Jiao Ji. After exchanging greetings with the Master, he asked, pointing at Iron Monk Tao, "Who is this?"

"He just gave me information about a good client. We're in business!"

The three men entered Big Characters Jiao Ji's home. The Master took some loose pieces of silver from his waistband so that Jiao Ji could buy wine and meat for the three to share. After eating, Iron Monk Tao went out to make inquiries. When he returned, he gave this report: "For your information, about twenty loads of miscellaneous things have already been carried into the city, but Squire Wan's daughter Wan Xiuniang, her brother Squire Wan Junior, and a servant called Zhou Ji will be arriving at Wulitou at about sundown before the city gate closes. So, there will be three people, two horses, and a load of valuables."

At this report, the Master said, "Follow me, Iron Monk!" And the three men, each carrying a broadsword, went to the woods in Wulitou to wait for the procession.

Sure enough, at about sundown, Squire Wan Junior, Wan Xiuniang, Zhou Ji the servant, and two grooms reached Wulitou on their way to the city. As they drew near the woods, they saw

A cluster of clouds when viewed from afar,
Drops of rain when seen at close range.
Dragons and snakes wriggling their long bodies,
Making sounds that shake the cold, rainy sky.

The company of five had hardly entered the woods when a loud voice rang out from the trees crying, "The three hundred worthy men of the Purple Gold Mountains, do not come out, so as not to frighten the young master and the young lady!" With that, three men emerged, each carrying a broadsword. The five travelers were so scared that their souls took flight through the tops of their heads and their spirits escaped via the soles of their feet. The two grooms took to their heels and ran for dear life, leaving behind Wan Xiuniang, Squire Wan Junior, and the servant Zhou Ji.

One of the three men said, "We're not going to kill you. Just stand and deliver!"

By Squire Wan Junior's order, Zhou Ji handed a twenty-five-tael ingot of silver to the man. (*Not a small amount of money.*)

Big Characters Jiao Ji burst out, "You swine! You mean we are worth only one ingot of your silver!"

He swung his broadsword high, fixed his eyes on Zhou Ji, and was just about to bring it down when Squire Wan Junior and Wan Xiuniang said, "If you want, venerable warriors, you may take everything we have here."

Placing the carrying pole of the load on his shoulders, Big Characters Jiao Ji was about to enter the woods when Squire Wan Junior cried out, "Iron Monk, so you're the one who's robbing us!"

In alarm, Big Characters Jiao Ji put down the load and thought to himself, "This is bad! If we let them go, they'll report to the Xiangyang prefectural yamen tomorrow and have Iron Monk arrested. What will happen to me and the Master?" He rushed over to Squire Wan Junior and, his broadsword raised high, cried, "Here you go!" As for the young master,

His body limp as flying willow catkins,
His life hangs by a thread as thin as a lotus fiber.

Big Characters Jiao Ji killed Squire Wan Junior and the servant Zhou Ji with his broadsword. He dragged the two bodies into the woods and then picked up his load again. Iron Monk Tao took the reins of the young master's horse, and the Master went to lead Wan Xiuniang's horse. "Venerable warriors," pleaded Wan Xiuniang, "please spare my life."

That night, they all went to Big Characters Jiao Ji's house. In the darkness of the night, they knocked on the door of a wineshop, entered, and bought some wine and food. After the meal, they divided the valuables into three portions, one for Iron Monk Tao, one for Jiao Ji, and one for the Master.

"Now that the things have been divided up, I want to keep Wan Xiuniang for myself. She'll be the lady of the camp," said the Master. So, Wan Xiuniang, the only survivor, was kept in Jiao Ji's house, where she bided her time, cajoling the men with sweet words. (*By swallowing minor insults while planning a major revenge, Wan Xiuniang shows she is a woman of great worth.*)

The days went by. The Master spent his time either drinking wine or eating meat in Jiao Ji's house or went out to waylay travelers and rob them of their valuables. One day, he drank himself into a stupor. Truly,

Three cups of wine went right through his heart,
Two peach blossoms rose on his cheeks.

Wan Xiuniang asked, "You always call yourself 'the Master,' 'the Master.' Even dogs and horses can be distinguished by the color of their hair. How can people have no names? After all, you are my husband. May I make so bold as to ask the Master's name?"

Exhilarated by the wine, the man said, pointing at his legs, "Yes, I am a man to be reckoned with in Xiangyang Prefecture. If you don't know me for who I am, let me tell you something. You'll be so impressed you'll lose your mind." So saying, he rolled up his pants to reveal some characters tattooed on his legs. "This is my name. Ten Dragons Miao Zhong. Now you know." But, truly,

There are ears within the walls
And eyes outside the windows.

Big Characters Jiao Ji overheard the conversation from the other side of the window. He thought, "Look at this Master Miao, older brother of mine! Why should he tell her his name? Doesn't he have better things to do?" Bursting in, he said aloud, "Brother, now you'll have to push that cow!" In the robbers' jargon, to kill a person is to "push a cow." Jiao Ji was telling Ten Dragons Miao Zhong to kill Wan Xiuniang. Indeed,

Hoe up the roots when you weed,
So that the weeds won't come up again.
If weeds are not removed by the roots,
They'll grow back again, come next spring.

Turning a deaf ear to Jiao Ji, Miao Zhong said to him, "We divided everything equally among us, except this woman, whom I've kept for myself. And now you are so jealous that you want to bump her off. I'm only making her a lady of the camp. What harm can there be?"

Jiao Ji countered, "Someday, this woman will be a source of trouble, and I'll be done for!"

One day, after waiting until he saw Miao Zhong go out through the door, Jiao Ji said to himself, "I've told this brother of mine several times to push that cow, but he just won't listen. Since he puts it off day after day, I'd better do it for him, to remove a source of future trouble." Holding in his bosom a sheathed knife with a short handle and a long, thin, sharp blade, Jiao Ji walked into the room where Wan Xiuniang was sitting. With the knife raised high in his right hand, he held Wan Xiuniang with his left and was about to bring the knife down when a man grabbed his wrist from behind. "So you really want to do it. Don't you have any regard for me?" said the man.

Jiao Ji turned around and saw that it was none other than Ten Dragons Miao Zhong, who continued, "Turning her out of your house will be enough. Why kill her?" (*Actually, he'd be in greater danger if she left the house. Miao Zhong is quite mistaken.*) At these words, Jiao Ji relented. As the day drew to an end,

The red wheel sinks in the west;
The jade hare rises in the east.
The beauty retires to her room, candle in hand;
The angler by the river calls it a day.
The fireflies light up the meadow;
The moon shines through the clouds in the sky.

At about the first watch of the night, Miao Zhong said, "This is no place for you, woman. Haven't you noticed that they've been trying to kill you at every opportunity?"

"Oh, what am I going to do?"

"Easy." Miao Zhong then placed her on his back and walked until they reached a farmstead at the first light of dawn.

He put Wan Xiuniang down and knocked at the gate. A voice called out from within, "Coming!" A moment later, a farmhand appeared, and Miao Zhong said to him, "Tell your master that Master Miao is here at the gate." The farmhand went in to announce the visitors, after which a man emerged from the house. What was the man wearing? Behold:

A brick-shaped cap tied at the back,
A floral green silk vest over his shoulders,
A pair of pants tied at the waist,
A pair of silk shoes in the latest fashion.

After exchanging bows, the two men brought Wan Xiuniang into the main hall, where the three sat down in their proper seats as host and guests. Miao Zhong said, "Brother, I really shouldn't burden you with the care of this person."

"That's perfectly all right," said the host.

After drinking a few cups of wine and eating breakfast with the host, Miao Zhong departed. The host led Wan Xiuniang into the study and said to her, "Do you know that Ten Dragons Mr. Miao has sold you to me?" At these words, Wan Xiuniang burst into tears. There is a lyric poem set to the tune of "Partridge Sky" that says:

The tiny pearls fall, one by one,
Clear autumn dewdrops shining on the cheeks.
They speckle the Xiang River bamboo,
Their sadness causes long walls to crumble.

Her thoughts are on love, fickle or tender;
Her heart sick with grief, she plays the zither.
Her handkerchief bears evidence
Of new tearstains, adding to the old ones.

Weeping, Wan Xiuniang thought to herself, "That swine Miao Zhong! He robbed me of my money, killed my older brother and Zhou Ji the servant, soiled my body, and now, out of the blue, he sells me! How can I go on living!"

A few days later, when everyone was asleep on a dismal, moonless night, Wan Xiuniang slipped out the back gate into the garden, where she prayed, her face raised to the sky: "My father, Squire Wan, must have been less than a reasonable man. That's why I've been put through so much misery, to end up like this. That brute Miao Zhong! He robbed me, killed my brother and servant, soiled my body, and sold me!" She took off her vest, threw it over the branch of a big mulberry tree, tied it into a noose, and said, "My brother and Zhou Ji, your souls being not yet far off, please wait for me by the Gate of the Dead. I belong to Xiangyang Prefecture, in life and in death."

She was about to put her neck through the noose when a strongly built man carrying a broadsword suddenly emerged, faintly visible in the darkness, from behind an ornamental rock. Pointing to Xiuniang, he said, "Don't make a sound! I heard everything you said. Stop trying to kill yourself. I'll get you out of here, all right?"

"That would be wonderful. What is your name, brave man?"

"I am Yin Zong, known to all as Filial Son Yin Zong because of my devotion to my eighty-year-old mother. I came here to steal some things so that I can sell them to support my mother. It's fate that I should run into you. As the proverb says, 'Whenever you see a wrong, draw your sword and set it right.' Let me get you out of here. You'll be quite safe. Don't be afraid." (*There are gentlemen among robbers, and robbers among gentlemen.*)

Yin Zong placed Wan Xiuniang on his shoulders and went up to the garden wall. With a mighty thrust from his shoulders, she landed on top of the wall. Using his sword as a pole, he vaulted over the wall and helped her down. He had just set her squarely on his shoulders when a brush-pen-shaped lance appeared out of nowhere, clearly visible in the darkness. A voice cried out, "Here it goes," and the lance flew right toward Yin Zong's heart but then broke with a snap. This is what had happened: A patrolman had been making his rounds on the other side of the wall when he saw a big man with a knife vault over the wall and put a woman on his back. The patrolman thrust his lance forward, but Yin Zong dodged, and the lance lodged in the wall. While the patrolman was struggling to pull out the lance, Yin Zong ran off with Wan Xiuniang on his back, his broadsword in hand.

While they were making their way to his home, Yin Zong told Wan Xiuniang, "My mother doesn't like strangers in the house. So, when you get to my home, you'll have to tell her about what has happened."

"All right," said Wan Xiuniang.

When she heard the much-awaited footsteps of her son, Yin Zong's mother said, "So, my son's back!" She opened the door and reached out for him, delighted to see that he appeared to be carrying some stolen goods on his back. Upon realizing that he was transporting a woman, she picked up a staff and began hitting him, without bothering to ask for an explanation. It was not until she had hit him three or four times that she said, "I told you to steal something for me. Didn't you have anything better to do than bring home a woman?"

Thus beaten, Yin Zong dared not speak up. Having witnessed the beating, Wan Xiuniang also grew afraid. Yin Zong put her down and made her bow to his mother. Wan Xiuniang then told the old lady what had happened, adding, "I'm very grateful to Yin Zong for saving my life."

"Why didn't you mention this earlier?" said the old lady.

Yin Zong then requested permission to escort Wan Xiuniang home.

"How are you going to do that?" asked the old lady.

Yin Zong explained, "All along the way, we'll claim to be brother and sister, and we'll announce ourselves as such when we stay at inns."

"Let me tell you something," said the old lady as she went into her room. When she reemerged, she had in her hands an old, much patched red vest, which she put on Wan Xiuniang. To Yin Zong, she said, pointing a finger at him, "You'll be seeing me when you see this vest. Remember not to do anything foolish to this woman." (*A good mother.*) After Wan Xiuniang bade farewell to the old lady, Yin Zong put her on his back and set off for Xiangyang Prefecture.

That evening, they entered the first inn they saw and asked for a room and a meal. Wan Xiuniang slept in the bed, while Yin Zong slept on the floor in front of the bed. At about the third watch of the night, Wan Xiuniang lay awake, thinking, "By his kindness in saving my life, Yin Zong is like a parent who has given me another life. I'll have to marry him as a way of showing my gratitude."

She got down from the bed, gently shook Yin Zong awake, and said, "Older brother, I'd like to have a word with you. You saved my life, but I have nothing with which to thank you. I wonder what you might think of an idea of mine."

Picking up his broadsword, Yin Zong replied, "You're not thinking of doing anything foolish?" (*An upright man.*)

Wan Xiuniang thought, "I'll marry him when I get home. Surely he's not one to do anything foolish." As he was a filial son accustomed to obeying his mother,

Yin Zong was indeed not one to do anything foolish. But seeing how fierce he looked, Wan Xiuniang said instead, "Brother, when we get to Xiangyang Prefecture, I'm afraid you'll have to see my parents."

"It won't come to that. Don't worry. When we get there, I'll turn back, and you go home by yourself."

The next day, Yin Zong resumed the journey, carrying Wan Xiuniang on his back. When they were only about five to seven li from Xiangyang, truly,

They saw the city wall looming ahead
And heard string and pipe music borne on the wind.

As they drew near the city, a rain suddenly began to fall.

Clouds gathered in the northeast;
A fog rolled in from the southwest.
In a trice, a rain came pelting down,
Like a river descending from above.

There was no shelter to be found in the persistent rain, so Yin Zong continued onward, with Wan Xiuniang on his back. When a farmstead came into view, they headed for it to take shelter from the rain. Because they went to this farmstead,

She fell back into misery when almost free;
He became a graveless ghost in an alien land.

Yin Zong was doing nothing short of driving a cartful of his luckless bones right into a well ten thousand feet deep, for this was the very farmstead belonging to Big Characters Jiao Ji. When she recognized the house, Wan Xiuniang was dumbfounded, at a loss what to do. The sight of Wan Xiuniang also confused Jiao Ji. While he was debating with himself whether or not to ask why she was here, a man who was more than half drunk was seen approaching with a broadsword in his hand. Wan Xiuniang burst out, "Older Brother, that's the very Ten Dragons Miao Zhong who abducted me!"

At this revelation, Yin Zong dashed toward Miao Zhong, his hand on his broadsword, and Miao Zhong stepped forward to meet him, broadsword in hand. The fact of the matter was that Yin Zong was not going to be defeated for three reasons: First, Miao Zhong was drunk. Second, Miao Zhong had been caught off guard, whereas Yin Zong was prepared to kill. Third, Miao Zhong, being on the wrong side of the law, was panic prone. Knowing that he was no match for Yin Zong, Miao Zhong turned and, sword in hand, showed a clean pair of heels. Yin Zong gave chase, holding onto his own sword. After about a li, Miao Zhong came to a fence in the fields and climbed over it. (*Don't ever go after a man in desperate straits.*) Yin Zong was so intent on running after Miao Zhong that he was unaware of Big Characters Jiao Ji following behind, similarly equipped with a broadsword. Yin Zong was struck dead. Truly,

The mantis stalks the cicada,
Unaware of the evil-intentioned oriole;
In its turn, the oriole stalks the mantis,
Unaware of the catapult aimed at itself.

How was Yin Zong to fend off two men?

Before long, Jiao Ji turned back, followed by Miao Zhong. The latter put down his broadsword and picked up a pointed knife with a short handle and a long, sharp blade with his right hand. With his left hand, he grabbed Wan Xiuniang by her upper garment and cursed, "You slut! It's all your fault that I was almost killed by that man. Now take a couple of stabs from my knife!" Truly,

With a hand that had crushed many a flower,
He was about to break off the prettiest plum twig.

At the sight of Miao Zhong's knife raised high in the air, Wan Xiuniang had a sudden flash of inspiration. She held his wrist and said, "Stop! You've got it all wrong! You don't know the facts! I had no idea who that big man was or what kind of a man he was either. He put me on his back and carried me off without a word of explanation. When he happened to head in the direction of this house, I recognized it as Jiao Ji's home, so I deliberately told him to approach the house, meaning to look for you. Now wouldn't you be making a mistake if you killed me?" (*How quick-witted she is in a desperate situation!*)

"You've got a point there," said Miao Zhong. As he put his knife back into its sheath, he remarked teasingly, "So, I almost wronged you!" Before he had quite finished, Wan Xiuniang seized him with her left hand and boxed him on the ear with her right hand. It was as loud as a thunderclap. Miao Zhong

Opened his eyes wide and
Gnashed his teeth in a rage.

To the angry Miao Zhong, Wan Xiuniang said, "You brute! I have an eighty-year-old mother at home. By joining Jiao Ji in killing me, you will come to no good end!" With that, she fell flat on the ground. Only then did Miao Zhong realize that Yin Zhong had attached his soul to Xiuniang's body. Right away, he helped her up and revived her. Nothing more of note happened.

In the meantime, Squire Wan learned that his son and Zhou Ji the servant had been murdered, their bodies abandoned in the Wulitou woods outside the city. He also found out that the robbers had made off with goods worth more than ten thousand in cash and that Wan Xiuniang had disappeared. The squire reported the case to the Xiangyang prefectural yamen. A thousand strings of cash were offered as a reward for the capture of the murderers and robbers, but no trace of them was found. Squire Wan added a thousand strings of his own, but several months went by without a clue. The reward offered by the prefectural yamen and Squire Wan increased to three thousand strings of cash in total. "Wanted" posters were put up, but still, the criminals were not found.

Squire Wan had a neighbor, an old man of seventy-odd years who had a son nicknamed Brother He. One day, the old man said, "Brother He, if you go on being as lazy as you are, you'll never make anything of yourself. Now, why don't you go to a dealer today and buy some miniature mountain pavilions to sell?"

Carrying two bags across his shoulders, and two hundred to three hundred in cash in his pocket, Brother He went to see Jiao Ji the dealer to buy some goods that he could sell. What did he buy?

Miniature mountain pavilions, temples, pagodas, stone bridges, screens,
and human figurines.

After buying the items, Brother He said, "I need more pavilions of better design."

Big Characters Jiao Ji replied, "Just go to the corner outside the window and take your pick."

So Brother He went outside. He was busily picking toy pavilions when he heard a voice on the other side of the window whispering, "Brother He!"

He thought the voice resembled that of Squire Wan's daughter and asked, "Who's that?"

"It's me, Wan Xiuniang."

"What are you doing here, young lady?"

"It's a long story. Iron Monk Tao led the others in abducting me and bringing me here. When you go back, please tell my parents to have the authorities send police to arrest Big Characters Jiao Ji, Ten Dragons Miao Zhong, and that Iron Monk Tao. Let me give you something to show my parents." So saying, she untied an embroidered sachet that she had with her, slid it through the window, and turned away. (*Xiuniang plans her every move with care.*)

Brother He caught it and hid it under his waistband. As soon as he had paid Jiao Ji for the items, he picked up his load and was ready to go when Jiao Ji asked, "Were you talking with someone by the window, you lowlife? Who was it?"

Brother He was so frightened that

The eight pieces of his skull opened up;
Half a bucket of ice and snow poured in.

Putting down his load of goods, he said to Jiao Ji, "What did you see that made you think I was talking with someone?"

Jiao Ji stretched his neck to look inside the window but saw no one there, whereupon Brother He picked up his load and left. With never a pause, he went straight to the city and threw the load into the river, miniature pavilions and all. In great strides, his arms waving in the air, he strutted his way back home.

"Where are the mountain pavilions?" his father demanded, noticing his empty hands.

"I dumped them into the river."

"Where's the load?"

"I threw it into the river."

"Where's the carrying pole?"

"In the river, too!"

His father flared up. "Now this boy needs a beating! What do you mean by doing that?"

"You're in for a reward of three thousand strings of cash!"

"How's that?"

"I saw Wang Xiuniang, Squire Wan's daughter."

"Don't let your tongue run away with you! But where is she?"

At this point, Brother He took out the embroidered sachet and showed it to his father. The two then went together to Squire Wan's house. After hearing their account and seeing the sachet, Squire Wan called for his wife, who recognized her daughter's needlework on the sachet. The entire family burst into sobs. "Don't cry," said the squire before going with Brother He to the prefectural yamen to report the case. Without a moment's delay, the authorities dispatched more than twenty locally recruited soldiers, all armed, to arrest the criminals. Brother He was told to lead them to Miao Zhong's house. They signed their pledge in court, chanted a farewell, and set out on their mission. Truly,

Everyone was as fierce as a tiger;
All were as ferocious as dragons.
Rain gear, hemp sandals, and bags on their shoulders,
Spears, forks, swords, bows, and arrows in hand,
They stopped only for food and drink;
They rested by night and traveled by day.
Passing apricot blossom villages
And ferry crossings with patches of tender green,
They pressed onward like black hawks after young swallows,
Like hungry tigers after helpless sheep.

Upon arriving at Miao Zhong's farmstead, Brother He told the officers, "Don't do anything yet. Let me go in first and find out how things are."

When he had been gone for quite a while, the officers consulted one another, saying, "Miao Zhong must have got wind of this and hidden himself somewhere." But Brother He came back at this point. He whispered to the men, "We'll have to think of a trick to make him come out."

After searching all through and around the house without finding any trace of the man, the officers said, "Doesn't that Miao Zhong always act like a parent to Brother He whenever the boy comes to his house? What could have happened this time?" They put their heads together and came up with a trick. They sent a man to set fire to Miao Zhong's house so that Miao Zhong's whereabouts would then be exposed. As soon as he saw the officers setting fire to the house, Miao Zhong came out of hiding and raced off in a westerly direction, broadsword in hand. The officers gave chase, like

Black hawks chasing a desperate wild goose,
White falcons pouncing on a turtledove.

Terrified, Ten Dragons Miao Zhong sprinted into a grove of trees. There, before he had taken ten steps, he saw a big man with bloodstains all over his body waiting for him, holding a broadsword in his hand. It was none other than Filial Son Yin Zong, whom he had murdered. Indeed,

Take this advice: Never make enemies.
You're bound to run into them, face to face.

Recognizing Yin Zong, Miao Zhong tried to slip away, but Yin Zong blocked his path. Miao Zhong could not turn back, either, because the officers had caught up with him. They tied up Miao Zhong as well as Big Characters Jiao Ji and teahouse waiter Iron Monk Tao and marched them to the Xiangyang prefectural yamen, where they were taken into the office of interrogation. Under torture, all three confessed.

On that same day, Big Characters Jiao Ji, Ten Dragons Miao Zhong, and teahouse waiter Iron Monk Tao were taken under guard to the marketplace to be executed in accordance with the law. Brother He received the reward of three thousand strings of cash. Squire Wan, out of gratitude for Filial Son Yin Zong, sent for Yin's mother and offered to support her in his home for the rest of her life. (*A most just thing to do.*) He then filed a request with the yamen and, using his own funds, had a temple erected in Yin Zong's honor at Wulitou, outside the Xiangyang prefectural seat. The Temple of Filial Piety and Righteousness in Wulitou outside of Xiangyang is this very one, a historic site that has never been short of worshipers making offerings. This story has been titled "Miniature Pavilions" and "The Story of Ten Dragons, Iron Monk Tao, and Filial Son Yin Zong." A later poet wrote these well-chosen words:

Squire Wan's meanness led to the tragedy;
Iron Monk Tao did a foul deed in desperation.
Xiuniang endured misery to seek revenge;
Filial Son Yin Zong died and was honored as a god.

38

Jiang Shuzhen Dies in Fulfillment of a Love Bird Prophecy

The love in eyes and hearts never dies;
Furtively, the lovers arrange their trysts.
With marriage beyond reach in this lifetime on earth,
I am seized with feelings of gloom.
Throughout the long nights, my shawl keeps my knees warm;
In low spirits, I play with my jade hairpin.
The cherry blossoms gone, the pear blossoms bloom;
Both are stricken with the gut-wrenching grief of youth.

The above poem is about passion and physical charm, which are, in fact, one and the same in both substance and function. Thus, when physical charm pleases the eye, passion arises from the heart. With passion and physical charm reinforcing each other, the eye and the heart find themselves in greater accord. This is a fact that no worthy gentleman has ever been able to ignore since time immemorial. Someone in Jin times said, "Passion is at its highest in people like me."[1] Also, Monk Huiyuan said, "Passion and physical charm go together, the way a magnet and a needle do. If this applies even to inanimate objects, how much truer is it for one like me, who goes about his daily work immersed in passion?"[2]

Now, why all this talk about passion and physical charm? Well, because this brings me to a story about a Mr. Wu Gongye of Linhuai County [in what is now Anhui Province], who was an adjutant in the Henan prefectural yamen during the Xiantong reign period [860–73]. He had a beloved concubine named Feiyan, née Bu, who was so delicate in beauty and bearing that she appeared hardly able to withstand the weight of her silk and satin clothes. Being also proficient in the music of the Qin region [in present-day Shanxi and Gansu Provinces] and well versed in poetry and prose, she was much treasured by Gongye. Next to their house lived a Zhao family from Tianshui County [in what is now Gansu Province], also of a distinguished status. The son of the family, Zhao Xiang, was a handsome young man with literary talent.

One day, he caught sight of Feiyan through a crack in the south fence wall, a sight that made him lovesick. His spirits sank, and his appetite vanished. He gave Gongye's doorkeeper a handsome bribe and told him to convey his sentiments to Feiyan. The doorkeeper was reluctant at first, but the bribe helped him make up his mind. (*Is there anything under the sun that bribery cannot ruin?*) He so instructed his wife, who seized a convenient moment and conveyed Zhao Xiang's sentiments to Feiyan. Feiyan smiled but did not give a verbal response. Upon hearing the report from the doorkeeper's wife, Zhao Xiang went into such raptures that he hardly knew what to do. He took a piece of fancy stationery paper and wrote on it the following quatrain:

The green paled, the red dimmed, an evening mist arose;
In my small yard I nurse my sorrows, all alone.
To whom can I talk in the deep, lovely night?
The Milky Way parts the stars in the moonlit sky. (Words of love.)

He sealed the letter and asked the doorkeeper's wife to deliver it to Feiyan. After reading it, Feiyan sighed for a considerable while before saying to the doorkeeper's wife, "I've also caught a glimpse of Mr. Zhao, a most handsome man. It's my misfortune that I won't be able to marry such a man in this life. My husband is an uncouth military man with no outstanding qualities." By way of a reply, she wrote a quatrain on a piece of gold-traced stationery with floral patterns. The poem said,

Spring swallows build their nests on the eaves;
Love birds by the water never fly alone.
Ruefully I watch maidens of Peach Blossom Spring
Casually send their lovers home midst the flowers.

She sealed the poem and had the doorkeeper's wife take it to Zhao Xiang, who, upon reading it, said joyfully, "My wish will be granted." He then spent his time sitting quietly, burning incense, praying, and waiting.

One evening several days later, the doorkeeper's wife walked hurriedly up to him, greeted him jovially, and said, "Mr. Zhao, are you ready to see the beauty?"

Astonished, Zhao Xiang shot a series of questions at her, and she relayed the following message from Feiyan: "My husband is on duty tonight at the yamen. This is a good opportunity. My back garden is connected to your front yard, and I will be waiting for you, if you have not changed your mind."

Soon, it grew pitch-dark. Zhao Xiang climbed up the wall on a ladder, to find that Feiyan had already stacked two stools, one atop the other, on her side of the wall for his convenience. Once he was on the other side, a gorgeously dressed Feiyan came out to lead him to her chamber, where they went to bed, hand in hand, and fulfilled their desires to the utmost.

At dawn, Zhao Xiang said, holding Feiyan's hands, "With your beauty matching my talent, I have already vowed to the gods to devote the rest of my life to your pleasure." With that, he stealthily went back the way he had come. Henceforth, at least once every ten days, he slipped into the backyard for a tryst at which they brought their love to fulfillment, believing they were observed by none and aided by humans and gods.

After a year had gone by in this fashion, it so happened that Feiyan beat her maid on several occasions for some trivial offenses. Resentful, the maid seized an opportunity to inform on her to Gongye. (*Is there anything in the world that anger cannot ruin?*)

"Keep quiet!" said Gongye. "Let me see for myself."

When his turn for night duty came up again, he secretly asked for a leave of absence. When darkness fell, he left for the yamen as usual but turned back and hid behind the gate. At the strike of the evening watch, he tiptoed along the wall to the backyard, where he saw Feiyan leaning against the window, moaning softly, and Zhao Xiang ogling her over the wall. In a rage, Gongye dashed forward to get Zhao Xiang, who sensed danger and fled. Gongye tried to grab him but managed only to tear off a piece of his shirt. He went back into the house and summoned Feiyan for questioning. She turned pale but refused to tell the truth. His rage mounting, Gongye tied her to a post and flogged her till blood flowed, but Feiyan said only, "I loved him in life, and I shall have no regrets in death." With that, she drank a cup of water and died. (*Poor thing!*)

As for Zhao Xiang, he left home and lived the life of a fugitive, using a disguise and an alias so as to avoid trouble. How sad that the rain stopped, the clouds dispersed, the flowers withered, and the moon waned! Those like Zhao Xiang who have enough good sense to extricate themselves from the tiger's mouth and get out of harm's way may well be prone to repentance. (*But Zhao Xiang would know no peace for the rest of his life.*[3])

Now, let me tell of another young man, one without much sense, who also got himself involved in an adulterous affair with a woman that ended in tragedy after many days and nights of joy. Lives were taken by the sword, and souls traveled to the netherworld. He left his mother and his wife with no means of support, his son crying from the cold of the severe winter, and his daughter whimpering with hunger the whole day long. Come to think of it, when all's calm and quiet, was the affair worth it if she was to bring him to such ruin? (*An observation quite to the point.*) Truly,

> *Beauty is but a sword in disguise*
> *Which kills off all dissolute men.*

Storyteller, where did that woman live? What was her name?

Well, she was born of a Jiang family in a village outside of Wulin Gate, Hangzhou Prefecture, Zhejiang. Her pet name was Shuzhen, and she was a girl fair to look upon, with cheeks as pink as peach blossoms and eyebrows as fine and arching as willow leaves. Born with a sharp mind and deft hands, she was most adept at embroidery, able to fashion clothes out of snow and clouds. She was also a romantically inclined girl and had a capacity for wine, too. (*Good description of lowly women. An effective pen.*)

When Shuzhen came of age, her parents began to seek marriage proposals for her but could not find the right one. In her longing for romance, she commiserated with spring and felt deep melancholy over wasting her youth in a loveless life. She did not even bother to roll up her curtains, to the regret of the flitting pairs of young swallows. She confined herself lazily to her chamber, in no mood to listen to the chirping of the orioles. When would her wish ever be granted? I have composed ten lyric poems to the sad tune of "Vinegar Gourd," to be dispersed throughout the story to describe the girl's feelings as the story develops. Please oblige me, my accompanist. Listen to the song before I continue with the story:

Her eyes two pools of sparkling water;
Her golden-lily feet only three inches long.
Her tiny waist lithe as a willow in the spring wind;
Her charms more endearing than those of Hong'er.[4]
The sight of such a bewitching girl
Is enough to send any man into raptures.

Now, why did no distinguished families, no young men of high birth, no scholars or wealthy merchants ever make a proposal of marriage to the Jiang family for their daughter Shuzhen, as pretty and as smart as she was? Well, in fact, the girl was of a queer disposition, much given to painting her eyebrows, shadowing her eyes, and applying heavy rouge and powder. With her long hair done up in a high knot, courtesan style, she spent her time striking poses in her tight-fitting clothes, leaning against the railings, looking as if she was lost in reverie or wreathing her face with smiles for passing pedestrians. Thus she came to be despised by all and sundry in the neighborhood, and the days went relentlessly by, leaving her still unbetrothed in her twenties.

Next door to her family lived a boy called Aqiao, who had not yet quite grown up. He often went to the Jiangs' house to play, little knowing that Shuzhen had set her leering eyes on him some time ago. Since Aqiao had not reached puberty, his parents took nothing amiss and let him visit freely. One day, Aqiao happened to come by while Shuzhen's parents were away. The young woman tricked him into her room and forcibly had her way with him. Suddenly, rapid knocks were heard on the door. Aqiao scurried away in alarm, and Shuzhen's parents were none the wiser upon their return.

As for Shuzhen, she had been burning with desire for such a long time that she found it hard to control herself after this first taste of fulfillment. Aqiao was so shaken upon returning home that he gave up the ghost. (*One life gone.*) For all her heart-piercing grief upon hearing the news, the young woman dared not show it on her face. And now, I beg my partner to accompany me on my next song:

Her fine brows furrowed, her heart heavy with sorrow,
She grieved over the death of the one in her heart.
All too soon, the clouds and rain dispersed;[5]
She missed him sorely after their last encounter.
Overwhelmed by emotions that filled the sky,
She looked forward to seeing him in her dreams.

After Aqiao's death, the young woman's spirits sank. She said to herself, "I'm the one who drove him to an early grave." Day after day, she could not put her mind at ease. In a trice, another month went by.

She was at her toilette one morning when her parents saw her and noticed that she did not look her usual self and was not talking sense. The old man remarked to his wife, "Could it be that Shuzhen has done something she shouldn't have done?" Little did they realize that their daughter's youth was already fading, much like butterflies and bees lose their color after mating, that the flower was beginning to shed its petals and the willow was past its prime.

The mother and father blamed each other. Afraid that their kith and kin would laugh at them, they observed, "As the proverb says, 'A daughter of marriageable age is not to be kept at home.' One who is kept at home is like a package of smuggled salt that you should dispose of as soon as possible. Otherwise, if you wait until a scandal breaks out, it won't reflect well on you." Having thus made up their minds, they asked an Auntie Wang to be the matchmaker, saying, "We won't be too picky. We'll try to be more accommodating and just marry her off."

One day, Auntie Wang brought a marriage proposal from Li Erlang of a neighboring village. Li Erlang, a farmhand more than forty years of age, was looking for no other qualities in a wife than beauty. After Miss Jiang crossed his threshold, the new couple got along very well.

In the twinkling of an eye, more than ten years went by. The nightly torments left Li Erlang so exhausted that he lost all interest in that business when he was only in his fifties. (*Old men with young wives, take warning from this!*) However, the young woman, now in the prime of her life, was so addicted to her pleasures that she started an affair with the tutor hired by her husband's family. No sooner had Li Erlang found out about the affair than a chronic illness flared up, and he died. (*Two lives gone.*) So Shuzhen had two human lives on her hands. I beg my partner to accompany me again on my next song:

Her married life lasted more than ten years;
She had three partners in passion.
Out of the blue, calamity struck,
Landing her in dire misery.
A pair of phoenixes now parted,
She leans tearfully against the railings, wordless.

Li Erlang's older brother, Li Dalang, fired the tutor and buried his brother's coffin on a chosen day. As required, Shuzhen was in mourning for three years. Knowing what she had done, the Li family kept her under watch, but the woman dared not do anything wild, because of her guilty feelings. Those were days of immense suffering for her. Members of the Li family paid no attention to her needs, caring not if her stomach was full or empty. After more than a year, Li Dalang saw no good reason for keeping her any longer and decided to send her back to her parents so as to forestall any more scandals that would disgrace the family. So he summoned the matchmaker to announce the marriage null and void and ousted Shuzhen without allowing her to take any of her belongings. Feeling as free as a bird out of the cage and a fish out of the net, she did not mind the loss of her possessions. Upon her return home, her parents felt obliged to let her stay, but they treated her none too politely, ordering her about as they would a servant. Even so, she had no complaints.

One day, a Mr. Zhang passed the house and happened to catch a glimpse of her. He was smitten. He sought the services of a matchmaker and proposed that Shuzhen become his second wife, his first wife having died. Shuzhen's parents gave their consent, for they were only too glad to push her out of the house. Mr. Zhang, a traveling merchant who was more often on the road than at home, did not investigate her background but rushed into preparations for gifts and a feast, and, on a chosen auspicious day, the wedding took place. It would have been all right if the woman had not gone to Mr. Zhang, but as she did, she was:

Like pigs and sheep on their way to the slaughterhouse,
With each step she drew nearer to her death.

That night, the bride and groom sat at the grand feast, in the light of carved candles amid the fragrance of the hall. Under cover of the embroidered brocade quilt, both revealed what had certainly not been unused before. I beg my partner to accompany me on my next song:

With the moon joyously at its fullest,
And the flowers cheerfully in bloom,
Hand in hand, they merrily go to bed.
Their desires fulfilled, they drift off to sleep,
Relaxed and soothed from head to toe,
Overjoyed by this second chance at married life.

After the wedding night, the two sat shoulder to shoulder during the day and slept thigh to thigh at night, as happy in their union as fish in water, as inseparable as lacquer and glue. One forgot all about her late husband's tender love; the other could hardly recall the face of his deceased wife. The woman was impressed by the man's wealth; the man was captivated by the woman's charms.

After living in this manner for one month, Mr. Zhang rose from bed one morning and told his servant to pack his luggage, for he had to travel to Deqing to collect debts. Over Shuzhen's objections, he got ready for the journey. As the tears trickled down her cheeks, Mr. Zhang said, "This isn't necessary between husband and wife." With that, they took leave of each other.

About half a month after his departure, Shuzhen, who had not enjoyed her newlywed life to an extent that made up for her prolonged celibacy, began to find her loneliness too hard to bear. Listlessly, she went to the door to look around and saw, in the shop across the street, a young man in his thirties, handsome and graceful of bearing. She asked a servant, Aman, who the man was. Aman replied, "It's Zhu Bingzhong, owner of the shop and a very nice man. Everybody calls him Second Brother Zhu."

The woman went upstairs to retire for the night without bothering to eat supper. A canal ran by her house, and under her window was a berth for boats. At about the second watch of the night, a fisherman's impromptu song came faintly to her ears. She listened intently and heard these lines:

With twenty gone, twenty-one sets in;
How stupid not to have some romance!
After your beauty is faded and gone,
No man will come to you, however hard you try.

Her desires stirring again, Shuzhen often went to lean against the door. Zhu Bingzhong came over from time to time for a few flirtatious exchanges. Their eyes conveyed their admiration for each other, but to their chagrin, they were never able to have a good talk. I beg my partner to accompany me in the following song:

His cheeks full and glowing,
His hair long and shiny,
He spent half his life on wine and romance;
He told nothing but lies to people's faces.
He stayed away from honor and dignity
And busied himself with clandestine love affairs.

Shuzhen yearned for Zhu Bingzhong with all her heart, but she could find no opportunity to do anything about it. One day, Mr. Zhang returned from his debt-collecting trip. Husband and wife greeted each other and engaged in the usual small talk necessitated by their days of separation. Wearing an ever so slightly displeased look, Shuzhen forced herself to play up to him, but she had her whole heart set on Zhu Bingzhong.

Mr. Zhang stayed at home for more than a month, until mid-winter, when he began purchasing goods in preparation for the upcoming New Year festival. Then he hired a boat and set out again, the boat laden with goods. But the transactions did not turn out well, as all the goods were given out on credit while old debts remained outstanding. With the New Year approaching, he was unable to return home for the holidays and contented himself with sending money home for household expenditures.

Let us leave him for the moment and come to Zhu Bingzhong, who took advantage of the husband's absence to pay a visit to the woman, ostensibly to offer his New Year's greetings. After a few cups of wine, they felt quite disposed to engage in some amorous adventure, but with too many visitors coming and going, Shuzhen slipped him an invitation to a rendezvous on the night of the Lantern Festival.[6] Bingzhong accepted and took leave of her.

In the snap of a finger, the thirteenth day of the first month of the year rolled around. It was the first day of the festival, when lanterns were hung, and every household celebrated the occasion by beating gongs and drums and playing flutes and string instruments. Sightseers sang and tapped the ground with their feet to mark the rhythm; graceful maidens danced, fluttering their long sleeves. Lanterns were piled up like hills that rose to the sky. Strands of fragrant incense drifted over the gaily decorated streets. The houses and gardens were aglow with candles. The towers and pavilions glittered under the lanterns. I beg my partner to accompany me in my next song:

Amid charming strains of music,
Water lilies bloom in the ponds.
The streets and fairs swarm with people,
Laughter fills the town joyous with the advent of spring.
Lovers wait for each other by the lanterns,
Afraid they will be missed if they turn away.

That night, Bingzhong eagerly changed into nicer clothes and shoes and strutted up and down the streets. Shuzhen also displayed herself at her door. Inwardly delighted to be seeing each other, they were determined to plunge into action without delay. All too unexpectedly, Shuzhen's mother, out to view the lanterns, dropped by to see her. Shuzhen had no choice but to invite the old lady in and put her up for the night. Bingzhong waited until night fell and gloomily returned home to sleep. The next night went by in the same way. When he happened to run into Shuzhen, he asked her why she had failed to keep the appointment. While he was speaking, he moved closer and kissed her on the lips before bidding her good-bye. (*The proverb says "The road to happiness never runs smooth." It applies to this case of debauchery as well!*)

Soon thereafter, as she offered wine to her mother, the latter remarked, noticing her listlessness, "Now that you've raised your station in life, you should be content with what you have and try to be a credit to your parents." Little did she know that her daughter had arranged an assignation that she had failed to keep for two consecutive evenings out of sheer bad luck.

The next morning, Shuzhen bought two boxes of pastry, hired a sedan-chair, and saw her mother off. As evening began to close in, Bingzhong slipped into her home when the coast was clear, and went up the stairs. Without bothering to light the lamp, Shuzhen took off her clothes and joined him in a union of delight. So far, the men with whom she had indulged herself were either too young or too old, with little knowledge of the secrets of lovemaking. This new experience shattered her and left her with a feeling of floating lightness, the sweetness of which was beyond words. Zhu Bingzhong, being the rake that he was, knew all there was to know about the ten tricks of the trade as far as women were concerned. Which ten?

First, act wild. Second, don't begrudge time and effort. Third, be generous with sweet, honeyed words. Fourth, be soft and gentle. Fifth, be persistent. Sixth, put the lance to good use. Seventh, act the fool. Eighth, have friends. Ninth, dress well. Tenth, be all affability. In order to captivate a bewitching woman, anything less than all ten tricks would not do.

But let us get on with our story. After Bingzhong left, Mr. Zhang came back again. Shuzhen was left to suffer the pangs of stifled longing, which would not go away unless she saw her lover again. I beg my partner to accompany me in my next song:

The army taps announced the onset of evening,
Bringing tears of sadness down the cheeks.
The longing traveled to the corners of the earth,
Making the heart itch in mysterious ways.
Unable to be in his arms,
She found herself weighed down with sorrow.

Having enjoyed herself to the fullest the other night, Shuzhen had asked for another rendezvous, hoping that the pleasure would last tens of nights. When her husband returned home all to unexpectedly, she was plunged into such low spirits that she fell ill with a headache and a stomachache. Her bones burned, but her body felt cold. Mr. Zhang had been eagerly looking forward to coming home for some rest and diversion. Witnessing his wife's illness, he became so worried that he engaged physicians to treat her and priests to make offerings to the gods. He tasted the medicinal soup before serving it to her and attended her day and night without ever taking off his clothes for a good sleep, working harder than he did on his business trips.

In the meantime, thoughts of Shuzhen made Bingzhong restless. On some excuse, he went to see Mr. Zhang, saying, "I've been remiss in my services to you, sir. I heard yesterday that you had returned home. That's why I'm here to pay you my respects and also to invite you to my humble home for lunch tomorrow. I will lay out some simple fare by way of welcome. Please do not turn me down!"

The next day, Mr. Zhang duly went to Bingzhong's house for dinner, in the course of which Bingzhong had his wife and daughter ply Mr. Zhang with so much wine that he drank himself into a stupor and had to be supported by his arms when he went back home. Mr. Zhang then reciprocated with an invitation to Bingzhong, and so the comings and goings went on. (*He gave in order to take. He did not expect reciprocation.*)

Whenever she learned that Bingzhong would be at the table, Shuzhen would talk and laugh, all her illness forgotten. If he did not show up, she would moan and scream, to the irritation of the neighbors. Mr. Zhang was hoping she would get better, but instead, her condition worsened day by day. As soon as she closed her eyes, Aqiao and Second Brother Li appeared, demanding that she pay them back with her life. As they grew fiercer and fiercer, the woman got afraid. Finding it difficult to tell the truth, she said to her husband, "Please consult a fortune-teller as to when I will recover."

Accordingly, Mr. Zhang sought the services of a fortune-teller, who did a divination and said, "This is an almost hopeless case. She has on her hands the deaths of two men, one young and one old. Actually, the grievances go back to a previous life. Tonight, you may prepare some offerings in the way of wine, fruit, and paper clothes for the dead and lay them out in a westerly direction at midnight. If you pray hard enough, she may have a chance. Otherwise, her time has come." I beg my partner to accompany me in my next song:

They come to taunt me in my misery
Whenever I'm about to drift off to sleep.
In my illness, my vision goes blurry;
My gaunt frame can hardly hold my perturbed thoughts.
When am I ever to be left alone,
Never to see those foes of mine again? (Not badly written.)

Mr. Zhang was in the middle of his sacrificial services when Shuzhen saw Aqiao and Li Erlang again. Clapping their hands, they said, "We complained against you to heaven and are here to take your life, but, out of consideration for your current husband's sincere pleas on your behalf, we'll give you until the fifth day of the fifth month. We'll see you then, through the help of a certain Zhang, when you are with a certain man." With that, they suddenly disappeared.

That very night, Shuzhen began to feel better. Gradually she regained her health, much to Mr. Zhang's joy. Of this, we shall speak no further.

With Bingzhong frequently visiting the house and bringing gifts, Mr. Zhang began to have misgivings, but he could not be sure. One day, upon returning home from a trip to the city to collect some goods, he stepped through the door and saw Shuzhen and Bingzhong sitting hand in hand. Mr. Zhang recoiled and made some noise, whereupon Bingzhong came out to greet him. Bingzhong and Shuzhen had no idea they had been seen. Mr. Zhang had already been more than half inclined to suspect that something was amiss because of Bingzhong's attentiveness. This encounter fully confirmed his suspicions. He thought to himself, "If I ever catch them in the act, I'll make sure that their dead bodies won't even have a place to be buried!"

He then set off for Deqing on business, arriving on the first day of the fifth month. After depositing his luggage at an inn, he went to a shop and bought a knife, which he then strapped to his waist. On the fourth day of the month, he hurried home under cover of night and hid, but let us leave him there for now.

In the meantime, Shuzhen, burning with desire, sent over one invitation after another for Bingzhong, who was at home nursing some minor illness. On the fifth day of the month, Aman the servant went again to invite him to a rendezvous. Bingzhong forced himself to go.

At Shuzhen's house, a feast has been laid out upstairs, with products of the river as well as the land. There were two plates of fried yellow croakers, two vessels of sautéed pheasants, cups of wine flavored with sweet flag, pyramid-shaped dumplings made of sweet rice, and more dishes of vegetables and fruits than can be enumerated here. The two drank to their hearts' content, totally oblivious to everything around them. I beg my partner to accompany me in the next song:

The cups filled to the brim with green wine,
The candles aglow with bright red flames,
The flowers merging in shadow in the moonlit yard,
They went on till they were the worse for drink.
Forgetting themselves in merry laughter,
They had no idea they'd soon be seen.

In the midst of the drinking, Bingzhong felt his ears burning, his eyelids throbbing, and his heart and flesh quivering. He rose from his seat and asked to be excused. The woman flared up. "No wonder you've been turning down my invitations day after day! How can you treat me so shabbily! So you have a wife. Don't I have a husband? Let me tell you my idea of imitating a pair of mandarin ducks. These are love birds that stay together all the time, whether flying, sleeping, or eating. If you and I can't be a couple in this life, we'll be one in our next lives."

In the olden days, there was a Han Pin who had a most beautiful wife. Both killed themselves when the king tried to take her away by force. In anger, the king had them buried in two separate graves. Later, two trees grew from the graves and merged into one. On top of the tree was seen a pair of mandarin ducks that later flew away, crying sadly. Now, this talk about turning into mandarin ducks would soon prove prophetic. This was a woman who would indulge in wanton debauchery as soon as she recovered from an illness. Truly,

Cats will always steal chickens;
Whores will always steal men.

Knife in hand, Mr. Zhang tiptoed to the door and climbed up a tree to listen to what was going on. The flirtatious talk he heard so enraged him that he threw a brick into the window. Shuzhen blew out the lamp and quieted down. After the third brick, she told Bingzhong to go to sleep first, adding, "I'll go take a quick look." (*Good detail.*) Aman the servant led the way, holding a candle, and opened the front gate, but nothing suspicious was seen. The woman cried out, "Today being the Dragon Boat Festival, who would begrudge themselves a few cups of *xionghuang* wine?"[7]

Before she could go on, Mr. Zhang leaped down from the tree and roared, "You slut! With whom were you drinking at this time of the night?"

Trembling all over with fear, the woman could only manage to say, "No! No! No!"

"Follow me upstairs and let me take a look. Everything will be fine if there's no one up there. What are you afraid of?"

At this point, Shuzhen saw Aqiao and Second Brother Li coming toward her again. Knowing that this must be the moment of her death, she stretched out her neck in anticipation of the fatal blow. (*Second Brother Li was fully justified in coming to demand her life. Why should Aqiao tag along?*)

In alarm, Bingzhong, got down from the bed, completely naked, and prostrated himself, saying, "I deserve death! I deserve death! But I'd be happy to offer you all my possessions and my daughter. Please have pity on my aged mother, my young wife, and my little children!"

Turning a deaf ear to his pleas (*A real man!*), Mr. Zhang swung down his knife. Two heads rolled to the ground amid spurting streams of blood. Truly,

They knew not that love would turn to hate;
They know now that lust will bring them death.

When Shuzhen had been ill in bed, she had heard Aqiao and Second Brother Li say, "On the fifth of the fifth month, we'll see you again, through the help of a certain Zhang, when you are with a certain man." Sure enough, she was killed by Mr. Zhang on the fifth day of the fifth month. "A certain man" was a reference to Bingzhong. How fearsome that spiritual beings never fail to foretell the coming of calamity or fortune!

It is a truism that scholars who flaunt their talent lack moral character, and women who flaunt their charms overflow with passion. If they knew how to behave themselves and exercise caution, they could all qualify as gentlemen and ladies of class. Wouldn't that be nice? May all husbands and wives throughout the land remain devoted to each other! Those who have erred should mend their ways; those who have not should be on their guard. It is never too late to observe propriety and decorum. Dear audience, to bring to a conclusion this story about death in fulfillment of a love bird prophecy, let me beg my partner to accompany me in the following song:

The deadly intent of the bricks was all too clear;
The man's entry frightened them even more.
With the sword went all tender feelings of the past

For the one who was unrepentant even to this hour.
With three men dead and gone,
Truly it was retribution divine.

There is also a lyric poem to the tune of “Song of the Southern Country”:

Cuckoos lament the aging of spring;
How sad that the beauty is gone for good.
The lovers perished by the flashing knife;
To the Nine Springs the aggrieved ghosts wafted their way.

The struggle on the verge of death was long and hard,
A result of the karma of previous years.
The scenery the same, the people gone,
The moon waxes and wanes in loving eternity.

39

The Stars of Fortune, Rank, and Longevity Return to Heaven

Those wishing to be immortal, be advised:
Eternal life is nothing but a lie.
Stay away from lust, maintain your good health,
Deceive none, and an immortal you will become.

I cite the above quatrain because this story is about a man who, in spite of twenty years of assiduous study by his window day and night, failed repeatedly at the imperial civil service examinations and, since he thought he was not meant for an official career, accepted his fate and set his heart on becoming an immortal. It was a matter of time, fortune, and fate. This happened in the autumnal eighth month of the fourth year in the Jingde reign period [1004–8] under Emperor Zhenzong, the third emperor of the great Song dynasty. The gentleman of our story was, by now, making a living as a fisherman on the river. There are four things to be said about a fisherman:

He leans backward to pull up the net;
He beats the boat's side to drive in the fish.
He angles peacefully by the shore;
He dances when he casts his net.

Our gentleman lived in Jiangzhou, of Dingjiang District, by the Xunyang River outside of Jiujiang Gate, which was the east gate of Jiangzhou.

The ten-thousand-li Yangzi River sweeps along
And roars like thunder as it flows east to the sea.
With the cold waters defending the city,
There is no need to feed a mighty army.

On the fourteenth night of the eighth month, our gentleman released his fishing boat from its mooring, punted away from the shore, and rowed to the middle of the river, which was brightly lit by the moon. He picked up the net and cast it three times in a row without catching so much as a fish scale. Suddenly, he heard a voice crying, "Liu Bendao, Liu Bendao, why does a worthy man like you not pursue honor and glory but resigns himself to fishing?"

Astonished that he was being addressed in such a familiar way, by his surname plus his given name, he hauled in his net and looked around. Failing to see the slightest trace of a man, he cast the net one more time, and again the voice called out. As before, there was no one in sight. This happened three times. He gave up and rowed his boat back to shore.

The following night, the fifteenth night of the month, when he again rowed the boat to the middle of the river, he heard his name called out as before. Growing impatient, he put down his net and listened intently. The voice came from behind him. He rowed in that direction and traced the voice to the reeds, but when he entered the reeds, he found no one. How very strange! He rowed out of the reeds and into the middle of the river again and cast his net. Feeling the net grow heavy in his hands, he pulled it out of the water, and to his surprise and joy, he saw in the net a five-foot-long golden carp with a red tail.

"Heaven and earth be praised!" said Bendao. "If I sell it in the market tomorrow, I'll get enough food to last me three to five days." He secured the boat to the shore with a rope and put the carp in the water-filled compartment below the deck so as to keep it alive. He then went into the cabin, took off his clothes, and got into bed, but feeling hungry and thirsty, he looked around the boat for something in the way of food and drink, of which there was none. What was to be done? He tossed and turned and thought of buying some wine at the village wineshop of a Mr. Zhang. He picked up a gourd used for holding wine and went ashore, the punt pole under his left arm and the gourd in his right hand.

As he walked along the river in the moonlight, he said to himself, "I wonder if Mr. Zhang has gone to bed or not. If not, I'll knock at his door and go in to buy wine. But if he has gone to sleep, I'll have to spend the night hungry and thirsty." After following the many twists and turns of the road for more than half a li, he saw a house looming ahead. It was Mr. Zhang's house. Upon reaching the door, he peeked inside to see if the house was still lit. And indeed he saw that it was. There is a lyric poem to the tune of "Moon over the West River" in praise of the snuff of the candlewick:

It is not the spring rain that makes it fall,
Nor the east wind that blows it out.
A natural red blossom, it is lovelier
Than those that take hard work to grow.

No butterfly can land on its flame;
No wandering bee will draw near its petals.
In the boudoir, in the quiet of the night,
It keeps the lady company in her dreams of spring.

Finding Mr. Zhang's house with candles still lit, Bendao called out, "Would you still happen to have wine for sale, Mr. Zhang? If you've gone to bed, I won't bother you, but if you haven't, please sell me some."

"This old man is still up," replied Mr. Zhang. So saying, he opened the door, took Mr. Liu's gourd, asked him how much he wanted, and went inside. When he reemerged with the gourd, now filled with wine, he said, "I do still have wine all right, but it's cold."

Bendao said, "I have no money with me now. Tomorrow, after I sell the fish, I'll come back to pay you."

"That's all right," said Mr. Zhang as he closed the door.

Carrying the punt pole under one arm and the gourd in the other hand, Bendao started back to the boat. Hunger got the better of him, and he began drinking the wine even though it was cold. By the time he reached his boat, he had already consumed one fifth of the gourd's contents.

In the bright moonlight, he saw a man not even three feet tall wearing a ball-shaped gauze hat and a wide-sleeved green silk robe. As soon as he saw Bendao, the man burst out in loud sobs. Covering his face with his sleeves, he said, "You captured all my children and grandchildren!"

Bendao was flabbergasted at the sight of this man who looked more like a ghost than any person one was likely to see in these parts. He put down his gourd and swung his pole at the man, crying out, "Here it goes!" As he did, sparks flew about, accompanied by a splashing sound.

Bendao took a good look around. Instead of being on his way to immortality, he almost ended up a stray ghost by the river and a corpse in the waves. There is a poem in testimony:

Many men of worth admire the immortals.
When will they, too, land on Penglai Island?[1]
But immortality lies in the human heart;
Just listen to the song "Fishermen's Pride."
Few fishermen ever learn this truth,
But who ever will if not shown the way?
Those who seek the fish, look no farther;
The magpie bridge leads to immortality.

Bendao could see no trace of the man under three feet tall wearing a ball-shaped gauze hat and wide-sleeved green silk robe. How extraordinary!

Drawing near the spot where he had moored his boat, he gave a mournful shriek. It had disappeared. "Who could have stolen my boat?" he wondered. He looked across the river but there was no sign of life in the dead silence, nor was there a single boat to be seen anywhere. Where was he to spend the rest of the night? He said to himself, "My boat could not have been stolen. I never lost it before in all these years as a fisherman. How strange that it should have disappeared today! If it's the work of a thief, he's from either the lower reaches or the upper reaches of the river."

Instead of going downstream to look for his boat, he drank up the wine in the gourd, tossed the empty gourd aside, and began to walk along the shore. He walked from the second watch until the third watch of the night but saw not the slightest trace of the boat. "Now, where am I going to spend the rest of the night?" he asked himself. He walked blindly ahead without the least knowledge of where he was going in these unfamiliar parts.

A country house came into view, and he went toward it. When he reached the door, he put down his pole, tried to look in, and saw candlelight inside. Since he didn't know how to gain admission to the house, he thought of crying out but hesitated because he did not know who lived in the house. But then again, if he did not cry out, he would have no place to stay for the night. So in the end, he called, "Is anybody home? I am Bendao, a fisherman searching for my lost boat. I have no place to stay for the rest of the night. Would you please let me stay here until tomorrow morning?"

"Coming! Just a moment please!" came a woman's voice from inside the house. She opened the door. Bendao lowered his head, folded his hands, and bowed deeply. The woman returned the greeting, saying, "Please come in, sir. You can stay for the night."

Bendao followed her in with words of thanks, his pole under his arm. After closing the door, the woman led him into the main hall, where she offered him a seat and asked his name. "I'm afraid you might be hungry, sir," said she kindly. "Shall I serve you some wine and food?"

"Thank you. If you could manage to put me up somewhere for the night, I'll be ever so grateful."

"That can easily be done." Before she had quite finished speaking, a voice was heard from outside. "Aya! Aya! I didn't do anything to him, but he had to whack me like that! That man will surely come to this house of mine and ask to be put up for the night."

Alarmed at these words, Bendao said, "Madam, who is outside?"

"It's my older brother."

Bendao ducked into a shadowed spot to observe, and the woman went to open the door. As she called out a greeting to her older brother, he exclaimed, "Aya! Aya! Close the door, Sister, and follow me in." The woman closed the door and offered her brother a seat in the main hall. Upon seeing the man in the main hall, Bendao cried out in anguish, "My time is up!" It was truly a case of "Like pigs and sheep on their way to the slaughterhouse / With each step he draws nearer to his death," as evidenced by the following poem:

He jilted his wife and married another,
One who loved not the son who wasn't her own.

But the first wife survived the second one;
Once an enemy, always an enemy.

Bendao saw that the man in the main hall was none other than the one less than three feet tall wearing a ball-shaped gauze hat and a wide-sleeved green silk robe. "Didn't my blow with the punt pole send him tumbling into the river? Didn't he die? How can I stay in *his* house for the night?" Without bothering to say anything to the woman, Bendao sneaked out the door, the pole under his arm, and ran downriver.

In the meantime, the man in the house said to his sister, "Give me a piece of resin and a bowl of warm wine to ease the pain in my back."

In a little while, the woman brought what he wanted and asked, "What happened to you?"

"Let me tell you. I didn't do anything to that man. I was standing by the river when I saw that fellow coming back with wine. I covered my face and burst into loud sobs, saying, 'You captured all my children and grandchildren.' That brute then hit me with his pole, but I changed into a beam of fire and dived into the water. After he went up the shore, I hid his fishing boat. Unable to find his boat anywhere, he walked along the shore all the way upriver. I don't think he has anywhere to spend the night unless it's in this house. Has he shown up yet, sister?"

"What kind of man is he?"

"He's a fisherman called Liu Bendao."

The woman thought, "So, that gentleman is the one who hit my brother. Well, why don't I cover up for him?" Out loud, she said, "Yes, he did come here, asking to be put up for the night, but I didn't let him stay. He went away. Now, you've had a hard day, Brother. Let me get the bed ready for you."

Along the shore, Liu Bendao forged ahead in great haste from the third watch of the night until what he thought was the fifth watch. His feet sore, his legs aching, he saw a big rock in the moonlight and put his pole down to take a rest. Before long, he heard hurried steps and a voice calling out, "Liu Bendao! Stop! Wait for me!"

Bendao gave a cry of anguish. "Could it be that man, here to seek revenge for the blow I gave him?" He stood up, his pole at the ready.

Soon, as the figure came nearer, he saw that it was the woman from the country house, wearing white clothes. She walked up to him, carrying a parcel, and said, "Why did you go like that? I couldn't find you, so I put my brother to bed and then came to be with you. Don't be afraid. I'm not a ghost or an evil spirit. I'm a regular human being. Look at the seams in my clothes and the shadow I cast under the moon, and listen to my voice! I came all this way to catch up with you."

Bendao put down his pole and asked, "Is there something you came such a distance in the night to tell me?"

"Are you married? If you are, I'll serve you as a concubine. If not, I'll be your wife. I have enough money in the parcel for you to live a good life. What do you say?"

Bendao thought that such a pretty woman plus a parcel filled with valuables were all he could ever wish for. Looking at her, he said, "Thank you. I'm not married."

So saying, he tossed his pole into the river and walked with her until daybreak all the way to Jiangzhou.

Since she was now his wife, the woman said, "Husband, where are we going to settle down?"

"Don't worry. I'll find a place."

While they were walking around in the city, they saw a shop with a sign that said "Gu Yilang's Inn." Bendao walked up and asked, "Who is Gu Yilang?"

The man he had addressed replied, "I am."

"I quarreled with my father, who then drove me and my wife out. We have no place to go and would like to rent a small room from you for a stay of about three to five days. Our relatives will be mediating on our behalf. So when we're reconciled with my father, we'll pay you and go back."

"But where is your wife?" asked Gu Yilang.

"Wife!" Bendao called out. "Come here and meet Mr. Gu."

Gu Yilang led Bendao and his wife to the third room in the south wing of his inn, opened the door, and gave them the key. Bendao was delighted with the room. After lighting a fire and eating their meal, they sold some of the woman's jewelry and bought trunks, bedding, and clothes.

They had stayed for about half a year at the inn, when Bendao said to his wife, "The way we spend money, even a mountain of gold could have disappeared."

"Don't worry!" The woman burst out laughing. She took an object from a trunk and showed it to her husband, saying, "This will last us for the rest of our lives." Indeed,

Don't accuse men of not knowing better;
Women, in fact, are truly smarter.

The woman had taken out a divination tray. When he saw it, Bendao asked his wife what predestined bond between them had brought them together.

The woman launched into this explanation: "My father, when alive, was the prefect of Jiangzhou, named Qi Wenshu. My pet name is Shounu. When my father's term of office expired, we left and were unfortunately caught in a storm while traveling by water. Both my parents died, and so did the servants. The man you beat—the one less than three feet tall wearing a ball-shaped gauze hat and a wide-sleeved green gauze robe—rescued me and took me to his house. That's how I came to honor him as my older brother. Your boat, which you couldn't find, was hidden by him. When he asked me if you had come to the house to stay for the night, I told him a lie because I wanted to marry you.

"You wonder how I've come by this divination tray. Well, in my childhood, I learned three things from my father: First, reading and writing. Second, drawing magic figures and making holy water. Third, telling fortunes and doing divinations. Now, this divination tray will come in handy. Let's go out with Gu Yilang and find a busy marketplace where I can open a fortune-telling shop and make a decent living."

Bendao said thankfully, "I owe everything to you, my good and able wife!"

Right away, they took some money and went with Gu Yilang to South Marketplace. There, they found a spot where they could set up their fortune-telling shop. They bought paper, ink sticks, brush-pens, and ink slabs, hung up a shop sign, and chose an auspicious day on which to open the business. Gu Yilang sat in the shop for a considerable while with Bendao and his wife, who now called herself the Lady in White, before leaving. No clients came that day, nor were they any more successful the next day. By the afternoon of the third day, still with no patrons, Bendao's wife remarked, "I wonder why there's been no business for three days in a row. Someone must be working against me. Go out and see what's going on, and then come back to tell me."

Bendao rose and checked out the neighboring shops but found nothing suspicious. Afterward, he left the marketplace and proceeded to the street, where he saw a crowd. He approached and peered over the onlookers' shoulders. A man with a medicine ladle in his hand was intoning a poem by way of starting his speech:

A small hill that stands five li high
Has paths that lead north, south, east, and west.
Many of those who lose their bearings
Have regained the right path by following my finger.

"Dear audience," he went on to say, "I am a Daoist priest from Mount Wangong. There are three reasons why I left the mountain for Jiangzhou. Now, let this poor priest tell you, gentlemen of inquisitive minds, what the three reasons are. First, having attained proficiency in the skill of alchemy after thirteen years of spiritual cultivation in the mountains, I am here to save people. Second, to find an object. Third, to save everyone in the city of Jiangzhou."

The audience was astounded. The priest went on, laughing, "Without having bought any of my medicine, all of you are already seeing the thing I'm looking for. Do you want to know where it is?" (*In the very person of Bendao.*) Waving above the throng at Bendao, the priest called out, "Come here, young man!"

As Bendao stared at the priest, the latter repeated, "Come here! I have something to tell you." Fearfully, Bendao made his way through the crowd. Clapping his hands, the priest said, "Come and save everyone in the city of Jiangzhou! This poor priest has seen that thing. You may well ask, where is it? It's right here, in the form of this young man."

Everyone was aghast. How could this young man be a thing? The priest continued, "Now, listen up. Young man, there's something dark hidden in your brow, a sign that some evil spirit is haunting you. Tell me the truth."

After Bendao gave an account of how he had met his wife, the priest said, "Listen, everyone! The thing I told you about is none other than that woman! Let me save this man." He took a magic figure out of the yellow parcel on the ground and gave it to Bendao, saying, "Now, go back to the inn, and when you get there, pretend to be drunk and go immediately to your room and to bed. The woman will come back at night. At the third watch of the night, press this figure onto her body, and she'll change into her true form." Thus instructed, Bendao returned to the inn instead of the shop and, pleading drunkenness, went to his own room to sleep.

After waiting in vain for Bendao, the woman closed up shop when evening came. Back at the inn, she asked Gu Yilang in an irritated tone, "Has my husband come back?"

"Your husband got drunk and has been sleeping in your room for quite some time now."

The woman burst out laughing, "So that's what it is." As soon as she laid eyes on Bendao, she gave a shout, startling Bendao. "What a thing you did!" she said. "In all the time we've been married, have I ever done anything to hurt you? Why did you have to believe someone who's determined to turn us against each other? I told you to find out if anyone had been doing anything against my shop in the last three days, and you had to believe a cursed priest and go to bed pretending to be drunk, meaning to press some magic figure on me so as to see me in my true form. I am Prefect Qi's daughter, not an evil spirit! How could you believe such lies and try to help him destroy me! Now, give me that magic figure, and I'll still be your wife. If not, I'll leave you right now."

Bendao took the magic figure from his bosom and gave it to her. After dinner, they went to bed and slept through the night.

The next morning, they rose and ate breakfast. Before leaving the house, the woman said, "Wait! Instead of tending to the shop today, I'll go with you to seek out that beggar of a priest and ask him why he has to use a magic figure to turn husband and wife against each other. Also, I want you to watch me beat him at his own game."

Bendao led the way to South Marketplace, where they saw a crowd gathered around the priest. While the priest was in the middle of an excited speech, the woman parted the crowd with her hands and cried, "You beggar of a priest! Why don't you do your begging somewhere else instead of using some magic figure to try to turn my husband against me? You also told him to put it on me and see me in my true form." Clapping her hands, she continued, "I am the daughter of Commissioner Qi, the former prefect. You all know who my father was. How can I be some evil spirit? Hey, priest! If you play your tricks well, fight it out with me in front of everybody here, and claim victory. If I'm better than you are, then I'll be the winner."

In a rage, the priest picked up his sword and swung it right at the woman's head. The onlookers thought she had been cut down by the sword, but she stood unscathed and raised a finger. The crowd cried out in shock. There is a poem that bears witness:

An evening wind from the east sprang up in the universe.
The alchemist's stove fireless, the wine cups few,
Worthy men failing at their lives' ambitions
Read ancient books by the lamp from time to time.

With her finger raised, the woman cried out, "Stop!" Lo and behold, the priest froze, unable to bring down the sword or raise his hand. The woman said, "My husband and I were happily going about our lives when you gave him a magic figure to destroy me, and now that you can't do anything to me, what do you have to say?"

The priest pleaded, "Madam, please forgive this poor priest! I gave you offense in a moment of foolishness. Please forgive me!" The onlookers burst out laughing. They all turned to the woman with placating words, and she said, "Out of respect for all of you, I'll let that beggar of a priest go." She murmured an incantation, and the sword fell to the ground, to the merriment of the spectators. The priest threaded his way through the throng and was gone. But before the crowd had quite dispersed, the priest reappeared. Could he be coming back to attack the woman? No, he had come to pick up his sword. That done, he left.

After that, the woman's shop was packed with clients from morning to night. She was so busy telling fortunes, performing divinations, drawing magic figures, and giving out holy water that she had no time to spare even for refreshments. Her fame began to spread.

One day, a man leading a sedan-chair came to issue an invitation. "I am a servant of Commissioner Zhao of Jiangzhou. Mr. Zhao Junior has been ill for quite some time. I've been instructed to invite you to see him. This sedan-chair is at your service."

The woman gave her husband a few words of instructions and told him to go back to the inn. She then mounted the sedan-chair and set off for Mr. Zhao's house. She arrived and was shown into the garden, where she saw the young master in a pavilion, talking to himself and smelling of wine. A crowd gathered by the garden gate to watch the Lady in White perform her magic. After her incantations, a strong wind sprang up.

It comes and goes without shape or form;
At its will, flowers bloom and wither.
It sneaks its way up the flower stems.
To whom does it give the stolen fragrance? I wonder.

When the wind died down, a woman in yellow was seen, saying angrily, "Who is trying to make things difficult for me? The temerity!" At the sight of the Lady in White, she bowed deeply and said, "So it's you, my younger sister."

"Why has my older sister come down from the sky?" asked the Lady in White. "But why are you here?"

"I'm here at the invitation of Commissioner Zhao to cure his son and drive away the evil spirit."

Everything would have been all right if the woman had not heard this, but as she did, she said, her eyes opening wide, her jaw firmly set, "You can't even save your husband, let alone other people."

With a gust of wind, the woman in yellow was gone. The Lady in White cured the young master right there in the garden. Commissioner Zhao thanked her with some gifts and had a messenger take them over to Gu Yilang's inn. Upon arriving at the inn, the woman tipped the messenger and dismissed him before she asked Gu Yilang, "Is my husband in the room?"

"Let me tell you something," said Gu Yilang. "A woman in yellow came in, picked him up, opened the skylight, and departed in a southwesterly direction."

"That's all right," said the Lady in White. She shouted, "Rise!" A cloud appeared under her feet. She then rose into the air and began to chase the woman in yellow. When she caught up with her, she cried, "Give me back my husband!"

The one in yellow saw her and shouted, "Down!" She let Liu Bendao down and turned to do battle with the Lady in White.

Bendao did not bother to be concerned about his wife but kept walking until he came to a temple. Seeing a monk standing at the door, Bendao, who was exhausted, asked, "Your Reverence, may I take a rest in the temple?"

The monk replied, "We're busy today! A benefactor is coming to offer us donations." While he spoke, several loads of firewood, several buckets of sauce, and several baskets of rice came into view. There were also fragrant candles, paper utensils for the dead, and money for the prayer services. Under an umbrella, still some distance away, was the same man less than three feet tall wearing a ball-shaped gauze hat and a wide-sleeved green silk robe whom Bendao had encountered before.

As soon as Bendao set eyes on the man, he took to his heels, but the man caught up with him. Holding Bendao tightly, he said, "You are the very person who hit me with a pole! Now that you're in my hands, I'm going to gouge out your heart and liver and eat them with wine."

At this critical moment, the Lady in White appeared. She called out to the man, "Older Brother! Don't be angry! He's my husband."

Before she had quite finished, the woman in yellow also arrived, crying, "Older Brother! Don't listen to her. He's by no means a real husband. Since he hit you, he is also our enemy!"

While the four were tugging and pulling at one another, all tangled up in a heap, an old man walked out of the temple and exclaimed sharply, "Where are your manners? You beasts! Change!"

Immediately the woman in yellow turned into a yellow deer, the man in green changed into a green turtle, and the woman in white became a white crane. The old man, the god of longevity, mounted the white crane and rose into the air. Bendao mounted the yellow deer and followed the god of longevity. With the turtle leading the way, they rose all the way to the sky. (*Liu Bendao had been demoted from his position as an official in the realm of the immortals and was made a poor scholar. That's why the crane and the deer were not afraid of him. The only one with whom he did not get along was the green turtle.*)

Liu Bendao had been an official in the division of longevity in the realm of the immortals. Because he liked playing with the crane, the deer, and the turtle, and neglected his duties, he had been banished to the mortal world, where he became a poverty-stricken scholar. Now that his term of banishment had expired, the god of longevity led him back to heaven. That temple, called the Temple to the God of Longevity, still stands to this day by Xunyang River in Jiangzhou. The poem says,

An immortal untainted by the dust of this world,
He lived with a crane and a deer in the fairyland.
By failing to reveal his true identity,
He misled goodness knows how many mortals.

40

An Iron Tree at Jingyang Palace Subdues Demons

Spring ushers in a riot of colors:
Peach blossoms pink, plums white, and willows green.
Horse carriages come and go at leisure,
Bringing the east wind to the forbidden city.

Finish the wine, intone poems to our hearts' content,
And forget all about fame and fortune.
In reminiscing about past events,
We recall Jingyang's conquest of the water demon.[1]

When the primeval chaos had cleared away and humans and all other living beings on earth began to multiply, there emerged three leading sages who founded three religions. What are the three religions?

One is Confucianism, founded by Confucius, who edited the Six Classics and laid down rules that were to last till the end of time.[2] He is the teacher of all the emperors and kings and the patriarch of all literary writings. This is one.

There is also Buddhism. The Buddha Śākyamuni of the west, born in the kingdom of Śrāvastī [in present-day Nepal] of King Śuddhodana of the Kshatriya caste, illuminated the entire world with his wisdom. His six-foot-tall gilded body was poised upon golden lotus flowers that rose out of the ground, and he could transform himself into whatever shape and size he wanted. For his work of redeeming all living creatures, he was given the epithet Teacher of Heaven and Humans. This is another religion.

Then, there is Daoism. It was founded by Laozi, progenitor of the vital force that gave birth to the sky and the earth, the buddhas and the immortals. Called the Supreme God of Masters of Iron and the Primeval Yang, he metamorphosed into the innumerable grains of sand of the mortal world. In the forty-eighth year of the reign of King Tang of the Shang dynasty, he presented himself to the mortal world again, transforming himself into a pill, which, filled with the essence of the sun, maneuvered itself into the mouth of the Jade Maiden. Soon after she swallowed it, the Jade Maiden knew she was pregnant. In the ninth year of King Wuding's reign, after an eighty-one-year pregnancy, she gave birth through her ribcage to a baby who came to be called Laozi [Old Child] because his hair was white at birth. Having been born under a plum tree, he assumed the surname Li [Plum] and the given name Er, courtesy name Boyang. Later, when he rode on a green buffalo out of the Hangu Pass, Officer Yin Xi, who guarded the pass, knew from the purple aura above him that he was no ordinary man. He sought from Laozi the five-thousand-character *Daodejing* [Tao te ching], which has been handed down from generation to generation. Laozi then went to the desert, where he attained immortality through spiritual cultivation. He now resides in the Grand Pure Fairyland under the title The Daode Heavenly Venerable One. So, that is another religion.

Of the founders of the three religions, only Laozi, the patriarch of Daoism, lives in the Grand Pure Fairyland, where wispy, curling, colorful clouds emit an auspicious air. Once, on the occasion of his birthday, a grand gathering of immortals took place in the palace on the thirty-third layer of heaven. Thousands upon thousands of immortals from the Zhongnan Mountains, the Penglai Mountains, the Langyuan Mountains, the thirty-six caves, and the seventy-two blessed lands descended on the scene of the festivities, borne by wafting clouds and riding on colorful divine birds, white cranes, red dragons, and red phoenixes. One after another, they offered their congratulations along with poems written for the occasion, and they kowtowed, prostrating themselves on the ground in ritualistic tribute. There is in evidence a lyric poem, "Song of the Water Dragon":

Thronging with red clouds and purple canopies,
The palace is filled with dignitaries.
Black cranes and green buffalo come and go
Amid clouds of never-fading colors.
A grand birthday banquet it is,
To honor the Daodejing of eternal fame.

The banquet for the divine immortals
Offers fruits never seen in the world below:
Dates large as melons, peaches of ten thousand years,
And lotus roots ripened over one thousand years.
His age equals that of the universe,
As eternal as the deep, vast oceans.

Delighted by this grand assembly of immortals, present to offer him congratulations, the Venerable Laozi had a banquet set out in their honor. When the company was well warmed with wine, the god of the Gold Star left his seat and said, "Has anyone here heard about what is happening in Jiangxi in the South Jambudvipa Continent? Jiangxi used to be under the jurisdiction of Yuzhang. Four hundred years from now, the region will be dominated by a demon flood-dragon that no one will be able to subdue. By that time, thousands of li of land will be submerged in water."

The Venerable Laozi said, "Yes, I've heard about this. Four hundred years from now, a wizard named Xu Xun will make a name for himself in West Hill in Jiangxi, a hill that is surrounded by water on all sides and is shaped like a coiling dragon and a crouching tiger. He will lead the immortals in wiping out the demons. Now, we must send someone down to the mortal world to choose human beings of impeccable moral integrity and teach them the Daoist arts, so that by the time Xu Xun appears, he will inherit a well-grounded tradition."

Among the guests was an immortal called Wei Hongkang, courtesy name Bochong, King of Filial Piety and Brotherly Love. He stood up and announced, "I have observed in the world down below, a man named Lan Qi, who is a perfect paragon of virtue. Moreover, he has the essence of an immortal within him and will therefore be highly receptive to Daoist arts. He can then transmit the arts to the immortal Reverend Mother, who will, in her turn, teach Xu Xun. Through this chain of person-to-person transmission, Jiangxi will be saved from sinking into the sea. What do you think, everyone?"

"A good idea! A good idea!" said Laozi.

Thereupon, the company of immortals escorted the King of Filial Piety and Brotherly Love to the Jade Emperor's palace in the third layer of heaven. They reported the matter to the Jade Emperor, who approved the request and ordered that officials of the palace give the necessary divine imperial edict to the King of Filial Piety and Brotherly Love. Bidding farewell to the immortals, the king rose on an auspicious cloud. In a trice, he found himself in the world of mortals.

During the Western Han dynasty, there lived a man called Lan Qi, courtesy name Ziyue, in Jiuyuanli of Gaoping, Qufu County, Yanzhou Prefecture. At the time of which we speak, he was already two hundred years old, with white hair and a ruddy complexion, guiding the more than one hundred members of his family in spiritual cultivation. They treated all people with kindness and bore no malice toward any living being. To all and sundry, he was known as Mr. Lan, for no one was presumptuous enough to call him by his given and courtesy names. There was a children's song that said, "Mr. Lan, Mr. Lan, he's connected to heaven, he's saluted by red dragons, he's listed among the stars." That he was an immortal was taken for granted.

One day, Mr. Lan was sitting at a table when a man wearing a casual head-wrap, a Daoist robe, and a pair of cloud-patterned shoes and carrying in his hands a bamboo drum and clappers walked up to him with graceful, unhurried steps. Impressed by the man's air of a Daoist immortal, Mr. Lan rushed down the steps to greet him. After they had seated themselves in their respective places as host and guest and tea was served, Mr. Lan ventured, "May I ask your honorable name?"

The man replied, "I am an immortal from the stars, known as the King of Filial Piety and Brotherly Love, and I am touring the mortal world from the Heaven of Exalted Purity. I'm visiting you, sir, because I have long heard about your devotion to spiritual cultivation and filial piety."

At these words, Mr. Lan bowed deeply and said, "This poor old man is but a lowly mortal being. My devotion to spiritual cultivation and filial piety is limited only to myself. Having done nothing to inspire people throughout the four seas, I hardly deserve the honor of this visit."

Raising Mr. Lan, the King of Filial Piety and Brotherly Love said, "Please sit! Let me tell you about the essence of filial piety and brotherly love."

Mr. Lan half rose from his seat and said, "I beg to be enlightened."

The King of Filial Piety and Brotherly Love launched into the following speech: "The Primordial Vital Force being the Great Way based in the sun, it is the King of Filial Immortals. The First Vital Force being the Profound Way based in the moon, it is the King of Filial Sagaciousness. The Cosmic Vital Force, being the Way of Filial Piety based in the stars, is the King of Filial Piety. When filial piety reaches the heavens, it lends brightness to the sun and the moon. When filial piety reaches the earth, all things on earth grow and thrive. When filial piety reaches the people, benevolence becomes the rule of the land. That is why phoenixes descended to salute the sage-king Shun and Emperor Wen of the Han dynasty, both paragons of filial piety.[3] That is why Jiang Shi and Wang Xiang were blessed with fish to present to their mothers.[4] These examples go to show that filial piety applies to all categories of people, from the emperor down to the lowliest commoner.

"You, sir, having devoted three lifetimes to spiritual cultivation, have achieved perfection and earned yourself a place in the moon with the First Vital Force and the title King of Filial Sagaciousness. Four hundred years from now, in the Jin dynasty, a true immortal named Xu Xun will be born, who will propagate the Way of Filial Piety as the head of all immortals. He will find his place in the sun with the Primordial Vital Force and become King of Filial Immortals."

Thereupon, the King of Filial Piety and Brotherly Love gave Mr. Lan the secrets of immortality, some alchemists' gold pills, magic mirrors, copper and iron tablets (*Copper and iron tablets are instruments for spiritual cultivation*), and incantations originating from the Realm of Exalted Purity that could be used for swift subjugation of demons. He added, "This method is not to be shared lightly with others. You may pass it on only to the morally impeccable Reverend Mother of Huangtang, in Danyang. You may tell her to instruct in her turn young Xu Xun of the Jin dynasty, who, in his eagerness to learn to achieve immortality, will then impart it to Wu Meng and others. With such a sequence, those wishing to transcend the mortal world will find no lack of guidance."

That said, the King of Filial Piety and Brotherly Love rose into the sky on an auspicious cloud as Mr. Lan bowed farewell. Henceforth, Mr. Lan delved into the secrets of the copper and iron tablets and began his alchemical experiments in a chosen spot. The following passage is a description of the alchemical process:

> Black lead is the essence of the sky; white gold the pith of the earth. The black contains the yang of water; the white the vital force of fire. The black

> and the white shoot back and forth, to push yin and yang to their rightful places. The two elements share the same nature and belong to the same category according to *The Book of Alchemy*. The black takes the white as its sky; the white takes the black as its earth. When the yin and the yang become a swirl of chaos, bright golden lotus flowers emerge. The wondrous moonlight fills the cinnabar field,[5] the glow of the rosy clouds brightens the mind. Do not block the aperture to the sky; do not allow the vital force to leak and lose its purity. Practice well the incantations; carefully tend to the temperature. To produce the divine out of the common is the very noblest of all callings. There will be one male product a day, each with a matching partner.

Every member of Mr. Lan's family took his alchemical pills. As a result, those hoary with age regained their black hair, and the tender young abstained from the five grains without feeling hungry. When the news spread, all and sundry knew that the Lans were ready to ascend to the Heaven of Exalted Purity.

There lived, at the time, a fire dragon, the terror of the Yangzi River, that possessed great magical powers. It also heard that Mr. Lan had attained the Way, that he was to pass on his knowledge, and that all its descendants were to be wiped out. With the fire dragon in the lead, an army of turtle generals, shrimp soldiers, crab commanders, and other like creatures sallied forth with the rising tide and laid siege to Mr. Lan's house. When the deafening battle cries assailed Mr. Lan's ears, he wondered what the pandemonium could be all about. He opened the door to see and was shocked at what met his eyes.

Clouds of black smoke and raging fires swirled out of the 480,000 pores in the body of the Red Boy,[6] burning like the thirty-six gold bricks in the hands of General Radiance. If in Xianyang, they would have lasted for more than three months;[7] if on Mount Kun, they would have destroyed all the jade and rocks. Could this be a scene from Zhou Yu's Battle of the Red Cliffs?[8] Or a sight from the wise Zhuge Liang's burning of the grain storage barn at Bowang?[9]

The fire came not from heaven or earth, or humans or ghosts, or the God of Thunder. It came from the mouth of a fire dragon of the Yangzi River. While Mr. Lan's frightened family members shrieked mournfully, Mr. Lan said, knowing this to be the work of a fire dragon, "You accursed beast! Why are you doing this to my family? I have certainly given you no reason for it!"

"Give me your gold pills, magic mirrors, copper and iron tablets, and scriptures," replied the accursed dragon. "If you do, I'll stop. If not, I'll burn up your entire clan."

"The gold pills, magic mirrors, and other things were given to me by the King of Filial Piety and Brotherly Love. How can I hand them to you just like that?"

Against the leaping flames of the fire, a turtle general stepped forward. A most grotesque creature it was, carrying its shield on its back and gesticulating wildly in an exaggerated show of force. Opening wide his immortal eyes, Mr. Lan saw that it was but a miserable turtle, nothing to be taken seriously. The shrimp soldiers jumped up and down, and the crab commanders crawled sideways, all wearing armor and brandishing steel forks. Mr. Lan took a good look with his immortal eyes and saw that they were nothing but a bunch of worthless shrimp and crabs. Dismissing them out of hand, he trimmed his long fingernail on a middle finger, blew his immortal breath on this three-inch nail clipping, and chanted an incantation, thereby changing the clipping into a three-foot-long sword. There is a poem in testimony:

Hard and solid though made of neither steel nor iron,
The precious sword shines with bone-chilling light.
Never smelted or tempered,
It yet has an aura unmatched by Dragon Spring.[10]
It glitters with the color of frost and snow,
An amazing sight that awes every beholder.
Named Lotus, it lies in a colored glazed case,
Its carved handle aglow with golden rings.
Blessed with the essence of gold by the immortals,
It outshines even Ganjiang and Moye.[11]
Glistening like the bright scales of a green snake,
The handle looks like layers of green turtle scales.
Its cold rays of light ascend to the stars;
Its resounding boom sounds like a dragon's roar.
Through the air and into the fire it flies,
Will the demon be able to fend it off?

Mr. Lan tossed the sword that he had conjured into the air, and, with a swishing sound, it somersaulted right into the flames. As it lunged left and right and swung up and down, chopping and cleaving, the monsters ran pell-mell for their lives. The turtle general drew its head back under its shell and scurried away. Where did it go? All the way to the rocks at the mouth of the Xiajiang River, where it is still hiding today, never daring to stick its head out again. (*The writing style resembles that of* The Journey to the West.) A shrimp soldier hopped along, dragging its two iron forks behind it. Where did it go? All the way to the cracks in the rocks under Luoyang Bridge, where it is still hiding, never daring to straighten its back. A crab general, its impregnable armor notwithstanding, crawled this way and that in panic, dragging its two iron forks behind it. Although it had eight legs, it could not move faster and was caught by the sword. With a crackling sound, the sword cut it in half. Out of its belly and onto the ground flowed something neither red nor white, neither yellow nor black, something that looked like pus but was not pus, something that resembled blood, but was not blood. Truly,

To a crab's antics we turn a scornful eye,
For how much longer can it run amok?

Now realizing that Mr. Lan had more magic power than it could ever hope to match, the fire dragon said to itself with a sigh, "As they say, 'The children will have their share of heaven's blessings, whatever the parents' plans.' Let my children and grandchildren enjoy whatever good fortune comes their way and cope with whatever misfortune befalls them. Why should I worry so much?" So, it raced back to the Yangzi River and hid itself in the depth of the water. Mr. Lan and his family, several tens of them, ascended to heaven, where the Jade Emperor granted Mr. Lan the title King of Filial Sagacity, and there we shall leave them.

Now, in a place called Huangtang, in Danyang Prefecture, Jinling, there was a female immortal with the courtesy name Yueying. Through assiduous spiritual cultivation, she attained the Dao and lived so long that she forgot how old she was. Throughout the hundreds of years that the generations of her neighbors had known her, her teeth were as firm and her hair as black as ever. All the neighbors called her Reverend Mother.

One day, she was passing by the marketplace when she saw a child crouched on the ground, crying bitterly. To her questions, the child replied, "My parents abandoned me here when we were fleeing from a war." Out of compassion for the poor orphan, Reverend Mother took the boy under her care.

As he grew older, she began to teach him to read. He turned out to be of extraordinary intelligence and soon learned all there was to know under the sun. An elderly gentleman who lived in the neighborhood offered his daughter for marriage. When Reverend Mother asked the boy for his opinion, he said, "I am not some mortal being of this world. I am the King of Filial Sagacity, who lives in the moon, here to impart the Way to you, Mother, by order of the King of Filial Piety and Brotherly Love of the stars. I am here in the shape of a boy to redeem my mother. So, please don't bring up the subject of marriage again. You may erect a high altar for me by which I may transmit the knowledge to you, so that you can ascend to the Heaven of Exalted Purity."

Pleasantly surprised by these words, Reverend Mother had an altar built in Huangtang, where the boy imparted to her what he had learned from the King of Filial Piety and Brotherly Love. When Reverend Mother had acquired the Way, the King of Filial Sagacity transferred to her all that he had obtained from the King of Filial Piety and Brotherly Love, including the gold pills, magic mirrors, copper and iron tablets, and the orthodox method of killing demons in three to five steps.

To the boy, Reverend Mother said, "In terms of the family relationship, I am the mother, and you are the son, but today, you are the teacher, and I am the student."

She was about to sink to her knees in a deep bow when the King of Filial Sagacity said, "Let's stay mother and son, instead of teacher and student." So he refused to accept any bows but added, "What I have passed on to you must be kept an absolute secret and is not to be divulged to anyone. In the future, during the Jin dynasty, there will be two men, a Xu Xun and a Wu Meng, who will devote themselves to spiritual devotion in their aspiration to become immortals. Their names will be in the immortals' registry book, but Xu Xun will be the one to acquire the Way first. According to the ranks assigned to immortals as recorded in *The Jade Emperor's Registry Book,* Wu Meng will be a royal inspector, and Xu Xun will be a first emissary, concurrently the grand historian, and the supervisor of all immortals. You, Mother, may pass on the Way to Xu Xun and have him impart it to Wu Meng. In that way, the order of seniority will not be disrupted." That said, the King of Filial Sagacity bade farewell to his mother, rose into the air, and was gone. There is a poem in evidence:

He comes and goes on clouds rather than carriages;
He stands aloof from beings of this mortal world.
Afraid that the immortal arts might be lost,
He tries to keep intact the line of succession.

Now, during the reign of Emperor Ling [r. 168–90] of the Han dynasty, with ten eunuchs wielding power in the court, the good and the loyal were thrown into prison, and slander and flattery became the order of the day. The scourge spread across the four seas, bringing untold misery to the people. The discontent of the people moved the gods, who brought about two disasters, a prolonged rain followed by a prolonged drought. The rain lasted for a good five months until the eye saw nothing but water everywhere and no smoke rose from the kitchen chimneys. After the flood subsided, drought followed. For years, not a drop of rain fell. Crop seedlings died, grass and trees withered. How tragic that the people had to worry about where their next meal would come from and had nothing except their summer clothes to protect themselves against the cold of winter. Truly, if there are treacherous officials at the imperial court, thieves will run amok in the villages, nothing will grow in the fields, and trees will be stripped of bark. The young will flee in all directions, and the old will die in the gutter.

In Xudu at that time, there lived a man called Xu Yan, courtesy name Ruyu. A descendant of Xu You of Yingyang,[12] he was a most kindly man and a good physician who had been made a member of the Imperial College of Physicians. In those lean years, he spent all of his family's funds on the preparation of thousands of what he called "hunger staying pills" and gave them out freely to all those in need. Each pill was enough to ward off hunger for more than forty days. A remarkable number of people were thus able to survive the famine.

In the Chuping reign period under Emperor Xian of the Han dynasty, with the Yellow Turbans rising in rebellion, Xudu again found itself suffering through a lean year. With one peck of rice selling for a thousand in cash, everyone had the sallow and emaciated look of starvation. By this time, Xu Yan had died. His son, Xu Su, who had a sizable family fortune, donated all the grain in his barn to the local inhabitants and led the entire family to take refuge in his chosen place, Nanchang of Yuzhang, south of the Yangzi River. The god responsible for investigations informed the Jade Emperor about the good deeds performed by the two generations of the

Xu family, adding, "If the Xus are not richly rewarded, people will see no point in doing good deeds!"

The Jade Emperor agreed and had the immortal judge check the registry book to see which immortal was due for reincarnation into the mortal world. The judge did as ordered and reported, "In the Jin dynasty, there will be a demon dragon spirit south of the Yangzi River who will wreak havoc among the populace and breed in great numbers. It's the turn of the immortal of the Jade Cave to descend to the mortal world to pass on to the female immortal Reverend Mother the demon subjugation method that will exterminate the demon dragon and its clan for the benefit of the people."

Upon hearing this, the Jade Emperor summoned the Immortal of the Jade Cave and ordered that he change into a golden phoenix holding a precious pearl in its beak and descend to the mortal world for reincarnation into Xu Su's family. There is a poem in evidence:

The Jade Emperor himself issued the order;
Divine clouds bore the phoenix, the pearl in its beak.
An immortal was born into an earthly home,
A joyous occasion for the good and kind Xus.

In the third month of the second year of the Chiwu reign period [238–51], under Sun Quan of the state of Wu, Xu Su's wife, He-shi, had a dream one night, in which a golden phoenix descended into the yard and dropped the pearl it held in its beak onto He-shi's palm. Delighted, He-shi played with the pearl and put it in her mouth. Before she knew it, the pearl slid all the way down into her belly, and she became pregnant. Xu Su was both overjoyed and worried, overjoyed because they were more than thirty years old and were still without children and worried because He-shi had never had a child before and might have difficulties with childbirth.

There was a fortune-teller by Guangrun Gate with the nickname Never-erring Diviner, whose prophecies were miraculously accurate. "Why not listen to his predictions about the pregnancy, whatever they might turn out to be?" thought Xu Su to himself. So, he straightened his clothes and his hat and headed straight for Guangrun Gate.

The fortune-teller was so busy, with one patron after another, that Squire Xu found it impossible to thread his way through the packed crowd. He remained standing until his legs felt numb, but still, his turn did not come. He saw nothing for it but to cry out, "Mr. Never-erring Diviner!" Hearing someone call him by his nickname, the fortune-teller thought that it must be an old friend of his, and said eagerly, "Please come in! Come in!"

Squire Xu pushed his way through the crowd. After an exchange of greetings, Squire Xu said, "I am Xu Su, here to ask for a prophecy about my wife's pregnancy. Please tell me whether the child will be a boy or a girl, and whether or not the pregnancy portends well."

The fortune-teller lit joss sticks, chanted a signal to begin, and intoned the following quatrain:

> *"To the Six-*ding *goddesses I devoutly appeal;*[13]
> *To King Wen's wondrous trigrams I resort.*[14]
> *Omens good or bad, please tell everything;*
> *Be sure not to yield to human will."*

After stating the name and the purpose of the divination, the fortune-teller tossed a copper coin six times. Finally, a divinatory symbol that read "Peace in heaven and on earth" came up. The fortune-teller said, "Congratulations! You'll have a boy, one that will bring you great joy." He wrote the following quatrain in explanation:

> *With rich blessings upon your wife*
> *And the green dragon in dominance,*
> *In autumn, a son destined for greatness will be born,*
> *And the mother's recovery will be worry-free.*

Greatly delighted at this prophecy, Squire Xu took the paper and thanked the fortune-teller with several tens of cash. Upon hearing his account, the squire's wife, He-shi, felt a little relieved.

Time flew by like an arrow. Soon, the Mid-autumn Festival rolled around. That night, the clear sky was lit by a lambent moon. Squire Xu and his wife were so fascinated by the view that they stayed up later than was their wont. Before they knew it, the second watch of the night came to an end. As the drum began to strike, announcing the third watch, the moon suddenly emitted rays of unusual brilliance, and celestial music arose from the sky. With a spasm of her belly, He-shi gave birth to a baby amid a shining red light and an extraordinary fragrance that permeated the chamber. Truly,

> *Amid five-colored clouds appeared a phoenix;*
> *From the ninth heaven came a unicorn.*

The next morning, the neighbors all came to offer their congratulations. The baby was none other than the Sage of our story, and a well-shaped baby he was.

The boy possessed an extraordinary intelligence and showed an understanding of proper decorum when he was only three years old. His parents named him Xun, courtesy name Jingzhi. When he began his studies under a tutor at ten years of age, he was able to read ten lines at a glance and write characters and compose essays without even being taught. No mortal being was competent enough to teach him. ([Illegible.]) Consequently, the Sage abandoned his studies and turned his attention to the cultivation of the spirit required to achieve immortality, although he was frustrated that he could find no teacher.

One day, a man named Hu Yun, courtesy name Ziyuan, came to visit him. Hu

Yun had been a schoolmate of his since childhood and was a close friend, whom he had not seen in a long time. The Sage rushed out to greet him with extended hands. As they reminisced about the old days, Ziyuan noticed that the Sage revealed an admiration for immortals. "My brother," observed Ziyuan, "am I to understand that a talented young man like you wishes to be a man beyond the clouds?"

"I'm ashamed to say that I have indeed been thinking about the transience of mortal life and would like to search for a way to achieve immortality. Too bad there isn't anyone to enlighten me!"

"I happen to have been thinking along the same lines. I once visited a Daoist friend, Mr. Zhan Wei, of Yunyang. He said that in Xining Prefecture there is a Wu Meng, courtesy name Shiyun, who had been recommended, on the strength of his filial piety and moral integrity, to a post in the Wu state. He later became magistrate of Luoyang but has since resigned and returned to his hometown, where he obtained a magic formula from Ding Yi, an immortal, and set about smelting immortality pills every day. He then heard that Bao Jing, prefect of Nanhai, was a man well versed in the arts of Daoism, and so, he went to Bao Jing and obtained a secret formula. On his way back to Yuzhang, a raging storm sprang up in midriver. He drew a line in the water with a white-feather fan, and a road appeared. As soon as he reached the end of the road, taking leisurely steps, it changed back into water. Witnesses were astounded at the sight. Henceforth, the Daoist arts began to gain popularity, and his disciples multiplied. I've long wished to join them, but I can't leave my aging mother alone. If you don't mind the hardships of the journey, why don't you go and learn from him?"

The Sage was delighted beyond measure. "Much obliged for the advice!" he said. As soon as Ziyuan left, the Sage bade farewell to his parents, packed up his belongings, and set off for Xining in search of Mr. Wu. There is a poem in praise of him:

The road to immortality is beyond reach;
Make no attempt without proper guidance.
Thanks to Mr. Hu's kind advice,
He took the first step toward achieving the Way.

Now, back to the story. Determined to seek out the teacher, the Sage withstood the tribulations of the journey and arrived at Mr. Wu's residence in a matter of days. He wrote a visiting card presenting himself as a disciple and asked the doorkeeper to announce him. At the sight of the visiting card, which read "Xu Xun, a disciple from Yuzhang," Mr. Wu exclaimed in astonishment, "This is a man who knows the Way!" Right away, he went out to greet the Sage.

Thinking it too much of an honor to be greeted thus by a ninety-one-year-old man, the forty-one-year-old Sage said, "Your Reverence, I beg to be taken on as a disciple of yours."

"I have only a rudimentary knowledge of the Way myself and can hardly claim to be a teacher. But since you've made the trip, I should, by rights, impart to you everything I know. I'd hardly dare keep anything for myself, nor would I be so presumptuous as to list you among my students." Henceforth, he addressed the Sage as "Mr. Xu," and honored him as a distinguished guest. The Sage also showed Mr. Wu great respect and never put on any airs.

One day in the main hall, in the course of their conversation about issues relating to immortality, the Sage said, "Where there is life, there is death. This is an eternal truth. But I see people who do not age and people who do not die. I wonder what makes that possible?"

Mr. Wu replied, "Life comes from an act of sexual intercourse, when the yin and the yang merge. The vital force grows in the fetus until, after three hundred days, a divine light enters the full-size fetus, which then leaves the mother's body. After five thousand days, at fifteen years of age, the yin and the yang arrive at a balance, much like the light of the morning sun. After that, if no attention is paid to the cultivation of the spirit, the yang will be lost. With the vital force gone, illness, old age, death, and suffering set in."

"But what can be done to prevent the onset of illness, old age, death, and suffering?" asked the Sage.

"One needs to cultivate the spirit so as to stave them off and achieve immortality, and once that is accomplished, to ascend to heaven."

"I know that to die is to become a ghost and to achieve the Way is to become an immortal. But how do immortals manage to ascend to heaven?"

"Those who have only yin but no yang become ghosts. Those who have only yang but no yin become immortals. Those in whom yin and yang stay juxtaposed are mortal beings. So, mortal beings can become either immortals or ghosts. There are five categories of immortals and three methods by which to achieve immortality. The choice is up to the mortal being."

"What are the three methods and the five categories?"

"The three methods are the minor one, the middle one, and the superior one. The five categories of immortals are ghost immortals, human immortals, earth immortals, divine immortals, and heavenly immortals.

"Ghost immortals are those who indulge their passions in youth instead of devoting themselves to the cultivation of the spirit. They do this to such an extent that their shape is reduced to that of a dead tree, and with hearts that are nothing but heaps of burned-out ashes, they die of illnesses, although their souls linger and become evil spirits that wreak havoc on people. They are called ghost immortals because they essentially remain ghosts.

"Human immortals are those who, in cultivating the spirit, concentrate on minor things and neglect major goals. While abstaining from the five flavors of food, they remain ignorant of the six cosmic essences.[15] While freeing themselves from the seven human emotions, they fail to observe the ten commandments.[16] While practicing the art of generating saliva, they sneer at the method of breathing out the stale air and taking in the fresh. While fortifying themselves with tonics, they laugh at those who keep a light diet. To benefit from women's yin force is not the same as abstention from sexual intercourse. To seek nourishment from women's milk is different from engaging in alchemy. Those who belong to this category acquire only a few tricks out of the vastness of Daoist arts, just enough to live in contentment and prolong their lives. They are called human immortals because they essentially remain humans.

"As for earth immortals, they are not quite heavenly immortals or divine immortals. They also confine themselves to the minor method I mentioned above. They understand the union of water and fire and the role of dragon and tiger[17] in the art of alchemy and manufacture immortality pills that enable them to live forever on earth. They are called earth immortals because they are earthbound.

"As for divine immortals, they loathe the earth immortals' earthbound way of living and acquire the middle method, by which they take away lead, add mercury, and apply the essence of gold to the top and jade liquid to the middle, until, with the five vital forces having merged and the three yang elements having come together, they complete the process and change their bodies so that all the yin departs and nothing but the yang remains. By then, they can assume multiple bodily forms and become immortals who transcend the mortal world and attain divinity. Graciously, they bid farewell to the mundane world and take up residence on the three fairy islands. They are called divine immortals because of their divine nature.

"Now, heavenly immortals are those who, tired of living on the three islands as the divine immortals do, acquire the superior method by which they successfully perform alchemical transmutations inside as well as outside the body. Having achieved the Way and performed good deeds in the mortal world, they are now well qualified to receive celestial mandates so they may take up residence in heaven. They are called heavenly immortals because they reside in heaven. Of everything that needs to be done to achieve immortality, alchemy is of the first importance. I have here twenty-two songs of the immortals. Remember them well.

"Before the beginning of immortality pills:

When the universe was still in primeval gloom,
The Venerable Mother of Laozi
Gave instructions to the saintly master
To cultivate his spirit and achieve immortality.

How immortality pills began:

The essence of immortality pills,
Born of heaven, earth, and humans in high antiquity,
Hiding in lakes, ponds, and mountains,
Was plucked by the wise to make the pills.

The father of immortality pills:

It flew up the mulberry tree in the morning
When a myriad of sunbeams brightened the universe.
When blended with the essence of the moon,
It was ready for brewing in the cauldron.

The mother of immortality pills:

In the sparkling, crystal-clear starry night,
The sun and the moon fought until morning
And produced an elixir of eternal life
That had no equal in the universe.

The embryo of immortality pills:

Fostered by the essence of the sun and moon,
The embryos are fed by water, mercury, and sand
At the ratio of one to three to three,
And the right proportion follows all the way.

The omens of immortality pills:

Three days after the embryos are formed,
Good omens begin to assert themselves:
A red glow rises high into the skies
Amid music of five tones and six tempos.

The substance of immortality pills:

Almost unrecognizable in their purple light,
They're shaped like pearls the size of millet grains.
Form is indeed emptiness;
Emptiness is indeed form.

The efficacy of immortality pills:

The pills mature after ten months in the fetuses.
Take one pill a day for a hundred days, and
You will transmute shape and bones
And attain eternal life.

The sanctity of immortality pills:

The rosy-cloud patterned tripod took nine years to build;
When water and fire are added to the chemicals,
Dried dead bones will rise to life,
And forlorn souls will awake to the world.

The chamber of the cauldron:

Right in the middle of the cauldron
Is the void called the chamber,
Where the magic substance that is produced
Changes into precious gold liquid.

The cauldron of immortality pills:

With a strong wall surrounding the cauldron,
Water, fire and gold are protected within and without.
At the right time, out of the gold fetus,
Was born Pangu, creator of the universe.

The hearth for immortality pills:

With bending pipes shaped like the fairy islands,
With fences and shields installed for protection,
The golden hearth smelts lead and mercury,
One from the tiger, the other from the dragon.

The fire of the furnace:

The heat must vary in degree
To match the twelve time periods of the day.
In reducing the lead and adding mercury,
Remember not to go to excess.

The water in immortality pills:

All containers are equally good.
Neither too much nor too little,
The water must be neutral and mild
In order to produce the magic golden substance.

The awe-inspiring quality of immortality pills:

Their red glow rises high into the sky,
Lighting up the Big Dipper's seven stars.
All the deities of heaven and earth
Bow to them in humble submission.

The key to immortality pills:

Heaven, earth, and humans, all have their secrets;
Stars, mountains, rivers, sovereigns,
And all the spirits of the three realms
Are converted to the truth of the Way.

The colors of immortality pills:

The colors are arranged in neat order;
Green, red, white, and yellow in the middle,
They attract nothing but the auspicious
In their divine serenity.

The uses of immortality pills:

Real earth, real lead, and real mercury;
White is extracted from black, blue from red.
All is done by the water and the fire
That move about in tranquillity.

The mixing process for immortality pills:

The yin and the yang, the male and the female,
Merge and mix as the cauldron brews
The marrow of dragons and tigers
Over fire tended by the cosmos.

The nature of immortality pills:

The marrow of dragons and tigers
Works with a magic second to none.
Merging the essence of the two
Completes the smelting process.

The auspice of immortality pills:

Infinitely small and large at the same time,
It contains the sky and earth, east, south, north, and west;
All three realms of the universe
Are embraced in pearls the size of millet grain.

The completion of immortality pills:

The Jade Emperor asks for the one
Destined to impart the right method.
No mundane being is to be given
This one chance in ten thousand karmas.

The Sage said, "Thank you so much for pointing out the Way for me! May I ask, of the five categories of immortals, to which category do you belong?"

Mr. Wu replied, "Being but a benighted country boor, I have learned only the minor method and am therefore an earth immortal. Though I know what needs to be done to become both a divine immortal and a heavenly one, I lack the wherewithal to get there."

Thereupon he imparted the secret alchemical formula and the White Cloud magic symbols to the Sage. With a grateful kowtow, the Sage took leave of Mr. Wu and went back home.

Loathing the hustle and bustle of the town in which he lived, the Sage wanted to find a scenic mountain area to serve as his residence. He heard of a Guo Pu, courtesy name Jingchun, in Runan [in present-day Henan Province], who was most knowledgeable on matters relating to yin, yang, and fengshui and was in the habit of touring rivers and lakes. Out of respect for him, the Sage decided to pay him a visit.

One day, Guo Pu rose bright and early and, upon hearing the cries of a crow coming from a southeasterly direction, performed a divination. "At noontime today," he concluded, "an immortal with the surname Xu will visit me and ask about choosing a place of residence."

Sure enough, at noontime, a page boy announced the arrival of a visitor. Guo Pu hastened out to meet the man. After an exchange of greetings, they took seats as host and guest, respectively. Guo Pu asked, "Aren't you Mr. Xu, here to ask me for a divination as to your future place of residence?"

"How did you know, sir?"

"That's what I learned from my divination this morning. Am I correct?"

"Yes," replied the Sage, whereupon he introduced himself and stated the purpose of his visit.

Guo Pu said, "With your refined and unearthly look, you are clearly not a person bound to this mortal world. Even the most opulent place is not good enough for you. Could it be the land of the immortals that interests you?"

"Well, in the olden times, Lü Dongbin took up residence in the Lu Mountains and achieved immortality, and Guigu lived in the Yunmeng Marshes before he attained the Way. Are there no such blessed places any more?"

Guo Pu replied, "Yes, there are, but first, you need to see all such places that are available."

Accordingly, Guo Pu had his servants pack for him and set off with the Sage to tour the counties south of the Yangzi River in search of famous mountains.

One day, when approaching Mount Lu, Guo Pu remarked, "This mountain certainly is high and majestic. Its lake runs east, its crest is topped by purple clouds, and for generations, it has produced immortals who ascended to heaven. But this mountain, by it shape, belongs to the earth phase of the five phases[18], and your surname Xu, which is of the tone *yu* in the five tones of music[19], belongs to the phase of water. Water and earth being conflicting elements, that mountain is not for you, except as a place to rest temporarily on your travels."

When they arrived at Banghu, in Poyang, Raozhou Prefecture, Guo Pu said, "This is a place destined for greatness, but it's not for you either."

"This is a place where the wind seems to blow away all vital force. How can it be destined for greatness?"

Guo Pu answered, "When assessing fengshui, there is the overall, intuitive view and the specific, guided view. In the first view, one observes the overall picture of the mountains and rivers with one's own eyes. In the second view, one goes by the eight trigrams and the positions of the stars. A place destined for greatness is secretly blessed by heaven and earth and protected by divine beings. One not meant to enjoy the blessings of the land will not see what lies beneath the surface. This is exactly what's meant by the proverb 'Blessed lands are reserved for blessed people.'"

"Why don't you leave something behind in this blessed place as a future proof of your prophecy?"

At this suggestion, Guo Pu wrote a poem to serve as proof in times to come. The poem says,

While touring south of the Yangzi River,
Divine signs are seen only in Banghu.
Wild geese announce the nightly watches;
Fish and turtles bow daily to the king.
The fire dragon sits in his throne, hidden from view.
Water from the southeast flows into Lake Poyang.
Those blessed ones who come here after me
Will enjoy blissful lives for hundreds of years.

After leaving Lake Poyang, Mr. Xu and Guo Pu made their way to Mount Qiwu in Yichun, where lived a man named Wang Shuo, who was well-read in astrology and the theory of the five phases. When he saw Xu and Guo climbing up the mountain, he recognized in them the makings of extraordinary men and invited them into his house. After obtaining their names, he put them up for the night in his western pavilion and treated them with the utmost hospitality.

Out of gratitude, the Sage said to him, "You have such an air of distinction that I'll impart my formula to you," whereupon he told Wang Shuo his formula for achieving immortality.

Guo Pu suggested, "This area being so scenic with its hills and waters, why don't you build a monastery in which to pursue spiritual cultivation?"

Wang Shuo followed this advice and had a monastery built. The Sage wrote "Monastery for Immortals" as an inscription for the horizontal board over the door frame. Wang Shuo was grateful beyond measure. Mr. Xu and Gao Pu took their leave of him and continued on with their journey.

Upon reaching a place called Golden Fields at West Hill, Hongdu, they saw a towering mountain, jutting peaks, lively green dragons, majestic white tigers, and clean sand along curving riverbanks. At the top of the mountain soared dark green pine trees, and at its foot stood verdant bamboo grooves. In the foreground stretched soft grass in the shape of dragon's whiskers, and in the back were withered camphor trees in the form of antlers. There came to one's ears the graceful cries of phoenixes, the intermittent chirps of cranes, the ferocious roar of tigers, and the timid calls of deer. The mountain was craggier than Mount Tiantai of Zhejiang, more jagged than Mount Wuyi of Fujian, more intriguing than Mount Jiuhua of Anhui, more picturesque than Mount Emei of Sichuan, sharper in contour than Mount Wudang of Chu, shapelier than Mount Zhongnan of Shanxi, more tortuous than Mount Tai of Shandong, and more verdant than Mount Luofu of Guangdong. It was indeed a scenic spot without peer and the most famous mountain west of the Yangzi River. Harboring the cosmic essence of the ages, it was truly a residence fit for the immortals.

Now, back to the story. Upon reaching the foot of the mountain, Guo Pu looked around in all directions. After setting his compass and examining it, he laughed out loud, rubbing his palms, and launched into the following speech: "Of all the places whose fengshui I have studied, I have never come across one so wonderful. If seeking riches and honor, one will experience rises and falls here. If looking for a hermitage, then this is the very place. The mounds are thick and round, and sit on deep foundations. With three peaks standing like a wall and clouds surrounding all four sides like a lock, it could not serve a hermit's purposes better. In most cases, when assessing fengshui, one must also examine the physiognomy of those who live in the place, to see if their physical features conform with the topographical features. (*In my part of the country, it's precisely because the fengshui masters ignore human features that their prophecies mostly fall flat.*) Moreover, the west mountain belongs to the phase of metal, but your surname Xu, being of the tone *yu* in the five tones of music, belongs to the phase of water. Metal is a phase that fosters water, which makes this mountain an ideal habitat, better than anywhere else, for those destined to have eternal life. I wonder who owns this place?"

A woodcutter nearby said, pointing, "This is all the property of the venerable Mr. Jin."

"Judging by the way you refer to him as 'the venerable Mr. Jin,'" said the Sage, "he must be a good man."

Mr. Xu and Guo Pu went to visit Mr. Jin, who came out joyfully to meet them, greeting them as cordially as if they were old friends.

"May I ask where you've come from, my venerable guests?"

Guo Pu replied, "I am Guo Pu, and I have a rudimentary knowledge of the theory of yin and yang. This is my friend Xu Xun, who is equally interested in Daoist pursuits. We are traveling past your estate in our search for a hermitage for Mr. Xu. Impressed by the divine scenery of this place, he would like to buy a house here for purposes of spiritual cultivation. Would you, sir, be so kind as to give your consent?"

"I'm only afraid that what I have is too small for Mr. Xu's purposes. If you would not be disdainful, I'd be happy to give you several *mu* of the poor land around this humble cottage."

The Sage said, "Please give me a price. I'll accept whatever you say."

"A true gentleman's word is worth ten thousand taels of gold. Being a straightforward man, I've never had a need to draw up a document." Thereupon, he obtained from the Sage a coin of a large denomination, broke it in half, kept one half for himself, and gave the other half back to the Sage, who thanked him with a kowtow. The guests and the host then took leave of each other.

Thereafter, the Sage bade farewell to Guo Pu, and on a chosen auspicious day, he took his parents, his wife, and several tens of other members of the clan all the way to the west mountain, had houses built, and took up residence there. Later, Mr. Jin gained the title Lord of Lands. His house is today's Yulong Longevity Palace.

Every day, the Sage engaged in his alchemical experiments. In due course, he produced gold pills that could change stones into gold and, when taken orally, halted the aging process and extended life expectancy. By using the pills in his charitable work, he became known far and near as a virtuous and just man.

After Emperor Wu of the Jin dynasty brought peace to the Shu region in the west and the Wu region in the east, the reunified empire was given the new reign title Taikang [280–90]. Acting on a memorial submitted by Shan Tao, secretary of the Ministry of Personnel, the emperor issued a decree, soliciting nominations for official posts on the basis of virtue, filial piety, and competence. Fan Ning, prefect of Yuzhang, impressed by the Sage's filial devotion to his parents, his friendliness with his neighbors, and his disdain for material wealth, recommended him as a candidate. Emperor Wu sent a messenger with an imperial decree granting the Sage the post of magistrate of Jingyang County, in Shu. The Sage wrote a memorial in reply, declining the assignment because he could not bring himself to leave his aged parents. The emperor turned down his request and ordered the prefect to urge the Sage to take up his post. The Sage dragged his feet but finally, the following year, resignedly bade farewell to his parents and his wife and set off on the journey.

The Sage had two older sisters. The older of the two was a widow, her husband, Mr. Xu of Nanchang, having died early, leaving behind a son Xu Lie, courtesy name Daowei, who served his mother with great devotion. Wishing to provide his widowed sister with better living quarters, the Sage had arranged to have a house built for her to the west of his own house. Accordingly, the mother and son were able to hear the Sage's explanations of the Way. Just before he departed, the Sage said to his sister, "Our parents being advanced in age and my wife knowing very little about affairs of the world, could you, my good sister, please take charge of the household on my behalf? If hermits pass by, treat them courteously. As for your son Xu Lie, I would like to reward him for his kindness and filial piety by taking him with me."

"My good brother," replied his sister, "you go along to your post! I'll take care of the household. Don't worry!"

Before she had finished, a young boy walked up and, with a deep bow, addressed the Sage. "Brother Xu Lie and I are both your nephews. Why are you taking only him and not me?"

The Sage saw that it was his second sister's son, surname Zhongli, given name

Jia, courtesy name Gongyang. A native of Xili, Ivory Mountain, Xinjian County, he had lost his parents early in his childhood and had been living with the Sage all these years. He had a magnanimous mind and a gentle, kind nature. The Sage agreed to take him on the trip. The two cousins thus came under the Sage's edifying influence, which stood them in good stead later in their endeavor to acquire the qualities of immortals.

The Sage then called for his wife, Lady Zhou, and said to her, "I have no interest in rank and honor, but if I continue to reject the emperor's repeated appointments, I'll be accused of defying him. It's always been said that you can't be loyal to the emperor and to your parents at the same time. As my parents are advanced in age, you should serve them day and night, protect them from the severities of the weather, and perform the duties of a filial daughter-in-law. In addition, our children are still young and need to be taught well. There's also your duty to be frugal and hardworking around the house."

"As you say!" replied his wife.

With that, he bowed his farewell and set off on his journey. Of this, no more need be said.

Earlier, before the Sage assumed his post, there was a famine in the Shu [Sichuan] region, and the people were too poor to pay taxes. After assuming his post, the Sage came under such pressure from his superiors that he used his pills to change rocks into gold and had the gold buried quietly in the backyard of the county yamen. (*This makes me wish even more that immortals could be officials!*) All those apprehended for failing to pay taxes were brought to the Sage, who asked them, "Why don't you pay the taxes that you owe the imperial court?"

The poor villagers replied, "We would never dream of evading our tax duties to the state. But owing to the famine, we have nothing with which to pay the taxes."

"In that case," said the Sage, "my judgment is that you perform corvée by digging a pond in the backyard of the county yamen. If you dig up anything of worth, surrender it to me as payment of your taxes."

Greatly relieved, the villagers proceeded to the backyard to dig a pond. As they dug, they all came upon pieces of gold and were able to pay their taxes. Thus, they were spared the misery of migration. As word got around, people from neighboring counties swarmed to the Sage's county, expanding the local population. According to the local chronicles, Jingyang [flag, sun] County, in Hanzhou, was called Deyang [virtue, sun] County after the Sage ascended to heaven, in commemoration of the kind deeds he had done for the people. Thanks to his golden touch, the area remains rich to this day, but let us not digress.

At the time, a plague broke out in the area, taking a heavy toll on human lives, but, wherever the Sage delivered his magic figures, the sick immediately regained their health. Out of compassion for the sick in other counties, the Sage had bamboo poles erected by the streams along the borders and burned his magic figures there. After the sick drank the water, all recovered. The elderly, children, and women who were too weak to make the trip had the water brought back to them, and they were all cured. A poet in the Sage's county had this to say in praise of him:

The hundred-li fields were under good governance;
The ten thousand houses lay under a gentle breeze.
He ruled with scrupulous justice and fairness;
His reputation was as spotless as pure ice.
His magic expelled illness from the counties;
His buried gold rid the land of poverty.
The Sage's good deeds are felt to this day,
As attested by the temples to his name.

Now, in Chengdu Prefecture, there lived a man called Chen Xun, courtesy name Xiaoju. Through recommendations for his filial piety and moral integrity, he was assigned to the post of assistant prefect of Yizhou. Having heard that the Sage who had been passing on Wu Meng's Daoist formula was now the magistrate of Jingyang County, doing kind deeds for the people, he offered the Sage his services as a clerk. In this way, he would benefit from daily contact with the Sage and from his teachings. Impressed by Chen Xun's refined manners and his rosy complexion, the Sage granted his request. Later, as he observed Chen's distinct air of a Daoist destined for immortality, the Sage took him on as a disciple and had him attend to the alchemical cauldron. Then another man came along, named Zhou Guang, courtesy name Huichang. He was a native of Luling, a descendant of General Zhou Yu of the state of Wu.[20] On his tour of Mount Yuntai in Sichuan, he learned the basics of Celestial Master Zhang's[21] method of demon subjugation and, having heard about the Sage's mastery of the Daoist arts, made his way to Jingyang County to honor the Sage as his master and submit himself to the latter's teachings. The Sage accepted him and put him in charge of the thunder platform. Henceforth, the two disciples learned the wonderful secrets of immortality.

As the days went by, the Sage began to have more disciples at his post in Jingyang. He spent his leisure hours mostly in explaining the Way to his group of disciples.

After the Jin dynasty had enjoyed many years of peace, five foreign tribes began to make forceful incursions into the central plains of China. Which five?

Liu Yuan [d. 310], the Hun who occupied Jinyang; Shi Le [274–333], of the Jie tribe, who took Shangdang; Yao Yizhong, a Qiang who was based in Fufeng; Fu Hong, of the Di tribe in Linwei; and Murong Wei [269–333], of the Xianbei tribe in Changli.[22]

Since the days of the Han and Wei dynasties [220–80], vanquished tribes had been settled in areas well within the Great Wall. Jiang Tong, attendant to the crown prince, had advised Emperor Wu to relocate them to the borders so as to forestall future trouble, but Emperor Wu had turned a deaf ear. And now, the tribes were indeed wreaking havoc on the Jin dynasty. The crown prince, now Emperor Hui, was a stupid man, and his mother, the empress dowager, ruled the court with an iron hand, killing court ministers at will. The Sage said to his disciples, "As they say, 'Serve only when the sovereign is wise. Otherwise, retire and live in seclusion.'" So he resigned from his post and returned to the east.

As the news spread, the populace turned out onto the streets and held the wheels of his carriage, begging him to stay. Amid the earth-shaking wails of grief, the Sage also broke down in tears. To the gathered masses, he said, "It's not that I want to abandon you, but the land will soon be engulfed in chaos. I have to protect myself. Please take good care of yourselves!"

Sadly, the throng escorted him on his journey, some for about a hundred li, and some for several hundred li. Some even escorted him all the way to his home and refused to leave.

Upon seeing one another, the Sage, his parents, his wife, his children, and the whole family rejoiced at the happy reunion. Right away, they put together some hay on an empty lot east of the house and built a camp of cottages for the people from Sichuan who had followed the Sage. Those who stayed took on the Sage's surname and came to be known as people of the "Xu Camp."

Lady Zhou, the Sage's wife, said to him, "Our daughter is of a marriageable age now. It's time to pick a good husband for her."

The Sage replied, "This has been on my mind for quite some time."

Among his disciples, there was a Huang Renlan, courtesy name Ziting, a native of Jiancheng, who was the son of Chief Imperial Inspector Huang Fu. A loyal, trustworthy, pure-hearted, and earnest man, he had the makings of an immortal worthy of the knowledge of the Way. The Sage had another disciple, Zhou Guang, serve as matchmaker. After Renlan had reported the matter to his parents, an auspicious day was chosen and gifts were prepared for the wedding ceremony, which was to take place in the Sage's house.

A month after the wedding, Renlan asked the Sage for permission to go with his wife to visit his parents. His wife being a paragon of wifely virtues, Renlan told her to stay with his parents and serve them, whereas he returned reverently to the Sage to continue his pursuit of immortality.

Having heard that the Sage had resigned from his post and gone back home, Wu Meng, who was more than one hundred and twenty years of age, traveled all the way from Xi'an to see him. The Sage straightened his clothes and went out to greet him. After they had sat down and reminisced about the old days, the Sage ordered a house built to the west of his house for Mr. Wu.

One day, in a strong gust of wind, Mr. Wu drew a magic figure and tossed it onto the roof. In a trice, a blue bird was seen picking the magic figure up in its beak and flying away. The wind died down instantly. The Sage asked, "What omens did the wind bring?"

Mr. Wu replied, "A boat was crossing South Lake when the wind sprang up. A man in the boat appealed to heaven for help. That was why I put a stop to it."

In a few days, a man wearing a thick robe, a large belt, and a hat entered the Sage's house and, with a bow, addressed the two sages as follows: "I am Peng Kang, courtesy name Wuyang, a native of Lanling. Through recommendations, I attained an official post early in my youth and rose to be counselor of the Grand Secretariat of the Jin court. I had a premonition that the land was going to be ravaged by chaos and resigned, pleading ill health. Having heard about Mr. Xu's kind deeds and mastery of the Daoist arts, I came to ask him to accept me as a disciple. Yesterday, when I was crossing South Lake, my boat almost capsized in a gust of wind. As soon as I cried out to heaven for help, a blue bird flew over, and the wind died down. How fortunate I am to be able to see you today!"

When the Sage recounted what Mr. Wu had done with his magic figure, Peng Kang was grateful beyond measure. He brought his whole family to the city of Yuzhang. Noticing that the Sage had a son who was still unbetrothed, he offered his daughter as a candidate. The Sage gave his consent. Henceforth, Peng Kang was treated with much respect and was taught all the secret formulas of immortality that the Sage possessed. There is a poem by Master Dongming that says:

A high post in the imperial court
Was abandoned in favor of the Way.
If not for feelings of kinship,
How would Peng ever have ascended to heaven?

By now, the Sage had learned Wu Meng's arts but not yet the Reverend Mother's method of demon subjugation. The god of the Gold Star offered the Jade Emperor this advice: "In Nanchang County, a demon dragon will wreak havoc on the people. Now there is a Xu Xun, a reincarnation of Jade Cave Sage, who is destined to subdue the Demon Dragon. Please send a celestial messenger to award him a divine demon-subjugation sword that will help him eliminate the demon and save the people from the scourge."

Upon hearing these words, the Jade Emperor summoned two girls and gave each a divine sword. He then told them to go to a place called Bailin, where they were to present the swords to Xu Xun and relay to him the Jade Emperor's order that he subdue the demon for the well-being of the people.

The Sage took the swords with a deep bow. By the time he looked up again, the girls were already high up in the sky on a cloud. A later poet had this to say:

Tempered in the furnace by raging fire,
The shining swords could cut through the hardest steel.
The Jade Maidens gave them to the immortal;
Henceforth the rivers would reek of stench.

South of the Yangzi River, there was a monster called the Demon Dragon, who began life in human form as a talented scholar named Zhang Ku. He was crossing the river in a boat when he was caught in a strong gust of wind. His boat capsized, and he fell into the water. He hung onto a plank of wood and drifted to a sand beach. To allay his hunger, he swallowed a bright bead that he happened to see. The bead was by no means an ordinary bead but an egg produced by a fire dragon. Zhang Ku's hunger vanished after he swallowed the bead, and he found himself able to swim.

More than a month later, he underwent a transformation. Scales appeared all over his body, and only his head remained human. This monster could do nothing but play in the water, jumping into giant waves to watch the fish and dragons or diving down into deep pools to watch the shrimp and turtles swim about. Then, the fire dragon spotted him and thought the young monster was its son. The fire dragon blew its breath on the young monster and taught him magic power.

Once the young monster was back on shore, he found he was able to change into any shape he wanted, summon wind and rain, hold the mist, and move the clouds. When he was in a cheerful frame of mind, he would take on human form and debauch women of the mortal world, and when in a foul mood, into evil spirits that flooded the land and destroyed houses, drank human blood, capsized boats, and snatched valuables. A truly major scourge he became. He went on to have six sons and, in several tens of years, they had multiplied into a clan one thousand strong. As there were many flood dragons in the clan, they often thought of turning several counties in Jiangxi into a sea.

One day, the Sage was making immortality pills on a mountain in Aicheng when one of the flood dragons caused a flood, intending to wash away his furnace room. In a rage, the Sage summoned celestial warriors, who captured the flood dragon. The Sage then impaled it on a rock—which still exists to this day—and killed it with his sword. Now, after hearing about the death of a member of his clan, the Demon Dragon rallied his kith and kin, both old and young, big and small, who rushed forth at his first call for support. The Demon Dragon said, "That abominable Xu Xun means to destroy us. If this offense goes unavenged, I will have lived this life in vain!"

Members of his clan, who called him either Grandpa or Uncle or Older Brother, said, "Don't worry. We'll go and bring that Xu Xun to you. We'll cut his corpse into ten thousand pieces in revenge."

The Demon Dragon said, "I heard that Xu Xun has gained considerable magic power through Wu Meng. We need someone really good."

A long snake spirit said, "Older Brother, let me go!"

"Yes, you are the right one," said the Demon Dragon, giving his approval.

With the long snake spirit leading the way, about a hundred flood dragons burst onto Xu Xun's estate and, spreading themselves out in a single straight row, cried, "Xu Xun, do you dare battle us?"

At the sight of the bunch of flood dragons, the Sage said, sword in hand, "You cursed beasts! How dare you fight me with what little power you have!"

The long snake spirit replied, "Listen!

"With an awe-inspiring scaled coat of mail,
I display my magic in tournaments.
With my open jaws, I can swallow an elephant;
Three years of breathing exercise will make me a dragon.
I need only open my mouth to make a fog,
I need only raise my head to stir up a wind.
I can stretch out as long as ninety thousand li
And coil my way up the tallest peak of Kunlun."

While the long snake spirit boasted of his prowess, the flood dragons hopped up and down, shrieking, "You shouldn't have killed a member of our clan. We're not through with you yet!"

The Sage said, "I'm afraid my sword won't spare you, you foul beasts!"

Working one of his magic tricks, the long snake spirit conjured up a strong gust of wind. Lo and behold:

It comes without form and shape, but the howl is deafening.
With a crash here and a clatter there,
It shakes the gate of heaven and the axis of earth
And vexes even the fairies in the ninth layer of heaven.
As it churns seas and rivers in a riot of colors,
The dragon kings of the four seas huddle in terror.
As thunder growls, as lightning flashes,
Grains of sand whirl, stones and pebbles fly,
Till all is as dark as the dawn of a spring day.
Under the dismal clouds and fog,
Ancient trees are blown to the ground
In darkness hardly relieved by the villagers' lamps.
As it screams its way back and forth, left and right,
Ten thousand tiles fly off the roofs of grand palaces.
As it sweeps away everything in its path,
Not a hair is left in the tiger and wolf dens.
For all Zong Que's ambitions,[23]
He would not dare ride this wind and cleave these waves.
For all Lie Yukou's agility,[24]
He would not dare challenge this wind for days on end.
Truly, dust and sand darken the land;
Few would answer a knock at the door.
With willows and other trees all gone,
Why go on to tear away the roofs?

What a strong wind it was! Sword in hand, the Sage said sharply, "God of Wind, it's time you stopped this wind!" In a trice, the wind died down, but the demons conjured up a rainstorm.

Stones in the shapes of swallows and birds flew about;
Rain poured from the clouds and the sky,
Though it was not to relieve the drought.
Pitter-patter, the rain beat on the withered leaves
And scattered them about.
Drip-drip, it fell on the lotus flowers in the pond
And ruffled their pink petals.
The ditches overflowed with water,
Which quickly bore away Gao Feng's wheat crop;[25]
The eave gutters spilled enough water
To wash clean the weapons of Zhou Wu's soldiers.[26]
This was not the much-needed rain prayed for through lizards[27]
But the saliva of whales and salamanders.
Truly, kitchen fires died down in thatched cottages.
In courtyards aglow with pear blossoms,
Dreams ended in panic.
The canals were swollen with muddy water and swimming fish;
Cranes could not walk on ground too slippery with moss.

A raging storm it was indeed! Sword in hand, the Sage again ordered sharply, "God of Rain, it's time you stopped this rainstorm!" In an instant, the rain stopped. Not even half a drop could be seen anymore. In a mighty show of his magic power, the Sage charged into the long snake spirit's ranks, and as his two swords swung high, he cut it in half. Terrified at the death of the long snake spirit, the flood dragons ran pell-mell for their lives. The Sage caught up with them and did away with all of them. He then headed straight for the flood dragon's abode to seek out the Demon Dragon.

Having heard about the long snake spirit's death and the heavy casualties among its underlings, the Demon Dragon was determined not to give up. A crowd of a thousand flood dragons rallied by the Demon Dragon cursed the Sage in a medley of voices, saying, "You cursed Daoist! Why have you come to bully us in our home?" With some calling up winds, some summoning rain, some conjuring up a fog, some bringing on clouds, some generating smoke, and some lighting fires, they charged en masse at the Sage. The Sage swung his two swords left and right, but how much could he do when there were so many of them? Moreover, not yet having learned the Reverend Mother's method of flying, he was still an earthbound immortal. The Demon Dragon, which was capable of bodily transformations, shot all the way up to the sky and changed into an eagle. Truly,

Its talons as sharp as copper nails,
Its beak as hard as an iron drill,
It unfurled its wings like a roc, ready to soar.
From the clouds, it cried at the top of its voice;

It stood on the treetops, raising its head high.
The birds and sparrows scurried to hide;
No bird dared stand in its way.

Its wings spread wide against the sky, the eagle dived down and flung a wing against the Sage's face. His face covered with blood, the Sage was about to cut it down with his swords when it rose again into the sky. The Sage saw no alternative but to return home. The flood dragons, which had suffered heavy casualties, also withdrew and returned home.

Having witnessed the Demon Dragon's immense magical powers, the Sage paid Mr. Wu a respectful visit, to ask for a way of subduing the demon. Mr. Wu said, "The Demon Dragon has been a scourge of the people for so long that I, too, have been meaning to get rid of him, but he's too powerful for me. Now that you've beaten the flood dragons, the Demon Dragon will surely be mad with anger and seek to do greater evil. That will be the end of the Jiangnan region south of the Yangzi River."

"What's to be done?"

"I recently heard that in a place called Huangtang, in Danyang County, Zhenjiang Prefecture, there is a female immortal known as the Reverend Mother who is a master of the Daoist arts. Let's go to see her, honor her as our teacher, learn her arts, and then come back and wipe out that demon. We should have enough time."

Delighted by this suggestion, the Sage packed and followed Mr. Wu to Huangtang, where they saw the Reverend Mother.

"Who are you two gentlemen? How can I help you?" asked the Reverend Mother.

The Sage replied, "I am Xu Xun, and this gentleman is Wu Meng. We are here because we wish to eliminate the Demon Dragon who is a scourge of the people in the Jiangnan region south of the Yangzi River, but he has greater magic power than we do. We have long heard that you, Reverend Mother, have limitless power, so we came here to beg you to teach us your secret formula, to fulfill the greatest wish of our lives." With that, the two men prostrated themselves on the floor.

"Please rise," said the Reverend Mother. "Listen, you are by no means ordinary people. Both your names are listed in the heavenly registry. A long time ago, the King of Filial Piety and Brotherly Love descended from the Realm of Exalted Purity to Mr. Lan's house in Qufu County, in Shandong, and told Mr. Lan that in a future Jin dynasty, there would be an immortal called Xu Xun, who was to inherit his method. This Xu Xun would be the head of all immortals. With these words, he gave Mr. Lan gold pills, magic mirrors, and copper and iron tablets and taught him the method of subduing demons while flying. He then ordered Mr. Lan to teach it to me, and I was supposed to wait for you. This all happened four hundred years ago. Now that you are here, I will of course pass it on to you."

On a chosen auspicious day, in a solemn ritual proper for the occasion, she gave

Mr. Xu the copper and iron tablets, the golden pills, the magic mirrors, the method of demon subjugation, the art of flying, and secret formulae and magic figures of all descriptions. The Clear and Bright method and the Five Thunders method still in existence today were both imparted to Mr. Xu by the Reverend Mother. The Reverend Mother then turned to Mr. Wu and said, "You used to be Mr. Xu's mentor, but now, with Mr. Xu destined to inherit the formulae of the King of Filial Piety and Brotherly Love, you will have to step back and honor him as your teacher."

Having learned all that he had come to learn, the Sage was about to return when he thought to himself, "Since I have had the good fortune to be taught by the Reverend Mother, I will pay her yearly visits in the future to show my respect as a disciple."

Before he was able to express this thought in words, the Reverend Mother knew what he was going to say. "I am returning to the place where the Jade Emperor resides," she said. "You don't have to pay me visits." So saying, she picked up a blade of lemongrass and tossed it in a southerly direction. As the windborne blade of grass wafted through the air, the Reverend Mother said to the Sage, "Go tens of li south of where you live and see where that blade of lemongrass has landed. You may build a temple to me on that very spot. One visit to the temple every autumn will suffice." No sooner had she finished speaking than a celestial carriage appeared in midair. Immediately, she rose into the air and was gone.

Mr. Wu and the Sage bowed their farewells skyward before returning to their abode. They then set off in search of the lemongrass. It was not until they had traveled forty li south of West Hill that they found it in the form of a thriving thicket that had grown from the single blade of grass. The two had a temple erected right there on the spot, named it the Yellow Hall, and engaged craftsmen to build a statue of the Reverend Mother. They maintained a strict schedule of worship services and made a commitment to visit the temple every year on the third day of the eighth month to pay homage. This is the very temple that is known today as Chongzhen Temple, and the ritual of annual homage is still being observed.

In the Yellow Hall, the Sage had an altar built, where, as instructed by the Reverend Mother, he imparted the secrets to Mr. Wu, who now reversed his role and honored the Sage as his mentor.

After they had both mastered the arts of flying and bodily transformation, they returned to Xiaojiang, where they found lodging at an inn. Impressed by their otherworldly appearance, the innkeeper, Madam Song, treated them with the utmost hospitality and did not charge them for their room and board. Out of gratitude for her deference, the two gentlemen asked her for brush-pens and ink and painted a pine tree on the wall before they departed. After they left, the pine tree turned green, as if fully alive. When the wind blew, its branches swayed to and fro. When lit by the moon, its needles turned a paler green. On damp days, it glittered as if with dew. Curious spectators numbered in the thousands daily. With all of them leaving a tip before departing, Madam Song became fabulously rich. Later, when the river rose and destroyed the embankment, the inn was washed away, but that wall remained intact.

Now, back to the Demon Dragon, who was filled with wrath over the casualties that the Sage had inflicted on members of his clan. Having heard that Mr. Wu and the Sage were in the Yellow Hall pursuing their studies, he ordered the flood dragons to wreak havoc on Mr. Wu's hometown. Upon returning to Xining, the Sage's nostrils were assailed by the flood dragons' foul odor. Pointing an accusing finger at the local god, he said, "Being the chief of all the deities of this county, how can you condone their wanton behavior?"

The local god said, "Those monsters are too powerful for this humble deity." While the god was offering profuse apologies, the Demon Dragon saw that the Sage had returned. Immediately, he rallied the flood dragons and roused waves several tens of feet high. How intimidating were the surging and spouting sheets of waves?

First came rumbles that shook the valleys,
Then a set of waves that burst sky-high.
They roared like awe-inspiring thunder
And churned like furious wind-blown snowstorms.
The soaring waves swallowed up the roads;
The raging waters spouted high against cliff rocks.
The frothy foam was as delicate as jade;
The rolling sound was as musical as plucked chords.
Like pieces of jade splashed against the crags,
Eddies spun around down below.
As the currents ran their tortuous course,
The surging waves rose all the way to the sky.

Fearing that the ferocious waters would do damage to the local people and their houses and crops, the Sage drew a magic figure in the air with his sword and called out, "God of Water, let the waters subside!"

To the Sage's seething indignation, the God of Water failed to make the water die down as quickly as was expected. "Isn't it often said that it's impossible to take back spilled water? Be easy on me!" the God of Water said in his own defense.

The Sage looked as if he was on the point of chastising the God of Water, so the god took fright, and in a trice, the river sank to its previous level along the banks.

Sword in hand, the Sage charged at the Demon Dragon, who stepped forward in the shape of a lance-wielding yaksha charged with the task of safeguarding the seas.[28] A ferocious fight it was:

The Sage swung his swords; the demon parried with his lance.
The frosty light of the swords shone with sparks of fire;
The aura of the sharp lance rose to the gloomy clouds.

One was a demon born in the Yangzi River;
The other was an immortal sent by heaven.
One violated the divine laws, flaunting his prowess;
The other fought evil and disasters, wielding Daoist power.
The immortal pushed back the evil mist;
The demon conjured up waves of dust.
Both strove hard to win the battle
For the millions of Nanchang people.

Witnessing the fierce fight between the Demon Dragon and the Sage, the flood dragons stepped forward in unison to help the Demon Dragon. (*The first major victory against the flood dragons.*) All of a sudden, an eerie sandstorm came on, called up to blur the Sage's vision. Behold:

Like fog or smoke, the sand swirled through the air
Before spinning down to the ground.
In the vast expanse of whiteness,
Eyes could hardly stay open;
In the wide-spreading darkness,
Finding one's way was too great a challenge.
Woodchoppers couldn't see their companions;
Fairies picking medicinal herbs couldn't find their way home.
The sand grains wafted gently through the air,
Some like finely ground wheat, some like coarser sesame seeds.
The world misted over, the hilltops lost to view;
The sky became blurry, the sun blocked.
By no means the kind of dust kicked up by horses
Nor the kind of fine sand that pads fancy carriages,
This was sand that showed no mercy
And whipped at the eyes till one saw stars.

As the flood dragons gave a single battle cry in the swirling sandstorm, the Sage blew a puff of his immortal's breath. The puff turned into a powerful gust of wind that blew the sand the other way.

From his high vantage point, Mr. Wu saw that the demons were indeed in possession of remarkable magic power. He worked up a thunder in the palm of his hand and threw it toward the sky. Though wind, clouds, thunder, and rain are things that give flood dragons delight, Mr. Wu's thunder was a magic one designed to subjugate demons. Behold:

Generated from a palm, it shook the clouds.
As it rolled, inspiring awe, it lit up the fire god's flames
And pushed along the thunder god's chariot wheels.
Its rumbling sounded like drumbeats that shook the sky and earth.

Its roar sounded like cannons that echoed through the army barracks.
It made Liu Bei drop his chopsticks;[29]
It made Cai Yuanzhong circle his mother's tomb.[30]
With no time to cover their ears before it comes,
All are transfixed with fear.
Truly, the immortal's hand emanated magic power;
The demons' hearts trembled in terror.

As the thunder burst upon their ears—loud enough to shake the sky, the earth, the seas, and the mountains—the demons were so frightened that their souls took flight. Failing to parry the Sage's glistening swords, chilly with the air of death, the Demon Dragon changed again from yaksha into goodness knows what and disappeared.

With the Demon Dragon gone, the Sage chased after the flood dragons, which ran helter-skelter in all directions. The Sage followed two of them all the way to Ezhu, where they suddenly vanished. Seeing three old men standing by the road, the Sage asked, "Have you three gentlemen seen the evil flood dragons that I have been chasing? When they got here, they suddenly disappeared."

The old men said, pointing, "Could they be hiding under the bridge over there?"

The Sage betook himself accordingly to the bridge, where he shouted angry words at the flood dragons, his sword at the ready. Terrified, the flood dragons scurried into the river and hid themselves at the bottom of an abyss. The Sage drew several magic figures to drive them out. Unable to remain in their hiding place, the flood dragons emerged, only to be cut down by the Sage. The river was dyed red. These two flood dragons were the Demon Dragon's sons. (*So, two sons are gone.*) Even to this day, there are in Ezhu a temple to the Three Sage Kings, a bridge called Dragon Subjugation Bridge, and an abyss named the Dragon's Nest. And the place where the flood dragons were killed is called Dragon Source.

Upon returning to Xining, the Sage locked the door of the local god's temple with a brass padlock, angry at the latter's incompetence, and forbade the local people to make sacrificial offerings there. To this day, the front door of the local god's temple in Fenning County is still more often closed than open, and few sacrificial items are offered by the local populace. The Sage then ordered that the people worship the Mao brothers as minor deities. These were the very three men who had pointed out to the Sage the flood dragons' hiding place under the bridge. Later, they were granted titles as dukes of Yeyou. Their temple has never been short of worshipers making offerings.

To Mr. Wu, the Sage said, "The Demon Dragon is at large, and the flood dragons have scattered. I am determined to seek them all out and exterminate them."

"Having just returned from Jinling, you must first of all pay respects to your parents," said Mr. Wu. "As for the demons, with you here, they won't dare be as rampant as before. You can get rid of them in good time."

As they came to Miaozhen Cave in Fengcheng County, the Sage said, "Let me block this cave because the flood dragons will surely make it one of their haunts." He picked up the branch of a big fir tree, drew a magic figure on it, and used it as a padlock. The branch remains to this day, free from decay.

They passed Fengxin County and came upon a creek that never ran dry. It was called Hidden Creek and was also known as Flood Dragon Hole. The Sage commented, "This must be another hiding place for the flood dragons." He split open the huge rock by the side of the creek with his divine swords and drew a magic figure to block the creek. The rock, henceforth known as Flood Dragon Subjugation Rock, stands to this day.

They then went through Xinjian County, where there was a Tanzao Lake, which was full of leeches. The creatures were slaves of the flood dragons and would wriggle into the fields to suck human blood. In disgust, the Sage tossed a pill into the lake, and all the leeches were annihilated once and for all. The lake is now called Leech Pill Lake.

The Sage then returned to his home in West Hill and saw his parents, to the joy of the whole family, but of this, we shall speak no further.

Now that the Sage had defeated the Demon Dragon time and again, his fame for his magic powers and good deeds spread far and wide. Those who sought to be his disciples numbered in the thousands. Unable to accept them all, the Sage made hundreds of beautiful women out of charcoal and placed them at night in the applicants' rooms. The following morning, only ten men were untainted with charcoal. (*So, feminine beauty is nothing but charcoal. Those tainted with it are unaware of being victims.*) What follows is a list of the first six disciples:

Chen Xun, courtesy name Xiaoju, a native of Chengdu.

Zhou Guang, courtesy name Huichang, a native of Luling.

Huang Renlan, courtesy name Ziting, a native of Jiancheng and the Sage's son-in-law.

Peng Kang, courtesy name Wuyang, a native of Lanling, whose daughter married the Sage's son.

Xu Lie, courtesy name Daowei, a native of Nanchang and the Sage's nephew.

Zhongli Jia, courtesy name Gongyang, a native of Xinjian and the Sage's nephew.

They were joined later by the following four disciples:

Zeng Heng, courtesy name Dianguo, a native of Sishui, whose refined looks and sharp intelligence deeply impressed Sun Deng.[31] He had been diligently applying himself to the study of Daoism, making trips south of the Yangzi River while maintaining his residence at Zhenyang Temple in Fengcheng, Yuzhang. After hearing of the Sage's fame, he came to be his disciple.

Shi He, courtesy name Daoyang, a native of Julu, who became a Daoist

> acolyte early in his youth and was studying Laozi's school of Daoism at Fengxian Temple, Muyangyuan of the Eastern Sea. After he had learned the breathing method from an immortal during an excursion to the Siming Mountains, he was able to abstain from consuming grains and could engage the services of ghosts and deities. In admiration of the Sage's fame, he journeyed on foot to the Sage's abode to be a disciple.
>
> Gan Zhan, courtesy name Bowu, a native of Fengcheng, who was disposed to cultivate the inner spirit rather than pursue official posts, was determined to learn the Daoist arts from the Sage.
>
> Shi Cen, courtesy name Taiyu, a native of Pei County, whose father, Shi Shuo, had served as an official in the Wu region and was therefore living in Chiwu County, Jiujiang. He was a man of powerful physique, courage, and strength. Having heard about the Sage's meritorious deeds in killing the flood dragons, he joyfully came to follow the Sage. The Sage entrusted him and Gan Zhan with the care of the divine swords and made both men his personal attendants.

The Sage praised these ten men for staying away from the charcoal women and took them with him in his travels across the land, subjugating flood dragons and snakes. They were the ones who would rise to heaven later in the story. Those who had been tainted by charcoal were so ashamed of themselves that they took themselves off. The Charcoal Women marketplace exists to this day.

To Shi Cen and Xu Lie, the Sage said, "The demons wreaking havoc even as I speak can transform themselves in unpredictable ways. The two of you may go to Boyang Lake and track them down."

They gladly accepted the order and departed, their swords drawn. It was night when they arrived at Boyang Lake, where they ascended a stone platform and looked around for demons. This is the very Overlook Platform, mistakenly called Fishing Platform, that remains to this day at the mouth of the Yao River. At the sight of an object that resembled a snake, its head raised high, its tail stretching several tens of li, Shi Cen asked, "Could this be a demon?" With that, he brought his sword down and cut it in half. The next morning, they saw that it was a mountain called Mount Centipede, now cut in half. The mountain, which bears witness to the deed of the immortal, stands to this day. Shi Cen said to Xu Lie, "In the darkness of the night, I thought this mountain was a demon, but I've been proved wrong. Let's move on and search elsewhere."

Having suffered defeat at the Sage's hands and lost two sons and many other members of his clan, the Demon Dragon burned with hatred for the Sage. Gnashing his teeth in rage, he called a clan meeting, where he expressed the wish to go to Little Sister-in-law Pond to ask the Old Dragon to help him take revenge. The flood dragons said, "That's a good idea." Thereupon the Demon Dragon dived straight into Little Sister-in-Law Pond, and a deep pond it was. As a popular saying goes, "Big Sister-in-Law Pond is ten thousand feet in width; Little Sister-in-Law is ten thousand feet in depth." Hence the name Little Sister-in-Law Pond. The Demon Dragon plunged to the very bottom of the pond. Behold:

The water rises to the sky; the waves lap against the shore.
In midstream stands Little Sister-in-Law Rock,
The mainstay of the river;
Underneath lies a pond that holds an eternal palace,
The abode of the Old Dragon.
The roof is covered with paired green tiles
Surrounded by glistening fan-shaped peacock tails.
The hall is adorned with green jade curtains;
In the middle is a round-armed chair covered with tiger skin.
On the chair sits the Old Dragon,
With dragon maids in attendance at the foot of the steps,
Dragon soldiers at their posts throughout the palace,
Yakshas guarding the doorways,
And dragon sons and grandsons standing in line on the dais.
Truly, it is a sight second to none in the heart of the river,
A palace without equal in the world of water.

Now, a word about the Old Dragon's background. It was this very dragon that the Yellow Emperor had ridden on his way to heaven after making a brass tripod at Mount Jing. As punishment for the dragon's greed and malice, the Lady of the Nine Heavens had him arrested and sent to the chief arhat, who kept him for a thousand years in an alms bowl, but the dragon remained as greedy and malicious as ever. After descending to earth, he ate Zhang Guolao's[32] donkey and wounded the eight precious horses of King Mu of the Zhou dynasty. An indignant Zhu Manping[33] learned ways of killing dragons and was determined to capture him, but the dragon hid in an orange in the backyard of a house in the Sichuan region. When two old men playing chess talked about making dried dragon meat of him (*What an imagination!*), he betook himself to Gepi, where he ran into Fei Changfang,[34] and was given a good whack with Fei's staff. In pain, the dragon scurried off to Huayang Cave, only to be hacked in the head with Wu Chuo's[35] merciless ax. What a luckless dragon! Even though his head was none the worse for it, the pearl tied to his neck was gone, which meant that he could never go back to heaven again. So he ingratiated himself with the goddess Little Sister-in-Law and was given this ten-thousand-foot-deep pond, where he had a grand palace built for himself.

Now, let's resume our story. The Demon Dragon ran into the palace, flung himself at the Old Dragon's feet, and sobbed out his tale of woe. After delivering this account of Xu Xun killing his sons and other members of his clan and now hot on his trail, he burst into violent wails of grief. There was not a dry eye among the entire audience.

The Old Dragon said, "As they say, 'Just as the fox saddens at the death of the hare, one feels for one's own kind.' Since Xu Xun is such a hateful brute, let me get him, and you may have your revenge."

The Demon Dragon said, "But with the Reverend Mother's flying method plus two demon-subjugation swords from the Jade Maiden, he has such great magical power that you can't take him lightly."

"Whatever flying method he has, he can't beat me in flying. Whatever demon-subjugation swords he has, he can't touch me!" So saying, the Old Dragon changed himself into a celestial god, with three heads, six arms, a black face, and protruding teeth. Behold:

A heavy suit of mail over his body, a sharp iron fork in his hand.
The gold helmet on his head shines under the rosy clouds;
His mighty horse is rearing to go.
A valiant warrior indeed, an awe-inspiring sight,
His heart set on revenge on behalf of others,
He strikes terror into all who set eyes on him.

The Old Dragon's new attire drew enthusiastic applause from the yakshas, commanders, and soldiers, and all present cheered, "Wonderful!"

The Demon Dragon followed suit. With a shake of his body, he, too, changed into a celestial god. How did he look? Behold:

His cheeks as black as those of the God of Monkey,
In stature, as tall as Marshal Deng.[36]
Holding Zhang Fei's[37] *eight-foot lance,*
He has the posture of no less a god than Marshal Wang.[38]
Spitting fire from his mouth, as did Sage Ge,
And emanating the aura of Bodhisatta Huaguang from his head,
He is a goodly sight to see,
For he was not what he used to be.

Thus transformed, he won applause and cheers from all and sundry throughout the palace.

Together, the two monsters spun themselves around in a whirlwind before heading for the shore. With the Old Dragon on the left and the Demon Dragon on the right, the flood dragons stood in battle array, ready to meet the Sage head-on. Let us leave them there for the moment.

Shi Cen and Xu Lie, while looking out from their vantage point, noticed that the air reeked of evil spirits. Completely indifferent to the enemies' power and overwhelming numbers, they jumped from the high ground, swords in hand, filled with youthful courage and determined to fight it out with the demons. Though they had learned the Sage's secret formulae, they were hopelessly outnumbered. After fighting three rounds, they had difficulty warding off the flood dragons and took flight. The Old Dragon and the Demon Dragon chased after them.

Shi Cen returned to the Sage's abode in defeat. His account of what had happened enraged the Sage, who picked up his two precious swords and, along with Gan Zhan and Shi He, traveled on an auspicious cloud to the battleground. When the Demon Dragon saw the Sage, his feelings could be captured by the saying "When enemies meet face to face, their eyes blaze with anger." Picking up his lance, he charged at the Sage. The Old Dragon also charged, his iron fork at the ready. Exercising his magic power, the great Sage repelled their attacks left and right with his two swords. Behold:

One sword parries the lance in relentless ferocity;
The other sword fearlessly fends off the iron fork.
A blow from one is like the raging Lüliang waterfall;
A cut from the other is like an avalanche in the Sichuan mountains.
In a display of power, one is like a falcon among crows;
In a show of might, the other is like a tiger pouncing on lambs.
One kills like wind blowing away withered flowers,
Until heads roll like petals on the ground;
The other kills like waves sweeping the land,
Until soil, dust, and all end up in the sea.
Truly, with hands that can overturn sky and earth,
He wipes out demons that wreak havoc on the land.

Locked in battle with the Sage, with neither side gaining the upper hand, the two dragons suddenly leaped into the air, ready to call forth a rainstorm to whip up sand and stones so as to disorient and capture the sage. But by this time, the Sage, who already knew the art of mounting the clouds and riding the mist, also rose into the air, caught up with the dragons, and resumed combat.

A good while later, they all descended to earth again and continued to fight. The flood dragons observed that the two dragons were gradually succumbing to the Sage and charged forward. Shi He and Gan Zhan, sharp swords in hand, also plunged into the melee. With the Sage and his two disciples rampaging through the enemy ranks, the dragons could hardly fend them off. As his strength failed him, the Old Dragon found that the Sage had wounded one of his three heads and cut off one of his six arms. Changing himself into a cool breeze, he fled.

Witnessing the Old Dragon's defeat, the Demon Dragon took fright. Afraid that the Sage would capture him, he also changed into a cool breeze and fled in a westerly direction. The flood dragons ran for their lives, dispersing themselves every which way. Some changed into grasshoppers, hopping in the wheat fields; some into green flies, buzzing on the date trees; some into earthworms, wriggling through the rice paddies; some into bees, noisily gathering nectar from the flowers; some into dragonflies, flitting about among the clouds; and some into crickets, hiding quietly beneath the ridges in plowed fields. The Sage happened to walk past one of those ridges while pursuing the demons. He suddenly lost his footing and inadvertently kicked away part of the ridge. What should he see emanating from the gouged earth but a wisp of vapor signifying the presence of a demon! Alarmed, he looked down and saw a cricket hiding inside. He swung his sword and cut the cricket in half. It turned out to be the Demon Dragon's fifth son. (*Three sons have now perished by the sword.*) A later poet had this to say:

How laughable that the demons didn't know better
Than to fight the immortal!
With his merciless sword drawn high in the air,
He killed the fifth son of the Demon Dragon.

After killing the Demon Dragon's fifth son, the Sage hastened to hunt down the Demon Dragon himself but could find no trace of him.

The Sage returned to Yuzhang with his two disciples. Mr. Wu said to him, "The flood dragons are still flourishing. They have not been exterminated. Since he has their support, the Demon Dragon is not going to give up. The best course of action is to eliminate his underlings so that, alone and powerless, he can be easily captured. This is what meant by the saying 'When shooting a man, aim at his horse first.'"

"How right you are!" said the Sage. With Shi Cen, Gan Zhan, Chen Xun, Xu Lie, Zhongli Jia, and other disciples, he again went in pursuit of the flood dragons. Afraid that the Demon Dragon would attack his hometown, he left Wu Meng and Peng Kang there for defense. And so, the Sage and his group of disciples went over hill and dale, through deep ponds, and across long bridges and large lakes to hunt down the flood dragons.

One day, the Sage came to a place called Xinwu. There, he saw a flood dragon change itself into a water buffalo, preparing to raise a flood that would drown the local residents. It blew out one breath, and the water rose one foot. With two breaths, the water rose two feet. In anger, the Sage drew his sword, but the flood dragon was so terrified by the sight of him that it jumped into a pond. The Sage put up a stone tablet on the spot and wrote an essay that placed a curse on the flood dragon. The essay said:

> Having attained immortality by order of the Universe, to live as long as the ever-cycling kalpas and the sky and the earth, I have power that is limitless and most profound. In assiduous cultivation of my spirit, I shall ascend to heaven in broad daylight. With my divine swords descending to the ground and my magic figures rising to the sky, demons are stricken with terror, and evil spirits hide themselves from view.

The pond, henceforth called Dragon Subjugation Pond, exists to this day, as does the stone tablet.

One day, coming upon a place called Haihun during his travels, the Sage heard that a giant python had made a mountain in the vicinity of its home. The breath it blew into the air traveled for several li in the shape of a cloud, which then swallowed all the people and animals caught in it. The python was also much given to capsizing boats in rivers and lakes, wreaking havoc on the people. Looking out from the top of North Hill, Shi Cen noticed the evil miasma in the air and said with a sigh, "What have the people done to deserve such misery?"

When he asked the Sage for permission to kill the python, the latter cautioned him in these words: "From what I've heard, the poison of this beast is most lethal. Everyone who comes into contact with its breath is sure to die. Let's wait for a more opportune moment before doing anything."

A considerable time later, a red crow flew by. The Sage said, "Now is the moment for action." It is said that a red crow heralds the advent of the gods of the sky and the earth and is therefore a signal that the moment has come for the subjugation of evil spirits. Later, a temple was erected on the spot and was given two names—Biding Time and Red Crow.

But, to continue with the story, the Sage led a group of his disciples to the python's cave. Abruptly, the monster leaped out of the depths of its cave and raised its head until its neck was several tens of feet long. Its eyes blazing like torches, its open mouth like a basin filled with blood, its scales like shining coins, it blew an evil breath. Behold:

Opaque as the fog conjured up by Chiyou,[39]
Murky as the dust storm that reminds one of Yuangui,[40]
The black particles, like those formed in the Han palace,
Fly back and forth, up and down, like dark clouds over Mount Tai.
They block out hills, the sun, the moon, and the stars.
They spread far, killing everyone in their way.
Truly, the evil python's breath travels three thousand li;
Even the air a thousand li away reeks of its foul smell.

With one exhalation of the Sage's immortal breath, the python's foul breath was gone. The Sage and his disciples held their swords high, and the local residents started waving flags, beating drums, and uttering earth-shaking battle cries to help frighten the python. But the evil python showed no sign of fear and charged at the Sage, who then conjured up a thunder and flung it head-on at the python while pointing his divine swords at it. The python stopped in its tracks. Shi Cen and Gan Zhan dashed forward. With Shi's feet on the python's head and Gan standing on its tail, the Sage slashed its jaws, and Chen Xun cut it right through the middle. Its belly burst open, and a small python several feet long emerged from it. Shi was about to kill it when the Sage stopped him, saying, "This one hasn't yet even seen the light of day from inside the belly of its mother and is not guilty of any crime against humans. Don't kill it." He then said sternly to the small python, "Go now, beast! I'm letting you off, but don't do anything to harm people!"

In terror, the small python ran for six or seven li. Only when it heard a great commotion did it turn around to look at its mother. Today, that spot is called the Port of the Python's Son. To the disciples' requests to give chase and kill the small python, the Sage replied, "If we do that after we have already let it go, where's the mercy in our hearts?"

Thus it was that the small python managed to reach the river. A temple still stands on this spot at Wucheng, Xinjian. Most responsive to prayers, it received the name Temple of Efficacious and Manifest Succor and Benevolence from Emperor Zhenzong [r. 998–1023] of the Song dynasty but is better known to all and sundry as the Temple of the Young Dragon King. The bones of the mother python, gathered together, formed an islet, which is called today the Islet of Bones.

In his travels in Haihun, the Sage left behind six altars. These six, plus the one he had before while he was biding his time, were the altar of transformation, the altar of prayer, the altar of magic figures, the altar of ornamental columns, the altar of the purple sun, the altar of the crane sun, and the altar of the naming of sages. The seven altars were spread out in the shape of the Big Dipper so as to subjugate future demons. All seven have since been made either temples or monasteries.

With the giant python out of the way, the Sage washed the blood of the monster off his swords, honed their blades, and struck a stone with them to test their sharpness. The pond where he cleaned his swords and the rock on which he tested their sharpness still exist in Xinjian. He said to his disciples, "The flood dragons have not been wiped out. The Demon Dragon, being as smart as he is, surely knows where I am. Should he take advantage of my absence to attack my hometown, I'm afraid that Wu and Peng won't be able to subdue him. Let's leave this place and go back."

The valiant warrior Shi Cen said, "With so many demons around here, let's spend a few more days trying to find them and kill them before we leave. Wouldn't that be better?"

The Sage replied, "I've been away for so long that I'm afraid the flood dragons in my town have rallied again. We should be on our way as soon as possible so we can destroy them all." Accordingly, they all left Haihun. Out of gratitude for the Sage's kind deeds, the local residents erected a temple to him and made seasonal offerings, but of this, no more.

Sure enough, the Demon Dragon hated the Sage with every fiber of his being. He planned to take advantage of the Sage's absence to submerge Yuzhang in the sea as revenge for his defeat. He gathered together the seven hundred to eight hundred flood dragons who had survived the assaults and said to them, "Last night, the moon moved close to the Bi star, heralding a rainstorm. By late afternoon today, the sky will be overcast, and a violent storm will sweep through this region. Why don't we take the opportunity to sink Yuzhang under the sea?" It was the noon hour when he said this.

It so happened that while the Demon Dragon was saying those words, Wu Meng and Peng Kang looked out from the height of West Hill and saw the sky overcast with an aura that indicated a massive demonic presence. They commented, "So, the demons have rallied here while Master Xu is away looking for them."

Before the words were quite out of their mouths, the local gods of Yuzhang appeared before Wu, saying, "The Demon Dragon has again rallied about eight hundred flood dragons to sink Jiangxi in the sea. They'll make their move late this afternoon when the rainstorm begins. Residents who heard about this came to our temples to kowtow and ask for protection. As we see it, we can help them if Jiangxi were not swept into the sea, but if this were to happen, it would truly be as the proverb says, 'A clay statue of Buddha crossing a river is hardly able to save itself, let alone everyone else.' Please help us."

Alarmed by this account, Wu hastened down the hill with Peng and said to him, "Now, you go ahead with your sword and summon the celestial warriors after you first patrol around the river."

After Peng left, Wu mounted a nine-constellation altar, took a five-thunder command tablet, and, holding a seven-constellation precious sword in one hand, filled a bowl with the pure water that came out of the mouths of five dragons. He then intoned an incantation that began "May the cosmos and the nine dragons help the Sage triumph over evil," cited a divine formula, and traced with his feet on the ground the imagined outline of the Big Dipper. Then he tossed a message to the god on yearly duty in the Jade Emperor's palace so that he could transmit it to the God of the Sun in the sun palace. The message requested the God of the Sun to postpone the sinking of the sun by six hours and make the sun reverse its course as it did when Duke Luyang pointed his lance at it and hold its position as it did when the duke of Yu pointed his dagger at it.[41]

He then tossed a message to the god on monthly duty at the Jade Emperor's palace, to be transmitted to the God of the Moon in the moon palace. The message asked the God of the Moon to postpone the rising of the moon that night by four hours and to make the full moon cast its lambent light over all corners of the earth from the moment it rose above the sea and emerged from the clouds. ([Illegible])

He tossed another message to the god on daily duty at the Jade Emperor's palace, to be transmitted to the God of Wind. This message asked the God of Wind to let the wind rest for the night and not give even one howl or puff of breath, nor cross the river and whip up dragon-head waves or blow up dust from horses' hooves, scatter withered leaves from trees, and drive white clouds out from the mountains.

Then he tossed a message to the god on hourly duty at the Jade Emperor's palace, to be passed on to the God of Rain. This message requested the God of the Rain to hold back the rain for the night and not let the raindrops destroy plantain leaves and wash away mosses, nor let it pour down ink from the black fog on the bald mountains, swell the wind-driven waves that the god of waves could churn up in the sea, and make deafening noises like those heard in the battle between Xiang Yu and Zhang Han.[42]

Another message went to the fleet-footed God of Running for him to deliver to the God of Thunder, asking the latter to hide the five thunders for the night and not blow his bugle, let out the bolts, or send the rumbles that shake the mountains, nor to drum by the Gate of Yu or make the sky spin and the earth tremble.

The last message went to the Messenger God, to be delivered to the God of Clouds, asking the latter to hold back the clouds for the night and not allow them to cover the vast sky, block out the rivers and mountains, carry the phoenixes and the dragons, or evoke the nostalgia of travelers to the Taihang Mountains and give dreams to King Xiang at Wu Gorge.[43]

Having sent out all the messages, Mr. Wu told the local gods to report to the Sage with all the speed they could muster so that the Sage could rush back to Yuzhang and subdue the demons without delay. This done, Wu took up his sword to do battle with the flood dragons. More of this later.

In the meantime, the Demon Dragon was waiting for the hour when the sun would yield to the moon so that he could summon the wind, rain, clouds, and thunder to submerge the whole county of Yuzhang in the sea. Yet, however anxiously he waited for the hour to arrive, the sun kept shining brightly from its early afternoon position. When he ordered it to set, it did not budge, as if tied to its place in the sky by a rope. The Demon Dragon then tried to make the moon rise, but it, too, stayed where it was, as if someone were holding it tight. Losing all patience, the Demon Dragon ordered all the flood dragons to summon the wind, whether it was the right hour or not. But the God of Wind, under instructions from Wu, called out from midair, "Demon Dragon! You have become such a monster that I'm not going to obey your order for wind!"

Having failed to call forth the wind, the Demon Dragon turned to the God of Thunder for help, little knowing that this god had also received orders from Wu. As the God of Thunder remained silent, the Demon Dragon exclaimed, "God of Thunder! You have never failed to give me at least a thousand peals of thunder whenever I asked. Why are you so quiet today? Have you lost your voice?"

The God of Thunder replied, "No, I haven't lost my voice, but you have certainly lost your mind!"

The Demon Dragon could do nothing else but call out, "God of Clouds! Give me clouds, and be quick about it!"

Under orders from Wu, the God of Clouds had rolled up all the clouds that were scattered above the hills and valleys and had hidden them in a secret place. Why would he give in and release them now? There was not even a streak of cloud across the clear sky, where the God of Clouds was heard merrily singing, "I call back the sunset clouds over the ten-thousand-li Yangzi River."

Realizing that the God of Clouds was determined not to oblige him, the Demon Dragon turned to the God of Rain, little knowing that the latter, too, had received orders from Wu. Not even half a drop of rain was going to fall, let alone thousands upon thousands of them.

With the sun refusing to sink, the moon to rise, the wind to blow, the rain to fall, the thunder to rumble, and the clouds to gather, the Demon Dragon burned with rage. He said to the flood dragons, "I don't believe that tiny Yuzhang County can't be sunk beneath the sea without winds, clouds, thunder, and rain." With that, he spread out the scales covering his body, flipped head over tail, and sank the area outside Zhangjiang Gate of Jiangxi tens of feet under the ground. At the sight, Wu quickly raised high his precious sword and, riding an auspicious cloud, charged straight at the Demon Dragon. While the two were thus engaged, Peng rushed over to help, his sword drawn high. The Demon Dragon called for his underlings to join him in the fierce battle outside the city gate, and they came in one great swarm. Some changed into numerous wasps and fiercely attacked Wu and Peng in the face, while others turned into long, wriggling snakes and coiled around the two men's feet. The Demon Dragon transformed himself into the shape of Buddha's giant warrior attendant. Brandishing a gold dagger-ax, he got into a good fight with Wu and Peng. An impressive sight it was, with Wu and Peng holding the frenzied wasps at bay, their swords swishing above their heads like snowflakes; fighting off the long snakes at their feet, their swords swirling about in the pattern of the twisted roots of a withered tree; and fending off the Demon Dragon, their swords flitting about the middle like somersaulting sparrow hawks.

They fought from early afternoon all the way to sundown. Suddenly, the Sage arrived, followed by a group of his disciples. "Xu Xun is here!" he bellowed. "Would you accursed beasts dare do violence to me?"

The flood dragons took fright, but the Demon Dragon, his jaw set firmly at the sight of the Sage, was determined to exact his vengeance. (*This will be the fourth major victory over the flood dragons.*)

The Demon Dragon announced to the flood dragons, "At this darkest hour, for you as well as for me, whether we live or to die depends on what we do now!"

With zest, the flood dragons replied, "Being members of the same clan, we'll surely fight for our lives and live together if we win or die together if we lose."

And so, they joined the Demon Dragon and fought with all their might against the Sage. How do we know it was a good fight?

Dark clouds blotted out the sun;
The air of death permeated the sky.
Heaven and earth turned upside down;
The gods grieved, and ghosts wept.
The immortal had boundless magic power;
The evil one was equally endowed.
One was a monster from a pond ten thousand feet deep,
Brandishing a gold dagger-ax;
The other was an immortal from the ninth layer of heaven,
Wielding precious swords.

One moved with shimmering layers of scales;
The other made good use of his skills of transfiguration.
One needed only a puff of his demon breath
To make fog and clouds appear.
The other needed only a puff of his immortal breath
To make the sky clear again.
One led his flood dragon offspring in fighting the immortal,
Like the eight-hundred-thousand-strong Cao army at the Red Cliffs;[44]
The other led his disciples in subjugating evil,
Like the twenty-eight Han warriors at Kunyang.[45]
One churned the rivers and seas, stirring up the waves;
The other shook the pillars and axes of the universe, invoking thunder.
One was intent on revenge for members of his clan;
The other was bent on destroying the scourge that plagued the people.
Truly, the two sides fought with all their might,
Using their magic powers.
The stronger will win; the weaker will lose.

Now, the Demon Dragon charged with all his might at the Sage, who was determined to capture him and put an end to this source of all trouble once and for all. The flood dragons, however, were horror-stricken. The Sage's disciples, wielding their swords, cut them down, some killing one or two, some killing three or four, some even five or six. The foul-smelling blood spurted out, dyeing everything red. With one blow of Zhou Guang's sword, the second son of the Demon Dragon perished. (*So, four of his sons have died.*) All the surviving flood dragons changed shape and fled, leaving only the Demon Dragon to fight the Sage alone. Turning his head and seeing none of his underlings with him, the Demon Dragon jumped up on a cloud, changed himself into a gust of black wind, and was gone. The Sage quickly gave chase, but the monster was already out of sight.

On the way back with his disciples, the Sage said to Wu Meng, "If it hadn't been for your magic power, millions of human lives would have been lost in the flood!"

Wu replied, "It was you who put the flood dragons to flight. Otherwise, my life would have been in danger as well."

As for the Demon Dragon, after so many defeats and such heavy casualties among his underlings, he was left with only two sons out of six. All the flood dragons, afraid that the Sage would be after them next, changed into human form, except three, two of whom were the Demon Dragon's sons and one his grandson. These three hid in the rivers of Xinjian, but the rest of the flood dragons changed and dispersed into the towns and marketplaces of different countries so as to stay out of danger.

One day, Zeng Heng, one of the sage's disciples, went into the city, where two young men with extraordinary looks bowed to him with great respect and asked, "Might you be one of Mr. Xu's disciples?"

"Yes," replied Zeng. "Who might you be?"

"We live in Chang'an. We are from families with a long history of devotion to good works. Though we live far from here, we've heard about Mr. Xu's magic powers and the divine swords that he uses to kill evil spirits. But what exactly do his divine swords do?"

"My master's divine swords can do everything. When pointed at the sky, they rend it asunder. When pointed at the earth, they split it open. When pointed at the stars, they make them fall from their places in the sky. When pointed at the rivers, they reverse the currents. No evil spirit can fend them off, and no monster can defend against them. When drawn from their sheaths, they shine like cold frost and chilly snow. Wherever their glow is seen, ghosts weep and deities are distressed. They're truly a treasure bestowed by heaven."

"Is anything in this mortal world immune to your master's divine swords?"

Zeng said in jest, "The only two things that are immune are winter melon and bottle gourd. Nothing else."

Having heard this, the two young men bade him farewell and departed. Zeng had no idea that they were actually flood dragons in human form. The two hastened to share the news about winter melons and bottle gourds with other flood dragons.

One day, the Sage gave his divine swords to his disciples Shi Cen and Gan Zhan, telling them to search for flood dragons and exterminate them. With Shi and Gan hot on their heels, the flood dragons, in desperation, all changed into bottle gourds and winter melons and floated on the river. The Sage mounted the crest of Xiu Peak, looked around with his divine eyes, and called out to Shi and Gan, "Those things floating on the river are not gourds and melons but flood dragons, the ones we did not kill. You may step onto the surface of the water and get rid of them."

Swiftly, they landed on the water and swung their swords vigorously at the bottle gourds. (*The fifth major victory over the flood dragons.*) Being light and buoyant, the melons and gourds just dipped under the water when struck by the swords instead of bursting open. While Shi and Gan were fretting, an immortal passing by stopped in midair to watch and soon ordered that a local deity change himself into a parrot. With the parrot crying overhead, "Go from the bottom up! From the bottom up!" Shi suddenly understood and drove his sword upward from underneath the melons and gourds. Of about seven hundred flood dragons in the river, none survived, vines, roots, and all. The clear green water became turbid red waves. Only three of the flood dragons, those that had not changed their form, were unhurt.

Seeing that the flood dragons had been annihilated, the Sage rewarded the parrot with a crown, which parrots of this day still wear. A later poet had this to say in praise of the Sage's extermination of the flood dragons:

The divine swords, nemeses of all demons,
Slashed melons and gourds on the green waves.
The demons, bent on flooding the town,
Ended up dead in the heart of the river.

Of the Demon Dragon's six sons, four were killed. The flood dragons, more than a thousand in all, were exterminated except for three—the Demon Dragon's third son, his sixth son, and his oldest grandson—who survived by hiding in the rivers of Xinjian County. Upon hearing that the Sage had wiped out all their kin, the Demon Dragon's two sons burst into loud sobs. "With our father's whereabouts unknown, we two are the only surviving sons of a total of six. Our children, six hundred to seven hundred in all, plus other kith and kin, added up to more than a thousand. Now that all of them are gone, killed by that Xu Xun, we two and a nephew are all that remain. With his immense magic power, Xu Xun is not going to let us live. Let's hide in places like Fujian before deciding what to do next." They were about to set out on their journey when the Sage and his disciples Gan Zhan and Shi Cen came into view. Frantically, the three flood dragons scurried away.

Noticing a column of vapor rising into the sky, a vapor that signified the presence of demons, the Sage pointed in that direction, saying to Gan and Shi, "There are more flood dragons. Let's pursue them and destroy them all."

Quietly, the three sped ahead and caught up with the flood dragons. Swinging his sword, Shi Cen cut the tail off one and kept running after them, as far as Yanping Prefecture, Fujian, where one of the three flood dragons dived into a deep pond called Chayang Nine-Li Pond.

The Sage called the local residents together and said to them, "I am Xu Xun of Yuzhang, here because we've been chasing an evil flood dragon that has hidden itself in this pond. I shall now plant a bamboo between the rocks at the edge of the pond. The bamboo will keep the evil one in there so that it can't come out to harm the people. Remember, all of you, not to cut down the bamboo." With that, he planted the bamboo and said to the flood dragon, "If the bamboo dies, you may gain a new life, but as long as the bamboo lives, you shall not leave this pond."

To this day, a single bamboo stands on that very spot at the edge of the pond. As soon as it begins to wither, a shoot comes up, and so the cycle continues. Called Sage Xu's Bamboo, it remains a single bamboo.

Merchants traveling back and forth on boats have reported sightings of a tailless flood dragon. As for the second flood dragon, the Sage and his two disciples Gan and Shi chased it all the way to Chong'an County in Jianning Prefecture, Fujian. An abbot called Abbot All Benevolence was reciting the sutra in the hall in Huaiyu Temple when a young man walked up to him and entreated him, saying, "I am the Demon Dragon's son. Xu Xun exterminated my whole family and has chased me all the way here. Please take pity on me and save my life. I will surely repay you handsomely later on."

"As far as I know," said the abbot, "Xu Xun of Yuzhang is a great master of the Daoist arts and has eyes of such divine perception that there's no place in this monastery you can hide."

"Your Reverence, should you be willing to save me out of compassion, I'll change myself into a grain of millet and hide in your palm. When Xu Xun comes into the monastery, if you recite your sutra with your palms joined together, I'm sure nothing will happen to me."

The abbot agreed. The young man changed himself into a grain of millet hidden in the abbot's palm.

Soon, the Sage led Gan and Shi to the temple. "I am Xu Xun of Yuzhang," said the Sage to the abbot. "I am here in pursuit of an evil flood dragon. Where is he? Please make him come out to see me."

The abbot did not answer but kept reciting the sutra, his hands joined palm to palm. Little knowing that the flood dragon was hiding in the abbot's palm, the Sage searched for it in vain. He went outside to search the neighborhood, also to no avail.

"The evil one must have left," said Shi Cen. "Let's go search elsewhere."

When he believed the Sage to be a safe distance away from the temple, the flood dragon changed back into a young man and said with a thankful bow to the abbot, "I have little with which to repay this enormous debt of gratitude to Your Reverence for saving my life, but could you order that the temple bells and drums not be struck for seven days and nights, so that I can do something by way of thanks?"

The abbot agreed and told his disciples and everyone else in the temple to comply with the young man's wish.

On the third day, a violent gust of bone-chilling wind sprang up around the temple, disturbing the soil and trees. In great alarm, the abbot said to the monks, "I just knew that the Demon Dragon's son was by no means a good sort. After I saved his life, he told us not to strike the bells and drums for seven days and nights, and today, only the third day, things are already beginning to go wrong. He must have been lying to me. If we don't strike the bells and drums, he will not only fail to repay the debt of gratitude but also ruin us. By then, regrets will be too late."

With that, he ordered the monks to strike the grand bell on the eastern tower. They struck it one hundred and eight times, filling the air with echoes. Truly, they were like the calls of whales in the Brahma's Palace that could be heard by merchants on their boats in the middle of the night. Then, the monks beat the painted drum on the western tower three times, rat-a-tat. Truly, it was like thunder booming over the clouds and a giant turtle roaring among the waves of the sea.

Startled at the sounds of the bell and the drum, the flood dragon changed back into a young man. He returned to the temple and said to the abbot, "A couple of days ago, I asked you not to strike the bells and drums for seven days because I wanted to change the hilly area surrounding the temple into a vast expanse of fertile land. This was to be my way of repaying my debt of gratitude to you for saving my life. In the last three days, I've had only enough time to flatten the hills slightly and make the springs run. But before I could accomplish more, Your Reverence had bells struck and drums beaten. I wonder why." (*Why didn't he tell the abbot the truth in the first place so as not to arouse suspicions as to his motive?*)

The abbot replied that he had done so because of the violent wind that had shaken the earth and hills. The young man heaved sigh upon sigh. The abbot then sent men out to check what had been done. They found that the steep spots had been flattened into cultivable land watered by ever-flowing springs. To this day, Huaiyu Temple is surrounded by a thousand acres of flat fertile land, the work of a grateful flood dragon.

Now, after leaving the temple and still not spotting the flood dragon anywhere, the Sage climbed to a high vantage point and saw that the air over the temple was still astir with evil. He turned back to the temple with Gan and Shi. Knowing that the Sage was coming back, the flood dragon changed into a monk and took leave of the abbot, saying, "The thousands of members of our clan have all been exterminated by Xu Xun. Of the six sons, four have died, and I have no idea if my father is alive or not. I'm going to mend my ways and enter the Buddhist order." With that, he took tearful leave of the abbot.

When the Sage came back to the temple and observed that the evil vapor had left the grounds, he followed its trail all the way to a place called Yedun in Jianyang. Far ahead, he saw a monk, who he knew must be the flood dragon. With Gan and Shi following him, he quickened his pace and caught up with the monk. Gan and Shi were about to kill him, but the Sage hastened to stop them, saying sharply, "Don't! He may have done evil things before, but in changing himself into a monk, he has most probably determined to mend his ways." Raising his voice, he said sternly, "Accursed beast! I am letting you off, but you must devote yourself to good deeds, cultivate your spirit, and do no harm to people. Remember well this line: 'Stop at the first lake you see and take up residence on Mount Yang.'" Having said that, the Sage let the flood dragon go.

"Accursed beast!" shouted Gan Zhan. "My master has spared your life, so you must never do harm to people again!"

"Accursed beast!" shouted Shi Cen. "If you don't follow my master's instructions but persist in your evil ways, I'll capture you as easily as I turn over my palm."

In shame, the monk ran helter-skelter all the way from Yedun to a village with a mountain standing in front of it. Seeing a herd-boy, the monk asked, "What is this place called?"

The herd-boy replied, "This is Lake Gui. The mountain ahead is Mount Yang."

The monk was ecstatic. "The Sage said, 'Stop at the first lake you see and take up residence on Mount Yang,'" he said to himself. "Now, this place exactly fits both parts of that line. So, let me take up residence here."

He rested at the side of the road between two rice paddies, and a spring of ever-flowing water rose on that spot. The place came to be called Dragon's Cave, later changed to Encountering Dragon Cave. The dragon monk entered the Buddhist order on Mount Yang and assumed the Buddhist name Abbot Ancient Plum. He then had a monastery built and called it Mount Yang Monastery. There being no water supply around at the time, Ancient Plum pointed randomly at rocks with his fingers, and spring water spouted forth wherever he pointed. The monastery came to be in possession of large tracts of crop-yielding land. The monastery and the land exist to this day. The Sage had a temple built in Yedun and called it the Sage's Temple. It faced Mount Yang and kept Ancient Plum's monastery in submission. The Sage's Temple still stands today.

Now, the Sage went in pursuit of the other flood dragon, son of the Demon Dragon's oldest son and therefore the Demon Dragon's oldest grandson. This flood dragon hid himself in Nantai, in Fuzhou, and left no trace of himself anywhere. The Sage ordered Gan and Shi to search for him all around, while he himself stood on a rock and cast a fishing rod into the water. Suddenly, he felt a tug on the rod and pulled it up with such force that the rock on which he stood split open. The rock exists to this day and is called Fishing for Dragon Rock. At the moment the rock split open, there emerged from the water a giant spiral shell twenty to thirty feet in height, from which a woman stepped out.

"You are an evil spirit!" exclaimed the Sage. With both knees on the ground, the woman said, "I am the third daughter of the god of the South Sea. Having heard of your fame as the master of Daoist arts, I came here on the shell boat to ask that you teach me the ways of spiritual cultivation."

The Sage pointed toward Mount Gaogai as a place for spiritual cultivation. He said, "There are bitter ginseng and licorice roots on that mountain. If you throw these herbs into the well at the top of the mountain and drink the water of the well every day, you'll become an immortal in due course."

He ordered the woman back into the spiral shell, and blew the shell across the surface of the water with one gentle puff of breath until it reached the foot of Mount Gaogai. Then the shell changed into a big rock, which still stands today. The woman climbed the mountain to pick bitter ginseng, licorice roots, and other herbs.

She threw them into the well every day and drank the water from the well until she achieved immortality as the Sage had said and departed. To this day, those villagers who become sick need only drink water from this well to regain their good health.

Now, Shi and Gan returned to report to the Sage that they had seen no flood dragons, whereupon the Sage ascended the very crest of the mountain and saw a barely discernible stream of evil vapor rising from the well of Kaiyuan Temple in the city of Fuzhou. He said to his disciples, "The flood dragon is in that well." He made his way to the temple and placed an iron statue of the Buddha on the well to block the exit. The statue remains to this day.

After having thus subjugated the three flood dragons, the Sage returned to Yuzhang with Gan Zhan and Shi Cen to search for the Demon Dragon and exterminate him. (*The six sons and one grandson are now all out of the way.*) A later poet had this to say in praise of the Sage:

From afar, he went to southern Fujian;
Riding the mist and clouds, he sought out flood dragons.
Leaving his name and traces everywhere,
He is worshiped by all posterity.

As told above, the Demon Dragon failed to flood Yuzhang County. On the contrary, his kith and kin, by changing themselves into melons and gourds, had been destroyed by the Sage. Of his six sons, four had been killed, and nothing was known about the fate of the remaining two sons and grandson. The more he thought about it, the more he chafed with vexation. He saw no choice but to return to the Yangzi River to his father, the Fire Dragon.

As he sobbed out his tale of woe, the Fire Dragon said, "Four hundred years ago, the King of Filial Piety and Brotherly Love imparted the arts to Mr. Lan, who then passed them on to Reverend Mother, who, in her turn, taught them to Xu Xun. I know all about Xu Xun's background. The trouble you are having dates back many years. This is why I had once led my turtle commander, shrimp soldiers, and crab generals and demanded that Mr. Lan give me the gold pills, magic mirrors, and copper and iron tablets, but Mr. Lan routed me. I was no match for Mr. Lan even when I was young and energetic. How am I to stand up against Xu Xun when I'm so old and rickety! You'll have to do it yourself."

The Demon Dragon said with a sigh, "There are people who say this is a world where fathers abandon their sons, and now I know how true that is!"

The Fire Dragon lashed out, "You beast! I used to have so many grandsons. It was you, good-for-nothing, who lost them all, and now you turn around and blame me!" So saying, he threw his son out.

Aggrieved that his father refused to help him, the Demon Dragon burst into loud wails of grief on the riverbank, wails that caught the attention of the third son of Aoqin, Dragon King of the South Sea. The dragon prince, fully armored, sword in hand, was patrolling the Yangzi River by order of his father, along with a yaksha on patrol duty. Recognizing the Fire Dragon's son, the prince hastened to ask, "Why are you crying here?"

The Demon Dragon replied, "All my kith and kin, numbering more than a thousand, have been killed by Xu Xun, and my father refuses to help me. Being as wretched as a stray dog, how can I not help crying?"

"As the ancients said, 'Families should not be exterminated down to the last one.' How could Xu Xun have killed so many of your clan? He believes he has no match in our water palace. Now, don't you worry, brother. Let me put my magic power to work and capture him so as to redress the wrongs he has done to you."

"But Xu Xun is equipped with the Reverend Mother's flying method and precious swords from a fairy maiden. His magic power is too great to be taken lightly."

The prince replied, "In the palace, we have an iron pestle called the As-You-Wish Pestle, and we used to have an iron rod called the As-You-Wish Rod. They can grow to be as thick as rafters or shrink to the size of a needle if you so wish. They can be thirty to forty feet or one to two inches in length. That's why they are called 'As-You-Wish.' Both treasures belong to Father, but the Monkey King[46] took away the rod, and goodness knows how many demons and monsters he killed with it. The pestle has never been put to use. Actually, I have it with me. Let me try it out on that Xu Xun. If it doesn't hurt him, I'll say he's really good."

"When was the pestle made?"

"When the universe first came into being. King Pangu chipped several sheets of rock from Mount Kunlun and made a furnace out of them. He then cut down a big tree in the Moon Palace and burned a lot of black charcoal. With tens of thousands of pieces of pig iron from Mount Sumeru and the samadhi fire from the Sun Palace, he had Nüwa, the goddess who smelted rocks, tend the furnace for forty-nine days.[47] He then had the rain god sprinkle rain on it, the wind god fan it, the god of the Gold Star protect it, and the fire god watch the flames. That was how the pestle came into being. It can be as big or small, as long or short, as you wish. Even more wonderful, when it is tossed into midair, it can multiply into ten, and the ten into a hundred, the hundred into a thousand, and the thousand into ten thousand. And it can change its shape, too."

"Where is it now?"

The prince took it out of his ear. With one shake in the wind, it grew as thick as a rafter. Two shakes, and it grew as long as a bamboo pole. The Demon Dragon was wild with joy. "Xu Xun may be able to dodge a few blows with his magic power, but his disciples won't be able to do the same!"

Observing that the prince was determined to seek revenge on behalf of the Demon Dragon, the yaksha offered this advice: "Without an order from His Majesty, how can Your Highness use any weapon on your own authority? Should His Majesty learn about this, it may not reflect well on you."

"My mind is made up," said the prince. "If you are willing to help me, go with me. If not, you may return to the South Sea."

Unwilling to help, the yaksha turned back. The prince, grimly determined, headed straight for Yuzhang to capture Xu Xun and seek revenge for the Demon Dragon. How did the prince look? Behold:

Layer upon layer of solid turtle shells,
A neat bandolier of kelp across the chest,
Riding a seahorse, he looked like a guard at the heavenly gate.
He kicked up pebbles as he advanced.
He whipped up swirling grains of sand as he flew.
He swore to capture the powerful immortal
With a rope made of heavenly hemp.

Swords in hand, the Sage and his disciples Gan and Shi were about to set off in search of the Demon Dragon when the third son of the Dragon King cried out,

"Xu Xun! Xu Xun! How can you be so heartless as to have exterminated a family of more than a thousand? How dare you look down upon the Dragon King? Let me fight it out with you, if only just to make you acknowledge my power."

With his all-knowing eyes, the Sage saw that it was the third son of the Dragon King. "Your father does a good job taking care of the South Sea," said the Sage. "Too bad he has you for a son! Now, go back home, so that you won't have any regrets later!"

"One who kills someone else's father will have his own father killed. One who kills someone else's brother will have his own brother killed," retorted the prince. "I will never allow any member of the aquatic clan to be bullied like this by you!"

So saying, he aimed his sword at the Sage. The Sage also raised his swords to meet the prince's. A fierce fight ensued.

One was a leading immortal from the ninth layer of heaven;
The other a dragon prince commanding the four seas.
One was a master of the Daoist arts,
Able to swallow clouds and inhale mist;
The other was proficient in the martial arts,
Able to make thunder and lightning.
One had the Reverend Mother as his mentor—
What greater claim to magic power could there be?
The other called the Dragon King his father—
What higher status could be imagined?
One wielded precious swords
That glistened like winter frost as they swung back and forth;
The other brandished an iron pestle
That clattered like New Year's eve firecrackers as it lunged left and right.
With both having met their match in each other,
Victory was hard to predict.
With both equally skilled,
None was the winner or the loser.

Sword against sword, the Sage and the prince fought for two hours, with neither winning or losing. Shi Cen said to his fellow disciples, "The Dragon King's son is so skilled that I'm afraid our master won't be able to subdue him easily. Let's all join him!"

Seeing the Sage's disciples coming at him, the prince took the iron pestle out of his ear, shook it a couple of times, and tossed it into the air. A wondrous pestle it was! It multiplied into ten, then a hundred, then a thousand, and then ten thousand pestles, spinning about in the air like so many willow catkins and flitting up and down like so many dragonflies, banging together like so many pestles at the command of Prime Minister Pan's son [reference unidentified]. Look at the Sage's disciples! Hardly had one fended off a pestle in front of his face than another came knocking against the back of his head. Scarcely had one warded off a pestle at the back of his head than another came thumping at his chest. The moment one had pushed the pestle away from his chest, another came and thwacked his shoulder. In terror, the disciples turned on their heels and fled. But the wondrous Sage was truly a consummate master of magic power. Wherever his precious swords pointed—whether to the east, west, south, or north—the pestles came tumbling down. Yet, regardless of his virtuosity, victory was still out of reach because there were just too many pestles.

Up in the sky, the Bodhisattva Guanyin heard about this. She said, "Dragon King Aoqin is so very kind and compassionate, but this wayward son of his is helping an evil spirit. Let me take away his As-You-Wish pestle, because Xu Xun can't do much about it, however great a master he is." So saying, she rose on an auspicious clouds, took off a ribbon from her clothes, made it into a loop, and gathered in all the thousands upon thousands of pestles. With his weapons gone, the prince took fright and fled.

The Demon Dragon greeted him and asked, "So, did you put Xu Xun to rout?"

"I was about to when a woman whisked off my pestle with some kind of loop, and I have no idea where to get it back."

"It was the Bodhisattva Guanyin who did it," said the Demon Dragon. Before the words were quite out of his mouth, the Sage appeared on the scene. At the sight, the Demon Dragon changed into a column of black wind and disappeared. The prince resentfully picked up his sword and stepped forward for another round of fighting. Having already suffered a defeat, he found his courage failing him.

In the second round, the Sage held off the prince's sword with the sword in his left hand and was about to kill the prince with the sword in his right hand when a voice called out from behind him: "Stop! Stay your hand!" The Sage raised his eyes and saw that it was the Bodhisattva Guanyin. He held back his sword. The bodhisattva said, "This is the third son of Dragon King Aoqin. He should be sentenced to death for having abetted the Demon Dragon without good reason. However, his father is most kind and compassionate. If the son is killed, and in my presence, too, the Dragon King will blame me for failing to save his son. That would put me in an awkward position." So the Sage gave up the idea.

In the meantime, the yaksha on river duty had returned to the Dragon King's palace and given the king a detailed account of how the prince was aiding the Demon Dragon. The Dragon King stamped his feet and cursed, "What a disobedient son I have!"

Aoshun, Dragon King of the East Sea, Aoguang, Dragon King of the West Sea, and Aorun, Dragon King of the North Sea, were all visiting Aoqing, and they commented, "By fighting Xu Xun, that little beast is acting like the Lord of Ge setting himself against Tang.[48] By abetting the Demon Dragon, he's doing what the Lord of Chong did in aiding the evil King Zhou in his tyrannical rule.[49] Such behavior is not to be tolerated."

"I don't need a son like that!" said Aoqin. With that, he picked up a sharp sword and gave it to the yaksha, instructing him to deliver it to the prince along with a written decree demanding the prince's suicide.

Bearing the decree and the sword, the yaksha went to the third son. Upon hearing the purpose of the yaksha's visit, the prince was frightened out of his wits. He fell on his knees and cried out to the Bodhisattva Guanyin, "Oh, Bodhisattva! In your compassion, please persuade my father to let me go this time!"

"I'm afraid your father is not likely to change his mind," replied the bodhisattva. "I suggest that you hide yourself in Eagle Fear Ravine in Snake Coil Valley. In three hundred years, when Tripitaka of the Tang dynasty is ready to go to the West on a pilgrimage for Buddhist scriptures, I'll change you into a mule as a punishment, so you may follow him to India and carry the scriptures back.[50] After you thus atone for your crime with a good deed, I will talk with your father. By that time, he may be willing to forgive you."

His eyes brimming over with tears, the prince took leave of the bodhisattva and made his way to Eagle Fear Ravine. The bodhisattva gave the yaksha the iron pestle, which she had recovered, and told him to return it to the Dragon King. The Sage also took leave of the bodhisattva and went back to Yuzhang, and there we shall leave him for now.

After bidding the Sage farewell, the bodhisattva started her journey back to Potala Rock, but on her way, the Demon Dragon threw himself at her feet, stating in the most plaintive tone that he wished to make peace with the Sage, mend his ways, and never harm people again. Moved by the sincerity of his words, the bodhisattva went to Yuzhang to see the Sage.

"What orders does the great bodhisattva have for me?" asked the Sage.

"My only mission is to bring you a message from the Demon Dragon. He wishes to make peace with you and mend his ways. Would you grant his wish?"

"If he wants peace, tell him to make a hundred canals tonight before the roosters crow tomorrow morning. I won't grant his wish if he's short even one canal."

After the bodhisattva had gone, Wu Meng, a disciple of the Sage's, offered this advice: "I don't think that accursed beast has had a real change of heart. You can't say yes to him."

The Sage replied, "I know. But much of Jiangxi is easily flooded in the rainy spring season. I just want him to make a hundred canals that will provide outlets for the water. I don't mean to make peace with him. I'll tell the local god to prevent him from completing the job. If he can't get to a hundred, he won't be forgiven, and I'll still be able to keep my word to the bodhisattva." (*The Sage could well have granted the Demon Dragon his wish and let him live while keeping him under submission, as with the two flood dragons. But perhaps the Sage means to imitate Zhuge Liang and make the Demon Dragon truly submissive before letting him go?*)[51]

In the meantime, the Demon Dragon greeted the bodhisattva and asked her for the Sage's reaction. Upon hearing the Sage's demand, the Demon Dragon was greatly delighted.

That very night, he put all his magic power to work, and by the fourth watch of the night, he had made ninety-nine canals, as counted by the local god. Alarmed, the god faked a rooster's crows, and all the roosters in the neighborhood echoed him. The Demon Dragon was flabbergasted. Knowing he was not going to be forgiven, he changed himself into a young man and fled to Huguang before the first light of dawn. When the day broke, the Sage counted the canals and found that one was missing and the roosters had already crowed. He knew this was the work of the local god. After making arrangements for the giving of rewards with his disciples, the Sage hastily went in search of the Demon Dragon, but the beast was nowhere to be seen. Later, a new county was established at the mouth of the river and is called today Hukou County, in Nankang.

In the meantime, the Demon Dragon fled to Huanggang County in Huangzhou Prefecture and transformed himself into a young teacher in search of a school. It so happened that a rich old man named Shi Ren was looking for a teacher for his more than ten grandchildren. The Demon Dragon made his way to the old man's home and announced, "I am Zeng Liang from Yuzhang, here to seek a teaching job in your establishment."

Inwardly delighted by the young man's refined looks and respectful manners, Mr. Shi decided to test his scholarship, saying, "According to an old custom of this region, before a teaching job is offered, the applicant is usually tested either through writing an essay or through supplying matching lines to given phrases. I have in mind a line for you to match."

"What is the line?"

"Here it goes: Add four dots to the character *zeng* and you become a worthy gentleman from the region of Lu."

The Demon Dragon countered, "Allow me to cite your grandsons in my matching line: 'Add one horizontal line to the character *shi* and they become top officials of the Ministry of Personnel."

Mr. Shi was impressed by the ingenious match. Pleased beyond measure, he went on to say, "With your remarkable talent, I'm afraid you'll be shortchanged, for I offer but a modest salary for this teaching job."

"Actually, I will just be pursuing my own studies in your house. Remuneration is not what I seek."

Thereupon, Mr. Shi chose a day on which to open the school. After the grandsons had made ceremonial bows to the new teacher, school began. With the Demon Dragon answering the pupils' questions and clearly explicating the texts, the Shi children made great progress in their studies, but this is of no concern to us.

Failing to find the Demon Dragon after the canals had been made, the Sage went to Huguang with Gan Zhan and Shi Cen to look for his traces. Suddenly, the Sage saw a streak of evil vapor rising from an establishment belonging to the Shi family in a village in Huanggang County. With his two disciples, the Sage headed straight to the Shi establishment, where, upon seeing some pupils in the schoolhouse, he realized that the Demon Dragon had changed himself into a teacher.

"Where is your teacher?" the Sage asked the boys.

"He's gone to bathe."

"Where is he bathing?"

"In the ravine."

"How can he bathe in cold water in this the eleventh month of the year?"

"Since he is so heavily built, he often needs to immerse himself in water, in cold and hot weather alike. Sometimes he's away for as long as four to six hours."

The Sage and his disciples sat in the room, waiting to capture the Demon Dragon upon his return. Raising his head, the Sage saw a couplet on a pillar:

Orphan Zhao never forgot Tu'an Gu, his hateful nemesis;[52]
Wu Zixu whipped King Ping's corpse to vent his hatred.[53]

On the wall, there was another poem that read:

How woeful my fate over the past year,
With my sons and grandsons dispersed and gone!
My ambition rides the waves of the East Sea;
My rage towers over the trees by West River.
In hatred, I gnash my teeth and nurse old grudges;
In outbursts, I pick up my brush and write new poems.
For a grown man not to achieve his ambition
Is to waste the life bestowed by heaven.

Alarmed upon reading the lines, the Sage said to his disciples, "The couplet and the poem are both about revenge. If this demon is not gotten rid of, he'll be a major source of trouble. You must do all you can to capture him."

Before the Sage had quite finished speaking, Mr. Shi came into the schoolhouse to watch his grandchildren study. It being the depths of winter, he wore a sheepskin cape over his shoulders and a warm hat on his head. As he entered, walking in his leisurely manner, he was impressed by the Sage's extraordinarily refined looks. Eagerly, he saluted the Sage and said, "May I ask where you are from?"

"I am a native of Yuzhang, here to visit a friend."

Turning to the children, Mr. Shi said, "Why didn't you announce the arrival of guests?" He then invited the Sage and the two disciples to his house, where tea was served. After tea, Mr. Shi asked the Sage's name.

"My name is Xu Xun. These are my disciples, Shi Cen and Gan Zhan."

"I've heard that there is a Mr. Xu who wiped out the flood dragons with his immense magic power. Might that be you?"

"Yes."

Mr. Shi immediately left his seat and bowed deeply. Out of respect for Shi's seniority in age, the Sage hastened to return the courtesy.

"What might be the purpose of your visit?" asked Mr. Shi.

"The one who teaches your grandchildren is none other than the Demon Dragon in human form. I've been following his tracks and am here to capture him." (*Another attempt to subdue the Demon Dragon.*)

In consternation, Mr. Shi said, "No wonder the teacher takes daily baths in the ravine in both hot and cold weather. The water used to be shallow where he takes his baths, but it's an unfathomably deep pond now."

"You are lucky to have me here. Otherwise, in a matter of days, there will be a river where this house now stands, and you'll perish in the belly of some fish."

"But how is that demon to be caught?" asked Mr. Shi.

"That demon is capable of any number of physical transformations. If he's on guard against me, it will be difficult to catch him. Luckily for us, he may not be aware of my presence here at this moment. So if he wants to change, he'll need water. Now, please make sure there is no water in any of the water jars, buckets, basins, bowls, and plates throughout the house, so as to prevent him from changing. I'll then capture him easily."

After Mr. Shi had given the instructions, the Demon Dragon returned from his bathing trip. Upon seeing him, the Sage roared, "Accursed beast! Where do you think you are going?"

The Demon Dragon was aghast. He searched frantically for water but found none throughout the house except for a few drops left in an ink slab, and that was enough. He disappeared into it, leaving no trace of himself behind. (*This is a lesson to be thorough in whatever one does.*) A later poet had this to say:

What a sly demon it was indeed!
The story of the ink slab is told even to this day.
Had it mended its evil ways,
It would have been summoned to heaven.

Grateful to the Sage for driving the Demon Dragon away, Mr. Shi invited him to stay for a few days and showered him with every hospitality. The Sage said, "The Demon Dragon having lived here for so long, I fear that he might submerge this place in water. Please give me a piece of fir. I'll write a magic figure on it and drive it into the ground. That will be enough to keep the Demon Dragon under subjugation."

The Sage put the piece of wood bearing the magic figure in place. Afterward, grateful for Mr. Shi's hospitality, he took out a magic pill and used it to change stones into gold worth more than three hundred taels.

After they had taken thankful leave of their host, Shi Cen remarked, "I wonder where the Demon Dragon is hiding. Let's search Huguang and get rid of him once and for all."

The Sage said, "Having seen us here, he might well have gone to Yuzhang to flood the town. We should go back to Yuzhang and look for traces of him. If he's not there, we can always go elsewhere without losing much time." So the master and two disciples made for home.

In the meantime, after disappearing into the few drops of water in the ink slab, the Demon Dragon changed himself into a handsome young man and fled to Changsha Prefecture, where he heard that Prefect Jia Yu had a most beautiful daughter. How beautiful?

Her eyebrows like kingfisher feathers,
Her skin creamy and delicate.
Her teeth like white gourd seeds,
Her hands shaped like tender new leaves.
Her cheeks rosy as peach blossoms,
Her hair arranged like a bun of golden phoenix filaments.
Her eyes as sparkling as ripples of autumn water,
Her fingers as delicate as new bamboo shoots.
Speak not of Wang Qiang of the Han palace,
Xishi of the Wu state, Feiyan of the Zhao clan,
And Consort Yang of the Tang house![54]
Her gold pendants tinkled to the swaying of her willow waist;
Her jadelike limbs moved to the rhythm of her lotus steps.
The moon goddess hardly measured up to her;
The fairy maidens on ninth heaven were by no means her match.

So the Demon Dragon sought to make the acquaintance of Prefect Jia Yu.

"Who might you be?" asked the prefect.

"I am Shen Lang, a native of Jinling. I have been well-versed in the classics since an early age. However, I was not able to advance my scholarly career and instead ended up being a traveling merchant. During a business trip to South Guangdong, I came upon several precious pearls, which, being of no use to ordinary people, I am now offering to you. Please accept them."

"You must have had a hard time getting these pearls. Moreover, I don't know you. How could I dream of accepting such an overwhelming gift?"

And so, the prefect declined the offer time and again. But Shen Lang was so persistent that the prefect had no choice but to accept and invite him to stay on as a houseguest for several days. Much impressed by Shen Lang's courteous manners, good looks, and mastery of the arts of music, chess, calligraphy, and painting as well as his skill with bows and arrows and dagger-axes, the prefect offered to marry his daughter to the young man. Shen Lang bowed his thanks and bribed the prefect's trusted followers liberally with precious jewels until all praised him for his generosity. On a chosen auspicious day, the prefect married his daughter to Shen Lang, but of this, no more need be said.

After being married in the Jia mansion, Shen Lang would, with the prefect's permission, take a business trip each year when spring was about to give way to summer and return when autumn was yielding to winter, his boat laden with rare treasures.

"What a nice son-in-law I have!" the prefect exulted. Little did he know that his son-in-law was a flood dragon, who was bringing back the possessions of travelers whom he had robbed by capsizing their boats in the spring and summer floods.

In the three years of his marriage, Shen Lang fathered three sons. One day, in the midst of his reflections, Shen Lang was seized with wrath. "My clan had lived in Yuzhang for generations, but now, by killing all my children and other members of the clan, more than a thousand in all, Xu Xun has destroyed my base and made me homeless. Hiding here hasn't lessened my frustration. It's been a long time now. Xu Xun should have forgotten me. I'll go back to Yuzhang to flood the town and drown Xu Xun and all his clan. Only such a revenge will restore my peace of mind." Thinking thus, he went to see the prefect.

"What is it you want to say, my good son-in-law?"

"This warm spring weather is the right time for me to go on a business trip, so I'm here to bid you farewell. Please take good care of my wife and children."

"Go ahead, don't worry! Come back early if you make enough profit." And so, they took leave of each other.

It was the seventh year of the Yongjia reign period [307–13] of the Jin dynasty, and the Sage and his disciples Gan Zhan and Shi Cen had spent three years searching everywhere for the Demon Dragon. Never finding a trace of him, they put him out of their thoughts, little knowing that the Demon Dragon was coming to them, courting death. One day, a page boy announced a visitor, a handsome and well-dressed young man, who had come to see the Sage.

After inviting the visitor in, the Sage asked, "Which part of the country do you come from?"

"I am Shen Lang, a native of Jinling. I have long heard that, with your hands that can turn around the sky and the earth and your subjugation of the Demon Dragon, you are second to none in the whole wide world. I am here for no other purpose than to make the acquaintance of such a great man."

"In fact, I feel quite ashamed about this undeserved reputation, since I have not been able to subdue the Demon Dragon."

After the Sage had spoken these words, the young man departed. When the Sage returned after seeing the guest off, Gan and Shi asked, "Who *was* that young man?"

"None other than the Demon Dragon," replied the Sage. "He came to sound me out."

"How could you tell?"

"I detected an evilness about him, and he had quite a foul smell. That's how I know."

"In that case, you should have caught him and killed him. Why did you let him go?"

"I have tried four times before, but each time, he changed his form and got away. This time, by pretending not to know the truth, I'll be able to catch him off guard."

Shi Cen said, "I wonder where he has gone? We two would be happy to go and get rid of him."

Looking around with his all-seeing eyes, the Sage said, "He's now at a riverbank, in the form of a yellow ox lying on the sandy beach of our town. Let me change into a black ox and fight it out with him. You two may take up your swords and watch the fight, but make sure you aren't seen. When you think his strength is beginning to wear out, draw your swords and cut him down. He'll surely be finished this time." (*The sixth attempt at subduing the Demon Dragon.*) With that, the Sage changed into a black ox and ran off. Truly,

Its four hooves hard as those of a mountain tiger,
Its two horns majestic as those of a sea dragon,
To the sandy beach it went, ready for battle.
Great indeed was the magic power of the Sage.

The Sage went to the sandy beach in the shape of a black ox and engaged the yellow ox in battle. After about four hours, Gan and Shi walked up on tiptoe. Observing that the yellow ox was showing signs of fatigue, Shi Cen drew his sword and hit it in its left thigh. Gan also wielded his sword and managed to cut into one of its horns. As it ran off into a well south of the city, the horn fell off. To this day, opposite Madang lies a Yellow Ox Islet, where the horn, after becoming an evil spirit, often changed itself into an ox to raid the boats of merchants passing by, but of this, no more.

The Sage said to Gan and Shi, "Since the Demon Dragon jumped into this well, it must be his nest. I'll have the gods lead the way for me. You two can come after. Let's follow his tracks all the way to his nest, capture him, and finish him off to forestall all future trouble." With that, the Sage jumped into the well, followed by Shi and Gan.

As the gods led the Sage forward, they saw that, though narrow at the mouth, the well contained a veritable world of its own. Through a hole here and an aperture there, one could see that all the streets were linked in the same way as the twenty-four streets of the pleasure quarters of the city of Hangzhou, and that all the coves were connected like the thirty-six coves of Dragon Hole Port. It is often said that a frog in a well has a limited view of the world, but that's because frogs have never been to this well from which to see the vastness of this world.

As the Sage followed the gods, his eyes happened to rest on a cylindrical object that, neither long nor short, resembled a pestle. Gan Zhan picked it up and saw that it was a linchpin. He asked the Sage, "How did a linchpin for a wheel come to be in a well?"

The Sage replied, "In the Western Han dynasty, there was a man named Chen Zun who, each time he entertained guests, had the habit of closing his door and throwing their carriage linchpins into the well so that none could leave, not even those with urgent matters demanding their attention. The linchpins were not returned to his guests until the feasts were over. But on one occasion, a linchpin could not be found. So, this is where the water has borne it."

After several li, they sighted a square object that looked quite intriguing. Shi Cen picked it up and found that it was a box used for keeping seals. When asked, the Sage replied, "In the Eastern Han dynasty, there was a eunuch, Zhang Rang, who took the emperor hostage and brought him up north to the river's edge, where he threw the imperial jade seal into the well, and nothing has been heard of it since. Later, Sun Jian saw a five-colored column of vapor rise into the sky from the Nanli Palace of Luoyang, and recognizing it as indicating the presence of some treasure, he ordered the well to be dredged. When he came upon the jade seal, he kept it but left the box where it was, and this is the very one.[55]

Another few li farther on, a bright, white object with a curved mouth and a big belly came into view. Gan picked it up and found it to be a silver vase. He asked the Sage, who responded, "I've heard a woman intone these lines: 'I tried to grind my jade hairpin on a stone, but the hairpin snapped in the middle. I tried to draw my silver vase from the well, but the thread broke before the vase rose to the top.' So my guess is that this is the very silver vase the woman was pulling up when the thread snapped, and that's how the vase ended up here."

At this point, the god who was guiding them spoke up. "The Demon Dragon has been gone for some time now," he cautioned. "The Sage must make haste. Please do not waste time telling stories from history."

Accordingly, the Sage ordered that his disciples quicken their pace. As they proceeded, aquatic animals that saw them were scared out of their wits. The catfish's jaws dropped, the softshell turtles withdrew their heads, the shrimp bent over as far as they could, the silver carp did nothing but wave their tails. Paying them no heed, the Sage followed the god through twists and turns until, just at the moment when he thought they had come to a dead end, the Jia Yu Well of Changsha came into view.

"So, this is where the nest is," said the Sage as he bid his guide farewell and approached the well to capture the Demon Dragon.

But that evil spirit had already left the well. Once again taking the form of Shen Lang, he had returned to Prefect Jia's establishment, where the whole family was shocked to see him in such a wretched state. When the prefect asked what had happened to him, Shen Lang gave this story: "I made quite a lot of profit on this trip, but as bad luck would have it, I ran into a group of bandits on the way back. They took all my possessions and wounded me in my left temple and left hip. The pain is really more than I can bear."

The sight of the sword-inflicted wounds pained the prefect. Immediately, he had a house servant hire a physician.

The Sage disguised himself as a physician, while Gan and Shi posed as his apprentices. Now, this physician:

Had skills that were nothing less than divine
And knew all there was to know about the various herbs.
When seeing patients, he observed their complexions,
Listened to the sounds they made,
Asked them their symptoms, and felt their pulses.
When writing prescriptions,
He put to use his profound medical knowledge.
A Tang-style cap on his head,
A Daoist's cape over his shoulders,
He radiated an ethereal elegance.
Waving a feather fan,
Carrying a medicine gourd on his back,
He was a picture of grace.
He had only to feel the pulse to diagnose the illness.
He had only to raise a hand
To cure broken limbs and illnesses at all stages
And bring the dead back to life.
Indeed, he was a Bianque of the Spring and Autumn Period[56]
Born again in the Eastern Jin times,
And a Shennong[57] *of antiquity*
Reappearing in the West River region.
Called the divine physician throughout the ages,
He had a heart that overflowed with compassion.

Disguised as a physician, the Sage was engaged by the house servant of the Jia establishment. After exchanging greetings with the Sage in the hall, Prefect Jia said, "Bandits wounded my son-in-law on the left temple and left hip while he was on a business trip. Do you have any effective medicine to cure him? I'll reward you handsomely to show my gratitude."

"If the wounds were inflicted with a sword," said the Sage, "I know a miraculous way to heal them." (*The seventh attempt at subduing the Demon Dragon.*)

Greatly delighted, the prefect sent for Shen Lang. The Demon Dragon was lying in his room at the time and asked the servant, "Is the physician alone?"

"No, he's accompanied by two apprentices."

Suspecting that it was the Sage, the evil one refused to leave his room. His wife Jia-shi urged, "The physician is out there in the hall. Why don't you go?"

"What do you know?" retorted Shen Lang. "The physician may do me good, but he may also do me harm."

Jia-shi was at a loss as to what to do. When Shen Lang did not appear, the prefect went to his son-in-law's room to summon the young man. The Sage followed behind. As soon as he entered Shen Lang's room, the Sage called out severely, "Accursed beast! Do you dare to evade me again?"

In desperation, the Demon Dragon showed his true shape and wriggled out of his room, little knowing that the Sage had already set the cosmic net around him. He fell into the net and was caught. The Sage then sprayed holy water on Shen Lang's three sons, who instantly changed into small flood dragons. The Sage then drew his sword and slew all three of them. Jia-shi, the prefect's daughter, was on the point of attempting a bodily change when Shi Cen captured her, to the horror of the prefect. The Sage said, "Shen Lang is the Demon Dragon. He became your son-in-law by taking on human form. I am Xu Xun of Yuzhang. I have been following his trail. Now that he's been captured, your daughter, having also become a flood dragon, deserves a blow from my sword."

Prefect Jia and his wife fell to their knees in front of the Sage and pleaded, "It's not my daughter's fault that she was contaminated by the evil flood dragon. Please have pity and forgive her!"

The Sage made the young woman take a magic potion, which stopped her transformation. He said to the prefect, "Wherever flood dragons take up residence, there is water underneath. Your house is now standing on only one foot of soil, beneath which there is nothing but water. You will have to move quickly to some other location to escape danger."

The prefect's whole family was flabbergasted. They hastily moved to higher ground. In a matter of days, the mansion they formerly inhabited sank into an unfathomably deep pond, known today as Pond Zhao of Changsha.

Shi Cen picked the Demon Dragon out of the cosmic net and was about to apply his sword when the Sage said, "To slay that accursed one is easy enough. The difficulty was in attempting to capture him. I believe the Jiangxi region is full of flood dragons' nests underneath a thin layer of soil. To the south of the city, there is a bottomless well with water that rises and ebbs with the river. It would be better to deal with him by trussing him up and taking him to that well. I'll put an iron tree in the well and tie that beast to it, so that future flood dragons will take warning from his suffering and refrain from doing evil."

"Good idea!" said Gan Zhan. So they tied up the Demon Dragon and took him back to Yuzhang. There, the Sage summoned celestial soldiers, who made a tree out of iron and put it in the well to the south of the city. With iron chains and locks that kept the fengshui under control, the Sage had the Demon Dragon tightly bound to the tree, and intoned the following incantation:

> *"Should the iron tree burst into bloom, the demon will break free, and I will come again. As long as the tree stays as it is, the evil spirit will remain in subjugation, the water demons powerless, and the town out of harm's way."*

He also wrote the following epigraph:

With the iron tree guarding Hongzhou, peace will reign for ten thousand years. This place will be spared from whatever turmoil may engulf all other places and enjoy modest harvests when drought plagues all other regions.

Wu Quanjie of the Yuan dynasty had a poem that said,

The eight ropes hold the earth in crisscross fashion;
A well determines the rivers' water level.
Yuzhang, a blessed place made by heaven,
Is the mainstay that holds the sky through the ages.

The Sage also made iron tablets and placed them in Boyang Lake to subdue any demons that might be present. He also made an iron lid, which he put over Yuan Pond in Luling. To this day, one of his swords still lies by the pond. He then erected an altar at the top of Mount Tiaoyao. All these things he did so as to forestall the rise of future demons.

By subjugating the demon, the Sage performed an immensely laudable service. In the second year of the Taining reign period [323–25], under Emperor Ming of the Jin dynasty, General Wang Dun, courtesy name Chuzhong, the garrison commander of Wuchang, rose in rebellion and marched his troops inland. When he was stationed at Lake Dongting, the Sage and Mr. Wu went to see him in an attempt to stop his advances and preserve the Jin house. Guo Pu being an adviser to Wang Dun, the three men enjoyed a reunion.

Guo said to the Sage, "By subjugating the flood dragons, you have achieved the greatest merit possible. Moreover, as signs of the presence of an immortal have been on the wane in the Xishan region, that must mean you will soon be ascending to heaven." The Sage thanked him.

One day, Guo Pu took the Sage and Wu to see Wang Dun, who, greatly delighted at the sight of the three men, ordered that a feast be laid out. When well warmed with wine, Wang Dun said, "I had a dream last night in which I saw a tree piercing the sky. I wonder what it could portend?"

The Sage replied, "A tree piercing the sky makes up the character *wei,* meaning 'not.' So you should not be making any ill-considered moves."

Mr. Wu chimed in, "My master's words are always full of prophetic wisdom. Please bear them in mind."

Wang Dun was displeased. At his order, Guo Pu performed a divination for him and said, "This says that function overpowers essence, which means that your endeavor will only end in failure."

"How long am I going to live?" asked Wang Dun in vexation.

Guo Pu replied, "If you do something ambitious, you won't have long to live, but if you return to Wuchang, you will have a long life ahead of you."

Wang Dun flared up. "How long are *you* going to live?"

"My span of life ends today," replied Guo Pu.

In a towering rage, Wang Dun ordered that his armed guards seize Guo Pu and kill him, and so they did. Flinging their wine cups into the air, the Sage and Mr. Wu changed into a pair of white cranes and flew around the rafters. Wang Dun raised his eyes to look at the cranes, but both of them were gone.

With Guo Pu dead, the Guo family set about making arrangements for the funeral. Three days after the funeral had taken place, Guo Pu was seen in the marketplace, properly dressed and greeting friends and relatives as if nothing had happened. Not believing what he had heard, Wang Dun ordered that the coffin be pried open so he could see for himself. Sure enough, there was no corpse inside. Only then did he realize that Guo Pu had achieved immortality. (*Of the five ways to attain immortality, Guo Pu's was the one called "Release by metal," which means to be released from mortality by means of a weapon.*) Thereafter, Wang Dun did indeed fail in his armed rebellion and died as soon as he returned to Wuchang, where his corpse was dismembered, and all because he had refused to follow the advice of the three masters.

Now, Mr. Wu invited the Sage to follow him to Jinling and take a pleasure trip to view the mountains and waters. They engaged a boat to go back to Yuzhang but came up against a persistent adverse wind. The boatmen said, "With such a strong southerly wind in midsummer weather, the boat can't move an inch. What's to be done?"

The Sage said, "Let me do it for you, but you'll have to sit tight with closed eyes. Do not, on any account, open your eyes to steal a look."

With Mr. Wu standing at the bow, the Sage took over the boatmen's job and summoned two black dragons to help the boat along. As they passed Chiyang, he printed the seal of the Heavenly God of Thunder on the rock cliff of West Hill in order to keep water monsters away. To this day, the cliff still bears traces of the seal. Gradually, the boat began to rise in the air. In a trice, it flew over the crest of the Lushan Mountains to Cloud Peak. Eager to look into the caves, the Sage and Wu kept the boat so close to the mountainside that it scratched the trees, making loud noises. The boatmen, their curiosity getting the better of them, opened their eyes. Instantly, the boat came to a standstill right there on top of the mountain, and its mast fell into the deep valley below. The place where the boat stopped is now called Iron Boat Peak, and the broken rock underneath is part of its mast. The Sage said to the boatmen, "You didn't do as I said, and now look at what you've gotten yourselves into. How are you going to find your way back home?"

The boatmen kowtowed to him and implored him to deliver them, whereupon the Sage gave them a magic potion that would protect them from hunger while they lived in seclusion under Purple Cloud Peak. The Sage and Mr. Wu each rose on the back of a dragon and flew back to Yuzhang, where they resumed their lives as hermits and spent their days explicating the Daoist truth to disciples. In their longing for immortality, they wrote this poem:

The cosmic cycles go round and round as if on wings,
In this mortal world among human beings,
What is there to do?
Don't fights for fame and profit lead one to the grave anyway?
Whoever knows the true taste of a romantic life?
Better to take shelter in a golden wine vessel
And drink and sing till the sun sinks in the west.
A cinnabar pond for a jade dragon,
And a vast world measured in small ladlefuls.
Take me not for a benighted one;
My drunken laughter fills the sky and earth.

For their disciples, they wrote the following words of admonition in explanation of the eight virtues:

> Loyalty, filial piety, integrity, caution, magnanimity, independence from want, tolerance, and endurance. Loyalty keeps one from cheating, filial piety prevents disobedience, integrity guards against greed, caution obviates loss. Attainment of these virtues will be a major spiritual accomplishment. Magnanimity wins hearts; independence from want ensures a decent living; tolerance enables one to mix readily with others; endurance gives one peace of mind. Treat people with courteousness, and all grievances will be washed away. All of you disciples, bear the above in mind in whatever you do, in stillness or in motion. The least aberration is punishable by court trial and death.

The kings of the sky, earth, and water and the god of the Gold Star announced that the Sage had been the Immortal of the Jade Cave before descending to earth and recommended him to the Jade Emperor for his highly meritorious deeds in subjugating demons for the benefit of humanity. In their recommendation, they also included the names of some of his disciples, including Wu Meng, for their achievement of the Way by supporting their master. After consulting one another, they presented the memorial to the Jade Emperor, who then approved the request and granted Xu Xun the titles Celestial Envoy and Envoy of Wisdom as well as the title King Xiaoxian. Titles were also conferred upon Xu Xun's ancestors. The celestial messengers Cui Ziwen and Duan Qiuzhong delivered the Jade Emperor's decree to Xu Xun, giving him the date of his ascension to heaven in acknowledgement of his good deeds. It being the second year of the Ningkang reign period [373–76] under Emperor Xiaowu of the Jin dynasty, the Sage was one hundred and thirty-six years old when the two celestial messengers descended to earth with the Jade Emperor's decree.

On the first day of the eighth month, at the sight of a cloud carriage with a large entourage descending from the sky into his courtyard, the Sage went out to pay homage to the visitors. The two celestial messengers said, "By the Jade Emperor's order, we are here to deliver to you His Majesty's decree. You may prepare some fragrant carved candles, adjust your clothes and cap, and kneel down in front of the steps to listen." The decree read as follows:

> To Xu Xun, a student aspiring to attain immortality:
>
> Having applied thyself assiduously to the cultivation of thy spirit before the many kalpas to come, thou hast learned all there is to know about the truths of the universe and mastered all the doctrines. By alleviating the suffering of those in disaster areas and eliminating demons and evil spirits for the benefit of the people, thou hast earned thyself a prominent place in the registry of immortals. Upon recommendation, thou art hereby granted the titles of Celestial Envoy, Envoy of Wisdom, and King Xiaoxian and bestowed a robe of purple feathers, a celestial banner, and a jade staff. Thou shalt ascend to heaven with thy family at the hour of noon on the fifteenth day of the eighth month. Thou needst only follow the instructions of the decree due on that day.

When the decree had been read, the Sage bowed twice and ascended the steps to receive it. Then he invited the two messengers to take seats of honor and asked them their names. One replied, "I am Cui Ziwen. He is Duan Qiuzhong. We are both celestial messengers."

"What have I done to deserve the honor of having the Jade Emperor send you down to earth?"

"You have achieved sufficient merit through spiritual devotion and good works performed on behalf of humanity. Yesterday, you were recommended by the gods to the Jade Emperor for the attainment of immortality. We are here to greet you and give you advance notice." With that, they mounted their dragon carriage and departed.

Now that the Sage had received notice from heaven, Wu Meng and other disciples as well as the local elders and relatives all knew that his departure was imminent. Every day, they gave him farewell drinking parties. At one of these gatherings, the Sage announced: "To attain immortality, the important thing is to do good deeds before thinking of claiming credit for them. (*Excellent advice.*) One thousand two hundred and forty years after I am gone, more than eight hundred people among the five hills of Yuzhang will attain immortality. Their mentor will be a native of Yuzhang who will zealously impart my teachings. When branches of the pine tree in front of my altar are brushed against the ground and a sandbar large enough to cover the mouth of a well appears in the middle of the river, that will be the moment."

Later, there arose this saying, "When the dragon meets the sand, immortals shall be made." The spot where the dragon and the sand met is by the west bank of the Zhang River, within view of the city, as is recorded in *The Records of the Dragon and the Sand.* Pan Qingyi wrote this poem titled "Watching the Dragon and the Sand":

Throngs of people of the five hills
Watch for the pine branches and the sandbar.

Before the dragon and the sand actually meet,
The terrain has already changed.
Where waves used to swell,
Half has become tilled land.
The land follows the curves of the river
And the unbroken lines of the rolling hills.

When the fifteenth day of the eighth month came around, the neighbors, relatives, friends, and disciples of the Sage, be they old or young, were called together for a grand gathering. At mid day, there came the distant sound of music accompanying the auspicious clouds that moved slowly toward the gathering. It was the celestial messengers Cui Ziwen and Duan Qiuzhong, this time riding a feather-canopied dragon carriage preceded and followed by an entourage of celestial boys and maidens, officials, generals, clerks, and soldiers. As the Sage bowed in greeting, the two messengers read aloud the Jade Emperor's decree:

> To Xu Xun, student aspiring to attain immortality:
>
> Having attained perfection in thy spiritual cultivation, thou art hereby ordered to follow the Qian Shan Stars of Civil Virtue, who have brought gold pills to the lower world, to ascend to heaven, together with thy family and thy house. The heavenly guardians shall light the way with golden fire bells, with no remission in their duty. Thy great-grandfather Xu You is hereby granted the title Supervisor of the Fairy Palace; thy grandfather Xu Yan, the title Taiwei Commander; thy grandmother, Lady Taiwei; thy father Xu Su, the title Immortal of Zhongyue; and thy mother Zhang-shi, the title Lady Zhongyue. This decree is to be executed immediately upon delivery.

The Sage bowed again and received the decree. Cui Ziwen said, "Of your many disciples, only Chen Xun, Zeng Heng, Zhou Guang, Shi He, Huang Renlan and his father, and Xu Lie and his mother, forty-two people in all, can join you. The others will have their own days of ascension. They cannot all follow you this time."

With that, he invited the Sage to mount the dragon carriage. Forty-two people in all rose to heaven with him.

Those neighbors and disciples who were not allowed to join him hung on to the axles of the wheels, loath to see him go. Their cries shook the sky, but their wish to follow was not to be granted. The Sage said, "There is no lack of ways in which to achieve immortality. If you all adhere to filial piety and render good services to the people, you will surely be duly rewarded."

Xu Jian, a grandson of the Sage's, said in a plaintive tone, "There being nothing to remind future generations of you who are ascending to heaven, please leave us some memento to remember you by."

Thereupon, the Sage left behind a bell that he had used in his spiritual cultivation as well as a stone box, saying, "As the world changes, these will become things of the past."

A servant of the Sage's, a certain Xu Da, was buying rice with his wife at West Hill when he heard about his master's rise to heaven. Immediately, he started back, but in his haste, his carriage overturned, spilling the rice. All the grains of rice sprouted and became seedlings. To this day, the hill is called Spilt Rice Hill and the town is called Growing Rice Town.

To Xu Da's sobbed appeal to follow his master, the Sage responded by teaching him ways of becoming an earthbound immortal, believing him to be destined for no more than that. The servant and his wife henceforth took up residence at West Hill as hermits. After the Sage had risen to heaven—along with the whole family and the house, with chickens and dogs and all—the celestial soldiers pushed a rat down because it was unclean. Its intestines fell out as it thumped against the earth, but it remained alive. Those who witnessed the scene attributed the rat's escape from death to the grace of heaven. Next fell a pestle for a medicinal mortar, a grain grinder, and a chicken cage, all of which landed about ten li southeast of the house. Xu Xun's wife dropped a gold hairpin, and to this day, that place is called Spot Where Lady Xu Dropped Her Hairpin. A contemporary had this to say in praise of the Sage's rise to heaven with his entire family and the house:

Sage Xu's compassion is widely admired;
His kind deeds will never be forgotten.
With his family, he rose to the sky;
His meritorious service moved heaven.

The Sage flew into the distance and gradually passed from sight. Only auspicious rosy clouds were seen floating in the sky, and an extraordinary fragrance permeated the air throughout the area within one hundred li. Suddenly, a red brocade curtain wafted into view and hovered over the ground where the Sage had lived.

While he was flying past the Qiwu Mountains of Yichun County, Yuanzhou Prefecture, the Sage sent down two boys dressed in green to tell Wang Shuo about his ascension to heaven by order of the Jade Emperor and to bid him farewell. As he led his whole family in kowtowing, Wang Shuo pleaded, "I have been following the methods that you, my master, have kindly taught me for a long time now. Please take me along!"

The Sage replied, "You are not yet ready for anything more than prolongation of your allotted life span. I cannot take you along." With that, he threw a blade of lemongrass onto the ground and told the two boys to hand it to Wang Shuo, adding, "The lemongrass has an extraordinary fragrance. If you plant it in this spot, let it grow, and use it as an herbal supplement, you'll be able to live a long life. Its sweetness nourishes the flesh, its pungency nourishes the joints, its bitterness nourishes the vital force, its saltiness strengthens the bones, its smoothness lubricates the skin, its sourness is good for the tendons. If you put it in fine wine and drink the mixture, you will surely notice the effects." With that, he took leave of Wang Shuo.

Wang Shuo followed the Sage's instructions and planted the lemongrass, let it grow, drank the wine mixture, and lived to be three hundred years old. The Yuxu Temple that stands in Linjiang Prefecture is the very place where Wang Shuo's residence used to be, and the wondrous lemongrass is still there.

After the Sage rose to heaven, the neighbors and Xu Jian, his consanguineous grandson, erected an altar on the spot of his ascension. They inscribed the one hundred and twenty poems he had left behind onto bamboo slips and put the slips inside a giant bamboo tube so that people could pick one when seeking to settle disputes. His bell, his medicine grinder, his pestle, and his stone box were all placed reverentially onto the altar, which later became a temple. Because a red brocade curtain had flown over this spot, it came to be called Flying Curtain Temple.

When the Sage arrived in the celestial palace, the Jade Emperor mounted his throne, while Cui Ziwen and Duan Qiuzhong instructed the Sage and his disciples to wait for the Jade Emperor's order granting them an audience. Upon receiving the order, the Sage went in, bowed according to proper etiquette, and prostrated himself at the foot of the golden steps that led to the throne. He presented a memorial to the Jade Emperor and said, "Your humble subject Xu Xun is of but mediocre ability and inferior nature. All that I have done in the way of spreading holy water, drawing magic figures, and subjugating demons is attributable to the efforts of my eleven disciples, but only Chen Xun, Zeng Heng, Zhou Guang, Shi He, Huang Renlan, and Xu Lie have, by Your Majesty's blessing, risen to heaven. Wu Meng, Shi Cen, Gan Zhan, Zhong Lijia, and Peng Kang have not been so blessed. This is indeed a pity. Please give them your blessings as well, Your Majesty, and summon them to the celestial palace in consummation of their quest for the Way."

The Jade Emperor granted his request and dispatched Zhou Guang to deliver the decree that Wu Meng and the four others rise to heaven on the same day. Accordingly, Zhou Guang took respectful leave of the Jade Emperor and went on his mission.

It was the first day of the ninth month in the second year of the Ningkang reign period in the Jin dynasty. Wu Meng was one hundred and eighty-six years old. Displeased that he had not been allowed to rise to heaven with the Sage, he was in the middle of a journey with four fellow disciples—Shi Cen, Gan Zhan, Zhong Lijia, and Peng Kang. They were returning to Xining to pursue further spiritual cultivation when Wu Meng saw Zhou Guang descending from the sky, decree in hand. After an exchange of greetings, he asked Zhou what had brought him to the mortal world. Zhou Guang replied, "The Master told the Jade Emperor that he had benefited greatly from the help of friends who had not been allowed to rise to heaven, and he entreated the Jade Emperor to extend his grace to them. And so, the Jade Emperor sent me down with his decree, ordering that all five of you rise to heaven in consummation of your pursuit of the Way."

Immensely delighted by these words, all five rose to heaven in broad daylight on white deer carriages. The Immortal Wu Village and the Immortal Temple of our day mark the spot where the ascension took place. Of the Sage's more than three thousand followers, only eleven, including Wu Meng, rose to heaven on the basis of their worthy service and virtue. The Sage took all the disciples to an audience with the Jade Emperor, who conferred titles on them. Afterward, the Sage led them to pay their respects to Patriarch Wei Hongkang, King of Filial Piety, Brotherly Love, and Wisdom; Grand Master Lan, King of Filial Sagacity; and the Sage's mentor, Reverend Mother. They also thanked the kings of the sky, earth, and water and the god of the Gold Star for their recommendations, after which the Sage recommended his friends Hu Yun of Xudu and Zhan Cui of Yunyang to the Jade Emperor for their devotion to the Dao. The Jade Emperor conferred upon both men the title Sage, but this is of no concern to us.

After his ascension, the Sage had many opportunities to put his magic power to use. The evil Emperor Yang of the Sui dynasty [r. 605–17] had Buddhist temples burned and Flying Curtain Temple destroyed. During the Yongchun reign period [682–83] under Emperor Gaozong of the Tang dynasty, the Sage ordered Sage Hu Huichao to rebuild them. By Song times, Emperors Taizong and Renzong graced Flying Curtain Temple with letters of praise. During Emperor Zhenzong's reign, the name of the temple was changed to Yulong Palace. In the second year of the Zhenghe reign period [1111–18] in the Song dynasty, Emperor Huizong was afflicted with a vicious boil on his face. While he was napping during the day, he dreamed he saw a Daoist priest wearing a tall crown and a scarlet robe with patterns of the sun, the moon, and the stars. Approaching in the direction of Donghua Gate, the priest drew near the steps at the foot of the throne, led by two boys with swords in their hands. Suspecting that he was not a Daoist priest of the mortal world, the emperor asked, "Who are you?"

"I am Xu Xun, in charge of administrative affairs in the nine heavens. I am on my way to the state of Liao by order of the Lord on High. Passing by my old country, I learned about Your Majesty's illness and came to see for myself."

"This boil of mine is a poisonous one. No prescription has done any good. Do you have anything that will work?"

With a small ladle, the priest dispensed one pill the size of a mungbean, blew a puff of breath on it, and applied it to Emperor Huizong's boil. As he bowed his farewell, he said, "My humble former residence by West Hill in Hongdu has fallen into decay. Please do me the great honor of taking a look at it."

Suddenly, the emperor woke up. Feeling a soothing cool on his face, he stroked his cheek and found that the boil was gone. He ordered a minister to take up a map and inspect the region mentioned by the Sage. As Sage Xu Jingyang's former residence was indeed found by West Hill of Hongzhou, the emperor decreed that Yulong Palace be renovated and made habitable so that Sage Xu could use it during his sojourns on earth. The word "longevity" was added to the name of the palace. A new statue of the Sage was erected, and he was given a new title: Sage with Divine Power. All the objects Sage Xu had left behind were under the protection of celestial guardians and were not to be touched.

The cypress the Sage had planted by hand in front of the palace often portended, by its thriving or withering, the rise or decline of the imperial court. When brewed in a soup, the leaves of the tree could cure all illnesses.

Yan Zhuan of Tang, prefect of Hongzhou, did not believe the story about an iron tree in the well. He ordered that the tree, if it existed, be dug up. As soon as the work started, the weather changed. Thunder rolled, as violent winds swept the waves of the river high and shook the city walls. Only a considerable while after the terrified prefect had kowtowed in repentance did the storm begin to subside.

The prefect then had the Sage's bell taken by force and placed in a Buddhist monastery, where it gave only a dull thump when struck, as if it were made of earth or wood. When he dozed off in his seat, the prefect saw a god reproaching him. Upon awaking, he had the bell sent back to its place in Yulong Palace.

As for the medicine grinder and the pestle, a later prefect, Xu Deng, ordered that they be brought to his house for his inspection, but, before he had a chance to examine them, they flew back to the palace. As for the stone box, after usurping the post of prefect of Hongzhou, Zhang San'an of the Tang dynasty had its lid pried open, only to see these characters, written in vermilion: "This box will be pried open in five hundred years by Zhang Shan'an the rebel." In fear, Zhang Shan'an rubbed at the characters, trying to obliterate them, but to no avail. He hid the lid, but the same characters remained at the bottom of the box.

During the Jianyan reign period [1127–31], under Emperor Gaozong of Song, the Jurchens wreaked havoc along the lower Yangzi Valley. As they were about to set fire to Yulong Palace, water spouted from the gutters and put out the fire. The Jurchens fled in alarm.

Successive emperors paid their respects to the Sage's palace and kept it in good repair. The Sage, for his part, frequently came to the country to cure illnesses. During the Zhongde reign period [1506–22], Zhu Quan, the prince of Ning, rose in rebellion. When he approached the palace, the Sage sent down from heaven the following lines:

In threes and twos, and twos and threes,
He slaughtered people south of the river.
When the lotus withers, the chrysanthemum blooms;
The Ming dynasty still lives on.

Later, the rebellion was indeed suppressed. So many of the Sage's prophecies turned out to be accurate that a later poet had this to say:

The good book in gold and jade is not to be had;
Seek, instead, the Sage's eight-character teachings.
Consider how he achieved the highest merits
And sails through the danger-infested seas.

Notes

Introduction

1. For a detailed discussion of the *Sanyan* and its influence on Chinese fictions, as well as a bibliography of relevant works, see Feng Menglong, *Stories Old and New: A Ming Dynasty Collection,* trans. Shuhui Yang and Yunqin Yang (Seattle: University of Washington Press, 2000), xv–xxvi, 778–794.

2. Lu Shulun, "Feng Menglong," in his *Feng Menglong sanlun* (Shanghai: Shanghai guji, 1993), 7.

3. Pi-ching Hsu, "Celebrating the Emotional Self" (Ph.D. diss., University of Minnesota, 1994), 48.

4. Quoted in Lu Shulun, "Feng Menglong," 92.

5. The facsimile edition of *Feng Menglong quanji* (Complete works of Feng Menglong), published by Shanghai Guji Chubanshe in 1993, contains forty-three volumes that, when stacked together, are more than six feet tall.

6. Patrick Hanan, *The Chinese Vernacular Story* (Cambridge: Harvard University Press, 1981), 80–81.

7. Hanan, *Chinese Vernacular Story,* 80–81.

8. The moralistic and didactic tone of the three *Sanyan* titles (*Illustrious Words to Instruct the World, Comprehensive Words to Warn the World,* and *Constant Words to Awaken the World*) can probably also be understood in the same light.

9. Y. W. Ma, "Feng Meng-lung," in William Nienhauser, ed., *The Indiana Companion to Traditional Chinese Literature* (Bloomington: Indiana University Press, 1986), 381.

10. Hanan, *Chinese Vernacular Story,* 104; and Patrick Hanan, *The Chinese Short Story: Studies in Dating, Authorship, and Composition* (Cambridge: Harvard University Press, 1973), 76–86.

11. In his "Preface to *Art Song Prosody*" (Qulü xu), Feng complains that "the most abused literary genres today are classical poetry and prose." In his preface to *Hill Songs,* he also says that "although there is an abundance of false poetry and prose, there are no false folk songs." See Guo Shaoyu, *Zhongguo lidai wenlun xuan* (Shanghai: Shanghai guji, 1979), 3:194, 231.

12. Cyril Birch, "Feng Meng-lung and the *Ku Chin Hsiao Shuo,*" in *Bulletin of the School of Oriental and African Studies* 18 (1956): 82.

13. Patrick Hanan, "The Nature of Ling Meng-ch'u's Fiction," in Andrew Plaks, ed., *Chinese Narrative: Critical and Theoretical Essays* (Princeton, N.J.: Princeton University Press, 1977), 87.

14. Hanan, "Nature of Ling Meng-ch'u's Fiction," 87.

15. David Rolston, *Traditional Chinese Fiction and Fiction Commentary* (Stanford, Calif.: Stanford University Press, 1997), 232. Rolston also says that the simulated storyteller can be seen "as a functional attempt to deal with the absence of the 'author' in early vernacular fiction."

16. The word *huaben* was adopted as the regular term for the traditional Chinese vernacular short story only in the twentieth century. On its early usage as simply "story," rather than "prompt-book," see Charles Wivell, "The Term '*Hua-pen,*'" in David Buxbaum and Frederick Mote, eds., *Transition and Permanence: Chinese History and Culture* (Hong Kong: Cathay Press, 1972), 295–306. The prompt-book theory has been criticized from another angle: because professional storytellers were more likely to have re-

lied on abstracts or notes in the classical language, the earliest extant *huaben* texts were perhaps also meant for reading, rather than reciting, as were their later imitations; see André Lévy, "*Hua-pen,*" in Nienhauser, ed., *Indiana Companion,* 443.

17. See W. L. Idema, "Storytelling and the Short Story in China," in *T'oung Pao* 59 (1973): 3, 35–39.

18. W. L. Idema, "Some Remarks and Speculations Concerning *P'ing-hua,*" rpt. in his *Chinese Vernacular Fiction: The Formative Period* (Leiden: E. J. Brill, 1974), 72.

19. See, for example, Yang Xianyi and Gladys Yang, trans., *The Courtesan's Jewel Box* (Beijing: Foreign Languages Press, 1981).

20. See Hu Wanchuan, "*Sanyan* xu ji meipi de zuozhe wenti," rpt. in his *Huaben yu caizi jiaren xiaoshuo zhi yanjiu* (Taipei: Da'an, 1994), 123–38.

Preface

1. The Six Classics are *The Book of Songs, The Book of History, The Book of Rites, The Book of Music, The Book of Changes,* and *The Spring and Autumn Annals.*

2. "Daren fu" and "Zixu fu" are by the famous poet Sima Xiangru (179–117 B.C.E.). "Daren fu," about the fictional character Daren, is a satire of Emperor Wudi (r. 140–87 B.C.E.) of the Han dynasty. "Zixu fu," about the fictional characters Zixu, Wuyou, and Wangchi, is a criticism of the extravagances of the imperial court.

3. Qixiashan (Hill amid Rosy Clouds) is probably a reference to the Qixiashan located to the northeast of the city of Nanjing.

1. Yu Boya Smashes His Zither in Gratitude to an Appreciative Friend

1. For more on the friendship between Guan and Bao, see the prologue story of story 8 in Feng Menglong, *Stories Old and New: A Ming Dynasty Collection,* trans. Shuhui Yang and Yunqin Yang (Seattle: University of Washington Press, 2000).

2. During the Ming dynasty, Huguang consisted of present-day Hubei and Hunan Provinces. Yingdu was northwest of modern Jiangling, Hubei.

3. Fuxi was one of the legendary Three Sovereigns whose reign supposedly began around 2800 B.C.E.

4. The five planets are Venus, Jupiter, Mercury, Mars, and Saturn.

5. The thirty-three layers of heaven, *trayastrimsas,* is a Buddhist concept.

6. A year was divided into seventy-two units, called *hou,* with each *hou* consisting of five days.

7. The Jasper Pool is a legendary abode of the gods at the top of the Kunlun mountains in western China.

8. The eight solar terms of the year are the Beginning of Spring, the Beginning of Summer, the Beginning of Autumn, the Beginning of Winter, the Spring Equinox, the Summer Solstice, the Autumn Equinox, and the Winter Solstice.

9. Golden Boys and Jade Maidens are page boys and maids who serve Daoist immortals.

10. The dragon's pond and the phoenix's pool are the two holes at the back of the zither.

11. Yao and Shun were legendary sage-kings who ruled in antiquity.

12. "While your parents are alive, do not travel far" is from *The Analects,* 4:19.

13. Jinyang is now Jinyuanzhen, to the southwest of the city of Taiyuan, Shanxi.

14. "If you do, you should always make your whereabouts known to them" is the sentence that follows "While your parents are alive, do not travel far" in *The Analects,* 4:19.

15. "Nine Springs" is a term for the netherworld.

16. The reader will remember that they met in autumn.

17. "The phoenix's tail" is a reference to the zither.

2. Zhuang Zhou Drums on a Bowl and Attains the Great Dao

1. The cangue, a form of punishment, is a wooden collar usually three or four feet square.

It is placed around the neck and sometimes also confines the hands of an offender.

2. Zhang Jiazhen, prime minister in the Tang dynasty, wished to have Guo Tuanzhen as a son-in-law. He positioned his five daughters behind a curtain, with each daughter holding one end of a red thread and leaving the other end of the thread exposed on the other side of the curtain. Guo Tuanzhen was to pick up one of the red threads at random and take as his wife whichever girl happened to hold the other end. Hence the metaphor of red thread for marriages.

According to legend, the Old Man Under the Moon, the god of marriages, has a bag full of red strings with which he ties would-be couples together by their ankles.

3. Zhuang Zhou or Zhuangzi (ca. 369–286 B.C.E.) was a leading Daoist philosopher. A Daoist classic, *Zhuangzi,* bears his name.

4. According to Buddhism, the six sensory organs are the eye, ear, nose, tongue, body, and mind, receptors of sight, sound, smell, taste, touch, and idea, respectively.

5. "The six senses," pronounced "lu gen" in Feng's native Wu dialect, is a homophone of "green roots," a reference to the green seedlings in the first line.

Dao (the Way), also romanized Tao, is a homophone of *dao,* the word for "rice plants."

6. When transplanting rice seedlings, the Chinese farmer puts the seedlings down in the rice paddy one at a time, backing up a step with each plant, and thus gradually moves backward as the seedlings are planted.

7. The state of Song covered what are now the eastern part of Henan and neighboring portions of Shandong, Jiangsu, and Anhui.

8. According to some historians, Qiyuan was located north of what is now the city of Shangqiu, Henan; according to others, it was north of what is now Dingyuan County, Anhui.

9. The Jasper Pool is a legendary abode of the gods atop the Kunlun mountains in western China.

10. The *Daodejing,* also romanized *Tao te ching,* is the best-known text in classical Daoist philosophy.

11. In the first year of the Tianbao reign period (742), Emperor Xuanzong of the Tang dynasty gave Zhuangzi the posthumous title Sage of Nanhua, and the Daoist classic *Zhuangzi* also came to be known as *The Book of Nanhua.*

12. According to legend, while he was leaving China in search of some distant and secluded land, Laozi stopped at the frontier at Hangu Pass, where the warden asked the sage to write a book for him. Laozi granted the request, and the result is the five-thousand-character *Daodejing.*

13. Wu Qi (d. 381 B.C.E.) was a military strategist in the state of Lu during the Warring States period. When the state of Qi launched an attack against Lu, the king of Lu was inclined to make Wu commander in chief but hesitated because Wu's wife was a native of Qi. Thereupon, Wu killed his wife and won the promotion.

14. Xun Can, of the state of Wei in the Three Kingdoms period, died of grief soon after the death of his beloved wife.

3. Three Times Wang Anshi Tries to Battle Academician Su

This story has been translated as "Wang Anshih Thrice Corners Su Tung-p'o," in John Lyman Bishop, *The Colloquial Short Story in China: A Study of the San-Yen Collections,* Harvard-Yenching Institute Series 14 (Cambridge: Harvard University Press, 1956).

1. King Jie of the Xia dynasty and King Zhou of the Shang dynasty were the last rulers of their dynasties. Both are believed to have been despots.

2. For more on Shi Chong's fabulous wealth and precipitous downfall, see story 36 in Feng Menglong, *Stories Old and New: A Ming Dynasty Collection,* trans. Shuhui Yang and Yunqin Yang (Seattle: University of Washington Press, 2000).

3. Yan Hui (521–490 B.C.E.) was one of Confucius's students. He is mentioned by the woodcutter Zhong Ziqi, who recites a poem about the student in story 1.

4. Li Bai (701–762), also romanized as Li Po, was one of China's greatest poets.

Cao Zhi (192–232), courtesy name Zijian, was a poet of the state of Wei in the Three Kingdoms period.

Wang Anshi (1021–1086) was a famous man of letters and a political reformer who, as prime minister, promulgated a series of controversial reforms in public service, agriculture, trade and commerce, governmental finance, public works, education, and the military. Story 4 in this collection is a criticism of his reforms.

5. "Chirping turtledoves" (*ming jiu*) appears in *The Book of Songs* as *shijiu* (cuckoo).

6. Ouyang Xiu (1007–1072) was a great historian, epigraphist, statesman, poet, and essayist.

7. The term "Huguang," referring to today's Hunan and Hubei Provinces, was used during the Ming and Qing dynasties.

8. Yangxian is present-day Yixing, Jiangsu, a region that produced tea of superior quality.

9. The Double Ninth Festival falls on the ninth day of the ninth lunar month. It is a Chinese tradition to drink chrysanthemum wine on this day.

10. Yanyu Rock was dynamited in 1958.

11. The Eastern Capital (Dongjing) of the Song dynasty is now Kaifeng, Henan.

12. This is most probably a reference to *Commentary on The Waterways,* written by Li Daoyuan of the Northern Wei dynasty. Though it claims to be but a commentary on *The Waterways,* which is attributed to Guo Pu (276–324), it actually constitutes a much more important work of geography in itself.

13. Empress Wu Zetian (r. 684–704) of the Tang dynasty was the only female sovereign in Chinese history.

Xue Aocao, originally named Feng Xiaobao, was a much favored male companion of Empress Wu Zetian's.

14. "Clouds and rain" is a metaphor for sexual encounters. The term was first used in the prose poem "Gao-tang fu," attributed to Song Yu (ca. 290–ca. 223 B.C.E.).

15. No such book exists.

16. *Zuodui* can also mean "to be hostile and difficult."

17. Confucius is said to have honored Xiang Tuo, a seven-year-old boy, as his teacher because he was unable to answer the boy's questions.

4. *In the Hall Halfway-up-the-Hill, the Stubborn One Dies of Grief*

This story has been translated as "The Stubborn Chancellor," in Richard F. S. Yang, ed. and trans., *Eight Colloquial Tales of the Sung, Thirteenth Century China* (Taipei: China Post, 1972).

1. The Gold Valley Garden belonged to Shi Chong, an immensely rich man of the Jin dynasty. For more on Shi Chong and his fabulous wealth, see story 36 in Feng Menglong, *Stories Old and New: A Ming Dynasty Collection,* trans. Shuhui Yang and Yunqin Yang (Seattle: University of Washington Press, 2000).

2. Han Xin (d. 196 B.C.E.) helped Liu Bang found the Han dynasty but was later killed by order of Empress Lü and Prime Minister Xiao He on suspicion of disloyalty to the court.

3. In the Spring and Autumn period, Lord Mu of the state of Qin arranged a grand gathering of the lords of seventeen states at Lintong, where Wu Zixu of the state of Chu lifted a mighty cauldron in a show of strength. Lord Mu of Qin was so awestruck that he gave up his ambitions of annexation.

4. This quatrain is a slightly altered version of the last four lines of "Fangyan," a poem by Bai Juyi (772–846), a well-known Tang dynasty poet. Stories about the duke of Zhou and Wang Mang follow in the text.

5. The empress, wife of Emperor Yuan (r. 48–34 B.C.E.), was Wang Mang's aunt.

6. Ouyang Xiu (1007–1072) was a great historian, epigraphist, statesman, poet, and essayist.

Han Wei, Wen Yanbo, and Ouyang Xiu all opposed Wang Anshi's policies.

7. Yao and Shun were legendary sage-kings.

8. Gao Yao and Kui were good officials under Shun. Yi Yin and the duke of Zhou (Ji Dan) were known as good prime ministers of the Zhou dynasty.

9. Su Xun (1009–1066) was the father of Su Shi. For more on Su Shi, see story 3.

10. Under the crop loans policy, the government lent farmers funds in the planting season at an interest rate much lower than the usurious rate charged in the private market and was paid back after the autumn harvest.

The local goods transportation policy allowed products needed by the government to be bought locally, with a portion to be stored for future local needs in lean years and the rest to be transported to state depots throughout the empire. This measure was intended to adjust supply and demand and to bring down prices.

Under the militia policy, the people were supposed to ensure their own security by creating peasant militias, which were organized in units of ten families and were regularly trained and supplied with arms. This measure was supposed to reduce the swollen numbers of the regular armies.

The market trading policy made goods stored in government warehouses available to merchants on credit, with interest charged when the accounts were settled. The reason for this measure was to curb the merchants' monopoly on goods.

Under the horse care law, the government assigned people to take care of the horses it provided for the military establishment in exchange for exemption from taxes.

The land-grids policy specified that taxable land was to be gridded into squares of five thousand feet on each side. Within each square, soil productivity was classified into five grades, and taxes were assessed accordingly.

Under the guild tax policy, merchants belonging to guilds were allowed to pay taxes in cash rather than in kind.

11. Prayer services for the dead begin with a ritual performed to invite the presence of the Buddha, and upon completion of the service, paper is burned to send the Buddha away.

12. The cangue is a wooden collar usually three or four feet square. It is placed around the neck and sometimes also confines the hands of an offender.

13. The seat of Jiangning Prefecture is present-day Nanjing.

14. Guabu, named for Mount Guabu, is located southeast of Liuhe, Jiangsu.

15. On Yao, Shun, Yi Yin, and the duke of Zhou, see notes 7 and 8.

16. Before Wang Anshi became prime minister, he defended a youngster who had killed the man who robbed him of his quail. Wang argued that the youngster did not deserve the death penalty.

17. One day, while viewing the flowers and fishing in the palace garden, Wang Anshi ate up all the fish-bait in the golden plate by mistake.

18. All the men named here—Han Qi, Fu Bi, Sima Guang, Lü Hui, and Su Shi—were officials who fiercely opposed Wang Anshi's policies. For more on Su Shi, see story 3.

19. Fu Bi, Han Qi, and Sima Guang opposed Wang Anshi's policies.

20. Lü Huiqing was much trusted by Wang Anshi but later turned against Wang and criticized him in the severest terms.

21. According to Chinese mythology, Fengmeng learned archery from Yi but later killed Yi because he could not tolerate the thought that, on account of Yi, he was not the best archer in the universe.

22. "Nine Springs" is a term for the netherworld.

23. During the Jingkang reign period (1126), Emperors Huizong and Qinzong were captured by the Jurchens, and the Northern Song dynasty perished.

5. Lü Yu Returns the Silver and Brings about Family Reunion

1. According to "The Biography of Mao Bao" in *The History of the Jin Dynasty,* Mao Bao, prefect of Yuzhou, had under his command a soldier who bought a white turtle, raised it, and then put it back into the river. Later, when the army to which that soldier belonged was defeated in a battle, the soldier threw himself into the river, only to be saved and carried to shore by the very turtle he had raised. The reference here is based on a later version of the story, *Taiping yulan*, a reference book published in 983 during the Song dynasty,

in which Mao Bao himself saves the turtle and consequently receives a major promotion in his career.

2. It is said that during the Song dynasty, a certain Song Jiao made a small bridge out of pieces of bamboo after a rainstorm and thus saved the many ants in the puddle in front of his house. Because of this act of kindness, he later won first honors as a *zhuangyuan* in the imperial civil service examinations.

3. Deng Tong of the Western Han dynasty was an immensely rich man who was granted permission by Emperor Wen (r. 179–157 B.C.E.) to mint copper coins for the use of his own family. He later lost favor with the new emperor and died of hunger in prison. For more on Deng Tong, see story 9 in Feng Menglong, *Stories Old and New: A Ming Dynasty Collection,* trans. Shuhui Yang and Yunqin Yang (Seattle: University of Washington Press, 2000).

4. Guo Kuang of the Eastern Han dynasty, brother-in-law of Emperor Guangwu (r. 25–57), received so many gifts from the emperor that his house came to be known as "The Gold Vault."

5. Shi Chong was an extremely wealthy man during the Jin dynasty. For more on Shi Chong, see story 36 in Feng, *Stories Old and New.*

6. Lü Yan, courtesy name Lü Dongbin, also known as Lü Chunyang, is one of the Eight Immortals in the Daoist legends.

7. A *dou* is a unit of dry measure for grain, now roughly equivalent to one peck.

8. Guan Ning and Hua Xin of the Three Kingdoms period were working in the vegetable garden when they saw an ingot of gold on the ground. Guan Ning ignored it as he would a stone. Hua Xin picked it up but just as soon put it down again.

Pei Du (765–839) was touring a temple one day when he found two waistbands made of jade and a waistband made of rhinoceros horn. They belonged to a woman who had obtained them as a loan with which to redeem her father from prison. Pei Du returned the waistbands to her, an act that was believed to have earned him merit in the other world and accounted for his attaining the post of prime minister later in his life. For more on Pei Du, see story 9 in Feng, *Stories Old and New.*

6. Yu Liang Writes Poems and Wins Recognition from the Emperor

1. Zhang Liang, courtesy name Zifang (d. 189 B.C.E.), took refuge in Xiapi, Xuzhou, after a failed attempt to assassinate the First Emperor of the Qin dynasty. Later, he served as adviser to Liu Bang, founder of the Han dynasty.

2. Yi Yin, an adviser to King Tang, founder of the Shang dynasty, was of humble origin and a native of the state of Youxin near what is now Kaifeng, Henan.

3. Lü Wang—popularly known as Taigong Wang, Jiang Taigong, or Jiang Ziya—was a military strategist who did not rise to eminence until he was accosted by King Wen of the Zhou dynasty (ca. 1027–956 B.C.E.) while fishing by Panxi Creek, which flowed into the Wei River. He was already about eighty years old.

4. In his youth, Han Xin (d. 196 B.C.E.) was challenged by a ruffian and made to crawl between his legs. He later helped Liu Bang found the Han dynasty. For more on Han Xin, see note 2 of story 4.

5. Lü Mengzheng of the Song dynasty was a *zhuangyuan* (winner of highest honors in the civil service examinations).

6. Pei Du (765–839) was prime minister during the Tang dynasty. For more on Pei Du, see note 8 of story 5 and story 9 in Feng Menglong, *Stories Old and New,* trans. Shuhui Yang and Yunqin Yang (Seattle: University of Washington Press, 2000).

7. Qi and Chu were states during the Warring States period. Qi covered present-day northern Shandong and southeastern Hebei, and Chu comprised present-day Hubei, northern Hunan, and other regions along the lower and middle reaches of the Yangzi River.

8. Zou Yang and Mei Gao were famous men of letters of the Western Han dynasty.

9. "Mr. Fantasy" (Zixu fu) is a criticism of the extravagances of the imperial court.

10. During the Warring States period, the state of Qi came under attack by Chi of the state of Chu, and Fazhang, the crown prince of Qi, was disguised as a servant and took refuge in Grand Historian Jiao's household. Jiao's daughter, impressed by the prince's refined looks, surreptitiously gave him clothes and extra portions of food. In 279 B.C.E., General Tian Shan retook more than seventy towns in Qi and made Fazhang the new king of Qi; Grand Historian Jiao's daughter became queen. Jiao said, "She is no longer my daughter, for she brought disgrace to the family by marrying herself off without the proper matchmaking procedures." He never saw his daughter again.

11. This comment refers to the story of Han Xin (see note 4), who was fishing when an old woman washing clothes by the river noticed that he looked hungry and gave him some food. After he rose to power and became commander in chief under Liu Bang, Han Xin sought out the old woman and gave her a reward of a thousand pieces of gold.

12. In a vinegar fumigation ritual, red-hot coal is thrown into vinegar, and the resulting vapors are supposed to drive away bad luck.

13. A "lyric" (*ci*) poem differs from a "poem" (*shi*) mainly in that it is written to fit an existing tune.

14. The four treasures of the scholar's study are brush-pen, ink slab, inkstone, and paper.

15. In fact, during the Song dynasty, the imperial civil service examinations were held in three rounds: at the prefectural level, the provincial level, and the palace level. The local-level examinations were not added until the Yuan dynasty and became widespread practice during the Ming dynasty.

7. Chen Kechang Becomes an Immortal during the Dragon Boat Festival

This story has been translated as "P'u-sa Man," in Richard F.S. Yang, ed. and trans., *Eight Colloquial Tales of the Sung, Thirteenth Century China* (Taipei: China Post, 1972).

1. Heavenly Stems and Earthly Branches are two sets of signs. One is taken from each set to form sixty pairs designating years, months, and days.

2. This is the eve of the Dragon Boat Festival, which falls on the fifth day of the fifth month every year.

3. *Zongzi* is a pyramid-shaped dumpling made of glutinous rice that is wrapped in bamboo or reed leaves; it is eaten during the Dragon Boat Festival.

4. Prince Wu Yi was actually Empress Wushi's brother.

5. The Monk of Tang was Tripitaka Xuanzang (602–664). A great translator of Buddhist scriptures, he studied in India and had a major influence on the development of Buddhism in China. In this context, however, "the Monk of Tang" is a reference to any monk.

6. Qu Yuan (ca. 340–278 B.C.E.) is the model loyal minister in traditional Chinese culture. Frustrated because his ruler repeatedly ignored his strategic advice, he drowned himself in the Miluo River.

7. The eight characters of the astrological chart are two characters for the hour of birth (one for the Heavenly Stem, one for the Earthly Branch), two for the day, two for the month, and two for the year.

8. In Buddhist mythology, King Yama is the king of hell and judge of souls.

9. The God of Mount Tai, or the East Mountain God, is the Daoist counterpart of King Yama.

10. During the Song dynasty, Shamen Island, located east of what is now Shandong Province, was a place of exile for most convicts whose death sentences had been commuted.

11. In Buddhist terminology, to go to the west is to die.

12. The fire of *samadhi* is the fire that consumed the body of the Buddha when he entered nirvana.

13. The Tusita Heaven is the fourth layer of heaven in the Buddhist belief.

8. *Artisan Cui's Love Is Cursed in Life and in Death.*

Story 8 has been translated by C. Lung as "Artisan Ts'ui and His Ghost Wife," in *Traditional Chinese Stories: Themes and Variations,* ed. Y. W. Ma and Joseph S. M. Lau (Boston: Cheng and Tsui, 1986), and as "The Jade Worker," in *The Courtesan's Jewel Box: Chinese Stories of the Tenth–Twelfth Centuries,* trans. Yang Xianyi and Gladys Yang (Beijing: Foreign Languages Press, 1981). In the original edition, a note appended to the title reads "The Song dynasty text was titled 'The Jade Bodhisattva.'"

1. Lady Huang is often identified as Sun Daoxun, a Song dynasty poet.

2. Wang Anshi (1021–1086) was a famous man of letters and political reformer. For more on Wang Anshi, see stories 3 and 4.

3. Su Shi, or Su Dongpo, (1037–1101), was one of China's greatest men of letters. For more on Su Shi, see story 3.

4. Qin Guan (1049–1100), courtesy name Shaoyou, was a famous *ci* poet.

5. Shao Yong (1011–1077), courtesy name Yaofu, was a Northern Song philosopher.

6. This is probably a reference to Zeng Gongliang, courtesy name Zhongming, who held posts in the Grand Secretariat and the Privy Military Council under Emperor Renzong of the Song dynasty.

7. Zhu Dunrun (1081–1159), courtesy name Xizhen, was a Southern Song *ci* poet.

8. Legend has it that the soul of Du Yu, king of Sichuan in high antiquity, changed into a cuckoo and would not stop its mournful cries until it coughed up blood.

9. Su Xiaoxiao of Suzhou was a famous courtesan with literary talents during the Southern Song dynasty.

10. "Plum rain" refers to the kind of intermittent drizzle that occurs during the rainy season in the middle and lower reaches of the Yangzi River.

11. "The southern shore" (*nanpu*) is an expression taken from "Nine Songs" by Qu Yuan (ca. 340–ca. 278 B.C.E.) and is often used in reference to places where lovers part.

12. Wang Yansou (1042–1092), courtesy name Yanlin, was an official in the Privy Military Council.

13. The prince of Xian'an was the famous general Han Shizhong (1089–1151), who repelled invading Jurchen troops.

14. During the Tang, Song, and Yuan dynasties, the *muhurta* doll—usually made of clay, wood, or wax in the shape of a child—was often offered as a gift on the Double Seventh Festival. The festival is held on the seventh day of the seventh month and celebrates the annual meeting of the Herdboy and Weaving Maiden stars, which are said to cross the Milky Way on a bridge formed by magpies. The term *muhurta* is derived from Mahoraga, a Buddhist deity with a human body and a snake's head.

15. Baosi was the favorite concubine of King You (r. 781–771 B.C.E.) of the Zhou dynasty. In order to win a smile from her, King You lit the beacon fires on Mount Li, which were intended to signal distress to the feudal lords. Believing the king to be in danger, the lords came rushing to the rescue with their troops, only to find upon arrival that nothing was amiss. Baosi exploded with mirth. Later, when western tribes raised armies and invaded the empire, none of the lords bothered to come to the king's aid, and King You perished at the foot of Mount Li.

16. Zhou Yu was a military strategist under Sun Quan (182–252), king of Wu, who once reigned over the entire region southeast of the Yangzi River. In a famous battle at Red Cliff, Sun Quan joined forces with Liu Bei, an adversary, and routed their common enemy, the powerful Cao Cao.

17. The Wutong god is a fire god in Daoist beliefs.

18. Song Wuji is revered in Daoism as a fire god who rides a red donkey.

19. General Liu is Liu Qi (1098–1162), a famous general known for his valor in fighting the Jurchen invaders. He was a native of Deshun County in what is now Jingning, in Gansu

Province, not a native of Xiongwu County, as the storyteller asserts.

20. In the summer of 1140, Liu Qi led thirty-seven thousand soldiers in a major battle against the Jurchen army at Shunchang, present-day Fuyang in Anhui Province, and routed the invaders.

21. Prince Yang of He was Yang Cunzhong, a well-known commander of the Southern Song army. He was posthumously awarded the title Prince of He.

22. A military pledge is a usually voluntary written statement signed by a military officer that pledges willingness to be executed if the pledger is unable to accomplish a given mission.

9. "Li the Banished Immortal" Writes in Drunkenness to Impress the Barbarians

1. The Caishi Cliffs, or Caishi Ji, are east of what is now Ma'anshan, Anhui Province. This is where Li Bai is believed to have drowned when, in a drunken state, he tried to embrace the moon's reflection in the water.

2. Li Hao (351–417) was the founder of the Western Liang state in West Gansu. He ruled from 400 to 417.

3. Du Fu (712–770) was one of the most celebrated poets in the history of Chinese literature.

4. Vimalakirti is said to have been a contemporary of Sakyamuni and to have visited China.

5. Chao Cuo (200–154 B.C.E.) was an eminent political figure of the Western Han dynasty.

Dong Zhongshu (179–104 B.C.E.) was an important philosopher.

6. He Zhizhang (659–ca. 744) was a famous Tang dynasty poet.

7. *Kodu* is possibly the Korean equivalent of the Chinese term *jutou* (huge head).

8. The center of Parhae, which was overrun by the Khitan in the tenth century, was in the Songhua River drainage of northeastern China; its capital was the present-day city of Dunhua in China's Jilin Province.

9. When You Kaesomun died in 666, he was succeeded by his son Namsaeng, but, while Namsaeng was on a tour of inspection, his younger brothers Namgon and Namsan took over the court. Afraid to return to Pyongyang, Namsaeng appealed to the Tang emperor, who, with the support of Silla, sent troops and subdued Koguryo.

10. Dongfang Shuo (154–93 B.C.E.) was a great man of letters of the Western Han dynasty. Stories about his wisdom and fortune–telling skills abound.

11. Guo Ziyi (697–781) later became prime minister.

12. Tao Qian, courtesy name Yuanming (365–427), was a famous poet and essayist. Refusing to "stoop low for the sake of five piculs of rice," he resigned from his post and spent the rest of his life as a recluse, farming in his native village.

"Be gone, and let me drift into wine-rapt sleep" was written not by Tao Yuanming but by Li Bai himself. It appears in the poem "A Drink with My Hermit Friend in the Mountains."

13. "Clouds and rain" is a metaphor for sexual encounters. The term was first used in the prose poem "Gao tang fu," attributed to Song Yu (ca. 290–ca. 223 B.C.E.).

14. Zhao Feiyan (d. 1 B.C.E.) was a court lady in the service of Emperor Cheng (r. 32–6 B.C.E.) of the Han dynasty and was later made empress.

15. "*Dongwu*" or "*Dongwu yinxing*" is the title of a tune used in poems collected by Yuefu, an official conservatory set up during the Han dynasty. *Dongwu* poems often lament the brevity of life and the transience of fame and glory.

10. Secretary Qian Leaves Poems on the Swallow Tower

1. The *zhe*, or *zhezi*, a dance introduced from Central Asia, was popular during the Tang dynasty.

2. Wuning was a commandery during the

Tang dynasty. Its seat was Xuzhou in what is now Shandong Province.

3. Bai Juyi (772–846) was one of the most influential poets of the mid-Tang.

4. These three poems, with slight variations, were written not by Guan Panpan but by Zhang Zhongsu, a male contemporary of Bai Juyi's.

5. Mount Yu, located on the border of Jiangxi and Guangdong, is famous for its abundance of plum blossoms.

6. According to "The Biography of Gongsun Hong," in *Han shu* (The history of the Han), Gongsun Hong, while serving as prime minister under Emperor Wu of the Han dynasty, was in the habit of admitting his untitled friends through an eastern door (*dongge*), which can also be understood as the "East Hall." There is no record of Gongsun's "East Hall" being reduced to a stable.

7. Qian Yi (ca. 978–1034) was a Song dynasty man of letters.

Qian Liu (852–932), a native of Hangzhou, was king of Wu and Yue from 907 to 932. For more on his life, see story 21 in Feng Menglong, *Stories Old and New: A Ming Dynasty Collection,* trans. Shuhui Yang and Yunqin Yang (Seattle: University of Washington Press, 2000).

8. This is a reference to Zhang Jianfeng.

9. "Nine Springs" is a term for the netherworld.

11. A Shirt Reunites Magistrate Su with His Family

1. Bai Juyi (772–846) was one of the most influential poets of the mid-Tang. For more on Bai Juyi, see story 10.

2. Su Shi, (1037–1101), or Su Dongpo, was one of China's greatest men of letters. For a poem by Su Dongpo, see story 8, and for a story about the scholar, see story 3.

3. Du Kang is believed to have been the earliest brewer of wine in China.

4. The goddess of the Wu Mountains is the one who conjures up "clouds and rain." The term is a metaphor for sexual encounters.

5. Sima Xiangru (179–117 B.C.E.), one of the most celebrated prose poem (*fu*) writers in the history of Chinese literature, is also known for his romance with Zhuo Wenjun. The two eloped after their first meeting. See the prologue story of story 6.

6. Li Jing (571–649) was a military strategist who helped Emperor Taizong conquer the western tribes and found the Tang dynasty.

7. These are the eight immortals (seven male and one female) in popular Daoist legends.

8. Liu Kan, Emperor Ping (r. 1 B.C.E.–6 C.E.) of the Western Han dynasty, was poisoned by Wang Mang, usurper of the throne.

9. Li Bai (701–762) was one of the greatest poets of China. For more on Li Bai, see story 9.

10. Legend has it that a young man called Weisheng, waiting in vain for his loved one at their agreed-upon spot under a bridge, held on to the bridge post even after the water began to rise and drowned.

11. Xishi, a beauty of the state of Yue in the Warring States period, is believed to have caused the defeat of Fuchai, king of Wu.

12. Shi Chong, see note 5 of story 5.

13. On Deng Tong, see note 3 of story 5.

14. Xiang Yu (232–202 B.C.E.) was a major rival of Liu Bang's in contending for the throne. Liu Bang later became the first emperor of the Han dynasty.

15. On Zhou Yu, see note 16 of story 8.

16. Ming dynasty officials underwent performance appraisals once every three years. Promotions or demotions were based on the results.

17. The Jing and Wei Rivers are both tributaries of the Yellow River. Where they merge, the clear water of the Jing does not mix with the muddy water of the Wei.

18. The Hall of Loyalty and Justice is the gathering place of the outlaws depicted as heroes in the Ming dynasty novel *Outlaws of the Marsh*, traditionally attributed to Shi Nai'an.

19. A narrative that trails off in phrases such as "This and this must be done" is a convention used in vernacular stories to create suspense until the actions to which they allude take place.

20. In ancient China, convicted criminals were usually executed in autumn.

21. Cheng Ying and Gongsun Chujiu are characters in the famous play *Orphan of the Zhao Clan*, which is set during the reign of Duke Jing of the state of Jin in the Spring and Autumn period. Tu'an Gu killed the entire clan of Prime Minister Zhao Dun, except Zhao Dun's daughter-in-law, who fled and gave birth to a son, Zhao Wu. Cheng Ying and Gongsun Chujiu, retainers of the Zhao family, saved the orphan, who later sought revenge against Tu'an Gu. This story was retold in French by Voltaire.

22. When he was a fugitive from the state of Chu during the Spring and Autumn period, Wu Zixu once begged for food from a girl washing gauze by the river. As he took leave of her, he told her not to tell anyone that she had seen him. As proof of her trustworthiness, she threw herself into the river and drowned. For more on Wu Zixu, see note 3 of story 4.

23. Legend has it that Qi was conceived when his mother Jiang Yuan was standing on the footprints of a giant. Out of fear, she abandoned the newborn baby boy in the fields, only to take him back after three days when he was found to be still alive, protected by the wings of a hundred birds. Hence, his name Qi (The Abandoned). Later, King Yao appointed him to take charge of agricultural matters, and he came to be known as Houji.

24. Legend has it that Yi Yin, prime minister under King Tang of the Shang dynasty, was born in a hollow mulberry tree and that his mother had changed into this tree after she had drowned.

25. A *juren* is one who has passed the imperial civil service examinations at the provincial level.

26. Emperor Lie is most probably Emperor Zhaolie, the posthumous title of Liu Bei (162–223), founder of the kingdom of Shu in the Three Kingdoms period (220–265).

27. A *yaksha* is usually a malevolent spirit in the Buddhist belief.

28. For the meaning of tying a red thread to the feet, see notes 2 and 3 of story 2.

29. When selecting his sons-in-law, Dou Yi, an official in the Sui dynasty, had two peacocks drawn on his door. Those candidates who were able to hit the peacocks in the eye with their arrows stood a good chance of being selected.

12. A Double Mirror Brings Fan the Loach and His Wife Together Again

This story has been translated by Earl Wieman as "Loach Fan's Double Mirror" in *Traditional Chinese Stories: Themes and Variations*, ed. Y. W. Ma and Joseph Lau S.M. (Boston: Cheng and Tsui, 1986).

1. Legend has it that when pursued by the Jurchens, Zhao Gou, prince of Kang (later to become Emperor Gaozong), took refuge in a temple. After he crossed the river on horseback and threw off his pursuers, he found that the horse he was riding was the clay horse he had seen in the temple. It had been sent to help him by the god of the temple.

2. Bianjing, also called the Eastern Capital, is present-day Kaifeng, Henan.

3. According to legend, Zhang Hua (232–300) saw an aura over Fengcheng that spoke of hidden precious swords. After he appointed Lei Huan prefect of Fengcheng, Lei dug up a pair of swords and presented one to Zhang, keeping the other for himself. After both men died, the swords were seen at Yanping Ferry, where they joined together and changed into two dragons.

4. A picul equals 133.33 pounds.

5. Zhang Jun (1097–1164), courtesy name Deyuan, a native of Sichuan, was an official in the Privy Military Council.

Yue Fei (1103–1142) is revered as a national hero in China for his accomplishments in repelling the advances of Jurchen (Jin) invaders.

Zhang Jun (1086–1154), courtesy name Boying, a native of Gansu, fought the Jurchens with Yue Fei but later joined in the conspiracy against Yue Fei.

Zhang Rong was a fisherman turned military official known for his deeds in fighting the Jurchens.

Wu Jie (1093–1139), courtesy name Jinqing, was a general in the Song army.

Wu Ling (1102–1167), courtesy name Tangqing, was Wu Jie's brother.

6. Han Shizhong (1089–1151) was a famous general best remembered for successfully repelling the attacks of invading Jurchen troops. He is featured as the prince of Xian'an, in story 8.

7. Yang Yao (d. 1135) was the leader of a peasant rebellion in the Dongting Lake region.

13. Judge Bao Solves a Case through a Ghost That Appeared Thrice

This story has been translated as "The Ghost Came Thrice," in *Lazy Dragon: Chinese Stories from the Ming Dynasty*, trans. Yang Xianyi and Gladys Yang (Hong Kong: Joint Publishing Company, 1981).

1. Gan Luo was a native of the state of Qin during the Warring States period. He was granted a royal title at the age of twelve for his meritorious service to the state.

Ziya is Jiang Ziya, or Lü Wang, also popularly known as Taigong Wang or Jiang Taigong. He was a Zhou dynasty military strategist who did not rise to eminence until he was about eighty years old.

2. Peng Zu was a legendary figure in the time of the sage king Yao (before 2100 B.C.E.) who was said to have lived for eight hundred years.

Yan Hui (521–490 B.C.E.) was a student of Confucius. For more about Yan Hui, see story 1.

3. Fan Dan (112–185), an erudite scholar on the classics, was also known for his poverty.

For more on Shi Chong's wealth and downfall, see story 36 in Feng Menglong, *Stories Old and New*, trans. Shuhui Yang and Yunqin Yang (Seattle: University of Washington Press, 2000).

4. Zhang Dun (1035–1105), courtesy name Zihou, was a court official committed to Wang Anshi's reforms.

5. The five phases are water, fire, wood, metal, and earth. The eight characters of the astrological chart are two characters for the year of birth (one for the Heavenly Stem, one for the Earthly Branch), two for the month, two for the day, and two for the hour. Phases and characters combined are used to tell one's fortune.

6. Dongfang Shuo (154–93 B.C.E.) was a great man of letters of the Western Han dynasty. Stories about his wisdom and fortune-telling skills abound.

7. The Tai'e sword is believed to have been cast by the legendary ironsmiths Ganjian and Ouyezi in the Spring and Autumn period.

8. In fortune-tellers' parlance, a white tiger symbolizes misfortune.

9. A story in *Liezi* tells of a woodsman in the state of Zheng who forgot where he had hidden the deer he had killed and thought he had dreamed about it. Another man heard about this, found the deer, and took it home. Then the woodsman dreamed he remembered the place where he had hidden the deer and also saw the man who had taken the deer. The two men brought the case to court. When asked for his judgment, the prime minister said, "I can't tell what is dream and what is not." The mention of "Qin" suggests an allusion to Prime Minister Zhao Gao of the Qin dynasty. He demanded absolute obedience by pointing at a deer, calling it a horse, and killing everyone who disagreed. Feng Menglong may have confused the two stories.

10. Zhuangzi or Zhuang Zhou (ca. 369–286 B.C.E.) was a Daoist philosopher. According to the *Zhuangzi*, he once dreamed he was a butterfly that did not know it was Zhuang Zhou. When he awoke suddenly, he found himself Zhuang Zhou again but did not know whether he was Zhuang Zhou who had dreamed he was a butterfly or a butterfly dreaming it was Zhuang Zhou. For more about Zhuang Zhou, see story 2.

11. "Green" (*qing*) is a homophone of the character for "clear," implying in this context that the case is to be solved.

14. A Mangy Priest Exorcises a Den of Ghosts

This story has been translated by Morgan T. Jones as "A Mangy Taoist Exorcises Ghosts," in *Traditional Chinese Stories: Themes and Variations* ed. Y. W. Ma and Joseph S. M. Lau (Boston: Cheng and Tsui, 1986). In the original edition, a note appended to the title reads

"The Song dynasty text was titled 'A Den of Ghosts of West Hill.'"

1. "Clouds and rain" is a metaphor for sexual encounters; it was first used in a prose poem attributed to Song Yu (ca. 290–ca. 223 B.C.E.).

2. This poem was written by Shen Tang, courtesy name Gongshu, not Wenshu.

3. Chen Ke, courtesy name Chen Zigao, was a *ci* poet of the Northern Song dynasty.

The Cold Food Festival, a day in April on which no fire is lit for cooking, originated during the Spring and Autumn period in commemoration of Jiezitui the hermit. When searching for Jiezitui, Duke Wen of Jin ordered that a fire be lit on the mountain where the hermit was living, hoping to drive him out of his quarters, but Jiezitui held on to a tree and burned to death.

4. Li Yi'an is Li Qingzhao (1084–1151), China's greatest woman poet. This poem, however, was written not by her but by Zeng Yu of the Northern Song dynasty.

5. *Nanpu* (the southern bank) is often used to denote a place where people bid each other farewell.

6. "Dongyang" is a reference to Shen Yue (441–513), a man of letters of the Liang dynasty in the Southern Dynasties period. He once served as prefect of Dongyang.

7. The Precious Moon Chan Master was a monk-poet in the Southern Song dynasty.

8. Ouyang Xiu (1007–1072) was a great historian, epigraphist, statesman, poet, and essayist.

9. The Clear and Bright Festival, usually falling one day after the Cold Food Festival (see note 3), is a day on which people visit the graves of their ancestors.

10. Chao Buzhi (1053–1110), courtesy name Wujiu, was a *ci* poet in the Northern Song dynasty.

11. Liu Yong (d. 1053), courtesy name Qiqing, was a famous Northern Song *ci* poet. For more on Liu Yong, see story 12 in Feng Menglong, *Stories Old and New: A Ming Dynasty Collection,* trans. Shuhui Yang and Yunqin Yang (Seattle: University of Washington Press, 2000).

12. Yan Jidao (ca. 1040–1112 or 1031–1106), courtesy name Shuyuan, was a Northern Song poet whose poems were mostly of a melancholy nature.

13. Lady Wei was the wife of Zeng Bu (1036–1107), a Northern Song dynasty official under the reformer Wang Anshi.

14. Kang Yuzhi (d. ca. 1162), courtesy name Boke, was a scholar-official and *ci* poet.

15. Qin Guan (1049–1100), courtesy name Shaoyou, was a famous *ci* poet.

16. According to legend, the soul of Du Yu, king of Sichuan in high antiquity, changed into a cuckoo and would not stop its mournful cries until it coughed up blood.

17. Huang Tingjian (1045–1105), courtesy name Luzhi, was a famous Song dynasty poet.

18. Zhou Bangyan (1056–1121), courtesy name Meicheng, was a Northern Song *ci* poet.

19. Grand Preceptor Qin is Qin Hui (1090–1155), prime minister for nineteen years during the Song dynasty.

20. The three departments are the Department of State Affairs, the Secretariat, and the Chancellery.

21. The six ministries are the Ministries of Personnel, Revenue, Rites, War, Justice, and Works.

22. The "green plum" comes from the phrase "green plums and a bamboo horse," which refers to a girl and a boy with an innocent affection for each other playing together.

23. In the Song dynasty, a bridegroom-to-be visited the bride-to-be on a chosen day bearing gifts and, if pleased with her, stuck a hairpin in her hair.

15. Clerk Jin Rewards Xiutong with a Pretty Maidservant

1. The Xuandu Temple referred to in two of Liu Yuxi's poems is not the Xuanmiao Temple of Suzhou but is located south of Chang'an, the capital (present-day Xi'an in Shaanxi Province).

2. Zhenwu or Xuanwu was a legendary figure of the Han dynasty who was said to have crossed the Eastern Sea and received a double-edged sword from a god. He then went into the mountains, from which he later ascended

to heaven. Because he watched over the northern region by order of the Lord on High, the title Xuanwu became identified with the serpent-entwined tortoise that symbolizes the north.

3. A green dragon symbolizes good luck, and a white tiger, misfortune.

16. The Young Lady Gives the Young Man a Gift of Money

This story has been translated as "The Honest Clerk," in *The Courtesan's Jewel Box: Chinese Stories of the Tenth–Twelfth Centuries,* trans. Yang Xianyi and Gladys Yang (Beijing: Foreign Languages Press, 1981). In the original edition, a note appended to the title reads "Originally titled 'Zhang Zhicheng the Manager Escapes an Extraordinary Calamity.'"

1. Jade Maidens and Golden Boys are maids and page boys who serve the Daoist immortals.

2. The Weaving Maiden is a star on one side of the Milky Way, and her husband, the Herdboy star, is on the other side. They are able to meet only once a year, on the seventh day of the seventh month, when magpies form a bridge across the river.

17. The Luckless Scholar Rises Suddenly in Life

1. Lü Mengzheng (944–1011), prime minister for three terms under Emperors Taizong and Zhenzong of the Song dynasty, had suffered great poverty earlier in his life. See the prologue story about Lü and a melon in story 18, in Feng Menglong, *Stories Old and New: A Ming Dynasty Collection,* trans. Shuhui Yang and Yunqin Yang (Seattle: University of Washington Press, 2000).

2. Zhu Maichen (d. 115 B.C.E.) started his career as an official quite late in life. See the prologue story about his wife divorcing him in story 27, in Feng, *Stories Old and New.*

3. There was no Ganlu reign period in the Tang dynasty. The author might have been thinking of the "Ganlu Incident" of 835, in which Prime Minister Li Xun, under Emperor Wenzong of the Tang dynasty, led a failed attempt to bring down the eunuch clique in the imperial court. There were, however, several reign periods called Ganlu in other dynasties, including one from 53 to 50 B.C.E. under Emperor Xuandi of the Han dynasty.

4. Han Xin (d. 196 B.C.E.) later helped Liu Bang found the Han dynasty. For more on Han Xin, see note 2 of story 4.

Before he rose to power, Su Qin (d. 317 B.C.E.) of the Warring States period was shunned by his kinsmen for returning home impoverished after a prolonged journey to find employment.

5. Yan Ziyuan is Yan Hui (521–490 B.C.E.), one of Confucius's students. For more about Yan Hui, see story 1.

Yu Shinan (558–638) was a famous calligrapher of the Tang dynasty. "Having learned by heart enough books to fill five carriages" was what he said, not about himself, but in praise of Liang Renfang of the Southern dynasty.

6. The eight characters of the astrological chart are two for the hour of birth, two for the day, two for the month, and two for the year.

7. The five phases are water, fire, wood, metal, and earth. The five planets are Mercury (water), Mars (fire), Jupiter (wood), Venus (metal), and Saturn (earth).

8. Literally, "When your time comes, the wind will send you to the Pavilion of Prince Teng." This is from a Tang dynasty legend about Wang Bo (640–676), a famous poet and master of prose. He was on his way to visit his father in Jiangxi when a gust of wind blew him to the prefect's banquet in the Pavilion of Prince Teng in the city of Nanchang by West River, and that was how he came to write his best-known piece, "A Preface to the Poem 'Pavilion of Prince Teng.'"

9. Literally, "When your time goes, a thunderbolt will smash the stone tablet of Jianfu Temple." This is from the following Song dynasty story: When the famous essayist and poet Fan Zhongyan (989–1052) was prefect of Raozhou, a poverty-stricken scholar went to seek his help. Fan Zhongyan offered to make him one thousand rubbings of a Jianfu Temple stone tablet with inscriptions by the most pop-

ular calligrapher of the day, Ouyang Xun, and each rubbing would be worth a thousand in cash. On the very night before the rubbings were to be done, the stone tablet was destroyed by a thunderbolt.

10. Wu Yuan, courtesy name Zixu (d. 484 B.C.E.), was a member of the aristocracy in the state of Wu during the Spring and Autumn period. For a time, he was so impoverished that he was reduced to being a beggar. See also note 3 of story 4 and note 22 of story 11.

It is said that in his days of poverty, Lü Mengzheng (see note 1 above) used to join the monks at meals whenever he heard the meal bell of the nearby monastery. The monks grew so sick of him that they took to ringing the bell only after they had already eaten.

11. This is a reference to the old woman who gave food to Han Xin (see note 4) when she noticed that he looked hungry. For more on this story, see note 11 of story 6.

12. "Wind and clouds" is a metaphor for a scholar's receiving recognition from the imperial government.

18. A Former Protégé Repays His Patron unto the Third Generation

1. Gan Luo was a native of the state of Qin during the Warring States period.

2. Jiang Taigong was a military strategist during the Zhou dynasty who achieved eminence when he was about eighty years old.

3. Dong Zhongshu (179–104 B.C.E.) was an important philosopher.

Sima Xiangru (179–117 B.C.E.) was one of the most celebrated *fu* (prose poem) writers in the history of Chinese literature. For more on Sima Ziangru, see the prologue story of story 6.

4. Jieyu, the madman of Chu, advised Confucius to give up trying to save the land. See *The Analects,* 18.5.

5. According to a Han dynasty story, the king of the state of She (now pronounced as Ye) was very fond of drawings of dragons, but one day, when a true dragon appeared in his window, he was frightened out of his wits.

6. Su Qin (d. 317 B.C.E.) returned home impoverished after a long journey seeking employment.

7. Before he became the first emperor of the Han dynasty, Liu Bang (256–195 B.C.E.) enlisted the services of Han Xin (d. 196 B.C.E.) and built a platform for a grand ceremony honoring him as commander in chief. On Han Xin, see also notes 4 and 11 of story 6.

8. The model loyal minister Qu Yuan (ca. 340–278 B.C.E.) drowned himself in the Miluo River, frustrated because his ruler repeatedly ignored his advice.

9. The Four Books are *The Great Learning, The Doctrine of the Mean, The Analects* of *Confucius,* and *Mencius.*

10. "Xianyu" is a very rare surname.

19. With a White Falcon, Young Master Cui Brings an Evil Spirit upon Himself

This story has been translated as "The White Hawk of Ts'ui, the Magistrate's Son, Led to Demons," in *Eight Colloquial Tales of the Sung, Thirteenth Century China,* trans. Richard F. S. Yang (Taipei: China Post, 1972). In the original edition, a note appended to the title reads "Titled 'The Three Evil Spirits of Mount Ding' in an ancient version. Also known as 'The White Falcon from Silla.'"

1. Bingzhou, in present-day Shanxi, was famous for its sharp scissors.

2. The Double Seventh Festival falls on the seventh day of the seventh month, when the Weaving Maiden Star is believed to meet her husband, the Herdboy Star, by crossing a bridge formed by magpies across the Silver River (Milky Way).

3. The prince of Ning, Li Xian, a skilled flute player, was actually Emperor Xuanzong's older brother, not his younger brother.

4. Zhao Feiyen, (d. 1 B.C.E.) was the favorite of Emperor Cheng of the Han dynasty and later became empress. For more on Zhao Feiyen, see story 9.

5. Zhang Fei (d. 221) was a brave warrior and, together with Guan Yu, a sworn brother of Liu Bei's (162–223), founded the kingdom of

Shu in the Three Kingdoms period. According to *The Romance of the Three Kingdoms* (Sanguo yanyi), his thunderous shouts from Changban Bridge stopped the advances of Cao Cao's troops and scared Xiahou Jie, a subordinate of Cao Cao's, to death.

6. Wang Yanzhang (863–923), courtesy name Xianming, was a valiant warrior of the Later Liang dynasty in the Five Dynasties period.

7. Li Bai (701–762) was one of China's greatest poets. For more on Li Bai, see story 9.

8. Liu Ling (221–300) was one of the Seven Sages of the Bamboo Grove during the Western Jin dynasty.

9. This is a reference to the four old hermits of the Shang Mountains in the early Han dynasty.

10. Once, when offering sacrifices to the gods on Mount Tai, the First Emperor of the Qin dynasty was caught in the rain and took shelter under a pine tree. Later, he gave the pine tree the title Grand Master of the Fifth Grade.

11. Wu Daozi was a famous painter of the Tang dynasty and was often commissioned by Emperor Xuanzong (r. 673–756) to paint in the palace.

12. Kuai Wentong, also known as Kuai Tong, was a sophist of the earlier Han dynasty.

13. In a horse chess game, all thirty chess pieces, fifteen on each side, are horses.

14. Chen Shubao (553–604), king of the Chen dynasty during the Southern Dynasties period, was a talented poet, albeit an incompetent ruler obsessed with feminine beauty.

15. King Zhou was a notorious despot and the last king of the Shang dynasty.

20. *The Golden Eel Brings Calamity to Officer Ji*

1. A crow symbolizes misfortune, and a magpie good luck.

2. Xiao He (d. 193 B.C.E.), prime minister under the first emperor of the Han dynasty, formulated the larger part of the Han penal code.

3. For the story about Li Yuan saving a snake, read story 34 in Feng Menglong, *Stories Old and New: A Ming Dynasty Collection,* trans. Shuhui Yang and Yunqin Yang (Seattle: University of Washington Press, 2000).

4. Sun Simiao (581–682) was a famous physician and author of medical literature. Legend has it that he saved a snake that happened to be the Dragon King's son who had assumed the shape of a snake. The grateful Dragon King gave Sun Simiao a thousand prescriptions.

21. *Emperor Taizu Escorts Jingniang on a One-Thousand-Li Journey*

This story has been translated by Lorraine S. Y. Lieu and the editors as "The Sung Founder Escorts Ching-niang One Thousand Li," in *Traditional Chinese Stories: Themes and Variations,* ed. Y. W. Ma and Joseph S. M. Lau (Boston: Cheng and Tsui, 1986).

1. Legend has it that there is a hare in the moon and a three-foot crow in the sun. Hence, the moon is called the Jade Hare, and the sun the Gold Crow.

2. The Nine Regions are believed to have been established by King Yu in high antiquity. The term is often used as another name for China.

King Tang founded the Shang dynasty.

3. Emperor Wu of Wei was Cao Cao (155–220), courtesy name Mengde.

4. In the first year of the Jingde reign period (1004–7) under Emperor Zhenzong, the Liao swept south against the Song. Kou Zhun (961–1023), the prime minister, led an expedition to Chanyuan (in present-day Henan) and killed the leading Liao general. However, the advocates of appeasement prevailed and negotiated peace in a document known historically as the Treaty of Chanyuan.

5. Han Tuozhou (1151–1207) was a powerful minister during the reign of Emperor Ningzong of the Song dynasty. He was a staunch supporter of Yue Fei (1103–1142), who is revered for fighting against the Jurchen (Jin) invaders. In 1206, Han Tuozhou was defeated by the Jurchen troops, and in the following year, he was killed and his head offered to the Jurchens in a bid for peace.

Jia Sidao (1213–1275) was an evil minister in the Song court. For more on his life and death, see story 22 in Feng Menglong, *Stories Old and New: A Ming Dynasty Collection,* trans. Shuhui Yang and Yunqin Yang (Seattle: University of Washington Press, 2000).

6. Empress Lü-shi (241–180 B.C.E.) was the wife of Liu Bang, founder of the Han dynasty.

Empress Wu Zetian (r. 684–704) was the only female sovereign in Chinese history.

7. Zhao Feiyan (d. 1 B.C.E.) was a court lady in the service of Emperor Cheng (r. 32–6 B.C.E.) of the Han dynasty. She later was made empress.

Yang Yuhuan (719–756) was a favorite consort of Emperor Xuanzong (r. 712–55) of the Tang dynasty. For more on Consort Yang, see story 9.

8. Empresses Gao, Cao, Xiang, and Meng were the wives of Song emperors Renzong, Yingzong, Shenzong, and Zhezhong, respectively.

9. Toward the end of the Five Dynasties period, when the Northern Han and the Qidan (Khitan) joined forces in a southward invasion, Zhao Kuangyin led the Zhou dynasty troops in a counterattack, but Zhao maneuvred to have the troops mutiny when they reached Chen Bridge, which was located near present-day Kaifeng, Henan. A robe of the imperial yellow color was thrown over Zhao Kuangyin, and he was declared the emperor of the new Song dynasty.

10. Xishi, a beauty of the state of Yue in the Warring States period, was said to have looked even more attractive when she was ill.

11. For an account of Consort Yang cutting her hair to show her loyalty to Emperor Xuanzong, see story 19.

12. Lady Ming was Wang Zhaojun, a court lady, who was married off in 33 B.C.E. to a Tartar king.

13. Cai Yan, courtesy name Cai Wenji (b. ca. 178), popularly believed to be a talented poet, was abducted around the year 192 by Tartar troops and later lived among them for twelve years. She was eventually ransomed and brought back to Han territory.

14. The Northern Mountain is also known as Mount Heng, which is located in Yangqu County at the border between Hebei Province and Shanxi Province.

15. Guan Yu, courtesy name Yunchang, a sworn brother of Liu Bei's (162–223), is revered to this day as a central figure in the folk pantheon and embodies fidelity to commitments. Together with Zhang Fei (d. 221), he helped Liu Bei found the Kingdom of Shu.

16. Hongfo was a courtesan in the service of Yang Su, prime minister of the Sui dynasty, when she abandoned him and followed Li Jing (571–649), a military strategist. She later proved to be of great value to him in his career. For more on Li Jing, see note 6 of story 11.

17. Liuxia Hui (Hui of Liuxia), a court official of the state of Lu in the Spring and Autumn period, was known for his stoic indifference to sexual temptation.

18. Wumengzi was the wife of Duke Zhao of the state of Lu during the Spring and Autumn period. As both she and her husband were descendants of the royal house of the Zhou dynasty, they bore the same family name of Ji. At the time, those bearing the same family name were prohibited from marrying each other.

19. As the story goes, one stormy night in the state of Lu, a widow whose house was destroyed by the storm asked her neighbor if he could put her up for the night, but he turned a deaf ear to her.

20. Lord Guo was Guo Wei (904–954), founder of the Later Zhou dynasty. For more on Guo Wei, see story 15 in Feng, *Stories Old and New.*

21. Emperor Shizong was Chai Rong, the second emperor of the Later Zhou dynasty, who ruled from 954 to 959.

22. This is a reference to Empress Lü, wife of Liu Bang of the Han dynasty, and Empress Wu Zetian of the Tang dynasty.

22. Young Mr. Song Reunites with His Family by Means of a Tattered Felt Hat

This story has been translated as "The Tattered Felt Hat," in *The Courtesan's Jewel Box: Chinese*

Stories of the Tenth–Twelfth Centuries, trans. Yang Xianyi and Gladys Yang (Beijing: Foreign Languages Press, 1981).

1. In imperial China, scrolls bearing emperors' decrees were wrapped in yellow cloth and carried on the backs of imperial messengers.

2. Jizha of Yanling, prince of Wu during the Warring States period, was traveling through the state of Xu when the king of Xu expressed much admiration for his sword. When Jizha passed by Xu again on his way back, he learned that the king had died, whereupon he hung his sword on a tree by the king's grave before returning home.

3. The aristocrat Wu Zixu, reduced to poverty at one point in his life, eked out a living by playing the flute on the streets. For more on Wu Zixu, see note 10 of story 17.

4. For the story of Han Xin and the woman washing clothes by the river, see note 11 of story 6.

5. Cao Zhi (192–232) was a highly talented poet of the state of Wei in the Three Kingdoms period.

6. Pan Yue (265–?), courtesy name Anren but more often known as Pan An, personifies male beauty.

7. As told in the *Book of Poems,* after Gongbo died an early death, his widow Gongjiang vowed never to remarry.

8. *Ruyi* (literally, "as you wish") is a symbol of good luck.

23. Mr. Le Junior Searches for His Wife at the Risk of His Life

1. Sea Gate (Haimen) in Zhejiang is where the Qiantang River flows into the sea.

2. In the Spring and Autumn period, Wu Zixu, a member of the aristocracy in the state of Wu, was ordered by Fuchai, king of Wu, to take his own life as punishment for his remonstrances against the king's policies. Legend has it that his remains, cast into the Qiantang River after his death, became the god of the tides. Hence the association of his angry soul with the surging waves of the rising tide.

3. Leizhou (Thunder Prefecture), in Guangdong, is known for its frequent thunderstorms. The thunderstorms of late spring were believed to be the ritual in which the Thunder God changed his drums.

Legends about the huge Changle Cave in Guangde, in present-day Anhui, have become lost. Judging from the first line in the next paragraph ("The first three wonders occur only once a year"), this must be a reference to a unique natural phenomenon associated with the cave.

Dengzhou is present-day Penglai, in Shandong Province.

4. Rakshasas are malignant spirits in Hindu mythology.

5. Huang Chao (d. 884) led a major peasant rebellion toward the end of the Tang dynasty.

6. Qian Liu (852–932), a native of Hangzhou, was king of Wu and Yue from 907 to 932. For another, slightly different version of Qian Liu's life, see story 21 in Feng Menglong, *Stories Old and New: a Ming Dynasty Collection,* trans. Shuhui Yang and Yunqin Yang (Seattle: University of Washington Press, 2000).

7. In Hinduism, a kalpa is the length of time of a complete cosmic cycle, from the origination to the destruction of a world system.

8. Su Shi (1037–1101), or Su Dongpo, is one of the greatest men of letters in the history of Chinese literature. See also story 3.

9. During the Clear and Bright Festival, which usually falls in early April, people visit the graves of their ancestors.

10. On the red thread of marriage, see note 2 of story 2.

11. This is a reference to a story in *Stories about the Pillow,* by Shen Jiji of the Tang dynasty. In it, a man, while sleeping on a porcelain pillow given to him by an old man, dreams of a life of fame and fortune. When he wakes up, the yellow millet on the stove is still cooking.

12. According to legend, every year, on the seventh day of the seventh month, magpies form a bridge across the Milky Way so that the Herdboy and Weaving Maiden stars can cross the sky and meet.

13. The four treasures of the scholar's study are brush-pen, ink slab, inkstone, and paper.

14. See note 2 of this story.

15. The duke of Bowang is Zhang Jian (d. 114 B.C.E.), famous for his diplomatic missions along the Silk Road. Legend has it that on one of his expeditions, his raft took him to the Milky Way, where he met the Weaving Maiden star.

24. Yutangchun Reunites with Her Husband in Her Distress

1. It was the custom in brothels for the prostitutes to address the procuress as "Mother."

2. Lord Guan (d. 220), or Guan Yu, a sworn brother of Liu Bei's in the Three Kingdoms period, is revered to this day as a central figure in the folk pantheon and is the embodiment of fidelity to commitments.

3. Li Yaxian and Zheng Yuanhe are characters in the Yuan *zaju* play *The Winding River* and the Ming romance "Story of the Embroidered Blouse," both of which are based on "The Story of Li Wa," by Bai Xingjian of the Tang dynasty.

4. According to *The Romance of the Three Kingdoms,* Zhou Yu (175–210), military adviser to Sun Quan of Wu, devised a plan to capture Liu Bei, Sun's rival, by offering him Sun's sister as wife so as to lure him to the Wu region to pick up the bride. But Liu Bei's military adviser, the great strategist Zhuge Liang, saw through the plot and beat Zhou Yu at his own game by having Liu Bei successfully take away the bride and return to his own territory safe and sound. Zhou Yu led his troops in a chase but was defeated by Liu Bei's general, Zhang Fei. This story is invariably cited in reference to situations whereby one ends up suffering a double loss through actions intended to produce a gain.

5. On Zheng Yuanhe, see note 3.

6. "Nine Springs" is a term for the netherworld.

7. Actually, Yutangchun is better known in traditional opera as Su San. The aria "Su San Leaves the Prison" is so famous that the prison where she supposedly stayed is a tourist attraction.

Yutangchun is the name she uses as a courtesan, but her real name is Su San.

25. Squire Gui Repents at the Last Moment

1. Chen Zhong and Lei Yi of the Eastern Han dynasty were known for their devoted friendship that lasted throughout their lifetimes.

2. On the friendship between Guan and Bao, see the first paragraph of story 1.

3. There was no Dashun reign period in the Yuan dynasty. There was only a Tianshun reign period that lasted less than a year (1328).

4. Feng Menglong himself was a native of Suzhou.

5. Yang Weizhen (1296–1370), sobriquet Tieya, was a famous calligrapher of the Yuan dynasty.

6. Yang Huo of the state of Lu in the Spring and Autumn period wished to visit Confucius, but his request was denied. So, after making sure one day that Confucius was not at home, Yang Huo went ahead and left a steamed piglet at Confucius's home as a gift.

7. Fang Guozhen (1319–1374) was a salt smuggler who later bribed his way into officialdom during the Yuan dynasty. He surrendered to Zhu Yuanzhang, the first emperor of the Ming dynasty.

8. On Zhou Yu's ruse, see note 4 of story 24.

26. Scholar Tang Gains a Wife after One Smile

1. Tang Yin was a great painter and calligrapher of the Ming dynasty. The Metropolitan Museum of Art in New York City has collections of his work on permanent display.

2. These were officials responsible for scrutinizing and criticizing policy decisions of the imperial court.

3. Mount Mao is in southwest Jiangsu Province.

4. Hong Fo, a maidservant, eloped with Li Jing (571–649), a guest in the home of her employer, and later helped Li Jing attain exalted status in the newly founded Tang dynasty.

Zhuo Wenjun, daughter of an immensely rich family of the Han dynasty, eloped with

Sima Xiangru (179–117 B.C.E.), who was then a poverty-stricken young man but later rose to great prominence. For more about the elopement of Zhuo Wenjun and Sima Xiangru, see the prologue story of story 6.

5. Huayang Cave in present-day Jiangsu Province is believed to be inhabited by Daoist immortals.

6. On Hong Fo, see note 4 above.

7. Zhu Jia, a knight-errant in the Lu region at the beginning of the Han dynasty, sheltered Ji Bu when the new emperor Liu Bang put a price on Ji Bu's head. Only by working as a slave in Zhu Jia's household was Ji Bu, a former general under Xiangyu (Liu Bang's rival for the throne), able to avoid capture.

8. Wen Zhengming (1470–1559), sobriquet Resident of Hengshan, was a famous calligrapher and painter during the Ming dynasty.

9. Zhu Yunming (1460–1526), courtesy name Xizhe and sobriquet Zhishan, was a famous calligrapher during the Ming dynasty.

27. Fake Immortals Throw Guanghua Temple into an Uproar

1. Feng Menglong may have made a mistake here. According to *Xihu youlan zhi* (Travel notes about West Lake), the temple dedicated to the Five Gods of Wuxian was built on the old site of the temple dedicated to Bodhisattva Huaguang. But toward the end of this story, the Five Gods of Wuxian merge into one single god, the god of Wuxian, who, in turn, becomes Bodhisattva Huaguang.

2. The five phases (metal, wood, water, fire, and earth) represent a theory by which ancient Chinese philosophers explained the origin of the world.

3. The Five Gods of Wutong are five brothers and are believed to be evil spirits according to folk mythology in areas south of the lower reaches of the Yangzi River.

4. Lü Dongbin, of a scholarly bent, is one of the Eight Immortals in Daoist mythology.

5. The four treasures of the scholar's study are brush-pen, ink stick, ink slab, and paper.

6. It was in Feiyin Pavilion, in Yueyang, Hunan, that Lü Dongbin was inducted as an immortal by Han Zhongli, another immortal in Daoist mythology.

7. "Mount Wu" here is a reference to the goddess of Mount Wu, the mythical figure that gave rise to the expression "clouds and rain," a metaphor for sexual encounters.

8. This is a reference to Chen Shubao (553–604), king of Chen during the Southern dynasties, who was known for his debauchery and his erotic songs, such as "Jade Tress and Flowers in the Rear Court." *Houting* (rear court) may be a reference to male homosexual sex.

9. Yang Guang (569–618), Emperor Suiyang of the Sui dynasty, was one of the most notorious despots in Chinese history.

10. He Xiangu is the only female among the Eight Immortals in Daoist mythology.

11. The goddess of the Luo River is said to have made love with Cao Zhi, a highly talented poet of the state of Wei in the Three Kingdoms period, and then given him her girdle pendant as a keepsake. "Clouds and rain" is a metaphor for sexual encounters.

12. Zhang Sanfeng was a famous Daoist priest of the Ming dynasty.

28. Madam White Is Kept Forever under Thunder Peak Tower

This story has been translated by Diana Yu as "Eternal Prisoner under the Thunder Peak Pagoda," in *Traditional Chinese Stories: Themes and Variations,* ed. Y. W. Ma and Joseph S. M. Lau, (Boston: Cheng and Tsui, 1991).

1. Bianzhou, or Bianjing, present-day Kaifeng in Henan Province, was the capital of the Song dynasty before the court moved south to Hangzhou.

2. Lin Bu (967–1029), courtesy name Junfu, was a Song dynasty poet, posthumously given the title Hejing.

3. Bai Juyi (772–846) was a well-known Tang dynasty poet. He is featured in story 10.

4. Su Shi (1037–1101), also called Su Dongpo, was a famous scholar of the Song dynasty. For more on Su Shi, see story 3.

5. The Qingming Festival is the Clear and

Bright Festival, a day on which people visit their ancestors' graves.

6. These baskets hold paper coins, paper horses, and other items for the deceased to use in the underworld.

7. Animal blood is believed to have the power to combat sorcery.

8. *Jiangxiang,* rendered here as "fragrant wood", is *Acronychia pedunculata,* a small forest tree in the Rutaceae family.

9. This is wine seasoned with *xionghuang* (realgar), which is usually drunk at the Dragon Boat Festival, the fifth day of the fifth lunar month, to detoxify the body.

10. King Yama is the ruler of hell.

29. Zhang Hao Meets Yingying at Lingering Fragrance Pavilion

1. Dengtu is the title character in the poem "Mr. Dengtu," by Song Yu (ca. 290–ca. 223 B.C.E.).

2. The Wushan Mountains are associated with the goddess who gave rise to the expression "clouds and rain," a metaphor for sexual encounters.

3. This story is a parody of the Tang dynasty's "The Biography of Yingying" and *The West Chamber* by Wang Shifu of the Yuan dynasty. In both works, it is the man, Zhang Junrui, who scales a wall to see his lover Cui Yingying. Hence the reference to the reversal of roles.

4. The Divine Maiden is the goddess of the Wushan Mountains. See note 2 above.

Legend has it that during the Eastern Han Dynasty, when Liu Chen and Ruan Zhao were on a trip to collect medicinal herbs, they had an amorous encounter with two fairy maidens in the Cave of Peach Blossoms on the Tiantai Mountains.

5. It is said that the Yellow Emperor had a dream in which he toured the legendary country of Huaxu. Thus, "Huaxu" came to be synonymous with "dream."

6. According to legend, two goddesses of the Han River encountered a man called Zheng Jiaofu at the foot of the Hangao Mountains (in present-day Hubei Province) and gave him their jade pendants as tokens of love.

7. Jia Wu, daughter of Jia Chong, a court minister of the Western Jin dynasty, fell in love with Han Shou, a subordinate of her father's, and surreptitiously gave Han the incense that her father had received as a gift from the emperor.

8. Zhuo Wenjun and Sima Xiangru (179–117 B.C.E.), one of China's most celebrated prose poets, eloped after their first meeting. For more on Zhuo Wenjun and Sima Xiangru, see the prologue story of story 6.

9. On Jia Wu and Han Shou, see note 7 above.

10. Cui Yingying and Zhang Junrui are characters in "The Biography of Yingying" and *The West Chamber.* See note 3 above.

30. Wu Qing Meets Ai'ai by Golden Bright Pond

1. This is a reference to the story about the love between Zhu Wen, a scholar in the Eastern Capital of the Song dynasty, and a female ghost.

2. For the story about Han Shihou (or Han Sihou) meeting the ghost of his deceased wife, see story 24 in Feng Menglong, *Stories Old and New: A Ming Dynasty Collection,* trans. Shuhui Yang and Yunqin Yang (Seattle: University of Washington Press, 2000).

3. These were the four wise old men with white hair and eyebrows who lived in the Shang Mountains toward the end of the Qin dynasty and into the early Han dynasty.

4. This is a reference to Lü Wang, popularly known as Taigong Wang or Jiang Taigong, of the Zhou dynasty. He rose to eminence when he was about eighty years old.

5. Tao Gu, courtesy name Xiushi, of the Song dynasty served successively as secretary of the Bureaus of Rites, Justice, and Revenue.

6. "The balcony" is a metaphor for a lovers' tryst. It was first used in the prose poem "Gao tang fu," attributed to Song Yu (ca. 290–ca. 223 B.C.E.).

7. A green dragon symbolizes luck, and a white tiger symbolizes misfortune.

8. In Daoist myth, Goddess Shangyuan is the youngest daughter of the Queen Mother of the West.

9. The six preliminaries are that the groom's family (1) give presents to the prospective bride's family to make the offer of marriage; (2) obtain written documentation of the prospective bride's name and date of birth; (3) secure through divination a good omen endorsing the marriage; (4) send betrothal gifts to the bride's family; (5) seek approval from the bride's family of an auspicious date for the wedding; and (6) send the groom in person to bring the bride home.

10. The three animals were the ox, sheep, and pig.

31. Zhao Chun'er Restores Prosperity to the Cao Farmstead

1. A *pipa* is a four-stringed lute.

2. Lady Liang was Liang Hongyu, a former prostitute who married Han Shizhong before he became a general.

Han Shizhong (1089–1151), a famous general, is remembered for repelling the attacks of invading Jurchen troops.

3. The *xiezhi* is a legendary animal said to be capable of distinguishing right from wrong. Hence its adoption as a symbol to adorn the robes of government officials.

32. Du Shiniang Sinks Her Jewel Box in Anger

This story has been translated as "The Courtesan's Jewel Box," in *The Courtesan's Jewel Box: Chinese Stories of the Tenth–Twelfh Centuries,* trans. Yang Xianyi and Gladys Yang (Beijing: Foreign Languages Press, 1981), and as "Tu Shih-niang Sinks the Jewel Box in Anger," in *Traditional Chinese Stories: Themes and Variations,* ed. Y. W. Ma and Joseph S. M. Lau (Boston: Cheng and Tsui, 1991).

1. Toyotomi Hideyoshi (1536–1598), *kanpaku* (prime minister) of Japan, invaded Korea during the Chinese Wanli reign period under Emperor Shenzong and was defeated by Ming troops.

2. Bo Cheng'en, deputy commander of Xixia in northwestern China, rebelled in 1592, together with his father. The rebellion was put down later in the same year.

Yang Yinglong, pacification commissioner of Bozhou (present-day Zunyi, Guizhou Province), rebelled in 1597. The rebellion was suppressed in 1600.

3. In the Ming dynasty, the "two capitals" were Beijing and Nanjing.

4. Zhuo Wenjun was renowned for her beauty, intelligence, and musical talent. For her elopement with the celebrated writer Sima Xiangru (179–117 B.C.E.), see the prologue story of story 6.

5. Fan Su was a maid employed in the household of the famous Tang dynasty poet Bai Juyi (772–846), who wrote the line "Fan Su's cherry of a mouth."

6. Zhong Kui (formerly translated as Chung Kuei) is a deity who can drive away evil spirits in Chinese folklore.

7. A white tiger symbolizes bad luck.

8. Shi Hui, courtesy name Junmei, a native of Hangzhou, is believed to be the author of the play *Bai yue ting* (Moon pavilion).

9. Gao Qi (1336–1374), courtesy name Jidi, was a poet and a historian who was put to death by the first Ming emperor, Zhu Yuanzhang.

33. Qiao Yanjie's Concubine Ruins the Family

1. There was no Shanghai County at the time the story is supposed to have taken place. Shanghai County was not established until the Yuan dynasty.

34. Wang Jiaoluan's One Hundred Years of Sorrow

1. According to ancient legends, a crow with three feet lives in the sun, and a jade hare lives in the moon.

2. In a Song dynasty story, Wang Kui, a scholar, benefited from financial help he received from his lover, a prostitute named Jiao Guiying. Wang jilted Jiao after he won first honors on the

civil service examinations and married someone else. Jiao Guiying took her own life and, as a ghost, wreaked vengeance on Wang Kui.

3. According to "The Story of Huo Xiaoyu," by Jiang Fang of the Tang dynasty, Huo Xiaoyu was a prostitute in love with a man called Li Yi. When the man later obtained an official post, he got rid of her and married someone else. Xiaoyu took revenge after her death.

4. The term "clouds and rain" is a metaphor for sexual encounters.

5. The Herdboy and Weaving Maiden stars are separated by the Milky Way. They are able to meet only once a year across a bridge formed by magpies.

6. Han Shou was loved by the daughter of his superior, the court minister Jia Chong of the Western Jin dynasty.

7. The reference is to Cui Yingying, female protagonist of the famous play *The Western Chamber,* by Wang Shifu. Cui Yingying's mother reneges on her promise to marry her to Zhang Gong, whereupon Zhang plays the lute on a moonlit night to express his feelings to Cui Yingying.

8. On Zhang Gong, see previous note. Cui Yingying's mother only allowed Zhang Gong and Yingying to address each other as brother and sister.

Shen Chun is the male protagonist of *The Story of Jiaohong,* by Song Meidong of the Yuan dynasty. He fell in love with his cousin Wang Jiaoniang, but Wang's father refused to let them marry. In the end, the lovers died brokenhearted.

9. See note 5 above.

10. Miss Jiang, of the state of Qi, was married to Chong'er (697–628 B.C.E.), prince of Jin, when he was in exile in Qi. Miss Jiang encouraged Chong'er to return to his native state of Jin to assume power, advising him not to be content with the status quo. She plotted with Chong'er's major adviser to get Chong'er drunk and had him driven out of Qi. Later, Chong'er returned to Jin and reigned as King Wen from 636 to 628 B.C.E.

11. According to *The Book of Poems,* when Gongjiang's husband, Gongbo, died an early death, she vowed never to remarry.

12. Min Jian was a student of Confucius's who was known for his filial piety.

13. During the Tang dynasty, Suiyang (in what is now Henan) was besieged by the troops of An Lushan the rebel (d. 757). Nan Jiyun (d. 757), one of the defenders of Suiyang, was sent by his superior Zhang Xun (709–757) to seek help from Helan Jinming, but Helan turned him down. Suiyang fell, and Zhang Xun and Nan Jiyun both perished.

35. Prefect Kuang Solves the Case of the Dead Baby

This story has been translated by C. T. Hsia and Susan Arnold Zonana as "The Case of the Dead Infant," in *Traditional Chinese Stories: Themes and Variations,* ed. Y.W. Ma and Joseph S. M. Lau (Boston: Cheng and Tsui, 1991). In the original edition, a note appended to the title reads "Originally titled 'How Prefect Kuang Solves the Case of the Dead Baby by the Road.'"

1. For more on Abbot Yutong and Red Lotus, see story 29 in Feng Menglong, *Stories Old and New: A Ming Dynasty Collection,* trans. Shuhui Yang and Yunqin Yang (Seattle: University of Washington Press, 2000).

2. There are seven classes of Buddhist disciples: the monk, the female observer of all the commandments, the novice, the male and the female observers of the minor commandments, and the male and the female observers of the five commandments. See *A Dictionary of Chinese Buddhist Terms* by Soothill (Delhi: Motilal Banarsidass, 1987).

3. Guye, a mountain in present-day Shanxi Province, is said to be an abode of fairies.

4. Wine seasoned with *xionghuang* (realgar) is usually drunk at the Dragon Boat Festival to detoxify the body.

5. Kuang Zhong (1383–1443), the title character of this story, about whose wisdom and personal integrity many stories were told, served as prefect of Suzhou, from 1430 until his death in 1443.

6. Judge Bao (999–1062), as prefect of Kaifeng, gained such fame as a wise and fair dis-

penser of justice that stories about him abound in folklore and traditional drama.

36. The King of the Honey Locust Grove Assumes Human Shape

1. Xichuan is roughly the same as present-day Sichuan.

2. In Buddhist mythology, King Yama is the king of hell and, in popular belief, passes judgment on the dead in order to determine their reincarnations.

3. Lantian is a mountain located to the southeast of Lantian County, Shaanxi Province. It is famous for its jade.

4. A yaksha is usually an evil spirit in the Buddhist belief.

37. Wan Xiuniang Takes Revenge through Toy Pavilions

1. Xichuan is roughly the same as present-day Sichuan.

2. A thin fabric made of yellow grass was specific to the region of Suzhou in the Song dynasty.

3. A yaksha is usually an evil spirit in the Buddhist belief.

38. Jiang Shuzhen Dies in Fulfillment of a Love Bird Prophecy

1. This quotation is attributed to Wang Yen in "Biography of Wang Yen," in *Jin shu* (History of the Jin dynasty).

2. Monk Huiyuan (334–416) spent more than thirty years of his life in Donglin Temple on the Lu Mountains in Jiangxi Province. He was honored as the patriarch by the Pure Land School.

3. The prologue story has been translated by Jeanne Kelly in its unabridged form as "The Tragedy of Pu Fei-yen," in *Traditional Chinese Stories: Themes and Variations,* ed. Y. W. Ma and Joseph S. M. Lau (Boston: Cheng and Tsui, 1991).

4. Hong'er was a famous courtesan in the Tang dynasty.

5. The term "clouds and rain" is a metaphor for sexual encounters.

6. The Lantern Festival falls on the fifteenth day of the first lunar month of the year.

7. Wine seasoned with *xionghuang* (realgar) is usually drunk at the Dragon Boat Festival to detoxify the body.

39. The Stars of Fortune, Rank, and Longevity Return to Heaven

1. Penglai Island is believed to be an abode of the immortals.

40. An Iron Tree at Jingyang Palace Subdues Demons

1. Jingyang is Xu Xun (239–374), courtesy name Jingzhi, the main character of this story. A Daoist priest in the Eastern Jin dynasty, he is often referred to as Xu Jingyang because he was a prefect of Jingyang County in present-day Hubei Province, where his efforts to bring the waters under control gave rise to stories about his magic power. The stories later became part of Daoist mythology. During the Song dynasty, he was given the posthumous title Divine and Wondrous Sage.

2. The Six Classics are *The Book of Songs, The Book of History, The Book of Rites, The Book of Music, The Book of Changes,* and *The Spring and Autumn Annals.*

3. Shun was a legendary king who ruled in antiquity. Emperor Wen was Liu Heng (r. 179–156 B.C.E.).

4. Jiang Shi and his wife, of the Eastern Han dynasty, served Jiang's mother, who loved eating fish, with such devotion that heaven rewarded them with a spring right next to their house. Two carp leaped out of this spring every morning.

Wang Xiang of the Jin dynasty was a most filial son to his stepmother. To satisfy her craving for carp when she was ill, he took off his clothes and lay down on the ice in the depths of winter. Heaven was moved. The ice melted, and fish leaped out.

5. In Daoist terminology, the "cinnabar field" is the lower part of the abdomen, about three inches below the navel.

6. The Red Boy is a character in the famous Ming dynasty novel *The Journey to the West.* Son of the Demon Bull King and the Iron-Fan Princess, he walks on fiery wheels and fights the Monkey King with his fire power.

7. Xiangyang, capital of the Qin dynasty, smoldered for three months after being looted and burned by the rebel Xiang Yu's troops.

8. In the Battle at the Red Cliff (208), Zhou Yu, strategist for Sun Quan (who founded Wu, 220–80), joined Zhuge Liang, strategist for Liu Bei (who founded Shu Han, 221–63), in defeating Cao Cao (whose son founded Wei, 220–65) by setting fire to Cao Cao's troops.

9. Zhuge Liang, courtesy name Kongming (181–234), strategist for Liu Bei (see previous note), had the storage barn for his own troops set on fire in order to lure the enemy, Xiahou Chun. The battle ended in Xiahou's defeat.

10. Dragon Spring is the name of a legendary sword.

11. Ganjiang and Moye, husband and wife in the ancient state of Wu during the Spring and Autumn Period, were such skillful sword makers that their names came to be synonyms for precious swords.

12. Xu You is the one to whom the sage-king Yao, who ruled in antiquity, wished to pass on the throne, but he repeatedly declined the offer.

13. *Ding* is the fourth of the ten Heavenly Stems, which are used in combination with the ten Earthly Branches to designate years, months, days, and hours. "Six-*ding*" here refers to *ding* plus six of the Earthly Branches—*mao, si, wei, you, hai,* and *chou* (i.e. *ding mao, ding si,* etc).

14. King Wen of the Zhou dynasty was a tribal leader in the late Shang dynasty. He is said to be adept in the use of trigrams in performing divinations.

15. The six cosmic essences are those generated by dawn in spring, sunset in autumn, noontime in summer, and midnight in winter and by the sky and the earth.

16. The ten commandments are (1) One must not disobey one's parents and teachers; (2) One must not kill live beings; (3) One must not rebel against the sovereign of the state, (4) One must not take liberties with one's female kith and kin as well as other women, (5) One must not vilify the Dao and the Daoist classics, (6) One must have one's body covered when in the vicinity of the altar, (7) One must not bully the poor and the humble and commit robbery, (8) One must not abandon the elderly and the sick, (9) One must not drink to excess and engage in verbal abuse, (10) One must not commit acts of violence and show off one's power.

17. In Daoist alchemical terms, the dragon represents mercury and the tiger represents lead. Both are used for mixing immortality elixir.

18. The five phases are water, fire, wood, metal, and earth.

19. Chinese musicians in ancient times used a pentatonic scale with only five notes (corresponding to 1, 2, 3, 5, 6, in Western numbered musical notation) and named them GONG, SHANG, JIAO, ZHI, and YU.

20. On Zhou Yu, see note 8 above.

21. Celestial Master Zhang is Zhang Daoling (34–156), founder of the Five Piculs of Rice sect of Daoism. For more on Zhang Daoling, see story 13 of Feng Menglong, *Stories Old and New: A Ming Dynasty Collection,* trans. Shuhui Yang and Yunqin Yang (Seattle: University of Washington Press, 2000).

22. Liu Yuan, of mixed Han and Hun descent, was the founder of the state of Han; Shi Le founded the state of Zhao; Yao Yizhong's son was the founder of the Later Qin; Fu Hong's son founded the Former Qin; and Murong Wei's son founded the state of Yan.

23. Zong Que (d. 465), courtesy name Yuangan, a native of Nieyang of Nanyang in present-day Henan Province, is known for his military exploits and for his childhood wish, expressed to his uncle, to "ride the wind and cleave the waves."

24. Lie Yukou, or Liezi, of the Warring States period, was said to have achieved immortality as a Daoist sage and was able to ride the winds and fly.

25. Gao Feng of the Eastern Han dynasty was so dedicated to his studies that one day, while trying to keep an eye on the wheat field as his wife had told him, he became so absorbed in his reading that all the wheat was washed away by a sudden rainstorm without his ever being aware of it.

26. It is said that on the first day of a military campaign, King Wu, the first king of the Western Zhou dynasty, sought to reassure those who thought the rain a bad omen by saying, "This rain is sent by heaven to wash our weapons clean."

27. In ancient times, lizards were believed to have the power to bring rain. They were often collected and put in jars for rituals in which people prayed for rain.

28. A yaksha is usually an evil spirit in the Buddhist belief.

29. Liu Bei (161–223) founded the Shu Han kingdom of the Three Kingdoms period. In chapter 21 of the Ming dynasty novel *The Romance of the Three Kingdoms* (San guo yan yi), Liu Bei was engaged in a conversation with his rival, Cao Cao, when the latter said, "You and I are the greatest heroes of our time." Liu Bei was so alarmed that he dropped his spoon and chopsticks, but he was able to attribute his consternation to a sudden thunderbolt that struck while Cao Cao was making that comment.

30. Cai Yuanzhong was Cai Shun, courtesy name Junzhong (not Yuanzhong), of the Later Han dynasty, who was known for his filial devotion to his mother. As his mother had always been afraid of thunder, he made a point of walking around her grave every time a storm came, to comfort her soul.

31. Sun Deng was a hermit in the state of Wei toward the end of the Three Kingdoms period (220–80) and the beginning of the Western Jin dynasty (265–317).

32. In the Daoist belief, Zhang Guolao is one of the Eight Immortals. For more on Zhang Guolao, see story 31 in Feng Menglong, *Stories Old and New.*

33. Zhu Manping was Zhu Pingman, who, according to legend, spent three years and all his money learning how to kill dragons but never put what he had learned into practice.

34. Fei Changfang, a native of Runan during the Later Han dynasty, was a necromancer said to have a staff with which he whacked demons and evil spirits.

35. According to legend, Wu Chuo, a Daoist, was picking medicinal herbs at the mouth of the Huayang Cave when he saw a little boy with three large pearls in his hand playing under a pine tree. When Wu Chuo asked him who his parents were, the boy ran into the cave and changed into a dragon, with the pearls stuck in its left ear. Wu Chuo hacked at it with his ax. The dragon's left ear fell off, but the pearls disappeared.

36. In Daoist belief, Marshal Deng is a thunder god.

37. Zhang Fei (d. 221) was a brave warrior of the Three Kingdoms period and a sworn brother of Liu Bei, founder of the Shu Han Kingdom.

38. Marshal Wang is believed to be a celestial fire god.

39. Chiyou, legendary leader of the Jiuli tribes, is said to have conjured up a thick fog in a fight at Zhuolu (in present-day Hebei Province) against the Yellow Emperor, legendary ancestor of the Chinese, in order to disorient the Yellow Emperor's troops. But with the aid of the compass chariot, the Yellow Emperor chased down Chiyou and won final victory.

40. Yuangui (289–340) is Yu Liang, courtesy name Yuangui, a powerful official in the court of three consecutive emperors of the Eastern Jin dynasty. Wang Dao (276–339), the prime minister, detested Yuangui's overbearing ways and often raised a fan to cover his head whenever a wind arose, saying, "Now here comes Yuangui with all the dust!"

41. Luyang Wenzi, better known as Duke Luyang, of the state of Chu in the Spring and Autumn period, was fighting with Han Gou when the sun began to set. As soon as Luyang pointed his lance at it, the sun reversed its course and rose back into the sky.

According to legend, the duke of Yu in high

antiquity was fighting with Xia when the sun began to set. When the duke pointed his sword at it, the sun reversed its course and remained fixed in the sky.

42. Xiang Yu (232–202 B.C.E.) led the uprising that overthrew the Qin dynasty. Zhang Han was a general in the Qin army. In a fierce battle fought at Julu, Zhang Han surrendered to Xiang Yu.

43. According to the prose poem "Gao tang fu," attributed to Song Yu (ca. 290–ca. 223 B.C.E.), King Xiang of Chu dreamed of having a sexual encounter with the goddess of Wu Gorge.

44. On the Battle at the Red Cliff, see note 8 above.

45. Liu Xiu (6 B.C.E.–57 C.E.) led twenty-eight generals in a major battle against the troops of Wang Mang (45 B.C.E.–23 C.E.). Liu Xiu later became Emperor Guangwu (r. 25–28) of the Eastern Han dynasty.

46. The Monkey King is a much beloved character in the Ming dynasty novel *A Journey to the West.*

47. Nüwa, a principal character in Chinese mythology, is the goddess who smelted stones of five colors with which to patch up the sky after it had been damaged.

48. The lord of the state of Ge during the Xia dynasty set himself against Tang and was defeated. Tang later founded the Shang dynasty.

49. King Zhou was the last king of the Shang dynasty.

50. For the story about Tripitaka's pilgrimage to India, see Cheng'en Wu, *The Journey to the West,* trans. and ed. Anthony Yu, (Chicago: University of Chicago Press, 1973–78).

51. Zhuge Liang (181–234), courtesy name Kongming, was adviser to Liu Bei, who founded the Shu Han Kingdom in the Three Kingdoms period. He captured Meng Huo, chieftain of the tribes living in what is now Yunnan, seven times but released him each time so that Meng Huo would sincerely acknowledge his defeat rather than simply submit grudgingly.

52. In the famous play *Orphan of the Zhao Clan,* set during the reign of Duke Jing of the state of Jin in the Spring and Autumn period, Tu'an Gu killed the entire clan of Prime Minister Zhao Dun except for Zhao Dun's daughter-in-law, who fled and gave birth to a son, Zhao Wu. Cheng Ying and Gongsun Chujiu, retainers of the Zhao family, saved the orphan, who later sought revenge against Tu'an Gu. This play was rewritten in French by Voltaire in 1754 as "L'Orphelin de la Chine" in O'Euvres Complètes de Voltaire, ed. Loius Moland (Paris: Garnier, 1877–1885, vol. 5, pp. 289–358). It was performed on stage in Paris in 1775.

53. Wu Zixu (d. 484 B.C.E.), whose father and brother were both killed by King Ping of the state of Chu, later vented his hatred by whipping King Ping's corpse three hundred times.

54. Wang Qiang, or Wang Zhaojun, was a lady-in-waiting at the Western Han court. She volunteered to marry a Hun chief in 33 B.C.E. Xishi was a famous beauty in the late Spring and Autumn period. Zhao Feiyan (d. 1 B.C.E.) was a court lady in the service of Emperor Cheng (r. 32–6 B.C.E.) of the Han dynasty and was later made empress. Consort Yang, or Yang Yuhuan (719–755), was Emperor Xuanzong's favorite concubine. She is featured in story 9 and story 19.

55. For more on this story, see chapter 6 in [Kuan-chung Lo], *Three Kingdoms: A Historical Novel,* trans. Moss Roberts (Berkeley: University of California Press; Beijing: Foreign Languages Press, 1991).

56. Bianque (ca. 407–ca 310 B.C.E.) was a medical scientist and developed the method of pulse diagnosis.

57. Shennong was a legendary ruler of ancient China who is said to have introduced agriculture and herbal medicine to China.